By Terry Brooks

Shannara
First King of Shannara
The Sword of Shannara
The Elfstones of Shannara
The Wishsong of Shannara

The Heritage of Shannara
The Scions of Shannara
The Druid of Shannara
The Elf Queen of Shannara
The Talismans of Shannara

The Voyage of the Jerle Shannara
Ilse Witch
Antrax
Morgawr

High Druid of Shannara
Jarka Ruus
Tanequil
Straken

Genesis of Shannara
Armageddon's Children
The Elves of Cintra
The Gypsy Morph

Legends of Shannara
Bearers of the Black Staff
The Measure of the Magic

The World of Shannara

The Magic Kingdom of Landover
Magic Kingdom for Sale—Sold!
The Black Unicorn
Wizard at Large
The Tangle Box
Witches' Brew
A Princess of Landover

The Word and the Void
Running with the Demon
A Knight of the Word
Angel Fire East

Sometimes the Magic Works: Lessons from a Writing Life

THE
HIGH DRUID
OF
SHANNARA
TRILOGY

BALLANTINE BOOKS • NEW YORK

THE
HIGH DRUID
OF
SHANNARA
TRILOGY

TERRY
BROOKS

High Druid of Shannara: Jarka Ruus, copyright © 2003 by Terry Brooks
High Druid of Shannara: Tanequil, copyright © 2004 by Terry Brooks
High Druid of Shannara: Straken, copyright © 2005 by Terry Brooks

Published in the United States by Del Rey,
an imprint of The Random House Publishing Group,
a division of Random House, Inc., New York.

DEL REY is a registered trademark and the Del Rey colophon is
a trademark of Random House, Inc.

The novels contained in this omnibus were each published separately by
Del Rey, an imprint of The Random House Publishing Group, a division of
Random House, Inc., in 2003, 2004, and 2005.

Endpaper maps by Russ Charpentier

ISBN 978-0-345-52895-7

Printed in the United States of America on acid-free paper

www.delreybooks.com

2 4 6 8 9 7 5 3 1

First Edition

CONTENTS

JARKA RUUS

For Judine,
my favorite traveling companion,
at the start of another journey.

ONE

She sat alone in her chambers, draped in twilight's shadows and evening's solitude, her thoughts darker than the night descending and heavier than the weight of all Paranor. She retired early these days, ostensibly to work but mostly to think, to ponder on the disappointment of today's failures and the bleakness of tomorrow's prospects. It was silent in the high tower, and the silence gave her a momentary respite from the struggle between herself and those she would lead. It lasted briefly, only so long as she remained secluded, but without its small daily comfort she sometimes thought she would have gone mad with despair.

She was no longer a girl, no longer even young, though she retained her youthful looks, her pale translucent skin still unblemished and unlined, her startling blue eyes clear, and her movements steady and certain. When she looked in the mirror, which she did infrequently now as then, she saw the girl she had been twenty years earlier, as if aging had been miraculously stayed. But while her body stayed young, her spirit grew old. Responsibility aged her more quickly than time. Only the Druid Sleep, should she avail herself of it, would stay the wearing of her heart, and she would not choose that remedy anytime soon. She could not. She was the Ard Rhys of the Third Druid Council, the High Druid of Paranor, and while she remained in that office, sleep of any kind was in short supply.

Her gaze drifted to the windows of her chamber, looking west to where the sun was already gone behind the horizon, and the light it cast skyward in the wake of its descent a dim glow beginning to fail. She thought her own star was setting, as well, its light fading, its time passing, its chances slipping away. She would change that if she could, but she no longer believed she knew the way.

She heard Tagwen before she saw him, his footfalls light and cautious in the hallway beyond her open door, his concern for her evident in the softness of his approach.

"Come, Tagwen," she called as he neared.

He came through the door and stopped just inside, not presuming to venture farther, respecting this place that was hers and hers alone. He was growing old, as well, nearly twenty years of service behind him, the only assistant she had ever had, his time at Paranor a mirror of her own. His stocky, gnarled body was still strong, but his movements were slowing and she could see the way he winced when his joints tightened and cramped after too much use. There was kindness in his eyes, and it had drawn her to him from the first, an indication of the nature of the man inside. Tagwen served because he respected what she was doing, what she meant to the Four Lands, and he never judged her by her successes or failures, even when there were so many more of the latter than the former.

"Mistress," he said in his rough, gravel-laced voice, his seamed, bearded face dipping momentarily into shadow as he bowed. It was an odd, stiff gesture he had affected from the beginning. He leaned forward as if to share a confidence that others might try to overhear. "Kermadec is here."

She rose at once. "He will not come inside," she said, making it a statement of fact.

Tagwen shook his head. "He waits at the north gate and asks if you will speak with him." The Dwarf's lips tightened in somber reflection. "He says it is urgent."

She reached for her cloak and threw it about her shoulders. She went by him, touching his shoulder reassuringly as she passed. She went out the door and down the hallway to begin her descent. Within the stairwell, beyond the sound of her own soft footfalls, she heard voices rise up from below, the sounds of conversations adrift on the air. She tried to make out what they said, but could not. They would be speaking of her; they did so almost incessantly. They would be asking why she continued as their leader, why she presumed that she could achieve anything after so many failures, why she could not recognize that her time was past and another should take her place. Some would be whispering that she ought to be forced out, one way or another. Some would be advocating stronger action.

Druid intrigues. The halls of Paranor were rife with them, and she could not put a stop to it. At Walker's command, she had formed this Third Council on her return to the Four Lands from Parkasia. She had accepted her role as leader, her destiny as guide to those she had recruited, her responsibility for rebuilding the legacy of the Druids as knowledge givers to the Races. She had formed the heart of this new order with those few sent under duress by the Elven King Kylen Elessedil at his brother Ahren's insistence. Others had come from other lands and other Races, drawn by the prospect of exploring magic's uses. That had been twenty years ago, when there was fresh hope and everything seemed possible. Time and an inability to effect any measurable change in the thinking and attitudes of the governing bodies of those lands and Races had leeched most of that away. What remained was a desperate insistence on clinging to her belief that she was not meant to give up.

But that alone was not enough. It would never be enough. Not for someone who had come out of darkness so complete that any chance at redemption had seemed hopeless. Not for Grianne Ohmsford, who had once been the Ilse Witch and had made herself Ard Rhys to atone for it.

She reached the lower levels of the Keep, the great halls that connected the meeting rooms with the living quarters of those she had brought to Paranor. A handful of these Druids came into view, shadows sliding along the walls like spilled oil in the light of the flameless lamps that lit the corridors. Some nodded to her; one or two spoke. Most simply cast hurried glances and passed on. They feared and mistrusted her, these Druids she had accepted into her order. They could not seem to help themselves, and she could not find the heart to blame them.

Terek Molt walked out of a room and grunted his unfriendly greeting, outwardly bold and challenging. But she could sense his real feelings, and she knew he feared her. Hated her more than feared her, though. It was the same with Traunt Rowan and Iridia Eleri and one or two more. Shadea a'Ru was beyond even that, her venomous glances so openly hostile that there was no longer any communication between them, a situation that it seemed nothing could help.

Grianne closed her eyes against what she was feeling and wondered what she was going to do about these vipers—what she could do that would not have repercussions beyond anything she was prepared to accept.

Young Trefen Morys passed her with a wave and a smile, his face guileless and welcoming, his enthusiasm evident. He was a bright light in an otherwise darkened firmament, and she was grateful for his presence. Some within the order still believed in her. She had never expected friendship or even compassion from those who came to her, but she had hoped for loyalty and a sense of responsibility toward the office she held. She had been foolish to think that way, and she no longer did so. Perhaps it was not inaccurate to say that now she merely hoped that reason might prevail.

"Mistress," Gerand Cera greeted in his soft voice as he bowed her past him, his tall form lean and sinuous, his angular features sleepy and dangerous.

There were too many of them. She could not watch out for all of them adequately. She put herself at risk every time she walked these halls—here in the one place she should be safe, in the order she had founded. It was insane.

She cleared the front hall and went out into the night, passed through a series of interconnected courtyards to the north gates, and ordered the guard to let her through. The Trolls on watch, impassive and silent, did as they were told. She did not know their names, only that they were there at Kermadec's behest, which was enough to keep her reassured of their loyalty. Whatever else happened in this steadily eroding company of the once faithful, the Trolls would stand with her.

Would that prove necessary? She would not have thought so a month ago. That she asked the question now demonstrated how uncertain matters had become.

She walked to the edge of the bluff, to the wall of trees that marked the beginning of the forest beyond, and stopped. An owl glided through the darkness, a silent hunter. She felt a sudden connection with him so strong that she could almost envision flying away as he did, leaving everything behind, returning to the darkness and its solitude.

She brushed the thought aside, an indulgence she could not

afford, and whistled softly. Moments later, a figure detached itself from the darkness almost in front of her and came forward.

"Mistress," the Maturen greeted, dropping to one knee and bowing deeply.

"Kermadec, you great bear," she replied, stepping forward to put her arms around him. "How good it is to see you."

Of the few friends she possessed, Kermadec was perhaps the best. She had known him since the founding of the order, when she had gone into the Northland to ask for the support of the Troll tribes. No one had ever thought to do that, and her request was cause enough for a convening of a council of the nations. She did not waste the opportunity she had been given. She told them of her mission, of her role as Ard Rhys of a new Druid Council, the third since Galaphile's time. She declared that this new order would accept members from all nations, the Trolls included. No prejudices would be allowed; the past would play no part in the present. The Druids were beginning anew, and for the order to succeed, all the Races must participate.

Kermadec had stepped forward almost at once, offering the support of his sizeable nation, of its people and resources. Prompted by her gesture and his understanding of its importance to the Races, his decision was made even before the council of nations had met. His Rock Trolls were not imbued with a strong belief in magic, but it would be their honor to serve as her personal guard. Give them an opportunity to demonstrate their reliability and skill, and she would not regret it.

Nor had she ever done so. Kermadec had stayed five years, and in that time became her close friend. More than once, he had solved a problem that might otherwise have troubled her. Even after he had left for home again, his service complete, he had remained in charge of choosing the Trolls that followed in his footsteps. Some had doubted the wisdom of allowing Trolls inside the walls at all, let alone as personal guards to the Ard Rhys. But she had walked in darker places than these and had allied herself with creatures far more dangerous. She did not think of any Race as predisposed toward either good or evil; she saw them all only as being composed of creatures that might be persuaded to choose one over the other.

Just as she saw the members of her Druid order, she thought, though she might wish it otherwise.

"Kermadec," she said again, the relief in her voice clearly evident.

"You should let me rid you of them all," he said softly, one great hand coming to rest on her slim shoulder. "You should wash them away like yesterday's sweat and start anew."

She nodded. "If it were that easy, I should call on you to help me. But I can't start over. It would be perceived as weakness by the governments of the nations I court. There can be no weakness in an Ard Rhys in these times." She patted his hand. "Rise and walk with me."

They left the bluff and moved back into the trees, perfectly comfortable with each other and the night. The sights and sounds of Paranor disappeared, and the silence of the forest wrapped them close. The air was cool and gentle, the wind a soft whisper in the new spring leaves, bearing the scent of woods and water. It would be summer before long, and the smells would change again.

"What brings you here?" she asked him finally, knowing he would wait for her to ask before speaking of it.

He shook his head. "Something troubling. Something you may understand better than I do."

Even for a Rock Troll, Kermadec was huge, towering over her at close to seven feet, his powerful body sheathed in a barklike skin. He was all muscle and bone, strong enough to rip small trees out at the roots. She had never known a Troll to possess the strength and quickness of Kermadec. But there was much more to him. A Maturen of thirty years, he was the sort of person others turned to instinctively in times of trouble. Solid and capable, he had served his nation with a distinction and compassion that belied the ferocious history of his Race. In the not so distant past, the Trolls had marched against Men and Elves and Dwarves with the single-minded intent of smashing them back into the earth. During the Wars of the Races, ruled by their feral and warlike nature, they had allied themselves with the darker forces in the world. But that was the past, and in the present, where it mattered most, they were no longer so easily bent to service in a cause that reason would never embrace.

"You have come a long way to see me, Kermadec," she said. "It must be something important."

"That remains for you to decide," he said softly. "I myself haven't seen what I am about to reveal, so it is hard for me to judge. I think it will be equally hard for you."

"Tell me."

He slowed to a stop in the darkness and turned to face her. "There is strange activity in the ruins of the Skull Kingdom, mistress. The reports come not from Rock Trolls, who will not go into that forbidden place, but from other creatures, ones who will, ones who make a living in part by telling of what they see. What they see now is reminiscent of other, darker times."

"The Warlock Lord's domain, once," she observed. "A bad place still, all broken walls and scattered bones. Traces of evil linger in the smells and taste of the land. What do these creatures tell you they see?"

"Smoke and mirrors, of a sort. Fires lit in darkness and turned cold by daylight's arrival. Small explosions of light that suggest something besides wood might be burning. Acrid smells that have no other source than the fires. Black smudges on flat stones that have the look of altars. Markings on those stones that might be symbols. Such events were sporadic at first, but now occur almost nightly. Strange things that of themselves alone do not trouble me, but taken all together do."

He breathed in and exhaled. "One thing more. Some among those who come to us say there are wraiths visible at the edges of the mist and smoke, things not of substance and not yet entirely formed, but recognizable as something more than the imagination. They flutter like caged birds seeking to be free."

Grianne went cold, aware of the possibilities that the sightings suggested. Something was being conjured up by use of magic, something that wasn't natural to this world and that was being summoned to serve an unknown purpose.

"How reliable are these stories?"

He shrugged. "They come from Gnomes for the most part, the only ones who go into that part of the world. They do so because they are drawn to what they perceive in their superstitions as sacred. They perform their rituals in those places because they feel it will lend them power. How reliable are they?" He paused. "I think there is weight to what they say they see."

She thought a moment. Another strangeness to add to an already overcrowded agenda of strangenesses. She did not like the sound of this one, because if magic was at work, whatever its reason, its source might lie uncomfortably close to home. Druids had the use of magic and were the most likely suspects, but their use of it in places beyond Paranor was forbidden. There were other possibilities, but this was the one she could not afford to ignore.

"Is there a pattern to these happenings?" she asked. "A timing to the fires and their leavings?"

He shook his head. "None that anyone has discerned. We could ask the Gnomes to watch for it, to mark the intervals."

"Which will take time," she pointed out. "Time best spent

looking into it myself." She pursed her lips. "That is what you came to ask me to do, isn't it? Take a look for myself?"

He nodded. "Yes, mistress. But I will go with you. Not alone into that country—ever—would I go. But with you beside me, I would brave the netherworld and its shades."

Be careful of what you boast of doing, Kermadec, she thought. *Boasts have a way of coming back to haunt you.*

She thought of what she had committed herself to do in the days ahead. Meetings with various Druids to rework studies that members of the order would undertake. Those could wait. Overseeing the repairs to the library that concealed the Druid Histories—that one could not happen without her presence, but could wait, as well. A delegation from the Federation was due to arrive in three days; the Prime Minister of the Coalition was reputed to lead it. But she could be back in time for that if she left at once.

She must go, she knew. She could not afford to leave the matter unattended to. It was the sort of thing that could mushroom into trouble on a much larger scale. Even by her appearance, she might dissuade those involved from pursuing their conjuring. Once they knew that she was aware of them, they might go to ground again.

It was the best she could hope for. Besides, it gave her an opportunity to escape Paranor and its madness for a few days. In the interval, perhaps a way to contend with the intrigues might occur to her. Time and distance often triggered fresh insights; perhaps that would happen here.

"Let me tell Tagwen," she said to Kermadec, "and we'll be off."

Two

They departed Paranor at midnight, flying north out of the Druid forestlands with a full moon to light their way, riding the edge of their expectations just ahead of their doubts and fears. They chose to use Grianne's War Shrike, Chaser, to make the journey, rather than a Druid airship, thinking that the Shrike would draw less attention and be less cumbersome. An airship required a crew, and a crew required explanations. Grianne preferred to keep secret what she was investigating until she better understood what it meant.

Tagwen accepted the news of her sudden and mysterious departure stoically, but she read disapproval and concern in his eyes. He was desperate for her to tell him something more, a hint of what she was about so that if the need arose, he might be able to help. But she thought it best he know only that she would be gone for a few days and he must see to her affairs as best he could. There would be questions, demands perhaps, but he couldn't reveal what he didn't know. She braced his shoulders firmly with her hands, smiled her approval and reassurance, and slipped away.

It went without saying that Tagwen would make no mention of Kermadec unless she failed to return; a visit from the Rock Troll was always to be kept secret. There were too many who disapproved of the relationship, and the Dwarf understood the importance of not throwing fuel on a fire already dangerously hot. Grianne could depend on Tagwen to use good judgment in such matters. It was one of his strongest attributes; his exercise of discretion and common sense was easily the equal of her own. Had he the inclination or the talent, he would have made a good Druid. That accolade bestowed, she was just as happy to have him be what he was.

The flight took the rest of the night and most of the following day, a long, steady sweep out of Callahorn and across the Streleheim to the peaks of the Knife Edge and the Razors, where the ruins of the Skull Kingdom lay scattered in the valley between. As she guided Chaser onward, the rush of air in her ears wrapping her in its mindless sound, she had plenty of time to think. Her thoughts were both of what lay ahead and behind. But while the former merely intrigued, the latter haunted.

Her efforts at this new life had started so promisingly. She had returned to the Four Lands with such confidence, her identity regained, her life remade, the lies that had misled her replaced by truths. She had found her lost brother Bek, whom she had never thought to see again. She had broken the chains that the Morgawr had forged to hold her. She had fought and destroyed the warlock with her brother at her side. She had done this so that she might be given a chance at the redemption she had never thought to find. The dying touch of a Druid, his blood on her forehead marking her as his successor, had set her on her path. It was a destiny she would never have chosen for herself but that she had come to believe was right and had therefore embraced.

Walker, a shade with a shade's vision, had reappeared to her at the Hadeshorn, and given her his blessing. Druids dead and gone passed in review, their shades materializing from the ether, rising out of the roiling waters, infusing her with their knowledge and a share of their collective power. She would rebuild their order, resuming the task that Walker had undertaken for himself and failed to complete. She would summon members of all the Races to a Third Druid Council and from it found a new order, one in which the dictates of a single Druid would no longer be all that stood between civilization and anarchy, between reason and madness. For too long, one Druid had been required to make the difference. Those few who had done so—Bremen, Allanon, and Walker—had persevered because there had been no one else and no other way. She would change that.

Such dreams. Such hopes.

Ahren Elessedil had talked his brother, the Elven King Kylen Elessedil, into supplying the first of the new order, two handfuls of Elves Ahren had led to Paranor personally. After Kylen discovered he had been tricked, that Walker was dead and the hated Ilse Witch had replaced him, he had sought to recall those he had sent. But it was too late; the Elves who had come were committed to her and beyond his reach. In retaliation he attempted to poison the minds of the leaders of the other Races against her at every opportunity. That did not prove to be too difficult with Sen Dunsidan, by then Prime Minister of the Federation, who already feared and detested her. But the Dwarves and Trolls were less easily persuaded, especially after she made the effort to go directly to them, to speak in council, and to insist that she would place the order at their disposal so far as it was possible to do so. Remember what the Druids were created to do, she kept reminding them. If you seek a source of strength in the cause of peace and goodwill among all nations, the Druids are the ones to whom you should turn.

For a time, they did so. Members of both Races came to her,

and some from Callahorn, as well, for they had heard good things about her from the Rover Captain Redden Alt Mer and from the Highlander Quentin Leah, men they respected. Besides, once they learned that the Federation did not support her, they were inclined to think that was reason enough for them to do so. The war between the Federation and the Free-born was still being fought, mighty armies still locked in combat on the Prekkendorran, leaders still waging a war that had been waged since the passing of Allanon—a war pitting unification against independence, territorial rights against free will. The Free-born wanted Callahorn to be its own country; the Federation wanted it to be a part of the Southland. At times it had been both, at times neither.

There was more to it, of course, as there always is in the case of wars between nations. But that was the justification most often given by those involved, and into the breach left by the absence of any sensible attempt to examine the matter stepped the Ard Rhys.

It was a fateful decision, but one she did not see how she could avoid. The Federation–Free-born war was a ragged wound that would not heal. If the Races were ever to be brought together again, if the Druids were to be able to turn their attention to bettering the lives of the people of the Four Lands, this war must first be ended.

So, even as she struggled to strike a balance in the diversity of temperaments and needs of those who came to Paranor to study the Druid ways, she was attempting, as well, to find a way to resolve the conflict between the Federation and the Free-born. It involved dealing with the two leaders who hated her most—Kylen Elessedil of the Elves and Sen Dunsidan of the Federation. It required that she put aside her own prejudices and find a way to get past theirs. She was able to do this in large part not through fear or intimidation but by making herself appear indispensable to them. After all, the Druids were still in possession of knowledge denied common men, more so than ever since the events in Parkasia. Neither man knew for certain what knowledge she had gained from the Old World that might prove invaluable. Neither understood how little of that knowledge she actually possessed. But perception is often more persuasive than truth. Without the Druids to offer support, each worried that crucial ground would be lost to the other. Without her help, each believed he risked allowing the other a chance to grow more powerful at his expense. Sen Dunsidan had always been a politician. Once he understood that she did not intend to revert to her ways as the Ilse Witch or hold against him his temporary alliance with the Morgawr, he was more than willing to see what she had to offer. Kylen Elessedil followed along for no better reason than to keep pace with his enemy.

Grianne played at this game because it was the only choice she had. She was as good at it now as she had been when she was the Ilse Witch and manipulation was second nature. It was a slow process. Mostly, she settled for crumbs in exchange for the prospect of a full loaf. At times, brought close by promises made and fitfully kept, she thought she would succeed in her efforts, her goal no more than a meeting away. Just a truce between the two would have opened the door to a more permanent solution. Both were strong men, and a small concession by one might have been enough to encourage the other to grant the same. She maneuvered them both toward making that concession, gaining time and credibility as she did so, making herself the center of their thinking as they edged toward a resolution to a war no one really wanted.

Then Kylen Elessedil was killed on the Prekkendorran, the blame for it was laid at her doorstep, and in an instant everything she had worked for nearly six years to achieve was lost.

When they stopped at midmorning to rest Chaser, Kermadec reopened the wound.

"Has that boy King come to his senses yet, mistress?" he asked in a tone of voice that suggested he already knew the answer.

She shook her head. Kellen Elessedil was his father's son and, if it was possible, liked her even less than his father had. Worse, he blamed her for his father's death, a mindset she seemed unable to change.

"He's a fool. He'll die in the same way, fighting for something that to right-thinking men makes no sense at all." Kermadec snorted softly. "They say Rock Trolls are warlike, but history suggests that we are no worse than Men and Elves and in these times perhaps better. At least we do not carry on wars for fifty years."

"You could argue the Federation–Free-born war has been going on for much longer than that," she said.

"However long, it is still too long." Kermadec stretched his massive arms over his head and yawned. "What is the point?"

It was a rhetorical question and she didn't bother to attempt an answer. It had been a dozen years since her efforts at finding a solution had broken down, and since then she had been preoccupied with troubles much closer to home.

"You are due for a change of guards," Kermadec offered, handing her his aleskin. "Maybe you should think about a change of Druids at the same time."

"Dismiss them all and start over?" She had heard this argument from him before. Kermadec saw things in simple terms; he thought she would be better off if she did so, too. "I can't do that."

"So you keep saying."

"Dismissing the order now would be perceived as weakness on my part. Even dismissing the handful of troublemakers who plague me most would have that effect. The nations look for an excuse to proclaim the Druid Council a failure, especially Sen Dunsidan and Kellen Elessedil. I cannot give them one. Besides, if I had to start over at this point, no one would come to Paranor to aid me. All would shun the Druids. I have to make do with things as they are."

Kermadec took back the aleskin and looked out over the countryside. They were just at the edge of the Streleheim, facing north toward the misty, rugged silhouette of the Knife Edge. The day was bright and warm, and it promised another clear, moonlit night in which to explore the ruins of the Skull Kingdom. "You might think about the impracticality of that before you give up on my suggestion."

She had thought about alternatives frequently of late, although her thinking was more along the lines of restructuring and reordering so as to isolate those most troublesome. But even there she had to be careful not to suggest an appearance of weakness to the others or they would begin to shift allegiance in ways that would undo her entirely.

At times, she thought it might be best if she simply gave them all what they wanted, if she resigned her position and departed for good. Let another struggle with the problem. Let someone else take on her responsibilities and her obligations as Ard Rhys. But she knew she couldn't do that. No one else had been asked to shoulder those responsibilities and obligations; they had been given to her, and nothing had happened to change that. She could not simply walk away. She had no authority to do so. If Walker's shade should appear to tell her it was time, she would be gone in a heartbeat— though perhaps not without disappointment at having failed to accomplish her task. But neither Walker's nor the shade of any other Druid had come to her. Until she was discharged, she could not go. The dissatisfaction of others was not enough to set her free.

Her solution to the problem would have been much easier if she were still the Ilse Witch. She would have made an example of the more troublesome members of her order and cowed the rest by doing so. She would not have hesitated to eliminate her problems in a way that would have appalled even Kermadec. But she had lived enough of that life, and she would never go back to it. An Ard Rhys must find other, better ways to act.

By late afternoon, they had crossed the Streleheim and flown through the lower wall of the Knife Edge into the jagged landscape of the Skull Kingdom. She felt a change in the air long before she saw one on the ground. Even aboard Chaser, several hundred feet up, she could sense it. The air became dead and old, smelling and tasting of devastation and rot. There was no life here, not of a sort anyone could recognize. The mountain was gone, brought down by cataclysmic forces on the heads of those who had worked their evil within it, reduced to a jumble of rocks within which little grew and less found shelter or forage. It was a ruined land, colorless and barren even now, a thousand years later, and it was likely to be a thousand more before that changed. Even in the wake of a volcano's eruption, in the path of the resultant lava flow, life eventually returned, determined and resilient. But not here. Here, life was denied.

Ignoring the look and feel of the place, even though it settled about them with oppressive insistence, they circled the ruins in search of the site where the fires and the flashes had been observed. After about an hour they found it at one end of a long shelf of rock balanced amid a cluster of spikes that jutted like bones from the earth. A ring of stones encircled a fire pit left blackened and slick from whatever had been burned. When Grianne first saw it from the air, she could not imagine how anyone could even manage to get to it, let alone make use of it. Rock barriers rose all about, the crevices between them deep and wide, the edges sharp as glass. Then she amended her thinking. It would take a Shrike or a Roc or a small, highly maneuverable airship to gain access, but access could be gained. Which had been used in this instance? She stored the question away to be pondered later.

Guiding Chaser to one end of the shelf, they dismounted and walked back for a closer look.

"Sacrifices of some sort," Kermadec observed, glancing around uneasily, his big shoulders swinging left and right, as if he were caged. He did not like being there, she knew, even with her. The place held bad memories for Trolls, even after so long. The Warlock Lord might be dead and gone, but the feel of him lingered. In the history of the Trolls, no one had done more damage to the nation's psyche. Trolls were not superstitious in the manner of Gnomes, but they believed in the transference of evil from the dead to the living. They believed because they had experienced it, and they were wary of it happening again.

She closed her eyes and cast about with her other senses for a moment, trying to read in the air what had happened here. She tracked the leavings of a powerful magic, the workings of a sorcery that was not meant to heal or succor. A summoning of some sort, she read in the bits and pieces that remained. To what end, though? She could not determine, though the smells told of something dying, and not quickly. She looked down at the fire pit and read in the greasy smears dark purpose in the sacrifices clearly made.

"This isn't good," she said softly.

He stepped close. "What do you find, mistress?"

"Nothing yet. Nothing certain." She looked up at him, into his flat, expressionless features. "Perhaps tonight, when darkness cloaks the thing that finds this dead place so attractive, we shall find out."

She tethered Chaser some distance away, back in the rocks where he couldn't be seen, giving him food and water and speaking soothing words to steady him against what might happen later. Afterward, she ate a cold dinner with Kermadec, watching the light fade from the sky and the twilight descend in a flat, colorless wash that enveloped like smoke. There was no sunset, no change in the look of the land and sky save an almost rushed transition from light to dark. The sensation it generated in Grianne was one of possibility draining into despair.

She pushed such dark thoughts away but could not change her feelings for the place. It was wretched ground for living things, a wasteland in which she did not belong. The pervasive feelings of hopelessness and isolation gave notice that for some transgressions there could be no redemption. If she lived another thousand years, she did not think to see a rebirth of life in the Skull Kingdom. Perhaps, given the types of life that might find purchase in such a land, it was for the best.

"Sleep," she told Kermadec. "I will keep watch the first half of the night."

He grunted agreement and was asleep in seconds. She envied him a rest that came so easily. She watched him for a time, his rough skin looking smooth in the darkness, his hairless body and nearly featureless face giving him the appearance of a smoothly faceted shape hewn from stone. Sleek—that was the way he struck her. Like a moor cat, big and powerful and smooth. She liked him better than almost anyone. Not so much for the way he looked as for the way he was. Direct and uncomplicated. That wasn't to say he was slow-witted or combative; he was neither. But Kermadec didn't complicate matters by overanalyzing and debating. When something needed doing, he spent as little time and effort as was possible in getting it done. He had a code of conduct that served him well, and she did not think he had ever varied from it. She wished her own life could be as straightforward.

Time slipped away, and Grianne watched the moon rise and

the stars paint the sky in a wash of white pinpricks. The rocks around her remained silent. The fire pit, its rings of rocks looking like hunched Gnomes in the gloom, sat cold and untended. Perhaps nothing would happen this night, the one night she was here to see it happen. Perhaps whoever built the fires and created the flashes had sensed her presence and would stay away. She wondered if she could force herself to keep watch another night if nothing happened on this one. She had no good reason to do so; her presence now was generated mostly by her instinctive reaction to the possibilities of what she feared might happen, not to what actually had.

Then, as midnight approached, the fire pit abruptly flared to life. It did so without warning or reason. No one had appeared to tend it; no fuel had been laid or tinder struck. It burned sharp and fierce on nothing more than air, and Grianne was on her feet at once.

"Kermadec!"

The Rock Troll awoke and rose to stand beside her, staring at the phenomenon without speaking. The intensity of the fire increased and diminished as if the flames were breathing, as if the air were changing in some indefinable way, first lending strength to the invisible fuel, then leeching it away. All around, illuminated by tendrils of light, the jumbled rocks became ghostly spectators. Grianne eased forward cautiously, just a step or two at a time, eyes shifting back and forth among the shadows in an effort to find what was out there. Something had to be; something had to have initiated the blaze. But she could detect no life, no sign of anything living save Kermadec and herself. Someone had lit the flames from another place, someone or something that did not need to be present to work whatever magic was intended.

"Mistress!" Kermadec hissed.

Flashes of light appeared in the air above the fire, sudden flares of brightness that suggested small explosions. But they made no sound and left no residue of smoke or ash, as if giant fireflies in the darkness. They were moving in circular fashion, widening their sweep and rising higher as their numbers increased. Below, unchanged, the fire continued to burn.

Grianne reached out with her magic to explore this mix of burning air and flameless light, using the wishsong to investigate what was there that she wasn't seeing. She found other magic at once, concentrated and powerful, dispatched from another place to this one. It was as she had thought. She detected, as well, that something was responding to it, something that was able to find purchase in this ruined land where it might not have been able to do so in one less poisoned. It was not something she could put a name to, but it was there nevertheless, pressing up against the fire and the light.

A face in the window, she thought suddenly.

Perhaps not just from somewhere in this world, but from another plane of existence altogether.

She probed harder with her magic, trying to break through to whatever was out there, to generate a response that would reveal something more. Her efforts were rewarded almost at once. Something small and dark appeared at the edges of the light, like a wraith come out of the netherworld, not altogether shapeless, but lacking any clear definition. It slid in and out of the light like a child playing hide and seek, first here, then there, never quite revealing itself altogether, never quite showing what it was.

Kermadec was whispering hurriedly, anxiously, telling her to back away, to give herself more space. It wasn't safe to be so close, he was saying. She ignored him; she was caught up in the link she had established between the foreign magic and her own. Something was there, quick and insubstantial, just out of reach.

And then all at once it wasn't hiding anymore. It was there, right in front of her, its face turned full into hers, edges and angles caught in the light. She caught her breath in spite of herself. The face was vaguely human, but in no other way recognizable. Malevolence masked its features in a way she had not thought possible, so darkly threatening, so hate-filled and remorseless, that even in her time as the Ilse Witch, she had not experienced its like. Dark shadows draped it like strands of thick hair, shifting with the light, changing the look of it from instant to instant. Eyes glimmered like blue ice, cool and appraising. There was recognition in those eyes; whoever was there, hiding in the light, knew who she was.

Grianne lashed out at the face with ferocious intent, surprising even herself with her vehemence. She felt such loathing, such rage, that she could not stop herself from reacting, and the deed was done before she could think better of it. Her magic exploded into the face, which disappeared instantly, taking with it the flashes and the burning air, leaving only darkness and the lingering smell of expended magic.

She compressed her lips tightly, fighting back the snarl forming on them, consumed by the feelings this thing had generated. It was all she could do to pull herself together and turn back to an obviously unnerved Kermadec.

"Are you all right?" he asked at once.

She nodded. "But I wasn't for a moment, old bear. That thing radiated such evil that I think letting it come even that near was a serious mistake. If I didn't know better, I would say it lured me here."

Which it had, she knew at once, though she would not say so to him. It had known she would come, would respond to its advances, and would step close enough to feel it. It wanted her to know it was there. But why? What did it want? Where did it hide that she could not find it, and that it could not do more than it had?

"Do we stay here another night?" the Rock Troll asked cautiously.

She shook her head. "I think we've seen all we are going to see. We'll fly to Paranor at first light. I'll find better answers back there to what is happening."

THREE

"We've talked enough!" Shadea a'Ru snapped irritably. "How much more talking does it need? This is the best chance we'll get!"

No one said anything in response. No one cared to be the first to speak. She was a big woman, and she dominated with her size as much as with the force of her personality. Fully six feet tall, broad-shouldered and strong, she had fought in the front lines on the Prekkendorran for two years, and none of them had survived anything nearly as terrible as that. The contrasting hues of her sun-browned skin, smooth and dusky, and wind-blown blond hair, short-cropped and uncombed, gave her a look of good health and vitality. When she stepped into any room, heads turned in her direction and conversation slowed.

Here, however, the reaction was different. Here, they all knew her too well to be much more than cautious. She looked from face to face, her calculating blue eyes searching out signs of doubt or hesitation, challenging them to try to hide it from her. Their responses were as different as they were. Terek Molt disdained even to look at her, his flat, hard features directed toward the doorway of the room that concealed their secret meeting. Iridia Eleri's stunningly perfect features had a cool, distant look. Neither Dwarf nor Elf had ever demonstrated any hesitation in their joint endeavor. Either would have undertaken the effort alone long ago but for Shadea's insistence on unity.

Traunt Rowan and Pyson Wence glanced uneasily at each other. The problem lay with the Southlander and the Gnome. *Cowards,* she thought angrily, though she knew better than to say so to their faces.

"Act in haste, regret at leisure, Shadea," the former offered softly, shrugging.

She wanted to kill him. He was the only one of them who would dare to speak to her like that, and he did so for no better reason than to demonstrate that she could push him only so far before he would dig in his heels. He wanted this as much as she did, as all of them did, but he was too cautious for his own good. It came out of being the child of Federation functionaries; the fewer chances you took in that world, the better off you were.

"Please don't fall back on platitudes to justify your reluctance to do what is necessary!" she snapped in reply. "You're better than that, Traunt. Smarter than that. We can nose this matter about like a dog with an old bone for as long as you wish, but it won't change a thing. Nothing will happen to improve matters unless we make it happen."

"She smells out plots like ours," Pyson Wence said, his small hands gesturing for emphasis. "Step wrong with her, and you might find yourself down here for good!"

They were deep underground in the cellars of Paranor, gathered in one of the rooms used primarily for storage. The room smelled of dust and the air was cold and stale to the taste. Stone walls locked them away beneath tons of rock and earth, a safehold that few ever bothered to visit save to retrieve stores. It was the one place in Paranor where some degree of privacy was assured.

They had been meeting for almost a year, just the five of them. Shadea a'Ru had carefully selected the other four, discovering where their loyalties lay, then approached them one by one. Each shared her distaste for the Ard Rhys. One hated her openly. All wanted her gone, if for widely differing reasons. To some extent, they complemented each other, each bringing an attribute to the endeavor that the others lacked. The Southlander, Traunt Rowan, was strong of heart and body, more than a match even for Shadea—a warrior seeking to put right what he perceived as wrong. The Elven sorceress, Iridia Eleri, was cold of heart and hot of temper, but quick-witted and intuitive, as well. Her ability to stanch her emotions masked the dark truths that had set her on this path. The Dwarf, Terek Mott, while stolid and taciturn in the manner of Dwarves, was hungry for power and anxious to find a way to get past the Ard Rhys' rules and restrictions so that he could claim the destiny he so desperately craved. Pyson Wence, so frail and helpless-looking, was a snake trapped in a supplicant's body, a rare combination of treacherous instinct and decisive purpose. No superstitious tribal pagan, he wielded his magic in a cold and calculating fashion.

Had the Ard Rhys any inkling of their true dispositions when she accepted them into the order? Shadea a'Ru could not be certain. It was possible, if only because Grianne Ohmsford herself had been such a dark creature for so long—the Ilse Witch, the Morgawr's tool. She had found redemption, she believed, and so thought others could find it, as well. She was mistaken on both counts, but that was to the advantage of those gathered in this room, those who waited only on fate to provide them with the chance they needed to be rid of her.

As perhaps it did here, if their impatient leader could gain the pledge of support she required.

"You want her gone, don't you?" she asked Pyson Wence pointedly. "Dead or otherwise, but gone?" She looked around. "How about the rest of you? Changed your minds about her? Decided you like having her as Ard Rhys? Come! Speak up!"

"No one in this room and few outside of it want Grianne Ohmsford as Ard Rhys, Shadea." Traunt Rowan looked bored. "We've covered this ground before, all of it. What keeps us from acting is the possibility of failure—a very real possibility, I might point out. Failure means no second chance. So before you start berating us for our reluctance, try to see the reality of the situation a little more clearly. When we act against her, we had better be very certain that we will succeed."

The weight of her stare settled on him and she did not remove it for long seconds. The others shifted uncomfortably, but they said nothing for fear her eyes would seek them out instead. Traunt Rowan, to his credit, held her gaze, but she could see the uncertainty mirrored in his eyes. She might do anything; that was her reputation. If you provoked Shadea a'Ru—something not at all hard to do—you did so at great risk. One who had tested her had already disappeared. Everyone suspected that she might have caused that disappearance, even the Ard Rhys, but no one could prove it.

"I would not summon you with such urgency," she said, speaking to Traunt, but including all of them with a quick shift of her eyes, "if I did not have a way to dispose of her that would pose no risk at all to any of us. I am aware of the possibility of failure. No matter how carefully we plan and execute, something can always go wrong. The trick is to make certain that even if that happens, no suspicion or blame will fall on us. But in this instance, I do not think we will fail. I think we will succeed better than we had hoped. Are you ready to hear me out?"

All nodded or at least kept quiet. Terek Molt never agreed or disagreed with anything. He simply stayed or walked away. Dwarves were given to physical gestures over words, which suited her fine. They were given to directness, as well, and it was good to have at least one of those among so many dissemblers.

"Wait!" Iridia hissed suddenly, one hand lifting sharply.

She rose from her bench, crossed the room to the door, and put her ear against it. The door was ironbound oak two inches thick and sealed with magic to prevent even the faintest echo of their voices from escaping. None of them cared to have even the smallest whisper drift beyond this chamber. The Ard Rhys already suspected they were plotting against her; what saved them was that others were doing so, as well. There was no time for Grianne to deal with all of them. Still, if she was ever to discover the particulars of this specific plot, they would be dealt with swiftly and thoroughly. The Ard Rhys might claim to no longer be the Ilse Witch, but she could revert in the blink of an eye. Not even Shadea a'Ru cared to go up against her if that happened.

That was a good part of the problem, of course. That Grianne Ohmsford was not simply the Ard Rhys, but that she was the Ilse Witch, too. It was not something any who had come to Paranor to join the Druid order could ignore. The past was the past, but it was always with you. She might claim to be a changed woman, having taken up the Ard Rhys mantle at the behest of Walker Boh, having been given the blessing of Druids dead and gone, and having pledged herself to reestablish the Druid Council as a viable force in the Four Lands. She might claim to be committed to helping the Races become strong, independent, and peaceful neighbors, to putting an end to the war between the Free-born and the

Federation, and to reintroducing a mix of science and magic into the world for the betterment of all men and women. She might claim anything she wished, but that didn't change what everyone knew about her past. It didn't erase what she had done. In some cases, nothing could. It was too close, too personal—as with Traunt Rowan and Iridia Eleri, the two among these conspirators who sought vengeance for acts committed by the Ilse Witch and forgotten by the Ard Rhys. The others were simply hungry to employ their magic and sate their ambitions in ways that were forbidden. But for each, to realize desires meant getting rid of Grianne.

This tension didn't start and end with the five gathered in secret here. It manifested itself in other splinter groups, as well, all of them working to achieve something secret, all of them with goals and hungers that were in some way in conflict with the Third Druid Council as Grianne Ohmsford had conceived it. It wasn't a question of *if* she would be done away with; it was merely a question of *when*.

And a question of who would prove clever and bold enough to make it happen, of course. And then be strong enough to take charge of the order, once she was gone and a new Ard Rhys was needed.

Some part of Shadea a'Ru, some tiny bit of reason shoved far back into the darker corners of her consciousness, accepted that not all of those who had come to Paranor to begin life as Druids felt as she did. Some admired Grianne and believed her right for the position—strong, determined, tested, and unafraid. But Shadea a'Ru would not allow herself to think well of those because to do so might give credibility to their loyalty, and she believed that to be a weakness she could not afford. Better to see them as sycophants and deceivers and to plan for their removal, as well, once the path was clear to do so.

Iridia was still standing by the door, listening. Everyone was waiting on her now, watching silently. "What is it?" Shadea asked finally, irritated and impatient.

The sorceress stepped back and stared at the portal as if it were an enemy that needed dispatching. Her distrust of everyone and everything ran deep and unchecked. Even Shadea herself merited Iridia's suspicion. She was beautiful and talented, but deeply flawed. Her personal demons ran loose through her predatory mind, and someday they were going to turn on her.

"I heard something moving," she said, turning away, dismissing the matter. "I just wanted to be certain the warding was still in place."

"You set it yourself," Shadea pointed out.

Iridia did not look at her. "It could have been tampered with. Better to be sure." She returned to the bench and sat down. For a moment, she said nothing more. Then she glanced up at Shadea, as if remembering her. "What were you saying?"

"She was saying she has found a way to solve our problem with the Ard Rhys." Traunt Rowan picked up the loose thread of the conversation with his calming voice. "Without posing any danger to us."

"There is a potion I have a chance to obtain," Shadea told them. "Mixed with a spell, it produces a magic strong enough to work against anyone, no matter how well prepared they are. The potion is called liquid night. Together with the spell, it will dispatch the intended victim to another place. It doesn't kill them; they simply disappear. No blame attaches because there is no body. There isn't even a residue to tell any searchers what happened. Everything disappears in a few hours, victim and magic alike."

Pyson shook his head. "There is no such magic. I know most, have read about the ones I do not know, and I have never heard of liquid night."

"That is because it isn't from this world," Shadea said. "It is from the world into which I am sending the Ard Rhys."

They stared at her with a mix of expressions. "What world would that be?" Traunt Rowan asked finally.

She shook her head. "Oh, no, Traunt. I don't give you anything more until after I have your word that you are committed to me and to what I am proposing. I am the one who sought the potion out, and I intend to keep the particulars my own. All you need to know is that once I have implemented it, you will never see the Ard Rhys again."

"But she will not be dead," Pyson Wence persisted doubtfully. "If she is not dead, there is always a chance she can find her way back. She has more lives than a cat. You know her history, Shadea. She is not like anyone else. I like her no better than you, but I respect her ability to stay alive."

Shadea nodded in agreement. *Idiot.* "She won't be coming back from where I intend to send her, Pyson. No one comes back from where she will be going. Besides, she won't stay alive long enough to do much about her situation in any case. There are things there far more dangerous than the Ilse Witch. Once gone, she will never come back."

They were intrigued, interested, but still hesitant. Except for Terek Molt, who was nodding vigorously. "Do it, I say. If you have a way to eliminate her, woman, do it!"

"When will this happen?" Iridia asked.

"When she returns, two or three nights from now. I can have everything in place before then. It will happen while she sleeps, so smoothly and silently that she will not wake again in this world."

"If you have this all ready, or can make it ready, why do you have need of us?" Traunt Rowan asked. "This was begun as a joint endeavor, but it seems to me that you have taken over the effort yourself. We no longer have anything you need."

She had been anticipating the question and was pleased to know that she was still able to keep one step ahead of them. "It might seem that way if you didn't think it through carefully," she said. "This effort will not succeed if we don't look beyond eliminating Grianne Ohmsford."

"You would have us make you Ard Rhys in her place," Traunt Rowan declared softly. "Wouldn't you?"

She nodded. "I am best suited for it. I command the most respect among those who must be convinced of the necessity of choosing a new Ard Rhys quickly. But do not be fooled, Traunt. I do not see myself as another Grianne Ohmsford, a leader standing alone and apart, needing no one. This is exactly what set us against her in the first place. She isolates herself. She sees herself as wiser and more capable, better able to determine what is best for everyone. If I were to take that route, how would I be any different?"

"You oversimplify," Pyson Wence said. "Our dislike for the Ard Rhys goes well beyond the way she holds herself above us."

"Indeed," she agreed. "But inaccessibility and the appearance of isolation will doom whoever stands for the position of Ard Rhys, once Grianne is gone. I need all of you to support me if I am to succeed. You each represent a faction of the order—you, Pyson, of Gnomes; Terek Molt, of Dwarves; Traunt, of Southlanders; and Iridia, of Elves. Not all of each, by any means, but a sizeable number. You are among the strongest of your respective Races, and you can bring support to me as such. I cannot serve as Ard Rhys and achieve what we have decided upon without your help."

"Why should you be Ard Rhys?" Terek Molt snapped suddenly, his sullen features tightening.

She kept her temper. Speaking out like this was his nature. "Because the order would not have you, Terek. They might have

Traunt Rowan, but none of the rest of you. And Traunt is not interested." She looked purposefully at him. "Are you?"

He shook his head, his lips pursing with disdain. "I have no
need to be leader of the order—only to see it set upon the right
path, one determined by someone other than her."

Grianne Ohmsford, he meant, but would not speak her name.
In his own quiet way, he hated her most. If Shadea had found a
way that would allow him to kill her himself, he would have accepted it without question. She often wondered what he thought
things would be like for him after Grianne was gone. What would
there be left for him to do after having burned so much energy and
devoted so much time to seeing her dispatched?

"Where have you found this potion?" Pyson Wence asked.
"Liquid night? If not from this world, if instead from this place you
refuse to reveal, how did you come by it?"

She shook her head. "No answers until I have your commitment, Pyson. It is sufficient to say that it will do what is needed."

"Someone gave it to you?" he continued. "You have a secret
ally? Another who serves our cause? Are you keeping other secrets,
Shadea?"

She was, of course, but he would never find them out. "No
more questions from you, no more answers from me," she told
him, told them all. "I want your oath, your Druid oath, your word
and your bond. Everything that you hold sacred stands behind it,
and we all bear witness to what you say. If I do this, if I rid you of
the Ard Rhys, then will you support my bid to be the new leader
of the order? Will you stand with me to the death to see finished
what we seek to do?"

Iridia Eleri rose, cold eyes sweeping the room. "You have my
oath. Let her burn a thousand years in her own magic's fire!"

Terek Molt grunted approvingly. "She's earned banishment a

thousand times over, and I care nothing for where she gets banished to. Get it done, Shadea. Put this creature out of our lives!"

There was a long silence. Traunt Rowan was clearly thinking, head lowered, hands clasped. Pyson Wence, sitting beside him, glanced over, then looked at Shadea, frowning.

"If you can do as you say, then I have no quarrel with your effort." His eyes shifted from face to face. "But if Shadea exaggerates in any way, if the power of the magic she proposes to use is less than what she thinks it is, then I want to be certain she does not exaggerate, as well, her certainty that nothing of this can come back to haunt us."

"How could it do that, Pyson?" she spit at him. "Would it bear our names spelled out upon its liquid surface? Would it somehow speak them aloud?"

He shrugged. "Would it, Shadea?"

"It is a potion supplemented by a spell. The potion does not originate in this world. The spell is one familiar to dozens and available to all who care to read and study on it. Nothing of either attaches to us. Stop equivocating! If you want out of this business, there is the door that brought you in. Pass back through, and you have your release."

Not that he would ever live to reach it, she thought darkly, waiting on him. Not that he would take half a dozen steps before she burned him to cinders. It was too late for backing away. Too late for anything but going forward.

Maybe Pyson knew this, for he made no move to rise, showed no inclination to do anything but ponder her words. He was so settled in place, so loose and comfortable with his legs tucked under and his arms folded into his robes that it seemed to her, infuriatingly so, that he might be thinking of a nap.

"I'll give you my oath, Shadea," he said finally. "But—" He

paused, cocking his head to one side, his sharp Gnome features thoughtful. "But I think my oath must be conditional on discovering where it is that you propose to send the Ard Rhys. If it isn't sufficiently far away or secure, I intend to tell you so and back out."

There were murmurs of assent to this, but Shadea ignored them, knowing that what she had in mind for Grianne Ohmsford would please them all. Once they heard, there would be no more mutterings. "What of you, Traunt?" she asked the Southlander. "You've said nothing."

"I have been thinking." He smiled faintly. "Thinking about how much we are entrusting you with. It seems to me that more than one of us ought to be involved in this effort—not just in the planning, but in the execution. It would require a stronger commitment, which is what you are looking for. It would give us all a sense of participation beyond what you have proposed so far."

"It would also entail a greater risk," she pointed out, not liking where his suggestion was going. "Two stand a greater chance of being detected than one. Whoever administers the potion and the spell must approach the Ard Rhys secretly. Stealth and quickness will determine success or failure."

"Two can move as quietly as one," he argued, shrugging. "Moreover, if one falters, the other can still act. It offers us a measure of protection."

"I don't intend to falter," she said coldly, openly angry.

"We'll draw straws to see who goes with you," Iridia said, siding with Rowan.

Both Pyson Wence and Terek Molt nodded in assent. Shadea knew when she was up against a wall. She was not going to get them to back off without arousing suspicion. "All right," she agreed. "But only one."

She rose and walked to a stack of crates containing serving ware packed in straw and drew out four strands. Breaking off three, she evened them between her fingers and offered them to the others. Terek Molt snatched the first. It was short. Iridia drew a short straw, as well.

The other two looked at each other, hesitating. Then Traunt Rowan picked from the remaining two straws. His was the long one.

"How fitting," Shadea sneered, "since taking part was your idea. Now give me your word, Traunt. Your oath and your promise as a Druid to stand with me no matter what."

He nodded, unruffled. "You always had that, Shadea, from the moment you told me what you intended and recruited me to your cause. I am as committed as you will ever be."

Perhaps, she thought. *But we will never know for sure because there is no way to test such a claim.* For her purposes it was sufficient that he was committed to support her as the new Ard Rhys after Grianne was dispatched. Once she held that office, and despite what she had told them to gain their support, they would all become expendable. Her plans were greater than they knew and did not include them.

"We are agreed then," she said, looking from face to face, seeking again any sign of hesitation.

"We are agreed," Traunt Rowan affirmed. "Now tell us where you intend to imprison the Ard Rhys. Where can you send her that she cannot find a way back to haunt us?"

Shadea a'Ru smiled at the looks on their faces when she told them.

FOUR

§

en Dunsidan was a cautious man. He had always had reason to be cautious, but he had more reason these days since he had more to lose. His life's accomplishments were impressive, but the price exacted in exchange had been severe and permanent. It wasn't the sort of price one could measure in terms of wealth. If it had been only money, he would not have been as cautious as he was. The price levied against him was a piece of his soul here and a part of his sanity there. The price was psychological and emotional, and it left him bereft of almost anything resembling peace of mind.

Not that he had ever possessed much of that in any case. Even in the days when he was only Minister of Defense of the Federation and in the thrall of the Ilse Witch, he had compromised himself in almost every way imaginable to advance his position and increase his power. Peace of mind was a benefit that did not accrue to those who lacked moral restraint. He was cautious back then, as well, but not nearly as much so as now. He saw himself as invincible in those days, too clever for anyone to outsmart or outmaneuver, too powerful to be challenged. Harm might come to lesser men, but not to him. Even the Ilse Witch, for all her disdain and aloofness, was wary of him. He knew how she saw him—how most saw him. A snake, coiled and ready to strike. He did not take offense. He liked the image. Snakes were not cautious. Others were cautious of snakes. It was beneficial to instill a sense of uneasiness in those with whom he was compelled to deal.

Caution came to him after he broke off his relationship with the Ilse Witch—betrayed her, in fact—and allied himself with the Morgawr, her warlock mentor. It was the smart thing to do. The Morgawr was the more powerful of the two and the more likely to succeed in their battle to destroy each other. Moreover, the warlock was the one who was willing to give Sen Dunsidan what he wanted most in exchange for his support—a chance at becoming Prime Minister. Two men stood in Sen Dunsidan's way, and the Morgawr had them killed in what appeared to be for one an accident, and for the other, natural causes.

But what the Morgawr claimed from him in the bargain was much more than he had ever expected to pay. The Morgawr forced Sen Dunsidan to watch as he turned living men into the walking dead, creatures without wills of their own, things that did only as they were told. Worse, he forced Sen Dunsidan to participate in the atrocity, to bring the men to him under false pretenses and to witness their destruction. When it was finished and the Morgawr had gone, Sen Dunsidan was a changed man. Even after becoming Prime Minister, even after gaining enough power that no one dared to challenge him, he never felt safe. Devastated by watching what had been done to those men, by being an accomplice to it, he could not regain the sense of invincibility he had once thought he would never lose. Worse, he could not take any comfort in what he had gained. He could not stop thinking about those men. He became obsessed with his own vulnerability; his need to protect himself against falling victim to what he had witnessed dominated his thinking. Emotions already blunted by his lesser crimes were turned to stone. His heart hardened and his soul shriveled. He no longer felt anything for anyone other than himself, and what he felt for himself was mostly fear.

With the passing of the years, he grew steadily more unsettled, responding to fears he could not control.

Tonight was one of those times.

He sat waiting impatiently in a reading chair that did not face the doorway of the room, but a blank wall. The room itself was in a place he had never thought he would visit. He was at Paranor, a guest of the Druids and, more particularly, of his onetime nemesis, Grianne Ohmsford. Twenty years ago, when she had returned from the airship voyage she had undertaken in search of a lost magic from another time, he had thought himself a dead man. She had destroyed his ally, the Morgawr, and would certainly have determined that he had supplied the Federation ships and men under the warlock's command. Had she been the Ilse Witch still, had something not happened to change her while she was away, she would have killed him at once. Instead, she had ignored him, retreating to the confines of Paranor, secluded with the shades of dead Druids, and had done nothing.

At first, he had thought she was playing a game with him and had waited stoically for the inevitable. But after a time, he began to hear rumors of a new Druid order and an Ard Rhys who would lead it. He heard that the Ilse Witch had forsaken her name and disclaimed her past, that she was no longer who or what she had been. It was too outlandish to credit seriously, the sort of rumor that invariably proved false. But men and women from all the Races were traveling to Paranor to seek a place in the Third Druid Council, and he began to wonder.

And then the impossible happened. She summoned him to a

meeting on neutral ground to discuss their relationship. He went because he saw no reason not to. If she wanted him dead, she would find a way to make him so, and hiding in his compound in Arishaig, or anywhere else in the Four Lands, wasn't going to save him. To his astonishment, she told him that the past was behind them both and it was time to consider the future. There would be no more dealings of the sort that had taken place before. There would be no recriminations for what was done. She sought instead to open lines of communication between Paranor and the Federation that would facilitate a productive sharing of ideas and solutions to problems of mutual concern—like the war on the Prekkendorran, for instance. She would give him what help she could in his new position as Prime Minister, sharing knowledge that would aid the people he led. In turn, he would help her restore the credibility and effectiveness of the Druids throughout the Four Lands.

It had taken him a while to adjust to the new relationship, but in the end it gave him back the life he had thought forfeited and so he was willing to make that adjustment. There had been other meetings over the years, many of them, with visits to Paranor by him and to Arishaig by her. Discussions had been held and trades made and, all in all, they had gotten along well enough.

Which never once stopped him from trying to find a way to kill her, of course. It was impossible for him not to think of doing so. Whoever she claimed she was, Ilse Witch or Ard Rhys, she was too dangerous to be allowed to live; nothing prevented her from reverting at some point to the creature she had been, casting off her new guise, her new identity. More to the point, he knew he could never control her. If he couldn't control her, he couldn't control the Druids, and controlling the Druids was essential if he was to govern the Four Lands. That was his ambition and his intention, and he meant to see it fulfilled. Only the Free-born stood in his way, but eliminating the Free-born meant finding a way to subvert the Druids. They claimed not to be siding with anyone in the Federation–Free-born conflict, but it was clear enough that however the war on the Prekkendorran turned out, the Ard Rhys was never going to allow either side to crush the other.

Sen Dunsidan had decided long ago that crushing his enemies was the only way to survive them. Leaving them alive after you had defeated them only gave them another chance to come after you. If they were dead and gone, you had nothing to worry about.

So he was in Paranor for yet another meeting with Grianne Ohmsford, for discussions concerning the Prekkendorran and the war with the Free-born and whatever else she cared to talk about, and none of it mattered to him because the meeting would never happen. It was scheduled to take place in the morning, but by then the Ard Rhys would be dead.

Or would wish she was.

It had taken a long time to find a way to eliminate her, and it had come about in a most unlikely way from a most unlikely source. Assassination had always been an alternative, but her instincts were so acute that she could sense that sort of thing almost without making an effort. Her magic was formidable, the wishsong of the Ohmsford legends, passed down through the bloodline, stronger in her than in almost any other member of her family, made so by her training and her life as the Ilse Witch. You might try to catch her off guard and kill her, but you would have a better chance at growing wings and learning to fly.

He had looked for other ways to rid himself of her, but no other solution immediately presented itself. Employing another magic to overcome her own was the logical approach, but he didn't know any magic and wasn't equipped to wield it if he did. Finding an ally who could act in his place was the logical solution, but with the death of the Morgawr and the formation of the Third

Druid Council, he no longer had direct dealings with magic wielders save for the one he wanted to eliminate.

Then help arrived from an unexpected source, not much more than a year ago, and he had not only his ally, but a spy in the Druid camp. The spy gave him a pair of much needed eyes and ears to monitor the Ard Rhys' movements. Sooner or later, he believed, he would find a way to get past her defenses, as well.

Now, he had found that way at last. Tonight, he would test it—without risk to himself, without danger of discovery. If it worked, Grianne Ohmsford would no longer be a problem. By morning, the world would be a different place.

Yet he was uneasy, not quite believing it would happen, afraid that his complicity in the deaths of all those men years ago at the hands of the Morgawr would take form somehow this night and devour him. It did not seem ridiculous that it might happen; it seemed almost inevitable. There was a price to be paid for what he had done, and sooner or later someone would appear to collect it.

He was thinking of that as the wall across from him slid silently open and Shadea a'Ru stepped into the room.

Grianne Ohmsford sat at the writing table in her chambers, making notes for her meeting with Sen Dunsidan, preparing herself for the bargaining that would take place. It was always a matter of give and take with the Prime Minister, a question of how much she was willing to give versus how much he was attempting to take. He had changed over the years in some ways but, when bargaining, still sought to extract more than the other party was prepared to give. A politician to the end, he remained outwardly friendly and forthright while inwardly thinking of ways to cut his opponent's throat.

Literally, in her case.

She knew how he felt about her. To him, she was still the Ilse Witch and that would never change. He was afraid of her, no matter how hard she tried to convince him that her time as the Morgawr's creature was at an end. She might be Ard Rhys of the Third Druid Council, but that was not how he saw her. Because he could not change old habits, she knew his fear would rule his thinking. That meant he would be looking for a way to eliminate her.

She didn't mind that. He had always been looking for ways to eliminate her, from the moment they had formed that first alliance, nearly twenty-five years ago. That was how Sen Dunsidan dealt with allies and enemies alike; he used them to the extent he could while searching for ways to render them ineffective, which often meant eliminating them altogether once they had served their purpose. In some cases he had been successful, but he had never posed a threat to her. He did not possess the tools to cause her harm, lacking both magic and allies to accomplish that end. Alone, he could do nothing.

Besides, he was the least of her worries. She had other, more dangerous enemies with which to contend, others with equally strong motives for seeing her dispatched, others living closer to home.

She didn't like thinking of it. So much hard work had gone into re-forming the Druid order, and now it was a nest of vipers. It wasn't what she had intended or envisioned, but there it was. Kermadec was right. Her position grew more tenuous with the passing of every day, and if the erosion of her authority continued, she would lose control completely. If that happened, she would have failed, and she could not bear even to think of that.

She returned her thoughts to Sen Dunsidan and the more immediate concerns of tomorrow's meeting. She was seeking a truce in the battle on the Prekkendorran, one by both Federation and Free-born, one that would result in a stand-down of both armies.

And that might lead to a gradual reduction in forces and a chance at peace. But neither side was showing much interest in the idea, even though after nearly fifty years of conflict it seemed almost inconceivable to her that they could think of anything else. Most of the people who had initiated the struggle were dead and gone. Only the inheritors were left, men and women who probably didn't have any real idea of the circumstances that had triggered the war.

Not that any of them cared, she thought darkly. War was often its own excuse.

A knock at the door announced the arrival of Tagwen. She bid him enter. The Dwarf shuffled in under a load of books and papers, which he deposited on the working table to one side, where she could pick through them. They were the detritus of her previous efforts to persuade Sen Dunsidan and the Federation to her cause. Tagwen studied the stack forlornly for a moment, then looked at her.

"Is he settled in his chambers?" she asked.

"Quite comfortably. He should be. He has the best rooms in the Keep." Tagwen didn't like Sen Dunsidan, a fact he didn't bother to hide from her, though he was careful to hide it from others. "I left him to his ale and cogitation. More of the former, less of the latter, unless I miss my guess."

She smiled in spite of herself. She rose and stretched. "Everyone is advised of tomorrow's gatherings?"

He nodded. "You meet privately with the Prime Minister after breakfast, then he addresses the full council, then he meets with a select few—you know them all and they know one other—and then you sit down for some serious bargaining, which will once again probably result in nothing much being decided."

She gave him a hard look. "Thank you for your optimism. What would I do without it?"

"I prefer reality to fantasy," he said, huffing through his beard as he met her gaze squarely. "Better for you if you did the same now and then. And I am not talking about your meeting with the Prime Minister."

"Have you been trading opinions with Kermadec again?"

"The Maturen sees things far more clearly than some people. He doesn't waste time on looking for ways to smooth things over when he sees it is a waste of effort. You ought to listen to him."

She nodded. "I do. I just can't always follow his advice. I am not in a position to do so. You know that."

Looking back at the stack of documents on the table, then at the half-eaten dinner sitting cold on the plates he had brought earlier, Tagwen didn't say anything for a moment. "He wants to know if you've decided yet when you are leaving." Tagwen looked back at her.

She walked to the window and looked out at the moonlit sky. Her rooms in the high tower were so far above the forest that wrapped the Keep that the trees seemed a black ocean stretching away to the Dragon's Teeth. She had decided that she would go to the Hadeshorn to seek the advice of Walker's shade about what she had seen in the ruins of the Skull Kingdom. Shades did not always give direct answers to questions of that sort, but they sometimes revealed insights into what was being sought. Someone or something was behind those fires that burned on air and in those strange flashes of light, and the magic invoked had come from a source she did not recognize. Walker's shade might at least be willing to tell her about it.

Wanting to see the business through and to make certain she stayed safe in the process, Kermadec had offered to go with her. She was happy for his company.

"As soon as the Prime Minister departs," she answered. "I would guess he will not stay after tomorrow night. Everything will have been said by then."

"Everything has been said already," Tagwen said.

"Perhaps it just needs saying again."

The Dwarf gestured toward the door. "Traunt Rowan is outside. He wants to speak with you. I told him you did not have time for him tonight, but he was quite insistent."

She nodded. Another thorn poking at her from the Druid bramble bush. She liked Rowan, admired his determination and willingness to work hard, but she knew that he did not like her. Sometimes she wondered at the source of his dislike, but she had never broached the subject with him. If she started asking everyone who disliked her why that was so, she would not have time for anything else. It pained her to think that so many in the order could not get past their bad feelings toward her. On the other hand, it said something about their resolve that they had come to study with her anyway.

"Send him in, Tagwen," she said. "I can give him a few minutes."

Tagwen went without a word, but his parting look suggested he thought she was making a mistake. She smiled. It wouldn't be her first.

She glanced at herself in the mirror that hung by the door, reassuring herself she was still presentable so late at night. Or maybe to reassure herself that she had not faded away into her thoughts, become a ghost woman.

Traunt Rowan knocked and entered at her bidding. He was tall and broad-shouldered and in his black robes looked less a Druid than a warlock. His strong features had a calm, distant expression that belied the intensity he brought to every meeting. She had been fooled by it at first, but knew better now. Rowan never did anything haphazardly or halfway. If he ever overcame his resentment of her, he would be a valuable ally.

He bowed stiffly, a formality only. "Thank you for seeing me," he said. "What I have to say is important."

"Say it then."

She did not offer him a seat or anything to drink. He was all business and would have refused both. When he was with her, he was mostly anxious to be gone again.

"I think you should resign your office," he said.

She stared at him, speechless in the face of such audacity.

"I don't say this to attack you," he continued. "Or because I don't respect what you have done. I say it because I think it will help the order if you do as I suggest. You are a smart woman. You understand the situation well enough. There are too many at Paranor who do not think you should lead them. There are too many here who cannot forget your past. Or forgive you of it. I admit I am one of them. Such prejudice hamstrings your efforts at accomplishing almost anything you undertake. If you were no longer leader, the prejudice would be removed. Another might do better."

She nodded slowly. "I don't think you intend putting yourself forward as Ard Rhys, Traunt Rowan. Who, then?"

He took a deep breath. "Whomever you name," he said finally.

It took him some effort to concede her this, and she wondered at its source. He was close with those vipers Shadea a'Ru and Iridia Eleri, who he knew she would never support, yet he had named neither. Why?

"You were chosen to form this order," he continued, his voice calm and persuasive. "No one could argue that you haven't done what you set out to do in bringing it to life. But perhaps you were not meant to lead it. Perhaps your purpose ended once the Third Council came into being. Another role might work better, one less visible in the larger scheme of things. Have you considered that?"

She had. She had considered every scenario that might break the logjam the Third Council found itself enmeshed in. But she still did not judge any other alternative acceptable under the present circumstances. Things were too unsettled for her to step down, too uncertain for her to let another take her place. To begin with, there wasn't anyone strong enough of whom she approved. The factions already established within the order would tear almost anyone else apart. Anarchy would claim the Third Council and destroy it. She could not allow that.

"I admire and appreciate your honesty and your boldness," she told him. "Not many would have dared to come to me with this suggestion. I don't know that I can do what you ask, but I will consider it."

He nodded, clearly unhappy. "I have never told you what brought me to Paranor, but I think you need to hear it now. It is no secret that we are not friends. You have probably already guessed that it has something to do with your past. My parents were Federation officials who became victims of your manipulations when you were the Ilse Witch. They were destroyed politically because of you. The reasons no longer matter. The fact remains that they died broken and despised even by their closest friends. Dannon and Cela Scio. They were members of the Coalition Council, at one time. Do you remember them?"

She shook her head.

He shrugged. "It doesn't matter. I took my mother's family name so no one here, especially you, would make the connection. My purpose in coming was to see to it that you did not subvert the Druid Council in the same way you had subverted other political bodies—to make sure that you really were Ard Rhys and not still Ilse Witch. I was willing to let go of the past if you had changed. I thought that might be enough. But it isn't. You are still linked to your past in the minds of too many, both inside and outside Paranor's walls. You are rendered ineffective by acts you committed before you became Ard Rhys. That won't change; it can never change. I have stayed on as a Druid only because I believe you must be made to leave."

The heat of anger rose in her face, a faint blush she could not prevent. "Your opinion does not necessarily represent that of the majority. Nor is it necessarily right."

"Resign your office," he repeated. His expression was suddenly hard and fixed. "Do so now, tonight. Announce it to all. Time does not allow for extended deliberation on the matter."

She stared at him in surprise. He was practically ordering her to leave. "Time allows for more deliberation than you seem willing to afford me. I said I would consider your demand, Traunt Rowan. That will have to be enough."

He shook his head. "It isn't nearly enough. I should have come to you long before this. Pay attention to me, Ard Rhys. Events have a way of piling up and stealing away our choices."

"Do they do so here? What are you trying to say? Why is this so urgent? Tell me."

For a moment, he hesitated as if thinking he might, then simply turned away and went out the door, slamming it behind him with such force that she felt the vibrations in the stone beneath her feet.

"Have you brought it?" Shadea a'Ru demanded as she stepped out of the darkness of the hidden passageway into the light of the room.

Sen Dunsidan regarded her with bemusement. "Good evening to you, too."

She took her time closing the wall panel behind her, watched it slide smoothly back into place, and let her temper cool. As impatient as she was to get on with things, it would do her no good to argue with Dunsidan at this point.

"My apologies," she said, turning back to him with a smile. "I am more than a little nervous about all this, as you might guess. I am also anxious to get it over with."

He nodded. "Understandable, Shadea. But haste often results in mistakes, and we can't afford to have any here."

She gritted her teeth against what she was tempted to say and let the moment pass. They were never going to have much of a relationship, Sen Dunsidan and she. The one they had was one of convenience and nothing more. As much as she wanted the Ard Rhys out of the way, she was only slightly less anxious to be rid of him. He was a treacherous, self-serving snake, a man who had built his career on the misfortunes and failings of others. She had heard the stories about his despicable uses of children and women, and she believed them all. Once Grianne Ohmsford was eliminated, she would turn her attention to him. But for the moment, they must remain allies, and she would play that game as best she could.

"There won't be any mistakes," she said.

She moved over to the table with the wine carafe and poured herself a glass. His room was rich with tapestries and rugs, with wine and sweets, and with good smells. It contrasted sharply with her spare and unassuming quarters some floors below. She felt no jealousy; finery and comforts were a sign of weakness. They made demands that caused one to lose focus on what really mattered. She would not allow that in herself, but was more than willing to allow it in him. It would make it easier to break him down and destroy him when the time to do so arrived.

"How do you know that the potion you have brought me works as you think? What if you have been betrayed?"

She watched for a reaction. He merely shrugged. "I haven't tested it myself, but I am assured it is lethally effective."

"Assured by whom?" she asked. "Who gave you this 'liquid

night,' Prime Minister?" she pressed. "You didn't mix it up yourself. Such a potion requires magic, and you have none. Who do you know who has such magic? Did someone at Paranor assist you? Someone not allied with me? Do you play us against each other?"

His leonine features lifted slightly. "I don't discuss my alliances. What does it matter, anyway? If it doesn't work, what have you lost? Only a little of your time. I will have lost your trust completely. I am the one at risk, Shadea."

He lifted his own wineglass and toasted her. "But it will work. By morning, the Ard Rhys will be a memory and all the talk will be of you, the new Ard Rhys. I know something of how this works, Shadea. I know because it happened to me when I coveted the position of Prime Minister. The order will be frightened and confused. It will be looking for direction and for someone to supply it. No one else has the backing you possess. The matter will be settled quickly. I salute you, Ard Rhys to be."

She ignored his patronizing, wondering how she could find out who had given him the potion. She would find out, she had decided. But short of torturing him on the spot, she would not find out immediately. She would have to bide her time, something at which she had gotten quite good.

"Let's not get ahead of ourselves, Prime Minister." She finished the wine and set down her glass. "What will you do when the news comes? Stay or go?"

"I will depart immediately, the expected reaction for a head of state when someone as important as the Ard Rhys disappears. It will give you a chance to consolidate your power before we have our meeting to arrange an alliance. Perhaps by then you will have discovered evidence of Free-born participation in the matter, and I will be able to use that discovery as a lever for pressing the war."

"Something you intend to do by any means possible." She made it a statement of fact.

He smiled. "The fortunes of war are about to change for the Free-born and their allies, Shadea. With your support, the change will come about much more quickly."

She nodded. The room, with its rich smells and opulent feel, was beginning to wear on her. As was this fool. "We have our understanding, Prime Minister. No need to discuss it again. No need to talk further at all, this night. Do you have it?"

He rose and walked to the bookcase at the far side of the room, moved several of the books aside, and extracted a small glass bottle with its stopper set firmly in place. The contents of the bottle were as black as a moonless night. Nothing of the room's light reflected from the surface of either the bottle or its contents.

"Liquid night," he declared, and handed her the bottle.

She took it gingerly and studied it a moment. The liquid night had an opaque texture to it that reminded her of chalk or black earth. It made her feel decidedly uneasy.

She looked back at him. "This is all there is?"

"A little is all that is needed. Nevertheless, use the whole of it. Do it while she sleeps. Do not let even a single drop touch your skin. Then carry the bottle away and destroy it. There will be no trace of what has happened, no sign of anything different. But the Ard Rhys will be gone. As if she had never been."

"You make it sound so easy," Shadea said, giving him a sharp look.

"It will be easy, if you do it right." He stared back at her. "You will be able to do it right, Shadea, won't you?"

"If there is any treachery attached to this gift, Prime Minister," she said carefully, "it will come home to roost on your doorstep."

He reached over for a set of notes he had been writing and began leafing through them. "A word of caution. The Ard Rhys has a brother who possesses the gift, as well. His magic is said to be the equal of hers. You might want to consider what he will do when he discovers that his sister is missing. I understand he went through quite a lot to save her during that airship journey west twenty years back, when he discovered they were related. If not for him, she would still be the Ilse Witch. That makes her an investment he might not be quick to give up on."

"He has little contact with her these days," she replied irritably. "He has little to do with her at all."

He shrugged. "Sometimes a little is all that is necessary where families are concerned. Brothers and sisters are funny that way. You, of all people, should understand that." His smile was smug and indulgent. "It just seems to me that where a potential problem exists, you would be smart to find a solution early."

He studied her momentarily, then lowered his gaze to his notes. "Good night, Shadea. Good luck."

She held her ground a moment longer, thinking how easy it would be to kill him. Then she tucked the bottle into her dark robes, turned away without another word, touched the wall to release the hidden catch, and left him behind.

F I V E

When she was behind the wall panel and out of Sen Dunsidan's room, Shadea a'Ru stood in the darkness of the passageway beyond and breathed deeply to calm herself. Any encounter with the Prime Minister was unsettling, but it was the task that lay ahead that gave her pause now. She touched the hard outline of the bottle inside her robes, to reassure herself that it was safely under her control, then gathered her thoughts. It would have to be done that night, while the Ard Rhys slept. She believed herself safe in her chambers, and she had been until that night. Rock Trolls under the command of Kermadec stood at her doorway day and night, and her own magic warded the chamber against intruders. The passageways that honeycombed the Keep behind its stone walls had been closed off long ago so that, aside from the windows, there was only one way in or out.

But Shadea had found a way to get around all that. The Rock Trolls outside the door were of no use if the attack came from within, which it would. The magic that warded the chamber was of no use if the attack was not something it could protect against, and in this case it wasn't. Finally, although the passageways had been closed off some time back, Shadea had opened a few very recently in expectation of what was planned for that night. She had started with the passageway leading to Sen Dunsidan's quarters, so that they could meet secretly. She had ended with the passageway that led to the chambers of the Ard Rhys. The latter had taken her nearly two weeks because not only was it physically sealed, but it was warded with magic, as well. She had broken down that magic, a painfully slow process, then restored it at its perimeter to give the appearance of still being intact.

She stared into the darkness around her, her eyes adjusting, her thoughts settling. Everything was in place. Everything was as ready as it was ever going to be. Her careful planning and preparation were about to be rewarded.

She allowed herself a fierce, predatory smile and started walking.

Shadea a'Ru had experienced a hard life, but she thought herself the better for having survived its vicissitudes and misfortunes. Surviving had made her strong of body and tough of mind. Without those attributes, she would not be where she was, planning to accomplish something that others could only muse about privately. Terek Molt aside, all the others had enjoyed privileged upbringings with advantages that she had never even come close to enjoying. She didn't resent it or feel cheated because of it; she reveled in it.

She was orphaned by the age of eight, her mother dead in childbirth and her father killed on the Prekkendorran. Shadea and her siblings were separated and sent to live with the families of various relatives, but she ran away at ten and never saw any of them again. She was big for her age and initially awkward, but she was always strong. As she grew, the awkwardness disappeared and her strength increased. She lived in the streets of Dechtera for five years, staying alive by her wits and her daring and the occasional kindness of others.

At fifteen, already close to six feet tall and the physical equal of anyone her age, she began hanging out at the Federation barracks, doing odd jobs for the soldiers. A few thought to test her resistance to their unwanted advances, for she was striking by then, but after they discovered she not only was big and strong but knew how to fight, they left her alone. A few took the time to teach her to use weapons. She was a quick study and naturally gifted. By the time she was twenty, she was already more accomplished than the men she had learned from. At twenty-four, she had served two years on the front lines of the Prekkendorran and gained the respect of everyone who knew about her.

She met the cripple the following year. He was of indeterminate origin, so gnarled and deformed that it was impossible to label his Race. She never learned his name, but names were never important in their relationship. He was a practitioner of the magic arts, primarily a weaver of spells. He was infatuated with her for reasons she never fully understood, and he was willing to trade what he knew for the pleasure of her company. It was an easy bargain for her to make. She stayed with him only one year, time that passed so quickly that in retrospect it always seemed impossible to her that it had really been that long. His health was already failing when they met, and by the end of the year he was dead. But before he died, he taught her what he knew about magic, which was considerable. He was a teacher in search of a student, but he was careful in making his choices. He must have watched her for a time, she decided afterwards, measuring her strengths, determining whether or not she would be worth the effort. Once he had decided that she was and further determined that she was not repelled by his looks, he gave her his full attention for the time that was left him.

He never told her why he decided to spend his last few months teaching her. He must have known he was dying. She thought that maybe it helped him to have a purpose in his life rather than simply waiting for the inevitable. She thought that he took pleasure in watching his own deteriorating skills put to use by someone still young and strong. Perhaps teaching was all he knew to do in his final years, and so he did it. Perhaps he found in her company something that was sustaining and comforting. Perhaps he simply didn't want to die alone. It was hard to tell, but she accepted his gift without questioning it.

Her natural affinity for summoning and employing magic was immediately apparent to both of them. She was able to grasp and employ the subtle art of spell weaving almost from the beginning, her comprehension of the ways in which words and hand movements worked together enabling her to cast simple spells from their first session. The old man was delighted and actually clapped his hands. She progressed rapidly from there, all of it, at first, a mystery that offered such possibilities that she could not help imagining the secrets she would uncover.

After he died, held in her arms as he breathed his last, comforted in the way he deserved to be, she studied alone for several years, closeted away in quarters not far from her Federation soldier friends, whom she still spent time with regularly. But the Federation no longer held any interest for her. It was too regimented, too structured, and she was in need of freedom. She saw that her future lay elsewhere.

Her break with Federation life came about in an unexpected way. She stayed too long and perhaps spoke too freely of leaving. Some took exception, men she knew only casually and didn't much care for. One night, they drugged her and took her out of the city to an abandoned shack on the Rappahalladran's banks.

There, they held her prisoner for two days and violated her in unspeakable ways, and when they were finished with her they threw her into a river to drown. Tougher than they suspected, dragging herself to safety through sheer force of will, she survived.

When she had recovered her strength, she went back into the city, hunted them down one by one, and killed them all.

She fled afterwards, because the dead men most certainly had relatives and friends. There had been enough talk that sooner or later some of them would come looking for her. Besides, the incident had soured her on the city and the Federation and her life in general. It was time for her to go somewhere else. She had heard about the Third Druid Council and thought she might find a home there, but she didn't want to ask for admission into the order until she was certain they would not turn her away. So she went west into the Wilderun and the town of Grimpen Ward, the last refuge of fugitives and castoffs of all kinds, thinking to isolate herself and work on her magic skills until she had perfected them. Few came looking for those who hid in Grimpen Ward, where all hid secrets of one sort or another and none wanted the past revealed.

She stayed there until her twenty-eighth birthday, keeping apart from the other denizens, practicing her art with the single-mindedness that defined her personality. She expanded her field of study from potions and spells to the uses of earth power and the elements, particularly the summoning up of shades and dead things that could be made to do her bidding and to offer their insights. Her skills sharpened, but her emotional character deadened proportionately. She had never had trouble killing when it was required; now killing became a means to her magic's ends. Killing was inherent to the unlocking of many of the forms of power she sought to master. Whether of animals or humans, killing was a part of the rituals she embraced. There were other, safer ways in which to proceed, but none so quick or far-reaching in their results. She let herself become seduced. She hastened to her self-destruction.

By the time she met Iridia Eleri, an outcast and a sorceress like herself, she was deep in the throes of dark magic's lure and hungry for a larger taste. Iridia was already half-mad with her own twisted needs, her own secrets, and they formed a friendship based on mutual cravings. Magic could give them everything they desired, they believed; they needed only to master its complexities.

They decided together to go to Paranor and seek admission into the Druid order. They made the journey in a fever, but when they put forth their applications were careful to hide the inner madnesses that drove them. The Ard Rhys was surprisingly easy to fool. She was distracted by the demands of her undertaking as leader of the order, and her primary concern was to find talented individuals willing to serve the Druid cause. Shadea a'Ru and Iridia Eleri seemed to be what she was seeking. What she failed to perceive was that both women dissembled; they were willing to embrace the Druid cause, but only in so far as it was necessary for them to do so and then only for reasons that were peculiarly their own.

After the first three years of service, it was clear to both sorceresses that although Grianne Ohmsford possessed great power, she no longer commanded the authority of the Ilse Witch. She had allowed herself to become weakened by the constraints she had imposed on herself in casting off her past life. She was unwilling to take the risks or make the sacrifices that the witch would have been quick to understand were necessary. Neither Shadea nor Iridia had such compunctions. The order was foundering, and its chances of gaining control over the Races were diminishing daily. Shadea, in particular, was determined to take control of the order and to lead it in the direction she knew it needed to go. Having decided that there was only one way that could happen, she was quick to put

aside her oaths of loyalty to the Ard Rhys and to take up the mantle of active dissident.

For five years, Shadea had searched for a way to fufill her ambitions, to topple Grianne Ohmsford and to make herself Ard
Rhys. This night, it was finally going to happen.

Her steps quickened as she followed the musty passageway to
its secret exit, two floors farther down in a storeroom in which
bedding and pallets were kept. Excitement radiated from her smooth,
strong face, a palpable hunger that was fierce and alive. She would
not falter, she would not fail. If the potion was good, her goal
would be achieved and the waiting would end.

If it failed, she hoped only to escape long enough to return to
Sen Dunsidan and cut out his heart.

Grianne Ohmsford put aside her notes and writings, her rec-
ords of past meetings with the Prime Minister, her summaries of
efforts undertaken and mostly failed, and prepared herself for
bed. Tagwen appeared long enough to brew her a cup of sleeping tea, which she took regularly these days, and to straighten up
her room. He fussed about for a time, waiting for her to say something to him, which she finally did. She asked if he had taken Kermadec something to eat, which he had. Trolls took pride in their
independence and resourcefulness, and it was not customary for
them ever to ask for anything while traveling. It had to be offered
voluntarily. This habit was born out of custom and a history of being at war with almost everyone, and it wasn't likely to change
anytime soon.

Tagwen also reported that the Trolls guarding her room were
in place, something he did every night as a reassurance to her, but

to which she paid hardly any attention. She did not feel threatened at Paranor, her prickly relationship with some of the more
overtly hostile members of the order notwithstanding. Guards and
stone walls, warding spells and watchful eyes were not what would
save her in any case, should the need for saving arise. Instincts and
premonitions were what protected her, her own resources and not
those of others. Years spent as the Ilse Witch had sharpened both
to a razor's edge, and she did not think time spent as the Ard Rhys
had dulled either.

"Wake me early, Tagwen," she asked him as he prepared to
leave.

"I won't need to," he responded. "You will be awake before me.
You always are. Good night, mistress."

He went out quietly, closing the door behind him as if it were
made of glass. She smiled to herself, wondering what she would do
without him. For someone so small and seemingly inconsequen-
tial, he was in many respects the most important member of the
order.

She wandered over to her tea, sat down, and began to sip the
hot mix gingerly. As it cooled, she finished it off, hardly aware of
what she was doing, her thoughts on the coming meetings and on
the ramifications of what she hoped to accomplish. She let her
thoughts stray momentarily to Traunt Rowan and his strangely urgent request, but she quickly moved on to other matters. Resign-
ing her position was out of the question. She thought she would
elevate one or two members of the order to positions of greater
importance, among them Trefen Morys, who had demonstrated
repeatedly that he merited advancement. Gerand Cera was another possibility, but she wasn't sure yet where he stood on the
matter of her continuing as Ard Rhys. She toyed with the idea of
elevating Traunt Rowan, in spite of his attitude toward her. It
might serve to distance him from Shadea a'Ru and Iridia Eleri,

something that could only help him. They were the women with the most talent in the order, and neither could be trusted for a moment. Sooner or later, they would have to be dealt with.

Her eyes grew heavy with the drink, and she moved to her bed, slipped off her robe, and climbed beneath the covers. Her last thoughts were of the strange happenings in the ruins of the Skull Kingdom and her determination to discover who had initiated them. A visit to the Hadeshorn and the shades of the Druids might provide insight into the matter, and she had already made the necessary arrangements for the journey. As soon as the meetings with Sen Dunsidan were completed, she would depart with Kermadec, perhaps even telling Tagwen where she was going, just to see the look of disapproval on his face.

She was too tired even to blow out the candles on her writing desk, and so drifted off to sleep with the light of both still flickering brightly in the overlay of the chamber's deep shadows.

Night settled over Paranor, silent and velvet black under a wash of light from moon and stars that spilled from a cloudless sky. Most of the Druids were asleep, only a few who liked working late at night still awake in their rooms and study chambers, keeping to themselves. The Troll watch was in place, not only at the door of the Ard Rhys but at the gates of the Keep, as well. There was no real concern for anyone's safety, no anticipation of the sort of danger that had existed in the time of the Warlock Lord, but the Trolls were careful anyway. Complacency had undone the Druids and their protectors in the past.

Shadea a'Ru stole through the walls of the high tower, following the twists and turns of the secret passageway that led to the sleeping chamber of the Ard Rhys. It was well after midnight, and she knew no better opportunity would offer itself than the one she acted on now. She had swept the musty corridor of magic once again only two days earlier, during the Ard Rhys' absence, and she was quite certain Grianne had not had an opportunity to reset her wardings in the short time since her return. The sorceress moved slowly in the gloom, generating a small finger of magic light to keep from stumbling. She must make no sound in her approach, offer nothing that would alert the sleeping Ard Rhys to her presence. She must maintain the presence of a tiny mouse.

She was sweating freely, her body heat elevated by the closeness of the passageway and her excitement. She was not afraid. She was never afraid. It wasn't that she was reckless or foolish; it was that she understood the nature of risk. Failure in dangerous situations came about because of poor planning or bad luck. The former was something you could control, and if you kept your wits about you, sometimes the latter, as well. She had learned that for people like her, orphans and disadvantaged souls, gains were achieved mostly through risk. That was the nature of her lot in life, and she had long ago accepted it.

The night's activities would measure that acceptance in a way it hadn't been measured before. If she succeeded, she would have a chance at gaining everything she had wanted for so long. If she failed, she would likely be dead.

That was acceptable to Shadea a'Ru. For what was at stake, that was a price worth wagering.

She wondered anew at the source of the liquid night. It bothered her that it had come into the possession of someone who did not himself possess magic. Sen Dunsidan was a high-ranking official in a powerful government, but he lacked the skills and resources to obtain something so powerful on his own. He must have had help, and she didn't like it that help of a magical sort had not come from her. It meant he had another option and might choose to use it down the road, and that could prove dangerous to her. Still, he needed her. Without her, he could not hope to gain control of the Druid order, and without that, his plans for the Free-born could not succeed.

Ahead, the last stairway led upward to the tower chamber where Grianne Ohmsford slept. Shadea slowed automatically, her movements, her thinking, even her breathing, and calmed herself. Soundlessly, she climbed the stone steps to the landing beyond, then stood just outside the section of wall that opened into forbidden territory. She tested the fabric of warding she had left in place and found it undisturbed. The Ard Rhys had not bothered to see if anyone had tampered with her magic. She still thought herself safe.

A fierce rush of anticipation surged through Shadea as she reached into her robes and extracted the bottle of liquid night. Silence concealed her movements, extending from the place she stood to the chamber beyond and then to the Keep beyond that. Dreams and slumber blanketed the rooms of Paranor, where the occupants lay unmoving and unaware. She listened, satisfied, and set the bottle on the floor in front of her.

She was ready.

Carefully, she constructed a series of spells and incantations, setting them atop one another in the space before the door. One after another, she created them with movements and words. No one saw or heard. No one could. She breathed as if there was not enough air to waste on breathing, creating an intricate pattern of small, cautious inhales and exhales. Her life force became a part of her efforts, aiding and supporting. She kept her concentration fixed on the task at hand, neither wavering nor hesitating, working steadily and diligently at her task.

It took her almost an hour to complete the conjurings. Then she knelt before the wall and opened the skin of magic she had left in place, giving herself clear access to the secret doorway and the chamber beyond. She could hear the sound of her heart pumping her blood through her body. It seemed to her that she could hear the Ard Rhys breathing on the other side of the wall, deep in sleep but capable of waking in an instant.

She prepared to remove the stopper from the bottle of liquid night.

Her hands began to shake.

For just a second she faltered, thinking suddenly that she was daring too much; that she was overreaching herself; that her failure to accomplish what she was attempting to undertake was assured; that the moment she tried to place the liquid inside the bedchamber, the Ard Rhys would wake and discover her treachery; that she would have been smarter simply to feed the Ard Rhys poison and be done with it; that this more sophisticated execution would never work. How could it?

Furious with herself, she crushed her hesitation and doubt as if they were annoying insects buzzing in her ears.

She pulled the stopper from the bottle and poured it into the funnel she had created in the last conjuring of magic, sending both the liquid night and the spells that directed it into the chamber beyond.

There, it was done, she told herself, replacing the stopper once more.

She rocked back on her heels to wait.

Grianne Ohmsford woke just long enough to recognize that something was dreadfully wrong, that an alien magic had bypassed her wardings and entered her room. She threw up her defensive magic instantly, but it was already too late. The room was moving—or she was moving in it—consumed by a blackness that transcended anything she had ever known. She fought to get free of it, but could not make herself move. She tried to cry out, but no sound came forth. She was trapped, immobilized and helpless. The blackness was enveloping her, sweeping her away, bearing her off like a death shroud wound about a corpse on its way to interment, clinging and impenetrable and final.

She felt the shroud slowly begin to tighten.

Shades! she swore silently as she realized what was happening, and then the blackness was in her mouth and nose and ears, was inside her body and her mind. She struggled until her strength was gone and with it her hope, and then she lost consciousness.

Still hidden in the passageway behind the wall of the bedchamber, Shadea a'Ru listened to the faint, sudden sounds of movement on the other side, then to the enveloping silence that followed. She was desperate for a look inside, but didn't dare to open the passageway door for fear of what she would find. She held her breath, listening as the silence lengthened.

Then a finger of blackness wormed its way under the door, the leading edge of a clutch of ragged tendrils. They twisted and groped as if seeking to snare her, as if the Ard Rhys was not enough, and Shadea stepped back quickly, poised to flee. She did not know what it was—some residue of the liquid night, perhaps—but she wasn't about to find out. The fingers stretched a bit farther, crooking toward her, then slowly retreated and disappeared back beneath the door.

Shadea a'Ru was sweating heavily, the tunic beneath her Druid robes drenched. Something had happened in the Ard Rhys' bedchamber, something that was the result of what Shadea had done—of that much, she was certain. But she could not know the particulars right away—not until morning, perhaps. No matter how desperate she was to find them out, she could do nothing but go back the way she had come and wait.

She exhaled heavily, quickly, a fear she had never felt suddenly caressing her in an all-too-familiar fashion. She backed away, still watching the door, retreating cautiously down the steps she had climbed more than an hour earlier, listening, listening.

By the time she reached the landing below and turned into the passageway leading out of the Keep's stone walls, it was all she could do to keep from running.

S I X

In spite of the chill she experienced even coming near the bed-chamber, Shadea a'Ru made certain she was among the first to discover that the leader of the Druid order was missing. She was there, waiting to speak to Grianne, when Tagwen appeared with breakfast. Employing her most subservient manner, she requested an audience at the Ard Rhys' convenience. Tagwen gave her his patented nod of agreement, the one that said he would act on her request immediately while at the same time wishing she would dis-appear into the earth, and entered the chamber. As he went inside, Shadea caught a glimpse of the room and saw nothing out of the ordinary.

Maybe, she thought suddenly, nothing had happened after all. Maybe the liquid night had failed.

But a moment later the Dwarf reappeared, looking confused and not a little concerned. Had the Ard Rhys gone out already? he asked the Troll guard. They said she had not, that she had been in her room all night. When Tagwen hesitated, clearly uncertain about what to do next, Shadea stepped into the breach and took over.

"Where is your mistress?" she demanded of the Trolls. "Why isn't she in her room? Have you let something happen to her?"

Without waiting for the response she knew they couldn't give, she brushed past Tagwen and went in, glancing around quickly. The bed was unmade, the covers rumpled and tossed. Last night's sleeping tea was set to one side, the cup empty. Notes for the meeting with Sen Dunsidan lay stacked neatly on her writing table, ready for use. A surreptitious glance at the wall behind which she had hidden and fed the liquid night into the chamber revealed nothing. There was no trace of the potion and none of Grianne Ohmsford, either. There was no indication at all of what had actually happened.

She spun back to face Tagwen, who had entered behind her, a furious look on his rough face. "Where is she, Tagwen?" she snapped, bringing him up short. "What's wrong?"

"Nothing is wrong!" he replied defensively, moving at once to the writing table to snatch up Grianne's notes. "You can't be in here, Shadea!"

"If nothing is wrong, then where is the Ard Rhys?" she demanded, ignoring his protest. "Why isn't she in her room?"

"I don't know," he admitted, a prickly tone to his words, placing himself squarely in her path. "But I don't see that it is your concern in any case."

"It is the concern of all of us, Tagwen. She doesn't belong to you alone. When did you see her last?"

The Dwarf looked mortified. "Just before midnight. She took her tea and was going to bed." He looked around doubtfully. "She must have gone out."

"Without the Troll watch seeing her?" Shadea looked around as if to make sure the Ard Rhys wasn't somewhere plainly in view, then declared, "We need to make a search at once."

"You can't do that!" he exclaimed, appalled. "You don't know that anything has happened to her! There's no reason for a search!"

"There is every reason," she declared firmly. "But we'll keep it quiet for the moment. You and I are the only ones who need know of this until we make certain nothing is amiss. Or would you prefer we stand around doing nothing?"

Clearly at a loss as to what to do, he made no response to her unspoken accusation. Already she was assuming command of the Keep, and he could do nothing to prevent it. He didn't fully realize yet what was happening; his concern for the Ard Rhys was clouding his judgment. Had he been thinking clearly, he might have wondered at how quick Shadea was to act. She smiled inwardly at his obvious confusion. He would do better to forget the Ard Rhys and worry about himself. But he would come to that particular realization too late.

Under the supervision of the sorceress, the Troll watch conducted a search for the Ard Rhys. It took less than an hour and revealed exactly what Shadea had been hoping for: No trace of Grianne Ohmsford was to be found anywhere. At its conclusion, she demanded to know what Tagwen was going to do.

"You were the last one to see her, Tagwen, and she is your responsibility in any case. That is why you were selected to be her personal assistant."

Tagwen looked crushed. "I don't know what could have happened to her. She wouldn't leave Paranor without telling me. She was preparing for this morning's meeting with the Prime Minister just last night, when I brought her tea and said good night. I don't understand it!"

He was clearly holding himself responsible, even though there was no reason for him to do so save out of loyalty to his mistress. That was what Shadea was counting on. "Well, Tagwen, let's not panic," she soothed. "It isn't time yet for the meeting. She may have slipped away to do some thinking on it. She comes and goes like that now and then, doesn't she? Using her magic so no one can tell what she's about?"

Tagwen nodded doubtfully. "Sometimes."

"Perhaps she has done so here. You wait for her in her chambers and I will look for her myself. I will use my own magic in an effort to trace her movements. Perhaps I can read something of them in the air." She patted his shoulder. "Don't worry, she'll turn up."

With that false reassurance to placate him, she departed the bedchamber and went to the rooms of her confederates. One by one, she advised them that the plan was working. As expected, there was some grumbling from each over her decision to act alone, but their discontent was more than offset by their euphoria. The Ard Rhys was dispatched. Now they must begin to gain control of the Druids and the Keep. Once it became known that the Ard Rhys had disappeared, confusion and indecision would quickly settle over Paranor. A vacuum would open with the loss of Grianne Ohmsford's leadership, and no one would want to be too quick to step into it. Shadea's name must be the first mentioned as the logical choice, in part premised on her early involvement and willingness to take action. It must appear that of all those who might be called upon to take charge, she was the one in the best position to do so.

For that to happen, she must not only have verbal support from her allies, but also have demonstrated her ability to serve. The best way to accomplish that was to offer up a scapegoat to bear responsibility for what had happened to the Ard Rhys. Someone must be made to bear the blame, and she had already decided who that would be. Her confederates were to spread the rumor that the Ard Rhys had been murdered and that the Rock Trolls who guarded her were in some way responsible. There was no proof nor could there be, of course, but in the heat of the moment, many would find reason to believe it was true. A word here and there was all that was required. With enough talk, momentum would build in favor of that explanation, and it would take on the appearance of logic.

A fierce rush of elation surged through Shadea as she left her allies and made her way back through the corridors of the Keep to the bedchamber of the Ard Rhys. It was happening just as Sen Dunsidan had promised, as she had hoped, as fate had whispered to her time and again. She was meant to lead the order. She was meant to wield its power.

"Shadea a'Ru, Ard Rhys!" she whispered to the walls and shadows marking her passage.

She found herself wondering if Grianne Ohmsford had awakened yet and discovered where she was. Perhaps the hapless Ard Rhys would not get a chance to come awake, but while she still slept would be set upon by the denizens of the place to which she had been dispatched. Perhaps she was already dead.

Shadea wished she could be there to see it for herself.

Tagwen had served the Ard Rhys for almost the whole of her time as leader of the Third Druid Council, and he believed that he knew her as well as anyone alive. Even though he was her close friend and confidant, he understood that she could not tell him everything. No one who commanded the responsibility and power that she did could afford to trust completely in anyone. But he believed that when she wished to talk out her problems, to reveal her concerns to another human being, she thought of him first. So he found it disturbing that she would slip out of her quarters during the night without telling him. The longer he thought about it, the more uncomfortable he grew. Shadea a'Ru, as much as he disliked and distrusted her, might be right to worry. That his mistress wasn't back for her breakfast on a day in which she had such an important meeting was very unlike her.

A practical man, Tagwen understood the implications of her absence. She would not cast the day's meeting aside without good reason. She would never act out of haste or panic; she thought everything through first, considering the ramifications of her choices. If she had left her quarters voluntarily, there would be good reason for it. If she had chosen not to confide in him, there would be good reason for that, as well. But if she did not resurface soon, he had to accept that words like *voluntary* and *choice* had nothing to do with the matter and that something bad had happened to her.

He sat in her chambers for what felt like an endless amount of time, his uneasiness and discomfort growing, his patience slipping. He could hear the sounds of increased activity in the hallways beyond, a clear indication that the Druids were beginning to discover that something was wrong. Shadea had not returned from her search, a search he was not at all confident would succeed in any case, given the Ard Rhys' opinion of her. He walked around the room, looking at everything, trying to make some sense of what had happened. He didn't like the look of the unmade bed, the appearance of which suggested she had departed in a rush.

But no one could get into the room, he told himself in trying to shake off his fear that she had been attacked. The Troll watch was fiercely loyal, and the Ard Rhys had installed warding spells all through the walls to protect herself. If something bad had happened to her, there would be some sign of a struggle. Besides, no enemy could slip into Paranor without being detected. Wouldn't the watch have seen and sounded an alarm?

Unless, of course, the enemy was someone already within the walls. He rubbed his beard furiously as he considered the possibility. There were some who might take action against her, however misguided. Shadea a'Ru was one. But how likely was that, given the risk of failure and discovery? Any Druid who tried such a thing would have to be mad! He shook his head. It didn't bear thinking on too closely. Not yet, at least.

Suddenly it occurred to him that she might have gone to see Kermadec. The Rock Troll was still camped outside the walls of the Keep, waiting to depart to wherever it was that the Ard Rhys had decided to go. Something important was happening in connection with these mysterious comings and goings, the one planned for the next day and the one just finished a day earlier, so it was not so farfetched to wonder if perhaps his mistress was off pursuing that business again.

He was on his feet and moving toward the doorway when Shadea reappeared from the hallway and stepped inside.

"Nothing," she said, shaking her head in frustration. "I searched everywhere in the Keep and on the grounds outside, and there is no trace of her that isn't at least a day old. I don't like it, Tagwen." She looked at him thoughtfully. "How reliable is this Troll Kermadec?"

Tagwen was horrified. "Entirely. He is a trusted friend, has been so forever." He allowed his indignation to show. "Much more so than some others I might name."

"Yet he is responsible for choosing her guard, including the two who stood watch last night and now have no idea where she is." She cocked her head. "He was the last to see her outside these walls, wasn't he? Don't bother to deny it; she was seen. What was that meeting about?"

The Dwarf was furious. "None of your business, Shadea! I don't discuss the affairs of the Ard Rhys without her permission—with you or anyone else! Wait for her return to ask such questions!"

She gave him an indulgent look. "Perhaps I should ask Kermadec in her absence, since you seem unwilling to do so. Why don't you ask him to come up to her chambers to discuss what has happened?"

Tagwen realized two things immediately. First, that Kermadec would never set foot inside the Keep. He had made that plain enough quite some time ago, and he was not about to change his mind for Shadea a'Ru, whom he distrusted anyway. Second, if he were foolish enough to accept the invitation nevertheless, perhaps out of concern for the Ard Rhys, he would not come out again. Shadea a'Ru was looking for someone to blame for the Ard Rhys' disappearance. Tagwen felt that instinctively. Why she felt it was necessary—or her responsibility—was beyond him, but what was happening was clear.

The Rock Trolls had never been a popular choice as protectors of the Druids. Elves had been used traditionally, a practice begun by Galaphile during the First Druid Council. An Elf himself, Galaphile had felt more comfortable relying on his own people in the wake of the destruction of the Old World and a thousand years of barbarism. Elven Hunters had warded the Druids until the fall of Paranor at the hands of the Warlock Lord. When the Third Council was convened, it was thought that Elves would be called upon again. But the Ard Rhys did not trust Kylen Elessedil sufficiently to rely on him to choose her protectors. By the time of his death, she was already committed to Kermadec and his Rock Trolls. Perhaps she felt more comfortable with them because her relationship with Kermadec did not owe anything to politics. She liked the independence of the Trolls; they gave their allegiance only when they felt it necessary and did not give it lightly. If they were your allies, you could rely on them.

None of that history would help the situation if Shadea managed to manipulate it, as she obviously intended. The Rock Trolls had responsibility for the safety of the Ard Rhys, and the Ard Rhys had disappeared right under their noses. It wouldn't take much effort for the sorceress to convince the order that the blame should be laid squarely at their feet.

Tagwen glared at Shadea. "Kermadec won't come inside; you know that."

"I do," she agreed. "But if he doesn't, then I will take that as proof of his complicity in whatever has happened and dismiss him along with all of his Trolls. I don't want them guarding the rest of us if they can't do any better job of it than they did with the Ard Rhys." She paused, a finger lifting to rest lightly on one cheek. "Refusing to come into the Keep suggests he is hiding something, Tagwen. If he isn't, he should tell us so—all of us, who depend on him for our safety. Tell him I said he should explain himself, if he can."

"Who gave you the right to tell anyone what to do, Shadea a'Ru?" the Dwarf demanded, standing his ground. "You don't command the Druid order."

She smiled. "Someone has to, in the Ard Rhys' absence. My name has already been put forth. I will serve as best I can, but serve I will. I can do no less." She looked past him at the empty room. "Go on, Tagwen. Do what I tell you."

He started to object again, to say something so terrible it would leave no doubt about how he felt. Then he realized that an unguarded response might be exactly what she was hoping for. Something bad was going on, and he was beginning to believe that Shadea had a part in it.

He held his tongue. Better to keep his head. Better to stay free. Someone needed to tell Kermadec what was happening, to warn him of the danger.

Nodding curtly, he went out the door and down the hallway, his eyes downcast, his face flushed. A part of him wanted to run out of there as fast as he could and not come back. He was suddenly afraid, looking about as he went at the faces of those he passed, seeing suspicion and doubt and in some cases outright anger. As Shadea had said, the word was already out. Schemes were being hatched and alliances formed. If the Ard Rhys did not resurface soon, everything was going to go Shadea's way.

On impulse, he made a short detour to the Rock Troll living quarters in the north courtyard and asked one of the watch commanders to bring a dozen of his men to the north gates on orders of the Ard Rhys. The commander did not argue. Tagwen had carried messages of this sort to him before from time to time; there was nothing unusual about this one.

Once outside the walls of the keep, Tagwen went to the edge of the forest and called for Kermadec. He knew the Maturen was camped somewhere just beyond the north gates. Waiting, he rubbed his beard and folded his arms across his burly chest, trying to think what he could do to stop Shadea from taking control.

"Bristle Beard!" Kermadec called with a laugh. His guttural tongue was rough-edged and resonant as he stepped out of the trees and stretched out his hand in greeting. "What's the matter with you? You look as if you swallowed something sour. Could your day be going better, old Dwarf?"

Tagwen clasped hands with the Troll. "It could. But yours isn't looking so good, either." He glanced quickly over his shoulder. "Better listen carefully to me, Kermadec. I don't know how much time we've got, but it isn't much."

Quickly, he explained what had happened to the Ard Rhys, then what had brought him down to find Kermadec. The Rock Troll listened silently and without interrupting, then looked up expectantly as his watch commander and a dozen fully armed Trolls appeared through the gates.

"I thought it best that you not be left alone, whatever you decide," Tagwen explained. "I don't like what's happening in there.

Shadea is manipulating things in a way that suggests she intends to take control of the order. When the Ard Rhys reappears, this will stop quick enough, but in the meantime I think you are at some risk."

The Maturen nodded. "Shadea a'Ru wouldn't dare this if she didn't have reason to believe it would succeed. That isn't good. I don't know what's become of the Ard Rhys, but she hasn't been down here since she went inside after our return. I don't suppose it will hurt to tell you we were in the ruins of the Skull Kingdom, looking into rumors of strange fires and shadow movements. We saw something of them while we were there, a clear indication of magic at work. The Ard Rhys intended to visit the shades of the Druids at the Hadeshorn to ask their advice on the matter. But I don't think she would have gone there without me. Or at least without letting me know."

"Or me either, though she might not tell me as much as you about what she was doing." Tagwen looked put-upon. "But she wouldn't just leave."

"Something has happened to her, then," Kermadec said, anger reflected in his blunt features. "It may have something to do with what we witnessed in the Knife Edge. Or it may have something to do with what's happening here. I don't trust Shadea or her friends. Or a whole lot of the others, for that matter. Druids in name only, no friends to the Ard Rhys or to the Druid cause."

Tagwen hugged himself. "I don't know what to do, Kermadec," he admitted.

The Rock Troll walked over to the watch commander and spoke quietly with him for a moment. The watch commander listened, nodded, and disappeared with his men back inside the walls. Kermadec returned to Tagwen.

"I'm pulling all the Trolls out of the Keep and down to the gates. We will stand watch there for another few days. If the Ard

Rhys returns, things can go back to where they were. If she doesn't and we're dismissed, we'll go. As long as we hold the gates, we can keep ourselves safe. Shadea can order us out, but she can't do much more than that."

"Don't be too sure of that. She has command of powerful magic, Kermadec. Even your Trolls will be at risk." The Dwarf paused. "You won't go inside, will you? Promise me you won't."

Kermadec grunted. "Oh, come now, Tagwen. You know what would happen if I did. Shadea and her bunch would have me in irons quicker than you could blink. It would suit them perfectly to announce that I was responsible for the disappearance of the Ard Rhys. Neither truth nor common sense would prove much of an obstacle to the expediency of having me locked up until things could be sorted out. Besides, the matter is likely already decided. I'm to be cast as the villain, even if no proof is ever offered. Wiser heads would prevail in different circumstances, but not here. I told the Ard Rhys she would be better off dismissing the whole lot of them and starting over. But she wouldn't listen. She never does." He shook his head. "I can't help thinking that her stubbornness has something to do with what's happened to her."

"I wouldn't argue the point," Tagwen said. He was wishing he had been more insistent about her precautions while inside the walls. He was wishing he had stayed in her bedchamber last night to keep watch.

"I think I might go back into the ruins of Skull Mountain and take another look around," Kermadec announced. His blunt features tightened, eyes shifting away from the Dwarf. "I might see something more, might find something. I don't think I can sit around here doing nothing. My men don't need me; they know what to do."

"You don't want to go into the Skull Kingdom alone," Tagwen

said, shaking his head for emphasis. "It's too dangerous up there. You've said so yourself, many times."

The Maturen nodded. "Then I won't go alone. I'll take someone with me, someone who's a match for spirits and dark magic. But what about you, Bristle Beard? You can't go back inside, either. Shadea will have you in irons, as well, as soon as she thinks of it. Or worse. You're in some danger, too."

Tagwen stared at him. He hadn't considered the possibility of anything happening to himself. But he remembered the looks cast his way by some of the Druids he had passed. Anyone capable of making the Ard Rhys disappear wouldn't have much trouble doing the same with him. It might be convenient if he did, given the fact that he was likely to raise a considerable fuss if they tried to name a new Ard Rhys.

Which, he supposed, was exactly what Shadea a'Ru was trying to do right that minute. He was dismayed at the prospect. He could do nothing to prevent it.

"I'll go with you," he said, not much liking the idea of visiting the Skull Kingdom but liking less the idea of staying on alone at Paranor.

Kermadec shook his head. "I have a better idea. The Ard Rhys has a brother living at a way station called Patch Run on the Rainbow Lake. The family operates an airship service that hires out to fly expeditions into remote regions of the Four Lands. He and his Rover wife are airship pilots."

"I know," Tagwen interrupted. "The Ard Rhys told me about them. His name is Bek."

"The point is, the brother has the use of magic, too. He and his sister are pretty close, even though they don't see all that much of each other these days. Someone ought to tell him what's happened. He might be able to use his magic to find her."

Tagwen nodded doubtfully. "It's worth a try, I guess. Even if she shows up in the meantime, maybe he can talk some sense into her about what's happening at Paranor. We don't seem to be able to."

The big Troll reached down and placed his hands on the Dwarf's sturdy shoulders. "Don't be gloomy, old friend. The Ard Rhys has a lot of experience at staying alive."

Tagwen nodded, wondering if that was what matters had come to, that his mistress was fighting for her life.

"Let's find her," the Maturen said quietly. "Let's bring her safely home."

Shadea had dismissed the Trolls standing guard at the door of the Ard Rhys' bedchamber and was conducting a thorough search of the rooms, just in case anything incriminating or useful was lying about, when Iridia Eleri appeared. The Elven sorceress's cold, perfect features radiated triumph, and she gave her coconspirator a satisfied nod.

"We have approached them all and won them over, or at least the larger part of them," Iridia said. "Most have committed to supporting you as temporary Ard Rhys until this matter can be sorted out. Almost all are suspicious of the Trolls, wondering how they could have kept adequate watch and still let this happen. There is enough confusion and doubt that they are ready to blame anyone at whom a willing finger points." She glanced around. "Have you found anything?"

Shadea shook her head. "Tagwen took her notes when he left to convey my message to Kermadec. I didn't see him do so or I would have stopped him. He may have taken more than that, but it doesn't matter. We have what we want. Neither he nor the Troll will be back inside."

"Don't be too sure." Iridia's strange eyes had a hard look to them, as if her thoughts were of darker things still. "The Trolls have withdrawn from the Keep and massed at the gates, taking up watch. It looks like they are expecting trouble, but intend to hold their place for as long as they can."

Shadea a'Ru nodded slowly, staring back at Iridia, thinking that nothing was easy, not even now. "We'll let them be for the moment. After I've been named Ard Rhys, I'll deal with them myself."

"Kermadec isn't with them. I don't know where he's gone. Tagwen has disappeared, as well. We might want to think about finding them." Iridia stepped close, her voice dropping to a near whisper. "We might want to think about another possible hindrance to our plans. Her brother, the one who lives below the Rainbow Lake—if he finds out what has happened, he might decide to do something about it. He has her magic and strong ties with the Rovers. He could cause a lot of trouble for us."

Sen Dunsidan had said the same thing. For a moment Shadea wondered at the coincidence, then dismissed it as nothing more. It was a logical consideration for all of them, one she might have been too quick to dismiss before.

"Do we know where her brother can be found?"

Iridia nodded. "A way station called Patch Run."

Shadea took her arm and smiled. "Let's send someone to tell him ourselves."

SEVEN

Penderrin Ohmsford came out of his crouch in the forward compartment of the cat-28's starboard pontoon, rocked back on his heels, and surveyed his handiwork. He had just finished resplicing both sets of radian draws off the single mast to stacked sets of parse tubes mounted fore and aft on both pontoons, giving the small sailing vessel almost double the power of anything flying in her class. The stacked tubes were his own design, conceived late one night as he lay thinking about what he might do to make her faster. He was always thinking about ways to improve her, his passion for airships and flying easily a match for that of the other members of his family, and when your uncle was Redden Alt Mer, that was saying something.

He had built the cat two years earlier at the beginning of his apprenticeship with his father. It was the first major project he had undertaken on his own. It was a rite of passage experience that demonstrated he should no longer be considered a boy, although he was still only in his teens. The vessel he chose to construct was a twenty-eight-foot catamaran—thus the cat-28 designation.

It was a racing vessel, not a fighting ship, its decking mostly sloped and its gunwales low, its pontoons only slightly curved and lacking rams, and its sleeping compartment set into the decking right below the pilot box and barely large enough to lie down in. Its single mast was rigged with a mainsail and a jib, and all of its spares and gear were stored in holds in the pontoons.

It was a fast ship to begin with, but Penderrin was not the sort to take something as it was and leave it alone. Even with his parents' larger airships, the ones outfitted for long-term expeditions and rough weather, he was always experimenting with ways to make them better. He had been living around airships all his life, and working on them had become second nature. He wished his parents would let him fly more, would give him a chance at the larger ships, especially *Swift Sure*, their favorite, the one they were on now, somewhere out in the Wolfsktaag Mountains. But like all parents, they seemed convinced that it was better to bring him along slowly and to make certain he was old enough before he was allowed to do the things he had learned to do years earlier.

His full name was Penderrin, but everyone called him Pen except for his mother, who insisted on calling him Penderrin because it was the name she had chosen and she liked the sound of it. And his uncle, who called him Little Red, for reasons that had something to do with his mother and their early years together. Pen's long hair was a dusky auburn, a mix between his mother's flaming red tresses and his father's dark ones, so he supposed Little Red was an apt nickname, even if it irritated him to be called something his mother was once called. But he liked his uncle, who his mother had told him to call Big Red, so he was willing to put up with a few things he wouldn't have tolerated otherwise. At least his uncle let him do some of the things his parents wouldn't, including piloting the big airships that flew the Blue Divide. His blue eyes brightened. In another couple of months, he would get a chance to visit Big Red in the coastal town of March Brume and fly with him again. It was something he was looking forward to.

He stood up and surveyed the cat-28 one more time, making sure everything was as it should be. For now, he would have to satisfy himself with flying his single-mast, small to be sure, but quick and sturdy, and best of all, *his*. He would test her out in the morning to make certain the splicings were done properly and the controls for feeding the ambient light down through the radian draws operating as they should. It was tricky business, splitting off draws to channel energy to more than one parse tube, but he had mastered the art sufficiently that he felt confident this latest effort would work.

He glanced at the late afternoon sky, noting that the heavy mist lying over the Rainbow Lake had thickened with the approach of storm clouds out of the north. The sun had disappeared entirely, not even visible as the hazy ball it had been earlier. Nightfall was approaching and the light was failing fast. There would be no sunset this day. If the storm didn't blow through that night, visibility would be down to nothing by morning and he would have to find something to do besides test out his splicing.

"Rat droppings," he muttered. He didn't like waiting for anything.

He finished putting his tools back into their box and jumped down off the cat-28. It was in dry dock, tethered close to the ground and out of the water until he was ready to take her out for her test run. If a storm was coming, he had to make ready for it, although the cat was secure enough and *Steady Right*, the other big expedition airship, was anchored in a sheltered part of the cove. With his parents gone east, he was responsible for taking care of the airships and equipment until they returned, which wasn't likely to happen for at least another two months. It was all familiar territory to him, though. He had looked after things since he was twelve, and he knew what was needed in almost any situation.

What he missed when his parents were away was being out there with them. It reminded him that they still thought of him as a boy.

He carried the toolbox into the work shed and shut and barred the double doors. He was average in size and appearance, neither big nor small, his most striking feature his long auburn hair, which he kept tied back with brightly colored scarves in the Rover fashion. But the commonness of his physical makeup hid an extraordinary determination and an insatiable curiosity. Pen Ohmsford made it a point to find out about things that others simply accepted or ignored and then to learn everything he could and not forget it. Knowledge was power in any world, whether you were fifteen or fifty. The more he knew, the more he could accomplish, and Pen was heavily committed to accomplishing something important.

In his family, you almost had to be—especially if you didn't have the wishsong to fall back on.

He regretted its absence sometimes, but his regret was always momentary. After all, his mother didn't have any magic either; she was beautiful and talented enough that it probably didn't matter. His father rarely used his magic, though he had been born with it and been forced to rely on it extensively before Pen was born.

But his aunt? Well, his aunt, of course, was the Ard Rhys, Grianne Ohmsford, whose use of magic was legendary and who had used it almost every day of her life since the time she had become the Ilse Witch. She was so closely defined by her magic that the two were virtually inseparable.

He knew the stories. All of them. His parents weren't the sort to try to hide secrets about themselves or anyone else in the family, so they talked to him freely about his aunt. He knew what she had been and why. He understood the anger and antipathy her name invoked in many quarters. His uncle Redden would barely give her the time of day, although he had grudgingly admitted once to Pen that if not for her, the remnants of the crew of the *Jerle Shannara*, including himself and Pen's parents, would never have returned alive. His parents were more charitable, if cautious. His father, in particular, clearly loved his sister and thought her misunderstood. But they had chosen different paths in life, and he rarely saw her.

Pen had seen her only twice, most recently when she had come on his birthday to visit the family. Cool and aloof, she had nevertheless taken time to fly with him aboard her airship and talk about his life at Patch Run. She had made a point of asking if he sensed any growth of the wishsong's magic inside his body, but had not seemed disappointed when he told her he didn't. Her own magic was never in evidence. Other people talked about it, but not her. She seemed to regard it as a condition that was best left undiscussed. Pen had respected her wishes, and even now he did not think it was a subject he would talk to her about, ever, unless she brought it up first.

Still, magic's presence marked the history of the Ohmsford family, all the way back to the time of Wil Ohmsford, so it was hard to ignore, whether you had the use of it or not. Pen knew that it tended to skip whole generations of Ohmsfords, so it was not as if he was the first not to possess it. His father said it was entirely possible that it was thinning out in the bloodline with the passage of the years and the increase in the number of generations of Ohmsfords who had inherited it. It might be that it was fading away altogether. His mother said it didn't matter, that there were more important attributes to possess than the use of magic. Pen, she insisted, was the better for not having to deal with its demands and was exactly who he was meant to be.

Lots of talk and reasoning had been given over to the subject, and all of it was meant to make Pen feel better, which mostly he did. He wasn't the sort to worry about what he didn't have.

Except that he didn't have his parents' blessing to go with

them on their expeditions yet, and he was getting impatient at being left home in the manner of the family dog.

He walked down to the cove and did a quick check of *Steady Right*, tightening the anchor ropes and cinch lines so that if a blow did materialize, nothing would be lost. He glanced out over the Rainbow Lake when he was finished, its vast expanse stretching away until it disappeared into a haze of clouds and twilight, its colors drained away by the approach of heavy weather. On clear days, those fabled rainbows were always visible, a trick of mist and light. On clear days, he could see through those rainbows all the way to the Runne Mountains. Such days gave him the measure of his freedom. He was allowed the run of the lake, his own private backyard, vast and wonderful, but forbidden to go beyond. His invisible tether stretched to its far shores and not a single inch farther.

He wondered sometimes if he would have been given more freedom if he had been born with the wishsong, but he supposed not. His parents weren't likely to think him any better able to look after himself because he had the use of magic. If anything, they might be even stricter. It was all in the way they saw him. He would be old enough to do the things he couldn't do now when they decided he was old enough and not before.

But then, how old had his father been when he had sailed aboard the *Jerle Shannara*? How old, when he had crossed the Blue Divide to the continent of Parkasia? Not much older than Pen, and his adoptive parents, Coran and Liria Leah, had given him permission to go. Admittedly, the circumstances compelling their agreement had been unusual, but the principle regarding a boy's age and maturity was the same.

Well, that was then and this was now. He knew he couldn't compare the two. Bek Ohmsford had possessed the magic of the wishsong, and without it he probably wouldn't have survived the journey. It made Pen want to know how *that* felt. He would have liked to have the use of the wishsong for maybe a day or two, just to see what it was like. He wondered how it would feel to do the things that his father and aunt could do. Had done. He was curious in spite of himself, a natural reaction to the way things could have been versus the way they were. He just thought it would be interesting to try it out in some way, to put it to some small use. Magic had its attractions, like it or not.

His father talked about it as if possessing it wasn't all that wonderful, as if it was something of a burden. Easy for his father to say. Easy for anyone who had the use of it to say to someone who didn't.

Of course, Pen had his own gift, the one that seemed to have come out of nowhere after he was born, the one that allowed him to connect with living things in a way no one else could. Except for humans—he couldn't do it with them. But with plants and animals, he could. He could always tell what they were feeling or thinking. He could empathize with them. He didn't even have to work at it. He could just pay attention to what was going on around him and know things others couldn't.

He could communicate with them, too. Not speak their language exactly, but read and interpret their sounds and movements and respond in a similar way. He could make them understand the connection they shared, even if he clearly wasn't of their species.

He supposed that could be considered a form of magic, but he wasn't sure he wanted to designate it as such. It wasn't very useful. It was all well and good to know from gulls that a storm front was building in the west or from ground squirrels that a nut source was dwindling or from a beech tree that the soil that fed its roots was losing its nutrients. It could be interesting to tell a deer just by the way you held yourself that you meant no harm. But he hadn't found much point in all that. His parents knew about it, and they told him that it was special and might turn out to be important one day, but he couldn't see how.

His uncle Redden wanted him to read the seas when they went fishing, when they flew out over the Blue Divide. Big Red wanted to know what the gulls and dolphins were seeing that might tell him where to steer. Pen was glad to oblige, but it made him feel a bit like a hunting dog.

He grinned in spite of himself. There was that image again. A dog. The family dog, a hunting dog. Maybe in his next life, that was what he would be. He didn't know if he liked the idea or not, but it was amusing to think about.

The wind was whipping across the lake, snapping the line of pennants attached atop the trees bracketing the cove entrance to measure velocity, a clear indication that a storm was indeed approaching. He was just turning away to go inside when he caught sight of something far out on the water. It was nothing more than a spot, but it had appeared all at once, materializing out of the mist. He stopped where he was and stared at it, trying to decide if it was a boat. It took him several minutes to confirm that it was. Not much of a boat, however. Something like a skiff or a punt, little and prone to capsizing.

Why would anyone be out in a boat like that in such weather?

He waited for the boat to come closer and tried to decide if it was headed for Patch Run. It soon became apparent it was. It skipped and slewed on the roughening waters, a cork adrift, propelled by a single sail and a captain who clearly did not know a whole lot about sailing in good weather, let alone bad. Pen shook his head in a mix of wonder and admiration. Whoever was in that boat wasn't lacking in courage, although good sense might be in short supply.

The little boat—it was a skiff, Pen determined—whipped off the lake and into the cove, its single occupant hunched at the tiller. He was a Dwarf, gray-bearded and sturdy in build, cloaked against the wind and cold, working the lines of the sail as if trying to figure out what to do to get his craft ashore. Pen walked down to the edge of the water by the docks, waited until his visitor was close enough, then threw him a line. The Dwarf grasped it as a drowning man might, and Pen pulled him into the pilings and tied him off.

"Many thanks!" the Dwarf gasped, breathing heavily as he took Pen's hand and hauled himself out of the skiff and onto the dock. "I'm all worn out!"

"I expect so," Pen replied, looking him over critically. "Crossing the lake in this weather couldn't have been easy."

"It didn't start out like this. It was sunny and bright when I set off this morning." The Dwarf straightened his rumpled, drenched clothing and rubbed his hands briskly. "I didn't realize this storm was coming up."

The boy smiled. "If you don't mind my saying so, only a crazy man would sail a ratty old skiff like this one in *any* weather."

"Or a desperate one. Is this Patch Run? Are you an Ohmsford?"

Pen nodded. "I'm Pen. My parents are Bek and Rue. Are you looking for them?"

The Dwarf nodded and stuck out his hand. "Tagwen, personal assistant to your aunt, the Ard Rhys. We've never met, but I know something about you from her. She says you're a smart boy and a first-rate sailor. I could have used you in coming here."

Pen shook the Dwarf's hand. "My aunt sent you?"

"Not exactly. I've come on my own." He glanced past Pen toward the house and outbuildings. "Not to be rude, but I need to talk to your parents right away. I don't have much time to waste. I think I was followed. Can you take me up to them?"

"They're not here," Pen said. "They're off on an expedition in the Wolfsktaag and won't be back for weeks. Is there something I can do to help? How about some hot cider?"

"They're not here?" Tagwen repeated. He seemed dismayed. "Could you find them, if you had to? Could you fly me to where they are? I didn't expect this, I really didn't. I should have thought it through better, but all I knew was to get here as quickly as I could."

He glanced over his shoulder, whether at the lake and the approaching storm Pen couldn't tell. "I don't think I can find my parents while they're in the Wolfsktaag," the boy said. "I've never even been there. Anyway, I can't leave home."

"I've never been there, either," Tagwen allowed, "and I'm a Dwarf. I was born and raised in Culhaven, and other than coming to Paranor to serve the Ard Rhys, I've never really been much of anywhere."

Pen grinned in spite of himself. He liked the strange little man. "How on earth did you find your way here, then? How did you manage to sail that skiff all this way from the north shore? If you get out in the middle of Rainbow Lake on days like this, you can't see anything but mist in all directions."

Tagwen reached into his pocket, fished around, and pulled out a small metal cylinder. "Compass," he advised. "I learned to read it at Paranor while exploring the forest that surrounds the Keep. It was all I had to rely on, coming down through the Dragon's Teeth and the Borderlands. I don't like flying, so I decided to come on horseback. When I got to the lake, I had to find a boat. I bought this one, but I don't think I chose very well. Listen, Pen, I'm sorry to be so insistent about this, but are you sure you can't find your parents?"

He looked so distressed that Pen wanted to say he could, but he knew his parents used the wishsong to hide their presence in

dangerous places like the Wolfsktaag, the better to keep themselves and their passengers safe. Even if he knew where to begin to
look, he doubted that he could locate them while they were using
magic.

"What is this all about, anyway?" he asked, still unsure what
the Dwarf wanted. "Why is all this so urgent?"

Tagwen drew a deep breath and exhaled so vehemently that
Pen took a step back. "She's disappeared!" the Dwarf exclaimed.
"Your aunt, three nights ago. Something happened to her, and I
don't think it's something good. It hasn't been safe for her at Paranor for some time; I warned her about this over and over. Then she
went into the Skull Kingdom with Kermadec to investigate some
disturbance there, and when she came back, there was supposed
to be a meeting with the Prime Minister—another snake in the
grass—but sometime during the night, she just vanished, and now
I don't know what to do!"

Pen stared at him. He didn't know who Kermadec or the Prime
Minister were, but he could follow enough of what the Dwarf said
to know that his aunt was in trouble. "How could she disappear
from her own room?" he asked. "Doesn't she have guards? She told
me she did. Rock Trolls, she said. Big ones."

"They're all big." Tagwen sighed. "I don't know how she disappeared; she just did. I thought that maybe your parents could help
find her since I've done everything I can think to do. Perhaps your
father could use his magic to track her, to discover where she's
gone. Or been taken."

Pen thought about it. His father could do that; he had done it
before, though only once when Pen was with him, when their
family dog disappeared in the Duln. His father probably could
track Grianne, although only if she left a trail and hadn't just gone
up in a puff of smoke or something. Where the Ard Rhys was concerned, anything was possible.

Tagwen rubbed his beard impatiently. "Is there anything you can do to help me or must I go alone to find them?"

"You can't find them on your own!" Pen exclaimed. "You wouldn't have one chance in a thousand! You barely managed to sail across Rainbow Lake in that skiff!"

Tagwen drew himself up. "The point is, I have to do something besides sit around hoping the Ard Rhys will show up again. Because I don't think she will. I've pretty much reconciled myself to it."

"All right, but maybe there's another way, something else we can do." Pen shrugged. "We just have to think of what it is."

"Well, we'd better think of it pretty fast. I told you I don't have much time. I'm pretty sure I was followed. By Druids, I should point out, who don't want your aunt back, whether or not they're responsible for her disappearance in the first place. I expect they have decided I might be more trouble than I'm worth and would be better off 'disappeared' somewhere, as well."

He paused dramatically. "On the other hand, it is possible that they don't care about me one way or the other, but are coming down here to see about you and your parents. They know about your father's magic, just as I do. You can decide for yourself what use they might choose to make of it, should they find your parents before I do."

Pen was taken aback. He didn't even know those people, Druids with whom his family had not been involved even in the slightest. That was his aunt's world, not theirs. But it seemed that Tagwen believed the two were not as separate as Pen had believed.

He wondered what he should do. His choices were somewhat limited. He could either tell Tagwen that he was unable to help, confined to this way station by direct order of his parents, who had made it quite clear he was forbidden to go anywhere while they were away and made him promise he would remember that—

or he could break his word. It might be in a good cause to chance the latter, but he didn't care for the odds of his explaining it to his parents if he was successful in helping the Dwarf find them. That's if nothing else happened on the way to doing so, which was far from certain given the distance he must travel and the dangers he was likely to encounter.

He sighed wearily. "Let me think about this. Come up to the house for a glass of hot cider, and we can talk about it."

But the Dwarf's face had gone white. "I appreciate the offer, Pen, but it comes too late. Have a look."

He pointed out across the lake. An airship was making its way toward them through the drifting curtains of mist—a big, sleek three-master, as black as midnight. Frozen by the vessel's unexpected appearance and the consequences it heralded, Pen stared. All of a sudden, he wished his parents were there.

"Whose is it?" he asked Tagwen.

"It is a Druid ship."

Pen shook his head, watching the vessel's slow, steady approach, feeling knots of doubt begin to twist sharply in his stomach. "Maybe they're just . . ."

He trailed off, unable to finish the thought.

Tagwen stepped close, a smell of dampness and wood smoke emanating from his clothing. "Tell you what. You can wait here and find out what they want if you wish, but I think I will be moving along. Maybe I won't go out the way I came in, however. Do you have a horse you can let me borrow?"

Pen turned to look at him. There was no mistaking the mix of determination and fear he saw in the Dwarf's eyes. Tagwen wasn't taking any chances. He had made up his mind about the ship and its inhabitants, and he did not intend for them to find him. Whatever Pen decided to do, the Dwarf was getting out.

The boy looked back across the lake at the airship, and in the wake of the uneasiness that its dark and wicked look generated, his indecision faded.

"We don't have any horses," he said, taking a deep breath to steady himself. "How about a small airship and someone to sail her, instead?"

EIGHT

In that single instant, Penderrin Ohmsford's life was changed forever. Given what had happened already at Paranor, it might have been changed in any event, but likely not in the way his decision to go with Tagwen changed it. Later, he would remember thinking at the time that making the decision felt like a shifting of the world, not so much in the noisy manner of an earthquake but in the quiet way of the light deepening at sunset. He would remember thinking, as well, that he could do nothing about it because his family's safety was involved and he couldn't ignore the danger to them just to protect himself.

He took hold of Tagwen's arm and propelled him up from the landing to the dry dock where the cat-28 was tethered, telling the Dwarf to get aboard. There was no time to outfit her in the right way, to gather supplies and equipment of the sort a proper expedition required. He had her packed with spare parts, so that he could fix her if something went wrong out on the lake, but that was about it. He took just a moment to run into the shed for his toolbox, grabbing up a water container and some dried foodstuffs that he kept around to nibble on, then bolted back out the door.

He wondered for just an instant how big a mistake he was making. Then he dismissed the thought completely because he had no time or patience for it. Hesitation in circumstances like these always led to trouble, and he thought he probably had trouble enough with things just the way they were.

"Strap that safety line around your waist!" he called up to Tagwen, tossing the bag of foodstuffs and the water container onto the deck. "Stuff these into one of the holds in the pontoons!"

He worked his way swiftly from one tethering line to the next, loosening the knots from the securing pins and tossing the rope ends back onto the cat's decking. He did not look out again at the approaching airship, but he felt the weight of its shadow. He knew he had to get airborne and away before it got much closer or he would not be able to gain the protective concealment of the Highland mists and the low-slung clouds that would hide his escape. With luck, they might not even see him leaving, but he could not count on that.

When all the lines were unknotted save the one that secured the bow, he paused to look around the compound and tried to think if he was forgetting anything. A bow and arrows, he thought, and he rushed back into the shed to take a set from the weapons cupboard, along with a brace of long knives.

Rushing out again, he climbed aboard the cat-28, finding Tagwen, arms wrapped protectively about his knees, already strapped in and hunkered down in the aft hold of the starboard pontoon. It looked so comical that Pen wanted to laugh, but he resisted the impulse, instead scurrying to raise the sails to draw down whatever ambient light this gray day offered. There would be energy stored in the parse tubes, but the diapson crystals were small and not designed for long-term storage, so he could not rely on that alone to elude the larger ship.

He found himself wondering suddenly if its occupants would even bother coming after him. After all, they couldn't know who he was or what he was about. They were likely just to land and walk up to the house in the mistaken belief that the presence of *Steady Right* indicated that his family was still in residence. By the time they found out differently, he would be far away.

But what if Tagwen was wrong? What if the Druids were actually there to help in some way? Maybe those aboard the approaching ship were not among his aunt's enemies, but her friends. They might have come for the same reason Tagwen had come—to seek help from his father in tracking down the Ard Rhys. This could all be a big mistake.

He glanced at the Dwarf. Tagwen was staring out at the lake, his eyes wide. "We're too late, Pen," he whispered.

Pen wheeled around. The big airship was right on top of them, sliding through the entry to the cove to hover over the water in front of the docks. It had advanced much more quickly than Pen would have believed possible, which indicated all too clearly how powerful and fast it really was. It might even be a match for *Swift Sure*, although he didn't think the airship existed this side of the Blue Divide that was that fast.

He saw her name carved into her great, curved rams, bold and etched in gold. *Galaphile*.

"That's her airship!" Tagwen exclaimed in dismay. "Your aunt's! They're using her own ship!"

"Get down!" Pen hissed at Tagwen. "Hide!"

The Dwarf ducked below the gunwales of the pontoon, and Pen threw a canvas over him, concealing him from view. He had no idea what he was going to do, but whatever it was, there was no point in taking chances until he found out if the Dwarf was right about who these visitors were.

There was also no point in pretending that he didn't see them, so he turned to watch the *Galaphile*'s dark hull settle heavily into the waters of the cove. The skies over Rainbow Lake were darkening steadily with thunderheads and rainsqualls. It was going to be a bad storm when it hit. If he was going to make a run for it, he was going to have to do so soon.

He watched as a long boat was lowered over the starboard pontoon. Half a dozen passengers sat hooded and cloaked within, dark figures in the late afternoon gloom. Several took up oars and began to row, pointing the boat toward the docks. Pen caught a glimpse of their lifted faces as they strained against the oars. Gnomes, swarthy and sharp-featured, yellow eyes glittering and cold.

Something about the Gnomes convinced him instantly that Tagwen was right. He couldn't say exactly why, because he had encountered Gnomes before at Patch Run and on his travels about the lake. He stepped into the pilot box, unhooded the parse tubes stacked on both sides of the cat, and pushed the controls to the port and starboard thrusters forward just far enough to nudge the diapson crystals awake.

"Whatever happens," he whispered to Tagwen, his head lowered to hide his words, "don't let them know you're there."

"You'd better worry about yourself," came the muffled reply.

The long boat had landed, and its occupants were climbing onto the dock and walking toward the compound, spreading out in all directions right away, a maneuver clearly intended to cut off anyone trying to get around behind them. Pen was terrified by then, standing alone on the deck of the cat-28, the brace of long knives strapped about his waist and the bow and arrows at his feet pathetically inadequate for mounting any kind of a defense. He couldn't begin to fight off men like those. Funny, he thought, how quickly he had given up on the possibility that they might be friendly.

One of them separated from the others and came toward him. This man wasn't a Gnome, and he wasn't wrapped in their mottled green and brown cloaks. This man wore the dark robes of a Druid. He was a Dwarf, and as he pulled back his hood to give himself a better field of vision, Pen immediately thought him twice as dangerous as the Gnomes. He had the stocky, square build of all Dwarves, the blunt, thick hands and the heavy features. But he was tall for a Dwarf, standing well over five feet, and his face looked as if it had been chiseled from rough stone, all ridges and valleys, nothing smooth or soft. His razor-edged eyes found the boy, and Pen could feel them probing him like knives.

But Pen stood his ground. There was nothing else to do except to run, and he knew that would be a big mistake.

"Can I help you?" he called out as the other neared.

The Dwarf came right up to the cat and climbed aboard without being invited, an act that in some quarters was considered piracy. Pen waited, fighting to control his terror, catching sight of the heavy blades the Dwarf wore strapped beneath his robes.

"Going somewhere?" the Dwarf asked him bluntly, glancing around in a perfunctory manner, then back at Pen.

"Home," Pen answered. "I'm done for the day."

He thought he kept his voice from shaking, but if he hadn't, there was nothing he could do to steady it that he wasn't already doing.

"Is this the Ohmsford place?" the Dwarf asked, squaring up before him, much too close for comfort. Behind him, the Gnomes were beginning to poke around in the shed and under the canvas-sheltered stores and equipment. "Bek Ohmsford?"

Pen nodded. "He's away, gone east on an expedition. I don't expect him back for weeks."

The Dwarf studied him wordlessly for a moment, eyes searching his, measuring. Pen waited, his heart frozen in his chest, his breathing stopped. He didn't know what to do. He understood now why Tagwen had been so afraid. The Dwarf's gaze made Pen feel as if wild animals were picking him apart.

"Left you to look after things?" the Dwarf pressed.

Pen nodded again, not bothering with an answer this time.

"He must have some faith in you, boy. You don't look very old." He paused, a lengthy silence. "I'm told Ohmsford has a boy about your age. Penderrin. That wouldn't be you, would it?"

Pen grinned disarmingly. "No, but he's my friend. He's up there at the house, right now."

He pointed, and when the Dwarf turned to look, Pen shoved him so hard the Dwarf lost his balance, tumbled off the deck of the cat, and fell to the ground. Pen didn't think about it; he just did it, an act of desperation. He leapt into the pilot box and shoved the thruster levers all the way forward, unhooding the parse tubes completely. The response from the cat was instantaneous. It lurched as if it had been struck from behind, bucking from the surge of power fed into the crystals, snapping the bowline as if it were string, and careening directly toward the *Galaphile*.

Pen, braced in the pilot box and hanging on to the controls for dear life, had only an instant to respond to the danger. He pulled back on the port thrusters, swinging the cat left to sweep past the foremast of the Druid airship, coming so close that he might have reached out to touch her. Shouts and cries followed after him, then a volley of arrows and sling stones. The whang and snap of them caused him to crouch deep in the box, gasps escaping him in little rushes as arrows embedded themselves in the wood frame of his momentary shelter. The cat shot out over the waters of the cove and surged through an opening in the conifers to Rainbow Lake and the approaching storm.

What had he done?

There was no time to consider the matter and little time for much of anything else. He caught a glimpse of Tagwen flinging off the canvas covering and peering back at the flurry of activity on-shore, where the Dwarf and the Gnomes were rushing for the long boat. Pen's heart was pounding so hard he could hear it inside his ears. It would take them only minutes to reach the *Galaphile*, and then they would be coming after him. As big and fast as the Druid airship was, they would quickly run him to earth.

If they caught him now . . .

He didn't bother finishing the thought. There was no time for thinking about anything but flying the cat. He gave her all the power the diapson crystals could deliver, bringing her up to a little over two hundred feet, then turning her east down the lakeshore toward the distant Highlands and the heavy mists that draped those rugged hills. Concealment could be found there, a way to lose pursuit, his best hope for finding a way to escape.

"Do you know who that was?" Tagwen gasped from his shelter, peeking frantic-eyed over the gunwales. "That was Terek Molt! He would have cut you to ribbons! Still might, Penderrin Ohms-ford! Can this ship fly any faster?"

Pen didn't bother with an answer. The Highlands were still some distance away, and a quick glance over his shoulder revealed the dark rams of the *Galaphile* nosing into view out of the cove, al-ready in pursuit. Those Gnomes were sailors; they knew what they were doing. He had hoped that they were land creatures filling in, but he should have known better. Druids wouldn't bother using anyone who wasn't good at what was needed.

"If Terek Molt is behind this, then I was right about the Ard

Rhys!" Tagwen shouted, and then disappeared back down into the pontoon hold.

Pen canted the mainsail to take advantage of the storm wind howling across the water. The cat was buffeted and shaken by its force, but propelled forward, as well, riding the back of sharp, hard gusts. Rain was falling steadily, picking up strength as clouds closed about. The storm would help to hide them, but Pen didn't want to be caught out on the lake when it struck. A blow of that magnitude could knock a cat-28 right out of the skies.

He took her down to less than a hundred feet off the surface of the water, hugging the shore as he fought to regain land. They were well beyond the Duln and the mouth of the Rappahalladran, the Highlands already visible on their right, rugged and mist-shrouded under a ceiling of clouds hung so low that the horizon had disappeared.

"Penderrin!" Tagwen shouted in warning.

Pen turned and found the *Galaphile* looming out of the rain and mist, closing the distance between them far too quickly. How much time had passed since they fled from her? It didn't seemed like any time at all. Pen glanced ahead, then angled the cat to starboard, heading directly off water and inland, seeking the cover of the Highlands. If he could gain the hills, he would look for a place to set down, somewhere leafy and shadowed where he couldn't be seen from the air. But if one didn't present itself immediately, he would have to keep flying. On balance, his situation seemed hopeless, his chances so poor he couldn't imagine what he had been thinking to try running in the first place. What if Terek Molt had the use of magic to track them, just like his aunt? Druids had all sorts of magic they could call upon.

Pen, on the other hand, had none at all.

Straight into the mists he flew, recklessly disregarding what might be hidden there. Cliffs and rocky outcroppings dotted the coastline, dangerous obstacles for any craft and disastrous for one as small as his. He had flown the hills repeatedly over the years, but not in such poor weather and not under such desperate circumstances. He kept his eyes locked on the movement of the clouds and mist and listened to the sound of the wind as it shifted. White curtains enveloped him, closing everything away. In seconds, he was alone in an impenetrable haze of rain and mist.

The rain increased, and he was soon soaked through. There hadn't been time to grab anything to protect himself against the weather, so he couldn't do much to ease his discomfort. A glance over his shoulder revealed no sign of the *Galaphile*, so he performed a quick compass check and turned east again, changing direction. He was hoping the Druid airship would continue to follow the course he had just abandoned. He thought about taking the cat higher to reduce the odds of colliding with the cliffs, but he couldn't chance it; the higher he rose, the thinner the mists and the greater the risk of discovery. His pursuers were too close.

He dropped his speed and edged ahead, watching cliffs appear and fade to either side through the curtain of rain and mist, angling the cat gingerly between the gaps. The intensity of the storm was increasing, buffeting his craft more heavily now and threatening its stability. He pushed the thrust levers forward again, increasing power to counter the wind. Fat raindrops hammered off the wood decking like pebbles. He had already released the stays and dropped the mainsail to the deck in a heap, otherwise the wind would rip it to shreds. He was so cold by then that he was shivering. Visibility was reduced to almost nothing. If things got any worse, he was going to have to set down.

Time slipped away on ghost steps. Watching and listening, he waited for danger signals to register. He was far enough inland that he was behind the hills that formed the coastal barrier, gaining some measure of protection from the onslaught of the storm. It was rough going even there, but he no longer feared he would be forced down.

He hunched his shoulders and took a deep breath to calm himself. He felt his pulse slow. There was still no sign of the *Galaphile*.

He was beginning to think he had gotten away altogether when abruptly the Druid airship appeared right in front of him, *Galaphile* emerging from the haze like an apparition out of the netherworld, huge and forbidding. Pen gasped in spite of himself, shocked by the suddenness of it, then swung the cat hard to starboard to come in behind and under the bigger ship, hoping against hope that no one aboard her had caught sight of him.

But someone had. The *Galaphile* immediately began to come about, then to drop rapidly, intent on crushing the cat beneath its hull, smashing it in midair, and sending its passengers tumbling into the hills below. The boy countered the maneuver with the only option left to him, slamming all the thrust levers forward at once, expending every bit of power the diapson crystals could muster, in an effort to get clear. The little craft lunged forward, surging through the mist and rain like a frightened bird, throwing Pen back against the pilot box wall.

Down came the *Galaphile*, dropping toward her like a stone. For just an instant—the cat a little too slow, the warship a little too close—Pen was certain they were not going to get clear. The cat's mast snapped as the warship hull caught its tip, and the little ship lurched and dropped beneath the weight of the larger craft. Pieces of mast and rigging collapsed all around Pen, splintering the walls of the pilot box. The boy dropped to his knees and ducked his head as debris rained down on him. The cat shuddered from the blow, but then abruptly broke free with a scraping and splintering of wood. Lifting away as the bigger ship continued to drop, it ran hard and fast under the full power of its crystals until it disappeared into the mist.

Pen rose cautiously from behind the walls of the pilot box. The shattered mast had snapped off midway up; the top half had fallen away completely, and the lower half was bent at a rakish angle across the rim of the box. Pen had to steer with the remnant of the mast practically in his face, but he was so grateful to have escaped that he scarcely noticed. He was breathing hard, and his hands were fastened on the control levers in a death grip.

"What happened?" Tagwen demanded in a strangled gasp.

"Nothing," Pen answered, refusing to look at him. His hands on the levers and his eyes on the mist kept him from shaking too badly. He swallowed hard. "Get down. Stay out of sight."

Night arrived, and the storm began to diminish. The winds died away and the rain slowed to a drizzle. Mist and clouds still masked the horizon in all directions, but the buffeting the cat had experienced earlier was gone. With darkness to help conceal them, Pen felt marginally safer. The *Galaphile* had not reappeared, and he was beginning to think that their last encounter had happened solely by chance. Otherwise, she would have found him again by then. He knew he was grasping at straws, but straws were all he had.

He told Tagwen that he could come up on deck, and after hesitating, the Dwarf did so. Pen gave him the controls to hold and dragged out an all-weather cloak from a storage bin to throw over his soaked clothes. The temperature was dropping quickly, even though the winds had died away and the rains slowed, and he needed to stay warm. He was navigating by compass readings, unable to catch more than a brief glimpse of the land below and nothing of the stars above. At least he was no longer simply running away; he was flying toward something, as well. Having fled

Patch Run, his plan was to undertake a search for his parents in the Wolfsktaag Mountains as Tagwen had suggested. It wouldn't be easy, and it might not even be possible, but it was all he could think to do. If he could manage to locate them, Tagwen could explain what had brought him to Patch Run, Pen could relate what had happened since, and they could decide what to do from there. The whole business would be safely out of Pen's hands, which was the only sensible place for it to be.

Riding through the empty, misted night, cold and miserable, he found himself missing his parents in a way he would not have believed possible a day earlier. It made him realize how much of a boy he still was. He didn't like to think of himself that way, but it was hard to pretend he was all grown up when he felt the way he did. All he wanted was to find his father and mother and go home again. No more running away and hiding from terrifying Dwarf Druids and their Gnome strongmen. No more flying blind in a damaged ship through strange lands.

All of which served to remind him of how much trouble he was really in. Sooner or later he was going to have to set down to make repairs to the cat's damaged mast and then take a look around to determine how far east the storm had blown him. All that was left for him to do was to decide how long he would wait before doing so.

In the end, the decision was made for him. He must have expended more power than he thought, or perhaps had less to start with, because sometime around midnight the diapson crystals began to give out. He knew at once what was happening when the ship began to stall, slowing sharply and dipping its bow in fits and starts. Enough power remained to land, and he did so at once. With Tagwen shouting in his ear, demanding to know what was wrong, he put the cat into a slow glide and eased her downward in search of somewhere flat and open to land.

He had no idea where he was but was relieved to find patchy stretches of forest clearings bordering the recognizable expanse of Rainbow Lake only a few miles to the north, and he steered the failing cat in that direction. He took a quick look about, peering through the mist, but saw nothing of their pursuers. Maybe things were going to work out, after all.

A broad, dark stretch of ground opened ahead of him, and he took the cat toward it. He was almost on the ground when he realized it was a marsh. Angling the nose of the cat up sharply, he skipped over the bog and settled down hard at the very edge of a thick stand of trees east. The cat slammed into the ground, skidded wildly for a moment, and then bumped up against a tree trunk and stopped.

"Haven't you had any practice landing this thing!" Tagwen demanded irritably, hauling himself out of the hold into which he had tumbled.

Pen finished hooding the parse tubes and bringing the thrust levers all the way back. "Don't be so grumpy. We're lucky to be down in one piece. Smooth landings are for undamaged ships."

Tagwen huffed, then looked around. "Where are we?"

Pen shook his head, peering over the lip of the pilot box at the broken mast and damaged rigging. "Don't know."

"Well, wherever it is, I don't much care for the look of it."

"The Highlands have rough features, but they're safe enough. At least, that's what my parents say."

The Dwarf climbed back onto the deck and stood staring out at the night. "This doesn't look like the Highlands to me."

Pen glanced up at once. A quick survey of the surrounding countryside confirmed Tagwen's assessment. Instead of hills and valleys, the terrain consisted of low, flat stretches of marshy ground abutting heavy stands of forest that soon turned into a solid wall to the east. Rainbow Lake was still there, glimmering dully in the misty dark, but nothing else seemed quite right.

He looked at the black trunks of the massive trees ahead of them, many of them well over a hundred feet tall. There were no trees like those in the Highlands. A chill ran through him, and it was from more than the damp and the cold. This wasn't Leah. The storm had blown them right through the Highlands and into the country beyond—country so dangerous that his parents had forbidden him to go into it under any circumstances.

He was inside the Black Oaks.

NINE

They could do nothing about their situation that night, so they hunkered down to wait for morning. The cat couldn't fly until there was power for the diapson crystals, and there wouldn't be power for the crystals until there was light from which to draw it. Even then, the problem wasn't solved, because they needed to rig the mainsail and radian draws to absorb the ambient light into the crystals, and they couldn't do that on any kind of permanent basis without a mast. They couldn't replace the mast until it was light enough to see to go into the Black Oaks—a whole other kind of problem—to find a tree suitable for the purpose. Then they had to cut down the tree, haul it back to the airship, shape it, attach the iron clips and stays that would hold it and the rigging in place, and put it up.

Pen, sunk down in a funk that defied his best efforts to dispel it, estimated conservatively that such an operation might take as long as three days. In the meantime, they were grounded in one of the most dangerous places in the entire Southland.

Nor could they do much to ease their physical discomfort. Soaked through and chilled to the bone, they might have welcomed even a little warmth. But a fire was out of the question while the *Galaphile* was hunting them, and Pen could not use the diapson crystals to generate even the smallest amount of heat because all their stored power was exhausted. He had not had time to pack the right provisions for this experience, so the best they could do for shelter was to strip off their wet clothes, crawl into the sleeping space under the pilothouse, and wrap up in spare sails to try to stay warm.

But only one of them could do this at a time because the other needed to stay topside and keep watch. Even Tagwen saw the wisdom in that. The *Galaphile* was of obvious concern, but the creatures that lived in the Black Oaks offered a more immediate threat. Gray wolves ran in packs large enough to challenge even a moor cat. The swamps were filled with snakes and dragon beasts. There were rumors of even larger, more dangerous things, some in the Black Oaks, some out in the Mist Marsh bordering it to the northeast. While they had weapons with which to defend themselves, neither Pen nor Tagwen was particularly anxious to test them out.

Things could be worse, Pen thought darkly as they sat staring at each other and the night, but not by much and not in any way he could immediately identify.

"Is there any food?" Tagwen asked glumly.

They were sitting inside the pilot box, talking about what they would do when morning came. The sky was clearing, the first stars and a hint of moonlight visible now through the broken clouds. Pen knew it was well after midnight, the beginning of a new day.

Wordlessly, he retrieved the pack of dried stores he had snatched up on his way out of the work shed and handed it to the Dwarf. Tagwen rummaged around inside and produced some dried beef and a rather sorry-looking hunk of cheese. He split both and handed half to the boy. Pen accepted his meal wordlessly and began to eat.

What was he doing out in the middle of nowhere, completely disabled? How had he ever let this happen?

"We should get some sleep," he said wearily.

"I'll keep watch," Tagwen offered, working his knife across the cheese rind. "I'm more rested than you are, after that storm."

Pen didn't argue; he was exhausted. "All right." He yawned.

"I don't sleep much anyway," Tagwen continued. "I used to stay awake for hours sometimes while your aunt was sleeping, just sitting there with her. I was always there for her when she was sick. I liked doing that—just sitting there. It made me feel I was doing something to help her, something besides keeping her affairs organized."

"What is she like?" Pen asked suddenly.

The Dwarf looked at him. "You've spent time with her."

"Not very much. Not enough to know her well. She doesn't let you know her well. She keeps you at a distance."

"She does that even to me. I can tell you that she lives with her past more than most. She's haunted by it, Penderrin. She hates who she was and what she did as the Ilse Witch. She would do anything to take it all back and start over. I don't think anyone understands that. The Druids mostly think she hasn't changed all that much, that once you have the kind of magic she does, you don't regret anything. They think she's the same underneath, that she just masks it from them."

"I don't know what she was like before," Pen said. "But I think she is a good person now. She doesn't want to get close, but she wants to help. She tries to be kind. At least, that's how she was with me, and she didn't even know me then. What do you think has happened to her?"

Tagwen shook his head. "Whatever it is, I think it has something to do with Terek Molt and Shadea a'Ru and the rest of their little group of traitors. At first I thought it had something to do with her trip into the Northland a few days before she disappeared, but I don't think that now."

He took a few minutes to explain what he knew about Grianne Ohmsford's journey into the ruins of the Skull Kingdom with the Maturen Kermadec, then segued right into a dissertation about the cliques of Druid troublemakers who had made things so difficult for the Ard Rhys at Paranor. The boy listened attentively, thinking that there was a lot about his aunt that he didn't know, much of it because his parents never discussed it. He was seeing her in an entirely new light now, and his admiration for her was growing.

"I would have walked away from all that a long time ago," he said. "I think Kermadec is right. She should just start over."

Tagwen shrugged. "Well, it's all to do with politics and appearances, Pen. If she were free to act as she chose without consequences, I expect there would be some very surprised Druids when she was finished."

Pen was silent for a moment, contemplating the ramifications of what he had just learned. If someone had acted against his aunt, as powerful as she was, and that same someone was responsible for sending Terek Molt and those gimlet-eyed Gnomes after him, then he was in a world of trouble—much more than he had thought he was. He wondered what was at stake that would cause someone to take such drastic action. If it was Shadea a'Ru, then perhaps the lure of becoming Ard Rhys was enough. But given his aunt's dark history, he thought it more likely that it had something to do with revenge or misguided loyalties or fanatical beliefs. Those who committed atrocities always seemed to do so out of a misconceived sense of righteousness and the greater good.

"Do you think she's dead, Tagwen?" he asked impulsively.

It was a terrible thing to ask the Dwarf, who was beside himself with feelings of guilt and despair already, and Pen regretted asking the question as soon as it was out of his mouth. But boys ask those kinds of questions, and Pen was no exception.

"I don't care to think about it," the Dwarf said quietly.

Pen cringed at the sadness he heard in the other's voice. "It was a stupid question."

Tagwen nodded noncommittally. "Go to sleep, Pen," he said, nudging him with his boot. "There's nothing more to be done this night."

Pen nodded. There didn't seem to be. He wasn't at all certain how much could be done on waking, but at least a new day might grace him with a better attitude. The damp and cold had leeched all the good feelings out of him. The running and hiding had stolen his confidence. They would both come back with the advent of a new day, just as they always did with a little rest and a little time.

He rose and stepped out of the pilot box, ducked down into the sleeping compartment, and rolled himself into a square of sailcloth. He was asleep almost at once.

He dreamed that night, and his dreams were dark and frightening. He was fleeing through a forest, the trunks huge and black, whipping past him in a blur as he ran. He was running as fast as he could, but he knew it wasn't fast enough to escape what was chasing him. It was close behind him, its shadow looming over him, and if he was to look back at it, even for a moment, he would be doomed. He didn't know what was back there, only that it was something terrible. All he could do was run from it and hope that eventually he would find a way to escape.

But his fear overcame his reason, and he turned to look—just a glimpse, nothing more. The moment he did so, he knew he was doomed. A massive airship hovered right above him, dropping slowly, preparing to crush him. The airship had eyes as cold as those of a snake, razor-sharp fangs, and a long, wicked tongue that licked out at him. The ship was alive, but it was what lay inside, what he couldn't see from where he was on the ground, that really terrified him. What waited in the bowels of the airship was what would have him after the ship had crushed him into the earth. He would still be alive, but he would wish he wasn't.

With the airship so close he could feel its wood brush against his hunched back, he threw himself to one side into a deep ravine, and then he was falling, falling . . .

He woke with a start, sitting up so abruptly he bumped his head against the decking of the pilot box. Pain ratcheted through him and tears flooded his eyes. He sat holding his head for a moment, trying to clear his thoughts, to make the nightmare go away. But it lingered, stronger than before, pressing down on him, as if it were still happening in real life.

Consumed by this unreasonable, yet nevertheless unshakable fear, he crawled from the sleeping space onto the deck of the cat, breathing in the night air to clear his head. It was still dark, but the clouds had dissipated and the sky was bright with stars and moon. Sitting with his back against the wall of the pilot box, he glanced at the darkness, listened to the silence, and tried to shake off the effects of the dream.

Then he rose to look forward over the pilot box wall and saw the *Galaphile* flying directly toward him.

He felt his heart stop, and his breath caught in his throat, tightening down into a hard knot of fear. He could not quite believe what he was seeing, even though it was right in front of him and unmistakable. He caught a glimpse of Tagwen asleep inside the pilot box, oblivious to the danger. Pen wanted to reach out and wake him, but he could not make himself move. He just stood there, staring helplessly as the massive bulk of the airship grew larger and larger, bearing down on him like the airship in his dream, preparing to crush the life out of him.

And then abruptly, it changed course.

There was no reason for it. If anyone was on deck searching for them, they would have been seen. The moonlight was too clear and bright for any other result. Yet the *Galaphile* swung sharply to port and away, flying back toward the shoreline of Rainbow Lake, an act so unexpected and improbable that it left Pen open-mouthed.

"Tagwen!" he whispered harshly, groping for the other's shoulder.

The Dwarf awoke with a start, scrambling into a sitting position as he struggled to figure out what was happening. Pen steadied him with his hand, drew his attention, then pointed at the retreating airship. Tagwen stared at it, confusion and shock mirrored on his rough features.

"It was right in front of us," Pen explained, keeping his voice to a whisper. "I had a dream about it, came up on deck, and there it was! Right there! It had us, Tagwen. It couldn't have missed us, sitting out like this in the moonlight, even at night. But it did. All at once, it just turned and flew off."

He knelt next to the Dwarf, taking quick, short breaths, feeling light-headed. "What happened? Why didn't it see us?"

"Perhaps it didn't recognize you," a voice replied from behind them.

For the second time in only minutes, Pen experienced heart failure, jumping with the unexpected sound, almost falling over Tagwen, who was just as startled. Crouched in one corner of the pilot box, man and boy turned to see who had spoken.

An old man stood looking at them, an ancient so bent and

gnarled that it seemed impossible he could have managed to climb aboard. He braced himself with a polished black staff that glistened like deep waters in moonlight, and his robes were so white they gleamed like the moon itself. Long gray hair and a heavy beard fell about his chest and shoulders, and his eyes had an oddly childlike twinkle to them, as if the old man had never quite grown up all the way.

Pen, recovering from the shock of finding him there, said, "Why wouldn't they recognize us?"

"Sometimes things don't look quite the way we expect them to," the old man said. "Especially at night, when shadows drape the world and mask the truth."

"We were right out in the open," Pen persisted. He stood up again, deciding there was nothing to be afraid of. He looked at the ancient's strange eyes, finding himself drawn to something reflected in them, something that reminded him of himself, though he couldn't say what. "Did you do something to make them not see us?"

The old man smiled. "Penderrin Ohmsford. I knew your father, years ago. He came looking for something, too. I helped him find what it was. Now, it seems, it is your turn."

"My turn?" Pen stared at him. "How do you know who I am? My father didn't tell you, did he? No, this was before I was born, wasn't it?"

The old man nodded, amused. "Your father was still a boy, just as you are now."

Tagwen struggled to his feet, straightening his rumpled clothes and squaring his stocky body away. "Who are you?" he asked boldly. "What are you doing out here? How do you know so much about Pen and his father?"

"So many questions," the old man said softly. "Life is full of them, and we spend it seeking their answers, first of one, then of another. It is our passion, as thinking creatures, to do so. Do you not know me, Tagwen? You are of the Dwarf people, and the Dwarf people have known me for centuries."

But it was Pen who answered, hesitating only a moment before saying, "I know who you are. The King of the Silver River. My father told me of you—how you came to him when he was traveling with my uncle, Quentin Leah, into the Eastland. You showed him a vision of my aunt, before he knew she was his sister. You gave him a phoenix stone to help protect him on his journey across the Blue Divide."

All who resided in the Four Lands knew the legend of the King of the Silver River, though not all believed it. He was said to be a Faerie creature, as old as the Word itself, come into being at the same time and made part of the world in its infancy. The last of his kind, he was caretaker of wondrous gardens hidden somewhere in the Silver River country, a place where no humans were allowed. He was seen now and then by travelers, always in different forms. Sometimes he would give aid to them when they were lost or in peril. He had done as much for several generations of Ohmsfords, going all the way back to Shea and Flick, in the time of the Druid Allanon. Others in the Four Lands might doubt his existence, but those like Bek, who had encountered him, and Pen, who had heard his father's story, did not.

"Well spoken, Penderrin," the old man said. "You are clearly your father's son. What we must determine now is if your courage is a match for his." He came forward in a sort of half shuffle, stopping at the pilot box steps. "Are you brave enough to undertake a journey to find your missing aunt and bring her safely home again?"

Pen glanced quickly at Tagwen, searching for reassurance and finding only surprise and confusion. It was what he should have expected. No one could answer such a question for him.

"She badly needs you to do this," the King of the Silver River assured him. "She is trapped in a very dangerous place, and she cannot get home again without your help. No one can save her but you, Penderrin. It is an odd set of circumstances that makes this so, but it is the way of things nevertheless."

Tagwen grunted. "This boy is the only one who can help the Ard Rhys? No one else? What about his parents? What about his father, Bek Ohmsford? He has the same magic as his sister, a very powerful magic, to assist him. Surely, he should be the one to make this journey."

The old man leaned more heavily on the black staff and cocked his head as if seriously considering the question. His gaze was distant and just a little sad.

"Often, it is the least likely among us who is in a position to accomplish the most. It is so here. Bek Ohmsford cannot help his sister this time. Penderrin is just a boy, and it would seem impossible that a boy would be best able to save so powerful a wielder of magic as Grianne Ohmsford, Ard Rhys and Ilse Witch. Certainly those who have sent her to her prison would never think it possible. Perhaps that is why they have overlooked him. In truth, they think it is his parents they need to fear, and so seek them out, just as you do."

"I knew it!" Tagwen exclaimed angrily. "It was Shadea a'Ru and Terek Molt and the rest of them! They've done this to her!"

He was practically beside himself, and Pen felt compelled to put a cautioning hand on his shoulder, but the Dwarf barely seemed aware of him. He stamped his foot furiously. "Vipers! Treacherous snakes! Kermadec was right all along! She should have rid herself of the lot of them long ago and none of this would have happened!"

The King of the Silver River passed his hand in front of the Dwarf's eyes, causing him to sigh heavily and grow calm again. "It isn't as simple as that, Tagwen. In fact, there are others responsible, as well, others who are from different places and pursue different goals. But the most dangerous of those who would see the Ard Rhys destroyed is someone of whom the others are not even aware. That one plays the others as a master does his puppets, pulling the strings that guide their actions. Wheels within wheels, secrets yet unrecognized. The danger is far greater than it appears, and it threatens far more than the life of the Ard Rhys. Yet she is the key to restoring a balance, to making things right again. She must be returned to the Four Lands in order for everything else that is necessary to happen." He looked at Penderrin. "You alone can bring that to pass."

Pen sighed, thinking that only a day ago he was wondering how to best pass the time in Patch Run until his parents returned. He had been anxious for an adventure, eager to be with them in the Wolfsktaag, to be a part of their lives as guides of an expedition. Now he was being recruited to undertake an expedition of his own, one that appeared to be far more dangerous than theirs. How quickly things changed.

"What is it you want me to do?" he asked.

The King of the Silver River climbed the steps to the pilot box, not in a weary shuffle, but in a smooth, effortless glide. One wrinkled hand came to rest on the boy's shoulder. "You must abandon your efforts to find your parents; they cannot help you in this. If it were possible for them to do so, I would have gone to them first. I shall speak with them in any case to warn them of the danger from your enemies. But your parents' time is past, Penderrin; it is your time now. You must go in search of your aunt without them, and you must do so at once."

"Then I shall go with him," Tagwen declared bravely. "Finding the Ard Rhys is my responsibility, too."

The King of the Silver River glanced at him appraisingly, then nodded. "You will make a good and loyal companion, Tagwen," he said. His eyes shifted back to Pen. "Such companions will be needed. Find them where you will, but choose them with caution."

He leaned forward, and his thin, aged voice lowered until it was almost a whisper. "Listen carefully. A potion has been used against the Ard Rhys, a magic of great power. The potion is called liquid night. It has imprisoned your aunt in another place, one that cannot be reached by ordinary means. A talisman to negate its magic is needed. The required talisman is a darkwand. It is a conjuring stick and must be fashioned by hand from the limb of a tree called a tanequil. The tanequil is sentient; it is a living, breathing creature. It will give up a limb only if it is persuaded of the need for doing so. It must act freely. Taking the limb by force will destroy the magic that it bears. Someone must communicate with the tanequil in a language it can comprehend. Someone must explain to it why its limb is so important. Penderrin, you have the gift of magic, the talent with which you were born, to do this."

Pen was speechless. He was being told that his little magic, which he had repeatedly dismissed as being virtually useless, was suddenly his most important possession. He could hardly believe it, but the old man's words bore weight, and he could not bring himself to dismiss them out of hand.

"How will I know what to do?" he asked. Even if he wasn't sure yet whether he would go—and he most certainly wasn't—he had to know what was needed if he did. "How will I know what language to speak to it or how to shape this darkwand from its limb?"

The King of the Silver River smiled. "I cannot tell you that. No one can. But you will know, Penderrin. When it is time, you will know. You will understand what to do, and you will find a way to do it."

"Well, we have to find this tree first," Tagwen interjected, huffing doubtfully. "How do we do that? Is it far away?"

"The tanequil grows in a forest on an island deep in the

Charnal Mountains. To reach it, you must pass through gardens that were once the center of an ancient city called Stridegate. Trolls and Urdas inhabit the surrounding forests and foothills. They will know the way to enter and pass through."

Pen shook his head. "I don't know if I can do this." He looked at Tagwen. "I've never even been out of the Borderlands."

"I don't know if you can, either," Tagwen replied. His bearded face was scrunched up like crumpled paper. "But I think you have to try, Pen. What else can you do? You can't abandon her."

He was right, of course, but Pen was beset with doubts. The Charnal Mountains were more dangerous than the Black Oaks, and to try to penetrate them with as little experience as he had and not even a sense of where to go seemed foolish.

The King of the Silver River sighed with what seemed deep regret. "Life offers few certainties, Penderrin. This journey is not one of them. Hear me out, for there is more to know. What I have told you is only a first step. Your journey begins with your search for the tanequil. It begins with your shaping of a darkwand. But it ends in another place altogether. The darkwand must be taken to Paranor and the chamber of the Ard Rhys. There, the talisman's magic will give you passage through the curtain of liquid night to where the Ard Rhys has been imprisoned. Only you, Penderrin, and you alone. No other may go with you. Not even Tagwen. When you find your aunt, the darkwand will give you passage back again—you, because you bear the wand, and your aunt, because the magic of the wand negates that of the liquid night."

He paused. "But remember, no other may pass. The magic's thread is slender and fragile, and it cannot be rewoven or lengthened to accommodate others. Passage over allows passage back, but there can be no deviations. There can be no exceptions."

Pen was not at all sure why the other was making such a point of this, but he thought it was in reference to something very spe-

cific, something that the old man did not want to reveal in greater
detail. That was in keeping with what he knew to be true about
the ways of the ancients, the Faerie creatures who were the first
people. They spoke in riddles and always held something back. It
was in their nature, very much as it was in the nature of the Druids,
and that would never change.

What should he do?

He looked into the eyes of the old man, then at Tagwen's
rough face, and then off into the night, where possibilities were
still shaping themselves and dreams still held sway. He had never
been put in a position where so much depended on a decision and
the decision must be made so quickly.

Then, almost without thinking about it, he put aside his objections and concerns as secondary to his aunt's needs. He stood
staring down at the wooden deck of the pilot box for a moment,
measuring the depth of his commitment. It all came down to the
same thing, he supposed. If their positions were reversed, would
his aunt do for him what he was being asked to do for her? Even
without knowing her any better than he did, he was certain of the
answer.

"All right," he said softly, "I'll go."

He looked up again. The King of the Silver River nodded.
"And you will come back again, Penderrin. I see it in your eyes,
just as I saw it more than twenty years ago in your father's."

Pen took a deep breath, thinking that what was mirrored in his
eyes was probably more on the order of bewilderment. So much
had happened so quickly, and he was not sure yet that he understood it all or even that he ever would. He wished he had more
confidence in himself, but he supposed you got that only by testing yourself against your doubts.

"Where has my aunt been imprisoned?" he asked the old man
suddenly. "Where do I have to go to find her?"

The King of the Silver River went very still then, so still that at first it seemed as if he had been turned to stone and could not speak. He took a long time to consider the boy's question, his ancient face a mask of conflicting emotions. The silence deepened and turned brittle with suspense.

The longer Pen waited for a response, the more certain he became that he would wish he hadn't asked.

He was not mistaken.

When the King of the Silver River had gone, Penderrin slept, exhausted by the day's ordeal. He woke again to sunshine and blue sky, to soft breezes blowing off the Rainbow Lake, and to birdsong and crickets. Tagwen was already hard at work, clearing away the debris from their landing. Pen joined the Dwarf in his efforts, neither of them saying much as they labored. They cut away the mast, then found a suitable tree from which to fashion a new one. It took them most of the day to shape it, then set it in place. By the time it was firmly attached to the cat, the sun had gone west and the shadows were lengthening.

They ate dinner on the deck of the airship, a patched-together meal of foodstuffs left aboard from an earlier outing, fresh water and foraged greens. Fish would have helped, but they would have had to eat it raw since neither was willing to risk a fire. They had not seen the *Galaphile* since the previous night, and they believed themselves safe from it there in the lands of the King of the Silver River, but there was no point in taking chances.

Dinner was almost finished before Pen spoke about the previous night. By then, he had spent the better part of the day thinking it through, repeating the words of the King of the Silver River in his mind, trying to make them seem real.

"Did it all happen the way I think it did, Tagwen?" he asked finally, almost afraid of what he was going to hear. "I didn't imagine it?"

"Not unless I imagined it, too," the Dwarf replied.

"Then I agreed to go find my aunt?"

"And me with you."

Pen shook his head helplessly. "What have I done? I'm not up to this. I don't even know where to make a start."

Tagwen laughed softly. "I've been giving it some thought, since I saw how dazed you were last night. One of us needed to keep a clear head. You may have the means to secure this darkwand, but I have the means to look out for us. I think I know what we need to do first."

"You do?" Pen didn't bother to hide his surprise. "What?"

The Dwarf grinned and pointed toward the setting sun. "We go west, Penderrin, to the Elven village of Emberen."

T E N

She awoke to the sound of weasel voices, raspy and sly, the words indistinguishable one from the other. The voices giggled and snickered, little taunts intended to disparage her, to make her feel vulnerable and weak. She listened to them from within layers of cotton that wrapped about her like a chrysalis. The voices hissed with laughter. She was a nameless corpse, they whispered, an empty shell from which the life had been leeched away, a body consigned to the earth's dark breast for burial.

She fought against a sudden stab of panic. She was Grianne Ohmsford, she told herself in an act of reassurance. She was alive and well. She was only dreaming. She was asleep in her bed, and she remembered . . .

She drew a sharp, frightened breath, and her certainties were gone as quickly as the voices, disappeared like smoke.

Something had happened.

Still wrapped in cotton that filled her head and mouth, that bound up her thoughts and clogged her reason, she tried to move her arms and legs. She could do so, but only with great effort. She was terribly weak and her body was responding as if she had slept not for one night but for a hundred. She brought one hand to her breast and found she was still wearing her nightclothes, but no blankets covered her. The air smelled stale and dead, and she could not feel even the smallest trace of a breeze. Yet where she slept within the towers of Paranor, there was always a breeze and the air smelled of the trees, fresh and green.

Where was she?

The softness of her sleeping pad and comforter were gone. She felt hard ground beneath her bare arms; she smelled the earth. Her panic returned, threatening to overwhelm her, but she forced it down. She had no patience for it and no intention of giving it power over her. She was not harmed; she was still whole. Deep breaths, one after the other, calmed and steadied her.

She opened her eyes, peeling back the layers of deep sleep into which she had sunk, squinting into hazy gray light. It was night still. She was staring at a darkened sky that domed overhead in a vast leaden canopy. Yet something was wrong. The sky was cloudless, but empty of moon and stars. Nor was the sun in evidence. The world was cast in the sullen tones of a storm's approach, shrouded in layers of silence, in hushed tones of expectation.

It must be twilight, she decided. She had slept longer than she thought. The sun was down, the moon not yet up, and the stars not yet out—that would explain the strange sky.

The weasel voices were gone, a figment of her imagination. She listened for them and heard nothing, either in her mind or in the real world. But there was no birdsong either, or buzzing of insects, or rustle of wind in the trees, or ripple of water in a stream, or any sound at all save the pounding of her heart.

It took her a while, but she finally forced herself to move, rolling to her side and then into a sitting position, wrapping her arms about her drawn-up knees to keep herself in place. Slowly,

her vision sharpened from a watery haze to clarity, and the spinning that had begun when she levered herself upright faded.

She looked around. She sat in a ragged, blasted landscape, surrounded by trees that were wintry and thick with withered leaves.
The trees had the look of blight about them, sickened so that they
could no longer thrive. Because she was sitting on a high piece of
ground overlooking several valleys and, further out, a river, she
could see that the forest extended for miles in all directions, bleak
and unchanging. Farther out still, at the edges of her vision, mountains loomed stark and barren against the skyline.

Paranor was nowhere in evidence. Nor was there any sign of
anything else man-made—no buildings, no bridges, no traffic on
the river, not even a road. No people. No life. Seemingly, she was
alone in this empty, alien world.

And yet . . .

She took a second look around, a more careful look, seeing
her surroundings with a fresh eye and, to her surprise, recognizing
what she saw. At first, she couldn't believe it. She was still struggling with the idea that somehow she had been transported in her
sleep—drug induced, she was certain—to a strange and terrible
place, all for reasons that were not yet apparent. Disoriented and
confused, she had misread what was now patently clear. The land
she was looking at, although now turned lifeless and empty, was
the land she had gone to sleep in last night.

She was still in Callahorn, in the Four Lands.

Yet it was not the Callahorn she knew and, from what she
could see of it, only a ruined shell of the Four Lands.

She sat staring off into the distance, her gaze shifting from feature to feature to make certain. She took note of the Dragon's
Teeth, their jagged outline unmistakable, as familiar to her by then
as her own face. And there, a glimpse of the Mermidon, south and

west where the mountains broke apart. The plateau on which she sat was where the Druid's Keep had stood. North, south, east, and west, the geography was just as it had been for thousands of years.

But blasted and leeched of life, a corpse of the sort she had thought herself to be on waking.

And where was Paranor?

She could reach only one conclusion. Either she had awakened in the aftermath of the Great Wars or gone into a future in which a similar catastrophe had occurred. But that was impossible.

She checked herself carefully to make certain she was all in one piece, and having done so, managed to get to her feet. Her dizziness and the sluggish feel of waking from a deep sleep had worn off, and her strength was beginning to return. She gave it a few more minutes, still puzzling through her situation, still trying to make sense of it. She couldn't, of course. There was no way to do so without knowing both where she was and how she had gotten there.

She realized she was hungry, and she started to look for food. In her world, the one she had left behind that looked like this one but apparently wasn't, there would have been berry bushes in a clearing near a stream not far from where she stood. While Ard Rhys, she had gone there from time to time to pick the fruit, a private, secret indulgence about which only Tagwen knew.

But it was unlikely that such sweet fruit grew anywhere in this world. Her hunger would have to wait.

She started to walk through the trees, looking for water. As she walked, she listened futilely for the sounds of other life. What sort of world was she in where there were no birds? Were there any people, any creatures at all? Was it possible that she was the only living thing there? The forest was empty and dead, smelling of its own decay. The gray light was unchanging and oppressive, and the sky remained empty of sun, moon, or stars. Even of clouds. The dark, ruined world felt incomplete, as if it were only a faintly cast shadow of the real world.

She found a stream finally, but the water looked so foul she decided against drinking it. She sat down again, her back against a blighted oak, and looked off into the shadowed trees, into the distance, reasoning out what had happened. Clearly, she hadn't come on her own; someone had caused her to be transported. She could safely assume it had not been done for her benefit. Most likely, given the number of enemies she had made, it had been done to get her out of the way. Further, it had been done using magic, because there was no other explanation for how something so difficult could have been accomplished. Yet no one she knew possessed such magic. Not even she could transport people to other places.

So perhaps it had been accomplished by someone who was not of her world, but of another.

But what world would that be? Surely not *this* one.

She gave up thinking about it finally, deciding that she should walk to the edge of the bluff for a better look around. Something else must exist in the place, another creature, another life form. If she could find it, whatever it was, she might be able to determine where she was. If she could do that, she would have a better idea of how to get back to where she belonged.

The walk took her only a short time, though it left her winded and fatigued. She wasn't herself yet, and she would have to be careful how she expended her energy until she was. Thin and diaphanous, her nightclothes billowed about her as she walked. They were warm enough for the moment, but totally inadequate for the task at hand. They would deteriorate quickly. Yet where would she find anything to replace them?

When she stood again upon the heights, close to the bluff

edge and still in the shadow of the lifeless trees, she began a slow scan of the countryside, searching for movement that would identify life.

She was in the middle of this search, completely absorbed in her efforts, when the Dracha appeared. Her concentration was so intense that at first she didn't even know it was there. But in its eagerness to reach her, it stepped upon some twigs and gave itself away. Even so, it was on her so quickly that she barely had time to react. At the last possible moment, she threw herself to one side as it lunged for her, leathery wings spread wide, jaws snapping. She managed to avoid the jaws, but one wing caught her a glancing blow and sent her spinning. The breath left her lungs as she slammed into a tree trunk, and the air before her eyes danced with dark spots.

A Dracha, she thought in disbelief. *It can't be. It's not possible. They don't exist anymore.*

But there it was nevertheless, wheeling about to come at her again. It was big for a Dracha, fully twenty feet long from nose to tail and wing tip to wing tip, sinuous body heavily muscled and covered with glistening scales, back ridged with spines and razor-edged plates, legs crooked and claw-tipped.

Knowing she was dead if she didn't act quickly, she righted herself against the tree trunk and screamed the magic of the wishsong at the beast. Her voice was hoarse and raw from her long sleep, the magic badly managed and scattershot at best, but it was enough. It caught up the Dracha and threw it away as if it were made of straw. The creature hissed and shrieked, enraged at what was being done to it. She saw the fury mirrored in its lidded yellow eyes. She saw it in the twist and snap of its scaly body as it tumbled away into the trees.

Then her voice gave out; she was still too weak to sustain the magic for more than a few seconds. She staggered to her feet, watching as the damaged beast hauled itself upright, dazed and battered, but still dangerous. It turned toward her, eyes glistening from the shadow of its horned brow, the sound of its breathing heavy and thick with anger. Long neck extended, it flicked its tongue out from between rows of dagger-sharp teeth. It stared at her balefully for a long moment, weighing its options. She held her ground, staring back. If she tried to run, it would be on her in seconds. All she could do was to run her bluff and hope it worked.

For a moment, she was certain it wouldn't. The Dracha was too furious even to think of backing away. It would come for her because that was its nature. It was a dragon and dragons were relentless. It would not back away until one of them was dead.

But then it surprised her. Perhaps it decided she wasn't worth the trouble after all, that she was too dangerous, that there was easier prey. It spat venom, came toward her a few steps in menacing fashion, then turned away almost disdainfully and disappeared into the trees.

She took a deep breath to steady herself. A Dracha. There hadn't been Drachas in the world in thousands of years, not since the time of Faerie. There were dragons still, though only a few, hidden in the mountains, in deep caves and bottomless crevices, in places far beyond the reach of men. But no Drachas—no small flying dragons of that sort.

She took a long moment to consider what encountering one meant. Her thinking shifted. There were no dragons in the aftermath of the Great Wars. There were barely any humans. Was she somewhere farther back in time, before the age of humans, when only Faerie creatures existed? That would explain the presence of the Dracha and the absence of Paranor. It would explain why the geography of the world about her looked so familiar, yet was devoid of buildings like Paranor. There would have been no buildings and no people in the first age, when the world was still new, populated by Faerie creatures that required no shelter save that provided by nature.

But had the age of Faerie been so bleak? She hadn't thought so from her readings. She had not imagined it possible. That world was newly made and fresh. This world was dying.

A rustle in the branches overhead drew her attention. The sound was so slight that she almost missed it. But her encounter with the Dracha had put her on guard, and so she glanced up and caught sight of the creature. She stepped back automatically, tensing in expectation of a second attack, but what she found instead of another Dracha was some sort of monkey. It skittered through the trees on spindly limbs, flashes of its hairy, gnarled form appearing through breaks in the ragged boughs. Having been seen, it was trying frantically to escape.

Impulsively, she yelled at it. She didn't pause to think about what she was doing, merely acted on an instinctive need to stop whatever it was from getting away. She was successful. Startled by the sound of her voice, the creature lost its grip and fell, tumbling end over end through the limbs to land with an audible grunt not a dozen yards from where she stood.

It lay dazed and twitching as she walked over to it, and she glanced about as she approached in case it had friends in hiding. But no others appeared, and this one seemed barely able to draw breath after its long fall. It lay on its side, panting heavily, face upturned to the sky. She changed her mind about it as she got closer; it wasn't a monkey, after all. It was hard to say what it was. What it most resembled was a Spider Gnome, but it wasn't that, either. Whatever it was, it was easily the ugliest creature she had ever seen. It was barely four feet tall. Its body was all out of proportion, with bony protrusions and elongated limbs. Coarse black hair sprouted in thick patches from the top of its head and from its dark, leathery skin through rents in its worn pants and tunic.

It recovered and struggled up, still trying to get away from her. She grabbed it by the scruff of the neck and held it fast, holding it away from her as it tried to bite her, using teeth that were considerably sharper than her own. She shook it hard and hissed at it, and it quit trying to bite. It hung limply in her grasp for a moment, then began to chatter wildly. It spoke a language she didn't recognize, but the cadence and tonal repetition suggested it might be a derivation of the tongues with which she was familiar. She shook her head to show she didn't understand. The creature just kept talking, faster now, gesturing wildly. She answered, trying various Gnome dialects. It paused to listen, then shook its own head in reply and began to chatter again. It was so animated that it was bobbing up and down as it spoke, giving it the look of a disjointed puppet, its limbs manipulated by hidden strings.

She set it down and released it, pointing at it in warning to keep it from trying to flee again. It frowned at her and folded its arms over its chest, managing to look defiant and frightened at the same time. She tried a handful of Dwarf and Troll dialects, but it didn't seem to understand those, either. Each time, it would stop and listen to her words, then start chattering away in its own language, as if through insistence and repetition she could be made to understand.

Finally, it plopped down in the grass, arms folded over its chest, eyes turned away, mouth set in a disapproving line. She saw the knife at its waist for the first time, an odd-shaped narrow blade that curved and was serrated at the tip. She saw a small pouch attached to a belt, both decorated with beads sewn into the leather. The pockets cut into the sides of its worn pants were sculpted with thread. Whatever species it was, it was advanced beyond the Spider Gnome level. By the same token, it wasn't a member of any race she could put a name to.

She gave up on the Dwarf and Troll dialects and was about to give up on the creature, as well, thinking that it was hopeless, that she should leave it and move on, go hunt for something else. Then she decided, rather impulsively, to try speaking to it in the Elven language, even though the creature looked nothing like an Elf. But the Elves were the oldest species in the world and their language had been around the longest. The response was immediate. The creature shifted to a variation of what she was speaking at once, and she could understand him clearly.

"Stupid woman!" it snapped, the words strange-sounding in the odd dialect, but comprehensible. "Yelling at me like that. Look what you did to me! Look how far I fell! I could have broken every bone in my body!"

He rubbed his arms as if for emphasis, daring her to contradict him. She narrowed her gaze at him. "You should watch what you say to me. If I don't like what I hear, I might break every bone anyway."

He grimaced. "I could hurt you, if I wanted. You ought to be afraid of me." His odd face scrunched up, and his tongue licked out like a cat's, revealing the razor-sharp teeth. "Who are you? Are you a witch?"

She shook her head. "No, I am Ard Rhys of Paranor. I am a Druid. Where am I?"

He stared blankly at her. "What's wrong with you? Why don't you know where you are? Are you lost?" He didn't wait for an answer. "Tell me what you did to that Dracha. Magic, wasn't it? I've never seen anything like that. If you aren't a witch, you must be a sorceress or a Straken. Are you a Straken?"

There was another name she hadn't encountered outside of the

Druid Histories. Strakens were powerful magic wielders out of the world of Faerie, gone for thousands of years. Like the Dracha.

"Is this the Faerie world?" she asked, beginning to think it must be.

The spindly creature stared at her, head cocked. "This is the land of the Jarka Ruus. You're inside the Dragon Line, above Pashanon. You must know that! Where is it you come from?"

"Paranor. Callahorn. The Four Lands."

She paused with each name, searching his eyes for recognition and finding none. But the words *Jarka Ruus* meant something to her. She had heard them before, though she couldn't remember where. "What are you?" she asked him. "What Race do you belong to? Are you a Troll?"

"Ulk Bog," he announced proudly. He smiled, showing all his considerable teeth. "But I don't have a home at present because I'm traveling. This country is too dangerous. Dragons everywhere, all sorts, and they like to eat my kind. Of course, I try to eat their eggs, so I guess it's fair they should try to eat me. But they're much bigger than I am, for the most part, so I have to be careful. Anyway, I don't want to stay here anymore. Where are you going?"

She didn't have the faintest idea, of course, since she didn't even know where she was. She wasn't at all sure she was going anywhere until she figured out what had happened to her. Nevertheless, she pointed west, if only to satisfy him, at the same time trying to figure out how to extract some useful information.

"Ah, Huka Flats. Good choice. Soft earth for burrows and tender rats to eat." He hitched up his belt. "Maybe I should go with you, since you don't seem to know the way. I know it. I've been everywhere."

Ulk Bogs had disappeared with the world of Faerie, as well, she was thinking. Everything suggested she had gone back in time to the beginning of things, back before Men were created. The idea was so ridiculous that she kept searching for a better answer, but nothing else suggested itself.

"Are there lots of dragons here in the Dragon Line?" she pressed. "Big ones, as well as the Drachas?"

"You *are* a stranger, aren't you?" he said. He was growing bolder again, more confident. He puffed out his narrow chest. "Of course there are big ones. Wyverns and Frost Dragons. Fire Drakes, too, though not so many of those. Some live right down here in the forests, like the Drachas. You have to watch out for them all the time. That's how I happened to be up in that—"

He stopped himself quickly, looking away into the trees. "Well, how I was, uh . . . how I was . . ."

"That Dracha I encountered was hunting you, wasn't it?" she guessed. She leaned close. "Don't lie to me, little rodent."

The Ulk Bog sneered at her. "It wasn't my fault it found you instead of me. I didn't do anything to make it come after you. I was just trying to hide in the trees, because Drachas don't climb and they can't fly close in where there are branches that might get in the way of their wings, so I . . ."

She held out her hand beseechingly and stopped him midsentence. She doubted he was telling the truth, but then again she wasn't sure he would recognize the truth if it bit him on the nose. There wasn't much about Ulk Bogs in the Druid Histories, but if they were all like this one, they were pretty good at shifting blame.

"Never mind," she told him. "It doesn't matter."

She cast about for help from any quarter, but there was none to be found. She was alone and stuck with this fast-talking creature unless she set him free, which she wasn't ready to do quite yet. She still might learn something from him if she gave herself a chance. Even by just letting him rattle on, she might stumble over something that would help.

"Tell me your name," she said.

He drew himself up. "Weka Dart. What's yours?"

"Grianne." She abandoned the Ard Rhys designation because it clearly meant nothing to him. "Tell me more about the Dragon Line. Have there ever been any buildings up here on this bluff? A castle, perhaps?"

He laughed. "Dragons don't need buildings! They rule this territory of the Jarka Ruus. Everything else stays away. If you want buildings, you need to go down onto the plains where the Straken live. Your kind."

My kind. She remembered suddenly that they were speaking in the Elven tongue—an ancient dialect, but Elven nevertheless, a Faerie language. The Elves were the original people, the only true Faerie Race to survive the Great Wars. There had been Elves forever in the world. If this was the past, even if she was all the way back to the time of the Word, there would be Elves.

"Tell me, Weka Dart," she said. "Are there Elves close by? Where do the Elves live?"

The look he gave her was filled with disdain. "Are you stupid? There are no Elves here! Elves are forbidden! We cast them out, back when we made this world! *Jarka Ruus ba'enthal corpa u'pahs!*"

She had no idea what he was saying, but she got the message anyway. "But there must be Elves. You are speaking in the Elven tongue."

He became enraged. "I speak Ulk Bog, *my* tongue, *my* language, and it does not sound anything at all like Elfish! I will hurt you if you say that again, whether you are Straken or not! No one can call an Ulk Bog an Elf! We are the free peoples, the world of the *ca'rel orren pu'u!* Jarka Ruus!"

For a moment she was afraid he was going to attack her; his face was twisted in fury, and his breathing had turned quick and dangerous. She could not imagine why he was reacting that way. If he knew about the Elves, this must be the Old World, and the

Elves had always been a part of it, not separate from it, not until after the war when the bad Faerie creatures had been exiled to—

She went still, realization flooding through her, so dark it threatened to bury her in an avalanche of horror. No, she must be mistaken, she thought. But she remembered now the origin of the words *Jarka Ruus*. She had never heard them spoken; she had read them. They were words from the Druid Histories—Elven words, whether Weka Dart liked it or not. They meant *banished peoples*, and they had been used first in a time before the Four Lands existed, long ago in the beginning, when the war fought between good and evil Faerie creatures reached its climax.

But she had to be certain. "Ulk Bog," she said to him. "You say there are dragons. Are there giants, as well? Are there demonspawn and goblins? Are there warlocks and witches and ogres?"

He nodded at once. "Of course."

She took a deep breath. "Are there Furies?"

He grinned at her with unsettling purpose. "Everywhere."

She was frozen by that single word. *Everywhere.* Furies. No Elves, only monsters that preyed on each other and those more helpless. The Ellcrys had shut them all away thousands of years ago in a place that no human had ever gone into.

Until now.

She exhaled slowly. She was inside the Forbidding.

ELEVEN

"What's wrong with you?" Weka Dart asked, leaning forward for a closer look, his ferret face wrinkling with something that could have been either suspicion or distaste. "Are you going to be sick? You look as if you might be thinking about it."

She barely heard him. She was stunned to the point of being unable to speak. *Inside the Forbidding!* The words roared in her ears like the howl of a high wind, blotting out every other sound and leaving her wrapped in confusion and disbelief. It was such an impossible idea that she could not bring herself to quit looking for a way to dismiss it. No one had ever been inside the Forbidding. There was no way to get inside, for that matter. The barrier was made strong enough to keep the demons and their kind inside, but it had a similar effect on those without. There was no congress between them, not even the smallest contact.

Once, five hundred years ago, the barrier had ruptured with the failing of the Ellcrys. Grianne's ancestor Wil Ohmsford had been instrumental in helping an Elven girl named Amberle, the

Chosen of the tree, find the Bloodfire to create a new Ellcrys and restore the barrier. But other than that one time, there was no instance in recorded history of demons or humans crossing over from one realm into the other. There was simply no way for it to happen.

Yet happen it had, because she was inside the Forbidding, and she could argue against it all she wanted, but it was so. If there were Furies here, there could be no mistaking it. Weka Dart was an Ulk Bog, and all the Ulk Bogs of ancient times, of Faerie, had been sent into the Forbidding along with the other creatures who were indiscriminately predatory. The things that lived inside the Forbidding were savage and raw, unable to function in a climate of civilized behavior, unable to overcome their instincts for killing. She understood the darkness that drove such creatures, for as the Ilse Witch it had driven her, as well. When the darkness took hold, becoming the hard edge of emotions best kept buried and unexamined, there was no act a creature could not justify.

"Do you want some water? I can run for some, not far. I don't like the way you look. Did that Dracha bite you? Are you poisoned?"

Weka Dart was pressed so close to her now that his sharp features were only inches from her own. She saw the warts and blemishes on his dark skin, where the hair failed to cover them. She saw the sharpness of his teeth and heard the hissing of his breath. It was like looking closely at a weasel.

"Back away from me," she said, and he did so instantly, cowering slightly at the harsh sound of her voice. "There's nothing wrong with me, Ulk Bog. I was thinking."

Thinking of how desperate her circumstances had become. No situation she could imagine was worse. Being inside the Forbidding was a death sentence. She did not know who had found the means to place her there or how she would ever get out again, but

she was the Ard Rhys, even there, and she held herself together
with an iron will forged in countless struggles she had survived and
her enemies had not.

She took another deep breath and looked around to reassure
herself that the geography of the land about her was what she remembered it to be. It hadn't changed. The Dragon's Teeth formed
a barrier on three sides, allowing small glimpses of grasslands
and rivers beyond, all of it familiar, while north the Streleheim
stretched away in bleak, misty emptiness.

She tried to reason it through. If she was inside the Forbidding,
then the Forbidding was not another place entirely; it was the
same place on a different plane of existence, an alternate world
and history, one that had progressed little since the time of Faerie.
Her world had seen an entire civilization rise and fall in a holo-
caust of power gone mad. This one had failed to progress beyond
the time of its creation out of Elven magic, thousands of years ago.
One had seen Races created out of myth, out of a time when they
were real, made new again by the changes wrought in the survivors of the Great Wars. The other had seen its denizens frozen
in time, until the myth was reality born of nightmare.

No wonder Weka Dart and probably most of those who lived
here spoke a variation of the Elven tongue she knew from her
studies. Once, all creatures had spoken the same tongue, born of
the Word's magic, given life and a chance at unity that they had
tossed away.

"Have you always been the banished people?" she asked Weka
Dart. "Do you keep histories of this? Does anyone?"

"Strakens and warlocks keep our histories, but they do not
agree on what it is," the Ulk Bog responded. He rubbed his sharp
chin and sneered. "They like to change it to suit their own purposes. Liars and cheats, all! But those like myself who are not burdened with magic know the truth. The history is the history! It is

not just what anyone says! Jarka Ruus have been here a thousand, thousand years, since they chose to be rid of the Elves and their kind, to come here and be free!"

A reasonable interpretation, she thought, for creatures that did not want to see themselves as exiled, but as self-determinative. The irony was that they still referred to themselves as Jarka Ruus— the banished people. Perhaps it was in the nature of all people that they should reinvent themselves to keep their pride and dignity intact. Monsters and demonkind had the same need for self-respect as humans.

She stopped herself in midthought, aware that she had missed something. "Are there others here like me?" she asked, thinking that since she had been sent here out of her own world, perhaps others had, as well.

"Strakens? Of course!"

"No, not Strakens. Humans."

He stared at her. "What are humans?"

"People who look like me. Smooth-skinned." She tried to fig-ure out what else she could say. "Anyone who looks like me."

He looked uneasy. "Like you? Some, not many. Strakens and warlocks and witches can look like anything with their magic." He rubbed his hands together nervously and looked about. "Can we go? That Dracha probably has friends. It might have gone to fetch them. Drachas are smart, and even a Straken as powerful as you can't stand against a pack of them."

She stared him down. He knew something that he wasn't telling her, something important. She could see it in the shift of his eyes and hear it in his voice. But she decided to let it go for the moment. He was right about not lingering. It was too dangerous to stay anywhere for long inside a place like the Forbidding. Every-thing here was hunter or prey in its turn, and she could not afford to be seen as the latter.

She cast about again, trying to decide on a direction. She would have to choose one, whether it would take her anywhere useful or not. She had to get moving, away from this haven for dragons. Geographically, this world was the same as her own. She could use that, if she could just think how. Something about the similarity between the two should suggest a solution, a place to go, a way to survive.

She would have liked to use her magic, but she couldn't think of a way in which that would be helpful. The wishsong could do many things, but it didn't allow for opening doors between worlds. Besides, she was pretty sure that if she used it for that purpose, the amount of magic required would almost certainly attract unwanted attention.

Then, abruptly, she had her answer. She should have seen it at once. If the Forbidding was a mirror of her own world, it would have an equivalent to the Hadeshorn and perhaps a gateway to the Druids. If she could raise their shades here, as she would have been able to do there, she might be able to discover what she should do. As a working idea, it had promise. Besides, since it was the only idea she had, it was worth a try.

She looked at Weka Dart. "I'm going east, below the Dragon's . . . below the mountains."

The Ulk Bog furrowed his brow and said something unintelligible, clearly unhappy.

"You don't have to come with me. I can go alone."

She hoped he would agree with her, thinking that he would be of little help in any case. But Weka Dart, still not looking at her, still frowning, shook his head. "You may need me to help you find your way, being a stranger. The land is unsafe for strangers. It doesn't get any better where you want to go. Safer west, but I suppose you have your reasons for not going there right away. Maybe later."

He looked up suddenly, eyes narrowed. "But you don't want to go east. You want to go south through the mountains. I know you call them something else, but here they are called the Dragon Line. We should go below them before we go east. Too dangerous to try to go back the way I have come."

He was so eager to have her do what he wanted that she was immediately suspicious.

"We can take one of the passes," he continued quickly. "That will put us in Pashanon. There are cities and villages. Fortresses, too. Do you know someone there? Another Straken, perhaps?"

Clearly he was hiding something, but she had already made up her mind to go the way he was suggesting, and she decided to let it drop for now.

"Listen to me, Weka Dart," she said quietly, kneeling so that she could look him the eye. She held him frozen in place with the force of her gaze, a prisoner to her eyes. "You are not to call me a Straken again. Is that understood?"

He nodded hurriedly, mouth twisting, gimlet eyes bright and eager. "You are in disguise?" he guessed.

She nodded. "I want my identity kept secret. If you travel with me, you must agree. You must call me Grianne."

He laughed, a rather scary sound, all rough edges and rasps. "I will do exactly as you wish, so long as you do not knock me out of any more trees!"

She straightened. Maybe this would work out, after all. Maybe she would find a way out of here. "Let's be off," she said.

Without waiting for his response, she started away.

They walked all day—or more accurately, she walked while he scurried, a sort of crablike motion that employed all four limbs and carried him from one side to the other in a wide-ranging

and aimless pattern. She was astonished by his energy, which was
boundless, and by his seeming unawareness of the fact that he was
covering twice as much ground as was necessary for no reason.
She decided, after watching him scramble about for several hours,
that it must be genetic to Ulk Bogs. She knew very little about the
species, having only touched on the subject in her reading of the
Druid Histories, and so had little to go on. Nevertheless, in this
case observation seemed enough.

The country they traveled through was both familiar and
strange to her, its geographical features similar to those of her own
world, but not the same. The differences were often small, ones
she could not specifically identify but only sense. It was not surprising to her that the world of the Forbidding, impacted by an alternate history, would not reflect everything exactly. In her world,
the topography had been altered by the destructive effects of the
Great Wars. The basic landmarks were identifiably the same—the
mountains, passes, bluffs, rivers, and lakes—but certain features
were changed. The landscape gave her the impression that she was
revisiting a familiar place, yet seeing everything in an entirely new
light.

They did not encounter any other dragons. They saw huge
birds flying overhead, ones that were neither Rocs nor Shrikes,
and Weka Dart told her they were Harpies. She could not make
out their women's faces, but could picture them in her mind—
narrow and severe, sharp and cunning. Harpies were mythical in
her world, thought to be nothing more than the creation of ancient storytellers. But they were among the creatures banished in
the time of the creation of the Forbidding, and so only the stories
remained. To see one here, real and dangerously close, made her
think about all the other dangerous things that were here, as well,
creatures that would hunt her for food or sport or for no reason at
all. It was an unpleasant prospect.

It had the effect, however, of distracting her. Since her awakening and realization of what had happened to her, she had given little thought to the problems she had left behind; they were distant and just then beyond her control. In a sense, it was liberating. The Druid Council, fractured by its contentious members and constant scheming, was a world away, and would have to get on without her as best it could. She hadn't been able to say that in almost twenty years, and there was a certain relief in being able to do so now.

The weather inside the Forbidding never changed, earth and sky rendered gray and colorless by an absence of sunlight and a heavy, unbroken ceiling of clouds that in the distance flashed with lightning and rumbled with thunder. Sunset was little more than a deepening of the gray they had traveled through all day. Vegetation everywhere had a blighted and wintry look to it, as if sickened by the soil in which it grew. Nothing of the world suggested that living things were welcome or encouraged. Everything whispered of death.

By day's end, they had reached the southern mouth of one of the passes leading out of the mountains and were looking down from the foothills into the plains that Weka Dart called Pashanon, which in her world would be Callahorn. Burnt, stunted grasses grew in clumps over miles of hardpan earth and barren hills that stretched away from countless miles through a scattering of high, windswept plateaus.

"We need a safe place to sleep," the Ulk Bog declared in his odd, phlegmy voice, casting about for what he wanted. "Ah, there!"

He pointed to a huge chestnut set back from the bluff at the edge of a stand of trees that marched upward into the foothills like soldiers.

"We have to sleep in a tree?" she asked him doubtfully.

He gave her a wicked grin. "Try sleeping on the ground, Straken, and see what friends you make during the night."

She was not happy that he was still calling her *Straken* after she had warned him, but she supposed there was no help for it. He addressed her as he saw her, and nothing she said was likely to change that.

"Is it safer in the trees?" she asked.

"Mostly. We are less visible in the trees and the worst of the things that hunt at night don't climb. Except for vine serpents." He grinned, his teeth flashing like daggers. "But there are not so many of those this high up." He started away into the trees. "Wait here."

He was gone for some time, but when he returned, he was carrying an odd assortment of roots and berries, which he deposited at her feet triumphantly. He clearly thought that this was what she would want to eat, and she decided not to disappoint him. She thanked him, cleaned the food as best she could, and ate it, grateful for the nourishment. Afterwards, he directed her to a small stream. The water seemed clean enough to drink, and so she did.

She was aware of the light failing around her, of the darkness settling in, heavy and enfolding. The silence of the day was deepening, as well, as if what little noise she had been able to discern on her travels had gone into hiding. The look and feel of the land around her was changing from gloom to murk, the kind of darkness she understood, the kind in which predators flourished. But the darkness here had a different feel to it. Partly, it was the absence of moon and stars. Yet the smell and taste of the night air were different, too, fetid and rotting, and it carried on its breath the scents of carrion and blood. She felt a tightening in her stomach, a response of her magic to unseen dangers.

"Better get up into that tree now," Weka Dart urged, looking skittish and uneasy as he led her back from the stream, his side-to-side movements becoming quick feints.

She was aware that he hadn't eaten anything of what he had brought her, and she asked him about it. His response was a grunt of indifference. They climbed the chestnut and settled themselves in a broad cradle formed by a conjoining of branches. Any sort of rest seemed out of the question, she thought, feeling the roughness of the bark digging into her back. She glanced down at her nightgown and found it tattered and falling away. Another day of this, and she would be naked. She had to find some clothes.

"Tomorrow," he told her, on being asked what she should do. "Villages and camps ahead. Clothes can be found. But you're a Straken—can't you make clothes with magic?"

She told him no. He seemed confused by this. The hair on the nape of his neck bristled. "Magic can do anything! I've seen it myself! Are you trying to trick me?"

"Magic cannot do everything. I should know." She gave him a sharp look. "Anyway, why would I want to trick you? What reason would I have for doing so?"

His face tightened. "Everyone knows Strakens have their own reasons for doing things. They like tricking other creatures. They like to see them squirm." He was squirming himself, the fingers of his hands twisting into knots. "You'd better not try to trick me!"

She laughed in spite of herself. "You seem awfully concerned about being tricked. Why would that be, I wonder? A guilty conscience, perhaps?"

His eyes were furious. "I have a right to look out for myself! Strakens are not to be trusted!"

"I am not a Straken, Weka Dart," she said again. "I've told you that already. Pay attention to me this time. Look at me. I am not a Straken. I am an Ard Rhys. Say it."

He did so, rather reluctantly. He seemed determined that whether she admitted it or not, she was a Straken and not to be trusted, which made it odd that he had chosen to ally himself with her. Or rather, she corrected, choose her as a traveling companion. Clearly, if he felt as he did about Strakens, he would not travel with her if he could avoid it. It made her wonder what he was after.

"I should cover our tracks before the big things start to hunt," he announced suddenly, and disappeared down the trunk of the tree before she could stop him.

He was gone a long time, and when he returned he was gnawing on something he held in one hand. It was hard to tell what it might have been, but it looked as if it was the remains of a ferret or rat. All that was left were the hindquarters. There was blood on the Ulk Bog's mouth and face, and a wicked glint in his eyes. "Tasty," he said.

"You look happy enough," she observed, meeting his challenging stare. She had seen much worse than this, if he thought to shock her.

"Fresh meat," he declared. "Nothing already dead. I'm no scavenger."

He consumed what was left with relish, teeth tearing the raw meat into bite-size shreds that he quickly gulped down. Finished, he wiped his mouth with the back of his hand, licked his fingers, and belched. "Time for sleep," he announced.

He stretched himself out on one of the limbs, looking as if sleep would come easily. "Where are your people, Weka Dart?" she asked him, too uncomfortable herself even to think of sleeping.

"Back where I came from. Still living in their burrows. They are a shortsighted, unimaginative bunch. Not like me. That's why I left. I decided there was more for me in life than burrows and roots. But not if I remained with them."

What a liar, she thought. Even the way he spoke the words gave him away. He must think she would believe anything. It made her angry. "Where is it you intend to go?" she pressed, keeping her anger carefully hidden.

He smacked his lips. "Oh, that's for me to know. I have plans for myself. I may tell you when I get to know you better."

"Won't you be missed?" She had put up with this Ulk Bog's deceptions long enough and had decided to do something about it. He was relaxed and unsuspecting. It was a good time to teach him a lesson. She began to hum softly, bringing up the magic of the wishsong and layering it about him. "Parents? Brothers and sisters?"

He shrugged, yawned. "No family. No friends, either, for that matter. Not ones I care about leaving behind. Ulk Bogs are a stupid lot, most of them. Can't see beyond their ground roots and mushrooms."

"Roots can be tender and mushrooms sweet," she ventured, the magic beginning to insinuate itself into his thinking. "You were quick enough to bring them to me. Why don't you eat them?"

He laughed foolishly, the magic taking hold. He had no defense against it. A Druid would have brushed her efforts aside effortlessly, but Weka Dart didn't even know what she was doing to him. "I could tell you were the sort that ate roots and berries. Not me. I need meat, fresh meat. Keeps me strong. Makes me dangerous!"

She had a strong hold over him now, so she began to press harder. "Not eating roots was what got you in trouble in the first place, wasn't it?" she asked, guessing at the truth, reading it in his poor attempt at lying. "What sort of fresh meat did you eat? It must have been something that was forbidden to Ulk Bogs."

"More foolishness!" he snapped defensively. "What difference did it make? They weren't even ours! They were tender, and I only ate a few! There were plenty more where those came from! But you would have thought I had eaten my own children!"

"Instead of someone else's?"

"Another tribe's offspring, useless to everyone! Weren't even missed for a long time!"

"But when they were missed? . . ."

"All my fault, not even a chance at an explanation!"

"So they drove you out."

"I left before they could. It was clear what they intended for me, and I saw no reason to endure it. Stupid burrow people! Rodents! They are food for bigger things themselves, little more than rats to dragons and ogres and such! If you don't want to be prey, you have to be predator! I told them this, I told them! What good did it do? What reward did I get? A promise of punishment if I stayed and no more babies to eat. Impossible! I had a taste for them by then. I couldn't give them up just because the others didn't feel the same way I did!"

He stopped suddenly and stared at her, wild-eyed. "Why did I tell you that? I didn't want to tell you that! Not any of it! But I did! How did that happen? What did you do to me?"

"I helped you come to terms with the truth, little man," she said softly. "I don't like liars and deceivers. I was one myself, and I know them for what they are. You were perfectly willing for me to believe that you are traveling about to see the world. But the truth is that you are running away, perhaps from other Ulk Bogs searching for you because you ate their babies. You want me to protect you, but you don't want to tell me why. All this talk about my tricking you has got to do mostly with you tricking me."

"You used magic on me! You are a Straken, just as I said!"

"I am not a Straken . . ."

But Weka Dart was having none of it. He was so incensed he didn't even try to listen to the rest of what she was going to say, leaping to his feet, hissing and spitting like a scorched cat, and baring his teeth at her as if to attack. Then down the tree trunk he skittered, still raging at her, leaping away with a final epithet and disappearing into the dark.

She waited for him to return, unable to believe that he wouldn't.

Staying with her seemed too important for him to allow his pride to stand in the way. But after a while, when he failed to reappear, she gave up listening for him, deciding that she was better off without him in any case. Anything that would eat its own kind, whatever the reason, was not suitable company. If he stayed, she would have to watch him every minute, always wondering when he might turn on her. Let him go off on his own and be done with it.

But in the ensuing silence, she became aware again of how different she felt inside the Forbidding. For as much as that world resembled the one she had come from, it was not the same. Where before she had always been comfortable in the darkness, here she was uneasy. The night had a decidedly different feel. Smells, tastes, and sounds were just strange enough to bother her, to make her think that she must watch her every step. She was convinced she could make her way to that world's version of the Hadeshorn, if it existed, and attempt a summoning of the shades of the Druids. But was she ready for the things she might meet along the way? It was one thing to face down a Dracha, but another altogether to stand against a pack of Furies. She was powerful in her world, but how powerful was she in the Forbidding?

She stared out into the blackness, not at all certain she wanted to find out the answer.

T W E L V E

"Concentrate," he said, his disembodied voice coming from just over her left shoulder, soft and reassuring. "Remember what you are trying to do. Slow and steady. Keep the air moving at the same speed all the time. Breathe through your mind as well as your lungs."

She thought that an odd, but accurate way of expressing what was needed, and she did her best to comply. Using her skills, she exhaled and then blew the air in a steady, concentrated stream across the clearing to the leaf that hung suspended midair twenty yards away. She watched the leaf hover like a bug, vibrating slightly in response to the gentle currents, reacting to the fingers of magic she was using to control it. A small skill, in the larger scheme of things, but one that took her farther than she had gone before. She was getting better at using the magic, at perfecting the Druidic talents he sought to teach her, but she was still not as good as either of them wanted her to be.

"Now, lift gently," Ahren Elessedil instructed, still keeping out of her line of sight, not wishing to distract her any more than was necessary. He understood the delicacy of what she was doing. He preferred that she learn the sophisticated maneuvers first. The ones that relied on power and weight would come later and more easily.

Khyber Elessedil moved the leaf higher, taking it up another two feet until it was well out of reach of anyone standing under it. It was harder keeping it aloft, the wind currents stronger at the increased height, the force of gravity working with more insistence. She felt impatient with the exercise, as she did with so many, but she was determined to succeed. It was not easy for the daughter and sister of Elven Kings to persevere, knowing it would be much easier simply to accept the path her father, and now her brother, had laid out for her. But though she was born into the royal family, she had never felt a part of court life, and she did not think that was likely to change.

A bird flew by, bright orange and black-tipped at its wings and beak. Distracted by its beauty, she lost her concentration, and the leaf fluttered to the earth and lay still.

Her uncle came up beside her and placed his hand on her shoulder. "He was beautiful, wasn't he? Such a brilliant orange."

She nodded, angry and disappointed with herself. "I'll never learn anything if I keep letting myself be distracted by beautiful birds!"

"You'll never find any joy in life if you don't." He came around and stood facing her. "Don't be so hard on yourself. This takes time. It takes practice. I didn't learn it all at once either."

Warmed by his reassurances, she smiled in spite of herself. They were remarkably alike in personality, both possessed of quiet determination and strong emotions. Their dark features and hair gave them a similar appearance as well, and of late Khyber was as tall as her uncle, having grown the past year, edging toward womanhood, toward the marriageable age her brother welcomed and she loathed. Fine for him to want to marry her off so that she would be out of his hair, but that didn't make it right for her. She loved her brother, but he was nothing like her. In fact, aside from her mother, the member of the family she was closest to was standing right in front of her.

No one wanted to hear that, of course, since her uncle was not welcome in Arborlon. He had become, over the course of the years, the member of the family that the others were ashamed to acknowledge. They would have locked him away if he had been foolish enough to try to make a life with them, but Ahren Elessedil had decided to go another way a long time ago.

He patted her shoulder and glanced at the sky through the heavy canopy of tree limbs. "Midday. Why don't we have something to eat before we continue? It is easier to concentrate when your stomach isn't rumbling."

Which hers was, she realized with embarrassment. Sometimes she could barely tolerate herself, a vessel for shortcomings and ungovernable urges that betrayed her at every turn.

She followed him back through the woods to the village, her strides matching his, thinking that food would be good and his company over a glass of ale even better. She loved talking with her uncle—just talking with him. He was so interesting; he had done so many things in his life. He was not yet forty, and he was recognized everywhere as a Druid of immense importance and power. The Ard Rhys herself considered him indispensable, and she had visited him many times over the years, although Khyber had never been fortunate enough to be present when she did. Ahren Elessedil had sailed on the *Jerle Shannara* with the Ard Rhys, her brother Bek, and a handful of others whose names were now legendary. He had been one of the fortunate ones to survive. If not for him, the Ard Rhys might have failed in her efforts to restore the Druid Council at Paranor. It was his support of Grianne Ohmsford that had cost Ahren his place at court, that had earned him rebuke and exile from first his brother and now his brother's son. He had deserved neither, in her opinion, but she was alone in her support and was herself increasingly isolated by the male members of the Elessedil house.

Well, it hardly mattered in her uncle's case, given the use to which he had put his life. He had gone to Paranor with the first of the new Druids and studied the Druidic arts with the Ard Rhys. He was not blessed with natural talent, his sole use of magic previously confined to the Elfstones he had retrieved on his long-ago voyage. But he was a quick study and had an affinity for tapping into earth magic, which was at the heart of all Druid studies. He learned quickly, becoming strong enough to take his talent back into the Westland fifteen years ago, to the village of Emberen, where he had devoted his life to caring for the land and its people. He was good at what he did, and all had benefited greatly, no matter what the others in her family thought.

The problem, of course, was that none of them could get past what they perceived as Ahren's betrayal of his father, who had died at the hands of assassins dispatched by the Ard Rhys, when she was still the Ilse Witch. They could not forgive Ahren for tricking his elder brother, who became King afterwards, into sending Elves to serve as Druids under the woman who had killed their father. That he would be a part of such subterfuge, knowing as he did the truth of things, proved to be incendiary, once it was discovered. An order of exile was issued immediately, and all were forbidden even to speak his name. By then, he was already gone, of course, studying with the Ard Rhys and those he had brought to serve her, the first of many who would come to Paranor. Even the fact that the Ard Rhys had been transformed so utterly by the power of the Sword of Shannara made no difference to the Elessedils. Nothing would satisfy them, short of seeing her dead and gone. That would change when enough time had passed and enough new Kings had ascended the Elessedil throne, but change of that sort was very slow.

"How much longer will you be able to stay with me?" Ahren asked her suddenly.

She laughed. "Anxious for me to be gone, now that you've seen how inept I am?"

"You have put your finger on it," he agreed. "Nevertheless, I am concerned about your brother's response to your increasingly frequent visits."

Kellen hated her visits to Emberen, but even as King he could not do much to prevent them. She had told him as much, suggesting that he had enough to worry about with the war on the Prekkendorran. He had inherited the war after their father was killed, and Kellen had made it his life's mission to see it concluded with a Free-born victory—something that at present looked none too likely. Between governing the Elves and waging his pet war, Kellen had little time for her. She knew he hated his uncle, but he ignored Ahren because it was easier than taking more direct action. Of course, Kellen didn't yet realize the nature of her visits. If he discovered what she was up to—or, more to the point, *when* he discovered it—he would put a stop to things in a heartbeat. But by then, she hoped, she would be a student at Paranor and beyond his reach. She hadn't told her uncle yet, but she thought he must suspect as much. She was not in line for the throne, since her brother had produced male heirs and the line of succession ran down the male side of the family ladder until it stopped and females were all that were left. So it shouldn't matter to the rest of her family what she did so long as she stayed out of the way.

For the moment, she was willing to accept that compromise,

having little interest in Arborlon and family in any event, though there were times when her resolve was sorely tested.

"My brother is off visiting the Prekkendorran," she said, brushing Ahren's concerns aside. "He gives little thought to me. For the most part, he doesn't even know where I am. He doesn't know now, as a matter of fact."

Ahren looked at her. "Does anyone?"

"Mother."

He nodded. "Your passion for the Druidic arts, for elemental magic's secrets, can't sit well with her. She sees you married and producing grandchildren."

Khyber grunted. "She sees poorly these days. But then I don't do much to enlighten her. She would only worry, and Kellen gives her reason enough for that. Besides, she has grandchildren—my brother's sons, good, stout, warrior lads, all three. They fill her grandmotherly needs nicely."

They walked into the village and down the single road that formed its center, to Ahren's small cottage at the far end. He had built it himself and continued to work on it from time to time, telling her he found working with his hands relaxing. He kept a project in the works at all times, the better perhaps to get through the demands of his service to the Westland. At present, he was installing a new roof, a shingle-shake overlay that required hand-splitting new shingles to replace the old. It was taxing and time-consuming, which she supposed was just what he wanted.

They sat at a small outdoor table in the sunlight and ate cheese, apples, and bread washed down with cold ale from his earth cellar. Food and drink always tasted better in Emberen than at home. It had to do with the company, but also with the life of the village. In Emberen she was just Khyber to everyone she knew, not Princess or Highness or some other deferential term. Nothing was expected of her save common courtesy and decent manners.

She was just like everyone else, or as much so as was possible in a world of inequities.

Her command of the Druid magic set her apart, of course, just as it did Ahren. Well, not as much so as Ahren, who was more highly skilled in its use. But the point was that the villagers regarded the use of elemental magic as a trade, a craft of great value and some mystery but, ultimately, of much good. Her uncle had never done anything to persuade them otherwise, and she intended to follow in his steps. She knew the history of magic in the Four Lands, both within and without the family. All too often, magic had caused great harm, sometimes unintentionally. In many places, it was still mistrusted and feared. But with the formation of the new Druid Council, the Ard Rhys had mandated that magic's use embody caution and healing in order for it to be sanctioned. In spite of her checkered past—or perhaps because of it—she had dedicated the Druid order to that end. Khyber had witnessed the results of that commitment in the nature of the service undertaken by Druids like her uncle, who had left Paranor and gone out into the Four Lands to work with its people. The effect of their efforts was apparent. Slowly, but surely, the use of elemental magic was being accepted everywhere.

She would undertake such a mission, as well, one day soon. She would study at Paranor and then go out into the Four Lands to apply her skills. She was determined to make something of her life beyond what the others in her family had envisioned. It was her life, after all, not theirs. She would live it the way she chose.

"I want to work with the stones again this afternoon," she announced, thinking suddenly of something else entirely and feeling a sudden heat rise to her face.

One of their lessons was in the cracking open of rocks by touch and thought applied in precise combination, a technique in which envisioning a result leads to its happening. A Druid could manage it, just as easily as tearing paper between fingers. She hadn't found the skill for it herself, but she was determined it would be hers.

"We can do that," he agreed. "So long as you swear to me that you are not violating any promises or arousing any concerns by being here."

"Nothing out of the ordinary. I have another week before my brother returns and looks to find everything the way he left it. I will be back by then."

But not before you show me what you know about what I carry, she thought to herself. *My secret, for now, but I will reveal it to you before I leave and you will teach me to make use of it.*

Her heart pounded at the prospect. She was uncertain how her request would be received—uncertain, for that matter, of his reaction to what she had done. She had taken an enormous chance, but she had learned a long time ago that if you didn't take chances now and then in a royal family, nothing ever was permitted you that you really wanted. Mostly, her family wanted to keep her safe and compliant, and she had never wanted to be either of those.

It was surprising to her that after all these years, any of them really thought she would ever be docile. When she was little, she was her brother's worst nightmare. Kellen was older and stronger, but she was always the more daring. She learned everything first and learned it quicker. She was the better rider, her bond with horses instinctual and passionate. She was better with weapons, able to battle him to a draw when he was a head taller and she barely strong enough to wield the practice blades. When he was intent on his studies of court practices and statesmanship, she was off wandering the forests and river country that surrounded her home. At eight, she ran away and got as far as the Sarandanon before a family of wheat farmers recognized her and brought her back. At twelve, she had already flown in an airship all the way to Callahorn, stowed away in the hold until she was discovered.

And all that didn't even touch on the times she had disguised herself as an Elven Hunter to go off on dangerous forays into country so wild that if her father had been alive, she would have been locked in her rooms for a month when she was brought back.

But he wasn't alive, by then; he was dead, killed on the Prekkendorran. Her brother was King, and he was still intimidated by her. He gave her a lecture that would have scorched paint in a rainstorm before turning his mind to less troublesome concerns, but a lecture was nothing to her.

She brushed back her thick, unruly hair. Sometimes she thought she should just cut it all off and be done with it, but her mother would have reacted to that much the same way she would have reacted if Khyber had announced she was going to marry a Troll. There was no point in antagonizing her mother, who was her sole source of support and confidence.

She finished off her cheese and bread, watching her uncle surreptitiously. It was hard to know what he was thinking. His expression never really changed, the result of his Druid discipline, which taught that emotions must be contained if magic was to be successfully wielded. She wanted to tell him what she had done when he was in a good mood. But how could she know? She grimaced. She recognized what she was doing. She was procrastinating. She should just tell him. Right here. Right now.

Nevertheless, she did not. She finished her glass of ale, rose, and began to clear the table of plates and glasses. It was one of the small services she could perform on her visits, and she liked doing something for her uncle that no one else would. He lived alone, and some said he did so because he preferred it that way. He had been in love a long time ago with a seer on the *Jerle Shannara*, though he had never said as much when speaking of her. He had been only a boy himself in those days, younger even than she was now, and much more sheltered. The seer had been killed on the voyage, and Khyber was fairly sure he had never gotten over it. She had done something important for him, something that had helped him grow into the man he was, although once again he never said exactly what that something was.

Since then, there had been only one other woman—a sorceress, who had loved him desperately. Khyber had seen them together, and it was frightening how determined the other woman was that Ahren Elessedil should be hers. But he had decided otherwise and never spoke of her now. Apparently, she was as exiled from his life as he was from Arborlon's.

"Have you ever thought about returning to Paranor?" she asked impulsively, pausing on her way into the house with the dishes.

He looked at her. "Now and then. But I think I belong here, in the Westland. Paranor is a place for study and Druid politics. Neither is for me. What are you really asking, Khyber?"

She made a face. "Nothing. I just wondered if you ever missed the company of other Druids, the ones who still remain at Paranor."

"You mean her," he said, his smile sad and ironic. He was too quick, she thought. He could read her mind. "No," he said. "That's done."

"I just think it would help if you had someone living here with you. Someone to help you. So you wouldn't be lonely."

It sounded stupid, even to her. He laughed. "Well, it wouldn't be her, in any case. She isn't the kind to help others when she has herself to worry about. Why are you so eager to see me partnered? I don't see you looking around for someone to marry."

She stalked into the house without replying, thinking that her good intentions were wasted on her uncle. He was right about her, of course, but that was beside the point. She was too young to marry, and he would soon be too old and too set in his ways. In fact, he already was, she decided. There was no room in his life for anything but his work. She didn't know why she thought that it might be otherwise. He would live alone until he died, and she might as well accept it. She would just have to do the best she could for him on her visits and hope he got by the rest of the time.

She had just returned for the rest of the dishes when she heard a shout from the other end of the village, and Elves came running out of their houses and workshops, looking skyward.

"An airship," Ahren said, getting to his feet at once.

No airships ever came to Emberen. It was too small and too isolated. There was only one road, and much of the year it was sodden and rutted and virtually impassable by wagon or cart. Khyber always came on horseback, knowing that she could be assured of getting in and out again that way. Flying vessels in that part of the world were rare. Some of the Elves who lived in the village had never even seen one.

She followed Ahren down the road and through the village toward the sound of the shouting, joining the flow of the crowd and trying to make out the ship through the heavy canopy of limbs. She had no idea where it might find a place to land in woods as heavy as those surrounding Emberen, but she supposed there must be a large enough clearing somewhere nearby. Ahren was striding ahead, gray Druid robes whipping about his ankles, and she thought from the purposeful nature of his walk that he was concerned that whoever had taken the trouble to fly an airship to Emberen might not have their best interests at heart. A rush of excitement flooded through her at the prospect of whom it might be.

Maybe the routine of her studies was about to take an unexpected, but rather more interesting turn.

The crowd reached the end of the road and turned down a pathway that led into the trees. Overhead, she caught a glimpse of movement. The airship appeared momentarily and was gone again, circling the trees. It wasn't very big—a skiff at best.

She broke into a narrow clearing just as the airship started down, a slow looping motion that brought it in line with a narrow opening in the forest canopy. She could see it clearly by then, a small skiff of the sort favored by Southlanders who did their flying across the inland lakes. Even though it was coming down at a precipitous decline, she didn't think that its power had failed. Nevertheless, given the tightness of the space, the pilot was taking a dangerous risk. Whoever was flying had better be pretty good or the airship would end up in pieces in the trees.

"They're landing!" someone belatedly cried out in surprise.

As the pilot continued to maneuver toward the slot, the Elves scattered back into the trees, pointing and shouting. Khyber stood her ground, not wanting to miss the details of the landing. She had flown on airships, but never seen one landed in a space so small. She wanted to see how it was done. She wanted to see if the pilot could do it.

She got more than she bargained for. It appeared the craft would touch down before it reached her, but at the last minute it lurched drunkenly, skipped across the forest floor, and came right at her. If Ahren hadn't yanked her out of the way and thrown her down, she might have been struck by the pieces of metal that broke loose and flew wildly in all directions. The little skiff slammed into the ground, tore open huge ruts with its pontoons, and came to a halt not twenty feet from where she crouched.

Ahren released his grip on her arm and stood her back up. "You need to pay better attention, Khyber," he said quietly.

She rubbed her arm and shrugged carelessly. "Sorry, Uncle Ahren. I just wanted to watch."

The Elves began to filter out of the trees for a look at the airship's occupants, one of whom, a boy who was younger than she was, stood on the skiff's deck, surveying the damage and shaking his head. She stared. Was he the one who had been flying the skiff? This boy? Then a second head popped up from one of the storage holds in the starboard pontoon, a Dwarf who looked as if he didn't know whether to strangle the boy or embrace him.

"Is that Tagwen?" Ahren whispered in disbelief. "Shades, I think it is. What is he doing here?"

With Khyber right beside him, he hurried forward to find out.

THIRTEEN

Penderrin Ohmsford hauled himself out of the pilot box, brushed off his rumpled clothes, and surveyed the little skiff with no small sense of satisfaction. Another vessel would have broken apart on impact, coming in as fast and as hard as she had. That they were down safely at all was a miracle, but he had survived tougher landings and had never really been in doubt about the outcome.

Tagwen did not share that reaction. The Dwarf was incensed as he climbed out of the storage bin into which he had fallen, and pointed a shaking finger at the boy.

"What's the matter with you? Are you trying to kill us? I thought you said you could fly this thing! Didn't you tell me you could? Why your aunt thinks you are so good at flying escapes me! I could have done a better job myself!"

His beard was matted with leaves and twigs and dirt clots, and a rather large leaf stuck out of his hair like a feather, but he failed to notice, the full weight of his attention given over to Pen.

Pen shrugged. "We're down and we're safe, and we're walking away," he pointed out. "I think that ought to be good enough."

"Well, it isn't good enough!" Tagwen snapped.

"Well, why not?"

"Because we should be dead! This time we were lucky! What about next time? What about the time after that? I'm supposed to be able to depend on you! I said I would come with you in search of the Ard Rhys, but I didn't say I would commit suicide!"

"I don't see why you're so angry!" Pen snapped, made angry himself by the other's irascible behavior.

"Tagwen, is that you? As I live and breathe, it is! Well met!"

The shout came from one side, drawing their attention and putting an end to their arguing. The speaker was an Elf about the same age as Pen's father, but with a more careworn face and with an even slighter build. A girl walked beside him, darker complected and more intense. Her eyes were riveted on Pen, and he had the feeling that she was making up her mind about him before she even knew who he was. Then she smiled when she saw him looking back at her, a disarming, warm grin that made him regret his hasty conclusion.

"Tagwen!" the speaker exclaimed again, reaching up to take the Dwarf's hand. "What are you doing out here? And on an airship?"

"Desperate times require desperate acts," Tagwen advised philosophically. He extended his own hand, and they shook. "I must say, flying with this boy is as desperate as I care to get." He paused, glancing over at Pen ruefully. "Although I will admit, in all fairness, that he has saved my life several times on our journey."

He reached out a hand and guided Pen to the forefront. "Penderrin Ohmsford, this is Ahren Elessedil. You might have heard your father speak of him."

"Ah, young Pen!" the Elf greeted enthusiastically, shaking his hand, as well. "I haven't seen you since you were too tiny to walk. You probably don't remember me."

"My father does indeed speak of you all the time," Pen agreed. "My mother, as well."

"They were good friends to me on our voyage west, Pen. If not for your father's help, I would not have returned." He gestured toward the girl. "This is my niece, Khyber, my brother's daughter. She visits from Arborlon."

"Hello again, Khyber." Tagwen nodded to her. "You have grown up."

"Not all that far," she replied, her eyes staying on Pen. "That was a spectacular landing," she said. "I didn't think you were going to make it down."

Tagwen went crimson again, the disapproving frown returning to his bluff features, so Pen jumped down from the decking with a mumbled thanks and quickly added, "Tagwen's right. I was lucky."

"I think it was more than that," she said. "How long have you been flying airships?"

"Enough about airships!" the Dwarf huffed, noticing for the first time the debris in his beard and brushing it clean with furious strokes. "We have other things to talk about." He lowered his voice. "Prince Ahren, can we go somewhere more private?"

Elves were gathered all around by then, come out of the trees to take a closer look at the airship and its occupants. Children were already scurrying around the pontoons and under the decking, making small excited noises amid squeals of delight. A few of the braver ones were even trying to climb aboard while their parents pulled them back.

"My cottage is just up the road, Tagwen," Ahren Elessedil said. "We can clean you up and give you something to eat and drink. Khyber makes the best mango black tea in the Westland, a secret she won't share even with me." He gave the girl a wink. "Leave the skiff. She'll be all right where she is. She's an object of curiosity, but the villagers won't harm her."

"I don't care whether they harm her or not!" Tagwen groused. "I've had more than enough of her for one day, thanks very much!"

They walked back through the village, Ahren Elessedil leading with Tagwen at his side, Pen following with Khyber. No one said very much, respecting the Dwarf's wishes that they wait until they were in private to talk. Pen was thinking that even though Tagwen had insisted the Elven Prince-turned-Druid could help them in their search for the Ard Rhys, Ahren didn't look up to it. If anything, he looked too soft and frail for the physical demands of such an endeavor. A strong wind might blow him away, the boy thought. But looks were misleading. Ahren Elessedil had survived the voyage of the *Jerle Shannara* when more than twenty others had not, and he wasn't a Druid then. Tagwen had warned Pen not to judge Ahren too quickly, that what was visible on the surface was not necessarily representative of the man inside. Pen hoped he was right.

"Your father is Bek Ohmsford?" Khyber Elessedil asked him.

He nodded. "Do you know the story from your uncle?"

"All of it. It is the most famous story of this generation. My family doesn't much care for it because they hold your aunt responsible for my grandfather's assassination and Uncle Ahren responsible for helping her escape them and found the new Druid order at Paranor. My brother is the worst. I don't agree with any of them. That's why I'm here. I am training with my uncle to be a Druid. In secret."

"Your family doesn't know?"

She shook her head. "They think I come here only to visit, so they leave me alone. They don't know the truth."

He stepped a little closer, lowering his voice. "My parents don't know where I am. They think I am still back in Patch Run."

"What will they do when they find out you're not?"

He smiled. "Track me down. They can do it, too. But they won't find out for a while. They're off in the Anar on an expedition, guiding customers hunting and fishing. They won't get back for weeks. So they won't know."

She smiled back. "Looks like we have something in common."

They reached Ahren's cottage, where the Druid provided Pen and Tagwen with fresh clothes, a bucket of water, and cloths with which to wash up. The pair did so, and returned to find that Khyber had prepared the promised black tea and set out some cheese and bread, as well. Since neither had eaten since early morning, when they had set out from somewhere below the Mermidon, they devoured the food hungrily and drank down the entire pot of tea.

When they were finished, Tagwen rocked back in his seat, glanced across the table at Ahren to be certain he was listening, and said, "I'll tell you why we've come now, but it might not be something you want to share with Khyber." He gave her a pointed look. "No offense is meant, young lady, but the truth is you might be better off not knowing what we have to say. There is some danger involved."

The girl looked at her uncle, who shrugged. "I am not much good at keeping secrets from Khyber," he said, smiling. "In any case, she would have it out of me before the sun was down. If you don't mind, I'll let her stay to hear your story."

Tagwen nodded. "She can quit listening when she decides she doesn't want to hear any more. I'll leave it at that."

Leaning forward, arms resting on the tabletop, bearded face scrunched up so that he looked as if he was about to undertake

the most difficult task of his life, he began his story. He related
the events surrounding the disappearance of the Ard Rhys, the
dismissal of Kermadec and his Rock Trolls, his own decision to seek
help from Grianne's brother, his arrival at Patch Run and meeting
with Pen, and their subsequent flight from Terek Molt and the crew
of the Druid airship *Galaphile*. He ended with the unexpected appearance of the King of the Silver River, come out of nowhere to
save them from Terek Molt and to tell them of what they must do.

The longer Tagwen's story went on, the more ridiculous it
sounded to Pen and the more foolish he felt for coming even that far.
What the King of the Silver River expected him to do—even if you
accepted that it really was the King of the Silver River and not some
malevolent shade—was patently impossible. For a boy with no practical magic to go alone into the Forbidding was so arrogant and pig-
headed that no right-thinking person would even consider it. Pen
didn't have to know the particulars of what lay behind the Faerie
magic that closed away the creatures of the Forbidding to know that
he had virtually no chance of surviving a journey inside. He might be
able to find and secure the darkwand from the tanequil—though that
was debatable, as well—but he saw no way he could reasonably expect to rescue the Ard Rhys once he had done so.

By the time Tagwen had concluded, Pen could not bring himself to look at Ahren Elessedil. He imagined himself in the other's
shoes, thinking that he would dismiss this whole business in a
heartbeat. The Dwarf had been so certain Ahren would help them,
but looking at it now, Pen couldn't see any reason why.

He glanced over at the Druid in spite of himself and found the
other staring back.

"This is a terrible responsibility you have been given, Penderrin," Ahren Elessedil said quietly. "I am surprised you found the
courage to accept it."

Pen stared. It was not what he had expected the Druid to say.

"I was just thinking that it might have been a good idea to think it through a little more."

"Are you worried that you acted in haste? Or that you might have been tricked in some way because it all sounds so incredible?" The Elf nodded. "I remember feeling that way more than once during my time on the *Jerle Shannara*. I don't think you can avoid such feelings. Maybe second-guessing what you choose to do in difficult situations is necessary if you are to find peace of mind. Blind acceptance of what you believe to be the dictates of fate and circumstance is dangerous."

"Do you think it really was the King of the Silver River?" Pen asked impulsively.

The Druid pursed his lips. "Your father met him years ago, on his way to Arborlon. He told me of the meeting later; he described it. Not so much how the King of the Silver River looked—that wouldn't matter anyway because he can change his appearance. He described how it happened and how it made him feel. Your experience sounds as if it was the same. Yes, Pen, I think it was him."

He glanced at Khyber, who was staring at Pen with rapt attention. "Khyber believes it was, don't you, Khyber?"

She nodded at once. "I believe it all. But what are we going to do about it, Uncle Ahren? Sorry, what are *you* going to do about it?" she corrected herself.

"I told the boy to come here," Tagwen confessed, straightening. "It's my fault we have involved you in this. But I know how you feel about the Ard Rhys, and I couldn't think of anyone else to turn to. I don't think we can do this on our own. We managed to get this far on grit and luck." He grimaced. "I can't imagine how we will get all the way into the Charnals alone."

"But we can if we have to," Pen added quickly.

Tagwen shot him a withering glance. "You have more confidence in what we can accomplish than I do, Penderrin."

Ahren Elessedil smiled ruefully. "Confidence isn't to be discouraged, Tagwen. Nor overrated, Penderrin. Remember—we seek a balance in all things."

"But you will help them, won't you?" Khyber pressed eagerly.

"Of course, I will help. The Ard Rhys has been both mentor and friend to me; I would never abandon her or those who feel about her as I do." He paused, looking again at Tagwen. "But much of what you have told me is troublesome. I think there is still a great deal about this business that we don't know. Shadea a'Ru, Terek Molt, and those others are dangerous, but they lack sufficient power to imprison the Ard Rhys within the Forbidding. It took the magic of an entire Elven nation to create the Forbidding in the first place. Nothing passes through the barrier except when the Ellcrys fails. She doesn't do so now, so far as I know."

He glanced at Khyber for confirmation. "She was well when I departed Arborlon a week ago," she said.

"She wouldn't have declined so precipitously without our hearing about it," Ahren continued. "No, some other force is at work here—something hidden from us. We may not find out what it is until we reach the Ard Rhys, but we must be wary of it."

He paused. "A more immediate problem is that those who have worked against the Ard Rhys will be searching for Pen. They will not stop simply because he has escaped them once. Perhaps they realize that he has the potential to help her. Perhaps they are simply looking to tie up loose ends. The King of the Silver River helped you escape once, Pen, but he will not be able to help you a second time. You are beyond his reach now."

"They were searching for my father when they came to Patch Run," Pen pointed out. "Maybe they will forget about me and go after him."

The Druid shook his head. "They will keep looking. Eventually, they will find you. So we must act quickly. Do you have any idea at all where in the Charnals the tanequil can be found?"

Pen shook his head. "Only what the King of the Silver River told us—that it grows on an island beyond the ruins of a city called Stridegate and that Urdas and Trolls might help us find the way. Nothing more than that."

"I can use earth magic to try to seek it out through lines of power and air currents," the Druid mused, looking off into the woods, as if he might find the answer in the trees. "But that approach is uncertain. We need something more definite."

"What you need," Khyber declared suddenly, "are the Elfstones, the seeking stones."

Pen knew the stories of the Elfstones, which had been given by the Druid Allanon to Shea Ohmsford to aid him in his search for the Sword of Shannara and then had been held for many years by other members of the Ohmsford family. They had been returned to the Elven people during the reign of Wren Elessedil, an Ohmsford cousin, and remained there until they disappeared with Kael Elessedil fifty years earlier. Ahren Elessedil had recovered them on the voyage of the *Jerle Shannara* and given them to his brother in exchange for help in forming the Third Druid Council.

Ahren frowned. "What do you know of the Elfstones, Khyber?"

"Enough, from listening to my father and brother. They spoke of them often, before my father's death, usually when they thought I couldn't hear. They believed the Stones could be used as a weapon against the Federation."

The Druid thought about it a moment. "Well, I won't deny that the Elfstones would help us. But I don't have possession of them or any reasonable hope of persuading your brother to lend them to me. We will have to find another way."

"Maybe not." Khyber reached in her tunic and produced a

small pouch. With a determined, almost defiant look, she held it out. "I took them from their hiding place because I wanted you to teach me how to use them. I was going to tell you later, when I found the right way to do so, because I knew you would be angry with me. But I guess I can't wait any longer, so here they are. If you want to be angry, go ahead."

She thrust them at her startled uncle, who immediately said, "Khyber, you have gone too far."

Her lips compressed defiantly. "My brother refuses even to look at them since our father died. They serve no purpose being locked away. Besides, I have as much right to use them as any other member of the family. The Elfstones belong to all the Elves. The Elessedils are caretakers and nothing more. Someone has to learn to use them. Why not me?"

"Because you are not King of the Elves and do not have his permission!" Ahren snapped, balancing the pouch in his palm as if weighing the option of throwing it into the trees. "What will happen when Kellen finds out what you have done? You won't be making any more trips to Emberen!"

Khyber shrugged. "He won't find out. I replaced the Elfstones with pebbles. As I said, he never even looks at them. In any case, that's not what's important. What's important is the Ard Rhys. Uncle Ahren, we can use the Elfstones! We can find the tanequil with their magic! You know we can! Don't you want to help Pen and Tagwen?"

Ahren Elessedil flushed angrily, his composure beginning to slip. "Don't twist my words, Khyber. I know what matters. I also know a great deal more about the use of the Elfstones than you do. They are a dangerous magic. Using them has consequences you know nothing about. Ask Penderrin about his family history. Why in the world did you think I would agree to this? What makes you think you should be the one who knows how to use them?"

"Because no one else dares!" she snapped. "No one but me! If I am to be a Druid, I should know how magic works in all its forms. You teach me earth magic, and that can have consequences, as well. Aren't I careful with the earth magic? Don't you think I would be careful with the Elfstones, too? Don't you trust me? Anyway, things have changed. I have given you the Stones so that you can help Pen and Tagwen. Are you going to do so or not?"

She glared at him, and Pen found himself holding his breath in astonishment. He would never have dared to talk to the Druid that way. Whatever bond she shared with her uncle, it was much stronger than he had imagined. She wasn't afraid of him at all—not intimidated in the least. He risked a quick glance at Tagwen, who seemed equally surprised.

"If you use the Elfstones, you can discover if what the King of the Silver River told Pen is true," she continued insistently. "You can see whether or not there is even a tanequil to be found. Then we can at least know whether there is a chance of helping the Ard Rhys by looking for it."

It was hard to argue with logic like that, and Ahren Elessedil didn't even try. He gave his niece a final look of reproof, then opened the pouch and poured the contents into his hands. The Elfstones glimmered a deep blue in the midday sun, their facets mirroring the world about them in prismatic colors. There were three of them, perfectly formed, flawless, and beautiful. Pen remembered the legends. One Elfstone each for the heart, mind, and body, together forming a whole that responded to the strength of the user. Only those born of Elven blood could use them, and only if they were freely given or claimed by the user. Once, they had belonged to the Ohmsfords, and it was Wil Ohmsford's inadvisable but necessary use of them to help the Elven girl Amberle that had altered his body and passed on to his scions the magic that was dying out with Pen.

"I will use the Stones, Khyber," Ahren Elessedil said, "because you are right in believing that only by using them can we be certain that the tanequil is real. If the Elfstones reveal it to us, then we know the journey to reach it should be made. But understand something else. I spoke of consequences. By using the Stones, I risk revealing our intentions to Shadea a'Ru and her allies. The Elfstones are a powerful magic, and its release will be detected. When that happens, those we seek to escape will come looking."

"They will come anyway, Uncle Ahren," Khyber pointed out defensively. "You just said so."

Ahren nodded. "But now they will come sooner. By nightfall, in all probability. We will no longer have time to think about what we are going to do. The decision will have been made. We will have to leave Emberen—Penderrin, Tagwen, and myself in search of the tanequil, and you back to Arborlon."

Khyber Elessedil shook her head at once. "I'm going with you. I have no other choice. Uncle Ahren, please, let me finish before you say anything! You are going to take the Elfstones with you because you know you will need them again. Since I can't return home without them, I will have to go, as well. But there is another reason, an even better one. If something happens to you, neither Pen nor Tagwen can use the Stones because they aren't Elves. That leaves me, if you teach me how. I know it isn't what you want. I know you don't like the idea. But you know it's necessary. Finding and rescuing the Ard Rhys is what matters."

She paused. "I want this, Uncle Ahren. I want to help. I want to do something besides sit around in Arborlon and wait for my family to marry me off. I want my life to matter. Please. Let me come."

He studied her for a moment, then turned to Tagwen. "Is there any other Druid at Paranor that we can trust to come with us?"

Tagwen frowned and pulled absently at his beard. "If you're

asking me if there is anyone I can be sure of, the answer is no. I trust some more than others, but at this point I don't know how deep the conspiracy goes. You know how things are as well as I do." He squared his shoulders. "I think we ought to take her with us. She's older than this boy and she's able. We might need her. I don't like to think about it, but something could happen to any of us. The rest have to be able to carry on."

Ahren Elessedil shook his head in dismay. "I regret agreeing to let you listen to this conversation in the first place, Khyber. This isn't something you should be involved in."

"It isn't something any of us should be involved in," she replied. "But we all are, aren't we? Let me come."

He took a long time making up his mind, and Pen was certain that he was going to say no. Pen's parents would have said no to him, had they been in a position to do so. Parents didn't want their children taking the sort of risks involved here. Parents wanted their children safe at home. He didn't think it was any different with uncles and nieces.

"All right," Ahren said finally, surprising them all. "You can come with us—mostly because I can't think of what else to do with you. Sending you home will just get you in worse trouble, and whatever trouble comes of this ought to be mine. But you must agree to do as I say, Khyber. Whatever I tell you to do on this journey, you do it. No arguments, no excuses. I know you; I know how you think. Give me your word."

She nodded eagerly. "You have it."

Ahren sighed, tightened his fingers about the Elfstones, rose from the table, and stretched out his arm. His eyes closed in concentration, but his face remained calm. "Stand back from me," he said softly. "Watch carefully what the magic shows. Remember it well."

Not certain what to expect, they backed away from him, eyes

riveted on his outstretched hand. Slowly his fingers opened to the light. His concentration deepened. The seconds crawled past.

Then abruptly, light exploded from the crystals in a deep cerulean starburst, brightened until the sun itself disappeared behind the enveloping blue, then shot away into the distance in a blinding flare. It arced away through the trees and beyond, through mountains and hills and the curve of the earth itself. Some of what they saw was recognizable—the Dragon's Teeth and the Charnals, the Mermidon and the Chard Rush, even the sweep of the Streleheim and the dismal emptiness of the Malg. Forests came and went, one a shelter for gardens that eclipsed in beauty and complexity anything they had ever seen, a profusion of flowers and silvery waterfalls painted against a shimmering backdrop of green.

When the light finally came to rest, somewhere so far away that the distance could barely be calculated, it was illuminating a strange tree. The tree was huge, larger than the black oaks of Callahorn, broad-limbed and wide-leafed. Its bark was smooth, a mottled black and gray. Its leaves were deepest green with an orange border. The tree was bathed in dappled sunlight and surrounded by a dense forest of more familiar trees—oaks, elms, hickories, maples, and the like. Beyond the trees, nothing was visible. The tree seemed incredibly old, even in the wash of the Elfstones' light, and Pen felt certain as he looked upon it that it was as old as Faerie. He could feel its intelligence, even in what was no more than a vision. He could sense its life force, slow and rhythmic as a quiet heartbeat.

The blue light held steady for a moment, then flared once and was gone, leaving the watchers staring at nothing, half-blind and stunned by the suddenness and intensity of the experience. They blinked at each other in the ensuing silence, the image of the tree and it surroundings still vivid in their minds.

Ahren Elessedil closed his fingers about the Elfstones. "Now we know," he said.

"Or think we do," Tagwen grumbled.

Pen swallowed against a sudden tightness in his throat. He was dizzy at what seeing the tree had made him feel, deep inside where instincts governed thought. "No, Tagwen, that was it," he said softly. "I could *feel* it. That was the tanequil."

Ahren Elessedil nodded. "We are settled on what we must do." He dumped the Elfstones back into their pouch and tucked the pouch into his tunic. "Time slips away, and it doesn't favor us by doing so. Let's move quickly."

FOURTEEN

Midday at Paranor was dark and forbidding, the skies gone black with storm clouds and the air as still as death. There had been no sunlight all day, only a hazy glow at sunrise before the enveloping clouds screened even that away. Birds had long since gone to roost in sheltering havens, and the winds had died away to nothing. The world was hushed and waiting in expectation of thunder and lightning and fury.

Shadea a'Ru glanced through the open window of her chambers, her face a mirror of the weather. She should have felt triumph and satisfaction, a reward for her successes. She had dispatched Grianne Ohmsford into the Forbidding and taken her place. The Druid Council, albeit with some reluctance and after considerable debate, had named her Ard Rhys. Her cohorts controlled all the major positions on the council, and Sen Dunsidan, as Prime Minister of the Federation, had officially recognized her as head of the order. The Rock Trolls under Kermadec had been dismissed and sent home in disgrace, blamed for the disappearance of the Ard Rhys and, in more than a few corners, suspected as the cause for it, as well. Everything had worked out perfectly, exactly as she had hoped and planned.

Except for that boy.

She ran her fingers distractedly through her chopped-off blond hair, letting the short ends slip through her fingers like the loose threads of her perfect plan. It was all because of Terek Molt, who was the most reliable of her coconspirators and the one Druid she thought she could depend upon. To let that boy—that slip of a boy—make a fool of him like that was unforgivable. It was bad enough that none of them had thought to lock up Tagwen, who they should have known would not sit idly by and do nothing after his beloved Ard Rhys disappeared, but to lose the boy, as well, was too much. She should have taken care of the matter herself, but it was impossible for her to do everything.

She stalked to the door and stood staring at it a moment, thinking to go out again to calm herself. She had walked the corridors earlier, an intimidating presence to the Druids she now commanded. They would obey her because she was Ard Rhys, but also because they were afraid of her. No one would challenge her openly while she had the backing of Molt and the others and the Ard Rhys was gone, though some would plot behind her back, just as they had plotted against Grianne Ohmsford. She could do nothing about them until they tried to act, but she could let them know she was watching and waiting to catch them out.

She walked back to the window and looked out again. The first sharp gusts of wind were rippling the tree limbs, signaling the approach of the rainstorm. She had half a mind to put all of them out into it, every last Druid—to make them hike to the Kennon Pass and back again as an exercise in deprivation and humility. Some of them might not come back, and it wouldn't make her unhappy if they didn't.

Her thoughts returned to Tagwen and the boy. They might

have escaped her for the moment, she thought, but sooner or later she would find them again. The parents, as well. She had Druids and airships looking for all of them and had put out the word to all corners of the Four Lands. She had kept it simple. The ones she sought were members of Grianne Ohmsford's family and they were in danger. Help could be given them at Paranor, where their Druid protectors would keep them safe. Anyone seeing them was to send word. As incentive, she had offered a substantial reward. Most would ignore the offer, but the greedy among them would look around. Someone would see the boy and his Dwarf companion and report them. And when they were found, she would deal with them herself.

She was contemplating the satisfaction that enterprise would give her, when a sharp knock sounded, and without bothering to wait for her to respond, Terek Molt barged in.

"What do you think you are doing?" she snapped at him. "Rooms have doors for a reason, Molt!"

"We've found them," he rumbled in his deep, subterranean voice, ignoring her. "West, across the Mermidon."

She started. "Tagwen and the boy?"

"Only moments ago, someone used Elfstone magic. It was visible on the scrye waters in the cold chamber. Iridia was there to see it. There is no mistaking what it is."

The cold chamber was where the Druids read the lines of power that crisscrossed the Four Lands. The scrye waters were the table of liquid on which all uses of magic revealed themselves as ripples that indicated the extent of the power expended. Grianne Ohmsford herself had implemented it at Paranor more than a dozen years ago, a tool she had employed as the Ilse Witch.

"Elfstones?" she asked. She did not yet understand the connection.

"Of course, Shadea," he said, smiling with such satisfaction that she wanted to tear his face off. "They've escaped us and gone for help from the one Druid who might actually give it."

"The Elven Prince!" she hissed. "But he doesn't have the use of the Elfstones. His brother keeps them."

"Not so well protected that he couldn't get to them if he chose. He would do so to save the Ard Rhys. No, it has to be him. The readings come from that part of the Westland where he keeps his home. Tagwen would know to go there and take the boy with him."

"I am surprised they chanced using the Stones. Ahren Elessedil must know we will be watching for any use of magic."

"But how else can he find the Ard Rhys?" Molt pointed out. "He has no choice but to use the Stones."

She nodded slowly, thinking it through. "True enough. He can't know what we've done to her, even if he suspects we're responsible, unless he uses the Stones." She hesitated. "Wait. Did you say that Iridia was the one who discovered this use?"

Terek Molt's laugh was low and rough. "I thought of that, too. I asked her if she was certain. She insisted there was no mistake. It was Elfstone magic. I told her she had better be sure, since you would question it. She is waiting to speak with you in the cold chamber." He paused, a faint smile twisting his mouth at the corners. "She wants to be the one to go after him."

"I would expect nothing less. Such a fool."

She walked to the window and stared out at the darkening skies. She could not leave the matter to Iridia, but then Terek Molt had not proved particularly adept at settling things, either. She should do this herself, yet she did not think it wise to leave Paranor just yet. She was too newly settled in as Ard Rhys. Someone else must make certain that Tagwen and the boy, and now Ahren Elessedil, as well, did not succeed in their efforts.

"Perhaps we should let this matter lie," Terek Molt said quietly.

"After all, even if they know what we have done with the Ard Rhys, there is nothing they can do to help her."

"Is that so?" she asked without bothering to look at him. "Are you so certain?"

"Certain enough."

"You assume too much. Besides, they can cause us a great deal of trouble, even if they cannot reach her. I don't want to chance it. Better that we remove them from the picture."

"That could cause us more trouble still. Others will know what we have done. Killing a boy and an old man is one thing. Killing a Druid is something else again. That's what you intend, isn't it?"

"I intend to do whatever is necessary to make certain our efforts do not fail. I expect you to do likewise." She turned back to him. "Ready the *Galaphile*, but do not tell Iridia. I don't trust her in this matter, not where Ahren Elessedil is concerned. She may think she can blind herself to her feelings, but I don't care to chance it. Better that she remain here. I will tell her after you are gone. Given the look of the weather, you won't leave today. If the storm passes by nightfall, leave then."

He turned for the door.

"Stay a moment," she said. "I have more to say to you. Heed me well. Are you listening, Terek?"

The Dwarf turned back slowly, brow darkening in anticipation of what he knew was coming. "Speak your mind, woman."

"First," she said, walking over to stand directly in front of him, "don't come into this room again until you are invited. Not for any reason."

She waited for his response. He grunted and shrugged.

"Second, don't fail me again. I would not be pleased if you did."

He laughed. "I am less concerned about pleasing you than pleasing myself, so spare me your threats. The matter of finding and dispatching the boy and the old man has become personal.

I don't like to be tricked. They used magic of some sort or I would have had them. I intend to see that accounts between us are settled."

She held his fierce gaze a moment, then nodded. "Fair enough. But that may not prove to be so easy now that you must contend with Ahren Elessedil, as well. Dispatching him may prove troublesome, even for you. So I am sending someone to help."

The Dwarf glowered at her. "Who? If not Iridia . . ."

"Another Druid would only muck up the waters. You don't need another Druid to get this business settled." She paused. "I'm going to send Aphasia Wye."

Terek Molt turned his head aside, though barely, and spit very deliberately on her carpet. "No."

"This isn't open to debate."

"I won't put that monster on any ship I command. Get someone else, if you think you can."

"I don't want anyone else. If I wanted someone else, I wouldn't be talking with you! Where is your backbone? Are you afraid? Think how it will it look if you stay behind after failing so badly the first time. Some will see it as a weakness, and you can't afford that." She drew her robes about her in a dismissive fashion. "Be smart about this, Druid. You are the best of the lot and you know it. I depend on you. Don't make me question my faith in you."

"You've never had faith in anyone but yourself, Shadea."

"Think what you want. What matters is that you understand that Aphasia Wye is coming with you. Stop worrying. He won't dare to cross you."

The Dwarf snorted derisively. "Aphasia Wye will cross anyone if opportunity allows for it. He's a monster, Shadea. There isn't anything that creature won't do—or anyone he won't do it to. Shades, we don't even know what he really is!"

She laughed. "He's the most efficient assassin I have ever seen!

What more do you want him to be? I don't care what sex or race or breed he is! I don't care how loathsome you find him! You're not partnering with him! You're putting him to work! Stop whining!"

Terek Molt was seething, his chiseled face turned red, the muscles of his forearms knotted. He was as dangerous at that moment as she had ever seen him, and if she was foolish enough to give him an opening, he would kill her before she could blink. But she faced him down, keeping his eyes locked on hers and making him see that no matter how dangerous he was, she was more dangerous still.

"Don't even think it, Dwarf," she hissed softly. "Remember who I am."

He glared at her a moment longer, then looked away, furious still, but no longer threatening. "Someday you will go too far with me, Shadea." His voice was eerily calm. "Be careful of that day."

"Perhaps," she replied, reaching past him to open the door. "But until then, you will listen to me when I tell you what to do. Go ready the airship. When the storm passes, you will sail at once."

His big hands tightened into fists as he considered saying something more. Then, without doing so, he turned his back on her and walked away.

She waited until he was well away and her frustration with his recalcitrance had faded before she departed for the cold chamber to find Iridia Eleri. The sorceress would not be happy with what Shadea intended to tell her. Unfortunately, disappointing Iridia was unavoidable, because the sorceress was only as reliable as her control over her feelings about Ahren Elessedil, which meant she was not reliable at all. Iridia had set her mind on the matter long ago, and Shadea was not going to be able to change it, even if she tried.

Love was like that.

Denial only sharpened its edges.

Shadea entered the cold chamber and found Iridia standing at the broad stone basin set in its center, bending close as she read the movement of its contents. The scrye waters were shallow and deep green, shielded from the elements by the walls of the tower and the sides of the basin. Disturbances came solely from magic channeled through the earth's lines of power. Just then they manifested themselves as concentric ripples fanning out from a point just west of center. Iridia's slender hands moved in time to the ripples, as if to trace their liquid ridges back to her doomed love. Her perfect features radiated her intensity, a mix of light and dark, pale skin and black hair. Her Elven features were drawn taut by her concentration, emphasizing what could be both passionate and cruel about her. Shadea stood in the doorway and watched her for a long time, observing. Iridia, captive to her memories and her dreams, didn't even know Shadea was there. It was possible that the madness Iridia had always seemed so close to embracing was finally coming to her.

"Iridia!" she called sharply.

The sorceress turned at once. "Have you heard?"

Shadea walked over to her. "Terek told me of it. Is there no chance that you are mistaken?"

The delicate features hardened. "What do you take me for? I don't make mistakes of that sort. It was Elfstone magic, which means it could be him. I want to make certain of it, Shadea. You will have to send someone in any case. It should be me."

Shadea shook her head. "It should be anyone but you. What will you do if you find him and he looks at you and you cannot act? Don't tell me it cannot happen because I know better. I was there, Iridia, when you lost him. You were inconsolable for weeks. He was the one you wanted—the one you will always want."

"I don't deny that!" she snapped. "But that part of my life is over. I am committed to our efforts here. If he stands in our way, if he acts to help *her*, then I want him dead! I have the right to watch him die. I ask nothing more than that. If he is to be killed, I want to be there to see it. I want my face to be the last face he sees in this life!"

Shadea sighed. "You only think you want that. What you want is for him to take you back again, to tell you that he loves you still, despite what has happened. If he were to do so, you would abandon your cause and us in a heartbeat. No, wait, Iridia—don't lie to yourself. You would, and you know it. Why wouldn't you? I don't condemn it. I would do the same in your place."

"You would do nothing of the sort," the other woman sneered. "You have never loved anyone but yourself. Don't pretend to understand me. I know love compels me, but it compels me in ways other than those you seem so quick to attribute. Love doesn't compel me to embrace him; it compels me to see him suffer!"

"Yes, but not at your hands." Shadea moved away, gazing out the tower window at the enfolding darkness and roiling storm clouds. Outside, the wind began to howl and the rain to fall in heavy curtains that lashed the stone walls.

"Better at my hands, where we can be certain of the result, than at the hands of Terek Molt, who has already failed us once!"

"Better at another's hands entirely. I am sending Aphasia Wye to make certain the job is done right."

She glimpsed Iridia's face out of the corner of her eye, and the look confirmed what she had already decided about the other's feelings for Ahren Elessedil.

"Iridia," she said softly, turning back. "Distance yourself from this matter. Leave it to others to determine what is needed. You have suffered enough at the hands of the Elven Prince. He has betrayed you already and would do so again. His loyalty is to her, not to you. That will never change. To place yourself in a position where you must test your resolve is foolish and dangerous. It asks too much of you."

The sorceress stiffened, her lips tightening to a thin, hard line, her perfect features cast in iron. "And you think too little of me. I am not a fool, Shadea. I am your equal and in some ways your better. I have experiences you do not; don't be so quick to dismiss me as a lovesick child."

"I would never do that."

"You not only would, you do!" Iridia's glare would have melted iron. "If Ahren Elessedil has used the Elfstones to try to help that woman, I want him dead as much as you do. But I want to see it happen. I want to watch him die!"

"Do you?" Shadea a'Ru paused. "I would have thought you'd had enough of that sort of thing. How many more of those you profess not to love, but secretly do, must you watch die before you are satisfied?"

Iridia's face went white. "What are you talking about?" There was an unmistakable warning in her words.

Shadea ignored it, her gaze cold and empty. "The baby, Iridia. You remember the baby, don't you? You didn't love her, either."

For a long moment Iridia neither moved nor spoke, but simply stared at Shadea, the look on her face one of mixed incredulity and rage. Then both drained away with frightening swiftness, leaving her features calm and dispassionate. "Do what you want," she said.

She turned and walked away without looking at Shadea. As she went through the door, she said softly, "I hate you. I'll see you dead, too."

As Iridia disappeared down the tower stairs, Shadea glanced after her, thinking for just a moment that she should go after her, then deciding otherwise. She knew the sorceress. Iridia was quick to anger, but she would think the situation through and realize she was being foolish. It was better to let her be for now.

She looked down at the scrye waters in the basin. The ripples had disappeared; the surface had gone completely still.

Ahren Elessedil would be made to vanish just as swiftly.

One last task remained to her, the one she dreaded most. She had no more love for Aphasia Wye than did Terek Molt, but she found him useful in carrying out assignments that others would either refuse or mishandle. She had already seen enough of the latter in the hunting down of Grianne Ohmsford's family, and the task would get no easier with Ahren Elessedil added to the mix. Terek Molt might protest her decision, but it was a matter of common sense and expediency. One Druid of her inner circle was all she cared to spare for the venture, and one was probably not enough.

As she passed through the towers and hallways of the Keep, by sleeping rooms and meditation chambers, the resting and the restless, her mind focused on the task ahead. She wanted the business over, but not before she had accomplished what was necessary. She had given the matter considerable thought since Terek Molt's return. It was a mistake—her mistake, unfortunately—to have thought of the Patch Run Ohmsfords as ordinary people. The boy and his parents might not be Druids, but that did not render them commonplace. The magic that was in their blood, and their long history of surviving against impossible odds, made them dangerous. It would require a special effort to overcome both, one that she would not underestimate again.

It would help that she had the services of Aphasia Wye. But something more was needed.

She descended the winding stairways of the Keep into its depths, into the cellars and dungeons that lay far underground in the bedrock, dark places where the Druids seldom ventured. Her destination was known only to her, now that Grianne Ohmsford was gone, a place she had discovered some years ago while shadowing the Ard Rhys in an effort to discover her secrets. She had been good at shadowing even then, having developed the skill in her early years when the uses of magic were first revealing themselves to her. It was dangerous to challenge Grianne Ohmsford's instincts, but she managed it with the aid of a fine-grained, odorless dust that rendered the other's tracks visible in a wash of prismatic light. Layering the dust in the dark places she knew the other sometimes went, she would wait for her return before sneaking back down to read the trail. She had gotten lucky once or twice, but never again as lucky as with what she now sought to retrieve.

She entered the deep center of the Keep, the heart of the fortress, down where the earth's heat lifted out of its churning magma to warm the rooms above. She found it interesting that the Druids would build their home atop a volcanic fissure that might erupt and destroy them one day. But the Druids lived in harmony with the earth's elements and found strength in what was raw and new. She understood and appreciated that. A proximity to the sharp edge that divided life and death was compelling for her, as well.

The passageways narrowed and darkened further. So far down, there was no need for space or light. She thought that some of the corridors had not been walked in a thousand years, that some of the cells and rooms they fed into had not seen life in thousands more. But she sought nothing of life that day, only of death. She moved in silence, listening for sounds of the spirit creature that lived in the pit beneath the Keep and warded Paranor and its magic. It slept now and would slumber until awakened. So long as the Druids kept occupancy and life, it would lie dormant. She knew the stories of its protective efforts. The stories were legend. They did not frighten her, however. Rather, they intrigued her. One day, she would come down to take a closer look at it. Spirits were something she understood.

She pondered for a moment the circumstances that had led her to that moment. She had no regrets about how she had achieved her position, but she would have preferred that it be otherwise. She wasn't evil, just practical. She was the right choice to be Ard Rhys, the better person for the title, but that did not mean she was happy with the way she had obtained it. Climbing over the backs of others to get what you wanted was suited more to politicians and to royalty than to students of magic. She would have preferred to face Grianne Ohmsford in combat, but a decision based on the outcome of trial by magic would not have been accepted by the others—neither her allies nor her enemies. Druids, for all their examination and study, were conservative by nature. History had taught them that independence and disobedience led to disaster, so they preferred that matters progress in an orderly fashion.

That couldn't happen here. Not with the Ilse Witch as Ard Rhys and the fate of the order hanging in the balance. Shadea had understood that from the beginning. Unlike the others, she had chosen to act.

She reached a heavy iron door at the end of a corridor and stopped. Placing her fingers on a set of symbols cut into the metal, she closed her eyes and pressed in deliberate sequence. It had taken her a while to unlock the puzzle, but in the end she had done so. Tumblers clicked and a bolt slid back. The door opened.

Inside, the room was round and dark save for a single, flameless lamp set in a raised stanchion at the chamber's center. Heavy stone blocks encircled a mosaic floor in which runes had been carved in intricate patterns that suggested story panels. There was only the one door leading in and no windows. There were no openings in either the walls or floor. The ceiling domed away in shadowed darkness.

A tomb for the dead and their possessions, Shadea thought. A space where things were placed with a strong expectation that one day they would be forgotten.

She walked to the stanchion, stood with the heel of her right boot pressed against one edge of its square base and fitted into an invisible depression beneath, then walked straight ahead until she reached the wall. Placing the palms of both hands flat against the stone at waist height, she worked the tips of her fingers around until she found the hidden depressions in the stone, then pushed.

A heavy panel swung open on hidden hinges, revealing a deep, ink-black chamber.

Her smile said everything about her expectations for what waited within.

She entered without the use of fresh light, relying on the faint glow of the lamp behind her. Her eyes adjusted quickly, and she saw what she had come for. She walked over to a low pedestal set against one wall, opened the iron box sitting on top of it, and took out the velvet pouch that rested within. She handled it carefully, the way she might a deadly snake, taking care not to grip it too strongly but to balance it in the palms of her hands. Even more carefully still, she reached inside to extract what was hidden there.

Slowly, gingerly, she drew out the Stiehl.

It was the most deadly weapon in the world, a blade forged in the time of Faerie in the furnaces of the Grint Trolls. Infused with lethal strains of arcane fire magic, it could penetrate anything, no matter how thick or strong. Nothing could stand against it. It had been in the hands of the assassin Pe Ell in the time of the Shadowen and Walker Boh, and he had used it to kill the daughter of the King of the Silver River. The Druid had recovered it afterwards and hidden it here. No one had known where it was since. No one, but Grianne Ohmsford and now Shadea.

She held it by its handle, feeling the markings that signified its name where they were carved into the bone plates. The blade gleamed silver bright, its surface smooth and flawless. It had survived thousands of years without a mark. Grianne had kept it concealed for the same reasons as Walker Boh—it was too dangerous to reveal. It was an assassin's weapon, a killer's tool.

It belonged, Shadea told herself, in a killer's hands, in an assassin's sheath. It belonged in the hands of a master. She would see that it found its way there. She would see that it was put to the use for which it was intended. The lives it snuffed would be well spent.

She sighed. She wasn't being evil, she told herself for a second time that afternoon. She was just being practical.

She put the Stiehl away, closed the chamber anew, and climbed out of Paranor's dark cellars to the light above.

F I F T E E N

With the decision made to go in search of the tanequil, Ahren Elessedil arranged for horses to transport the party on the first leg of their journey, and within an hour they were mounted and riding out of Emberen. Seemingly unconcerned about its contents, the Druid didn't even bother to close up his cottage, leaving everything pretty much the way it was. Pen had the feeling that the Druid wasn't much attached to possessions and, in the tradition of Druids who did service in the field, thought them mostly superfluous. The boy didn't pretend to understand this, having worked hard for everything he had, but he supposed that his own attachments were mostly the result of habit and not because he valued his belongings all that much. Still, he had to fight a strong urge to go back and lock up.

They rode south along the main roadway, stopping frequently to say good-bye to the villagers, Ahren making a point of telling everyone he spoke to that they would be gone for several weeks. Pen thought it odd that he would make the information public and was further confused when they departed in the wrong direction and a dozen miles outside the village turned not east toward the Charnals, but west.

When he finally gathered up courage enough to ask what they were doing, Ahren Elessedil smiled. "Confusing the enemy, I hope. If they come to Emberen, which I expect they will, the villagers will tell them we left heading south. If they track us that way, they will find that we have turned west. But they will lose our trail when we reach the Rill Song because we will leave the horses there and catch a barge downriver to the Innisbore and the inland port of Syioned. At Syioned, we will find an airship to take us where we really want to go."

"An airship?" Pen asked.

"An airship offers speed on a direct line and doesn't leave tracks. If I'd had one at my disposal in Emberen, we would have taken it from there. But horses will have to do for now." He laughed. "You should see your face, young Pen!"

They rode all that day and most of the next through the Westland forests before reaching the Rill Song and a way station that offered the use of barge transport downriver. The weather stayed warm and bright, the storm that was lashing Paranor and the Druid's Keep having passed north a day earlier. They rode steadily, stopping only to eat and sleep, and in that time Pen managed to find discomfort in ways he hadn't dreamed possible. Horses were not a regular part of his life, so riding for such long stretches left him aching from neck to ankles. Having done little riding himself, Tagwen didn't fare much better. Both Elves seemed untroubled by the effort, but on the first evening Khyber took time to give the Dwarf and the boy a liniment she carried in her pack to ease their pain.

Leaving the horses behind at the way station, they boarded the barge late in the afternoon of the second day and set out anew. The Rill Song was deep and wide at that time of the year, and they had no trouble making headway on its turgid waters. When darkness set in, they navigated by moonlight so bright it might have been the middle of the day. Ahren could have tied up on the riverbank and let them all sleep, but he seemed anxious to continue on while light permitted and so they did. Pen was just as happy. He did not care to chance another run-in with Terek Molt.

The following day, they passed below Arborlon, its treetop spires just visible over the lip of the Carolan. The storied Elfitch, the heavily fortified ramp that gave access to traffic coming in from the west, rose like a coiled snake from the eastern bank of the river to the bluff. Elves worked their way through the switchbacks and gates, a steady stream of commerce coming from and going to the Sarandanon. Pen found himself thinking about the battle fought between the Elves and their allies and the demons from the Forbidding almost five hundred years earlier. He stared at the Elfitch as they sailed past, trying to imagine the strength of its iron being tested against the frenzy of the demons. Thousands had died in that struggle. The legendary Border Legion had been decimated. The Elves had lost one out of every three able men. Their King, Eventine Elessedil, had been killed.

Pen wondered if another battle of the same sort was waiting down the road—if in spite of what Khyber said, the Ellcrys was failing again and the demons had found another doorway out of their prison.

They passed other boats on the river, and now and again they saw airships sailing overhead, a mix of warships on their way to the Prekkendorran and freighters on their way to less angry places. The weather stayed sunny and warm. There was no sign of the *Galaphile*. There was no sign of trouble of any sort. Pen began to think that maybe things weren't so bad.

Three days later, they reached the Innisbore, a body of water so vast that even if sun had broken through the clouds long enough to burn away the mists that lay in ragged strips across her choppy surface, the far shores would still have been out of view. It was late in the day when they maneuvered their barge into the landing area just beyond the mouth of the river, arranged for its docking and transport back upriver, and began the two-mile walk up the lake's eastern bank to the city of Syioned. Thunderheads were forming up again to the west, another storm beginning to build in that midseason time of storms. That they were common-place at this time of the year didn't make them any less inconvenient, Pen thought. If one struck while they were grounded, they would not be able to fly out until it passed. That could take up to several days. Impulsively, Pen asked Ahren if they might be able to leave yet that day, but the Druid told him they didn't even have a ship arranged as yet and probably wouldn't before week's end.

Pen settled into a funk that matched the approaching weather. He didn't like delays, especially where flying was concerned. He was already itching to get back in the air. That was his life at Patch Run, and although he understood he had left that life behind, he couldn't pretend he didn't want it back. Traveling by horse and barge and on foot was all well and good, but flying was what he craved. The sooner he got back in the air, the better he would feel about himself.

But just then, patience was needed. Deep twilight had settled in by the time they reached the outskirts of the city, and his stomach was rumbling. They found an inn on a side street not far off the road leading in that served food and offered rooms. It was sufficiently far off the beaten track that Ahren Elessedil felt comfortable with staying there for the night. They ate at a table in the back of the common room, and by the time they were finished, Pen's eyes were heavy with sleep.

He didn't remember going up to his room afterwards. He didn't remember stripping off his clothes and tumbling into the bed. All he remembered, thinking back on it, was the sound of the rain beating on the shingled roof as the storm arrived.

"It doesn't look like it's ever going to stop," Pen observed glumly, staring out the window of the inn.

The rain fell in sheets as it had been doing all night, flooding the roadways and turning low-lying stretches of waterfront into small inlets. The glass of the window he looked through was sufficiently obscured that he couldn't see more than a dozen yards. Not much of anyone was moving about outside. Nothing was flying. Pen was not happy.

Khyber studied the gaming board in front of her, nodding absently at his comment. "Give it time, Pen. Storms out here are worse than they are inland. But they pass." She moved a piece to confront one of his. "If you're worried about pursuit, just remember that if we can't fly, neither can they."

"I don't like being grounded like this," he growled. "I feel trapped." He took her piece with one of his own. He thought about Ahren Elessedil and Tagwen. "How long have they been gone now?"

She shrugged, eyes on the board. The Druid and the Dwarf had gone out early that morning in search of passage. With no one flying, the airship Captains would be gathered at their favorite inns and ale houses, passing the time while they waited to get back in the air. A few among them might be looking for business, and out of those there had to be at least one that the Druid would consider hiring. In their situation, discretion was as important as speed, and he wasn't going to sign on with anyone with whom he didn't feel comfortable. He wanted one of the Rovers, accomplished mercenaries who knew how to keep their mouths shut. Syioned was a regular stop for transport from the coast and continuing farther inland to the landlocked cities. Rover Captains made the run all the time, and more than a few of them would be here now.

Pen and Khyber had been told to stay at the inn, out of sight and trouble. The Druid was worried that someone would notice them and remember later, when those who hunted them found their way to the port. The less they were seen, the better. Especially Pen, with his distinctive long red hair. The inn was crowded, but those gathered were clustered in private groups and engaged in their own conversations. Not much attention was being paid to anyone else.

"When did you start flying airships?" Khyber asked. She looked up at him. "You must have been doing it a long time."

He nodded. "Since I can remember. My mother always flew and my father, as well, after he met her. They took me with them everywhere after I was born, even when I was a baby. I remember learning to steer when I was barely old enough to stand on an up-ended crate and look over the pilot box railing."

"I wanted to fly," she said, "but my father, when he was alive, and after he died, my brother, insisted that someone always go with me. In a big warship with lots of the Home Guard for protection, I might add. Even after I began traveling out on my own, old enough to know how to take care of myself, I wasn't allowed to go by airship."

He shrugged. "You haven't missed that much."

She laughed. "What a terrible liar you are, Penderrin! You can't possibly believe that! You're the one who can't wait to get back up in the skies! Admit it!"

"Okay, I admit it." He was laughing, too. "But you can make up for what you've missed. I could show you."

He moved another piece, and she responded. She was good at the game, but not nearly as good as he was. He had an innate sense of what she was going to do even before she did. She studied the board intently, aware that she was being backed into a corner.

"Have you thought about the fact that your father and my uncle Ahren were about the same age we are now when they sailed on the *Jerle Shannara?*" she said.

"More than once."

"Do your parents ever talk about what it was like?"

"Once in a while, a lot of their friends died on that voyage, and I don't think they like to remember it." He looked at her. "How about your uncle? Does he ever say anything?"

She shook her head, her brow creasing. "He doesn't like to talk about it, either. Because of the seer, I think. He was in love with her, though he won't say so now. It's too painful for him." She cocked her head. "Are you afraid of what we're doing, Pen?"

He leaned back, thinking about it. Was he afraid? What did he feel? He hadn't really stopped to think about it. Or maybe hadn't allowed himself, afraid of what he might discover.

"No," he answered, then immediately grimaced. "All right, yes, but only in a general sort of way. I don't know enough to be afraid of anything specific yet. Except for that Druid, that Dwarf. He was pretty scary. I'm afraid of him."

She brushed back strands of dark hair that had fallen forward over her face as she bent to the board. "I'm not afraid. I know some magic, so I can protect us if I have to. Uncle Ahren knows a lot of magic, though he doesn't show it. I think he's probably a match for anyone. We'll be all right."

"Glad you think so."

"Don't you have some of your father's magic? He had the magic of the wishsong, like your aunt Grianne, didn't he?"

Pen nodded. "True. But he didn't pass it on to me. I think the bloodline has grown thin after all these years. He's probably the last. Just as well, he'd tell you. He doesn't trust it. He uses it now and then, but not much. He's just as happy I don't have any."

"It might help if you did."

Pen paused, considering whether or not he should tell her about the talent he did have. "Maybe."

"You could protect yourself a little better. From those renegade Druids and their magic. From what you might come upon inside the Forbidding. Don't you think so?"

He didn't reply. They went back to the game, moving pieces until only eight remained on the board. Pen knew by then that he would win, but he let the game continue anyway. Playing it helped pass the time.

"Do you remember what Tagwen said about the tanequil giving me the darkwand if I could find it?" he asked her finally. He leaned forward over the board as if concentrating, deliberately lowering his voice. "It's because I do have magic."

She leaned in to meet him, their foreheads almost touching. Her Elven features sharpened with surprise. "What sort of magic? The wishsong? But you said not."

"No. Something else. Something different." He fiddled with one of the pieces, then took his hand away. "I can sense what living things are thinking, what they are going to do and why. Not people. Birds and animals and plants. When they make sounds, noises or cries or whatever, I can understand what they are saying. Sometimes, I can make the sounds back, answer them."

She cocked one eyebrow. "That seems to me like it could be pretty important. I don't know how exactly, but I think it could be. Have you told Uncle Ahren?"

He shook his head. "Not yet."

"Well, you should. He ought to know, Pen. He's a Druid. He might know something about it that you don't, maybe a way you can use it that will help us." She paused, studying his face. "Are you afraid to tell him? You can trust him, you know."

"I know." His eyes locked on hers. "I just don't talk about it much. I never have."

They went back to playing, the sound of the rain beating against the window increasing in intensity. All around them, voices and laughter fought to hold their ground. The flames of the lamps on the walls and the candles on the tables fluttered like tiny flags as the wind slipped through cracks and crevices in the wood boarding and gusted through the open door every time someone entered or left.

"I'll tell him when he comes back," Pen said finally. He moved his assault piece to confront her control. "Stand down. You lose, Khyber."

They played another game and were in the middle of a third when the door opened to admit a drenched Ahren Elessedil and Tagwen. Shedding water from their all-weather cloaks like ducks come ashore, they hurried over to the boy and girl. "Get your things together," Ahren told them quietly, bending down so that rainwater dripped on the tabletop. "We've found a ship."

They gathered up their gear, strapped their packs over their shoulders, and departed the inn for the ship that the Druid had engaged. Better that they settle in at once so they could be ready to leave when the storm abated, the Druid advised. They had to walk from the side street on which the inn was situated back to the main roadway and down to the docks, then along the waterfront to where the ship was tied up at the pier. As they slogged through the downpour, Ahren Elessedil provided the details.

"The ship is the *Skatelow*. Appropriate name for its uses, I'd guess. Low and sleek in her hull, raked mast, lots of rigging on the decks. She can't carry much in the way of passengers or freight with all the sail she stores, but she can probably outrun almost anything flying."

"Made for our uses," Tagwen grunted, his words nearly drowned out by a sudden gust of wind.

"Not much in the way of comforts, but adequate for our needs," the Druid continued. "Her Captain is a Rover named Gar Hatch. I don't know anything about him other than what I've learned from talking with him and what a few on the waterfront tell me. He's got a reputation for being willing to try anything, and they all say he can go places no one else would even think of trying. If I read him correctly, he's done a lot of what we're after—carrying passengers who want to keep it quiet. He's charming, but there's some snake in him, as well, so watch what you say. He knows we want to go east to the Lazareen, but that's all I've given him to work with. What he cares about most is the money he will get, and I've satisfied him on that count."

"The Lazareen?" Khyber asked.

"An inland lake at the foot of the Charnals, the first step of our journey. That's all the Rover knows of our plans just yet."

They walked on for a while, not speaking, heads bent against the wind and rain. Pen was not only wet, he was cold. He had been out in the weather a lot aboard airships and knew how to dress for it, but in his haste to leave the inn this afternoon, he hadn't given much thought to his personal comfort. He was regretting that oversight now.

"Penderrin."

Ahren Elessedil had dropped back to walk beside him, letting Khyber and Tagwen go on ahead. Pen hitched up his pack and moved closer so that he could hear. The rain obscured the Druid's face and ran off his shoulders in sheets.

"I took the liberty of telling Captain Hatch that you had extensive airship experience," he said. "I'm afraid I put you on the spot rather deliberately." The hood shifted, and Pen caught a glimpse of his Elven features, somber and intense. "I don't trust this fellow entirely; he's a mercenary, and mercenaries always look out for themselves first. But he was the best I could do, and I didn't want to delay our departure. The longer we wait, the better the chance that those hunting us will get wind of where we are."

Pen nodded. "I understand."

The Druid leaned closer. "The reason I told Hatch about your experience is so that he knows at least one of us can determine if he's doing what he's supposed to. I don't want him telling us one thing and doing something else. I don't want him thinking he can put one over on us. I don't say that would happen, but I want to guard against it. I don't know that much about airships; I never did. Your father was the pilot and your mother the navigator when it was needed. I was always just a passenger. That's never changed. Khyber and Tagwen know even less than I do. In fact, I think it's something of a miracle that Tagwen managed to reach you on his own."

"I thought that, too, after he told me what he'd done." Pen blinked away the rain that swept into his eyes.

"Stay alert on our journey, Pen," Ahren said. "Don't make it obvious, but keep an eye on what's happening with the navigation of the ship. If anything looks wrong, tell me. I'll deal with it. Can you do that?"

"I can do it."

"Gar Hatch doesn't know who we are, but that doesn't mean he won't find out. If he does, he might be tempted to make use of that information. The Druids are already looking for you. They've put it about that because of what happened to your aunt, you might be in danger, as well, and should be protected. If you're seen, word is to be sent to them immediately."

He hunched his shoulders against the wind. "I gave him only first names, thinking it safe enough at the time, but now I wish I hadn't given him even that. News of the Druid search didn't reach Syioned until this morning, but now that it has, Hatch may hear of it. He isn't a stupid man. Be very careful, Pen."

He moved away again into the rain, his cloaked form dark and shadowy in the gloom. Pen stared after him, slowing.

Be very careful. Easily said, he thought; not so easily done.

Aware suddenly that he was falling behind, he hurried to catch up with the others.

SIXTEEN

The storm raged on through the rest of the day and all that night, but by daybreak it had begun to diminish. By the time the general population of Syioned was stirring awake, the *Skatelow* had cast off her moorings and was under way.

Pen and his companions had been huddled belowdecks since boarding, trying their best to sleep through the storm's fury, and they had not had more than a rain-drenched glimpse of their vessel. Now, with the skies clearing and the sun a bright wash in the east, they came on deck to look around.

Their transport was a sloop, a new design for airships, although a very old one for sailing ships. Ahren Elessedil had described it accurately. It was low and flat and clearly built for speed. A single mast and spars were rigged to fly a mainsail, foresail, and flying jib. In his travels, Pen hadn't seen much of the latter, another sailing ship feature that had been converted for airship usage. A broad, billowing sail that traditionally captured the wind off the bow and gave the vessel extra thrust, the jib was used by airships to absorb a wider swath of ambient light that could be converted to energy by the diapson crystals that powered the ship. The *Skatelow* lacked the pontoons that serviced most of the older airships of the catamaran design, relying instead on its pilot's sailing skills and the flatness of its hull to keep it steady in the air.

Pen liked the *Skatelow* right away. It had been modified from its original design considerably to eliminate anything that might slow its flight. Except for the mast and rigging, everything else was tucked away belowdecks or in storage bins. Even the pilot box was recessed into the hull to cut back on drag. Everything was sleek and smooth, the ship a great swift bird that could hunt or run as needed. It was powered by eight diapson crystals, the most in use for a ship of only seventy-odd feet. Anything more and the thrust might have torn her apart. Even with eight, the Captain had to know what he was doing.

Gar Hatch did, and he let Pen know it right from the first. Pen had been abovedecks less than five minutes when the Captain of the *Skatelow* hailed him over.

"Penderrin!" he called out from the pilot box. "Stand to, lad! Give an old sailor an ear to bend!"

Obediently, Pen walked down the deck to the box and climbed in beside Gar Hatch. The Rover was a big man, heavy and square through his midsection with huge arms and legs—a tree trunk of a man. Bushy hair sprouted from his face and head, even from his sizeable ears, giving him the appearance of a great woolly bear. When he spoke he had a tendency to rear back, his stomach thrust out and his chin tucked so far into his beard that his mouth disappeared entirely. What remained visible were his sharp, hawkish eyes, bright and dangerous.

"You're a sailor yourself, I'm told," he said, his deep, rough voice rising from somewhere inside his beard. His breath smelled of fish and sea salt. "Been so since you were a small lad, an early

old salt. Spent years sailing airships big and small about Rainbow
Lake and the rivers that feed her. Good for you!"

"My parents are the real sailors," Pen said. "I learned what I know
from them. They take customers on expeditions into the Eastland."
He stopped himself quickly. Remembering Ahren Elessedil's ad-
monishment, he was aware that he had already said more than he
should have. "I just fly with them once in a while and look after the
ships in dock," he finished carefully.

Gar Hatch didn't seem to notice. "Grew up that way myself,"
he said. "Learned what I know from my father and uncles, sailors
all. On the coast, off the Blue Divide, whichever way the wind
blew. We flew the big ships mostly, but I had my own skiff when I
was your age. Got one of those yourself, your uncle tells me."

My uncle? "Yes, that's right," Pen answered quickly. "A cat-28. I
built it myself."

"Did you now? Good for you, Penderrin!" The Rover laughed,
his belly shaking with the effort. "Best way to learn about airships
is to build one. Haven't got the skills for that myself, but I've
helped those who do. I learned keel from mast quick enough that
way, so when I flew I understood if the lady didn't like the way she
was being treated."

Pen grinned. "I like this ship. I've never flown one, but I've seen
them and I know how they're made. This one is made to fly fast.
Have you run out the string on her?"

Hatch roared. "That's the lad! Ask what matters, and no beating around the main mast! Sure, I've had her thrusters all the way
open, and let me tell you, Penderrin, she can fly faster than fast!
Nothing alive can catch her, save for the big birds off the coast,
and they might have to work some to do it. She's a glutton for
speed, this one. You're right, though. I gave her all her curves, all
her smooth limbs and soft lines. She's my lady, she is."

He paused. "You've never flown a sloop, did you say? Lad, that's unconscionable! Do you want to try now?"

Pen could hardly contain his excitement. "You'd let me?"

"A sailor like yourself, born to the air?" Hatch leaned forward, his fish breath in Pen's face. "Take the helm, Captain Pen."

Despite Ahren Elessedil's warnings about the big man, Pen was desperate to fly the sloop, so he put aside his misgivings. It wouldn't hurt to accept the offer, he told himself. He was just going to test his skills a bit, try out the controls, and see if he could manage the vessel. He had flown other airships of the same sort, some much bigger. *Skatelow* couldn't be that much more difficult.

Gar Hatch backed away, and Pen stepped up to the helm. He glanced down quickly, noting thrusters, lifts, banking levers, and the like, all familiar to him, though located in somewhat different positions than he was used to. The compass was set dead center above the half wheel that managed the keel rudder.

"There you be, young Pen," the Rover Captain declared cheerfully. "A fine and proper set of controls for a fine and proper young sailor. Give her a try, lad."

Pen did so, easing into things slowly, carefully, setting trim before taking the airship a little higher with the lifts. She nosed upward, but he felt the tension in her hull, then a slight shaking. He frowned as he worked to steady her. It wasn't as easy as he had thought. Everything was the same, but the sloop's responses were less certain than he would have liked. He adjusted the thrusters and felt her shake some more. An effort at resetting trim proved unsuccessful. He eased the power back, glancing over at Gar Hatch.

The Rover's sharp eyes were glittering. "Not so easy as it looks, is it?" he asked, and Pen could see he wasn't expecting an argument. "Flying a sloop is not the same as flying a cat-28 or even a warship with pontoons and rams for stability. A sloop needs tender loving care from a master who knows her needs."

He smiled, but even through the heavy growth of beard Pen could see the teeth behind. He realized with a sinking feeling that Hatch had been testing him. Knowing how difficult it would be for someone unfamiliar with the sloop to sail her, he had enticed Pen into trying so that he could judge the boy's skills. The Rover was one step ahead of Ahren Elessedil; he knew that Pen had been asked to check up on him, even without having been present at the conversation. Now he had Pen's measure, and the boy had helped him take it.

Gar Hatch stepped forward and took back the ship's controls, easing Pen out of the way without seeming to do so.

"You keep in mind, Penderrin," he said softly, looking over at the boy as he steadied the vessel anew, "that there's only one Captain on this ship. Do that and we'll get along fine. Now out of the box you go. Back down on the deck with the others. That's a good lad."

Pen left without a word, burning with frustration and shame, so furious with himself that he could have spit. But there was no help for it, and he refused to give Garth Hatch the satisfaction of seeing him react. Fighting to control himself, he stood alone at the starboard rail, his gaze directed resolutely forward even though he could feel the Rover Captain's eyes on his back. He should have paid better attention to Ahren Elessedil's warning. But that was water over the dam. What mattered was how well he remembered the lesson he had just been taught. Well enough, he promised himself. The next time Gar Hatch tried to make a fool of him, things would turn out differently.

* * *

It was late in the afternoon of that same day when Cinnaminson came on deck. She climbed up through the hatchway leading from the narrow sleeping quarters below, stepping into the crimson light of the sunset like a shade. Pen was sitting with Khyber at the aft rail, still stewing over the way he had let himself be fooled by Gar Hatch, when he saw her. He did not know where she had come from or what she was doing there. He had thought that besides the four who had booked passage there were only Hatch and two crewmen. Now this apparition had appeared. He stopped talking in midsentence, causing Khyber, who had not been paying close attention, to look up from her writing and follow his gaze.

She was only a girl, no older than Pen, younger than Khyber, her slender form wrapped in something soft gray and green that might have been a long robe and shimmered like the sea. She looked to have woken from a deep sleep, her short, sandy blond hair disheveled and her face tilting toward the light as if to make certain of the time. Pen thought her beautiful, although he would later revise that judgment to striking, and sometime later to captivating. Her features were delicate, but unremarkable and not quite perfect. Still, they intrigued him. What mattered more was the way she moved, not looking at anything while seemingly aware of all. She glided rather than walked, the soft whisper of her gown marking her passage as she came toward them.

It was when she had almost reached them that Pen saw her eyes. They were milky white and empty, staring straight ahead at nothing. She was blind.

Pen did not know who she was. He did not know her name. What he did know was that he would never forget her.

"Are you our passengers?" she asked them, looking off into a space they did not quite occupy.

Pen nodded, then realized she couldn't see him. "Yes, two of them, anyway. I'm Pen and this is Khyber." He had presence of mind enough, though just barely, to remember to use only first names.

"I'm Cinnaminson," she told them. "I'm Gar Hatch's daughter."

She stretched out her hand and waited for them to take it, which they did, one after the other. Her smile was winsome and a bit fragile, Pen thought, hesitant and protective at the same time, which seemed right for her condition. But there was strength to her, too. She was not afraid to come up against what she couldn't see.

"Traveling to the Charnals," she said, making it a statement of fact. "I like that part of the world. I like the feel of the mountain air, the smell and taste of it. Snowmelt and evergreens and ice."

"Do you always come on these trips?" Khyber asked, looking doubtful about the whole business.

"Oh, yes. Ever since I was eight years old. I always go. Papa wouldn't fly anywhere without me." She laughed softly, milky eyes squinting with amusement. "I am an old salt, he tells me, a child of the air and sea."

Khyber arched a questioning eyebrow at Pen. "I am surprised he would allow you aboard at so young an age when you could not see to help yourself. It seems dangerous."

"I see well enough," the girl replied. "Not so much with my eyes as with my other senses. Besides, I know every inch of the *Skatelow*. I am not in any real danger."

She sat down beside them, moving effortlessly to find a place between them, her gray and green robes settling about her like sea foam. "You don't fly, do you, Khyber?"

"No. But Pen does. He was born to airships."

Her gaze shifted, not quite finding him. "Don't tell my father. He doesn't like it when other flyers come aboard. He's very jealous of what's his."

Pen thought, without having any better reason to do so than

the way she said it, that she was including herself in that assessment. "Too late," he told her. "He found out from my uncle and already made a point of letting me know how lacking I am in real skills."

Her smile dropped. "I'm sorry, Pen. I would have warned you if I had known. Papa can be very hard."

"Is he hard on you?"

The smile returned, less certain. "I am his most important crew member," she said, not quite answering the question. She hesitated. "He wouldn't want me to tell you this, but I will anyway. I am his navigator."

Pen and Khyber exchanged a quick glance. "How do you manage that?" the Elven girl asked. "I didn't think you could navigate if you couldn't see."

The milky eyes shifted slightly toward the sound of Khyber's voice. "I don't see with my eyes. I see with my other senses." She bit her lip. "I can do things to help Papa that don't require sight." Again, she paused. "You mustn't tell Papa I told you any of this. He wouldn't like it."

"Why wouldn't he like it?" Pen asked.

"Papa worries about outsiders, people other than Rovers. He doesn't trust them."

Nor do we trust him, Pen thought. Not a good situation.

"I still don't understand this navigation business," Khyber pressed, her brow furrowing. "Tell us something more about how you help your father."

"Cinnaminson!"

All three turned in the direction of the voice. Gar Hatch had turned around in the pilot box and caught sight of them. He looked furious. "Come help your Papa, little girl," he ordered brusquely. "You've sailor work to do."

She stood up at once. "Coming, Papa." She glanced down quickly. "Say nothing!" she whispered.

She left without another word, walking straight to the pilot box and climbing in. Pen watched to see what would happen and wasn't sure if he was relieved or disappointed when nothing did. Gar Hatch put his hand on his daughter's shoulder, patted it briefly, and turned back to steering the vessel. Cinnaminson remained standing beside him.

"What do you make of that?" he asked Khyber.

"A bad business that we should stay out of," she answered. She regarded him thoughtfully. "I think we ought to cut your hair. That long red mane is too recognizable. Maybe we should dye it, too."

She put down her writing tools and went off to find her scissors.

They were told at the evening meal that, after dark, passengers were not allowed topside until morning. It was a rule of long standing aboard the *Skatelow* and the Captain's express order. The reason given was concern for safety; a fall at night from the ship's sleek decking would almost certainly result in death. It was better if everyone but the crew stayed below. Ahren Elessedil assured the Rover that the order would be obeyed, and Pen went to bed with every intention of breaking it.

He woke sometime after midnight and slipped from his bed on cat's paws, brushing absently at his newly shorn hair, grimacing at the roughness of its feel. Hardly anything was left of it; Khyber had done a thorough job. He glanced at Tagwen, who was snoring loudly in the berth above him. Clearly, the Dwarf would not wake. Ahren and Khyber shared a cabin down the hall, so he was less

concerned about them. He took several deep breaths to settle himself, then moved to the door. He stood there for a moment, listening, but heard nothing. When he stepped outside, the corridor was
empty. Other than the creaking of the rigging and the soft rustle
of the mainsail in the almost dead night air, everything was silent.

He went down the corridor and up the stairway, stopping often
to listen. Having done that sort of thing any number of times before, he was not particularly worried about getting caught, but he
did not care to be embarrassed by Gar Hatch again. So he went
slowly and cautiously, and when he reached the head of the stairs
and found the hatchway open, he stopped yet again.

Above, not far from where he stood, he heard voices. It took
him only seconds to recognize whose they were.

". . . not fair that I never get to talk to anyone. I don't tell them
anything about us, Papa. I just like hearing about their lives."

"Their lives don't matter to us, girl," Gar Hatch responded,
firmly but not unkindly. "They aren't of our people and you won't
see them again after this journey."

"Then what does it matter if I talk to them?"

"It matters in ways you don't understand because you are still a
child. You must listen to me. Be pleasant to them. Be helpful when
it is needed. But do not go out of your way to speak to them. That
is a direct order, sailor."

There was silence after that. Pen remained standing where he
was, listening. He wanted to peek outside, but he was afraid that if
he did, he would be seen. The moon was three-quarters full and
the sky clear. There was too much light to take a chance. He wondered what was going on up there that he wasn't supposed to see.
As far as he could tell from what he was hearing, nothing at all.

"I'm going below to sleep for a few hours," Hatch announced
suddenly. "You take the helm, Cinnaminson. Keep her on course,
no deviations. There's no weather on the horizon, so the sail should

be smooth enough. You know what to do. Come get me if there's trouble. Good girl. I'll come back before dawn."

Pen retreated down the steps as swiftly as he could manage, reached his cabin and stepped inside. He stood with his back against the door and listened as Gar Hatch trudged past toward the Captain's quarters. The Rover's footsteps receded, a door opened and closed, and everything was silent again save Tagwen's snoring.

For a moment, Pen determined to go topside again. But he was nervous about it now, afraid that Hatch might come back and catch him. What had he said? *You take the helm, Cinnaminson?* How could she do that if she was blind? Was she up there all alone, steering the airship and charting their course when she couldn't see? That didn't seem possible, and yet . . .

He stood awhile longer, debating what to do. In the end, he went back to bed. Khyber was right. It was none of his business, and he shouldn't mix in it. Ahren wouldn't like it if he jeopardized their safety through his interference. He couldn't afford to antagonize Hatch while they depended on him.

Perhaps, he thought, he would just ask Cinnaminson the next time he saw her. If she would speak to him, that was.

He went back to bed to think about it some more and was asleep in moments.

SEVENTEEN

They flew north out of the Westland, then turned east across the Streleheim Plains down the corridor that lay between the Dragon's Teeth and the Knife Edge Mountains. It was a shipping lane used by almost everyone traveling west and east above Callahorn, and they passed other airships at regular intervals. The weather remained good, the skies clear and calm, the days warm and dry, the nights deep and cool, and there were no more storms. The *Skatelow* kept a steady pace, but not a fast one, staying low and hugging the forestline above Paranor. She sailed at night as well as during the day, and Gar Hatch put her down only twice in three days for fresh water and brief repairs.

Pen spoke with Cinnaminson every day, several times a day, and there was no indication from her behavior that she was trying to avoid him. In fact, she seemed eager to search him out, although she never did so in a way that suggested she was disobeying her father's wishes. Pen, for his part, tried to make their meetings seem to those who might observe to be about something other than their growing friendship. But he didn't even try to pretend to her that he wasn't interested. He was captivated, and even at his young age he could not mistake what he was feeling for her. He was excited just at the prospect of seeing her, and every day brought new opportunities to do so. He looked forward to those moments with an anticipation that made him ache.

But he never asked her about that first night. The more he thought about doing so, the less comfortable he felt. In the first place, he had been spying on her, and he didn't want her to know that. Nor could he think of a way to broach the subject without seeming to pry. It wasn't his place to ask her what she was doing for her father. At best, it would make her uncomfortable because anything she told him would be a betrayal. He still wanted to know how she could sail an airship despite being blind, but he decided it would have to be her idea to tell him.

He had plenty of time to indulge his newfound attraction for her. Tagwen was often airsick and seldom appeared topside. He was a Dwarf, he pointed out sourly, and he belonged on the ground. Khyber had resumed her Druid studies and spent most of her time with her uncle. Pen would see them sitting across from each other on the decking, heads bent close in conversation, the girl taking notes and making animated gestures that indicated she was trying to understand what he was teaching. Much of the time, they remained in their cabin, freer to engage in open discussion than when the Rovers were present. Khyber, always intense, seemed more so now that they had set out, perhaps appreciating better than Pen did the weight of the task she had agreed to shoulder.

But Pen, too, spent much of his time thinking about why he was there, a passenger aboard an airship bound for the Charnals and country few had ever explored. He no longer questioned whether what he was doing was the right thing. He no longer even questioned the motives of the King of the Silver River in sending him. He just accepted it and concentrated instead on how he was going to get through in one piece. If he allowed himself to think about the larger picture, it was too overwhelming to contemplate. So much was expected of him, and he had no reason to believe those expectations were justified. He found he could manage better if he considered things incrementally. Step one was escaping the *Galaphile* and Terek Molt. He'd done that. Step two was reaching Emberen and enlisting help from Ahren Elessedil. He'd done that, too. Step three was embarking on the journey east.

When he got to step four, however, things became a little less clear. Finding the tanequil was the goal, but he had the feeling that there were a few other steps in between and he would not find out what they were right away. Only time would reveal them, and it would not do to try to plan too far ahead. That he was making the journey on faith in the first place helped him accept that, but it didn't make him any less anxious about the outcome.

Spending time with Cinnaminson relaxed him most. He understood it was an indulgence, one that was difficult to justify given the seriousness of his purpose. But he understood, as well, that something was needed to distract him from his doubts and fears, and turning his thoughts to Cinnaminson helped. He wasn't foolish enough to expect that this infatuation would grow into something more. He knew it would be finished when they reached their destination and disembarked from the airship. But it did no good to think in those terms. Better to allow a little light into a darkened room than to worry about what would happen once it faded.

On the third day, they were sitting in the bow where he was pretending to write and she to listen to what he had written, their backs to the pilot box and Gar Hatch.

"Can you tell me where you are going?" she asked him quietly.

"I can tell you anything, Cinnaminson."

"Not anything. You know you can't do that."

He nodded to himself. She understood some things better than he did. "We go into the Charnals, looking for the ruins of an ancient city. Ahren wants to look for something there."

"But he brings you and Khyber and Tagwen to help him," she said. "An odd company for such an effort."

Her fingers brushed his wrist, a soft swirl that made him itch all the way down to his toes. "I won't lie to you," he said finally. "There's more to this. I'm sworn to secrecy."

"Better that you tell me so than deceive me. I have traveled with enough passengers to know when they keep secrets. My father is paid to keep it so. But I want to know that you will be safe when you leave me. I want to know that I might see you again someday."

His hand closed on hers, and he stared into her milky, empty eyes. She did not see him, but he could feel her watching in other ways. He studied her face, the lines and curves and softness, the way the light fell against her skin. He loved to look at her. He could not have told anyone why, just that he did. "You will see me again," he said quietly.

"Will you come find me?" she asked him.

"I will."

"Even if I am flying somewhere on the *Skatelow*, you will look for me?"

He felt his throat tighten. "I don't think I could do otherwise," he said. "I think I have to."

Then, without thinking about who might be watching, he leaned forward and kissed her on the mouth. She kissed him back without hesitation. It was a thrilling, tantalizing kiss, and he immediately wanted more. But he was playing a dangerous game, and contemplating the way it might end tempered his enthusiasm sufficiently that he kept himself in check.

He broke away, not daring to look back at the pilot box. "Sorry," he said.

"Don't be sorry," she answered at once, leaning into his shoulder, head lowered so that her hair brushed his bare arm. "I wanted you to do that."

"Your father won't like it."

"My father wasn't looking."

Unable to help himself, he glanced over his shoulder. Gar Hatch was turned away, working on placing lines at the rear of the box. She was right; he hadn't seen anything.

Pen looked back at her. "How did you know that?"

She gave him a smile that reached all the way into his heart. "I just did," she said, and kissed him again.

"I wish you'd stop following Cinnaminson around like an eager puppy," Khyber told him late that same day while they were sitting together at the bow of the *Skatelow*. She brushed back her thick dark hair and stared out at a sky lit purple and rose, her brow furrowed by deep lines of condemnation.

"I like her," he said.

"As anyone can plainly see, including her father. Even Uncle Ahren has noticed, and he usually doesn't bother with such nonsense."

He frowned. "Nonsense?"

"Well, it is. Do you have any idea what you're doing? You're going to get us in a lot of trouble if you aren't careful."

"You don't know everything."

"I know what I see. What everyone sees. I don't think you've thought this through. Or if you have, you've managed to leave out the important parts. You know how her father feels about outsiders. He doesn't want anything to do with us beyond taking our money. Rovers live by a different code of behavior than the rest of us. Everyone knows that. So why do you persist in nosing around after Cinnaminson?"

He looked sharply at her. "Stop it, Khyber."

"Stop what? Stop telling you the truth?"

"You don't have to be so mean about it! Have you forgotten that my mother is a Rover?"

They glared at each other, each silently daring the other to say something more, each refusing to give ground. Pen knew Khyber was right about Cinnaminson, even if he wouldn't admit it. He knew he shouldn't be interested in her, even in a casual way and certainly not in the way he was. But he didn't know what he could do about it. It wasn't as if he had chosen for it to happen. It just had. Now he was stuck with his feelings, and he couldn't cast them aside or bundle them up and stick them in a locker. He was way beyond that, and besides, he wasn't at all sure he wanted to change things anyway.

"We're being careful," he said finally.

She snorted. "How, exactly? Are there things happening between the two of you that I'm not seeing? I certainly hope not, because what I am seeing is already way too much."

He wheeled on her. "Just because your brother wants to marry you off and you don't like the idea doesn't mean the rest of us have to feel the same way about things!"

"Oh, are you thinking of marrying her?"

"That's not what I mean!" He was furious now. "I mean I don't have to be as close-minded as you obviously are! I don't have to be like you!"

"Keep your voice down!" she hissed.

Behind them, Gar Hatch stood in the pilot box. Pen shot him a quick look, but he didn't seem to notice the boy. His eyes were directed forward, toward the horizon.

"You're being unreasonable!" Pen hissed back at her. "We're just friends!"

She started to reply, then stopped herself. Her face softened, her anger faded, and she nodded slowly. "All right, Pen. Let's drop the matter. What right do I have to tell you how to behave, anyway? Ask my family how well behaved I've been. I haven't the right to lecture you."

He sighed wearily, looking out over the bow toward the approaching night. "I know I shouldn't be doing this. I know I should just stay away from her. I know that."

Khyber put her hand on his shoulder and squeezed. "But you can't and you won't and I don't have the right to ask you to do so. I wouldn't want you telling me what to do if our positions were reversed. But I worry, anyway. I don't want you disappearing over the side of the ship one night just because you smiled at this girl once too often. Everything we're doing depends on you. We can't afford to lose you. Just keep that in mind when you're thinking about how pretty she looks."

He exhaled sharply. "You don't have to worry about that. I can't stop thinking about it. That's part of the reason I like being with her. She helps me forget for a little while."

They didn't say anything for a long time as they looked out at the skyline, listened to the cries of the seabirds and the hum of the ship's rigging. The western sky had gone shadowed and gray with the setting of the sun, and the first star had appeared in the north.

"Just be careful," Khyber said finally.

He nodded, but did not answer.

The fourth day of travel dawned gray and sullen with storm clouds layered all across the northwest horizon, roiling and wind-swept as they bore down on the Streleheim. Pen came on deck at first light to find Gar Hatch and both Rover crewmen hard at work taking down the sails, tightening the rigging, and lashing in place or carrying below everything that might be lost in the blow. Cinnaminson was standing in the pilot box, her face lifted as if to taste the raindrops that had begun to fall.

He thought at first to go to her, then decided against it. There was no reason to do so, and it would call needless attention to his infatuation. Instead, familiar enough with what was needed to be able to help, he went to help the crewmen secure the vessel. They glanced at him doubtfully as he joined them in their work, but said nothing to discourage it. Behind him, Ahren and Khyber appeared, as well, standing in the hatchway, stopped by a wind that had begun to howl through the rigging like a banshee.

"Get below!" Gar Hatch bellowed at them. His gaze shifted to Pen. "Penderrin! Take Cinnaminson down with them, then come back on deck! We need your strong back and skilled hands, lad! This is a heavy blow we're facing down!"

Pen dropped what he was doing and raced at once to the pilot's box, slipping precariously on decking slick with dampness. He heard Cinnaminson shouting at him as he reached her, but her words were lost in the shrieks and howls of the wind. Shouting back that everything would be all right, he took her arm and steered her out of the pilot box and over to the hatchway, bending his head against the sudden gusts that swept into him. Again, she tried to say something, but he couldn't make it out. Ahren was waiting to receive her, and Pen turned back at once to help the beleaguered Rovers.

"Safety lines!" Gar Hatch roared from the pilot box, where he had taken over the controls.

Pen found one coiled about a clasp on the mainmast and snapped the harness in place around his waist. The *Skatelow* was dropping swiftly toward the plains as Gar Hatch sought shelter. The Rover Captain had to set her down or she would be knocked out of the sky. But finding a place that would offer protection from the wind and rain was not so easy when it was impossible to see clearly for more than a dozen yards.

The sails were down by then, so the boy hurried forward to secure the anchor ropes and hatch covers. Rain began to fall in sheets, a deluge that soaked Pen in only seconds. He had not worn his weather cloak on deck, and his pants and tunic offered no protection at all. He ignored the drenching, blinking away the torrent of water that spilled out of his hair and into his eyes, fighting to reach his objective. Still descending toward the plains, a stricken bird in search of a roost, the airship was shaking from the force of the wind.

Pen had almost reached the bow when the other end of his safety harness whipped past him like a snake, shooting out through the railing and over the side. It took him a moment to realize what had happened, that it had somehow come free, and his hesitation cost him his footing as the snap of the line jerked him off his feet. He went down on his back, his hands grasping for something to hold on to as he began to slide toward the open railing, skidding on rain-slick decking, unable to stop himself. He had only a moment to wonder how the line had come loose before he was tumbling over the side.

He would have fallen to his death if he had not caught hold of one of the stanchions, and even so, the effort of stopping himself nearly dislocated his arms. He hung helplessly over the side, legs dangling and arms stretched to the breaking point. For a second, he thought he would not be able to hold on. The airship was lurching and heaving as the wind whipped at it, and it felt as if everything was about to let go.

"Penderrin!" he heard Gar Hatch scream.

He looked across the decking through the rain to where the Rover Captain stood braced in the pilot box with a coiled line gripped in both hands. Catching the boy's eye, he gave the line a heave that sent it flying all the way forward and across the railing, not six feet from where Pen hung suspended. Working the line with both hands, Gar Hatch whipsawed it back and forth across the railing until it fell over Pen's shoulder.

"Grab on!" the big man shouted.

The boy hesitated. There was no reason for his safety line to have come loose unless someone had released the locking pin. The man best in position to do that was the one offering to help him now. If he wanted Pen dead, all he had to do was wait for him to grab the line, then release it. Pen would be over the side and gone. Was that what Gar Hatch intended for him? Was he incensed enough about Cinnaminson to kill Pen?

The airship shuddered violently, and Gar Hatch was thrown to one side in the box. "Hurry, lad!" he cried out.

Pen released his grip on the stanchion, one hand at a time, and transferred his weight to the rope the big man had thrown him. As he hung from it, the line the only thing keeping him from tumbling away, he experienced a terrible certainty that he had made a mistake and was going to pay for it with his life.

Then Gar Hatch began to haul on the rope, and Pen felt himself being lifted back over the side of the vessel and onto the deck. In seconds, he was back aboard and flat on his stomach as he crawled toward the pilot box, his heart still in his throat.

Gar Hatch extended his hand over the side of the box and pulled him in effortlessly, dark eyes glittering. "There, now! Safe again! That was close, Penderrin! What happened to your line? Did you check to see that it was secure at the masthead before buckling in?"

Pen had to admit he had not. "No. I didn't think there was any need."

"Haste is a dangerous enemy aboard an airship," the Rover Captain declared, tucking his chin into his beard. "You want to be careful how you go, especially in weather like this. Good thing I was watching out for you, lad." His eyes narrowed. "Good thing, too, I decided you were worth the trouble of saving. Another man with another daughter might have thought otherwise. You want to remember that." He gave Pen a none-too-gentle shove. "Down you go with the others till this is over. Better think on what I just said while you're there."

Pen made his way out of the pilot box and across the decking to the hatchway, a cold place opening in the pit of his stomach. Behind him, he heard the Rover Captain laugh.

EIGHTEEN

"Safety lines don't come loose for no reason at all," Khyber Elessedil whispered, poking him in the chest to emphasize her point. "They don't get put away with one end left unattached, either."

Outside, the wind hammered and the rain beat against the wooden hull of the *Skatelow* as if to collapse it to kindling.

"I thought that, too," Pen answered, shaking his head. The cold feeling wouldn't leave him. It had found a home, deep inside, and even being down in the companionway and out of the weather didn't ease its chill. "But I couldn't argue about it with him, because he was right—I hadn't checked it."

They were huddled together in his tiny cabin, talking in low voices and casting cautious looks at the closed door as they did so. Creaks and groans filled the silences, reminders of the precariousness of their situation. Overhead, they heard the heavy boots of the Rover crewmen as they moved about the decking, making sure the airship didn't break free of her moorings. They had landed only minutes ago in the lee of an oak grove at the edge of

Paranor's forests, anchored about five feet off the ground while they rode out the storm. Gar Hatch had come below immediately and taken Cinnaminson to his cabin. Ahren and Tagwen were in the Druid's quarters already by then, the Dwarf sicker than Pen had seen a man in some time.

Khyber frowned. "It doesn't matter what he says anyway. The point is, we know how he feels. I doubt that he cared all that much whether you went over the side or not. A fall would have been an unfortunate accident, but accidents happen. Carelessness on your part, he'd say, exactly what he warned you against earlier. He doesn't have to answer for your failure to listen. But saving you works even better. It lets him make clear to you how vulnerable you are. He's made his point. Now you know for sure not to come near his daughter anymore."

She paused. "You do know that now, don't you?"

He sighed. "Stop trying to tell me what to do, Khyber."

"Someone has to tell you! You don't seem capable of figuring things out on your own!" She scowled and went silent, and they both looked away, listening to the wind howl across the decking. "I'm just trying to keep you from getting killed, Pen."

"I know."

"What was Cinnaminson trying to tell you when you were bringing her down? Did you find out?"

"Just to be careful, to watch out for myself, that's all."

"She knew. She was trying to warn you." Khyber shook her head. "I wish this trip was over. I wish we were rid of these people."

He nodded, thinking at the same time that he wished he were rid of everyone but Cinnaminson. It didn't seem fair that a simple friendship should put him in so much danger. He still couldn't quite bring himself to believe it, although he had no illusions about what Gar Hatch might be capable of. Khyber was right about what happened topside. He might never know if Hatch intended for him to go over the side, but he knew for certain that he had been warned.

"Well, the trip will be over soon enough," he muttered, suddenly bone weary and heartsick. "Probably nothing else will happen now anyway."

Khyber exhaled sharply. "I wouldn't bet on it."

Although he didn't say so, Pen guessed he wouldn't, either.

The storm passed around midday, the winds dying down and the rain ending, and the *Skatelow* resumed her journey east. By then, she was above the Jannisson Pass, leaving Paranor and Callahorn and sliding north along the foothills fronting the Charnals and the Eastland. The weather turned sultry, and the skies were clouded over and gray for as far as the eye could see. Water birds soared overhead from the mountain lakes and rivers, white flashes against the gloom, their cries eerie and chilling. Far to the east and south, the departing storm clouds formed a dark wall splintered by flashes of lightning.

Except for the still-airsick Tagwen, everyone was back on deck by then, looking out at the distant mountains, catching the first glimpses of their destination. It was another day's journey to the Lazareen, but Pen felt a shift in his thinking anyway. His time with Cinnaminson was growing short, for after the Lazareen there was only another day's flying before they left the airship. He marveled that only yesterday it seemed as if they had all the time in the world, and now it seemed that they had almost none. Part of his attitude was fostered by what had happened earlier, but even that wouldn't have discouraged him entirely, had they had another week to spend together. But he could do nothing to pro-long their journey's ending, could change nothing about parting from Cinnaminson.

They flew up the corridor leading off the Streleheim toward the Malg Swamp, a misty flat smudge across the landscape on their left, the terrain in dark counterpoint to the rolling green foothills on their right. Gar Hatch took the airship lower, trying to avoid the heavier mix of clouds and mist that layered the sky with a thick ceiling between swamp and mountains. As they neared the Malg, the water birds disappeared, replaced by swarms of insects that defied winds and airspeed to attack the ship's passengers in angry clouds. Gar Hatch swore loudly and took his vessel up until finally the insects dropped away.

Pen spit dead gnats from his mouth and wiped them from his nostrils and eyes. Cinnaminson appeared next to him, moving over from the pilot box with unerring directional sense, never wa-vering in her passage, and he was reminded again of how, even blind, she seemed able to see what was going on around her.

He was about to ask her what her father had said to her in his cabin, but before he could do so, he heard something in the cry of a heron that winged past so close it felt as if he could reach out and touch it. He looked at it sharply, hearing in its call a warning he could not mistake. Something had frightened the bird, and that did not happen easily with herons.

He scanned the horizon, then saw the dark swarm of dots soar-ing out of a deep canyon cut into the rugged foothills.

Birds, he thought at once. Big ones. Rocs or Shrikes.

But they didn't fly like birds. There was no wing movement, and their shapes were all wrong.

They were airships.

"Captain!" he shouted over to Gar Hatch and pointed.

For a long second, the big man just stared at the shapes, then he turned back with a dark look on his face. "Cinnaminson, get below and stay there. Take the other young lady with you. Penderrin, come into the pilot box. I'll need you."

Without bothering to wait for a reply, Gar began shouting at the Rover crewmen, both of whom jumped in response. Within moments, they were hoisting every scrap of sail they could manage, a clear indication that whatever was coming, Gar Hatch intended to run from it.

Cinnaminson was already descending through the hatchway, but Khyber was having none of it. "I'm staying," she declared firmly. "I can help."

"Go below," Ahren Elessedil ordered her at once. "The Captain commands on this ship. If I need you, I'll call. Stay ready. Pen, let's find out what is happening."

Be careful, Khyber mouthed silently to the boy as she disappeared from view.

Together, Pen and the Druid hurried over to the pilot box and climbed inside. Gar Hatch was setting the control levers, readying them for when the sails were all in place. He scowled at Pen and the Druid as if they might be responsible.

"Put on your safety lines," he ordered. "Check both ends of yours, young Penderrin. We've no time for mistakes here."

Pen held his tongue, doing as he was told, buckling himself into his harness and testing the links. Ahren Elessedil did the same.

"Sometimes I wonder if it's worth it, making these runs," Gar Hatch growled. He nodded toward the approaching dots. "Those are flits. Single-passenger airships, bothersome little gnats. Quick and highly maneuverable. Gnome raiders use them, and that's who those boys likely are. They want to bring us down for whatever we've got aboard. They'll do it, too, if they get close enough. I wouldn't worry normally, but that storm took something out of the *Skatelow*. She's faster than they are when she's working right, but she's down in her power about three-quarters and I haven't the time to do the work necessary to bring her back up again until we reach the Lazareen."

"We can't outrun them?" Ahren asked.

Gar Hatch shook his head. "I don't think so. If we get far enough ahead of them, they might lose interest. If they know the ship, they might fall off. If not . . ."

He shrugged. "Still, there's other ways."

He yelled at the crewmen to make certain they were ready, then shoved the thruster levers all the way forward. The *Skatelow* shuddered with the sudden input of power from the radian draws and shot ahead, lifting skyward at the same time. Hatch worked the controls with swiftness and precision, and Pen could see that he had been down that road before. Even so, the flits were getting closer, growing larger and beginning to take shape. Pen saw the Gnomes who were crouched in their tiny frames, faces wizened and burnt by wind and sun. Gloved hands worked the levers that changed the direction of the single-mast sail, a billowing square that could be partially reefed or let out to change direction and thrust. At present, all sails were wind-filled, catching the light, powering the flits ahead at full speed.

Pen could already see that the *Skatelow* had no chance of out-running them. The angle of attack and her injuries from the storm didn't allow for it. The flits would be on them in moments.

"Penderrin, lad," Gar Hatch said almost calmly. "Do you think you know enough by now to take the helm and keep her running full out?"

The boy nodded at once. "I think so."

"She's yours, then," the Rover said, stepping aside. "You look like you might have fought a battle or two in your time," he said to Ahren. "How are you with rail slings?"

They went out of the pilot box, safety harnesses trailing after them, and worked their way across the deck to either side of the mainmast. A Rover crewman joined each of them, and in teams they began to set up the rail slings, pulling the catapults out of storage bins and setting the pivot ends into slots cut into the deck. Pen had never seen a rail sling before, but he understood their function right away. Built like heavy crossbows, they sat on swivels that could be pointed in any direction over the railings. A hand winch cranked back a sling in which sat a missile the size of a fist. When the sling was released, the missile hurtled out into the void, hopefully striking something in the process.

Hitting a moving target with one of those weapons while flying in an airship was virtually impossible, unless the target was huge, in which case no damage was likely to occur. But used against a swarm of targets, like the flits, a rail sling might have some success. Miss one flit and you still had a chance at half a dozen more.

The rail slings were barely in place and loaded when the first of the flits reached them. The flits by themselves were useless as weapons, too small and fragile to ram a larger vessel or to shear off a mast. The Gnomes' intent was to sever the radian draws or rigging or to shred the ambient-light sheaths. They did this by using poles with razor-sharp blades bound about the business end.

In seconds, the flits were everywhere, coming at the *Skatelow* from every direction. Pen kept the airship steady and straight, knowing that this offered Gar Hatch and Ahren Elessedil their best chance at bringing down their attackers. The rail slings were firing by then, and a few of the tiny ships went down, sails holed or masts shattered, plummeting earthward like stricken birds. One either miscalculated or failed for some other reason and crashed into the *Skatelow's* hull, shattering on impact. Another became tangled in the bigger ship's rigging and crashed to the deck, where its pilot was seized by one of the Rovers and thrown overboard.

But the flits were inflicting damage on the *Skatelow*, as well. Several of her rigging lines had already been severed, and one radian draw was frayed almost to the breaking point. The mainsail had a dozen rents in the canvas, and the flit that had become tangled in the rigging had brought down several spars. The *Skatelow* was still flying, but Pen felt the unevenness of her effort.

When the frayed draw finally snapped, he switched off power to the crystal it fed and transferred what remained to the others. But the airship was shaking and bucking and no longer responded smoothly.

"Hold her steady!" Gar Hatch bellowed angrily.

Another flit whipped past Pen, the pole and blade sweeping down at his head, and he barely managed to duck away from it. Sensing the ship was in trouble and its crew unable to do any more to help her or themselves, the raiders were growing bolder. One good strike on one more essential component, and the vessel would not be able to stay in the air. She would fail quickly, and then she would be theirs.

They were deep into Northland country by that time, flying close to the Malg, and mist had closed about them in a heavy curtain that reduced their vision to almost nothing. The flit attacks seemed to materialize from nowhere as they winged out of the haze and then disappeared back into it again. How the Gnome pilots could find their way under such conditions was beyond Pen. He was struggling to see anything.

"Take her up!" Hatch shouted at him.

He did so, lifting her nose into the soup just as a Gnome raider came right across the bow. The flit simply disintegrated, but pieces of it ricocheted everywhere, severing lines forward and starboard and cutting loose the flying jib. The *Skatelow* slewed sideways in response, and Pen could no longer make her do anything. Gar Hatch abandoned his rail sling and clawed his way back across the deck to regain the controls.

In the midst of that chaos, with the *Skatelow* beginning to fall and the flits attacking like hornets, Ahren Elessedil stepped away from his rail sling, stood at the center of the airship's deck, and raised his arms skyward, his robes billowing like dark sails. For a moment he stood without moving, a statue at rest, eyes closed, head lifted. His face was calm and relaxed, as if he had found peace within himself and left the madness behind.

Then his hands began to weave like snakes and his voice to chant, the sound low and guttural and unrecognizable as his.

Gar Hatch had hauled himself into the pilot box and taken over the controls from Pen with an angry grunt. His hands were flying over the levers and wheels, but when he looked up long enough to catch sight of Ahren Elessedil, he froze. "What in the name of sea salt and common sense is the man doing?" he demanded.

The boy shook his head. He knew. "Saving us," he answered.

Behind them, Khyber had come out on deck, grasping the hatchway frame to hold herself steady, and was shouting at her uncle in disbelief.

Gnome raiders, bladed poles lowered to skewer him, were darting at the Druid from all directions. But try as they might, they could not get close enough to do so. Mist obscured their vision and gusts of wind knocked them aside, the mix roiling faster and faster, taking on the shape of a massive funnel. Heads began to turn in response. Aboard the *Skatelow*, the Rovers were shouting. Astride the flits, there wasn't the time or energy to spare for it. The mist and wind had become a deadly whirlpool surrounding the airships and then closing on them.

Ahren Elessedil's arms were stretched above his head, as if he sought to grasp something that was just out of reach. The funnel cloud of mist and wind continued to tighten. It caught the outermost flits and engulfed them. One minute they were there, fighting to stay aloft, and the next they were gone. The rest tried to flee, banking their tiny ships in all directions, seeking a means of escape. Some came right at the *Skatelow* and Ahren Elessedil, but they could not get close enough to strike at either. One by one, they were plucked from the sky by the funnel. One by one, they disappeared until all were gone.

The Druid lowered his arms, the mist dissipated, the winds died, and the whirlwind vanished, as well. Not a flit remained in the sky. Everything was the way it had been before the attack, the air hazy and gray but calm. The *Skatelow* sailed on, wounded but able to continue. In the distance, a sliver of sunlight broke through the clouds.

Ahren Elessedil walked back over to the pilot box and beckoned to Pen. "Let's help clear the decks and put away the rail slings," he said. He glanced at Gar Hatch. "Odd weather we're having, isn't it? No one would ever believe such strange things could happen. A man would be crazy even to suggest it."

Pen smiled inwardly. The Druid knew something about giving warnings, as well. Which was a good thing, he supposed, since now everyone aboard knew what he was.

NINETEEN

L ate in the morning of the following day, they arrived at Anatcherae, the inland port on the Lazareen that serviced all traffic passing north along the corridor formed by the Charnal Mountains to the east and the Knife Edge Mountains to the west. They reached their destination more quickly than anticipated because tailwinds filled and sunshine fed the sails and because Gar Hatch had been able to complete repairs to the damaged radian draw before nightfall of the previous day. It was a smooth flight the entire way after their escape from the flits, with no further trouble arising to impede their passage.

Anatcherae was an old city built by a mix of Trolls and Bordermen following the Second War of the Races, when Southlanders were mostly keeping to themselves below Callahorn but trade was flourishing everywhere else. A sprawling, ramshackle outpost in its early days, it grew quickly, the principal port servicing trappers and traders coming out of the Anar, Callahorn, and everywhere the Troll nations made their homes. It had become a major city, though still with the look and feel of a frontier town, its buildings spread out along the southwest shore of the lake, timber and shingle structures that were torn down and replaced as the need arose and without much thought to permanency. Even though the greater part of the populace lived in the city, most did not intend to make Anatcherae their final stop along life's road and so did not build for the long term.

The *Skatelow* set down at the waterfront docks, where warehouses and barns loomed like low, squat beasts bent down for a drink at the Lazareen's dark waters, their mouths open to receive what the lake would deliver. Airships crowded the waterfront, most of them large freighters and warships. Traffic leaving the docks passed down roads flanked by ale houses, pleasure dens, and inns of various descriptions. Shops and homes lay farther inland, away from the bustle and din of the docks, back from the raw edge of seaport life.

Standing on deck while the harbormaster towed the *Skatelow* to her assigned slip, Pen took a moment to glance over his shoulder in the other direction, back across the lake. The Lazareen was legendary. A broad, slate-gray body of water that seldom changed color in any weather, it was believed to run several thousand feet deep. Rumor had it that in some places it reached all the way to the netherworld and thereby provided the souls of the dead a doorway to the domain of the living. Mountains framed its rugged banks to the east and south, walls of stone that kept those souls contained. Dozens of rivers had their origins in snowmelt glaciers thousands of feet higher up, the confluence of their waters tumbling through canyons and defiles to feed the lake. Cold winds blew down out of snowy heights to mix with the warmer air of the flats and create a swirling mist that clung to the shorelines like gray moss. Pen did not like the Lazareen, he decided. It had

the look and feel of the Mist Marsh, a place the boy was all too familiar with and wished never to visit again.

The *Skatelow* eased up against the dock, and the Rovers set
about securing her. When Gar Hatch came over to speak with
Ahren, Pen listened in.

"I'll be needing several days to make repairs before we continue on," the Rover Captain advised in a gruff voice, hitching up
his pants to emphasize that work lay ahead. "Maybe more. Once
that's done, we'll continue on to where you need to go, and then
I'll be dropping you off and saying good-bye."

"I don't think we discussed being dropped, Captain," the Druid
said, frowning. "I think the agreement was that you would wait until we came out again from our search."

"That was then, this is now. The agreement is changed." Gar
Hatch spit over the side. "Others need a little business done, as
well, and rely on me to conduct it for them. I require my ship
to do so. I can't make a living while she sits idle. You don't pay
enough for that. Give me a time and a place, and I'll come back for
you. My Captain's word on it."

"There isn't any way of knowing when we'll be finished. We
can increase your purse, if it's a matter of money."

The Rover shook his head. "Sorry, mate. This isn't about
money."

Ahren Elessedil smiled. "You are a Rover, Gar Hatch. It's always about money."

The big man laughed and glanced over at Pen. "You listening
close, young Penderrin? Here's a man who knows the way of the
world. He's right, too. Everything is about money, one way or
the other." He looked back at the Druid. "Still, I can't let myself be
tied down for so long. You might not even come back from wherever it is you're going. I've seen already the sort of business you do,

and it isn't reassuring to puzzle on. So I'm dropping you and that's the end of it."

The Druid nodded. "I could find other passage and cancel our agreement here and now, Captain Hatch. I would be justified."

"You could try," the big man amended. "But you won't find anyone else to take you where you want to go that knows the ways of that country like I do. You won't find anyone who can sail the mists and the night like I can. Maybe most important of all, you won't find anyone who can keep his mouth shut about who you are and what you're doing. You might want to bear that in mind."

"But can I trust you? I find I have serious doubts."

Gar Hatch smiled and inclined his head. "Put aside your doubts, sir. My word is good."

The irony of that statement probably did not escape the Druid, but he let it pass. "Three days, Captain. That's as long as I'll give you to do your business here. We leave on the fourth. We'll find lodgings ashore and check back with you. I won't press for you to wait on us, if you've decided against it. But there will be no further changes to our agreement, and I expect a close watch on the tongues of your people. Don't disappoint me."

He went down the hatchway to his cabin to bring up Tagwen. Khyber was already on the dock, looking around eagerly.

Pen sensed Gar Hatch staring at him and met his stare, refusing to look away when it lingered too long. The big man laughed. "You've been a revelation for me, Penderrin. A treasure and a find."

"Can I say good-bye to Cinnaminson?" Pen asked.

He hadn't seen her since the attack of the flits. Gar Hatch had kept her shut away in his cabin, not even allowing her to come on deck at night, advising his passengers that she was ill. Pen had thought several times to sneak down and see for himself, but each time he thought to try, Gar Hatch was somewhere close, watching.

It was his last chance until they reboarded in three days' time, and anything could happen between now and then. Hatch could promise what he wished, but that didn't mean it was likely to happen.

The Rover Captain smiled. "Better you don't, lad. What she's got might be catching. Wouldn't do to have you come down with a fever while you're resting in port. Your uncle is mad enough at me already. You'll see her when you come back aboard."

I'll never see her again, Pen thought. But he could do nothing about it short of forcing a confrontation, and he was aware how much trouble that would cause.

He turned away without a word, shouldered his pack, and started down the ladder. He was halfway to the pier when he heard his name called.

"Pen, wait!"

Cinnaminson appeared at the railing, blind eyes staring downward without finding him. He started back up the ladder and stopped when he was close enough to see Gar Hatch glaring at him in the background.

"I'm feeling better now, Pen," she said, giving him a small wave and a smaller smile. "I just wanted to say good-bye." Then she whispered so softly that only he could hear, "Come back tonight."

She turned away quickly and went to her father, who took her by the arm and steered her below again, not bothering with even a glance at Pen. The boy stood watching until they were out of sight, then went down the ladder with his heart in his throat.

With Ahren Elessedil leading, the four companions walked down through the center of the city, mingling with the crowds as they searched for a likely place to secure lodging for the days ahead. Pen could barely make himself concentrate on the task at hand, his mind still on Cinnaminson and her whispered words. *Come back tonight.* He was intoxicated by them, made light-headed at the prospect of what they meant, chilled by the prospect of the danger at which they hinted. He wasn't afraid, though. He was fearless when it came to her. He understood that by even considering a secret return, he was risking not only his own safety but also the success of his undertaking. Yet he couldn't help himself. He had to go to her.

It took them the better part of an hour to find what Ahren was looking for, a small, prosperous inn just off one of the main roadways, one that was better kept than those closer to the docks, one frequented by other travelers than sailors. It was called Fisherman's Lie. It sat on a corner that opened onto a small plaza and was wrapped by a veranda that fronted both streets. Broad double doors opened into the common room, where travelers sat to visit and drink glasses of ale. Tables and benches and a long serving bar took up most of the available space. Flowers grew in boxes under the windowsills, and baskets hung from the veranda and eaves, splashes of color to brighten the clapboard facade.

Ahren left the other three on the porch while he went inside to take rooms. The less they were all seen together, the less likely it was that anyone would make the connection to the four the Druids were hunting. Since Khyber had cut Pen's hair short and bound his head in a scarf, none of them was particularly noticeable. But there was no point in taking chances. Those tempted by the money the Druids offered would be looking hard.

The Elf emerged in moments with the rooms secured. They went into the dining room after that and sat at a table in the back while waiting for their food. Sipping at glasses of cold ale, they talked about their situation.

"Hatch knows who I am," Ahren said quietly, eyes scanning

the mostly empty room as he spoke. "Or at least he knows *what* I am. He might not know my name yet, but there is a good chance he will find out. Or if not him, then one of the crewmen. All of them will be asking around, talking with other Rovers."

"Maybe not," Pen offered hopefully. "You might have scared him out of it."

Ahren smiled. "Not likely. Not that man. If he finds out who we are, he will look for a way to turn it to his advantage. It's his nature. So we have to be very careful until we set sail again. That's why I didn't tell him where he could find us. He mustn't know. If he betrays us, our enemies will still have to search us out. That won't be easy in a city of this size."

"We should just leave him right here and now and be done with it!" Tagwen snapped. He scowled into his glass. "Take him up on his offer. That way we can stop worrying about him."

"But not about getting to where we have to go," Ahren replied. "I don't trust him, either, but he is right when he says we will have trouble finding anyone else to fly us into the Charnals. Even by looking, we risk giving ourselves away. Say what you want about Hatch, he knows how to sail. His reputation is one of getting in and out of tight places. We need that. I think we have to stick with him."

"One of us could watch the *Skatelow* and see who comes and goes," Khyber suggested.

Her uncle shook his head. "That's too risky and too time-consuming. Besides, any one of them could give us away. We can't watch them all. Better to keep our heads down and wait this out. I will speak with Hatch each day to see how matters stand. If he lies to me, I will know. The rest of you will remain here, inside, out of sight. No one leaves the inn without permission until it is time to sail. Agreed?"

All of them nodded, but Pen knew it was an agreement he was going to break.

He waited until it was dark and Tagwen was asleep before slipping out of his bed. He crossed the room in his bare feet, boots in hand, and went through the door without a sound. Instead of leaving by the inn's front entrance, he went out the back, taking the rear stairs to the street. Cloaked and hooded, he went quickly toward the waterfront. The night air was clear and sharp, turned cold after sunset, and the sky was bright with stars. It was close to midnight, but the streets were still bustling with activity, the denizens of the ale houses and pleasure dens just beginning their night's fun. Many were sailors, come from all over, a mix of travelers passing through. None of them looked at him. None spoke.

He was taking a chance, risking everything. He was neither happy nor sad about it, felt neither guilt nor satisfaction. Such things didn't matter to a boy who thought he was in love. What mattered was that Cinnaminson was waiting, and the thought of her drove every other consideration from his mind. His excitement gave him courage and determination. It gave him a sense of invulnerability. Whatever happened, he was a match for it. His certainty was so complete that he never stopped to question whether his bravado might be playing him false. On that night, there was no place in his heart for rational thinking.

He reached the waterfront and began working his way down the docks. New ships had arrived, some of them bigger than anything he had ever seen. He looked closely for the *Galaphile* as he went, but did not see her. Nor did he see Terek Molt or any other Druids. Loading and unloading went on about him, unceasing, unending, and all seemed as it should.

When he reached the *Skatelow*, he moved into the shadows across from her, staying well back from the light. There was no sign of life aboard. Even the storm lamps were extinguished. The boarding ladder was pulled up, signaling that visitors were unwelcome. On the piers to either side, similarly darkened ships lay at rest, sleeping birds awaiting the dawn.

Pen eased along the wall of the warehouse that fronted the slip, then moved just to the edge of the light that pooled down from the lamps hung over the entrance doors. He stood there, undecided, searching the contours of the *Skatelow* for signs of life.

Then he saw her. She appeared all at once, beckoning to him, knowing somehow that he was there. He took a chance, his throat tightening with anticipation. He stepped into the light, crossed the dock to the mooring slip, and stopped just below where she stood.

"Cinnaminson," he said.

Her blind gaze shifted and her hair shimmered in the moonlight. "Wait," she whispered. She moved at once to the ladder and dropped it over the side. "Come up. They're all in town at the ale houses and won't be back before dawn. We're alone."

He did as she said, climbing the ladder and hauling himself aboard. He stood on the decking in front of her, and she reached to take his hands. "I knew you would come," she said.

"I couldn't stay away."

She released his hands and pulled the ladder back aboard. "Sit with me over here, out of the light. If they come, they need me to lower the ladder to let them aboard. By then, you can be over the side."

She led him to the far side of the pilot box, where the shadows were deepest, and they sat down with their shoulders touching and their backs to the low wall. Her milky eyes turned to find him.

"Let's not tell each other any lies tonight," she whispered. "Let's tell each other only truths."

He nodded. "All right. Who goes first?"

"I do. It was my idea." She leaned close. "Papa knows who you are, Penderrin Ohmsford. He knew Ahren Elessedil was a Druid after what happened during the flit attack, and he found out the rest from asking around the docks. He didn't give you away, or let on that you were passengers on the *Skatelow*, but he knows."

Her smooth features were tight with trepidation and uncertainty, her chin lifted as if to take a blow. Pen touched her cheek. "Ahren told us this might happen. It isn't unexpected. But he had to reveal himself if he was to save us."

"Papa knows this, and he doesn't forget such favors. I don't think he intends you harm. But I don't always understand how he thinks, either." She took his hands again. "Will you tell me where you are staying? So that if I discover you are in danger, I can warn you?"

He hesitated. It was the one thing he had been ordered not to reveal, no matter what. He had promised to keep it a secret. And now Cinnaminson was asking him to violate his trust. It was a terrible moment, and his decision was made impulsively.

"We are lodged at Fisherman's Lie, about half a mile into the city." He squeezed her fingers. "But how will you find us, even if you need to? You'll have to ask for help, and that's too dangerous."

She smiled. "Let me tell you another truth, Penderrin. I can find you anytime I want, because even though I am blind, I can see with my mind. I have always been able to do so. It is the way I was born—with a different kind of sight. I travel with Papa because I can see better than he can in darkness and in mist and fog, bad weather, storms of all sorts. I can navigate by seeing with my mind what is hidden to his eyes. That's why he can go into places others cannot—across the Lazareen, into the Slags, places cloaked by weather and gloom. It's like a picture that appears behind my eyes of everything around me. It doesn't work so well in daylight, although I can see well enough to find my way about. But at night, it is clear and sharp. Papa didn't know I could do this, at first. When Mama died, he began taking me to sea rather than leaving me with her relatives. He never liked them or they him. Having me travel with him was less trouble than finding someone he trusted to raise me at home. I was still very young. I thought I was being given a chance to prove I was worth keeping. I wanted him to love me so that he wouldn't give me up. So I showed him how I could read the sky when no one else could. He understood my gift, and he began using me to navigate. I let him do so because it made me feel secure. I was useful, and so I believed he would keep me."

She paused. "Papa doesn't want anyone to know this. Only the two men who serve as crew know, and they are his cousins. Both are sworn to secrecy. He is protective of me; I am his daughter and helpmeet. But I am also his good-luck charm. Sometimes, he isn't clear on the difference. I think he loves me, but he doesn't know what loving someone really means."

She reached out and cupped his face in her hands. "There. I've given you a gift—a truth no one else has ever heard."

He took her hands in his own and squeezed them gently. "You've kept this to yourself a long time. Why are you telling someone now, after so long? Why disobey your father's wishes like that? I wouldn't have minded if you had kept it secret."

She freed her hands, and her fingers brushed at her hair and face like tiny wings. "I am tired of not being able to talk about it with anyone. Not talking about it is like pretending I am someone other than who I really am. I have been looking for someone to tell this to. I chose you because I think we are the same. We are both keeping secrets."

"I guess that's so," he said. He sat back against the pilot box wall. "Now it's my turn to tell you a secret. I hardly know where to begin, I have so many. You know who I am, but you don't know what I am doing here."

"I can guess," she said. "The Ard Rhys is your aunt. You are here because of her. But the Druids say you are in danger. They say that what happened to her might happen to you if you are not found and brought to them. Is that true?"

He shook his head. "I'm in danger, but mostly from them. Some of them are responsible for what's happened to her. If they find me, I might end up the same way. I escaped them when they came looking for me in Patch Run. So now I'm running away."

"Are you looking for your parents?"

"I'm looking for my aunt. It's complicated." He paused. "We promised to tell each other truths tonight, so let me tell you one. You have a kind of magic that no one else has. So do I. Like you, I was born with it. It is probably a part of the magic my father inherited, something that's been passed down through the Ohmsford bloodline for generations. Only, mine is different."

He exhaled softly, searching for a way to explain. "I can tell what plants and animals are feeling and sometimes thinking. They don't talk to me exactly, but they communicate anyway. They tell me things with their sounds and movements. For instance, I know if they're afraid or angry and what causes them to be so."

"Your gift is not so different from my own," she said. "You can see things that are hidden from other people and you can see them without using your eyes. We are alike, aren't we?"

He leaned forward. "Except that I am free and you are not. Why is that, Cinnaminson? Could you leave your father if you wanted? Could you go somewhere else and have a different life?"

It was such an impulsive question that he surprised himself by asking it. Worse, he had nothing beyond encouragement to offer if she answered yes. What could he do to help her in his present circumstances? He couldn't take her with him, not where he was going. He couldn't offer to aid her while Ahren was so determined not to aggravate Gar Hatch.

She laughed softly. "Such a bold question, Penderrin. What should I do? Leave my Papa and run away with you? A blind girl and a fugitive boy?"

"I guess it sounds silly," he admitted. "I shouldn't have asked."

"Why not?" she pressed, surprising him. "Do you care for me?"

"You don't have to ask that."

"Then you must care *about* me, too. So it seems right to want an answer. I like it that you do. Yes, I want a different life. I have looked for it. But you are the first to whom I have talked about it. You are the first to ask."

He stared at her face, at her smooth features, at the smile that curved her lips, at her strange blank eyes. What he felt for her in that instant transcended love. He might say that he loved her, but he didn't know all that much about love, so saying it wouldn't mean anything. It was only a word to him; he was still only a boy. But this other feeling, the one that was more than love, encompassed whole worlds. It whispered of connection and sharing, of confidences and truths like the ones they had told each other tonight. It promised small moments that would never be forgotten and larger ones that could change lives.

What could he give her that would tell her this? He struggled to find an answer, lost in a sea of confusing emotions. Her hands were holding his again, her fingers making small circles against his skin. She wasn't saying anything. She was waiting for him to speak first.

"If you were to decide you wanted to leave your father, I would help you," he said finally. "If you wanted to come away with me, I would let you. I don't know how that could happen. I only know that I would find a way."

She lowered her head just enough that the shadows grazed her face and hid her expression. "Would you come for me wherever I was, Pen? It is a bold thing to ask, but I am asking it anyway. Would you come for me?"

"Wherever you are, whenever you have need," he whispered.

She smiled, her face lifting back into the light. "That is all I need to know." She sat back and turned her face to the starlit sky. "Enough of making promises and telling truths. Let's just sit together for a little while and listen to the night."

They did so, side by side, not saying anything, their hands in their laps, their shoulders and hips touching. The sounds of the waterfront rolled over them in small bursts and slow meanderings, brief intrusions from a place that seemed far away. The night turned colder, and Pen wrapped them both in his cloak, putting his arm around her to lend his warmth, feeling her small form melt against him.

After a time, she leaned over and kissed him on the cheek. "You must leave now. It grows late. They will return. Go back to your room and sleep." She kissed him again. "Come again tomorrow, if you can. I will be waiting."

He rose and walked with her to the ladder, scanning the dock for signs of approaching Rovers. The docks were empty now. She lowered the ladder for him, and he climbed down. He stood looking up at her as she pulled it away again, then he turned and went down the waterfront.

Cinnaminson.

Nothing in his life, he knew, would ever be the same again.

TWENTY

Grianne Ohmsford woke to a morning so dismal and gray that it might have drifted out of the marshy depths of the Malg Swamp, an apparition come in search of the unfortunate Jarka Ruus. It felt alive and hungry. It had a shape and feel. The air it breathed smelled of fetid water and brushed at the skin with greasy, insistent fingers. The clouds that formed its hair were so low in the sky as to be indistinguishable from the misty beard that curled about its ragged face. Everything about it whispered of hidden danger and lost souls. In its presence, heartbeats quickened with the uneasy and certain knowledge that death, when it appeared, would be quick and unexpected.

The Ard Rhys was cramped from sleeping in the cradle of tree limbs, her body aching and stiff. She had slept, though she did not pretend to understand how, and she had kept her perch and not fallen as she had feared she would. Climbing down through brume that would have discouraged even the most intrepid seabird, she caught sight of the tracks that crisscrossed the earth directly below, and decided she had been lucky to have survived the night with no more than her sore muscles. Weka Dart had been right to warn her against trying to make her bed on the ground.

She glanced around, scanning the mist and gloom for some sign of the devious little Ulk Bog, thinking he might have come back during the night, even as mad at her as he had been when he left. After all, he had gone to a lot of trouble to persuade her to allow him to accompany her, and she found it hard to believe that he would toss it all away because of a perceived slight. He didn't seem the type who would allow insults to get in the way of ambitions. She still wasn't sure what he was after, only that he was after something. But there was no sign of him, so she accepted that he had gone his own way after all.

Just as well, she told herself.

Except that she didn't know the country, and that put her at a disadvantage. She knew in general how she should go, given that the Forbidding mirrored the Four Lands. She could estimate the location of the Hadeshorn from what she knew of its location in her own world. But the mist was confusing, and her sense of direction skewed by the different land formations. Worse, she would have to risk encountering the monsters that inhabited the Forbidding, without knowing who and what they were. At least Weka Dart had knowledge of the things she needed to avoid.

But there was no help for it. Nor help for her lack of food and water. She would have to forage for both as she traveled, hoping that she would recognize the former when she saw it. Water should be less of a problem, although just then she didn't want to assume anything.

She stretched her aching limbs and looked down at herself. Ragged and dirty, she was a mess. Her clothes were almost in shreds, her pale skin showing through the gaps in ways that didn't please her. She wrapped her tattered nightdress closer and told herself she would have to find something else to wear soon or she would be naked as well as starving and lost. She couldn't travel much farther without boots, either. Her feet were already scraped and bleeding, and she hadn't even gotten to the rocky climb to the Hadeshorn.

When I find out who did this to me . . .

She was about to set out when there was movement in the trees to one side and Weka Dart, bristle-haired and spindly-limbed, emerged carrying a cloth-wrapped package in both arms. He caught sight of her and stopped, his sharp teeth showing as he smiled broadly.

"Ah, Grianne of the trees. Sleep well, did you? You don't look so bad for having spent the night aboveground. See all the tracks?" He gestured. "Now you understand what I was telling you."

She stared at him without answering, undecided if she was happy about having him back.

His cunning features scrunched with disappointment. "Don't look at me like that! You should be pleased to see me. How far would you get without me? You don't know anything about this part of the world, anyone can tell that. You need me to guide you."

"I thought you were finished with me," she said.

He shrugged. "I changed my mind. I decided to forgive you. After all, you have a right to know about me, so you did what Strakens do and used your magic to find out. It isn't any different than what any creature of habit would do. Here, I brought you some clothes."

He came forward and dumped the bundle at her feet. She bent down and picked through it, finding leather boots, a loose-fitting cotton shirt, pants, a belt and knife, and the great cloak in which he had wrapped them. All were in good condition and close enough in size to fit her comfortably. She had no idea where he had found them and didn't think she should ask.

"Put them on," he urged.

"Turn your back," she replied.

It was silly, given that an Ulk Bog would not be interested about her that way, but she wanted to assert her authority before he got the wrong idea about who was in charge. If he was going to accompany her on the rest of her journey, as it appeared he was determined to do, she had better set him straight on the nature of their relationship immediately.

She removed the nightdress and put on the clothes, watching him fidget as he stared off into the trees. "I want to know why you insist on coming with me," she told him. "And don't tell me it's because you want to help a stranger find her way."

He threw up his hands. "Can't anyone do a good turn for you without being questioned about it?"

"In your case, no. You don't seem the type to do good turns unless there is something in it for you. So let's be honest about it. What is it that you want from me? Maybe it isn't anything I'll mind giving up, if it means you can get me to where I want to go." She finished buttoning the tunic. "You can turn around now."

He did so, looking sour-faced and ill-used. "I thought Strakens could tell what normal people are thinking. Why don't you just use your magic to find out what I want?"

She didn't bother with an answer, waiting patiently on him. He pouted. "You already know the reason. You just weren't paying attention when I told you. Too self-absorbed, I suspect."

"Tell me again."

He pouted harder. "I got in some trouble with my tribe. I had to flee for my life. They might still be chasing me. Alone, I'm not much good against a lot of the things that are Jarka Ruus. I know how to find my way and mostly how to avoid them, though. So I thought we could help each other." He folded his arms defiantly. "There, are you satisfied, Grianne of the curious mind and endless questions?"

He was being insolent, but she let it go. "I am. For now. But in the future, you will tell me the truth about your motives and your plans, little rodent, or I will feed you to the bigger things you seek to avoid. I don't like surprises. I want to know what you are thinking about. No secret plans, or our bargain is off."

"Then you agree that we should travel together?" he asked. He was positively gleeful. "That you will watch out for me?" He caught himself. "Well, that we will watch out for each other?"

"Let's just start walking," she said, and turned away.

They walked all that day, traveling east below the Dragon Line and across the grasslands and foothills of the Pashanon. The weather stayed gray and misty, the sun never more than a faint brightness high above them, the world they journeyed through composed of brume and shadows. The air was damp and chilly, a discomforting presence that made Grianne grateful for the clothes and boots that Weka Dart had brought her. The grasslands and hills were coated with moisture that never quite evaporated, yet the land remained barren and lifeless. The absence of small birds and little animals was unnerving, and even the insects tended to be of the buzzing, biting variety. Grasses grew thick and hardy, sawtooth and razorblade spears that were a washed-out green and mottled gray. Trees were stunted and gnarled below the Dragon Line, and many were little more than skeletons. The waters of the ponds and streams were stagnant and algae-laced. Everywhere they traveled and everywhere she looked, the world seemed to be sick and dying.

Yet the Jarka Ruus had existed for thousands of years. She tried to imagine a lifetime in such a world and failed. It frightened her to think of being trapped there for long. If she had not believed that she would find a way out, she would have been devastated.

But she never wavered in her certainty that she would. Those who had sent her there had made a mistake in letting her live. They might think themselves rid of her, but she would prove them wrong.

Her thoughts drifted frequently to the cause of her predicament. It was impossible for her to know exactly who had transported her, but she could make an educated guess or two. What baffled her was why they hadn't simply killed her and been done with it. It was what she would have done to them when she was the Ilse Witch. Leaving a dangerous enemy alive to come looking for you later, no matter how difficult the task, was always risky. So why had they let her live? It would have been no more difficult for them to kill her than to send her into the Forbidding. It made her think something else was happening, a reason for her enemies to keep her alive and imprisoned. It also made her ponder anew the source of the power it had taken to put her here. It was more than even the most powerful of the Druids possessed. It was beyond anything that existed in her world.

It was a power, she was beginning to think, that might have come from the Forbidding itself.

Her ruminations kept her occupied for much of her journey. Weka Dart continued to skitter about, dodging sideways and occasionally climbing up and down trees and rock formations, but always moving. He did not talk much, for which she was grateful; absorbed, apparently, in keeping an eye out for the things they should avoid.

There were a great number of those, and they encountered many of them on their way. Ogres and giants stomped through the grasslands, mindless behemoths, dim-sighted and single-minded, with great shoulders hunched and massive arms dragging. Harpies flew overhead, winged shrews that screamed and spit venom at each other and anything below. A scattering of dragons came

and went, smaller for the most part and different from the Drachas. Various forms of Faerie creatures were glimpsed, as well, particularly kobolds, which seemed to live in large numbers in that
region.

Once, they saw a village of Gormies, far in the distance, a
mud and grass huddle of shelters cut like caves into a hillside.
Walls fronted the village and spikes jutted out of the earth in
pointed warning. The Gormies themselves, ferret-eyed and wiry,
crept about their enclosure like shades.

"What would frighten an entire village of those little terrors?"
she asked Weka Dart.

He laughed and growled deep in his throat. "Wait and see."

She did so, and a few hours later she had her answer. They had
just crested a small rise, catching sight of a valley that stretched
away to the east when Weka Dart wheeled around suddenly,
hissing, *"Down, down!"* She dropped at once, flattening herself
against the earth, pressing into tufts of the spiky grass that grew
everywhere, her breathing turned sharp and quick. The Ulk Bog,
stretched out beside her, wormed forward just far enough that he
could see something that was still hidden from her.

"Watch," he whispered over his shoulder.

She did so, peering into the valley, waiting. The minutes passed
and nothing happened. Then an ogre of monstrous size lumbered
into view, hunched over and shouldering a massive club. It was
young, Grianne guessed, coarse hair black along its spine and
across its shoulders, and its thick skin leathery and smooth. It was
shaking its head from side to side and brushing at the air as if to
ward off gnats or flies. But she saw neither.

"What is it doing?" she whispered.

Weka Dart's eyes were bright. "Listen."

She did, and then she heard it, too—a high-pitched, keening sound that seemed to come from everywhere at once. It was

clearly bothering the ogre, who was grunting with annoyance, lifting its head every so often in a futile effort to search out the source. The sound intensified steadily, turning to a wail that cut right to the bone, raw and harsh and filled with pain.

Finally, the ogre stopped walking altogether, turning this way and that, blunt features twisted into an ugly knot. Grianne flattened herself further. The ogre was looking for something on which to vent its irritation, and she had no desire to provide it with a target. Weka Dart lay motionless, as well, but she saw the knowing smile at the corners of his mouth. There was anticipation in that smile, and she did not care for the look of it.

Suddenly, small, four-legged creatures began to appear, coming out of the grasses and from behind the rocks, a handful at first and then dozens. Their sharp-featured cat faces and sleek, sinuous shapes were unmistakable; she recognized them at once, even though she had never seen one before. Furies. She had read about them in the Druid Histories. Only once since their imprisonment had they broken through the Forbidding, doing battle with Allanon and nearly killing him. They were creatures of madness and mindless destruction, the worst of the many bad things imprisoned in this world. They attacked in swarms and were drawn to their victims by a hunger for blood. In the world of the Jarka Ruus, everything avoided them.

They closed now on the ogre, coming at it from all directions, so many that she could no longer count them. The ogre waited on them, its small, piggish eyes already anticipating the damage it would inflict on the creatures. Perhaps because it was young, it did not realize the danger it was in.

When they attacked, leaping blindly at the ogre, it smashed them like flies, wielding club and fists with equal effect. The Furies were smaller and their bodies unprotected, and those it found could not save themselves. But there were too many for the ogre to stop, and soon they had broken through its defenses, biting and tearing at its massive body with teeth and claws. Bits of flesh and patches of hair came away, and in moments the ogre was slashed and bleeding from head to foot. It fought on, killing Furies as long as it could, struggling to stay upright.

But in the end, they pulled it down, severing ligaments and tendons, shredding muscle and flesh, draining its blood and its strength until it was helpless. Bellowing in rage and despair, it disappeared beneath their relentless onslaught, blanketed in a squirming, heaving mass of furry bodies, borne to the earth until its life was gone.

Grianne, who had witnessed many terrible and violent deaths in her own world, nevertheless cringed at this one. The ogre meant nothing to her, and yet she was horrified by what had happened to it. She wanted to look away when the ogre was reduced to its final shudders and gasps, but she could not. It took a tap on her arm from Weka Dart to recall her to her senses.

"This way," the Ulk Bog whispered, "while they are busy."

They crawled through the grasses along the top of the rise and then down the reverse slope until they were out of sight. Once concealed from view, they stood and began walking, neither speaking, concentrating on the sounds that came from the other side of the hill.

When they were far enough away that they could no longer be heard, even by cat ears, Weka Dart turned to her. "Better they find it than us," he said with a wicked smile.

She nodded in agreement. But she did not feel good about it.

They slept that night in the trees again, and Grianne did not offer any objections. She understood how vulnerable they were to the creatures that roamed the Pashanon under cover of darkness.

Many she had not even seen, but a single viewing of the Furies was enough to persuade her. The trees offered little enough protection, she guessed, but she would take what she could find.

In her dreams that night, she saw the ogre die again, the scene replaying itself in various forms. Sometimes she was simply a spectator, a passive viewer to the death scene. At other times, she was the victim, feeling the teeth and claws of the cat things tear into her, flailing and helpless beneath their attack, thrashing awake in a cold sweat. At other times still, she was a participant, one of the Furies, assisting in the destruction of another hapless creature, driven by bloodlust and hatred, by feelings she thought she had left behind when she had ceased to be the Ilse Witch.

She woke tired and out of sorts, but she kept it to herself as they continued their travels east, walking the grasslands through another dismal and oppressive day. They followed the banks of what would have been the Mermidon in her world. She didn't bother to ask Weka Dart for its name, content to be left alone while he sidled back and forth about her at his own pace. It rained on that day, and even with the great cloak to protect her, she was soon drenched. They saw little of the land's denizens and no sign of the Furies, and for that she was grateful.

On the afternoon of the third day, they reached a break in the Dragon Line that she recognized as the mouth of the pass leading to the Hadeshorn and the Valley of Shale. A twisting, dark defile, it wound upward into the cliffs and disappeared into the mists.

"Do you know this place?" she asked Weka Dart. Rain dripped off her hood and into her face, and she brushed it out of her eyes. "Have you been here before?"

He shook his head. "Never." He glanced up into the dark mass of rocks. "It doesn't look like a place anyone would want to go."

"It is where I am going," she said. "You needn't. Do you want to wait for me here?"

He shook his head quickly. "I'd better stay with you. In case you need me."

They began to climb, working their way through the rubble-strewn foothills until they had reached the base of the mountains. There, the terrain turned steeper and more treacherous. There were no signs of passage, no marks on the rocks or wearing down of the earth. The pathway she knew to be there in her own world was not there in the Forbidding, and she was forced to blaze it on her own. Perhaps no one had ever come that way before. Weka Dart trailed her with less enthusiasm than he had displayed on the flats, grumbling and muttering the entire way. She ignored him. It had been his choice to come. She was no happier than he was to have to break the trail.

It was not long before they heard the wailing. The sound was unmistakable, a low moaning that might have been just the wind or something alive and in pain. It rose and fell in steady cadence, trailing off entirely at times, only to return seconds later. She tried to ignore it but found it impossible to do so. Changes in pitch and tone set her teeth on edge. The sound raked the rocks of the pass, tunneled deep into its crevices, and slithered down its gaps. Weka Dart hissed in dismay and frustration and covered his ears with his hands. When she looked back at him, his teeth were bared.

The shadows appeared soon after that, sliding out of splits in the walls and from behind rocks. They were not cast as shadows should be, but moved independently of the light, separating themselves from solid objects in ways that should not have been possible. They flowed across the pass, crooked black stains that tracked her progress like predators. When they touched her, their blackness trailed across her skin with icy fingers.

She knew instinctively what was happening. She was being told to turn back. She could feel the warning in the touch of the shadows and hear it in the sound of the wailing. But she ignored it, as she knew she must, and continued on.

By nightfall, they reached a break in the rocks that opened through a thick curtain of gloom and mist to a hole in the sky. Grianne Ohmsford stared in surprise, then realized that the sky was ink black and empty of stars or moon. There was simply nothing there. She walked forward, unable to believe she was seeing correctly.

Beyond the break in the rocks, where the mist and gloom fell away, she found herself standing on a rise that looked out over the Valley of Shale.

It was as she remembered it and yet not. The sharp-edged ebony stones were the same, strewn across the empty slopes like shards of polished glass. But a wall of mist enclosed the valley, a wall so deep and so high that she could see nothing save the black hole of the sky above. The mountains had vanished. The world had disappeared.

All that remained was the Hadeshorn, pooled at the bottom of the valley, its still waters shimmering dully in the deep gloom. Its flat, mirrored surface gave off a faintly greenish light that reflected from the pieces of stone. Mist rose off its surface like steam, but no warmth was to be found in those waters. Even from where she stood, Grianne could feel that the lake was as cold as winter and as lethal as death. Nothing lived there that hadn't crossed over into the netherworld long ago.

Weka Dart scuttled up behind her and peered about. "This place is evil. Why are we here?"

"Because answers to my questions are to be found in the waters of that lake," she replied.

"Well, ask your questions quickly then, and let's be gone!"

The wailing began anew, low and insistent, seeping from the stones and filtering through the air. The shadows reappeared, taking form this time, some familiar, some not, swirling about them like phantoms come to haunt. There were no voices, no faces, no human presence, and yet it seemed as if life might be embodied in the shadows and in the wailing, bereft of substance and soul, trapped in the ether. The sounds and the shadows responded to each other, speeding and slowing, rising and falling, a symbiosis that reflected a terrible dependence.

"Straken, do what you must, but do it quickly!" Weka Dart urged, and there was fear in his voice.

She nodded without looking at him. There was no reason to wait, nothing to be gained by deliberation. She could not know what waited for her when she summoned the spirits of the dead. It might be different here than in the Four Lands. It might be lethal.

It might be her only hope.

Resolved, she started down.

TWENTY-ONE

S he felt the presence of the dead almost immediately. They had assumed the forms of the shadows that flitted about her and taken on the voices that wailed from the rocks. They were a part of the air she breathed. As she descended the slopes, she found them all about her, pressing close, trying to recapture something of the corporeal existence they had left behind in crossing over into the netherworld. Shades felt that absence, she knew. Even dead, they remembered the substance of life.

This phenomenon would not have happened in her own world, where shades were confined to the depths of the Hadeshorn and no trespass into the world of the living was allowed. But in the Forbidding, more latitude seemed to be given to the dead, and though not yet summoned from the afterlife, they were already loose in the valley.

She sensed another aberration, as well. The shades that visited her were not friendly. At best, they were hostile toward all living things, but she sensed a specific antipathy toward herself. She could not determine the reason for that right away. They did not know her personally or possess a specific grudge that would explain their attitude, and yet there was no mistaking it. She felt it prodding at her, small barbs that did not sting so much as scratch. There was disdain and frustration in those scratches; there was outright dislike. Something about her was angering these shades, and although she sought to discover a reason for it, she could not. Shades were difficult to read, their emotions not connected to the physical and therefore not easily understood.

She considered using her magic to push them away, to give herself space in which to breathe. But within the Forbidding, her magic could have unforeseen consequences, and she did not want to risk losing a chance to speak with the shades of the Druids. Her purpose in coming there was to summon them, and she could not afford to be distracted from that effort. The lesser shades were annoying but manageable.

Even so, her journey to the floor of the valley seemed endless. The shades rubbed on her nerves like sandpaper. Their whispers and icy touches left her unsettled and anxious. She felt something of her old self rise in response, an urge to crush them like dried leaves, a desire to scatter them beneath her boot heels. It was what she would have done once upon a time and not given it a second thought. But she was no longer the Ilse Witch, and nothing would ever make her be so again.

She glanced back at Weka Dart. He sat cross-legged on the rise, hands over his ears, face knotted in determination. He was hanging on, but it was taking everything he had to do so.

By the time she reached the edge of the lake, the shadows were draped all about her, frozen scraps of silk burning with death's chill. The wailing was so pervasive that she could hear nothing else, not even the crunching of her boots on the loose stone. The shades had crowded in from every side, gathering strength in numbers until they had enveloped her. She was being suffocated, punished for ignoring their warning. If she failed to rid herself of them quickly, she would be overwhelmed.

She stared momentarily at the calm waters of the lake, at its columns of steam, fingers of mist risen straight from the nether-world. She knew better than to touch those waters. In her own world, they were deadly to living things, although Druids could survive them. Here, even Druids might be at risk.

Gathering her wits and focusing her determination, she raised her arms and began the weaving motion that would call forth the Druid dead. When the waters of the lake began to stir in response, she added the words that were needed. Slowly, the waters began to churn, the steam columns to geyser, and the lake itself to groan like a sleeping giant come awake. The shades already present fell away, taking with them their wailing and their icy touches, leaving dead space and silence in their wake.

Once rid of her most bothersome distraction, Grianne brought the full force of her power to bear. Using her skills and her experience, she bore down on this other world's Hadeshorn, manipulating it as she would its twin in the Four Lands, summoning the shades that would serve her cause, beckoning them from the depths to the surface, drawing them with her call. The lake surged and heaved with sudden convulsions, and its greenish waters turned dark and menacing. Waterspouts erupted with booming coughs, angry and violent. The lake hissed and spit like a venomous snake.

Her throat tightened and her mouth went dry. Something was wrong. There was resentment in the lake's response. There was resistance. That was not the way it was supposed to be. When the gateway to the netherworld was opened properly, there should be a lowering of barriers that invited a joining. The shades sought for it; it was their one chance to touch even briefly on what they had lost. The lake that gave them that chance had no reason to complain. But it was doing so here. It was more than disgruntled; it was enraged.

Had it been so long since a summoning had occurred in that world that the lake failed to recognize it for what it was? Was it possible there had never been a summoning before?

She gave herself only a moment to consider all that before refocusing on the task at hand. She had come too far to turn back and would not have done so if she could have. She had made her decision and she would be the equal of whatever happened. It was not bravado or foolhardiness that drove her; it was the certainty that it was her one and only chance to find a way out of this prison.

It took everything she had to maintain her concentration. Her instincts were screaming at her to back away, to cease her efforts. The air was filled with sounds and sensations that grated on her resolve and wore at her courage. The Hadeshorn was roiling by then, a volcanic pit threatening to explode with every new gesture she made, with every new word she spoke. Her magic, she saw, was anathema there, stirring the currents that led to the netherworld in the manner of fire on parchment, incendiary and destructive.

Still she continued, implacable and unyielding, as hard as the stone upon which she stood.

Then the shades began to rise in looping spirals, their transparent forms linked by the trailing iridescence that poured out of their trapped souls. Like shooting stars, they soared from the waters and lifted into the air, bright flashes against the night's firmament. They writhed and wailed piteously, giving vent to the travesty of their imprisonment, their outrage a mirror of her own. They spun like sparks showered from a fire grown too hot, released in an explosion of heat. But from where she stood on the shore, she felt only a deep, abiding cold that permeated the air and left her exposed skin freezing.

Where was Walker? Where was Allanon? Where was the help she so badly needed?

She bore down, ignoring the cold air and damp spray, the terrible wailing and the debilitating infusion of fear and doubt. She hardened herself as she had been taught to do in darker times, cloaking herself in her magic and her determination, fighting to keep her hold over the lake and its inhabitants. She had opened the door to the world of the dead to seek answers to her questions, and she would not close it again until she found what she had come for.

Her search ended when her strength was almost gone. A Druid shade surged out of the roiling waters like a leviathan, huge and threatening, scattering lesser shades as if they were krill on which it might feed. Dark robes billowed out, the edges frayed and torn, the opening of its hood a black hole that had no bottom. The lake's greenish light filtered through rents in its empty form, carving intricate patterns that threw strange shadows everywhere.

Grianne Ohmsford stepped backwards in shock.

It's too big! Too massive!

The shade wheeled toward her soundlessly, drawing all the light into itself, extinguishing the smaller shades around it. Within the hood, red eyes flared to life and burned with unmistakable rage. She felt it watching her, measuring her. It advanced as it did so, coming on like a juggernaut that meant to crush her. As powerful as she was, as skilled at magic's uses, she was dwarfed by this presence. She could not decide who it was. Not Walker, she knew. She had spoken with his shade enough times to know how it felt when he appeared. Allanon, perhaps. Yes, Allanon, darkest of them all.

But this dark?

She waited as the shade skimmed across the lake's boiling surface to reach her, growing steadily in size. It gave her no hint of whom it was nor spoke even a single word. It simply advanced, enigmatic and intimidating, testing her resolve to stand fast. She could not look away from it. She was transfixed.

When it was close enough that it had blotted out the entirety of the sky behind it, it stopped, hovering above the Hadeshorn, its dark form riddled and tattered. Grianne brought her arms down now, lowering them slowly, carefully, keeping her eyes fixed on the crimson orbs that burned out of the impenetrable gap in the shade's hood.

—Do you know me, Straken—

Its voice was as empty and cold as the death that had stolen away its life. Her stomach lurched in sudden recognition. Sweat beaded her forehead, though the rest of her was as cold as that voice. She knew who it was. She knew it instinctively. It wasn't Allanon. Or Bremen. Or even Galaphile. Not here, inside the Forbidding. She had forgotten the importance of where she was. She was in a place where only creatures *exiled* from the world of Faerie belonged. She was in a place where only those who felt at home with such creatures would come.

Even from the world of the dead.

What sort of shade would such creatures draw? Only one, she realized belatedly.

The shade of the rebel Druid Brona.

It was the Warlock Lord.

After Grianne Ohmsford had been stolen away as a child and begun her training as the Ilse Witch, fear was the first emotion she had learned to control. It wasn't easy at first. Her family had been killed and she was hunted still. She had no friends save her rescuer, the Morgawr, and he was as dark as anything she had ever imagined. He was impatient and demanding, as well, and when she did not perform as he required, he made certain she realized the consequences of failure. It took her years to get past her fears, to harden herself sufficiently that in the end she was afraid of nothing, not even him.

But she was afraid now. The fear returned in paralyzing waves that stole away her strength and rooted her in place. It was the Warlock Lord she had summoned, the most powerful and dangerous creature that had ever lived. What could she hope to do with him?

The huge apparition rolled toward her once more, easing across the turgid waters.

–Speak my name–

She could not. She could do nothing but stare. She had summoned the Druids' worst enemy, their most implacable foe, to ask for help that she couldn't possibly hope to receive. It was the worst mistake she had ever made, and she had made many. She had not imagined that anyone but Walker would appear, just as he always did when she came to the Hadeshorn. But it was not the Hadeshorn of her world, but of the Forbidding, and it made perfect sense that in the world of the Jarka Ruus, of the banished people, of the despised and the hated, Brona's would be the shade that would respond to any summons.

She sensed his impatience; he would not wait much longer for her response. If she failed to give it, he would depart, returning to the netherworld and stealing away her last hope. Refusing to speak with him was pointless. He would already know who she was and what she was doing there. He would know what she was seeking.

"No one speaks your name," she said.

—You will. You will dare anything, Ilse Witch. Haven't you always—

She cringed inwardly but kept her face expressionless. "You are Brona," she said. "You are the Warlock Lord."

—I am as you name me, Straken. The name causes you to be afraid. It causes you to question what you have done. As it should. Tell me. Why do you summon me—

She mustered her courage, telling herself that he was dead, only a shade, and incapable of harming her physically. Alive, he would have been a very real threat. Dead, he was a threat only if she allowed him to be. If she kept him at bay and controlled her emotions, she was safe enough. She told herself that, but she was not entirely sure. It was not the Four Lands, after all. She was in another world, and the rules might be different.

"I am lost, and I want to go home again."

—You carry your home inside you, dark and tattered as the robes I wear. You bear it in your heart, a sorry, empty vessel. Ask me something better—

Behind him, the lake rumbled in discontent, and a scattering of lesser shades reappeared at the edges of the Warlock Lord's dark form, hovering cautiously.

"Who sent me here?" she asked him.

He made a sound that could have been laughter or something more terrible. Beneath his ragged form, the waters hissed and steamed.

—Not those you suspect, foolish girl—

"Not other Druids? They didn't send me?"

—They are pawns—

Pawns? It made her pause. "Who then?"

The dark form shifted anew, blowing spray and cold into her face, sending shivers down her spine.

—Ask me something more interesting—

Frustrated, she took a moment to think. Shades were notorious for giving vague or incomplete answers to the living. The trick was in determining from those answers what was real and what was false. It would be doubly hard here.

"Why are you even speaking with me?" she asked impulsively. "I am Ard Rhys of the Druids, your enemies in life."

—You are not what you see yourself to be. You are a changeling who dissembles and pretends. You hide whom you really are inside. Others fail to see it, but I know the truth. I speak to you because you are not like them. You are like me—

Although it made her cold inside, she dismissed the comparison out of hand; she understood well enough its source. He was not the first to see her that way nor would he be the last. "How do I get home again? How do I find my way back?"

—You cannot. Someone must find you—

Her heart sank, but she forged ahead anyway. "No one will ever find me here. No one can even get to me."

—You are already found. Someone already comes—

"Here? For me?" She felt her heart jump. "Who does this?"

—A boy—

That stopped her in her tracks. "What boy?"

—He is your way back. When he comes for you, you must be ready to go with him—

A boy. She took a deep breath, her throat tightening with the effort. A boy. There was more to this, there had to be, but she knew he wouldn't tell her what it was. He would make her wait, because that was the nature of the game he played. Besides, the future was uncertain, even for a shade. He could not tell her if the boy would succeed or fail. He could tell her only that the boy was coming. He would let her imagine the rest. She must go another way.

She pulled her cloak closer about her, aware suddenly of how cold she was. It was his presence, the nearness of his evil. Even in death, it was there, in the spray off the lake, in the currents of the air, in the darkness pressing down on her. Death, come alive in the form of his shade, gave power to what he was.

—Ask me something more—

His restlessness had returned, and she was in danger of losing him. But she didn't know where to go next. "Where will I find this boy?"

—At the doorway through which you entered. You waste my time. Ask me something that matters. Is it possible that you are as stupid as you are pathetic—

She stiffened. He was taunting her and it was working. "Tell me why I am still alive. What reason was there for imprisoning rather than killing me?"

She was certain that he laughed, the sound so raw it made her cringe with embarrassment and rage. The lake's waters spit in response to the sound, and the greenish light that radiated from beneath pulsed with energy.

—To serve the needs of the one who brought you here—

"What needs are those?"

—You ask the wrong question. Ask the right one—

Her mind worked furiously, thinking it through. "Why am I inside the Forbidding?" she asked finally.

Again, the laughter, but cool and soft this time, barely a whisper on the wind.

—That is better, little Straken. You are inside the Forbidding so that the one who brought you here could get out—

She caught her breath. Get out? Someone had gotten out? An exchange, she thought. Of course. The power that had imprisoned her belonged to the thing that sought to escape, not to someone from her own world. Something powerful had wanted out, something clever enough to manipulate those it needed in the Four Lands, and it had found a way through her.

The shade's voice cut through her thoughts, commanding her attention.

–Heed me. You understand some, but not all. Here is the truth you must embrace, if you are to survive long enough to learn the rest. You cannot cast off your true self. You gain power through acceptance of your destiny. Bury your emotions with your foolish ambitions for the Druid Council. Become who you were meant to be, Ilse Witch. Your magic can make you powerful, even here. Your skills can give you domination. Use both. Wield them as weapons and destroy any that challenge you. If not, you will be destroyed, in turn–

"I am not the Ilse Witch," she replied.

–Nor am I, then, the Warlock Lord. I have watched you grow. You were powerful once. You disdained that power for foolish reasons. Had you stayed strong, you would not have been sent here like this. But you have grown weak. Death's cold hand is on you. Your time grows short–

The shade threw out one hand, and a wind howled across the lake, whipping at its robes and sending Grianne to her knees. The lesser shades scattered once more, disappearing into the darkness, lost. The lake boiled anew, spitting and rumbling, a cauldron of discontent, and the Warlock Lord began to retreat back toward its center, burning eyes still fixed on her. She tried to stand again, but the wind beat her down, and it was all she could do to meet that terrible gaze from her kneeling position. So much hatred in those featureless orbs—not for her alone, but for everything that lived. Even in death and from the netherworld, it sought release.

"I am Ard Rhys!" she screamed at it in frustration.

The shade did not respond. It reached the center of the lake and sank from sight, its black form vanishing with the quickness of a shadow exposed to light, gone in an instant, leaving only the lake and the sound of the wailing. Waterspouts exploded into the night, and Grianne backed away on her knees, buffeted by the relentless force of the wind. As she backed away, she fell, tearing her clothing and scraping her knees on the rocks. Shadows fell across her, cast by things she couldn't see. She lowered her head, closed her eyes, and pulled her hood tight against her ears.

I am Ard Rhys!

Then abruptly, everything went still. The wind died, the wailing faded, and the lake quieted once more. She kept her head lowered a moment, then lifted it cautiously. The valley was empty of movement and sound, of anything but a flicker of greenish light that emanated from the depths of the lake and reflected off the crushed stone.

Overhead, the sky was still black and empty of stars. All about the valley's rim, the wall of mist pressed close.

She rose, battered of body and emotions, drained of strength and spirit, and walked away.

TWENTY-TWO

Penderrin Ohmsford had thought he would sneak off to see Cinnaminson again the following night and perhaps the night after that, as well, if the *Skatelow* was still in port. His initial assignation had infused him with such joy and excitement that he could hardly wait for the next one to take place. He knew it was wrong to give so much attention to Cinnaminson when he should be thinking about finding his missing aunt. But the latter was far away, the former all too close. He couldn't seem to help himself; in a struggle of emotions, his sense of responsibility finished a distant second to his passion. All that mattered was that he be with Cinnaminson.

Having thought of little else all that day, he managed to slip away again the next night, only to find that her father and the other two Rovers were still aboard. He stood dockside in the shadows, watching them smoke on deck and listening to their voices. He waited a long time for them to leave, but when it became clear they had no intention of doing so, he gave up and returned to the inn.

The second night was even more frustrating. A new storm moved in, more ferocious than the one they had encountered several days earlier, drenching Anatcherae and halting all traffic for the next twenty-four hours. The rain was so bad that even on the ground visibility was reduced to almost nothing. Pen knew no one would be venturing out in weather like this, including the Rovers aboard the *Skatelow*. There was no point in even thinking about meeting with Cinnaminson.

So he was forced to make do with daydreams, which could not replace the real thing but which at least gave him an outlet for his frustrations. Sitting around at the Fisherman's Lie for hours at a time, sometimes with Khyber, sometimes with Ahren and Tagwen, but mostly alone, he passed the time thinking of ways he could separate her from her father, bring her with him when he returned home, and build a life for the two of them. It was such fantasy that even he knew it didn't bear looking at too closely. He was just a boy and she only a girl, and neither of them had any experience at falling in love. But Pen didn't care. He knew how he felt, and that was enough.

Khyber kept him company much of the time, but she spent hours alone in her room working on her Druid disciplines and exercises, practicing movements and words, and tending to her studies. Ahren worked with her each day, but he was gone much of the time, scouting for news of their pursuers and checking on Gar Hatch's progress with the *Skatelow*. Tagwen surfaced now and again, but mostly he kept to his room. He was less sociable than he had been when it had just been the two of them, and Pen thought it was due in part to his discomfort with life outside of Paranor. Tagwen was used to carrying out his duties for the Ard Rhys in the claustrophobic company of the Druids, and his time at the inn was too unstructured. What he did when he was alone was a mystery, although Pen caught him writing in a notebook on two occasions, and the Dwarf confessed to keeping a diary of their progress to help pass the time. That made as much sense to Pen as what he was doing, moping around about Cinnaminson, so he left the Dwarf alone.

Khyber, on the other hand, chided both of them mercilessly. More driven and disciplined than either, she found their lack of purpose irritating, and took every opportunity to suggest that they ought to do better with their time. Tagwen was incensed, but Pen just ignored her. He was beginning to see her as the big sister he didn't have but had often imagined. She was pushy and insistent, and she thought everyone should see things the way she did. Having talked with her about her life, Pen understood her motivation. She had been forced to fight for everything she had, a young Elven Princess whose life had been charted out for her by her family without any consideration at all for what she wanted. It had only become worse for her after her father's death and her brother's ascension to the throne. Just to come visit with Ahren had required a great deal of fortitude and determination. He could not imagine what would happen to her when her brother found out she was with them.

In any case, by the third day everyone was growing impatient. Pen and his companions were still stuck inside at the inn, and Gar Hatch had given Ahren no indication as to when they were going to set sail again. The rains had subsided, but a rise in the temperature had caused a deep fog bank to settle over the Lazareen and the surrounding lakeshore, the port of Anatcherae included. Visibility continued to hamper travel, and the dockside was quiet.

By midafternoon, with their lunch finished and the prospect of another day in port looming ever closer, Ahren announced that he was going down to the waterfront to tell Hatch that whether he liked it or not they would set sail at dawn. The Rover's reputation was that he could sail in any weather and under any conditions. It was time to prove it. The Druid was clearly displeased, his patience with Gar Hatch exhausted. Pen exchanged a knowing look with Khyber when Ahren told them to pack and be ready to leave when he returned. The boy did not think that Hatch would be given a chance to offer any more excuses. He wished, however, that he had been able to tell Ahren Elessedil what Cinnaminson had told him—that her father knew who they were, knew of their purpose, and might be making plans of his own. He could not say anything, however, without giving away the fact that he had disobeyed the Druid. He rationalized his decision to keep quiet by telling himself that Ahren already suspected Hatch of knowing the truth, which was almost the same as knowing it for a fact, so that the Druid was prepared for it anyway.

Still, it unsettled him to be keeping secrets from his friends. It wasn't that he didn't trust the Druid and his niece and the Dwarf; he did. It was just that once he didn't tell them, later, he didn't know how, and it became easier not to do so at all. It wasn't as if he *couldn't* tell them, when it became necessary. If it ever did. Maybe it never would.

So he kept what he knew about Gar Hatch to himself as Ahren Elessedil went out the door. He plopped down in a wooden chair by the window, alone for the moment, and stared out into the mist. He allowed himself to think briefly of Cinnaminson, then turned his attention for the first time in several days to the more important matter of reaching the tanequil. He was beginning to wonder not so much if he could do so, which he firmly believed he could, but if he could do so in time. His aunt was trapped inside the Forbidding, and he knew enough about what was locked away there to realize that even an Ard Rhys might have trouble staying alive. He knew she was powerful, that her magic had made her one of the most feared humans in the Four Lands. He knew, as well, that she was a survivor, that her entire life had been spent finding

ways to stay alive when others either wished her dead or were ac-
tively looking for ways to make it happen. She would not be killed
easily, even by the monsters that dwelled within the Forbidding.

But she was alone and friendless there and that would put
her at a decided disadvantage. Sooner or later, that disadvantage
would begin to tell. How many days had she been trapped in there
already? At least two weeks, and that was just the beginning of the
time that it would take for him to reach her. Under the best of
conditions, he thought, he would need another week or two to
find the tanequil. Then he had to persuade it to fashion the darkwand. Then he had to return to Paranor, get inside the Keep, and
use the wand to cross over into the Forbidding.

How much time would all that require? Two months? More?
Just listing the steps necessary for the rescue demonstrated how
impossible the task was. She would be dead before he could reach
her. Perhaps she was already dead.

He stopped himself angrily. What was he thinking? The King
of the Silver River would not bother sending him if he had no
chance of success; there would be no point in making the journey.
No, his aunt was alive and she would stay alive until he reached
her. She would die only if he talked himself out of going on.

If he persuaded himself he should quit.

As he was trying to do now.

He took a deep breath and leaned back in his chair. He would
not think like that again, he promised himself. He would do what
he knew he should and continue on, right up until the moment
that it became impossible for him to do so. That was what was expected of him; it was what he expected of himself.

Then Khyber appeared, sat down without a word, pulled out
her folding game board, and cocked an inquisitive eyebrow at him.
He smiled in spite of himself.

"I'll give it a try," he said.

*   *   *

Several hours passed and Ahren Elessedil did not return. As dusk approached and the shadows lengthened, rain began to fall once more, a steady, obstinate drizzle that dampened the mist but did nothing to dispel it. Pen went into the common room with Khyber and Tagwen to eat. Mindful of the need to stay anonymous, they took a table in a back corner, well away from the door and the stream of traffic entering and leaving. The Druids were still hunting them, the word still abroad that money would be paid for anyone who brought Pen to their attention. Perhaps they should have worried more about Gar Hatch's mercenary tendencies, since Rovers were always on the lookout for an easy opportunity to increase their fortunes. But Ahren had not seemed concerned, and Khyber had insisted that because the Druid was paying Hatch a great deal more than the Rover could get by turning them in, it made better sense for Hatch to stay loyal to them.

"I don't like it that he's been gone so long," Tagwen growled softly, giving Khyber a hard look. "You don't think something might have happened to him, do you?"

She shook her head. "I think if it had, we would have heard. Word would have spread by now."

"Then where is he?"

Pen took a long pull on his mug of ale. "He might have decided we'd get out of here quicker if he stayed around to supervise Hatch in making the necessary preparations. I don't think he believes the Captain has done all that well on his own."

Tagwen grunted, took a piece of bread from his plate and shoved it into his mouth in one monstrous bite. "Mmmff ummfatt wff."

The boy cocked his head. "I didn't quite catch that." Khyber was shaking her head in disgust.

The Dwarf swallowed. "I said, maybe one of us should go and see."

"That would be you," Khyber snapped irritably, "since Pen and I are forbidden to go outside the walls of this grim little lie-down. Do you want to leave now?"

They went back to eating in silence, turning their attention to steaming plates of fresh fish that the server had brought over from the kitchen. Tagwen rubbed his hands together enthusiastically, any plans for going down to the waterfront put aside for the moment. While eating, they finished off the ale pitcher, and an impatient Khyber rose and walked to the serving bar to get another.

She was waiting for a refill when the doors to the inn banged open and Terek Molt walked into the room, trailed by half a dozen of his Gnome Hunters.

Heads turned to watch them enter, and conversations died. Pen put down his fork and knife and glanced quickly at Tagwen. The Dwarf hadn't seen their enemy yet, but now he caught the look on the boy's face and turned. "Oh, no," he whispered.

They were trapped. The Gnome Hunters were already spreading out, moving through the crowded room like wraiths. Two remained stationed at the only door leading to the street. Pen thought of fleeing through the kitchen, but he didn't know if it led outside or not. His mind raced, seeking a way of escape. Maybe Molt didn't know they were there. He didn't seem to. He was standing in the middle of the room, black cloak shedding water on the wooden floor, hard eyes scanning the room. It was dark back here. He might not see them.

Cows might fly, too.

When the Druid's gaze finally settled on him, Pen went cold all the way down to his feet. There was no mistaking what he saw in that gaze. He wondered how the Druid had found them, how he had come to Anatcherae when they had been so careful to leave no trail. He glanced quickly at the serving bar and saw Khyber preparing to return to the table. She didn't know who Molt was, having never seen him; she didn't realize the danger they were in. He had to warn her, but there was no way for him to do so without giving her away.

It was too late anyway. Terek Molt stalked over to their table and stopped when he was still a few feet away. "You've led me a chase," he said softly. "But it's ended now. Get to your feet and come with me. Don't cause any trouble or it will be the worse for you. I don't much care what it takes to bring you back to Paranor."

Tagwen shook his head stubbornly. "We're not coming with you. Not this boy and not me. We don't want your protection."

The Druid's smile was quick and hard. "I'm not offering protection, Tagwen. I'm offering you a chance to stay alive, nothing more. Don't mistake what this is about. Where is Ahren Elessedil?"

Neither Pen nor Tagwen answered. If Terek Molt didn't know, that meant the Elf was still free. That, in turn, meant there was a chance.

"Get to your feet," the Druid said a second time.

"We know what you've done with the Ard Rhys," Tagwen declared, raising his voice so that those around could hear him clearly. "We know what you'll do with us, too. We're not coming."

There was a muttering in the room, and Terek Molt's hard eyes grew angry. "Enough of this, little men. Get up and walk out of here or I'll drag you out."

A Troll roughly the size of a barn pushed away from the serving bar and took a step forward. His blunt features tightened, one hand resting on a huge mace hanging from his belt. "Leave the boy and the old man alone," he ordered.

Terek Molt turned slowly to face him, away from the still-open doors to the inn, his concentration divided between the Troll and his quarry, so he didn't see Ahren Elessedil step out of the night. "Stay out of this," Molt said to the Troll.

At that point, Khyber pushed away from the bar. Carrying the pitcher of ale in both hands, she crossed the room directly toward the table at which Pen and Tagwen were sitting. Terek Molt glanced sharply at her, but she averted her eyes, as if not daring to look at him, and he started to turn back. "Get up," he said to Pen and Tagwen.

Khyber, from less than six feet away, threw the pitcher of ale all over him.

The room exploded with shouts, its occupants leaping to their feet in a whirl of sudden movement. Chairs and tables were over-turned, and glassware went crashing to the floor. The Troll had his mace free and was swinging it at Terek Molt, who rolled out of the way just in time. But when he came to his feet to strike back, Ahren's Druid magic threw him across the room and against the wall, where he lay in a crumpled heap, screaming in fury. Gnome Hunters came at Khyber, but her hands were already lifted and weaving, and the Gnomes stumbled all over themselves in their ef-forts to stay upright.

"This way!" she shouted at Pen and Tagwen, and broke for the kitchen.

The boy and the Dwarf didn't stop to ask if she knew what she was doing; they just went after her. The room was in chaos by then, its occupants surging up against one another in their efforts to get clear, most of them trying to reach the front door. The Gnome Hunters, still fighting to regain their equilibrium after Khyber's attack, were bowled over in the rush. A moment later, the lights went out, and the room was engulfed in blackness. Pen and Tagwen were in the kitchen by then, with Khyber just ahead, flinging open the back door that led to the street. Without a back-ward glance, they plunged into the rain and fog and darkness.

The streets were crowded, and it was difficult to move ahead at a brisk walk, let alone a run. Pen struggled to keep Khyber in sight, Tagwen pushing up against him from behind, both of them jostling and shoving to break free of the knots of people hindering their flight. Ahren Elessedil had disappeared, but Pen thought he must be somewhere close. Behind them, Fisherman's Lie was still in an uproar, shouts turning to cries of pain and anger, the windows breaking out, the entire place in blackness. Pen realized they had left everything behind in their escape, but knew there was no help for it. What mattered was getting away. What counted for something was staying alive.

A burly dockworker shouldered Pen aside effortlessly. As the boy staggered, he felt something rip through his cloak, scoring his left arm. He heard the dockworker gasp and felt him clutch at his arm. As he tried to wrench free, he saw a dagger protruding from the man's chest, the blade buried to the hilt. The man fell heavily into the boy, his dead eyes open and staring.

Pen looked around in shock and caught sight of something big scurrying along the peaks of the roofs, something cloaked and hooded and shadowy. Terek Molt, he thought at once, then realized that there hadn't been time for the Druid to get out of the inn and come after them. The figure on the roof was much larger than Molt in any case, and it didn't move like him. It moved like some huge insect.

It was coming down, toward the dead man and Pen.

"Penderrin!" Khyber called back to him.

He turned at the sound of her voice and began to run anew. Behind him, he heard gasps as the crowd realized what had happened to the dockworker. He didn't glance back to see if they were looking at him. He wasn't about to stop anyway. He wasn't going to do anything but keep running.

They angled down a maze of narrow side streets, grunting and shoving their way clear of passersby, until they finally reached the waterfront. Pen's arm was throbbing, and he glanced down in the light of the dockside lamps and saw blood soaking through his sleeve. The dagger had cut him from shoulder to elbow, the blade so sharp that even the heavy cloak had failed to blunt it.

Who had attacked him? He knew he had been the target, not that dockworker. If the worker hadn't shoved him aside at just the right moment, Pen would be the one lying in the street back there.

Glancing over his shoulder, he saw the shadowy figure giving chase, working its way swiftly along the warehouse roofs, scuttling along in the manner of a spider, arms and legs cocked out from its low-slung body.

It was coming too fast for him to outrun it.

"Khyber!" he shouted in sudden fear.

The girl wheeled back, saw the figure, as well, and thrust out both arms in a warding gesture. The magic caught the figure in mid-leap and sent it spinning out of sight.

"What was that?" she shouted at him.

He didn't reply. He had no idea what it was. He just knew he didn't want to see it again. Maybe he wouldn't. Maybe the fall had killed it. Or injured it badly enough that it couldn't keep after them.

As they began to run again, he glanced back worriedly. He was right to do so. His pursuer was atop the roofs once more, leaping and bounding from one building to the next, coming fast.

"Khyber!" He grabbed her arm and pointed.

She turned a second time, saw the figure, lifted her arms to summon the magic, and immediately it disappeared. They stood looking for it, but it was as if the night and rain and mist had swallowed it whole. That hadn't happened, of course; it was still out there, coming for him. Only it was on the ground, lost in the shadows.

The hairs on the back of Pen's neck pricked up. He backed toward the water, away from the buildings.

"Run!" Khyber hissed at him.

He did so, Tagwen beside him, their boots pounding on the wooden planks of the docks, the rain and mist a thick curtain all about them. Pen glanced toward the warehouses as he fled, searching for his pursuer. There was no one to be seen. But it was there, still chasing him. He could feel it. If it got close enough, it would use that dagger again. Or another like it. It would send its blade hurtling out of the darkness, and he would be dead before he knew what had happened. His lungs burned and his legs ached from running, but he didn't slow. He had never been so scared. It was one thing to stand up to an enemy in the light, face-to-face. It was another to be stalked by something he couldn't even see.

They reached the *Skatelow* and clambered aboard in a rush. Not until they were crouched down behind the pilot box did Pen quit feeling as if a fresh blade was already winging its way out of the gloom toward his unprotected back. Scanning the lamplit shadows of the docks, he found no sign of his mysterious hunter. But he was scared enough that he was going to stay right where he was, with his back to the open water.

"What *was* that?" Khyber asked him for the second time, her breathing quick and labored.

Pen scanned the darkness, searching. "I don't know. I don't even know where it came from. Did you see what it did?"

"Killed that man," she whispered.

"But it meant to kill you, didn't it?" Tagwen's rough face pressed forward so that their eyes met.

"I think it did," Pen answered, watching the mist shift along the dock front and down the side streets like a serpent. Shadows moved everywhere he looked. "I think it's still out there."

Ahren Elessedil, already on board, was speaking heatedly with Gar Hatch. Ahren's clothes were disheveled and rain-soaked and his face flushed. He glanced over at the three hiding behind the pilot box wall, a hint of uncertainty in his blue eyes, then turned back to the Rover Captain, ordering him to cast off their mooring lines. But Hatch refused to do so, folding his arms across his chest and planting his feet. They weren't ready, he said. They hadn't finished their repairs.

"They've found you, haven't they?" he sneered. "The Druids? You think I don't know who you are or what you are about? I want no part of this. You can't pay me enough to take you farther. Get off my ship!"

His Rover crewmen moved closer, ready to act on his behalf. From somewhere farther down the docks, shouts arose. The other pursuit—Pen had forgotten about Terek Molt and his Gnome Hunters.

"There!" Tagwen hissed suddenly, pointing left. "Something moved by that building!"

They peered into the gloom. Pen's heart was hammering in his chest, blood pounding in his ears. He was cold and hot at the same time, so afraid that he was holding his breath.

Then a huge shadow burst into view, leaping from the dockside onto the deck of the airship in a single bound, an impossible distance. It landed in a skid, its crooked limbs scrambling to find purchase on the smooth, damp wooden planking. Ahren Elessedil and Gar Hatch, startled, turned to look at it, both of them frozen in surprise. Pen caught the sudden flash of a blade, wicked and bright, but he couldn't make himself move, either. It was Khyber who leapt up, screaming in challenge. Hands outstretched, she summoned elemental magic in the form of a wind that picked up the dark form while it was still trying to regain its balance and threw it back over the side of the vessel into the cold lake waters.

Pen and Tagwen rushed to the side of the airship and peered down. The dark figure was gone.

On the dockside, the shouts were coming closer. Torchlight flickered through the mist. "Cast off," Ahren Elessedil snapped at Gar Hatch, "or I'll put you and your crew over the side and do it myself!"

The Rover Captain hesitated for just an instant, as if perhaps he would test this threat, then wheeled about, ordering his men to release the lines. The ropes fell away, and the airship began to drift from the dock. Pen continued to scan the waters into which the dark thing had fallen, not convinced it had given up, not persuaded it wasn't going to come at him again.

"Safety lines!" Gar Hatch snapped.

The *Skatelow* began to rise and the lake to drop away. Pen exhaled sharply. Still nothing. He glanced at Tagwen. The Dwarf's rugged features reflected his fear. His eyes shifted to find the boy's and he shook his head.

"Safety lines!" Hatch repeated angrily. "Young Pen! If you can spare the time, would you bring Cinnaminson into the pilot box before you secure yourself?"

Pen waved his response. He took a final look over the side before heading for the hatchway. The lake had disappeared beneath a sea of shifting mist.

Then they were flying into the night, a solitary island in the deepening gloom, leaving Anatcherae and its horrors behind.

TWENTY-THREE

Darkness had fallen, stealing away the last of the daylight. Heavy fog closed on the airship, enfolding it in a swirling gray haze. There was no difference now between up or down or even sideways to those who sailed aboard the *Skatelow*. Everything looked the same. The day had been dreary to begin with, washed of color and empty of sunshine, but the night was worse. The clouds were so thickly massed overhead that there was not even the smallest hint of stars or moon. Below, the waters of the Lazareen had vanished as if drained from an unplugged basin. The lights of Anatcherae had vanished minutes after their departure. The world had disappeared.

Pen brought Cinnaminson to her father. She squeezed Pen's hand as he led her along the corridor from her cabin and up the stairway to the deck, but neither of them spoke. There was too much to say and no time to say it. In the pilot box, she moved obediently to her father's side, saying as she did so, "I'm here, Papa." Pen was dismissed, told to go below, and he moved away. But he lingered at the hatchway with Khyber and Ahren, staring out into the impenetrable fog, into the depthless night. If Cinnaminson wasn't able to navigate blind, he was thinking, they were in trouble. There wasn't even the smallest landmark on which they could fix, no sky to read, no point of reference to track. There was nothing out there at all.

"She's her father's compass, isn't she?" Ahren asked him quietly. "His eyes in the darkness?"

He nodded, looking at the Druid in surprise. "How did you know?"

"It was nosed about at the docks in Syioned. Some say she's his good-luck charm. Some say she can see in darkness, even though she's blind in daylight. None of them have it right. I saw the way she moved the first few days we were aboard. She can sense the position of things in her mind, their location, their look and feel."

"She said she sees the stars in her mind, even in mist and rain like this. That's how she navigates."

"A gift," Ahren Elessedil murmured. "But her father thinks it belongs to him because she is his child."

Pen nodded. "He thinks *she* belongs to him."

They could hear her speaking softly to her father, giving him instructions, a heading to take, a course to follow. His hands moved smoothly over the controls in response, turning the airship slightly to starboard, bringing up her bow as he did so, easing ahead through the gloom. In a less stressful situation, he might have noticed them watching and immediately ordered them below so that they would not discover his secret. He might have refused to proceed at all. But that night he was so preoccupied that he didn't even know they were there.

The mist thickened the farther away from land they flew, swirling like witch's brew around the airship, alive with strange shadows and unexpected movement. There was no wind, and yet the haze roiled as if there were. Pen felt uneasy at the phenomenon, not understanding how it could occur. He glanced again at Ahren Elessedil, but the Druid was staring straight ahead, his concentration focused on something else.

He was listening.

Pen listened, as well, but he could hear nothing beyond the creaking of the ship's rigging. He looked to Khyber, but she shook her head to indicate that she didn't hear anything, either.

Then Pen froze. There was something after all. At first, he wasn't sure what it was. It sounded a little like breathing, deep and low, like a sleeping man exhaling, only not that, either. He furrowed his brow in concentration, trying to place it. It must be the wind, he thought. The wind, sweeping over the hull or through the rigging or along the decks. But he knew it wasn't.

The sound grew louder, crept closer, as if a sleeping giant had woken and was coming over for a look. Pen glanced quickly at Ahren, but the Druid's gaze was intense and fixed, directed outward into the mist, searching.

"Uncle?" Khyber whispered, and there was an unmistakable hint of fear in her voice.

He nodded without looking at her. "It is the lake," he said. "It is alive."

Pen had no idea what that meant, but he didn't like the sound of it. Lakes weren't alive in the sense that they could breathe, so why did it sound as if this one was? He tried to pick up a rhythm to the sound, but it was unsteady and sporadic, harsh and labored. The ship sailed into the teeth of it, sliding smoothly through the fog, down the giant's throat and into its belly. Pen could see it in his mind. He tried to change the picture to something less threatening, but could not.

Then abruptly, ethereal forms appeared, incomplete and hazy, riding the windless mist. They brought the sound with them, carried it in their shadowy, insubstantial bodies, bits and pieces echoing all about them as they moved. Pen shrank back as several approached, sliding over the railing and across the airship's rain-slick deck. Cinnaminson gasped and her father swore angrily, swatting ineffectually at the wraith forms.

"The dead come to visit us," Ahren Elessedil said quietly. "This is the Lazareen, the prison of the dead who have not found their way to the netherworld and still wander the Four Lands."

"What do they want?" Khyber whispered.

Ahren shook his head. "I don't know."

The shades were all around the *Skatelow*, sweeping through her rigging like birds. The breathing grew louder, filling their ears, a windstorm of trouble building to something terrible. Slowly, steadily, vibrations began to shake the airship, causing the rigging to hum and the spars to rattle. Pen felt them all the way down to his bones. Seconds later, its pitch shifted to a frightening howl, a wail that engulfed them in an avalanche of sound. Pen went to his knees, racked with pain. The wail tightened like a vise around his head, crushing his ineffectual defenses. In the pilot box, in a futile effort to keep the sound at bay, Cinnaminson doubled over, her hands clapped over her ears. Gar Hatch was howling in fury, fighting to remain in control of the airship but losing the battle.

"Do something!" Khyber screamed at everyone and no one in particular, her eyes squeezed shut, her face twisted.

Like the legendary Sirens, the shades were driving the humans aboard the *Skatelow* mad. Their voices would paralyze the sailors, strip them of their sanity, and leave them catatonic. Already, Pen could feel himself losing control, his efforts at protecting his hearing and his mind failing. If he had the wishsong, he thought, he might have a way to fight back. But he had no defense against this, no magic to combat it. Nor did any of them, except perhaps . . .

He glanced quickly at Ahren Elessedil. The Druid was standing rigid and white-faced against the onslaught, hands weaving, lips moving, calling on his magic to save them. It was a terrible choice he was making, Pen knew. Using magic would give them away to the *Galaphile* in an instant. It would lead Terek Molt and his Gnome Hunters right to them. But what other choice did they have? The boy dropped to his knees, fighting to keep from screaming, the wailing so frenzied and wild that the deck planking was vibrating.

Then abruptly, everything went perfectly still, and they were enfolded in a silence so deep and vast that it felt as if they were packed in cotton wadding and buried in the ground. Around them, the mist continued to swirl and the shades to fly, but the wailing was no longer heard.

Pen got to his feet hesitantly, watching as the others did the same.

"We're safe, but we've given ourselves away," Ahren said quietly. He looked drained of strength, his face drawn and worn.

"Maybe they didn't come after us," Khyber offered.

Her uncle did not respond. Instead, he moved away from them, crossing the deck to the pilot box. After a moment's hesitation, Pen and Khyber followed. Gar Hatch turned at their approach, his hard face twisting with anger. "This is your doing, Druid!" he snapped. "Get below and stay there!"

"Cinnaminson," Ahren Elessedil said to the girl, ignoring her father. She swung toward the sound of his voice, her pale face damp with mist, her blind eyes wide. "We have to hide. Can you find a place for us to do so?"

"Don't answer him!" Gar Hatch roared. He swung down out of the pilot box and advanced on the Druid. "Let her be! She's blind, in case you hadn't noticed! How do you expect her to help?"

Ahren Elessedil's hand lifted in a warding gesture. "Don't come any closer, Captain," he said. Gar Hatch stopped, shaking with rage.

"Let's not pretend we both don't know what she can and can't do. She's your eyes in this muck. She can see better than either of us. If she can't, then send her below and steer this ship yourself! Because a Druid warship tracks us, and if you don't find a way off this lake, and find it quickly, it will be on top of us!"

Gar Hatch came forward another step, his fists knotted. "I should never have brought you aboard! I should never have agreed to help you! I do, and look what it costs me! You take my daughter, you take my ship, and you will probably cost me my life!"

Ahren stood his ground. "Don't be stupid. I take nothing from you but your services, and I paid for those. Among them, like it or not, is your daughter's talent. Now give her your permission to find a place for us to hide before it is too late!"

Hatch started to say something, then his eyes widened in shock as the huge, ironclad rams of the *Galaphile* surged out of the fog bank.

"Cinnaminson!" he shouted, leaping into the pilot box and seizing the controls.

He dropped the nose of the *Skatelow* so hard and so fast that Pen and his companions slid forward into the side of the pilot box, grabbing onto railings and ropes and anything else that would catch them. The airship plummeted, then leveled out and shot forward into the haze, all in seconds. As quick as that, they were alone again, the *Galaphile* vanished back into the fog.

"Which way?" Gar Hatch demanded of his daughter.

Her voice steady, Cinnaminson centered herself on the console, both hands gripping the railing, and began to give her father instructions, calling out headings. Pen, Khyber, and Ahren Elessedil righted themselves and snapped their safety harnesses in place, keeping close to the pilot box to watch what was happening. Gar Hatch ignored them, speaking only to his daughter, listening to her replies and making the necessary adjustments in the setting of the *Skatelow's* course.

Pen looked over his shoulder, then skyward, searching the mist for the *Galaphile*. She was nowhere to be seen. But she was close at hand. He sensed her, massive and deadly, an implacable hunter in search of her prey. He felt her bulk pressing down through the haze, looking to crush him over the Lazareen the way she would have crushed him over the Rainbow Lake almost three weeks ago.

He was aware suddenly that the shades had vanished, gone back into the shroud of mist and gloom they had swum through moments earlier, sunk down into the waters of the Lazareen.

"Why didn't the dead go after Terek Molt?" he asked Ahren suddenly. "Why didn't they attack the *Galaphile*, too?"

The Druid glanced over. "Because Molt protects his vessel with Druid magic, something he can afford to do and we cannot." He paused, hands knuckle-white about the pilot box railing, droplets of water beaded on his narrow Elven features. "Besides, Penderrin, he may have summoned the dead in the first place. He has that power."

"Shades," the boy whispered, and the word was like a prayer.

They sailed ahead in silence, an island once more in the mist and fog, a rabbit in flight from a fox. All eyes searched the gloom for the *Galaphile*, while Cinnaminson called out course headings and Gar Hatch made the airship respond. The wind picked up again, set loose as they reached the Lazareen's center, and the haze began to dissipate. Below, the lake waters were choppy and dark, the sound of their waves clear in the fog's silence.

Ahren Elessedil leaned over the pilot box railing. "Where do we sail?" he asked Gar Hatch.

"The Slags," the big man answered dully. "There's plenty of places to hide in there, places we will never be found. We just need to clear the lake."

Pen touched the Druid's arm and looked at him questioningly.

"Wetlands," the Druid said. "Miles and miles of them, stretching all along the northeastern shoreline. Swamp and flood plain, cypress and cedar. A tangle of old growth and grasses blanketed with mist and filled with quicksand that can swallow whole ships. Dangerous, even if you know what you're doing." He nodded toward Hatch. "He's made the right choice."

She has, Pen corrected silently. For it was Cinnaminson who set their course, through whose mind's eye they sought their way and in whose hands they placed their trust.

The mist continued to thin, the sky above opening to a scattering of stars, the lake below silver-tipped and shimmering. Their cover would be gone in a few minutes, and Pen saw no sign of the shore. The mist still hung in thick curtains in the distance, so he assumed the shore was there. But it was a long way off, and the wind was in their face, slowing their passage.

Then, all at once, clouds blew in, and rain began to fall, sweeping across the decking in a cold, black wash, and quickly they were soaked through. It poured for a time, thunder booming in the distance, and then just as suddenly it stopped again. At the same moment, the wind died to nothing.

"Twenty degrees starboard," Cinnaminson told her father. "We'll find better speed on that heading. Oh," she gasped suddenly, "behind us, Papa!"

They all swung about in response and found the *Galaphile* emerging from the remnants of the fog bank, sails furled and lashed, the warship flying on the power of her diapson crystals. She was moving fast, surging through the night, bearing down on them like a tidal wave.

Gar Hatch threw the thruster levers all the way forward and yelled to his Rover crewmen to drop the mainsail. Pen saw the reason for it at once; the mainsail was a drag on the ship in that windless air and would be of less help if the wind resumed from the east. The *Skatelow* was better off flying on stored power, as well, though she could not begin to match the speed of the *Galaphile*. Still, she was the smaller, lighter craft and, if she was lucky, might be able to outmaneuver her pursuer.

The chase was under way in earnest; the fog that had offered concealment only moments earlier all but vanished. Pen did not care for what he saw as he watched the *Galaphile* draw closer. As fast as she was coming, the *Skatelow* could not outrun her. The Lazareen stretched away in all directions, vast and unchanging, and there was no sign of the shoreline they so desperately needed to reach. Clever maneuvers would get them only so far. Cinnaminson was still calling out tacks and headings, and Gar Hatch worked the controls frantically in response, trying to catch a bit of stray wind here, to skip off a sudden gust of air there. But neither could do anything to change their situation. The *Galaphile* continued to close steadily.

Then a fresh rainsquall washed over them, and Ahren Elessedil, seeing his chance, stepped away from the railing, arms raised skyward, and called on his magic to change the squall's direction, sending it whipping toward the Druid warship. It caught the *Galaphile* head-on, but by then it had changed into sleet so thick and heavy that it enveloped the bigger ship and swallowed it whole. Clinging to the *Galaphile* in a white swirling mass, it coated the decking and masts with ice, turning the airship to a bone-bleached corpse.

Now the *Skatelow* began to pull away. Burdened by the weight of the ice, the *Galaphile* was foundering. Pen saw flashes of red fire sweeping her masts and spars, Druid magic attempting to burn away the frigid coating. The fire had an eerie look to it, flaring from within the storm cloud like dragon eyes, like embers in a forge.

Ahead, the fog bank drew nearer.

Ahren collapsed next to Pen and Khyber, his lean face drawn and pale, his eyes haunted. He was close to exhaustion. "Find us a place to hide, Cinnaminson," he breathed softly. "Find it quickly."

Pressed against the pilot box wall, rain-soaked and cold, Pen peered in at the girl. She stood rigid and unmoving at the forward railing, her face lifted. She was speaking so low that Pen could not make out the words, but Gar Hatch was listening intently, bent close to her, his burly form hunched down within his cloak. He had dropped the *Skatelow* so close to the Lazareen that she was almost skimming the surface. Pen heard the chop of the lake waters, steady and rough. The wind was back, whipping about them from first one direction and then the other, sweeping down out of the Charnals, cold and bleak.

Then they were sliding into the mist again, its gray shroud wrapping about and closing them away. Everything disappeared, vanished in an instant.

"Starboard five degrees, Papa," Cinnaminson called out sharply. "Altitude, quickly!"

Blinded by the murky haze, Pen could only hear tree branches scrape the underside of the hull as the *Skatelow* nosed upward again—a shrieking, a rending of wood, then silence once more. The airship leveled off. Pen was gripping the pilot box railing so hard his hands hurt. Khyber was crouched right beside him, her eyes tightly closed, her breathing quick and hurried.

"There, Papa!" Cinnaminson cried out suddenly. "Ahead of us, an inlet! Bring her down quickly!"

The *Skatelow* dipped abruptly, and Pen experienced a momentary sensation of falling, then the airship steadied and settled. Again there was contact, but softer, a rustling of damp grasses and reeds rather than a scraping of tree limbs. He smelled the fetid wetland waters and the stink of swamp gas rising to meet them; he heard a quick scattering of wings.

Then the *Skatelow* settled with a small splash and a lurch, sliding through water and mist and darkness, and everything went
still.

"I was so frightened," she whispered to him, her blind gaze
settling on his face, her head held just so, as if she were seeing him
with her milky eyes instead of her mind.

"You didn't look frightened," he whispered back. He squeezed
her hands. "You looked calmer than any of us."

"I don't know how I looked. I only know how I felt. I kept
thinking that all it would take was one mistake for us to be caught.
Especially when that warship appeared and was chasing us."

Pen glanced skyward, finding only mist and gloom, no sign of
the *Galaphile* or anything else. Around them, the waters of the wetlands lapped softly against the hull of the *Skatelow*. Even though he
couldn't see them, he heard the rustle of the limbs from the big
trees that Cinnaminson told him were all about them. For anyone
to find the *Skatelow* there, they would have to land right on top of
it. From above, even if the air were clear instead of like soup, they
were invisible. Their concealment was perfect and complete.

Two hours had passed since their landing, and in that time
the others had gone to sleep, save for the Rover who kept watch
from the bow. Pen stood with Cinnaminson in the pilot box, looking out into the haze, barely able to see the man who stood only
twenty yards away. Before that night, the boy would not have
been allowed on deck at all. But maybe the rules were no longer
so important to Gar Hatch since he and Ahren Elessedil knew
each other's secrets and neither was fooling the other about how
things stood. Pen didn't think the Rover Captain's opinion of him
had changed; he didn't think Hatch wanted him around his daugh-

ter. But maybe he had decided to put up with it for the time being, since their time together was growing short. Whatever the case, Pen would take what he could get.

"What are you thinking?" she asked him, brushing damp strands of her sandy blond hair away from her face.

"That your father is generous to allow us to be on deck alone like this. Perhaps he thinks better of me now."

"Now that he knows who you are and who's hunting you? Oh, yes. I expect he would like to be best friends. I expect he wants to invite you home to live with him." She gave him a smirk.

Pen sighed. "I deserved that."

She leaned close. "Listen to me, Penderrin." She put her lips right up against his ear, her words a whisper. "He may have given you away in Anatcherae. I don't know that he did, but he may have. He is a good man, but he panics when he's frightened. I've seen it before. He loses his perspective. He misplaces his common sense."

"If he betrayed us to Terek Molt . . ."

"He did so because he was afraid," she finished for him. "If he is backed into a corner, he will not always do the sensible thing. That might have happened here. I wasn't with him on the waterfront, and I didn't see who he talked to. That Druid might have found him and forced him to talk. You know they can. They can tell if you are lying. My father might have given you up to save his family and his ship."

"And for the money they are offering."

She backed away a few inches so that he could see her face again. "What matters now is that if he has done it once, he might try to do it again. Even out here. I don't want that to happen. I want you to stay safe."

He closed his eyes. "And I want you to come with me," he whispered, still feeling the softness of her mouth against his face.

"I want you to come now, not later. Tell me you will, Cinnaminson. I don't want to leave you behind."

She lowered her head and let it rest on his shoulder. "Do you love me, Penderrin?"

"Yes," he said. He hadn't used the word before, even to himself, even in the silence of his mind. *Love*. He hadn't allowed himself to define what he was feeling. But as much as it was possible for him to do so, still young and inexperienced, he was willing to try. "I do love you," he said.

She burrowed her face in his neck. "I wanted to hear you say it. I wanted you to speak the words."

"You have to come with me," he insisted again. "I won't leave you behind."

She shook her head. "We're children, Pen."

"No," he said. "Not anymore."

He could sense her weighing her response. A dark certainty swept through him, and he closed his eyes against what he knew was coming. He was such a fool. He was asking her to leave her father, the man who had raised and cared for her, the strongest presence in her life. Why would she do that? Worse, he was asking her to accompany him to a place where no one in their right mind would go. She didn't know that, but he did. He knew how dangerous it was going to be.

"I'm sorry, Cinnaminson," he said quickly. "I don't know what I was thinking. I don't have the right to ask you to come with me. I was being selfish. You have to stay with your father for now. What we decided before was right—that when it was time, I would come for you. But this isn't the time. This is too sudden."

She lifted her head from his shoulder and faced him, her expression filled with wonder. In the dim light and with the mist damp and glistening against her skin, she looked so young. How old was she? He hadn't even thought to ask.

"You told me in Anatcherae that you would come for me and take me with you whenever I was ready to go," she said. "Is that still true. Do you love me enough to do that?"

"Yes," he said.

"Then I want you to take me with you when we get to where we are going. I want you to take me now."

He stared at her in disbelief. "Now? But I thought—"

"It's time, Pen. My father will understand. I will make him understand. I have served him long enough. I don't want to be his navigator anymore. I want a different life. I have been looking for that life for a long time. I think I have found it. I want to be with you."

She reached out and touched his face, tracing its ridges and planes. "You said you love me. I love you, too."

She hugged him then, long and hard. He closed his eyes, feeling her warmth seep through him. He loved her desperately, and he did not think for a moment that his age or his inexperience had blinded him to what that meant. He had no idea how he could protect her when he could barely manage to protect himself, but he would find a way.

"It will be all right," he whispered to her.

But he knew that he spoke the words mostly to reassure himself.

TWENTY-FOUR

At daybreak, Pen and his companions got a better look at the Slags, and it wasn't encouraging. The wetlands had the look of a monstrous jungle, an impenetrable tangle of trees, vines, reeds, and swamp grasses, all rising out of a mix of algae-skinned waterways that stretched away as far as the eye could see. The eye couldn't see all that far, of course, since the mist of the previous night did not dissipate with the sun's rising, but continued to layer the Slags in a heavy, gray blanket. Swirling in and out of the undergrowth like a living thing, snaking its way through the twisted, dark limbs of the trees and across the spiky carpet of grasses, it formed a wall that promised that any form of travel that didn't involve flying would be slow and dangerous.

Ahren Elessedil took one good look at the morass surrounding the *Skatelow*, glanced up at a ceiling of clouds and mist hung so low that it scraped the airship's mast tip, and shook his head. No one would find them in this, he was thinking. But they might never find their way out again, either.

"Here's how we go," Gar Hatch said, seeing the look on his face. It was warmer in the Slags, and the Rover was bare-chested and shiny with the mist's dampness. His muscles rippled as he climbed out of the pilot box and stood facing the Elf. "It isn't as bad as it looks, first off. Bad enough, though, that it warrants caution if we stay on the water, and that's what we'll mostly do. We'll drop the mast, lighten our load as best we can, and work our way east through the channels, except where flying is the only way through. It's slow, but it's sure. That big warship won't ever find us down here."

Pen wasn't so sure, but Gar Hatch was Captain and no one was going to second-guess him. So they all pitched in to help take down the mainmast, laying it out along the decking, folding up the sails and spars and tucking them away, and tossing overboard the extra supplies they could afford to let go. It took most of the morning to accomplish this, and they worked as silently as they could manage; sounds carry long distances in places like the Slags.

But they saw no sign of the *Galaphile*, and by midday they were sailing along the connecting waterways and across the flooded lowlands, easing through tight channels bracketed by gnarled trunks and beneath bowers of limbs and vines intertwined so thickly that they formed dark tunnels. Three times they were forced to take to the air, lifting off gently, opening the parse tubes just enough to skate the treetops to the next open space, then landing and continuing on. It was slow going, as Hatch had promised, but they made steady time, and the journey progressed without incident.

It might have been otherwise, had the Rover Captain not been familiar with the waters. Twice he brought the airship to a standstill in waters that ran deeper than most, and in the distance Pen watched massive shapes slide just beneath the surface, stirring ripples that spread outward in great concentric circles. Once, something huge surfaced just behind a screen of trees and brush, thrashing with such force that several of the trees toppled and the waters churned and rocked with the force of its movement. Yet nothing came close to the airship, for Hatch seemed to know when to stop and wait and when to go on.

By nightfall, they were deep in the wetlands, though much farther east than when they had started out, and there was still no sign of their pursuit. When asked of their progress, Hatch replied that they were a little more than halfway through. By the next night, if their luck continued to hold, they would reach the far side.

That couldn't happen any too soon for Pen. He was already sick of the Slags, of the smell and taste of the air, of the grayness of the light, unfriendly and wearing, of the sickness he felt lurking in the fetid waters, waiting to infect whoever was unfortunate enough to breathe it in. This was no place for people of any persuasion. Even on an airship, Pen felt vulnerable.

But perhaps his anticipation of what was going to happen when it was time to leave the *Skatelow* was working on him, as well. Taking Cinnaminson from her father was not going to be pleasant. He did not for a moment doubt that he could do it, did not once question that he could do whatever was necessary. But thinking about it made him uneasy. Gar Hatch was a dangerous man, and Pen did not underestimate him. He thought that Cinnaminson's fears about what might have happened in Anatcherae were well founded. Gar Hatch probably did betray them to Terek Molt. He probably thought they would never live to reach the *Skatelow* to finish this voyage and that was why he was so distressed when Ahren Elessedil reappeared and ordered him to set sail. It wasn't unfinished repairs or stocking of supplies that had upset him; it was the fact that he had been forced to go at all.

What would he do when he found out that his daughter, his most valuable asset in his business, was leaving him to go with Pen? He would do something. The boy was certain of it.

On the other hand, Pen hadn't done much to help matters along from his end, either. He hadn't said a word to his three companions about what he and Cinnaminson had agreed upon. He didn't know how. Certainly, Tagwen and Khyber would never support him. The Dwarf would do nothing that would jeopardize their efforts to reach the Ard Rhys, and the Elven girl already thought his involvement with Cinnaminson was a big mistake. Only Ahren Elessedil was likely to demonstrate any compassion, any willingness to grant his request. But he didn't know how best to approach the Druid. So he had delayed all day, thinking each time he considered speaking that he would do so later.

Well, later was here. It was nightfall, dinner behind them by now, and the next day was all the time he had left. He couldn't wait much longer; he couldn't chance being turned down with no further opportunity to press his demand.

But before he could act on his thinking, Gar Hatch wandered over in the twilight and said, "I'd like to speak with you a moment, young Penderrin. Alone."

He took the boy up into the pilot box, separating him from the others. Pen forced himself to stay calm, to not glance over at Ahren and Khyber, to resist the urge to check how close they were if he needed rescuing. He knew what was coming. He had not thought Cinnaminson would be so quick to tell her father, but then there was no reason why she should wait. He wished fleetingly, however, that she had told him she had done so.

Standing before Pen, the misty light so bad by now that the

boy could barely make out his features, Gar Hatch shook his bearded head slowly.

"My girl tells me she's leaving the ship," he said softly. "Leaving with you. Is this so?"

Pen had given no thought at all to what he would say when this moment happened, and now he was speechless. He forced himself to look into the other's hard eyes. "It is."

"She says you love her. True?"

"Yes. I do."

The big man regarded him silently for a moment, as if deciding whether to toss him overboard. "You're sure about this, are you, Penderrin? You're awfully young and you don't know my girl very well yet. It might be better to wait on this."

Pen took a deep breath. "I think we know each other well enough. I know we're young, but we aren't children. We're ready."

Another long moment of silence followed. The big man studied him carefully, and Pen felt the weight of his gaze. He wanted to say something more, but he couldn't think of anything that would make it any easier. So he kept still.

"Well," the other said finally, "it seems you've made up your minds, the two of you. I don't think I can stop you without causing hard feelings, and I'm not one for doing that. I think it's a mistake, Penderrin, but if you have decided to try it, then I won't stand in your way. You seem a good lad. I know Cinnaminson has grown weary of life on the *Skatelow*. She wants more for herself, a different way of life. She's entitled. Do you think you can take care of her as well as I have?"

Pen nodded. "I will do my best. I think we will take care of each other."

Hatch grunted. "Easier said than done, lad. If you fail her, I'll come looking for you. You know that, don't you?"

"I won't fail her."

"I don't care who your family is or what sort of magic they can call on to use against poor men like myself," he continued, ignoring Pen. "I'll come looking for you, and you can be sure I will find you."

Pen didn't care for the threat, but he supposed it was the Rover Captain's way of venting his disappointment at what was happening. Besides, he didn't think there would ever be cause for the big man to act on it.

"I understand," he replied.

"Best that you do. I won't say I'm the least bit happy about this. I'm not. I won't say I think it will work out for you. I don't. But I will give you your chance with her, Penderrin, and hold you to your word. I just hope I won't ever have cause to regret doing so."

"You won't."

"Go on, then." The big man gestured toward Ahren and Khyber, who stood talking at the port railing. "Go back to your friends. We have a full day of sailing tomorrow, and you want to be rested for it."

Pen left the pilot box in a state of some confusion. He had not expected Gar Hatch to be so accommodating, and it bothered him. He hadn't lodged more than a mild protest, hadn't tried to talk Pen out of it, hadn't even gone to Ahren Elessedil to voice his disapproval. Perhaps Cinnaminson had persuaded him not to do any of those things, but that didn't seem likely to Pen. Maybe, he thought suddenly, Hatch was waiting for the Druid to put an end to their plans. Maybe he knew how unreceptive Pen's companions would be and was waiting for them to put a stop to things.

But that didn't feel right, either. Gar Hatch wasn't the sort to count on someone else to solve his problems. That kind of behavior wasn't a part of the Rover ethic, and certainly not in keeping with the big man's personality.

Pen looked around for Cinnaminson, but didn't see her. She would be up on deck later, perhaps, but since they were not flying that night, she might be asleep. Pen glanced at Ahren and Khyber. He should tell the Druid now what was happening, give him some time to think about it before he responded. But just as he started over, Tagwen appeared from belowdecks to join them, grumbling about sleeping in tight, airless spaces that rocked and swayed. The boy took a moment longer to consider what he should do and decided to wait. First thing in the morning, he would speak with Ahren Elessedil. That would be soon enough. He would be persuasive, he told himself. The Druid would agree.

Feeling a little tired and oddly out of sorts, he took Gar Hatch's advice and went down to his cabin to sleep.

He awoke to shouting, to what was obviously an alarm. Bounding up instantly, still half-asleep, he tried to orient himself. Across the way, Tagwen was looking similarly disoriented, staring blankly into space from his hammock, eyes bleary and unfocused. The shouting died into harsh whispers that were audible nevertheless, even from belowdecks. Boots thudded across the planking from one railing to the other, then stopped. Silence descended, deep and unexpected. Pen could not decide what was happening and worried that by the time he did, it would be too late to matter. With a hushed plea to Tagwen to follow as quickly as he could, he pulled on his boots and went out the cabin door.

The corridor was empty as he hurried down its short length to the ladder leading up and climbed swiftly toward the light, straining to hear something more. When he pushed open the hatch, he found the dawn had arrived with a deep, heavy fog that crawled through the trees and over the decks of the *Skatelow*. At first he didn't see anyone, then found Gar Hatch, the two Rover crewmen, Ahren Elessedil and Khyber standing at the bow, peering everywhere at once, and he hurried over to join them.

"One of the crewmen caught a glimpse of the *Galaphile* just moments ago, right overhead, flying north," the Druid whispered. "He called out a warning, which might have given us away. We're waiting to see if she comes back around."

They stood in a knot, scanning the misty gray, watching for movement. Long minutes passed, and nothing appeared.

"There's a channel just ahead that tunnels through these trees," Gar Hatch said quietly. "It goes on for several miles through heavy foliage. Once we get in there, we can't be seen from the sky. It's our best chance to lose them."

They pulled up the fore and aft anchors and set out. Breakfast was forgotten. All that mattered was getting the ship under cover. Everyone but Cinnaminson was on deck now. Pen thought to go look for her, but decided it would be wrong to leave in the midst of the crisis. He might be needed; Hatch might require help piloting the craft. He stayed close, watching as the Rover Captain took the *Skatelow* through a series of connecting lakes spiked with grasses and studded with dead tree trunks, easing her carefully along, all the while with one eye on the brume-thickened sky. The Rover crewmen moved forward, taking readings with weighted lines, hand-signaling warnings when shallows or submerged logs appeared in front of them. No one said a word.

The channel appeared without warning, a black hole through an interwoven network of limbs and gnarled trunks. It had the look of a giant's hungry maw as they sailed into it, and the temperature dropped immediately once they were inside. Pen shivered.

Overhead, he caught small glimpses of sky, but mostly the dark canopy of limbs was all that was visible. The channel was wide enough to allow passage, though the *Skatelow* wouldn't have been able to get through if her mast had been up. As it was, the Rover crewmen had to use poles to push her away from the tangle of tree roots that grew on either side and keep her centered in the deeper water. It was too dark for Pen to see exactly what they were doing, but he was certain they could not have done it without Hatch. He seemed to know what was needed at every turn, and kept them moving ahead smoothly.

Still Cinnaminson didn't appear. Pen glanced over his shoulder repeatedly, but there was no sign of her. He began to worry anew.

Ahead, the tunnel opened back into the light.

Gar Hatch called him into the pilot box. "Take the helm, young Penderrin. I need to be at the bow for this."

Pen did as he was told. Hatch went forward to stand with his men, the three of them using poles to ease the *Skatelow* along the channel, pointing her toward the opening. Now and again, he would signal the boy to swing the rudder to starboard or port.

They were almost through when there was a scraping sound and a violent lurch. Pen was thrown backwards into the railing, and for an instant he thought that whatever had happened, he had done something wrong. But as he stood up and hurried forward, he realized he hadn't done anything he hadn't been told to do.

Gar Hatch was peering over the side of the airship into the murky waters, shaking his head. "That one's new," he muttered to no one in particular, then pointed out the massive log that the airship had run up on. He glanced up at the canopy of trees. "Too tight a fit to try to fly her. We'll have to float her off and pull her through by hand."

Hatch went back up into the pilot box, advising Pen that he

would take the controls. There was no admonition in his voice, so Pen didn't argue. Together with Tagwen, Ahren Elessedil, and the two crewmen, Pen climbed down onto the tangled knot of tree roots and moved forward of the airship's bow. Using ropes lashed about iron cleats, they began to pull the *Skatelow* ahead, easing her over the fallen trunk. Eventually the airship gained just enough lift from Gar Hatch's skilled handling to break free of the log and begin crawling along the swamp's green surface once more.

It was backbreaking work. Bugs of all sorts swarmed about their faces, clouding their vision, and the root tangle on which they were forced to stand was slick with moss and damp with mist and offered uncertain footing. All of them went down at one point or another, skidding and sliding into the swamp water, fighting to keep from going under. But, slowly, they maneuvered the *Skatelow* down the last few yards of the channel, easing her toward the open bay, where the light brightened and the brume thinned.

"Move back!" Gar Hatch shouted abruptly. "Release the ropes!"

Pen, Tagwen, and Ahren Elessedil did as they were ordered and watched the airship sail by, the hull momentarily blocking from view the Rover crewmen who were working across the way. When Pen glanced over again in the wake of the ship's passing, the crewmen were gone.

It took the boy a second to realize what was happening.

"Ahren!" he shouted in warning. "We've been tricked!"

He was too late. The *Skatelow* began to pick up speed, moving into the center of the bay. Then Khyber Elessedil came flying over the side and landed in the murky waters with a huge splash. The faces of the crewmen appeared, and they waved tauntingly at the men on shore. Tagwen was shouting at Ahren Elessedil to do something, but the Druid only stood there, shaking his head, grim-faced and angry. There was nothing he could do, Pen realized, without using magic that would alert the *Galaphile*.

Slowly, the *Skatelow* began to lift away, to rise into the mist, to disappear. In seconds, she was gone.

At the center of the lake, Khyber Elessedil pounded at the water in frustration.

TWENTY-FIVE

No one said anything for a few moments, Pen, Tagwen, and Ahren Elessedil standing together at the edge of the bay like statues, staring with a mix of disbelief and frustration at the point where the *Skatelow* had disappeared into the mist.

"I knew we couldn't trust that man," Tagwen muttered finally.

At the center of the bay, Khyber Elessedil had given up pounding the water and was swimming toward them. Her strokes cleaved the greenish waters smoothly and easily.

"You can't trust Rovers," Tagwen went on bitterly. "Not any of them. Don't know why we thought we could trust Hatch."

"We didn't trust him," Ahren Elessedil pointed out. "We just didn't watch him closely enough. We let him outsmart us."

This is my fault, Pen thought. I caused this. Gar Hatch didn't abandon them because of anything the others had done or even because of the *Galaphile* and the Druids. He had abandoned them so that Pen couldn't take Cinnaminson away from him. That was why he had been so accommodating. That was why he didn't argue the matter more strongly. He didn't care what either Pen or his daughter intended. He was going to put a stop to it in any case.

Khyber reached the edge of the bay and stood up with some difficulty, water cascading off her drenched clothes. Anger radiated from her like heat from a forge as she stalked ashore to join them. "Why did he do that?" she snapped furiously. "What was the point of abandoning us now when we were so close to leaving him anyway?"

"It's because of me," Pen said at once, and they all turned to look at him. "I'm responsible."

He revealed to them what he and Cinnaminson had decided, how she had told her father, and what her father had obviously decided to do about it. He apologized over and over for not confiding in them and admitted that, by deciding to take the girl off the airship, he was thinking of himself and not of them or even of what they had come to do. He was embarrassed and disappointed, and it was all he could do to get through it without breaking down.

Khyber glared at him when he was finished. "You are an idiot, Penderrin Ohmsford."

Pen bit back his angry reply, thinking that he had better just take whatever they had to say to him and be done with it.

"That doesn't help us, Khyber," her uncle said softly. "Pen loves this girl and he was trying to help her. I don't think we can fault him for his good intentions. He might have handled it better, but at the time he did the best he could. It's easy to second-guess him now."

"You might want to ask yourself what Hatch will do to her now that he knows what she intended and no outsiders are about to interfere," Tagwen said to Pen.

Pen had already thought of that, and he didn't like the conclusion he had reached. Gar Hatch would not be happy with his daughter and would not trust her again anytime soon. He would make a virtual prisoner of her, and once again, it was his fault.

Khyber stalked away. She stopped a short distance off and stood looking out at the bay with her hands on her hips, then wheeled back suddenly. "Sorry I snapped at you, Pen. Gar Hatch is a sneak and a coward to do this. But the matter isn't finished. We'll see him again, somewhere down the road. He'll be the one who goes over the side of that airship the next time, I promise you!"

"Meanwhile, what are we supposed to do?" Tagwen asked, looking from one face to the next. "How do we get out of here?"

Ahren Elessedil glanced around thoughtfully, then shrugged. "We walk."

"Walk!" Tagwen was aghast. "We can't walk out of here! You've seen this morass, this pit of vipers and swamp rats! If something doesn't eat us, we'll be sucked down in the quicksand! Besides, it will take us days, and that's only if we don't get lost, which we will!"

The Druid nodded. "The alternative is to use magic. I could summon a Roc to carry us out. But if I do that, I will give us away to Terek Molt. He will reach us long before any help does."

Tagwen scrunched up his face and folded his arms across his chest. "I'm just saying I don't think we can walk out of here, no matter how determined we are."

"There might be another way," Pen interjected quickly. "One that's a little quicker and safer."

Ahren Elessedil turned to him, surprise mirrored in his blue eyes. "All right, Pen, let's hear what it is."

"I hope it's a better idea than his last one," Tagwen grumbled before Pen could speak, and set his jaw firmly as he prepared to pass judgment.

*   *   *

He showed them how to build the raft, using heavier logs for the hull, slender limbs for the cradle, and reeds for binding. It needed to be only big enough to support the four of them, so a platform measuring ten feet by ten feet was adequate. The materials were easy enough to find, even in the Slags, though not so easy to shape, mostly because they lacked the requisite tools and had to make do with long knives. On more than one occasion Pen had built similar rafts before and knew something about how to construct them so that they wouldn't fall apart midjourney. Working in pairs, they gathered the logs and limbs for the platform and carried them to a flat piece of earth on which they could lay them out and lash them together.

They worked through the morning, and by midday they were finished. The raft was crude, but it was strong enough to support them and light enough to allow for portage. Most important, it floated. They had no supplies, nothing but the clothes they wore and the weapons they carried, so after crafting poles to push their vessel through the swamp, they set out.

It was slow going, even with the raft to carry them, the swamp a morass of weed-choked bays and logjammed channels that they were forced to backtrack through and portage around repeatedly. Even so, they made much better progress than they would have afoot. For just the second time since they had set out, Pen was able to make practical use of his magic, to intuit from the sounds and movements of the plants, birds, and animals around them the dangers that lay waiting. Calling out directions to the other three as they worked the poles, he concentrated on keeping them clear of submerged debris that might have damaged their craft and well away from the more dangerous creatures that lived in the Slags— some of them huge and aggressive. By staying close to the shoreline and out of the deeper water, they were able to avoid any confrontations, and Pen was able to tell himself that he was making at least partial amends for his part in contributing to the fix they were in.

By nightfall, they were exhausted and still deep in the Slags. Pen's pocket compass had kept them on the right heading, of that much he was certain, but how much actual progress they had made was debatable. Since none of them knew exactly where they were, it was impossible to judge how far they still had to go. Nothing about the wetland had changed, the mist was thick and unbroken, the waterways extended off in all directions, and the undergrowth was identical to what they had left behind six hours earlier.

There was nothing to eat or drink, so after agreeing to split the watch into four shifts they went to sleep, hungry and thirsty and frustrated.

During the night, it rained. Pen, who was on watch at the time, used his cloak to catch enough drinking water that they were able to satisfy at least one need. After the rain stopped and the water was consumed, Khyber and Tagwen went back to sleep, but Ahren Elessedil chose to sit up with the boy.

"Are you worried about Cinnaminson?" Ahren asked when they were settled down together at the edge of the raft, their backs to the sleepers, their cloaks wrapped about them. It was surprisingly cold at night in the Slags.

The boy stared out into the dark without answering. Then he sighed. "I can't do anything to help her. I can help us, but not her. She's smart and she's capable, but her father is too much for her. He sees her as a valuable possession, something he almost lost. I don't know what he will do."

The Druid folded himself deeper into his robes. "I don't think he will do anything. I think he believes he made an example of us, so she won't cross him again. He doesn't think we will get out of here alive, Pen. Or if we do, that we will escape the *Galaphile*."

Pen pulled his knees up to his chest and lowered his chin between them. "Maybe he's right."

"Oh?"

"It's just that we're not getting anywhere." The boy tightened his hands into fists and lowered his voice to a whisper. "We aren't any closer to helping Aunt Grianne than we were when we started out. How long can she stay alive inside the Forbidding? How much time does she have?"

Ahren Elessedil shook his head. "A lot more than anyone else I can think of. She's a survivor, Pen. She can endure more hardships than most. It doesn't matter where she is or what she is up against, she will find a way to stay alive. Don't lose heart. Remember who she is."

The boy shook his head. "What if she has to go back to being who she *was*? What if that's the only way she can survive? I listened to my parents talk about what she was like, when they thought I wasn't listening. She shouldn't have to be made to do those kinds of things again."

The Druid gave him a thin smile. "I don't think that's what has you worried."

The boy frowned. "What do you mean?"

"I don't think you are worried about whether we will reach the Ard Rhys in time to be of help. I think you are worried about whether you will be able to do what is needed when the time comes. I think you are worried about failing."

Pen was instantly furious, but he kept his tongue in check as he looked out again into the mist and gloom, thinking it through, weighing the Druid's words. Slowly, he felt his anger soften.

"You're right," he admitted finally. "I don't think I can save her. I don't see how I can manage it. I'm not strong or talented enough. I don't have magic like my father. I'm nothing special. I'm just ordinary." He looked at the Druid. "What am I going to do if that isn't enough?"

Ahren Elessedil pursed his lips. "I was your age when I sailed on the *Jerle Shannara*. Just a boy. My brother sent me because he was secretly hoping I wouldn't come back. Ostensibly, I was sent to regain possession of the Elfstones, but mostly I was sent with the expectation that I would be killed. But I wasn't, and when I found the Elfstones, I was able to use them. I didn't think such a thing was possible. I ran from my first battle, so frightened I barely knew what I was doing. I hid until someone found me, someone who was able to tell me what I am telling you—that you will do your best and your best might surprise you."

"But you just said you had the Elfstones to rely on. I don't."

"But you do have magic. Don't underrate it. You don't know how important it might turn out to be. But that isn't what will make the difference when it matters. It is the strength of your heart. It is your determination."

He leaned forward. "Remember this, Penderrin. You are the one who was chosen to save the Ard Rhys. That was not a mistake. The King of the Silver River sees the future better than anyone, better even than the shades of the Druids. He would not have come to you if you were not the right person to undertake this quest."

Pen searched Ahren's eyes uncertainly. "I wish I could believe that."

"I wished the same thing twenty years ago. But you have to take it on faith. You have to believe that it will happen. You have to make it come true. No one can do it for you."

Pen nodded. Words of wisdom, well meant, but he didn't find them helpful. All he could think about was how ill equipped he was to rescue anyone from a place like the Forbidding.

"I still think it would have been better to send you," he said quietly. "I still don't understand why the King of the Silver River decided on me."

"Because he knows more about you than you know yourself," the Druid answered. He rose and stretched. "The watch is mine now. Go to sleep. You need to rest, to be ready to help us again tomorrow. We aren't out of danger yet. We are depending on you."

Pen moved away without comment, sliding to one side, joining Khyber and Tagwen at the other end of the raft, where both were sleeping fitfully. He lay down and pulled his cloak closer, resting his head in the crook of his arm. He didn't sleep right away, but stared out into the misty gloom, the swirling of the haze hypnotic and suggestive of other things. His thoughts drifted to the events that had brought him to that place and time and then to Ahren Elessedil's encouraging words. That he should believe so strongly in Pen was surprising, especially after how badly the boy had handled the matter of Cinnaminson and Gar Hatch. But Pen could tell when someone was lying to him, and he did not sense falsehood in the other's words. The Druid saw him as the rescuer he had been charged with being. Pen would find a way, he believed, even if the boy did not yet know what that way was.

Pen breathed deeply, feeling a calmness settle through him. Weariness played a part in that, but there was peace, as well.

If my father was here, he would have spoken those same words to me, he thought.

There was comfort in knowing that. He closed his eyes and slept.

They woke to a dawn shrouded in mist and gloom, their bodies aching with the cold and damp. Once again, there was nothing to eat or drink, so they put their hunger and thirst aside and set out. As they poled through the murky waters, stands of swamp grass clutched at them with anxious tendrils. Everywhere, shadows stretched across the water and through the trees, snakes they didn't want to wake. No one spoke. Chilled by the swamp's gray emptiness, they retreated inside themselves. Their determination kept them going. Somewhere up ahead was an end to the morass, and there was only one way to reach it.

At midday they were confronted by a huge stretch of open water surrounded by vine-draped trees and clogged by heavy swamp grass. Islands dotted the lake, grassy hummocks littered with rotting logs. Overhead, mist swirled like thick soup in a kettle, sunlight weakened by its oily mix, a hazy wash that spilled gossamer-pale through the heavy branches of the trees.

They stopped poling and stared out across the marshy, ragged expanse. The islands jutted from the water like reptile eyes. Pen looked at Ahren Elessedil and shook his head. He didn't like the feel of the lake and did not care to try to cross it. Ripples at its center hinted at the presence of things best avoided.

"Follow the lakeshore," the Druid said, glancing at the sky. "Stay under the cover of the trees. Watch the surface of the water for movement."

They chose to veer left, where the shallows were not as densely clogged with grasses and deadwood. Poling along some twenty feet offshore, Pen kept one eye on the broad expanse of the lake, scanning for ripples. He knew the others were depending on his instincts to keep them safe. Out on the open water, trailers of mist skimmed the viscous surface. A sudden squall came and went like a ghost. The air felt heavy and thick, and condensation dripped from the trees in a slow, steady rhythm. Within the shadowy interior of the woods surrounding the lake, the silence was deep and oppressive.

At the lake's center, something huge lifted in a shadowy parting of waters and was gone again, silent as smoke. Pen glanced at
Khyber, who was poling next to him on the raft. He saw the fierce
concentration in her eyes waver.

They had gone some distance when the shoreline receded into
a deep bay overhung with vines that dipped all the way to the water's dark surface. Cautiously, they maneuvered under the canopy,
sliding through the still waters with barely a whisper of movement, eyes searching. The hairs on the back of Pen's neck prickled
in warning. Something felt wrong. Then he realized what it was.
He wasn't hearing anything from the life around him, not a sound,
not a single movement, nothing.

A vine brushed against his face, sliding away almost reluctantly, leaving a glistening trail of slime on his skin. He wiped the
sticky stuff from his face, grimacing, and glanced upward. A huge
mass of similar vines was writhing and twisting directly overhead.
Not quite sure what he was looking at, he stared in disbelief, then
in fear.

"Ahren," he whispered.

Too late. The vines dropped down like snakes to encircle them,
a cascade of long arms and supple fingers, tentacles of all sizes and
shapes, attacking with such ferocity and purpose that they had no
time even to think of reaching for their weapons. His arms pinned
to his sides, Pen was swept off the raft and into the air. Tagwen
flew past him, similarly wrapped about. The boy looked up and
saw so many of the vines entwined in the forest canopy that it felt
as if he were being drawn into a basket of snakes.

Then he saw something else, something much worse. Within
the masses of tentacles were mouths, huge beaked maws that
clacked and snapped and pulsed with life. Like squids, he thought,
waiting to feed. It had taken only seconds for the vines to immobilize him, only seconds more for them to lift him toward the wait-

ing mouths, all of it so quick he barely had time to comprehend what was happening. Now he fought like a wild man, kicking and screaming, determined to break free. But the vines held him securely, and slowly, inexorably, they drew him in.

Then spears of fire thrust into the beaks and tentacles from below, their flames a brilliant azure, burning through the shadows and gloom. The vines shuddered violently, shaking Pen with such force that he lost all sense of which way was up. An instant later, they released him altogether, dropping him stunned and disoriented into the swamp. He struck with an impact that jarred his bones and knocked the breath from his body, and he was underwater almost instantly, fighting to right himself, to reach air again.

He broke the surface with a gasp, thrashing against a clutch of weeds, seeing scythes of blue fire slash through the canopy in broad sweeps, smelling wood and plants burn, hearing the hiss and crackle of their destruction, tasting smoke and ash on the air. Overhead, the canopy was alive with twisting vines, some of them aflame, others batting wildly at burning neighbors. He saw Ahren Elessedil standing on the raft, both hands thrust skyward, his elemental magic the source of the fire, summoned from the ether and released from his fingers in jagged darts.

"Pen!" someone yelled.

Khyber had surfaced next to the raft and was hanging on one end, trying to balance the uneven platform so that her uncle could defend them. The swamp waters had turned choppy and rough, and it was all the Druid could do to keep from being tossed overboard. Pen swam to their aid, seizing the end of the raft opposite the Elven girl, the vines whipping all about him.

An instant later, Tagwen dropped out of the canopy, his bearded face a mask of confusion and terror as he plunged into the murky waters and then surfaced next to Pen.

"Push us out into the bay!" Ahren Elessedil shouted, dropping to one knee as his tiny platform tilted precariously.

Kicking strongly, Pen and Khyber propelled the raft toward open water, fighting to get clear of the deadly trap. Tagwen hung on tenaciously, and Ahren continued to send shards of fire into the clutching vines, which were still trying to get at him but were unable to break past his defenses. Smoke billowed and roiled in heavy clouds, mingling with swamp mist to form an impenetrable curtain. From somewhere distant, the frightened cries of water birds rose.

When at last they were far enough from the vines to pause in their efforts, Pen and Khyber crawled onto the raft beside Ahren Elessedil, pulled Tagwen up after them, and collapsed, gasping for breath. For several long seconds, no one said anything, their eyes fixed on the smoky mass of tree vines now some distance off.

"We were lucky," Pen said finally.

"Don't be stupid!" Khyber snapped in reply. "Look what we've done! We've given ourselves away!"

Pen stared at her, recognition setting in. She was right. He had forgotten what Ahren Elessedil had said about how using magic would reveal their presence to those who hunted them. Ahren had saved them, but he had betrayed them, as well. Terek Molt would know exactly where they were. The *Galaphile* would track them to the bay.

"What can we do?" he asked in dismay.

Khyber turned to her uncle. "How much time do we have, Uncle Ahren?"

The Druid shook his head. "Not much. They will come for us quickly." He climbed to his knees and looked around. Everything was clouded with smoke. "If they are close, we won't even have time to get off this bay."

"We can hide!" Pen suggested hurriedly, glancing skyward for movement, for any sign of their pursuers. "Perhaps on one of the islands. We can sink the raft . . ."

Ahren shook his head. "No, Penderrin. We need to go ashore and find a place to make a stand. We need space in which to move and solid ground on which to do it." He handed the boy one of the two remaining poles. "Try to get us ashore, Pen. Choose a direction. Do the best you can, but do it quickly."

With Ahren working on the opposite side, Pen began poling toward shore once more, farther down from where the vines still thrashed and burned, farther along in the direction they had been heading. They made good time, borne on the crest of a tide stirred by their battle with the vines, a tide that swept them east. But Pen sensed that however swiftly they moved, it wasn't going to be swift enough.

This is all my fault, he kept thinking. *Again.*

The haze continued thick and unbroken, layering the surface of the water in a roiling blanket that stank of burning wood and leaves. Slowly, the bay went quiet again, the waters turning slate black and oily once more, a dark reflection of the shadows creeping in from the shoreline. Pen poled furiously, thinking that if they could just reach a safe place to land, they might lose themselves in the trees. It would not be easy to find them in this jungle, this swamp, this morass, not even for Terek Molt. All they needed to do was gain the shore.

They did so, finally. They beached on a mud bank fronting a thick stand of cypress, tangled all about with vines and banked with heavy grasses. They pulled their raft ashore, hauled it back into the trees, and set out walking. The silence of the Slags closed about them, deep and pervasive, an intrusive and brooding companion. Pen could hear the sound of his breathing. He could feel the pumping of his heart.

Still there was no sign of their pursuers.

We're going to escape them after all, he thought in sudden relief.

They walked for several hours, well past midday and deep into the afternoon. The shoreline snaked in and out of the trees, and they stayed at its edge, keeping a sharp eye out for more of the deadly vines and any sign of movement on the bay waters. They did not talk, their efforts concentrated on putting one foot in front of the other, Ahren Elessedil setting a pace that even Pen, who was accustomed to long treks, found difficult to match.

It was late in the afternoon, the shadows of twilight beginning to lengthen out of the west, when they found the eastern end of the lake. It swung south in a broad curve, the ground lifting to a wall of old growth through which dozens of waterways opened. Pen searched the gloom ahead without finding anything reassuring, then took a moment to read his compass, affirming what Ahren, with his Druidic senses, had already determined. They were on course, but not yet clear of the swamp.

Then sudden brightness flared behind them, dispersing the mist and brightening the gloom as if dawn had broken. They wheeled back as one, shielding their eyes. It looked as if the swamp were boiling from a volcanic eruption, its waters churning, steaming with an intense heat. The dark prow of an airship nosed through the fading haze like a great lumbering bear, slowly settling toward the waters of the bay, black nose sniffing the air. Pen fought to keep from shaking with the chill that swept through him.

The *Galaphile* had found them.

TWENTY-SIX

The huge curved horns of the *Galaphile's* bow swung slowly about to point like a compass needle toward the four who stood frozen on the muddy shoreline. There was no mistaking that she had found what she was searching for. Through the fading screen of mist and twilight's deepening shadows, the vessel settled onto the reed-choked surface of the bay, not fifty yards away, and slowly began to advance. Her sails were furled and her masts and spars as bare and black as charred bones. She had the stark, blasted look of a specter.

"What do we do?" Khyber hissed.

"We can run," Pen answered at once, already poised to do so. "There's still time to gain the trees, get deep into the woods, split up if we have to . . ."

He trailed off hopelessly. It was pointless to talk about running away. Ahren had already said that it was too late to hide, so running would not help, either. The *Galaphile* had already found them once; even if they ran, it would have no trouble doing so again. Terek Molt would track them down like rabbits. They were going

to have to make a stand, even without an airship in which to maneuver or weapons with which to fight. Ahren Elessedil's Druid
magic and whatever resources the rest of them could muster were
going to have to be enough.

What other choice do we have? Pen thought in despair.

The *Galaphile* had come to a stop at the edge of the shoreline, advanced as close to the mud bank as her draft would allow.
Atop her decks, dark figures moved, taking up positions along the
railing. Gnome Hunters. Pen saw the glittering surfaces of their
blades. Perhaps the Gnome Hunters simply meant to kill them,
having no need to do otherwise.

"Do you see how she shimmers?" Ahren Elessedil asked them
suddenly. His voice was eerily calm. "The ship, about her hull and
rigging? Do you see?"

Pen looked with the others. At first, he couldn't make it out,
but then slowly his eyes adjusted to the heavy twilight and he saw
a sort of glow that pulsed all about the warship, an aura of glistening dampness.

"What is it?" Khyber whispered, brushing back her mop of
dark hair, twisting loose strands of it in her fingers.

"Magic," her uncle answered softly. "Terek Molt is sheathing
the *Galaphile* in magic to protect her from an attack. He is wary of
what we did to him last time, of another storm, of the elements I
can summon to disrupt his efforts."

The Druid exhaled slowly. "He has made a mistake. He has
given us a chance."

A rope ladder was lowered over the side of the airship, one end
dropping through a railing gap and into the water. A solitary figure
began to descend. Even from a distance and through the heavy
gloom, there was no doubt about who it was.

Pen glanced up again at the cloaked figures lining the *Gala-*

phile's railing. All their weapons were pointed at himself and his companions.

"Khyber," Ahren Elessedil called softly.

When she looked over, he passed her something, a quick exchange that was barely noticeable. Pen caught a glimpse of the small pouch as her hand opened just far enough to permit her to see that it was the Elfstones she had been given. Her quick intake of breath was audible.

"Listen carefully," her uncle said without looking at her, his eyes fixed on Terek Molt, who was almost to the water now. "When I tell you, use the Elfstones against the *Galaphile*. Do as you have been taught. Open your mind, summon their power, and direct it at the airship."

Khyber was already shaking her head, her Elven features taut with dismay. "It won't work, Uncle Ahren! The magic is only good against other magic—magic that threatens the holder of the stones! You taught me that yourself! The *Galaphile* is an airship, wood and iron only!"

"She is," the Druid agreed. "But thanks to Terek Molt, the magic that sheathes her is not. It is his magic, Druid magic. Trust me, Khyber. It is our only chance. I am skilled, but Terek Molt was trained as a warrior Druid and is more powerful than I am. Do as I say. Watch for my signal. Do not reveal that you have the Elfstones before then. Do nothing to demonstrate that you are a danger to him. If you do, if you give yourself away too early, even to help me, we are finished."

Pen glanced at Khyber. The Elven girl's eyes glittered with fear. "I've never even tried to use the Elfstones," she said. "I don't know what it takes to summon the magic. What if I can't do so now?"

Ahren Elessedil smiled. "You can and you will, Khyber. You

have the training and the resolve. Do not doubt yourself. Be brave. Trust the magic and your instincts. That will be enough."

Terek Molt stepped down off the ladder and into the shallow water, turning to face them. His black robes billowed out behind him as he approached, his blocky form squared toward Ahren Elessedil. He radiated confidence and disdain, the set of his dark form signaling his intent in a way that was unmistakable.

"Move to one side, Khyber," Ahren said quietly, his voice taking on an edge. "Remember what I said. Watch for my signal. Pen, Tagwen, back out of the way."

The boy and the Dwarf retreated at once, happy to put as much distance as possible between themselves and Terek Molt. The warrior Druid's chiseled face glanced in their direction, a slight lifting of his chin the only indication that he noticed them at all. But even that small movement was enough to let Pen see the rage that was reflected in the flat, cold eyes.

When he was twenty feet from the Elf, he stopped. "Give up the boy. He belongs to us now. You can keep the old man and the girl as compensation for your trouble. Take them and go."

Ahren Elessedil shook his head. "I don't think I care to take you up on your offer. I think we will all stay together."

Terek Molt nodded. "Then you will all come with me. Either way, it makes no difference."

"Ultimatums are the last resort of desperate men."

"Don't play games with me, outcast."

"What has happened to you, Terek Molt, that you would betray the Ard Rhys and the order this way? You were a good man once."

The Dwarf's face darkened. "I am a better man than you, Ahren Elessedil. I am no cat's paw, underling fool in league with a monster. I am no tool at the beck and call of a witch!"

"Are you not?"

"I'll say this once. I got tired of the Ard Rhys—of her disruptive presence and her self-centered ways. I got tired of watching her fail time and again at the simplest of tasks. She was never right for the position. She should never have assumed it. Others are better suited to lead the Druid Council to the places it needs to go. Others, who do not share her history."

"A full council vote might have been a better way to go. At least that approach would have lent a semblance of respectability to your efforts and not painted all of you as betrayers and cowards. Perhaps enough others on the Druid Council might have agreed with you that all this would not have been necessary." The Elven Prince paused. "Perhaps it still might be so, were someone of character to pursue it."

He made it sound so reasonable, as if treachery could be undone and made right, as if the conversation was between two old friends who were discussing a thorny issue that each hoped to resolve. "Is it too late to bring her back?" he asked the other.

The Dwarf's face darkened. "Why bring her back when she is safely out of the way? What does it matter to you, in any case? You have been gone from the council and her life for years. You are an outcast from your own people. Is that why you think so highly of her—because she is like you?"

"I think better of Grianne Ohmsford than I do of Shadea a'Ru," the Elf replied.

"You can tell her so yourself, once we are returned to Paranor." Terek Molt came forward another step, black cloak billowing. One hand lifted and a gloved finger pointed. "Enough talk. I have chased you for as long as I care to; I am weary of the aggravation. You might have gotten away from me if those Rovers hadn't stranded you in this swamp and then betrayed you to us. Does that surprise you? We caught up with them early yesterday, trying to slip past us in their pathetic little vessel. That Captain was quick enough to tell us everything once he saw how things stood. So we knew where you were, and it was just a matter of waiting for you to show yourselves. Using magic was a mistake. It led us right to you."

Ahren nodded. "Unavoidable. What have you done with the *Skatelow* and her crew?"

The Dwarf spit to one side. "Rover vermin. I sent them on their way, back to where they came from. I had no need of them once they gave you up. They'll be halfway home by now and better off than those who so foolishly sought to use their services." He looked past the other now to Pen. "I am done talking. Bring the boy. No more arguments. No further delays."

Ahren Elessedil's hands had been tucked within his cloak. Now he brought them out again, balled into fists and bright with his magic's blue glow. Terek Molt stiffened, but did not give ground. "Do not be a fool," he said quietly.

"I don't think Pen should go with you," Ahren Elessedil said. "I think you intend him harm, whether you admit to it or not. Druids are meant to protect, and protect him I shall. You have forgotten your teachings, Terek Molt. If you take one step nearer, I shall help you remember them."

The Dwarf shook his head slowly. His gloved hands flared with magic of his own. "You are no match for me, Elessedil. If you test me, you will be found wanting. You will be destroyed. Step aside. Give the boy to me and be done with this."

They faced each other across the short stretch of mud and shallow water, two identically cloaked forms born of the same order but gone on separate paths. Elf and Dwarf, faces hard as stone, eyes locked as if bound together by iron threads, poised in a manner that suggested there would be no backing down and no quarter given. Pen found himself tensed and ready, as well, but he did not know what he would do when doing something became necessary. He could not think of anything that would help, any difference he could make. Yet he knew he would try.

"Your ship," Ahren Elessedil said suddenly to Terek Molt, and nodded in the direction of the *Galaphile*.

The Dwarf turned to look, did so without thinking, and in that instant Ahren attacked, raising both hands and dispatching the elemental magic that he commanded in a burst of Druid fire. But it was not the other man he targeted; it was the warship, his elemental magic striking the vessel with such force that it was rocked from bow to stern. The infuriated Dwarf struck back instantly, his own fire hammering into the Druid. Ahren Elessedil had just enough time to throw up a shield before the other's magic knocked him completely off his feet and sent him sprawling in the mud.

It was a terrible blow, yet Ahren Elessedil was up again immediately, fighting off the warrior Druid's second thrust, steadying his defenses. Now arrows and darts cast down by the Gnome Hunters who were gathered at the railing of the *Galaphile* began to rain on the beleaguered Elf. Pen and Tagwen threw themselves out of the way as a few stray missiles nearly skewered them, then began crawling toward the protective shelter of the trees. Khyber screamed in rage, bringing up her own small Druid-enhanced magic to protect herself, and crouched down close by Ahren, poised to strike but still waiting on her uncle's command.

Ahren Elessedil was fighting for his life, down on his knees with his hands extended and his palms facing out, as if in a futile effort to ward off what was happening. His protective shield was eroding under the onslaught of Terek Molt's attack, melting like ice under searing heat. Yet once again, he chose to strike not at the Dwarf, but at the warship, diverting precious power from his defenses. Pen could not understand what the Elf was thinking. Ahren already knew that the ship was protected, that it was a

waste of time and effort to try to damage her. Why was he persist-
ing in this method of attack?

Yet suddenly, improbably, the *Galaphile* began to shudder, massive hull and ram-shaped pontoons rocking as if caught in a storm
instead of resting in shallow water. Something of what Ahren
was doing was making a difference, after all. Terek Molt seemed
to sense it, as well, and redoubled his efforts. Druid fire exploded
out of his fingers and into the Elf, staggering him, crumpling his
shield. Pen heard Ahren call out to Khyber, the signal for which
she had been waiting, and immediately she had the Elfstones
in hand, arms outthrust. Brilliant blue light built about her fist,
widening in a sphere that caused the boy to shield his eyes.

Then the magic exploded from her clenched fingers in a massive rush that swept over the *Galaphile* like a tidal wave. For a single
instant the Druid warship was lit like a star, blazing with light, and
then it burst into flames. It didn't catch fire in just one place or
even a dozen. It caught fire everywhere at once, transformed into
a giant torch. With a monstrous whoosh it detonated in a fireball
that rose hundreds of feet into the misty swamp sky, carrying with
it the Gnome Hunters, bearing away a twisting, writhing Terek
Molt, as well, the latter sucked into the vortex. A roar erupted from
the conflagration, burning with such fury that it scorched Pen and
Tagwen a hundred yards away, sweeping through the whole of the
Slags.

In seconds, the *Galaphile* and all who had sailed her were gone.

Pen looked up from where he lay flattened against the mud
and scorched grasses. Smoke rising from his blackened form,
Ahren Elessedil lay sprawled on his back at the shoreline. Khyber
knelt in shock some yards away, her arms lowered, the power of

the Elfstones gone dormant once more. Her head drooped, as if she had taken a blow, and the boy could see her eyes blinking rapidly. She was shaking all over.

He forced himself to his feet. "Tagwen," he called over to the Dwarf, finding him through eyes half-blinded by smoke and ash. Tagwen looked up at him from where he was huddled in a muddied depression, his eyes wide and scared. "Get up. We have to help them."

The boy staggered across the flats, head lowered against the heat of the still-fiery bay. Flames and ash-smeared waters were all that remained of the *Galaphile*. Pen glanced at the charred mix, baffled and awed by what had taken place, trying unsuccessfully to make sense of it.

He reached Khyber and knelt beside her. He touched her shoulder. "Khyber," he said softly.

She did not look up or stop shaking, so he put his lips to her ear, whispering, "Khyber, it's all right, it's over. Look at me. I need to know you can hear me. You're all right."

"So much power," she whispered suddenly. She stopped shaking then, her body going perfectly still. A long sigh escaped her lips. She lifted her head and looked out across the fiery surface of the wetlands. "I couldn't stop it, Pen. Once it started, I couldn't stop it."

"I know," he said, understanding now something of what had transpired. "It's all over."

He helped her to her feet, and they stumbled together to where Tagwen knelt beside Ahren Elessedil. Pen knew at a glance that the Druid was dying. A handful of arrows and darts had pierced him, and his body was blackened and smoking from the explosion. But his eyes were open and calm, and he watched their approach with a steady gaze.

Khyber gasped as she saw him, then dropped to her knees and began to cry, her hands clasped helplessly in her lap, her head shaking slowly from side to side.

The Druid reached out with one charred hand and touched her wrist. "Terek Molt tied his magic to the *Galaphile*," he whispered, his voice dry and cracked with pain. "To protect her. When I attacked, he strengthened the connection until he was too committed to withdraw it. The Elfstones couldn't tell the difference. To them, the *Galaphile* was a weapon, an extension of Molt. So it consumed them both."

"I could have helped you!"

"No, Khyber." He coughed and blood flecked his burned lips. "He couldn't be allowed to know that you had the Elfstones. Otherwise, he would have destroyed you."

"Instead, he destroyed you!" She was crying so hard that she could barely make herself understood.

The ruined face tilted slightly in response. "I misjudged the extent of my invulnerability. Still, it is a reasonable trade." He swallowed thickly. "The Elfstones are yours now. Use them with caution. Your command of their power . . ." He trailed off, the words catching in this throat. "You've seen the nature of your abilities. Strong. Your heart, mind, body—very powerful. But the Stones are more powerful still. Be wary. They will rule you if you are not careful. There is danger in using them. Remember."

She lifted her tear-streaked face and looked over at Pen. "We have to help him!"

She was almost hysterical. Pen was frightened, unable to think of what to say to her. There was nothing they could do. Surely she could see that. But she looked so wild that he was afraid she might try something anyway, something dangerous.

Ahren Elessedil's hand tightened on her wrist. "No, Khyber," he said. He waited until she looked back at him, until she met his terrible burned gaze. "There is nothing to be done. It is finished for me. I'm sorry."

His eyes shifted slowly to Pen. "Penderrin. Twenty years ago, when I sailed on the *Jerle Shannara* with your father, a young girl gave up her life for me. She did so because she believed I was meant to do something important. I would like to think this is part of what she saved me for. Make something good come out of this. Do what you were sent here to do. Find the Ard Rhys and bring her back."

He took several sharp, rattling breaths, his eyes holding the boy's as he struggled to speak. "Ahren?" Pen whispered.

"Promise me."

The Druid's eyes became fixed and staring, and he quit breathing. Pen could not look away, finding in that terrible gaze strength of purpose he would not have believed possible. He reached out and touched the Druid's charred face, then closed those dead eyes and sat back again. He looked over at Khyber, who was crying silently into her hands, then at Tagwen.

"I never thought anything like this would happen," the Dwarf said quietly. "I thought he would be the one to get us safely through."

Pen nodded, looking out over the burning lake at the flames licking at the twilight darkness, staining sky and earth the color of blood. The surface of the water burned silently, steadily, a fiery mirror reflected against a backdrop of shadow-striped trees. Smoke mingled with mist and mist with clouds, and everything was hazy and surreal. The world had an alien feel to it, as if nothing the boy was seeing was familiar.

"What are we going to do?" Tagwen asked softly. He shook his head slowly, as if there were no answer to his question.

Penderrin Ohmsford looked over again at Khyber. She was no longer crying. Her head was lifted and her dark features were a mask of resolve. He could tell from the way she was looking back at him that there would be no more tears.

The boy turned to the Dwarf. "We're going to do what he asked of us," he said. "We're going to go on."

Shadea a'Ru stalked from the Druid Council without sparing even a glance back at those fools who expected it, her eyes directed straight ahead. She would not give them the satisfaction. She would give them nothing. She was seething with rage and frustration, but she would not let even a hint of it escape. Let them suspect what they wished about her true feelings; their suspicions were the least of her problems.

Her stride lengthening, she shouldered past the few grouped by the doors leading out, using her size and weight to brush them aside, and turned down the hallway toward the stairs leading up to her rooms. It was a kindness she bestowed on them, leaving so abruptly. Had she hesitated longer, she might have killed one of them.

Surely that would have been more satisfying than anything else that had happened.

She had spent the entire afternoon trying to convince the Council of the necessity of taking a stand on the war between the Federation and the Free-born. She had insisted that no progress in the efforts of the Druid order could be made until the war was concluded. It was inevitable, she argued, that the Federation, superior in men and materials, would emerge as the eventual victor. Better that it happen now, so that the rebuilding could begin, so that the work of the Druids could commence in earnest. Callahorn was Southland territory in any event, inhabited mostly by members of the Race of Man and naturally aligned with the interests of the Federation. Let them have it. Make that the condition to ending the war. The Free-born were a rebel outfit at best, consumed by their foolish insistence on keeping Callahorn for themselves. Remove the tacit support of the Druids and the rebels would collapse.

She did not tell the Council, of course, that she had made a bargain with Sen Dunsidan to help him secure control over the Borderlands. She did not tell them that Federation control of Callahorn was the price of his support of her and her efforts to expand the authority and influence of the order. That wasn't something they needed to know. It was enough that she was proposing a reasonable, commonsense solution to a problem that had plagued the order since the day of its inception.

But the Council had balked at adopting her proposal, its members led in their opposition by that snake Gerand Cera, who had insisted that a thorough study of the consequences of such drastic action was needed first. The matter was not as simple as the Ard Rhys was trying to make it seem, his argument went. Elven interests would be impacted by the outcome of the Federation–Free-born war in a significant way, as well. Once he had mentioned the Elves, it was only moments before the Dwarves were insisting that their interests were important too. Soon, everyone was arguing. Clever of him. Without repudiating the suggestion outright, he had managed to defer any action on it until a later date, all with an eye toward his own special interests, she was certain.

Very well. He had won this day, but there would be another—although not necessarily for him. He was becoming something of a nuisance, one that she would have to deal with soon. If he could not be brought into line, he would have to be removed.

For the moment, she had more pressing concerns. Sen Dunsidan would arrive in three days, and he would expect to hear that she had secured the Council's approval for Federation occupation of Callahorn along with its open repudiation of Free-born claims to the land. He would be expecting a joint announcement of solidarity on the matter, one that would clearly indicate to the Free-born that their cause was lost. His expectations would not be met. She would have to tell him that the matter was not settled, that he would have to be patient. He would not like that, but he would have to live with it. He was used to disappointment; he would survive.

She began to climb the stairs to the tower, conscious of the darkness pressing in from without, filtering through the windows to cast its shadows in the flickering torchlight. Nighttime already, and she had not yet eaten.

She was halfway up when Traunt Rowan appeared at the top of the stairs on his way down. She could tell at once that something was wrong.

"You had better come, Shadea," he told her quietly, waiting until she had reached him, then turning back the way he had come. "The cold chamber."

She fell in beside him, angry without yet knowing why. "Has Molt failed yet again?"

"Someone has. The scrye waters indicate a massive collision of magics somewhere east of Anatcherae. The *Galaphile* is gone."

"Gone?" She stared at him. "Gone where?"

"Destroyed. Obliterated."

Her fists clenched in fury. "How could Molt allow such a thing to happen?" Her mind spun with possibilities. "When was our last report from him?"

"Yesterday." Rowan wouldn't look at her. "The message indicated he was in pursuit of the boy and the others and had caught up with them in Anatcherae. That would have been two days ago."

She forced herself to stay calm, to think it through. Courier birds released from the *Galaphile* brought her regular messages from Molt, indicating where he was and what he was doing. Nothing in yesterday's message suggested the Dwarf was in any trouble, let alone the sort that would cause a Druid warship to be destroyed. Magic of such power was unusual, and it would have to have been employed in just the right way. The Elfstones? Perhaps. But Ahren Elessedil was not a warrior Druid or trained in battle the way Molt was. It was inconceivable that he would have prevailed in a confrontation.

They entered the cold chamber to find Iridia Eleri standing at the basin, staring down at the scrye waters with haunted eyes, arms folded across her rigid body. Her eyes snapped up at their entry, and the haunted look gave way to one of rage.

"If you had sent me, this wouldn't have happened!" she hissed at Shadea, making no effort to hide her feelings.

Shadea ignored her, walking over to the basin and looking down. Heavy ripples emanated from a point at the eastern shore of the Lazareen, perhaps somewhere within the Slags. She knew that country. Dangerous to anyone, no matter how well armed or prepared. There was no mistaking what she was reading in the waters. The nature of the ripples clearly indicated a massive explosion, one instigated by a use of magic. The little blip that had served as a beacon for the *Galaphile* was gone. Traunt Rowan was not mistaken in what he had told her.

"There's no way of knowing who survived this," she said, mostly to herself.

"Not without sending someone to find out," Traunt Rowan said.

Iridia spun around the end of the basin and came face-to-face with Shadea. Although smaller of frame and stature, Iridia looked as if she intended to attack the bigger woman. Shadea took a step back in spite of herself.

"This is on your head," Iridia snapped, her words as sharp-edged as daggers, her voice freezing the air. She was shaking with rage. "You are responsible for this travesty, you and your insistence on doing whatever you choose to do. What do you need with the rest of us, Shadea? What have you ever needed with us? I thought you my friend, once. I thought we were sisters. But you are incapable of friendship or loyalty or caring of any sort. You are as much a monster as that creature you summoned to bear the Stiehl. And I am no better. I have been one of your monsters, one of those who act in your behalf. I have been your tool."

She shook her head slowly. "No more. Not ever again."

She held the other's gaze for a moment longer, then turned and walked from the room. Unimpressed, Shadea watched her go. She thought it unfortunate that Iridia could no longer sort things out in a reasonable manner. Her attachment to Ahren Elessedil had left her emotionally unstable, and Shadea found herself hoping that the Elven Prince had gone the way of the *Galaphile*. Then, perhaps, Iridia would come back to herself.

Shadea looked over at Traunt Rowan. "Are you of a like mind?"

The Druid shrugged. "I am no one's tool, and I do what I choose. Iridia's problems are her own. On the other hand, I question the wisdom of your decision to send Terek Molt after that boy. I don't see the benefit to it. It distracts us from what matters."

"What matters is making certain no one finds a way to bring the Ard Rhys back!" she snapped at him. "Why can't you see that? All of you are so certain it can't be done. But remember who she is. Others thought her dead and gone, as well, and lived to regret it."

"No one can go into the Forbidding—"

"Hssst! Don't even speak the word!" She leaned close. "It is bad enough that Ahren Elessedil and the boy know what has happened, and it would be a mistake for us to think that they do not. They will seek a way to reach her. Successful or not, they will not forgive us for what we have done. This matter will not resolve itself while they live. If you think otherwise, say so now!"

He stared at her in silence, then shook his head. "I think as you do."

Shadea wasn't sure she believed him, but it was enough of an affirmation for now. She looked back at the scrye waters. Another message would arrive by tomorrow if Terek Molt was still alive. If not, then she could only hope that he had taken the boy, the Elven Prince, and that sycophant Tagwen with him to the grave. Then she could stop thinking about all of them and concentrate on what was happening at Paranor.

It occurred to her suddenly that she had forgotten about Aphasia Wye, dispatched with the Stiehl, as Iridia had reminded her, to eliminate the boy and his protectors. What of him? Even if the *Galaphile* was destroyed, even if Terek Molt was dead, perhaps the assassin was still carrying through on his task. Nothing would stop him once he set his mind to it. The only character flaw she had ever discovered was his troublesome streak of independence. On a whim, he might abandon the whole project.

She stared down again at the scrye waters, studying the diminishing series of ripples that marked the passing of the *Galaphile*.

With Aphasia Wye, she thought, you never knew.

Iridia Eleri strode blindly from the cold chamber and down the hallway beyond, so furious she could barely make herself think.

Tears leaked from the corners of her eyes, a series of ragged, glistening tracks on her perfect features. Had she stayed a moment longer, she would not have been able to hold them back. She stopped now, turning into a deep alcove in the empty hallway, and cried freely for several minutes, her body racked with sobs, her world collapsed about her. She knew what Shadea only suspected. Ahren Elessedil was dead. The voice had told her so.

When she stopped crying, she stood motionless in the alcove's darkness and forced herself to confront the truth. She had lied to herself, lied to them all. She was still in love with Ahren. She had always been in love with him and always would be. Shadea might sneer and the others might doubt, but it was so. It didn't even matter that he was dead. She loved him anyway.

What she could not bear was that he had not loved her in turn.

She stared into space, the words echoing in her mind. The voice had promised that this would change, that with time and patience, he would love her. The voice had promised from the very beginning, when it had first summoned her and offered its help. The voice was persuasive and comforting, and so she had listened and believed. Ahren could be hers, and for that she would do anything.

And had.

She closed her eyes against a wave of memories that paraded through her mind like specters. A flood of emotion followed on their heels. The sadness she felt for the man she had left in order to pursue Ahren. The emptiness she had experienced when she had given birth to and then abandoned the man's baby. The humiliation she had endured when Grianne Ohmsford had discovered what she had done. The terrible hurt she had suffered when Ahren had told her that in spite of everything, they could not be together, that his life was meant to go another way. The rage she had called upon to ally herself with Shadea and the others in their determination to rid the Druids of Grianne Ohmsford. The hatred she had nurtured for the Ard Rhys, the person most responsible for her misery.

The sense of devastation and irreparable loss she felt now, with Ahren Elessedil forever beyond her reach.

—But it need not be so—

Her eyes snapped open and she took a quick breath. The voice was back, come to comfort her anew. She nearly began crying again, so grateful was she to hear it. How much she depended on it. Just the sound of it was enough to give her fresh hope, new strength.

—He can still be yours—

She nodded at the darkness, wanting it to be true. But how could it? Ahren was dead, the voice had already told her so. There was no way to bring him back, no way to restore life to his shattered body. She could join him, of course. She could end her own life and reunite with him in death. She believed that was possible and even preferable to what life offered without him. Maybe she would have that, anyway. Now that she had broken with Shadea, it would not take the other long to decide to eliminate her.

—You need not die to have him back—

She had always trusted the voice, and she had never had cause to regret it. From the beginning, when it had summoned her north to the ruins of the Skull Kingdom and she had built the fires and made the sacrifices that had brought it into being, she had known it spoke the truth. It was a small thing for her to help it, when it was doing so much to help her. Shadea had believed from the first that she was the guiding force behind the conspiracy to eliminate the Ard Rhys, that she was the one who had sought out and found the means to carry out the act through her connection with Sen Dunsidan. The Federation Prime Minister, in turn, believed that he was the one who was determining the course of events, that his promises and gifts to Iridia, after she had approached him, had subverted her and made her his spy within the Druid camp. But she was the one to whom the voice spoke. She was the one who had brought it out of the darkness and into the light. She was the one to whom it had given the liquid night and the means by which she could gain some small measure of revenge against the woman who had turned Ahren Elessedil against her through scurrilous subterfuge and self-serving advice.

The others could think what they wished. She was the one who had made everything possible.

—I am here, Iridia—

She felt a surge of expectation and joy. She had waited for it, longed for it, the time when the voice took form, as it had promised it would, to give her back her place in the world. It would happen after the exile of the Ard Rhys, it had told her. Once the High Druid was gone, the voice could come out of hiding. It could take form and become for Iridia the friend and confidant she had once thought Shadea might be.

—I can be more than that, Iridia. I can be him—

Not quite willing to believe that she had heard the words correctly, she felt her heart lurch. She stood frozen in the darkness of the alcove, listening to their echo in the silence. *I can be him.* Was that possible? The voice was a chameleon, a changeling, capable of wondrous things. But could it bring back the dead? Could it make Ahren Elessedil whole again? Was the voice capable of that?

—Walk to me. In the cellars—

She left the alcove at once and proceeded to the main staircase, descending in a rush, her footfalls tiny and lost in the cavernous passage. No other Druid was abroad; most were gathered in the dining hall, the rest in their rooms or libraries. It felt to her as if she were alone in the world, free of its constraints and discriminations. She had never been well liked, never a part of anything, always alone. It was because of her childhood, where she had been set apart by her skills and the mistrust of those who recognized them. Even her parents had looked on her with growing suspicion and doubt, distancing themselves and their other children, sending her away early to study with an old woman who was said to understand such magic. The old woman did not, but living with her gave Iridia space and time to grow as she wished, to hone her talents, to gain a better understanding of what they offered. She needed no mentor to help her with this. She needed only herself.

Ten years she lived with the old woman, a crone of demands and false promises that would have eroded a less determined student. But Iridia only smiled and agreed and acquiesced to all, pretending obedience and waiting until she was alone to do what she wished. The old woman was no match for her, and when it was time, Iridia led her abusive and demanding benefactor to the well out back and pushed her in. For three days and nights, the crone screamed for help that never came.

Iridia turned down the lower hallway to the cellar doors at the north end of the Keep, knowing instinctively that was where she was meant to go, that was where the voice would be waiting. Shadows draped the heavy stones of the floors she passed across, her own the only one moving. No guards warded the passageways or walked the walls of Paranor now; the Druids alone kept watch, and theirs was a desultory, disinterested effort. In the time of the Warlock Lord, the keep would have fallen already.

At the heavy, ironbound doors leading down, the Elven sorceress paused to look back. No one was in sight; no one had followed. Shadea might have thought to try, but had not made the attempt. Just as well, Iridia thought. That would have complicated things. She wanted no one to intrude on her meeting.

—Hurry, Iridia. I am anxious—

As was she, flushed with unexpected passion. She was like a young, foolish girl, filled with wild emotion and desperate need. The voice had never failed her, and now it was going to give her the thing she desired most. It made her feel heady, as if she could dare anything, as if anything were possible. She pushed through the cellar doors in a rush, taking one of the torches from the brackets just inside, lighting it with a sweep of her fingers and a spray of magic, and started downward once more.

This time, her descent was much longer and darker, the stairwell windowless and narrow as it tunneled into the deep earth beneath the castle foundation. The air was damp and stale, smelling of long years of confinement and ageless dust. Her footsteps on the stone steps matched the sound of her breathing, quick and hurried. When this was finished, she thought, she would leave Paranor and go far away, taking Ahren with her so that they could build a life together free of everything that had gone before. It was what she would have done in the first place, had the Ard Rhys not poisoned Ahren against her. Ahren claimed Grianne had nothing to do with his dismissal of her, but Iridia knew better. His claim that he had never loved her, did not feel for her as she did for him, was a lie forged in the furnace of his anger at what *she*, who would always be the Ilse Witch, had told him. For that alone, she had deserved banishment to the Forbidding, and much worse.

At the bottom of the stairs, a rotunda formed a hub for a dozen passageways leading in different directions. Iridia chose the one from which the voice was calling, certain of its location, of its presence. Holding out the torch to chase back the darkness, she went down the passageway, a silent presence in a silent tomb. The catacombs were used infrequently, which had something to do with the past, with the history of the Keep, though Iridia had never cared enough to find out what that history was. It was the place she met with her coconspirators, but not a place she visited otherwise. It was enough that she would do so for the last time tonight.

A hundred feet down the corridor, a door stood open, the room beyond as black as pitch.

—I am here—

Iridia stepped inside, the torchlight flooding the room with its yellow glow. Her eyes searched swiftly. Four blank walls, a floor, and a ceiling. The room was empty.

"Where are you?" she asked, unable to keep the desperation from her voice.

—In the air, Iridia. In the ether you breathe. In darkness and in light. In all things. Close your eyes. Can you feel me—

She squeezed her eyes shut and exhaled slowly. It was true. She could feel his presence. He was there, all about her. "Yes," she whispered.

—It is time to give you what you were promised for helping me. To give you Ahren Elessedil, whole and complete again. To give you peace and love and joy. It is time, Iridia. Are you ready—

"Yes," she breathed, tears flowing once more, gratitude flooding through her. "Oh, please."

—Extinguish your torch and lay it on the floor—

She hesitated, not liking the prospect of being left in darkness. But her need for Ahren overcame her doubts, and she did as the voice had commanded. The torchlight went out and she was left standing in the heavy darkness.

—Close your eyes, Iridia. Stretch out your arms. I will come to you, into your embrace, no longer a voice, but a man. I will be him. For you, Iridia. Forever. Enfold me with your love and your desire. Accept me—

She would not have thought to do otherwise, though she still did not see how it could happen. But the persuasiveness of the voice was sufficient to make her believe. Again, she did as she was told. She closed her eyes and opened her arms.

Almost instantly, she felt a presence. It was only a faint sense of movement at first, a stirring of the air. Warmth followed, an infusion that spread through her like the flush of expectation she had experienced earlier. She felt a tingling, and her breath quickened at the prospect of what waited.

Then he was there, in her arms, Ahren Elessedil come back to life. Though she had never held him and did not know how it would feel, she knew at once that it was him. Her arms came about him gratefully, and she breathed in his smell and pressed her body against his. He responded at once, pliant and anxious, the part of her that was missing, the part that would make her whole.

"Ahren," she whispered.

He moved closer still, so close that it felt as if he were a part of her. She could feel them joining, becoming one. He was melting into her, entering her, becoming a part of her physically. She started in shock, then instinctively tried to resist what was happening. But it was too late, he was already fused to her as metals in a forge locked together to form a single skeletal frame.

Then the pain surged through her, so intense that when she began screaming she could not stop. Raw and sharp, pulsing with razors and knife points, it riddled her from head to foot, and her scream turned into a shriek that lasted until her voice gave out and her mind snapped.

Then she ceased to think or feel anything.

It was later that evening when Shadea a'Ru passed down the corridor of the north tower on her way to her chambers and encountered Iridia coming from the opposite direction. She approached the Elven sorceress warily, remembering how they had left things in the cold chamber earlier. One hand snapped free a dirk from the sheath bound to her wrist beneath her tunic sleeve. She had endured enough of Iridia's unpredictable behavior. If there was to be a confrontation, she wanted it to be done with quickly.

The other woman came right up to her, but there was no anger or resentment or challenge of any sort in her green eyes. Her perfect features were composed, and there was an air of new determination about her.

"I behaved poorly this afternoon," she said, coming to a stop several feet away. "I apologize."

Shadea was immediately suspicious. She didn't like the abrupt switch. It wasn't like Iridia to forgive so readily. Not her, not anyone. Nevertheless, she nodded agreeably. "We will put it behind us."

"That would be best for everyone," Iridia said as she turned away.

She walked past Shadea and continued down the hallway without looking back. Shadea stayed where she was, watching until the other was out of sight, all the time wondering what was going on.

TWENTY-EIGHT

They chose not to bury Ahren Elessedil's remains, but to burn them. A wetland was a poor place to dig a grave, and they had only their long knives to attempt the task. Besides, Khyber was not happy with the idea of leaving her uncle interred in a mud flat where rains and erosion might soon uncover him and leave him food for scavengers.

Working by light provided mostly from the still-burning swamp waters, they collected deadwood, piled it high on the mud bank where he had fought and died, and placed him on it. Khyber sang a Druid funeral song, one she had learned from her uncle, one that spoke of the purpose of a life well lived and an afterlife where hopes were fulfilled and rebirth possible. She used her magic to ignite the dry wood, and soon it was burning. They stood together, watching as it consumed her uncle's body, turning it to ash and smoke.

When it was finished, they moved into the trees and slept, exhausted physically and emotionally, not bothering to mount a

watch against the things that dwelled in the Slags. They shared a
sense of inevitability that night, that what would happen to them
was not within their control, that if their strongest member could
be taken from them so abruptly, their own efforts at protecting
themselves would make little difference.

They woke unharmed and in a better frame of mind, the trauma
of the previous day far enough behind them that they could think
about what was going to happen next. The day was typical of the
Slags, all grayness and mist and sunless, fetid air. The fires of
the funeral pyre and the doomed *Galaphile* were extinguished finally,
and only dark smears of ash remained to mark their passing. Looking
out over the bay, Pen caught sight of heavy ripples that indicated the
movement of something big beneath the dark surface. Life went on.

With nothing to eat or drink, the three companions huddled
down in the chilly dawn light to discuss what they would do.

"Perhaps we should think about going back," Tagwen offered
solemnly. "Don't misunderstand me. I'm not suggesting we give
up—just that we not continue on as we are. After all, we are in a
rather desperate situation. We are lost, grounded, and weaponless.
I know what Ahren told us to do, but it might not be the best
thing. We might be better off doing what I started out to do in
the first place—finding Penderrin's parents and seeking their help.
With Pen's father's magic and an airship, we will have a better
chance of getting to where we want to go."

To Pen's eyes, the Dwarf looked a wreck. His clothes were
hanging raggedly from his once stout frame, his face was haggard
and worn, and his eyes had a jumpy, nervous look to them. The
gruff, determined air he had brought with him to Patch Run had
vanished in the chase across the Lazareen and through the Slags.
There was more than a hint of desperation about him.

But, then, he might be describing any of them, Pen thought.

He need only look at his own reflection in the waters of the bay to see that was so.

"I don't know where my parents are," he said to the Dwarf. "I'm not sure we can find them."

"Besides, it would take as much effort to go back as to go on," Khyber pointed out. "At least out here we are safe from the Druids who hunt us. With the *Galaphile* destroyed, the closest enemies are eliminated. Unless we give ourselves away again, the rest can't find us once we're out of the area."

"Oh, they can find us, don't you doubt it!" Tagwen snapped. "They are resourceful and skilled. I should know. And Shadea a'Ru is a demon. She won't give up, even with the *Galaphile* gone. Maybe *especially* with it gone, since she will blame us for its destruction. And for Terek Molt's death."

Khyber glared at him. "Well, they won't find us right away. If we can get out of this swamp, we can find help among the Trolls. Didn't you say that Kermadec lives in the Taupo Rough country? Surely he will help us."

"He will help us if he is still alive, but given the way things are going, I wouldn't say that's at all certain!" Tagwen was not to be placated. "I don't know how you expect to find him when you don't know where you are yourself! And you say we will be all right if we don't use the Elfstones, but if we don't use the Stones, we might not find our way out of here! And remember this— Ahren Elessedil thought he wouldn't have to use the Elfstones, either, but he did have to, didn't he?"

He was nearly in tears, the tough old Dwarf, and for a moment it appeared he would break down completely. He looked away in embarrassment and frustration, then rose and stalked down to the edge of the bay, where he stood for a time looking out into the mist. Pen and Khyber exchanged glances, but said nothing.

When Tagwen returned, he was calm again, his rough features composed and determined. "You're right," he announced without preamble. "We should go on. Going back would be a mistake."

"Will Kermadec help us if we can find him?" Pen asked at once.

The Dwarf nodded. "He is devoted to the Ard Rhys. He will do whatever he can to help. He is a good and brave man."

"Then we have our plan," Khyber declared. "But we will be careful how we go, Tagwen," she assured the Dwarf. "We won't be careless. Uncle Ahren gave us a chance to complete this journey. We won't waste that gift."

"Then we'd better think about moving away from here right now," Pen declared. "If they can track us from our use of magic, they won't have much trouble finding us here. Not after the expenditure of magic used to destroy the *Galaphile*."

Khyber stood up. "Once we're back in the trees, we won't be so easy to track." She paused. "I just wish I knew how much farther we had to go."

"Then why don't you find out?" Pen asked. She stared at him. "Use the Elfstones. What difference does it make if you use them now? We've already given ourselves away. Before we set out, let's see where it is that we're going. Then maybe we won't have to use the Stones again."

"The boy is right," Tagwen said at once. "Go ahead. Let's see where we are."

They stood in a ragged group at the shore's edge while Khyber took out the Elfstones and balanced them in her hand. They stared at the glittering talismans for a moment, transfixed by their brightness and their promise. Without saying so, they were all thinking the same thing. So much depended on what the Stones revealed. If they were too deep in the Slags to avoid its snares and predators, then they might have to use the magic again, even if it gave them away. But if they were close to the wetland border, they might have a chance to escape undetected.

Khyber closed her fingers about the talismans and held them out in the direction of the sunrise. Long moments passed, and nothing happened.

"They're not responding," she said. Her voice was strained and rough. "I can't make them work."

"Don't be afraid, Khyber," Pen said.

"I'm not afraid!" she snapped.

"Yes, you are. But don't be. I'm frightened enough for the both of us."

She glanced over at him, saw the look on his face, and smiled in spite of herself. She dropped her arm to her side. "All right," she said. "Let me try again."

She took a deep, steadying breath, exhaled slowly, and held out the Stones. Her eyes closed. An instant later, the magic flared from her fist, gathered itself in a blaze of fire, and shot out into the gloom like a beast at hunt. Slicing through trees and brush and grass, through the whole of the Slags, it flared in sharp relief against a backdrop of hills leading into mountains, of green fields brightened by wildflowers, of streams and waterfalls, and of dazzling sunshine.

The picture shimmered bright and clear for a moment longer, then vanished as if it had never been, leaving them encased once more in mist and gloom. They stood looking off in the direction it had shown for a moment, savoring the memory, the promise, then looked at one another appraisingly.

"It's not all that far," Pen declared bravely, although in truth he had no idea how far it was. "We can make it."

"Of course, we can," Tagwen agreed, screwing up his worn countenance into a mask of resolve.

"It can't be more than another day," Khyber added, pocketing the Elfstones. "We can be there by sunset."

They began walking, turning back into the trees and leaving the mist-shrouded bay and its dark memories behind. It was slow going, their passage obstructed by fallen trees, heavy brush, and endless stretches of swamp water. They had to be especially careful of the latter because many hid patches of quicksand that would have swallowed them without a trace. Pen used his magic once more, reaching out to the life of the swamp to discover what it was thinking and doing. Though he couldn't see what he was hearing for the most part, he was able to detect the presence of small birds, rodents, insects, and even a smattering of water creatures. Each told him something of what was happening around them. He was able to discover more than once dangers that threatened. He was able to tell from moods and responses between species the paths they should follow and those they should avoid.

They walked all day, yet by sunset it felt as if they hadn't gone anywhere. Everything looked exactly the same as it had hours earlier. Nor was there any apparent end in sight, the gloom and mist and wetlands stretching on endlessly in all directions. If anything, the swamp had thickened and tightened about them, stealing away a little more of the light and air, eroding their hopes that they might get clear soon.

When they stopped for the night, Pen used his compass a final time to check their direction. It seemed as if they were going the right way, but he was beginning to wonder if the compass was working. His concerns were fostered in part by the way in which the light seemed not to change in any direction, the gloom and haze so thick that it was getting harder and harder to tell which way the sun was moving through the hidden sky.

"We might be lost," he admitted to them. "I can't be sure any more."

"We're not lost," Khyber insisted. "Tomorrow, we will be through."

But Pen wasn't convinced. He took the first watch and sat brooding while the others slept, replaying the events of the past few days in his mind, a nagging concern that he couldn't identify tugging at his already dwindling confidence. Something wasn't right about the way they were looking at things, but he couldn't put his finger on it. As the darkness deepened and the minutes slipped by, he found himself going further afield with his thinking, working his way back through the entire journey, from the moment Tagwen had first appeared with news of his aunt's disappearance. Remembering how he had been forced to flee his home triggered memories of his parents and made him aware of how much he missed them and wished they were with him. He had always been an independent sort, raised to be that way, but this was the farthest he had ever been from home. It was also the most threatened he had ever felt. He knew of the dangerous creatures that dwelled in the places he visited regularly on his skiff journeys, but most of those he was encountering now were entirely new. Some of them didn't even have a name.

And just like that, he realized what was bothering him. It was his inability to account for what had become of the mysterious hunter that had chased him through the streets of Anatcherae on the night he had fled Terek Molt.

He took a long moment to think it through. His pursuer had come after him outside Fisherman's Lie, when the little company had fled into the streets to reach the safety of the *Skatelow*. A man had died right in front of him, killed by a dagger thrown from the rooftops and intended for him. During all of this, he had caught only brief glimpses of the wielder, just enough to suggest it wasn't entirely human.

What had happened to it?

It would be comforting to think that it had died aboard the *Galaphile*, consumed in the inferno that had claimed the ship, the Gnome Hunters, and Terek Molt. But Pen didn't think that was what had happened. It didn't feel right to him. The thing that had chased him through the streets wouldn't have been caught off guard like that. If it was still with Terek Molt at the time the *Galaphile* had found them, it would have been off the ship and stalking him anew. It would have survived.

It would be out there now.

In spite of the fact that he was virtually certain it wasn't, he looked around cautiously, peering into the darkness as if something might reveal itself. He even took time to read his magic's response to the sounds of the night creatures surrounding him, to the insects and birds and beasts that inhabited the swamp gloom, searching for anything that would warn him of danger. When he had satisfied himself that he was not threatened, that the hunter he feared might be lurking out there, invisible and deadly, was not, he took a deep breath and exhaled softly, feeling comforted for the moment, at least.

He sat listening, nevertheless, through the rest of his watch.

When his watch was finished, he took a long time falling asleep.

On waking the following morning, Pen said nothing to Khyber and Tagwen of his concerns. There was nothing to be gained by doing so. Everyone was already on edge, and adding to the tension could not help the situation. Besides, the hunter of Anatcherae's dark streets might have been a denizen of the port city rather than a tool of Terek Molt's. If the hunter had been the Druid's creature, then it stood to reason that it would have been used in tracking them down and disposing of them long since. The Druid wouldn't have confronted them himself when he had his creature to do the job for him.

It was solid reasoning, but it didn't make Pen feel any better and in the end it didn't convince him that his problems with his mysterious enemy were finished. Just because he couldn't account for its whereabouts didn't mean he was rid of it. But he kept that unsettling thought to himself, knowing that what mattered just then was getting clear of the Slags.

They worked all day at doing so, picking their way through a quagmire of tangled roots, choking reeds, quicksand, sinkholes, and mud flats thick with biting insects and gnats. They still hadn't had anything to eat or drink since they had lost their raft in the attack of those vines, and the lack of nourishment was beginning to tell. Tagwen was experiencing stomach cramps, Khyber was fighting off dizzy spells, and Pen felt feverish. All three were weaker, and progress had slowed noticeably. If they didn't find food and drink soon, they were going to be in serious trouble.

It was midafternoon when they entered a sprawling wilderness of scrub-choked trees that stretched in both directions until it could no longer be seen. Threaded by tendrils of mist and layered with shadows, the woods were so vast that there wasn't any hope of finding a way around. In any case, they were too exhausted to do anything but go forward, and so they did. Pushing into the tangle, they soon found themselves forced to proceed in single file, the trees grown so close together and the spaces between so clogged with brambles and scrub that any other formation was impossible. Weaving between the trunks and stalks, they slogged through pools of swamp water and sucking mud, using roots and limbs for handholds. Overhead, flying squirrels and birds darted through the dank foliage, and on the uncertain ground snakes slithered and rodents scurried in silent, dark flashes. Now and then, they caught glimpses of larger creatures sliding ridge-backed and deadly through deeper water.

"I thought it couldn't get any worse," Tagwen grumbled at one point, his beard a nest of brambles. "Is there any end to this place?"

As they continued on, Pen began to worry about what would happen if they were caught in that tangle when darkness fell. If that happened, they would have to climb a tree and spend the night aloft. He didn't care for the prospect of watching the limbs for big snakes all night, but he didn't see that they would have any alternative. He began to make promises to himself about the sort of life he would lead if they could just reach better ground before dark.

It was gratifying when they did, if only momentarily. They slogged out of a heavy stretch of mud-soaked grasses and reeds and climbed an embankment to what seemed to be an island in the midst of the swamp, a low forestland amid the damp. Pen, leading the way, heaved a sigh of relief as he stepped onto the first solid ground he had felt beneath his feet in days, then immediately froze.

Directly to his left, not ten yards away, was the biggest moor cat he had ever seen in his life. He was not unfamiliar with moor cats, so coming on one unexpectedly was not in and of itself shocking. But that particular cat froze him in his tracks and sent a lurch through his stomach that he felt all the way to his toes. For starters, it was huge—not just big in the way of all moor cats, but gigantic. It wasn't lean and sleek; it was muscled and burly, a veteran of battles that had left its mottled, dark body crisscrossed with scars. It loomed up before him like a Koden gone down on all fours, the thick ruff around its neck giving it a bearish look. Its face was striking, as well, marked with a black band across its eyes that made it look as if it was wearing a mask.

Pen hadn't sensed it, hadn't detected it at all. He was searching for things that might threaten them, connected to the life around him, and still he hadn't known the cat was there. It must have been waiting for them, biding its time, letting them come to it.

Seeing Pen, the moor cat pricked its ears forward and its luminous eyes widened into amber lanterns. It made a coughing sound, deep and booming, and instantly the entire swamp went still.

Khyber Elessedil gave a strangled gasp. "Shades," she managed to whisper.

Pen's eyes were locked on the moor cat, trying to read its intentions. It didn't seem to have any, mostly finding them curious. Suddenly its eyes narrowed and its muzzle drew back in warning, and Pen glanced back to find Khyber slowly withdrawing the pouch with the Elfstones from her pocket.

"Put those away!" he hissed at her. "They're useless anyway!"

She hesitated. Then, slowly, the Elfstones disappeared back into her clothing. Flushed and angry, she glared at him. "I hope you have a better plan, Penderrin!"

Tagwen looked as if he hoped the same thing, but the truth was Pen didn't have a plan at all beyond trying to avoid a confrontation. It appeared that the cat and the humans each intended to go through the same patch of ground. One or the other was going to have to give way.

The big cat growled, more a grunt than a cough. Though Pen

could tell it was not intended as a threatening sound, it came across as one nevertheless, causing his companions to back away hurriedly. The boy motioned for them to stand their ground, not to make any movements that suggested they were trying to run. Movements of that sort would bring the moor cat down on them instantly. The trick was to appear unafraid, but not threatening. A neat trick, if they could figure out how to make it work.

The moor cat was growing restless, its huge head lowering to sniff the ground expectantly.

Better try something, Pen thought.

Relying on his magic to guide him, he made a rough, low coughing sound at the cat, a sound meant to communicate his intentions, one he knew instinctively would be understood. The moor cat straightened immediately, head lifting, eyes bright.

"What are you doing?" Khyber hissed at him.

Pen wasn't sure, but it seemed to be working. He made a few more sounds, all of them nonspecific but indicative of his desire to be friendly. *We're no threat,* he was saying to the cat. *We're just like you, even if we look and smell a little different.*

Intrigued, the moor cat answered with a series of huffing noises that came from deep within its throat. Pen was working furiously now, taking in the sounds and translating them into words and phrases, into deciphering the nature of the big animal's interest in them. The moor cat wanted reassurance that Pen and his companions were passing through to other places and had no intention of trying to usurp its territory. There was an unmistakable challenge in the sounds, a testing for antagonistic intent. Pen responded at once, doing his best to create a semblance of the coughing sounds, demonstrating that he and his companions were on their way to their own home, that a challenge to the moor cat's territory was of no interest.

He acted instinctively, almost without thinking about what he was doing. His magic guided him, leading him to say and do what was needed to connect with the moor cat. He was surprised by how easily the sounds came to him, at the certainty he had of what they were communicating to the cat. The huge beast seemed to be listening to him.

"Is he actually talking with that beast?" Tagwen whispered to Khyber.

"Shhhh!" was her quick, irritated response.

Then all of a sudden the moor cat started toward Pen, its great head swinging from side to side, its huge eyes gleaming. It stopped right in front of him and leaned in to sniff his face and then his body. It was so big it stood eye to eye with him, equal in height but dominant in every other respect. Pen stood perfectly still, frozen with shock and fright. Running or fighting never entered his mind. He swallowed hard and closed his eyes, letting the cat explore him, feeling the heat of its breath on his skin, hearing the sound of its breathing.

Finally, the cat stepped away, satisfied. It circled back the way it had come, then turned in the direction it had been going and disappeared into the trees without even a glance in their direction, and was gone.

Pen and his companions stood statue-still for long minutes, waiting for it to return. When at last it became apparent that it did not intend to, Pen exhaled heavily and looked from Khyber to Tagwen. The expressions on their faces almost certainly mirrored the one on his own, a mixture of heart-stopping awe and deep relief. With one hand he brushed nervously at his mop of reddish hair, which was finally beginning to grow out again, and realized he was coated with sweat.

"I don't care ever to have that experience again," Tagwen declared, doing his best to keep his voice from shaking. "Ever."

Khyber glanced in the direction of the departed moor cat. "We need to go that way, too," she pointed out.

Pen nodded. "Yes, we do."

Tagwen stared at them, horror-stricken, then straightened very deliberately. "Very well. But let's rest up a bit before we do."

And before they could object, he sat down quickly.

TWENTY-NINE

They trooped on for the remainder of the afternoon, fighting through scrub-growth woods and a new stretch of swamp laced with mud holes and waterways, everything encased in mist and gloom and crosshatched with shadows. The light lasted for another three hours and then began to fail rapidly. Still, they slogged ahead, reduced to putting one foot in front of the other, to pushing on when it would have been much easier not to.

It was almost too dark to see when Khyber realized that the feel of the ground had changed and the air no longer smelled of damp and rot but of grass and leaves. She stopped abruptly, causing Tagwen, who was walking behind her with his head down, to bump into her. Ahead, Pen heard the sudden oaths and quick apologies and turned around to see what was happening.

"We're out of the Slags," Khyber announced, still not quite believing it. "Look around. We're out."

She insisted they stop for the night, so bone weary and mentally exhausted from the events of the past few days, so in need of sleep that she barely managed to find a patch of soft grass within a stand of oaks before she was asleep. Her last memory was of the sky, empty for the first time in days of mist and clouds, clear and bright with moonglow and stars.

She dreamed that night of her uncle, a shadowy figure who called to her in words she could not quite make out from a place she could not quite reach. She spent her dream trying and failing to get close enough to discover what he was saying. The dream world was shadowy and uneven in its feel, the landscape misty and changing. It was filled with dark creatures that hovered close without ever quite coming into view. It was a place she did not want to be, and she was grateful when she woke the next morning to bright sunlight and blue sky.

Pen was already awake and returned from foraging for food, and it was the cooking fire he had built that brought her out of her dream. Somehow, the boy had snared a rabbit, which he was skinning, dug up some root vegetables, and picked several handfuls of berries. Added to the fresh stream water he had collected, it made the best meal Khyber could remember in years and gave her a welcome and much needed sense of renewal.

They set out shortly after, heading east and north into the hilly country that fronted the Charnals, determined to find Taupo Rough and the Troll Maturen, Kermadec. None of them had ever been in that part of the world or knew enough about it to be able to discern much more than the general direction they should take. Taupo Rough lay at the foot of the mountains somewhere north of the Slags. The best they could do was to use the pocket compass and head in that direction, trusting that sooner or later they would come across someone to help them. The Rock Trolls were a tribal people and there was some animosity between tribes, but the Trolls were not at war with the other Races just then and there was no reason to think they posed a threat to travelers in their country. At least, that was what Khyber hoped.

She gave it some thought on setting out, but they had little choice in the matter and therefore little reason to dwell on the unpleasant possibilities if they were wrong. Tagwen seemed to think that whatever Rock Trolls they encountered would be of help once they heard Kermadec's name. Maybe that was so. Khyber was so grateful to be clear of the Slags that she was willing to risk almost anything. Even the simple fact of no longer being shrouded by the wetland's gloom and mist gave her a large measure of relief.

But it was more than that, of course. It was the leaving behind of the place in which Ahren Elessedil had died. It was the sense that maybe she could come to terms with his death if she could put time and distance between herself and its memory. She had persuaded herself to continue on without him, but accepting that he was really gone was much more difficult. Losing him had left her devastated. He had been more than an uncle to her; he had been the father she had lost when she was still a child. He had been her confidant and her best and most dependable friend. As compensation for her anguish, she told herself that he was still there, a spirit presence, and that he would look out for her in death even as he had in life. It was wishful thinking, but shades were real and sometimes they helped the living, and she needed to think it could happen here because she had serious doubts about herself. She did not believe that her meager talents with Druid magic were going to be enough to see them through the remainder of their journey, no matter what reassurances Ahren had offered her. Even her use of the Elfstones was suspect. She had managed to bring the magic to bear in the battle against Terek Molt, but that had been facilitated by her uncle's sacrifice. She still shivered at the memory of the Elfstone power coursing through her, vast and unchecked, and she did not know that she could make herself summon it again, even to defend herself. In truth, she did not know what she might do if she was threatened, and the uncertainty could prove as dangerous as the threat itself. It was one thing to talk as if she possessed both resolve and confidence, but it was something else again to demonstrate it. She wished she had a way of testing herself. But she didn't, and that was that.

They walked on through the morning, and she felt a little better for doing so. Time and distance helped to blunt her sadness if not her uncertainty. Given the nature of their journey thus far, she would take what she could get.

"Did you see him?" Pen asked her when they stopped at midday to drink from a stream and to eat what remained of the roots the boy had foraged that morning.

She stared at him. "See who?"

"The cat. It's tracking us."

"The moor cat?"

Tagwen, sitting a little bit farther away, turned at once. His eyes were big and frightened. "Why would it be doing that? Is it hunting us?"

Pen shook his head. "I don't think so. But it is definitely following us. I saw it several times, back in the trees, trying to keep out of sight, following a course parallel to our own. I think it's just interested."

"Interested?" the Dwarf croaked.

"You can't mistake that masked face," Pen went on, oblivious to the other's look of terror. He grinned suddenly at Khyber, a little boy about to share a secret. "I've decided to call it Bandit. It looks like one, doesn't it?"

Khyber didn't care what the moor cat looked like, nor did she care for the idea of it tracking them into the mountains. She had always thought moor cats pretty much stayed in the swamps and forests and clear of the higher elevations. She hoped theirs would lose interest as they climbed.

They trekked on through the remainder of the day, through hill country dotted with woods and crisscrossed by streams that pooled in lakes at the lower elevations, bright mirrors reflecting sunlight and clouds. The hours drifted away, and although they covered a fair amount of ground, they did not encounter any of the region's inhabitants. Darkness began to fall and the shadows of the trees to lengthen about them, and still they had not seen a single Troll.

"Is that moor cat still out there?" Khyber asked Pen at one point.

"Oh, sure," the boy answered at once. "Still watching us, sort of like a stray dog. Do you want me to call it over?"

They made camp in the lee of a forested bluff, finding shelter in a grove of pine by a stream that tumbled down out of the rocks. Behind them, the hill country they had trekked through all day sloped gently away through woods and grasslands until it disappeared into the twilight shadows. Although Pen made a valiant effort to catch something, he was unsuccessful; there was nothing to eat. They drank stream water and chewed strips of bark from a small fig tree.

"Don't worry," Pen reassured his companions. "I'll go hunting at sunrise. I'll catch something."

They sat back to watch the stars come out, listening to the silence fill with night sounds. No one spoke. Khyber felt an emptiness that extended from the darkness down into her heart. She could not put a name to it, but it was there nevertheless. After a moment, she rose and walked off into the trees, wanting to be alone in case she cried. She felt so unbearably sad that she could hardly manage to keep from breaking down. The feeling had come over her insidiously, as if to remind her of how badly things had gone for them and how desperate their circumstances were. She might argue that they were all right, that they would find their way, but it wasn't what she felt. What she felt was utter abandonment and complete hopelessness. No matter what they tried or where they went, things would never get any better for them. They would struggle, but in the end they would fail.

Away from her companions, unable to help herself, she sat down and cried, bursting into tears all at once. She wished she had never come on the journey. She wished she had never left home. Everything that had happened was because of her insistence on looking for a stupid tree that Pen thought he had been sent to find but might well have simply dreamed up. Uncle Ahren was dead because of her intractability and her foolish, selfish need to find a way out of her pointless life. Well, she had accomplished her goal. She could never go back to Arborlon, never go home again. Not after stealing the Elfstones. Not after letting her uncle die. She bore the burden of her guilt like a fifty-pound weight slung across her shoulders, and she had nowhere to set it down. She hated herself.

In the midst of her silent diatribe, she realized that someone was looking at her.

Or something.

Huge, lantern eyes peered at her from out of the blackness. It was the moor cat.

"Get out of here!" she snapped in fury, not stopping to think about what she was doing.

The eyes stayed where they were. She glared at them, hating that the cat was watching her, that it had seen her break down and cry, that it had caught her at her worst. For no reason that made any sense at all, she was embarrassed by it. Even if it was only an animal that had witnessed it, her behavior made her feel foolish. She took several deep breaths to steady herself and sat back. The cat wasn't going to move until it felt like it, so there wasn't much point in railing at it. She found herself wondering once again what it was doing there. Curiosity, Pen had thought. Could be. She kissed at it, whispered a few words of greeting, and gave it a wave. The cat stared without blinking or moving.

Then all at once, it was gone again. Like smoke caught in the wind, it simply disappeared. She waited a moment to be sure, then rose and walked back to where Pen and Tagwen were already asleep. The first watch was hers, it seemed. Just as well since she wasn't at all tired. She sat down next to them and wrapped her arms about her knees. It was chilly so high up, much more so than in the Slags. She wished she had a blanket. Maybe they could find supplies in the morning. There had to be a settlement somewhere close by.

With her legs drawn up to her chest and her chin resting on her knees, she listened to the sounds of Pen and Tagwen breathing and stared out into the night.

Intending to wake one of her companions to share the watch, but failing to do so, she dozed off sometime after midnight. When she came awake again, it was with the sudden and frightening realization that things were not as they should be. It wasn't the silence or the darkness or even the sound of the wind rustling the leaves like old parchment. What caught her attention as her eyes snapped open and her head jerked up was the dark movement that crept like a stain across the forest earth in front of her. For a moment, she thought it was alive, and leapt to her feet, backing away instinctively. But then she recognized its flat, fragmented shape and realized it was a shadow cast from something passing overhead.

She looked up and saw the *Skatelow*.

She couldn't believe it at first, thinking that she must be mistaken, that her eyes were playing tricks on her. It wasn't possible that the *Skatelow* could be there, flying those skies, so many miles east of where it should be. But the shape was so distinctive that Khyber quickly accepted that it was her, come after them for a reason that was not immediately apparent. For come after them she had, the Elven girl reasoned, or she would not be here at all.

Particularly since she was flying straight toward them.

But there was something not quite right about her, a look to her that was foreign and vaguely frightening. She carried only her mainsail; its canvas billowed out in the rush of the wind, yet there were yards of rigging stretched bare and stark from decking to spars like spiderwebbing.

Khyber stared, transfixed, not yet fully awake and not yet come to terms with what she was seeing.

The *Skatelow* passed overhead and when she had gone a short distance beyond where the Elven girl stood watching, somewhere above the bluff east, she wheeled back and slid across the star-scattered firmament a second time, more slowly, as if searching.

Then, abruptly, she started to come down, making a slow and cautious descent toward the grasslands that lay just beyond the woods in which Khyber and her companions slept. As she did so, Khyber saw what she had missed before. Three ropes dangled in a ragged line from the yardarm, pulled taut by the weight of the bodies attached.

"Pen!" Khyber hissed, reaching down quickly to shake the boy awake, galvanized by sudden shock and a rush of fear.

Penderrin Ohmsford jerked upright at once, eyes darting in all directions at once. "What is it?"

Wordlessly, she hauled him to his feet and pointed, leaving Tagwen still stretched out and asleep at her feet. Together, they watched the *Skatelow* settle toward the grasslands, a ghost ship dark and ragged against the moonlit sky, the bodies at the ends of the ropes swaying like gourds from vines. The light caught those bodies clearly by then, illuminating them sufficiently for Khyber to identify Gar Hatch and his crewmen, faces empty, mouths hanging open, eyes wide and staring. There was a wizened, drawn cast to their features, as if the juices had been drained from them, leaving only skin and bones.

"What's happened?" Pen breathed.

Then his fingers tightened sharply about her arm, and he pointed. She saw it at once. Cinnaminson stood in the pilot box, a thin, frail figure against the skyline, her head lifted into the wind, her clothing whipping against her body, her arms hanging limply at her sides. One end of a chain was attached to a collar about her neck; the other was wound about the pilot box railing.

Khyber scanned the decks of the sloop from end to end, but no one else was visible. No one was sailing the airship, no one acting as Captain and crew, no one visible aboard save the three dead men and the chained girl.

Then Khyber saw something move across the billowing mainsail, high up in the rigging, a dark shadow caught in a swath of moonlight. The shadow skittered down the lines like a spider over its webbing, limbs outstretched and crooked as it swung from strand to strand. Nothing more of it was visible; its head and body were cloaked and hooded, its features hidden. It was there for just an instant, then gone, disappeared behind the sail and back into the shadows.

Khyber took a deep breath. It was the thing that had chased

them through the streets of Anatcherae—the thing that had tried to kill Pen.

A shiver ran down Khyber's back when Cinnaminson turned her head slightly in their direction, as if seeing them as clearly as they saw her. In that instant, her features were clearly revealed,and such anguish and horror were mirrored there that Khyber went cold all the way to her bones. Then the Rover girl looked away again and pointed north. The thing that hung from the mainmast moved quickly in response, leaping through the rigging, changing the set of the sail, the tautness of the radian draws, and thereby the direction of the airship. The *Skatelow* began to lift away again, turning north in the direction Cinnaminson had pointed. The crooked-legged thing darted back across the moonlight, then fastened itself in place against the mast, hunching down like a huge lizard on a pole.

Seconds later, the airship disappeared behind the rise of the bluff, and the sky was empty again.

In the dark aftermath, Khyber exhaled sharply and exchanged a hurried look with Pen. Then she jumped in fright as Tagwen stood up suddenly next to her, rubbing at his bleary eyes. "What's wrong?" he asked.

"Don't do that again!" she snapped furiously, her hands shaking.

They told him what they had seen, pointing north at the empty sky. A look of disbelief crossed his rough features, and he shook his head, blinking away the last of his sleep. "Are you certain of this? You didn't dream it? It wasn't just the clouds?"

"It's tracking us," Pen answered, his voice dismal and lost-sounding. "It's killed Gar Hatch and his Rover cousins, and now it's using Cinnaminson to hunt us."

"But how did it get aboard the *Skatelow*?"

No one could answer him. Khyber stared at the empty sky,

trying to reason it through. Was there a connection between the creature and the Druids? Could it have gotten aboard the *Skatelow* while the *Galaphile* had the Rover airship in tow? That would mean Terek Molt had deliberately lied to them about sending the *Skatelow* safely on her way. But why do that? For that matter, why bother to put the creature aboard the *Skatelow* at all if the Druid intended to hunt Penderrin on his own anyway?

Whatever the answer, someone was going to an awful lot of trouble to prevent the boy from attempting to rescue his aunt. So someone must think he had a very good chance of succeeding, even if the boy himself thought he had very little. It was an intriguing conclusion, and it gave her unexpected reason for hope.

Pen was staring at her. "Do you think the Elfstones could be used against whatever's got Cinnaminson?"

She gave him a doubtful look. "We don't even know what it is, Pen. It might be human, and the Elfstones would be useless."

"It doesn't look it."

"Whatever it is, we're not going to fight it if we don't have to." She motioned toward the bluff. "Let's get out of here. We can stop and eat when it gets light. I don't want to chance it coming back again."

Pen stood his ground, his mouth a tight line. "Did you see the way she looked at us?"

Khyber hesitated.

"She saw us. She knew we were here. Yet she turned the ship the other way." His voice was shaking. "She's being made to track us, Khyber. Maybe her life depends on whether or not that thing finds us. Yet she steered it away. She saved us."

Tagwen shook his bearded head. "You don't know that, young Pen. You might be mistaken."

The boy kept staring at Khyber. She had a sinking feeling in her stomach as she realized what he was about to ask. She had to stop him, even if it meant lying to him about what she had seen. But she could not bring herself to do that. That was the coward's way out. Ahren would not have lied in that situation. He would have told Pen the truth.

"We can't do this," she said.

"We have to!" he snapped. His face had an angry, almost furious look. "She saved us, Khyber! Now we have to save her!"

"What are you talking about?" Tagwen demanded. "Save who?"

"She's not our concern," Khyber pressed. "Our concern is with your aunt, the Ard Rhys."

"Our concern is with whoever needs our help! What's wrong with you?"

They faced each other in stony silence. Even Tagwen had gone quiet, looking quickly from one face to the other.

"We don't have any way of saving her," Khyber said finally. "We don't know anything about that creature, nothing about what it will take to overcome it. If we guess wrong, we'll all be dead."

Pen straightened and looked off to the north. "I'm going, whether you go with me or not. I'm not leaving her. I have to live with myself when this is over. I can't do that if something happens to her that I might have prevented." He glanced back at her, the angry look suddenly pleading. "She isn't the enemy, Khyber."

"I know that."

"Then help me."

She stared at him without answering.

"Khyber, I'm begging you."

He wasn't asking Tagwen; he was asking her. With Ahren Elessedil dead, she'd become the unofficial leader. She was the one with the Elfstones and the magic. She was the one with the lore. She thought about the choices she had made on the journey and how badly many of them had turned out. If she made the wrong

lock Lord. Yet the memory of them haunted her, voices whispering at the back of her thoughts, damp fingers trailing lightly across
her unprotected skin, an insidious presence.

The sun was rising, turning the eastern horizon the color of
ashes, gray and damp against the departing night. Another day of
low clouds and threatening skies. Another day of colorless gloom.
She felt her already battered spirits sink at the prospect. She
wanted out of this miserable place, out of this world of savagery
and despair. She pondered on the words of Brona's shade. *A boy
is coming.* The pronouncement confounded her, no matter how
often she repeated the words in her mind. What boy? Why a boy
in the first place? It made no sense to her, and she kept thinking that it must be a puzzle of some sort, the secret to which she
must find a way to unlock. Shades were famous for speaking in riddles, for teasing with half-truths. Perhaps that was what had happened here.

She stopped for a moment and closed her eyes, feeling dizzy
and weak. Her encounter with the Warlock Lord's shade had left
her battered of mind and body, light-headed and unsteady. She
could feel an aching not only in her muscles and joints, but also
in her heart. Just standing in the presence of the shade had left
her sickened. Its poison had permeated the air she breathed and
the ground she walked. It had infused the entire valley, though she
had not been aware of it until now. Evil—in its rawest, most lethal
form—had infected her. Though she had resisted the Warlock
Lord's offer to embrace it, it had claimed her anyway. She wouldn't
die from it, she thought, but she would be a long time ridding herself of its feel.

The dizziness passed, and she walked on. A boy, she kept
thinking. And she must wait for him. She could do nothing from
this end, nothing that would set her free. She did not believe
it; there was always something you could do to help yourself in

any situation. There was always more than one way in or out of any place, even this one. She need only find what it was. But even as she told herself it was so, she found reason to doubt the words. No one—until now—had ever found a way out of the Forbidding, not after thousands of years. No one had ever found a way in, once the wall of magic was set in place. It was a prison that did not allow for escape.

It was light by the time she reached the base of the mountains: the same sooty gray light that seemed to mark every day, the clouds slung low against the earth, fused with mist and darkened by the threat of rain. Weka Dart was sitting on a rock at the trailhead, chin in his hands, looking south across the flats, but he leapt to his feet on hearing her approach and was waiting eagerly as she came up to him.

"I thought you weren't coming back, Straken," he announced, not bothering to hide the relief in his voice. "That shade, so terrible, so threatening! It didn't want you?"

She shook her head. "Nor you, so you needn't have run away."

He bristled with indignation. "I didn't run! I chose to wait for you here!" His cunning features tightened as he prepared to lie. "I realized that you could not afford to be disturbed during your summoning and decided to come back down here to keep watch against . . . whatever might intrude." He spit. "It worked, didn't it? Were you bothered in any way? Hah! I thought as much!"

She almost laughed. The truth wasn't in the little Ulk Bog, but she didn't find herself angry or even disappointed. It was simply his nature, and there was no point in hoping for anything else. Candor was not a quality she was likely to see much of in Weka Dart.

"If I had thought you needed protection from that shade, if I had not believed you to be a Straken of great power and experience, I would have stayed to see that you were kept safe!" he con-tinued hurriedly, clearly not knowing when to stop. "But since there was no reason for worry, I came down here, where I knew I could be of more use to you. Tell me. What shade was it you spoke with?"

She sighed. "A warlock of immense power."

"But its power was no greater than yours or you would not have dared summon it. What did it tell you?"

She sat down next to him. "It told me I must go back to where you found me."

Instantly, his demeanor changed. "No, no!" he insisted at once. "You mustn't go back there!"

She stared at him in surprise. His distress was reflected on his rough features, revealed by the way the furrows on his brow deep-ened and knotted and his mouth tightened.

He seemed to realize he had overreacted. "What I mean to say is that you've already barely escaped a Dracha. What reason would you have to risk another encounter? I thought we had decided we would go to . . . I thought . . ."

He trailed off. "What did we decide, exactly? Why did we come here? You never said."

She nodded, amused by his confusion as much as troubled by his distress. "We came here so that I could speak with a shade, Weka Dart. I was not given a choice as to which one."

The Ulk Bog nodded eagerly. "But you did speak with one. What did you ask it? Why did it tell you to go back to where you had come from? What was its reason for doing so? It must be try-ing to trick you, perhaps to see you hurt!"

She considered her answer carefully. "I don't think it wants me hurt. Not in the way you suggest. What I asked was how to find my way home again."

Weka Dart bounded up from the rock to face her. "But you won't reach your home from there! You were lost already when I found you! Anyway, that place is too dangerous! There are dragons everywhere, some worse than that Dracha you encountered!" He was practically jumping up and down now, his hands balled into fists. "Why do you have to go back there to find your way home? Can't you find it from somewhere else?"

She shook her head, watching him carefully. "No, I can't. Why are you so upset? Are you frightened for yourself? If so, don't come with me. I can find my own way. Go west, where you were headed when you met me."

"I don't want to go west!" He practically screamed the words at her. "I want to stay with you!"

"Well, if you want to stay with me, you have to go back to where you found me. What's wrong with you? Are you afraid I can't protect you from those hunting you? Is that what this is all about?"

He flew at her in a rage, catching himself just before he got within reach, wheeling away again, then stamping the earth with both feet until she thought he was in danger of breaking his legs. "Aren't you listening to me?" he screamed at her. "Don't you believe me? You can't go back there!"

She came to her feet, ready for another attack. "Are you coming with me or not? Make up your mind."

He hissed at her like a snake, his face twisted into a grotesque mask, and his fingers extended like claws. She was so astounded by the transformation that for a moment she thought she had better summon the magic and immobilize him before he lost all control. But then he seemed to get hold of himself, going so still that he was frozen in his bizarrely aggressive pose. He took a deep breath, blew it out, wrenched his fiery gaze away from her and directed it out onto the flats.

"Do what you want, Grianne of the foolish heart," he said quietly. "Go to whatever doom awaits you, whatever fate. But I will not be caught up in the net, as well. No, I will not come with you."

Without another word, he stalked away, moving off at a rapid pace, no longer darting from side to side as he had done all the way there, but proceeding straight ahead, south into the Pashanon. She watched him incredulously, not quite believing he was giving up so easily, certain he would turn around and come back after he had gotten far enough away to make his point.

But he did not turn around or come back. He kept walking, and she kept watching him until he was out of sight.

She found a stream from which to drink, then began retracing her steps west. She was near exhaustion from her encounter with the shade of Brona, but she didn't think she should try to sleep until she reached less open country. She was hungry, as well, but as usual there was no food to be found. She thought she might find some ground roots when she reached the forests again, but there was no way to be certain. Grudgingly, she admitted that having Weka Dart along would have solved the problem, but the Ulk Bog just wasn't worth the trouble. It wasn't entirely his fault, of course. He couldn't understand what she was trying to do, and that frustrated him. It was better that he was gone.

Nevertheless, she couldn't help puzzling over his extreme reluctance to return to where he had found her. He was adamant about avoiding that place, and she thought there was more to it than his fear of encountering the tribal members he had fled. Something else was going on, something he was keeping to himself. Had she wanted to, she could have used her magic to force it out of him, but she no longer did things like that just to satisfy her curiosity. That approach to problem solving belonged to the Ilse Witch, and she was careful to keep it in the past.

Her trek, though across open, mostly unencumbered ground, quickly tired her, and by midday she was having trouble concentrating. The oppressive grayness closed about her in a deep gloom, and tracking the sun through the screen of clouds took more than a little effort. Sometimes, there was no indication of where it was in the sky, and she could only guess at its progress. Sometimes, she felt as if there were no sun at all.

It was wearing on her, this prison to which she had been consigned. It was breaking down her confidence and her determination. The erosion was incremental, but she could feel it happening. Even the prospect of rescue seemed remote and gave her no real encouragement. Too much relied on chance and the efforts of others. She didn't like that. She had never trusted either.

She was approaching the hill country where they had encountered the Furies two days earlier, and she decided to turn north toward the mountains again. Her memories of the death of that ogre were too fresh to ignore, and she thought that if she stayed close to the base of the cliffs, she might have better luck escaping notice. She didn't know enough about Furies to have a clear idea of how to avoid them, but she suspected that staying out in the open was not wise. Better to take her chances where there was a chance for finding cover if the need arose.

Her choice yielded unexpected benefits. She found fresh water and an odd tree that bore a round orange and yellow fruit that, while bitter, was edible. She ate the fruit, sitting by the stream in the shadow of the tree and looking out into the blighted landscape. She felt light-headed and heavy-eyed afterwards, a condition she attributed to lack of rest. She would feel better by the next morning. At least, she reminded herself, she was still alive.

Did any of those she had left behind believe her so? Or did they think her dead and gone?

She took a moment to picture what it must have been like when she disappeared. Tagwen and Kermadec would have been frantic, but there would have been nothing they could do. Nothing anyone could do, the Druids included. Only a handful, at most, knew what had really happened, those few who had orchestrated her imprisonment. But how much did they understand of what they had done? Not as much as they thought, perhaps. The shade of the Warlock Lord had called them pawns. It was the creature from the Forbidding who controlled them all.

A creature of immense power and great cunning, an enemy perhaps even more dangerous than the Morgawr, it had found a way to reach across the barrier of the Forbidding and subvert at least one of her Druids to its cause. It had tricked that Druid into helping it make possible the exchange of an Ard Rhys for a monster. Perhaps she had been party to the effort, as well. It was possible that her journey to the ruins of the Skull Kingdom with Kermadec was prompted by the thing's need to connect with her. It was possible she had been lured there to make that happen. She could remember the malevolent, dark look of it when it had shown itself. She could still feel the evil that emanated from it. It was not difficult to believe that it had gained a hold over her just from that single, brief encounter.

What did it intend to do, there in the Four Lands, outside the Forbidding for the first time in thousands of years? That it had escaped would not be enough. It was after something more.

Before she set out again, she used her magic to probe the surrounding countryside. It was a precaution, nothing more. She hadn't seen anything move all day, not even in the sky. She felt alone in the world, and the thought was immensely depressing because for all intents and purposes, that was exactly what she was. It didn't make any difference who or what she encountered;

the best she could hope for was another Weka Dart. Everything locked within the Forbidding was a potential enemy, and that wasn't going to change.

She walked on through the remainder of the afternoon without incident, and her spirits lifted marginally. Perhaps she would find a way out of this situation in spite of her doubts. Perhaps someone really was coming to rescue her.

Nightfall was approaching when she heard a strange metallic chirp that reminded her of birdsong. She was so surprised by the sound that she stopped where she was and listened until she heard it again, then started to walk in the direction from which it had come, curious. She reached a grove of shaggy, moss-grown trees when she heard it a third time and saw a flash of something bright red within the shadows. She didn't care for the sickly color of the gnarled trunks, almost a fire-scorched black and gray, or for the way in which the moss draped the limbs like a badly torn shroud, but the sound and the flash of red were simply too intriguing to ignore.

She moved into the grove warily, and almost at once she caught sight of the bird, a fiery crimson splash in the gloom. What was it doing here? It was tiny, too small to be obviously dangerous, but she knew better than to take anything for granted. She eased closer, probing with her magic for hidden dangers. The bird sang again, a quick, high note that was so pure and true she almost cried at the sound.

She was right underneath it, peering up into the branches, when the ground beneath her feet was yanked out from under her and a net whipped tightly about her flailing arms and legs and hauled her up into the trees in a collapsed, gasping bundle. She fought to break free, tearing at the netting, screaming in rage and frustration. But almost instantly fumes flooded her nostrils and mouth, thick, toxic and mind numbing.

Her last thought before she lapsed into unconsciousness was that she had been a fool.

She woke to a rolling, shaking motion that jerked her back and forth against the chains that secured her arms and legs to wooden walls and iron bars. The chains allowed her to move just enough to turn from side to side, but not completely around. Nor was there enough play in the lengths to allow her to reach her head or body. She rested on a bed of straw inside a wheeled wooden cage being pulled by two huge, broad-back horned animals that looked a little like bulls but were clearly something more. A second cage preceded her own and a third jolted along behind. There might have been more; she couldn't see.

Her joints ached and her head throbbed. When she tried to clear her mouth of its dryness, she found she was securely gagged.

She closed her eyes, gathering her strength, taking a moment to remember how she had come to this. The birdsong. Then the bird itself. A lure, she realized now, clever and seductive. She had let herself be trapped by one of the oldest tricks in the world. Her magic had failed to detect the snare. That was odd, but not impossible. The snare was sophisticated. Whoever had set it had taken great pains to hide it. That suggested that the trapper was expecting its prey to have the use of magic, which in turn suggested the trapper was looking for someone like her.

She opened her eyes and peered around. The landscape was blighted and gray with shadows, and the air smelled of deadwood and old earth. Through the bars, she could see a handful of lupine forms loping silently through the graying daylight, massive four-legged beasts with shaggy ruffs. Tongues lolled and breath steamed, even though the day was warm. When one of them caught her looking, it lunged at her, snapping at the iron bars and snarling furiously when it failed to reach her.

A tall, rawboned creature wearing leather half-pants and a tunic appeared suddenly at the side of the cage, peering in at her. Coarse black hair formed a topknot on a nearly pointed head, and a beard fringed a face that was as elongated and sharp-featured as a child's drawing of a Spider Gnome. It chattered at her with high-pitched sounds that reminded her vaguely of Weka Dart. But the language was different. She stared at it mutely, and the creature stared back. Then it was gone.

She glanced around, trying to get her bearings. To her dismay, she saw the Dragon Line fading into the gloom and mist behind her. She was headed south, away from her original destination.

Away from the mysterious boy who was coming to save her.

TANEQUIL

To the Big Island Book Bunch—
Abby, Amanda, Beth, Brian, Eric, Gerard, Judine, Kathy,
Kevin, Lloyd, Nan, Paul, Russell, Val, and Yvette—
who still believe that a good book
is the best entertainment of all.

O N E

Sen Dunsidan, Prime Minister of the Federation, paused to look back over his shoulder as he reached his sleeping chambers.

There was no one there who shouldn't be. His personal guard at the bedroom doorway, the sentries on watch at both ends of the hallway—no one else. There never was. But that didn't stop him from checking every night. His eyes scanned the torchlit corridor carefully. It didn't hurt to make certain. It only made sense to be careful.

He entered and closed the door softly behind him. The warm glow and sweet candle smells that greeted him were reassuring. He was the most powerful man in the Southland, but not the most popular. That hadn't bothered him before the coming of the Ilse Witch, but it hadn't stopped bothering him since. Even though she was finally gone, banished to a realm of dark madness and bloodlust from which no one had ever escaped, he did not feel safe.

He stood for a moment and regarded his reflection in the full-length mirror that was backed against the wall opposite his bed. The mirror had been placed there for other reasons: for a witnessing of satisfactions and indulgences that might as well have happened in another lifetime, so distant did they seem to him now. He could have them still, of course, but he knew they would give him no pleasure.

Hardly anything pleasured him these days. His life had become an exercise conducted with equal measures of grim determination and iron will. Political practicalities and expediencies motivated everything he did. Every act, every word had ramifications that reached beyond the immediate. There was no time or place for anything else. In truth, there was no need.

His reflection stared back at him, and he was mildly shocked to see how old he had become. When had that happened? He was in the prime of his life, sound of mind and body, at the apex of his career, arguably the most important man in the Four Lands. Yet look what he had become. His hair had gone almost white. His face, once smooth and handsome, was lined and careworn. There were shadows in places where his worries had gathered like stains. He stood slightly stooped, where once he had stood erect. Nothing about him reflected confidence or strength. He seemed to himself a shell from which the contents of life had been drained.

He turned away. Fear and self-loathing would do that. He had never recovered from what the Morgawr had put him through the night he had drained the lives from all those Free-born captives brought out of the Federation prisons. He had never forgotten what it had felt like to watch them become the living dead, creatures for which life had no meaning beyond that assigned by the warlock. Even after the Morgawr had been destroyed, the memory of that night lingered, a whisper of the madness waiting to consume him if he strayed too far from the safety of the pretense and dissembling that kept him sane.

Becoming Prime Minister had imbued him with a certain measure of respect from those he led, but it was less willingly bestowed these days than it had been in the beginning, when his people still had hope that he might accomplish something. That hope had long since vanished into the rocks and earth of the Prekkendorran, where so many had shed their blood and lost their lives. It had vanished with his failure not only to end the war that had consumed the Four Lands for the better part of three decades, but even to bring it closer to a meaningful conclusion. It had vanished in his failure to enhance the prestige of the Federation in the eyes of those for whom the Southland mattered, leaving bitterness and disappointment as the only legacy he could expect should he die on the morrow.

He walked to his bed and sat down, reached automatically for the goblet that had been placed on his bedside table, and filled it from the pitcher of wine that accompanied it. He took a long drink, thinking that at least he had managed to rid himself of the intolerable presence of Grianne Ohmsford. The hated Ilse Witch was gone at last. With Shadea a'Ru as his ally, even as treacherous as she was, he had a reasonable chance of ending the stalemates that had confronted him at every turn for the last twenty years. Theirs was a shared vision of the world's future, one in which Federation and Druids controlled the destinies and dictated the fates of all the Races. Together, they would find a way to bring an end to the Free-born–Federation war and a beginning to Southland dominance.

Although it hadn't happened yet, and nothing he could point to suggested it would happen anytime soon. Shadea's failure to bring the Druid Council into line was particularly galling. He was beginning to wonder if their alliance was one-sided. She had the benefit of his open support and he, as yet, had nothing.

Thus, he was forced to look over his shoulder still, because doubt lingered and resistance to his leadership grew.

He had just emptied his goblet and was thinking of filling it anew when a knock sounded at his door. He jumped in spite of himself. Once, an unexpected silence would have startled him. Those he feared most, the Ilse Witch and the Morgawr, would not have bothered to knock. Now every little sound caused the iron bands that wrapped his chest and heart to tighten further. He gave them a moment to loosen, then stood, setting the empty goblet carefully on the table beside him.

"Who is it?"

"Apologies, Prime Minister," came the voice of his Captain of the Guard. "A visitor wishes a word with you, one of your engineers. He insists it is most urgent, and from the look of him, I would judge it to be so." A pause. "He is unarmed and alone."

Dunsidan straightened. An engineer? At this time of night? He had a number of them working on his airships, all of them assigned to find ways to make the component pieces of his fleet work more efficiently. But few, if any, would presume to try to talk to him directly, especially so late at night. He was immediately suspicious, but reconsidered as he realized that an attempt to see him under these conditions indicated a certain amount of desperation. He was intrigued. He put aside his reservations and irritation and stepped to the door.

"Enter."

The engineer slid through the doorway in the manner of a ferret to its hole. He was a small man who lacked any distinguishing physical characteristics. The way he held himself as he faced Sen Dunsidan suggested that he was a man who recognized that it was important not to overstep. "Prime Minister," he said, bowing low and waiting.

"You have something urgent to speak to me about?"

"Yes, Prime Minister. My name is Orek. Etan Orek. I have served as an airship engineer for more than twenty years. I am your most loyal servant and admirer, Prime Minister, and so I knew that I must come directly to you when I made my discovery."

He was still bent over, not presuming to address Sen Dunsidan as an equal. There was a cringing quality to his posture that bothered the Prime Minister, but he forced himself to ignore it. "Stand up and look at me."

Etan Orek did so, though his effort at meeting Sen Dunsidan's practiced gaze failed, his eyes preferring to fix on the other's belt buckle. "I apologize for disturbing you."

"What sort of discovery have you made, Engineer Orek? I gather this has something to do with your work on my airships?"

The other nodded quickly. "Oh, yes, Prime Minister, it does. I have been working on diapson crystals, trying to find ways to enhance their performance as converters of ambient light to energy. That has been my task for the better part of the past five years."

"And so?"

Orek hesitated. "My lord," he said, switching to the more formal and deferential title, "I think it best if I show you rather than tell you. I think you will better understand." He brushed at his mop of unruly dark hair and rubbed his hands together nervously. "Would it be too much of an imposition to ask you to come with me to my work station? I know it is late, but I think you will not be disappointed."

For a moment, Sen Dunsidan considered the possibility that this might be an assassination attempt. But he dismissed the idea. His enemies would surely come up with a better plan than this if they were serious about eliminating him. This little man was too fearful to be the instrument of a Prime Minister's death. His presence was the result of something else, and much as he hated to admit it, Sen Dunsidan was increasingly interested in finding out what it was.

"You realize that if this is a waste of my time, there will be unpleasant consequences," he said softly.

Etan Orek's eyes snapped up to meet his, suddenly bold. "I am hoping that a reward will be more in order than a punishment, Prime Minister."

Dunsidan smiled in spite of himself. The little man was greedy, a quality he appreciated in those who sought his favor. Fair enough. He would give him his chance at fame and fortune. "Lead the way, Engineer. Let us see what you have discovered."

They went out the door of the bedchamber and into the hallway beyond. Instantly, Sen Dunsidan's personal guard fell into step behind them, warding his back against attack, lending him fresh confidence just by their presence. There had never been an assassination attempt against him, although he had uncovered a few plots that might have led to one. Each time, those involved had been made to disappear, always with an explanation passed quietly by word of mouth. The message to everyone was made clear: Even talk of removing the Prime Minister from office would be regarded as treason and dealt with accordingly.

Still, Sen Dunsidan was not so complacent as to think that an attempt would not be made eventually. He would be a fool to think otherwise, given the restless state of his government and the discontent of his people. If an assassination attempt were successful, those responsible would not be condemned for their acts. Those who took his place would reward them.

It was a narrow, twisting path he trod, and he was aware of the dangers it held. A healthy measure of caution was always advisable.

Yet that night he did not feel such caution necessary. He couldn't explain his conclusion, other than to tell himself that his instincts did not require it, and his instincts were almost always correct. This little man he followed, this Etan Orek, was after something other than the removal of the Prime Minister. He had come forward very deliberately when few others would have dared to do so, and for him to do that, he had to have very specific plans and, in all likelihood, a very specific goal. It would be interesting to discover both, even if it proved necessary to kill him afterwards.

They passed through the Prime Minister's residential halls to the front entry, where another set of black-cloaked guards stood waiting, backs straight, pikes gleaming in the torchlight.

"Bring the coach around," Sen Dunsidan ordered.

He stood waiting just inside the door with Etan Orek, watching as the other shifted anxiously from foot to foot and cast his eyes everywhere but on his host. Every so often, it appeared he might speak, but then he apparently thought better of it. Just as well. What would they talk about, after all? It wasn't as if they were friends. After tonight, they would probably never speak again. One of them might even be dead.

By the time the coach rolled into the courtyard beyond the iron-bound entry doors, Sen Dunsidan was growing impatient with the entire business. It was taking a lot of effort to do what his engineer had asked, and there was no reason in the world to think the trouble would be worthwhile. But he had come this far, and there was no point in dismissing the matter until he knew for certain that it merited dismissal. Stranger things had happened over the years. He would wait before passing final judgment.

They boarded the coach, his guards taking up positions on the running board to either side and on the front and rear seats outside the cab. The horses snorted in response to the driver's commands, and the coach lurched ahead through the darkness. The compound was quiet, and only the lights that burned in a scattering of windows indicated the presence of the other ministers of the Coalition Council and their families. Outside the compound walls, the streets roughened, smells sharpened, and sounds rose as a result of the greater numbers housed there. Overhead, the moon was a bright, unclouded orb in the firmament, shining down on Arishaig with such intensity that the city lay clearly revealed.

On nights like this, the Prime Minister thought darkly, magic often happened. The trick was in recognizing if such magic was good or bad.

At the airship field, on the north edge of the city, Etan Orek directed them to one of the smaller buildings, a block-shaped affair that sat beyond the others and clearly was not used to house anything so grand as a flying vessel. A sentry on watch came out to greet them. Clearly confused and intimidated by the unexpected appearance of the Prime Minister, he nevertheless hastened ahead of the entourage to unlock the doors to the building.

Once there, the engineer led the way, indicating a long corridor barely lit by lamps at each end, the spaces between dark stains and shadowed indentations. Two of Sen Dunsidan's guards moved ahead, taking note of each place in which an assassin might hide, close on the heels of an impatient Etan Orek.

Halfway down a second corridor, the engineer stopped before a small door and gestured. "In here, Prime Minister."

He opened the door and let the guards enter first, their bulky forms disappearing at once into shadow. Inside, they fired torches set in wall brackets, and by the time Sen Dunsidan entered, the room was brightly lit.

The Prime Minister looked around doubtfully. The room was a maze of tables and workbenches piled high with pieces of equipment and materials. Racks of tools hung from the walls, and shards of metal of all sizes and shapes littered the floor. He saw several crates of diapson crystals, the lids pried open, the crystals' faceted surfaces winking in the flicker of the torchlight. Everything in the room seemed to have been scattered about in haphazard fashion and with little concern for what it might take to find it later.

Sen Dunsidan looked at Etan Orek. "Well, Engineer Orek?"

"My lord," the other replied, bowing his way forward until he stood very close—too close for the Prime Minister's comfort. "It would be better if you saw this alone," he whispered.

Sen Dunsidan leaned forward slightly. "Send my guards away, you mean? Isn't that asking a little bit more than you should?"

The little man nodded. "I swear to you, Prime Minister, you will be perfectly safe." The sharp eyes glanced up quickly. "I swear."

Sen Dunsidan said nothing.

"Keep them with you, if you feel the need," the other continued quickly, then paused. "But you may have to kill them later, if you do."

Dunsidan stared at him. "Nothing you could show me would merit such treatment of the men in whose hands I daily place my life. You presume too much, Engineer."

Again, the little man nodded. "I implore you. Send them away. Just outside the door will do. Just so they don't see what I have to show you." His breathing had quickened. "You will still have them within call. They can be at your side in a moment, should you feel you need them. But they will also be safely away, should you decide you don't."

For a long moment, Sen Dunsidan held the other's gaze without speaking, then nodded. "As you wish, little man. But don't be fooled into thinking I have no way to defend myself should you try to play me false. If I even think you are trying to betray me, I will strike you dead before you can blink."

Etan Orek nodded. An unmistakable mix of fear and anticipation glittered in his eyes. Whatever it was, this business was important to him. He was willing to risk everything to see it through. Such passion worried Sen Dunsidan, but he refused to let it rule him. "Guards," he called. "Leave us. Close the door. Wait just outside, where you can hear me if I summon you."

The guards did as they were told. Once, there would have been hesitation at such a request. Now, after having survived a handful of unpleasant examples resulting from such hesitation, they obeyed without question. It was the way Sen Dunsidan preferred them.

When the door was closed, he turned again to Etan Orek. "This had best be worth my time, Engineer. My patience is growing short."

The little man nodded vigorously, running his hand through his dark hair as he led the way to the far end of the room and a long table piled high with debris. Grinning conspiratorially, he began to clean away the debris, revealing a long black box sectioned into three pieces.

"I have been careful to keep my work hidden from everyone," he explained quickly. "I was afraid they might steal it. Or worse, sell it to the enemy. You never know."

He finished clearing the table of everything but the box, then faced Sen Dunsidan once more. "My assigned task for the past three years has been to seek new and better ways in which to convert ambient light into energy. The purpose, as I am sure you are aware, is to increase the thrust of the vessels in combat conditions, so that they might better outmaneuver their attackers. All my efforts to readapt a single crystal failed. The conversion is a function of the crystal's composition, its shaping and its placement in the parse tube. A single crystal has a finite capability for conversion of light into energy, and there is nothing I have found that will alter that."

He nodded, as if to reassure himself that he was right about this. "So I abandoned that approach and began to experiment with multiple crystals. You see, Prime Minister, I reasoned that if one crystal will produce a certain amount of energy, then two working together might double that figure. The trick, of course, is in finding how to channel the ambient light from one crystal to the next without losing power."

Sen Dunsidan nodded, suddenly interested. He thought he understood now why Etan Orek had been so anxious to bring him there. Somehow, the engineer had solved the dilemma that had plagued the Federation for years. He had found a way to increase the power generated by the diapson crystals used in his airships.

"At first," the other went on, "all of my attempts failed. The crystals, when I found a way to place them so that their facets transferred their converted energy from one to the other, simply exploded in the tubes. The additional power was too much for any one of them to handle. So then I began working to combine more than two, attempting to find a different way to channel their energy in a manner that was not so direct and less likely to incur damage."

"You were successful?" Sen Dunsidan could not contain himself. Etan Orek's insistence on dragging out this business was wearing on him. "You found a way to increase the amount of thrust?"

The little man shook his head and smiled. "I found something else. Something better."

He walked over to the torches and extinguished them one by one until only those by the door were still burning. Then he moved to the box and raised its hinged lid, revealing a series of diapson crystals of varying sizes and shapes that were nested in metal cradles throughout the three sections of the box. The crystals had been arranged in sequence from small to large and in lines, but each one was blocked front and back by a shield carefully cut to its individual size. Narrow rods that crisscrossed the chambers like spiderwebs connected all the shields.

Orek stepped aside so that Sen Dunsidan could peer inside. The Prime Minister did so, but could make no sense of what he was seeing. "This is what you brought me to see?" he snapped.

"No, Prime Minister," the other replied. "I brought you to see this."

He pointed to the far end of the room, where a piece of heavy metal armor was fixed to the wall. Then he pointed down again toward the very rear of the box, where dark canvas draped an object Sen Dunsidan had overlooked.

Etan Orek smiled. "Watch, my lord."

He lifted away the canvas to reveal a diapson crystal that looked something like a multifaceted pyramid. The instant the canvas was removed, the pyramid began to glow a dull orange. "You see?" Orek pressed. "It begins to gather ambient light. Now, watch!"

Seconds later, he fastened his fingers about the crisscrossed rods and snatched away the network of shields.

Instantly, light erupted from the pyramid crystal and ricocheted through all the other crystals in the box, brightening them one by one with the same dull orange glow. Swiftly the light built, traveling down the length of the box from crystal to crystal, gathering power.

Then, with an audible explosion, the light shot through a narrow aperture at the front of the box in a thin ribbon of fire that struck the piece of armor at the far end of the room. The metal erupted in a shower of sparks and flames and then began to melt as the light burned a fist-size hole right through its center and into the wall beyond.

Swiftly, Etan Orek pulled on a rod attached to the cradle in which the rear crystal rested, taking it out of line in the sequence. At once, the other crystals began to lose their power and their light began to fail. The engineer waited a few moments, then dropped the connecting shields back into place and re-covered the rear crystal with the canvas.

He turned to Sen Dunsidan and did not miss the look of shock on the Prime Minister's face. "You see?" he repeated eagerly. "You see what it is?"

"A weapon," Dunsidan whispered, still not quite believing what he had witnessed. At the far end of the room, the piece of target metal was still red-hot and smoking. As he stared at it, he envisioned a Free-born airship in its place. "A weapon," he repeated.

Etan Orek stepped close. "I have told no one else. Only you, my lord. I knew you would want it that way."

Sen Dunsidan nodded quickly, recovering his composure. "You did well. You will have your reward and your recognition." He looked at the engineer. "How many of these do we have?"

The engineer looked pained. "Only the one, Prime Minister. I have not been able to build another yet. It takes time to calculate the proper angle and refraction needed. No two crystals are exactly alike, so each of these boxes will have to be built separately."

He paused. "But one may be more than enough to do what is needed. Consider. To power the crystals in this box, I used only the torchlight by the doorway, a small and feeble source. Think of the power that you will have at your command when the crystals are exposed to bright sunlight. Think of the range and sweep when you increase the field of fire. Did you notice? The light does not burn the aperture at the front of the box. That is because it is glass-fused, and the light does not burn the glass as it does the metal. It heats it, singes it, but does not destroy it. We control the power of our weapon accordingly."

Sen Dunsidan was barely listening, his thoughts racing ahead to what the discovery meant, to its vast possibilities, to the certainty he felt that in one bold stroke he could change the course of history. He was breathing hard, and it required an effort for him to calm himself enough to address his immediate concerns.

"You will tell no one of this, Etan Orek," he instructed. "I will give you space and materials and a guard to allow you to work undisturbed. If you require help, you shall have it. You will report your progress to me and to me alone. Your superiors will be instructed that you have been assigned to a project of a personal nature. I want you to build me as many of these weapons as you can. Swiftly. If one is all you can manage, then one will have to do. But others would be most desirable and would enhance your reputation even further."

He placed his hand on the engineer's narrow shoulder. "I see greatness in you. I see a life of fame and fortune. I see a position of responsibility that shall transcend anything you have ever dreamed about. Believe me, the importance of what you have accomplished is impossible to exaggerate."

Etan Orek actually blushed. "Thank you, Prime Minister. Thank you, indeed!"

Sen Dunsidan patted his shoulder reassuringly and departed the room. His waiting guards fell into step as he passed. Two he left stationed at the workroom door with strict orders to allow no one but himself to enter or leave. The engineer was to be kept under lock and key. He was to take his meals in his workroom. He was to sleep there as well. He was to be allowed to come out once a day for an hour when everyone else had gone home, but at no other time.

He was in his coach and riding back toward his bedchamber

when he decided he would not have Etan Orek killed right away. He would keep him alive until he had constructed at least a handful of these marvelous weapons. He would keep him alive until after the Free-born army had been smashed and the Prekkendorran reclaimed.

Six weeks ought to be just long enough.

T W O

awn's faint silver tinge was creeping over the eastern horizon in a dull wash when Shadea a'Ru heard the tinkle of the bell. She was already awake, sitting at the desk in the chambers reserved for the Ard Rhys of the Druid Council, the chambers that had once belonged to Grianne Ohmsford but now belonged to her. She was already awake because she could not sleep, preoccupied by her ever-shifting plans for the order and troubled by her inability to bring them to pass.

Her lack of success wasn't entirely unexpected, of course. Even though the Ilse Witch had been enormously unpopular with the Druids in general, Shadea was not much better liked. She had alienated almost as many members of the order as her predecessor, using her superior talents and physical prowess to intimidate and bully when she would have been better advised to use more subtle means. Now it was taking all of her efforts to persuade her followers that she had changed her ways and would be for them the understanding, concerned leader they all foolishly believed they needed.

In the meantime, the order languished. She had secured her hold on the office of the High Druid through the aid of her allies, especially Traunt Rowan and Pyson Wence, either of whom was better suited to the role of diplomat than she was and who together had worked tirelessly to bring as many Druids into line as they could manage. But the effectiveness of the Druid Council continued to be limited, its shadow no more intimidating or impressive than it had been with Grianne Ohmsford at its head. Still regarding the order with distrust and disdain in equal measures, none of the nations or their governments spent a moment to consider the position of the Druids on any of the issues affecting the Four Lands. The sole exception was the Federation—but that was only because she had made Sen Dunsidan her ally early on, giving him the promise of the order's backing to put a favorable end to the war on the Prekkendorran. Even the Prime Minister was in scant evidence these days, however, the leader of the powerful Federation having retired to Arishaig with scarcely a word of communication since his announcement of support for her as acting Ard Rhys.

That was not out of character for Sen Dunsidan, of course. His history as leader of the Coalition Council was notable for his behind-the-scenes manipulations and judicious absences. Long had he coveted his position; it was no secret. He had gotten it because his rivals had died mysteriously, both on the same day, a coincidence too obvious to ignore. But in the years since he had realized his goal, he seemed less satisfied. Once a very public man, he now appeared rarely and only when it was unavoidable. She had endured his sly and condescending attitude on more than one occasion. But he seemed less sure of himself these days, less driven, and she thought that his secrets were beginning to erode his once unshakable confidence.

Nevertheless, he was a valuable ally. If he chose to hide out in Arishaig, it was of no matter so long as his support of her was made open and obvious to all. The trick was in finding a way to persuade him to accommodate her.

For now, there was the matter of the bell and what it signified. She rose from her desk and walked to the alcove window that opened north. On the ledge just outside the frame, she had constructed a platform and secured a wire cage for her carrier birds, the same species that Grianne Ohmsford had used when the chambers had been hers. The sound of the bell meant that the one she was expecting had finally returned.

She opened the window and peered inside the wire enclosure. The fierce, dark face of the arrow swift peered back at her, its sleek, swept-back wings folded into the sides of its distinctively narrow body, its right leg bound with the tiny message tube. She reached into the cage and stroked the bird familiarly, speaking soothingly, calming it. The birds imprinted on their owners early and never shifted their allegiance. She had been forced to destroy all her predecessor's birds because they were useless to her. Their loyalty was legendary, and like creatures that mate for life, they would not accept a new master.

After a moment, she slipped the tube from the swift's leg and brought it into the light. Unfastening the tip, she pulled out the tiny piece of paper inside and carefully unrolled it.

The familiar block printing confirmed what she had suspected for days:

GALAPHILE DESTROYED. TEREK MOLT AND
AHREN ELESSEDIL DEAD. I TRACK THE BOY.

The scrye waters had told them already of the destruction of the *Galaphile*, and she had assumed that Terek Molt was gone, as well, especially since there had been no word from him since. That Ahren Elessedil was dead was the first positive piece of news she had received on the matter. She was more than pleased to have Grianne Ohmsford's strongest ally out of the way.

I track the boy.

She felt a shiver of excitement at the words. Aphasia Wye still hunted Penderrin Ohmsford. The boy was doomed. Once Aphasia began to hunt, there was no escape. It was only a matter of time. She had feared the assassin had perished in the conflagration that had consumed the *Galaphile*, and after days with no communication, she had dispatched the arrow swift to seek him out. It did not matter to her how he had survived, only that he had.

She carried the tiny message back to her writing table and fed it into the flame of the candle. The paper blackened and curled and turned to ash. She bore the charred fragments back to the window, blew them into dust, and watched them drift away on the wind.

Aphasia Wye.

She had found him quite by accident, an outcast and recluse living at the edge of the teeming, squalid hovels that encircled the city of Dechtera. She had been in the last year of her service with the Federation, a big, strong woman with little fear and a burning ambition. Her introduction to Aphasia Wye came about because she was looking for a certain deserter from the army, a man she knew well enough to dislike and stay clear of in other circumstances. But a rumor of his presence in the tenement sections of the city having surfaced, she was assigned to find and bring him back. She was given no choice in the matter.

Aphasia Wye, however, had found him first. A street child of unknown origins, Aphasia had grown up as something of a legend to those who populated the dark undersurface of Dechtera. At some point in his early life, he had been badly disfigured, but not before he had been so severely mistreated that the damage to his physical appearance could not begin to approach the damage to his psyche. Emotionally and psychologically, he dwelled in a realm few others had ever occupied, dark and soulless and empty of feeling. If he had a code of conduct, Shadea had never been able to figure out what it was. That it involved killing as a ritual cleansing was something she learned when she went looking for the deserter. That it was quixotic and arbitrary became clear when she discovered that Aphasia felt an unexpected connection to her.

His attraction to her might have had something to do with their similar backgrounds as orphans and children of the street, outcasts who had been forced to make their own way in the world. It might have had something to do with their mutual acceptance of violence as a way of life. When she found out what he had done to the deserter, her only response had been to ask for a piece of the man to prove that he was dead. She had not sought an explanation of the circumstances. She had neither approved nor disapproved of the act. That might have impressed him.

Then again, he might have recognized that she was drawn to him, finding his disfigurement, both external and internal, oddly attractive, as if surviving such damage was proof of his resiliency, of his worth. That he was repulsive to look upon, all crook-limbed and spiderlike, did not matter to her. Nor did his penchant for mutilating and eviscerating his victims, which might well have reflected his own lack of self-esteem. In the world of the Federation army, strength of heart and body counted for more than strength of character or physical appearance. Judgments were passed daily on the former and seldom on the latter. She found Aphasia Wye admirable for his talents and cared nothing for the package in which those talents came wrapped. Killing was an art, and this man, this odd creature of the streets and darkness, had elevated it to a special form.

She visited with him regularly after that, talking of death and dying, of killing and surviving, and their conversations confirmed that they were more alike than might appear to be the case on the face of things. He spoke in short, halting sentences, his voice the sound of crushed glass and dry leaves, intense and tinged with bitterness. He had no time for words with most people yet found them pleasant when shared with her. He didn't say so, but she could feel it. He lacked friends, lacked a home, lacked anything approaching a normal existence, gnawing at the edges of civilization the way a rodent would a garbage pit.

At first, she couldn't determine anything about his way of life. What did he do to stay alive? How did he spend his time? He wouldn't reveal such things, and she knew better than to press. It wasn't until he was sure of her, until he felt the connection between them to be strong enough, that he told her. He was a weapon for those who needed one and could afford to pay. He was a poison so lethal that no one he touched lived beyond that moment. Those who needed him found him through word of mouth spread on the streets. He came to them when he chose; they were never allowed to find him.

He was an assassin, although he didn't call himself that yet.

Two years later, after she had decided to leave the Federation and pursue her ambitions elsewhere, she had been drugged and violated by a handful of men who wanted to make an example of her.

Left for dead, she had recovered, tracked them down, and killed them all. Aphasia Wye had helped her find them, though he knew better than to deprive her of the pleasure she took in watching them die. Afterwards, she had fled Dechtera and the Southland for the protective isolation of Grimpen Ward and the Wilderun. Deep in the Westland, she had continued her study of magic in preparation for her journey to Paranor, where she intended to become one of the new Druids.

Within two months of her arrival, Aphasia Wye appeared in Grimpen Ward, as well. How he found her was a mystery she never solved; nor did it matter. In truth, she was glad to see him. He had followed her, he said, because he wanted to see what she was going to do. It was an odd way of putting things, but she understood. He wanted to share in the violence and upheaval in which she almost certainly intended to immerse herself. He understood her as well as she understood herself. There would be killing and death in her life no matter where she went or what she did. It was in her nature. It was in his, as well.

He did not live with her, or anywhere that would suggest they shared a relationship. He stayed on the periphery of her existence, surfacing only when she put out word for him or when he sensed, as he was capable of doing, her need for him. When she met Iridia, Aphasia Wye was the first person she introduced to the Elven sorceress. It was a test of sorts. If Iridia was disturbed by Wye, she would be of little use in more repellent situations. Iridia barely gave the assassin a second glance. She was made of the same stuff as Shadea and driven by the same relentless hunger.

So the three of them had coexisted in Grimpen Ward until Shadea had come east to Paranor, bringing Iridia with her. Aphasia Wye had been left behind very deliberately so as not to complicate her induction into the Druid Council. Later, when she was firmly established and there was need, she had sent for him. The others who had joined her conspiracy against the Ard Rhys—Terek Molt, Pyson Wence, and Traunt Rowan—instinctively disliked and mistrusted her dangerous friend. Molt called him a monster from the first. Wence called him worse. Rowan, who had heard of him during his time in the Southland, kept his thoughts to himself. But when mention of Aphasia Wye was made in his presence, his face betrayed him every time.

All in all, it made Shadea a'Ru very happy to find them so unsettled by a man who answered only to her.

She turned from the window of her sleeping chamber and walked back to her desk. There was a great deal she did not know about Aphasia Wye. In truth, he unsettled her, as well, at times. There was something subhuman about him, something so primal that it was irreconcilable with human nature. It was his gift to be so, a gift she was quick to take advantage of when confronted with difficult situations. Remorseless and inexorable, he never failed. She would have used him against the Ard Rhys had she not believed Grianne Ohmsford the more dangerous of the two and the one person besides herself who would be a match for him.

But against the boy . . .

She bent down to blow out the candles.

It was late in the day, the assignment of duties given out and the members of the Druid Council dismissed to their rooms, when Traunt Rowan and Pyson Wence appeared at the door to her chambers. She had not seen them since that morning, when she had advised them of the message from Aphasia Wye. Their response had been guarded—perhaps out of a sense of resignation that the unpleasant task of capturing the young boy was going to be carried out after all; perhaps out of a sense of futility they felt regarding the whole business. Neither had been overly supportive of the endeavor. It was as if they believed that eliminating Grianne Ohmsford was all that mattered, that beyond her removal lay green pastures and blue skies. *They lack the fire of old,* she thought, *the passion that brought them into my circle of influence.* But she didn't worry. They were still committed enough to do what was needed and not likely to disappear in a pointless rage as Iridia had done.

Besides, she was already making plans for new alliances that would eliminate the necessity of maintaining the old.

"A message just reached us, Shadea," Traunt Rowan began as soon as he had closed the door behind them. "We have found the boy's parents."

She felt a surge of elation. Everything was finally falling into place. Once they had the parents under their control, they could rest easy. There was no one else who would pursue the matter of the Ard Rhys' disappearance, no one who cared enough to become involved. Kermadec might still be out there, or Tagwen, but neither possessed the magic of Bek Ohmsford. He was the one who was dangerous.

"Where?" she asked.

"In the Eastland. We have been searching that area ever since Molt discovered from the boy that his parents were on an expedition in the Anar. But no one had seen or heard anything until a week ago. Then a trader working the supply route along the Pass of Jade on the lower edge of Darklin Reach sold some goods to a man and woman piloting an airship named *Swift Sure*. They are the ones we seek."

"A week ago?" Shadea frowned.

"Ah, but here is the thing," Pyson Wence interrupted eagerly. "All this time we have been searching for them in the Wolfsktaag Mountains, because that is where we assumed they were going. But that isn't where they have been! They have been exploring the Ravenshorn, farther east and so deep into the Anar that no word has reached them of our search. We are fortunate, Shadea, that they still have no idea of what has happened to their son or we would have lost them for sure."

"Have they no idea now?"

Wence shook his head. "None. We learned of it by accident, our spies making inquiries everywhere until they found the trader. He, of course, had no idea of the value of his information and gave it willingly to those who did. So now we have their location. What do we do?"

She walked to her window and stood looking out, thinking it through. She must be careful; unlike the boy, Bek Ohmsford possessed enough magic to incinerate anyone foolish enough to give him reason to do so. He would not be easily disposed of. He must be brought to Paranor if it was to be done properly.

She turned back to them and gestured at Traunt Rowan. "Take the *Athabasca* and go east. Find our spies and get what additional information you can. Then find the boy's parents."

"Am I to kill them for you?" the other asked, not quite managing to keep the disdain from his voice.

She walked over to him and stood close. "Do you lack the stomach for it, Traunt? Are you too weak to see this matter through?"

There was a long pause as she held his gaze. To his credit, he did not look away. He was conflicted perhaps, but determined, too.

"I have never pretended to support what you are doing, Shadea," he said carefully. "I would not have bothered with either the boy or his parents, but the decision was not given to me to make. Now that we are committed, I will do what is needed. But I won't pretend that it makes me happy."

She nodded, satisfied. "This is what you do then. Tell them that the Ard Rhys has disappeared and we are seeking her. Tell them that their son has gone looking for her, and we are seeking him, too. If they come with you to Paranor, perhaps they can help find both. None of this is a lie, and in this instance the truth is preferable. No one is to die outside these walls if we can help it."

Traunt Rowan nodded slowly. "You will keep them alive just long enough to help you do . . . what?"

"To help us find the boy, if it becomes necessary, and perhaps to help us make certain that Grianne Ohmsford is safely locked away within the Forbidding. If we can trick Bek Ohmsford into using his magic to seek them out, we can be assured that our efforts to eliminate the Ohmsford threat will succeed."

"I think we should kill him and be done with it," Pyson Wence declared, brushing her suggestion aside. "He is too dangerous."

She laughed. "Are you such a coward, Pyson? We have eliminated our greatest enemy, our most dangerous foe. What do we care for someone as unskilled as her brother? He isn't even a Druid! He doesn't practice his magic. He chooses to ignore it entirely. I don't think we need spare too much concern for his abilities. We are Druids of some power ourselves, as I recall."

The small man flushed at the rebuke but, like Traunt Rowan before him, did not look away. "You take too many chances, Shadea. We are not as powerful as you pretend. Look at how things stand with the Council. We barely control it. Our grip is so tenuous that it could slip entirely upon a single misstep. Instead of hunting down Grianne Ohmsford's relatives and playing games with them, we should be consolidating our power and strengthening our hold on the Council. With Molt dead and Iridia gone off on her own, we need more allies. There are allies to be had, of that I am certain. But they won't come without persuasion and enticement."

"I am aware of this," she replied evenly, keeping her anger in check. He was such a fool. "But watching our backs is our first order of business just now. We mustn't let any of those who have strong feelings for the former Ard Rhys become a threat."

There was a strained silence as they faced each other. Then Pyson Wence shrugged. "As you wish, Shadea. You are our leader. But remember—we are your conscience, Traunt and I. Don't be too quick to dismiss us."

I will do worse than that soon enough, little rat, she thought. "I would never dismiss you without first listening carefully to what you have to say, Pyson," she said. "Your advice is always welcome. I depend on you to offer it freely." She smiled. "Are we done?"

She waited until they had closed the door behind them before sitting down to write the note. Traunt Rowan would depart Paranor for the Ravenshorn at first light, both he and Pyson Wence having agreed to accept her decision on the fate of the Ohmsfords. In truth, they didn't care one way or the other about the Ohmsford family, so long as they could feel they had put some distance between themselves and any bloodletting. They were strong enough when it came to manipulation and deceit, but not so good when it came to killing. That was her province—hers and Aphasia Wye's.

She sometimes thought how much easier her life would have been if she had never come to Paranor. Perhaps that would have been the wiser move. She would not be Ard Rhys of the order, but neither would she be forced to bear the burden of its members' confusion and indecision. She could have practiced her magic alone, or even with Iridia as her partner, and accomplished much. But she had been desirous of more than that, greedy for the unmatchable power that came from leading those who could most affect the destiny of the Four Lands. Sen Dunsidan might think that the Federation was the future of the world, but she knew differently.

Nevertheless, there were times when she wished she could simply eliminate all the Druids and do everything herself. Things would be accomplished more quickly and efficiently. Events would progress with less conflict and argument. She was tired of shouldering the responsibility while being questioned at every turn by those she depended on to support her. They were a burden she would gladly shed when the time was right for it.

She wrote the note swiftly, having already decided on its contents while listening to the prattling of Pyson Wence. The time for hesitation was through. If they weren't strong enough to do what was needed, she would be strong enough for them.

When the note was finished, she read it back to herself.

WHEN YOU FIND THE BOY,
DON'T BOTHER WITH BRINGING HIM BACK.
KILL HIM AT ONCE.

She rolled up the paper and placed it into the tube she had retrieved from the arrow swift earlier in the day. Walking over to the window, she reached into the bird's cage and refastened the tube to its leg. The sharp-beaked face turned toward her as she did so, the bright eyes fixing on her. *Yes, little warrior,* she thought, *you are a far better friend to me than those who just left. Too bad you can't replace them.*

When the tube was securely fastened, she withdrew the swift from its cage and tossed it into the air. It was gone from sight in moments, winging its way north into the twilight. It would fly all night and all the next day, a hardy, dependable courier. Wherever Aphasia Wye was, the arrow swift would find him.

She took a moment to think about what she had done. She had imposed a death sentence on the boy. That had not been her original intent, but her thinking about the Ohmsfords had changed since she had begun her search for them. She needed to simplify things, and the simplest way of dealing with the Ohmsfords was to kill them all and be done with it. She might tell Traunt Rowan and Pyson Wence otherwise, might suggest there was another way, but she knew differently. She wanted all doors that might lead to Grianne Ohmsford permanently locked and sealed.

By this time next week, that job would be done.

THREE

Tagwen crossed his arms, tucked his bearded chin into his chest, and gave a frustrated growl.

"If this isn't the most ill-considered idea I have ever come across, I can't think what is!" He was losing what little remained of his patience. "Why do we think there's even the possibility of making it work? How long have we been at it now? Three hours, Penderrin! And we still haven't a clue about what to do."

The boy listened to him wearily, admitted to himself that Tagwen was right, and promptly continued talking it through.

"Khyber is right about not relying on the Elfstones. We can't do that unless we're certain that this creature has the use of magic, as well, magic that the Elfstones can react to. I haven't seen anything that suggests it does. It might not be human, but that doesn't mean it relies on magic. If it does, and we find that out, then Khyber can use the Elfstones to disable it. But otherwise, we need to find a different way to gain an advantage."

"Well, we have seen how fast it can move," the Elven girl said. "It's much quicker and more agile than we are, so we can't expect to gain an advantage there."

"What if we could find a way to slow it down?"

The Dwarf grunted disdainfully. "Now, there is a brilliant idea! Maybe we could hobble it with ropes or chains. Maybe we could drop it into quicksand or mud. Maybe we could lure it into a bottomless pit or off a cliff. There must be dozens of each in these mountains. All we need do is catch it napping and take it prisoner!"

"Stop, Tagwen," Khyber said quietly. "This isn't helping."

They stared at each other in uneasy silence, brows furrowed in a mix of concentration and frustration, a little more of the latter revealed on Tagwen's bluff face than on the those of the other two. The night before, the *Skatelow* had appeared in the sky above the foothills west of the Charnals. Twelve hours had passed since the horrifying discovery that the creature from Anatcherae had commandeered the airship, killed Gar Hatch and his Rovers, and taken Cinnaminson prisoner. No one had slept since, though they had pretended at it. Now that daylight had returned, they were sitting in the sunshine on a mountainside trying to decide what to do next. Mostly, they were arguing about how best to help Cinnaminson. Pen might have persuaded his companions that they should not abandon her, but that didn't mean he'd persuaded them there was a way to save her.

"It would be less mobile if we could lead it into a confined space," Khyber suggested.

"Or force it to climb a tree or a cliff face," Pen added, "where it couldn't use its speed or agility."

"A ledge or defile, narrow and slippery."

"Why don't we find a way to force it to swim out to us!" Tagwen snapped irritably. "It probably doesn't swim very well. Then we could drown it when it got close. Bash it over the head with an oar or something. Where's the nearest big lake?" He blew out his breath in a huff. "Haven't we covered this ground already? What are the chances of making this happen? What in the world is going to persuade this creature to go anywhere we want it to go!"

"We have to find a way to lure it off the ship," Pen declared, looking from the Dwarf to the Elf and back again. "Off the ship and away from Cinnaminson. We have to separate them if we are to free her."

"Oh, that shouldn't be so hard," Tagwen mumbled. "All we need is the right bait."

His face changed instantly as he realized the territory he had mistakenly entered. "I didn't mean that! I didn't! Don't even think about it, Penderrin. Whatever else happens, you have to keep safe. If anything happens to you, the Ard Rhys has no chance of being saved. I know how you feel about this girl, but you should feel more strongly still about what you have been sent to do. You can't risk yourself!"

"Tagwen, calm down," the boy told him. "Who said anything about risking myself? I'm just looking for a way to tip the balance in our favor long enough to free Cinnaminson and make an escape. In order to do the former, we need to separate her from her captor. In order to do the latter, we need to get control of the ship."

"Get him off the ship and away from Cinnaminson, then get us on the ship and safely away," Khyber summarized. She stared at him. "That doesn't seem like something that is likely to happen in the ordinary course of events."

"Well then, we will change the course of events," Pen declared. "This thing might be faster and stronger than we are, but it isn't necessarily smarter. We can outthink it. We can find a way to trick it into making a mistake."

Tagwen got to his feet, making a rude noise that left no doubt about his opinion of this proclamation. "I've had enough of this. I need to take a walk, young Penderrin, young Khyber. I need to leave this conversation behind and clear my head. I was secretary and personal assistant to the Ard Rhys when we began this odyssey, and I haven't left that life far enough behind to feel comfortable with this one. I applaud your efforts in trying to save Cinnaminson, but I cannot think how they will lead to anything. If, while I am gone, you come up with the solution to this dilemma, I will be happy to hear all about it on my return."

He gave them a perfunctory bow, one stiff with impatience and dismay, and walked away.

They watched him go in silence, and it wasn't until he was well

TERRY BROOKS   435

out of sight and hearing that Khyber said, "He may be looking at this with clearer eyes than we are."

Pen bristled instantly. "I suppose you think we should give up, too? Just leave her to that monster and go on our way?"

The Elven girl shook her head. "I don't think that at all. When I told you I would help, I meant it. But I'm beginning to wonder what sort of help we can provide. Maybe we would be smarter to continue on to Taupo Rough and ask help from Kermadec and his Trolls. Whatever this thing is, the Rock Trolls are likely a better match for it than we are."

"You might be right," Pen agreed. "But in order to find out, we have to go all the way to Taupo Rough, then persuade Kermadec to help, then come back this way again and find the *Skatelow*, which is flying while we're on the ground. I don't much care for our chances there, either. If we don't do something right now, it will probably be too late. This creature won't bother keeping Cinnaminson around if it's not to its own advantage."

He was remembering how Cinnaminson, blind but privy to a sort of inner mind-vision that sighted people did not possess, had deliberately led her captor away from the spot where Pen and his companions were hiding in the rocks. He could not be certain that she had known he was there, but Pen felt in his heart that she had. Her courage astonished him, and he was terrified that it might have cost her life.

"All right." Khyber straightened and leaned forward. "Let's try it again. We know what we need to do. We need to get this thing off the *Skatelow* and away from Cinnaminson. We need to keep it off long enough to take over the airship, get airborne, and escape. How much time would that take if you were piloting?"

Pen thought, running his hand through his red hair. "A few minutes, no more, if the power lines haven't been disconnected. Even then, not long. A reconnect from any draw to any parse tube would be enough to get off the ground. Cut the ropes, engage the thrusters, open the draws, and you're away. We wouldn't have to worry about Cinnaminson until after we were airborne."

"All we need to figure out, then, is what it will take to get our cloaked friend off the ship." She considered. "Besides you."

"But I am exactly what it *will* take, Khyber," he said quietly. "You know that. I'm what it's after. We know that much from Anatcherae. We don't know the reason, but we know I'm what it's come for." He took a deep breath. "Don't look at me that way. I know what I told Tagwen."

"Good. That means you know as well that you are talking nonsense. Tagwen was right to warn you against latching on to any plan that exposed you to risk. That isn't why you came on this journey, Pen. You are the reason for everything that's happened, and you don't have the right to put yourself in a position where you could be killed."

"That isn't what I'm suggesting!" He couldn't keep the irritation from his voice. "The trick is to make sure that by becoming bait, I can still get away when I need to. The trick is in getting the monster off the *Skatelow* and me on, all at the same time. But I don't see any other way of making that happen if we can't deceive this thing into thinking it has a chance to get its hands on me."

Khyber sighed. "You assume that getting its hands on you is its goal. What if it simply wants to kill you? It came close to doing that in Anatcherae."

Pen looked down and rubbed his eyes. "I've been thinking about that. I don't think it *was* trying to kill me. I think it was trying to scare me. I think it was hoping I would freeze in place and it would be on me before anyone could help. It wants me for its prisoner, to take me to whoever sent it."

He saw the look of doubt that crossed her face and went on hurriedly. "All right, maybe it was trying to injure me or slow me down. It's possible."

She shook her head. "What's possible is that you are no longer in touch with reality. Your feelings for this girl have muddled your thinking. You're starting to invent possibilities that have no basis in fact or common sense. You have to stop this, Pen."

He suppressed the sharp reply that struggled to break free and looked off across the mountainside. They were wasting time, going nowhere, and it was his fault. What they were supposed to be doing was traveling to Taupo Rough to find Kermadec, so that he could reach the ruins of Stridegate and the island of the tanequil, gain possession of a limb from the tree, fashion it into a darkwand, return to Paranor, get through the Forbidding, and somehow rescue his aunt, Grianne Ohmsford, the Ard Rhys! Even without speaking the words aloud, he was left breathless—and left with a feeling of urgency for getting on with what he was supposed to do.

Yet here he was, doing none of it. Instead, he was insisting on rescuing Cinnaminson, and it was admittedly for selfish reasons. He looked up at the clear blue sky, then down at the foothills that banked and leveled to the shores of the Rabb. He felt a momentary stab of panic as he realized that Khyber was right in her analysis; he *was* grasping at straws.

But he couldn't bear to think of leaving Cinnaminson in the hands of that spidery creature, not feeling as he did about her.

There has to be a way.

Why couldn't he think of what it was?

Why couldn't he think of *something*?

Shouldn't his magic be able to help him? He had been chosen for this journey expressly because his magic would give him a way to communicate with the tanequil. If it would allow him to do that, shouldn't he be able to find a way to use it here? It had possibilities he had never dreamed of; the King of the Silver River had revealed as much. One of those possibilities ought to be available for use here. If he could think of it. If he could get past the feeling that his magic was small and insignificant, no matter what anyone said—spirit creature or human. If he could persuade himself that it was good for something more than drawing the interest of moor cats like Bandit and reading the danger signs in the flight of cliff birds. If he could just do that, he ought to be able to use it to help Cinnaminson.

He was looking for a place to restart the conversation with Khyber when Tagwen walked back out of the rocks, brushing off his hands and looking less owlish than earlier.

"You can't imagine what I just found," he said. Pen and Khyber exchanged a quizzical glance. "Broad-leaf rampion. Hardly ever find it in low country. Prefers higher elevations, cooler climates. No snow, mind you, but a hint of frost seems to favor it."

Both the boy and the Elf girl stared at him. He looked quickly from one to the other. "Never heard of it? It's a plant. Not very big, but fibrous. It secretes a sticky resin from splits in its skin. You break off stalks, crush them up, fire the whole mess to release the resin, separate it from the plant material, mix it with wort moss and albus root, cook it all until it thickens, and you know what you get?"

He grinned through his beard with such glee that it was almost frightening. "Tar, my young friends. Very sticky tar."

So now they had a means, of sorts, of gaining an advantage over their enemy. If they could manage to lure it into a patch of that tar, everything it touched would stick to it, including the ground itself, and it would quickly become so bogged down with debris that it would have great difficulty functioning. Better still, if they could find a way to bring it into contact with something as immovable as a tree, it wouldn't be able to function at all.

They spent the remainder of the morning distilling resin from the plant and turning it into a small batch of tar. They were able to find the albus root and wort moss needed to make the mix, and they cooked it over a smokeless fire using an indented stone for a bowl. When it was ready, they formed it into a ball, allowed it to cool, and wrapped it in young broad leaves tied together with strips of leather. The tar smelled awful, and they had to consider the problem of disguising its presence as well as tricking the creature on the *Skatelow* into stepping into it.

"This won't work," Khyber declared, wrinkling her nose against the stench as the three of them stared down at the steaming pouch. "The creature will spot this in a heartbeat and go right around it."

Pen was inclined to agree, but he didn't say so. At least the leaf-wrap was holding together, although it didn't look any too secure.

"If it's distracted, it might not notice the smell," he said.

"There's not very much of it to work with, either," the Elven girl continued doubtfully. "Not enough to cover more than maybe two square feet, and that's stretching it. How are we going to get it to step into a space that small?"

"Why worry about it?" Tagwen asked, throwing up his hands. "We don't know how to find this thing anyway, so the matter of applying the tar unobtrusively and in sufficient amounts to render the creature helpless is of very little consequence!"

"We'll find it," Pen declared grimly.

They started walking north, the direction the *Skatelow* had flown. Pen reasoned that the creature knew Cinnaminson's talent was most effective in the dark. It probably preferred to hunt at night anyway, since that was the only time they had ever seen it. They had been keeping watch for the *Skatelow* since sunrise, but hadn't seen anything other than birds and clouds. Pen felt pretty certain that the airship wouldn't reappear until nightfall.

As they traveled, they discussed how they were going to lure their hunter into the tar once they found it and attracted its attention. There were all sorts of problems about accomplishing this. In order to get it into the tar, they would have to spread the tar around, then lead the creature to it and hope it stepped blindly in. It didn't seem too likely that this would happen; the thing hunting them was smart enough to avoid such an obvious trap. More to the point, one of them was going to have to act as bait, and the only one who would do was Pen. But neither Khyber nor Tagwen would hear of that, so another way had to be found.

It was midafternoon, and they were high on the slopes leading up to the Charnals, when they finally began to put a workable plan together. By then they were beginning to think about food again, remembering how good the rabbit Pen had caught two days before had tasted and wishing they had saved a bit of it. They had water from the mountain streams and had found roots and berries to chew on, but none of it was as satisfying as that rabbit.

"We can build a fire," Khyber said. "That will attract attention from a long distance. The creature on the *Skatelow* won't miss it. But we won't be there. We'll bundle up some sticks and leaves to look like sleepers, but we'll be hiding back in the rocks."

Pen nodded. "We need to find the right place, one where the creature will have to land in a certain spot and approach in a certain way. It has to seem to the creature that we think we are protected but really aren't. It has to think it's smarter than we are."

"That shouldn't be too hard," Tagwen declared with a snort. "It *is* smarter than we are."

"An open space leading to a gap in the rocks would be ideal," Pen went on, ignoring him. "We can coat the ground and rock sides with the tar. Even if it just brushes up against it, that would help." He looked over at Tagwen. "Does this stuff stay sticky when it gets cold?"

The Dwarf shook his head. "It stiffens up. We have to keep it warm. Frost is a problem, too. If it frosts, the tar will harden and lose its stickiness."

There were so many variables in the plan that it was tough to keep them all straight, and Pen was growing increasingly worried that he was going to miss at least one of them. But there was nothing he could do about it except to continue talking the scheme over with Khyber and Tagwen, hoping that, together, they could keep everything straight.

The afternoon slipped away, and the shadows were beginning to lengthen when Khyber suddenly gripped Pen's arm and said, "There! That's what we're looking for."

She was pointing across a sparsely wooded valley to a meadow that fronted a heavy cluster of rocks leading up into the mountains. The rocks were threaded by a tangle of passages that gave the cluster the look of a complicated maze. The maze lifted toward the base of a cliff face that dropped sharply for several hundred feet from a high plateau.

"You're right," Pen agreed. "Let's have a closer look before it gets dark."

They went down through the valley, into the trees, and along a series of ravines and gullies that rains and snowmelt had carved into the slope, watching the sun slide steadily lower on the horizon. East, the sky was already dark behind the mountains, and a three-quarter moon was on the rise. Night birds were winging through the growing gloom, and night sounds were beginning to surface. A wind had picked up, bitter and chill as it blew down out of the higher elevations.

They were almost through the trees when Pen drew up short and pointed back the way they had come. "Did you see something move just then?" he asked.

The Dwarf and the girl peered through the dark wall of trunks and the pooling shadows. "I didn't see anything," Khyber said.

Tagwen shook his head as well. "Shadows, maybe. The wind."

Pen nodded. "Maybe."

They went on quickly and were out of the trees and across the meadow in moments, heading for the rocks. Pen saw at once that it was exactly what they had hoped to find. The meadow sloped gently upward into a jumble of boulders too high and too deep to see over. There were passages leading into the rocks, but most of them ended within a dozen yards. Only one led all the way through, traversing small clearings in which sparse stands of evergreens and scrub blocked clear passage. It was possible to get through, but not without maneuvering over and around various obstacles and making the correct choices from among the narrow defiles. Best of all, one of the choices led to an outcropping at the edge of the woods they had just come through—and it was elevated enough to allow them to see over the rim of the maze to the meadow below.

"We build our fire in one of these clearings, make our sleeping dummies, and hide out here." Pen had it all worked out. "An airship can spot our fire if she comes anywhere within miles, but we can spot the airship, too. We can tell if she's the *Skatelow*. We can see her land, we can watch what happens. Once the creature comes into the rocks, we slip down off the outcropping, skirt the trees, and come at the ship from outside. It's perfect."

Neither the girl nor the Dwarf cared to comment on that bold declaration, so it was left hanging in the stillness of the twilight, where, even to Pen, it sounded a bit ridiculous.

They went back through the maze to a clearing where the opening from the meadow was so narrow it was necessary to turn sideways to squeeze through. Pen looked around speculatively, then found what he was looking for. On the other side of the clearing, deeper in, was a rocky alcove where someone could hide and watch the opening.

"One of us will hide here," he said, facing them. "When our friend from the *Skatelow* comes through that opening, the tar gets thrown at it. The leaves will split on impact, so the tar will go all over. It will take the creature a moment or two at least to figure out what happened. By then, we'll be heading for the airship."

Tagwen actually laughed. "That is a terrible plan, young Penderrin. I suppose you believe that you should be the one who throws the tar, don't you?"

"Tagwen has a point," Khyber agreed quickly. "Your plan won't work."

Pen glowered at her. "Why not? What's wrong with it?"

The Elven girl held his angry gaze. "In the first place, we have already established that you are the one individual who is indispensable to the success of the search for the Ard Rhys. So you can't be put at risk. In the second place, you are the only one who can fly the airship. So you have to get aboard if we're to fly out of here. In the third place, we still don't know what this thing is. We don't know if it's human or not. We don't know if it has the use of magic. That's too many variables for you to deal with. I'm the one who has the Elfstones. I also have a modicum of magic I can call upon if I need to. I'm faster than you are on foot. I'm expendable. I have to be the one who confronts it."

"If you miss," Tagwen said darkly, "you had better be fast indeed."

"All the more reason why you and Pen have to be moving toward the *Skatelow* the moment it enters the rocks. You have to be airborne before it can recover and decide it has been tricked, whatever the result of my efforts. If it gets back through that maze and out into the meadow before you board and cut the lines, we're dead."

There was a long silence as they considered the chances of this happening. Pen shook his head. "What if it brings Cinnaminson into the rocks with it?"

Khyber stared at him without answering. She didn't need to tell him what he already knew.

"I don't like it," Tagwen growled. "I don't like any of it."

But the matter was decided.

F O U R

Night descended across the rugged slopes of the Charnals like a silky black curtain pricked by a thousand silver needles. The clarity of the sky was stunning, a brilliant wash of light that gave visibility for miles from where Khyber Elessedil sat staring northward in the company of Penderrin and Tagwen. The purity of the mountain air was in sharp contrast to the murkiness of Anatcherae on the Lazareen or even to Syioned's storm-washed isolation on the Innisbore. There was a hushed quality to the darkness, the sounds of the world left far below on the hilltops and grasslands, unable to rise so high or penetrate so deeply. Here, she felt soothed and comforted. Here, rebirth of the sort that the world always needed was possible.

They had done what they could to prepare for the *Skatelow*'s appearance. They had built their fire, a bright flicker of orange just below where they sat hiding, feeding it sufficient wood so that it would burn for hours before it needed replenishing. They had placed the tar ball close enough to protect it from the cold so that it would stay sticky inside its leafy wrapping. They had built their straw men, scarecrows made of debris and covered with their cloaks. They had spent time working on the look of them, on the setting of positions, placing them just far enough away so as not to be immediately recognizable for what they really were, but close enough to suggest the possibility of sleeping travelers. They had done this before the sun had disappeared into the hills west, before twilight faded and darkness arrived. They had studied all the possible routes of approach and escape, marked well the path from where they hid to where the fire burned and from where they hid to where the tree line would lead them back to the meadow.

They were as ready, she supposed, as they were ever going to be. She wished they could do more, but they had done all they could think to do and would have to be content with that.

The plan was unchanged save for one aspect. Instead of hiding down in the rocks ahead of time, she was waiting with Pen and Tagwen until the *Skatelow* made her approach. That way she would know better when to make ready. Her plan was simple—wait for the creature to appear, toss the tar from her hiding place in the rocks, and run. By then, Pen and Tagwen would already be aboard the *Skatelow* and flying to meet her. If they were unable to land again, they would simply drop her a line and whisk her away.

It all sounded simple, but she was already having her doubts. For one thing, the tar ball was heavy and unwieldy. It was going to take a mighty throw to get it to fly more than twenty feet. That meant letting their hunter get awfully close. And it was going to be difficult to be accurate. The tar was squishy and crudely formed; it wasn't going to be like throwing a rock or a wooden ball. She was also thinking back to how fast the creature had moved along the rooftops of Anatcherae, and she didn't think she could outrun it if the tar didn't slow it down.

Of course, she would use her Druid skills to help in the effort, an implementation of a little magic to help with speed and direction and control. But her skills were untested for the most part and never in circumstances as dire as these. She would have to get everything right.

She sighed wearily. It didn't do much good to think about those things because she knew she couldn't change any of them. Most plans involved an element of luck. She was going to have to hope she had a lot of it with this one.

She listened to the breathing of her companions in the stillness, to the soft scrape of their boots on the rocks as they shifted position. Pen was lying down, and Tagwen was sitting with his head between his knees. Both were dozing. She didn't blame them. It was nearing midnight, and there had been no sign of the airship. She was beginning to think that it had gone another way, even though Pen insisted the creature would return to search the only area they could reasonably be expected to cover on foot. Cinnaminson might attempt to steer it away from them, but it would know approximately where to look no matter what she said. So far it hadn't appeared, however, and Khyber was growing impatient.

And cold. Without her cloak to keep warm, she was shivering. This whole journey had been a disaster as far as she was concerned. But she was the one who had encouraged it, insisting that Uncle Ahren take them all under his Druid's wing and bring them in search of the tree that would give Pen entrance into the Forbidding. She was the one who had said they had an obligation to help the Ard Rhys.

She felt her throat tighten, and her eyes filled with tears as she thought of Ahren Elessedil, dead in the Slags. Her mentor, her surrogate father, her best friend—gone, killed by another Druid. Druids at war with Druids—it was an abomination. She had wanted so badly to be one of them, but now she wasn't sure. Ahren was dead, Grianne Ohmsford was locked in the Forbidding, and the very order she had so desperately wanted to join was responsible for all of it. She had learned a little of how to employ elemental magic, but so far it hadn't proved very useful. She carried the Elfstones, but they weren't really hers. In plain language, she was a rank amateur, a thief, and a runaway, and she was risking her life to achieve something she wasn't sure she believed in.

She gave vent to her disappointment and despair, crying silently, keeping her face turned away from the other two so as not to wake them. She stopped after a few moments, deciding she had been self-indulgent enough, and composed herself. She could not afford to waste time. The decision had been made, the journey had been undertaken, and there was no turning back. She had believed rescuing the Ard Rhys was the right thing to do when she had started out, and nothing had changed. The loss of her uncle was staggering, but she knew that if he were there he would tell her not to give up, to remember what was at stake, to be brave and to trust in what her instincts and common sense told her was true. He had come through worse on the voyage of the *Jerle Shannara*. He had found strength in recognition of his own failures and his ability to confront them. A boy younger than she was now, he had remade himself into a man. She must do no less for herself, if she was to be deserving of his trust.

Absorbed in her thoughts, she very nearly missed seeing the sleek, dark shape of the *Skatelow* as it appeared on the horizon and turned toward them.

"Pen!" she hissed frantically. "Tagwen!"

They jerked awake, the Dwarf starting so violently that he nearly rolled off his perch. She seized his shoulder to steady him, then pointed out to where the airship sailed through the starlit sky like a dark phantom. "That's her," Pen whispered.

"I'm going down," Khyber announced, climbing to her feet. "Don't forget. Once you see that thing leave the airship, move into the trees. Even if it brings Cinnaminson into the rocks, Pen. No matter what."

She didn't hear his response, if he gave one, and she didn't look back at him. She couldn't worry about him anymore. He was going to have to do his part, just as she was going to have to do hers, and that meant he was going to have to put all thoughts of Cinnaminson behind him. She wasn't sure he could do that, but it was out of her control.

Her heart was beating rapidly and her face felt flushed as she hurried through the maze toward the fire, blood singing through her veins. She forced herself to focus on the task ahead, picturing herself flinging the tar ball at the creature, imagining it coated in black goo. She glanced skyward once or twice, but she was too deep in the rocks to see what was happening with the *Skatelow*. The creature hunting them had to have seen the fire. Patience, she told herself. It was coming.

She reached the clearing and retrieved the tar ball from beside the fire. The tar was warm and pliable through its leafy wrapping, in perfect condition for its intended use. She turned back to her hiding place and stepped inside. The crevice was deeply shadowed and slightly elevated from the fire and the three cloaked forms stretched out around it. She could see everything that might happen and not be seen herself. Moon and stars lit the open space, revealing the opening to the passageway through which the creature would enter the clearing. But the angle of the moon left her own hiding place in the rocks shadowed and dark.

She hefted the tar in her hands and settled back to wait.

If she had been a little more proficient with her magic, she might have floated the tar out over the entry point, as Ahren had taught her to do with a leaf, dropping it on the creature when it appeared. But that required skill and timing she did not yet possess, and she could not afford to miss on her one opportunity. Thinking of her inability to use her magic made her wish she had studied longer and harder when she'd had the chance, when Ahren was still there to teach her. Who would teach her now? There was only so much she could do for herself, and now no one in the Druid ranks whom she could turn to.

If she even got the chance to try.

The minutes passed. The darkness was deep and silent, a sweeping shroud lying soft and gentle across the world. Nothing moved. The clearing remained empty.

The longer she stood there waiting, the more certain she became that the whole plan was doomed to fail. The thing that hunted them was quick and agile. Her chances of actually hitting it were poor, and her chances of escaping afterwards were poorer still. She began to think of ways in which she could use her small magic to slow it down—something, anything she could do to get far enough ahead of it that it couldn't catch her. A cold certainty began to creep through her that she didn't possess the necessary tools. She was just learning magic, just beginning to make the sort of progress that would lead her to a command of real power.

Maybe she could use the Elfstones. Maybe the thing was possessed of magic, after all. They had been referring to it as *creature* rather than *human being* all along. It certainly looked to be so from the brief glimpses they had caught of it in Anatcherae. So maybe the Stones would work against it.

Or she could try summoning the wind that she had used to sweep it off the deck of the *Skatelow*. The wind had worked once. There wasn't any reason it shouldn't work again. That was a magic she could safely command. That was a weapon she could put to use.

She waited some more. The minutes dragged by. The creature did not appear.

Something was wrong. It had been too long. It should have been here by now, if it was coming. She hated that she couldn't see what was happening beyond the clearing. It left her blind and helpless to do anything but stand there and hope they had guessed right about what the creature would do. But what if they hadn't?

Her eyes scanned the clearing, probing the passage opening at the far side. Still nothing moved.

Then a soft scrape sounded right above her hiding place, and a small shower of dust descended in a tiny cloud.

Her breath caught in her throat. It was right above her.

She froze, caught off guard completely. *Right above me.* Did it know she was there? She waited, trying to regain control of her muscles, listening to the silence, anticipating so many bad possibilities that she wanted to scream to relieve the tension.

Then she saw it, creeping along the rim of the rocks to her right, circling the clearing like a big spider, cloaked and hooded, as silent as the dark into which it had blended so easily. She realized at once the mistake they had made. They had assumed it would come at them on the ground because that's what they would have done in its place. But the thing wasn't like them. In Anatcherae, it had used the rooftops. Aboard the *Skatelow*, it had hung from the rigging. It liked the advantage of height. It had used it here, coming into the maze not through the twisting passageways, but over the tops of the boulders, leaping and crawling like the insect it resembled.

Do something!

It was still moving, slowly and just a few yards at a time, studying the fire and the bundled forms. It might have sensed something was wrong or it might simply have been making sure it wasn't missing anything. Whatever the case, if she was going to use the tar, she had to do it while the thing was still within striking distance. It would see her the moment she moved, of course. She would have to step out from her hiding place, and it would see her.

She realized suddenly that this wasn't going to work. She wouldn't be fast or accurate enough. It could drop down in those rocks much faster than she could move. It was looking for a trap, and it would spot her the moment she left the shadows.

What else can I do?

The question echoed in her mind in a hopeless wail of despair.

Then all at once the creature wheeled about, looking off to the south, toward the trees below the meadow, toward the path that Pen and Tagwen were already surely taking to reach the *Skatelow*. It froze in place, tensed and staring. A second later it was gone, bounding over the rocks and out of view, moving so swiftly that it seemed simply to disappear.

She stood staring after it for a second, realizing what it intended, immobilized by her sense of failure and helplessness to prevent it from succeeding. She was too far away to reach them, too far away to get back to where they were.

There was only one chance. Breaking from her hiding place in a rush, she raced across the clearing and through the passageway that led out to the meadow and the airship.

After Khyber Elessedil disappeared into the rocks, Pen sat with Tagwen and watched as the *Skatelow* moved steadily closer to their hiding place and then finally started to descend toward the meadow. Even with the bright moon and stars to aid him, he could not make out what was happening aboard the airship. As the vessel landed, he searched for Cinnaminson and her captor without success. A cold premonition began to seep through him that it was too late for her; that the thing that had taken her prisoner had decided she was not worth the trouble. His premonition was not eased when he saw the

shadowy form of the creature slide over the side of the vessel to tie
her off and then start toward the rocks in a skittering crawl.

"We have to go, Penderrin." Tagwen nudged him.

He took a moment longer to scan the decks of the *Skatelow* for
any sign of the girl, but all he could make out were the desiccated
forms of Gar Hatch and his crew, still hung from the rigging. He
swallowed and forced himself to look away.

She'll be all right, he told himself. *It won't have done anything to her yet,
not this quickly.* But his words sounded hollow and false.

They descended from their hiding place in a crouch, staying
back from the light and any view from the meadow. Pen glanced
through the rocks only once to make certain the creature was still
heading toward the fire, caught a glimpse of its dark, skittering form,
and turned his concentration to the task at hand. It took them a
few minutes to get through the back end of the maze and down to
the forest edge, where they could begin to make their way out to the
meadow.

They moved swiftly then, anxious to reach the airship and take
control of her. The moonlight brightened their way, and they made
good progress skirting the tree line, but their path was circuitous and
it took them longer than Pen had thought it would. The minutes
seemed to fly by and still they hadn't reached the opening between
the trees and rocks that would get them out onto the flats.

"Do you hear anything?" he whispered to Tagwen at one point,
but the Dwarf only shook his head.

Finally, the meadow came into view ahead of them, its grasses
silver-tipped and spiky in the moonlight. They began to move away
from the maze, but still Pen couldn't see the *Skatelow.* He glanced
toward the rocks, catching a quick glimpse of the fire's orange glow
rising from their midst, dull and smoky against the darkness. The
creature must be all the way in by now, but he still hadn't heard anything. Any minute, Khyber would throw the tar into its face. They
had to move faster. They had to get to Cinnaminson.

"Tagwen," he whispered again, looking back to catch the other's
eye, beckoning him to hurry.

He was just turning away again when he caught sight of a spidery shape leaping across the boulder tops and coming toward them with frantic purpose. At first he didn't comprehend what he was seeing. Then he let out a gasp of recognition.

"Tagwen!" he shouted. "Run!"

They bolted ahead, galvanized by the boy's frantic cry, the Dwarf not yet fully understanding what had happened but accepting that it was not good. They tore down along the tree line and into a vale that fronted the meadow. In the distance the *Skatelow* was visible, silhouetted against the skyline, dark and silent. Pen turned toward it, taking a quick glance sideways into the rocks as he did so. The creature was still coming for them, moving swiftly across the crest of the maze, leaping smoothly and easily from boulder to boulder, closing the distance between them with frightening ease.

It's too close, Pen thought in horror. *It's coming too fast!*

"Faster, Tagwen!" he cried.

The Dwarf had seen the creature as well and was running as fast as his stout legs could manage, but he was woefully slow and already falling behind. Pen glanced back, saw his companion dropping away, and slowed. He wouldn't leave Tagwen, not even to save himself. He reached for his knife, readying himself.

Where is Khyber?

Its cloak billowing behind it like a sail, the creature leapt from the edge of the rocks to the open ground, landing in a crouch that only barely slowed it as it came at the boy and the Dwarf on all fours. Crooked limbs akimbo, head lowered within its concealing hood, it rushed them in a scuttling sideways charge.

"Pen!" Khyber screamed in warning, appearing abruptly out of the maze, rushing into the meadow and turning toward them.

Then a huge, dark form catapulted out of the trees behind them, a blur of gray and black that rippled and surged like the darkest ocean wave. Hugging the ground in a long, lean shadowy flow, it intercepted the creature so quickly that it was on top of it before the other knew what was happening. With shrieks that caused the hair on the back of Pen's neck to stand straight up, the two collided and went tumbling head over hindquarters through the long grass. Roars and snarls and a terrible, high-pitched keening followed as both scrambled up, clots of earth and grass flying in all directions.

"Bandit!" Pen breathed in disbelief, the name catching in his throat as the massive moor cat's masked face wheeled into the light, muzzle drawn back, dagger teeth gleaming.

The creature was up as well, and moonlight flashed off a strange knife held in one gnarled hand, its blade as silver as the crest of waves caught in sunlight, its edges smooth and deadly. In the glow of moon and stars, Pen could see it clearly, and he knew at once from its unnatural brilliance that it was a thing of magic.

Bandit never hesitated. Enraged by whatever animal instincts the creature had provoked, determined to see the thing torn apart before backing away, it closed on its enemy with a scream that froze Pen's blood. In a knot of rippling fur and billowing cloak, the antagonists tumbled through the grass once more, locked in a death grip that neither would release.

"Bandit!" Pen cried out frantically, seeing the knife flash as it rose and fell in short, choppy thrusts.

"Run, Penderrin!" Tagwen shouted at him, pulling on his arm for emphasis. "We can't wait!"

The boy obeyed, knowing there was nothing he could do to affect the battle between the creature and the moor cat. Remembering Cinnaminson, he tore his eyes away from the struggle. With Tagwen panting next to him, he raced for the *Skatelow*. Bandit had been following them all this time, he thought in wonder. Had the moor cat come into the high country solely because of their chance meeting and his few halting attempts at communication? He couldn't believe it.

Behind him, he heard grunts and gasps, snarls and spitting, sounds of damage inflicted and damage received.

They were almost to the airship when he forced himself to look back again. The creature was staggering after them, coming as swiftly as its damaged limbs could manage, its cloak shredded. Bandit lay stretched on the ground behind it, unmoving. Damp, glistening patches of blood coated its still body. Tears filled his eyes, and the boy made himself run even faster.

Khyber was already aboard the airship, hacking at the anchor ropes with her long knife, freeing the vessel of her moorings. Pen climbed the ladder so fast he couldn't remember later whether his feet had even touched the rungs. His eyes searched everywhere. There was no sign of Cinnaminson.

"Get us out of here!" Khyber screamed at him. "It's coming!"

Pen leapt into the pilot box, fingers flying over the controls. He unhooded the diapson crystals as an exhausted Tagwen tumbled onto the deck, gasping for breath. Khyber cut away the last of the anchoring lines. On the plains below, their pursuer was closing on the ship in a terrible, hobbling rush, the bloodied knife lifted into the moonlight, a low wail that sounded like a dog in pain rising from the dark opening of its hood. Pen threw the thruster levers forward, feeding power to the parse tubes, and the *Skatelow* lurched and began to rise.

They were too slow. The creature caught the low end of the rope ladder with one hand and held on, lifting away with the airship.

"Tagwen!" Pen cried out frantically.

The Dwarf heaved to his knees, looked over the side, and saw the dark thing below, one hand gripping the ladder, the other the strange knife. Grunting with the effort, he began yanking on the brace of wooden pins that held the ladder in place. Below, the creature swayed in the wind, got a better grip on the rope, and began to climb. One of the pins came free, and Tagwen threw it aside. The ladder dropped to an unnatural angle, and the creature spit out something so terrifying that for a moment the Dwarf froze in place.

"Tagwen, the other pin!" Khyber howled at him, crawling across the listing deck.

The creature had both hands back in place now and was climbing swiftly. At what might have been the last possible moment, the Elven girl shouted out something in Elfish and flung out both hands in a warding gesture. The last pin erupted from its seating in an explosion of wooden splinters and flew off into the night.

The rope ladder and the creature fell away without a sound.

Tagwen and Khyber peered over the side, searching. The landscape below had turned to forest and hills that were dark and shadowy. There was no sign of the creature.

In the meadow farther back, Bandit's still form was a dark stain on the silvery grasses.

As soon as they were safely airborne and the airship was flying at a steady rate of speed, Pen asked Tagwen to take over the controls. "Just keep her sailing as she is and you won't have any trouble. I have to take a look below."

Tagwen nodded without comment. "I can go with you," Khyber offered quickly. "It might be better—"

Pen held up his hand to stop her from saying any more. "No, Khyber. I need to do this by myself."

Without looking at her, he climbed out of the pilot box and walked to the rear hatchway. The door was open, and moonlight brightened the stairs leading down into the shadowed corridor below. All he could see in his mind was Bandit's bloodstained body, an indelible image that dominated every possibility he could imagine for Cinnaminson's fate. He purposely had not looked again on the corpses of Gar Hatch and his crewmen, trying to hold himself together against what he might find.

He paused at the top of the stairs, listened to the silence, then took a deep breath and started down.

At the bottom of the steps he stopped again, peering ahead into the gloom. Nothing moved. No sound reached his ears. He fought back against the panic rising inside, determined not to give way to it. He moved ahead cautiously, the sound of his own breathing so loud that it felt as if every other possible sound was blocked away. At each door, he paused long enough to look inside before continuing on. There was no one in the storerooms or sleeping chambers that the members of the little company had occupied on their journey out of Syioned.

The door to the Captain's quarters stood ajar at the end of the corridor. It was the only place left to look. Pen couldn't decide at this point if he wanted to do so or not. He couldn't decide which was worse—knowing or not knowing.

He pushed the door open and stepped through. Shadows cloaked the chamber in layers of blackness, concealing and disguising in equal measure. Pen stared around blindly, searching the inky gloom.

Then he saw her. She lay stretched on the bed, bound hand and foot with ropes and chained to the wall. Her face was turned away, and her pale blond hair spilled across the bedding like scattered silk.

"Cinnaminson," he whispered.

He went to her quickly, turned her over, and took away the gag that covered her mouth. "Cinnaminson," he repeated, more urgently this time.

Her milky eyes opened, and she exhaled softly. "I knew you would come," she whispered.

On deck, Khyber stood next to Tagwen in the pilot box. She had thought to take down the bodies of the Rovers, then decided to leave that job for later. The night air was cool and clear, and it felt good on her face as the airship sailed the feather-soft skies.

"You should go see if he's all right," Tagwen said.

She shook her head, brushing away strands of her dark hair. "I should stay right where I am."

"I don't hear anything. Do you?"

She shook her head a second time. "Nothing."

They were silent again for a moment, then Tagwen said, "Did you see what happened back there in the meadow?"

She nodded. "I saw. I don't understand it, though. That cat must have tracked us all the way out of the Slags. Why would it do that? Moor cats don't like high country like this. They don't ever come up here. But that one did. Because of Pen, I think. Because of the way he spoke to it back there, or how he connected to it, or something."

Tagwen snorted. "That's not the strangest part. It's what happened afterwards, when it attacked that creature. It gave up its life to save the boy. To save all of us. Why would it do that?"

She touched the controls lightly, fingering without adjusting, needing to make contact with the metal. "I don't know." She glanced over at him. "Maybe Pen's magic does more than he realizes. If it moved that cat the way it seems to have, it isn't just a way of communicating or of reading behavior."

"Doesn't seem so."

Again they fell silent. Ahead, stars filled the horizon with diamondlike brilliance, myriads spread across the dark firmament, numbers beyond imagining.

"I don't think we killed it," she said finally.

Tagwen nodded slowly. "I don't think so, either."

"It will come after us. It won't give up."

"I don't suppose it will."

She looked out into the night. "It's probably already tracking us."

Tagwen snorted and rubbed at his beard irritably. "I hope it has a long walk ahead of it."

Pen could feel Cinnaminson trembling as she told him the story. "They caught us coming back across the Slags. They were in a Druid ship, the *Galaphile,* and they snared us with grappling hooks and came aboard. One of them was a Dwarf; I could tell by his voice and movements. He wanted to know where you were, what we had done with you. Papa was terrified. I could feel it. I knew from what had happened in the swamp how frightened he was of them. He didn't even try to lie. He told them he had abandoned you after finding out who you really were. He gave them your descriptions and identities. I couldn't do anything about it."

She took a deep breath and pressed him closer. "I couldn't do anything about any of it!" she whispered and began to cry again.

He had freed her hands and feet, and he was sitting with her on the bed, holding her, stroking her hair, waiting for her to stop shaking. He let her cry now, knowing she needed the release, that it would help to calm her. She seemed to be all right physically, but emotionally she was close to collapse.

"They left as soon as they got directions from my father on where to find you. The other one must have come aboard while this was happening. We never saw it until they left, and then all of a sudden it was there. It didn't say anything and we couldn't see who it was, wrapped in that cloak and hood. It didn't look or move like a human, but I think it is. It spoke to me a few times, a strange voice, hoarse and rough, like someone talking through heavy cloth. I don't know its name; it never gave it."

He touched her face. "We dropped whoever it was over the side of the *Skatelow* as she was rising. We tricked it off, and it was trying to get back aboard, but we managed to cut the ladder loose as it was climbing up. I think it might be dead."

She shook her head at once, her face rigid with terror. "It isn't dead. It isn't. I would know. I would feel it! You haven't spent three days with it like I did, Penderrin. You haven't felt it touch you. You haven't heard that voice. You haven't been through what I've been through. You don't know!"

He pressed her close again. "Tell me, then. Tell me everything."

"It made us prisoners. I don't know how it managed, but I never heard anything. No one even had a chance to struggle. I was locked away below, but I heard everything. It tortured Papa and the others and then it killed them. It took a long time. I could hear them screaming, could hear the sounds of—"

She broke off, gasping. "I'll never forget. Never. I can still hear it." Her fingers were digging into Pen's arms. She took a deep breath. "When it was over, the . . . thing came for me. I thought I was next. But it knew about my sight, about how I could see things in my mind. That was what it wanted. It told me to find you. I was so afraid that I did what I was told because I didn't want to die. I did everything right up until I found you, and then I turned us another way. I don't know why. I don't know how I found the courage. I thought I was dead, then."

"We saw you lead it away," Pen whispered. "We knew what you had done. So we came after you."

"If you hadn't . . ."

She shuddered once and began to cry again. "I can't believe Papa is gone."

Pen thought of Gar Hatch and his cousins hanging from the

rigging like scarecrows, food for scavengers. He'd have to cut them down and dispose of them before she was allowed on deck. Maybe she couldn't see with her eyes, but she could see in other ways. He didn't want that to happen.

"Tell me what this is all about," she whispered. "Please, Pen. I need to know why Papa's gone."

Pen told her, starting at the beginning with the disappearance of the Ard Rhys, detailing his own flight west to find Ahren Elessedil and their journey before they had found Gar Hatch and the *Skatelow*. He told her how he had come to be in this situation, what he was expected to do and why, and where they were heading now. He confided his doubts and fears to her, admitted his sense of inadequacy, and revealed his reasons for continuing on nevertheless. As he spoke, she stopped shaking and grew quiet in his arms. Her horror of what had happened seemed to drain away, and the calmness he had been awaiting settled over her.

When he was finished, she lifted her head from his shoulder. "You are much braver than I am," she said. "I am ashamed of myself."

He didn't know what to say. "I think we take our courage from each other."

She nodded and closed her eyes. "I want to sleep awhile, Pen. I haven't slept in three days. Would it be all right if I did?"

He covered her with blankets, kissed her on the forehead, and waited for her to fall asleep. It only took a few minutes. He stood looking down at her afterwards, thinking that finding her alive was the most precious gift he had ever received and he must find a way to protect it. He had lost her once; he would not do so again.

His resolve on that point would be tested at some time, he knew. What would he do when that happened? Would he give up his life for her as Bandit had for him? Did he love her enough to do that? There was no way to know until he was faced with the choice. He could tell himself anything, make any promise he wished, but promises were only words until more than words were required.

He paused at the doorway and stared into space. He knew how much she would depend on him. She would need him to be there for her. But that worked both ways. Because of how he felt about her, he depended on her to be there for him, too. He might be only a boy and she even younger than Khyber, but that didn't change the truth of things.

They would need to be strong for each other if they were to keep each other safe.

He closed the door softly behind him as he went out.

F I V E

The day's heat still clung to the foothills below the Ravenshorn, sultry and thick in the waning of the afternoon
light, when Rue Meridian said in a surprised voice, "That
looks like an airship coming toward us."

Bek Ohmsford turned and caught sight of the black dot out on
the western horizon, backlit by the deep glow of the setting sun.
Even though he wasn't sure what he was looking at, he took her at
her word. Her eyes had always been better than his.

He glanced at her admiringly. He couldn't help himself. He still
loved her as much now as he had when he had met her some twenty
years earlier. He had been just an impressionable boy back then, and
she, older by several years and a good deal of life experience, a
woman. Circumstances and events had contrived to make falling in
love the inevitable result of their meeting, and all these years later
that surprised him still.

She remained strong and beautiful, undiminished in any way by
time's passing, a rare and impossibly wondrous treasure. Blessed with
dark red hair and bright green eyes, a tall rangy body, and a personality that was famously mercurial, she constantly surprised him with
her contradictions. Born a Rover girl, she had flown airships with her
brother, fought on the Prekkendorran, journeyed to the then un-

known continent of Parkasia, and returned to marry and stay with a man whose world was so different from hers that he could not begin to measure the gap between them. She might have chosen another way, something closer to the life she had abandoned for him, but she had not done so, nor voiced a moment's regret. As wild and free as her life had been, it seemed impossible to him that she had given it up, but she had done so in a heartbeat.

Together, they had settled in Patch Run and started their airship exploration business. They had wanted a son, and one had been born to them within the first year. Penderrin to her, Pen to him, Little Red to his footloose Rover uncle, Redden Alt Mer, he was everything they had hoped for. Having Pen in her life changed Rue noticeably, and all for the good. She became more grounded and settled. She found greater pleasure in her home and its comforts. Always ready to sail away, she nevertheless wanted time with her baby, her son, to prepare him to face the larger world. She taught him, played with him, and loved him better than anyone or anything but Bek. As a consequence, Bek loved her better, as well.

She caught him looking at her and smiled. "I love you, too," she said.

Bound to each other initially by the experiences they had shared during their journey aboard the *Jerle Shannara*, they discovered that they also shared an important similarity in their otherwise disparate backgrounds: Both had lost their parents young. Bek had been raised by Coran and Liria Leah, Quentin's parents, and Rue by her brother. It was their mutual decision that Pen would know his parents better than they had known theirs. From the beginning it was their intention that he should share in all aspects of their life together, including their business. He became a part of it early, learning to fly airships, to maintain and repair them, to understand their components and the functions they served. Pen was a quick study, and it was no stretch for him to master the intricacies of navigation and aerodynamics. By the time he was twelve, he was already designing airships as a hobby. By the time he was fourteen, he had built his first vessel.

He wanted to fly with them on their trips, of course, but he was not yet ready for that. It was a source of great disappointment to him. But he was young, and disappointments didn't last.

Bek shaded his eyes with his hand to cut the glare of the setting sun. He was of medium height, not as tall as she was, but broader through the shoulders, his hair and eyes dark and his skin browned by the sun. Always quick and agile, he was nevertheless beginning to feel the inevitable effects of sliding into his middle years. His less-than-perfect eyesight, he thought, was the first indication of what lay ahead.

"I think that's a Druid ship," Rue said quietly.

He peered at what was now definitely identifiable as an airship, but he still couldn't tell what sort it was. "What would a Druid airship be doing out here?"

She glanced at him, and he could tell that whatever she was thinking, it wasn't good. They were miles into the Central Anar, in wilderness that few ventured into who weren't in the trapping, trading, or exploration business. The Ravenshorn Mountains were mostly unsettled and infrequently traveled other than by the Gnome tribes that called them home. A Druid airship so far out would be coming for a very definite purpose and on business that couldn't wait.

Bek looked at their passengers, who were sitting around a map, talking about where they wanted to go next. Two from the Borderlands, three from the deep Southland, and a Dwarf—all had signed on to see country that they had only heard about. They were five weeks out of Patch Run, where Bek and Rue had begun a series of stops to pick up their customers and take on supplies. They had three weeks left in the Eastland before they started back.

"Your sister?" Rue suggested, nodding toward the airship.

He shook his head. "I don't know. Maybe."

He didn't want to voice what worried him most. One of the reasons a Druid airship would come for them was that something had happened to Pen. Word would reach Grianne, and she would come to tell him herself. But he wouldn't let himself think like that, not just yet. This probably had something to do with the Ard Rhys or the state of the Four Lands.

They kept watch as the airship sailed toward them through the fading afternoon sunlight, moving unerringly toward their campsite. How it had located them was a mystery, since few knew of their intended destination. A Druid could find them with help, but only Bek's sister possessed sufficient magic to track them with no help at all. He could see now that it was indeed a Druid airship that approached, so he began to suspect that she was aboard.

The other members of the expedition had seen the ship and come over to stand with their guides. A few asked what she was doing there, but Bek just shrugged and said he had no idea. Then he asked them to move back into the campsite and closer to where *Swift Sure* was anchored, a precaution he would have taken in any event.

"Are you expecting trouble?" Rue asked him, cocking one eyebrow.

"No. I just want to be ready."

"We're always ready," she said.

"You are, at least."

She smiled. "That's why you were attracted to me. Don't you remember?"

The big airship eased out of the sky to the grassy shelf that fronted the encampment and overlooked the woodland country west. Anchor lines were dropped fore and aft, and a rope ladder was thrown over the side. Bek recognized the *Athabasca,* one of four ships-of-the-line in the Druid fleet, capable of great speed and power. He was impressed by her look. But not even a Druid ship could match the speed of *Swift Sure.*

A Druid began to climb down the ladder, dark-robed and hooded, swaying unsteadily as he carefully placed one foot below the other. A big man, Bek saw, powerfully built and strong, but unfamiliar with airships and flying. He stepped off the ladder, pulled back his hood to reveal his face, and started toward them. Bek had never seen him before, but then most of the Druids at Paranor were unfamiliar to him. Except for his sister and Ahren Elessedil, who was no longer at Paranor, he had met only one or two others over the years, and those he barely remembered. The Druid life was his sister's life, not his, and he had kept himself deliberately apart from it. Sometimes he felt badly that he was not doing more to help her in her work, but it was not work he had ever cared to involve himself in and so he thought it better not to pretend he did.

The man who approached was younger than they were, though not by much, and his careworn face suggested he might be aging in other ways. Their lives filled with secrets, their work clandestine and often unknowable, Druids always troubled Bek. It was a role that fit his sister well, the clothes of her life as the Ilse Witch, where she had perfected the art of subterfuge and dissembling. Such skills were necessary in the world of the Druids, even though intended for good and not for evil. Druids were not well liked in the Four Lands. It was not a prejudice he shared, understanding them as he did, but it was a fact of life. Power fostered fear, and fear mistrust. The Druid order was for many the genesis of all three.

"Aren't those Gnome Hunters crewing the *Athabasca*?" Rue asked suddenly. "Where are the Trolls?"

It was too late for speculation. "Bek Ohmsford?" the Druid asked as he came up to them. He held out his hand without waiting for a reply. "My name is Traunt Rowan."

He shook Bek's hand, then took Rue's as well. His grip was firm and reassuring. He spoke in even, measured tones that radiated sincerity and concern.

"I was sent by the Druid Council to bring you back with me to Paranor," he continued, looking at them in turn. "The Ard Rhys has disappeared. We don't know what happened to her, but she's gone, and we haven't been able to find out why."

Bek nodded. His sister had disappeared before, many times. She was known for going off without warning on undertakings she wished to keep secret. "You must have reason to be worried about her beyond what you've told me. She has gone her own way without advising others many times in her life. Why is this time any different?"

"Her personal assistant, Tagwen, always knows where she is. Or at least he knows when she is leaving. This time, he didn't know anything about what happened. Nor did the Troll guard. No one did. This is where matters become a bit more complicated. Tagwen was concerned enough that he sought out Ahren Elessedil to help search for her. Together, they traveled to Patch Run to find you. But they found you gone and spoke with your son instead. When they left, they took him with them. Now we can't find any of them."

Bek felt a stab of fear. Rue's fingers reached out to find his and tightened sharply. "How did you find all this out? You haven't received any messages, have you?"

The Druid shook his head. "None. We found out what we did by asking those who knew bits and pieces of the truth. Tagwen left word where he was going. We followed him to the Westland village of Emberen. We discovered that he spoke with Ahren Elessedil and that they left together. From there, we tracked them to Patch Run. But we don't know what happened after that. We only know that your son is gone, as well."

He grimaced. "I'm embarrassed we don't know more. We have been searching for them for days. We have been searching for you, too. We think that the disappearance of the Ard Rhys might indicate that her entire family is in danger. There is some indication of this being so. She has many enemies, and everyone knows you are close to her and are possessed of the Shannara magic, as well. Some of those enemies might consider you as dangerous to them as she is."

"Penderrin would never go off with anyone, even Ahren Elessedil, without leaving word for us," Rue broke in suddenly. "Did you look for a message?"

"We did," Traunt Rowan said. "We looked everywhere. But we didn't find one."

You searched our house, Bek thought. *That was bold. Why did you feel the need?*

"If Pen failed to leave a message, it was because he didn't have enough time to do so." Rue was sliding into her protective mother role, and Bek could see the anger in her eyes. "Why wasn't he offered your protection earlier?"

A flicker of irritation appeared on Traunt Rowan's handsome face and then quickly disappeared. "We did what we thought best at the time. We were a little disorganized, confused. We didn't know what had happened at that point."

"You still don't, it seems," she snapped.

The Druid turned to Bek. "If you will return with me to Paranor, perhaps we can find them together. We know you have a strong connection to your sister, that you share the use of her magic. We were hoping that you might find a way to apply your talents to help us with our search. If we can find either your sister or your son, we have a chance of finding both."

He hesitated. "I admit that we are growing desperate. We need a fresh approach. We need any help that we can get."

He sounded sincere and his plea had merit, but something troubled Bek. He couldn't put his finger on what it was, but he couldn't quite make himself dismiss it, either.

"What of the expedition?" he asked, trying to think it through.

"I will see that everything is taken care of. Another ship, paid for by the order, will fulfill your obligation to your passengers. With your permission, I will fly back with you aboard your airship to Paranor. The *Athabasca* can continue her search. We have all of our airships out looking, crisscrossing the Four Lands. I don't want to take any of them out of service until this matter is settled." He paused. "We are doing everything we can to find your son."

He directed this last comment at Rue in what was surely an effort to reassure her, but Bek was pretty certain it was too late for that.

"We have to find him, Bek," Rue said quickly. "We have to do whatever it takes."

She was right, of course. But that didn't mitigate his sense of uneasiness. Why would Pen, who was always so dependable, disappear without a word to anyone? Where would Ahren Elessedil have taken him that required such secrecy? Looking at it from every conceivable angle, he kept coming back to the same two possibilities—that his son had been forced to flee or that Traunt Rowan was lying.

"Let me talk with our passengers and tell them what's happening," he said to the Druid. "Then we'll come with you."

He took Rue's hand and led her over to where the six who had hired them were standing in the shadow of *Swift Sure*. Quickly, he told them a version of the truth—that an emergency had arisen that required them to leave immediately for home, that another airship with another Captain and crew familiar with expedition work would come to allow them to complete their outing. There were a few disappointed looks, but everyone took it well. None of them asked for their money back. They shook hands and wished one another well.

After giving a wave of reassurance to Traunt Rowan, Bek walked over to the crates of supplies stacked on the ground at the airship's stern and began checking through them. Rue, who had hesitated before following him over, bent close. "What are you doing?"

"Pretending that I'm doing something useful," he said. "Gaining us a little space and time so that we can think."

She joined him in poking through the crates, her eyes never leaving his face. "You don't trust him, either."

He glanced back at the Druid, who was leading their passengers over to the *Athabasca* in preparation for boarding. "Why do you think Tagwen felt the need to seek out Ahren Elessedil when there are more than a hundred other Druids at Paranor whom he could have turned to? Why would he choose to seek help outside Paranor's walls? That doesn't feel right."

"No," she agreed, "it doesn't."

"But let's assume he had a good reason for traveling all the way to Emberen to find Ahren. Why did Traunt Rowan and the other Druids suddenly feel a need to follow him? If they were worried about our family, why wouldn't they go straight to Patch Run to warn us? They've thrown Pen into the mix as a reason for their search, but they didn't know anything about a connection to us before they started looking for the other two."

Rue's mouth tightened. "He said Pen might be in danger, that we all might. But he never said from whom, did he?"

"I take your point. Whatever the case, I don't think we are being told the truth."

She straightened abruptly. "Then why are we going back to Paranor? If this is some sort of a trap, we shouldn't be so quick to step into it."

He shook his head. "They want something from us. If they didn't, they would have taken a different approach. Besides, if we don't go to Paranor, we lose our best chance of finding out what is really going on."

She brushed back loose strands of her long red hair and looked off into the distance. "I could make him tell us everything in about ten minutes if you left me alone with him."

Bek smiled in spite of himself. "He's a Druid, Rue. He's too powerful to play games with. Anyway, if we scare him, he won't be so eager to tell us anything. Even when he lies, he gives us small glimpses of the truth. Let's make use of that for now. We can skin him and hang him out to dry later."

She reached over and took his hand. "I want Penderrin safe, Bek. If this involves your sister, it probably involves her enemies, and her enemies are too dangerous for a boy to deal with." She glanced over at the Druid airship. "I hate it that we've become involved in her life again."

He straightened and took her in his arms. She let him do so, but her body remained stiff and angry as he held her. "Don't be too quick to blame this on Grianne," he whispered. "We don't know anything for sure yet. We don't even know that Pen is missing. All we know is what we've been told, and we can't really trust that."

She nodded and inclined her head into his shoulder. "What if he's telling the truth? We can't dismiss that possibility, either. Just because he hasn't told his story well doesn't mean it isn't true. We can't take chances with Pen's safety."

He pressed her against him reassuringly. "Nothing will happen to Pen. Remember who raised him. He isn't without resources or skills. If he's disappeared, it may be because he wants it that way. What we need to do is to discover the reason. But we have to go to Paranor to do that. Are you willing to take the chance?"

She backed out of his embrace, and he saw the familiar resolve reflected in her green eyes. "What do you think?"

SIX

S hadea a'Ru walked alone down the lower west corridor of the Druid's Keep, listening beyond the soft scrape of her footfalls for other sounds. The air was warm and stultifying outside the walls of the Keep, but cool and resonant inside. A barely audible whisper of faraway voices reverberated off the stone walls like motes of dust dancing in the light.

She listened to those voices carefully, but only to make certain they did not follow her.

They would be serving the noon meal now, and a period of rest would follow for those who cared to take advantage of it. Few would. The Druids she led knew there were consequences for any failure to complete their work. She kept them guessing as to what those consequences might be or when to expect them. She let them work without supervision or deadlines because her unpredictability was all the incentive they required. A little uncertainty and a few object lessons were strong motivators.

She did not visit acts of reprisal on those who disappointed her; she knew better than to do that. She did not use her office to punish outright. She had learned a long time ago that consequences must be administered in more subtle ways. A few well-chosen examples set the tone. She provided them early on, within days after gaining the position of Ard Rhys, a clear indication of her expectations. She chose two younger Druids, ones lacking in broad support, ones whose presence would not be missed. She called them into her office and simply dismissed them. She sent them home without offering them even the smallest clue as to how or why they had failed. They might apply for reinstatement, she advised, once they had determined the nature of their shortcomings. It was a fair and just approach to the strict demands of the order's disciplines, and no one could find fault with how she had handled things.

Yet the underlying message was unmistakable. If one failed, whether one understood how or why—one paid the price. The best way to avoid such consequences was to work hard and not make trouble.

Of course, the more powerful of the Druids were not so easily intimidated. Their dismissal would result in confrontations of the sort she was trying to avoid. Yet she was determined that they all be brought into line, that they be made to accept her leadership and her control. She did not require that they make a public display of their loyalty; she needed only to know it was understood that she was Ard Rhys in more than name.

Hence, this clandestine meeting with the most powerful of those whose support she required. If Gerand Cera would agree to back her openly, if she could gain his support for her efforts, then the rest would be easier to persuade. The problem was that Cera hated her almost as much as he had hated Grianne Ohmsford. If she was to have any success in gaining his support, she must first find a way to change his feelings.

She paused at the entry to a rotunda that served as a hub for a series of connecting corridors. Light from narrow slits cut high up in the circular walls reflected off the stone blocks, measuring sticks for the single stairway that led upward to the west watchtower and its parapets. She had chosen this remote and private spot to test Cera's resolve. If he feared to meet her there, alone and unprotected by his followers, he was not the ally she needed. If he appeared, it would reinforce her belief that he would serve the purpose she had set for him.

She needed a fresh ally. Terek Molt was dead, Iridia Eleri had abandoned Paranor, and Traunt Rowan and Pyson Wence were beginning to show signs of vacillation. Though the latter two did her bidding, they failed to command the respect and fear of the Dwarf and the sorceress. She was incensed about Iridia, who had simply disappeared after the death of her beloved Ahren Elessedil, but there was nothing Shadea could do about it. Searching for Iridia would consume time and resources. Worse, it would demonstrate weakness. Better to deal with her later.

She thought fleetingly of Traunt Rowan, who should by then have been deep in the Eastland and close to making contact with Bek Ohmsford and his wife. If he succeeded in bringing them to Paranor, she would have new leverage in her search for the boy and his companions should the unthinkable happen and Aphasia Wye fail. She would also have a means for reconfirming that Grianne Ohmsford was safely imprisoned within the Forbidding, where she could cause no further harm. The brother's magic could be put to that use. It was dangerous to use him that way, but it was a risk she felt she had to take. When she was done with him, when she had hunted down the boy and verified that his aunt was dead and gone, it would be easy enough to dispose of the entire Ohmsford family.

But first things first. She must concentrate on the task at hand, the manipulation of Gerand Cera. She glanced around the rotunda, their appointed meeting place. There was no sign of him.

"I am here, Shadea," he said from the shadows behind her.

She turned with a start. Tall and menacing in his black robes, he was standing just inside the same hallway she had come down. He must have followed her all the way to their meeting place, and she had not heard him do so. It was a clear demonstration of his skill, given so that she would not mistake his coming as an indication of weakness. It was typical of him; he had survived over the years by making certain no one ever misjudged what he was capable of doing.

"Gerand Cera," she greeted him, holding her ground.

He came up to her, lean and hatchet-faced, his nose and cheekbones narrow and chiseled, his mouth a thin line of disapproval. His expression was unreadable, as if his mind had emptied of thought and his heart of emotion. He was a formidable opponent, and there were few at Paranor who would dare to challenge him.

"Are we alone?" he asked.

He would already know the answer to that question, she thought. He only wanted to let her think he trusted her not to lie to him. "Of course. What I have to say to you is not meant for other ears."

"I didn't think so." He glanced around, as if come for the first time to a new place. "No one is likely to pass down these corridors, I suspect. Nevertheless, we are too much exposed to suit my taste. We should not be seen meeting like this, even by accident."

She nodded. "Come this way."

She led him into another of the passageways and from there into an unmanned guardroom fronting the outer wall.

"Here?" she asked. He nodded, and she closed the door behind them. "This should serve our needs."

He walked over to a bench set against the far wall and sat down. "Let me save you some time and effort, Shadea. You have summoned me because you require my help. Your own allies seem to be disappearing rather more rapidly than I think you anticipated in the wake of what's happened. Some won't be returning, I suspect. You are Ard Rhys in name, but your grip on the title is tenuous. Allies are necessary. I would be the one whose support you covet most. Am I right?"

She was angered by his presumptions, but kept her feelings in check. He was right, of course. That was one of his strengths—the ability to analyze a situation quickly and accurately. "Your support would be welcome," she acknowledged.

His sharp features tightened. "Why should I give it to you?"

"I could suggest the obvious—that it would be safer for you to have me as a friend than an enemy."

His smile was bitter. "You could never be a friend to me, Shadea. You could never be a friend to anyone you viewed as a potential rival. I accept that. I don't want you as a friend, in any case. As well, I don't want you as an enemy. Your successful elimination of Grianne Ohmsford demonstrates sufficient reason for that. Such an impressive piece of work. So unexpected. No one knows how you did it. Gone almost as if she never existed. Care to explain how you managed it?"

She shrugged. "As you said, you don't want me as your enemy."

"So, then, I can have you as neither friend nor enemy. Perhaps there is some middle ground?"

"Perhaps. Why don't we try to find it?" She walked over and sat down beside him, taking away the advantage of height to put them on an equal footing. "I do have need of your help. You have read the situation accurately. I have lost old allies; I need new ones. The Council follows me for now, but it may shift allegiance when the opportunity arises. I can do nothing to further the Druid cause until the problem is safely eliminated. Think what you want of me, but my goal in all of this is to make the order stronger and more effective. Under Grianne, we were wallowing in discontent and ineffectiveness. That has changed already, even in the few days she has been gone."

Gerand Cera arched one eyebrow. "How so?"

"I have gained the unqualified support of Sen Dunsidan and the Federation. That support goes beyond his openly professed acceptance of my stewardship of the order. A deeper understanding has been forged, one that will eventually give us control over him."

He nodded slowly. "He will crush the Free-born, and you will have the order stand by and let it happen. But how will you then gain control of him?"

She smiled. "What you need to know is that I do not intend to let things proceed in the disorderly fashion allowed by my predecessor. I intend to take action and to take it now. I will change the course of history, and I will make the Druid order the spearhead for that change."

"How ambitious of you," he said softly.

"I won't deny it. I am ambitious for both the order and myself. You can join me in this effort or you can continue to oppose me. If you join me, I will give you fresh standing in the order, a chance to advance at my side, equal in almost everything."

He laughed. "Until you no longer have need of me."

She held his gaze. "Or you of me?"

They stared at each other in silent appraisal, each measuring the other's hidden intent against the possibility of truth contained in the words already spoken. The silence lengthened and Shadea caught a hint of uncertainty in the other's black gaze.

"An alliance, then?" he said.

"A very close alliance. Personal as well as professional."

He stared at her. "You don't mean for us to become joined in *that* way, do you?" he asked softly.

She nodded slowly. "Oh, but I do. Why not? Don't tell me it hasn't crossed your mind. It crosses every man's mind, sooner or later. I see how they look at me. I know how they think. I am offering myself to you. I understand the risk of doing so, of course. But there are always risks. What I seek is an open and obvious alliance that no one in the order will dare to challenge."

"Well," he said, pursing his thin lips. "I didn't expect this. Do you find me so attractive?"

She shrugged. "Not in the way you might think. Attractive in a different way. Women and men don't always think alike about these things. Accept my offer, and I might even explain it to you one day."

He stared at her without answering, looking directly into her eyes and searching for what she was hiding. She let him hold her gaze, patient and unflinching. "You could move into my quarters, of course," she said. "You could sleep with me or not, as you choose. What matters is that others see us as a couple. We would be seen as joined in all things, not necessarily by proclamation, but otherwise openly so. I am Ard Rhys, but you would be my shadow half. Your word would be mine. We would advance the cause of the order to-gether."

He let his eyes drop to her body, then rose and walked away and stood looking at the wall. "I will not say I am not tempted. You understand me well enough to know I am. We both crave power in all its forms. Your submission would be immensely satisfying. But where does this lead? How does it end?"

She laughed openly. "Do you need to know in order to be per-suaded, Gerand Cera? Aren't you excited by the idea that neither of us can know how this will end, that it is a gamble we must accept? Life is risk! What is the point otherwise?"

He turned back to face her. "What of your other allies? How will they view this change of plans?"

She shrugged. "They will accept it. They haven't any choice. I am the one they answer to." She reached up to touch his cheek. "And now to you, as well, if you accept my offer."

He shook his head. "You would dispose of me in an instant, discard me with not a second thought."

"You would do the same with me," she countered. "We do not fool each other in any way about this arrangement. We make use of it until it no longer suits us, and then we see how things stand. It does not necessarily have to end in killing. It can end in any number of other ways. Are you so committed to my death that you cannot imagine any other possibility? Do I appear no different to you than Grianne Ohmsford did?"

He smiled. "You are different in more ways than I can count. I do not mistake you for her. But I do not mistake you for anything different from what you are, either. I would have to watch my back constantly were I to accept your proposal."

She put her hands on his narrow shoulders and drew him a step closer. "Oh, come now. What would be the purpose of making this offer if all I wanted was to see you dead? There are much less complicated ways to achieve that end. Once I have joined with you openly, it immediately becomes more difficult for me to dispose of you, doesn't it? Besides, what would be the reason? I need you alive and at my side if I am to achieve what I seek. You can see that, can't you?"

His lean features showed nothing, impassive and unrevealing as she pressed herself close and kissed him on the mouth. "Can't you?"

Then he was kissing her back, and she knew she had him.

Later that night, when the Druids of Paranor were asleep or at work in quarters kept open for that purpose, the night fallen in a thick black veil through skies so clouded that neither moon nor stars could penetrate, she slipped from her bed to walk the empty corridors and think. She spared only a single glance back at the sleeping and sated Gerand Cera before closing the door on him. Her seduction of her most dangerous enemy had been a success. It had even been enjoyable. She had not lied to him. She found him attractive enough. His menacing look and poisonous mind drew her much the way she thought the Ilse Witch must have felt drawn to snakes. They were treacherous by instinct and unpredictable by nature and one could not trust what they would do because they frequently did not know themselves. But they were fascinating, as well. She flushed with heat and passion imagining how it would feel to hold one close to her breast and feel its deceptively silky skin sliding against her own.

She slipped down the empty corridor outside her room, hugging the shadows as she moved to the stairwell that led upward into the central tower and the parapets that ringed it. She wore her nightgown and nothing more, disdainful of clothing, of armor and weapons, of trappings that hampered and slowed. She feared nothing in this world, so why should she care how she appeared or what she revealed? Convention and conformity were for others. She would be what she liked.

For now, Gerand Cera was hers. She knew he thought otherwise. He had taken her body and would think he had taken her mind in the bargain. He had allied himself with her so that he could gain a toehold on the steps of the office she warded. He was probably already planning how he would dispose of her. But she had known all that going in, had understood that he would accept her proposition only to get what he coveted most—the position she held. He would stay close to her so that he could more easily eliminate her.

But that was a blade that cut both ways. Keeping him close allowed her the same opportunities. His plans for her were no different than hers for him. Yet the bargain favored her. She was the one who would be seen to have united the Druids, to have pulled the two central factions together, so that there would no longer be bickering and dissatisfaction. She was the one who would be seen to have allowed common sense to prevail over pride. She was the one who would be seen as the real leader of the order, and Gerand Cera, though he might claim otherwise, would be only the consort of the Ard Rhys.

A consort, she had already decided, whose usefulness at Paranor would quickly run its course.

She climbed to the tower and walked out onto the parapet. A wind blew chilly and brisk out of the west, but anxious to feel something cold against her skin, she let it wash over her without shivering. She closed her eyes and breathed in the night, listening to its faint sounds, to its soft voice. She was at peace there, alone on the top of the Druid's Keep, her fortress, her world. She had won it, and she would keep it. Those who could help her might do so, but they had better know their place.

In the morning, Gerand Cera would address the Council. Ostensibly, he was to speak to the state of the Four Lands and the role of the Druids in monitoring its vicissitudes. But the true purpose of his speaking was to make clear that he was now allied with her, had become her consort, her shadow self. He would do so thinking to impress upon the listening Druids that he had gained control of her. None would believe it. It didn't matter what he said or did. None would believe.

If they did, they had better not let her find out.

SEVEN

I t was late in the day when *Swift Sure* sailed out of the shadows enfolding the Dragon's Teeth toward the brightly lit towers of Paranor, sharp-edged and spiraling against a horizon colored crimson and gold by the setting sun. Bek worked the rigging and sails in preparation for their arrival, while Rue stood in the pilot box, easing the big ship into position. It was a still, windless day, and sailing her required little in the way of skill, her steady progress reliant mostly on the power fed out of the diapson crystals. The journey had taken barely forty-eight hours, the weather clear and uncomplicated, the voyage made by flying day and night, the senior Ohmsfords taking turns at catching a few quick hours of sleep when needed. It was a schedule they were used to, having followed it on numerous occasions when there were weather reasons to do so. They might have anchored and slept in this instance, but both were anxious to get to their destination and find out the truth about Pen.

Of one thing they were quite certain. Traunt Rowan was holding something back, and whatever it was, it had everything to do with why they had been summoned.

Bek glanced over to where the Druid sat on a viewing bench with his back against the foremast and his safety line cinched tightly about his waist. He was not comfortable in the air, so he had spent much of his time in that position. He was friendly, though. He was more than willing to talk whenever they approached, always amenable to a discussion of the facts surrounding the disappearances of Grianne and Pen, seemingly anxious to help them find their family. Yet as Bek had observed at the start of this journey, it was what Traunt Rowan didn't say as much as what he did that kept giving him away. There was no mention still of why the Druids had decided to go in search of Tagwen after his departure from Paranor or why that pursuit had led them to Pen. There was no mention of what had become of the Troll guard that had served his sister so faithfully from the beginning of her term as Ard Rhys. Most important of all, he offered no suggestion as to what might have happened to Grianne.

Bek was aware that he might be overreacting to omissions that were nothing more than oversights on the part of a distraught messenger, omissions easily explained once broached. But Bek had always trusted his instincts on such things, and his instincts in this case warned him that something was not right. Because Rue felt the same way, he was inclined to keep his concerns to himself and to watch his back until he had a better understanding of what had happened.

As *Swift Sure* settled down inside the broad west court, where the Druid airships were anchored when not flying, it occurred to him that he had been to Paranor only twice before in his life. It was a shock to realize that he had not come more often than that, given that Grianne had been Ard Rhys for almost twenty years. But he understood the reason for it. Both times he had visited, he had been anxious to leave. The walls of the Keep closed in on him, shut him away and gave him a trapped and helpless feeling. The stone passageways reminded him of the underground lair of the Antrax. The dark forms of the Druids reminded him of the Morgawr and his Mwellrets. His time in Parkasia still haunted him, its memories unpleasantly vivid and troubling.

His sister had been anxious to explain what it was she was trying to achieve with the order, how she envisioned it serving the Four Lands. It was Walker Boh's dream she was seeking to fulfill, and she had dedicated her life to making it come true. But it was her vision she was following, not Bek's, and he had trouble finding reasons to believe in it as she did. He did not share Walker's belief in the importance of the Druids to the Races; he did not accept that a Druid Council would function any more effectively or wisely than the governments already established. He trusted his sister and believed her to be capable and committed. But she was still only one person, and however powerful she might think herself, she was diminished measurably by how she had lived her life as the Ilse Witch. Her exposure to the truth of who and what she was through contact with the Sword of Shannara had caused her psyche to suffer great damage. She might have woken from the coma into which she had fallen as a result of having faced up to that truth, but he wasn't sure she had come back from it whole.

Her responsibilities were so overwhelming and the response of those she sought to help so disdainful that he found himself wondering whether she might revert to the dark creature she had been before he found her. He hated himself for thinking that way, but he understood the pressure she was under and the weight of the task she had given herself. It was one thing to reestablish the Druid order; it was another to lead it. He wanted to tell her to let go, to come away with him. Even while she was explaining what it was she was trying to do, he wanted to urge her to stop. But, in the end, he said nothing. It was her life, not his. It was her decision.

Standing on the foredeck of *Swift Sure* as Rue set the big airship down on Druid soil, he found himself wondering if he would ever see Grianne again. His concerns had all been for Pen, but it was Grianne who had disappeared first and been gone longest. Because she had a history of such disappearances and because she had always returned from them, he had given little thought to what the most recent one might mean. But it was possible, even for an Ard Rhys, to venture too far into unfriendly territory and not be able to find a way out again. It was possible, even for Grianne, not to return.

He turned his attention to dropping the anchor lines then, as the airship touched the ground, climbing down the rope ladder to secure them. The air within the Druid walls felt hot and still. He smelled the dust and the dryness; he could breathe them in. Already, he was wishing he were somewhere else. Taking a deep breath to calm him-

self, he waited for Rue and Traunt Rowan to descend. It was pointless to dwell on his discomfort. He was here, and here he would remain until he found what he had come looking for.

With Rue beside him, he followed the Druid toward a pair of
massive double-entry doors at one end of the court. But before they
reached them, the doors opened and a small group of black-cloaked
figures emerged into the fading light. As they moved into the courtyard, their long shadows played against the earth like wraiths, faceless and bodiless within their coverings. A chill went up Bek's spine,
a warning to be careful. He had formidable magic at his command,
but his skills and experience were not the equal of these.

As the contingent approached them, Traunt Rowan turned back
to Bek and Rue. "Your arrival is much anticipated," he said with a deferential nod.

There were three of them, two leading the third, one of the two
a broad-shouldered woman of some size and obvious strength. She
pulled back her hood as she reached him, and he knew instinctively
from the strong features and military bearing that she was the leader.
"Bek Ohmsford," she said, extending her hand. "I am Shadea a'Ru,
Ard Rhys in your sister's absence."

She shook his hand quickly, took Rue's in turn, then nodded to
her companions. "My First of Order, Gerand Cera, and my assistant,
Pyson Wence."

Bek nodded to them in turn, the first tall, thin, and sharp-featured,
the second physically unintimidating, but with eyes that reminded
him of a hunting bird's. Deferring to the woman, neither spoke on
being introduced.

"What have you learned of our son?" Rue asked at once. "Have
you found him?"

"We haven't." Shadea met her gaze without flinching, something
a lot of men couldn't do. "We continue to search, of course, for both
your son and the Ard Rhys, but we have run out of places to look. If
you come with me, I will explain."

Without waiting for their agreement, she turned and started back
toward the Keep, her two companions and Traunt Rowan falling
quickly into step behind her. Bek glanced at Rue, shrugged, and they

followed as well. He was trying to remember if his sister had ever said anything about any of these Druids, but nothing came to mind. Aside from Ahren Elessedil, Tagwen was the only one he could remember her speaking about and the only one he could remember meeting. He wished now that he had paid better attention.

Inside the Keep, Shadea beckoned them forward to walk with her, and the other three Druids gave way as they moved ahead.

"The Ard Rhys disappeared after retiring to her chamber several weeks ago. She went into her room and never came out. There was no sign of a struggle when we found her missing. The Trolls on watch said she had not come out during the night and that they had heard nothing. I dismissed them anyway, simply as a precaution. We have many enemies, and they have many reasons to want us gone. The Trolls might have been subverted."

That was one explanation, Bek thought, though it didn't feel right. "I recall my sister saying more than once how much she depended on them, how reliable they were."

Shadea's sun-browned face turned his way sharply, and she brushed the short-cropped blond hair from her forehead. "She may have made a mistake by trusting them. We don't know."

"No one has seen her since? No one has sent any word of her?"

"None. Tagwen seemed to have an idea about what might have happened, but then he disappeared as well. We tracked him to Emberen and to Ahren Elessedil. Then we tracked them both to Patch Run. Apparently, when they left, they took your son with them. That was the last thing we discovered that's worth talking about. We still don't know why the Ard Rhys disappeared or where she might have gone. We don't know where your son, Tagwen, and Ahren Elessedil have gone, either. Our airships continue to search, but time slips away, and that doesn't favor our efforts. I am hopeful that by coming to Paranor, you can change things."

Bek felt Rue's hand tighten in his own. "How can I help you? I don't know anything about this."

Shadea a'Ru nodded. "It is no secret that you are extraordinarily close to your sister. The story of how you found each other twenty years ago is common knowledge. Your inherited magic drew you in

ways that nothing else could. It binds you irrevocably. I think we can
make use of that in finding her and very likely your son, as well. I'll
show you how."

They passed down the shadowed corridor and ascended a series
of stairs to the upper levels. In a broad, high-ceilinged hall that ran
down the center of the Keep, they encountered other Druids moving
about in small groups, carrying books and papers and conversing
with one another. A few looked them over as they passed, taking note
of the two who were clearly not of their order. But no one looked for
very long, turning quickly away when they caught sight of Shadea.

They are afraid of her, Bek thought.

He remembered that it had been the same when he had come to
visit his sister—the same looks, the same quick averting of faces
when she passed. Nothing had changed in her absence. It made him
wonder if it was the nature of the position or of the candidates drawn
to occupy it. It made him wonder why anyone would want it.

As they turned down a secondary passageway, one narrower and
less heavily traveled, a young Druid rushed into their midst, colliding with Bek in a flurry of confusion and knocking him to the floor.

"Sorry," he apologized quickly, reaching down to help Bek up
again. The papers he had dropped lay scattered everywhere about
them. "I didn't see you. I was in a hurry. My mistake. Are you all
right? Well, then. Again, sorry."

Their hands clasped, and Bek felt a tiny piece of paper pressed
into his palm. "There, no harm done," the young Druid declared, his
eyes meeting Bek's quickly before looking away. He apologized
again, this time to Shadea, and bent to retrieve his papers from the
floor. The big woman gave him a withering look and walked right on
past, beckoning the others to follow. Bek glanced down briefly at the
young Druid as he passed him. The other man did not look up.

As they continued on, Bek slid the piece of paper into his pocket.
He had never seen the young Druid before. He glanced over at Rue,
but she didn't seem to have noticed anything.

They climbed several sets of stairs and traversed several more
corridors before coming to a room set high in the Keep. Gnome
Hunters stood watch without, and the door was locked and barred.

The Gnomes moved aside quickly as Shadea stepped up and manipulated the locks. When the door was open, the Druids ushered the Ohmsfords inside.

Bek glanced around. The room was empty except for a huge basin of water that sat at its center. The basin bowl was shallow and broad, and the waters it contained were a very deep green. There were lines and markings drawn on the surface of the basin below the waters, bumps and ridges, as well. It was a map, he realized, moving over to get a closer look, a map of the Four Lands.

"This is where you can help us, Bek," Shadea a'Ru announced, moving up beside him. Rue had already taken up a position on his other side, and he could feel the anticipation radiating from her like body heat. "This room is called the cold chamber. The stone walls insulate the basin. The scrye waters in the basin monitor the lines of power that bind the earth. They reflect disturbances in those lines when a powerful magic is used. We study them in an effort to discover where magic is being used outside the purview of the order."

She turned to him. "We had thought to use the scrye waters to track your sister's movements after she disappeared, but there have been no disturbances that would indicate the use of her magic. Still, the waters will track such magic, even its most minuscule application, if their power to interpret is enhanced. If you were to apply the magic of the wishsong to that end, we might be able to discover where she is. I know you possess the power to control its effect on things. Will you use it here?"

Bek held her gaze a moment, trying to read what was behind it. She was asking him to do something very straightforward, but he was suspicious of her motives. Traunt Rowan's omissions and shadings still troubled him; his uneasiness about the circumstances surrounding the disappearances of his sister and son hadn't lessened. He was tired from lack of sleep and worry, and he didn't trust that he was thinking clearly.

"I know you want me to do this right away," he told her. "I want that, too. But I don't know that I can help you effectively until I am better rested. Application of the magic of the wishsong requires a steady concentration that I don't feel I can bring to bear just now.

What I would like to do is eat something and get some sleep, then try
in the morning, when I'm fresh."

"Bek!" Rue exploded angrily, gripping his shoulder so hard it hurt.
"This is our son and your sister we are trying to help! What do you
mean, you need to rest? You can rest later!"

Her words made him flinch, but he looked directly at her. "I'm
worried for them, too. But I don't want to make a mistake. I'm just not
sure I'm recovered enough from that fever to focus the way I need to.
Not without a little food and rest first."

He turned away from the surprise and confusion that flashed
sharply in her eyes. "Tomorrow, then?"

Clearly unhappy with the delay, Shadea a'Ru took a moment to
consider. Reluctantly, she nodded. "Tomorrow will be fine. Traunt
Rowan will see you to your sleeping chambers and arrange for food
to be brought. Rest well."

She swept out of the room without sparing him another glance,
a hint of disgust reflected on her strong features. The taller of the
two Druids who went with her turned briefly to study him, and Bek
did not care for what he saw in the dark eyes. Then they were gone,
and Traunt Rowan was saying something about arrangements for the
night. Bek didn't hear all of it; his attention was back on Rue, who
was looking at him in what he hoped was a less judgmental way.

"Come with me," the Druid ordered, his own face dark and troubled.

It took them only a few minutes to reach their sleeping chambers, which consisted of two rooms with a bed, a few furnishings, a
single door, high windows, and a pair of unfriendly looking Gnome
Hunters already positioned at the doors.

"To keep you safe," Traunt Rowan explained quickly. "We are
taking no chances with your family, even here. Until we find out
what has happened to the Ard Rhys and your son, we intend to keep
close watch over all of you. I will have dinner sent right up."

When he was gone and the door securely closed behind him, Bek
put a finger to his lips before Rue could say anything, shaking his
head in warning. He motioned about the room, to the walls and ceiling, to the vents and doors and windows, where other ears might be

listening. When she nodded her understanding, he took her in his arms and put his lips close to her ear.

"Are you all right?"

He felt her nod into his shoulder. Her mouth pressed against his ear. "What was all that about a fever? You haven't had a fever in months."

"An excuse to keep Shadea at bay," he whispered. "Something about all this isn't right. I need to think about what she's asking me to do."

Another nod. "I don't trust her, either. I don't trust any of them. They're lying about something."

"That young Druid who bumped into me in the hallway? That wasn't an accident. He gave me a note; I have it in my pocket. He pressed it into my hand while he was helping me get up. He didn't want Shadea and the others to see what he was doing. He took a big chance."

"Do you know him? Is he Grianne's friend?"

"I don't know who is or isn't her friend at this point."

"Have you looked at the note?"

He shook his head. "I was waiting until we got away from the others. I didn't want to take a chance that they might see me looking at it." He paused, looking past her to the stone walls. "Walk with me over to the window. Stand close so we can shield what we're doing."

He felt her hand press against his back. "Do you think they might be watching as well as listening? Here?"

He shook his head. He didn't know. But he wasn't about to chance it. The safety of his sister and his son were at stake, and some among the Druids might not have their best interests at heart, no matter what they said.

They moved over to the window. The sun was setting on the horizon, a bloodred orb hung against a cerulean sky. Shadows had lengthened into dark pools, and the moon was just visible along the northeast horizon. The air outside felt cool and fresh on their faces as they leaned out, resting their arms on the stone sill, hunched close together with their backs to the room.

Bek slipped the scrap of paper from its hiding place and laid it in front of them, keeping his hands cupped about it. They bent close. Four words were printed on it in block letters.

DO NOT TRUST THEM.

That was all. Bek studied the note a moment more, glanced at Rue, then pocketed it anew. When he had a chance to do so, he would destroy it. But he would have to be careful how he handled it. Druids could reconstruct messages from nothing more than ashes.

"Clearly, not everyone is in agreement about what has happened to my sister," he said. "The young Druid, for one."

"Maybe others, as well."

He laid his hand on her arm. "We can't trust anyone."

She nodded, her eyes shifting to find his. "What are we going to do?"

He smiled. "I was hoping you could tell me." He leaned over and kissed her forehead gently. "I really was."

In bed that night, wrapped in each other's arms, comforted by the darkness and the silence, they talked about it.

"Do you think they are listening still?" She said it with an edge to her voice that suggested what she might do to them if she discovered they were.

He stroked her hair. "I think they have better things to do."

"I hope they weren't watching when we bathed. That makes my skin crawl. But I can imagine that ferret-faced Druid doing it."

"No one watched us bathe."

She was silent a moment, pressed up against him. "At least the meal they gave us was decent. They didn't try to poison us."

"They have other plans for us. Poison doesn't figure into things until we've served our purpose."

He felt her face turn toward his own in the dark. "Which is? You have a hunch, don't you?"

His voice was already a whisper, but he lowered it further. "I've been thinking about it. Grianne disappeared for no discernible reason, but Tagwen went outside the order to find help. That suggests he didn't know who to trust among these Druids any more than we do. He knew he could trust Ahren, though. So he traveled to Emberen to ask for his help. Ahren would have given it willingly. That much I feel pretty certain about."

"Me, too."

"But then they went to Patch Run. Maybe they did so to look for us, but they found Pen, instead. So they asked Pen where we were. He probably told them and wanted to go with them. Somehow, he persuaded them that it was a good idea."

"Or they had to take him because they thought he was in danger."

"Right. But what happened then? Did they come looking for us? If they did, why didn't they find us? Pen would have been able to track us down. He would have known how. Ahren would have helped him, using Druid magic. Anyway, something happened to prevent that. So now these Druids who've brought us here are looking for them. And, ostensibly at least, for Grianne, as well. But they can't find them."

"They want us to find them," Rue whispered. "They want us to do their work for them. But maybe not to help. Maybe to do harm."

It made sense. While the Druids might profess that their intentions were honorable, there was good reason to think otherwise.

They were silent again for a time, pondering their fresh insight, trying to think through what they should do about it. Bek felt his wife tighten her grip on him. "We can't help them. We can't put Penderrin in any more danger than he is already in."

"I know."

"I hate it that he's become involved in this, in your sister's life, in Druid intrigues and gamesmanship."

"Don't underestimate Pen. He is smart and capable, and he has some experience in the world. He might not have magic to protect him, but he has his wits. Besides, if he's with Ahren, he's as protected as he would be with us."

"I wouldn't agree with that. Anyway, he shouldn't have to be protected in the first place."

He felt her anger building. "Rue, listen to me. We can't change what's happened. We don't even know for sure what that is. That's what we came to find out. Maybe we will, once we have a chance to talk with that young Druid. In the meantime, it doesn't do us any good to get too angry to think."

"What makes you think I'm angry?"

"Well—"

"Don't you think I have a right to be angry?"

"Well—"

"Are you suggesting I can't be angry and think at the same time?"

He hesitated, uncertain of his reply, then felt her begin to shake with suppressed laughter. "Very funny," he whispered.

She poked him in the ribs. "I thought so."

They lay quietly, listening to each other breathe. Bek ran his hands along his wife's ribs and down her legs. He could feel the ridges where scar tissue had formed over wounds she had suffered twenty years earlier aboard the *Jerle Shannara.* They were a testimony to her strength and resiliency, a reminder of how hard her early life had been. He had always believed her to be stronger than he was, tougher of mind and body both. He had never stopped thinking of her that way. Others might think that because he possessed the use of the wishsong's magic, he was the stronger. Some might even think that being the male in their partnership made him the stronger. But he knew better.

"I won't get angry until after I get Penderrin back," she said suddenly, her words so soft he could barely hear them. "I don't make any promises after that."

"I wouldn't expect it."

"We will get him back, Bek. I don't care what it takes."

"We'll get him back."

"How?"

"You asked me that earlier."

"You didn't answer."

"I was thinking. I'm still thinking."

"Well, hurry up. I'm worried."

He smiled at her insistence, but was glad she couldn't see him doing so. She was scared for her son, and he would not want her to mistake how he was treating the matter. He was worried, too. But he understood that what was needed was a calm, measured approach to untangling the puzzle surrounding Pen's and Grianne's disappearances. Rue's strength might lie in her determination, but his lay in keeping his wits.

"I'll hurry," he promised.

"I would appreciate that."

"I know."

"I love you."

"I love you, too."

Minutes later, they were asleep.

EIGHT

B ek and Rue were awake early, troubled enough by the challenges that lay ahead that the first inklings of light in the east were sufficient to bring them out of their fitful sleep. They washed and dressed and found breakfast waiting outside the door in the form of bread, cheese, fruit, and cold ale. When they retrieved the food tray, the hallway was deserted save for the Gnome Hunters, who were stationed across the hallway. Bek nodded agreeably but got no response.

"I don't think we are guests in the usual sense of the word," he told Rue as he closed the door.

Within an hour, Traunt Rowan was knocking, his eyes bright with anticipation. "Are you ready to try now, Bek?" he asked.

Bek was. He had a plan, although he hadn't confided it to Rue. He told her when they woke that he knew what to do, but that it was better if he kept it to himself. Her own response should not seem forced or planned. She must trust him even if it looked like he was doing something he should not. He understood what was needed. No one at Paranor could be trusted with Pen's or Grianne's whereabouts. If he was lucky enough to discover that information, it belonged to them and them alone.

He had explained it all in a whisper as they lay together in the deep gloom of early dawn, still wary of who might be listening, determined to make no mistake that would reveal their true intentions.

They left the sleeping chamber behind Traunt Rowan, who led them back down the hall and up the stairs to the cold chamber and the scrye waters. Bek held Rue's hand in his own, a reassurance that transcended physical presence and touched on emotional support. He could read her feelings in her touch, in the strength of her grip. He took his cue from those. He spoke with the Druid conversationally, asking if there was any news, if the airships searching for his sister and son had returned, if the day seemed a good one. He told Traunt Rowan that their sleeping arrangements were more than adequate, better than they had been used to over the past few weeks. He praised the food. He talked to put the other at ease. He talked to calm himself.

"Shadea is ready," Traunt Rowan advised him as they reached their destination, and Bek understood it to be a warning that he should be ready, as well.

The cold chamber felt frigid in the wake of the night's recent departure, the chill of the darkness still present. Bek shivered involuntarily as he entered the room, hunching his shoulders against the sudden change in temperature. Shadea a'Ru stood to one side, looking out the window at the sunrise, her broad shoulders wrapped in a scarlet cloak that fell all the way to the floor. When she turned, he saw that the clasp that fastened it bore the crest of the Druid order, the instantly recognizable emblem of the Eilt Druin. It flashed brightly as the light caught it momentarily, and Bek thought he caught a reflection of that hard brightness in Shadea's eyes as well.

"We are anxious to begin, Bek," she said perfunctorily, nodding to Rue, but not speaking to her. "Are you sufficiently rested now?"

"I am," Bek assured her. "Let's begin."

She beckoned him to stand with her at the basin. Bek moved over to peer down into the swirl of deep green waters, seeing fluctuations on their surface that seemed to have no discernible origin. He studied them for a moment, then glanced at Shadea expectantly. As he did so, he caught sight of Gerand Cera, who was standing back and to one side of him in the shadows. He wondered how many more were in hiding somewhere in that room. He wondered if he was going to be able to fool them all.

"You already understand what it is the scrye waters do," Shadea said. "If you can use your magic to connect with their impulses, you should be able to reach beyond what is visible for a more comprehensive reading. I am hopeful that your reach will extend to the magic that resides in your sister or perhaps your son. Any little trace, any clue revealed by doing so may prove helpful."

Helpful to whom? he thought. But he said nothing, only nodding in response.

"Would you move back from me a little?" he asked.

All of them, Rue included, stepped away from the basin to give him the space he needed. He took a deep breath and closed his eyes in concentration. He calmed himself, centered himself, and then lost himself in the deep silence that settled over the room. He would have only one chance, and if he wasn't convincing enough, he would be in the worst trouble of his life. These were Druids, he reminded himself for what must have been the hundredth time. Druids weren't easily fooled when it came to the use of magic.

On the other hand, none of them possessed or truly understood the magic of the wishsong. That was his edge, if he had any.

He waited until he could hear himself breathing in the stillness, then summoned the magic. He began with a low humming, a sound that mirrored a wind's whisper as it passed through the branches of the trees, soft and silky. He brought it out of its resting place and let it fill him with warmth. The cold of the room lessened and then disappeared. His concentration was so complete that the people around him disappeared as well. He was alone, lost in himself and in his magic.

When he opened his eyes again, he saw only the basin in front of him. He reached out with his hands and let them hover just above the deep green waters, so close he could almost feel the strange ripples that disturbed the otherwise placid surface. He moved his hands slowly, taking his time, not rushing the flow of the magic from his body. He watched the waters respond as he let the first tendrils stroke their surface. He felt them shudder at the intrusion.

He worked more swiftly then, enveloping the scrye waters in a broad swath intended to detect any obvious sign of Grianne or Pen. The former's presence would reveal itself immediately, so strong was the connection between them. Shadea had been right about that; their shared use of magic was a powerful link. But nothing showed itself; no sign of his sister surfaced. He kept searching, sending the wishsong's magic deep into the scrye waters, into the gridwork of the lines of power that crisscrossed the Four Lands, sifting and probing. He moved his hands in a slow, circular motion that took him in all directions, toward all of the possible places she might have gone.

Still nothing.

He was beginning to think that his efforts were a waste of time, a result he did not like to contemplate, when abruptly he touched on something. The surface of the scrye waters rippled in response, and he moved his focus away immediately so Shadea would not see. He continued his search in other areas, taking his time, trying to give an appearance of thoroughness. He must seem to be working hard at making the magic connect; he must not appear duplicitous. But it was harder now, because his instincts were to return to the place on the gridwork where he had found what he was looking for.

Time slipped away. Nothing further revealed itself. He let his hands sweep back to the point of connection, a testing of his previous discovery. Once again, the scrye waters rippled, and he felt the presence of wishsong magic. Moving his hands away, he marked the place in his mind, knowing now where to go and what to look for.

Then, preoccupied with his discovery and ready to break this off, he let his hands settle over the place on the gridwork that marked Paranor's solitary spires.

Instantly, the scrye waters boiled and steamed, then exploded in a massive geyser. Magic ripped through Bek, breaking down his defenses and his connection with the basin waters. He was caught completely unprepared, and the next thing he knew he was flat on his back on the floor, his clothing steaming and his hair singed.

"Bek!" Rue was at his side, cradling his head in her hands, bent close to his face. He blinked hard, trying to dispel the dizziness that was making the room spin and her voice echo. Had he lost consciousness? How long had he been lying there? "Look at me!" she said. "Can you see me? Can you hear what I'm saying?"

He nodded wordlessly. Their Druid hosts were gathered around him as well, crouched like vultures, faces a mix of hunger and expectation. He had planned to deceive them by creating a diversion with the wishsong's magic. He hadn't planned on it happening this way. His entire body throbbed and his head ached as if he had taken a physical beating.

"What did you see?" Shadea demanded of him, her eyes narrowed. "You must have seen something, felt something."

He shook his head. His tongue felt thick in his mouth, and his teeth were gritted against the pain. "Nothing," he mumbled as he worked his jaw muscles, trying to make them relax. "I don't know what happened. I was working the magic, just a general search. My hands passed over Paranor's location on the map. Then this."

He saw recognition in her eyes, a glint of satisfaction and exultation, a response that suggested she had found what she had been looking for and that it was not something she would ever reveal to him.

Then a veiled, guarded look took its place, and she smiled. "You came in contact with the magic that wards the Druid's Keep, Bek. It was a backlash of the protections we set in place for ourselves. Paranor was defending us. I should have warned you. Are you all right?"

"I'll need to rest myself a bit before I try again. I'm not done yet with my search."

"You shall have all the rest you need." She stood up, glancing at the other two. "He has done well, for his first attempt. He'll do even better next time. Traunt, take our guests back to their rooms. See that they have everything they need while Bek recovers. Food and drink and fresh clothing, perhaps a walk in the gardens later. On the morrow, Bek, we will try again."

She was gone from the room so quickly that he had no further chance to question her odd response. Still woozy, he drew himself up into a sitting position and hung his head between his knees.

"That was dramatic," Rue whispered as she placed his arm over her shoulders and helped him to stand. Traunt Rowan had moved ahead to open the door for them and was looking down the hallway after Shadea and Gerand Cera. "Did you intend to hurt yourself like that?"

"I didn't intend to hurt myself at all, if things had gone the way they were supposed to," he whispered back. He saw the look of surprise in her eyes and managed a tired smile. "I didn't plan any of that."

"What happened, then?"

"I don't know. Something I didn't expect. But it wasn't wasted effort, anyway."

She leaned close. "Penderrin?"

He nodded. "I think I found him."

He fell asleep almost immediately after reaching their bedchamber, too exhausted even to remove his clothes. He slept soundly until Rue woke him to make him eat something, and then he fell right back asleep. He dreamed, but his dreams were disjointed and strange, a collection of images from his past life and from other lives entirely, all connected in a way that made them surreal and unfathomable. He thought he was aware of Rue speaking to him more than once, but it wasn't enough to bring him out of the dreams.

When he woke again, the sun was setting. He was alone in the room, a tray of food sitting on the table by his bed. He ate, then washed and moved over to sit by the window and watch the sun disappear and the moon come up. Stars began to appear in the darkening sky north.

It was another half hour before Rue reappeared.

"You're awake," she said as she came through the doorway and saw him. "How do you feel?"

"As if I've been thrown off a cliff. But better than I felt earlier. The dizziness is gone; the aching isn't so bad. I expect I'll live. Where were you?"

"Traunt Rowan took me for a walk in the Druid gardens." She smiled. "They really are beautiful, and I would have loved to see more of them. But the walk turned into an inquisition. I spent most of my time fending off questions about Pen. The Druids don't know much about our son, but they seem awfully eager to learn. Too eager."

She kept her voice low, moving over to sit beside him on the bench. "On the other hand, I got a good look around. I have a better idea of how to get around than I did before. I thought we might want to know where all the doors and windows are, in case we end up having to get out of here quickly."

She put her arm around him. "You scared me this morning. Are you sure you're all right?"

He leaned over and kissed her, then put his lips against her ear. "I've been thinking while you were out," he whispered. "Thinking about this morning and what happened in the cold chamber. I have some ideas that might be worth considering."

"Tell me about Penderrin first," she insisted, putting her arms around him and drawing him close, her voice a whisper as well. "I've been waiting all day for you to be coherent enough to talk to me. You said you found him?"

He nodded into her shoulder. "In the Charnal Mountains. It happened too quickly for me to be sure exactly where he is; I couldn't take the time to find out without giving away what I was doing. But it was definitely him."

"Why would he be all the way up there?"

"I don't know." He took a deep breath. "Here's what I do know. I was doing a general search through the scrye waters for any sign of Pen or Grianne. I found Pen in the Charnals, like I said, but I moved away from the contact before Shadea or one of the others could tell what I was doing. Maybe they wouldn't have known anyway, but I didn't want to chance it. I purposely didn't search Paranor on the grid; after all, that was where Grianne was supposed to have disappeared. What was the point?"

"A question you might have answered differently if you had stopped to think about it," she said quietly.

He nodded. "True enough. Anyway, I worked my way back to Pen to make certain he was in the Charnals, that I hadn't made a mistake. Then I moved my hands away again, trying to decide what to do next. I let my concentration lapse, and my hands drifted back down over Paranor. That was when the scrye waters exploded and threw me away from the basin. Shadea claimed that Paranor's warding magic responded to my intrusion, defending the Keep. But I wasn't trying to intrude. I wasn't doing anything threatening. What I was doing was searching for Pen and Grianne, and I think the magic that wards Paranor reacted to that. I think it reacted because I found something it was trying to hide."

She was silent a moment. "But it wasn't Penderrin because he is somewhere in the Charnals. So it has to be Grianne."

"I think so. When she disappeared, Tagwen left Paranor without confiding in any of the Druids who might have helped him. I think the key to discovering what happened to my sister lies here, and that these Druids who claim to be her friends are covering it up."

"But you were brought here to find her. Why would they do that if they are trying to hide where she is?"

"I think we were brought here to find Pen and found Grianne by accident. Did you see Shadea's face when I explained what I was doing when the magic threw me back from the scrye waters? She was elated! I think it confirmed something she already knew about Grianne. It's Pen she's looking for, but she had to tell me to look for my sister, too, because it would have seemed odd not to."

Bek felt her shake her head slowly against his own. "I still don't understand what Penderrin has to do with all this. I still don't see why he's up in the Charnal Mountains, miles from everything."

He didn't make an immediate response. He didn't have the answers to those questions. His instincts told him that Pen was running away, that he had fled Patch Run to avoid capture, perhaps from these Druids, perhaps from someone else. What troubled him was that Pen would have come looking for them if he had been able to do so. He wouldn't have run off blindly, and he certainly wouldn't have gone into the Charnals without a very good reason.

He stared off into the growing dark. Pen was levelheaded and capable, but that didn't stop Bek from being frightened for his son. Pen was just a boy, and he lacked the life experience necessary to deal with this sort of danger. If he was being chased, there was always the possibility that he would panic.

"Bek, I just thought of something," Rue whispered. She moved so that they could see each other, her face so close to his that they were almost touching. "If Shadea knows the wishsong's magic exposed Grianne, she will expect it to expose Penderrin as well. You won't be able to pretend otherwise for long."

He nodded. "I thought of that."

"We can't allow that to happen. How are we going to prevent it?"

He leaned forward and kissed her on the mouth. "While they're sleeping, we're going to use the scrye waters and find him ourselves."

N I N E

Night had fallen across the Four Lands, and Arishaig was bright with the light of torches and candles when Sen Dunsidan made his way back from dinner to his sleeping chambers. The day had been productive. An address before the Coalition Council had produced a standing ovation following his carefully worded promise that he had found a way to resolve the war on the Prekkendorran quickly and favorably. Even those who would have liked to see his role in the Federation government diminished congratulated him afterwards for his courage and commitment. They were counting on him to fail, of course, but he was confident that he wouldn't.

This was due in part to an earlier visit to Etan Orek, who had completed all work on the first of what he was now calling his "fire launchers." He had mounted it on a swivel that allowed it to swing left and right at a ninety-degree firing angle and was equipped with a sighting system and recoil springs to keep it from disrupting the flight of an airship, once it was in place and operating. It was also equipped with controls to manipulate the amount of energy fed through the crystals and released from the mouth of the firing tube.

When Sen Dunsidan had tested it this time, the scope of its destructive capabilities had left him breathless with anticipation.

His excitement was only marginally diminished by news that no other weapons were yet complete. But after long hours of experimentation using different combinations of crystals, Orek was close to duplicating his first effort and expected to complete a second launcher before the week was out.

At the construction site for Federation airships, mercenary Rover designers and builders were at work on a huge new flagship, the *Dechtera,* which would carry Sen Dunsidan's secret weapon into battle when she was completed. He inspected their work and was satisfied with their progress. For the first time in a very long time, he could imagine a world dominated by the Federation.

His bedchamber was lit with candles, but deeply shadowed in its corners and alcoves when he entered, and he might not have seen her at all had she not immediately moved out into the light to greet him. His heart went directly to his throat in that instant, freezing his muscles and his voice so that he was rendered completely helpless. Then he recognized her, and he gave a quick, sharp sigh.

"Iridia," he said. He straightened himself, his composure recovered and his irritation fanned. "What are you doing here?"

"Waiting for you."

Iridia Eleri stepped forward, her slender body and white skin giving her an almost ethereal look. She was wrapped in a lightweight traveling cloak that hung open to the floor, and her dark hair fell in loose waves about her shoulders. He was captivated, as always, by her impossible beauty. He had not seen her in weeks, not since she had given him the liquid night that he, in turn, had given to Shadea a'Ru to eliminate Grianne Ohmsford and seize control of Paranor. She had been his spy within the Druid's Keep for some time, but it was not until she had provided the potion that she had proved her real value.

"Waiting for me for what reason?" he demanded. "It was our agreement that you would remain at Paranor and monitor the activities of our new Ard Rhys, so that I might have eyes and ears inside the Keep. It was our agreement that you would never come here."

The Elven sorceress shrugged. "The agreement has been changed."

He had never trusted her, never felt comfortable with what she was doing for him. He was more than willing to accept her offer of help and make use of her services as a spy. But she had been close to Shadea for too long for him to feel comfortable with the idea that she was ready to switch loyalties to him. It was one thing to betray Grianne Ohmsford, whom they all hated. It was another to betray a friend. Not that someone like Iridia would ever be bound too closely by friendship. But her machinations confused him. She would not tell him where she had gotten the liquid night. She would not tell him why she had chosen to pass it to Shadea through him rather than to give it to her friend directly. She would not explain her need for secrecy in working with him. Try as he might, he could not figure out what she would gain from all this. That sort of thing tended to bother a man whose life was built around understanding the nature of manipulations.

"You look tired, Sen Dunsidan," she said. "Are you tired?"

He shook his head. "I am irritated, Iridia. I don't like surprises and I don't like people who second-guess my decisions without speaking to me about it first. Why has our agreement been changed?"

She moved to one of the chairs flanking the windows looking out over the city and sat down. He could barely see her in the dim light, but he was aware suddenly that something was different about her.

"I have had a falling-out with Shadea," she said. "The damage cannot be repaired. She will no longer consult with me on things of any importance. She will seek to diminish me and ultimately to eliminate me completely. As a result, I cannot be effective as your spy."

"A falling-out?" he repeated.

"Of a sort that has nothing to do with our agreement. She does not know about you and me. She does not even suspect. What has caused the breach between us has to do with someone I once cared for deeply."

He had heard rumors about her involvement with another Druid, of a love affair that Grianne Ohmsford had put a stop to. Could this be whom she was talking about? But Shadea had not had anything to do with that business. He couldn't see the connection.

"So I came here," she finished, reaching for a goblet and pouring wine from the decanter that sat next to it.

"You came here to do what?" He moved forward a couple of steps to see her face better in the dim light, still trying to decide what was different about her.

She drank deeply of the wine, then set the goblet down and looked at him. "I came here to be your personal adviser. If I cannot be effective within the order, then I shall be effective from without. Our agreement still stands, Prime Minister. It has simply been altered. My usefulness must take another form. Since I can no longer spy on the Druid order, I shall advise you regarding it. I shall give you the kind of advice that no one else will, advice gained from having lived among them, of knowing how they think, of understanding what they will do. No one else can provide this."

He hesitated, finding her argument persuasive, but not quite trusting her motives.

"You need me to tell you what to expect from them," she said. "No one knows Shadea a'Ru better than I do. You have an alliance with her and with the order through her, but you need to know how to make use of it. I know how far she will allow herself to be pushed and in what directions. I know what will persuade her when persuasion is needed. I know her weaknesses far better than you do."

"I know her well enough to keep her at bay," he said.

She laughed softly. "You know her well enough to get yourself killed. If you think she will honor your agreement once she has no further use for it, you are a fool. She made it to gain credibility for the order and for herself. She will use you to see the Free-born smashed and the balance of power shifted, and then she will use you to gain control of the Federation, as well. Surely, you accept that this is so."

In fact, he did. He had known as much all along, although he didn't like thinking about it. He had accepted it as a necessary consequence of his alliance with her because he needed that alliance in order to end the stalemate on the Prekkendorran. Even with his new weapon, he was wary of the Druids, of their power as wielders of magic. What Iridia was telling him was nothing new, but it was making him take a fresh look at the realities.

"Your intent is to act as my adviser?" he repeated, trying to get used to the idea.

"Your Druid adviser. Your *personal* Druid adviser. No one else in all the Four Lands will have one, save you. That will give you a measure of respect that you could gain in no other way. It will give you stature for what needs doing."

"You would leave the order?"

She laughed again, and the sound sent a chill up his spine. It wasn't the laugh itself; it was the emptiness it suggested. "I have already left the order. Better to be your adviser in Arishaig than a whipping boy in Paranor. Understand me, Sen Dunsidan. I am a sorceress of great power. I was born with it; I was trained to use it. I am the equal of Shadea, though she might not think so. I might have been the equal of Grianne Ohmsford. I want for myself what you want— recognition and power. Yours will come with the Federation's victory over the Free-born. Mine will come when I have replaced Shadea as Ard Rhys. Together, we can make both happen more easily. Accept my offer."

He studied her without speaking. Could she have turned against him and become Shadea's spy? Could this be an elaborate charade, part of a plan to eliminate him? But, no, if Shadea wanted him dead, it would be easy enough to make him so. It would not require such a complicated approach. Besides, what use was he to Shadea if he was dead? Another from the Council would simply take his place, and she would risk losing her alliance with the Federation. He could think of no reason she would want that to happen.

He folded his arms across his chest. "Very well, Iridia. I accept. Your advice would be most welcome." He held up one finger. "But I hope this isn't a game you play with me. If I find that it is, I will have you killed without another thought. You might be a Druid, but you are still only made of flesh and blood."

Her pale face tilted slightly, as if she were seeing a strange animal. "Who was it who offered her services to you as your spy in the Druid camp? Who was it who told you of a way to dispose of Grianne Ohmsford without casting suspicion on yourself? Who brought you the liquid night? Who has stood by you every step of the way? Name another, besides me."

There was a coldness to the challenge that warned him against any answer but one. "Your point is well taken." He felt dangerously close to the edge of something he neither understood nor could control. What was it about her that was suddenly so troubling?

"I shall arrange rooms for you in my home," he added quickly, realizing that he was staring.

She didn't seem to notice. She rose and walked to the bedroom door. "Do not bother. I will look after myself. I am used to doing so." Then she turned. "When you have need of me, I shall be there."

She drew her cloak close about her and was gone.

Guards were stationed at the chamber doors and servants were at work farther down the hallway of the Prime Minister's residence, so the Moric waited until it was safely alone in an empty room at the back of the house before shedding its clothing and skin. It hated the stench of both and was anxious to return to the sewers, where it had been in hiding for several days while spying on the human Dunsidan. When the clothes and skin were removed, it folded them up and stuffed them into a bag under its cloak, strapping the bag over its sleek body. It would not wear them again until the next meeting. By then, it would be better able to bear the smell.

Relieved of its disguise and free to depart, it went out the window. It was three stories up, but since it had come in by climbing the wall, it had no difficulty leaving the same way. Using its claws to grip the stones, it went down like a lizard, crawling and skittering until it was back on the ground. From there, it scurried across the grounds and through the shadows to the edge of the compound, went over the wall, and faded into the night.

It had been in the city for the better part of a week, making itself familiar with its new surroundings. After coming out of the Forbidding, it had acted quickly to eliminate the human who had facilitated its crossing, absorbing it as a sponge would water, consuming flesh and bones and blood, but assimilating its memories and traits and keeping the skin to disguise itself. The Moric was a demon, but it was a changeling, as well. While most changelings could only pretend at being other creatures, however, the Moric could actually devour and become them. It was a useful ability, particularly here, in this world, where it would have been quickly noticed otherwise.

The woman's death had assured its secrecy, and her skin had given it a way out of the Druid safehold. Too many magic users resided there for the Moric to feel comfortable. It was powerful, but no match for large numbers. Besides, it had taken what it needed from the Druids. Misguided and corrupt, they had yielded to the temptations offered them and unwittingly opened the door that imprisoned it. So desperate were they to indulge their own greed that they had never stopped to think what it was they were really doing. How easily manipulated they had been! First the woman whose skin it inhabited, then those who shared her hatred of the one human it feared. Had she not been betrayed and sent into the Forbidding to take its place, it would still be locked away in the world of the Jarka Ruus. But the cunning and deception of the Straken Lord had deceived them all, and so for the first time in centuries, a demon was free.

Still, it would all be for nothing if the Moric did not accomplish what it had been sent to do. The human Dunsidan was the key. The Moric hadn't known as much when it had come to this city, its plans not yet fully formed, its intent for the most part to find a way to make use of its human disguise.

But yesterday it had discovered the project the human Dunsidan had sought to keep secret. It had learned of the weapon he had built and the hopes he harbored of using it against other humans. The Moric had watched as the man in charge played with the crystals. It had watched as Dunsidan used the weapon, burning through thick metal, twisting and destroying entire slabs in seconds. There was something of interest. The human thought to use the weapon as a tool of war. The Moric was not so shortsighted.

The city was sleeping, and the Moric was able to pass freely down its streets and alleyways. The few humans it encountered never saw it. It climbed the walls or hid in the darkness and waited for them to pass. It could have killed them easily and would have enjoyed doing so, but it was there for a different purpose and would not allow itself to be distracted. Its value lay not only in its adaptability, but also in its single-minded determination. There would be plenty of time for killing humans later, when its task was complete.

When it reached the entrance to its hiding place, it glanced around to be certain it was alone before going down through the grates. The smells of the sewer were sweet and welcome, and it hastened to reach the cold, dark catacombs through which they tunneled. It was the one place in that wretched world that reminded it of its own. It could feel at peace there. It could find comfort. One day, it promised, everything would be just like that.

The darkness was thick and deep beneath the earth, within the tunnels, and the Moric found a shelf submerged in several inches of fetid water and sewage and settled down to sleep.

TEN

They were still miles away when Grianne saw the fortress for the first time. It sat on a plateau that fell away hundreds of feet from a huge mountainside. Silhouetted against the empty horizon, black and stark within a swirling mix of gray mist and low-hung clouds, the fortresses' towers and parapets jutted sharp and hard-edged from the mottled rock as if they had blossomed like a cancer.

It was a huge, sprawling complex. She stared at it from the bed of straw on which she lay, her chains clanking softly as she rolled and swayed with the pitch of the wagon in which she was caged. They were moving in the direction of the fortress, and she felt certain that it was their destination. Whoever had made her a prisoner would be waiting there. She contemplated what that might mean as the strange caravan rolled on, the bull beasts snorting and huffing from their exertions, the wolves surging past in flashes of gray ruff and snarling muzzles, the creaking of ironbound wheels and leather harness mingling with the staccato snapping of whips and the odd croaking of wagon drivers she could not see. Dust filled the air, thick and choking, and she smelled its dryness and age. It made her choke, and she buried her face in her shoulder to breathe. Her body ached from being shackled, and her head throbbed from the ingestion of grit and the stench of the animals.

Once, when she was looking in the right direction, she saw the strange creature that seemed in charge of the little procession, its oddly elongated face peering in at her, topknot of coarse black hair swaying with its steps, bearded face intense and bright-eyed with interest. It did not speak to her as it had the first time it had approached, merely studied her a moment before moving on.

Exhausted and sick at heart, she dozed for a time, and when she woke again they were climbing a long, winding ramp that led to the fortress. It looked even bigger by then, looming up in a cluster of peaked roofs and crenellated walls, blacker than the soot of a wet fire and sharper-edged than a throwing knife. She sat up, bracing herself against the pitch and roll of the wagon, looking up the rampway to where a pair of massive, ironbound gates had opened to admit them. Creatures that reminded her of Weka Dart in the way they carried themselves scurried about on the tops of the walls and along the ramp itself, the metal of their weapons and armor glinting dully. The fortress was heavily defended, whoever its lord, and the only approach seemed to be up the fully exposed ramp.

She was reminded suddenly of Tyrsis, Callahorn's great fortress in the Four Lands. This keep could be a mirror of that one, and she suspected that it was situated on the same plateau in this world as Tyrsis was in her own. The similarities surprised her, and yet she knew that in the divergence of separate histories, some things would work out much the same. The use of geography in choosing natural positions of defense would surely be one.

The gates swallowed them up and closed behind them with a booming sound. Then there were faces all around her, sharp-featured and hungry looking, fringed in coarse hair and dominated by flat noses and pointed ears. Goblins, she realized, though she had never seen one. They had been banished into the Forbidding in the time of Faerie, she had read in the Druid Histories. Some of them grinned unpleasantly, revealing sharp, pointed teeth and black gums. They reached through the bars to touch her. The wolves snarled and snapped angrily at them, as if protecting a meal they would soon enjoy. The drivers she couldn't see flicked their whips and croaked. The air was filled with raucous sounds and fetid smells and, even inside the walls of the keep, clouds of dust.

The caravan rolled to a halt at a central tower, one ringed with walls that were spiked and barbed atop their parapets and through which the mouths of spear launchers protruded like serpent tongues. A flurry of activity announced their arrival as dozens more of the Goblins surrounded the wagons, some bearing lengths of rope and chain attached to slip-nooses and clamps and some bearing weapons. Grianne could no longer hear the snarls of the wolves; presumably the huge beasts had been locked outside the last wall they had passed through, their task as herders complete.

The creature with the topknot reappeared, coming out of the Goblin throng to unlock and open the door to her cage. She stood quietly as her keeper entered, thinking that if it got close enough, she might break its neck. But it kept its distance once inside, staying just out of her reach, working instead on the chains that held her fast, releasing them one at a time from the cage walls and passing the ends over to groups of Goblins waiting to receive them. It all seemed well rehearsed and smoothly accomplished, and she was given no opportunity to resist.

So she remained calm and let them do what they chose. She could wait. Her gag was left in place and her irons kept locked as she was led down out of the wagon. She was aware that her jailers held the chains taut so that she could be yanked over quickly if she tried to make a sudden move. It seemed clear to her that any effort at reaching for the gag in her mouth would trigger such a response. She couldn't know if they were aware of the wishsong's power and so were keeping her gagged because of it or if they were simply warding against the possibility of her employing any combination of utterances and gestures that might trigger an onslaught of magic.

She glanced once at the drivers of the wagons and found them to be creatures that resembled huge toads, perched on their seats with their hind legs tucked under them, short forearms gripping the reins to the bull beasts, widemouthed heads hunched forward, lidded eyes fixed and staring. They made no move to climb down off the seats.

They gave no indication that they had any interest at all in what was happening around them.

She saw that the cages ahead of and behind her were empty. She was the only object of transport.

The creature with the topknot appeared directly in front of her, its strange face blank and its flat eyes staring. It beckoned for her to follow, and she was assisted by the Goblins, who tugged none too gently on her chains to let her know what was required, allowing her to move but keeping her just the other side of being off balance. She straddle-walked after and through them, doing what was required of her, biding her time because that was all she could do.

Ahead of her, massive doors opened to the outer wall of the tower they had drawn up to, and she was led inside. The wall was several feet thick, and its doors were cross-braced with massive timbers and iron bars. Inside, the courtyard was barren and empty of life, a killing ground between the first wall and a second of equally imposing girth. Murder holes overlooked the entryway from walls and gatehouses on both sides. Topknot walked ahead, moving toward a second set of doors. The Goblins followed, half-dragging her with them.

The second set of doors opened into a large room ablaze with torchlight. A single stairway wound down out of the darkness ahead; it was the only other entry into the room. The air was cool and damp, and slicks of water shimmered on the floor and stained the walls. Chains hung from iron rings all about the room; at its center sat a chair similarly equipped. A torture room, Grianne decided, and she shivered involuntarily. At Topknot's direction, the Goblins moved her over to one wall, spread her legs, and fastened her ankle irons to rings embedded in the stone. Then a heavy leather belt was cinched tightly about her waist, and her wrists were chained to rings in the belt so that she could not lift her arms more than a few inches on either side.

Her mind raced. Had they brought her all this way just to kill her? Did they plan to torture her for information? She closed her eyes momentarily, and when she opened them again, the Goblins were on their knees, Topknot had gone into a deep bow, and the lord of the keep was coming down the stairway.

She knew it for a demon right away, though not one she recognized. It was big, taller than she was, and broad through the shoulders. It walked upright like a man and in general was proportioned as one, though the resemblance ended there. Its skin was black and spiky, with clusters of spines sticking out everywhere except its face, which was flat and devoid of expression, its features buried so completely that at first glance it seemed possessed only of cold blue eyes that fixed on her with glittering intensity. It wore no clothes, but an assortment of bladed weapons was strapped about its body, some shaped in ways she had never seen. In one hand it carried a strange collar.

When it got to within ten feet, it stopped and held out the collar. Topknot appeared as if by magic to take it, walked over to Grianne, and fastened it securely about her neck. Once it was in place, the angular creature looked back at its master.

"What you wear is called a conjure collar," said the demon that had brought it. To her surprise, it spoke in a language she recognized. "If you attempt to use your magic, it will cause you sufficient pain to make you wish you hadn't. If you disobey me in any way, it will punish you. Nod if you understand me."

She nodded. Topknot removed the gag. She coughed and spit to rid herself of the dryness and dust that were in her throat. Topknot studied her thoughtfully, then released the ankle chains as well.

"Get down on your knees and bow to me," the demon said.

She wasn't sure she had heard right and she stared in disbelief. The expressionless face looked away, and one clawed hand gestured languidly. Excruciating pain exploded all through her, radiating out from the collar like strands of barbed wire into her throat, her body, and her limbs. She screamed at the assault, unable to stop. Clutching herself, she dropped to her knees and lowered her head toward the demon.

"You will speak only when told to," it said. "Nod if you understand."

She nodded at once. The conjure collar no longer tore at her, but the pain lingered in small waves that rose and fell with every breath she took. She gasped with the effort required to endure it.

"When you speak to me, you will address me as *Master*. Nod if you understand."

She nodded.

"Would you like some water? You may answer."

Her jaw clenched in fury. "Yes, Master."

"Give her water, Hobstull." The demon's mouth was a thin, lip-less opening on the lower half of its flat, empty face. Its voice was raw and hoarse, suggestive of damage sustained by its vocal cords. There was no tonal inflection or hint of emotion.

Topknot brought her a cup filled with water that tasted of metal and smelled of swamp, but she drank it anyway. When she was finished, he backed away at once. She looked around. The Goblins had faded away. She was alone with Hobstull and the master of the keep.

"Do you know where you are?" the latter asked. "You may answer."

She nodded. The demon waved dismissively, and pain ratcheted through her once more, dropping her into a fetal position, where she lay moaning and sobbing. The demon studied her impassively, then came forward a step.

"Answer me as you have been taught. I want to hear you speak the words you were told to speak."

She squeezed her eyes shut against her humiliation and rage, fighting to keep from breaking down completely. "Yes, Master," she whispered.

"Do you know where you are? You may answer."

"Inside the Forbidding, Master." She opened her eyes again and looked up.

"Inside the world of the Jarka Ruus," the demon corrected softly. "Where I brought you to live."

She barely heard it; her head was buzzing with the aftereffects of the conjure collar's pain. The demon beckoned to Hobstull, who moved to fill the water cup once more, then hauled her to her knees so that she could drink again of the foul-tasting water. She accepted his gift wordlessly.

"You may thank me," the demon said.

She took a deep breath. "Thank you, Master."

The demon nodded. "Hobstull is not pleased with you. You made him work much harder than he intended when he left here three days ago. You made him feel inadequate. He is my Catcher, my finder and keeper of specimens. He is the one you must rely on for food and drink, so you don't want to upset him."

She looked briefly at Hobstull, who stared back at her with the same inquisitive look he had displayed earlier.

"Hobstull uses traps meant to lure his quarry by sounds, sights, and smells that speak to their deepest needs. He is very good at it. I have acquired many specimens as a result of his cleverness and perseverance. You are the latest and perhaps the most important. But you are still only a specimen. Do you understand?"

A specimen. She kept the anger from her face and voice with an effort. "Yes, Master."

"Good." The blue eyes glittered. "I am Tael Riverine, Straken Lord of Kraal Reach. I rule here. I rule everything from the Dragon Line north to the Quince south, from Huka Flats west to Brockenthrog Weir east. I rule you. Learn to accept this. I am your master, now and forever."

A pause. "Do you understand, Grianne Ohmsford, once Ard Rhys of the Druids?"

She felt her heart sink. She had been hoping desperately that her capture was by chance and not by design, that she would have a chance to gain her freedom after her captor's interest in her waned. But if the demon knew who she was, she was there because it had intended to bring her there, and there was no longer any chance of being set free.

"Yes, Master," she managed.

It saw the look on her face. "You didn't listen closely enough to what I said earlier, did you? You weren't paying attention."

She cringed in spite of herself, anticipating another rush of pain.

"I said that you are inside the world of the Jarka Ruus, that I brought you here to live. You are here because of me. You are here because I wished it to be so. Think back to your own world, to your visit to the ruins of the Skull Kingdom, where once the Warlock Lord ruled. Think back to the fires that ignited and burned without reason. Think back to the face you saw in those fires when you tried to probe them with your magic."

She knew at once what the demon was telling her. She remembered it all, especially the face that had appeared in the flames, coming out of hiding just long enough for her to see its features clearly.

It was this face. It was the face of the Straken Lord.

"You remember now, don't you?" the demon said. "Good." It gestured. "Get on your knees again and bow to me."

She did so, a chill settling through her as she realized how deeply in trouble she was.

"Take her, Hobstull," the Straken Lord ordered.

Without bothering to wait, the demon turned away and disappeared up the stairs into the gloom.

Hobstull walked over to where she knelt, clipped a fresh chain to a ring on the belt about her waist, and pulled her back to her feet. His eyes studied her for a moment, and then he tugged on the chain to indicate she was to follow. Moving to a heavy iron door concealed under the stairs, Hobstull led her through the opening and down a flight of worn, water-stained stone steps that lay beyond. She followed docilely, intent on conserving what was left of her strength for a time when she could put it to better use. She was thinking about her predicament. What she had been told by the shade of the Warlock Lord was confirmed. She was inside the Forbidding because the Straken Lord had arranged for a handful of Druids who hated her to be swayed into using magic that would put her here. Mostly, she was there because by being there something else had been set free. The Straken Lord hadn't admitted to it, but she was certain from what the shade of Brona had told her that it was so.

Yet it wasn't the Straken Lord that had crossed over into her world in response to the magic that had brought her here, but another demon, one she still knew nothing about.

Why hadn't the Straken Lord gone itself? Was the real purpose of the exchange to bring her in or to send the other demon out? The key to understanding everything was buried in the answer to that question.

At the bottom of the stairs, Hobstull turned back along a row of thick wooden doors into which tiny eye slits had been cut. As they passed those slits, she heard sounds emanating from within. Once or twice, blackened digits poked out tentatively, as if sampling her taste on the air she stirred in passing. Torches burned on the walls, creating a thick, smoky haze all along the corridor. Fresh air wafted down stone vents from somewhere above, but not enough to dispel the haze. The flames flickered and sputtered from the pitch-coated heads of the torches, casting her shadow against the stone walls as she passed. *Not a place from which many escape,* she thought.

She looked down at the chains she wore and saw herself as her captors did—an animal on a leash, a creature for display, a pet to amuse them, a curious specimen. In her own eyes, she had been reduced to the lowest level of existence possible, but in the eyes of her captors she was being treated exactly as she deserved. Men were less than animals in the world of the Jarka Ruus. Demons and demonkind were at the top of the food chain; Men were little more than an oddity. It was funny, but she had never thought about it before. She had never thought much about the Forbidding at all. It was a fact of life, but one so far removed from her day-to-day existence that it barely merited consideration.

Until now. Until it was all that mattered.

Hobstull stopped before one of the doors, inserted a key into the lock, and opened it. Leading her inside by the chain at her waist, he turned her about, unfastened the chain, and backed out the door. He looked at her again for a moment in that now-familiar way, then closed the door and locked it behind him.

Grianne Ohmsford, Ard Rhys of the Druid order, stared helplessly into the darkness that closed about her.

ELEVEN

Rigid with indecision, paralyzed by a sense of helplessness and loss, she stood without moving for a long time. The darkness and solitude of her prison only seemed to emphasize how desperate her circumstances had become. All that was familiar and dependable had been stripped away—her friends and family, her home and possessions, her entire world. The pain and humiliation she had been forced to suffer at the hands of the Straken Lord had shattered her confidence. Everything she had relied upon to sustain her, even her sense of how things worked, had vanished so completely that it seemed impossible in the wake of its passing to imagine ever getting it back again.

Finally, she sank to her knees on the stone floor of the cell and cried. She hadn't cried in a long time, and she wouldn't have cried now if she could have prevented it. Someone might hear and by hearing come to understand just how devastated she was. She had spent years learning how to keep any sense of weakness carefully hidden—first as the Ilse Witch and later as Ard Rhys. Since she had been a tiny child, she had fought to protect herself by hiding her feelings. But that method of self-protection, along with all the others she had been able to rely upon, had vanished.

When she was cried out, she rubbed her face against her shoulder to dry her eyes then stared blankly into the darkness. The slit in the heavy cell door admitted a small amount of light, and after a time her eyes adjusted to it sufficiently that she was able to see a little of her surroundings. Her cell was approximately ten feet square with a single bed covered with straw, a slop bucket, and a drain in the center of the room. There was nothing to eat and no water to drink. There were no covers for her bed. There was no place other than the bed to sit.

She tested the shackles that bound her wrists to the leather belt about her waist, then pulled on the belt as well. Both were tough and unyielding. She rolled her head to get a sense of the thickness of the conjure collar, but without being able to see it or put her hands on it, there was little she could determine. The clasps to both were behind her, where she could neither see nor reach them. Nothing in the cell would reflect their images. She took a deep, steadying breath and exhaled. There was no help anywhere.

She got to her feet again and walked to the door, peering through the slit into the corridor beyond. She could see parts of cell doors set into the far wall. Torchlight flickered and cast a mix of shadows and light, but there was no discernible pattern. She could hear faint sounds of movement and talking, but could not make out the sources of either. Smells permeated the air, and none of them was pleasant.

What am I going to do?

She turned away from the door and stared back into the darkness of her cell. No one who mattered knew where she was. The boy who was coming to rescue her—a boy!—had no idea where to look for her. Not that she thought it mattered. A boy wasn't going to make a difference anyway. No one was. Perhaps Weka Dart might have been able to help once upon a time; it was difficult to tell. But he certainly wouldn't be able to help now. The Ulk Bog had warned her against going back, almost as if he had known what would happen. The idea stopped her in midthought, a dark and suspicious voice in her subconscious. But she dismissed it quickly. It wasn't as if he had sent her to her doom. She had chosen her own way, and he had chosen his. She had done this to herself. Now any help from him was improbable at best. He was safely away and would stay so.

Questions nagged at her. What was she doing here? Why wasn't she already dead? The Straken Lord had brought her into the Forbidding, and it knew who she was. When she had been the Ilse Witch, she had disposed of her enemies swiftly and without hesitation, once they were in her power. A live enemy was always dangerous. So why was the demon keeping her imprisoned? Was there something about the transfer of its ally into the Four Lands in exchange for her that required it to keep her alive? She had not considered the possibility. Maybe the magic that had facilitated the transfer failed if either of them died in the other world. But did they both die in that situation? If so, then the Straken Lord had a vested interest in protecting her until its ally was ready to return.

She thought awhile about how that return might happen, but it was impossible to figure out without knowing what her counterpart had crossed over to accomplish.

Her thoughts drifted to other things, to the turmoil in the Four Lands, to the betrayal by her own Druids, and to concerns for her family. It was possible that those enemies who had dispatched her here would try to eliminate Bek, as well. Once he found out she was missing, her brother would come looking for her. Her enemies might try to stop him. It wouldn't be the first time that an enemy had come after members of the Ohmsford family with that idea in mind. The fact that she was Ard Rhys made the current generation of Ohmsfords targets in a way they hadn't been since the time of Shea Ohmsford and the Warlock Lord.

The longer she spent thinking about the ramifications of what had happened to her, the more determined she became. Her sense of indecision and confusion disappeared. Her fear turned to anger. She began to pull herself together, to regain the shattered pieces of her confidence. She no longer accepted her imprisonment as a condition about which she could do nothing. No one had ever imprisoned her and kept her so. She had not gotten so far in the world by giving in to her weaker emotions. She had not survived by giving up in seemingly impossible situations.

She tested the strength of the chains and belt again, this time trying to move the belt around her waist so that the buckle was more to the front. She was able to do this by sucking in her breath and jerking her hands all the way to the right. This brought the buckle around to her left side far enough that she could see how it was made. What she saw gave her hope. If she could find something to hook it on, she might be able to pull the leather tongue free of the metal clasp and then loosen it from the catch, as well.

A search of her cell walls, stone block by stone block, turned up nothing. What protuberances she discovered were too smooth or flat to be useful. She turned her attention to the door. The handle was a smooth metal grip fastened to the door at both ends. No help there. But on making a careful check of the hinges, she found a metal nail head on the lower hasp that had worked free from the wall just far enough to offer a possible hook.

She spent the next hour working the leather of the belt tongue, where it passed through the buckle, around the nail head and pulling it loose, inch by inch. All the while, she listened for the sounds of her jailers, for the soft scrape of boots on stone, for the tiniest creak of a door opening. She heard nothing.

At the end of the hour, she had freed tongue from buckle and was working on the catch. This was harder because the leather had to be pulled back much farther and with greater force. She struggled with it until she had exhausted herself, then tried again. Somewhere along the way her strength gave out and she fell asleep.

She woke to the sound of her cell door being opened. Hobstull appeared, blank-faced and empty-eyed, his topknot bobbing gently with his unhurried movements. He carried a tray on which rested a cup of water and some unidentifiable food. He set it by the door, glanced over at her perfunctorily, and went out again without speaking, closing and locking the door behind him.

When he was gone, she got to her feet and went over to the food. Because her hands were still chained to her waist, she could not use them to feed herself. She was forced to kneel and eat and drink like an animal. Her rage burned with a white-hot fury, but she made herself consume everything. She would need her strength for what lay ahead, and what lay ahead was freedom.

She began work again on the buckle as soon as she was done. She was stronger now, both physically and emotionally, and she stuck with the endeavor long after common sense told her it wasn't working. She did so because she couldn't think of anything better to do or any other plan to try. There were times, she knew from experience, when it was best just to continue on rather than to shift directions, even when it didn't seem as if you were getting anywhere. Your chances of success weren't always something you could measure accurately. Perseverance in the face of failure counted for something.

In the end, she was rewarded. Long hours later, the tongue at last pulled free of the troublesome catch, and the belt fell away from her waist. She held it in her hands, staring at it for a moment in shock, relief and fierce satisfaction surging through her. Her wrists were still bound by its chains, so she could not rid herself of it entirely, but she had a more complete range of motion than before and could lift her hands to her throat and the hated conjure collar.

But even as she started to search for the clasp that would open it, she hesitated. It was possible that any effort at trying to take off the collar would trigger a response of the sort that had laid her out earlier. It was also possible that the Straken Lord would be alerted to the fact that she had tampered with it. She could not afford for either to happen until she was safely away from the fortress. But if she left the collar in place, she could not use her magic to protect herself or to aid in making her escape. She would be imposing a severe handicap on herself before she even found a way out of her cell.

It was asking a lot. Maybe it was asking too much.

Reluctantly, she lowered her hands. She would leave the collar in place for the time being and take her chances.

She went back to working on the clasps and chains that bound her wrists to the belt. The iron from which they were made would not be easily bent, and she lacked the tools to do the job in any case.

She would have to get out of the cell before she could do anything more.

Then, suddenly, she heard the rough scrape of boots outside her door.

Immediately, she stepped to one side, fastening her hands about the heavy belt and drawing it close against her chest. A key turned, and the lock released with a soft snicking sound. Then the door opened, letting in a sudden flood of torchlight. A Goblin stepped through, already bending down to retrieve the food tray that Hobstull had left for her. Summoning every last ounce of strength she possessed, she hit it in the face with the belt, and it dropped without a sound. She thought she might have killed it, but she couldn't stop to worry about that. She dragged the Goblin to one side, where it wouldn't be seen from the doorway. Seizing the keys it carried, she peered through the door and found the corridor deserted.

Gripping the belt firmly, cradling it to her chest once more to mask the rattle of the chains that bound her to it, she went down the hallway in a controlled rush, taking just a moment to close the door behind her. She didn't know how soon her captors would find out she was free, but she didn't think she should count on it taking very long. By the time they did, she had to be outside the walls of the keep if she was to have any chance at all.

She reached the stairs and started up. She could hear the soft rustlings of other prisoners below, muted by the heavy wooden doors and thick stone walls. If they saw her, they might cry out. She moved quickly up the stairs, glancing behind as well as ahead, her heart hammering. She reached the landing at the top of the stairs and stopped. She couldn't hear anything. She pressed her ear against the door. Still nothing.

There was no help for it. She had to go out.

She turned the handle slowly. To her surprise, it gave way, and the latch clicked open. She peered cautiously through the open door to see what lay beyond. She could hardly believe her good fortune. The chamber was empty.

She slipped through the door and into the darkened space under the stairway. She was back in the room in which the Straken Lord had confronted her. She glanced around furtively, stepping out far enough to peer up into the darkness of the stairwell into which the demon had ascended. She couldn't see anything.

Across the room, the door leading out into the courtyard stood closed.

For the first time, she was at a loss as to what to do. If she went out the courtyard door, she would be completely exposed to the denizens of the fortress. Kraal Reach was crawling with demons and Goblins, and the chances of her getting through all the surrounding walls and gates to the outside were slim at best. She needed to find another way.

A disguise would help, she thought suddenly.

She glanced around the room, but there was nothing in sight. No cloaks or armor or anything to conceal who she was. There were no other doors besides the one she had come through and the one leading out. Her choices were clear. She could either take the stairs the Straken Lord had climbed or retrace her steps into the cells.

She felt a rising panic and quickly forced it down. She could not make herself go back. She would go up.

She began to climb the stairs.

She was halfway to the top when the door leading in from the courtyard opened and Hobstull appeared. She froze on the stairs, pressed against the wall, hoping the shadows were sufficiently deep to hide her. Hobstull closed the door and walked to the stairs leading down to the cells. Without glancing up, the Catcher went through the doorway and disappeared.

In minutes he would discover that she was gone.

Abandoning caution, she raced up the stairs to a dark corridor. She glanced all about for signs of the Straken Lord, but saw nothing. Slipping down the corridor as fast as she could manage while still keeping silent, she reached a rack on which hung a series of black cloaks. She snatched one off and flung it about her, then hurried on. She turned several corners as the corridor wound its way back into the tower, listening all the while for sounds of an alarm. But no alarm was given.

Finally, she arrived at a door that opened onto a walkway overlooking the fortress. She could see all of the keep's walls now, five concentric rings that enclosed increasingly larger courtyards and broader buildings the farther out she looked. The Pashanon was a hazy gray emptiness that spread away below the bluff, but the fortress itself teemed with life. She saw how completely trapped she was, how far she must go to reach safety, and she despaired. Without her magic to aid her and her hands free of the constricting chains, she could not hope to get away. Even a disguise would not be enough with so many demons and checkpoints to pass through.

She had to find a way to even the odds.

She glanced around furiously and found what she was looking for. Iron spikes protruded from slots in the battlements, a defense against intruders seeking to climb in. She walked to a cluster set far enough back that they weren't immediately visible to those passing below. Hooking the metal ring that bound the chain to the clasp on her right wrist about the closest spike, she began to twist it against its fastening. The clasp cut into her wrist until she was bleeding, but she continued to apply pressure, gritting her teeth against the pain.

At last, the ring snapped apart, and the chain and clasp fell away.

It took her even less time to free the left wrist, but cost her about the same amount of blood. Hugging her damaged wrists to her chest, letting the blood seep into her clothing, she searched for a way down. Finding nothing, she began to follow the walkway around the tower. There was still no alarm, something she found odd. Perhaps Hobstull hadn't gone to her cell after all. Perhaps the Catcher had gone into the cells for something else. She couldn't know.

She found a watchtower with a trapdoor and ladder leading down to the next floor. She climbed down quickly, found another trapdoor and another ladder, and climbed down that one, as well. From the courtyard below, she heard the chatter of the Goblins and, from somewhere beyond, the growls and snarls of the demonwolves. Too many enemies lay between her and safety. She hadn't a hope of getting past them all.

Her mind raced. Could there be a way underground, tunnels used by the defenders of the keep to move from wall to wall without exposing themselves, just as there was in Tyrsis, in her own world?

She went down the rest of the way, to the floor of the tower. There was nowhere else to go from there except outside or back into the main structure. Wrapping the cloak tightly about her body, she went out the door and into the courtyard. A scattering of Goblins was at work, but none of them even bothered to glance over at her. She walked swiftly across the open ground to the nearest door, opened it, and ducked inside.

Now she was in a building backed up against the next wall leading out, a storeroom for weapons and armor, and she passed through it to a door on the other side and down the corridor beyond. The corridor twisted and turned through the building as she followed it, and soon she was hopelessly lost. She kept searching for a stairway leading underground, but found none. Her plan of escape was rapidly coming apart.

Finally, she found a door that opened into the next courtyard. But there were demonwolves everywhere, prowling the grounds and lying in the shade, dozens of them, huge gray beasts with thick ruffs about their necks and jaws strong enough to snap a spear handle. She glanced at them just long enough to measure the danger before shutting the door. If she had the use of her magic, she wouldn't have worried. Without it, she was no match for them.

But she had to get across the courtyard if she was to escape. There wasn't any other way.

She opened the door and looked out again, searching for an overhead walkway that would connect the two walls. There wasn't one, or at least one that she could see. Nor was there any indication of any other way across.

She closed the door again and stood there, trying to think what she could do.

In the next instant, the cry of alarm she had been dreading rose from behind her, the thunder of a drum followed by the deep moan of a horn. She didn't mistake it for anything other than what it was, and without another thought, she went out the door and started across the courtyard for the far wall. Instantly, the demonwolves glanced over at her, but she didn't look back at them, keeping her eyes directed straight ahead, trying to act as if she belonged, moving for the closest escape.

Just a few minutes were all she needed.

Behind her, the warning continued to sound, and now Goblins were appearing all along the battlements atop the walls on either side, turning this way and that, searching. She kept moving, trying not to let her panic take control of her, trying to stay calm.

She reached the door and grasped the handle to open it. The door was locked.

Without pausing, she turned toward the next door down, walking quickly to reach it. But by then the demonwolves were moving, their suspicions aroused. Heads lowered, ruffs standing up like bunched quills, muzzles drawing back to reveal the rows of teeth concealed behind, they advanced on her. The first low growls and snarls came from their throats. Alerted by the sounds, a pair of Goblins on the wall behind her stopped to look down into the courtyard.

A huge wolf positioned itself directly in front of the door she was trying to reach and turned to face her. She stopped at once, a mistake. The wolf snarled defiantly, sensing that she was either afraid or intimidated. She turned back the other way, but more wolves were closing in, blocking her passage, and trapping her. On the walls, other Goblins were gathering, staring down at her.

She was finished, she knew, unless she used her magic.

She reached quickly for the conjure collar to release its clasp, but couldn't find the catch. Frantically, she searched its length for a buckle, for any telltale bit of metal. Nothing. The wolves drew closer, openly menacing now, teeth showing as they stalked her. The closest was no more than ten yards away. She had no choice. Even with the conjure collar in place, she would have to use her magic to defend herself.

"Haahhh!" she growled at the wolves, making a quick warding gesture that caused them to fall back.

She advanced on them as if she meant to punish them and, uncertain as to what she might do, they gave way to her. They were creatures of the Straken Lord, after all, and it had trained them to do its bidding. At some point, punishment had been a part of that training. As fierce as they were, they couldn't completely ignore the responses that had been conditioned in them.

Her audacity froze them in place, but only for a moment. It was enough. By then she was back at the first door she had tried, her one chance at escape. She was discovered, and if she couldn't get through the door, her captors would be on her in moments. She quit looking at the walls and the wolves. She ignored the shouts and growls that rose behind her. She quit thinking about anything but the door. Bracing herself, she summoned the magic of the wishsong to break free of her prison.

But the minute the first strains of the magic rose within her, the conjure collar reacted with blinding pain that seized her throat in a paralyzing grip and froze her vocal cords. The pain was instantaneous, and it rushed through her with relentless purpose, knocking her backwards with its force, sapping her strength and numbing her mind. Caught in the terrible grip of the collar's magic, she stiffened and screamed soundlessly, unable to help herself in any way.

She went down in a heap in the dusty courtyard, tumbling into blackness, lost to everything but the pain and an unmistakable sense of failure that trailed after her through the gathering dark like a death shroud.

in the *Skatelow*'s approach. No defensive maneuvers were being undertaken, and from what Pen could make out, there were few guards of any sort.

The boy knew almost nothing about Trolls. He had seen a few in his life, some of them had come to Patch Run to employ his parents. But his travels had not taken him into the deep Northland, where the tribes made their homes, and Trolls by and large did not venture south of their traditional homelands. He thought that he had heard his mother speak in the Troll tongue once or twice, but he couldn't be sure.

"Can we communicate with them?" he asked impulsively.

"I can speak a little of their language," Tagwen ventured. He shrugged. "It won't matter, once we find Kermadec."

If this is Taupo Rough and if Kermadec is here, Pen thought without saying so.

As he brought the ship slowly around toward the village, he called to memory what little he knew about the inhabitants. Trolls were nomadic by tradition, and frequently resettled themselves when their safety was compromised or their dissatisfaction with local conditions grew sufficiently strong. But because they were tribal, as well, they established territorial boundaries within the regions they traveled, and one tribe would never think of invading another's domain. Of such trespasses had the worst of the Troll Wars been born, wars that had died out years ago in the wake of the establishment of the First Druid Council. Galaphile and his Druids had made it their first priority to stabilize relations within the Races. They had accomplished that by setting themselves up as arbitrators and peacekeepers, developing a reputation for being fair-minded and nonjudgmental. The Trolls, who were the most fierce and warlike of the Races in those days, had accepted the Druids as mediators with surprising enthusiasm, anxious perhaps to find a way to put an end to the tribal bloodshed that had plagued them for so long. Trolls were creatures of habit, Pen's father had told him once. They embraced order and obedience within the tribal structure as good and necessary, and self-discipline was the highest quality to which a Troll could aspire.

There was more than one species of Troll living in the Northland, but by far the most numerous of the tribes were Rock Trolls. Physically larger and historically more warlike than the other tribes, they were found principally in the Charnals and the Kensrowe, preferring mountainous terrain with caves and tunnels rather than open encampments as safeholds. The Forest and River Trolls were smaller in size and numbers, and they were not nomadic in the way of Rock Trolls. The differences went on from there, but Pen couldn't remember them all. What he mostly remembered was that Rock Trolls reputedly made the finest weapons and armor in the Four Lands, and they knew how to use both when provoked.

"Someone's noticed us now," Khyber announced, nodding toward a handful of Troll warriors walking out to meet them.

Pen let the airship settle to the earth in an open space at one end of the plateau, well away from the village and its fortifications. Whatever happened, he did not want to give an impression of hostility. He shut down the thrusters, closed off the parse tubes, walked to the railing, tossed out the rope ladder, and climbed down to set the anchors. The others followed, with Tagwen in the lead, looking bluff and officious.

The Trolls came up to them, huge and forbidding giants, their barklike skin looking like armor beneath their clothing, their strange, flat-featured faces devoid of expression, but their eyes sharp and watchful.

One of them spoke to Tagwen in deep, guttural tones, a query of some sort, Pen thought. The Dwarf stared at the speaker blankly, then glanced hurriedly at Pen. The boy shook his head. "You're the one who says he speaks the language. Say something back to him."

Tagwen gave it a valiant try, but it came out sounding a little as if his last meal hadn't quite agreed with him. The Trolls looked at one another in confusion.

"Just use whatever Troll-speak you possess and ask him if Kermadec is here," snapped Khyber, impatient with the whole business. "Ask if this is Taupo Rough."

The Dwarf did so, or at least appeared to do so. Pen caught the words *Kermadec* and *Taupo Rough* amid all the garble, and the reception committee seemed to do the same. One of them nodded, beckoned for them to follow, and turned back toward the village. The other three fell into place about them like a stockade.

"I hope we haven't made another mistake," Khyber muttered to Pen as she glanced about uneasily.

Pen took Cinnaminson's hand and held it firmly in his own. The Rover girl did not pull away, but moved closer to him. "It doesn't look it, but this village is heavily defended," she whispered to him. "We can't see most of it. Most of it is hidden inside the mountains. I can feel the heat of furnaces and forges. I can feel movement in the earth radiating out from the rock."

The boy exhaled sharply. "Are these Trolls enemies?" he asked. "Are we in danger?"

She shook her head. "I can't tell. But they are prepared to do battle with something, and whatever it is, they mean to see it destroyed if it tries to attack them."

Pen nodded. "If we have to flee, I will stay right beside you."

She said nothing in reply, but squeezed his hand tightly.

They moved through the heavy stone walls that formed the outer fortifications into the village itself. Trolls turned to look at them, Trolls of all sizes and shapes, but their gazes were brief and didn't linger. A few young Trolls, barely five feet tall yet—though big when compared to Tagwen, who was not much more than that himself—fell into step beside them, casting interested glances at the outlanders. No one tried to speak to them, and no one did anything threatening. Pen studied the buildings as he walked, comparing them with those of Southland villages. The biggest difference was in the construction, which was almost entirely of rock and suggested that every building provided its own defense. Each unit had heavy iron-bound wooden doors and shutters, and weapons ports had been cut into the walls for use by the defenders. It had taken a lot of work to build the homes, and it seemed in direct contradiction to the nomadic tradition of the people who occupied them.

"We didn't do anything to protect the airship," Khyber whispered to him suddenly, a frown crossing her dark features.

Pen nodded. "I know. But what could we have done?"

"Sent Tagwen on ahead alone until we knew what to expect," she replied. "We aren't being very smart about this."

Pen didn't respond. "I don't sense any hostility," Cinnaminson said quietly. "We aren't threatened."

Khyber rolled her eyes as if to suggest that a blind Rover girl might not be the best judge but didn't pursue the matter.

They had just rounded the corner of a massive building that looked to be a storehouse rather than a home when a huge Rock Troll appeared in front of them, arms outstretched and voice booming out in familiar Dwarfish.

"Bristle Beard, you've found your way!" the Troll shouted, reaching down to pick up Tagwen and hold him out at arm's length as if he were no more than a toy. "It's good to see you safe and sound, little man!"

Tagwen was incensed. "Put me down at once, Kermadec. What are you thinking? A little decorum would be appreciated!"

The big Troll set him down at once, drawing back. "Oh, well then, sorry to have distressed you. I was only expressing my great joy at finding you in good health. It hasn't been a good time at Paranor, Tagwen."

"This does not come as news to me!" the Dwarf snapped. He cleared his throat officiously. "Here, let me introduce the others."

He did so, giving a quick explanation of who his companions were without yet getting into why they had all come together. Kermadec nodded to each at the mention of their names, his flat features somehow reflecting the pleasure he took in meeting them. There was an exuberance and expansiveness to the big man that transcended what Pen had heard of the Troll character, and he found himself liking their host right away.

"Penderrin," Kermadec said, taking the boy's hand in his own. It was like shaking hands with a rough piece of wood. "Your aunt and I are great friends, friends from as far back as the coming together of the Druid order, and I regret what has happened deeply. Your presence indicates that you intend to join me in doing something about it. You are most welcome."

He turned to Tagwen. "Now you must tell me all about what has happened since our parting at Paranor, and I will do the same. Come with me to my home, and we will have something to eat and drink while we talk. Is that an airship you flew in on, Bristle Beard? I thought you hated airships!"

Dismissing the Trolls who had guided them in from the *Skatelow*, Kermadec led them on through the village until they were almost to the cliff face against which it was backed. At that distance, Pen could see clearly the sophisticated network of walkways and ladders connecting the village to the caves and tunnels that riddled the cliff. He could also hear, for the first time, the sounds of hammers striking anvils and smell the fires of the furnaces that serviced them.

What was odd was that he couldn't see any smoke or ash.

He asked Kermadec about that, and the Troll pointed skyward. "The residue of the furnace fires goes into a vent system that carries it out the other side of the near peaks. It helps keep the air we breathe out here in the village clean. It also helps disguise what we do. You can't be sure where we keep the furnaces until you get this close. The furnaces are our lifeblood. Without the furnaces, we can't make the weapons and metal tools we trade to the other Races for the goods we need. Without the furnaces, we would revert to what we once were—raiders and worse. If anything happens to them, we are left without a way to make a living."

"What do you do with the furnaces when you move to another site?" the boy pressed. "You don't take them with you, do you?"

Kermadec laughed. "That would be a neat trick, young Penderrin. The furnaces are built right into the rock of the mountain. No, we shut them down, cool them off, and conceal them. We close off the entrances that lead to them, as well. And we set traps to discourage the uninvited. As long as I can remember, no one has ever bothered our furnaces."

"And there are those who would, I can promise you," Tagwen declared grimly.

Kermadec clapped him on the shoulder so hard he almost knocked him off his feet. "If they could, Bristle Beard. If they could."

"So you have other furnaces in other places?" Pen pressed.

"Half a dozen that have been constructed over the years, more if you count the ones we have abandoned as unsafe. We are a mobile people, but our villages are well established. We simply move back and forth among them, choosing the one that seems most advantageous with each migration. Just now, we are concerned about uninvited guests and so have chosen this village, with its superior defensive positioning."

Khyber glanced about. "You don't look all that ready to go to ground if you are attacked. No guards, no sign of anything out of the ordinary. We just sailed right in on the *Skatelow*."

"Only because we saw you coming from five miles off and identified your sloop as harmless." The dark eyes swept back to her and away again. "Don't mistake what you see, Khyber Elessedil. We keep close watch in all directions. We won't be easily surprised. If we are threatened, we can disappear into the caves behind the village in a matter of minutes, much quicker than an enemy can reach them. Once inside, we can survive for months on the provisions stored. Or we can escape through any number of back doors. And there are extensive fortifications inside the caves as well, in case an attack is pressed. Believe me, things are not entirely as they seem."

Which was in keeping with most of what they had encountered on their journey to reach Taupo Rough, so his guests decided to take him at his word.

A few minutes later, they were settled inside the big Troll's home, a sprawling affair occupied by his brothers, sisters, parents, and grandparents, as well as a child or two somehow connected with the rest. Kermadec explained, on completing introductions, that Trolls tended to house together in families, often living that way the whole of their lives. The house his family occupied had once belonged to another family, but that family had lost enough members over the years that they no longer needed anything quite so large. Since Kermadec's family had grown, they were offered the other family's home in exchange for their smaller one.

It was an odd approach to determining living conditions, but one that the Trolls seemed quite used to. Homes didn't seem to belong to any one person or family, but to the entire community. Pen thought that perhaps because Rock Trolls moved so often, they weren't quite so attached to their possessions, homes included, and were therefore able to share more freely.

Still, he was curious about all those people living together under one roof, and after being served a cold drink of black tea and herbs, he asked what determined if any member of the family moved away. Or didn't they? This produced an even odder and more complicated explanation of the Troll lifestyle. Trolls, Kermadec offered, did not maintain family units in the same way as the other Races. Trolls started out life as children in one family, but often ended up as children or even adults in another. When sickness or death rendered parents unable to raise their children, other parents stepped in. When a child or adult grew dissatisfied with a family situation, he or she could petition to move elsewhere, and frequently the move was allowed. It was thought better to accommodate that individual and try to ease the source of dissatisfaction than to allow the problem to fester. The move didn't happen until a thorough effort had been made to resolve the conflict.

Moreover, Troll parents did not regard their children as the exclusive property of the family and were not possessive of the responsibility for raising them. The care, nurturing, teaching, and disciplining of children was the responsibility of the entire village, and everyone was involved in the rearing process. Successes and failures were always shared; decisions and pronouncements were never left to one person. A Troll child started out life as the result of the union of two people, but reached adulthood as the result of the efforts of many.

"Well, that's enough for now about the social structure of Rock Trolls, young Penderrin," Kermadec declared, seating himself across from the boy and the others. "Tell me everything that's happened. Bristle Beard, you begin. Right from the time I left you at Paranor. Tell it all."

So they did, each of them speaking in turn, each of them adding a piece to the larger puzzle. Tagwen told of coming to find Pen's parents at Patch Run and finding only Pen. The boy related the details of their escape from Terek Molt, the subsequent encounter with the King of the Silver River, and the task he had been given—to travel to the ruins of the ancient city of Stridegate and the forest island of the tanequil. Tagwen then picked up the story once more to tell of their decision to seek help at Emberen from Ahren Elessedil. Much of it was difficult, especially Khyber's recitation of the events surrounding her uncle's death in the Slags. When it came Cinnaminson's turn to speak of the creature that had killed her father and her cousins aboard the *Skatelow*, she was forced to stop and compose herself several times. But both Elf and Rover made it through their tales, through the dark and terrible hurt they had experienced, to emerge, Pen thought, a little stronger than when they had started out.

Kermadec listened carefully and, when they had finished, shook his head in a mix of disgust and disbelief. "I knew our Grianne had placed too much faith in her ability to keep those Druid sorceresses from reverting to kind, Tagwen. Even an Ard Rhys can do only so much with black hearts and foul schemes."

He sighed. "But losing Ahren Elessedil? I never thought I would live to see that. I never thought anything could happen to him, as much as he had survived already. He was the best of them, Khyber, your uncle. The best of them all."

She nodded in acknowledgment of the kindness of his words. "I appreciate hearing that."

"And Cinnaminson." He turned to the Rover girl. "I am sorry for the death of your father, whatever the circumstances that brought it about. Your father is an irreplaceable loss. You have shown great courage and presence of mind in surviving the madness that consumed him. I will send my Trolls to see that he and his cousins are given burial."

He leaned forward. "Now, then. You have told me your tale; let me tell you mine. Maybe we can make some sense of this business once I do."

* * *

After leaving Tagwen at the Druid's Keep, Kermadec had traveled north on foot out of Paranor and across the Streleheim to the ruins of the kingdom of the Warlock Lord. He did not want to do this, but he had no better idea of where to begin his search for Grianne Ohmsford. Days earlier, he had accompanied the Ard Rhys to investigate rumors of apparitions and strange fires within those ruins and had encountered an impossibly dark and evil presence. The Maturen felt certain that there was a connection between that presence and the disappearance of the Ard Rhys, and he was hopeful that by taking a closer look at the site where the presence had revealed itself, he might discover something useful.

It was a long shot at best, and as Kermadec had made clear to Tagwen, the Troll people did not go into the Skull Kingdom for any but the best of reasons. Kermadec was brave, and there were few dangers that could turn him aside, but that was one of them. Rock Trolls had an inbred fear and distrust of the land where the Warlock Lord had ruled and been destroyed. Rock Trolls, in that time and place, had served the Warlock Lord, slaves and soldiers to help in the conquest and subjugation of the Four Lands. It had taken many years for the Trolls to recover from those monstrous times, years for them to be accepted again by the other Races. Grianne Ohmsford had done much to make that possible. If a journey to the forbidden land was what it would take to help her in turn, then so be it.

Nevertheless, he had determined that he would not go back there alone.

So he traveled first to a Gnome village situated below the River Lethe on the western borders of the Knife Edge, seeking a man he believed would know better how to protect against the danger he expected to encounter in the ruins. The man's name was Achen Wuhl, and he was a Gnome shaman of some repute in the tribe to which he belonged. He was old, perhaps ninety, and he had been a shaman the whole of his life, living with the Warst, a tribe that migrated across the Streleheim between the Kensrowe and the Charnals.

Kermadec had met Achen Wuhl twenty years before on an outing that had brought a company of his Trolls in contact with the Warst while the latter were under attack from Mutens. In most circumstances, Rock Trolls would have nothing to do with Gnomes because the two Races were traditionally at odds over territorial rights and migratory routes. But the Trolls hated Mutens worse than anything. Voiceless, soulless remnants of the Warlock Lord's dark magic, the Mutens survived in the Knife Edge in much the same way as the Werebeasts did within Olden Moor—by preying on the Gnomes who worshiped them as sacred spirits.

So Kermadec had broken the unwritten rule that forbids Trolls from interfering with the lives of Gnomes, and his company had come to the aid of those unfortunates who were being butchered by the Mutens because they had ventured too close to the monsters in a misguided effort to appease them. Among those rescued were women and children and the shaman, Achen Wuhl, who accepted the gift of his life from the Trolls with a promise that some day he would repay the favor. Kermadec had not claimed that promise before. He chose to claim it now.

With Achen Wuhl in tow, he journeyed back through the Knife Edge, carefully avoiding the caves of the Mutens, until he was back within the ruins of the Skull Kingdom at the site where Grianne Ohmsford and he had encountered the strange fires and the apparition. Without revealing the involvement of the Ard Rhys, he recounted to Wuhl the events of his earlier visit, suggesting that the apparition had appeared unbidden and that he was searching for its source. Together, they combed the ground surrounding the cold and blackened fire pit that had given birth to the presence, looking for something that would reveal its source. They found nothing. As nightfall approached, Kermadec suggested they leave and come back in the morning. But Achen Wuhl insisted that they stay. Once it was dark, the shaman would try to summon the apparition himself.

Kermadec felt that was a dangerous undertaking and that he should put a stop to it. But he was desperate to discover what had become of the Ard Rhys, and the shaman was still the only chance he had to unlock the secret. Achen Wuhl was a skilled conjurer and an experienced shaman. He would not be careless in his efforts. He might accomplish what Kermadec could not: find a link between the apparition and the Ard Rhys. Ignoring his instincts, which were screaming at him to get out of there, Kermadec convinced himself that the risk was necessary.

So they sat together in the growing dark, the old Gnome and the Troll Maturen, watching and waiting for something to happen. Darkness fell, and nothing did. Midnight came and went. The mountains were still and deep and seemingly empty of life.

Finally, with the moon down and the stars layered across the black firmament like scattered grains of brilliant white sand, the shaman rose from his place in the rocks. Motioning for Kermadec to remain where he was, he moved forward to where the fires had appeared last.

"I had a bad feeling about it right away, but I kept still," the big Troll told Pen and his companions. "I could still remember how that apparition made me feel, how dark and terrible was its visage, and I thought it would be better if we didn't see it again, ever. But the little man was determined; he had courage. So I let him go. I was thinking that this was the way I would reach your aunt, Pen. I was thinking that this was how I would discover where she was."

He shook his head at the memory. "Achen Wuhl brought up the fires right away, as if all he had to do was reach down to wherever they were hidden and summon them up. The fires flared and hissed right in front of him, bright flames burning with such intensity I could feel the heat from where I was sitting a dozen yards away. I heard the shaman muttering, saw the movement of his hands. I peered through the darkness to the flames, watching. *This is what I've been hoping for,* I kept thinking. *I'm going to find her, after all.*

"But then all of a sudden the flames just exploded. It was as if they found a fresh source of fuel, though there wasn't anything but the darkness for them to feed on. They shot upward a hundred feet, maybe more, all brilliant orange and yellow-tipped, crackling and hissing. It surprised me so, I almost fell over. But here's the odd thing. There wasn't any new heat. The fire burned with the same intensity, at the same temperature as before. Like magic."

He exhaled softly. "Something reached out of the flames and

wrapped itself about the old man. I don't know what it was. A part of the fire itself, I guess. It snatched him up and it pulled him in. He was gone in an instant, so fast I barely saw it happen. He never made a sound. He just disappeared. The flames consumed him. There was nothing left.

"Then I saw that face, the one the Ard Rhys and I had seen days earlier. I saw it in the fire, just for an instant. It was a dark and twisted thing, its eyes like a cat's, only blue and freezing cold. Those eyes were searching the darkness beyond the fire, hunting. I stumbled over myself trying to hide from them. I flattened myself against the rocks the best way I could. I never thought to do anything else. It was instinct that drove me, that warned me that if the eyes found me, I would go the way of the old man.

"So I hid. The face was there, the eyes searching for a moment more, and then both were gone. A second later, the flames were gone, too, collapsed into a black smear of ash burned into the stone of the pit. The heat died with the flames, and the night turned still and empty again.

"I stayed where I was for a few minutes more, then came out to look around. In the starlight, I could see what was left. Nothing. Nothing at all."

His voice trailed off and his gaze dropped to where his big hands knotted in his lap. In the silence, Pen could hear himself breathe.

"It was a trap," Kermadec said quietly. "It was a trap set to snare anyone who dared to search for the Ard Rhys. It got the old man. It could have gotten me just as easily. I came back to Taupo Rough alone. I will never go back to that place again."

"Does this mean you won't help us?" Pen asked him, impatient to know where Kermadec stood on the matter.

"Did I say that?" the Rock Troll exclaimed. "Did I say I wouldn't help you find this tree so that you can fashion your darkwand? Did I say I wouldn't help you reach the Ard Rhys and bring her out of the Forbidding? Shades, young Penderrin! Of course, I will help you! If I have to carry you to Stridegate and back again on my own shoulders, I will do so! All the Rock Trolls of Taupo Rough will carry you, if that's what's needed. We owe more than a little to your aunt for bringing us back into the mainstream of the Four Lands. She gave us trust and recognition when no other would, and we won't let that gift be for nothing. Whatever those black hearts at Paranor might pretend, we are still the Ard Rhys' protectors, and we will see her safe again or know the reason why!"

He stood up suddenly. "But I need to think on this a bit. The country into which you must go is dangerous—not that the rest of the Four Lands isn't, so long as Shadea a'Ru is acting Ard Rhys. But it's treacherous country all on its own, made more so by the presence of Urdas and some other things that have no name. We must make certain we keep you safe in your travels, those of you who decide to go."

He glanced sideways at Cinnaminson. "But there will be time for that later. For now, eat and rest. I'll set sentries to keep watch for the dark things tracking you, and I'll start the process of outfitting an expedition. But how will we travel? It's safest if we go on foot. Airships have difficulty getting through these mountains. The winds are unpredictable; they can send airships into the rocks as if they were pesky insects. But time is important, too, and travel afoot is slow."

He shook his head worriedly and went toward the door. "I'll think it through. Just ask, if you need something. There's plenty who speak the Dwarf tongue here. We'll celebrate your safe arrival tonight."

Then he was out the door and gone.

"I don't want you to leave me behind, Pen," Cinnaminson told him as soon as they were alone.

They had eaten, and Khyber and Tagwen had gone out to look around the village. The boy and the girl sat together in Kermadec's home, the other members of the big Troll's extended family coming and going silently about them, engaged in tasks of their own. It was after midday, and Pen was feeling the need to sleep again. But he couldn't sleep until this conversation was finished.

"I can't be responsible for putting you in any further danger," he replied, deliberately keeping his voice down so as not to attract attention.

Her face was anguished. "The thing that killed Papa still tracks us. It didn't die back there in that meadow. It will come after us. If it finds me, it will use me to find you—just like before. How can that be any less dangerous than what you might find where you are going?"

"You will be safe here," he insisted. "Kermadec's people are too well armed and this village too well fortified for anything to get to you. Even that thing we escaped. Besides, you don't know that it's still coming."

She kept her empty eyes fixed on the sound of his voice, as if she could actually see him speaking. "Yes, I do. It's coming."

He rose and walked to the open doorway of the room, stood there thinking, then came back to sit beside her.

"I'll have you sent home aboard the *Skatelow*. Someone in this village must know how to fly an airship. They will take you back into the Westland, to wherever you need to go. Kermadec will arrange it. I'll ask him to see that you are protected."

She stared at him for a long time, as if perhaps she hadn't heard right, then shook her head slowly. "Do you wish to be rid of me, Pen? Do you no longer need me in your life? I thought you said you cared about me. No, don't speak. Listen to me. You cannot send me home. I don't have a home to go back to. My home was with Papa, aboard the *Skatelow*. There isn't anyone else who matters now. Only you. My home is with you."

He looked down at his hands. "It's too dangerous."

She reached over and touched his cheek. "I know you are afraid for me. But you don't need to be. I'm blind, but I'm not helpless. You've seen that for yourself. You don't have to make me your responsibility. You only have to let me come with you."

"If I let you come with me, I make you my responsibility whether I like it or not!" he snapped. "Can't you see that?"

"What I see is that I can be of use to you." Her voice was desperate, almost pleading. "You need me! I can guide you where you are going in the same way I guided you across the Lazareen and through the Slags. No one else can see in the dark the way I can. No one else has my sight. I can help, Penderrin. Please! Don't leave me behind!"

"Of course, you're coming," Khyber Elessedil said quietly.

The Elven girl was standing in the doorway, watching them. They had been so wrapped up in their conversation, they hadn't heard her come back in.

"Khyber, you're not helping—"

"Don't lecture me, Pen. We don't need lectures, she and I. We share something that puts us in a better position to see what is needed here than you do. We've both lost someone important to us on this journey. We've lost a part of our family and, therefore, a part of ourselves. We could be diminished by this, but we won't let that happen, will we, Cinnaminson? We will use it to make us stronger. Neither of us would consider for a moment being left behind. If you think that I am better equipped to handle what lies ahead because I have the use of the Elfstones or that Cinnaminson is less able because her talent lies only in her mind-sight, then you need to think again!"

She was so vehement that Pen was left speechless. Of all the people he had expected to agree with him on the matter, Khyber was at the top of the list.

"Get out of here, Pen," the Elf girl ordered, gesturing toward the door. "Go find something to do. Cinnaminson and I need to talk. While we do, you think about what I just said. You think about whether what you are asking of her is reasonable or not. You think about everything that's happened while you're at it. Use your brain, if you can find a way to it through all your wrongheaded opinions."

She was angry, her face flushed and her gestures curt and threatening. Pen stood up slowly and glanced down at Cinnaminson. She was staring straight ahead; tears were leaking from the corners of her eyes, streaking her smooth face. He started to say something, then stopped himself.

As he left the room, he felt Khyber Elessedil glaring at him. He walked through the house, past the surreptitious glances of the Trolls, his gaze directed straight ahead. When he was outside again, he stopped and stared into space, wondering exactly what had just happened.

THIRTEEN

arkness had fallen over Paranor, deep and smothering, and the Druid's Keep was wrapped in silence. Within the fortress halls, the Druids came and went like wraiths; cloaked in black and hooded, they passed down halls that echoed softly with the scrape of slippers and the rustle of robes. Some cradled books and loose-leaf writings in their arms. Some carried materials for the tasks they had been given in the cause of the Druid order.

One carried nothing but a second cloak, neatly folded over one arm, so preoccupied that not a glance was spared for those it passed.

Bek Ohmsford looked up as the cloaked figure entered the room, and it took him a moment to realize it wasn't a Druid at all, but his wife. Rue Meridian came over to where he lay looking hot and feverish beneath his covers and laid the cloak at his feet.

She bent close to keep her voice a whisper. "I hope you don't feel as bad as you look."

He smiled. He was hot and sticky, and beads of sweat dotted his forehead. "I look terrible, don't I? That root you gave me really works. Traunt Rowan was here earlier to see how I was doing. I told him the fever had come back worse than before and was highly contagious. He was in and out of the room in seconds. No one has been back since. You found the robes, I see. No one saw you?"

She sat beside him, leaned over, and kissed his forehead. "Have a little faith, Bek. I am resourceful enough when it's needed. I just asked for them. I told the Druid I stopped that we would feel more comfortable being here if we were dressed as they were. Besides, it isn't me they're interested in. They watch me from around corners and through cracks in doors, but they don't pay close attention. You are the one who matters. So long as they think you intend to do what you were brought here to do, we won't have any trouble."

Bek nodded. "After tonight, we'll be more trouble than they thought possible. Hand me a cold cloth and towel."

She rose and did what he had asked. He sat up in the bed and began wiping himself down, washing away the sweat and grit, then drying off. The room was streaked with shadows, and the candles he had lit at sunset did little to chase the gloom. All the better, he thought, for what they had in mind.

"Did you have a chance to check out *Swift Sure?*"

She sat next to him again, keeping her voice low. There was still reason to worry that they were being listened to. "They cut loose the aft radian draws and locked down the thruster lever. I didn't see anything else. I pretended not to notice even that. I thought it better for them to think us unaware of their efforts. It might take us three minutes to make the necessary repairs. We can get away easily enough when we need to."

He finished cleaning himself, rose, and began to dress. He moved quickly and quietly, glancing over at the door every so often, listening to the silence that surrounded them. It was infectious, that silence. Everything about the Druid's Keep was measured in layers of silence, as if sound were an unwelcome intrusion. Perhaps it was, where power resided in such quantity and struggles to control it were all done through secret machinations and subtle deceits.

"I won't be sorry to be gone from here," she said. "Everything about this place is oppressive. How your sister stands it is a mystery to me. I wish her well, once we have her safely back from wherever she's gone, but mostly I wish her the wisdom to choose, then, to be somewhere else."

"I know." He glanced around. "I wish I had a weapon."

She reached beneath her robes, brought out a long knife, and handed it to him. "I retrieved it from the ship. I have my throwing knives, as well. But I don't think weapons are going to do us much good if we have to stand and fight."

"They might against those Gnome Hunters." He tucked the long knife into his belt, then reached for the other Druid robe. "Any sign of the young Druid?"

She shook her head. "Nothing."

They hadn't so much as caught a glimpse of him since he had slipped Bek the warning note on that first day. Bek had burned the note and had Rue scatter the ashes from one end of the Keep to the other, but he still didn't know who had tried to warn them or why. Clearly, the young Druid knew something about what was going on. He might know something about Pen, as well. But it was too risky to try to find out who he was. The best they could do was to keep watch for him, and so far he hadn't reappeared.

"You would think he would try to make further contact." Bek tightened the sash that bound the robe. "If he went to the trouble to contact us in the first place, he must want to help. He must be on my sister's side in all this."

"Maybe, but that doesn't mean he knows where she is or what's happened to her. He might not know anything other than what he's told us—that Shadea and the others are responsible. Maybe warning us was all he ever intended to do. It was enough to put us on guard."

Bek finished with his preparations and walked over to put his hands on her shoulders and draw her close. "You could wait for me aboard *Swift Sure*," he said. "I can do this alone."

"I think we had this discussion about twenty years ago, didn't we?" She leaned into him and kissed his mouth. "Let's just go."

They moved to the door and stood there for a moment listening. The Gnome Hunters assigned to the task of keeping watch were still stationed across the hallway, but they had been there for three days, and they were bored. It wouldn't take much effort to get past them.

Bek looked at his wife. "Ready?"

She nodded, pulling up the hood to her cloak. He did the same, then opened the door and stepped through. Already, he had the wishsong's magic working, a soft low hum that carried no farther than the ears of the guards. It whispered purposefully to form images in their minds. It told them that the cloaked figures leaving the room were Druids, easily recognizable as such by their robes, that they needn't bother with them and could look away.

By the time the guards looked back again, of course, the hallway was empty.

Bek and Rue moved swiftly to the stairs leading up to the cold chamber, turning into the stairwell before they could be seen. They had been fortunate in not encountering a single Druid on their way. If the Gnome Hunters at their sleeping room door didn't realize they had been duped, they stood a good chance of reaching their destination unnoticed.

They climbed the stone stairs to the next floor, sliding through shadows and pools of light as soundless and stealthy as foxes at hunt. This was a dangerous business, and they knew it. If they were discovered, their duplicity would be revealed and there would no longer be any chance of using the Druid's magic to find Pen. Worse, they probably would have to fight their way out of Paranor, and Bek wasn't sure they were up to it. It was one thing to have survived while traveling aboard the *Jerle Shannara*, while they were still young. It was another to test themselves when they hadn't fought a real battle in twenty years. Now was a poor time to find out if the magic of the wishsong could save them from the dangerous and experienced Shadea a'Ru.

In short, it would be best not to get caught.

At the top of the stairs, they stopped again while Bek peered around the corner and down the hallway. Nothing moved. The floor seemed deserted. There were no sleeping chambers on this floor, but a little farther on was the stairway that led to the north tower, which housed the quarters of the Ard Rhys. Shadea a'Ru would be there.

After a moment, they started down the corridor for the cold

chamber. The biggest danger they faced was that someone else would already be in the room when they got there. That would not only prevent them from carrying out their plan, but would require them to explain why they were there, unescorted and uninvited. It would be a difficult situation. At best, they would probably be forced to flee from the Keep.

But luck was with them. When they opened the door, they found the cold chamber empty. Rue took a moment to scan the corridor once more, making sure no one had seen them, then nodded to Bek to close the door. They stood inside in silence, the chilly air penetrating even the heavy fabric of the Druid robes. Rue shivered. Bek made a quick survey of the room, glancing toward the deep shadows, peering into the gathered gloom. No candles or torches were lit there, and they wouldn't risk lighting any. But a faint wash of light from moon and stars spilled through the high windows and reflected off the scrye waters in the stone basin, letting them see well enough to do their work.

Their plan wasn't complicated and didn't require much time. Bek had sensed Pen's presence in the Charnals during his initial effort to make contact, but he had lacked time and opportunity to pinpoint his son's location. Now, alone and undisturbed, he would use his magic on the waters to discover exactly where Pen was. Once he had accomplished that, they would slip back down through the Keep to *Swift Sure* and be on their way to retrieve him. The Druids might discover what had happened and try to follow, but their vessels were no match for *Swift Sure*, which was the fastest ship in the sky.

With Rue standing watch at the door, Bek moved to the basin and stood looking down at the scrye waters and the map of the Four Lands drawn on the surface of the bowl. The waters were still and untroubled, at rest save for where the faint pulse of the earth's magic crisscrossed the surface along the earth's lines of power. Bek studied their movements for a moment, then fixed his gaze on the Charnals and called up the wishsong. He did it quickly and quietly, directing the magic toward the area of the waters where he had sensed Pen to be the day before. He kept his concentration focused as he worked the magic deep into the basin, searching.

It took him only moments. His connection with his son was strong, born of his own history as a member of a family that had been connected by magic for centuries, and he found him almost instantly. He peered close, tightening down his search, marked the spot in his mind, and pulled the magic back again.

He went still, watching the scrye waters quiet and smooth once more, silver in the moonlight. He stepped away from the basin and turned back to Rue, nodding.

Together, they went out the doorway and back down the empty corridor toward the stairs. Neither spoke, unwilling to break the deep silence, to risk exposing themselves in any way. They would talk when they were aboard *Swift Sure* and safely away from this place.

On cat's paws, they descended the ancient stone stairs toward the torchlit corridor below, listening and watching.

They had just emerged from the stairwell into the corridor when the heavy metal-laced nets dropped over them, pinning them to the floor, and dozens of Gnome Hunters appeared all around them, crossbows notched and ready.

Pen had explored the Rock Troll village for what remained of the day. He'd been so tired he could barely keep his eyes open but was unable to sleep because of what had happened in Kermadec's home between himself and Cinnaminson. But Khyber's scathing attack on him, an attack he still didn't understand, really troubled him. Once or twice in his wanderings, he thought to return to the house and confront her, but he just couldn't make himself do it. He was embarrassed and hurt, in part because he didn't understand it, but mostly because it had happened in front of Cinnaminson.

So he forced himself to stay away until the evening celebration began, the welcome arranged for them by the members of the village, a feast with music and singing, neither of which he had ever associated with Trolls. But the music, consisting of pipes, drums, and a curious stringed instrument called a fiol, and the dancing, which was energetic and robust, brought him out of his mood sufficiently that by the time he had eaten two plates of rather wonderful food and drunk several pints of very strong ale, he was feeling pretty good again.

He even participated in the dancing, urged on by Kermadec and buttressed by the effects of the ale. He danced with whoever was nearest—men, women, and children alike—as there seemed to be little partnering in the Troll forms of dance, and he found himself thoroughly light-headed and happy by the time he was done.

Cinnaminson appeared with the others of his little group, and she sat with him during dinner and even danced with him briefly, but he couldn't find the right words to say to her, and so they didn't talk much. Tagwen was as taciturn as ever at first, though after a little of the ale he began to open up and pontificate endlessly on the virtues of hard work. Khyber smiled and clapped and spoke pleasantly to Pen, acting as if their earlier confrontation had never happened.

It was only when the evening was growing late, and his eyes were so heavy he was afraid he might fall over if he didn't sleep soon, that the Elven girl came over to sit beside him. He was alone at that point, sipping at his ale, listening to the music, and watching the Trolls dance in the firelight with what appeared to him to be boundless energy.

"I was too hard on you earlier," she said, putting her hand over his. "I didn't mean to scold. At the time, I was so mad, I just lashed out. I assumed you understood the problem, but thinking it through later, I realized you didn't."

He looked at her. "What problem?"

"If I tell you this, you must promise to keep it to yourself. Do you promise?"

He nodded. "All right."

"When I heard you tell Cinnaminson she couldn't come with us, all I could think about was how insensitive you were being to her situation. You saw it as common sense: If she came, she would be placed in danger again, and you wanted to keep her safe. I saw it through her eyes: You were casting her off as damaged and useless, no longer worthy of being a part of your life. She's in love with you, Penderrin. I warned you about this, but you paid no attention to me. You brought this on yourself, giving her so much of your time aboard ship, telling her how wonderful she was."

He bristled instantly. "I didn't say anything I didn't mean! Anyway, I don't see—"

She held up one hand in warning. "Don't say anything more until you hear me out. You *don't* see, indeed. If you did, we wouldn't be having this conversation. Now, listen. What do you think happened to her after that monster killed her father and the other two? Do you think she was left alone? Do you think that all that happened was that she was used to track you? It was bad enough that she had to lie trussed up and helpless belowdecks and listen to the cries of her father and cousins as they died; that was damage enough for an entire lifetime. But that wasn't the end of it."

He went cold. "What are you saying?"

Her dark eyes fixed on him. "I'm saying that she endured three days alone with that monster, and it wasn't satisfied with using her gift for night sight. It used her for other things, too. She told me. You didn't ask her if she had been abused physically, did you? It never even occurred to you that she might have been violated in other ways. This thing, this creature that took her, doesn't have any qualms about watching others suffer. It likes it. It enjoys inflicting pain. All kinds of pain."

He stared at her. He tried to say something, but the words lodged in his throat. A wave of nausea washed through him.

"So now she views herself as despicable." Khyber held his gaze. "When you tell her she can't go with you anymore, she sees it as an affirmation of what she already believes to be true about herself— that she is worthless, that no one could love her. It doesn't matter that you don't know the truth because she has kept it to herself. It's enough that *she* knows."

Pen looked off into the darkness, filled with sudden rage, filled with a need to exact revenge for what had happened, but impotent to do anything but sit and fume. The images that filled his mind were so terrible that he couldn't bear them. "I didn't realize what I was doing by telling her she couldn't come," he said quietly. "I didn't know."

She squeezed his hand. "I wish you still didn't know. I wish I didn't have to tell you. But you still care about the girl, don't you? So you need to know what's happened to her so that you can understand what she's going through. She's fragile in ways that you don't see. She might have mind-sight, but it's not sufficient protection against the monsters of this world and not enough to make up for the loss of her family. Her father, bad as he was, loved her, and she loved him. He was the support she could fall back on when things were too much for her. Who's going to offer her that support now?"

"I am," he said at once.

"Then you can't tell her you intend to leave her behind." Khyber's voice was fierce. "You can't make her safe that way, Pen. I know taking her is dangerous, but leaving her is worse."

They stared at each other in silence. In the background, the music and singing of the Troll revelers wafted through the darkness, rising above the firelight, echoing off the rock walls of the cliffs. Pen wanted to cry for what he was feeling, but no tears would come.

"I'll tell her she can come," he said finally. "I'll tell her I was wrong, that we need her."

She nodded. "Be careful what you say and how you say it. She wouldn't like it that I've told you what happened. She will probably want to tell you herself one day."

He nodded. "Thank you, Khyber. Thank you for telling me. Thank you for not letting me make a mistake I couldn't correct."

She got to her feet and stood looking at him. "I just did what I thought I had to do, Pen, but I have to tell you that it doesn't make me feel very good to have done it."

She turned and walked away.

Acting on whispered instructions from Shadea a'Ru, the Gnome Hunters removed the heavy mesh netting and bound and gagged Bek Ohmsford. He could have struggled or used magic to save himself, but he was terrified that if he did so, they would kill Rue. Bitter with disappointment and self-recrimination, he let them take him without a struggle.

"You aren't half so clever as you believe yourself to be," she said to him as the Gnomes carried him down into the cellars of the Keep. "I knew of your contact with your son the moment you made it. It was impossible to miss. I knew you were pretending at being ill earlier today, too, and that you would come back to the cold chamber to use the scrye waters again if you were given the chance. So I gave it to you."

She leaned over and tapped him lightly on the nose, a taunting gesture he couldn't fail to register. "You couldn't get a clear reading of where Penderrin was from your first contact; I saw that right away. So I knew you would have to come back and probe the scrye waters again when you thought we weren't around to see what you were searching for. Somehow, you found us out, didn't you? It was probably Traunt Rowan who gave us away. He lacks the finesse needed to fool someone as perceptive and experienced as you. Disappointing, if not entirely unexpected. At least I knew enough not to trust that you had been taken in by his explanation. I knew enough to read you the same way you must have read him."

She was silent for a time, staring straight ahead into the darkness, keeping pace with the guards who bore him. She took big, full strides that radiated power and determination. She looked taller and broader through the shoulders than he remembered, and there was a confidence about her that suggested she was equally comfortable with weapons or words. He did not know what his sister had done to antagonize her, but Shadea a'Ru was a formidable enemy.

"Your son has turned out to be a meddlesome boy, Bek," she continued after a while, "but no more so than Tagwen or the others who joined him to hunt for your sister. I took steps to put an end to their search, but until now they have managed to elude me. I tracked them all the way from Patch Run to the Elven village of Emberen and from there east to the Lazareen. Then, I lost them. But now, thanks to you, I know exactly where they are."

She smiled down at him, enjoying the dark look on his face. "Oh, you want to know how I know, since I wasn't in the cold chamber with you? Anticipating your nocturnal visit, I marked the scrye waters with a little magic of my own before you tampered with them. They will reveal to me exactly what they revealed to you. That should tell me everything I need to know about your son's whereabouts, I expect. Then I will find him and deal with him."

Bek listened with growing despair, aware of how completely he had been duped into doing just what Shadea had wanted him to do in the first place. Now he was a prisoner and unable to do anything to help either Pen or his sister. At least they were both alive. He could assume that much from what she had just told him. He could also assume she would try to change that.

They continued down until he smelled the damp and felt the cold of the deep underground. Somewhere not too far away, he heard water running. The heat of the Druid Fire was absent, as if that part of the Keep was far removed from the earth-warmed core.

Finally, they arrived at a corridor lined with heavy doors kept closed by iron bolts thrown through iron rings. His captors opened one of the doors and placed him in the tiny room beyond, a space barely larger than a closet. There was a wooden bed, straw, and a bucket. The floor, ceiling, and walls were rough and uneven and had been hollowed out of the bedrock.

They untied his arms and legs, but left his gag in place.

"Remove the gag when I am gone," Shadea said. "But first, listen to what I have to say. Behave yourself, and you might come out of this alive. I am locking your beloved wife up separately, in a place far away from you, somewhere you can't find her easily. I know stone walls and iron doors can't hold you, but they can hold her. If you try to escape, if your guards even *think* you are trying to escape, she will be killed at once. Do you understand?"

Bek nodded without speaking.

"Those guards will be stationed on each floor leading up, at each door, and they will communicate with each other regularly. If someone fails to answer, that will be the end of your chances of seeing your wife alive again. Behave yourself, and you and your family might still survive this."

She motioned the Gnome Hunters back into the corridor, followed them out, closed the door with a heavy thud, and threw the bolt.

Standing alone in the darkness and listening to their receding footsteps, Bek Ohmsford was certain of one thing. No matter what Shadea a'Ru said, if he didn't find a way to get out of there on his own, he wasn't getting out at all.

FOURTEEN

"I've been thinking about what I said to you yesterday," Pen said, sitting down beside Cinnaminson. It was midday, and he had been searching for her for almost an hour.

She kept her gaze directed straight ahead as her fingers worked the threads of the delicate scarf she was weaving on a tiny hand loom. How she could tell one color from the other was a mystery to him, but from the look of the completed portion, she was having no trouble doing so.

"I spoke without sufficient thought for what I was saying," he continued, watching her face for signs of a response. "You asked if I still cared about you, and I do. That was why I was so quick to tell you that you couldn't go with us. All I could think about was what it would mean to me if something more happened to you."

Still, she said nothing. They were seated high up in the bowl of the Gathering Place, the amphitheater used for elections when a Maturen was chosen, for presentations of music and song when there were celebrations and festivals, and for meetings of the entire population when it was necessary to make determinations that might affect the whole of the village. It sat well back against the cliffs and to the south end of the village, ringed by stone walls and hardy spruce, an oasis of calm in the otherwise bustling community.

It was deserted, save for the boy and the girl.

Pen sighed. "I want you to forget about what I said. You saved our lives back on the Lazareen, when the *Galaphile* was hunting us. You kept us from danger again in the Slags. You proved your value then, and I don't have any right to start questioning it now. I don't have any right to tell you what to do. You can decide for yourself."

"Have you been talking with Khyber?" she asked quietly.

"I've been thinking about what she said," he answered, avoiding the question. "She was so angry with me. It took me a while to sort it out." He brushed at his red hair, knotting it in his fingers. "I didn't know why she was so angry until I had thought about it for a while. I was presuming to speak for you when I didn't have the right. You asked me because you wanted my support. I should have realized that, and I should have given it."

She continued her weaving, her fingers moving smoothly and steadily, feeding in the colored threads and pulling them through, using the shuttle to separate and tighten down. He waited, not knowing what else to say, afraid he had already said too much.

"Do I have your support now?" she asked him finally.

"Yes."

"Do you want me to come with you? You, personally?"

"Yes, I do."

"Why? Tell me, Penderrin. Why do you want me to come with you?"

He hesitated. "I don't want this to be about you and me."

"But it is about you and me. It has been from the first day we met. Don't you know that?"

He nodded. "I guess I do. I just don't want to use that as the reason for your coming. But it is the reason. I want you to come because I want you to be with me. I don't want you anywhere else but with me."

She went still, her fingers motionless, her entire body frozen. He saw her differently in that instant, as if she had been captured in an indelible image, a portrait of such exquisite beauty and depth that he would never imagine her any other way. It made his heart ache to see her so. It made him want to do anything for her.

Without looking at him, she reached for him with her right hand, laying it feather-light across his own. "Then I will come," she said.

She went back to her weaving, silent once more, her attention on her work, her hand gone from his. He stared at her for a moment, wanting to say something more, but deciding against it. Just then, things were better left as they were.

He rose. "I think I should see how the *Skatelow* looks, now that they've moved her off the plains. I'll find you later."

She nodded, and he went down off the risers to one of the passageways that exited from the amphitheater floor to the ring of stone walls and spruce trees outside. From there, he walked down through the village to the south gates and passed out onto the flats, then worked his way back toward the cliffs until he reached the shallow defile into which the *Skatelow* had been pulled to conceal her from view. He did that without really being aware of anything but Cinnaminson. Her face, her body, her voice, her words, her smell, the movement of her hands as she wove the delicate scarf.

He was still thinking about her two hours later, happily lost in a mix of dreams and memories that gave him the first real peace he had known in days, when the Troll watch sounded the alarm.

Khyber Elessedil was standing with Tagwen outside Kermadec's home, listening while the little man held forth on the peculiarities of Troll life, when the horns began to wail and the drums to boom. The sounds were so unexpected and so earth shattering that for a moment she stood staring at the Dwarf, who stood staring back.

"What is that?" she managed finally.

He shook his burly head, his blunt fingers tugging at his beard anxiously as he glanced around. "Don't know. A warning?"

Trolls had begun running everywhere, all sizes and shapes, men, women, and children, entire families and households, charging out of buildings and down roads and alleyways with a single-mindedness that suggested they understood the sounds perfectly. After a moment, Khyber was able to discern a pattern to their movements that

suggested what was happening. The women and children were all retreating back through the village toward the cliffs, the biggest scoop-
ing up the smallest in squirming bundles. They took nothing else with
them, not one single implement or piece of clothing. They went without the slightest hesitation or thought for what they were doing, moving swiftly without seeming to look rushed.

They have practiced this often, Khyber thought.

The men, meanwhile, were all moving in the other direction,
down toward the front walls of the village, to the gates and ramparts
that served as protection and fortification. Some wore chain mail and
plate armor. All carried weapons. It didn't take a genius to figure out
what was happening.

Khyber rushed back inside the house for her short sword. When
she came out again, Kermadec was standing with Tagwen, huge and
forbidding in a towering iron helmet and a chain-mail chest and
shoulder guard.

"We're under attack," he advised, his words clipped and hard. She
had not heard him sound like that before. All of the heartiness and
openness was gone; his voice had gone tight and rough with anger
and menace. "Airships fly in from the south bearing Druid insignia.
We can assume the reason for their visit."

Khyber buckled on her sword, then felt for the reassuring presence of the Elfstones in her tunic pocket. She had no idea if she
would be required to use them, but she intended to be ready. She
glanced at Tagwen, who carried no weapons, then back at Kermadec. "How did they find us?"

The Rock Troll shook his big head. "No idea. The Druids have
ways of finding anyone, if they put their minds to it. I don't think
they followed you. If they had done so, they would have been here
sooner. I think they found you some other way."

He turned away from them to yell instructions to a squad of Troll
warriors passing by, gesturing toward the south wall, separating out
one and sending him in another direction. The village was alive with
movement; swarming with Trolls. It felt like controlled chaos.

"We're preparing a welcome for our uninvited guests," he said, turning back to them, changing once more to the Dwarf language. "We won't attack them until we hear what they have to say. We'll let them talk first."

"Perhaps they're friends," Khyber suggested hopefully, cringing at the loud snort Tagwen gave in response.

"Too many ships for that," Kermadec advised. "If they were friends, they would come in one ship, not in a dozen. They would send a representative ahead to announce their intentions. No, this is an assault force, come for a specific purpose." He glanced around. "Where are young Penderrin and the girl?"

Khyber stared at Tagwen. The Dwarf shook his head. Neither one had a clue.

Kermadec glanced skyward. "Too late to search for them now. Come with me! Hurry!"

At the sound of the battle horns and drums, Pen dropped off the *Skatelow's* decks to the ground and began to run. He needed no time to consider what he was doing or where he was going. He had left Cinnaminson inside the Gathering Place. She might still be there, alone and unprotected. She would not know what was happening. She would not know where to run.

He went through the south gates just as they were closing, bursting through the knot of Troll warriors bunched at the opening, huge armored shoulders and wide backs straining against the ironbound barriers and massive locks. Trolls were running everywhere, and the passageways of the village were all but completely blocked by Trolls hurrying toward the walls. Pen dodged past them, heading for the amphitheater and Cinnaminson. Shouts and cries rose all around him, their intensity and tone confirming what he already instinctively knew—the village was under attack. He would have liked to find Khyber and Tagwen to know more, but he would have to track them down later. First he had to reach Cinnaminson.

He gained a side street that was mostly deserted and led straight to his destination. He was running hard now, flushed with the heat of his efforts, a frantic warning sounding in his mind. *Don't lose her! Don't let anything happen to her!*

Ahead, the walls of the amphitheater loomed darkly through the ring of trees that surrounded the interior bowl. There was no movement at the entrance, no sign of life. Perhaps she had already gotten out. Perhaps one of the others had come to find her.

He glanced over his shoulder at the village walls, where Trolls were taking up positions all along the ramparts and at the gates. The central point of defense seemed to be the gates he had just passed through, the ones facing south down the broad corridor between the Razor Mountains west and the Charnals east. The reason for this became immediately apparent when he glanced skyward. A dozen black warships filled the horizon, flying down the gap directly toward Taupo Rough.

Shades!

He breathed the word in a whisper of fear as he burst into the tunnel leading into the amphitheater and nearly collided with Cinnaminson, who was trying to make her way out from the other end. She was careening from wall to wall, her hands clutching her ears to block out the sounds of the horns and drums.

"Cinnaminson!" he shouted as he reached her, grabbing her shoulders and pulling her against him.

"Pen!" she gasped in reply, burying her head in his shoulder. Her weaving materials and loom were gone, and he could feel her heart pounding. "I couldn't find my way out. The sounds disrupt my mindsight. It was too much for me."

"It's all right," he said, stroking her hair. Her breath was coming in quick, frantic bursts. "I'll get you back to the others. They must have gone into the mountains to hide. The sky is full of Druid warships, right outside the walls. We have to go. Can you walk?"

She nodded into his shoulder, then lifted her face to his. "I knew you would come for me."

He kissed her impulsively. "I'll always come for you. Always. Come on. Run!"

They hurried back through the tunnel to the streets outside. But as they reached the far end, Pen drew up short and pulled her back against the passageway wall, keeping hidden in the shadows.

One of the Druid airships was hovering just outside the village wall and across from their hiding place. Any attempt at escape would require them to cross open ground, where they would quickly be seen.

Pen bit his lip in frustration. They were trapped.

Khyber Elessedil crouched with Tagwen on the roof of a building some fifty yards back from the south gates. Both wore dark robes drawn close and hoods pulled up. They hid behind a half-wall facade that rose in front of them, situated where they could see and hear what was about to happen.

Kermadec stood on the ramparts above the south gates, surrounded by a squad of huge Trolls wearing body armor and insignia-crested helmets. The Maturen was watching as the Druid airships—their flags clearly visible now—formed a line just beyond the outer wall, intimidating black hulks hanging over the village like birds of prey. There was an unmistakable arrogance to their positioning, as if they were disdainful of anything the villagers might try to do to harm them. No attempt was being made to suggest that this was a friendly visit. Kermadec had been right: The Druids had come to threaten.

After the foremost airship had dropped almost to the ground, a single Druid descended the rope ladder and walked forward. He was a big man, and as he approached, he lowered his hood to reveal his face, a gesture clearly meant to identify himself to the Trolls.

"Traunt Rowan," Tagwen whispered to Khyber. "One of Shadea's bunch."

She watched the Southlander come almost to the gates before stopping, his eyes fixing on the Trolls standing atop them.

"Kermadec?" he called, his voice clearly audible in the near silence.

"I'm here, Traunt Rowan," the Maturen called back.

"Open your gates to us."

"I don't think so."

"Then bring out the boy, Pen Ohmsford, and you do not need to. Just the boy. The others can remain, if you want them to."

"You are a bold man, coming into our country and making demands as if it were your own." Kermadec's voice had taken on a decided edge. "You might want to give some thought to where you stand before you say anything else."

"Is the boy here?"

"What boy?"

There was a measured silence. "You are a fool to challenge us, Kermadec."

"The only fool I see is the one who serves Shadea a'Ru. The only fool I see is the one who betrayed the Ard Rhys in a way so foul and indefensible that it will surely lead to his destruction. Don't threaten me, Traunt Rowan! Don't threaten the Trolls of Taupo Rough! We were the defenders of the Druids for almost twenty years, before this dark time in your history, and we will one day be defenders of the Druids again. We know enough about you to be able to challenge you, if that is what is required. Turn your ships around and fly out of here while you still can. Don't mistake where you are."

Traunt Rowan folded his arms. "We have the boy's parents, Kermadec. We know that Ahren Elessedil is dead. You have no one who will stand with you in this. You are alone."

Khyber and Tagwen exchanged a quick, shocked glance. The Druids had Bek Ohmsford and his wife? How had that happened?

"He's lying," Tagwen hissed.

"Alone?" Kermadec laughed. "The Trolls are always alone. It is a condition of life to which we are not only accustomed, but one that we prefer. Threats of the sort you seem intent on making don't frighten us. If you have the parents, you don't need the boy, do you? Can the parents not give you everything you need? What is it that you need, by the way? You haven't said. What is it that a boy can give you that his parents can't? You speak as if you know, but I think, in fact, you don't. Explain yourself, and maybe I can be persuaded to do as you say."

Traunt Rowan stood unmoving on the flats, dark and solitary, anger radiating off him like heat. "We are to raze your village and kill you all, Kermadec, if you resist us. Those are my orders. I have brought Gnome Hunters to carry out those orders. I have brought Mutens, as well. Do you wish your village and people destroyed? Is that your intent?"

Kermadec seemed to be thinking it over. "My intent, Traunt Rowan," he said finally, his rough voice so dark with menace that Khyber immediately tensed, "is to see you and your raiders and your airships consumed by the fires of the netherworld that spawned you."

His arm swept up. Instantly, a hail of fire-tipped arrows arced out of the village and fell all across the flats beyond. In the next instant the flats exploded in gouts of fire that spread quickly down concealed channels in a crisscross pattern that blanketed the earth for two hundred yards. The flames leapt so high that one of the airships caught fire and was consumed immediately, the fire spreading up the bottom of its hull to find added fuel in yards of light sheaths strapped to its gunwales. The ship heaved in response to the blaze that consumed it, tried futilely to rise into the sky, then shuddered, blew apart, and fell in ruins onto the flats.

The other airships were backing away by then, powered up in response to the threat and lifting swiftly beyond the reach of the flames. Traunt Rowan had gone into a protective crouch, hands moving, his Druid magic sweeping about him. Now he, too, backed away, avoiding the flames as best he could, shielded well enough that he didn't seem threatened. His black robes swirled about him in a wind generated by the sudden heat as he reached an open spot, caught hold of the rope ladder once more, and began to climb.

The Trolls of Taupo Rough were attacking the airships using catapults now. The wooden machines were mounted all along the ramparts, their cradles flinging huge rocks through the smoke-filled air with deadly precision. Several found their marks, smashing through the hulls and sails of the airships, leaving gaping holes and ragged tears in the wood and fabric. One brought down a mast, collapsing it onto the deck and sending the airship into a spin that took it out of the fight.

The Gnome Hunters aboard the ships fought back with crossbows and slings, filling the sky with a cloud of deadly missiles. But the arrows and stones fell harmlessly, bouncing off heavy armor and rock walls and doing little damage to the well-protected Trolls.

For a moment, it seemed as if the battle was over almost before it had begun. The entire south end of the flats was on fire, grasses and scrub and whatever was in those trenches and holes burning fiercely. The Druid airships were in retreat, those not already down vanishing beyond the flames and smoke. Traunt Rowan had disappeared with them, his flagship turned about with the others.

But already Kermadec was coming down off the ramparts and signaling to his men to do the same. In dark, bulky knots, they began to retreat through the village toward the cliffs. Khyber and Tagwen climbed down from their hiding place, casting anxious glances toward the flats, where fresh trouble would appear. They had just gotten to the ground when Kermadec came charging up to them.

"We have to find that boy!" he snapped, turning momentarily to yell something to the Trolls charging past. "If we lose him now, this will all have been for nothing! Where do we look?"

"He might have found his way to the cliffs," Tagwen suggested quickly. "He might not need finding."

"I would have heard, if he were there. I left word to be informed when he showed himself. No, Bristle Beard, he's still out here in the village somewhere."

As they tried frantically to come up with something that would help, Khyber threw off the heavy concealing cloak, which was now more hindrance than help. As she did so, her fingers brushed across the small bulk of the Elfstones. She jammed her hand into her pocket and yanked them out. Now that the Druids had located them, there was no reason not to call upon the magic.

"I know how to find him," she said, dumping the blue stones into her palm. "Stand away from me."

They did so at once, neither choosing to question her command. Eyes closed, she retreated into her calming center, reaching for the magic. Ahren had trained her in that approach, so the effort was almost second nature. Even the presence of the Elfstone magic was no longer entirely unfamiliar after the Slags, and she recognized the sudden flush of heat that rose in response to her summons. Tendrils of life pulsed from her hand through her body, then back again, gathering speed and power, building in intensity. The magic of the Stones filled her, a wash of power finding a welcome home. She let it happen, left herself open to its need.

The blue light burst from the Elfstones and shot through the village streets and buildings, through stone and timbers, power that solid materials could not contain. The vision formed and tightened, and the three who watched saw them appear in the haze, the boy and the Rover girl, crouched in the shadow of a darkened tunnel.

"The amphitheater!" Kermadec shouted, and despite the encumbering weight of his massive armor, he began to run.

Pen Ohmsford had waited just an instant too long to make his break from the tunnel. When the fighting started, he stayed where he was, Cinnaminson close beside him, as fire erupted from outside the village walls in huge gouts and then catapults began launching boulders and Gnome Hunters retaliated with slings and crossbows. A hail of missiles clattered against the stone of the walls and buildings outside their hiding place, and the boy did not dare chance a break without better protection.

Then, abruptly, the fighting stopped as clouds of dark smoke rolled across the flats and began to seep into the village as well. Still Pen hesitated, unsure. He counted off twenty seconds, then took Cinnaminson's hand and pulled her after him.

"Run!" he ordered, breaking for the open street.

But the instant he showed himself, the huge bulk of an airship hove into view, slicing through the screen of smoke and flames. Gnome Hunters crowded the gunwales, crossbows and slings firing at everything that moved. Out in the open and unprotected, the boy and the Rover girl were instant targets. A flurry of darts whipped past them, striking the stone walls in a cacophony of tiny, violent explosions. One sliced through Pen's ribs, spinning him around. Another struck him in the arm and sent him sprawling against the closest wall.

"Pen, what's happening?" Cinnaminson cried, crouching on her hands and knees in the dirt, her face frantic with confusion and fear. Sling stones clattered all around her like hail.

"Get up!" he screamed, hauling her back to her feet, blood running down his arm and side. "Run!"

Searching for any sort of shelter that would deflect the deadly missiles, he tried to shield her as he pulled her after him. It seemed as if they were the only ones left in the village, the streets and buildings empty and the inhabitants all safely inside the tunnels and caves. But where were the tunnels? In what direction? Smoke obscured everything, and he had gotten turned around completely in his effort to escape.

A tiny alcove at the back of a building offered temporary shelter, and he shoved Cinnaminson inside, both of them gasping and bloodied.

I'm going to get us killed! he screamed at himself. *What am I supposed to do?*

Overhead, the Druid warship was swinging back around, searching for movement. They were safe for the moment, but trapped. Sooner or later, those Gnome Hunters would land and begin a search of the buildings. They couldn't stay where they were. They had to get out of there.

"Penderrin!" a familiar voice boomed, causing the boy to jump.

"Kermadec! We're here!"

He yanked Cinnaminson from their shelter and began to run toward the sound of the Rock Troll's voice, hugging the walls that best protected them as they went. Overhead, the smoke was building in thick black clouds, and the airship was a massive shadow wrapped in its haze. The Gnome Hunters were still firing blindly into the village, and the boy could feel bolts and arrows whistle past him as he ran.

Then Kermadec appeared in front of them, a huge armored behemoth. Without slowing, he snatched them up like children, tucking one under each arm. "Can't afford to lose you now," he said, pounding ahead like a great beast of burden. "Hold tight."

Gripped by one massive arm like a sack of grain, bouncing up and down with each footfall, Pen felt as if his eyes were going to be shaken loose from his head, but on balance he decided that was a small price to pay for being rescued. He closed his eyes to steady himself and waited patiently for the bouncing to stop.

F I F T E E N

When Kermadec set them down again, Pen and Cinnaminson were safely inside the caves that formed the Rock Troll fortress in the cliffs above the village. He had carried them in through an entrance concealed in the rocks, bundled them up a set of narrow stone steps to a door that opened after he'd manipulated various jagged outcroppings, then deposited them where they could spend a few moments regaining their equilibrium.

"We thought no one was coming," Cinnaminson offered, her face pale and her honey hair disheveled and coated with dust.

"Oh, it only took finding out where you were," the big Troll replied cheerfully. His strange, flat face glanced at her briefly. "You can thank the Elf girl for that. She had the magic, some blue gems that showed an image of you hiding in the tunnel of the Gathering Place."

The Elfstones, Pen thought. He had forgotten them entirely. *But of course she can use them now, when there is no longer any reason to guard against revealing our presence.*

"I remembered Cinnaminson and went back for her," Pen said. "But then after I found her, I got lost."

"Easy enough to do in our streets, young Penderrin. They were constructed to get you lost, if you weren't one of us. No need to say anything more about it. You're safe now, and that's what matters."

He released the locks on a concealed door and pulled it open to admit them to the safehold. Inside, it was controlled chaos of the same sort that Pen had experienced in the village on the approach of the Druid warships. Trolls bustled in all directions, each with a seemingly different task to accomplish. The chamber was huge, a monstrous cavern fully fifty feet high and more than a hundred across. Dozens of tunnels led away to places the boy could not see for the twists and turns in the corridors. But the openings to the left of where they stood formed a series of fortified redoubts in the cliff wall above Taupo Rough. Sunlight slanted through these overlooks in bright streamers, chasing back the shadows. Smaller cracks and crevices in the stone of the cliff wall admitted additional light. The combination of sunlit openings gave the chamber a peculiarly dappled look, but one that allowed the inhabitants to see clearly.

Kermadec refastened the locks on the concealed door, then added a pair of huge bars that slipped into iron cradles to further seal the entry. "That should keep out any unwanted visitors," he declared, brushing off his hands. He glanced around. "Come with me."

He led them to the left, to one of the redoubts, motioning the workers aside and moving to the edge of a thick protective wall of stone blocks that all but closed off the entry. He beckoned the boy and the girl forward and, when they were standing beside him at the fortifications, pointed outside. "I know you can't see what's out there, Rover girl, but young Penderrin can describe it to you in detail later. It's what's been sent to bring him back."

The Druid airships had repositioned just outside the walls of the village, hovering not far off the ground, but well back from the possibility of catapult attacks that might be launched from the cliffs. Dozens of Gnome Hunters were scurrying down rope ladders and up to the village walls, some carrying battering rams, some grappling hooks and ropes. They were already scaling the walls and forcing the gates. Behind them lumbered several dozen creatures that looked as

if they had been fashioned from wet mud hardened by the sun, creatures that resembled Trolls but lacked the proper proportions and
features, as if someone had concocted a batch of poor imitations.

"Mutens," Pen whispered.

"Our worst enemies. No brains, no feelings, no purpose. They
are one step above rocks on the evolutionary ladder. Magic controls them easily. In the old days, it was the Warlock Lord who controlled them. Now it is our Druid adversaries. The Ard Rhys would
weep."

He gestured toward the flats. "Those explosions earlier? We used
oil culled from the darker regions of the Malg, capped in barrels and
buried in the ground. Highly flammable. The Druids weren't expecting that. It gave us a chance to get safely away, once we knew that a
fight was our only recourse. But that's all the advantage we get from
down there. We fight now from up here, in our redoubt, for today at
least."

He touched their shoulders and led them back into the cavern.
"By tomorrow, we'll be gone from here. I need to make ready for our
departure, and you need to rest." He searched the cavern for a moment, then shouted. "Atalan!"

A burly troll with the blackest eyes Pen had ever seen lumbered
up to them. His dark gaze shifted from Kermadec to the boy and
girl, then back again. "I have work to do."

"Now you have new work to do. Take young Penderrin and his
friend and find their companions. Take them to one of the upper
chambers. See that they all have something to eat and drink and a
place to sleep. They will leave at first light. I'll select their escort."

The other Troll stepped closer. "What about me, Kermadec? Am
I to go?"

His voice was rough and surly; he made it sound more like a demand than a request. Kermadec gave him a long, measured look. "I
will give it some thought."

Then he turned back to Pen and Cinnaminson. "Atalan will see
to it that you are made comfortable. The three of you should get
along fine. You are all the same age, if not the same temperament."

He walked away without looking back, leaving the three staring after him. Atalan shook his head. "He treats me like a child. Who does he think he is?"

Neither Pen nor Cinnaminson was about to attempt an answer to that one, so they kept quiet. Pen was thinking they might have been better off if Kermadec had left them on their own. Atalan was still staring after the Maturen. Then he seemed to remember his charges. He gave them a cursory look and shrugged. "Come with me."

He led them through the main chamber to a set of steps cut into the rock and from there upstairs to a new level. He didn't speak for a time, trudging ahead with the movements of one resigned to a fate he didn't deserve. When they reached the top of the stairs, he glanced back at them.

"Do you have a brother?" he asked Pen. The boy shook his head. "Well, if you did, I would hope he would treat you better than Kermadec treats me. He was born earlier, but not necessarily smarter. He is Maturen now, but I will be Maturen one day, too."

He broke off and turned away, leading them into a series of narrow tunnels that twisted and turned through the rock. Several times, they encountered Trolls coming from the other direction, but not once did Atalan give way, bulling past the oncoming Trolls with an insistence that bordered on rudeness. He seemed of such an entirely different temperament than Kermadec that Pen could not come to terms with the idea that they were really brothers.

"So you are the reason for all this madness," Atalan offered at one point. "What is it about you that attracts this kind of attention from the Druids?"

Pen shook his head. "The Ard Rhys is my aunt."

"Your aunt?" Atalan seemed impressed. "Missing for several weeks now, isn't she? Do they think you know where she is?"

"I don't know what they think. Except that they don't want me hunting for her."

Atalan nodded. "That would explain why they want you so bad. It would explain why my brother is so intent on helping you, too. He thinks the Ard Rhys is the Word's own child. He thinks she can do no wrong. He forgets what she was before, a creature of darkness and murder. You know of this, don't you?"

Pen nodded. He was growing angry. "She was a creature of the Morgawr and not responsible for what she did," he answered in clipped tones.

Atalan glanced back once more. "If you say so."

They went on through the tunnels until they had reached a room far back in the cliff rock, where the light was dim and hazy and the noise of the activity taking place below was muted almost to silence.

The Rock Troll gestured. "Wait here."

He disappeared down another passageway, and when he was safely out of hearing, Pen said to Cinnaminson, "I don't think he likes us much."

She turned her milky gaze on him and smiled. "You don't like him, either. But this is mostly about his brother. You shouldn't take it personally."

He nodded, thinking it was easy to say, but hard to do. Especially when it was your family that was being attacked. But she was right, of course, so he put the matter aside. They sat together in the chamber, listening to the faraway sounds of the Trolls and waiting for something to happen.

When Atalan finally returned, he was carrying food and drink, which he deposited in front of them with barely a word before disappearing again. With nothing better to do, they began to eat. But it wasn't more than a few minutes later that Tagwen and Khyber appeared at the chamber entrance.

"Shades, Penderrin, can't you stay out of trouble for five minutes without someone keeping watch over you?" snapped the latter. "What happened to you out there? Are you all right, Cinnaminson?"

She rushed over to the Rover girl and embraced her warmly, giving Pen a dark look. Tagwen, standing at the entry with his arms folded over his burly chest, knit his brow in reproof and glared at him. Pen could tell already that nothing he said was going to make any difference.

Aboard the Druid flagship *Athabasca*, Traunt Rowan stood at the forward rail with Pyson Wence and watched the Gnome Hunters flood the abandoned Troll village. Already, the smell of smoke rising from fires and the sound of furniture being smashed had begun to reach them. Their orders, once it was determined that Kermadec intended to fight, were to destroy as much of Taupo Rough as possible and then lay siege to the cliffside redoubt. The Trolls might think themselves safe inside their rock fortress, but the Druid warships were equipped with catapults designed to breach such defenses. More to the point, the Trolls were outnumbered and constrained by the presence of their women and children. The Trolls might hold out for a day or even two, but in the end, they would be overrun.

"I don't like it that Shadea is so intent on finding this boy," Pyson Wence said quietly, his gimlet eyes shifting to find Rowan's dark face. "I don't like it that we're out here at all."

"Do you suspect that she wants us out of the way?" the Southlander asked, keeping his attention focused on the progress of the Gnomes. Wence had brought them to Paranor from among his own people, but they were under Rowan's immediate command in this operation. Pyson Wence was adept at many things, but he was not a soldier.

"I think she would like to see what happened to Terek Molt happen to us. I don't trust her."

"If you did, you would be unique."

"It troubles me that we have lost both Molt and Iridia in the span of a week's time. One dead and one disappeared, and now here we are, the last two of Shadea's company, dispatched from Paranor to hunt this boy while she cuddles with Gerand Cera and schemes to make the position of Ard Rhys a lifetime appointment."

Shadea's infatuation with Cera bothered Traunt Rowan, as well, but he wasn't convinced yet that it was real. Shadea was far too self-centered to make a pairing of equals with another Druid. She was up to something, and on first hearing of her alliance with Cera, he had decided to wait her out. She wasn't yet so firmly entrenched that she could afford to discard her old allies. It was unfortunate about Molt and Iridia, but what had happened to them was not directly Shadea's doing.

Her obsession with finding Pen Ohmsford was more troubling. It was the parents who should concern them, he thought, particularly Bek Ohmsford, who had the use of the magic of the wishsong, which was Grianne Ohmsford's principal weapon. Yet even though Shadea had locked the senior Ohmsfords in the cellars of the Keep, she wasn't satisfied. Before imprisoning them, she had tricked them into revealing their son's location so that she could continue to hunt him down. She was merely being safe, she insisted, but he thought it was something more.

Wheels within wheels. Games and more games. It was a part of the Druid culture, but he had never been comfortable with it. He was better at confronting problems in an open way, at meeting them head-on. It was one of the reasons he had gone to the Ard Rhys on that last night and asked her quite bluntly to resign her office. She might have been persuaded to do so, had he more time to convince her and had Shadea not been so anxious to use the liquid night. But Shadea was ambitious and manipulative; she was more representative of the Druid order at large. Traunt Rowan was more the exception. Oddly enough, it was one of the reasons he believed himself less vulnerable to Shadea's anger. She knew he was neither ambitious nor covetous; she knew he was content to let her lead. His goal from the beginning had been to remove Grianne Ohmsford as head of the order; it had never been to take her place. In their desire for advancement and acquisition of power, the others were more aggressive than he was. It put them in dangerous waters, while he stood safely on the shore.

He refocused his gaze on Taupo Rough. The Gnome attack force had reached the base of the cliff walls and was forming up for an all-out assault. Scaling ladders and grappling hooks were being brought forward, and shield walls were being prepared. When everything was in place, the attack on the redoubt would begin.

"I want you to go down into the village with your Hunters," he said suddenly to Pyson Wence. When the other gaped at him in disbelief, he added, "So that they can see we are committed to their efforts. I don't need you to lead any charges, Pyson. I need you to provide reassurance."

"Then you go!" the Gnome snapped.

"I would, but I have to command the airships when we begin to launch the catapults. I would leave you to handle this if you had any idea at all how to use a catapult. But you don't, so your place is on the ground, keeping your Gnome Hunters in line."

The Gnome Druid gave him a withering stare. "You don't command me, Traunt Rowan. No one commands me."

"Aboard this ship and on this expedition, I do," he responded calmly. "I have been given the responsibility for bringing back the boy. You were sent to aid me. So you must do as I instruct you to do. As you agreed to do by coming with me, I might add."

Pyson Wence did not move. "If I do so, what is to prevent you from leaving me behind? What if that is what Shadea has asked of you?"

His voice was petulant and accusatory. Traunt Rowan held his gaze. "Look at me, Pyson. Look closely. Do you see treachery in my eyes or hear it in my voice? Since when have you ever worried that I would betray any of us in this business?"

Long moments passed, their measure a blink of an eye to both as they stared each other down. "All right," Pyson Wence said finally. His narrow face reflected displeasure and disgust. "I will do as you ask. I will go down with my people. I trust you, if not Shadea."

He went over to the ladder and began to descend to the flats, his black robes billowing out behind him in the breeze. Traunt Rowan watched him in silence, thinking that if Pyson Wence had ever trusted anyone, it was a miracle.

Within the caverns of the Troll redoubt, Pen was sleeping soundly when a rough hand shook his shoulder and an equally rough voice said, "Wake up! You're leaving!"

He jerked upright, groggy and lethargic, trying to figure out where he was. When he caught sight of Atalan moving over to Tagwen to wake the Dwarf, he remembered. He had no idea how long he had slept, but it didn't feel as if it had been more than a few minutes. He rubbed his eyes and climbed to his feet. Khyber and Cinnaminson were standing by the cavern entry, staring out into the

corridor. Heavy booming shook the chamber, as if a giant were striking the cliff face with a huge hammer. From somewhere not too far
away, shouts and cries rose, the sounds of a battle being joined.

Pen moved over to the girls. "What's going on? What's happened?"

"The Druids and their Gnome Hunters are attacking the Trolls,"
Khyber answered. "Hear that pounding? They're using catapults to
launch huge boulders into the cliff walls to break down the Troll fortifications. Gnome Hunters are scaling the cliffs on ladders and
ropes, trying to breach the redoubt."

"Which they will do, sooner than later," Kermadec declared, appearing out of the corridor shadows. "They're determined about this,
it seems. We have to get you out now, before we lose the chance. All
awake and ready to go?" He swung around. "Atalan! Gather up their
things. Distribute them among the others. Hurry!"

Atalan hesitated. "Am I to go with you?"

"You are. Now join the others. Go!"

Black eyes glittering eagerly, Kermadec's brother snatched up
everything in sight belonging to the four companions and bolted
from the room. It was clear that he had taken on a new attitude.

Pen was less happy about the pending flight. "Kermadec," he said,
drawing the big Troll's attention. "I'm sorry about this. I shouldn't have
let Tagwen talk me into coming. Look what I've done."

To his surprise, Kermadec laughed. "Well, you can make that argument, Penderrin. You can say that this is all your fault. But the fact
remains that we need to bring back the Ard Rhys from where Shadea
and those others have sent her. Besides, what's happening now would
have happened sooner or later. There's no peace for the Trolls of
Taupo Rough while your aunt is lost to us. So don't blame yourself
for this. Blame her, if you want to blame anyone, for not listening to
me or Bristle Beard when we warned her to be more careful."

He beckoned Tagwen over and gathered all four around him.
"Now, listen. We haven't much time. Evacuation of the women and
children is already under way. All will be spirited away through tunnels that open onto the other side. The men will follow as soon as
they are out. Then a march will be undertaken to reach a new safe-

hold. We've done this before, and we are practiced at it. Everyone will just disappear. There won't even be a trail left. The Druids and the Gnomes will never know what happened.

"But first, we have to get you out. I've selected a dozen Trolls to provide escort. That includes Atalan and myself. You'll be as well looked after as possible. But we have to move quickly in the beginning, because as soon as it is discovered we are gone, Traunt Rowan is going to realize what we have done and bring his warships over the peaks and down the other side to search for us. He'll have the advantage from the air because we must cross the Klu Mountains to reach the Inkrim. That's a journey of perhaps a week on foot. A long time to be out in the open, but we haven't any choice."

He looked at each of them in turn, measuring. "Are you up to it? Are you ready to try?"

All nodded, but the Troll shook his head. His blunt features were tight. "Don't be too quick to sign on. If any of you wants to stay behind, now is the time to tell me. It won't be held against you. Not by me or by any of those who go with me." He paused. "Cinnaminson?"

She stiffened. "Why do you choose to start with me? Is it because I am blind?"

Kermadec reached out with his huge hand and placed it gently on her shoulder. "No, girl. I start with you because you have less of a stake in all this than the others do. It would be easiest for you to walk away."

"Once, that was so." She shook her head slowly. "Not anymore. My decision is made. I am going."

Kermadec looked at the other three. "Pen, you haven't any choice, so there's no reason to ask you. And Tagwen will go because he doesn't trust me to get the job done alone. What of you, Khyber Elessedil?"

She gave him a fierce look. "I will go because my uncle would have gone if he had lived. I stand now in his shoes."

Kermadec nodded his approval. "Then we're a company." He wheeled away. "Come with me."

He led them back down the corridor they had come through earlier, toward the shouting of fighters and the thunder of siege weapons. Pen felt his temperature rise and his hands begin to sweat as the sounds of battle reverberated through the mountain catacombs. He remembered how it had felt to be chased through the streets of the village, dodging arrows and sling stones, trying to stay safe. He did not care to experience that again, and yet it seemed as if that was exactly what was going to happen. He wished they had an airship and could simply fly away. He wanted to be back in the skies, where he felt safe.

The main chamber of the redoubt was filled with Trolls charging in all directions. The men stood at the walls where the cliffs opened to the village below, crouching behind their fortifications as boulders smashed into the rock and arrows whizzed past their heads. The women and children were making their way in small groups toward the back part of the cavern, then filing down a series of tunnels into the torchlit dark. The women, distinctive by their smoother skin and slender bodies, herded the tiny children like puppies, urging them along, carrying those too small to walk. They seemed calm on the face of things, moving deliberately and with purpose, evidencing none of the panic that Pen felt. Their self-control impressed the boy, and he tightened his own resolve.

With Kermadec leading the way, they hurried after the women and children. Dust was falling from the cavern ceiling as the pounding of the catapult missiles against the rock walls grew more insistent, the resulting reverberations deep and threatening. It felt as if the mountain might come down about them, broken in two by the constant hammering. Pen ducked his head instinctively and reached over to take Cinnaminson's hand. He did so as much for himself as for her, and was grateful when she squeezed his fingers reassuringly.

They were mingling with the women and children now, the latter staring up at him with curious, anxious eyes. He tried not to read accusation in those stares; the children wouldn't know that their upheaval was his fault. He smiled at them as he hurried past. He didn't know how else to tell them that he wanted them to think better of him than he thought of himself.

"Stay together!" Kermadec called back.

Silt rained down on Pen in a sudden shower, and he tripped over one of the children. Releasing Cinnaminson's hand, he paused to pick the child up, brushing off its tiny head, handing it back to the closest of the women. The woman took the child and smiled at him, her strange black eyes and smooth features drawing him in. Something in the look she gave him reminded him of his mother, and suddenly he missed her so that it made him ache. The shock was like a physical blow, and it left him stunned and momentarily disoriented. His world compressed to a tightness about his heart, where the things he needed most felt the farthest away.

Still struggling with his feelings, he hurried after the others.

S I X T E E N

They fled through the tunnels, away from Taupo Rough and deep into the mountain rock. At first they followed the women and children, a part of their steady flow down the boltholes, and then they broke away to follow a different set of tunnels and did not see them again. Pen and the rest of their small group moved swiftly and purposefully, sliding through the darkness with torches to light the way and a sense of urgency to keep them focused. The din of the battle they had escaped was audible for a time, then dimmed and faded, and they were left with the soft scrape and rustle of their own movements in the ensuing silence.

No one spoke. All of their efforts were concentrated on moving through the tunnels, on getting clear of the pursuit that was sure to follow. It might be that the Druids and their Gnome Hunters couldn't track them through the rock corridors, but Pen knew that Kermadec and his Trolls would not rely on that. He held Cinnaminson's hand as they went, drawing on the strength he found there, reassuring himself that she was with him. He didn't even try to tell himself that the contact was for her; he knew that she was better able to navigate the dark than he was. It was to keep his despair and loneliness at bay, for he was afraid that otherwise, without the feel of her, he would

give way to the dark emotions that threatened to overwhelm his failing sense of purpose and leave him drained of strength.

The eyes of those women and children haunted him, burned into
his memory, became ghosts in his mind. That wouldn't have happened had he felt less guilt over their fate. But he could not absolve
himself of the responsibility he felt, no matter what Kermadec might
say. Too much of what had transpired already on the journey was directly attributable to him. Fortunes altered, plans shattered, and lives
given up—that was pretty much the story for everyone with whom
he had come in contact since leaving Patch Run. It might not be his
fault and his involvement might not matter anyway in the long run,
but he could only see what was, not what might be. His presence was
the catalyst for everything that had happened. So much depended
on him, and the weight of it was terrifying.

"Keep right," Kermadec called over his shoulder, motioning
toward Pen and his companions. "Don't look down."

They entered a cavern that dropped away on the left into a black
hole so vast that it looked as if it could swallow whole villages. The
trail became a narrow ledge that hugged the wall of the cavern, and
the company pressed close to that wall as they edged forward. They
were strung out in single file, torches spaced along the ledge. Pen
could see for the first time the other Trolls who had joined them
somewhere along the way, a line of burly, dark shadows in the flicker
of the firelight. They wore no armor, only leather tunics and pants,
closed-toe sandals, and heavy cloaks. All carried weapons strapped
across their backs, along with packs of supplies. They moved pon-
derously, but with no visible effort or strain. They had the look of
massive rocks into which faces had been carved.

On the far side of the cavern, a tunnel opened into the rock wall,
and soon they were burrowing downward once more. They had
been descending steadily since they had set out, and if Pen was judging right, they were below the level of the village of Taupo Rough
by several hundred feet. He wanted to know where they were going, wanted to reach a place where he could ask, and wanted most
of all to get out in the open air again, where he could breathe. The

mountain and its darkness pressed down against him with suffocating force. He was a flier, born to the air, and he hated being closed away.

But the tunnels wound on, deep and dark passageways thick with stale air and tar smoke, dead feeling and tomblike. Pen closed his mind to them after a while, a defense against his distaste and the hint of fear that lay behind it. He whispered now and again to Cinnaminson, just so that he could hear her voice. Each time, she squeezed his hand, as if sensing his need to make contact.

When they finally emerged from the tunnels, it was late afternoon and the sun had disappeared behind the peaks west, the light gone gray and misty. A narrow wedge of sky was visible overhead, distant and thick with clouds. They were deep in a valley where the shadows were so heavily layered that the trees carpeting the slopes surrounding them seemed already given over to night. Mountains rose all about them in sheer cliffs and jagged edges. Pen stood with the others, breathing the fresh, cold air and thinking that he had somehow tunneled down to the bottom of the world and must now climb back out again before he lost his way forever.

Kermadec was speaking in his deep, calm voice with one of the Trolls at the front of the line, but the conversation was being conducted in his own tongue so that Pen could not understand it. When they were finished, the other Troll disappeared into the trees, and Kermadec walked over to the boy and his companions.

"Barek will scout ahead to make sure the way is safe. We will follow in a few minutes." He gestured toward the dense line of peaks that lay east. "These are the Klu. Part of the Charnals, but their own range, as well. To the extent that it's possible to do so, we'll travel at night from here on." He paused. "Is everyone all right?"

They nodded, all of them, but with nothing that approached enthusiasm. Pen was somewhat relieved to find that his companions had seemingly fared no better than he had within the tunnels and the dark.

Kermadec nodded. "We'll go on in a few minutes. We have to cross the valley floor before nightfall to be certain we're safe enough to get some sleep. Drink plenty of water. The air is dry here. You won't notice it until you pass out."

Pen and his friends did as the big Troll instructed, casting uneasy glances back at the opening to the tunnels from which they had emerged, then at the sky overhead where searching airships might appear at any second.

"It will take them a day or two just to discover we're gone," Tagwen announced confidently.

"Only if they are exceedingly stupid," Atalan shot back, overhearing as he walked past. He gave a dismissive shrug. "The fortifications will have been abandoned by now and our people moved on. We're being hunted already, little man."

Tagwen scowled deeply, not at all happy with being addressed in such familiar terms by the young Troll. After Atalan had moved away, Pen said quietly to the Dwarf, "His name is Atalan. He claims he's Kermadec's brother."

Tagwen shook his head. "Kermadec never spoke of a brother. He never spoke about his family at all. Whoever this fellow is, he's in need of some manners."

"I don't think he's overly fond of Kermadec, from what he said earlier. I think he resents Kermadec's position as Maturen."

The Dwarf snorted. "Kermadec is a force to be reckoned with, make no mistake. If we're to complete this journey in one piece, he is the one who will make it possible. His brother, if that's what he is, ought to know as much."

At Kermadec's command, they began walking east through the trees. Because they were already on the valley floor, travel was smooth and steady. The Trolls set the pace and chose the way, finding paths where there didn't seem to be any, moving everyone along, keeping watch on all sides. Pen felt much better out in the open again, and his earlier discomfort subsided and eventually disappeared. Things didn't seem so impossible when he didn't have an entire mountain pressing down on him. He gazed skyward and thought wistfully that if they could find an airship to convey them the rest of the way, things would be perfect.

But there would be no airships, of course. Kermadec had made it clear that airships were at risk in those mountains, and that travel afoot was much safer if their intent was to remain safely concealed from would-be pursuers. It was a choice that Pen might not have made, but they were in Kermadec's country, and the Rock Troll would know the best way to get to where they were going. Whatever else happened, Pen did not care to experience another encounter with the Druids who hunted him.

Ahead, the trees thinned as the valley floor opened up before them, and they crossed the central flats under a cover of clouds and mist and growing darkness. Diffuse and silvery, light from moon and stars began to filter through the haze, lending just enough brightness to enable the company to pick its way ahead without groping. Judging from the pace that Kermadec was setting, the Trolls knew the country well; there was no suggestion of hesitation as they progressed.

When they stopped to rest, just inside a thick stand of fir midway across the valley, Tagwen sat down next to Pen and leaned close.

"This is what you need to know about Kermadec, young Penderrin. It isn't the only story about him, but it is the one that I think says the most. Some years ago, when he was still a boy, he was taken on an outing with two dozen other young Trolls who were in the training stages of their wilderness survival education. All young Rock Trolls are given this instruction, boys and girls alike. Because they are a migratory people, it is presumed that at some point each of them will become separated from the tribe and be forced to find the way back alone, perhaps through dangerous country. Young Trolls are taken out twice a year beginning at the age of six or seven in order to learn what they need to know about doing so. The group in which Kermadec was included consisted of all ages and both sexes. For some, the littlest, it was the first time. It was autumn, and the green of summer was just changing to the bolder colors in the broad leaves. There was a bite to the night air."

His head lowered into shadow, Tagwen rubbed his beard. "Three handlers managed the two dozen, about average for a class of that size. They were hiking through the Razor Mountains across the valley from one of the villages several miles below the Lazareen. A two-week outing, give or take a few days—that was the intended duration. The country was familiar to them, mostly uninhabited, forested low mountains, some small lakes, streams, typical for the middle Northland and safely above the Skull Kingdom. Nothing too dangerous.

"Except that the unexpected happened. A band of renegade Forest Trolls, traditional enemies of the Rock Trolls and dangerous in their own right, stumbled across the group while it was descending a steep slope and recognized it for what it was. They began tracking it, deciding they would wait until their quarry was sleeping, kill the handlers, steal their supplies and weapons, and take the smallest children as slaves to sell to those who use children in that way. It wasn't much of a reason for such slaughter, but renegades don't usually need much of a reason to justify what they do."

He paused as Atalan stalked past, ignoring them as he had ignored them all day. Without a word of greeting, he moved over to talk with Kermadec. Tagwen glared at him balefully, then sighed. "I wish I could think better of him. I wish he would give me a reason."

He shook his head. "So, the Forest Trolls had their plan. But it failed because they weren't careful enough. The handlers spotted them and set about making an escape. That, too, failed. The Forest Trolls attacked, a dozen strong, and the two male handlers were killed along with one of the boys. Kermadec and the female handler managed to hide the rest of the children in a dense wood just as the sun was setting. The Forest Trolls spent all night hunting them, combing the wood in the dark. If they had been smarter, they might have thought better of the idea. But there were nine of them still alive after the battle with the handlers, and they thought there was safety in numbers. After all, these were only children they hunted."

He smiled. "I would have liked to have seen their faces when they found out otherwise. Kermadec was less a child than they thought, already big and strong, already as skilled as the adults. When he realized that the renegades weren't giving up, he slipped away from the other children and the woman handler, who was badly injured in the earlier skirmish, and began stalking the Forest Trolls. He caught them by surprise, and one by one, he killed four of them before the rest realized what was happening and backed off. But still they didn't give up. These were only children, after all. They waited until dawn, and they began to hunt again. A reasonable idea, but not when you're dealing with someone like Kermadec. He was waiting for them. He ambushed them and killed two more. This time, the rest fled for good.

"But that wasn't the end of it. Kermadec's little group was deep in the Razors, miles from their own tribe, and the woman handler was so weak she could no longer walk, let alone act as guide. So Kermadec led the rest of the children out of those mountains and back to the tribe. It took them four days. He carried the handler on his back the entire way, more than fifty miles. No one was left behind. All of them arrived home safe."

He paused. "Kermadec was fourteen years old when he did this." He arched one eyebrow at the boy. "That's the sort of man you've placed your trust in, should you be in any doubt about the matter."

They set out again shortly afterwards and walked the rest of the way across the valley into a deep wood that ran up the flank of the mountains and into the valleys and defiles in dark green fingers. The last of the light faded, and night drew in about them. By then, Kermadec had brought the Trolls and their charges to a grassy clearing by a stream that tumbled down out of the rocks into a high-banked pool that then spilled over to meander on across the valley west. They set camp, putting themselves safely within the cover of the fir and spruce and forgoing any sort of fire. They ate their dinner ration cold and rolled into their blankets to sleep without wasting further time.

But before they fell asleep, Khyber eased over next to Pen. Even in the darkness, he could see the troubled intensity of her dark eyes. "I've something to tell you, Pen. I'd forgotten earlier, in all the chaos, and when I remembered, I couldn't decide right away whether you should know. But I guess you should. I can't be sure if it's true, but Traunt Rowan told Kermadec that the Druids have made prisoners of your parents."

Her dark eyes studied him carefully. "I'm sorry. Especially if I made a mistake in telling you. Are you all right?"

He wasn't, of course. He wasn't anything close to all right. He felt hollowed out, drained of any good feelings he might have salvaged from their escape from Taupo Rough. It was bad enough that he carried the weight of his guilt from all of the others who had suffered on his behalf. He had thought his parents safe. The King of the Silver River had said he would warn them of the danger, that he would take steps to protect them. But perhaps that hadn't been enough and not even they were to be spared.

"It might have been a lie," she said. Her hand rested on his. "In fact, it probably is a lie. They would say anything to get to you. Even something as evil as that."

But it wasn't a lie. He knew it instinctively. It was the truth. Somehow, the Druids had lured his parents to Paranor and locked them away. What was expected of them, he couldn't be sure. But he was afraid for them because he thought that anyone connected with him, or with his aunt, was at risk. His impulse was to abandon the quest and go to them at once, to do anything that would help them. But of course, that was exactly what the Druids were hoping for, what they intended by giving out such information. He would not be helping his parents by giving in to his impulses. He could only help by finding his aunt and bringing her home again. She was the one who could save them all.

He remained awake long after the rest of them were asleep, trying to reassemble the shattered pieces of his confidence, trying to reassure himself that he wouldn't give way to what he was feeling.

They set out again at dawn, climbing out of the valley and into the jagged peaks of the Klu Mountains. The Klu were rugged, barren pinnacles that time and a shifting of the earth's crust had compressed as if they had been grasped by a giant's hand, the rock cracked and broken by the pressure, eroded by wind and water, and reshaped into strange formations that barely resembled the mountains they had once been. Narrow defiles and deep chasms split the rock at every turn, and passes were as likely to lead through stacked rocks and weather-carved fissures as along ledges or across slides. Nothing made sense about the Klu, which seemed to comprise an amalgam of every geological configuration that nature could devise.

As the day wore on and the air cooled at the higher elevations, the mist thickened about them. It did so slowly, but noticeably, so that Pen had time to realize that they would soon be climbing blindly into the rocks. It was not a pleasant prospect, given the treacherous terrain with its difficult and uncertain footing. But Kermadec pressed ahead, moving them along as quickly as conditions would allow, taking them off the flank of the mountains and into a series of defiles that twisted and wound through cliffs towering hundreds of feet above them.

The mist dissipated, but forward progress slowed. Loose stone littered the trail, and ice patches coated its surface. Wind howled overhead and down the gaps in the cliffs, buffeting them as they struggled to put one foot in front of the other without slipping. The path fell away to the left, the resulting cliff a sheer and unbroken drop that vanished into blackness.

Pen hugged the rock wall on his right, trying not to think of what would happen if he slipped, trying not to look down. He had managed to put his concern for his parents and his doubts about himself aside upon waking, but they nudged their way back into his thinking now, prompted by an increasing suspicion that their efforts on this day alone, their first day, were not going to be enough to get them to Stridegate. He watched Cinnaminson as she moved cautiously ahead of him, hands and feet finding the way. He would have taken her hand, done something to help her, but it was too dangerous on the narrow trail.

Then, abruptly, the mist gathered and settled down about them with such compacted heaviness that everything simply disappeared.

"Stay where you are!" Kermadec called back to them.

Pen froze on the trail, feeling the cold of the rock seep into him, listening to the wind die away to nothing, thinking that the worst had just happened. They were trapped, unable to go forward or back, exposed to the whim of the elements. It was probably close to midday. What would happen when it was night?

He reached out, groping, until he found Cinnaminson's hand

and took it in his own, then edged forward until he was just behind her. "Can you see anything that we can't?" he asked.

Her face turned to his, her lips cold when they pressed against his ear. "I can see a little of what lies ahead, but I don't know which way to go. There are too many choices. It all looks the same."

Pen thought. "Could you guide us if Kermadec told you what to look for?"

She gripped his arm. "I don't know. Maybe."

She sounded scared, but no more scared than he felt. And she was their best hope. He called to Kermadec, then eased his way forward past the others, leading Cinnaminson by the hand. He moved carefully, taking his time, one foot in front of the other, body pressed to the cliff wall. The mist was getting worse, visibility dropping to where he couldn't see more than a few yards ahead, and no wind appeared to blow it all away.

When he reached the Maturen, he explained his idea. Once Kermadec understood what the Rover girl was able to do, he agreed to let her try. He had never seen fog so bad and didn't care to wait it out. Exposed as they were, it was too dangerous to remain on the cliff trails. They needed to find shelter.

So with Cinnaminson leading them, using her special sight to see beyond the layers of mist, they began inching forward. It was slow going; Cinnaminson stopped often to explain what she was seeing so that Kermadec could advise her on which way to go. A maze of similar paths and trails awaited his decision, most of them leading to sudden drops or blank walls and only a few leading out. Pen wondered how far they were from safe ground and an easier passage, but wasn't sure he wanted to know the answer.

The mist got worse, and their progress slowed even more. Pen felt Cinnaminson hesitate more often, as if even her sight could not penetrate the haze. He turned his face into the mist, and the feel of it made him shiver. There was something wrong with its dampness and color, something that sent a whisper of warning rushing through his chilled body.

"Kermadec!" he called back. "Why is it getting worse?"

"Because the mist is Druid-formed," Khyber answered, an invisible presence somewhere behind him. "Because it isn't real. We saw this before, Pen, when we crossed the Lazareen. The ones who track us now must have sent it through the peaks to trap us. They must know what we are trying to do!"

"Can you get rid of it, Elven girl?" Kermadec called back. "Can you counter their magic with your own?"

A long pause. "If I do, I will give us away. They will track my magic to where we are. I expect that is what they are hoping for."

There was a long silence in the aftermath of this pronouncement, a silence filled with heavy breathing and a shuffling of feet.

"We can't just stand out here!" Atalan snapped angrily. "They'll find us anyway! Or the weather will. There's snow coming."

Cinnaminson leaned over to Pen and whispered in his ear. "I can't see anymore. My sight is gone. The Druid magic must be affecting it."

Pen leaned back against the rock, feeling the rough surface dig into his back. What could they do? If Cinnaminson couldn't find the way, they were trapped. But if Khyber used her magic to spring the trap, Traunt Rowan and his Gnome Hunters would be on them in minutes. They needed to find another way. But what way? A cave in which to hide? Even a deep crevice would be sufficient. Just something . . .

He turned his face into the rock, peering ahead, and felt something move against his cheek. He jerked away, looking back in surprise at a greenish gray patch on the stone.

Lichen.

But it had moved. He had felt it move. He hesitated, then placed his cheek against the patch again. Again, he felt it move. He wasn't sure if he was feeling it with his senses or his mind. It wasn't quite one or the other. He held his cheek against it and closed his eyes.

Warm.

The lichen was expressing what it felt, and his odd magic was reading its communication. He placed his cheek against it once more, feeling the faint movement of its tiny bristles, the expression of its tiny intelligence.

Warm.

He looked around quickly. Lichen grew all over these rocks in mottled greenish gray patches. He peered into the mist. Everything looked the same to him, but maybe not to the lichen. The lichen couldn't see, but it could feel. It was a plant. It sought the sun. That was what it was communicating to him. *Warm.* It was sensing the hidden sunlight.

Was there a way that he could use the lichen, a way that could help them get clear?

"Kermadec!" he said quickly, searching for the Maturen. The big man moved out of the haze past Cinnaminson. "What direction does the trail go, the one we need to follow?"

The big man bent down, his barked face as rugged as the mountains they were trapped in. "You look like you've seen a ghost."

"Just tell me. Which way?"

"Southeast. Why?"

"And the time? What time of day is it?"

"After noon by about an hour, I would guess. What are you asking, Penderrin?"

"Then north would be that way?" He pointed, and Kermadec nodded. "And south that way?" Again, the Rock Troll nodded. Pen took a deep breath. "Let me take the lead. I think I can get us out of here. If the trail leads down at some point, back to tree level, maybe we can get below this mist. Will you let me try?"

Kermadec eased him to the front of the line, and Pen began to move forward, running his hands along the patches of lichen that grew on the rock face. The afternoon sun would be south and west of them. He needed to lead them south and east to stay on the path. It was easy at first, because the trail only led in one direction and there were no choices to be made. But it quickly grew more difficult as the number of twists and turns increased and the path split, forcing him to read the lichen's response to his touch and then advance accordingly.

He couldn't be sure he was going the right way, not entirely, not while he was unable to see anything of his surroundings, the mist so thick and impenetrable it was like swimming underwater at night. But at least they were moving somewhere, rather than just standing out in the open with night coming on. It was better to take the chance, he told himself. It was better to do something than nothing.

Sometimes the lichen disappeared, and he was forced to continue on blindly until he found a new patch. Sometimes he found patches in places so cold and shadowy that they were locked down inside themselves and he could read nothing from them. Sometimes he was reduced to guessing at which way they should go, unable to be certain that he was interpreting the lichen's message clearly. It was slow, torturous work; the lichen's form of communication was much more subtle than that of a seagull or a deer. It wasn't a life-form of high intelligence, and what it gave to him was not much more than a tiny response to the environment that sustained it.

I can do this.

To their credit, the others in the little company left him alone. Once or twice, he thought he heard grumbling from somewhere behind, but it was always momentary and not directed at him. He never let it bother him, never let it break his concentration. Forgotten were the fears and doubts he had experienced the night before. He had something to do now, a purpose that was as much a lifeline as a duty. They were all here because of him, but now he was doing something to help. He wasn't just a charge to whom they were committed, to whom they must offer their protection. He was a member of the company, a part of the effort to find a way to their destination.

He ran his hands carefully over the lichen, feeling its tiny movement, its soft response. *Warm.* Reaching toward the sun, toward the light.

Deep and still, the mist continued to blanket them, and the light faded slowly with the passing of the day. Time was slipping away. He kept moving, kept his concentration focused. Cinnaminson hadn't spoken once since he had taken command. He understood. She couldn't do anything to help, her inner sight rendered useless by the onslaught of Druid magic. Like the others, she was relying on him.

I can do this.

It was nearing dark when at last they emerged from the mist and found the first sparse patches of grassy earth, uneven and rocky high meadows forming cradles of life among the barren peaks of the Klu.

Slowly the mist began to dissipate as they continued downhill. Then all at once it was gone, and they were standing in scrub and twilight at the edge of an alpine forest, the air clear enough for them to see one another once more.

Kermadec came over to Pen at once and clapped him on the shoulder. "Well done, young Penderrin. We owe you a measurable debt for this day's work."

The other Trolls, even Atalan, nodded their agreement, dark eyes communicating what words did not. Khyber was smiling. Even Tagwen muttered grudgingly that Pen was to be congratulated.

Cinnaminson didn't bother with words. She simply walked up to him and hugged him so tightly that the breath left his body.

It was the best he had felt in a long time.

SEVENTEEN

When Grianne Ohmsford regained consciousness, she was surprised to discover that she was still alive. In attempting her escape from Kraal Reach, she had fully expected that if she failed, Tael Riverine would have her put to death. It was what she would have done if their positions were reversed and she were still the Ilse Witch. Lying on the stone floor of her cell in a wash of pain and despair, she found her earlier assessment of her situation reaffirmed: She was being kept alive because the demon needed her that way.

But that was a dangerous supposition, and she quickly abandoned it for a less pleasant conclusion: The Straken Lord intended to make an example of her. Some form of punishment was to be administered.

When she could sit up again, she made a quick assessment of her situation and found that not everything was as it had been. The conjure collar was in place, but now her hands were shackled behind her back and to her waist and ankles so that while she could shuffle about on her knees, she could not stand upright. She had been moved to a different cell, one in which the front wall had been replaced with iron bars so that a jailer could sit on a chair across from her and watch her every movement. She was still not gagged, but there was little risk in allowing that. She already knew the consequences of attempting to use the magic of the wishsong.

Nevertheless, she began thinking about doing so almost immediately because she knew what was going to happen otherwise.

Still, time passed, and nothing did happen. She was spoon-fed and given water by hand through the bars. At first, she resisted, but in the end, hunger and thirst won out. Besides, after her initial assumption regarding her fate failed to prove out, she grew increasingly curious to find out why this was so. She wasn't being kept alive for no reason; the Straken Lord didn't admire her pluck. Her escape was in defiance of the rules she had been instructed to obey and a challenge to the demon's authority. She didn't think it likely that it would forgive her for that.

But the hours passed, then the days, and neither Tael Riverine nor its underling, Hobstull, appeared. She saw no one but the guards, cloaked and hooded silhouettes in the faint light of the torches that burned in wall brackets across from where she lay. Now and then, one would rise from its sitting place to feed her or to clean the messes she made when she was forced to relieve herself, but otherwise they ignored her. She spent her time trying to get comfortable, to shift her position often enough to prevent cramping and sores. She was only partially successful. She slept fitfully and for short periods of time, and because she was locked in a windowless cell deep within the rock of Kraal Reach, she never knew for certain what time it was. After a while, it no longer mattered. Nothing did. She felt her hopes sliding away. She felt her courage failing. Her one real chance at escape had failed, and she did not expect she would get another. All that remained for her was to prepare herself for whatever fate the Straken Lord intended.

Then, when sufficient time had lapsed that she had lost all track of it, Hobstull appeared. One moment, the corridor was empty save for the guard, and the next, the Catcher was standing there, staring at her in that peculiar way, head cocked, eyes contemplative. He didn't say or do anything. She stared back at him, as still as he was, waiting him out. A small surge of expectation gave her new strength. Finally, something was going to happen.

When he had satisfied himself, the Catcher opened the cell door and came inside. A pair of wizened Goblins stood crook-legged to either side of him, crossbows armed and pointed at her. *Don't move,* the sharpened bolts advised wordlessly. She didn't. She waited while Hobstull bent down and released the chains from her waist and ankles, leaving them in place about her wrists until he had helped her to stand. Then he released those, as well, moved her hands in front of her, and refastened the chains about her wrists. He stepped back, waiting to see how she would react, his strange eyes fixed on hers, then nodded. Taking the loose end of the chain that bound her wrists, he led her from the cell.

They went down the shadowy corridor to a set of stairs and began to climb, Hobstull leading, the Goblins trailing watchfully. Her mind raced. If they intended to kill her, she would have one final chance at escape when she got to where she was going. If they intended to punish her, she would have the same option. Perhaps she would live long enough to find out why they had kept her alive and left her alone for so long.

At the top of the stairs, she was taken down another corridor, then out through an entry warded by a heavy iron door and into a tiny courtyard walled in by buildings on four sides. The walls rose several dozen feet, leaving the courtyard bathed in cool shadows and resonant with the trapped echoes of voices that drifted in from more open places. She stood in the courtyard as Hobstull once again removed the chains from her wrists and this time left them off. The Catcher studied her in wordless appraisal, then went back through the door with the Goblins, leaving her alone.

She looked around. The walls were too smooth to be climbed. There were no doors save the one through which she had entered, and no windows at all. There were tiny slits that overlooked the courtyard from high above, too far to reach. Murder holes. She took a deep breath, walked over to one wall, and sat down against it. Overhead, clouds scudded through the gray sky like foam capping a rough sea, yellow-tinged and frothy. She saw a dark shape wing its way past, a Harpy perhaps. She smelled the decay of the land. Everything in this world felt ill used and tarnished. Everything felt as if it were dying.

Long minutes passed, and then the door to the courtyard opened again, and Tael Riverine appeared. It emerged into the pale courtyard light like a wraith risen from its midnight lair, so impenetrably black that its features were indistinguishable. It looked bigger than she remembered, but that might have been because its spikes were raised like the hackles on an angry dog, protruding everywhere in what felt to her like a warning. *Stay clear. Keep away.* It wore its weapons strapped on like body armor, studs and sharp edges glinting dully.

Its blue eyes fixed on her.

She climbed to her feet, unwilling to give even the appearance of weakness. It required noticeable effort to do so.

"You disobeyed me," it announced.

It gestured languidly, and instantly the familiar pain ripped through her, paralyzing her muscles and dropping her to her knees. She bent her head and clutched her body, trying to breathe.

"Disobedience is an unacceptable response to my commands," the demon continued, and gestured again.

This time, she collapsed altogether, her agony so excruciating she lay curled in a ball, sobbing. Her mind locked down and would not let her think of anything but the pain. She pressed her face in the dirt, feeling broken and helpless.

"Get on your knees," Tael Riverine ordered.

It took her a while to do so, but eventually she managed, still bent over at the waist, her arms wrapped protectively about her body.

"Look at me."

She did so, lifting her head from the veil of her dark hair, trying to hide the mix of fear and suffering that washed through her as she did so.

"Apologize for your disobedience."

"I am sorry, Master," she whispered.

The Straken Lord nodded, cold eyes glittering. "You are only sorry you were caught. I see it in your eyes. You do not respond well to discipline. It is not in your nature to choose obedience when you can avoid doing so."

It walked over to her, huge and forbidding, and reached down to haul her back to her feet, picking her up like a rag doll and propping her against the courtyard wall. She sagged slightly, but stayed upright, eyes locked on the demon's.

"I would have killed another for what you did," it said softly. "I would have taken my time doing so. I would have made the pain so unbearable that death would have come as a relief. Do you understand this?"

She swallowed. "Yes, Master."

"But you interest me."

It paused, and she waited for more, not yet understanding what that meant. Why would she be of any further interest? Other than the purpose she had already served in switching places with whatever creature the magic had set free from the Forbidding, what reason could the Straken Lord have for taking an interest in her?

"Do you know why you are here, inside the world of the Jarka Ruus?"

"No, Master."

The demon gestured angrily, and again the pain ratcheted through her, inducing a wave of nausea that caused her to wretch violently as she dropped to her knees. It was on her at once, hauling her upright and slamming her against the stone wall.

"Don't lie to me!" it hissed, fury etched on its flat features, rage mirrored in its strange eyes. "Do you think me such a fool? Speak!"

"I . . . won't lie again, Master," she gasped.

"You are intelligent. You are calculating. You are clever. You can pretend that you are not, but you will be disobeying me if you do and will be punished. Do you understand? Answer me."

"I understand, Master." Her stomach heaved, but she fought down the urge to empty it.

The Straken Lord nodded patiently. "Again, now. Do you know why you are here?"

"Yes, Master."

"Tell me."

"I was brought here so that something that lives in this world could be transported into my own."

"Very good. Do you know why I arranged for this?"

She took a deep, quieting breath. "No, Master."

The demon studied her carefully, then nodded. "Not yet, you don't. But you will, soon enough. You will understand everything, because that inquisitive mind of yours will mull it through until the answer surfaces. If not, I will tell you myself. If you stay alive long enough for me to do so."

If you stay alive. She closed her eyes and exhaled softly. What were the odds of that? She blinked, feeling the weight of his gaze on her, shifting from place to place, contemplative, curious. She was aware of how ragged and dirty she was, unwashed and uncombed, a used-up plaything. For an instant, she saw herself as worthless, of so little value that she deserved to be discarded without further consideration.

"You are a specimen," the Straken Lord said, as if reading her mind. "Hobstull finds you as interesting as I do. He makes more of a study of such things, so his opinion carries weight. He wishes to find out more about you, but I have forbidden him to use his knives just yet. Still, we both deserve an opportunity to see what sort of magic you wield. You do have magic, I know. It resides in you—a demon trait. His interest lies in that. He thinks you might be one of us."

She cringed at the idea. She was nothing like them. She was human. No matter what they thought or did to make her seem otherwise, she was human. But she said nothing, keeping what she was thinking hidden away inside.

"I intend to test you, Grianne Ohmsford, Ard-Rhys-that-was, my specimen of such promise." Its voice had turned oddly soft and soothing. "I intend to test you in a way that no one has ever been tested before. I want to see what you can do. I want to see how strong your survival instincts are."

As it spoke, its spikes lowered against its body, changing its look entirely. She stared in spite of herself, wondering what it was seeking from her that it didn't already have.

"This afternoon," it continued in the same compelling voice, "I will test you then. I will see how you respond."

Then it turned and disappeared through the door, leaving her breathless and pressed hard against the courtyard wall.

Hobstull returned with the Goblin guards moments later, and she was taken back to her cell. Although the chains were not put on again, three guards were stationed across from her cell with cross-bows pointed in her direction at all times. She sat quietly on the floor of her little room and thought about what the Straken Lord had told her. She would be tested. But what did that mean? Tested how? She did not think the answer would please her. She wished she could find some reassurance in still being alive, but her instincts told her that she would be foolish to do so.

Hobstull reappeared after a while with a basin of hot water, a clear indication that she was to clean herself up for whatever was going to happen next. He deposited sandals and a shift at her feet as well. She waited for him to leave, then turned her back on the Gob-lin guards, stripped off her rags, and used them to wash her aching body. Then she dressed in the sandals and shift and sat back down again to wait.

The wait was longer than she had expected. She had no accurate way of measuring, but she thought afterwards that it must have been several hours. When Hobstull led her back up the stairs and out of the tower and into the light, the day was edging rapidly toward nightfall, the gray of the sky gone darker and the endless clouds and mist dropped lower against the heights. The Catcher replaced the chains about her wrists, and a phalanx of Goblins surrounded her. She was taken across the courtyard through an outer wall to where a rolling cage similar to the one that had brought her to Kraal Reach was waiting. She was placed inside, and the chain that bound her was fastened to the bars. The Goblins formed ranks to either side of the cage, and Hobstull climbed onto the seat next to the driver. The driver snapped his whip over the heads of the massive horned crea-tures hitched up front, and the wheels began to roll.

They went out through a set of bigger, bulkier gates, heavy oak toughened with pitch and bound with iron plates. There demon-wolves joined the procession, panting and slavering, yellow eyes shifting to find her, their muzzles drawing back. She felt their hatred for her, read the warning in their snarls.

Down through the buildings of the fortress they wound, heading east into the growing darkness, toward the mountains against which the keep was backed. The earlier crowds had thinned to a wary-eyed few, some of them Goblins, some of them Gormies and kobolds, and some of them creatures she could not identify. When they were out-side the walls, they turned south, bending with the land toward a vast depression that dipped into the flats overlooking the country-side beyond. Scrubby and desolate, the depression was rippled by a maze of deep gullies and sharp ridges born out of massive erosion. They followed a cart path marked by wagon wheels and animal tracks, the dust rising in heavy clouds, the air hazy and gritty.

She sat quietly in the center of the cage, rocking back and forth to its uneven sway, one sleeve of her tunic held across her mouth to help keep the dust from her breathing passages. They had advanced far enough that when she looked back at the keep, its walls and tow-ers had shrunk to the size of a child's toy. She watched as the image grew smaller and less distinct and finally vanished entirely.

As they arrived on the valley floor, the roadway straightened and the landscape opened up again. The denizens of Kraal Reach, absent before, were now clustered everywhere she looked, fingers pointing, eyes and faces bright and eager, their conversations animated as they watched her pass. They understood more about what was going to happen than she did; that much was clear from their behavior. It was not a stretch to think that most of the city had come out to watch.

An embankment rose in front of them, a wall of earth more than thirty feet high. A pair of tall gates opened through the wall, and when the cage reached the other side, she found that the embank-ment wrapped around a bowl of earth and rocks that was perhaps a quarter mile wide from end to end. Seated atop the embankment were thousands of Kraal Reach's denizens, sharp-faced and gimlet-eyed, hunched over in their robes as they cheered and gestured in

greeting. It was not a comforting welcome; it was a welcome of dark
expectation and impatience, the kind reserved for those who would
provide a form of blood sport. Certain that her testing was to take
the form of combat against a carefully chosen opponent, she did not
like what she felt in that moment.

The wagon rolled to an unsteady stop in front of a set of tall risers formed of an iron framework and wooden slat seats. In the center
of a group of unidentifiable creatures hidden within robes and hoods
sat the Straken Lord. As the cage ceased its forward movement, the
demon rose and walked down to greet Hobstull. Heads lowered and
hackles raised, the wolves slunk away at his approach. The Goblin
guards stepped back and bowed low. Only Hobstull made no overt
movement of submission, his angular body unbent, his expressionless oval face lifted watchfully. The Straken Lord spoke softly to
him, then nodded at Grianne.

She took a deep, steadying breath as the Catcher approached
her, keys in hand. If she was going to attempt another escape, she
would have to do so now.

But she fought down the urge, telling herself to wait, to be patient. A wrong move would mean the end of her. She stayed quite
still while Hobstull opened the cage door and stepped inside, then
walked over to unlock the chains that bound her wrists. He stepped
back, beckoning her outside. She did as she was told, rising gingerly
to exit the cage and stand on the floor of the arena, facing the
Straken Lord.

"Bow to me," it ordered quietly.

She did so, deeply and slowly. It cost her nothing. She felt no respect for the creature, only a deep-seated wariness. She would do
what was required of her until the time was right. She was good at
waiting.

"Are you washed and rested?" the demon asked.

"Yes, Master."

"It is the time of your testing. Are you ready?"

"Yes, Master."

"The Jarka Ruus that are my subjects have come to watch. If you disappoint them by showing fear or cowardice, I will give you over to them to be killed. If you try to escape, I will kill you myself. You have only one choice. Complete the test successfully. Demonstrate that you are worthy of being kept alive."

She waited. She knew better than to speak without being spoken to, better than to ask questions. She held herself erect, her hands clasped before her, her fingers working slowly over her wrists, where the manacles had numbed the nerves.

The Straken Lord gestured, and the rolling cage was pulled away. With it went the Goblin guards and the demonwolves. Only Hobstull remained, bright eyes fixed on her. His specimen, awaiting her trial. She did not look at him. She would not give him the satisfaction.

"Walk out into the center of the arena," the Straken Lord ordered. The blue eyes glittered with an excitement she had not seen before. "There, you will find your opponent waiting. You may use any magic you possess to defeat it. You may call on any of your skills to protect yourself. So long as you do not attempt to escape this arena, the conjure collar will not be used against you. Your sole responsibility while you are here is to yourself. Your obligation is to survive. If you do, Ard-Rhys-that-was, your future is assured. There will be no need for further punishment. You will be given a place among us, one I shall choose for you, and it will be a place of honor. Now go."

She walked away at once, not daring to look at him another moment, afraid that the incredulity and disgust she was feeling would show through in spite of all that she was doing to hide it. What was the demon talking about? What could it think she would find to be honorable about life in this desolate prison world? All she wanted to do, all she lived for, was escape. The Straken Lord had an overblown opinion of what it could expect of her if it thought anything would change that, and she had no idea what fueled it.

She stared out into the flats as she walked, searching. There was nothing to see, no sign of movement in any quarter, no indication of any life. What sort of opponent had the demon chosen for her that an entire city would come out to see? What manner of creature was she expected to defeat in combat that would indicate she was worthy of keeping her life?

She glanced skyward momentarily, then out onto the horizon, thinking the attack might be coming from outside the arena. Nothing. She was aware that a hush had settled over the assembled denizens of Kraal Reach. They were waiting now, anticipating. All conversation had dropped to a barely audible whisper. Movement had stopped. All eyes were on her.

When the mewling sound began, soft and low, she had almost reached the center of the arena. She knew it for what it was immediately. A chill washed through her, causing her skin to shiver and the tiny hairs on the back of her neck to raise. She stopped at once, mouthing a single word voicelessly.

Furies.

She experienced an odd sense of calm. The uncertainty was gone, the waiting over. At least she could derive some small sense of satisfaction from knowing her opponent's identity. What better way to test her than with creatures like this? She breathed slowly, deeply, trying to steady herself. The mewling was rising steadily, building in intensity. She had only moments.

What shall I do?

Hers was the stronger weapon, her magic against their teeth and claws. Hers was the superior skill and cunning, her craft honed in a thousand battles. But the Furies were driven by instincts that did not value safety or self-preservation. A pack mentality ruled them when they found prey, and they would attack and keep attacking until either the enemy or they were destroyed. No quarter would be given and none asked. Furies knew only one way, and that way eschewed any identifiably rational behavior. She had been put into a den of madness, and the source of that madness was a legion of relentless, inexorable killers.

She tested the magic of the wishsong to see if the Straken Lord had told the truth about using it, thinking that if the demon had lied, she would be rendered unconscious fast enough that she wouldn't feel it when the Furies tore her to bits. But the magic blossomed at the end of her fingertips on command, gathering force, taking shape, waiting to be used, and the conjure collar gave no warning. Hope welled up within her at the realization that it would be an even battle. She would have her chance to survive.

A small chance.

She would have to kill all of them, if she was to walk away. Nothing short of that would save her. They would come at her in a rush, and they would keep coming until the life was bled out of them. Once, the task would have been a challenge she would have embraced, a struggle of dark magic against dark intent, the wellspring of the Ilse Witch's indomitable self-confidence. But she was no longer the Ilse Witch, and her desire for combat had fallen away with the identity she had shed.

Her strength must come from her life as the Ard Rhys.

What shall I do?

They began to appear, small shadows in the failing light, feline faces and slanted eyes, sinuous forms sliding from holes in the earth and from behind bits of scrub. Like ghosts, they materialized in the gloom, their mewling rising and falling in waves of expectation. They were all around her, perhaps a hundred of them. Too many for her to overcome, no matter how much magic she used, no matter how strong her determination. Like the ogre she had seen on her way to her confrontation with the shade of the Warlock Lord, she would fight with passion and fury, but in the end she would be pulled down.

Instantly, she began to rethink her strategy for surviving the confrontation. Strength alone would not be enough. Cunning was what would save her. Innovation and surprise. The unexpected might turn aside these little terrors. They were inching closer, some of them within twenty yards. She saw the madness glinting in their eyes. She felt the heat of their bloodlust. The longer she took to respond, the bolder they would grow. They were stalking her with a certain amount of caution now, but the testing would be finished all too soon, and then . . .

The testing.

Of who and what I am.

As swiftly as the thought was completed, she knew what she had to do. She didn't pause to consider the consequences or weigh the risks; she just did it. She reabsorbed the magic gathered at her fingertips, pulled it back inside, changed its form, and redistributed it throughout her body. The effect was instantaneous and irreversible. She lost control almost immediately, swept away by the magic's implacable response. Gasping in shock, she dropped into a crouch, her appearance changing as she did so, her form altering. The magic burned within her, turning her feverish as it stripped away her look and smell, her thinking, her reasoning, her conscience. She began to mewl like those that stalked her. Like those she confronted. Like a Fury. She made the change in a heartbeat, the magic sweeping across her until Grianne Ohmsford, Ard Rhys of the Third Druid Council, simply vanished from the valley floor.

What appeared in her place was another Fury, this one larger and more dangerous than its brethren, but clearly a twin.

The transformation was so unexpected that the other Furies drew back in shock. One moment, their prey was standing helpless before them. The next, it was gone, replaced by another thing, a recognizable presence that somehow wasn't exactly what they were, but close enough that it gave them pause.

She moved forward swiftly, cat-smooth and challenging, all spiky fur and menacing sounds, her eyes sweeping across those smaller replicas of herself, her teeth and claws bared and threatening. She hissed and spit as she swung about in uncontrollable rage. Where was her prey? Where was the human? She went so deep into her assumed form that she could anticipate the taste of blood in her mouth. She was so removed from her human side that she wanted to rip and tear at something—anything—that came within reach. She mewled her need to her cat kind, mirrors of herself, and they hissed and spit in reply.

Down through their midst she stalked, lost to herself, turned killer demon, no visible, recognizable part of her human side in evidence. She was all Fury now, a part of the pack, at one with the madness. If there had been something to attack, she would have done so, shredding it with relish, satisfying her newly minted primal need.

The other Furies rubbed against her as she passed, accepting her presence, her place among them. They circled and sniffed, taking in her smell, marking her as cats would. She responded in kind, moving through the landscape as if in a dream, afloat and not quite grounded by anything. She had a vague sense of things not being right, of seeming out of joint in place and time; she had a dim memory of having had another life that didn't square with this one. But her Fury self wouldn't give way to that other life, wouldn't let it intrude, and so she felt it slipping farther and farther away.

She cast frequent glances toward the embankment, where creatures she could eat if she could reach them buzzed and whispered among themselves, their voices raw sounding and enticing. She stalked toward them, drawn to them for a reason she couldn't identify. The other Furies ignored her, returning now to their dens, disappearing back into the earth like shadows in sunlight. The excitement was over, the chance for a kill gone. One by one they vanished, the happenings of earlier moments already forgotten.

She walked on, drawn by a craving she could neither understand nor resist. At first, it involved the creatures on the embankment, then only one of them, a singularly tall, dark, spiky being that was descending from its perch into the valley. Her ears pricked in expectation. Fresh prey. A meal. She eased forward, but the creature didn't turn aside or back away like her, it came on. She bared her teeth and flexed her claws. In a moment she would have it and then summon her brethren to the feast.

But all at once the spiky creature gestured at her, and pain ripped through her body, dropping her squirming and spitting on the earth. She tried to rise, and the pain returned, harsher and longer, flooding her with its razors and knives, stealing the last of her strength. She lay gasping as the black thing came over to her and stared down at her expressionlessly.

"Do you know me?" it demanded, blue eyes cold and brittle.

She did. It came back to her instantly, came back as the identity she had assumed fell away and her knowledge of who she was returned.

"Yes, Master," she whispered.

The Straken Lord nodded. "You have excelled in your testing. You have proved your worth. I am pleased."

The demon picked her up as if she were weightless and bore her from the arena to the thunderous roar of the assembled, to cheers and grunts and stamping of feet, to unmistakable acclaim. Yet she felt no euphoria; she felt only disgust and an appalling rage at what she had been forced to do. She had survived, as was her intention, but the cost could not be measured. It had taken more than she wanted to acknowledge, her emotional sanity compromised, her carefully constructed integrity destroyed. She had walked into the arena as the Ard Rhys, but she had emerged as something else. She had reverted to the monster she had once been. In the arena she had become the Ilse Witch again in everything but her heart, and that becoming could not be easily undone, if at all. She was blackened through and through by the change she had wrought in herself, by the adopting of the Fury persona.

She had made herself sick, and although it made her weep inside to acknowledge it, she did not think she would ever be well again.

EIGHTEEN

"Captain, he's calling for you."

Pied Sanderling, Captain of the Elven Home Guard, looked up from the maps he had been studying since rising early that morning and stared at the tent flap wordlessly. He had been expecting it, but he had hoped that somehow it might be avoided. He couldn't understand how the King could be so mistaken about something so obvious. But the King saw things differently, and perhaps that was why he was King, although Pied was inclined to think that being King was mostly an accident of birth.

Not that he had any room to talk. He was the King's first cousin, and that had played a significant part in his ascension through the ranks of the Home Guard and eventual selection as Captain. There had been Sanderlings standing with the Elessedil Kings for as long as anyone could remember. A Sanderling had stood beside Wren Elessedil when she had fought at the Valley of Rhenn and driven the Federation and its allies back into the deep Southland more than 150 years ago.

"Pied, are you there?" Drumundoon pressed anxiously.

Sanderling could picture his aide's young, anxious face with its fringe of black beard, high forehead, swept-back hair, and deeply slanted Elven features. Drum was already anticipating the worst,

imagining how it would be if it were left to him to face the King
alone, unable to explain what had become of his trusted cousin. But
that was Drumundoon, always seeing the goblet as being half empty,
always missing the silver lining behind any dark cloud. If he wasn't so
good at organizing and managing, wasn't so dependable, and wasn't
so impossibly loyal . . .

But he was, of course.

"One minute," he called to his aide, alleviating the other's fears.

He rose, stretched to relieve cramped muscles, and stared down
at the maps one final time. The whole of the Prekkendorran lay revealed in cartographic rendering, the positions of each army, Free-
born and Federation, painstakingly delineated. It had taken someone
a long time to do this, he thought. But it was a onetime job, since neither army had moved more than a few feet in over two years.

Until now, perhaps.

He reached for his weapons and began buckling them on. A
brace of long knives went about his waist, and a short sword was
strapped over one shoulder. He picked up his longbow as well, an
unusual weapon for a member of the Home Guard. Their primary
duty was to defend the King, which more often than not entailed
hand-to-hand combat. But Pied favored the longbow, a weapon both
versatile and reliable. Like most members of the Elven army, he had
done a tour of duty on the Prekkendorran, serving as an archer in the
ranks for six months, then as the leader of a long-range scouting unit
that spent the bulk of its time deep in enemy territory. Both assignments required extensive reliance on the longbow, and he had never
felt comfortable without it since. It was his work on the Prekkendorran that had gotten him noticed and appointed to the Home Guard
on his return. The longbow was his good-luck charm.

Besides, he was short and slight of build, and hand-to-hand combat with broadswords was never going to favor him. Skill and quickness were what he relied on, and the longbow was a weapon that
utilized both.

He glanced around his quarters to see if anything else needed
doing, decided it didn't, that he had stalled as long as he was able—

though not nearly long enough to suit him—threw on his cloak, and went out through the tent flap.

Drumundoon came to attention, a habit he couldn't seem to break, even when only the two of them were present. Tall and lanky, he towered over the shorter Sanderling. "Good morning, Captain."

"Good morning, Drum." Pied led the way as they moved down through the Elven camp toward the King's tent. He brushed back his mop of sandy hair and squinted up at the cloudless sky. "So he's made up his mind." He shook his head. "I wish he'd wait."

"You don't know what he's decided," Drumundoon ventured hopefully. "He might have decided not to try it."

"No." Pied shook his head. "He had his mind made up last night when I left him, and he's not changed it. I know him. He goes with his first impression of a plan, and he liked this one right from the start. It doesn't matter what the risks are. It doesn't matter that the source is suspect. All that matters is that it's bold and it favors his nature. Like his father, all he lives for is to break the stalemate and drive the Federation down off the heights and south again. He's obsessed with it." He shook his head again. "I can't reason with him."

"You have to try."

"Of course, I have to try. I am being summoned to try. He likes it when he can win these arguments. He forgets that he wins them solely because he is King. But that is the way things are, and I can't change them."

They walked in silence, wending their way through the Home Guard units encamped about the King's pavilion tent, where brightly colored banners flew bravely in the midday breeze, marking the territories they had occupied for months or, in some cases, for years. Elven Hunters came and went with the beginnings and endings of their tours of duty, but the camps remained, like markers in a landscape that had been trampled and pummeled and fought over for so long that nothing recognizable was left. The desolation depressed Pied, the barren earth and broken rock, the colors all brown and gray. He missed the green of his Westland home. He missed the lushness of the trees, the cool breeze off the Rill Song, and the sound of birds singing. He wanted it all back again. Wanted it now. But he would have to wait. Even though he had been there almost two months, he knew it would be another two at least before the King lost interest and went home again.

Still, he knew the situation—had known it from the moment he had accepted his appointment. A Captain of the Home Guard was the King's right hand, and where the King went, he went, too. This King was not a stay-at-home King. This King was restless.

"You sent Acrolace and Parn to see what they could discover?" he asked finally.

Drumundoon nodded. "Last night. They haven't returned. Can you stall until they do?"

"Probably not." He hunched his shoulders defensively. "I wish this wasn't being rushed so. I would feel better about things if a little more thought were being given to the probable consequences of guessing wrong. It bothers me that we are so eager to charge into things."

"The King," Drumundoon pointed out.

"The King, indeed. What sort of advice is he getting? If someone besides me would speak up, we might be able to bring him to his senses."

"There is no one but you." His aide smiled cheerfully. "His advisers, Ministers and otherwise, are all back in Arborlon, safely out of harm's way. You know that. They want no part of this foolishness. Half of them want no part of this war at all. This was always an Elessedil war more than it was an Elven war. First, it was the King's father, after his grandfather's death, and now it is the King. All of them have viewed it in the same way—a chance to expand Elven influence into other territories, to reassert Elven control over the rest of the Four Lands, to place the Elven people at the forefront of development and expansion."

Pied Sanderling grunted. "We have Druids for that. Let them be the ones to spread their influence."

"Cheek by jowl with the Federation. They have no time for the Free-born. Not since the disappearance of the Ard Rhys. Not that it would make any difference while Kellen Elessedil is King, in any case. He hates the Ard Rhys and her Druids. He blames them as his father blamed them for all the bad things that have happened to the Elves. There's no reasoning with him on the subject. He sees our future as leader of the Free-born, and that's the end of it."

Pied glanced over at him. "You never cease to amaze me. Your political sense is as astute as . . ." He paused.

"As your own, Captain," the other interjected quickly. "Don't pretend otherwise."

Well, whatever political sense we possess, it isn't going to get us out of our current predicament, Pied thought. *We could analyze the situation all we want and still be helpless to do anything about it.*

Ahead, the King's tent rose above those of his retinue. Kellen Elessedil never traveled lightly, always with baggage consisting of a great deal more than the clothes he wore. On this occasion, he had brought his sons along as well, something Sanderling regarded as particularly dangerous. The King wanted them to learn early about the realities of his office—as he saw it. That meant coming to the Prekkendorran to witness firsthand what war with the Federation was like—if you could call this impossible stalemate a war. At fifteen and thirteen, they were old enough to understand, the King had insisted, in spite of his wife's and Pied's pleas to the contrary. That he hadn't insisted Arling and the little girls come as well was the only true surprise of the whole business.

Sometimes, in his darker moments, Pied thought that the Elves had the wrong Elessedil as King. One of the others might have done a better job—say, the King's younger sister, Khyber. Headstrong and independent, she was forever sneaking around behind the King's back to visit her exiled uncle, which was a constant source of trouble. But she was true to her beliefs, chief of which was that Ahren Elessedil was the best of the lot and should never have been blamed for any of what had happened after the *Jerle Shannara* had returned.

Kellen thought otherwise, of course, as had his father. There was no reasoning with either one. There was no forgiveness in their hearts for perceived treachery, however misconstrued the judgment rendered.

"What can I say to him, Drum?" he asked quietly, their destination right in front of them now.

Drumundoon shook his head helplessly. He had no answer to that question. Pied marshaled his courage and resolve for what lay ahead, saluted the Home Guard on duty at the tent entry, nodded for Drum to wait, and entered.

Kellen Elessedil looked up from his own set of maps as his Captain of the Home Guard appeared through the tent opening, his young face eager and intense. Pied knew that look. It meant the King had decided on something and was impatient to act on it. It didn't take much thinking to know what would happen next.

"Good, you're here." The King's impatience was revealed in his tone of voice. "The reports from the scouts are all in. Guess what they tell me, cousin?"

"That you should attack."

The King smiled. "The Rover mercenaries have all pulled out, the whole bunch of them. Boarded their airships and flown off. They're on their way home, back to the coast, off the Prekkendorran. We've confirmed it. This isn't a stunt. Either they've quit or they've been dismissed, but either way, they're gone. The best pilots, the best craft, the best of everything, gone. The Federation is on its own."

Pied nodded. "Any idea as to why this happened? Have we heard of a rift between the Federation and the Rovers? Anything out of the ordinary, I mean. Now and then, some of them quit anyway. But not all of them at once. Why now?"

"You're suspicious?"

"Aren't you?"

The King laughed. "No, cousin. You're suspicious enough for both of us. You always have been. It's worrisome."

Kellen Elessedil was not one to sit when he could move, rest when he could work. He was a big man, taller than Pied and broader through the shoulders. There was nothing soft about him, his muscular body hardened by hours of exercise and training, his devotion to physical perfection legendary. He was so different from his grandfather and father in this respect that it was hard to believe they had come out of the same family. When they were children playing together at Arborlon, Kellen had always been better at every sport, every game. The only way to beat him, Pied had discovered early on, was to out-think him.

Nothing had changed.

"Part of my role as your protector is to suspect everything and everyone of being something other than what appearances suggest. So, yes, I am suspicious of this Rover withdrawal. I am suspicious of the Federation leaving itself so obviously vulnerable, of inviting us into its lair like the spider does the fly."

"They still have their armies, and their armies are formidable," the King pointed out quickly. He pushed back his long dark hair and knotted his hands. "They may think these are enough to keep us at bay. They know we would never launch a frontal attack against their lines, because if we did, they would smash us to pieces." He paused. "Which is why an aerial attack is so perfect. Look at the opportunity they've given us! Their fleet is big, but unwieldy. Their airship Captains are no match for ours. One quick strike and we can set fire to them all. Think of what that would mean!"

Pied shook his head. "I know what it would mean."

"Complete and unchallenged superiority of the skies," the King continued, so caught up in his vision that he was no longer even listening to his cousin. "Control of everything that flies. Once we have that, their ground forces no longer matter. We can ravage them at will, from too far up for them to do any real damage, from too far away for them to do anything but cover up. We can break them, Pied! I know we can!"

His face was flushed with excitement, his blue eyes bright and eager. Pied had seen him that way before. When they trained together with staffs and swords in hand-to-hand combat, it was the look he assumed when he believed he had gained the upper hand. What he had never learned was to distinguish the difference between when Pied really was in trouble and when he was only pretending at it in order to lure Kellen into making a mistake.

Nothing had changed about that, either.

Pied nodded agreeably, hiding his frustration. "You may be right. But just to be certain about all of this, I have sent two of my Home

Guards into the Federation camp to see what they can learn. I would like to wait for their return before we act."

The King frowned. "How long might that be?"

"Today, I should think. Tomorrow, at the latest."

Kellen shook his head. "Today, perhaps. Tomorrow, no. That's too long. By then, reserves might be called up and the odds made too great for us to chance a strike. The time to act is now, while the Federation fleet is diminished, while we are clearly superior in numbers and experience. Waiting is dangerous."

"Acting out of haste is more dangerous still." Pied stepped in with both feet, his eyes locked on his cousin's, watching as the other's face darkened angrily. "I know you want to attack now, but something about all this doesn't feel right. Better to wait and chance losing this opportunity than to seize it and find we have been tricked."

"Tricked how, Captain?" His cousin's tone of voice had turned dark and accusatory. "What exactly is it you fear?"

Pied shook his head. "You know I don't have an answer for that. I don't know enough about what the Federation's intentions might be. Which is why I want to wait—"

"No."

"—until we have a report—"

"No, cousin! No! There will be no waiting, no hesitation, no second-guessing what seems clear to everyone but you. None of my other advisers, commanders on the field and off, has voiced your concerns. Suppose you are correct. Suppose this is a trap. What risk do we take? We fly superior airships. We can outrun and outmaneuver our enemies at will. We cannot be hurt from the ground. At worst, we will find we were mistaken about the size of their fleet and be forced to retreat. We have done so before, and it has cost us nothing. Why would this time be any different?"

Because this time you are being invited *to act against them,* Pied wanted to say, but did not. He knew the argument was over and the matter settled. Kellen Elessedil was King of the Elves, and the King had the final word on everything.

"Cousin," the other soothed, stepping over to put his arm about him, "we have been friends a long time. I respect your opinion, which is why I asked you to come speak with me before I gave the command to proceed. I knew what you would say, but I wanted you to say it. I wanted you to question me, because frequently you are the only one who will. A King needs candid and reasoned advice from his advisers, and in most matters, no one gives better advice than you."

He gave Pied a small squeeze with his powerful arm. "That said, a King must listen to what his instincts tell him. He must not waver once his mind is made up. You know this."

He waited for Pied's response, so it was necessary to give it. "I know, my lord."

"I have made a commitment to turn the tide of this war once and for all, and now, at last, I have a way to do so. It would be cowardly of me to turn away a chance such as this merely because there are risks. It would be unforgivable."

"I know that, as well."

"Will you still come with me when we fly into battle?" The King stepped away, releasing his grip. "I won't ask it of you if you feel strongly about not going. Nor will I think less of you."

Pied arched one eyebrow at his cousin. "I am Captain of the Home Guard, my lord. Where you go, I must go, as well. That isn't open to debate. Don't make it seem as if it is."

The King's intense, considering gaze locked on him. "No, cousin, I guess it isn't. Not with someone as dedicated as you. And I wouldn't want it any other way." He paused. "I'll give this matter several hours more thought before acting. I had planned a late afternoon strike in any case, so that we can come at them from out of the twilight, out of the shadows. You may keep watch for your scouts until then. If they return in time, bring me whatever news you think matters. I promise I will listen. But if none comes, I will see you on the plains an hour before dusk."

Pied turned and started for the door. "One thing more," the King called after him. Pied turned. "I intend to take Kiris and Wencling with me." He must have seen the confusion in Pied's eyes. "Aboard the flagship, cousin. I want them to watch."

Pied stared. Kellen Elessedil was talking about his sons. About boys who were fifteen and thirteen. About taking them into the heart of an engagement with a dangerous enemy. "No," he said at once, before he could think better of it.

The King seemed unruffled. "They need to see what a battle is like, to understand what happens. They need to experience it for themselves, not just hear about it. They are future Kings, and this is a part of their training."

"They are too young for this, my lord. There will be other times, safer times, when the risk is not so great."

"The risk is always great in war, cousin," the King said, brushing his arguments aside.

Pied took a deep, steadying breath, picturing Arling's reaction once she found out what Kellen had done. "With any Elves-in-training, we expose them gradually to the dangers of war. We don't just throw them out on the battlefield—not unless we are desperate. We bring them along slowly. I think that is what is needed with Kiris and Wencling. Let them come on a few overflights first, ones in which combat is not a given."

Kellen Elessedil took a long moment to study him, as if seeing something he hadn't seen before, something he was not altogether pleased about. Then he said, softly, "I will think about it, cousin."

He motioned for Pied to go out, an odd gesture Pied had not seen before. But this was not the time for speculation. He departed quickly, happy to escape before Kellen could think of some further madness. Because he would, Pied knew. He was in that place where ideas came and went like silverfish, and each looked better than the one before, but never was.

Outside the tent, Drumundoon fell into step beside him, his tall form bent close as he said, "Did he listen to you?"

Pied nodded. "He listened. Then he ignored me. If I don't give him fresh reasons to call it off, the attack takes place at dusk. Worse, he intends to take his sons along for the ride."

Drumundoon exhaled sharply. "Has he lost his mind?"

"Arling would think so. I wish she were here to speak with him. She might have better luck than I."

Drumundoon shook his head. "I doubt it. He doesn't listen to her, either. Although he might, where those boys are concerned. What matters is that she left them in your charge. Yours, specifically. I was there when she did so. I heard the way she spoke to you. If anything happens to her sons, she will have your head."

Pied glanced at him. *Because I loved her once. Because I think she loved me, as well. You left that part out, Drum.*

He stalked off into the midday heat and tried not to think about it.

NINETEEN

By late afternoon, Acrolace and Parn had still not returned. It worried Pied, but he had learned long ago to live with the guilt associated with sending his Home Guard to spy on an enemy. It was obvious in any case that Acrolace and Parn were not going to return in time to be of any help in dissuading Kellen Elessedil from his ill-advised foray. The attack on the Federation fleet was going to happen whether he wanted it to or not, and he was just going to have to make the best of it. That was sometimes a soldier's lot, even if you were Captain of the Home Guard and cousin to the King.

Dressed in his battle gear, his weapons strapped about him once more, he called Drumundoon to his tent, and with the sun creeping toward the horizon through a screen of thin clouds and the daylight becoming diffuse and weak, they set out for the airship field.

"No word of any sort, Drum?"

The aide shook his head. "Nothing. I hear that the Federation is massing soldiers along its lines, looking to shore up the weaknesses brought about by the departure of the Rovers. That's the King's reading of the situation, at least. It reinforces what he already believes, which makes it attractive. It supports the decision he favors. Word is, he sees this war over and done within a week."

"Celebrating his victory before he's even engaged his enemy. How very like him." Pied shook his head. "Something is going on that we don't know about. I can feel it in my bones. This attack is a mistake. I have to find a way to stop it."

Drumundoon pursed his lips. "I don't know this for a fact, but I am given to understand that the King hasn't advised our allies as yet of his plans."

Pied came to an abrupt halt, staring at him. "What?"

"He intends to inform them just before he sets out, I'm told. That way, they can't stop him." His aide cocked an eyebrow at him. "He doesn't want to risk anything or anyone getting in his way. He knows he isn't commander of the Free-born army, that he isn't even commander of the airship fleet. But he is King of the Elves, and the Elves make up the greater part of the airship command, so in his mind, that's sufficient justification for striking out on his own."

Drumundoon glanced around warily, making sure no one else was listening. "Captain, he doesn't intend to ask for support from any quarter in this business. He intends this victory to belong solely to the Elves. Dwarves, Trolls, and Bordermen can share in it afterwards, once it has been realized, but ultimately it is the Elves who will bring it about. That's what they say he's decided."

Pied fumed. How had he not seen that coming? For more than two months, Kellen Elessedil had camped on the Prekkendorran with his Elven Hunters, an inspiring presence and little more on the face of things. But Kellen Elessedil was nothing if not driven. You could see it in his impatience with the failure of the Free-born army to effect any noticeable change in the status quo. Always anxious to be in the thick of things, always looking to see how matters so long stalemated might be resolved, the King was pressing his fellow commanders at every opportunity. The war was more than thirty years old, and the Elves were sick to death of it. The King saw it as his moral imperative to bring it to a conclusion, and no one could fault him for his commitment to do so. What was wrong with his approach was his insistence on doing it his way, on finding a solution that did not necessarily involve his Free-born allies. What was mistaken in his thinking was that the solution existed in simple terms;

that somehow the answer lay in a single brilliant military stroke, and that the finding of that answer had been left up to him.

Well, it was too late to try to explain it to him now, even supposing he would be willing to listen, which Pied was quite sure he would not.

He started walking again, more purposefully, a mix of irritation and concern flooding through him. King or not, Kellen Elessedil was overstepping his bounds, and it would come back to haunt them all. Drumundoon matched his strides to those of his Captain and kept his peace while he did so. Neither of them spoke. There had been enough talk already.

Pied surveyed the camp as they passed through it, taking careful note of what he saw. This section was mostly Elven; those farther on, east of where they walked, comprised Bordermen from the larger cities of Callahorn as well as Dwarves and Trolls, most of the latter mercenaries. The nominal leader of the army was an aged, though highly respected, Southlander named Droshen, but the real leader, the man who commanded the soldiers on the battlefield, was a Dwarf called Vaden Wick, a veteran of countless campaigns against the Gnome tribes before coming to the Prekkendorran. Just now, coordination of the various allied forces was loose, a condition brought about by the near inactivity of the armies on either side of the conflict over the past few years, an erosion of structure and discipline through constant changes in both ranks and command. The third generation of allies was fighting the war, and the toll was noticeable. It was assumed by most that the war would end only when the leaders finally grew so tired of it that they called it off by mutual agreement. No one thought it could be won on the battlefield. Not after so long. Not after so many failed attempts.

Except, of course, for a few who thought like Kellen Elessedil.

Pied was disconcerted by what he saw that evening. The obvious lack of discipline was worrisome. The looks on the faces of the men and women as they sat around their fires, playing games of chance and drinking ale, were more worrisome still. Disinterest and resignation were mirrored in those faces. That spoke to him clearly: No one believed in the war anymore. It said that everyone was sick of the fighting and dying. It said that keeping your head down and your mouth shut was all that would get you through. These men and women were waiting things out. They were waiting to go home.

He glanced around. No one drilled or trained. No one sharpened weapons or tightened straps on armor. There were Elven Hunters manning the walls at the front and there was a watch in place; that was enough. If something more was needed, it was somebody else's problem.

It was worse elsewhere, in the other armies, where discipline was even less in evidence. It wasn't that Bordermen, Dwarves, and Trolls weren't brave and capable; it was that they had no reason to think those attributes would be tested. The Federation army had squatted in place for almost two years without doing anything beyond sending out scouts and attempting an occasional foray into the Free-born lines. They were as indolent and disinterested in fighting as their enemies were. The mobilization of fresh forces along the Federation front in the wake of the departure of the Rover airships did not suggest to the Elves and their allies that their enemy's attitude had changed.

Pied glanced over at Drumundoon and gestured toward the encampment. "They don't seem to have much to do with their time, do they?"

Drum said nothing. There was nothing to say. He was of the same mind as his Captain. The Home Guard had a different approach to discipline than everyone else, but that was why they were Home Guard. The rest of the army regarded them as curiosities. They were a small unit assigned a single task—to protect the King. The way they conducted themselves, others believed, was mostly the result of the suspicion that the King was always watching them.

When they reached the heights, Pied paused. The front stretched along the plateau that comprised the Prekkendorran for more than two miles east and west through a series of broad flats segmented by twisting passes and ravines. At present, and for much of the past twenty years, the Free-born had occupied a pair of high bluffs bracketing a deep, wide pass that angled north all the way to the other side of the plateau before turning down through the foothills beyond.

Elves occupied the smaller bluff on the west; a mix of Bordermen, Dwarves, and Trolls, the larger one on the east. By placing archers and slingmen on either side of the gap, where it narrowed, they were able to ward against penetration. The Federation's only choice was to come at the allies from the front or sides and to do so from a highly vulnerable position.

The Federation had penetrated deep into the flats early on in the war, but once the allies had found the bluffs on which to set their defenses, the attack had stalled. Because the Federation was the invading force, the allies could afford to sit back and wait. It was the invader who must come to them, and by now they had constructed defenses of stone and timber that were believed to be sufficiently strong that it would cost the lives of thousands of men to achieve a breakthrough. It was generally agreed by both sides that another way must be found, and as yet it had not.

Pied studied the Federation lines, situated on the flats not half a mile away. A mass of dark figures crowded behind fortifications similar to their own. In the two months he had been on the front, they had not emerged from behind those walls. The most excitement he had experienced was the result of a pair of rather haphazard airship attacks on the Dwarf lines a mile farther down the front, which had been quickly driven back.

Were there more Federation soldiers at those walls than there had been a week ago? A mottled stain of black-and-silver uniforms spread away behind those fortifications for better than a mile, clusters of men settled about cooking fires and stacks of weapons. There was no drilling or training in evidence, no suggestion of an impending attack. Everything looked as it always looked.

But that didn't mean it was.

He shook his head. He didn't like anything he was seeing on either side of the front. He had been a soldier all his life, and he had learned to trust his instincts. They were screaming at him, telling him that the possibility of disaster was enormous and close at hand.

"Drum, I can't let him do this," he said quietly.

"The King?" His aide shook his head. "You can't stop him, Captain. You've already tried, and he won't listen. If you can't tell him something he doesn't already know, you'll just make him more determined."

Pied walked on, saying nothing. There had to be a way to stall, something he could say or do to win a reprieve. He had always been able to out-think Kellen; he ought to be able to do so now.

Ahead, the airfield came into view, settled in a swale at the center of the encampment east, close to the draw that separated the allied armies. There was noticeable activity, even from a distance. Ships were being readied for liftoff, crews scurrying across the decks and atop the rigging, tightening draws and loosening sails. Railguns were already fitted in place, and missiles were stacked in boxes beside them. Two dozen airships were set to fly, the larger part of the fleet, the best of the warships it comprised. The King was determined that the attack would succeed, holding nothing back against the possibility that it wouldn't.

As he descended from the higher flat, Pied caught sight of the King grouped with his airship commanders in a tight circle by the flagship *Ellenroh*, talking. The discussion appeared heated, but all the heat was coming from the King. His Captains were doing little more than listening.

Then Pied caught sight of Kiris and Wencling, standing off to one side of their father, and his heart sank. The King had decided to take his sons with him, after all. In spite of Pied's reservations. In spite of his advice. His nephews were looking at their feet, trying not to draw attention to themselves, staring ill at ease and out of place, and he guessed they didn't like the idea of being there any better than he did.

Taking a deep breath, he walked across the airfield and up to the King.

"Captain," the King greeted on catching sight of him. He would never use Pied's name or refer to their familiar relationship in a situation like this. "We are ready to depart. No word, I gather, from your scouts? No? Then we have no further reason to delay."

"My lord, I wish you would reconsider," Pied said quickly. "I would feel better for your safety if we waited just one more day. My scouts should return—"

"My safety is in good hands with these men," the King inter-rupted, an edge to his voice. "I thought we had settled this earlier, Captain. Was there something I said that wasn't clear to you?"

There was no mistaking the anger in his voice. He did not care to be challenged in front of his airship Captains and his sons and par-ticularly not about the coming attack. He was telling Pied he had gone as far as he was going to be allowed to go, and that he had bet-ter not try to go farther.

But Pied had no choice. Not if he was to keep his self-respect. "My lord, you made yourself perfectly clear. I respect your thinking. But I have been a soldier for a long time, and I have learned to trust my instincts. They tell me that something isn't right about what we're seeing—about the unexplained Rover departure and weaken-ing of the Federation fleet. Nor do I feel right about the mobilization reported along the Federation front. I know it seems to be in re-sponse to the Rover departure, but I think it might be something else. If I could suggest an alternative plan, my lord, I would ask you to take an exploratory flight to see—"

"Enough, Captain!" the King snapped, cutting him short. There was a hushed silence. The King was seething. "More than enough. You are Captain of the Home Guard. Limit yourself to that and leave the decision making to me!"

"As Captain of the Home Guard, I am responsible for your safety and must do everything in my power to protect you!" Pied snapped back. "I can't do that if you won't let me!"

The silence turned as frosty as midwinter in the Charnals. Pied caught a glimpse of the shocked faces of the King's sons, who stared at him in disbelief—Kiris, tall and dark like his father, and Wencling, fair and small like his mother. No one talked that way to their father, certainly not outside the family and not in public. Pied had crossed the line, but his conscience refused to let him back down.

Kellen Elessedil turned away. "Captains," he addressed his airship commanders, "prepare to set out. Board everyone. Make certain they know what is expected of them."

He gestured to a messenger standing off to one side. "Carry the message I gave you to Commanders Droshen and Wick. Go quickly and tell them to take whatever precautions they feel necessary in case of a counterattack. Make certain they know that I have already left."

When everyone was gone but his sons, he turned back to Pied. "You have abused your position as Captain of the Home Guard. As a consequence, you will not be coming with me. I don't trust you anymore. You've lost your nerve. I don't want my life or the lives of my family and soldiers in your hands. You are relieved of your duties. My safety is no longer your responsibility. Perhaps others, more capable of understanding the nature of your office, will serve me better."

He paused. "Just because my wife still favors you, a kindness she would do well to reconsider, doesn't give you the right to question me as you have just done—in front of my sons and my officers."

He turned to his sons, beckoned for them to follow, and stalked angrily toward the *Ellenroh*. Pied watched them go, stunned. He should say something more, he knew. He should make another attempt to stop him or maybe just try to explain himself better. But he couldn't make himself move.

He was still standing there when the airships lifted off like huge hunting birds and swung south toward the Federation lines.

Drumundoon, who had waited patiently in the background until Pied's attention had shifted away from the departing vessels, came up to him.

"He will change his mind, Captain," the aide said quietly. "He will realize he acted out of haste."

"Perhaps." There was an awkward silence as they faced each other. "I couldn't think of anything else to say, Drum. I just stood there and let him walk away from me."

His aide nodded and gave a faint smile. "Maybe there weren't any words left to be said."

They walked back across the airfield and into the Elven encampment in silence. Now and again, Pied cast anxious glances toward the Federation lines, where the first torches were being lit with twilight's approach. He could still see the Elven warships, dark smudges pinned against the sky. He searched for ground activity, but saw none. It was hard to tell, though, so far away and in poor light.

His thoughts drifted. He had grown up with Kellen Elessedil, and there were few men or women who knew him better. He should have been able to devise a more effective approach to dissuading him from making an ill-advised attack. He should have been able to avoid angering him so. Somehow things had gotten out of hand, and he was still struggling with the fact of it. He could see the faces of Kiris and Wencling in his mind, looking shocked and afraid, as if seeing what he hadn't seen, as if knowing secrets he should have known. He tried not to think what Arling would say once she discovered how badly he had let her down. If she would talk to him at all, he amended. She might not. She might dismiss him as swiftly as Kellen had.

"Captain," Drumundoon said suddenly, taking his arm.

A man was racing toward them from across the flats, one of his Home Guard. The man's name escaped him, though he knew it as well as his own. He struggled to remember it and failed.

"Phaile," Drum whispered, as if reading his mind.

Phaile reached them in a rush and saluted. "Acrolace has returned, Captain!" he exclaimed. His breath came in short, labored gasps. "She's badly injured! She says you are to come right away!"

They broke into a run, Phaile leading the way. Pied didn't bother questioning the man; Acrolace was the one he needed to see.

But the urgency of the summons frightened him.

They reached a cluster of Elves close to the edge of the bluff, just above the front of the Elven defensive line. Acrolace lay on the ground, the silver-and-black Federation tunic she had donned as a disguise stained and torn, her left arm ripped open all the way from shoulder to elbow. She was pale from loss of blood and rigid with pain. Her green eyes found his as he knelt beside her, and her fingers fastened on his wrist.

He bent close to hear her, his eyes never leaving hers. "What happened, Acrolace?" he whispered. "Where's Parn?"

She shook her head. "Dead." She swallowed thickly. "They have an airship . . ." She coughed, and blood bubbled on her lips. "Under heavy guard, no one allowed close. But . . . we got near enough . . ."

She trailed off, her eyes closing against pain or memory, he couldn't tell which. When she opened them again, he squeezed her hand. "What did you see?"

"A weapon mounted on the deck. Big. Something new." She inhaled sharply. "They're waiting for us, Captain. They know . . . we're coming. We heard them . . . say so."

She gave a long, slow sigh, and her hand released its grip on his. *A weapon*, he repeated silently.

"She's unconscious," one of the Healers said. "Better so."

Pied looked around quickly, trying not to panic. "Phaile," he said, spotting his Home Guard messenger. "Find Commander Fraxon. Tell him I said to expect a Federation attack. Tell him it will be massive, a push to break all the way through our lines. Tell him it will come at any time and to have his Elven Hunters ready. Hurry!"

He stood up. "Drum, call up all elements of the Home Guard and place them on the airfield. They are to hold it at all costs. All costs, Drum. Until I tell them to stand down."

His aide nodded, his long face as pale as Acrolace's. "Where will you be? What will you do?"

Pied was already hurrying away, his determination etched on his lean features. "I'm going after the King," he called over his shoulder. "This time he will have to listen to me!"

TWENTY

Pied Sanderling sprinted the length of the Elven encampment, bumping aside anyone who got in his way, knocking over equipment and stores, leaving in his wake a string of angry shouts and curses. His mind was already far ahead of his body, thinking of what he must do and how he must do it, aware of how futile his efforts were likely to be. A terrible certainty gripped him. He was going to be too late. No matter how quick he was, he wasn't going to be quick enough. The disaster he had feared had come to pass, and all the failed warnings in the world would not be enough to persuade him it was not his fault.

Run faster!

He reached the airfield winded and flushed, and as he tore down the embankment toward the airships, he searched frantically for someone he recognized among the few who hadn't gone with Kellen Elessedil. He found only a lone commander of a railgun sloop, a grizzled veteran named Markenstall. He barely knew the man, knew more of his reputation than of him. A brave man, dependable in a fight, a solid presence in the pilot box—that would suffice.

"Captain!" he shouted, rushing up to the older man. "Is your sloop fitted and ready?" He glanced at her name, carved into the stern. *Asashiel.*

Markenstall stared at him with a mix of surprise and doubt. Gray whiskers stuck out from the sides of his jaw, deep lines furrowed his weathered face, and his ears were tattered and scarred. He had the look of a man who had been in more than a few fights.

"Answer me, Captain!" Pied shouted at him.

The older man started sharply. "Ready and fitted as she can be, Captain Sanderling," he growled.

"Good. We're taking her up. Cast off."

Markenstall hesitated. "Captain, I'm not authorized to—"

"Listen carefully to me," Pied interrupted. "The King flies into a trap. One of my Home Guard nearly lost her life getting that news to me; another lies dead somewhere beyond our lines. I'm not about to let that be for nothing! There isn't time to seek authorization of any sort. If you want to save the King and those who went with him, we must leave at once!"

He cast a quick glance south, where the sky had turned deep blue in the twilight haze and the airships his gaze had followed earlier had disappeared from view. The dusk was thickening, the last of the sunlight a dim glow below the horizon west, the first stars beginning to brighten in the sky north. East, the moon was a silvery crescent lifting out of the Lower Anar.

His eyes flicked back to Markenstall. "Captain, please!"

The veteran studied him a moment longer, then nodded. "Very well. Get aboard." He turned to a pair of sailors sitting nearby. "Pon! Cresck! Off your duffs and get aboard! Take in the lines and anchors! Prepare to cast off!"

The two crewmen and the grizzled Captain were skilled at making quick departures, and the *Asashiel* was airborne in minutes, swinging south with the wind, tacking swiftly out across the flats and beyond the Free-born lines. Pied stood in the pilot box with Markenstall while the crewmen manned the railguns to either side, breeches opened and loaded, triggers unlocked. No one mistook the foray for anything but what Pied was certain it was going to turn out to be.

"Mind if I ask what it is you intend to do with a sloop and two railguns?" Markenstall asked once they were winging out over the desolate front, a hint of sarcasm in his voice.

Pied shook his head. "Whatever I can."

Ahead, the Federation lines were so dark they were virtually indistinguishable from the surrounding land. Pied thought he heard shouting, the sounds of sudden activity, but it was hard to tell with the rush of the wind and the whine of the rigging in his ears.

Then lightning split the darkness, brilliant and piercing, the bolt a horizontal rope stretched low and taut against the horizon. The bolt struck something that exploded instantly into a fiery ball, burning fragments pinwheeling into the darkness to fall like tiny firebrands to the earth. For just an instant, a cluster of airships was silhouetted against the brightness, masts and hulls stark and black.

"Shades!" Markenstall hissed. "What was that?"

Pied swiftly amended his earlier conclusion. It wasn't lightning after all. Not riding that low and that straight.

Then it flashed again, and there was another explosion, this one more violent than the first, and again the airships were revealed, scattering in all directions now, angling away from the fireball like frightened animals. An earth-shattering boom reverberated through the night, the shock waves so powerful that Pied could feel them even through the deck of the sloop.

He knew then what it was. It was the weapon Acrolace and Parn had discovered in the Federation camp. The trap had been sprung; Kellen Elessedil's airships were being destroyed, one by one. Pied was too late to give warning. He was too late to do anything but witness the consequences of the King's ill-considered, rash behavior.

"Faster, Captain," he said, catching hold of Markenstall's wiry arm. "We have to try to help."

It was a faint hope at best. There was little one airship could do to help another in the best of situations, which this most assuredly wasn't, and his was likely the weakest airship aloft. But he had to get a closer look. He had to know what the Elves and their allies were up against. If the King didn't get safely back, if none of them managed to get back . . .

He forced the thought away, hating himself for allowing it to surface. But another firebolt erupted and another airship caught fire, the flames turning masts and rigging into torches that illuminated the whole of the night sky. Stricken, the airship wheeled away from the attack, trying to stay aloft, to seek cover. But there was no cover in the skies and no place to hide when you were burning. A second strike turned it into a massive fireball. It blazed brightly for a moment, then fell apart and disappeared into the dark.

"Shades!" Markenstall whispered again in shocked disbelief.

They were close enough by then that Pied could make out the vague shapes of the Elven airships as they wheeled this way and that to avoid the huge Federation airship that was in pursuit. Her name, emblazoned across her upswept bow, was the *Dechtera*. The terrible weapon was affixed to her decking; Pied could just make out its armored bulk. Even as the shape of it registered, the man-made lightning exploded out of it again, crackling with energy and power, a terrible bright lance through the enfolding night, burning everything in its path. It caught pieces of two ships this time, nicking the hull of one, boring holes through the sails of another. It was firing blindly, Pied saw, unable to distinguish its targets clearly in the darkness. The moon was behind a bank of clouds, and the starlight was still too thin.

The Elven airships might have a chance if they fled now, if they turned around, if they raced for the safety of their own lines.

Incredibly, they did not. Instead, they attacked. It was suicide, but it was exactly what Kellen Elessedil would do, refusing to quit a battle, ready to die first. *He will get his wish here,* Pied thought in horror. The Federation weapon was firing into the Elven airships as they drew near enough to distinguish, and they were exploding one after the other. The King was trying to ram the Federation ship, to damage it sufficiently that it could be forced down, perhaps even made to crash. He was intent on salvaging something out of this disaster, but he could not seem to recognize that it was already too late for that.

"What in the name of everything sane is he doing?" Markenstall whispered in disbelief, recognizing at once the futility of the effort.

Committing suicide, Pied thought. Trying to ram the bigger ship in the mistaken belief that by doing so he could still save his fleet. But he wasn't even going to get close. Already, the *Dechtera* was firing at

the *Ellenroh,* a series of short, sharp bursts that set the Elven flagship
on fire in several places and brought down the foremast. Still, Kellen
came on, his railguns raking the enemy's decks. But the weapon that
was destroying his fleet was protected behind heavy metal shields
that the railguns could barely scratch. Another burst set the *Ellenroh*'s
mainsail afire, and now the airship was lurching badly, her sails gone
and one or more of her parse tubes damaged or blown away.

"No, Kellen," Pied whispered. "Land her! Get her down now before she—"

A fresh burst from the Federation weapon rocked the big Elven
flagship from bow to stern, striking with such force that it knocked her
backwards. The *Ellenroh* shuddered and bucked, then exploded in a
blinding ball of fire that consumed everything and everyone aboard.

In seconds she was gone.

Pied stared in stunned silence, unable to accept what he had witnessed. The King, gone. Kiris and Wencling, gone. The biggest warship in the Elven fleet together with every last one of the men and
women who crewed her, vanished.

"Captain Sanderling," Markenstall hissed in his ear, and he jerked
around in response. "What do we do?"

The *Dechtera* had turned her attention to what was left of the
Elven fleet—a handful of airships only, three of which were already
settling onto the flats. The plains were swarming with Federation soldiers marching toward the Elven lines, a dark stain that spread like
ink on old parchment. Thousands, Pied judged. He watched the
damaged airships fall into the mass of charging men. He watched
the men swarm up the sides of the ships and onto the decks. Then he
quit looking.

His eyes flicked back to the fleet, under attack once more from
the Federation killing machine. The *Dechtera* was moving after them,
overtaking them one at a time, burning them out of the sky the way
an archer might shoot down a flock of trapped geese. She shouldn't
have been able to do that, as big and cumbersome looking as she
was. She must be powered by an abnormally high number of crystals,
her stored energy capacity twice that of any other ship of the line.
Some of the Elven ships were dropping toward the plains now, try-

ing to use the enemy soldiers as cover so that they could not be fired
upon from above. But the tactic wasn't working. The weapon aboard
the big ship was too accurate to be deterred by the threat of what a
miss would mean. It simply took its time, burning away the Elven
ships whether they fled or tried to hide.

He looked at Markenstall. "We have to do something, Captain."

The older man nodded, but kept silent.

"Can you get behind that Federation ship? Can you come up at
her from below?"

The veteran stared at him. "What do you intend to do?"

"Disable her steering. Use the railguns to damage her rudders
and thrusters from underneath, where they can't do anything about
it without breaking off their attack and setting her down." He
paused. "We're small enough that they might not see us coming in
from behind."

Markenstall thought a moment. "Maybe. But if they do see us, we
won't have a chance. Railguns are only good from close in. From
more than fifty yards, we'll be so much target practice."

Pied glanced quickly at the skyline. The moon remained covered
by clouds, the light still something between dusk and full dark. Off
to their left, the *Dechtera* was hunting its Elven quarry like a big cat,
stealthy and sure, striking with bursts of white fire that filled the
night air with blinding explosions and the pungent, raw smell of ash
and smoke and death.

"We can't just sit here and let this slaughter continue," he said
quietly.

Markenstall adjusted the controls without a word, swung the
Asashiel toward the enemy camp, and sent her skimming over the
heads of the advancing Federation soldiers, who fired up at them
with bows and slings as they flew past. But they slipped through the
darkness unhindered and undamaged, and soon they were behind
their target, staying low so that they would not be silhouetted against
the horizon, approaching in a gradual ascent that kept them carefully masked from view.

But suddenly new airships began to lift off from the Federation
airfield, fresh reinforcements setting out to lend support to the

ground attack on the Free-born camp, their dark shapes like hunting birds as they swung about to place the sloop directly in their path.

"Captain," Pied exclaimed with a sharp intake of breath.

Markenstall nodded. "I see them. Warn the men on the railguns."

Pied left the pilot box in a rush, scuttling across the deck to Pon and Cresck, his safety harness dragging behind him, and alerted each of the crewmen of this new danger. He found himself wishing they had something besides railguns with which to work, but there was nothing to be done about that.

Moments later, he was back beside Markenstall. The night had gone black again, the moon disappeared once more behind the clouds, and the air turned brisk and chilly. Pied shivered in spite of himself, wishing he had thought to throw on warmer clothing.

He glanced out at the cluster of rising Federation airships. At least half a dozen were advancing in their direction.

"They're gaining on us," Markenstall announced. "I don't think they see us yet, but they will soon enough. We can't wait, Captain Sanderling. We have to take a chance."

"What do you mean?"

"We have to gain speed and altitude both, get above the heavier air and into the wind and closer to that ship." The other man paused. "We have to let them see us. If we don't, they're going to find us anyway. We don't have time to be clever or cautious about this."

Pied hesitated. He knew Markenstall was right, but he hated the thought of exposing the sloop when they had so few weapons with which to defend themselves. Once they were spotted, the other ships would be after them like cats after a mouse. That would give them only a single pass, barring a miracle, at their target.

"All right," he said. "Do your best. But find a way to get us close to that ship."

"Hold on," Markenstall said, and he pushed the thruster levers all the way forward.

The *Asashiel* bucked and shot ahead; the mouse was in flight. They rose swiftly into the sky, abandoning the comparative safety of the darkness for the revealing light of stars and moon—for the latter was emerging from behind the clouds. Fresh illumination bathed the

Prekkendorran in brilliant white light, revealing the hordes of attackers surging toward the Elven defensive lines. Already they were flooding the gap between the twin bluffs occupied by the Elves and their allies, breaking down the Elven fortifications and scrambling onto the airfield, where the last of the Elven airships were frantically lifting off. All across the battlefield, the remains of the destroyed ships burned fiercely, signal fires for the advancing army, encouragement for its soldiers. Pied saw the *Ellenroh's* hull, a charred, smoking wreck at the center of everything.

You should have listened to me, Kellen, Pied thought. He closed his eyes. *I should have found a way to make you listen.*

They were approaching their target now. The *Dechtera* was right ahead of them, her bulk blocking out an entire section of the sky. She was huge, a flying platform supported by four sets of pontoons with cross-bracing running all along her underside. Three masts flew yards of light sheaths, radian draws feeding banks of parse tubes housing the diapson crystals that powered her, metal shields opening and closing in sudden bursts of converted energy as the ship maneuvered first this way and then that, bringing the deadly weapon mounted on the foredeck to bear. No one aboard seemed to realize yet that the *Asashiel* was tracking her, all eyes were directed forward to where another Elven ship was under attack, a rope of fire burning through her, sizzling and exploding wood and metal in a booming cough that rocked the sloop with concussive force. Burning bodies flew over the railings of the stricken airship, tumbling to the earth like stricken fireflies.

Pied made a quick, agonizing survey. Only three Elven airships remained aloft of the twelve or so that had started out. The fleet was decimated.

"Quick, Captain!" he hissed at Markenstall. "Before we lose any more!"

The *Asashiel* was right below the *Dechtera* now, and Markenstall angled her to the port side, away from the approaching vessels that by now had surely spied them, giving his crew a chance to position the railguns where they could do the most damage. He, too, knew they would only have one pass. The big ship was moving forward in a slow, steady line, a fresh target already in sight, still oblivious to them. They were going to have a clean shot at her underside. The men on the railguns had swung their weapons into position and were sighting down the long barrels, waiting patiently.

Pied glanced over his shoulder. Their pursuers were closing on them, and he could see the frantic efforts of some of the crew to give warning to the men on the *Dechtera.*

"Release!" Markenstall shouted.

Both railguns discharged in the same instant, sending a hail of metal shards into the underside of the Federation ship, the missiles striking with explosive impact. Pied had just enough time to see two of the parse tubes disintegrate entirely and the main rudder collapse, and then Markenstall was swinging the *Asashiel* away, speeding out from under the damaged enemy, a tiny gnat in flight from a giant bird. They emerged from beneath the warship's shadow into a sky awash with moonlight and were immediately exposed. The railguns on the decking of the enemy swung toward them, but Markenstall dropped the sloop below their angle of fire, skimming the flats once more, content to take his chances with the missiles fired from the foot soldiers.

But it wasn't over yet. A line of white fire sizzled past their mainmast, snapping off one of the spars, burning away wood and sail and knocking the *Asashiel* sideways.

"Brace!" Markenstall shouted automatically, grabbing onto the railing to keep upright. Reaching for the thruster levers, he jammed them all the way forward, then sent the sloop into a stomach-churning dive.

"We should have taken a shot at that weapon, too!" Pied snapped at the veteran.

The Captain righted their wounded vessel not fifty feet above the flats and lurched away from the deadly Federation weapon. Pied glanced over his shoulder. The *Dechtera* hung silhouetted against the moonlit sky. She was still moving forward, but he saw that her course was fixed and undeviating. At least one, and possibly both, shots from the sloop's railguns had done the job; the steering was damaged, and the vessel was unable to come about.

He exhaled sharply. The big ship was slowing down. The other

Federation warships were coming up from behind, preparing to offer help. It occurred to him that now was the perfect time for that attack Kellen Elessedil had been so anxious to launch, the perfect opportunity to destroy that ship and the weapon she bore. But the bulk of the Elven fleet was in flames, and the ships of Callahorn were still on the ground somewhere east.

He looked down at the flats, swarming with Federation soldiers, then at the Elven defensive lines. He remembered the faces of the men and women he had seen earlier, weary and disinterested. He remembered the lack of discipline, evident everywhere. He was not encouraged. The Elven airfield had been overrun, the remainder of the fleet fled north. If their ground defenses held through the night, it would be a miracle. An impossible miracle, he amended, without help from the Free-born allies. And in the end, it might not matter anyway. By week's end, the *Dechtera* would be airborne again and would fly in support of the Federation attack, her terrible weapon primed and ready for use. What it had done to the Elven airships was nothing compared to what it would do to the Elven army.

The implications of his thinking did not escape him. The war on the Prekkendorran was about to take a disastrous turn, and he wasn't sure there was anything that could be done about it.

They were flying over the captured Elven airfield now, heading west toward the besieged Elven lines. "Captain," he called to Markenstall. The wind came up again in a sudden rush, tearing at his words. The veteran turned. "Can you fly us to where—"

He never finished. White fire lanced through the center of the airship in a searing rope of brightness that slammed the entire craft sideways with such force that Pied was thrown from the pilot box, catapulting over its railing. He caught a glimpse of the mast going up like a torch, the flames spurting skyward as the sails caught fire. Both railguns and crew disappeared into an explosion of sizzling light. The sloop lurched wildly, bucked, and began to drop.

"Markenstall!" he called weakly.

There was no response. His safety line was still attached to its ring inside the pilot box, but he was tangled so thoroughly in the rigging that he couldn't move. He tried to lift himself to see what was happening inside the box itself and failed. There was blood on his face, warm and sticky, running down his neck and arm. He had thought them safely away from the Federation warship and her terrible weapon. He had been mistaken. Its range must be enormous. Even from the better part of a mile away, it had managed to fix on them. Even now, after the fact, Pied could not imagine it.

He felt the sloop plunge earthward with sickening speed. He closed his eyes and waited for the impact.

It took Penderrin Ohmsford and his companions almost a week to navigate the maze of passes and defiles that wound through the Klu Mountains, although they did not again encounter the treacherous combination of mist and clouds that had very nearly prevented their initial escape from Taupo Rough. With Kermadec leading, steady and assured now in his choice of routes, they pressed on without needing to rely on Pen or Cinnaminson to find the way.

Nor did they see anything further of their Druid pursuers, although Tagwen was quick to point out, when the subject was raised, that not seeing them didn't mean they weren't out there. Once before they had thought themselves safe, only to discover how badly they were mistaken. If the Druids hunting them were doing so on orders from Shadea a'Ru, they were not likely to give up easily, the Dwarf insisted. But it was the use of the Elfstones that had brought Terek Molt and the *Galaphile* down on them in the Slags, Pen thought. As long as they were able to refrain from using the Stones, they should be able to keep Traunt Rowan and the *Ballindarroch* from finding them here. After all, he reasoned, if the Druid and his cohorts had magic that would enable them to find the little company, they certainly would have done so already. That they hadn't shown themselves even once suggested they were hunting blind.

Nevertheless, as the little company pressed on through the mountains, Pen found himself glancing skyward periodically to make certain he was not making a mistake.

It was late in the day, the sun already sinking into the jaws of the peaks west, when they climbed through a particularly nasty tangle of switchbacks to a ledge that overlooked the broadest, darkest valley Pen had ever encountered. It was difficult to judge exactly how big the valley was; from so high up there was no point of reference by which to measure accurately. Hundreds of square miles, perhaps? Even more? It sprawled in all directions, spilling out from its central cradle into passes and canyons like the fingers of a giant's spread hand. At its eastern end, farthest from where they stood, it simply disappeared into mist and twilight, so densely packed with trees and brush that its shadows overlapped to create the impression of a lake thick and black with deadwood and weeds.

Anything might live in a place that looks like this, Pen thought, and he shivered in spite of himself.

"The Inkrim," Kermadec announced, his voice flat and unemotional, a perfect match for his stolid Troll face. "Some say it is as old as the Races, and that the things that live there are older still. Some say there are things living down there that are as old as Faerie."

"Trees and dirt," Atalan muttered from behind Pen. "Nothing we haven't encountered before."

"And Urdas."

Atalan snorted. "Savages."

It seemed to Pen an odd comment coming from someone who looked vaguely like a walking tree stump, all bark and rough surfaces, as brutish and forbidding as anything that walked the Four Lands.

Kermadec must have thought the same. He looked at Atalan carefully. "Savages to us, but who are we to judge? In any event, I wouldn't be too quick to dismiss them. Urdas have lived in this valley since the destruction of the Old World. This is their ancestral home, and they regard it as sacred. Especially Stridegate. They will fight to protect it from outsiders. Like the Spider Gnomes on Toffer Ridge, they worship the creatures that share their abode, a symbiotic relationship, however one-sided, that influences their attitude toward intruders like us." He paused. "There are a lot of them down there, brother."

"Not enough to stop us, *brother*," Atalan replied, giving an edge to the last word that left no doubt about how he viewed the relationship. "We are the stronger force, no matter how few we are."

There was a hint of anger in Kermadec's eyes and a muttering among the other Rock Trolls. "You have never been down there," the Maturen said quietly. "I have. It isn't just trees and dirt. It isn't just Urdas, either. It is darkness of a different sort. Too many who thought as you do have disappeared into that darkness. If we are careless, we could end up the same way."

"Then we won't be careless, will we?" Atalan declared. His eyes flicked from his brother to Cinnaminson and Pen. "Lucky we have just the little people to help us. A blind girl who sees and a boy who speaks with lichen. What have we to fear?"

He shouldered his way forward and started down off the ledge, not bothering to see who might follow. Kermadec watched him go for a moment, then glanced back at the rest of the company and motioned them ahead.

The descent into the Inkrim was accomplished without incident. The trail down was not steep, though it was narrow and twisting, and at times even Pen, who was among the smallest, was forced to hug the cliff wall. The twilight deepened steadily all the while, and as it did so the valley came alive. Hushed before the change of light to dark, it began to hum and buzz with insect life. Night birds called out, their cries piercing and shrill as they took to the air in shadowy flocks, and Pen could hear grunts from ground animals, some recognizable, some not. He listened carefully as he walked and tried to sort them out. He searched for what sounded familiar amid the cacophony and failed.

At the bottom of the trail, the company made camp in a stand of fir. Even though they had reached the valley floor, they were still several thousand feet above sea level, cradled by the peaks of the Klu, and the air was clear and cold and the sky brilliant with stars and moonlight. As on past nights, Kermadec would not allow a fire. "Tomorrow," he promised. By then they would be deep enough into the territory of the Urdas that a fire would not draw Druid notice or, if spied, would not seem unusual to anyone searching for them. They would be risking discovery by the Urdas, of course, but that was a risk they were taking just by being there.

"The ruins of Stridegate lie much deeper in this valley, Pen," he told the boy later, when dinner had been consumed and they were sitting alone at the edge of the encampment. His blocky features were inscrutable, but his eyes were intense. "Two more days at least, and that's if we press ahead at a steady pace. I've been there, the one time I was in this valley before. I remember their look. It isn't a sight you are likely to forget."

"And the island?" Pen pressed. "The one that contains the tanequil?"

Overhearing their conversation, Khyber, Cinnaminson, and Tagwen had wandered over to join them. They sat down in a close circle, silent and attentive. Behind them, a pair of sentries had taken up positions just out of sight in the darkened trees. The rest of the Rock Trolls were settling in for the night, bulky forms lumbering through the darkness, the heavy clank and rasp of their weapons audible. Atalan was sitting not far away, hunched and unmoving, his back to his brother, his gaze directed into the forest dark.

"It is not an island of the sort you might imagine. It is surrounded not by water, but by a deep ravine choked with vines and trees. A single bridge spans its width, an ancient stone arch thousands of years old. It offers the only passage to the other side. But no one I know has ever crossed it."

"Why not?" Khyber asked at once.

Kermadec shook his head. "I am not superstitious in the manner of the Urdas, but I know the nature of the things that live within the Inkrim and I respect the power they wield. A warding stone placed on the near side of the bridge forbids passage. I try to pay attention to such things, when I can."

He paused. "I was told that others did not. Some attempted to cross anyway. There were rumors of a great treasure. A few used the stone arch. A few went down into the ravine with the intention of climbing out the other side. None were ever seen again."

"Then how are we to cross?" Khyber sounded suspicious and didn't bother keeping it from her voice. "Why are we any different than these others who couldn't?"

Kermadec shrugged. "I don't know that we are. I only know that we have to find out." He nodded toward Pen. "It is what is needed if we are to save the Ard Rhys."

He rose and walked back toward his sleeping Trolls. As he passed Atalan, he reached down and touched his shoulder. His brother glanced up and said something. Kermadec kept walking. A moment later, Atalan rose and followed him.

Khyber glanced at Pen and Tagwen, her brow furrowed. "I don't remember the Elfstones showing us anything about a bridge. I don't remember being warned about not being able to cross one."

"They don't always show you everything, do they?" Pen asked.

"I just think it odd that we're hearing about this for the first time now." She looked angry. "Did the King of the Silver River say anything to you about this?"

Pen shook his head. "Nothing." He wasn't any happier than she was about the bridge and its warning. "He told me to find the tanequil and ask it for a limb from which to fashion the darkwand, then to take the darkwand back to Paranor and use it to cross over into the Forbidding." His lips compressed. "Nothing about a bridge that no one is supposed to cross."

"What are the Trolls doing?" Cinnaminson asked suddenly, her blind eyes directed toward the encampment.

The other three turned to look. The Trolls were gathered in a circle, all of them, including Kermadec and Atalan. They were down on one knee, their blocky heads lowered, their palms flat against the ground, murmuring what seemed to be a chant. Now and then, one of them lifted a hand momentarily to touch fingertips to his forehead or lips.

"They are speaking to the valley," Tagwen said, pulling absently at his beard. "They are asking that it protect them against the dark spirits that live within it. It is an old custom among the Trolls, to seek the protection of the land they pass through and might have to fight upon."

Then, one by one, starting with Kermadec, the Trolls rose and walked around the circle, touching each Troll atop his head before returning to his place and kneeling to be touched in turn.

"Now they are pledging their lives in support of each other, promising that they will stand together as brothers should the spirits bless them with their protection and guidance." He cleared his throat. "I don't believe in this nonsense myself, but it seems to make them feel better."

The ritual continued for several minutes more. Then the Trolls rose and moved off, the sentries to their posts, the rest to their beds. Only Kermadec and Atalan remained where they were, talking quietly.

"Guess they've made their peace." Tagwen stretched and yawned. "I'm going to bed. Good night to all of you."

He moved off, and seconds later Khyber went, too. Pen sat alone with Cinnaminson in the darkness, their shoulders touching as they listened to the forest sounds.

"This valley is filled with spirits," the Rover girl said to him suddenly. Her fingers reached up to brush the air. "I can sense them all around, watching." She paused. "I think they might have been waiting for us. I don't know why they would do that, but they are very purposeful in their movements, very deliberate."

"Maybe they are here because they were called just now by the Trolls." Pen glanced at her. "Maybe they have come in response."

The girl nodded. "They might be here to offer protection. I don't sense hostility." She touched his hand. "I have an idea, Pen. Use your magic to ask them. You can communicate with living things of all sorts. Spirits are alive. See if they will speak to you."

He looked off into the velvet darkness, into the massed trees toward the black wall of the Inkrim, and wondered how to go about it. It began, in most cases, with whoever or whatever he was trying to communicate with making a sound or movement that he could interpret. A hawk might reveal its hunger or its desire for a mate through its cries. A rabbit might convey its fear by the way it looked at him. The way a small bird flew could reveal its urgency to reach its young. The brush of tree limbs or tall grasses against his face could tell him if they were in need of water. The movement of the wind told him of storms. He had once been warned of a wolf when a tiny ground squirrel darted through dried leaves.

But there was nothing to hear or see in this situation. Spirits did not always have a voice. They did not always take form. He would have to try something else.

He leaned forward and placed his hands against the earth, trying to read something from the feel of the ground. But after several minutes of patient concentration, there was still no response.

"No, Pen," Cinnaminson whispered suddenly, taking his hands and lifting them away. "These are spirits of the air. Reach up to them."

He did as she bid, holding up his hands with his fingers spread, as if to catch the feel of the wind. He held them steady, then moved them slowly about, groping for contact.

A moment later, he had it. Something brushed against his fingers ever so softly, just for a moment before it was gone. Then something else grazed his arm. He read purpose in those touchings; he found life. They were as gossamer as spider webbing and as ephemeral as birdsong, but they were old and therefore strong, too. They had lived a long time and seen a great deal. He could tell all that from a single touching, and it shocked him.

But they were gone as quickly as they had come, and they didn't return. After he told Cinnaminson what he had felt, he tried to reach for them several times more and could not find them.

"They are not ready for us to know them," the Rover girl said. "We must be patient. They will reveal themselves when they are ready."

Later, wrapped in his blanket, Pen thought for a long time before he drifted off to sleep about what form that revelation might take.

They set out at daybreak, moving into the heavy woods while the shadows still layered the earth in dark patches and the sunlight was a dim glow east through the canopy of the trees. The air was chilly and smelled of earth grown rich and fecund over time. The

night sounds were gone, replaced by morning birdsong and the soft
rustle of the wind through the leaves. The woods remained dark and
deep, as impenetrable to sight as a midnight pond, looking exactly
the same in all directions, the trees and grasses a wall against the outside world.

They traveled in single file, Kermadec leading, Atalan acting as
rear guard, and Pen and his companions placed squarely in the center of the line. The boy walked with Cinnaminson, his eyes sweeping the forest, his senses alert. He searched the shadows and treetops
for life, and more often than not, he found it. The Inkrim hummed
with activity, its life-forms a surprise at every turn. The birds were
often strange, colored and plumed in unfamiliar ways. There were
small ground animals that reminded him of squirrels and chipmunks,
but were something else. This valley and the creatures that lived
within it were old, Kermadec had said, and that suggested that their
origins could be found in the world that had existed before the Great
Wars. Certainly nothing of the world Pen knew seemed to have a
place here.

The day wore on and the sun lifted into the mountain sky, but little of its light penetrated to the forest floor. The night shadows remained thick and unbroken, and the air stayed cool and crisp. There
was a twilight feel to the valley, a peculiar absence of real daylight
and summer warmth. The woods produced their own climate, peculiarly suitable to this valley.

Now and then they would cross a trail. Narrow and poorly defined, the tracks meandered and ended abruptly, and there was little
about them to suggest that they might lead to anything. Kermadec
followed them when it was convenient to do so, but more often than
not kept to the off-trail breaks in the trees that offered easiest passage and clearest vision of their surroundings. He did not seem particularly concerned about what might be hiding from them and spent
no noticeable time searching the deep shadows. Perhaps his training
and experience reassured him that he would sense any danger lying
in wait. Perhaps it was his acceptance of the fact that in a place like
this, ancient and secretive, there was only so much you could do to
protect yourself.

Though he searched carefully at every turn, Pen did not see anything that day that seemed threatening. While at times the forest appeared dark and menacing, nothing dangerous ever materialized.

On the second day things changed.

They had enjoyed a fire and hot food the night before, the first of both in a week. They had drunk strong-flavored ale from skins the Trolls carried and slept undisturbed through the night. Rested and refreshed, they had set out again at dawn. This day looked very much like the first; the skies were more cloudy and the light paler, but the forests of the Inkrim seemed unchanged. Nevertheless, Pen felt a difference in things almost at once, a subtle distinction that at first lacked a source. It was only after he had been walking a while that he realized that the forest sounds were quieter, the wind softer, and the air warmer. Even these didn't seem to him to be the source of the problem, and he was plagued by a nagging certainty that he was missing something.

"Does everything seem all right to you?" he asked Cinnaminson finally.

"You sense them, too, don't you?" she replied at once. She was walking next to him, keeping close.

He stared at her, then glanced around quickly, scanning the forest shadows, the deep mottled black and green of the trunks and grasses, of the limbs and leaves. "Is someone there?"

"In the trees. Hiding. Watching. More than one."

He exhaled slowly. "I sensed them, but I didn't know what they were. How long have they been there?"

"Since we started out. They must have found us during the night." She brushed back loose strands of her honey-colored hair. "I thought they were the spirits of the air at first, the ones from last night. But these are creatures of flesh and blood." She paused. "They track us."

Pen took her hand and squeezed it. His eyes swept the trees. "Wait here. I'll tell Kermadec."

But Kermadec already knew. "Urdas," he advised, bending close to Pen to whisper the word. "Not many of them, but enough to keep us in sight without showing themselves. They're working in relays, small groups of them, each leapfrogging ahead of the others in turn to pick us up as we come past, bracketing us so that we don't get away."

Pen felt his heart quicken. "What do they want?"

The Maturen glanced over. His barklike features made him seem one with the trees. "They want to know what we are doing here. They will stay with us until they are sure."

Pen dropped back again, falling into step with Cinnaminson. "He says he knows about them. He says they are just watching us."

The Rover girl smiled. "Someone is watching them, too." Her blind eyes shifted to find his. "The spirits of the air didn't leave, after all. They are still out there."

The morning passed away, and the clouds massed and darkened overhead. A storm was blowing in, and it would bring a heavy rain. Kermadec began to look for shelter, but there were no caves or rocky overhangs to keep them dry. Instead, they crawled beneath the protective boughs of a huge fir, hunkering down when the cloudburst struck, staying put until the rains had slowed to a drizzle, then crawling out again, dampened and chilled, to begin walking once more.

That night, they camped in the lee of a lightning-split hardwood that had once risen hundreds of feet into the air and was now as dead as old cornstalks. Its leaves were gone and its limbs blackened and bare, charred bones on a skeleton. All around its shattered trunk, the ground was burned and denuded as well, and their fire cast its broken giant's shadow into the enfolding darkness. Kermadec doubled the watch, and Pen hardly slept at all. Overhead, clouds scudded across the stars and bats darted through the night like wraiths.

The third day dawned gray and damp, but the rains did not return. The company set out at daybreak, the Urdas tracking it from somewhere in the trees where Pen still could not see them, even if Kermadec could. Pen was tired and irritable from a restless night, and he was unnerved by the constant, unseen presence. His spirits lifted only marginally when Kermadec assured him that they were getting closer to their destination; seeing would be believing.

By midmorning, the look of the Inkrim had undergone a noticeable change. The trees had become massive and twisted, a forest of ancient behemoths that crowded out everything smaller and left the valley floor barren and stark. The gray light filtering through the clouds was diffused further by the canopy of leaves and branches. The forest was shadowy and gray at every turn, and the air had grown thin and stale. Birdsong and insect buzzing disappeared, and the ground animals faded away. There was a hushed quality to the landscape that reminded the boy of places where only dead things were found. He heard the sound of his own breathing as he walked. He could hear the beating of his heart.

"I don't like this place anymore," Cinnaminson whispered to him at one point, and took his hand in her own.

Sometime around midday, Pen saw the Urdas for the first time. They appeared all at once, coming out of the shadows, sliding from behind tree trunks, materializing out of nowhere. Even though he had never seen one before, he knew what they were immediately. They had a primitive, dangerous look to them. Physically, they appeared to be a cross between Trolls and Gnomes. Their bodies were small and wiry like those of the latter, but their skin was thick and barklike and their faces blunt and flat like the former. They were covered in a tangle of wiry hair, their Trollish features flat and expressionless. Short, muscular legs and long arms allowed them to move sideways in crab fashion as they shadowed the company on both sides through the ancient trees.

"Stay together," Kermadec called back over his shoulder. "Don't provoke them. They're only watching."

But more were appearing at every turn, gathering at the fringes of the hazy light in large clusters. Gradually, they began to surround the company. For the first time, Pen noticed the nature of the weapons they carried, a mix of short spears and odd-shaped flat objects that were hooked and sharpened on their ends and appeared to be designed for throwing.

"How far do we have to go?" Atalan called to his brother from his rear-guard position.

Kermadec glanced back and shook his head. "I'm not sure. It's been a long time. Another few miles, maybe. This forest runs all the way to the ruins of the city. Keep moving."

Moments later, more Urdas appeared directly in front of them, narrowing the way forward even farther. They were beginning to close in, Pen realized. He did a quick count; more than a hundred were set to block the way. The flat, dark faces were expressionless, but the way they hefted their weapons and the deliberate stances they had assumed suggested the nature of their intentions.

"Khyber Elessedil!" Kermadec called out. He beckoned her forward. The rest of the company closed in behind them, sensing that things were about to change. "Can you work a little Druid magic to make them move back?" the Maturen asked.

She frowned. "I can. But if I do that—"

"Yes, it may give us away to the Druids," he cut her short. "But if you don't, the Urdas are going to try to take us prisoner. They have made up their minds that we intend to invade the ruins, and they won't allow it. There are too many to fight. Magic offers us our best chance of escaping, even if you use just a little of it. They are afraid of what they don't understand."

She glanced back at Pen, giving him a look that suggested this was all his fault. "All right," she agreed. "I can scare them. Then what happens?"

Kermadec shrugged. "Then, we run. If we can get to the ruins, they won't follow us in. The ruins are sacred ground, forbidden to them. They'll leave us to the spirits."

Of which we already know there are some, Pen thought. But he understood they hadn't any better choice.

"Stand ready," Khyber said, her hands already beginning to weave in small circles.

An instant later, the air was filled with bits of fire that screamed and flew in all directions, a cloudburst of sound and light that sent the Urdas scrambling away in terror.

"Run!" Kermadec shouted.

The Trolls and their charges raced ahead through the trees and shadows. Kermadec led the way. As big as he was, he moved like a deer, leaping and bounding past scrambling Urdas and around ancient trunks with his war club swinging. Cinnaminson ran with Pen, holding his hand, letting him lead the way. The forest was open enough that she could do so, and he matched his pace to hers, quickly discovering she was almost as swift as he was.

Behind them, Tagwen lumbered mightily, his breath coming in short gasps, his stubby legs churning.

The whirlwind of fire darts lasted another few minutes, and then it faded, leaving a residue of smoke trails that lifted toward the canopy like tiny butterflies. It took a few minutes for the Urdas to collect themselves, and then they were in pursuit. They came through the trees in droves, small, wiry bodies leaping and scrambling, calling out in sudden, high shrieks that cut to the bone. Seconds later, their strange throwing weapons began to whiz through the air with deep humming sounds, slicing off small limbs and burying themselves in tree trunks. Had Pen and his companions been in the open and standing still, they would have been cut down in moments. Moving through the woods, they were less easy to hit. Nevertheless, Pen found himself running faster.

The chase wore on for a mile, then two. The Trolls were tireless, and Pen and his companions were driven by fear, so they managed to keep just ahead of the Urdas. When Tagwen faltered, one of the Trolls snatched him right off his feet, tucked him under one arm, and kept running. But the distance between hunter and hunted was closing fast. When Pen finally risked a quick glance over his shoulder, he found the Urdas right behind Atalan and the other two Trolls who were acting as rear guards. The throwing weapons mostly bounced off the Trolls like sticks, but Pen could see blood showing through rents in the leather tunics.

Then one of the Trolls running with Atalan caught a spear in the back of the neck above his protective vest, and he went down in a heap. Kermadec's brother turned instantly, shouted for help, and charged back into the pursuing Urdas with such ferocity that they were bowled over and scattered. Khyber wheeled around as well, words of magic tumbling from her lips, hands weaving. A fresh assault of fire darts flew at the Urdas, shrieking and burning. But this time the Urdas didn't flee. Ducking behind trees and flattening themselves to the ground, they simply waited out the barrage.

Atalan bent quickly over the fallen Troll. A moment later, he was back on his feet.

"Dead!" he snapped at no one in particular. Then, seeing Pen and Cinnaminson frozen in place and staring at him, he shouted, "Run, you fools!"

Everyone turned and began to race ahead once more. But the members of the company were winded, worn down by the chase and the never-ending number of pursuers. Already, more Urdas were after them, ignoring the fire darts, tearing through the trees and flinging their weapons with wild shrieks.

Then one of those weapons found Pen, catching him just behind the knees and toppling him in a wash of pain and blood.

It happened so fast that he was down on the ground almost before he realized what was happening. He had the presence of mind to let go of Cinnaminson as he was struck, so that she was not pulled down with him. But he tumbled hard, and when he tried to rise he found his legs would not work. Lying crippled on the ground, he would have died then if not for Atalan. The burly Rock Troll swept him up as he charged past, tucked him under his arm, pounded up to where Cinnaminson stood staring in petrified disbelief thinking she had lost Pen, and snatched her up as well.

"Can't be losing you now, little man," he hissed at Pen, racing after the others as missiles flew all around them. "Not after all the trouble you've caused us."

Somehow he eluded the Urda weapons flung at him, caught up to the others in the company, and matched their pace. Jounced and shaken in the crook of Atalan's arm, Pen was aware of how hard carrying him must be, how much strength it must require. But the Rock Troll didn't seem winded, just angry.

Ahead, more Urdas appeared, closing ranks in a line of dark, gnarled bodies. Beyond, the trees thinned, and the remains of rock walls and stone columns lifted against a backdrop of trees and mountains, their colors hazy in the grayish light. Kermadec yelled to his

Trolls, and five of them joined him in a tight formation of armored bodies and heavy clubs and axes. The rest of the company, including Atalan, fell into place behind him. There was no time to think about what they were doing; they were on top of the Urdas almost before Pen realized what they intended. The Trolls went through the Urda ranks as if they were made of paper. Weapons slashed and cut, but the Trolls fought past any resistance with ferocious purpose, and in seconds the entire company was through.

Again, the razor-sharp missiles flew after them, but this time they were thrown halfheartedly and to little effect. The effort to keep the intruders from the ruins had failed. Prevented by their beliefs from pursuing further, the Urdas clustered at the edge of the trees and screamed in fury. But by the time Kermadec and his Trolls had collapsed inside the first set of crumbling walls, putting Pen and his companions safely behind the protective stone barriers, the screaming had stopped.

In the ensuing silence, Pen Ohmsford listened to the pounding of his heart.

TWENTY-TWO

Lying on the ground beside a clearly winded Atalan, Pen managed to lift his head far enough to look back at his pursuers. A sea of staring eyes, the Urdas were hunkered down in knots all along the edge of the forest. The sudden silence was unnerving. It was as if they were waiting for something to happen, something they knew about that Pen and his companions did not. Pen looked over his shoulder into the ruins. Other than rubble, weeds, and a scattering of saplings that fronted the sprawl of walls of columns beyond, there was nothing to see.

"Savages," Atalan muttered.

Pen gave up on the Urdas and looked down at his legs. There was blood all over where the skin had been broken and the flesh gouged by Urda weapons. Cinnaminson moved over beside him, running her hands over his calves, exploring the wounds, her touch so gentle he could barely feel it. He marveled anew at how she could see so clearly what to do when she was unable to use her eyes. Her blind gaze found his face, as if she knew what he was thinking, and her sudden smile was so dazzling that it took his breath away.

"It doesn't feel as if the tendons have been severed or the bones broken," she said.

Beyond the walls of their shelter, the Urdas suddenly began to chant, breaking the momentary silence. The words of the chant were indistinguishable, but their purpose was clear.

"Look at them," Atalan growled. "Afraid to do anything more than stand out there and hope that by calling on their spirit guardians something bad will happen to us. Stupid."

"They do the only thing they know to do," Cinnaminson said quietly.

The Rock Troll glanced over at her, his gaze flat and unfriendly. "Don't make excuses for them, blind girl. They don't deserve it. They would have killed you."

"A blind girl understands something about the need for excuses," she replied, turning her empty eyes toward his face. "A blind girl perceives savagery differently than you do, I think."

Kermadec appeared and knelt down beside them. Without a word, he took out his hunting knife, cut off Pen's pant legs, and used the scraps of cloth to bind the wounds. "You can wash and dress this later, once we are deeper into the ruins and safely away from the Urdas."

Pen nodded. "I'll be all right."

Kermadec moved away again, and Pen looked over at Atalan. "I owe you my life," he said.

The burly Troll glanced at him, startled. His blunt features tightened. "You don't owe me anything, little man," he replied.

Then he rose with a grunt and walked away.

Perplexed, Pen stared after him. "What is wrong with him? Why is he so unfriendly?"

"He isn't sure how he feels about what he has just done," Cinnaminson answered. "He doesn't know why he did it." She touched his shoulder. "This doesn't have to do with you, Pen. It has to do with his brother and himself. I think almost everything does."

Pen thought about that for a time, sitting with his back to the wall and listening to the Urdas chant, and decided she was probably right. Atalan's relationship with his brother was complex and disturbing, and he didn't think there was much point in trying to understand it without knowing a good deal more than he did. He glanced over at Khyber Elessedil, who was sitting by herself, looking off into the ruins, and then at Tagwen, who sat with his head between his legs, as if he was sick to his stomach. Pen didn't like it that the four outlanders had become so dependent on the Trolls. He couldn't put his finger on why that bothered him so, but he thought it had more than a little to do with his uncertainty about Kermadec and Atalan. Rock Trolls were strange enough in their own right without the un-welcome addition of sibling conflict; it only heightened his uneasi-ness to think that at some point their safety might depend on how well the brothers could manage to get along. He knew how highly Tagwen thought of Kermadec, but Kermadec was only one man. They would have to depend on the other Trolls, as well, and that in-cluded Atalan.

How much did Atalan care about what happened to them?

It was an unfair question, of course. Atalan had just saved his life. There was no reason for him to be suspicious.

Nevertheless, he was.

Kermadec allowed them a short rest, then gathered them to-gether again. They knelt behind the wall at the edge of the ruins, lis-tening as the Urda chant rose and fell in a steady, monotonous rhythm.

"We're going now," he said quietly, ignoring the wailing. "I want us to be at the bridge by nightfall. We will make camp there, then cross in the morning, when it is light and we can see clearly. I don't think the Urdas will come after us. They are afraid of the spirits and won't chance angering them, no matter how badly they want to get their hands on us. They will rely on the spirits to punish us for them."

He paused. "Still, I don't want to take anything for granted. So we will leave quietly and in secret, just two or three of us at a time."

At the mention of spirits, Pen glanced at Cinnaminson, but the Rover girl was staring straight ahead.

"Young Penderrin," Kermadec said, causing Pen to jump. "You and your Rover girl will go first. I want you to keep a sharp watch for anything moving once we start inside. I've been here only once, years ago, and I barely got past these walls. What I know, I've heard from others, and none of it is reliable. I know of the bridge and the island. I know of the thing that sleeps in the ravine. But there may be other dangers, and I depend on you, with your special talents, to warn us of them."

Pen nodded. He noticed that Khyber looked relieved. The onus of having to risk using her Druid magic again had been lifted for the moment. As Kermadec finished his instructions to Pen and Cinnaminson and turned his attention to his Trolls, Pen moved over to the Elven girl. "Well done, Khyber," he said. "That was a clever bit of magic back there. You saved us all."

She nodded. "At a cost I don't care to contemplate."

"You think you gave us away? You think we were detected?"

She shrugged. "I don't know. I didn't use much magic, and what I did use is not so different from what can already be found in this valley. Elemental magic, in its purest form. The Inkrim is known to the Druids as a place of such magic. Ahren told me of it on the way." She hesitated. "I might not have attracted any attention at all. But I can't be sure. I can't really be sure about anything."

She shook her head. "Ahren would know, if he were here. He would do better at this."

Pen leaned close. "Don't talk like that. I know you miss him. I miss him, too. I know it would be easier if he were still alive." He lowered his gaze quickly when she wheeled on him, her eyes hot and angry, but he kept talking. "He gave you the responsibility for what happens to all of us. He knew what he was doing. You've saved us twice now, Khyber. I know we have placed ourselves in the hands of these Trolls, but it's you we depend on. It's you who really keeps us safe."

He lifted his gaze again. She was still staring at him, but the anger had drained away. "Sometimes I think you are older than you look, Penderrin," she said.

Kermadec was motioning that it was time to go. Pen reached over and squeezed Khyber's hand. "We'll be all right."

The Maturen led Pen and Cinnaminson away from the rest of the company and into the ruins, creeping across the open spaces behind the crumbling wall to gain the concealment of the undergrowth and rubble beyond. The terrain was uneven and difficult to navigate, and it took them some time to make their way through the weeds and debris. Pen turned his attention to his surroundings, searching out any indication of danger. All he sensed were insects, ground birds, and small animals. Stands of trees rose from the piles of broken stone in sparse clumps, casting shadows across the open spaces like wooden fingers, marking the progress of the sun west. There weren't more than a couple of hours of daylight left, and it was already obvious to the boy that Stridegate was much bigger than he had assumed. He saw bits and pieces of it poking out of the hills farther in and to either side of where they walked. He found himself wondering how old the city was and who had inhabited it. Once, it must have been enormous.

He kept his questions to himself. There would be a better time to ask them. He looked over at Cinnaminson, noted the concentration etched on her face, glanced back the way they had come, saw nothing of the others, and turned to what lay ahead.

They walked for a long time, more than an hour by his estimation, and Stridegate's look never changed. At times, he thought he detected movement, but he was never able to pinpoint its source or its nature. He wanted to ask Cinnaminson if she noticed anything, but he decided that if she did and if it was important, she would say something. The daylight was beginning to fade more rapidly by then, the shadows to lengthen and the sky to darken. Pen was growing hungry and wondered if they would be permitted a fire.

The others caught up with them shortly afterwards, appearing in small groups until the entire company had re-formed. Atalan, bringing up the rear, reported that there was no indication of pursuit by the Urdas, who seemed content to remain outside the ruins. He started to say something more, then glanced at Cinnaminson and turned away.

They continued on, walking into the twilight, watching the shadows lengthen and feeling the air turn brisk as the mountain breezes increased. The Inkrim closed them away, yet they could still catch glimpses of the jagged peaks of the Klu through a cloak of mist and clouds that wrapped the tips of the mountains. Pen felt the enormity of those peaks, their immutability, their weight and age. They made him feel small and vulnerable, and he wished more than once he were somewhere else.

Then, all at once, it seemed as if he were. The ruins underwent a sudden and dramatic change that brought the entire company to a shocked halt. They had reached the entrance to a wall that, while ancient and worn, was almost whole. But beyond that wall, all evidence of time's passing vanished. Spread out before them were gardens of such incredible beauty that it seemed as if they belonged to another place entirely. Blankets of columbine tumbled from rock walls. Fields of mountain violets, lupine, shooting stars, and paintbrush spread away in a dazzling mix of colors. Rhododendrons twenty feet high clustered against walls riddled with ferns and tiny yellow blossoms Pen had never seen. Clumps of pink-tipped heather grew everywhere.

There were fountains, ponds, and streams, too, their waters rippling and shimmering dark silver in the fading light. There were walkways formed of crushed stone and tile, set with benches of polished stone. There were shrines filled with strange images and inset with precious metals. There were columns of marble and granite. For as far as the eye could see, that part of Stridegate looked to have been untouched by time.

"How can this be?" Tagwen whispered, coming up to stand beside Pen. "Who could have done this?"

"Not those Urdas," Khyber whispered back.

Pen didn't hear them. He was listening to something else, something the others couldn't hear. It was a voice, deep and resonant. He couldn't locate its source, but he could hear it clearly. It was speaking to him. It was calling his name.

Kermadec and his Trolls were fanning out through the gardens, searching for hidden dangers, suspicious of what they were seeing. *As they should be*, Pen was thinking, still listening to the voice.

"Something lives here," Cinnaminson whispered, her smooth face lifting toward the light. "Something waits."

Pen shook his head slowly. The voice that called his name went silent. He was aware of something else then, perhaps the same thing that had attracted Cinnaminson's attention. It was close, but it was deep underground, he thought. It was huge and ancient. It was not human. He was sensing it through his magic at every turn. He was reading it from the things that grew in the gardens, from the small rustlings and movements of the plants and flowers, vines and grasses. They whispered of it. They responded to it. Insects and birds and animals, they carried knowledge of it. They could not give it a name or a description; they could only give it a presence.

Pen took a deep breath. "I sense it, too," he whispered.

Cinnaminson was already moving ahead into the gardens, her sun-browned face intense and her blind eyes sweeping over everything as if seeing what no one else could. She moved swiftly and determinedly, passing by Kermadec, who turned at her approach but did not try to stop her. Instead he joined her and beckoned for the others to follow.

Khyber was already hurrying after them. Pen stood rooted in place, still hesitating.

"There is something wrong here," Tagwen said uneasily, standing beside him. "These gardens are beautiful, but there is something wrong about them."

Pen felt it, too, although he couldn't explain it. "We'd better go."

They followed the others, Pen casting wary glances left and right, still searching for the voice, for the presence, for anything that would explain what they were seeing. But nothing appeared, and the gardens stretched on in a profusion of brilliant colors and sweet smells. Even in the enfolding twilight, they shimmered with a vibrancy that seemed so foreign to everything that had gone before that it was as if the travelers had entered a dream world.

Pen stared about in wonder. How could it be possible?

They caught up to the rest of the company, which was still following Cinnaminson. The Rover girl was walking as if she knew exactly where she was going, her head lifted into the breeze, her path steady and undeviating. It seemed to Pen as if she were listening to something. He wondered suddenly if the spirits of the air had returned, if she was responding to their voices.

Was that who he had sensed, as well?

The group reached a set of broad stone stairs that led upward until they disappeared into the twilight haze. Cinnaminson never paused. She began to climb the steps as soon as she reached them, and the rest of them had no choice but to follow if they were to see where she was going. Pen and Tagwen still trailed the larger group. The boy was beginning to sense something again, a stirring or a whisper, it was hard to tell. He put out feelers, reaching for what was clearly there, but although he could sense it easily, he could not identify it. There was something confusing about what he was finding; it was almost as if he lacked a frame of reference with which to understand it.

At the top of the stairs, the little company came to a halt behind Cinnaminson, who had stopped finally and was pointing ahead. The Rover girl's face was intense and she was breathing hard. Kermadec was trying to talk to her, but she wasn't responding. Pen, seeing what was happening, abandoned Tagwen and hurried forward.

"Cinnaminson," he said, taking her by the shoulders and turning her to face him.

Her young face was flushed with excitement. "We have to go there. We have to follow them," she said.

He looked in the direction she was pointing. An ancient stone arch, pitted by weather and time, bridged from the grassy area on which they stood to a forest of massive trees that sat atop a pinnacle of rock, a forested island surrounded by a deep ravine that ringed it like a moat, stretching away for as far as his eyes could see in the rapidly dimming daylight. The trees on the pinnacle were tall and straight and unbroken, rising hundreds of feet against the skyline, their bark mottled by greenish gray patches of moss. Their branches were deeply intertwined, forming a canopy so thick that it shut away the sky, but their trunks were widely spaced and the ground beneath opened through, clear and uncluttered by undergrowth. The forest backed away from the edge of the ravine in front of them until it joined with the curtain of the encroaching night.

Cinnaminson lowered her head against his shoulder, as if all the strength had gone out of her. "Did you hear them, too, Pen? Did you hear their voices?"

He wrapped her in his arms and stroked her long hair. "The spirits of the air?" he guessed. "The ones from before?"

She nodded. "From the edge of the gardens. Did you hear them?"

"I sensed them, but they spoke only to you." *Something else spoke to me.*

"No. It wasn't speaking. They didn't use words. But I knew what they wanted. For us to follow them. For us to cross to the island."

Pen looked again at the narrow stone arch and the forested pinnacle of rock beyond. The top of the pinnacle was mostly flat, though rock formations jutted from between the old growth and ravines split the forest floor. The interior of the woods was dark and shadowed in the failing light. It was difficult to tell how deep in it went.

"Is the tanequil in there?" he asked quietly. "Is this the place?"

She hesitated, then lifted her head to stare blindly at him. "Something is in there. Something is waiting."

Kermadec touched Pen on the shoulder and, when he turned, directed his attention to a flat-faced boulder into which symbols had been carved, the markings so worn they were almost unreadable.

"This is the warning of which I spoke," the Maturen advised. "Written in the Gnome language. Very old. It tells strangers that the place is forbidden. It warns that to cross the bridge is death." He looked at the boy. "We can't risk you going until we know. One of us will have to go first."

"No!" Cinnaminson said sharply. Her eyes were suddenly frantic. "No one is to cross but Pen and me. We alone are permitted entry. The spirits of the air insist!"

Atalan gave an audible snort and looked off into the trees. Tagwen began rubbing at his beard the way he did when he was anxious.

"They told you this?" Kermadec pressed her. "These spirits? You are not mistaken?"

"It doesn't matter," Khyber interrupted. "I'm going with them, whatever these spirits say. Ahren gave the responsibility of making this journey to me. He gave me the only real weapon we have. The Elfstones will protect us. And I have the use of Druid magic. Whatever threatens, I will be able to keep it at bay."

"No," Cinnaminson said again. She walked over to Khyber and embraced her. "Please, Khyber, no. The warning is clear. You cannot come with us. I wish you could. But whatever lies on the other side is for Pen alone."

"And for you, it seems," Khyber said quietly.

"And for me." Cinnaminson released her and stepped back. There were tears in her eyes. "I'm sorry. I don't understand why the spirits have chosen me. But my sense of what they want is very clear. Pen is to go and I am to go with him. But you cannot come. You must not."

"This could easily be a trap," Atalan pointed out, his flat face dark with suspicion as he swung back around again. "You are awfully trusting of invisible voices, Rover girl. If they have bad intentions, you will likely be dead before you know of them."

"He is right," Khyber agreed. "You are too trusting."

Cinnaminson shook her head. "They are not dangerous to us. They mean us no harm. I have felt them guiding us ever since we entered Stridegate. They are a presence meant to shelter us, not to cause us harm."

She turned to Kermadec. "Please. They have been waiting for us. They want something from us, but they won't tell us what it is until we cross the bridge." She hesitated. "What choice do we have but to do as they expect? Pen has come in search of the tanequil, and the Elfstones have shown it to be on this island. Doesn't he have to cross over and find out if it is really there?"

There was a long silence as the other members of the company looked at one another uneasily. Even the Rock Trolls, who spoke little of her language, seemed to sense what was happening. Already on edge from their encounter with the Urdas, they were suspicious of everything in this strange place. Stridegate belonged to the past, to a time dead and gone. They had intruded on that past by going there, and they were anxious to do what was needed and be gone again. Most looked to Kermadec, waiting on his decision.

Cinnaminson turned to Pen, her blind eyes empty, but her face bright with expectation. "You understand, don't you, Pen? You know what we have to do. Will you cross with me?"

The boy nodded. "I will." He looked at Kermadec. "There is nothing to be gained by sending someone on ahead. It would be a pointless sacrifice that would tell us nothing. Cinnaminson and I are the ones who must test the warning."

He could tell that the big Troll was unhappy with the idea, the impassive face giving away just enough to reveal his displeasure. The Maturen glanced at Tagwen and then Khyber, shaking his head. "I don't like it, but his point is well taken. We won't know anything if we don't let them try. We will have come all this way for nothing."

Atalan walked to the edge of the ravine and peered down. "It's deep enough that I cannot make out the bottom. Maybe there isn't one." He looked back at them. "If you fall off that bridge, boy, we will have come all this way for nothing, anyway."

"Tie a rope around his waist," Khyber suggested suddenly. "Tie one to each of them. It couldn't hurt."

They did so, the trolls knotting the ropes in place and taking up positions on both sides of the bridge, ready to haul back should it be required. Pen felt foolish, trussed as he was. He thought the effort pointless. If the spirits of the air or whatever else dwelled in that place wanted them dead, they were not going to be able to save themselves anyway.

He looked at Cinnaminson and wished she weren't involved. It was bad enough risking his life. He didn't care to risk hers, as well. It wasn't her fight. It had nothing to do with her. She was here because of him, and that was unforgivable.

"Pen." Khyber came up to him. "I will stand at the edge of the ravine when you cross. If anything threatens—anything at all—I will use the Druid magic and the Elfstones to help you." Her lips tightened. "I won't fail you."

He nodded and smiled. "You haven't yet, Khyber."

Cinnaminson took hold of his hand. Pen looked around at those assembled, those who had come with him on the quest. The trolls stared back, blank-faced and imperturbable. Tagwen was tugging on his beard, but he managed an encouraging nod. Khyber was already at the edge of the ravine, the Elfstones gripped in her hand, her dark face alert and watchful.

Pen took a deep breath and exhaled slowly. With Cinnaminson's hand in his own, he began to walk toward the bridge.

A s he approached, Pen was able to take a closer look at the bridge, and what he saw gave him pause. It was narrow, less than eight feet wide, and provided no handholds to protect against a fall. *You don't want to walk too close to the edge,* he thought. *You don't want to look down.*

But it was the nature of its construction that troubled him most. The bridge was formed of massive stone blocks cut and placed so precisely that the seams were barely noticeable. Each block was wedge shaped, with the narrow part pointed downward, the blocks carefully fitted and aligned so that the weight of each was buttressed by the others, the whole arranged to form the arch that spanned the ravine. There were no pins or supports or any kind. Stone abutments at each end wrapped the corners, serving as cradles to keep the stones tightly pressed together and immobile.

But the massive blocks each must have weighed thousands of pounds. How had they been shaped, carried, and placed across the ravine without underlying supports? They could not have just hung in midair, each in turn, while the rest were fitted. Pen could not fathom it. Even using pulleys and a block and tackle it would have been impossible to suspend the first stones while waiting to set the others. They were too big, too heavy, and too cumbersome.

There was something else to consider, he saw. These stones were not as old as those of the ruins themselves. They were smooth and not yet worn and pitted by weather and time as were the walls behind which Pen and his companions had hidden earlier. Stridegate was thousands of years old. The bridge was much newer. It had been constructed long after the city was destroyed and its inhabitants dead.

The implications of his reasoning caused him to shiver; they made him want to turn around right then and there and go back.

It would have taken at least one giant to construct this bridge. It would have taken technology that no longer existed in his world.

Or it would have taken a very powerful magic.

He didn't care for any of those possibilities. All were beyond anything the group had ever encountered. It dwarfed them, reducing their tiny defenses to a handful of pebbles. Even Khyber, with the magic of the Elfstones to aid her, would not be able to stand against something that could accomplish what he saw before him.

He stopped abruptly, not five feet from the bridge, and stood staring at it. Sensing his discomfort, Cinnaminson whispered, "Pen? What's wrong?"

He didn't know what to say in reply, how to explain. He wasn't sure he should try. He couldn't turn back, couldn't give up. The Ard Rhys needed him to go forward if she was to have any chance at all of escaping the Forbidding. Those he had come with needed him to cross if they were to realize any success from their efforts to bring him there. All other considerations, no matter how daunting, had to be put aside.

He was just a boy, but he knew instinctively what he must do.

"Nothing's wrong," he said, squeezing her hand reassuringly. "Don't worry."

He started forward again, leading her onto the bridge, reaching out with his senses into the twilight shadows that now draped everything from the forested pinnacle to the ravine that surrounded it to the bridge that reached to it. He used his tiny magic, his strange gift, to seek anything that might be waiting. Whispers came back to him, small rustlings and little hissings. They came from unidentifiable sources, from the impenetrable dark, from the void. He heard them, but could not make sense of them. He sorted through them swiftly, seeking just one that he might recognize.

Nothing.

He glanced over the side of the bridge into the ravine, into the pooled darkness. His gaze tightened. Was something moving down there?

He slowed, caution once again taking hold.

–Cross–

A chorus of voices spoke, all sounding the same, all whispering in perfect unison. They echoed in his mind, clear as the ringing of a bell. He started in shock, then glanced quickly at Cinnaminson.

"The spirits of the air," she said softly. "Can you can hear them, too?"

He nodded, surprised that he could, wondering why they were speaking to him, as well.

–Cross–

Fairy voices, soft and feminine. Telling him to come ahead, to do what they had brought him to do.

"Who are you?" he whispered.

–Aeriads. Spirits of the air–

"What is the matter?" Khyber called out to them, a disembodied voice from somewhere behind. "Are you all right?"

He waved back at her without looking.

–Cross–

The whispers urged him to obey, and he did so, not knowing why exactly, not understanding the nature of his readiness to do as they commanded, only knowing that he should. He moved slowly, one careful step at a time, climbing toward the apex of the stone arch, watching the island pinnacle draw steadily closer.

"Where do you come from?" he whispered, not really expecting an answer, but curious anyway.

–From our father and mother. From seedlings strewn far and wide. From wind and rain and time–

Surprised, Pen considered the words. He had no idea what they meant, but the word *seedlings* caught his attention.

"Are you children of the tanequil? Is the tree your father?"

–Our father and our mother. One lives in light; one dwells in dark. One has limbs; one has roots. They wait for you–

Pen shook his head. At the center of the bridge, at the apex of the stone arch, suspended above the dark void of the ravine, he was suddenly aware of something stirring down in the depths, down where he couldn't see. His senses warned him, but he could not trace that warning to anything specific. He just knew. He froze in response, feeling Cinnaminson do the same. She was aware of it, as well. It wasn't the rustle of grasses or the whisper of leaves. This was something much larger—like the heavy rub of a massive animal passing through brush or the drag of logs, cut and chained, through dry earth. But it wasn't localized like that, either. It was spread all through the ravine, twisting and turning along ruts and down sinkholes, oozing and burrowing through dirt and under loose stone.

Mirrored in the sharp glare of the setting sun, a vision flashed before his eyes. Out of that glare, a monstrous apparition took shape, vague and unformed, a thing of tentacles and feelers, of crushing strength and brutal response. He saw in its grip the bodies of humans and animals alike. He saw them break and bleed. He watched their struggles and heard their cries. He cringed from the vision, turning quickly away, closing his eyes to shut out the sights and sounds.

–Cross–

The ropes that had been bound about their waists fell away as if severed by knives. Shouts and cries ensued from those left behind, but quickly faded.

–Cross–

The voices of the aeriads called to him once more, firm and insistent. Keeping tight hold of Cinnaminson, he moved swiftly ahead, no longer even glancing toward the ravine. The shadows had thickened with the twilight, and it seemed as if, sinewy and rapacious, they were trying to climb from the ravine, out of the darkness and into the light. Pen walked more quickly still, trying to ignore their presence, to block away his perception of the thing below, to ignore the possibility that it was attempting to find him.

Then he was across, safely off the bridge, standing on the solid

rock of the pinnacle amid a fringe of trees and brush, just another of
the twilight shadows. He no longer sensed the thing in the ravine.
He no longer felt it coming for him. He breathed slowly and deeply,
steadying himself, pushing back his fear. He was all right. He was
safe.

He looked over at Cinnaminson, whose shadow-streaked face
was pale and drawn, etched with lines of fear. He squeezed her hand.
"We're across. It isn't coming anymore."

She nodded that she understood, but her tension would not be so
easily dispelled.

–Come–

The aeriads had no time or interest in fear, it seemed. Pen and
Cinnaminson started ahead once more, moving into the trees. Night
descended, the moon and stars appeared, and the texture of the light
changed. Slowly, their vision adjusted, and they were able to see well
enough to know how to place their feet. The trees closed about
them, towering old-growth giants, age-worn sentinels of that strange
place. Pen could almost feel them watching, waiting to see what he
and Cinnaminson would do. The forest was deep and still, and it was
living. Pen stepped lightly, gingerly, thinking it made a difference
where and how he walked. The earth was soft, carpeted with needles, damp and smelling of mulch and rot. He did not hear the
sounds of night birds or small animals. He did not see anything
move.

–Come–

The aeriads led them with whispered encouragement, leading
them through the forest, between the massive old trees, down the
ravines and across the ridges, over the rocky outcroppings and
around the steep drops. The path was circuitous and unknowable, a
thread that no one who hadn't traveled it many times before could
hope to find. Pen could not explain it, but he had the curious feeling that it might not even be possible to travel the same path twice,
that it might somehow be different each time. Even though comprised
of earth and rock, streams and trees—solid, knowable things—that
place felt as if it were ephemeral and ever shifting. There was a
changeling quality to it, a mutability that turned it from solid to liq-

uid, from a terrain of the physical to a dreamscape of the mind. Pen had the feeling that it wasn't a place you could go to if you weren't a guest of its maker.

It was a place, he thought suddenly, in which the King of the Silver River would feel at home.

He began to hear humming then, soft and insistent. He thought it was the wind at first, weaving through the branches of the trees, vibrating the leaves, but there didn't seem to be any wind. Then the humming changed to singing, the nature of the words indistinct but the sound clear and compelling.

"Cinnaminson?" he whispered.

She was smiling. "The aeriads are singing, Pen."

He listened to them, to the strange, echoing voices that seemed to come from both inside and outside his head, rising and falling in regular cadence, the sounds repeating, over and over.

"Can you understand them?" he asked, leaning close and speaking softly, afraid that his voice might do something to disturb the song, might break its spell.

She shook her head. "Isn't it beautiful? It makes me want to sing with them."

They continued on through the trees, deep into the forest, far away from the ravine and the thing that dwelled within it. Night had descended, and the world was a mix of tiny pieces of starlit sky glimpsed through breaks in the canopy. Pen could not be certain how far they had come, but it seemed much farther than should have been possible. The pinnacle, though large, was of a finite distance, certainly no more than a quarter of a mile across. Even allowing for all the climbing up and down and detours over rocky terrain, they shouldn't have been able to travel so far without reaching the opposite side.

But they walked on anyway, the time passing, the night settling in, silent and soft, the air warming, the light from moon and stars growing steadily brighter. After a time, Pen dropped Cinnaminson's hand, no longer afraid for her or himself, willing to believe that they had found a haven from the dangers that had tracked them for so many days. It was a conclusion based on a feeling, not rational cause.

But it felt as real to him as the earth he walked and the trees he navigated, and that was enough.

Finally, long after the moon had risen and they had walked well beyond any distance it should have taken to cross the pinnacle, the aeriads, who had been singing all the while, went suddenly still.

—Wait—

Pen and Cinnaminson did so, taking hands again without looking at each other, an act of reassurance that had become as familiar and comforting to them as a childhood hug. All about them, the ancient forest had gone still, the silence deep and penetrating, a presence as real as the sky and earth.

Ahead, a sudden, unexpected brightness shone through the trees, as if the moon had broken through the thick forest canopy to light a place previously hidden from view.

—Come—

They went forward once more, drawn by the invisible presence of the aeriads, trusting to fate and their invisible guides. Pen felt a strange sense of calmness, a peace of mind he hadn't known since Patch Run. Everything would be all right, he knew. Whatever awaited, everything would be all right.

Then they stepped from the trees into a clearing awash with moonlight. The canopy of the trees had pulled back, opening to the heavens as if in deference to the ancient tree that sat at the very center. It was massive by any standard, its trunk thick and gnarled and its limbs twisted and broad, lending it an otherworldly, surreal look among even the largest and strangest of the old growth that surrounded it. The moonlight revealed it clearly, particularly the odd colors that infused its bark and leaves—the former a peculiar mix of mottled black and gray, the latter deepest green bordered in bright orange. Pen could see the colors clearly, even in the darkness. He could see the way they mingled with each other, forming a strange pattern that glimmered against the deep black backdrop of the starry sky.

He had found the tanequil.

He had seen it only once, in the flare of the vision revealed by the Elfstones weeks before, when Ahren Elessedil had used the magic in the Elven village of Emberen to make certain that finding the tree was an attainable goal. He had seen it then, but the vision was nothing compared to what he was seeing in front of him. No vision could adequately capture the size and majesty of that giant. No vision could reveal how it made him feel to stand before it, dwarfed by its size and the sum of its years.

Dwarfed, he thought suddenly, by its intelligence.

He blinked in shocked surprise. He could feel the tanequil watching him. He felt it considering him, deciding what it would do with him now that he was there. It was a wild, irrational conclusion, one couched in premonition. Nevertheless, he was convinced of it. The tanequil was watching.

"Pen, I have to go now," Cinnaminson said suddenly, releasing his hand and stepping away. Her milky eyes shifted blindly. "The aeriads say I must go."

"Go where?" He was suddenly afraid. He wasn't sure if he was afraid for her or for himself; he only knew that he didn't want to be separated from her. "Why do you have to go?"

"So that you can be alone. So that you can do what you came here to do." Her smile was quick and dazzling, lighting up her face in a way that rendered her instantly beautiful. "The aeriads are going to show me what they look like. They brought me here so that I could see them. I won't be long."

He stared at her helplessly. "I don't want you to leave."

Her eyes shifted again, searching the space between them, making it seem as if she were trying to find a way to reach him. "You came to find the tanequil, Pen. You have done so. Make something good come out of that. Find what you need to help your aunt."

She hesitated a moment longer, then turned away. "I am coming," she said to the air, to something only she could hear. Her head lifted slightly. "Good luck, Pen."

He watched her disappear into the trees, sylphlike, a shadow quickly lost in the changing mix of light and dark, swallowed whole.

"Good luck," he echoed back, and was alone.

*   *   *

He stood motionless in front of the tanequil for a long time, unsure of where or how to begin, of what to do. The tree would give him one of its branches, if he could find a way to persuade it to do so. The branch could be shaped into something called a darkwand, if he could figure out how. The darkwand would give him access to the Forbidding and allow him to find and retrieve his imprisoned aunt and bring her home again, if he could reach Paranor and pass through the portal created by the potion called liquid night.

If. That word was everywhere. It loomed all about him like an impenetrable wall.

What should he do?

He waited some more, half hoping that the tree would try to communicate with him, that it would take the initiative and show him a way to speak with it. But after standing in front of it for what seemed an interminable amount of time, he gave up hoping. The effort to communicate would have to come from him. He was the supplicant; he was the one who was going to have to find a way to break through.

He had communicated with the aeriads just by speaking aloud. Would that work with the tanequil, as well?

"My name is Penderrin Ohmsford," he said. "Can you understand what I am saying?"

He felt foolish speaking that way, and he knew as soon as the words were out that there wasn't going to be any response. The tanequil was different from the aeriads. He was going to have to find a different way of speaking to it.

He walked up to the tree and placed his hands on its bark, running them slowly over the hard, rough surface. He was surprised at the warmth he found there, a pulsating heat that radiated outward to spread through his own body. He kept his hands in place as the heat entered him, thinking that might be the beginning of a way to connect.

But nothing more happened.

He took his hands away, staring upward into the thick nest of intertwined limbs. The orange-tipped leaves shimmered in the moonlight overhead, a rippling that reminded him of a sunset's glow on the surface of the Rainbow Lake. Rustling sounds emanated from that shimmer, soft and gentle, and he reached for them with his senses, drawing them in, trying to sort them out and make them into words.

But nothing revealed itself.

He moved back again, gaining some distance, hoping that by doing so he might also gain some perspective. But as he walked slowly around the tanequil, studying its shape, he began to doubt that such a thing was possible. From every angle, the tree appeared the same—ancient and huge, a knotted enigma a boy could never hope to untangle. It was a tree, and as such he understood some little bit about it. But it was a tree of such immensity—of size and shape and age and immutability, of innate intelligence and deep understanding—that it defied him. He recognized its power, but he could not begin to come to terms with it. The longer he tried to decide how it might be done, the more certain he became that it couldn't. The tanequil was too remote, too foreign, and too impenetrable for anyone possessed of less magic than a Druid.

Khyber, he thought, would be better suited for this. He wished suddenly that he had agreed to let her come.

But that was ridiculous. It wasn't Khyber who had been sent by the King of the Silver River. He was the one who had been told that he could find a way to communicate with the tree.

He sat down, crossing his legs before him, resting his chin in his hands, staring at its mottled trunk, and trying to think the problem through. There had to be a means for doing so. He might not know what it was yet, but he should be able to find it if he just thought about it long enough. Communication with living things came about in all sorts of unexpected ways. He had discovered that over the years; he knew it to be true. So there was a way to communicate with the tanequil too. There was a way to understand it and to make it understand him.

How do trees communicate?

He had no idea. Until then, he had never heard of one that did. Save for the legendary Ellcrys, when it spoke with the Chosen of the Elven people. But the Ellcrys was formed from a human who had willingly agreed to be transformed into a tree. So there was human nature buried somewhere deep within the Ellcrys. He wasn't sure the same could be said of the tanequil. He knew nothing of its history, nothing of how it had come into being. He could not presume that there was anything human about it.

He must find another way, then. It was a tree, and, as such, a plant. What did he know of plants and their relationship with the world? They were alive and took their nourishment from the soil. Some, like the tanequil, were very old, and because they could not move, they had to be very patient. They had endless amounts of time to think, and so they could reason in ways unknown to humans, who were never in one place long enough to give themselves over to reasoning as trees could.

He sighed, staring up into the branches. He was imbuing the tree with human characteristics. Should he be doing that? Did the tanequil think? Did it reason? Could it understand such concepts as patience? Did it do more than root and nourish as the eons passed and the world changed about it?

He thought for a time about the ways in which he understood other living things. Birds and animals he understood from their calls and cries, from the way they moved or didn't move. Insects communicated in much the same way, but without thought. Grasses and flowers possessed limited communicative skills, all in the form of instinctual responses to heat and cold, to wet and dry. Days earlier, in the Klu Mountains, he had read the responses of lichen to the sun's movement by touch . . .

He stopped himself. Would touch work here? He had tried placing his hands on the tanequil, but its bark was like an armor that protected it from the elements, designed specifically to shield it. It didn't take in nourishment or produce responses to the elements through its bark.

It did those things through its roots.

He stared at the tree. Was that the way to communicate with it— through its roots? How in the world was he supposed to do that, especially when those roots were buried dozens—perhaps hundreds—of feet underground? The prospect of digging down to find them seemed ridiculous. Surely that wasn't what he was intended to do if he wished to communicate with the tree.

If Cinnaminson were there, she might be able to offer a different perspective. In her blindness, sometimes she saw things more clearly than he did. He still didn't know why she had been ordered to leave him alone even though the aeriads had been so specific about her coming with him. Frustration and irritation warred with each other as he thought about it.

Suddenly, he was just tired. He didn't want to think anymore. He didn't want to do anything but rest. He couldn't remember how long it had been since he had slept.

He stretched out on the ground under the limbs of the ancient tree and closed his eyes. He needed only a few minutes, just long enough to clear his thinking, and then he would go back to work.

Overhead, the tanequil's branches formed a silvery green canopy in the moonlight, its strange webbing of orange lines shimmering softly. He had the distinct impression that time was slowing down, that his own breathing had become the measure of its passing. His tension and frustration drained out of him until nothing remained but the leaden ache of his body.

He closed his eyes and slept.

As he slept, he dreamed. His dream was of home and his parents. He was back in Patch Run, and his mother was telling him that magic wasn't important, that in some ways it was a burden. His father stood close by, using the wishsong to bring the buds of flowers into bloom. All around them, the sky was green and damp, and the air smelled of rain-soaked earth and leaves. Somewhere distant, an airship flew in silhouette against the sky, and he wished he were on it, safely aloft, safely away.

The scene changed, and he was hiding in a fortress, deep within its walls, down where only torchlight could penetrate the shadows and darkness. He crouched behind a wall, listening to sounds that came from the other side. He knew what was happening behind those walls, but he couldn't bring himself to look. His aunt, the Ard Rhys, was a prisoner of creatures so terrible that even to look at them was death. They were doing things to her best left to the imagination. Those things were meant to change her, to alter her mind, to make her something she didn't want to be. She was calling his name, begging him to help her, to save her from what was happening. Her cries were desperate, unbearable, filled with pain. She was all alone in that dark place, and he was the only one who could bring her back into the light.

But he couldn't move.

He could only sit there, listening . . .

He came awake again, eyes opening to a sunrise brightening through the heavy canopy of the tanequil in a flush of pink light. He stared at the limbs and the sky and the light, fighting back tears and a sense of desperation that threatened to overwhelm him. He lay without moving, waiting for both to pass, waiting to regain control of his emotions, to breathe easily again.

Something stroked the skin of his arms, soft and feathery. Little fingers were touching him, fairy hands or insect legs. They moved along the backs of his hands and wrists. But their movement was circular, a stroking that suggested an attempt to soothe or ease. He grew calm. His tears dried and his heartbeat slowed. He took deep, steadying breaths.

Without moving his hands or wrists, he raised himself carefully on his elbows.

Tiny roots sprouted from the ground all around him, little nests of them, some so slender they matched the hairs on his arm. They formed a bed, poking from the earth, weaving and touching, twisting and stroking. They were everywhere, though he felt them only where his skin was exposed. In front of him, the tanequil's limbs were swaying gently and its leaves shivering in time to the movement of the bed of roots that cradled him. He watched their undulation, watched the swaying of the tree, fascinated, mesmerized.

He lay back again and closed his eyes. The touching continued, and he lost himself in its hypnotic repetition. He reached out to it with his senses, embraced it, and made it a part of himself.

Then, deep within his consciousness, down where his heart beat and his life pulsed, he heard a deep, slow whisper, and even though it came from within himself, the voice wasn't his.

–Penderrin–

TWENTY-FOUR

A single word spoken. His name.

–Penderrin–

Only it wasn't spoken in the way that humans spoke. It didn't come from a mouth or even from an independent source. It came from the stroking of the tree roots against his skin, his magic extracting from that touch a communication meant solely for him.

–Penderrin–

The tanequil was speaking to him. He had been wrong about how communication with the tree would happen. It wasn't up to him to initiate contact; it was only up to him to be open to it. The tree would speak to him when it chose to. Trying to reach the tanequil on his terms was not going to work.

He lay against the earth, waiting for something more. But there were no further whispers, and he realized that the tiny fingerling roots were no longer stroking him. He rose to a sitting position and looked down. They were gone, all of them. He sat on a patch of sparse grass and bare earth from which no roots protruded and no sign of the ancient tree was in evidence.

He took a few moments to accept that the situation was not going to change, and then he rose and stood looking at the tree, trying to decide what to do next. Why had it stopped trying to communicate? Did it require something more from him? He couldn't think what else he could do that would help. To allow communication, he had opened himself up to the tree, reached out with his senses, engaged the magic that was his birthright, and it had happened. What more was there for him to do?

He circled the tree, squinting in the glare of the sunrise as the light fell across his face. The forest was silent and untroubled, a vast hall in which even the smallest sound could be heard. It was a sacred place, and he was a supplicant come in search of healing and direction. He stilled his mind and opened his thoughts, reaching to make a fresh connection, his eyes on the tree as he replayed in his mind the still-fresh whisper of his name.

Nothing happened.

After a time, he sat down again, taking up a new position on the other side of the tree, with his back to the sun. He watched the way the light played over the branches and leaves, illuminating fresh parts of the tree as the sun lifted out of the mountains into the sky. He tried speaking to the tree, tried engaging it with his magic, with his thinking, even by touching the earth in the hope that he might draw out the root tendrils. He did everything he could imagine that might stimulate the tree's consciousness.

Nothing worked.

Frustration washed through him. What had he done before that he was not doing now? Why wouldn't the tanequil continue their conversation? Perhaps, he thought, it was a question of patience. Trees had infinite amounts, and for them conversations might require a much longer period of time. Perhaps one word at a time was all that it could manage, and he must wait awhile for the next.

He didn't like that conclusion. He thought there must be a better one, a more sensible one. He went back to how things had begun, how he had been sleeping, dreaming of home, of the Ard Rhys . . .

He caught himself. Of the Ard Rhys, in danger, threatened because he could not help her, because he was incapable of acting. And then he had come awake in the sweat of his own fear and the roots of the tanequil had been reaching out to him. Responding, perhaps, to that fear, to his need to do something to help his aunt?

He lay down again on the earth, closed his eyes, and summoned pictures of his aunt in peril, jogging his memory, even though it was painful to do so, bringing to mind fresh images, fresh fears . . .

Almost immediately, the feathery touching begin again, a stroking of his skin that communicated a combination of reassurance and admonition. He remained still, giving himself over to the experience, but at the same time keeping his fears for his aunt at the forefront of his thoughts, the spark that he hoped would generate something more from the tree.

Hypnotically consuming, the stroking absorbed him. Lulled and calmed, he took a chance, speaking a single word in his mind.

—Tanequil—

—Penderrin. What do you require of me?—

The boy was so surprised by the response that he almost locked up, his mind going blank momentarily before he was able to construct an answer.

—A darkwand, so that I can reach my aunt, so that I can save her from the Forbidding—

—A darkwand formed of my body, of my limbs. What will you give me in exchange?—

Pen hesitated, surprised by the question. He had not thought to give the tanequil anything. The King of the Silver River had not mentioned anything about an exchange of gifts. Or was this something else? It might be that the tanequil was looking at a different sort of exchange entirely.

—What do you require?—

—What you ask of me. A part of yourself—

Pen took a deep, steadying breath, trying to stay focused on his aunt, on the Forbidding, on the journey he must make.

—What part of myself?—

As quickly as that, the stroking ended, the root tendrils withdrew, and the connection between them was broken once more. Pen lay where he was for a time, refocusing his thoughts on his aunt, stirring his emotions, and waiting for the words to come anew. They did not. He was left alone with his thoughts, his mind echoing with the words the tree had spoken and the silence that had replaced them.

Preoccupied with the crossing itself and with what waited, he had not thought to bring anything to eat with him when he crossed the bridge from Stridegate. He rose finally and went looking for food. He searched the forest about him, never moving too far from the tree, keeping the orange-tinged emerald canopy always in sight. But although he looked everywhere he could think to look, he found nothing save a tiny spill of water that trickled out of a fissure in a rock wall. He drank that, the water tasting of metal and earth.

He was about to return to the tanequil for another try at communicating with it when Cinnaminson appeared unexpectedly out of the trees, her face flushed with excitement as she rushed up to him.

"Penderrin," she gasped, "it was incredible!"

"Where have you been?" he asked, taking her by the shoulders. "I was worried about you."

She wrapped her arms around him and hugged him as if she had been gone for weeks, rather than hours. He could feel the soft hiss of her breath in his ear as she laughed. "Did you miss me?"

He nodded, confused by her strange excitement. "Are you all right?"

She pushed back from him so that they were face-to-face. Her smile reflected a child's wonder as she reached up to touch his cheek. "Pen, I saw everything. The aeriads showed me. I don't know how they managed it, but they let me see it all. They took shape and flew all around me, like tiny rainbow butterflies, changing colors and shimmering so brightly they seemed like pieces of the sun. It was so wonderful! Then they changed to become like me—girls, no older than I am! We danced and played! We laughed until I could hardly stand up! Do you know how long it has been since I laughed?"

He stared at her, shocked at the transformation. She had always been effusive, but she was alive now in a way he had never witnessed. It was as if she were being reborn into the world, made over by her encounter with the aeriads. He was surprised to find that he was vaguely jealous.

"Did you find out what they really are? Where they come from?"

She nodded. "They told me. They call themselves spirits of the air—aeriads—but they are much more. They call themselves seedlings, as well. They think of themselves as creatures of the tanequil, his children." She stopped herself. "Their children," she corrected. "I don't understand this part, but they think of the tanequil as both mother and father. The tree is both man and woman to them, able to be one or the other or both as needed." She shook her head. "I'm still learning."

Pen thought about the tanequil's voice in his head. Masculine, he reaffirmed, not feminine. Where was the mother side of the tree, then?

"Are you hungry?" she asked suddenly.

He nodded. "Starved. I've been looking for something to eat."

She took his hand. "Come with me."

She led the way through the trees, navigating the maze of ancient trunks as if her sight had miraculously been restored. There was no hesitation, no deviation. She seemed able to see even better than she had before, her strange gift enhanced perhaps by the magic of the place and its creatures.

She took him to a cluster of berry-laden bushes near a clear, spring-fed pool. The berries were rich and sweet, and he ate them hungrily, then drank the cool, clear water of the pool, which was nothing like the metallic trickle he had sampled earlier.

When they were finished, sitting next to each other on a grassy stretch by the pool, made lazy by the food and drink and the warmth of the sunlight through the trees, Pen asked, "How did you find this place? Did the aeriads show it to you?"

She nodded. "They seem to know what we need, Pen. They knew you were seeking the tanequil, and they led you to it. They knew that I needed to laugh again, and they made me. And they knew I needed to understand them, once they had revealed themselves, and they allowed me to do so. In part, at least." She paused, staring off into space. "They are so wonderful. I wish I could explain it better. They are free in a way I've never been. They can fly wherever they wish, be whatever they want, do whatever they choose. Sisters, of a sort—

though I don't think they really are. They seem to have come from different places, at different times."

"But they sound the same," he pointed out.

"They have become one, become a part of a whole. They are different, each of them, but they are the same, too."

He puzzled over that one for a moment, thinking of the way a family worked, then of something more cohesive, like a flock or a herd. But that didn't seem right, either. Finally, he settled on a school of fish, all swimming together and then changing direction at once.

"What do they want with you?" he asked finally.

"I don't think they want anything, Pen."

"Then why are they so interested in you? Why did they bring you here in the first place? Why are they telling you so much about themselves?"

She laughed, as if the answer should be obvious. "I think they just want someone to talk to. I think they know I will listen because I am interested in them."

She reached over and squeezed his hand. "Tell me about the tanequil. What have you learned?"

Strands of loose hair fell across her face as she leaned toward him, and he reached out to brush them away. "I did miss you, Cinnaminson," he said. "I don't like it when you're gone."

She smiled. "I missed you, too." Her face brightened. "Now tell me about the tanequil. Did you speak with it?"

"I spoke with it," he said. "It took me a while, but I found a way."

He told her everything that had happened, how it had taken him all night just to make contact, how it had then withdrawn until he had realized that his connection was premised upon its sensing of his need to help his aunt. He couldn't explain that, didn't understand it at all. But it was clear that the tree knew why he had come and what he had come for, and if he wanted to see the quest through, he was going to have to keep the needs of his aunt and his concerns for her safety foremost in his thoughts.

"But it was what it said last that bothers me most," he finished. "It

said that if I wanted to take a part of it—a limb from which to fashion the darkwand—then I must give it a part of myself in return.
When I asked what part it wanted, it quit talking to me."

Cinnaminson thought about it. "Perhaps it was just testing you.
Or perhaps it was speaking about something else. Maybe it wants a
part of you that's emotional or spiritual." She paused. "It can't be talking about an arm or leg."

Pen wasn't so sure. The entire business was strange enough that
he wasn't willing to rule out anything.

He looked off in the direction of the tree. "I should go back and
try to find out. This is taking longer than I thought it would."

"It is taking as long as it must," she corrected him gently. "Don't
be impatient. Don't let yourself become frustrated."

He nodded, shifting his gaze to study her. "What will you do?
Will you go back to the aeriads?"

"For now. I already know I can't be with you. You have to be
alone to speak with the tanequil. I will come looking for you
tonight."

She leaned over and kissed him lightly on the cheek, then on the
mouth. He kissed her back, not wanting to sever the connection, not
wanting her to go.

But when she rose and waved good-bye, her face still flushed
with excitement and expectation, he didn't try to stop her.

He returned to the tanequil in the warm hush of midday, the sun
spilling in faint, thin streamers through the thick canopy of the old
growth. Clouds scudded overhead in billowing white clusters, throwing shadows to the earth, and the skies were so blue they hurt his
eyes. A breeze blew through the trees, and the air was scented by
leaves and grasses sweet with summer warmth. It was the sort of day
when you felt that anything was possible.

He sat down in the space he had occupied the night before,
where the tree had first spoken to him, studied it for a time, then lay
down beneath it and closed his eyes. He gave himself time to relax,

then turned his thoughts to his aunt, to the Ard Rhys and her imprisonment inside the Forbidding, embracing the fear such thoughts
automatically generated.

And waited.

–Penderrin–

–Tanequil–

–You must have what you came for. You must take what you
need–

–What of giving you a part of myself? What of that?–

–You must do so–

He couldn't help himself. –Will I be crippled?–

–You will be enhanced–

–A part of me will be missing?–

–A part of you will be found–

There was no way to make sense of what he was being told. Pen
could not decide if he was about to make a good or a bad decision.
He could not read the consequences clearly.

–Are you afraid?–

–Yes–

–Fear for yourself has no place in what you would do. Your fear
must be for your aunt if you are to save her. A darkwand is born of
fear for another's safety. A darkwand responds to selfless need. Do
you wish to save your aunt?–

He swallowed hard. –I do–

–Then no sacrifice is too great, even that of your own life–

–Is that what is required?–

–What is required should not matter. Do you wish to proceed?–

He took a deep, steadying breath. Did he? How great a risk was
he taking? Things weren't working out the way he had expected.
The King of the Silver River had told him he must persuade the
tanequil to his cause. But the tanequil didn't seem interested in being
persuaded to anything. It seemed to have already made its decision,
and what mattered now was how far Pen was willing to go to allow
that decision to be implemented.

It was like being trapped in a cave with no light and having to find his way in darkness. There might be pits into which he could fall, and he had no way of knowing where they were.

–Do you wish me to give you what you came for, Penderrin?–

He closed his eyes. –I do–

–Then rise and come to me. Walk to me and place your hands on my body–

He opened his eyes and saw that the tiny roots had withdrawn once more, then rose and moved over to stand before the tree. Gingerly, he pressed his palms against its massive, rough trunk.

–Climb up into me–

He found handholds in the bark and began to climb. It was easier than he would have expected. The bark was strong and did not break off. The effort was considerable, but eventually he reached the lower branches and from there was able to continue on up through the sprawl of limbs as if climbing a ladder. He wasn't sure how high he was supposed to go, and so kept looking for some indication of where he was to stop. But he was deep within the canopy of the tree, its leaves forming a thick curtain about him, before it spoke to him again.

–Stop–

He stopped climbing and looked around. He was at a junction of branches where deep fissures had split the tree's trunk, forming crevices and boles in which birds or small animals might nest. The fissures were old, and in the wounds that had healed the skin had grown back over the soft heartwood, the bark wrapped about the openings anew.

–Look up–

He did so, turning his gaze skyward to the sea of limbs and leaves that spread away overhead.

–Reach up–

He did this, too, and his hand touched a limb that extended some six feet from the trunk, a limb that seemed too small and straight, that lacked twigs or even leaves. Heat radiated from the branch, sudden and unexpected, and Pen jerked away in surprise.

–Take hold–

Pen gripped the branch tentatively, feeling the heat course through his fingers and down his arm. The branch was vibrating, humming deeply as it did so, a strange, mournful sound.

Then the entire tree shook, and its trunk split apart where the branch sprouted, a sharp rending that sent pieces of bark and splinters of wood flying in all directions. Pen ducked his head and closed his eyes, keeping tight hold of the branch, rocking unsteadily with the tanequil's quaking. There was a deep, audible groan of darkest protest, and abruptly the branch came away in Pen's hands. The boy caught himself against the trunk and stared in shock. The tree had cracked wide open where the branch had broken off, and sap was leaking out in a steady stream. The sap was red and viscous and looked like blood. It ran down the trunk in thick rivulets. It dripped from the branch onto his arm.

He was studying it, his left hand braced against the tree for support, his fingers gripping one of the older splits, when the tree groaned again, deep and menacing, and the split closed over his fingers. He screamed in agony and jerked away, feeling flesh and bone tear free as he did so. He reacted at once, but was still too slow. When he stared down at his hand, he saw that his middle two fingers had been severed at the first knuckle. Blood dripped from the ragged wounds and ran down his hand. His finger bones shone white and raw.

Still clutching the tanequil's severed limb, Pen collapsed into a crook in the branches of the tree, pressing his injured hand against his chest, staining his clothing with his blood. For a moment, frozen by pain and shock, he couldn't move. Then, realizing the danger as his blood continued to well up, he tore free one sleeve of his tunic and wrapped the cloth about the stubs, compressing it into the wounds.

—A part of you for a part of me—

Pen nodded miserably. He didn't need to be reminded. The pain ratcheting through his hand and arm was reminder enough.

—Take my limb in your hand—

Holding his shirtsleeve-wrapped fingers tightly against his chest, he reached down with his right hand and took the tanequil's limb from his lap, where he had dropped it moments before. To his surprise, it was still warm and pulsating, as if it retained life, even though it had been severed from the tree.

–The wood of this limb comes from deep inside me, where my life is formed. The limb must be forced to the surface from the soft heartwood and forcibly severed. Such a sacrifice is necessary if a darkwand is to be shaped to the use you require. But you must give back what you are given if the sacrifice is to have value. A piece of your body. A piece of your heart. Remember this–

Pen closed his eyes and exhaled slowly. The loss of his fingers in exchange for the loss of the tanequil's limb. He wasn't likely to forget.

–Climb down from me. Carry my limb with you–

Pen cautiously made his way down from the tree, protecting his injured hand as he did so, cradling the limb in the crook of his arm. It was a long, tedious descent, and when he was still ten feet from the ground, he slipped and fell, striking the earth with force and jarring his hand. Fresh pain caused him to cry out. He was sweating heavily as he dragged himself to his feet and leaned back against the ancient trunk. His fingers throbbed, and the fabric wrapping them was soaked with his blood. He felt nauseous and weak.

–Move away from me and sit–

He lurched from the tree and found the patch of ground he had occupied before. He dropped heavily, crossed his legs before him, and bent his head to the earth as he felt everything begin to spin. He glimpsed the tanequil's root tendrils as they reemerged and began to stroke his clothing and boots. He pulled back his pant legs so that the roots could find his skin, so that the tree could make contact with him. He reached out with his own hand to touch them.

–Unwrap your fingers. Take the sap from the end of my limb and place it on your wounds–

Pen hesitated, then unwound the soiled cloth. The stubs of his fingers were red and inflamed, and blood was still leaking from them. He used his good hand to gather sap still oozing from the end of the tanequil's limb, and he rubbed it gingerly into his wounds. Almost instantly, they began to close, the bleeding to stop, and the flesh to heal. The pain, so intense only moments earlier, faded to a dull ache. He stared at his fingers in disbelief.

–Take your knife from your belt–

He did so, frightened anew of what would be asked of him.

–Close your eyes–

Again, he did so.

–You must shape the darkwand now, while the life of the wood is still strong–

He waited. He could not begin to carve the wood until he could see how to do so. He must be permitted to open his eyes. But no command to open them came. Instead, the nature of the touching changed, and communication that had come in the form of words now came in the form of images. He saw in his mind what he was meant to do, a clear and unmistakable direction.

Then something odd happened. He felt another hand on his, covering it, guiding it, and his own began to move in response. By feel alone, he began the cutting that would shape the limb into the darkwand. He should have been terrified that he would make a mistake. The cuts were often tiny and intricate. They were impossibly time-consuming. But the images were so clear and his sense of what was needed so strong that he never wavered in his efforts. And time did not seem to matter. It was as if time had stopped and he could use it in whatever manner or measure he deemed necessary to accomplish his task.

He worked through the remainder of the day and into the night. He did not eat or drink. He did not move from where he sat. His concentration was complete as he responded to the tree's steady, calm commands. Nothing distracted him; not the tiny itch of an insect's wings or the cool whisper of a breeze against his skin. He was in another world, another time, another life.

It was night when he finished, the moon risen and the stars come out, their light falling through the forest canopy in pale, thin streamers, the darkness about him deep and pervasive. The images stopped, the roots withdrew back into the earth, and he was alone in the silence. He opened his eyes and looked down at his lap.

The darkwand lay cradled in his hands, its six-foot length a rich mottled gray and black, the same colors as the tanequil's trunk, gleaming and smooth in a way that should have been impossible for newly carved wood. An intricate pattern of runes wrapped its surface, strange markings that Pen did not recognize and could not interpret. When they were turned to the moonlight, they gleamed as if lit by an inner fire. Pen could still feel unmistakable warmth emanating from the wood, the tanequil's life force firm and strong.

The boy unfolded his legs, which were cramped and sore. His mouth was so dry he could barely open it. He took a few minutes to gather his strength, then got to his feet and began hobbling toward the pool that Cinnaminson had showed him earlier. He carried the darkwand with him; he knew he would carry it everywhere from then on. Slowly, his legs regained their feeling and the cramps disappeared. He listened for signs of life as he walked, but there were none. Even as long as he had been sitting beneath the tree, he was still alone.

He wondered suddenly what had happened to Cinnaminson. She had told him she would come back to him at nightfall. She had promised.

He found the pool and dropped down on his hands and knees to drink. The water was cool and sweet, and he got back a little of his strength. When he had drunk his fill, he stood up again and looked around.

Where was Cinnaminson?

He exhaled in frustration. He didn't like it that she was still gone. He never liked it when she was gone. Losing her was worse than losing his fingers . . .

He stopped himself, remembering suddenly the sensation of another's hand guiding his as he shaped the tanequil's limb into the darkwand, one that allowed him to work blindly, his eyes closed, his reliance on touch alone.

A piece of your body. A piece of your heart.

A terrible certainty swept through him, harsh and implacable, so traumatizing that he could not give voice to it, but only whisper it in the silence of his mind. He thought he had understood. He hadn't. He assumed that the loss of his fingers was enough to balance the scales. It wasn't.

Something more was required.

Cinnaminson.

TWENTY-FIVE

S hadea a'Ru stood at the window of her sleeping chambers and
looked out from Paranor's towers over the forested sweep of
the land beyond. The sun was rising, a soft golden glow in the
east that silhouetted the jagged peaks of the Dragon's Teeth against
its bright backdrop and gave promise to the coming of a warm, lan-
guorous summer day.

Her lips compressed into a tight, angry line. It would not be such
a good day for her. And less so for some others.

She glanced down at the note she held in her hand, at the words
written on it, then looked away again. *Idiots!* She brushed absently at
her short, spiky blond hair and flexed her shoulders. Her muscles
were stiff and tight. She missed the training and fighting that had
been so central to her life when she had been a soldier in the Federation army. She missed the discipline and the routine. She had never
thought she would feel that way, but after weeks of struggling as Ard
Rhys of the Third Druid Order, she was ready to abandon it all for a
chance to go back to a time when things were less complicated and
more direct.

Her gaze drifted back to the note. It had arrived during the
night, while she slept, and she had found it on waking, tied to the leg
of the arrow swift. The bird's dark, fierce face had peered out at her

from its enclosure, almost daring her to reach inside. But it was her bird, one of the many she had appropriated and trained to carry her messages from her co-conspirators and servants in the plot against Grianne Ohmsford. Its countenance only mirrored the intensity that could be found in her own.

She knew the bird. *Split* was its name, chosen for the strange wedge in its tail feathers, an accident of birth. The arrow swift was one of those assigned to Traunt Rowan on his departure to the Northland; it had been sent by him.

She had reached inside for the message, untied it from Split's leg, withdrawn it from the cage, opened it, and her face had gone dark with rage immediately.

> THE BOY AND HIS COMPANIONS
> ESCAPED FROM TAUPO ROUGH.
> HAVE FOLLOWED THEM INTO THE KLU.

And lost them there, of course, though the writer had been careful not to say so.

She looked back at the message again, still furious with its contents and its incompetent sender. She had expected better of Traunt Rowen. She had expected better of Pyson Wence, as well, and better still of the two of them working together to track that boy!

She gritted her teeth. Why was it so difficult for anyone to find and hold him? The effort had cost Terek Molt his life. It had cost Aphasia Wye her respect, a respect she had thought nothing could diminish. What would it cost her this time? The lives of two more of her allies, men whose support she could scarcely afford to lose, even if they were proving less competent than she had imagined possible? Her respect for them had long since vanished, so there was no danger of losing that.

She crumpled the note in her hand, then set it in a small bowl on her desk, fired it with magic, and scattered the ashes out the window. She watched the breeze carry the ashes away and wished her anger and disappointment could be made to vanish as easily.

What was she going to have to do to finish this business?

For a moment, for just an instant, she toyed with the idea of breaking off the hunt entirely. It was requiring much more time and effort than she cared to spend and netting no favorable results at all. She had the boy's parents safely locked away in her dungeons. Couldn't she just wait for him to come for them? He would surely do so, once he found out where they were, and it would be easy enough to make him aware.

Her frustration building toward a headache, she rubbed at her temples with her fingers. The trouble with ignoring him was that she was almost certain she knew what he was doing. He was trying to find a way to reach his aunt. She had no idea how he planned to do that and believed it beyond his or anyone else's capability. But she could not chance being wrong. If he had found a way into the Forbidding, if he had discovered an avenue about which she knew nothing, then she had to stop him from using it. Because if he managed the impossible and actually reached Grianne Ohmsford from Paranor's side of the wall, he might find a way to guide her back again.

If that happened, Shadea knew she was finished. They were all finished, all who had conspired with her.

The chance of that happening was so small that it was scarcely measurable, but she knew better than to put anything past the Ohmsfords. Their history spoke for itself. They had survived impossible situations before, several generations of them. They were imbued with both magic and luck, and the combination had kept them from harm more times than anyone could count.

She could not afford to allow that to happen again.

So she would leave things as they were. She would allow Traunt Rowan and Pyson Wence to continue to hunt down the boy. Perhaps Aphasia Wye still tracked him as well, even though she had heard nothing from her assassin in days. One never knew about that creature. One could never predict.

The ashes of the burned note were gone, turned to dust and blown away. She breathed in the morning air, calming herself, reassuring herself that everything was going to be all right. In the next few days, she would journey to Arishaig to meet with Sen Dunsidan.

Gerand Cera shook his head in disagreement. "The Prime Minister doesn't have the use of magic."

"Perhaps he has acquired the aid of someone who does." Her eyes locked on his. "One of us."

He snorted. "Who? Who would want to give aid to Sen Dunsidan, knowing that you would view it as a—" He stopped himself. "Are you thinking of Iridia?"

"Do we know where she is? Did we ever find out where she went after she left here?"

Cera shook his head slowly. "No. But she wouldn't dare to betray us. She knows what would happen if she did."

She cringed at his use of the word *us*, at the implication that he was somehow a part of the decision-making process, when in fact he was little more than another obstacle. She glanced away to hide her disgust, then turned and walked to the window. She stood there for a moment, thinking.

"What do you intend to do?" he asked, rising and coming over to put his hands on her shoulders.

She felt the strength of those hands as they gripped her. They were possessive and commanding as they turned her about to face him. They suggested in no uncertain terms that he was the one in control. She smiled agreeably as he leaned down and kissed her mouth. She kissed him back, waited for the kiss to end, then broke away.

"I intend to drink my morning cup of tea before speaking with those in the order who will keep an eye on things in our absence."

He stared after her. "Our absence? Are we going somewhere?"

"To confront Sen Dunsidan, of course."

She had told him nothing of her plans to visit Arishaig before this. The reason was simple. She had not intended for him to go. She still didn't, but it was best to let him think she did.

"To confront him? In his own home, his own city, surrounded by his own people?" Gerand Cera considered the prospect. "A bold course of action, Shadea. How safe can we expect to be?"

She shrugged, pouring tea into cups, slipping into his the tiny pill she had been saving for that moment and watching it dissolve instantly. "We are Druids, Gerand. We can't afford to worry about being safe. We can't afford to be seen to be afraid."

She handed him his tea, stood in front of him as she sipped from her own, and watched with satisfaction as he drank.

"Sit with me on the bed." She took his arm and moved over. She pulled him down next to her. "Perhaps we needn't go down right away. The tea is making me warm all over. I need to find a way to cool off."

She smiled and sipped again. "Come, Gerand. Finish your tea. Don't keep me waiting."

He drank it in a single gulp and reached for her. His appetites were so pathetic, so predictable. She eased away playfully. He was still grinning when the drug took effect. An abrupt change came over his hatchet features. His face went slack and empty, and he lurched forward, falling onto his side.

That was quick, she thought. She rose and looked down at him, at the way his eyes rolled frantically from side to side as he tried to understand what was happening to him. She eased a pillow under his head, then reached for his legs and lifted them onto the bed so that he was lying stretched out along its length.

"Comfortable, Gerand? Much better to rest while this is happening." Knowing he could no longer reach for her, could no longer move at all for that matter, she bent over him. His lungs and his heart still worked, but not very efficiently. He barely had the strength of a baby.

"I've given you a drug," she explained, sitting next to him. "It saps the strength from your muscles and leaves you paralyzed. It only lasts a little while. There is no trace of its presence afterwards. Unlike poison, for example, which I considered using but decided against. After all, I can't afford to be seen as a murderess."

She leaned close. "You see what is to happen, I expect. Your eyes tell me you know. So now you no longer love me. Now, you despise me. Love is like that. It only lasts for as long as both parties require it, and then it becomes a burden, which is one reason I do not permit myself to love anyone too much. You should have learned that lesson a long time ago. I am surprised you didn't. Now you must learn it the hard way."

He was staring fixedly at her, and she read the hatred in his eyes. In contrast, his face was empty of expression, and it seemed as if the eyes must belong to someone else. Yet the eyes were really all that was left of him. Everything else had been stripped away by the drug.

She leaned down and kissed him lightly on the forehead. "Try not to think too harshly of me, Gerand. You would have done the same, if you had paid closer attention to how I looked at you."

Then she took the pillow from under his head, placed it firmly over his face, and pressed down on it with all of her considerable strength until he stopped breathing.

When the cell door closed and the locking bolts were thrown, Bek Ohmsford was engulfed in blackness. He sat down, waiting for his eyes to adjust, and after a time they did. A sliver of light crept under the door and through the seams on the latch side, permitting him just enough illumination to find his way around. The cell was tiny, and it didn't take him long to explore it. He found nothing that would help. The walls, floor, and ceiling were hewn from bedrock, and the only exit was through the barred door. The room contained only the bed, straw, and bucket he had seen upon being brought in. There were no implements that might be used for tunneling or prying. There were no fissures or seams on which to employ such a tool in any event. And there was nothing he could use for a weapon.

He sat on the bed and thought about his situation for a long time. If Shadea was to be believed—and he had no reason to assume she wasn't—there was a guard stationed on the other side of the door, watching for any attempt at escape. Down the hall and up the stairs, there would be others. A relay was in place to send word faster than he could run, should he attempt to break free. He couldn't know all the particulars, but he had to assume the guards had a form of communication that would allow them to know if one or more of their number had been overpowered.

Time passed, and eventually the door opened far enough to permit a Gnome Hunter to slide a tray of food inside before the locks

were thrown anew. Accustomed by then to the dark, Bek was blinded
by the sudden glare of torchlight and barely caught a glimpse of
what was happening before the door was closed again. He took that
into account as he continued to make his plans, sitting on the floor
of his cell and eating his meal. The food, he found, was reasonable;
apparently, Shadea didn't intend to do away with him through star-
vation. But he hadn't changed his mind that she intended to do away
with him in some manner.

He waited through three more meals, measuring the time it took
the Gnome to pull back the lock bolt, open the cell door, slide the
food tray inside, close the door, and throw the bolt again. It was clear
to him that any escape would have to come then. It would not be
possible to escape if he had to break down or lever open the door.
The noise such an effort would require, even if time and opportunity
allowed for it, would alert the Gnome Hunters immediately, and any
chance of surprise would be lost.

Even then, once he was through, what would he find on the
other side? At least one Gnome Hunter, but how many more would
be keeping him company? If he were Shadea, he would insist on at
least two, possibly more, being present anytime the cell door was
opened. That would eliminate the chance that he could successfully
overpower one guard without alerting the others.

He began positioning himself so that he could see something of
the hallway outside when the cell door was cracked, and through
two further meals, he tried to catch a glimpse of what was out there.
But it was impossible to see more than a little of what lay beyond,
never enough to be certain. He did catch sight of movement once, a
shadow thrown by torchlight that indicated the presence of another
man. But it was clear that he would have to make his break into the
hallway without knowing how many Gnomes he would find.

How could he do that and still make certain they could not
sound the alarm?

He puzzled it through with an increasing sense of desperation;
he needed to find a solution quickly, because time was slipping away
and with it his chances of freeing Rue and warning Penderrin. In

spite of what Shadea had learned of Taupo Rough, he had to assume that his son was still free and his exact whereabouts still undiscovered. But that could change in a hurry.

He decided in the end that what he must do was use the wishsong in a blanket assault, stunning everyone within hearing distance and giving him a chance to get up the steps to confront whomever he had missed. It was a long shot at best, one he did not much care to take. But sitting in his cell and waiting for the inevitable was madness. He hated putting Rue at risk, but he knew that she would want him to if it meant giving them a chance, however slim, of reaching Pen.

He decided to try for one more look, using the next feeding as a trial run for determining exactly where he should stand to get through the door to the guards. He waited patiently, using his time to run repeated rehearsals of what he would do, working and reworking his timing, his movements, everything that would be required of him.

When the door finally opened, he was standing just to the open side, watching the movements of the Gnome Hunter as he knelt to slide the food tray inside, counting the seconds from the time the door opened until it closed again. It took twelve seconds. He would have to act quickly. He would have to summon the wishsong and hold it within himself until the locks were thrown. Then he would have to sprint through the door, directing the magic down the hallway as he emerged, a quick and certain strike.

He sat in the darkness and thought about how little chance he had of making this plan work. Wasn't there a better one? Wasn't there something else he could do?

He was just finishing his meal when a piece of paper was slid under the door. He stared at it for a moment, then reached down to retrieve it. Bent close to the bottom of the door, where the thin light gave just enough illumination to allow him to make out the words, he read:

HELP IS COMING.

Bek recognized the writing immediately. It was the same hand that had penned the note he and Rue had received on their arrival at Paranor, the one that had warned them not to trust anyone. He had never discovered the identity of the writer, and in truth, he had forgotten all about the note until that moment.

Lying on the floor next to the crack beneath the cell door, he read it again. Could he believe it? Could he trust that the writer would be able to find a way to free him? How long could he afford to wait to find out?

He stared blindly into the darkness of his prison, searching for the answers.

TWENTY-SIX

He heard the voices first, soft and insistent, joined as one, humming and then singing, the words indecipherable, but their sound sharp and clear and compelling.

—Penderrin— she whispered from out of the confluence. —I've come back—

But it wasn't her voice, and he knew that when he looked, it wouldn't be her. It wouldn't be anybody at all.

—I said I would come back. I promised, didn't I—

He lay where he had fallen asleep near dawn, exhausted from searching for her after realizing where she might be and what she might have done. Frantic with worry, he had torn through the ancient forest like a madman, plunging through the dark trunks and layered shadows, calling her name until he was too tired to continue. Then, heartsick and drained of hope, he had collapsed. It couldn't be true, he kept telling himself. His suspicions were unfounded and fueled by his weariness and the shock of losing his fingers. It was all a lie of the mind, born of his misinterpretation of the tanequil's words, of the fears raised by the tree's dark reminder that its gift of the dark-wand required a like gift from him.

Of the body. Of the heart.

—Penderrin, wake up. Open your eyes—

But he kept his eyes closed, wrapped in the comforting darkness that not seeing her afforded, unwilling to let that last shred of hope fall away. He moved his damaged hand beneath him, feeling with his good fingers for the ones that were missing, finding the stumps healed over and the pain gone. It wasn't so bad, he supposed, losing parts of two fingers. Not for what he had been given in turn. Not for what it meant to his efforts at finding his aunt. Not for what it meant to the future of the Four Lands. It wasn't so bad.

But losing Cinnaminson was.

"Why did you do it?" he asked finally, his voice so soft that he could barely hear his own words.

Silence greeted his query, a long and empty sweep of time in which the voices grew quiet and the sounds of the forest slowly filled the void their departure created.

"Why, Cinnaminson?"

Still no answer. Suddenly fearful that he had lost her completely, he lifted his head and looked around. He was alone, sprawled on the grassy patch on which he had fallen asleep the night before, the darkwand resting on the ground beside him, its glossy length shimmering, its carved runes dark and mysterious.

"Cinnaminson?" he called.

—It was a chance for me to be something I couldn't otherwise be— She spoke to him from out of the air. —I am free from my body, Pen. Free from my blindness. Free in a way I could never be otherwise. I can fly everywhere. I can see what I could never see before. Not in the way I do now. I am not alone anymore. I have found a family. I have sisters. I have a mother and father—

He didn't know what to say. She sounded so happy, but her happiness made him feel miserable. He hated himself for his reaction, but he couldn't find a way to change it.

"It was your choice to do this?" he demanded, his words sounding woeful and plaintive, even to him.

—Of course, Penderrin. Did you think I was forced to become one of them? It was my choice to shed my body—

"But you knew I wouldn't be given the tanequil's branch any other way, didn't you?"

—I knew it was the right thing to do. Just as you did, when you agreed to come here to find the tree and to seek help in freeing your aunt—

"But you knew," he persisted, desperate to wring from her one small concession. "You knew that becoming an aeriad would help me. You knew that giving yourself to the tanequil was what it would take for the tanequil to give me its limb."

Her hesitation was momentary. —I knew—

She was moving all around him, a part of the ether, a disembodied voice buttressed by the soft singing and humming of her sister aeriads, her new family, her new life. He tried to see her in the sound of her voice, but he could not quite manage it. His memory of her was strong, but his efforts to form a picture from her voice alone were insufficient. He didn't want her back in still life; he wanted her back as a living, breathing human being, and the images he managed to conjure failed to capture her that way.

He sank back wearily. "When did you decide to do this?" His voice broke as despair threatened to overwhelm him. "Why didn't you tell me? Why didn't you talk to me about it?"

The singing rose and fell like a wave of emotion born on a shift in the wind. —What would I have said to you? That I love you so much that I cannot imagine life without you, but that I am old enough to understand that loving someone that much isn't always the only measuring stick for making a life with them? That choosing love should never be selfish—

"If you loved me that much . . ."

—I *love* you that much, Penderrin. Nothing has changed. I love you still. But you were sent here for another reason, one too important to sacrifice for anything—even for me. I know this. I knew it from the moment that I heard the aeriads speaking to me. They were telling me what was needed—not directly, not in so many words, but in the way they sang to me, in the sound of their voices. I knew—

He shook his head. "I don't think I can do this without you. I can't even think straight. I can barely move."

Matched by the voices of her sisters, soothing as a breeze on a hot summer day, her voice trilled with soft laughter. —Oh, Pen, it will pass! You will go on to do what you were sent to do! You will find your aunt and bring her home again. I am already a memory, already fading away—

He stared into space, into the place from where she spoke to him, trying to make himself accept what she was telling him, and failing.

The voices sighed and hummed and sighed some more. —Do not be sad, Penderrin— she whispered. —I am not sad. I am happy. You can hear it in my voice, can't you? I made a choice. The aeriads asked me to join them, to help you and myself. While you slept, I went with them from the surface of the earth to the Downbelow. From the sunlight and air world of Father Tanequil to the darkness and earth world of Mother Tanequil. She roots deep, Pen, to provide for her children, to give them life, to allow them the freedom she can never have. I saw the truth of what she is. Of what they both are. Joined as one—Father, the limbs; Mother, the roots. One lives aboveground, but the other must forever live below. She gets lonely. She needs company. I was a gift to her from Father Tanequil. But it was what I wanted. Perhaps he knew that when he sent me to her. Perhaps he knows us both better than we know ourselves. They are very old spirits, Pen. They were here when the world was born, when the Word was still young and the Faerie creatures newly made. We are children in their eyes—

"We are Men!" he snapped. "And they don't know what's right for us! They don't know anything about us because they aren't like us! Don't you see? We were manipulated! We were tricked!"

A long silence punctuated his angry words. —No, Pen. We did what we thought was best. Both of us. I don't regret it. I won't. We have the lives we have chosen, whether fate or the tanequil or some-thing larger pushed us to that choice—

He took a long slow breath to calm himself. She was wrong; he knew she was wrong. But there was nothing he could do about it. It was over and done with. He would have to live with it, although he couldn't imagine how he would ever do that.

"Did it hurt at all?" he asked quietly. "Your transformation? Was there any pain?"

–None, Pen–

"But what of your body? Did it just . . . ?"

He couldn't finish the thought, unable to bear the image it conjured—an image of her turning to dust, disintegrating.

Laughter greeted his failure, gentle and soothing. –Kept safe and unchanging in her arms, I sleep with Mother Tanequil, Pen, down within the earth, in the darkness and quiet, where she takes root. She nourishes me, so that I can live. If I were to die, I would cease to exist, even as an aeriad–

She is down in the ravine, he thought suddenly. He was finally beginning to understand. The tanequil was both male and female, mother and father to the aeriads, a trunk joining limbs at one end to roots at the other. Cinnaminson was in the keeping of the latter, down in the shadowy depths they had crossed over on the bridge. Down where something huge had stirred awake on their passing.

But still whole, she was telling him. Still alive in human form.

"Cinnaminson," he said, an idea coming to sudden life, a plan to implement it taking shape. "I need to see you again before I go. I need to say good-bye. It isn't enough just to hear your voice. It doesn't feel real to me. Can you take me to where you sleep?"

There was a long pause. –You cannot have me back, Pen. Mother Tanequil will not let me go. Not even if you beg–

She recognized his intentions all too well, but his mind was already made up. He was terrified of what he might find if he did it, half certain that she was already reduced to bones and dust, that her vision of herself as still being whole was a subterfuge fostered by the tree. But he couldn't leave without knowing, no matter how devastating the truth. If there was a way to set her free again, to take her with him . . .

"I won't do anything but make sure that you are safe," he lied. "I just need to see you one last time."

–This is a mistake– she trilled, her voice rising amid those of her sisters, sharp with rebuke. –You shouldn't ask it of me–

He took a deep breath. "But I am asking." He waited a moment. "Please, Cinnaminson."

The voices of the aeriads hummed, a long sustained chord that matched the sound of wind whispering through the leaves of trees, soft and resilient. He forced himself to keep silent, to say nothing more, to wait.

—I am afraid for you, Pen— she said finally.

"I am afraid for myself," he admitted.

A pause followed, and the humming died away.

—Come with me, then, if you must. If you can remember my warning—

He exhaled softly. He was not likely to forget.

On the far side of the ravine, Khyber Elessedil stood at the foot of the stone bridge, listening to the soft moan of the wind. She had been standing there for the better part of an hour, using her admittedly unskilled Druid senses to scan the forest for sign of Pen and Cinnaminson. It wasn't the first time she had done so, but the results were the same. She might as well have been casting about the Blue Divide for a sailor lost at sea, for all the good it was doing her.

One hand clutched the Elfstones. She kept them close on the theory that they might at some point prove useful in her search. They were doing her about as much good as her Druid skills.

Frustrated, she turned away. She hated feeling so helpless. Ever since the safety lines tied to Pen and Cinnaminson had dropped away as if severed by an invisible blade, she had known that the fate of her friends was out of her hands. More than once she had considered trying to cross over herself—and she wasn't afraid to try, in spite of the warning on the stone—but she didn't want to do anything that would jeopardize Pen's efforts to secure the darkwand.

She looked back into the gardens, her dazzlingly colorful prison. Trapped in all that beauty and unable to enjoy it, her concentration on Pen and on the island and on the Druids tracking them and on time running out—thinking about it all made her want to scream. But there was nothing she could do.

Nothing but wait.

She stalked over to where Kermadec sat talking with Tagwen,

trading stories of the old days, when Grianne Ohmsford was new to the position of Ard Rhys and they were just beginning in her service.

"Do you think there might be another way across?" she asked abruptly, kneeling next to them, her voice urgent. "Another bridge or a narrows we might vault?" She exhaled sharply. "I don't think I can stand waiting another minute without doing something."

Kermadec stared at her impassively. "There might be. If you want to take a look, you can. I can send Atalan or Barek with you."

She shook her head. "I can manage alone. I just need to do something besides stand around."

Tagwen frowned into his beard, but didn't say anything.

"You won't lose your way, will you, Elven girl?" the Maturen pressed. "I wouldn't want to have to come looking for you."

"I can find my way."

"If you discover anything, you will come back and tell us?" Tagwen pressed suddenly.

"Yes, yes!" she snapped. "I'm not going to do anything rash or foolish!" Her irritation got the better of her for a moment, and she took a deep breath. "I just want to see if that ravine goes all the way around or if there are other places to cross. I won't attempt anything on my own."

She didn't know if they believed her or not, but if they did, they ought to be less trusting. She fully intended to attempt a crossing if a place to make one could be found. She should have gone with Pen and Cinnaminson in the first place, but she had allowed her instincts to be overruled.

She stood up, giving them a bright smile. "I don't expect to be gone long. I probably won't get much beyond what we can see from standing right here, but it will make me feel better to have tried."

Their eyes fixed on her, as if searching for the truth behind her words, neither replied. She turned away quickly and started off, choosing to go south, where the gardens opened out toward a thinning woods and a set of hills. She could see the ravine as it snaked its way into those hills, disappearing finally into the horizon. In truth, she didn't have much hope that she would succeed in her quest. She mostly hoped that the distraction would help with the waiting.

She was so intent on her efforts to get clear of the others that she failed to detect with her normally reliable Druid training the shadowy form lying in wait directly ahead. She missed it entirely as it slipped away at her approach and circled back around toward the bridge.

Pen Ohmsford followed the low, vibrant humming of the aeriads as they led him on through the trees and back toward the dark cut of the ravine. The light casting his shadow before him as he walked, he could measure the direction they were taking from the slant of the sun's thin rays through the heavy canopy. He tried to hear Cinnaminson in the mix of aeriad voices, but he could not detect a noticeable difference in any of them. She was being assimilated into their order, and he could not stop himself from thinking that if he did not reach her soon, there would be no way to separate her from the others, even if her body was still intact.

Thinking of her body at rest beneath the earth in the cradle of the tanequil's roots made him wonder about the condition of the bodies of the other aeriads. For their spirits to survive in aeriad form, their bodies must be kept whole, as well. But how was that accomplished? He was feeling less and less certain about what it was he was going to find. He was starting to think that his request was a mistake.

Yet he kept on, drawn by the humming, by the promise it offered that he might still find a way to bring Cinnaminson back to him. Both hands gripped the polished length of the darkwand, the only weapon he possessed aside from his long knife. The darkwand was a talisman of magic meant to be used to breach the wall of the Forbidding. But it had come from the wood of the tree. Could it be used to penetrate the tangle of the tanequil's roots? Could it be employed in some way to free the Rover girl?

It was wishful thinking, seductive and empty of promise. There was nothing to suggest the darkwand would do him the slightest bit of good in his effort to bring Cinnaminson out of the ravine. But it

–Pen, no– Cinnaminson cried out, her voice separating suddenly from those of the other aeriads.

Instantly, the tanequil's roots began to shift, the rasp and scrape of fiber on earth and stone so menacing that Pen froze in midstride and brought the darkwand up like a shield. The wall had re-formed in front of him, barring him from getting any closer, telling him in no uncertain terms that he had transgressed. Tendrils stroked the exposed skin of his hands as the tree roots closest to him lifted out of the earth. In his mind, he could hear a hiss of warning, a sound so soft it was like the rustle of sand on old wood.

–Don't come any closer– It was the sound of a serpent's tongue sliding from a scaly mouth. –Go back to where you came from–

–Please, Pen– he heard Cinnaminson whisper. –Please, go away. Leave me where I am–

He wanted to ignore the warning, to go to her, to reach out to what was still real and substantive about her, to free her of that nightmare. The tanequil had given her the boundless world of an unfettered spirit, of the aeriads for whom it provided such freedom, but it was feeding on her, as well. He could tell that much just from looking. Did she realize that? Did she understand what was happening to her?

But he sensed, even as he asked these questions, that it didn't matter what she knew or how she might respond to knowing. What mattered was that she was content. She was the tree's captive, a slave to the roots that formed its feminine half, and they were not about to let her go for any reason. If he tried to take her, he would be killed. Then no one would know what had happened to her and no one would ever come to set her free.

He closed his eyes against what he was thinking, against his feelings of frustration and helplessness. He should do something, but there was nothing he could do. He had lost her all over again.

–Good-bye, Penderrin– he heard her say to him.

Her voice rose and fell to blend with the voices of the other aeriads before finally disappearing into them completely. Then the voices faded entirely, and she was gone.

Cinnaminson.

Aware of the sudden silence, he stood staring into space. Even the tree roots had gone still. Their tangled lengths lay limp and unmoving before him, a wall that he must breach. But he lacked the means to do so. He looked down at the darkwand, wondering anew if it might provide him the magic that was needed. But the purpose of the talisman was to help him gain access to Grianne Ohmsford, not to Cinnaminson. The darkwand could breach the wall of the Forbidding, but not the wall of the tanequil's roots. Nothing had happened to suggest otherwise. No magic had surfaced when his passage through the roots had been denied. No magic had emerged to help him.

His throat tightened as he realized that there was nothing more he could do. He would have to abandon his hopes of freeing her. He would have to leave her where she was. He would have to take the darkwand and travel to Paranor. He would have to attempt to cross over into the Forbidding and rescue the Ard Rhys. Cinnaminson had given herself to the tanequil so that he might do so. What was the point of her sacrifice if he failed to take advantage of it?

But it meant risking the possibility that he might never have a chance to come back for her.

He closed his eyes and took a deep breath. "Good-bye," he said softly to the darkness.

Then he turned away, walked back to the trail that had brought him down into the ravine, and began to climb.

The hand shook him gently awake, and Drumundoon's familiar voice whispered, "Captain, they're coming."

The Federation army. Preparing to attack.

Pied Sanderling opened his eyes to dawn's faint glow on the eastern horizon, scanned the maze of hills and ravines that surrounded him, and waited for the buzzing in his ears to quiet. Every muscle and joint in his body ached, but he couldn't very well complain. He was lucky to be alive at all.

He closed his eyes again, remembering. The explosion of fire, rocking the *Asashiel*, sweeping away railguns and deck crew. The plummet of the craft toward the earth as he clung to his safety line and called in vain for Markenstall. The impact of the airship as it slammed into a grove of wide-limbed conifers, breaking them apart, leaving him hanging from their shattered boughs. Miraculously, in one piece. No broken bones or severed limbs and no cuts or slashes deep enough to bleed him dry while he waited to be found.

And found he had been, almost at once, by Elven Home Guard in retreat from the airfield, who had watched his vessel fall out of the sky. His own troops, who had recognized him instantly and cut him down, pleading with him not to die, begging him to hold on until they could get help. He had been half-delirious then, burned and shocked, fighting demons that he imagined still flew overhead and hunted him as a hawk would a mouse seeking refuge where there was none to be found.

He had come around eventually, sometime during the long nighttime retreat through the cut to the hills north of the Prekkendorran, getting his first good look at the ragtag condition of his valiant Home Guard. Obedient to his orders, abandoned by Elven army regulars, they had stood alone against the hordes of Federation attackers that had swept across the airfield. The Home Guard had tried to hold their position, a hopeless task that, in the end, had failed. He had learned this much from Drumundoon, who had found him somehow during the night and stayed with him. He had learned, as well, that the Elven sector of the Prekkendorran was lost and that the Free-born allies, besieged on three sides, were in danger of being overrun. The battle was still being fought, a mix of Bordermen, Dwarves, and mercenaries fighting under the command of the charismatic Dwarf Vaden Wick. But disheartened by the death of their King, broken by the swiftness of their defeat, the Elves had abandoned the field.

"We need you, Captain," Drum had hissed at him, bent close so that only Pied could hear. "We need you desperately."

Pied could not quite understand why his aide was saying that. There was no longer anything he could do. He was a Captain of the Home Guard relieved of his command, reprimanded and humiliated by his King in a way that left no doubt about his future. Nothing could change that, especially with Kellen Elessedil dead and the Elven army scattered to the four winds.

But that was just the point, Drum had said. Kellen Elessedil *was* dead, and so was everyone who had heard him dismiss Pied as Captain of the Home Guard. The whole incident might never have happened, and in truth it would be best if everyone thought it hadn't. Look at how matters stood. Stow Fraxon, who commanded the Elven army regulars, was dead, killed in the Federation assault during the night. All of the airship commanders were dead. Most of the other commanders were scattered or lost. Of all Elven army units assigned to the Prekkendorran, only the Home Guard was still intact, and only Pied Sanderling was still with his command.

"We have Elven Hunters coming in from all over, Captain," Drum whispered. "They think you are their only hope, the only commander of the only unit still making a stand. Think about it. If they can't depend on you, who *can* they depend on? You still command, no matter what Kellen Elessedil might have said. Besides, a dead King can't do anything to save us from his mess. Only a live Captain of the Home Guard can do that."

Pied slept for a time, too tired to argue the point. When he woke, it was midday, and the Home Guard was deep in the tangle of hills north of the flats, pulling together the strays and the lost, linking up with other units that still looked to stand and fight somewhere, in spite of what had happened the night before. Most were in shock, but word had spread that Pied Sanderling had led a successful counterattack against the Federation and damaged the airship and weapon that had destroyed their fleet. While others had run, the Captain of the Home Guard had stood his ground. If there was any hope for the Elves, it lay with him.

Pied heard the talk, even though the words were whispered and the looks cast his way furtive. Drum hadn't exaggerated—everyone was depending on him. He might have been an ex-Captain of the Home Guard twenty-four hours earlier, but he was back in harness, like it or not. He could choose to set the record straight, but what good would that do? The Elven army needed confidence and determination; he knew better than most how to provide that, and he was in a position to do so. To forgo that responsibility would be to commit a violation of trust worse than anything Kellen Elessedil had ever imagined.

So he had called together his subcommanders and Lieutenants and devised a plan that would give them a chance to stall the Federation advance. In these hills, the Elves were a less visible target than on the flats or in the skies. Here, they could be more elusive as the terrain better suited their style of fighting. The Federation army was advancing on them with the intention of crushing any final resistance they might offer, then flanking and surrounding their Free-born allies. Putting a stop to their effort might very well determine the outcome of the entire war.

With a plan in place and the army regrouped, Drum had per-suaded Pied to go back to sleep. He was still battered from his tum-ble out of the sky, still exhausted enough that he needed to rest. Nothing he could do now was more important than what he would do when the Federation found them.

And now, he thought, opening his eyes once more to stare up into the still-darkened sky, *it has.*

He looked at Drumundoon. "Any sign of their airships?" He pushed himself up on one elbow with a grunt. The resulting aches and pains gave evidence of the time and distance he must travel still before he healed. "What about that big ship that was carrying their weapon?"

"No airships in sight at all," his aide responded, reaching down to pull him all the way up and handing him the chain-mail vest he al-ways wore in battle.

Pied stared in disbelief. "How in the world did you find this?"

"I never let go of it, Captain," the other man advised, giving him a wry smile. "I knew you'd be needing it when you came back."

That he believed Pied *would* come back spoke volumes about his faith in his commander. Pied pulled on the vest, buckled on the leather greaves and arm guards that Drum had also somehow sal-vaged, strapped on a short sword and long knife, and slung his bow and arrows across his back.

He shook his head. "You never cease to amaze me, Drum." He stretched, adjusted the armor and weapons, and nodded. "All right. Lead the way."

They went down through the camp to cheers and waves from the Elven Hunters and Home Guard. The ranks of the previous day had swelled to double and, in some cases, triple what they had been, units that had been broken and scattered re-formed and made whole again overnight. The day was clear and the sky cloudless, but the light was pale and silvery on the horizon, the sun still down behind the hills. When it lifted into view, it would blind those walking into it.

Accordingly, Pied had set his defensive line on a low rise that placed the Elves with their backs to the sun and required their enemies to come at them from out of a wide draw that was flanked by high hills on either side. The draw led out of a ten-mile-long cut that twisted through the twin plateaus of the Prekkendorran, a natural passage that seemed to those marching north to be the beginning of a clear opening to the land beyond. But the look was deceptive; after entering the draw, it became apparent that navigating a series of narrow defiles was then necessary to reach open terrain.

Pied was hoping that whoever was leading the Federation pursuit force did not realize that. It was a realistic hope, given the fact that no Federation force had penetrated that far north in almost fifty years. Airships scouting the Prekkendorran might have noticed the lay of the land, but surveys so far north would have been deemed unimportant or, even if made, long since forgotten or lost.

He put his archers on the flanking heights and his Home Guard and regulars within the draw in two ranks, splitting each into a series of triangles that could attack or retreat in sequence. He was counting on a shifting, three-sided Elven counterthrust to slow the expected full-frontal assault by the larger Federation force. He was counting on being able to turn the attacker's left flank into its main body. He was counting on the resulting confusion and the blinding sunrise to allow the Elves to inflict enough damage to force a retreat. The Federation, he believed, would be relying on superior numbers and brute strength to break the back of the Elven defense. Its perception would be that Elven morale was low after the previous night's debacle and that not much would be needed to put an end to whatever resistance remained.

In truth, Pied was not entirely certain that that wasn't exactly what would happen. He believed the Elves had recovered their pride and sense of purpose, but he also remembered his own assessment of two days earlier, when he had judged them ill prepared and poorly motivated. He had to hope that things had changed, that their defeat on the Prekkendorran, rather than disheartening them, had given them fresh courage.

But it was only in the heat of battle that he would discover which way the tide was running. By then, the die would be cast.

* * *

Sen Dunsidan stalked the perimeter of the cordoned-off shipyard where Federation workers were crawling all over the *Dechtera* in an effort to get her back in the skies. She had suffered damage to her steering mechanisms and several of her parse tubes, and he did not want to risk taking her up again until he was certain she was not in danger of going down behind Free-born lines, where his enemies could get their hands on his precious weapon. Nor did he want to risk the possibility of further damage if there was a way to protect against it. So he was impatiently biding his time while the airship engineers worked on repairs and improvements, all of them aware of what would happen if they failed in their efforts.

Sometimes he wished he were sufficiently skilled and knowledgeable to solve all of his problems himself, knowing that the job would get done quickly and efficiently. He hated relying on others, hated waiting to discover if they would succeed or fail, and hated the fact that members of the Coalition Council and the public alike would attribute their failures to him and their successes to anyone but.

Still, what was the point of being Prime Minister if you couldn't delegate and command the services of those you led?

He stopped his pacing and stared north. He could take considerable pleasure in what his leadership had accomplished so far. The trap he had set to snare the Elven warships had been more successful than even he had believed possible. In a single night, he had destroyed the bulk of the enemy fleet and killed the King and his sons in the process. The latter was an incredible stroke of good fortune, for it left the Elves not only without a fleet but without their titular leader and his chosen successors, as well. He couldn't imagine what had possessed Kellen Elessedil to do something so foolhardy, but he was grateful for the unexpected gift. Like his father before him, Kellen was given to rash acts. That his last had come when it could be capitalized on so completely was a sign to Sen Dunsidan that his fortunes were about to turn.

But not if he failed to finish the job. Not if he failed to destroy what remained of the Elven army so that he could surround and annihilate its allies. Not if he failed to get the *Dechtera* back into the skies.

He caught sight of Etan Orek scurrying across the platform that housed the weapon he had invented, checking fittings and surfaces, making certain that everything was sound. He had brought the little engineer out to the battlefield with him when he flew the *Dechtera* from the shipyards in Arishaig, deciding that he should be close by in case anything went wrong with the weapon once it was put into use.

A needless concern, as it turned out, but how was he to know? The prototype had performed as expected—better than expected, really, given the destruction it had wreaked on the Elves. It was the *Dechtera* that had fallen short of her goal. Still, a delay was not so costly at this point. The Federation army had penetrated the Free-born lines, taking command of the west plateau and sweeping all the way north into the hills in which the remnants of the Elven Hunters hid. The Free-born allies still held the east plateau, but they were surrounded on three sides. More to the point, they were confused and hesitant to counterattack. Having witnessed the destruction of the Elven fleet, they were terrified for the safety of their own. *As well they should be,* he thought. Because once the *Dechtera* was airborne again, it would be a simple matter to burn the allied vessels to cinders while they sat on the ground and cut apart the Free-born defensive lines to allow the Federation army passage through.

He was impatient for that. He wanted it to be over and done with. He wanted his victory in hand.

Beware, Sen Dunsidan, he cautioned himself as the adrenaline sent a fresh surge of heady, euphoric anticipation rushing through him. *Don't overstep. Don't overreact. Don't rush to your own doom.*

He had been a politician too long to indulge in rash behavior. Mistakes of that sort were for less experienced men and women, for the likes of those whose life spans he had cut short on more occasions than he cared to remember. Being a survivor meant being wary of premature celebration and incautious optimism. Being a survivor meant never taking anything for granted, never accepting anything at face value.

"Are your thoughts deep ones, Prime Minister?"

He whirled at the sound of Iridia Eleri's voice, surprised to find her standing right next to him. It frightened him that she could get so close without him hearing her approach. It angered him that she had been doing so repeatedly since he had agreed to accept her offer to act as his private adviser, as if their arrangement invited such intrusion. Worst of all, it reminded him of the way the Ilse Witch used to materialize in his bedchamber, a memory he would just as soon forget.

"My thoughts are my own, Iridia," he replied. "They are neither deep nor shallow, only practical. Have you something to offer, or are you just looking for new ways to stop my heart?"

If she was offended by his irritation, she kept it to herself. "I have something to offer, if you seek a way to end this war much more quickly than it will be ended otherwise."

He stared at her, transfixed by more than the possibility her words suggested. She was so pale in the moonlight that she seemed almost transparent, the cast of her skin as white as death, the darkness of her eyes in such sharp contrast they seemed opaque. She was dressed in a black robe, her slender body completely shrouded and her head hooded. Her face, peering from the hood's shadows, and her hands, clutching loosely at the robe's edges, gave disconcerting evidence that he was in the presence of a ghost.

It was not the first time he had experienced that feeling. There had been a look to Iridia of late that was so chillingly otherworldly, he had trouble at times believing she wasn't something less than human.

He pursed his lips at her. "I will end it quickly enough on my own, once the *Dechtera* is airborne again. My weapon will burn what remains of the Free-born fleet to cinders. I already hunt the remnants of the Elven army and will find them within the week, as well. Aren't you better off worrying about Shadea and her Druids than matters of war? Isn't that the task which you were assigned?"

It was a stinging rebuke, delivered as much out of distaste for her unwanted intervention as dismay over her lack of sophistication in battle tactics. But she seemed unmoved by his words, her expression empty of feeling.

"My task is to save you from yourself, Prime Minister. The Free-born have lost their ships on the Prekkendorran, but they can obtain others. Their army might be scattered and in momentary disarray, but it will regroup. You will not win this war through a single victory. You should know as much without my having to tell you."

Her words were so dismissive that he flushed in spite of himself. She was talking to him as if he were a child.

"This war has lasted fifty years," she continued, seemingly oblivious to his reaction. "It will not be ended on the Prekkendorran. It will not be won on any Southland battlefield. It will be won in the Westland. It will be won when you break the spirit of the Elves, because it is the Elves who are the backbone of the Free-born struggle. Break their spirit, and those who fight with them will be quick to seek peace."

He frowned. "I would have thought that the loss of their fleet and their King had accomplished that. Obviously, you don't agree. Have you something else in mind, a more persuasive way to bring them into line?"

"Much more persuasive."

He felt his patience ebb as he waited in vain for her to continue. "Am I expected to guess at what it is, or will you save me the trouble and simply tell me?"

She looked away from him, out over the shipyard to where the *Dechtera* sat dark and menacing in the moonlight, to where the shipyard workers continued to repair her. She was looking in that direction, but he had the feeling that she was looking at something else altogether, something hidden from him. He was struck again by the distant feel of her, the sense that she was not entirely where she appeared to be.

"You are not averse to killing, are you, Prime Minister?" she asked suddenly.

It was the way she asked the question that made him think she intended to trap him with his own words. He had developed a sixth sense about the use of such tactics over his years, and it had saved him from disaster more than once.

"Are you afraid to answer me?" she pressed.

"You know I am not afraid of killing."

"I know you believe that the ends justify the means. I know you believe that accomplishing your goals entitles you to take whatever steps are required. I know that you are the architect of the deaths of your predecessor and those who would have succeeded him. I know that you have participated in blood games of all sorts."

"Then speak your mind and quit playing games with me. My patience with you grows thin."

Her bloodless face lifted out of the hood's concealing shadows so that her dark eyes locked on his. "Listen closely, then. You waste needless time killing soldiers on the Prekkendorran. Killing soldiers means nothing to those who send them forth. If you want to break the spirit of the Elves, if you want to put an end to their resistance, you have to kill those whom the soldiers protect. You have to kill their women and children. You have to kill their old people and their infirm. You have to take the war from the battlefield into their homes."

Her voice was a hiss. "You have the weapon to do so, Prime Minister. Fly the *Dechtera* to Arborlon and use it. Burn their precious city and its people to ashes. Make them afraid to think of doing anything other than begging for your mercy."

She said it dispassionately, but her words transfixed him. He went hot and cold in turn, cowed at first by the prospect of such savagery, then excited by it. He was already perceived to be a monster, so there was little reason to pretend he wasn't. He did not care in the slightest about preserving the lives of those who opposed him, and the Elves had been a thorn in his side for twenty years. Why not cull their numbers sufficiently that they would not threaten again in his lifetime?

"But you are an Elf yourself," he said. "Why are you so willing to kill your own people?"

She made a sound that might have been meant as laughter. "I am *not* an Elf! I am a Druid! Just as you are a Prime Minister and not a Southlander. It is the power we wield that commands our loyalty, Sen Dunsidan, not some accident of birth."

She was right, of course. His nationality and Race meant nothing to him beyond the opportunities they provided for advancement.

"As a Druid, then," he snapped, "you must know that Shadea will not approve of this. She will be here to confer with me in two days. She is already distressed that I attacked the Free-born without first advising her. Once she discovers my new intention, she will put a stop to it. In appearances, at least, the Druids must seem impartial. She might back the Federation in its bid to reclaim the Borderlands, but she will never countenance genocide."

"Tell her nothing, then. Let her respond when it is over, after she has already openly declared her support of the Federation. Will anyone listen to her, no matter how loudly she protests?"

"In which case she will come looking for me, and not to offer congratulations."

The pale face looked away. "I will deal with her when she does."

He thought to question such boldness, for in the time he had known Iridia he had never once believed that she was a match for Shadea a'Ru. But perhaps things had changed. She sounded very sure of herself, and the steely resolve she brought to their alliance had given him reason to suspect she had grown more powerful.

"What is your decision, Prime Minister?" she pressed.

He was certain of one thing only. If he chose to pursue Iridia's course of action, questions of ethics were pointless. If he failed, questions of ethics would be the least of his problems. And if he succeeded, such questions would be whispered in private, because he would then have become the most powerful figure in the Four Lands. Not even the Druids would dare to challenge his authority.

It should have been an easy decision. Where power and influence were at stake, he had never hesitated in making his choice. Yet he hesitated here. Something felt wrong about this, perhaps a consequence he had not considered or a possibility he had overlooked. But whatever it was, it was definitely there, nagging at him. He could feel it deep inside where such things could not be ignored.

"Prime Minister?"

He gave the doubt another few seconds, and then he dismissed it. There was never gain without risk, and risk always raised doubts. He knew his own mind well enough to embrace what he must do. Without Grianne Ohmsford to worry about, he could afford to take chances he might not otherwise take. The loss of a few thousand lives was not worrying enough to deter him. There was more at stake than lives.

"We will fly to Arborlon," he said.

Dawn broke in a flare of brightness as the sun crested the rim of the hills and began to lift into the sky. The Elves were settled in, most hidden from view behind hummocks and rocks and in the shadows of the defiles, ranks formed and weapons at the ready. Already, they could hear the sound of the Federation army marching to the attack, the pounding of boots and the thumping of spears and swords against shields steady and rhythmic and unnerving. Flashes of light reflected off the flat surfaces of blades as the Federation soldiers wound through the cut and began the long, twisting trek across the flats to where their quarry waited.

Pied, standing with his Home Guard, scanned his ranks for movement and found none. The Elves had disappeared as only the Elves could. They would not be spied out by the Federation until it was too late. He wished he had the services of cavalry to ride at the Federation flanks, but foot soldiers would have to do. He wished he had the use of catapults and fire launchers, but slings and arrows would have to do. He would be outnumbered, perhaps by as much as five to one. He lacked practical experience commanding on a battlefield; he was Captain of the Home Guard, not a Commander of the Elven army. He was the highest-ranking officer present, and he had never been in a battle of such size.

There's a first time for everything, the old saying went. He just wished there wasn't so much at stake.

He looked down the ranks of those closest and found Drumundoon standing almost next to him, tall and gangly and looking oddly out of place in his battle gear. Drum wasn't meant to fight on the line; he was meant to serve behind it. Yet there was determination in his young face, and when he caught Pied looking at him, he winked.

Reason enough to believe in him, Pied thought. *Reason enough to believe in them all.*

He tightened his grip on his sword and settled deeper into the shadows.

TWENTY-EIGHT

G rianne Ohmsford lay with her face pressed against the stone floor of her cell, her eyes closed. She was trying to escape, even though there was nowhere to run. Torchlight from the hallway beyond intruded on the darkness in which she wished to hide. Low voices and the soft shuffling of boots nudged her out of her hiding places. Water dripped and the earth rumbled deep within its core, reminders of where she was. Like hungry preda-tors from the black holes into which she had tried to banish them, memories emerged and made her skin crawl.

But it was the mewling cries of the Furies, triggers to a mix of horror and madness from which there was no escape, that chased her down and found her out no matter how far inside herself she re-treated. She cringed from them, drawing up into a ball, becoming as small and still as possible, willing herself to disappear. But noth-ing helped. She had used her magic to become one of them, and she could not change back again. She mewled with them. She hissed and snarled with them. She spit with poisonous intent. She flexed her claws and drew back her muzzle. She rose to greet them, re-sponding to their summoning, a response she loathed but could not prevent.

She squeezed her eyes so tightly shut they hurt. She would have cried had there been tears to do so. Her world was a room six feet by ten feet, but it might as well have been the size of a coffin.

They had returned her to her cell from the arena in the same way they had brought her, in a cage and in chains, Goblins and demon-wolves surrounding her, Hobstull directing them. Back through the crowds and the blasted countryside. Back through the gloom and mist. Time had stopped, and her sense of herself and her place had disappeared. She was a captured beast. She was a lifetime removed from her role as Ard Rhys, and the Druids and Paranor were a dim memory. All the way back, she fought to regain her identity, but the rolling and the jouncing seemed only to exacerbate her confusion. It was easier to disappear into the role she had adopted than to try to follow the threads that might lead her out. It was simpler to embrace the primal creature she had awakened than to cast it aside.

They stripped and bathed her on her return, and she did not try to stop them. She stood naked and exposed and uncaring, gone so deep inside herself that she felt nothing of what they did to her. Cat sounds issued from her lips and her fingers flexed, but she did not see the way her captors drew back. She did not see them at all. She did not know they were there.

I am lost, she thought at one point. *I am destroyed, and I have done it to myself.*

Time passed, but little seemed to change. Guards came and went, the light dimmed and brightened as torches sputtered and were re-placed, food was delivered and taken away uneaten, and the demons that haunted her kept edging closer. She wanted to break their spell, to banish them along with the hissing and mewling of her Fury memories, but she could not gather together the will to do so.

One time only did she sleep. She did not know for how long, only that she did, and that when her dreams took the shape of her memories, she woke screaming.

The Straken Lord did not reappear. Hobstull stayed away. She did not know what they intended, but the longer she was left alone, the more certain she became that they had lost interest in her en-tirely. There was no use for such as her, for a woman who was will-ing to take the form of a monster, to assume the persona of a raver.

There was no place, even in the world of demons, for something that lacked any moral center or recognizable purpose. She saw herself as they did, a damaged and conflicted creature, a chameleon that could not distinguish between reality and fantasy, able to be either or both, but unable to tell the difference.

She felt herself sliding over the edge of sanity. It was happening gradually, just a few inches at a time, but there was no mistaking it. Each day, she felt her Ard Rhys self fall just a little farther away and her Fury self close about her just a little bit tighter. It grew easier to embrace the latter and reject the former. It grew more attractive to see herself as inhuman. If she was no better than one of the Furies, her life became less complicated. The madness seemed to ease and the conflict to diminish. As a Fury, she did not have to worry about where she was or how she had gotten there. She did not need to concern herself with the increasingly fuzzy distinctions between different worlds and lives. As a Fury, the world flattened and smoothed, and there was only killing and food and the lure of life with her cat kind.

She began seeing herself as an imprisoned animal. She began making cat sounds all the time, finding comfort in the soft mewling. She flexed her fingers and arched her back. She bit her cheek and tasted her own blood.

But she did not rise or eat. She did not move from where she lay. She refused to come out of the dark refuge of her delusions. She stayed safe and protected in her mind.

Then, as if from a dream, she heard someone calling to her. At first she thought she must have imagined it. No one would call to her, not here or anywhere else. No one would want to have anything to do with someone as terrible as she was.

But she heard the voice again, hushed and insistent. She heard it speak her name. Surprised, she stirred from her self-induced lethargy to listen for it, and heard it again.

"Grianne of the trees! Can you hear me? Why do you make those cat noises? Do you dream? Wake up!"

Her mind sharpened and her concentration coalesced, until the words became distinct and the voice recognizable. She knew the one who called to her, remembered him from another time and place.

She felt the pull of that familiarity, as if she were coming back from a long journey to someone she had left behind.

"Wake up, Straken! Stop squirming! What is wrong with you? Don't you hear me?"

Her breathing quickened, and a bit of the sluggishness fell away. She knew that voice. She knew it well. Something about it gave her fresh energy and a sense of renewed possibility. She tried to speak, choked on words that wouldn't come, and made unintelligible sounds instead.

"What are you doing, little cat thing? Have I wasted my time coming here? Are you not able to speak? Look at me!"

She did so, opening her eyes for the first time in days, breaking the crust of tears that had dried and sealed her lids, squinting against the unfamiliar brightness, reaching up to rub away the sleep and confusion. She stirred slowly, raised herself on one elbow, and looked toward the light that spilled from the hallway into her cell.

A Goblin sentry stood pressed against the cell bars, peering in at her. The torchlight cast his shadow across her like a shroud. She stared in confusion, feeling the lethargy and hopelessness return almost at once. This was no one. She was deceived. Her head lowered once more, and her eyes began to close.

"No! What are you doing? Straken! It's me!"

She looked up in time to see the Goblin pushing back the hood of his cloak to reveal his face. She peered at it out of a fog of exhaustion and uncertainty, watched it take shape, and struggled to make sense of what she was seeing.

"Weka Dart," she whispered.

She stared at him, not quite believing he was actually there. She had all but forgotten about the little Ulk Bog. Once he had abandoned her and she had fallen into the hands of the Straken Lord, she had not expected ever to see him again. That he was standing there was almost incomprehensible.

"You should have listened to me!" he hissed. "Didn't I tell you? Didn't I warn you not to go on without me?"

His sharp features were scrunched into a knot, giving him the look of a demented beast. His hair was standing straight out from his

head and neck, bristling and stiff. His sharp teeth flashed from behind his lips as he tried to smile and failed, and his fingers knotted on
the bars.

Her mind cleared a bit further, and she pushed back against the
urge to mewl and spit. "How did you find me?"

He stared at her as if she were mad. "You still don't know anything, do you? What kind of Straken are you?"

She shook her head. "The worst kind."

"You certainly look it." Weka Dart laughed. "I found you by paying attention to the world around me, something you seem to have
failed to master. But this isn't your world, is it? This isn't even remotely like it. So maybe you aren't to blame for anything more than
bad judgment."

He was telling her something, but she couldn't make sense of it.
"Was it good judgment that brought you here, then?"

The Ulk Bog spit. "I am not sure what it was. I heard in my travels what had happened to you, and I admit that I thought it best to
leave you to your fate. But then chance and inspiration intervened,
so here I am."

"Chance and inspiration?"

"I was crossing the Pashanon on my way to Huka Flats, the route
I had chosen for myself and advised you to take as well. As I traveled,
word reached me of your capture. Such things do not go unreported
in this land, and I keep my eyes and ears open. It was easy enough to
determine what had happened to you. The difficulty was in deciding
what I should do about it."

He puffed out his chest. "I will admit that at first I thought it best
simply to go on. You had dismissed me, after all. What did it matter
what became of you? You were rude to me. You insulted me. In the
end, you ignored my good advice and brought disaster on yourself. I
owed you nothing. No one could fault me if I chose to leave you to
your fate.

"But then, I reconsidered. After all, it wasn't your fault that you
were a stranger to this country, one lacking in good judgment and
common sense. You were to be pitied. I felt an obligation toward

you. I thought it over and made up my mind. I would come find you. I would see how you were. If you were nice to me, I would decide whether you deserved a second chance."

Even in her confused and debilitated state, of being not all of one thing or the other, she recognized that his words were lies. She could hear it in the way he spoke; she could see it in the rapid shifting of his eyes and body. As always, he was after something, but she had no idea what it was.

"How did you get down here?" she asked.

He gave a casual shrug. "I have my ways."

"Ways that allow you to get past the demonwolves and the Goblins that serve the Straken Lord?"

He sniffed. "I am not without skills."

She pulled herself into a sitting position and became aware for the first time in days how stiff and sore she was. She looked down at herself, first at the bruises and cuts on her arms and legs, then at the white shift she wore. She was much better dressed than when she had been taken to the arena. She glanced around. Her cell was cleaner, too.

Her focus narrowed sharply. Was she mistaken about the intentions of the Straken Lord? What was going on?

She looked at Weka Dart. "If you don't stop lying to me and tell me the truth," she said softly, "I might have to use my Straken magic on you, Ulk Bog."

He grinned, showing all his sharp teeth. "That might be a little difficult, since you wear a conjure collar."

He seemed to realize his mistake almost immediately, a change coming into his eyes and the self-satisfied look fading as his lips compressed in silent reprimand. "Conjure collars are not unknown to me," he said quickly. "I've seen them before."

In truth, she had forgotten about the collar until he reminded her of it, but he didn't know that and she wasn't about to tell him so. She held herself very still and continued to stare at him.

"I don't know who you are or what you want, Weka Dart," she said finally, "but you haven't told me one word of truth since we met.

This has all been a game for you, a game in which you seem to know all the rules while I know none. If you know what a conjure collar is, you know too much to be just a simple village creature traveling to a new part of the country. If you know how to bypass the Straken Lord's guards, you have skills and knowledge that suggest you are something more than you pretend. I have had enough of you. Either tell me the truth or leave me here to rot."

She held up one finger as he started to speak. "Be careful. If you are about to tell me another lie, think twice. I don't have much left to call my own, but I do have my sense of what is true and what isn't. You don't want to try to take that from me."

The Ulk Bog stared at her. Wary eyes studied her uncertainly; deep creases etched his wizened face.

He shook his head. "I don't know how much I should tell you," he said finally.

She sighed. "Why not tell me everything? What possible difference can it make now?"

"More than you think. Difference enough that I must consider carefully. You are right about me. You are right about my story. But you are in a stronger position than you believe. You have something I want. All I have to offer in exchange is the truth—and perhaps a way out of here. I can give you the one for the other. But I am afraid you will refuse me when you hear what I have to say. I am afraid you will hate me."

He spoke with such sincerity that for the first time since she had met him she was inclined to believe what he said. She did not understand how all that could be, but it didn't matter. What mattered was that he had said he might be able to help her escape. At that point, she would do anything; make any bargain, agree to any conditions to gain her freedom. Because if she remained where she was, she knew she was lost.

But she couldn't let him know that. She couldn't let him see her desperation. Giving Weka Dart that sort of power over her was too dangerous. He would take advantage of her as quickly as Tael Riverine had.

She took a deep breath. "Listen to me. You came here with the intention of trading or you wouldn't have come here at all. My word is good, Weka Dart. I keep my promises. So I will give you one now. If you tell me the truth about yourself, I will tell you if I can forgive you for your lies. Then you can decide if you still think it's worth it to try to trade what you want for my freedom."

She hauled herself to her feet and with some effort stumbled over to where he stood. "What's it to be, little Ulk Bog? A bargain or a good-bye? I don't really care anymore."

He stared at her some more, his yellow eyes flicking left and right, up and down, scanning the whole of her face, but never settling on any one part. She could see a glimmer of doubt and fear mirrored there. But she could also see hope.

He nodded. "Very well, Grianne of the many promises. I will tell you, even though I think all Strakens lie." He spit again and shook his head. "I know who you are and where you come from. I always did. I know because I was Catcher for Tael Riverine before Hobstull was. I would be Catcher still if the Straken Lord hadn't decided I had lost my skills. He was wrong, but there is no arguing with a Straken. So he replaced me. But not before he humiliated me in ways I will never discuss, so don't ask it of me."

He swallowed hard. "He took me in when I was driven from my tribe for eating my young. He cared nothing for any of that, only for what I could do for him. He recognized my skills and offered me a place at Kraal Reach as his Catcher. He knew that I would accept, that I had to because I could not survive alone and unprotected in the world of the Jarka Ruus. He gave me what I needed, but then he took everything back when he cast me out. So I vowed that I would take everything from him in turn."

His voice grew fierce. "The plans to bring you here have been in place for some time. Tael Riverine would swap you for his changeling creature, the Moric. Easy enough for a Straken of his power. I decided to disrupt his plans by getting to you first, which I did. I intended to take you away from him, to steal you out from under his nose. I intended to embarrass Hobstull and reveal him to the Straken Lord as a failure! Then I would produce you and regain my rightful place!"

He was breathing hard, his eyes become narrow slits, his throat working rapidly as he sought to gauge her reaction. She gave him nothing, listening blank-faced and empty-eyed, her talent as the Ilse Witch resurfacing from where she had kept it buried for twenty years. *So easy to call it up again,* she thought. *So easy to go back to being what I was.*

"My plan failed when you refused to come with me," Weka Dart continued. "Failed completely. I tried everything. But you were so insistent on going your own way! And I couldn't change your mind without giving myself away!" He shook his head. "So I let you go. I said, *If that is what she wants, then give it to her! See how well she does without you! Walk away from the Straken and nothing is lost!* I wasn't going to risk my life following after you when I knew what would happen. Hobstull was looking, and it was only a matter of time until he found you. He didn't know exactly where you would appear, only that you would. But I knew! I knew, because I have always been better able to read the signs of such things! I have always been the better Catcher!"

He spit the words out and flung himself away from the cell bars, dropping to the floor in a crouch, refusing to look at her. She watched him for a moment, her mind working through the choices his revelations had given her.

"Weka Dart," she said.

He stayed where he was.

"Look at me."

He refused, turned away, and hunched down.

"Look at me. Tell me what you see in my eyes."

Finally, he turned just enough to glance over his shoulder and make momentary eye contact, then looked away again.

"I am not angry with you," she said. "You did what I would have done if our positions had been reversed. In fact, once upon a time, when I was a different person living a different life, I did things much worse to others than what you have done to me."

He looked back at her once more.

"I don't hate you," she told him.

"You should." His teeth clicked as his jaws snapped shut.

"My hate is reserved for others more deserving and less forthcoming about their efforts to see me dead and gone." She gestured for him to come back. "Tell me the rest of what you know."

He stayed where he was a moment longer, then sighed, rose, and came back to stand in front of her. "You don't hate me? If you were free, you wouldn't try to kill me?"

She shook her head. "I don't hate you. Even if I had the chance to do so, I wouldn't try to kill you. Now tell me the rest. Do you know the Straken Lord's plans?"

The Ulk Bog nodded. "I was here at Kraal Reach when he was making them." He looked closely at her. "You still don't know what he intends? You haven't seen the way he looks at you?"

She went cold all the way to her bones, the little man's words conjuring up an image that froze her blood. "Tell me."

"He has been testing you to see if you are a suitable vessel to bear his children. He wishes to mate with you."

For the first time, she was really afraid. The demon was anathema to her. She could think of no worse fate than to be the mother of its children, the mother of demonkind, a bearer of monsters. She had never considered the possibility. She had never recognized that the Straken Lord had any interest in her beyond keeping her imprisoned and alive until its creature, the Moric, could do whatever it had been sent to do in her own world.

"This was the reason for bringing me here?" she managed to ask, working hard to keep her voice steady.

Weka Dart shook his head, his gimlet eyes glittering. "No. The idea must have occurred to him after you were his prisoner. His plans are much grander than that."

"How much grander?"

The Ulk Bog leaned close. "He has been searching for a way to send the Moric into your world for some time. But for that to happen, it was necessary to find someone in your world willing to help. He found those people, and he used them as his tool. Whoever they were had no idea what the Straken Lord intended, but were only interested in disposing of you. That was what your betrayer knew—that using the magic would banish you to the world of the Jarka Ruus. That, and nothing more. Your betrayers knew nothing of the exchange, nothing of the way the magic really worked, nothing of the trade that was necessary to bring you here. The Straken Lord was careful to keep that secret hidden."

As well it should have been, she thought. But she wasn't sure that knowing a trade was required would have stopped whoever was desperate enough to send her into the Forbidding.

"But why was I brought here if not to mate with Tael Riverine?" she pressed.

"You miss the point, Straken!" Weka Dart snapped. "Bringing you here was never what mattered! What mattered was sending the Moric into your world!"

She shook her head. "Why?"

"So that it could destroy the barrier that keeps us locked away! So that it could free the Jarka Ruus!"

Now she understood. The Moric had been sent to complete the task that the Dagda Mor had failed to accomplish more than five hundred years earlier—to break down the walls of the prison behind which the dark things of Faerie had been shut since before the dawn of Man.

Her mind raced. To do that, it would have to destroy the Ellcrys, the magic-born Elven tree that had been created to ward the Forbidding. How would it manage that, when the tree was always so closely guarded?

More important, how could she stop it from happening?

"Does the Moric have a way to destroy the barrier?" she asked Weka Dart.

He shook his head. "It was to find one once it crossed over into your world. It is very talented and very smart. It will have done so by now."

She ignored the fear that rushed through her at the thought that the Ulk Bog might be right. "Do you have a way to get me out of here?" she asked quickly.

On the landing above them, at the top of the stairway, a door opened and closed with a thud. Footsteps sounded on the stone steps, coming down.

"On the floor!" he hissed at her, and darted away.

She threw herself back down, sprawling in the same position in which he had found her, her heart pounding, her muscles tensed. *Don't move,* she told herself. *Don't do anything.*

The steps approached her cell and came to a stop. A silence settled in like morning mist.

Eyes closed, body still, she waited.

TWENTY-NINE

P en Ohmsford's ascent from the ravine was an endless slog. Burdened with self-recrimination and despair, it was all he could do to place one foot in front of the other. He kept thinking he should go back, should attempt one final time to free Cinnaminson, make one more plea or take one last stand. But he knew it was pointless even to think about doing so. Nothing would change until he had some better means of succeeding. Yet he couldn't stop thinking about it. He couldn't stop himself from feeling that he should have done more.

Lead-footed, he climbed through the hazy darkness, working his way up the narrow switchback trail, ducking under vines and brushing past brambles and scrub, leaning on his staff for support, his thoughts scattered all over the place. His grip about the rune-carved handle of the darkwand helped to center him, a reassurance that he had accomplished something in the midst of all the failures. Lives had been lost and hopes blown away like dried leaves in a strong wind, and he blamed himself for most of it. He should have done better, he kept telling himself, even though he could not think what more he might have done or exactly what he might have changed. Hindsight suggested possibilities, but hindsight was deceptive, sifted through a filter of distance and reason. Things were never so easy as they seemed later. They were mostly wild and confused and emotionally charged. Hindsight pretended otherwise.

But knowing so didn't make him feel any better. Knowing so only made him work harder to find a reason to believe he had failed.

He took some comfort in the fact that he had gotten to Stridegate at all, that he had confronted the tanequil and found a way to communicate with it, that he had secured the limb he needed and shaped it into the darkwand. He had gotten much farther with his quest than he had ever believed he would. He had never spoken of it, but he had always thought in the back of his mind that what the King of the Silver River had sent him to do was impossible. He had always thought that he was the wrong choice, a boy with little experience and few skills, a boy asked to do something that most grown men would not even attempt. He did not know what had persuaded him to try. He guessed it was the expectations of those who had accompanied him. He guessed it was his own need to prove himself.

These and other equally troubling thoughts roiled through his brain as he climbed, working along the tunnels of his conscience like worms, probing and sifting for explanations that would satisfy them. He tried to lay them to rest, but he only managed to settle with a few. The rest continued on, digging away, finding fresh food in his doubts and fears and frustrations, growing and fattening and taking up all the space his emotional well-being would allow.

He rested at one point, dropping down on his haunches with his back against the wall of the ravine, feeling the cold and damp of the earth seep through his clothing and enter his body, too tired to care. He leaned on the darkwand for support as he lowered his head and cried soundlessly, unable to help himself. He was not the hero and adventurer he had envisioned himself to be. He was just a boy who wanted to go home.

But he knew that wasn't something that was going to happen anytime soon, and it wasn't helping him to think that it might, so he quit crying, stood up, and began climbing once more. Overhead, the daylight was beginning to fail, a graying of the sky that signaled the onset of twilight. He needed to reach the top of the ravine so that he could cross the bridge before it was dark. It never occurred to him that he would have any trouble doing so; the tanequil would let him pass unmolested. It had taken from him already what it wanted.

The slope broadened and the trail cut away from the bridge into a thicket of scrub and grasses that quickly melded into the beginnings of the island forest. The way forward grew more difficult and the light continued to dim steadily. He continued on, eyes forward as he resisted the urge to look back, knowing he would see nothing if he did, that she was too far away from him now. His memories of her were firmly etched in his mind, and that was as much as he could hope for.

He was thirsty and wished he had something to drink, but that would have to wait. He was hungry, too. He hadn't eaten anything since . . . He tried to remember and couldn't. More than a day, he thought. Much more. His stomach rumbled and his head felt light from the ascent, but there was no help for it.

He rested again, pausing in the dark concealment of a stand of saplings to let the dizziness pass, and it was then that he realized he wasn't alone. It happened all at once. A mix of things warned him of his danger—things not so much external as internal, a sensing through his magic that the world about him wasn't quite right. He stood listening to the silence, took notice of the way the light shifted with the passing of clouds west across the sunset, caught the feel of the wind through the trees. His awareness was born of those mundane, ordinary observations, though he couldn't explain why. Something was there that hadn't been there earlier. Something he knew.

Or someone.

He felt a chill creep up his spine as he waited, trying to decide what he should do. His instincts told him that he was in danger, but they did not yet tell him what that danger was. If he moved, he might give himself away. If he stayed where he was, he might be found out anyway.

Finally, unable to think of anything else to do, he started forward, very slowly, a few steps at a time. Then he stopped and waited again, listening. Nothing. He took a deep breath and exhaled silently. If something was there, it was probably deeper in. His better choice was to skirt the rim of the island, above the ravine, until he reached the bridge and could then cross.

It occurred to him suddenly that he might be sensing someone from his own party, Khyber perhaps, grown impatient with his delay. But he didn't think Khyber would elicit the sort of response he was having; he wouldn't be made so uneasy by her presence. His reaction was surprising in any case, given the nature of his magic. Usually, he required contact with animals or birds or plants for such sensations to happen. Yet his response hadn't been triggered by any of those. It was coming from somewhere else entirely.

Move, he told himself silently, mouthing the word.

He started ahead, angling back toward the ravine. He could just make it out through the screen of the trees, the earth split wide and deep, a maw as black as night. An image formed, unbidden. *Cinnaminson.* He cast the troubling image aside angrily. *Move!*

To his left, farther into the trees and away from the ravine, something shifted. He saw it out of the corner of his eye and froze instantly. Leaves and grasses shivered, and the air stilled. Twilight had fallen in a gray mantle that blended shadows into strange patterns that gave everything the look of being alive.

He was aware suddenly that he was silhouetted against the horizon, easily identifiable by any eye. He thought to drop flat, but movement of that sort would give him away instantly. He stayed where he was, a statue, waiting.

In the trees, there was fresh movement. He saw it clearly this time, shadows separating and taking shape, the outline of a cloaked figure revealing itself. The figure crept through the maze of dark trunks and layered shadows like an animal, crouched down and moving on all fours.

Spiderlike.

He recognized it from their previous encounters. It was the thing that had chased him when he fled the seaport of Anatcherae to cross the Lazareen. It was the monster that had killed Gar Hatch and his crew and taken Cinnaminson.

It had tracked him all the way.

His heart sank. It was moving away from him, which meant it did not yet know exactly where he was. But it would find him soon enough, and when it did, he would have to face it. He wasn't going to have any choice. He knew it with a certainty that defied argument. He might try to run, to reach the bridge and cross to where his companions waited, but he would never make it. Flight wasn't going to save him. Not from this.

His fingers tightened on the darkwand, and he wondered again if it might possess a magic that could save him.

Then he wondered if anything could.

Khyber Elessedil had walked for the better part of two hours, following the dark line of the ravine through the trees, searching without success for a way across. At times, the gap narrowed, but never enough to suggest that trying to jump it or bridge it with a tree was going to work. Unchanging in its look as it twisted and turned and disappeared into the horizon, it angled on ahead of her as she stopped to consider whether to continue.

She glanced west, where the sun was dropping toward the jagged peaks of the Klu. No more than an hour or two of daylight remained. She sighed in exasperation. She did not want to give up, but she did not want to get caught out there alone in the dark, either. She looked ahead once more, then reluctantly turned around and started back. There was no help for it. Tomorrow, if Pen and Cinnaminson hadn't reappeared, she would consider going the other way, following the ravine north.

Or perhaps she would simply cross the bridge and find them, her promise to wait notwithstanding.

Perhaps enough was enough.

She trooped back through the trees and grasses, muttering to herself and thinking that they had all been ill served in the venture, starting with the questionable decision by the King of the Silver River to entrust the rescue of the Ard Rhys to Pen. Not that she doubted Pen's courage, but he was only a boy, much younger even than she and totally lacking in skills or magic. That he was still alive at all after what had happened to them was something of a miracle. Look how many of their company had died instead, including the most talented and experienced of them all.

But it didn't do her any good to think that way—to suggest that in some way Ahren Elessedil had died without reason—and she put the matter aside. Her doubts and fears could not be placed at the feet of others. If she was worried or afraid, she would have to find another way of dealing with it.

She thought it odd how things had changed since she had left Emberen. There, her chief concern had been in determining how and when to reveal to Ahren her theft of the Elfstones so that he wouldn't take them back until she had learned to use them. Now that the Elfstones were hers to keep for as long as she chose, she wanted nothing more than to be able to give them back.

Thinking she might as well wish she could fly for all the good it would do her, she kicked at the earth as she walked. She was in until the end, which meant at least until Pen had returned to Paranor and gone into the Forbidding to find his aunt. Even then, she would not be free to go home again until Pen reappeared safely. Probably, she should go with him. After all, they only had the word of the King of the Silver River that she couldn't, and there was good reason to question anything the Faerie creature had told them.

The sun slid down into the peaks, coloring the horizon in the wake of its passing, leaving the depthless bowl of the sky dark with night's approach. She cast wary glances left and right as she walked, using her Druid skills to make certain she was not being tracked by anything unfriendly. The Urdas might have chosen to come around the walls at the front of the ruins in an effort to get at them from the sides.

It was because her senses were pricked and her magic deployed that she found Pen. It happened unexpectedly, when she was nearing the bridge, her attention focused mostly on her return to her companions. She caught a whiff of his presence and slowed at once, casting all about. He wasn't immediately visible, but she could tell that he was still on the far side of the ravine, back in the trees. He was moving slowly and cautiously, as if wary of something.

When he appeared at the ravine's edge, her impression was confirmed. He was advancing in a crouch through a thin screen of trees, stopping frequently to look back into the deeper part of the forest. Each time he did so, he cocked his head as if listening for something. Or *to* something. She couldn't tell.

She thought to call out to him, but she was afraid that if she did so, she would give him away to whatever he was trying to avoid. So she waited, tracking his movements. She noticed a dark staff he was carrying, something new. Was it the darkwand? A rush of expectation surged through her. It must be. He had found what he had come for and was heading back.

She wondered suddenly what had become of Cinnaminson. Pen would never leave her behind, at least not without good reason. Perhaps he was trying to lead whatever pursued him away from the Rover girl. That sounded right.

As he edged ahead, she went with him, keeping low in the scrub and grasses, aware that the darkness was deepening and her ability to see lessening. There was no sign of the moon, and there were few stars in a clouded sky. Soon she wouldn't be able to see him at all.

Then a black shape appeared out of the trees behind the boy, a cloaked and hooded form that she knew immediately. It was the monster from Anatcherae. It had tracked them all that way, and now it was over there with Pen and had him alone. Her scalp crawled, and she felt a moment of panic. All she wanted to do was to rush to his rescue.

But she couldn't reach him. No one could.

Her fingers fumbled wildly for the Elfstones, but even as they closed about the talismans, she hesitated. There was no reason to think their magic would work against the creature. And there was no time to test it. She needed something else, something more reliable.

Her mind raced in search of a solution as the black thing crept closer to her friend.

Pen was still trying to decide what to do, still frozen by fear and indecision, when he heard the voices. At first he was certain that his hearing was playing tricks on him, that he was imagining things, that the loss of Cinnaminson had affected his mind. He cocked his head in response, trying to understand why the wind would sound as it did and why it would do so now.

—Follow—

The chorus whispered softly to him from out of the twilight before dancing away in a fading echo. The aeriads, and no mistake about it. Not Cinnaminson alone, but the entire chorus, a blend of identical voices as they called to him.

He stared into space, hesitant and confused.

—Follow. It comes—

He understood. They were speaking of the black thing back in the trees, the creature that was hunting him. They were trying to help him get away from it.

He began moving, obedient to the voices, thinking that in some way Cinnaminson was reaching out to him from her prison, giving him one more gift. He slipped silently through the trees and grasses, casting quick glances toward where he had last seen his pursuer. He could feel its presence. He could sense it as it tracked him. It had found his trail and was following him, but it did not yet realize how close Pen was. Once it cut across his most recent tracks, the ones leading out of the ravine, it would be on him in seconds.

How far, he wondered suddenly, was he from the bridge?

He looked for it in the fading light, but could not find it. He was right at the edge of the ravine then, skirting its rim as the voices beckoned him on. He peered down into its darkness, but nothing could be seen. He glanced across its span, as well, but there was nothing to see there, either. The voices whispered more urgently, redirecting his concentration. They were humming now, but he could detect in the rise and fall of their music the need they were trying to communicate to him. *Don't slow down*, they were saying. *Don't hesitate.*

He gripped the darkwand in both hands, moving ahead in a crouch, the twilight deepening swiftly toward nightfall. If he failed to reach the bridge quickly, he would be left in darkness. What chance would he have against his pursuer then?

He felt a sudden rush of panic, sweat forming on his brow and trickling down his spine, soaking through his tunic.

–Follow–

He did so, focusing his attention on the sound of the voices, the direction of their humming becoming his compass. He must trust in them. He must believe that it was Cinnaminson who guided him, the controlling voice among the many, no different now than before, when she had led him down into the ravine to find Mother Tanequil. She was watching out for him still. She was protecting him.

Behind him, he heard movement, a sudden rustling, and he turned to look. A shadow moved slowly through the trees, bent low, scrabbling on all fours, head close to the ground. An animal, tracking. It was moving slantwise to where he crouched at the edge of the ravine, not yet seeing him, but sensing his presence, realizing he was close. He froze, watching it creep through the grasses, appearing and disappearing. He felt his throat tighten and his mouth go dry. He had never been so afraid.

–Follow–

Mechanically, he started moving ahead again, his thoughts scattered, his mind on the consequences he would face if his pursuer caught up to him. He saw Bandit stretched lifeless on the grassy flats near Taupo Rough. He saw the desiccated bodies of Gar Hatch and his crew hanging from the spars of the *Skatelow*. He felt Cinnaminson shiver against him as she told him some of what she had endured as a captive. He felt his skin crawl as he imagined what it would be like for him if he were caught.

–Quickly–

No longer pretending that there was any time left, that he could afford to rely on stealth and caution to see him through, he began to run in a low crouch. His only chance was to reach the bridge and his companions. Surely Kermadec was a match for that monster. Surely Khyber could call on the Elfstones to stop it.

Please, please, someone must be able to help!

Then he heard the sudden, explosive sound of his pursuer coming fast, tearing through the trees, heedless of caution. He wheeled back to see the shadowy form bounding toward him, the glint of its strange weapon flashing in the darkness in small bursts of silver fire.

Pen backed toward the ravine's edge, lifting the darkwand to defend himself, a pitiful weapon employed in a hopeless effort.

–Stop. Do not move. Trust us–

What choice did he have? There was nowhere left to go. He waited helplessly, staff lifted, body tensed, not knowing what he was going to do, no longer able to think clearly, watching as his pursuer drew closer, grew larger, turned darker than the night about him. He could see its cloak and hood. He could see that they were shredded and blackened with blood, the result of its encounter with the moor cat days earlier. It looked ragged and wild, something left over from the netherworld. It came at him in a frenzy, screaming, the sound so chilling that the boy very nearly broke and ran in spite of the admonition of his protectors.

–Stand. Be strong–

Help me, he thought.

Then the monster was on top of him.

On the far side of the ravine, Khyber Elessedil watched Pen stop suddenly and turn back toward his pursuer, as if realizing that he had been discovered. Then the black-cloaked hunter leapt from cover and closed on the boy in a reckless, maddened rush. She was shocked by its ragged look, its clothing torn and crusted with muck, pieces of its cloak trailing behind it in long black streamers. It had clearly gone through some bad times to get there, but now, having arrived, its course of action was settled. Even from as far away as she was, she could see the flash of its knife as it attacked.

She had only a moment and only one thing she could think of to do. She threw up her hands, the Druid magic gathering in a sudden rush at her fingertips. *I know so little*, she was thinking. She needed more time, she needed better preparation, she needed Ahren to act for her, she needed so much and she wasn't going to be given any of it. She wasn't even going to be given a second chance if she failed with the first.

She braced herself against the earth, legs spread for balance, arms extended.

*   *   *

It felt to Pen as if a giant's hand had struck him, the force of the blow knocking him completely off his feet as his attacker leapt at him, knife sweeping through the space he had just vacated. But the back side of the giant's hand caught the attacker as well, flinging him away in an audible rush of wind that scattered dust and debris in all directions and ripped up clots of scrub and grass. Out flew the black-cloaked form toward the dark drop of the ravine, arms and legs flailing wildly. The hood fell away, and Pen saw his pursuer's face for the first time—a blasted, torn visage that was only barely human and reflected an unfathomable madness.

A fresh shriek ripped from its twisted mouth, one born not of fear or anguish, but of fury and a promise of terrible retribution. Still trying to escape, Pen scrambled backwards on all fours. His attacker's abnormally long limbs grappled for the roots that grew along the edge of the ravine, fingers catching hold, toes digging in. It caught itself and hung there, scrambling to find purchase, to get back atop the slope, its crazed eyes fixed on Pen.

Then a dirt-encrusted root snaked out of the ravine like a sea leviathan's tentacle and wrapped about the leg of the dangling creature, fastening tight. The black-cloaked form twisted and struggled as its grip was loosened. Another yank, and Pen's attacker was falling into the abyss, down into the blackness. It struck with an audible thud, and then the roots of Mother Tanequil were moving, sliding against each other in rough scrapings. Pen heard the sounds of flesh tearing, bones breaking, and blood exploding out of ruptured limbs.

A final shriek rose out of the ravine's depths.

And then there was only silence.

THIRTY

Pen sat facing the ravine, breathing so hard he thought his heart would give out. He stared down into the void, half expecting the hooded creature to reemerge, even knowing that this time it was dead and gone and never coming back. Stunned by the suddenness of its demise, not quite certain that he could trust what he had seen, he waited anyway.

When he lifted his gaze, he saw Khyber. She was standing on the other side of the ravine, arms extended, body braced. Her posture and the shocked look on her face revealed her part in what had happened. It was her Druid magic that had knocked him aside. She had used it there, as she had weeks earlier aboard the *Skatelow* in Anatcherae to sweep their hunter from the decks of the airship and into the waters of the Lazareen. Both times, she had saved his life.

He stared at her in disbelief and gratitude, then lifted his hand in a small wave. She straightened and waved back. They stayed where they were for a moment, looking at each other across the ravine, but from a greater distance, too, one measured by hardships endured and deadly encounters survived. Suddenly it made him feel close to her, enough so that he wanted to call out and tell her so. But the darkness was a curtain between them, and the night seemed poised to steal away his words, so he stayed silent.

She waved once more, pointed in the direction of the ruins, and started off into the darkness.

He watched her go, then gathered his strength, stood, and walked to the edge of the drop. He didn't want to look down, but he did so anyway. He peered into the blackness, telling himself that it was all right, that he didn't need to be afraid anymore, that the thing that had hunted him for so long was really dead. He stayed where he was for a long time, waiting for the bad memories and troubling emotions to settle, to lose their edge, to find a resting place inside.

When he had satisfied himself, he exhaled slowly and deliberately and turned away. He wondered if Cinnaminson was at peace with what had happened, as well, asleep in the arms of Mother Tanequil. He hoped she was.

He followed the rim of the ravine once more, stepping carefully along its border through the deepening night, the clouds drifting overhead in tattered dark strips, the stars a sprinkle of silver dust in the firmament. He had no idea what time it was. He scanned the horizon for the moon, hoping to use it to judge the hour, but he failed to find it. He couldn't seem to remember if it was waxing or waning, full or new. He couldn't remember when he had seen it last. He was tired, he knew. Too tired to think.

His thoughts scattered, and he found himself wondering if the aeriads had known that Khyber was across the ravine and ready to act to save him. He wondered if Cinnaminson was responsible, and if, being linked to the tanequil, she had asked the tree to aid him, too. Then it occurred to him that for the black-cloaked creature to reach the island to begin hunting him in the first place, the tanequil would have had to let it cross the bridge, thereby inviting it to its own doom.

He looked down at the darkwand. Having given up its limb in exchange for his fingers and Cinnaminson, had the tree become linked to him in a way he did not yet fully understand? It seemed clear that he was being kept safe at least until he was back across the bridge. It was no accident that he had been rescued that night. Khyber had not found him by chance. The aeriads had not led him to the edge of the ravine without knowing that Mother Tanequil was waiting.

How far did the protection of the tree reach?

He stopped and looked back into the darkness of the island forest. He wanted to know so much more than he did. He wanted to return to the tree to ask for the answers to his questions. But there was no point. His road lay ahead, on the other side of the ravine, back in the world of the Druids and Paranor.

And beyond, in the world of the Forbidding.

He began walking again, a steady march. The bridge was not far ahead. He saw a glow in the distance, fires lit within Stridegate's ruins. Kermadec and his Trolls were waiting. Khyber would be back. He was anxious suddenly to see them. He was tired of being alone. He needed their companionship; he needed the reassurance their numbers would provide.

He pushed through the screen of saplings fronting the bridge supports and stopped short.

Three huge warships hung anchored above the ruins, their massive black hulls reflecting dully in the light of bonfires lit all through Stridegate's flowered gardens. Shadows cast by the flames danced across through the carpeted beds and vine-covered walls, a swarm of shimmering black moths. Kermadec and his Rock Trolls sat weaponless and ringed by Gnome Hunters, their impassive faces lowered, their huge hands clenched about their knees as they faced away from their captors. Tagwen was crouched in their midst.

Directly across from Pen, on the far side of the bridge, stood a singular figure cloaked and hooded in black. At his appearance, the figure turned to face him.

Pen felt his heart sink and his euphoria fade.

The Druids had found them once more.

STRAKEN

In memory of Christina Michelle George and Caleb Alexander Delp
and
in celebration of readers like them everywhere

ONE

"Pen Ohmsford!" The black-cloaked figure called out to him from across the chasm that separated the island of the tanequil from the rest of the world. "We have been waiting for you!"

A male Druid. He came forward a few steps, pulling back his hood to reveal the strong, dark features of his face. Pen had never seen him before.

"Come across the bridge so that we can talk," the Druid said.

The firelight threw his shadow across the stone archway in a dark stain that spilled into the chasm, and the portent it fore-shadowed was unmistakable. Pen wished he hadn't rushed into the light so quickly, that he had been more careful. But he had thought himself past the worst of it. He had survived his encounter with the tanequil and received the gift of the darkwand, the talisman that would give him access into the Forbidding. He had lost two fingers in doing so, but he had come to believe that they were a small price to pay. Losing Cinnaminson was a much larger price, but he had ac-cepted that there was nothing he could do about it until after his aunt was safely returned, promising himself he would try to come back for her then. Finally, he had escaped the monster that had pur-sued them all the way from Anatcherae and knew it to be dead at last, pulled down into the chasm and crushed.

But now this.

His fingers tightened possessively around the darkwand, and he scanned the faces of the captive Trolls. All there, he saw. No one missing. No one even appeared hurt. They must have been caught completely by surprise not to have put up any fight. He wondered vaguely how that could have happened, how the Druids had found them at all, for that matter, but he guessed it was a pointless exercise.

A few of the Trolls were looking up now, Kermadec among them. The anger and disappointment on his face were unmistakable. He had failed Pen. They all had. The boy saw Tagwen there as well, almost hidden behind the massive bodies of his companions.

There was no sign of Khyber.

"Cross the bridge, Pen," the Druid repeated, not unkindly. "Don't make this any harder on yourself."

"I think I should stay where I am," Pen answered.

The Druid nodded, as if understanding him perfectly. "Well, you can do that, if you choose. I've read the warning on the stone, and I know better than to try to come across after you." He paused. "Tell me. If the danger is real, how did you manage to get over there without being harmed?"

Pen said nothing.

"What are you doing here, anyway? Trying to help your aunt? Did you think you might find her here?"

Pen stared back at him silently.

"We have your friends. All of them. You can see for yourself. We have your parents, as well, locked away at Paranor." His voice was patient, calm. "It doesn't do you any good to stay over there when those you care about are all over here. You can't help them by refusing to face up to your responsibilities."

My responsibilities, Pen repeated silently. What would this man know of his responsibilities? Why would he even care, save that he thought he could stop Pen from carrying them out?

A second Druid appeared beside the first, coming out of the darkness and into the light. This one was slender and small, a ferret-faced Gnome of particularly cunning looks, his eyes shifting swiftly from the first Druid to Pen and then back again. He muttered something, and the first Druid gave him a quick, angry look.

"How do I know you aren't lying about my parents?" Pen asked suddenly; it wasn't the first time he had heard the claim. He still didn't want to believe it.

The first Druid turned back to him. "Well, you don't. I can tell you that they were flying in a ship called *Swift Sure* when we brought them into the Keep. They helped us find you. Your father was worried about the disappearance of his sister, but more worried about you. That is how we found you, Pen."

Gone cold to the bone, the boy stared at him. The explanation made perfect sense. His father would have aided them without realizing what he was doing, thinking it was the right thing, that they were as concerned about his aunt as he was. The King of the Silver River was supposed to have warned his parents of the Druids, but perhaps he had failed. If so, his father wouldn't have known of their treachery. How could he?

Pen brushed back his tangled red hair while trying to think what to do.

"Let me put this to you another way," the taller Druid went on, moving slightly in front of the other. "My companion is less patient than I am, although he isn't volunteering to cross the bridge, either. But when morning comes, we will bring one of the airships across, and then we will have you, one way or the other. There are only so many places you can hide. This is all a big waste of time, given the way things eventually have to turn out."

Pen suspected that was true. But his freedom, however temporary, was the only bargaining chip he possessed. "Will you set my friends free, if I agree to come over?"

The Druid nodded. "My word on it. All of them. We have no use for them beyond persuading you to come with us. Once you cross over, they are free to go."

"What about my parents?"

The Druid nodded. "Once you are back at Paranor, they can go, too. In fact, once you've told us what we want to know, what your purpose is in coming here, you can go, too."

He was lying. He made it sound believable, exuding just the right amount of sincerity and reasonableness through his choice of words and tone of voice, but Pen knew the truth of things at once. The Druid would have done better to tell him something less soothing, but he supposed the man saw him as a boy and thought he would respond better to a lie than to the truth.

He paused to consider what he should do next. He had asked the questions that needed asking and gotten the answers he expected. It reconfirmed his suspicions about what would happen if he crossed the bridge to surrender to them. On the other hand, if he stayed where he was, they would capture him sooner or later, even if he went back down into the chasm, something he did not think he could do. Worse, he would be doing nothing to help his family and friends. If he was as concerned about responsibility as he liked to think, he would have to do more than go off and hide.

The decision was easier to make than he would have thought. He had to go to Paranor anyway if he was to use the darkwand to reach his aunt. Rescuing the Ard Rhys was what he had set out to do, and he couldn't do that if he didn't get inside the Druid's Keep. The Druids who had come for him were offering him a chance to do just that. He would have preferred going about it in a different way, but it all ended the same. The trick would be finding a way to keep the darkwand in his possession until he could get inside the chamber of the Ard Rhys.

He had no idea how he was going to do that.

"I want to speak with Tagwen," he called out. "Send him to the head of the bridge and move back so I can come across safely."

The Druids exchanged an uncertain glance. "When you surrender yourself, then we will let you talk with Tagwen," the taller one said.

Pen shook his head. "If you want me to surrender, you have to let me talk with Tagwen first. I want to hear from him what he thinks about your promises. I want to hear from him how good he thinks your word is. If you don't let me talk to him, I'm staying right here."

He watched their dark faces bend close and heard them confer in inaudible whispers. He could tell they didn't like the request and were trying to come up with a way to refuse it.

"If you think I will be so easy to find over here come morning, perhaps you should wait to try it and find out for yourselves," he said suddenly. "It might not be as easy as you think. That spider creature you sent to hunt me down? Or was it supposed to kill me? You did send it, didn't you?"

He asked the questions on impulse, not knowing how they

would answer, but suspecting. He was not disappointed. Both Druids stared at him in surprise. The one who did all the talking folded his arms into his cloak. "We didn't send him. But we know who did. We thought he was dead, killed in the Slags."

Pen shook his head, his eyes shifting to Tagwen, who was watching him alertly now, knowing he was up to something, anxious to find out what it was. "*He?* Not *it?*"

"Aphasia Wye. A man, but I grant you he looks more an insect than a human. Are you saying he isn't dead? Where is he?"

"No, he's dead. But he didn't die in the Slags. He tracked us all the way here. Last night, he crossed the bridge. Just as you want to do. Except that he found a way. Then he found me, but something else, too, and it killed him. If you want to see what that something is, fly your airship on over. I'll wait for you."

It was a bluff, but it was a bluff worth trying. Aphasia Wye was a predator of the first order—they might be hesitant to go up against something that had dispatched him. It cast Pen in a different light, giving him a more dangerous aspect, since he was alive and his hunter wasn't. He had to make them stop and think about whether it was worthwhile to refuse his request.

The taller Druid finished conferring with his companion and looked over. "All right, Pen. We'll let you speak with Tagwen. But no tricks, please. Anything that suggests you are acting in bad faith will put your Troll friends and your parents at risk. Don't test our limits. Have your talk, and then do what you know you have to do and surrender yourself to us."

Pen didn't know if he would do that or not, but it would help if he could talk with Tagwen about it first. He watched the Dwarf rise on the taller Druid's command and walk to the head of the bridge. He watched the Druids move back, signaling the Gnome Hunters to do the same. Pen waited until the area in front of the bridge was clear of everyone but the Dwarf, then stepped out onto the stone arch and walked across. He used the darkwand like a walking staff, leaning on it as if he were injured, pretending that was its purpose. Maybe they would let him keep it if they thought he had need of it to walk. Maybe pigs would learn to fly. He kept his eyes open for any unexpected movement, for shadows that didn't belong or sounds that were out of place. He used his small magic to test for warnings that might alert him to dangers he couldn't see. But nothing revealed it-self. He crossed unimpeded, captives and captors staying back, be-hind the fire, deeper into the gardens, away from the ravine's edge.

When he was at the far side, he dropped down into a crouch, using the bridge abutments as shelter. He didn't think they intended to kill him, but he couldn't be certain.

Tagwen moved close. "They caught us with our pants down, young Pen. We thought we were watching out for you, but we were looking too hard in the wrong direction." His bluff face wrinkled with distaste. "They had us under spear and arrow before we could mount a defense. Anything we might have done would have gotten us all killed. I'm sorry."

Pen put his hand on the Dwarf's stout shoulder. "You did the best you could, Tagwen. We've all done the best we could."

"Perhaps." He didn't sound convinced. His eyes searched the boy's face. "Are you all right? Were you telling the truth about that thing that was tracking us? Was it really over there with you? I thought we'd lost it once and for all when we entered the mountains. Is it finally dead?"

Pen nodded. "The tanequil killed it. It's a long story. But anything that crosses this bridge is in real danger. I'm alive because of this."

He nodded down at the darkwand, which was resting next to him on the bridge, flat against the stone, tucked into the shadows.

The Dwarf peered at it, then caught sight of Pen's damaged hand and looked up again quickly. "What happened to your fingers?"

"The tree took them in exchange for the staff. Blood for sap, flesh for bark, bones for wood. It was necessary. Don't think on it."

"Don't think on it?" Tagwen was appalled. He glanced quickly over Pen's shoulder into the darkness of the tanequil's island. "Where is Cinnaminson?"

Pen hesitated. "Staying behind. Safe, for now. Tagwen, listen to me. I have to do what they want. I have to go with them to Paranor."

Tagwen stared. "No, Penderrin. You won't come out of there alive. They don't intend to let you go. Nor your parents, either. You're being taken to Shadea a'Ru. She's behind what's happened to the Ard Rhys, and once she's questioned you about what you are doing and you tell her—which you will, make no mistake—you and your parents are finished. Don't doubt me on this."

Pen nodded. "I don't, Tagwen. But look at how things stand.

We're trapped here, all of us. Even without the Druids to deal with, we're stranded in these ruins, surrounded by Urdas. I have to get out if I'm to help my aunt, and the quicker the better. It's already been too long. If I don't get to Paranor and use the darkwand soon, it will be too late. And now I have a way. The Druids will take me faster than I could get there on my own. I know it's dangerous. I know what they intend for me. And for my parents. But I have to risk it."

"You're risking too much!" the Dwarf snapped. "You'll get there quick enough, all right. And then what? They won't let you into the chamber of the Ard Rhys. They won't let you make use of that talisman. Shadea will see you for the threat you are and do away with you before you have a chance to do anything!"

"Maybe. Maybe not." He looked off into the gardens, into the pale, shifting patterns of color and the dappled shadows cast by the Druids and Gnome Hunters in the firelight's glow. "In any case, it's the only choice that makes sense." He turned back to Tagwen. "If I agree to go with them, will that tall Druid keep his word and let you go? Is his word any good? Is he any better than the rest of them?"

Tagwen thought about it a moment. "Traunt Rowan. He's not as bad as the other one, Pyson Wence, and certainly not as bad as Shadea. But he joined them in the plot against your aunt." He shook his head. "She always thought he was principled, if misguided in his antipathy toward her. He might keep his word."

Pen nodded. "I'll have to chance it."

The Dwarf reached for him with both strong hands and gripped his shoulders. "Don't do this, Penderrin," he whispered.

Pen held his gaze. "If you were in my shoes, Tagwen, wouldn't you? To save her from the Forbidding, to give her a chance, wouldn't you do just what I'm doing?" Tagwen stared at him in silence. He gave the Dwarf a quick smile. "Of course you would. Don't say anything more. I've already said it to myself. We knew from the beginning that we would do whatever was necessary to reach her, no matter the risk. We knew it, even if we didn't talk about it. Nothing has changed. I have to go to Paranor. Then into the Forbidding."

He closed his eyes against the sudden panic that the words roused in him. The enormity of what he was going to attempt was overwhelming. He was just a boy. He wasn't gifted or skilled or anything useful. He was mostly just there when no one else was.

He took a deep breath. "Will you come after me? In case I don't find a way to get through? In case I get locked away in the dungeons and don't get my parents out? Will you try to do something about it?" He exhaled sharply. "Even if I do get through and find her, the Druids will be waiting for us when we get back. We'll need help, Tagwen."

The Dwarf tightened his grip. "We'll come for you. No matter how long it takes us, no matter where you are. We'll find a way to reach you. We'll be there for you when you need us."

Pen put his hands over those of the Dwarf's, pressing them down into his shoulders. "Get out of here any way you can, Tagwen. Don't stop for anything." He hesitated. "Don't try to reach Cinnaminson. She has to wait for me. She can't leave until I come back for her." He shook his head quickly, fighting back tears. "Don't ask me to explain. Just tell me you'll do what I've asked. All right?"

The Dwarf nodded. "All right."

"I can do this," Pen whispered, swallowing hard. "I know I can."

Tagwen's fingers tightened. "I know it, too. You've done everything else. Everything anyone could have asked of you."

"I'll find a way. Once I'm there, I'll find a way."

"There are some still loyal to your aunt," Tagwen said. "Keep an eye out. One of them might come to your aid."

Pen glanced down again at the darkwand. "What can I do about the staff? It's too big to hide, but I have to take it with me. I know they won't let me keep it, if they see it. But I can't afford to give it over to them, either."

From back in the shadows, the taller of the two Druids called out, "You should have said everything you intended to say by now, Pen. You should be finished and ready to honor your promise. Tell Tagwen to step back, and then you come forward to us!"

Pen stared toward the firelight, to the cluster of Troll prisoners huddled together, to the shadowy forms of the Gnome Hunters surrounding them, to the cloaked forms of the Druids. It had the look of another world, of a place and time he could barely imagine. He was still enmeshed in the world of the tanequil, of orange-tipped leaves and mottled bark, of massive limbs and roots, of a sentient being older than Man. His memories of the past two days were still so painfully fresh that they dominated his present and threatened to overwhelm his fragile determination.

He despaired.

"That's a pretty piece of work," Tagwen said suddenly, nodding down at the darkwand. "It might help if it wasn't so shiny."

He eased back on his heels and reached behind him for a handful of damp earth, then rubbed it along the length of the staff, clotting the runes, dulling the surface. He worked in the shadows, shielding his movements.

"If they take it away from you," he said, finishing up, "tell them you found it in the ruins. Tell them you don't know what it is. If they think it was given to you to help the Ard Rhys, you'll never see it again. You might keep it long enough to use it if they don't suspect what it's for."

Pen nodded. He stood up, one hand gripping the staff. He leaned on it once more, as if he needed its support. "Go back to them. Tell Kermadec to be ready. Khyber is still out there, somewhere. I saw her while coming back to you. She should have been here by now. She might be watching all this, and I don't know what she will do."

The Dwarf took a quick look around, as if thinking he might see her in the darkness, then nodded and rose, as well. Saying nothing, he returned to the Gnome Hunters and the encircled Rock Trolls, his head lowered. The Trolls watched him come, but did not rise to greet him. Pen waited until he was seated among them again, then looked over at the Druids, who were standing to one side.

"Do you promise my friends will not be harmed?" he asked again.

"Not by us or those who travel with us," the taller Druid replied, coming forward a step. "We'll leave them here when we depart. What happens to them after that is up to them."

It was the best Pen could hope for. He would have liked to have found a way to get them back to Taupo Rough, but he couldn't chance trying to make that happen. Kermadec was resourceful. He would find a way.

Pen glanced down at the darkwand. The dirt and mud that coated its length mostly hid its runes. Its smooth surface was dull. If he was lucky, they would not pay close attention to it. If they took it, he would have to find a way to get it back later.

His gaze shifted to the island of the tanequil, to the dark silent wall of the forest that concealed the sentient tree. He was leaving things unfinished here, he knew, and he might never have a chance to come back and set them right. The urge to act immediately threatened to overpower him, to turn him from his path to the Ard Rhys. He knew her so little, and Cinnaminson so well.

He took another deep, steadying breath and looked back at the waiting Druids. "I'm ready," he called out in what he hoped was a brave voice.

Then, using the staff as a crutch, he began to walk toward them.

TWO

From deep in the shadows at the edge of the gardens, Khyber Elessedil watched the drama unfold with a mix of anger and indecision.

"Oh, no, Pen," she whispered.

She had returned before him, seen the Druid airships hanging over the gardens like spiders from an invisible web, the Gnome Hunters ringing the captive members of her little company, the Druids watching the bridge, and she had determined that she must do something to warn the boy.

But she was too late. He appeared abruptly, incautiously revealing himself before he could think better of it and before she could stop him. She held back then to see what would happen, thinking that she must not act too hastily, that she did not know yet what to do. She could save one—the boy or the rest of the company—but not both, not without a great deal of luck she could not depend upon. Two Druids were more than she was able to handle on her own; her skills were too rudimentary, her knowledge too shallow. She would catch them unawares, but that would not give her enough of an edge to guarantee success.

No, she must wait.

She must bide her time.

And so she did, listening to the conversation that ensued between Pen and Traunt Rowan. She could divine the nature of their maneuverings, of their hidden intentions, from what they said and how they moved. She understood what was at stake, but not how the matter would be resolved. Desperately trying to concoct a plan that would allow her to act, knowing that sooner or later she must, she waited them out. When Tagwen was allowed to confer with Pen in private, she thought that then was the time to do whatever she could, but she was unable to make herself do so. Everything she considered promised to end badly. Everything depended on help that wasn't available. She prevaricated and waffled. Indecision froze her.

Until, finally, it was too late. Pen was coming down from the bridge to give himself up, counting on Traunt Rowan to honor his word about Tagwen and the Trolls, giving himself over to a fate he had already determined he must embrace. Anything to get to Paranor, he was thinking. She knew it without having to be told.

She watched him limp forward, leaning on his staff, his young face etched with lines of determination. He was sacrificing himself. For the Ard Rhys. For Tagwen. For Kermadec and his Rock Trolls. Even for her. He did not know where she was, only that she was out there somewhere, still free, perhaps still able to do something to help. But he wasn't looking for that help just then. His intention was to get to Paranor and hope that help could be found there.

The staff drew her attention. She had seen it before, when he was scurrying through the woods on the island of the tanequil. But then it had looked much brighter and better kept. She had thought it was the darkwand, the talisman he had come to find. The tree would have given it to him, persuaded in a way that only he knew, a way that the King of the Silver River said he would find when it was time. If it was the talisman, in fact. If . . .

But it was, of course. He had muddied the surface and was using it as a crutch to disguise what it really was. He was taking a desperate chance that neither of the Druids would think it anything more than a length of old wood. He could not go to Paranor without it, and go to Paranor he must, of course. That was his intention in giving himself up.

She saw it all clearly, a conclusion about which she felt so certain that she never questioned it. Brave Pen.

Seconds later, she was moving, sliding along the edge of the trees, making her way toward the closest of the airships. She must do what she could to help him, and to help him she must go where he was going. She must get aboard the airship, travel hidden to Paranor, then disembark in secret and find him before they discovered his intentions and put an end to them. Because they would, she knew. He was not clever or strong enough to fool them all. One of them would see through him.

Within the circle of light cast by the fire, the Druids had moved forward to intercept Pen. He did not resist them as Traunt Rowan took Pen's arm and guided him toward the *Athabasca*. Rowan's actions were almost paternal. He spoke softly to the boy, walking beside him in a way that suggested good intentions. He had not bothered yet with the staff, did not seem to care much about it at all. Pen was still limping, perhaps causing the Druid to think he was indeed injured and in need of support. The other one, his sly eyes fixed on them, trailed purposefully, and Khyber did not trust anything about him. If he had been the one to make the promise to release Tagwen and the Trolls, she would have acted at once, she told herself. There would have been no hesitation.

She reached the rope ladder that dangled from the airship she had chosen—not the one Pen was boarding, unfortunately—and went up it in a rush, not bothering to look back until she was aboard. There were Gnome Hunters forward against the railing, but their attentions were occupied with the events taking place below, and they took no notice of her. She slipped into the shadow of the mainmast, then over to the shelter of a rail sling set in place to port. From there, she could see Pen being led to the ladder of the other ship, the Druids shadowing him watchfully. She watched the Gnome Hunters drift through the light toward their ships like wraiths to their haunts. She saw Tagwen's rough features, sad and desperate, peer upward as Pen climbed the ladder. She saw Kermadec's strong hands knot together in a promise of certain action.

She could still stop it, she told herself. She could fling Druid Fire or elemental winds all through those Gnome Hunters and knock them sprawling. She could separate Pen from those Druids, burn away the ladder from below where he climbed, and give him a chance to flee. But it would not be settled then and there, and the consequences for those Trolls too slow to reach the shadows or the weapons of which they had been stripped would be ugly.

Remember. Pen is not trying to escape. He is trying to reach Paranor. He has made up his mind.

She pictured him anew as she had seen him from across the chasm not two hours earlier. She saw the monster Traunt Rowan had named Aphasia Wye. She saw Pen prepare to do what he could to stop it, even when there appeared there was nothing he could do. Facing what must have seemed to be certain death, he had not tried to flee or hide. He had stood there to meet it.

And would have, had she not been there to give him aid.

Perhaps he was relying on her now.

Perhaps he knew she would not abandon him; that because she had saved him once, his life was her responsibility. Old legends said that this was so. She had never believed it.

But somehow, at that moment, she did.

"Are you injured?" Traunt Rowan asked pleasantly, supporting Pen under his free arm, not looking at him as he talked, moving him steadily along toward the *Athabasca.*

Pen shrugged. "Nothing serious."

"Aphasia Wye?"

"I hurt it trying to get away from him."

"But no broken bones?"

Pen shook his head.

"You're lucky. If you hadn't gotten away from him, broken bones would have been the least of your problems."

The second Druid, the one Tagwen had named Pyson Wence, moved up suddenly on Pen's other side. "How *did* you get away from him?"

"I don't want to talk about it." He risked a quick look at Traunt Rowan, seemingly the friendlier of the two. "Not until we're away."

Pyson Wence seized his arm, the blunt fingers squeezing so hard he flinched. "I don't like your tone of voice, little man," he hissed. "What you want in this matter is of no concern to us."

Pen shrank from him. "I want to know my friends are safe before I tell you anything."

"Let him go, Pyson," the taller one whispered. "Unfriendly eyes are watching. We can wait."

The one called Pyson let him go. Pen tore away from Traunt Rowan and rubbed his injured arm. He kept his head down and his eyes averted. He didn't want to do anything to aggravate them until the airships were aloft and his friends free. He didn't know what to expect then, but he would have a story in place to tell them that might buy him some time.

They reached the ladder, and as he made an attempt to climb it while still holding the darkwand, Pyson Wence snatched it away and cast it aside. "You won't be needing any crutches from here on," he said.

Pen froze, hands on the ladder, one foot on the first rung. He couldn't leave the talisman behind.

Then Traunt Rowan walked over and picked it up. "He might have need of it, Pyson. I'll carry it up for him. Go on, Pen."

Pen exhaled sharply and began to climb, taking care to favor his supposedly injured leg as he went. He did not look down at the Druids. He did not slow until he was aboard the airship, when he turned to wait for them. They were aboard quickly, dark faces shadowed and unreadable in the faint diffusion of the now distant firelight. Below, the Gnome Hunters were moving to follow, all but those who ringed the prisoners.

Traunt Rowan moved over to Pen and handed him back his staff. "You wouldn't consider trying to use this as a weapon, would you?" he asked with an edgy smile.

Pen shook his head.

"Good. Now let's go below and get you settled in."

Instantly, Pen moved over to the railing, away from everyone. "Not until I see that my friends are going to be all right," he said. "I want to watch what happens next."

Pyson Wence's Gnomic features were dark with anger, but Traunt Rowan merely shrugged. "Stay where you are then."

He turned to Wence and nodded, and the latter issued orders to the Hunters who crewed the airships. The Hunters began scurrying about the decks and up the rigging, preparing the three ships to sail. With a last, dark look at Pen, Pyson Wence moved into the pilot box to stand next to the Athabasca's Captain, his face turned away from the boy.

Now only the few Gnomes guarding Tagwen and the Trolls remained, and one by one, weapons held at the ready, eyes fixed on the prisoners, they began to drift back toward the airships as well. Pen's companions sat quietly and watched their captors withdraw, making no attempt to stop them. Atalan was staring up at Pen, a strange look on his fierce face, one that suggested he couldn't quite believe what he was seeing. Tagwen was whispering to Kermadec, his head bent close to that of the Troll, their faces dark and intense.

Pen scanned the grounds at the edges of the firelight, where the walls caught the last of the flickering yellow glow, where the shadows encroached from the woods beyond. No sign of Khyber. But she had to be there. She had to be watching.

Then the *Athabasca* was lifting away, the other two airships following close behind, and the ruins of Stridegate were shrinking into the darkness. His former companions came to their feet and stood close together, looking after him. Quickly, their faces turned small and indistinct, and then disappeared. The ruins faded, as well, until all that remained was the tiny dot of the fire's heart.

When that disappeared and the island of the tanequil was nothing more than a dark lump silhouetted by starlight against the horizon, Traunt Rowan appeared at his side to take him below.

On the deck of the ship flying to starboard, Khyber Elessedil sat quietly in the concealing shadow of the aft port rail sling, watching the *Athabasca*. Pen had gone down the main hatchway and was no longer in view. The ruins of Stridegate had disappeared into the distance, and her companions with them. The glow of the fire had faded, and the position of the stars told her they were flying south along the edge of the Klu toward the Upper Anar, the vast sprawl of the Inkrim a dark lake below.

There was nothing she could do but wait.

When she was twelve, she had run away for the third time. On that occasion, intent on escaping her family and their dictatorial ways, she had stowed away aboard an airship flying to Callahorn. It wasn't that she didn't love them. It was that she didn't love what they had planned for her. Her brother and her father before him had very definite ideas about the ways in which an Elessedil Princess should conduct herself, and Khyber had trouble even seeing herself as a Princess. Her station in life was an accident of birth, and she could never quite bring herself to accept it as her due. She was always more comfortable with being someone and something else. Her family didn't like that. Her family let her know that rebelliousness would not be tolerated.

Her response had been to run away. She started at eight. At twelve, after two failed attempts, she had determined that this time she would succeed, that she would put herself permanently beyond their reach. Callahorn was Free-born land, and people of all Races were welcomed and accepted no matter who they were or where they came from. Everyone was treated the same. Royalty had been gone from the Borderlands for hundreds of years and wasn't likely to be coming back anytime soon. If she could get that far, she could disappear into the mix and never be found. At least, that was the way she saw it at twelve.

She got as far as her destination, but she was discovered by the Captain before she could disembark and was hauled back kicking and screaming yet again to her family. It was not a pleasant reunion. But she learned something valuable from that effort. She learned how to hide in plain sight. She learned that if you looked enough like you belonged, you stood a pretty good chance of being accepted. On that outing, she took on the look of a cabin boy or a very young crewmember, and to her surprise the crew never stopped to consider that she might be something else. Admittedly, she kept her exposure to a minimum, staying out of sight most of the time. But when she did surface, for food and water or just to breathe fresh air, she was able to move about without being stopped or questioned.

Aboard the Druid airship, she resolved to put this knowledge to good use. She had already appropriated one of the short cloaks worn by the Gnome Hunters who served as crew, using its hood to conceal her face. At night and in the absence of close scrutiny, she looked like one of them. She had already determined that by day, she would hide below, somewhere out of the way, somewhere the crew didn't often go. There were no Druids aboard the ship, so she had only the Gnomes to worry about. She knew airships well, and the configuration of the one she was on was familiar to her. Because the *Athabasca* was a warship, she offered plenty of hiding places. Because she was a Druid ship, everyone was trained to do their job and not ask questions.

Sitting by the rail sling as the ship flew into the night, pretending at inspecting its mechanism as the Gnome Hunter crewmen went impassively about their business, she considered her resources. She had the use of her Druid magic, although she possessed only a small arsenal and was largely unskilled in its use. She had the Elfstones, too. But, although powerful, they were of limited use. Mostly she had her wits and her determination, and she thought that those would probably end up serving her best.

Around her, things were settling down. The ship's course was set, her sails aloft, her rigging in place. Night enfolded all three vessels, rendering them starlit silhouettes against the horizon. She wished she were aboard Pen's ship so that she might reach him long enough to let him know he was not alone. But she knew that she was not likely to see him again before they reached Paranor. Even then, getting to him would be problematic. He would be celled and guarded, and he would be taken before Shadea a'Ru quickly once she knew he was there.

She leaned back against the rail sling. She realized she would have to reach Pen quickly once they landed or it might not be worth trying to reach him at all. The Druids would discover what he was up to, what he had come north to accomplish, and it would all be over quickly.

If he lived that long. Traunt Rowan and the other Druid might decide to dispatch him while they were returning. They might even have orders to that end.

She could not bear to think about it. Anyway, there was nothing she could do just yet. She could only wait. And hope.

She moved over to the provision hold, dropped through the hatchway quickly, found a shadowed place of concealment back among the spare light sheaths, and waited for sleep.

THREE

They took Pen Ohmsford to a storeroom that had been converted on one side into a sleeping space and told him that he was to stay there during the flight back to Paranor. His half of the room was furnished with a hammock, a clothes chest, a bench, a small table, and a lamp. The other half was piled high with coils of radian draws, spare light sheaths, casks of water and biscuits, and several crates of tools and caulking.

"Sorry we can't do better, but this is a warship and there isn't much in the way of accommodations," Traunt Rowan said.

They had sent three such airships to find him, Pen thought in response, which said more about their intentions for him than did the supposed dearth of decent accommodations. But he nodded because there wasn't much to be gained by doing anything else. He was their prisoner whether they said so or not.

They left him then, disappearing back through the doorway into the hallway beyond and closing the heavy storeroom door behind them. Pen heard the dull *snick* of the lock, further proof of his status. He waited until their footfalls had receded into silence, then sat down on the bench to think things through.

They had not taken away the darkwand, an oversight that surprised him. Having had it snatched away once already by Pyson Wence, he had been expecting to lose it again. But neither Druid had shown any further interest in the staff. He promised he would make them regret their carelessness, but then warned himself against making threats—even to himself—that he was in no position to carry out.

After giving it some consideration, he decided against trying to hide the staff. He could tuck it away amid all the stores, but they would notice it was missing the first time he limped about the room without it—and he would have to limp, at least for a day or two, to keep up the pretense that he was injured. No, hiding it would only call attention to it. They would find it quickly enough anyway, if they decided to look for it. It was better to just leave it lying out in plain sight and hope they paid no further attention.

He stuck it under the bench in a careless fashion and forced himself to pretend it didn't matter.

After a time, one of the Gnome Hunters brought him a plate of food and a cup of ale. He consumed both hungrily, realizing he was starved. It had been more than a day since he had eaten, and the rush of events was all that had kept him going. He needed sleep, too. After finishing the meal, he lay down to nap and was asleep in seconds.

He woke to the sound of the lock releasing, and another tray of food was brought inside and deposited on the floor. The Gnome Hunter barely looked at him as he backed out the door and locked it. Pen peered through the cracks of the shutters securing the single window opening into the storeroom. The sky was brilliant with either a sunrise or a sunset, depending on direction. He decided, after a moment's consideration, that it was a sunset. He had slept through an entire day.

He sat down and consumed his meal, thinking for the first time since he had been locked away of his friends back in the ruins of Stridegate. At least they were safe. Or safe from the Druids. They were still trapped by the Urdas and miles from any help. Kermadec would get them free, of course. Or Khyber, using her elemental magic to aid their efforts. But even after that it would take them a week to walk out and longer still to reach Paranor. Tagwen had meant well in promising they would come for him, but Pen knew that he couldn't depend on it. He had given them a chance at life by agreeing to leave with the Druids, but he had not given himself much hope in return. No matter what Tagwen had promised, Pen knew he was on his own.

He thought about what that meant. Barring unexpected help

from Druids still loyal to the Ard Rhys, he had to reach his aunt's chamber with the darkwand in hand and employ it quickly. That presupposed a lot of things that shouldn't be presupposed, the foremost of which was that he would be able to figure out how to use the talisman. He had no idea how it worked. He had no way of knowing what he had to do to summon its magic. Did he need to do *anything?* Or could he just stand there and wait to be whisked away?

The enormity of what he was hoping for left him momentarily shaken, and before he could pull himself together sufficiently to feel at least somewhat reassured that he would find a way out of his dilemma, the storeroom door opened, and his Druid captors reappeared.

He sat on his bench and stared at them, searching their faces for some indication of what to expect. Traunt Rowan seemed tense. Pyson Wence just looked angry. They moved into the room with an unmistakable air of authority, and Pen knew that the time for procrastination was over. Taking a deep breath, forcing himself not to look down at the darkwand where it lay on the floor beneath the bench, he came to his feet.

"I'm ready to tell you what you want to know," he said.

Best not to wait on the inevitable, he decided, and saw that his words had an instant calming effect on both, although the Gnome's brow remained dark and his eyes skeptical. "What is it that you think we want to know, little man?" he asked softly.

"You want to know what I'm doing out here. You want to know why I made such a long journey. You want to know if it has something to do with my aunt. Isn't that right?"

Pyson Wence started to answer, but Traunt Rowan held up one hand to silence him. His eyes fastened on Pen. "I think you prefer not to play games with us, young Pen, so I won't play games with you. The fact that you gave yourself up to save your friends tells me something about your character. I respect that. I won't waste any more time trying to convince you that everything in your life is going to be all right when this is over. As it happens, that isn't my decision. But you could help yourself—and your parents—considerably by doing just exactly what you propose. Tell us what we want to know, and I will see what I can do to help you. I have some influence in this matter. Shadea a'Ru is our leader, but Pyson and I are strong in our own right."

"Stronger than she thinks," the Gnome added, scowling at nothing, his eyes sweeping the room as if he was worried that someone might be listening.

"Let me repeat again that we didn't send Aphasia Wye to hunt you," Traunt Rowan continued. "We happen to agree with you. He was a monster. We're glad he's dead. But you need to understand that we think your aunt is a monster, too. A monster of another sort." He paused. "Do you know what we did with her?"

Pen nodded. "You sent her into the Forbidding."

He saw the surprise in both men's eyes. He knew more than they had thought he knew. "How do you know that?"

"She told me so," he said. "She came to me in a dream and told me she was being held prisoner by Druids. She asked me to help her. I didn't know what to think, but then Tagwen came to Patch Run and told me she had disappeared, so I decided to do what she had asked."

"Which was?"

"To travel to the ruins of Stridegate. To seek help that could only be found there."

Pyson Wence scowled. "What sort of help? Why would she ask help of you and not her brother?"

Pen's thoughts raced. "I don't know. Or, at least, I didn't know at first. I didn't think it was real. But I was afraid to ignore it, too."

"So you just decided to set out on your own?"

He took a deep breath. "Tagwen came to ask my father to help him find the Ard Rhys. Tagwen thought that my father could use his magic to discover where she had gone. But my father and mother were traveling, and I was the only one home. Then that other Druid appeared, the Dwarf, on the *Galaphile,* so we ran. He chased us all the way into the Black Oaks before we lost him. Then we flew my skiff to the Westland to ask Ahren Elessedil for help, and he got us a larger airship and took us north to Anatcherae. But the *Galaphile* found us again, and tracked us across the Lazareen and into the Slags, and there was a fight, and the *Galaphile* exploded and Ahren and the Dwarf were both killed."

He paused, trying to gauge their reaction. Did they believe any of this? He was trying to stay as close to the truth as possible without giving anything vital away.

"Terek Molt was always impatient," Pyson Wence growled, waving his hand dismissively. "This time it cost him more than he expected."

"What did you do after that, Pen?" Traunt Rowan asked.

"We continued north out of the Slags. We still had the airship. We flew all the way to Taupo Rough. We met Kermadec, and he agreed to guide us to Stridegate. Then you appeared and we started running again."

There was a long silence as the two men stared at him, weighing the truth in his story. Pen faced them squarely, meeting their eyes, willing them to believe.

"And all this time Aphasia Wye was hunting you?" the Southlander asked quietly.

Pen shook his head. "I didn't know anything about him, at first. He appeared for the first time in Anatcherae, after we had gotten away from the Dwarf. He chased us along the docks to the ship. Then we didn't see him until we were in the country beyond the Slags. He caught up to us again there. But we lost him. Then he appeared in the ruins. No one saw him that time but me. He crossed over to the island somehow, looking for me."

He paused. "If you didn't send him to find me, who did?"

Traunt Rowan pursed his lips. "Your aunt has many enemies, Pen. Not all of them are Druids."

An answer that wasn't an answer to the question, Pen thought.

"This doesn't feel right," Pyson Wence announced suddenly. "Aphasia Wye tracks you all the way to Stridegate, but twice you escape him along the way, something no one else has ever done. Then you confront him on the other side of a bridge that you say no one but you can cross, and you are able to kill him? You? A boy? Do you think we are fools?"

Pen shook his head quickly. "I didn't kill him. The spirits did. The ones who live on the island. They are called aeriads. They tricked him, lured him to the edge of the chasm. In the dark, he was confused. He fell, and the fall killed him. It is a long way to the bottom of the chasm. There are lots of rocks and tangled roots."

Pyson Wence was on him in a second, snatching him up by the front of his shirt and holding him pinned against the bulkhead. "Aphasia Wye could see better in the dark than most cats," the Gnome spit. "He was a skilled hunter. Nothing would have confused him. Nothing would have distracted him once he had the scent. Certainly not the dark! You are lying to us, little man!"

The Gnome's fist was jammed so tightly against Pen's throat that the boy could barely breathe, let alone talk. "It was the magic!" he finally managed to gasp.

Pyson Wence dropped him to the floor and kicked him hard. "Magic? What magic? Magic from these spirits you talk about? What sort of magic would they have that would stop Aphasia Wye? You're making this up, boy!"

Pen was shaking his head as hard as he could in denial, both hands clutching at his injured throat. "No, it's the truth! I didn't know they were there when I went to Stridegate. I didn't know anything except what my aunt told me in the dream. I was to go there and find out what I could do to help. So I went. The spirits were her means of communicating with me from within the Forbidding. She came to me on the island through them and told me that there was still a chance for her to escape so long as some of the Druids believed in her. She said that belief formed a connection to her and would help her find a way back!"

Pyson Wence kicked him harder still. "Belief in her? That's going to get her out of the Forbidding? That's what she told you?" He kicked Pen again, then looked over at Traunt Rowan. "Let's kill him now and be done with it!"

The tall Southlander seemed to consider the idea, then shook his head. "I don't think so." He walked over, moved the smaller man out of the way, then reached down and helped Pen back to his feet. Steering him by his shoulders, he led the boy back to the bench and sat him down.

Kneeling, he looked Pen squarely in the eye. "He's right about one thing," he said softly. "You're lying to us. I thought we agreed that there weren't to be any games played in this business."

Pen felt his throat tighten and his stomach clench. He thought for a minute he was going to be sick, but he kept it from happening by refusing to give them the satisfaction. "I wasn't lying!"

Traunt Rowan shook his head in disappointment. "Your aunt summoned you all the way to Stridegate to tell you that belief would help free her? Why didn't she just tell you that in your dream, Pen? For that matter, why didn't she just tell your father, who might have

been able to do something about it? Why choose to tell you, a boy
with no way to do much of anything without help?"

Pen looked down at his clenched hands. "All right. There was
something else. While I was on the island, I had to do something. I
had to find this tree, a kind of tree I had never seen before. I had to
find it and carve her name into its trunk. The tree bled sap into the
letters, and there was a kind of magic released. It was what saved me
from Aphasia Wye. It kept him from me, confused him, sent him off
into the dark so that he fell into the ravine. The magic was a part of
her, brought back from the Forbidding by the carving of her name. It
wasn't her body or mind or anything you could touch. It was her
spirit, I guess."

It was a plausible enough story, given the nature of magic and its
workings, much of which was elemental and released through nature's children. It even bordered on the truth.

Traunt Rowan smiled. "Strange, though. Your father couldn't do
all this? It had to be you. A boy not out of his teens, Pen?"

Pen nodded. "I have the use of a kind of magic my father doesn't.
It isn't much. I can understand the thinking and intent of birds and
plants and animals from their movements and sounds. It isn't communication exactly, but it's something like it. My aunt understood
that I would know how to carve the letters in the tree in a way that
wouldn't hurt it, that would allow it to permit her to reach through
the Forbidding."

A total lie this time, but he was too deep in to back away and he
needed to buttress his story with reasons for how things had come
about. He felt his credibility was slipping away, and he threw up his
hands in mock disgust.

"I don't understand it, either. You can believe me or not, I don't
care! But I love my aunt, and I did what I had to do to help her. I'd do
it again, if she asked me! She isn't a monster, no matter what you say."
He glared at Traunt Rowan fiercely. "I've had enough of this! You
don't believe anything I've told you! Fine! I don't have to tell you
anything else!"

From the other side of the room, Pyson Wence snorted. Traunt
Rowan remained where he was, studying Pen's face in a way that the
boy found disturbing. The Druid could tell he was lying, he realized.
He didn't know how he understood that, but he did.

"You might want to take those words back," the other said. "You heard Pyson. He thinks we should kill you and put the whole matter behind us. We already have your parents. It wouldn't be difficult to make them disappear as well. You can prevent this, but it doesn't seem as if you want to."

Pen shook his head. "Of course I want to! But I don't think I can prevent anything. You'll do what you want with all of us, no matter what I say! Besides, I've told you what I know."

"Everything you know?" Traunt Rowan pressed. "You've told us everything?"

Pen knew he was dead, sensed it in the way the other asked the question, could feel it right down to the soles of his feet. But there was nothing he could do to change things, not even if he wanted to.

He set his jaw. "Everything."

Traunt Rowan nodded slowly and started to rise. But as he did so he reached down for the muddied staff tucked under the bench beneath Pen's feet and pulled it free. "Well, then, it will come as something of a surprise to you to discover that this simple staff you have been using as a crutch for your injured leg is actually something more than it appears."

He held it out for Pen to inspect, keeping it just out of reach as he balanced it loosely in the palm of one hand. Pen felt all the strength go out of his body. He had thought the staff forgotten and his secret safe. He had thought the Druids fooled.

"You did think this just a simple staff, didn't you?" the other persisted.

Pyson Wence had come over to stand beside him now, his dark face furrowed in surprise. Apparently he had missed seeing what it was, even if Traunt Rowan had not. "What are you talking about?"

The Southlander ran his hands slowly up and down the length of wood, and as he did so the dried mud and dirt fell away and the surface turned bright and smooth, revealing the intricately carved network of runes hidden beneath. He blew gently to clean it of any remaining flecks of dust, then used one end of his sleeve to polish the wood.

"There," he said, smiling cheerfully at Pen. "You can see for yourself. What do you make of this? Pyson?" He glanced over at the other Druid. "Isn't this a surprise?"

Pyson Wence started for Pen, his face flushed with rage, but

Traunt Rowan held him back. "No, what are you doing? No need for that! You heard Pen; he didn't know what it was. He probably just picked it up while walking around the forest and kept it because he needed a crutch. Isn't that right, Pen?"

Pen said nothing, his eyes fixed on the other, watching him the way a mouse would a snake. Traunt Rowan had known all along. He had been leading Pen around by the nose, letting him fabricate whatever story he wished, because in the end he knew the one thing that counted—that what the boy was really hiding was the secret of the staff.

"Little man, I will see you hung from meat hooks and gutted before this matter is finished!" Pyson Wence hissed at him. His gaze shifted to Traunt Rowan. "What are we waiting for? Let me have him now, and we will know the truth of things quick enough!"

Traunt Rowan shook his head. "Not until Shadea is done with him. I don't want to have to explain to her why we failed to keep him alive long enough for her to question him." He smiled at Pen. "This isn't going to work out the way you wanted, Pen. Not for you or your parents. You shouldn't have tried to be so clever. You're only a boy, and boys always think themselves much more clever than they really are."

Pen was having trouble breathing. He knew he should say or do something, but he had no idea what it should be. It was all he could do to keep himself from falling apart completely.

Traunt Rowan watched him a moment longer, then shrugged. "Cat got your tongue?" He hefted the staff and tossed it to Pyson Wence. "What do you make of it, Pyson? Can you read the markings? Elfish, I think. Very old."

The Gnome studied the runes a moment, then shook his head impatiently. "Nothing I've ever seen. We might find something on it back at Paranor, in the books. What difference does it make?"

"I don't know. Pen, do you?" Traunt Rowan looked at him. "Anything about these markings look familiar? No?" He pursed his lips. "Maybe we should see if they're even real."

He took the staff out of Pyson's hands, dropped it carelessly to the floor, and pointed at it. Blue fire exploded from his fingers, engulfing the darkwand. Pen gasped in spite of himself, leapt to his feet, and tried to snatch the darkwand back. Almost casually, Traunt Rowan backhanded him into the wall so hard that he almost blacked out. On the floor, the darkwand jumped at the touch of the searing fire, but to his surprise refused to burn. The Druid tried again, the fire flashing from his fingers in a fresh wave, licking at and engulfing the wood. But again, nothing happened. When the fire ceased, the wood was left untouched.

Pyson Wence snatched up the darkwand and smashed it against the bulkhead, but the staff bounced away unmarked and unbroken.

"Magic, of a very powerful kind," Traunt Rowan declared softly, looking down at a dazed Pen. "Is this meant for the Ard Rhys, Pen? I have a feeling it is. A talisman of some sort, to be used to free her."

Pen tried to keep his expression blank, his feelings from showing on his face or reflecting in his eyes. He tried to pretend he didn't feel anything, that nothing that was happening mattered. But pain ratcheted through him as he slumped on the bench, his head throbbing with the blow he had taken, and his hopes for achieving anything of what he had set out to accomplish vanished.

"He doesn't want to talk now, but he will soon enough," Pyson Wence hissed. "Do you hear me, little man?"

Traunt Rowan stepped forward and yanked Pen off the bench, holding him up so that they were face-to-face. "He hears you, Pyson." He bent so close to the boy that their noses were almost touching. "Are you worried for your parents, Pen?" he whispered. "I worried for mine, too, but it wasn't enough to save them. You think Grianne Ohmsford is worth giving up your life for, but she isn't. She killed my parents, and in a way she will end up killing yours, as well, won't she? She is a monster, Pen. She always was and she always will be. Except that now she's where she belongs—with the other monsters."

He let go of the boy, shoving him back onto the bench. "You think about it while we fly to Paranor. You think about how much she really means to you."

He stepped back, flushed with the heat of his words. Then he turned and walked from the room, taking the staff and Pyson Wence with him.

In the ensuing silence, Pen was left alone to consider the fate that awaited him.

"What do you think you are doing?" a voice called out from behind Khyber, causing her to turn abruptly to face the speaker.

It was the sunset of the following day, and the light was weak and tinged with twilight, so she could not make him out clearly, other than to identify him as one of the Gnome crew. Of course, he couldn't make her out, either, so she was able to act before he could determine who she was. A quick movement of her fingers caused him to hear an unexpected noise, a sound he recognized as dangerous. When he was looking the other way, she brushed the air about her to create a screen of mist and walked away.

It was one of the small skills she had learned from Ahren Elessedil while aboard the *Skatelow* all those weeks ago. A lifetime ago, she thought. It made her sad, remembering. It made her wish she could change things, even though she knew she couldn't.

She glanced back at the Gnome Hunter, who was looking around in confusion, trying to figure out what had happened. It was the first time anyone had challenged her, but she had been prepared for the possibility. Still, she would have to be more careful. One sighting might go unreported. A second was more likely to draw attention.

They were flying south along the spine of the Charnals, come out of the Klu now and gone down below the Lazareen. Ahead, the bleak wasteland of the Skull Kingdom was a dark smudge against the extended green of the landscape stretching toward the southwest, where the light was a dim reddish gold band along the horizon. In another day, perhaps as early as the next evening, they would reach Paranor. The Druid warships were swift, and they flew unhindered and unconcerned through that dangerous country. Few enemies would dare to attack even a single Druid warship, let alone three.

She scanned the countryside below for a moment, then started for the starboard aft hatchway. The decks were mostly deserted, the crew below eating dinner, the night watch not yet come topside. Only the pilot and two crewmen were in view, and they were mostly passing time until they could eat and sleep.

She was at the hatchway when she saw the flash of light from the *Athabasca*, which was flying just ahead and to port. The light was sudden and intense, and it came from somewhere in the hold, below-decks, flaring out through cracks in the shutters, slivers of brilliance against the black. She recognized it as magic right away; it was too sharp-edged for firelight. She stared momentarily in shock, then watched it flash a second time.

But that was all. She waited, but it didn't come again. She listened for some indication of what had caused it, but heard nothing. She tried to read its origins using her own magic, probing the space between the vessels, but the air currents caused by the airships' movements swept away all traces.

Was it Pen?

She had no way of knowing. She wouldn't be able to tell anything until they landed at Paranor—perhaps not even then. She stared out at the dark bulk of the *Athabasca*. The ship was only a hundred yards away, but it might as well have been a hundred miles.

Disconsolate and frustrated, she dropped her gaze and slipped through the hatchway to try to get some sleep.

FOUR

Rue Meridian sat with her back against the cell's far wall, facing the locked door. Her prison, like Bek's, was deep beneath the walls and buildings of the Druid's Keep. There was only the single door. The door was solid metal, save for a flap at its bottom, which permitted her jailers to slide a tray of food inside without opening the door, and a series of slits at eye level, which let in slivers of torchlight from the hallway beyond. Within her cell were a wooden bed frame and mattress, a blanket, a slop bucket, and a broom. The broom was a mystery. Was she supposed to sweep up the cell when it got too dusty? Was she supposed to knock down cobwebs?

Since she had been shut away, she had not been allowed out. Not once, even for a moment. Nor had anyone come inside. She had heard the guards moving in the hallway, and she had looked out in an effort to see them once or twice. But the guards kept out of her line of sight and spoke in low enough tones that they were out of hearing, as well. They had not spoken to her through the door. Other than delivering her food and allowing her to slide the bucket out for emptying now and then, they had paid no attention to her at all. As far as she could determine, in the minds of her captors she had ceased to exist.

So she sat and waited for something to happen, all the while thinking of ways she might escape.

She thought constantly of her son, frantic for his safety. Her husband was resourceful and would be able to help himself. And she would be fine. But Pen lacked their experience and their skills; he would be at the mercy of whoever went to find him. She knew enough of Shadea a'Ru to appreciate how determined she was to eradicate the Ohmsfords. It wouldn't stop with Grianne, though she was the excuse for the purge. It would continue until the last Ohmsford was wiped from the face of the Four Lands.

Thinking of it left her furious. She had never trusted the Druids, never cared for their secretive ways and manipulative schemes. It had been bad enough when there was only one, and that one was Walker Boh. But now there were dozens of them, not only within the walls of Paranor, but scattered throughout the Four Lands, as well. She had always felt at risk, especially with Grianne as Ard Rhys. Her feelings for Bek's sister were unchanged. In her mind, Grianne would always be the Ilse Witch. Bek's assurances notwithstanding, she had never been convinced that Grianne's transformation from dark witch to white queen was real. Her attitude was not so different from that of many others. She could understand why some among the Druids were so eager to be rid of her.

But the real problem was her certainty that their connection with Grianne put them all in danger. It didn't matter that they were not close to the Ard Rhys and had nothing to do with the Druid order. It didn't matter that their lives were so different. Blood and history bound them inextricably. She had always known that the cauldron of mistrust and dislike Grianne stirred among those who were troubled by her position of power as Ard Rhys was in danger of spilling over onto the rest of them.

Her present circumstances seemed to bear that out.

She stared at the iron door and wished she had thought to stick a throwing knife into her boot. She wished she had any kind of weapon at all. She wished she had two minutes alone outside that door.

After a time, she dozed, drifting away on thoughts of her family and better times. In the near blackness of her prison, sleep was the only form of relief she could find.

She did not know how long she slept, only that it ended suddenly and unexpectedly. She awoke with a start, her sleep broken by an odd sound from beyond her cell. She blinked in confusion, sensing that what she had heard was the collapse of something. She sat up straight, listening for more.

Then a key twisted in the lock, metal scraping on metal, and the lock released with a sharp *snick*. She got to her feet quickly and took a deep breath to steady herself, to clear her sleep-fogged mind. She didn't know what to expect, didn't know how to prepare herself. She snatched up the broom, the only thing at hand that might serve as a weapon, and moved to stand close by the door.

The door opened, and a black-cloaked figure stepped through. One gloved hand came up quickly in warning as she started to move out of her crouch. "Wait!"

The hands rose to pull back the hood, and she found herself confronted by a young man with angular features and a quizzical expression. He blinked at her and smiled. "No need for that. I've come to help." He glanced over his shoulder into the hallway, his lank brown hair falling over his forehead and into his eyes. "Hurry. We haven't much time. They'll discover you've gone soon enough and they'll know where it is they must look."

Satisfied to be free, to have a chance at escaping the Keep, she went with him without questioning their destination. They slipped from the cell into the hallway, where she saw the collapsed form of the Gnome Hunter who had been keeping guard outside the door. There was no blood, no mark on him anywhere.

"A sleeping potion," whispered her rescuer, his young face brightening with pleasure. "Worked on the one at the top of the stairs, too. They have a warning system to prevent your escape that travels from the bottom up, but not from the top down. They expect any attempt at escape to come from you. They don't think you have any friends here."

"I didn't think so, either," she admitted, reaching down to snatch away the guard's dagger.

"Oh, yes," he replied quickly. "A few. Well, two of us, anyway. I am the one who slipped your husband that warning note when you first arrived. But I couldn't do more until now. Come, hurry!"

They moved silently down the shadowy corridor. Torchlight from brands set in wall brackets cast pools of yellowish light on the stone floor. She listened carefully for the sound of other movements as she went, but heard nothing. At the bottom of a circular ascent, her rescuer paused to peer upward into the dark hole of the stairwell. No light filtered down.

He glanced over. "I left the door closed against intrusion. No shift change is due for another hour, but you don't want to take chances."

He smiled his infectious smile again. "I'm Trefen Morys." He stuck out his hand, and she gave it a quick squeeze. "Bellizen and I are still loyal to the Ard Rhys. And to you and your husband, too."

"Where is Bek?" she asked quickly.

"Imprisoned, like you. I couldn't risk trying to reach him until you were free. They keep him closely watched, held in check by a warning that any attempt on his part to escape will result in your death. They are afraid of his magic. They think that if they keep him contained, you will not present a problem. So I freed you first, to take the pressure off while we break him free."

She nodded. "Sound reasoning, Trefen Morys."

He blushed. "I hope you will have a chance to tell that to my mistress." His brow furrowed. "When she disappeared, I knew that Shadea a'Ru and those who follow her had something to do with it, especially after they seized control of the order. Then Tagwen disappeared, and the word went out that they were looking for you and your son. It was all too clear that they meant to stop any effort at finding my mistress."

"Do you know where Pen is?" she asked quickly. "Have they found him? Have they brought him here?"

He shook his head. "There is no word of your son. I know he has not been brought here. I have been watching for him. We both have, Bellizen and I." He gripped her arm. "We have been waiting for the right time to set you free, but we could not chance it while Shadea and the others were all present at Paranor. But Shadea has gone south to meet with the Prime Minister of the Federation and will not return for several days. Her closest allies, Traunt Rowan and Pyson Wence, flew north days ago."

"In search of Pen?"

He nodded. "We will try to reach him first, once you are both free and we have control of your airship. Our usefulness here is ended. There is nothing more we can do to help my mistress. The order follows Shadea now, all but a handful. Already, they believe she is the leader the order requires and that my mistress was an unfortunate mistake. Whatever we can do to change their thinking, to find my mistress and stop Shadea, must happen elsewhere."

He pointed up the stairs. "We have to go. Follow me." He put a finger to his lips. "Quiet like a mouse, now."

They tiptoed up the stone risers, the young Druid leading the way. Rue had the Gnome dagger in her right hand, ready for use. She wished she had more than one, but the truth of the matter was that if they were discovered, a dozen daggers wouldn't be enough to save them. They must count on stealth and surprise to see them through.

At the top of the stairs, Trefen Morys eased open the iron-bound wooden door and peered through the crack. Glancing over his shoulder, he nodded and pushed through to the light beyond.

They were in a guardroom that served as a waypoint between the cellars and the rest of the Keep. Weapons and armor hung from racks on the walls, and open doors revealed storage closets filled with cloaks and boots. Torches burned in their racks, but the room was empty save for them.

Trefen Morys walked over to a pair of closed doors and opened them. A Gnome Hunter lay slumped on the floor. The young Druid nudged the Gnome with his boot, and when he didn't move closed the doors once more. Then he took one of the cloaks from its peg and handed it to Rue.

"Your husband is being held in another part of the Keep. They are taking no chances that one of you will have any chance of finding and rescuing the other. But I know where to go and how to get there. The trick will be in disposing of the Gnome Hunters who serve as guards. Make no mistake. They are Shadea a'Ru's men—mercenaries recruited and paid for by Pyson Wence to replace the Trolls. They have been ordered to kill both of you if there is any sort of escape attempt. So we have to keep them from finding out what has happened here until we reach your husband."

He paused. "One thing more you need to know. It is important that we do this now. Things are very bad here. Many Druids have been dismissed from the order and sent home. Others have simply disappeared, including some who were close to Shadea. Terek Molt has been gone for more than a month. Iridia Eleri disappeared two weeks ago. And right before Shadea left for Arishaig, her consort, Gerand Cera, was found dead. There wasn't a mark on him. No one says so, but we all think the same thing—she used him until he became expendable. It might be true of the others, as well."

He shook his head. "Yet most within the order still follow Shadea. However they feel about her secretly, they don't mistrust her in the same way they did the Ard Rhys. My mistress is shackled by her history as the Ilse Witch. She cannot escape it. Too many refuse to forgive her, even though she has changed. It doesn't matter that in the end, Shadea will prove a worse choice. They cannot see that she will destroy the order, that she will lead it to ruin because she lacks my mistress's passion for doing what is right."

"Isn't there a good chance that Grianne Ohmsford is already dead?" Rue asked. "Is there any reason to think she isn't?"

He shook his head vigorously. "If my mistress were dead, why would they work so hard at finding your son? What difference would it make to them where he had gone and what he was doing if she weren't still alive? No, they think he has found a way to reach her and if not stopped might well do so."

Rue heard the sound of footfalls in the corridor outside, and they both turned quickly. "Your cloak!" Trefen Morys hissed, pulling up his hood and tightening the folds.

But Rue knew it was too late for any sort of disguise. Stepping silently to one side of the entry as the steps approached, she waited for the door to open and the Gnome Hunter to step through, then brought the haft of the knife around in a powerful blow that caught the Gnome on his temple and dropped him like a stone.

"Help me," she said, kicking the door closed and taking the Gnome's arms.

Together they hauled the body to one of the closets, bound his arms and legs, gagged his mouth, and stuffed him inside. Without another word or more than a quick glance at each other, they went out through the door the Gnome had entered and down the corridor beyond, Trefen Morys leading the way. One corridor intersected with another, one set of stairs wound to a second, doors opened and closed into rooms, and so they made their way through the shadowy halls, pausing only to listen for voices or footsteps as they went. The minutes slipped away, and Rue was quickly lost. She didn't know that much about Paranor anyway, having visited only a handful of times and having never ventured much beyond the main halls that led to the council chambers and the rooms of the Ard Rhys. They were deep underground here, in a maze of passageways she had never seen and could never have navigated on her own. She could feel the cold permeating the rock. Even the central fires of the Keep's furnace, the fires that burned from deep underground at the earth's core, could not push back the chill.

Once or twice, Trefen Morys glanced back, and each time she nodded quickly for him to go on. She was thinking of Bek, just out of reach, but she was thinking about Penderrin, as well, much farther away and more vulnerable. She was thinking about her child and how she would never be able to live with herself if something were to happen to him.

Finally, Trefen Morys slowed, then stopped altogether, dropping into a crouch beneath the light of a torch burning in its wall bracket. Ahead, a door stood closed to whatever lay beyond.

"A pair of guards keeps watch there," he whispered, as she crouched next to him. "We have to silence them both. Beyond that room, stairs lead downward to a corridor of cells. Your husband is in one of them. A second pair of Gnome Hunters stands watch there— one at the bottom of the stairs, another in front of the cell that imprisons your husband. Any sort of warning will result in a swift response."

She nodded. "There won't be any warning."

"I was able to get another note to your husband several days ago, so that he would know that someone was looking to help him. He will know we are coming, and he will be ready, even if the Gnome Hunter at his cell door attempts to kill him. I don't know a great deal about his magic, but I gather it was a match for his sister's, so he will have a chance to survive this." He sighed. "I wish I could have done more."

She gave him a quick smile. "You have done all that could be expected of you, Trefen Morys. However this turns out, you can't be faulted for your efforts."

He took her arm as she started to rise. "Wait." He seemed suddenly nervous. "I have to tell you something. I am not a warrior Druid. I am not skilled in the use of weapons or magic as a substitute for weapons. I have magic, yes. But my studies are of rocks and soils."

She stared at him. "Rocks and soils?"

He nodded. "I have never killed anyone." He dropped his gaze. "I have never even hurt anyone. I don't know how to fight."

She took a deep breath. She had fought alone before and against great odds. But she had been much younger then, harder and more resilient, reckless about her safety in a way she no longer was. Not with the lives of her husband and son at stake as well as her own. She wished suddenly that her brother were there, that Redden Alt Mer were standing with her as he had on so many other occasions. Having Big Red with her would change the odds considerably. But she might just as well wish she could fly.

"You won't have to fight," she told Trefen Morys, reaching out to grip his arm reassuringly. She saw some of the tension drain from his young face. "Stay behind me and do what you can to protect yourself if you are threatened. I will dispose of the guards." Her grip tightened. "One thing you must promise me, though. If I fall, wounded or dead, you must continue on. You must do whatever you can to reach Bek. You must free him and then tell him what you have told me. He will know what to do. Will you do that?"

Trefen Morys nodded. "You have my word."

She looked down at the long knife she had taken from the Gnome Hunter and wished she had something more substantial with which to work. It had been twenty years since she had fought a battle like the one she was facing, and she knew she had lost the sharp edge of her survival instincts.

Could she do this?

A fierce resolution washed over her as she hefted the knife in her palm, watching the way the torchlight played across its polished surface. Some things you did because you had to.

"All right," she said, looking up at him. "I'm ready."

In a guarded crouch, they began to creep down the hall.

F I V E

Rue Meridian was leading the way, Trefen Morys hanging back. She reached the door to the guardroom, hesitated, glanced down at the latch, then back at the young Druid. He saw her questioning look and he nodded, motioning her to go ahead, indicating the door was not locked. She wasn't sure how he could know that, but had to believe him.

Taking a deep breath, she placed her hand over the heavy iron handle, twisted hard, and pushed.

Two Gnome Hunters looked up as she entered. One was at work on the broken handle of a short sword. The second stood across the room, leaning idly against the wall. Both hesitated, confused by the presence of the Druid behind her.

She had just enough time to register the open door across the room, and then the Gnome leaning against the wall made up his mind about her and reached for a pike.

Flinging the long knife underhanded with such force that the blade was buried in his chest all the way up to the hilt, she killed him before his hand could close on the pike's wooden shaft. The Gnome gave a sharp gasp and sank slowly down, hands clutching at the haft of the knife. By then, she was across the room and on top of the other one. He awkwardly struck at her with the broken sword, but she caught the flat of the blade on her forearms and knocked it aside.

She jammed her fingers into his throat, silencing his voice, and then struck him repeatedly on the side of his head with her fist. His eyes rolled back, and he collapsed and lay still.

Neither Gnome was moving. She found no pulse on either. She snatched a pair of daggers from a rack and stuck them in her belt, hesitated, then added a long knife. She turned to an ashen-faced Trefen Morys, who clearly hadn't exaggerated when he said he wasn't a fighter. She placed a warning finger to her lips and moved close. "Are you all right?" she whispered.

He nodded, his eyes big.

"Listen, then. I want you to go down the stairs ahead of me. The Gnomes won't react so quickly to the sight of a Druid. They will think Shadea or one of her allies sent you. When you reach the first, get him turned around so that his back is to me. Can you do that?"

He nodded again, breathing hard through his mouth.

"Don't worry," she said. "We'll be all right."

She steered him toward the open door across the room. Beyond, a set of narrow stairs spiraled downward into near darkness. She had to hope that no sound of the struggle that had just taken place had reached the ears of the guards below. It had been quick enough; there had been no cries of alarm. She paused at the top of the stairs and listened carefully.

Nothing.

She nodded to Trefen Morys and motioned him ahead. He moved reluctantly, woodenly, and she seized his shoulder to make certain he wasn't going into shock. He gasped in pain and glanced quickly at her, then took a deep breath and nodded that he was ready. She released him with a gentle shove and watched him start down.

She waited until he was out of sight around the bend in the stairs, then followed, creeping on cat's paws along the rough expanse of the curved wall, one of the daggers out and resting loosely in her hand. Halfway there, she thought. But the second pair might pose more of a challenge. She would have to silence them one at a time, and that wouldn't be easy. Bek might be ready or he might not, but the suddenness of a rescue like this one could throw your thinking off, no matter how formidable your skills. Bek was brave, but he did not have her experience at close combat. Though he had grown considerably during their journey to Parkasia, that had been twenty years ago and she was willing to bet that he had already forgotten much of what he had learned. Nor had he practiced with the wishsong in the intervening years. He had disdained to use it, preferring to leave that part of his life behind him. In spite of her own dislike and mistrust of the magic, she wished he had not been so insistent on ignoring his gift.

Well, that was the way of things, she supposed. Hindsight always suggested how you might have been better prepared.

She edged forward as the light grew slightly stronger near the bottom of the steps. Ahead, she heard Trefen Morys's voice and the responding growl of the Gnome Hunter on watch. She slid around the curve in the wall so that she could see them. The Gnome had his back to her. So far, so good.

She came up behind him swiftly and killed him with a single thrust of the dagger.

At which point Trefen Morys threw up. The retching sound reverberated down the corridor and instantly brought a sharp query from the near darkness. Leaping past the young Druid, Rue raced ahead, sliding free the other dagger as she ran, no longer bothering with stealth; speed was all that mattered. Ahead, there was movement at the edge of the light, and she saw the final guard peering at her through the smoky torchlit gloom, crossbow at the ready. She threw herself flat as the weapon swung up and heard the whir of the bolt as it shot past her, ricocheted off the stone walls, and fell harmlessly to the floor farther on. She was up and running again, watching her adversary wind back the string and insert another bolt with quick, practiced movements. This one was well trained, dangerous.

The crossbow came up, and she threw herself down a second time. But this time the Gnome did not fire at her. Instead, as soon as she was down he wheeled toward the cell door in front of him, grappling to release the heavy locking bolt. Rue was on her feet instantly, realizing at once what he intended. His orders in this situation were clear. She heard the locking bolt slide free and the cell door swing open. The guard brought up the crossbow a second time. She was still too far away to stop him, so she screamed at him, then hurtled the dagger as hard as she could. There wasn't enough force behind the throw to injure him, but the heavy blade ripped through his leather tunic, causing him to jerk back.

Then Bek Ohmsford was hurtling through the open cell door and slamming into the Gnome. The crossbow released, the bolt flew into the ceiling and dropped harmlessly. The Southlander and the Gnome went down in a heap, tumbling across the floor, arms and legs entangled. Rue put on a burst of speed, drawing the long knife from her belt. Ahead of her, the flat surface of a blade caught the light as it swept down. Someone cried out, and then she was on top of the fighters, screaming in rage, burying her own blade deep into the Gnome Hunter's back, driving it all the way through him.

The Gnome Hunter fell away, dead before his hands released their grip. Rue threw the body aside and knelt next to her husband, already seeing the red stain spreading across his tunic front. "No!" she hissed, and began trying to sort through the tangle of his clothes for the wound.

"Stop it, Rue!" He pushed her hands away, shaking his head. There was pain and frustration in his voice. "There's no time. We have to get out of here." He was already struggling to his feet, clutching his midsection. "I'm all right. He only scraped my ribs."

"It's more than that!" she snapped back. "Look at the blood!"

Trefen Morys came pounding up, his black robes flying out behind him. He looked at Bek and turned white. "How bad is it?"

Bek shook his head. "Not now. Which way out? Can you get us to *Swift Sure*?"

The young Druid nodded. "Bellizen should already be there. She will have secured it for us. Can you walk?"

Rue was tearing her robe into long strips, using the dagger to cut the fabric. Without comment, she began wrapping it tightly about Bek's midsection. He leaned into her and whispered as she did so, "I love you."

Then they were running, all three of them, back down the corridor past the dead men and fallen weapons, past the blood and vomit, and up the stairs, gaining the guardroom and the corridors beyond.

It was still quiet in the Keep, no warning yet raised, no alarm given. Then Trefen Morys took them a different way, using a series of narrow back stairways to gain the higher floors. Rue tried to help Bek, who was beginning to falter. His blood speckled the floor behind him as he ran. They were still in great danger, their escape reliant on reaching *Swift Sure* before the rest of the Gnome guards discovered their comrades.

Or they had the misfortune of stumbling across someone who would give them away—which was exactly what happened.

They had just reached the upper levels, where tall windows opened to hazy gray light and heavy clouds, when a lone Gnome Hunter came out of a room right next to them. Everyone froze for an instant, and then the Gnome was crying out. Rue buried her dagger in his chest, knocking him back into the room, but the damage had been done. The cry was immediately taken up, and the pursuit they had feared was mobilizing.

They began to run again, Bek's arm about Rue's shoulders, her arm about his waist. She felt the thick dampness of his blood seeping into her own clothing.

"It's not far!" Trefen Morys called back to them, leading the way. "Just ahead, through those doors!"

A pair of heavy, ironbound oak doors stood closed at the end of the corridor. But the sound of boots reverberated on the stone flooring from just out of sight behind the fugitives. *We're not going to make it,* Rue thought.

Gnome Hunters burst into view, rounding a corner of the hallway perhaps a hundred feet back. Too many to stand and face. Too many to overcome with conventional weapons. Rue glanced at Bek. His eyes were slits in a face gone pale and sweaty. His breathing was shallow and ragged. He was failing rapidly and in no position to use his magic.

Then they were at the double doors, and Trefen Morys was wrenching them open. Rue and Bek stumbled through, and the young Druid shoved the doors closed behind them and stepped back. "Wait!"

He mumbled something, his hands weaving. The locks on the doors melted and fused into a knot of iron, sealed shut.

He turned back to them and grinned triumphantly. "I know a little magic."

They were in the airship courtyard and *Swift Sure* hovered just off the ground not a hundred yards ahead, straining at her anchor ropes, her light sheaths rippling in the breeze and her radian draws taut. She was rigged for flying and ready to lift off. From the pilot box, a solitary figure dressed in black Druid robes jumped up and started waving.

"Bellizen!" Trefen Morys shouted.

The girl shouted back, then darted out of the box and down to the decking. A moment later, one end of a rope ladder flew over the side.

But in the same instant a clutch of Gnome Hunters appeared on the Keep's battlements behind them. They howled in anger when they saw what was happening. Still supporting a wounded Bek, Rue lurched toward the safety of the airship. Trefen Morys darted ahead. Then, seeing how badly his companions were struggling, he raced back to help, taking Bek's other arm and slinging it over his shoulder.

"Hurry!" he urged.

Rue didn't need to be told. Arrows fired from Gnome bows were falling all around them, sharpened heads clattering and skipping across the stones. Rue realized suddenly that she had no weapons of her own, that none of them had, that they had left everything behind in their battle to escape the cells.

She glanced ahead at *Swift Sure*, caught sight of the starboard rail sling in place on the bow, and felt a flutter of hope. "Does Bellizen know how to use airship weapons?" she shouted at Trefen Morys above the cry of the attacking guards. "Do you?"

The young Druid shook his head. "Neither of us does! We aren't trained in the use of weapons!"

A bad oversight, she thought. She took a deep breath. "Stay with Bek!" she ordered.

She dropped her husband's arm and sprinted for the airship ladder. She knew what she was doing. She was trying to save him, but she was also leaving him to his fate, abandoning him to the Gnome Hunters. He would never reach the airship if she failed. Both he and Trefen Morys would die.

But there wasn't any other way.

A crossbow bolt caught her in the thigh, passing so deep into her

flesh it jarred the bone. She cried out in pain, stumbled, righted herself and hobbled on. Arrows rained down all about her, but she was
only nicked until one caught her in the shoulder and spun her all the
way around. She continued to run, teeth clenched, hands knotted
into fists.

Just a little farther.

She leapt onto the rope ladder and clambered up the rungs in a
wash of razor-edged pain and suffocating heat that took her breath
away. She reached the top and Bellizen grabbed her arm and pulled
her past the railing and onto the deck. The Druid girl was no older
than Trefen Morys—younger still, Rue guessed. Short-cropped blue-
black hair formed a helmet about a face paler than Grianne Ohmsford's. Eyes as black as pools on a moonless night peered over. "What
do you need me to do?"

Rue hesitated. Gnome missiles thudded into the airship
decking, bristling from the planks and rails like quills. Impatient
with the failure of their bowmen to bring her down and infuriated by the efforts of Trefen Morys, Gnome Hunters were rap-
pelling down the Keep's walls on ropes. The young Druid had
shown enough presence of mind to use his Druid magic to cause
clouds of dust to swirl across the courtyard, hiding Bek and
himself. It was a clever strategy. But once those descending the
walls reached the ground, the pair would be found again quickly
enough.

And the rail sling, with its slow-cranking winch and single bolt,
wasn't going to be enough to stop them.

"Help me into the pilot box," she said, struggling to stand.

Bellizen was stronger than she looked, and she hauled Rue to her
feet, practically carrying her across the deck and up the three steps
into the pilot box. Fighting the waves of pain and nausea that threatened to undo her, Rue gripped the controls of the airship, unhooding the parse tubes to release the power stored in the diapson crystals
and readying the thruster levers.

"Cut the aft and forward anchor ropes," she ordered the girl.
"Then drop flat against the deck close by the rope ladder. But leave
the ladder down!"

Bellizen saw what she intended, jumped down the steps out
of the box, and raced off to cut the ropes. *Swift Sure* was already

straining against the lines, responding to the fresh power Rue was feeding her. In the courtyard, the haze of dust still obscured Bek and Trefen Morys, but the Gnome Hunters who had rappelled from the battlements were almost upon them. She shouted again at Bellizen, feeling the ship swing about as the aft anchor rope was cut, then lurch forward moments later as the bow anchor rope followed.

Swift Sure shot forward as if catapulted from a sling. Too much power! They would run Bek and the young Druid down! Rue hauled back on the thruster levers, reversing the flow of power through the parse tubes. The airship bucked and slowed, and she was suddenly in the thick of the dust cloud, arrows and crossbow bolts flying everywhere as shouts rose from the Gnomes charging across the courtyard.

"Bek!" she screamed.

The big airship swung about, clearing a space in the dust cloud, and she saw her husband and his rescuer almost underneath the hull. Bellizen was on her feet, calling down to them, directing them toward the ladder. They reached it in seconds and began to climb, Bek in the lead, Trefen Morys helping to boost him up. But they were too slow, each step taking too long. Bek, weak from loss of blood and exhaustion, was barely hanging on.

Frantic, Rue leapt from the pilot box onto the decking and charged forward to the rail sling. Cranking back the winch furiously, she inserted a bolt, swung the weapon about, and fired it into the clutch of Gnome Hunters just emerging from the haze. Three or four of them were knocked backwards like rag dolls. The rest, caught by surprise and not exactly sure what had just happened, dropped flat against the courtyard stones, trying to shield themselves. That gave Bek and Trefen Morys just enough time to gain the airship railing, where Bellizen was waiting to pull them aboard.

Rue dropped the handle of the rail sling and raced back for the pilot box. Leaping inside, she threw the thrusters to the left parse tubes forward and yanked the thrusters to the right parse tubes all the way back. *Swift Sure* swung violently about, turning toward the outer walls and the Dragon's Teeth, and Rue shoved all the thruster levers forward and tilted the tube noses up to gain lift.

An instant later, the airship exploded out of the courtyard and rose into the midday sky, leaving Paranor, with its Druids and Gnome Hunters and dark memories, behind.

S I X

Dawn broke on the Prekkendorran, a brilliant flare of golden light sweeping out of the eastern horizon down the twisting, broken maze of ridges and gullies where Pied Sanderling crouched. The sky was a cloudless canopy of brightening blue, the air still and cool, the light knife-sharp, etching the contours and folds of the land. It was a day created for the witnessing of great things.

The Federation army, a steady wave of silver and black visible through gaps in the shadow-dappled draw, approached like a winding snake toward the rise where the Elves waited. The scrape of their boots against the hardpan, and the clash of metal armor and weapons, signaled their arrival long before they came into view. In two days of steady marching, they had encountered only remnants of the force that had withstood their efforts to gain the heights for almost thirty years. Clearly, they felt they would encounter no meaningful opposition now that they had broken the back of the Elven army.

Maybe they will pay for their arrogance and overconfidence before the day is over, Pied thought. Or maybe such arrogance was justified, and he was the one who should take better stock of the situation. What reason did he have to think his ragtag force of Elves could defeat an army of regulars? Yet he knew that the Elves were determined, driven by rage at the losses they had suffered and by a humiliating sense of impotence at having been made to flee like cattle.

"Drum," he called quietly to his aide.

Drumundoon scooted over, staying low on the crest of the rise to keep hidden, his young face intense. "Captain?"

"What is this place called?"

Unable to answer, Drum shook his head. He crab-walked away, speaking to a handful of the Elven Hunters before coming back again. "It doesn't have a name. There's never been a reason to give it one."

Indeed, Pied thought. *Look at it.* A barren wasteland in which no one would want to live, a nature-ravaged stretch of earth which humans and animals passed through quickly on their way to somewhere more inviting. But it needed a name. His sense of his own mortality was strong that morning, and if he was to die there, he wanted to do so knowing where it happened.

"We will call it Elven Rock," he said. He gripped Drum by his shoulder. "It is here that the Elves become a rock against which all enemies are smashed. Pass the word."

Drum gave him a strange look, then turned and hurried off to do as he had been ordered. Pied watched him go, watched him stop and speak with groups of soldiers as he worked his way down the line, watched some of those soldiers nod in agreement, watched fresh determination etch their brows. They would fight hard, those men and women. They would not break easily.

Within the draw, the sounds of the Federation's approach deepened. The army was almost through. In moments, it would begin to emerge onto the flats leading up to the rise and the Elves.

Pied took a final look around at the defenses he had set, taking their measure one last time.

He could see nothing of the Elven bowmen hidden in the rocks and crevices in the heights to either side, where the draw opened onto the flats. There were more than two hundred, and they would have an unobstructed view of the Federation soldiers as they emerged from the shadows. Longbows were the order of the day, the favorite weapon of Elven bowmen, who disdained use of the bulkier, heavier crossbows. Erris Crewer, a Third Lieutenant, the highest-ranking officer left among them, commanded.

From his slightly higher vantage point, Pied caught glimpses of the Elven Hunters hidden in the deep folds of the ravines to his

right. Almost a quarter of his little army was concealed there, waiting for the summons that would bring it into battle on the Federation's left flank. The timing of that strike would determine the
outcome of the battle. The soldier who was to call for that strike was
a veteran Captain of the Home Guard who had served under Pied for
many years. Ti Auberen could be depended on, and Pied Sanderling
was depending on him heavily.

The bulk of the army, the Elven guards armed with swords and
short spears, was gathered about Pied, grouped in makeshift units
with newly designated commanders and lieutenants. Because they
were formed of remnants of decimated units, few had fought together before. That was a considerable disadvantage in close quarters, where one's life often depended on the experience and quick
thinking of those on either side. But most were familiar with the tri-
angle formations Pied had chosen to employ, so the Captain of the
Home Guard could only hope that in battle the men would remember to do what was needed to keep the units intact and the enemy
from breaking through.

Pied glanced up and down the lines to either side, checking for
readiness. He found it in the faces of most, and he knew that would
have to suffice. There was no time left for anything but hope and
trust. Alternating the advances of the triangles would give each unit
a short respite between strikes and a rear guard to buttress points
threatened with breakthrough. He had decided to hold two units in
reserve, keeping them back for when they were needed most. With
luck, they would not be needed at all, but he couldn't trust to luck in
the face of what was at stake.

These were the best of what remained; they were still alive and
they had not fled during the night. They had chosen to stay, to stand
with him against an enemy that had already routed them once. That
said something to him about their courage.

The first wave of the Federation attack force appeared from out
of the draw, marching in loose formation, shields up but swords
locked in place in the carry straps behind the shields. Their scouts
ranged to either side, but were still well below the ravines and rocks
in which the Elves hid. Had they chosen to come on ahead, doing
what scouts were supposed to do, they would have been disposed of.
Pied had no idea what the Federation commanders were thinking.

Perhaps that the Elves were too disorganized to make a stand. Perhaps that they would do so farther north. Perhaps that they were rallying with reinforcements in Callahorn.

Or perhaps they weren't thinking anything. Perhaps they were
just moving ahead, surprised themselves that after so many years the
stalemate was broken. Perhaps they were still coming to terms with
what that might mean.

Pied glanced behind him at the veteran archer he had chosen to
give the attack signal. The man's bow was strung and the whistle
arrow notched. Meeting his commander's eye, he nodded that he
was ready.

Pied took a deep breath. The sounds of the approaching army
filled his ears. Their boots stirred the dust from the flats and filled the
air with a light haze. Spear blades glinted in the sunlight, and coughs
and shouts emptied out the last of dawn's silence.

Patience, he willed himself. His hands closed more tightly about
his sword. *Another few seconds.*

He let the first ten rows of the Federation army clear the mouth
of the draw before he gave the hand signal to the archer at his back.
The archer dropped to one knee, drew back his bowstring, and released the signal arrow. Its shaft meticulously cored and its tip altered, the arrow caught the wind as it flew and made a shrieking
sound that could be heard for hundreds of yards. In the silence of the
early morning, it was deafening.

Instantly, the Elven bowmen released their arrows from both
sides of the advancing Federation force. A deep whine like the
buzzing of a thousand swarming bees replaced the shriek of the
warning arrow, and Pied's heart lurched. Positioned to fire in three alternating waves, his bowmen sent wave after wave of steel-tipped arrows raining down on the unprotected men. Screams and cries rose
on the morning air. Dozens of Federation soldiers were dead or injured before they could react. When those remaining realized what
was happening, they turned in all directions at once, and dozens
more fell. Caught in the open, they had no chance of escaping the
assault. Even using armor and shields to ward off the deadly killing
shafts, they were vulnerable. No matter where they turned or what
they did, some missiles still managed to get through.

Finally, someone in the ranks took control, and the remnants of
the stricken forward units formed up and charged the archers in

small groups, reinforced by soldiers still coming out of the draw— hundreds of them, flooding the flats with silver-and-black uniforms.

"Elessedil!" Pied Sanderling shouted the Elven war cry, leaping from his hiding place and raising his arm.

In a solid line, the front ranks of the Elven Hunters surged from their hiding places behind the rise and charged the Federation command, taking up Pied's war cry. The Southlanders, split apart in their efforts to reach the archers on their flanks, were caught by surprise. To their credit, they swung into defensive formation with practiced smoothness, but their ranks were already decimated, and there were gaps that could not be filled quickly enough. The Elves hammered through the front lines to the center, bowling over Federation soldiers who tried to stop them, pushing back the entire command.

But the soldiers of the Federation were well trained, and they regrouped quickly, first slowing, then stopping the assault, bracing behind dozens of oncoming ranks, behind weapons and armor, front ranks dropping to one knee and bracing the butts of their spears against the hardpan, rear ranks lowering spears over their shoulders. The Elves slammed into the wall but failed to break it, tried a second time and failed again.

Pied, still standing on the rise with the bulk of the Elven forces, signaled his archer a second time. A pair of arrows shrieked a command as they arced above the combatants. Not all heard the shrieking sound, but those who did signaled their fellows to pull back. Swiftly, the Elves disengaged, retreating on the run to the topmost part of the rise, moving past the six fighting triangles into which the remainder of the Elven foot soldiers had been formed.

It took only minutes for the first wave to retreat, but even in that short time, hundreds more Federation soldiers poured through the gap onto the flats, joining their fellows. It was a much larger force than Pied had envisioned, much larger than his Elves were equipped to handle, but there was nothing he could do about that. Lifting his sword a second time, he called out the Elessedil battle cry and sent his triangles into battle.

The triangles advanced as one. Shields locked and spears lowered, they presented bristling walls of steel tips. The triangles were formed into two lines, three triangles of eighty men each in front and three behind, the latter offset slightly to the right of the former, so that the leading points of each triangle filled all the gaps. As the triangles bore down on the Federation, Erris Crewer had the archers on the slopes rake the enemy soldiers once more, forcing them to cover up with their shields as they scrambled to re-form their shattered lines. Federation archers responded with crossbows, but they could not see their targets and were forced to fire blindly.

The men of the Federation re-formed their ranks once more, but many of those in the front lines had been downed by the initial attack and the gaps were hastily filled with reinforcements. The result was a reconfiguration of ranks where the soldiers were unfamiliar with each other and slow to act in concert or to a common purpose; it was all they could do to make ready to engage the advancing Elves. Their commanders struggled to unify them, but the chaos was so complete that no one could be heard.

Fifty yards from the Federation lines, the Elves shifted hard to the left, drawing the Federation squares about to face them. As the Federation lines turned to face the Free-born advance, their rear left flank was exposed. Ti Auberen, still hidden in the rocks with his men and waiting for his opportunity, was quick to act. Just before the triangles reached the Federation ranks, he brought his own soldiers out of hiding and attacked in a rush. Once again, the unexpectedness of the assault caught the Federation off guard. Having survived the first ambush, the Southlanders were not looking for a second. Ti Auberen's forces caught their rear ranks unprepared and vulnerable, and they smashed through before the surprised soldiers could even bring their weapons about to defend themselves.

Caught in a classic pincer movement, the Federation lines collapsed into pockets of men fighting to survive. The triangles came at them in a series of thrusts, first one rank and then the second, jabbing at them repeatedly, forcing them back and apart from each other. The Federation defense held only minutes against the Elves, then fell apart. The attack turned into a rout, the men in the front lines who tried to flee piling up against those still coming through the draw. Screams and cries filled the air as soldiers fell beneath the crush, trampled. The ground grew cluttered with dead and wounded; the flats turned into a slaughterhouse. The destruction of the Federation force was so complete that it became difficult for the Elves to advance across the body-strewn ground.

Finally, the surviving Southlanders broke free of the charnel house and began to retreat into the draw, the rear ranks falling back so that those still alive in the front could follow. Most of the latter never made it. The memory of their defeat on the Prekkendorran was still fresh in the minds of the Elven Hunters, and they were consumed by a killing lust that would not allow them to stop fighting, even when almost no one was left alive to oppose them.

"Signal a retreat," Pied ordered the archer at his elbow, exchanging a quick glance with Drumundoon.

The archer did so, three arrows whistling through the midmorning air, their shrieks mingling with those of the dead and dying men below. The Elven Hunters, streaked with blood and wild-eyed with battle fever, fell back reluctantly, leaving behind a tangle of dead men and an earth turned slick and matted with blood.

In the shadows of the draw, the last of the retreating Federation soldiers disappeared from view.

Thirty minutes later, Pied stood at the head of the rise with Ti Auberen and Erris Crewer, watching the details move through the carnage below, extracting the Elven dead and wounded. The sun was high in the sky by then, midday approaching, and the air was hot and still and thick with the smell of blood and death. Flies swarmed in black clouds. The men on the rise were making a conscious effort to breathe through their mouths.

"It's not finished," he said.

"No," Ti Auberen agreed, looking off into the hills as if he might catch sight of the enemy. He was a big man, broad-shouldered and lean, wearing his dark hair long and tied back. "But they will come at us another way."

Pied nodded. "They will regroup, reinforce, and come looking for us again, but not through that draw. There are other trails through these hills, tough to navigate, but usable. They will find one and try to get around behind us."

"But they won't underestimate us next time," Auberen added.

Pied thought about that a moment, then turned to Drumundoon, who was standing off to one side. "Drum, see if we have someone in the command who knows this country well enough to talk to us about its passes and trails."

Eager to be doing something other than standing around trying not to watch the burial teams, Drumundoon hurried off. Pied would have been happy to go with him.

"What about that airship?" Erris Crewer asked quietly. His blocky form shifted. "The one that destroyed the fleet?"

Pied shook his head. "I don't know how badly we damaged her. If they can make her fly, we're in trouble. We have no defense against her from the ground, and little enough from the air. We have to hope they can't use her yet."

"They might already be using her against Vaden Wick and our Free-born allies," Auberen growled. "If I was them, that's what I would do. Break us where we still hold, chase us back into the hills and then hunt us at leisure."

Pied considered the possibility. Auberen might be right. It made sense to finish the effort to drive the Free-born completely off the heights, to smash their defenses and claim the Prekkendorran themselves before worrying about the Elves, most of whom were already scattered to the four winds, his command notwithstanding. After all, how much trouble could his little force present in the larger scheme of things? Pied did not fool himself about their chances. They might have won this one battle, driven back one unit of the Federation. But the enemy forces were vast and close to home, where reinforcements were readily available. A sustained Federation effort at finding and engaging his Elves would eventually succeed, and when that happened, they were finished.

He exhaled softly, frustrated. They couldn't win the war, not with the way things stood. The best they could do was to avoid the forces hunting them long enough to link up with their allies. As their leader, it was up to him to find a way to make that happen. It was a tall order, one he was not sure anyone would be able to carry out, let alone a Captain of the Home Guard whose primary duty until two days ago had been to safeguard one man.

Drumundoon had reappeared with a smallish, nervous-looking Elf with lean features and quick, sharp eyes that darted everywhere.

"Captain," his aide said, "this is Whyl. He has served on the front for more than a year, working as a scout on both sides of the line, much of the time aboard airships. He has seen more of the terrain than most. I think he can help."

Pied nodded. "Tell me what you know about the passes that run through the Prekkendorran to these hills. Are there many?"

The Elven Hunter hunched his shoulders and pursed his thin lips. "Dozens."

"How many that a large force could negotiate, coming south to north?"

"Three, maybe four." The eyes skipped across Pied's face to the faces of his companions and back again. "You think they'll come at us again, Captain?"

"Maybe. Could they, if they wanted to, do you think? How would they come?"

Whyl thought about it. "Other than through the draw they just retreated down, they have only one other good choice. There's another cut through the hills to the west. It's wide and flat and open. But it will take them two or three days to reach it and get through, then come up to where we are."

"To the west," Pied repeated, thinking. "Nothing east?"

The Elf shrugged. "One trail, through scrub, forests, low country. Pretty dangerous. Lots of bogs and sinkholes. Cuts pretty close at its south end to where the Dwarves and Bordermen hold the east plateau. It would be risky for them to try it."

For them, but maybe not for us, Pied thought. The beginnings of a plan were taking shape. He nodded to Whyl. "Your help is appreciated. You may go back to your unit. But keep what we've said to yourself for now. Don't speak of it to anyone."

The Elven Hunter nodded and hurried off across the grass with several anxious glances back. In spite of his promise, he would tell his friends what had been said. In particular, he would tell them that their commander was anticipating another attack, one that might not turn out as well for the Elves as this one had. Word would spread quickly. Panic, if not squelched, would as well.

Pied turned back to Ti Auberen and Erris Crewer. "Form up the wounded—everyone who can't fight another battle right away. Detail enough men to carry those who can't walk. Use as few as you can manage, but enough so that they can travel afoot for several days. I want them to make for the Rappahalladran, then for the villages in the Duln. They will find wagons there to complete the rest of the journey home. With luck, they will come across an airship to transport them. Form up everyone else and prepare to march. We'll move east toward that pass Whyl mentioned, the tougher one that leads to the defensive position of our allies. Our best choice now is to try to link up with Vaden Wick before the enemy finds us again. There's some cover along the way. It may help shield us from Federation airships."

"Captain, if they send airships after us, whether it's the one with that weapon or not, we won't be able to hide this many men," Erris Crewer pointed out quietly.

Pied met his gaze. "Get on with it, Lieutenant. I want all burials completed and the wounded dispatched north within the hour. I want the rest of us heading east. Wait, not all of us. Detail two dozen men to stay behind to watch the pass in case the Federation decides to send scouts through to see if we're still here. We don't want them to find out too quickly that we've gone. All we need is a presence to keep them guessing. The men can use the time to create false trails. I want them to hold the pass for one day, then catch up to us. Put a Tracker or two in the mix. And bring up Whyl again, as well. We'll need what he knows about the country."

When they were gone, he walked over to Drumundoon. His aide shifted his lanky body from foot to foot. He looked dusty and tired, but he smiled at Pied anyway. "Not much help for some things, is there, Captain?"

"Drum, I need you to do something," Pied replied, taking the other's arm and steering him away from everyone else. "Word has to be sent to Arborlon of what's happened. Maybe it's already been done, but we can't know. The Elven High Council has to be told that the King and his sons are dead. More to the point, they have to be told to send reinforcements. More airships, more men to fly them. We don't stand a chance without their support. I want you to do this. Travel on foot until you can find horses. Then ride until you can find an airship. Take two of the Home Guard with you, just in case. Leave at once."

Drumundoon looked at him. "Arling will be Queen now," he said. "It will be her decision."

He was saying that she might not be favorably disposed toward Pied's suggestion, no matter what the High Council said. Nor toward Pied, for that matter, once she learned that he had failed to keep her sons safe. But there was nothing Pied could do about it without speaking to her. He had to hope she would allow him the opportunity, that something of what he believed she had once felt for him would persuade her to do what was right.

"Do the best you can, Drum," he said quietly. He placed his hand on the other's shoulder. "But do it quickly."

"I don't like leaving you, Captain," his aide replied, shaking his head slowly, looking down at his feet.

"I don't like having you leave me. But we don't always get to choose in these matters. I have to send someone I can depend upon to do this. There isn't anyone I depend on more than you."

He thought he saw Drumundoon actually blush, but it was hard to tell beneath the layers of dirt and sweat. Drum rubbed his fringe of black beard and nodded. "I'll do my best."

He was, as usual, as good as his word. By the time the wounded were loaded on litters and their bearers and caregivers ready to depart, Drum was already gone. Pied found himself wishing he could have given his friend something more than encouragement, but at least he was sending him out of the fighting. Drum was a good man, but he wasn't meant to stand in the front lines on a battlefield.

Maybe I'm not meant for this, either, Pied thought. *But here I am.*

He slung his longbow across his shoulders, cinched his quiver a notch tighter, and went off to meet his fate.

S E V E N

Darkness had settled across the cities of the Southland, but it was nothing compared to the darkness that had found a home in Shadea a'Ru's heart. She stood at a floor-to-ceiling window in a reception room deep inside Sen Dunsidan's compound, staring out at the lights of Arishaig. She had not moved from that spot, had barely changed her position, in more than an hour. She had gone deep inside herself, escaping the disagreeableness of the present, a Druid trick she had taught herself early on in her time at Paranor, when she had no friends and no future. It had served her well then; it was less effective now.

Behind her, the Captain of her Gnome Hunters stood with two of his men and watched her uneasily. He could feel the heat radiate from her. He felt her anger as she quietly seethed. He did not want to be present when she reached the boiling point, but there was nowhere else for him to go.

It had been a long day in more ways than one. They had arrived aboard the *Bremen* the previous night, only to be told that Sen Dunsidan had not yet returned from the Prekkendorran, where he was personally overseeing the destruction of the Elves. Shadea had been willing to forgive his failure to adhere to their schedule; the defeat of the Elves was a major blow to the Free-born hopes, and the Prime Minister would want to make certain things did not go awry. She had heard of the defeat of the Elven fleet, of the burning of their airships, and of the deaths of Kellen Elessedil and his young sons. She had heard of the subsequent rout of the Elven army and its frantic retreat into the hills north. Sen Dunsidan had accomplished something important, and he had done it without her help. She would grant him his victory, even though it rankled her that he had deliberately gone behind her back to achieve it. She had gone to bed in the quarters provided for her with the expectation that their meeting would take place promptly the next day.

She had been wrong. A day of touring the ministries, of speaking before the Coalition Council, and of deliberate delays had left her convinced that something she knew nothing about was happening. She could feel it in the attitude of the Ministers with whom she met—men and women who were civil and indulgent, but clearly disdainful of her, as well. They extended courtesies because they would do so even to their worst enemy on such a visit, but there was no warmth or sincerity in the efforts.

By nightfall, she had lost her patience with Sen Dunsidan entirely. She had been advised of his return several hours earlier, but then he had asked that she wait while he freshened himself for their meeting. She had kept her composure mostly by telling herself that it would only weaken her position with him to reveal the depths of her irritation. If he thought he could undo her so easily, he would be much more difficult to manage. And she already knew from the news of his victory on the Prekkendorran and the nature of her reception here that he would be difficult in any case.

A knock sounded on the door to the reception room and a functionary cautiously stepped just inside the opening. Shadea came out of her shell instantly, but let him stand where he was for a moment, her eyes directed out the window toward the city. Then, drawing herself up, she turned to face him.

"My lady," he said, bowing to her. "The Prime Minister apologizes for the delay and begs your indulgence for just a few minutes more. He is almost ready to receive you and asks that you wait—"

"I have waited long enough," she said quietly, cutting off the rest of what he was about to say.

The words were edged in steel so sharp that the functionary winced visibly. He hesitated, then tried to speak again, but Shadea's hand had lifted, her fingers had pointed in his direction, and suddenly his voice had failed completely. He gasped and tried again and again, but nothing would come out.

She crossed the room and stood before him. "Captain?" she said to the leader of her Gnome escort. His hard, weathered face appeared at her elbow. "Ready the *Bremen* for departure. Take your men with you. I will be along in a few minutes."

Her Captain of the Guard frowned. "It is not safe for you here alone, Mistress."

"Safer for me than for some," she answered. "Do as I say."

He left without further comment, taking his men with him, leaving her alone in the reception room with the still-voiceless functionary.

"As for you, little man," she said to him, "I have other plans. Do you wish your voice back?" The functionary nodded eagerly. "I thought as much. What service do you think I require of you if I am to grant you this favor?"

He didn't need to ask. He led her out through the doorway and down the hall. They passed dozens of guards, all armed and at watch, but none tried to stop them. Shadea had drawn her Druid robes tight about her, but within their folds, concealed from view, the fingers of her right hand flexed in a series of intricate moves, calling up magic to within easy reach, readying herself for the unexpected. She did not think she would have to use her magic, but she knew enough to be prepared in case she did. She could not trust Sen Dunsidan, could not rely on him to act honorably toward her, even as a guest of state. One thing she had learned about the Prime Minister of the Federation—he would do whatever he felt was necessary to get what he wanted.

The hallway ended at a pair of ornately carved double doors that stood open to the light. The room within was candlelit but draped in its corners and along its edges by deepest shadow. She heard Sen Dunsidan's voice, smooth and persuasive, a hiss against the silence. A snake's voice, she thought. But she knew how to draw the poison from his fangs.

The functionary turned toward her questioningly as they reached the door, uncertain of what he was expected to do next. She solved the problem for him by fastening one hand about his neck and marching him into the room in front of her.

Sen Dunsidan was seated on a couch to one side, sipping wine and speaking with a shadowy figure seated in the corner of the room where it was darkest. Shadea did a quick search of the chamber, found only the two and no one else present, swept up to Sen Dunsidan in a rush of black robes, and threw his functionary at his feet.

"Ready to receive me now, Prime Minister?" she asked softly. She eyed the glass of wine he held poised midway to drinking and smiled. "Go ahead. Finish it."

He did so, watching her carefully, clearly surprised by her appearance, but not altogether unprepared. A man like him was never entirely unprepared. She gestured at the functionary, who coughed out a few startled words, climbed quickly to his feet, and ran from the room.

"I was just about to come for you," Sen Dunsidan said, putting down the glass of wine and rising. "But I wanted to make certain of what I would say before we met."

"You have had time enough to make certain of what you will say for the next year. What seems to be the problem? Are you at a loss for words? Do you find your oratorical skills have suddenly deserted you?" She paused. "Or are you simply worried about how I might perceive your duplicity in acting without my knowledge in the matter of the Prekkendorran?"

The Prime Minister's face darkened. "I do not need to apologize for that. I acted when the opportunity presented itself, just as you would have done in my place. Had I waited to consult with you, the opportunity would have been forever lost. Don't presume to lecture me on how to conduct myself as leader of the Federation. I do what I must."

"Yes," she acknowledged. "And you tell me of it in your own good time, it seems. I do not judge you for your decision in attacking the Free-born. I judge you for your failure to inform me of it. It smacks of an independence that verges on rebellion. Have we come to a point where you think you no longer have need of an alliance with me? Or with the Druid order? Does your success whisper to you that you are sufficiently strong that you need ally yourself with no one? Is that the course you have chosen?"

She turned toward the shadowy figure in the corner. "Or do you take your counsel from someone else these days, someone you think may advise you better?"

There was a long silence. Then the figure in the corner rose, a slow languid movement of limbs and torso. "He seeks the counsel of someone who has his best interests at heart, Shadea."

"Iridia."

She breathed the name like a curse. Iridia Eleri—or at least a pale imitation of the Elven sorceress—stepped into the light. Whatever Shadea might have thought she would find, it wasn't this. There was no reason for Iridia to be present, not as an ally to Sen Dunsidan, not as a creature in thrall to the Prime Minister of the Federation. Even more shocking was how her onetime ally looked—bloodless and drained of life, thin to the point of emaciation, and hard-eyed in a way she had never seemed before. There was something wrong with her, but Shadea could not decide what it was.

"Did you think you had seen the last of me?" Iridia asked, her voice as bloodless as her face. "Did you think me safely away from Paranor and your Druid schemes?"

Shadea stared, not knowing what she thought, except that it wasn't this.

"You drove me from Paranor," Iridia continued in her flat, lifeless monotone. "You refused me any chance to gain revenge over the man who had wronged me. You took away my power. You stripped me of my pride. So I came here, to give my services to one who would better appreciate them."

Shadea looked back at Sen Dunsidan. He shrugged. "She acts as my personal adviser now. Her help has been invaluable to me. I hope you don't intend to try to rob me of it out of jealousy or a misguided sense of prior claims."

She grimaced. "Please, Prime Minister, try not to sound as stupid as you act. I don't care whom you bring into your confidence. Even her. She speaks the truth. She was banished when she failed to live up to her pledge to serve the order. She would not be welcomed back now even if she sought to return voluntarily. I certainly have no intention of trying to make her return by force. But you might think about her failure to serve one master and ask yourself how likely it is that she will successfully serve another."

"I think I am the best judge of how well a person will serve me, Shadea." Sen Dunsidan shrugged. "After all, I was smart enough to ally myself with you, wasn't I?"

"An alliance that no longer seems to have much merit, given what I see of your present situation."

The Prime Minister moved over to his couch and sat down again, his earnest expression only barely concealing the satisfaction she was certain he was feeling at her discomfort. She would have liked to wipe it away with her fingernails, but she wanted to see where things were going first.

"Our alliance still has value," he said, motioning for her to sit. She remained where she was. "As I said, I acted as I did on the Prekkendorran because the opportunity presented itself. But the war is not over, and I still have need of your support. And the support of the Druid order. If I am to successfully conclude the war with the Free-born, I must press north and west to force a resolution. I cannot do this without at least the tacit support of the Druids. By the same token, I know that you need my support, as well. You lack any other alliances. The Dwarves, the Elves, the Trolls, and the Bordermen all refuse to give you the allegiance you seek. They have not yet accepted you as Ard Rhys. For that matter, some within your own order have not accepted you."

She said nothing, holding her temper, showing nothing of what she was feeling. When the time was right, she would squash him like a bug—assuming Iridia let him live that long. Shadea was convinced that the sorceress was making use of him for her own needs and would keep him around only so long as was necessary.

"I don't say that you won't find a way to deal with these trouble-makers, Shadea," the Prime Minister continued. "But you must agree that it will make things considerably easier for you if we maintain our alliance rather than cast it aside. And, of course, it will make things easier for me, as well."

"Especially if your armies suffer another defeat like the one they suffered in the passes north of the Prekkendorran two days ago." She smiled. "How many men did you lose? More than a thousand? At the hands of some ragtag Elven castoffs you had driven from the heights?"

She enjoyed the look of surprise that appeared on his face, a look he tried without success to conceal. He had not expected her to know of the army's defeat, a secret he had tried hard to conceal from everyone. But there were no secrets that he could conceal from her.

"You had them beaten, Sen Dunsidan. You had them scattered and disheartened, and you let them drive your pursuit force into the ground. In all the years I served in the Federation army, I never heard of such stupidity. How could you let something like that happen?"

"Enough, Shadea. You have had your fun with me. Now let it alone. I intend to rectify matters on the Prekkendorran within a few days. When I am finished, the entire Free-born army will be in tatters, and my armies will be deep within their homelands."

"If I decide to let you do so." She kept Sen Dunsidan's eyes locked on her own, chained by the steel of her gaze. "I am not certain now that I should."

She saw the rage in those eyes, his hatred for her burning in them. She did not look away. The silence between them lengthened.

"You presume a great deal, Shadea," Iridia Eleri said suddenly.

Her voice was as cold as winter midnight and empty of feeling. Shadea was taken aback in spite of herself. Something about Iridia Eleri was not right. Something about her was changed, something deep and abiding, invisible to the eye, but there all the same.

She broke eye contact with Sen Dunsidan and glanced over. "It worries me that I may have allied myself and my order's cause with fools. I will presume what I must to remedy such a mistake." She studied Iridia a moment longer, then turned back to Sen Dunsidan. "Tell me, Prime Minister—must I do so here?"

Sen Dunsidan sighed. "I don't want you for an enemy, Shadea. You must know that. I need the Druid order to give its blessing to my efforts. I need to know you will not interfere with my plans. Surely you can see this?"

Shadea walked over to the wine pitcher, poured herself a glass, and drank deeply. She watched Iridia casually as she did so, trying to read something of what it was about her that was so troubling. It was in her eyes, she thought. It was in the way she looked out at the world. The problem was there.

"You need me," she said, "but not enough to tell me of your plans until after they are executed."

"I have kept nothing back from you that you couldn't find out on your own, it seems."

"Your attack on the Elven fleet, your destruction of their army, your own army's subsequent setback, your alliance with Iridia—what other secrets do you keep from me?"

He sighed. "What secrets do you think I keep, Shadea?"

"I haven't heard any mention of your new weapon, the one that so effectively destroyed the Elven fleet. An oversight?"

The Prime Minister shrugged. "It is a fire launcher, a pressure feed that sends burning liquid from a nozzle mounted on our airships into others, setting them aflame. A conventional weapon, good over short distances when properly manned. It is hardly worth mentioning."

What a pathetic liar, Shadea thought. "Which must be why you failed to mention it. Or is there something about it I might find objectionable? A forbidden use of magic, perhaps?"

"Magic?" Sen Dunsidan laughed. "Where would I get magic? Oh, you think Iridia might have given me something from the Druid storehouse, do you? Wouldn't that be useful! But, no, the weapon was developed long before Iridia appeared with her offer of support. She brings nothing of her Druid lore or of Druid magic to our relationship. Nothing that isn't her own, anyway. There is no betrayal of the Druids involved in the building of this weapon, Shadea. What are you worried about? The power of the Druids is more than a match for anything I have at my command. I have only my armies and my airships."

It was difficult to judge how deep the lie went, but it went sufficiently deep that Shadea was certain the weapon was much more powerful than he was suggesting and that he intended it for more than simple warfare. At some point, he would seek to use it against the Druids, because in his heart he could never be at rest until he had destroyed everyone who might threaten him. That was the demon that had driven him since he had begun his ascent to power all those years ago. It was a demon with which she had a fair amount of personal experience.

"Your plan," she said, "is to use this weapon against the remaining Free-born ground forces on the Prekkendorran? On the Dwarves and Bordermen?"

He nodded. "And on the remnants of the Elves who ambushed my pursuit force. The Free-born have nothing with which to combat it. The best they have been able to do is damage the airship that transports it, and that was a fluke." He sipped at his wine. "The war on the Prekkendorran is over, Shadea, the moment my airship returns to the skies. All I require to proceed is your clear support for my efforts. For the Federation's efforts," he corrected.

She walked over to the window, brushing past Iridia Eleri as if she weren't there, but feeling something so dark and empty as she did so that she wished she had avoided the sorceress entirely. Pausing at the window, she shuddered a moment in spite of herself. Whatever had happened to Iridia wasn't anything for the better.

She looked out at the city, considering her options, giving herself sufficient space and time to choose wisely. She made several decisions in that moment, but she spoke only of one.

She turned back to Sen Dunsidan. "The Druid order will support your efforts, Prime Minister. I will announce that support on my return to Paranor. But there are two conditions. First, you will speak before the Coalition Council tomorrow in support of my ascendancy to the position of Ard Rhys. You will make your support complete and unequivocal. No half measures, no politician's word games. Second, you will fly to Paranor within the week to speak before the Druid order so that all may hear your justification for the invasion of the other lands. You are good at explanations, Sen Dunsidan. You should be able to come up with one."

The Federation leader studied her, thinking through the ramifications of accepting her offer, as she knew he would, then nodded. "Agreed."

She walked back across the room, her eyes never leaving his, coming to a stop when she reached him. "A final word. Do not even think about trying to use your new weapon against me. Your hunger for power is vast, Sen Dunsidan, so I know the thought has crossed your mind. Control the Druids, and you control the Four Lands. But you lack the skill and the experience to manage such a task—even with your new ally to advise you."

She glanced at Iridia. "She is good at what she does, and once she was great. But she is only one person and nowhere near strong enough to challenge me. So keep a tight rein on your ambitions and do not forget your place in the pecking order. The Druids wield the real power in the Four Lands, just as they always have."

She looked back at him, waiting for his response. "I won't forget," he said quietly. "I won't forget anything."

He was making a thinly veiled threat, but she would allow that. A threat was only words until it was backed up by something more substantial than anything Sen Dunsidan could command.

She moved close to him, placing herself squarely between Iridia and himself. "Watch your back, Sen Dunsidan," she whispered.

Then she strode from the room without looking at either of them again and made her way through the halls of the compound buildings to board her airship and fly home.

"She is too dangerous," Sen Dunsidan declared, once she was gone. He faced Iridia Eleri in challenge. "Too dangerous for either of us. You would not argue the point, would you?"

She floated across the room into the darkness from which she had come and sat down again, cloaked in shadows. "I wouldn't worry about Shadea a'Ru, Sen Dunsidan."

He didn't care for the way she said it. "Well, I do worry about her, Iridia. If you choose to pretend she isn't a threat, that is up to you. But I intend to do something about her."

"I can protect you," she said.

"Perhaps. But if Shadea is dead, I won't need your protection."

There was a long silence. "Killing her won't be easy," she said. "And if you fail, she will know who to come looking for. Besides, who will you send to eliminate her? Who can you trust to make certain she is dead?"

He hesitated, unable to answer those questions.

"And we have other concerns at the moment." Iridia sounded sleepy and bored. "Your airship is nearly ready to fly again. You need to do what I told you. You need to take it into the Westland and attack the Elven home city of Arborlon. You need to convince the Elves they are not safe anywhere so that they will agree to abandon their alliance with the Free-born."

"If I smash the Free-born army first, I won't need to worry about persuading the Elves to abandon their alliance. There won't be anyone left for them to ally themselves with."

"An ill-advised course of action." He felt displeasure radiating from her words. "A waste of time and effort. You might smash this army, but they will simply raise another. You think too small, Sen Dunsidan. You must think in larger terms. Winning the war on the Prekkendorran will not happen until you win the war in their homes. Strike at their capital cities, and they will seek your peace quickly enough. Start with Arborlon, then fly on to the others. Soon, all resistance will end."

Her argument made sense, as it had the first time she had made it, but something about it bothered him. It felt to him as if she was saying one thing, but meaning another—as if she had thought the situation through better than he had and knew something about it he didn't. Besides, he could not ignore the defeat he had suffered in the Borderlands at the hands of the Elves. His army, so certain of victory after the destruction of the Elven airfleet, was stunned by the abrupt turnabout. He could not ignore what that meant to morale. If he didn't give the army a fresh reason to believe that the war was ending, it was hard to say what might happen.

"The best approach is still the one I settled on originally, Iridia. We attack the Free-born position on the east plateau of the Prekkendorran, using the airship and her weapon to break their defensive lines. Once they are scattered and the position overrun, the Federation will hold the entire Prekkendorran. Then I will do as you suggest and fly the *Dechtera* to Arborlon and attack the Elven home city."

She said nothing. She stared at him from out of the darkness, an all-but-invisible presence, faceless and silent. He waited for her to speak, but she didn't. Finally, he lost patience and rose. "I am going to bed. We can talk about this later. Think about what we can do to eliminate Shadea. I won't sleep soundly again until she's disposed of."

He walked quickly from the room, the weight of Iridia Eleri's eyes pressing against his exposed back.

EIGHT

A sudden lurch of the airship brought Khyber Elessedil awake, jarring her from sleep with such abruptness that for a moment she did not know where she was. Then her scattered thoughts came together, and she remembered. She was hiding in a locker in a forward storeroom that was filled with yards of light sheaths and coils of radian draws and heavy rigging. Rough voices sounded from somewhere outside the locker and she flinched anew. Gnome guards. She blinked uncertainly, listened as the voices drew nearer and the storeroom door banged open. She caught her breath as the Gnomes rummaged about, conversed in their guttural tongue, then departed once more.

She took a deep, steadying breath, squeezed free of the sail material into which she had wrapped herself, then opened the locker door cautiously and peered out.

Shadows draped the storeroom in heavy layers, the darkness broken by slender bands of moonlight spearing through cracks in the shutters that closed off the storeroom's solitary window. Reluctant to chance another encounter that might end less favorably, she had been hiding there since she had been discovered and almost caught the previous night. If she was discovered, she knew Pen would have no chance at all.

Not that he had much anyway. After watching the flare of magic explode from the hold of the *Athabasca* the previous night, she feared the worst had happened already.

She slipped from the locker and moved over to the shuttered opening, peering through its cracks into the night. The airship had landed inside a courtyard ringed by high walls and stark battlements interspersed with watchtowers. To one side, huge buildings rose against the moonlit sky like the squared-off sides of cliffs. They had landed and were inside Paranor. She glanced across the courtyard for the other airships, but at first saw only dark figures scurrying about the landing site, securing lines and fastening anchors. Lights appeared suddenly in windows in the buildings that formed the bulk of the Keep, and she heard locks release and a door open. Voices drifted on the night air, whispery and muffled. She needed to get out of the storeroom to find out what was going on, but she knew it was still too dangerous to do so.

Her patience ebbing swiftly, she forced herself to wait as the Gnome crew went about its business and finally disappeared altogether, save for a watch that patrolled the yard. That she knew because a Gnome Hunter strolled by the shuttered window, thickset and armed with a spear and short sword. There would be more stationed close by. Anchored farther down the length of the yard were other airships, their dark shapes barely identifiable in the shadow of the walls. Within the Keep, the lights remained aglow, bright squares framed by the windows through which they shone. She wondered how late it was, whether it was past midnight or not, whether it was approaching morning. She glanced at the sky, but could not tell from the position of the stars she could see.

When sufficient time had passed and her patience was exhausted, she opened the storeroom door and stepped out into the companionway. She stood listening for a long time, making certain she was alone. Satisfied at last that she was, she moved down the passageway and climbed on deck. Crouched in the shelter of the pilot box, just beyond the hatchway, she peered around the airship decking, then beyond to the courtyard. The *Athabasca* was anchored right next to her own ship, and the third ship was anchored just a little farther away. All appeared deserted.

But on the ground below, Gnome Hunters patrolled, slow-moving shadows in the night.

Khyber considered her situation. She could not get off the airship without alerting the watch. Yet she had to reach Pen. She assumed he had been taken inside the Keep, but could not know that for a fact without checking the *Athabasca* first. That would take time, however—time she felt she didn't have.

She studied the night sky, the position of the stars and moon, reading the time. It was after midnight and getting toward morning. The Druids would be asleep, but that would all change when it grew light. Any help she could offer Pen had to come soon.

But how could she reach him when she hadn't the faintest idea where he was? She had never been to Paranor; her time with Ahren was spent entirely in Emberen, his place of exile. He had deliberately chosen to stay away from the Druid's Keep and its politics. Since she had begun her studies with him, he had not gone back even once, and so she had never gone, either. It was something she had always meant to do, something she had assured herself would eventually happen.

Well, it had, but the circumstances were not what she would have hoped for.

She knew a little of the Keep's layout, having asked Ahren about it on several occasions, even persuading him once to draw her a rough map. But, in truth, she remembered little of the detail, and it was different being there, staring at its walls and buildings with no idea where to begin her search. She would need someone to help her find her way around, but she could not afford to ask for assistance because that would mean giving herself away.

The impossibility of her situation quickly became apparent. On starting out, she had thought that it would be easier, that a way to get to Pen would present itself. She had been wrong, and the boy was likely to pay the price for her presumption.

She shivered in response to her dark thoughts, and as her hands rubbed her arms and body to warm herself, they brushed against the small bulk of the Elfstones in her pocket.

She froze, her fingers closing over the talismans. She had forgotten about the Elfstones. Fresh hope warmed her chilly thoughts. She could use their magic to find Pen! The Stones would lead her straight to him!

And lead the Druids straight to her. Her hopes faded. Using the Elfstones would give her away instantly. Every Druid in the Keep was familiar with Elven magic. She would be detected in a heartbeat.

She released her grip on the Stones reluctantly and sank back against the pilothouse wall. The use of small magics was commonplace within the Druid's Keep. Small magics would not be noticed. But the Elfstones were a large magic that no one could mistake for anything other than what it was. Nothing could disguise the extent of their power. Another way would have to be found.

Another way, she thought, that utilized her skills and training as an apprentice Druid. A way that relied upon the lessons she had been taught by her mentor and best friend before his death. It was all she had left to call upon. It was what she would have to employ if she was to have any chance at all of saving Pen.

She went still inside as she measured herself for the task she was about to undertake. She had studied hard the skills that Ahren felt she should master. He had given her so little; their time was too short for more. But what he had given her would have to be enough. Most of what she could call upon relied on her ability to concentrate and to center herself. She had worked hard during the voyage to Anatcherae to become accomplished at both. She would put it to the test.

Gathering her resolve, she rose, moved over to the side of the airship, and looked down. The yard directly below her was empty. She went over the side quickly, down the rope ladder and onto the ground, not bothering to hide her descent or even her presence. Subtlety would not serve her well just then. The key to her success lay in boldness. She stood at the bottom of the ladder, looking around for the Gnome guards. Still wrapped and hooded by the cloak she had stolen earlier, at a distance she could pass for one of them. It was her best chance.

She picked out the guards in the darkness, then started toward the window-lit walls of the Keep as if it made no difference to her whether they were there or not.

Darkness served her purpose well. She was shadowed for much of the way by the hulls of the airships and then the walls of the parapets and buildings; she was just another solitary figure crossing the yard, no different in appearance from the others. One of the guards glanced her way as she advanced toward the doors she had spied ahead, but he made no attempt to challenge her. When another turned toward her in the making of his rounds, she released a quick bit of magic to create an unexpected noise behind him, causing him to turn back again. In the windows ahead, shadows passed through the light, their appearance unexpected and startling. She felt her throat tighten, but did not slow.

Keep going, she told herself.

She reached the doorway after what seemed an interminable length of time, pulled down on the handle to release the latch, and stepped inside.

A large anteroom, its ceiling cavernous and smoky with torch burn, its walls hung with heraldic pennants, opened into three long corridors that stretched away through pools of torchlight and layered shadows to lines of closed doors, high windows, and dark alcoves. She started forward and stopped. A pair of Gnome Hunters stood to either side of her, neither more than a dozen paces away, armed and gimlet-eyed as they watched her freeze in place.

She had no time to think and only a moment to react.

She threw back the hood to her cloak and fastened the one on the right with a dark glare. "Where have they taken him?"

The question was asked in Elfish, a language with which she did not think he would be familiar. She was right. He stared blankly at her, a hint of surprise shadowing his sharp features.

"The boy!" she snapped, speaking now in Callahorn's tongue, a Southland dialect everyone in the Borderlands spoke, accommodating him in a way that would demonstrate her superiority. "Where is he?"

She shifted her gaze quickly from the first Gnome to the second, her impatience evident, her sense of command clear. She radiated what she hoped was Druid authority, giving clear indication that as a member of the order, she was where she belonged and had a right to ask the questions she was asking. There was no reason to doubt her. All that was required was a quick, concise response.

Not surprisingly, the Gnomes had trouble supplying one. "The cells, I think," the second Gnome told her in the Southland dialect. He said something to the other in Gnomish, but his companion simply shrugged. "Yes, the cells. To be held until the Ard Rhys returns."

She nodded perfunctorily and marched past them down the central corridor, acting as if she knew exactly what she was doing, when in fact she had no idea at all. The cells? Where were the cells? Below

ground somewhere? She couldn't ask that, not of these guards. Someone else, maybe. She was inside and she had a destination, and that
was going to have to be enough.

A handful of doors farther down the corridor, she stepped into a
deeply shadowed alcove and stood breathing hard with her back
against the rough wall, her mind racing. Ahren would have known
what to do next if he were there. She must try to think the way
Ahren would. She squeezed her eyes shut against the pain that thinking of him cost her, then opened them quickly, determined not to
give way. The mechanics were easy. She needed to find her way to
the cells. To do that, she needed to find someone to tell her how.

She brushed at her short-cropped dark hair, squared her shoulders, then stepped back out into the corridor and began walking
deeper into the Keep.

Empty of life, the passageway tunneled ahead, her footsteps soft
echoes in the silence. She was aware that she still wore the Gnome
hunting cloak and that it would eventually draw unwanted attention.
Her first order of business was to replace it with a Druid robe. But
that was easier said than done. It wasn't as if there were robes hanging on hooks all up and down the hallway, Druids wandering about
from whom she might steal one.

But she got lucky. At a juncture of corridors much deeper inside
the Keep, just as she was despairing that she might wander the halls
of Paranor until sunrise, she came upon a study chamber with lights
burning and Druids at work. She paused just outside the doorway,
still within the corridor shadows, and peered inside. She could see
three dark-cloaked forms, hoods thrown back, bodies hunched over
books at tables, heads lowered in concentration.

She stood for a time, trying to decide what to do next. But she
couldn't think of anything that didn't involve going into the room for
a closer look around. That was too dangerous. She hesitated, undecided, and as she did so, she felt a finger tap her shoulder.

"Are you looking for someone?"

That she didn't jump out of her skin entirely was something of a
miracle. She even managed to turn around. A Druid stood behind
her, a questioning look on his scowling face. Bright green eyes
peered out from under heavy, furrowed brows. A Southlander. She
stared at him without speaking, her heart gone straight to her throat.

"Sorry," he said, not sounding sorry at all. "Didn't mean to frighten you. But you look like you don't know what you're doing here." He rubbed his smooth chin reflectively, then glanced at her robe and gave a disapproving frown. "Why are you wearing a Gnome Hunter's cloak? You know the rules."

She didn't, of course, but she nodded anyway. "I was working on the airships and wore the robe to keep from getting dirty. I forgot to take it off."

"Well, it's not allowed." He glanced past her into the study room. "Wait here."

He stepped inside, out of view, then returned a moment later and thrust a Druid robe into her hands. "Here, wear this until you can put on one of your own. The rules are clear."

She nodded her thanks, slipped off the Gnome cloak, and slipped on the proffered robe. "I've been away. I don't know all the new rules."

The Druid looked suddenly eager. "Did you come in one of those airships that just landed? Has something else happened?"

She hesitated. Something else? What was he talking about? "The airships brought in a boy," she said, deciding to measure his reaction.

"Ah, the Ohmsford boy." The Druid shook his head. "What a lot of bother. They've been looking for him for weeks. Nephew to the old Ard Rhys. They think the whole family is at risk, so they're bringing them here to keep them safe. Found the parents, but they couldn't find the boy. Until now."

"So the parents are here?" she tried.

"No, no, that's what I was talking about. They're gone. Disappeared with their ship two days ago. Flew off in something of a confrontation, I hear. Hard to say; the Gnomes won't talk about it with us. But there was a fight of some sort. No one knows. Shadea keeps such things secret from everyone but her closest advisers." He shrugged. "Typical."

Khyber took a deep breath. "Do you think she would be awake this late? I need to see her."

The Druid shook his head. "You don't know much about what's going on, do you? She isn't even here. She went to Arishaig and hasn't returned."

"As I said, I've been away," Khyber repeated. "All this is news to me." She had learned all she was going to learn and more than she had expected. She had to break this off. "Who would I speak to in her absence?"

The Druid frowned. "I don't know. Traunt Rowan or Pyson Wence, I suppose. Didn't you fly in with them? How did you get here?" The disapproving frown was back. "Where did you say you had been?"

But she was already moving away, giving him a perfunctory wave as she did so. She couldn't believe her luck. She knew now that the ringleader of the conspirators was away, so Pen would not be touched until she returned. That gave her a small measure of time in which to act. She also knew that Pen's parents were no longer prisoners in the Keep, so that the boy, if she could free him, would be able to go into the Forbidding without fear of reprisal against his captive family. But she had to find Pen quickly if he was to have his chance.

"Wait up! Stay where you are!"

She wheeled about, astonished to find the Druid she had thought left behind chasing after her down the corridor, black robes flying out behind him. One arm came up as if in challenge, a sense of urgency to the motion, his heavy brow furrowed more deeply than ever.

Having no choice but to deal with him, she stood her ground. "Who did you say you were?" he demanded, panting and out of breath as he reached her. "How is it you happen to have been aboard an airship bringing back the Ohmsford boy when . . ."

Khyber braced her feet, cocked her fist, and hit him so hard she knocked him backwards into the wall. She was on him instantly, hauling him up with one hand while putting a dagger to his throat with the other.

"Not another word," she hissed at him. "Not unless I tell you to speak. If you yell for help, I'll cut you chin-to-navel before you finish. Do you understand me?"

She had never seen such fear in another's eyes as she saw in his. His throat worked as he tried unsuccessfully to speak and finally settled for nodding.

"You don't know who I am and you don't want to," she told him softly, her eyes locking on his, making sure he did not misjudge her determination. "Behave yourself, do what you're told and you might stay alive. Now listen carefully. I want you to take me down to the cells where they keep the prisoners. Don't speak to anyone we pass on the way. Don't try signaling for help. Am I clear?"

She was only a girl, but the Druid she held pinned against the wall saw her as infinitely more dangerous than he was, and he nodded vigorously. "One thing more," she said to him. "I have the use of magic, just as you do. I understand its complexities. If you try to use your own, even secretly, I will know."

He found his voice again. "You've come for the Ohmsford boy."

She put her face inches from his own. "He means a lot to me. So much so that if something bad happens to him now, something much worse will happen to you. What I intend for him is safe passage out of here. If you interfere with me, I will kill you."

His face was bloodless, his eyes wide. "Don't hurt me."

"I won't if you don't make me. Now, which way?"

He pointed, his hand shaking. She pulled him away from the wall and marched him back down the cavernous hall, the dagger at his back, her free hand gripping his arm. They moved quickly, following the corridor to its end, turned into another, followed that for a time, then turned into a third. They passed no one on their way. They heard no movements or voices that would indicate the presence of others. What she was doing was madness, an impulsive act that could end badly for her, but at least she was getting to where she wanted to go. Someone would have had to tell her, and it might as well be someone under her control. Her eyes darted left and right as she walked, to every crevice and alcove, to every closed door. She kept waiting for her luck to run out. She kept waiting for things to go bad.

They reached a broad stairwell leading down and her prisoner hesitated.

"Keep moving," she whispered, nudging him with the tip of the dagger.

They descended carefully, Khyber watching the bend in the wall ahead for shadows cast by torchlight. None appeared. At the bottom of the stairwell, they reached an anteroom that served as a hub for five different corridors leading off like the spokes of a wheel.

A Gnome Hunter sat facing them from behind a table, his wizened face unreadable. Farther down the corridor at his back, torchlight cast the shadow of a second guard against the stone-block wall.

Keeping one hand firmly attached to her reluctant companion, Khyber moved over to the Gnome at the table. "We've been sent to speak with the boy," she said, again using the Callahorn dialect. "Where is he?"

The Gnome Hunter stared at her, clearly surprised by her demand. Then he shook his head. "No one sees him. I have my orders."

"Orders from Traunt Rowan," she snapped. "Who do you think sent us here? Now take us to the boy. Or do you want me to drag him down here to tell you for himself?"

The threat cut off whatever reply the Gnome was about to make, and he simply nodded. "Someone should tell me these things. I can't know them otherwise." He paused. "You just want to speak with the boy?"

She shrugged dismissively. "He won't be leaving his cell, if that's what you are asking."

He rose doubtfully, reached under the table to produce a ring of keys, and led them down the hallway. Khyber felt the beginnings of some resistance on the part of her reluctant companion and shoved him ahead.

"Don't," she whispered, the dagger digging into his back so hard he whimpered.

They passed the second guard on his way back. He glanced at Khyber and her companion without interest and moved on. She fought the urge to look over her shoulder at him when he was out of sight. Instead, she pulled the dagger away from the Druid and close to her body so that it was hidden in her robes, still keeping the fingers of her other hand tightly fastened to her prisoner's arm. She did not know how much longer she could hold him in check. Sooner or later, he was going to give way to his growing panic or to the temptation to run. If it happened now, while she was still out in the corridor with the Gnome Hunters, she was in trouble. Her plan to free Pen, born of opportunity and chance, was just beginning to take shape. She needed time to flesh it out, to think it through, to find a way to implement it fully. Getting to Pen was just the first step. The ones that followed would be much harder.

They reached the door of the cell, and the Gnome Hunter turned. "Do you want me to wait?"

She scowled. "I want you to go back to doing what you are paid to do and leave me to my work. I'll call you when I need you."

"I have to lock you in."

"Then do so. You are wasting my time."

The Gnome fiddled with the keys, slipped one clear of the others, inserted it into the lock, and turned it. The lock clicked, and the door opened with a squeal of metal fastenings.

As it did so, Khyber's prisoner wrenched free of her grip and ran screaming down the hall.

NINE

Khyber didn't stop to think, didn't do anything but respond to the disaster that was unfolding. She wheeled on the Gnome nearest, slammed the hilt of her dagger into his temple, and dropped him without a sound. As he collapsed, she turned back toward the fleeing Druid, her hands weaving, conjuring a magic with which she was familiar and on which she had depended before. In response to her summons, a sudden gust of wind exploded down the hallway, caught up her quarry before he had run a dozen yards, snatched him off his feet, and hurled him into the wall like a sack of wheat.

The remaining Gnome Hunter came racing toward her in response to the shouting and tumbling bodies, his weapons drawn. She used her magic again, picking him up off his feet and bearing him aloft as she had once done a simple leaf. Remembering to focus her efforts, she held him suspended in midair, kicking and squirming in a futile effort to break free. No failure of attention, no break in concentration. She was at her best in that moment, her uncle's attentive student in the way he had always wanted her to be. She reached the Gnome and dropped him to the floor in a ragged heap, kicking him so hard in the head that he did not move again.

Glancing back at the door to the cell, she called out. "Pen! Are you in there? Answer me!"

No response. Returning her attention to the bodies crumpled

about her, she used laces, bindings, and belts to secure them, then dragged them back up the hall and dropped them next to the Gnome with the keys. Peering inside the cell, she saw a bundled form lying at the back of the tiny room, trussed, gagged, and blindfolded.

"Shades!" she hissed under her breath.

She rushed into the room, bent to Pen Ohmsford, and began working to release his bonds. She freed his eyes first, looking to see if he was conscious. He blinked into the uncertain light and stared at her, wide-eyed. She grinned in response, then loosened the gag.

"I guess you didn't expect to see me again so soon, did you, Pen-derrin?"

"Khyber! How did you find me?"

The obvious relief mirrored in his boyish features made her smile broaden. "I saw what happened, slipped aboard one of the other airships, and flew into Paranor with you. Are you hurt?"

He shook his head. "Just get me free. I'll tell you everything."

She did so, using the dagger to cut through his bonds, then told him to wait while she hauled her three captives inside the cell and dumped them in a far corner. None of them moved even once while this was happening. "Let's see how *they* like being locked away in here," she muttered. "Come on, Pen."

"Help me walk, Khyber," he asked, struggling to rise.

They went out of the cell as quickly as his legs would permit, but his mobility was severely restricted by leg cramps and stiffness. He had been bound up in the airship for much of the flight back, then brought directly to the cell and left as he was. He had lost all the feeling in both legs and feet in that time, and it was slow to return.

"I thought I was finished," he admitted as he limped down the corridor, leaning heavily on her for support. "They caught me out, Khyber. I told them lies about what I was doing, but they saw through me and took the darkwand away. You saw that I had it, didn't you? From across the ravine? I took it with me from the tanequil's lair, kept it from that thing that tracked us from Anatcherae to Stridegate, kept it safe to use as I was instructed by the King of the Silver River, and they took it away!"

He was so distraught that he was practically crying. Khyber gave his shoulders a rough squeeze. "Then we'll just have to get it back, Pen."

They reached the end of the corridor, and she lowered the boy into the chair formerly occupied by the Gnome jailer, kneeling before him to rub some life back into his legs. "Now tell it all to me," she said.

He did, beginning with his crossing to the island of the tanequil with Cinnaminson and his efforts to communicate with the tree and hers to form a bond with the aeriads. He continued by describing his ordeal in gaining possession of the darkwand from Father Tanequil, Cinnaminson's seduction by the aeriads, his futile efforts to free her from the tree roots of Mother Tanequil, and his battle with the creature from Anatcherae. Finally, he explained how he had decided to surrender to the Druids both to help his captive friends and to reach Paranor, where he could use the darkwand at last to go into the Forbidding.

"I thought I could do it, Khyber. I thought they wouldn't know what the staff was, even if they took it from me. I was stupid. They knew it to be a talisman at once. They pretended ignorance, then mocked me for my foolishness."

"We will live to see them mocked for their own foolishness," she muttered, still rubbing his leg muscles. "Any better?"

He nodded. "I didn't know what had happened to you, except that I knew you were free. I thought you would be able to help Tagwen and Kermadec and the rest, even if the Druids took me. I never thought you would come after me."

"Let's hope the Druids were fooled, too. I don't think they know I'm here yet, but they will soon enough. Someone is bound to come looking to see how things stand. Or for a change of guards. We have to get moving right now. Can you stand?"

She helped him to his feet, where he took a moment to stretch his legs and stamp his feet. "That's better. The feeling's back." His face was drawn and weary, but determined, as well. "Traunt Rowan says Shadea will be back late tomorrow. I have time to get into the Forbidding before she does."

The Elven girl brushed back her short-cropped hair and grimaced. She had only been told by the Druid that Shadea was away. "There are a lot of others we have to worry about in her absence, though, so we don't want to get complacent. What is it you have to do, Pen?"

He moved close, then put his hand on her shoulder to steady himself. "Two things. I have to get the darkwand back from Traunt

Rowan, and then I must get inside the chamber of the Ard Rhys in order to enter the Forbidding. It shouldn't be too hard, except that I don't know how the magic of the darkwand works."

She exhaled heavily. "It sounds pretty hard to me. Which part do you view as being easy?"

"No, no, you don't understand. Now that I'm free, things are much easier. I can get to the darkwand and to the chamber of the Ard Rhys—I know I can do that much. Especially with you to help me." He grinned at the consternation that registered on her sharp features. "Really, I can. Listen a moment. Something happened in the shaping of the darkwand. Or maybe even before, when the tree broke off its limb and took my fingers, but certainly by the time I was done carving its runes into the wood. There was a joining of sorts, a binding of the staff to me. I didn't know about it, at first. I didn't realize what it was. But I do now. I am connected to the darkwand in the same way I am connected to the parts of my own body. I can feel its presence. I can feel its responses to my needs."

She shook her head. "I don't know about this, Pen. You're talking about a wooden staff—"

"I know where it is right now," he said, cutting her short. "I knew it as soon as they took it away from me and brought me down here. The runes are like a voice in my head, calling to me. They want me to find the staff. No matter where the Druids take it or how hard they try to hide it, the runes will tell me how to find it. I will always know where it is. All I have to do is follow its voice."

She wanted to say something about the reliability of voices in your head, but she forced herself to accept that what he was saying might be true. There had to be some kind of special connection between the boy and the staff or he wouldn't have been summoned to receive it in the first place.

"So you can go right to it, now that you're free?" she pressed.

"I can."

"And then take it to the chamber of the Ard Rhys, where she went into the Forbidding, and figure out how to go in after her?" Khyber gripped his face in both of her hands and squeezed. "This doesn't sound easy at all. We're inside Paranor, and every Druid in the Keep is looking for you—or will be soon. We have no friends here, Penderrin. We have no allies, only enemies and potential enemies. We have no magic that counts. I can use the Elfstones once we're backed into a corner and it doesn't matter anymore, but by then we're probably done for."

"We can do it, Khyber," he answered softly.

She stared into his eyes. "I think you believe that," she said. She shook her head and sighed. "In any case, what does it matter? We both know we're going to try. That is what we have been given to do and all we have left to do unless we try to go back to homes that aren't even ours anymore."

His enthusiasm faded suddenly. "My parents! What about my parents? The Druids still have them!"

"As a matter of fact, they don't. Your parents fled or escaped or whatever, but they're gone. I got that information from the Druid who brought me down here. So you don't have to worry about them."

His smile returned. "Then this is going to work. I know it."

She wanted to tell him that he was right, that it would. But it was a stretch to accept that all the steps he must take to reach Grianne Ohmsford and return with her would be the right ones and none missteps that would doom them both. He saw things in simple terms, in the terms of a boy who believed everything was still possible and no reach too great. She knew better. She had a stronger sense of the possible than he did, and that made her cautious of embracing rarefied hopes too warmly.

She took her hands away from his shoulders and tucked them into her robes. "Let's give it a try, Penderrin," she said.

Outfitted in Druids' robes, with weapons concealed and hoods pulled over their heads to shadow their faces, they went back up the stone stairwell to the upper corridors of Paranor. If Khyber had read the position of the stars correctly, it would be dawn in a few hours. She felt strongly that they had to complete their efforts by sunrise if they were to have any chance of succeeding. Once it grew light, they would have to hide. By the time it was dark again, everyone in the Keep would know that Pen was free and be looking for him. There would be little chance of succeeding after that.

Not that there was all that much chance of succeeding now.

She tried not to be negative in her thinking, but the odds against them were so enormous that she could not help herself. She reminded herself that the odds had been enormous from the beginning, and yet the two of them were still moving ahead, however slowly, still working their way toward their goal. They had lost good friends and strong allies, but even that hadn't been enough to stop them. She must take heart from that. She had come a long way from her forbidden Druid studies with her uncle in Emberen—and a longer way still from her rarefied life as an Elessedil Princess in Arborlon. She could barely remember what the latter had been like. Her worries at the prospect of being married off on the whim of her father or brother seemed to belong to another person altogether. She was so far removed from that time, so distanced from it by the events of the past few weeks, that it might never have existed.

And might not ever exist again, given her present situation.

She felt a moment of panic and fought to contain it. Uncle Ahren would calm her if he were there. He would tell her not to think beyond the moment, but to confront what frightened her and bring it under control. She tried doing that, isolating the source of her fear and putting it aside. But it was hard to give it a name or even a shape. Her fear was for something too large and too amorphous to define, an overwhelming sense of smallness and weakness and inexperience in the face of a tidal wave of power and dark intent. She might thrash and struggle. She might try whatever she could to break free of its grip. But in the end, it would have her anyway.

"We need to go farther up," Pen whispered suddenly, clutching at her arm, breaking the chains of the spell.

She gasped at his unexpected touch, caught her breath, then nodded quickly to conceal her shock. "Farther up," she repeated. She glanced around, surprised to discover that they had reached the top of the stairs. The corridor ahead stretched away into pools of torchlight and layered shadows, the silence as thick as cotton wadding. "Can you show me?"

He pointed diagonally upward into the darkness of the passageway, then looked back at her expectantly, excitement dancing in his eyes. He was enjoying himself. He wasn't even thinking about the danger—or if he was, he was discounting it in favor of his strong expectations for achieving the quest given him by the King of the Silver River. The realization made her smile inwardly, although she kept her face expressionless as she motioned for him to lead the way.

They walked down the passageway swiftly and silently, listening for voices or footfalls but hearing neither. Khyber was back to worrying about how they would regain the darkwand if they encountered any resistance. She would use her small Druid magic if she was forced to, but stealth and secrecy were better allies for as long as they could call on them for help. If they could get as far as the chambers of the Ard Rhys without being discovered, they had a reasonable chance of getting Pen through to the Forbidding, whether or not he knew how to use the magic of the staff, because such magic would reveal itself when it was time. It was in the nature of most magic to do so, and there was no reason to think it would be any different now.

And plenty of reasons to hope it wouldn't.

The first corridor turned left into a second corridor, and Pen, leading the way, stopped suddenly. "Khyber!" he hissed.

A pair of Gnome Hunters was coming toward them from out of the mix of light and shadows, spears resting on their shoulders, heads lowered in conversation. Their attentions on each other, they had not yet seen the boy and the Elven girl.

"Keep moving," she whispered, giving Pen a push. "Don't say anything when we pass. Keep your head lowered."

They walked toward the Gnomes at a steady pace, Khyber moving over to place herself between Pen and the guards, shielding him. She looked right through the Gnomes as they passed, a Druid preoccupied with more important things. It had the desired effect. The Gnomes, in turn, looked right through her.

Seconds later, they were alone again.

Pen turned them onto a broad stairway that wound upward into the Keep, and they began to climb. As they did so, the sound of voices reached them for the first time, coming from somewhere above. Khyber took Pen's arm to keep him moving. Hesitation was the enemy. At the top of the stairs, the corridor divided, one branch continuing on, the other angling left. A pair of Druids stood conversing not a dozen yards away, heads bent close, sharing possession of a book that one held while the other slowly paged through. The two gave Pen and Khyber only a cursory glance, and Pen turned down the corridor that ran left.

"It's not far now," he whispered.

Khyber nodded, feeling a renewed sense of trepidation. This would not be as easy as it seemed. There would be guards, probably watching over the darkwand, but certainly warding the sleeping chambers of the Ard Rhys. They would have to get past those guards and do so without a fight. How would they manage that?

There wasn't time to think it through. They were down the corridor, around a corner, and moving toward several Gnome Hunters stationed at the foot of a narrow staircase leading up into the highest reaches of the Keep. For an instant, Khyber considered turning back, withdrawing to a place where they could talk this through and decide how best to proceed. But it was already too late for that; the Gnomes had seen them coming and were turning toward them.

"The darkwand is up those stairs," Pen said quietly, sealing their fate. "In the chamber of the Ard Rhys."

Two of the Gnome Hunters moved forward to intercept them, one holding up his hand to slow their approach. "No one is allowed in this part of the Keep," he rumbled, speaking to them in a fractured Southland dialect.

Khyber stopped in front of him. "Traunt Rowan sent for us."

The Gnome hesitated. "I wasn't told."

"Is he up there?" she asked, gesturing toward the stairs.

"He has gone to bed. Do the same and come back again tomorrow when he is here."

She shook her head. "I have to leave something for him." She pointed at the stairs. "Up there."

Another Gnome drifted over. The three of them were staring at her. The remaining Gnomes were clumped together on the far side of the hall, engaged in their own conversation and not paying much attention to the first group. It was time to act. They could break past these three, she thought. They could gain the stairs before the guards could stop them.

She took a deep breath and exhaled slowly. That kind of thinking could get them killed.

She gestured at the Gnome. "You can come with me, if you need to make certain of what I will do. Surely you can allow me that?"

The Gnome had shifted his gaze to Pen and was studying him closely. "I don't know you," he said. "You're just a boy, too young to be a Druid. Why do you wear a Druid robe?"

Pen straightened. "I am an apprentice in training. I am nephew to Traunt Rowan himself and not a boy." He folded his arms across his chest. "I will tell him what you said."

"Tell him what you like," the Gnome grunted. He looked back at Khyber. "You can't go up there. Not tonight. I have my orders."

She stared at him with an intensity that would have melted iron, knowing she had pushed matters as far as she could, that her only options now were to turn around and go back or try to fight her way through. She glanced at Pen, saw that he was set to fight, put a hand on his shoulder to calm him, and said, "Let's go."

She walked him back down the corridor without looking at him, silencing his protests with a quick squeeze of his shoulder, her mind racing. She wasn't about to give up, not with what was at stake. But she needed a better approach than a straightforward attack on six armed Gnome Hunters.

When she was around the corner and out of their sight, she wheeled on Pen. "Don't worry, we're going back. But we need a plan for this. It won't help if we're injured or killed—especially you. You'll have all you can do just to stay alive on the other side."

"I can manage," he said.

She gave him a long, hard look. "I have to say this before the time to say anything has run out. What you encounter inside the Forbidding will be much worse than what you've encountered here. You will be all alone, and I haven't any idea how you will protect yourself from the things imprisoned in there. I can help you. I'm not Ahren, but I do have training in the use of Druid magic, enough so that I can be of use. More important, I have the Elfstones. I think you should take me with you."

He shook his head. "You know I can't do that."

"I know you *think* you can't. I know you were told you couldn't. But maybe we need to test what you were told. The King of the Silver River has misled you more than once. You have already sacrificed yourself in ways that you weren't expecting. What might you be expected to sacrifice this time? Maybe I can keep that from happening."

"No, Khyber," he said firmly. His mouth tightened into a thin line. "If you come with me—if you even can—no one will ever know what has happened to either one of us if I fail. But if you stay behind, you might be able to change things without me. You might find a different way to help, a better way."

She snorted. "There is no other way. You know that."

"No, I don't. I don't know anything. Neither do you. We're still learning what's possible." He paused. "I do know this much. The staff and I are bonded in a way that makes it very clear to me that in this one instance, at least, the King of the Silver River was right. I have to go alone. No one else is going to be allowed to go with me."

She stared at him. "You are so stubborn, Penderrin."

"You should know, Khyber. Who is more stubborn than you?"

"I wish you would change your mind." She folded her arms and waited, then gave him a cryptic nod. "Just remember not to put yourself in danger needlessly. Remember to be patient when you come up against things you can't get past. Don't be reckless, Pen. You are, sometimes. But you can't be in there."

She waited on his response. "I know," he said.

"You say it, but I'm not sure you mean it."

His lips tightened. "I mean it. I know what it will be like. I know it will be bad. But I have to think I have a chance or the King of the Silver River wouldn't be sending me in the first place. Maybe the darkwand will help protect me. In any case, I promise to be careful, Khyber. You'd do better to worry about yourself. You won't be much better off than me."

He was right. She would be alone in the Druid's Keep with no way out. She would be in as much danger as he was.

She put the matter aside. There was nothing either of them could do about what lay ahead. "Are you ready?"

"Are you?"

"I don't know."

"Do you have a plan, Khyber?"

"Just stick close."

With Pen at her shoulder, she moved back to the bend in the corridor and stopped just out of sight of the Gnome Hunters. She glanced both ways to be certain they were alone, then summoned magic in the form of a spark of light no larger than a firefly. It flared to life then danced in the palm of her hand. She held it for a moment, looked at Pen to be certain he was ready, then stepped out into the hallway and threw the spark at the Gnomes.

The spark flew down the corridor so quickly that it was on them before they knew what it was. One or two had just enough time to glance up before the spark exploded in a ball of fiery light that consumed them. But nothing burned. Instead, weapons, armor, iron stays, and clasps were turned to magnets that locked together instantly, becoming a clutch of metal pieces, pulling all six guards into a struggling heap.

"Now," Khyber hissed, yanking Pen out of the shadows.

They raced for the stairway, black robes flying out behind them, watching as the pile of hapless Gnome Hunters rolled and thrashed about the floor, trying to free themselves from one another. One or two saw the pair run by and yelled in warning, but could not do anything about it. Before even one of them had regained his feet, Khyber and Pen were past them and racing up the stairs.

By the time they reached the upper floor, Pen was leading the way, flying up the steps and across the floor as he turned down the hall. Rounding the corner of the stairwell, Khyber glanced back over her shoulder. No one was following, but the guards were cursing and screaming and the sporadic flash of her entangling magic revealed that it was still holding them fast. Help would arrive quickly, though. She ran after Pen, who was pulling futilely at the iron handles of a pair of wooden doors that were carved with intricate symbols.

"Locked!" he screamed in frustration.

Khyber pulled him aside, took a moment to study the locks, found the magic that bound them too much for her, and stepped back, motioning Pen behind her. Using a skill Ahren had taught her long ago, she attacked the fastenings on the hinges, where the securing magic was weakest, loosening the bolts that held them, ripping free the outer stays. In moments, the doors had collapsed in a thunderous crash, giving them access to the room beyond.

They rushed into the chamber, Pen wheeling left and right, desperately searching for the missing staff. "Khyber, I don't see it!"

"There," she said, pointing toward the ceiling.

The staff hung suspended from a hook, threaded through with ropes of magic, bound securely in place and out of reach.

"Can you get it down?" the boy pleaded.

She shook her head. She could feel her heart pounding as desperation flooded through her. "The magic is too strong for me, too complex. I'm not skilled enough to break it."

In frustration, he leapt for the staff, snatching at it with both hands. As he did so, the runes glowed like bits of fire, as if live coals were embedded in the polished wood. They were responding to his efforts to reach him, anxious for him to succeed.

"Pen, stop!" she exclaimed. "Let's try something."

She positioned herself beneath the darkwand, locked her hands together in front of her, palms-up, to form a cup, then said, "Step into my hands and I'll boost you up. Grab one end of the staff and whatever happens, don't let go."

He did as she asked, waiting until she had braced herself, then stepping into her locked fingers. He was much heavier than he looked, and it took all her strength to boost him up and then hold him in place as he groped for the staff.

"I have it!" he shouted after what seemed an endless amount of time.

She released him with a gasp and left him dangling from the ceiling, both hands holding on to the staff. The runes were burning so fiercely it looked as if the wood might spontaneously ignite. But Pen did not seem to feel any pain, and the threads that secured the staff were beginning to shimmer and lose their brightness.

"It's weakening, Pen! It's giving way!"

There was a flurry of movement and the sound of boots in the hallway beyond. She whirled, summoned her magic almost without thinking, and turned it on a rush of Gnome Hunters who suddenly appeared in the gap where the doors used to be. A burst of wind materialized right in front of them, a huge gust that caught them up and sent them tumbling back down the hallway in a jumble of grunts and cries.

Behind her, in the face of the talisman's need to serve Pen, the magic that chained the darkwand failed and the boy crashed to the floor. He scrambled up again almost at once.

"It worked, Khyber!" he exclaimed, beaming with excitement.

"Go," she told him, gesturing. "Do what you have to, but go now. They're coming."

She turned back to the doorway, stepped to the opening, and sent another gust of wind sweeping down the hall toward the Gnome Hunters and a single black-cloaked Druid who had joined them.

When she glanced over her shoulder, Pen was running his hands up and down the staff as the glowing runes radiated spears of brilliance that chased back the darkness in all directions and surrounded the boy in a halo of fire. "It's working, Khyber!" he shouted. "I can feel something pulling at me!"

She wasn't sure what he meant or even if he understood what was actually happening, but she couldn't do anything to help him in any case. Her attention reverted to the hallway, where something new was developing. A regrouping was taking place just out of her line of sight. She stepped to one side of the opening, trying to find shelter. She scanned the torchlit darkness beyond their refuge, searching for movement, readying herself for whatever was coming.

"Hurry, Penderrin!"

There was no response. When she glanced back to see what he was doing, he was gone.

"Good luck," she whispered.

In the next instant, something that might have been a huge fist slammed into her and sent her flying backwards through the last of the fading streaks of light from the darkwand's runes. All the breath went out of her as she struck the far wall and collapsed in a stunned heap.

Use the Elfstones, she thought, fumbling through her clothing for them.

Then the fist struck her again, exploding out of the darkness of the corridor through the gap in the wall, hammering her back a second time. She fell away from the blow like a rag doll, and all the light and sound went out of the world.

TEN

In a second, much darker world, in a stronger, more heavily warded Keep, in a place and time where life was measured by the thickness of sinew and iron and the durability of hope was as ephemeral as mist, another attempt at escape was hanging by a thread.

Grianne Ohmsford lay motionless on the floor of her cell, a ragged, broken creature, listening to the sounds of an approaching Goblin's heavy breathing. The guard it had come to relieve was dead, and in its place, sitting cloaked and hooded not ten feet from her cell door, was Weka Dart. Her would-be rescuer and the one creature in that wretched world who had demonstrated any compassion for her, he was also her betrayer and a liar of such monstrous proportions that it was impossible for her to know his intentions from one moment to the next.

Grianne Ohmsford, Ard Rhys of the Third Druid Order, had been reduced to a place in life where reliance on betrayers and liars was the best she could expect. How she had come to that end was still something of a mystery, although she knew the identities of those responsible. She knew, too, what was at stake, and it tethered her sanity and resourcefulness directly to a driving need to get clear of the dungeons and find her way back to her own world.

But once the Goblin caught sight of the poorly concealed Weka Dart—which it surely must—the alarm would be given and her last hope of ever escaping would be ended. She could not let that happen. Whatever her misgivings about the Ulk Bog, however uncertain his loyalty, he remained her one chance. Her expectations were reduced to little more than gambling on the mercurial nature of a creature she barely understood. It would have to be enough. Weka Dart would have to do.

She stirred, deliberately drawing the Goblin's attention. It turned toward her, hearing her scuffling sounds, her whimpers, her sudden gasps, watching her attempts to rise from the floor on which she had lain by then for the better part of three days. It grunted something at her, taking hold of the bars to the cell, leaning forward and peering in. She was an amusement that could keep it entertained during the long hours ahead, a curiosity to be enjoyed and, perhaps, even teased. She could see it in the Goblin's eyes. She could read it in the look on its face.

Then a shadow slipped behind the gnarled figure, swift as smoke on wind, and the Goblin inhaled sharply as a knife blade thrust through its throat and pinned it against the bars. Weka Dart held the Goblin in place until it was limp, then dropped it on the dungeon floor and kicked the body aside.

"They should all go the same way," the Ulk Bog hissed. There was a look in his eyes that Grianne hadn't seen before and wasn't sure she wanted to see again.

She pushed herself off the floor and limped over to the cell door. Her mouth was dry and her head was pounding. Her vision was blurred from too many days of no food and water and no real sleep. She was still impacted by her ordeal with the Furies, her impulses still governed by her need to be one with them, to mewl and spit and snarl. She fought those impulses, but the effort was debilitating.

"Open the door, Weka Dart!" she snapped at him. "Let me out! Hurry!"

She did not mean her words to sound so urgent, did not intend to appear so desperate. But her needs overpowered her intentions, and the truth escaped before she could contain it. She would do anything to escape. She would give anything to distance herself from the horror she had endured as the Straken Lord's prisoner.

But instead of opening the door, Weka Dart glanced sharply at her, an uncertain look in his yellow eyes.

"What are you waiting for?" she snapped. "Do you have a way to free me or not? Is our bargain still good? Will you honor it as you have said you would?"

"Our bargain is not complete," he growled. He reached into his pocket and produced an iron key, holding it up for her to see. "My end of the bargain is here—the key to your cell door. I can take off the conjure collar, as well. But what of your end of the bargain? What of the service I require of you?"

"Forgiveness? You already have that. I have told you that by telling me the truth, you have gained that forgiveness. I don't want revenge on you. I won't harm you when I'm free. You have my word!"

His strange, wizened face scrunched down farther on itself and the yellow eyes glittered. "Your forgiveness was the price for my truth. That bargain is made and done. This bargain is new, Grianne of the Straken Lord's jails. If I give you your freedom—from this cell and from the collar—you must give me what I need in turn."

She stared at him, realizing suddenly that he had failed to reveal as yet his reasons for coming back. Coming to her aid was not something the little Ulk Bog would do out of the kindness of his heart. He had abandoned her, cast her off as useless to him when she had refused to allow him to lead her where he wanted—which was right where she had ended up anyway. But he had lost his chance at reinstatement as Catcher with Tael Riverine, a loss that left him homeless and shunned. He had come back because he expected her to do something about it.

"I can't give you anything," she told him. "It isn't within my power to give you anything."

"Ah, Straken, you underestimate yourself. You are exactly the one who can help me, and it is for that reason that I will help you. A favor for a favor. I don't want much. I don't want anything more than what you want for yourself. Freedom. From these prisons and from this world. I want you to take me with you."

Take me with you. She stared at him. Take him out of the Forbidding, he meant. Take him back with her into her own world. Voluntarily release a creature that had been locked away by the Faerie world since before the dawn of Mankind.

"You want to come with me?" she asked him, still not certain she was hearing him right. "You want to leave the Forbidding and come back with me into my world?"

He licked his lips and nodded eagerly. "When you find a way to get free, you must free me, as well. I know that you were brought here against your wishes. I know that you are trapped. But I have seen what you can do. I think that you know a way back—or if you do not, that you will find one. I have seen how resourceful you are, much more so than any other Straken I have ever encountered. You may be a match for Tael Riverine himself!"

"I am a match for no one," she countered. "I don't know if I can help you. I don't know if I should."

He bristled at her words, stepping back from the cell door and hissing at her like a snake. "Then I don't know why I'm wasting my time! I don't know why I bothered coming here at all! You would rather stay in this cell than escape back into your own world? You would rather die here? Better that than help someone like me? Is that what you are saying? That I am not worthy of your efforts, that I don't deserve your help?"

He spit at her. "Free yourself, then!"

He wheeled and started to walk away. It took everything she had to refrain from calling out to him, from begging him to come back to her. But if he thought she needed him more than he needed her, she would be in his power, and that was a price she could not afford to pay.

He was halfway down the hall when he wheeled about, his face contorting in fury. "I came back for you!" he screamed so loudly that she jumped in spite of herself. "I risked everything to come back for you! I came to save you, and now you won't help me? One little thing I ask of you, Straken! One tiny, little thing!"

He came rushing back down the hall, sobbing uncontrollably, his shoulders shaking. "Nothing, for someone with your power! Nothing! Why won't you do it?"

She took a deep breath. "I can't be sure of my power here. I can't be sure of what it will do. What if taking you out of the Forbidding is more than I can manage?"

He shook his head slowly from side to side, as if her words made no sense. "Don't you understand, Grianne of the cat sounds? I was driven from my tribe for eating my children! They will never take me back! No Ulk Bog door will ever be open to me again! Losing the protection of Tael Riverine closed every other door, as well. Now all creatures are my enemies. I am shunned by everything that breathes.

I have nowhere to go and no one who will take me in. Better I was dead than to try to live like this!"

"But why bother with me, Weka Dart?" she pressed. "If you just wait, won't this demon that Tael Riverine has dispatched to my world break down the Forbidding and free you anyway?"

"Free me from what?" he screamed at her. "Free me from one prison so that I can go into another? Free me from one world in which I am outcast so that I can be outcast in another? I don't want the Straken Lord to succeed! I don't want the Forbidding destroyed! If your world becomes like the world of the Jarka Ruus, what difference will it make whether I escape into it or not!"

He pushed his face up against the bars. "You can help me, Straken. If I can help you, surely you can help me! How hard can it be for someone like you to give me what I want?"

In truth, she didn't know. What would it take to escape the Forbidding? Was the boy foreseen by the shade of the Warlock Lord real? Was he coming to set her free, or was the prophecy a cruel trick? She couldn't be certain, but it was the only hope she had. The shade of Brona had not lied about the truth behind the reason she had been sent into the world of the Jarka Ruus—Weka Dart had confirmed that. She was here so that a demon could be free, a demon that would destroy the wall of the Forbidding. If Brona's shade had told the truth about that, then it might well have been telling the truth about the mysterious boy.

So she must gamble on the words of a monster. She must accept the possibility that her only chance for escape was through the coming of a boy she didn't know. It didn't seem to her that Weka Dart's hopes for escape were any less realistic than her own. While she did not relish setting the Ulk Bog free in her world, it would be infinitely worse to refuse his bargain if it meant that she must stay imprisoned, as well.

"If you release me," she said, "I will try to find a way out of the world of the Jarka Ruus and back to my own world. If it is within my power to do so, I will take you with me. I can promise you nothing more."

"I have your word?"

"You do." She held up one cautionary finger. "But remember, I don't know yet that I can find a way back for either of us. I don't know that I can save us, even if you set me free. I don't know that I can find a way to stop the Moric from destroying the Forbidding. I don't know that."

He was already working the key to her cell into the lock. "You will find a way. I know you will."

He released her from the cell, then used a second, smaller key to unlatch the conjure collar. Stepping back, he handed her the collar, his wizened face bright with pleasure.

"I kept my keys to the cells and the collars from my days as Catcher," he said to her. "Tael Riverine never suspected I would dare to do such a thing."

"He has misjudged us both," she said. She cast the collar aside. She would never wear such a thing again or ever again be anyone's slave. "How do we get past all the guards and their demonwolves?" she asked as they stood facing each other in the empty hall.

He grinned, all his teeth showing. "We won't go that way. That way is death. We will go another way, a way I know that few others do. It is how I got into Kraal Reach to find you in the first place. I know secrets, little Straken. I know many secrets."

She didn't doubt him. But she refrained from saying anything, gesturing for him to lead the way. She was weak from her imprisonment and lack of nourishment, and she was already wondering how far she could go before her strength failed completely. She had no idea how long she had lain semicomatose in her delusional state in that cell, but it had to have been days. During that time, she had not eaten or drunk anything that she could remember. She had barely slept, suspended between sleeping and waking, beset by dreams and dark imaginings, still caught up in the subterfuge she had used to survive her ordeal in the arena of the Furies.

Some part of her was still there, she knew, amid the cat-things, unable to quite let go of the identity of the creature she had pretended so hard to be. Her magic was a powerful thing, and when it was employed as she had employed it in the arena, she could do or be anything. But the aftereffects were equally powerful and tended to cling to her psyche like the damp leavings of a sweat brought on by nightmares. She was Grianne Ohmsford again. She was Ard Rhys of the Third Druid Order once more. But she was also the Ilse Witch and the things the Ilse Witch could become. She had opened a door she had kept carefully closed for more than twenty years, and she was not sure what it would take to close it again.

They went down a corridor lined with doors that opened into cells like her own, some of them empty, some of them become containers for piles of bones and small lumps at which she chose not to look too closely. The corridor was silent and musty and empty of life. She heard Weka Dart's breathing and the scrape of his boots, but her own passage was soundless, a wraith's passage through darkest night.

The corridor ended at a set of narrow steps leading up, but Weka Dart took her into the shadows behind the stairs, where a rusted iron door was seated in the stone. He worked its ancient latch back and forth, a slow creaking in the deep silence, and at last the door opened into a wall of blackness.

"Very dark down here," the Ulk Bog announced solemnly.

He reached into the blackness to produce a torch, stuck its pitch-coated tip into the flames of one already lit in the corridor behind them, and caught it aflame. He gave the fire a moment to spread, then grinned at her once more and led the way forward.

She followed him down into the earth, down stairs eroded by centuries of footsteps and moisture, into depths so frigid that the cold cut right to the bone. The tunnels they traversed smelled of old damp and raw metal, and at times she saw what looked like frost on the rock but was, in fact, patches of lichen that glowed with a strange, bright radiance. Weka Dart's torch burned with smoky insistence, clogging the air with its distinctive smell, causing her to cough and finally forcing her to breathe through the sleeve of her tunic. There was no ventilation in the tunnels, and the smell of burning pitch trailed after them like a marker. If anyone thought to look for them down there, they would not have a hard time tracking them, she thought.

Weka Dart pressed on as if pursuit were not a concern, glancing back at her now and then to be certain she was keeping up, as if fearful he might lose her in the dark. Indeed, it wasn't an altogether unrealistic concern. She was already having trouble keeping up with him, even absent his tendency to roam as he had earlier in their travels. Her head ached from the cold and smoke, and her body was fatigued and shaky. She wished she had looked for something to eat or drink, but she had not even thought of that, so anxious had she been to get clear of the cells. In truth, she had not eaten or drunk in any reasonable way since she had come into the Forbidding, and the gradual erosion of her energy was finally making itself felt.

Time passed, more than she could keep track of, and the trek through the tunnels beneath Kraal Reach wore on. Clearly determined to take them through as swiftly as possible, Weka Dart did not stop or even slow. From time to time, he retrieved a fresh torch from a crevice she would have passed by without even seeing, lighting it from the old one so that they could continue. Their passage wound down crude steps cut into the stone, along narrow, twisting corridors in which they were forced to stoop, and through caves thick with stalactites dripping with mineral-rich water. After a time, the air warmed a bit, and Grianne stopped shivering. The floor of the tunnels began to rise; they were moving back toward the surface.

But still their journey continued with no end in sight.

Finally, as they were passing through yet another cavern, she stumbled and fell. She lay where she had fallen, her vision blurred and her muscles aching, too tired to rise.

"Are you hurt, Straken?" Weka Dart asked, trying in vain to pull her back to her feet.

"I am exhausted," she told him. "I have to rest."

He shook his head. "It is not safe here."

"I don't care. I have to rest."

She crawled along the floor of the cavern to an open space where she could stretch out. She was breathing so hard that the wheeze filled the silence of the cavern, frightening her with its intensity. Her head was spinning, and she felt as if all the strength had left her body.

"Do you have anything to eat?"

He produced a tuber of some sort, which she ate without questioning its strange taste, then accepted the water he produced from a gourd tucked in his clothing. She was beyond caring about the source of the offerings, beyond caring about anything but taking nourishment and going to sleep.

"I have traveled through these caverns often," he advised, glancing around at the darkness. He sat cross-legged before her and wedged the torch upright between two stones. "That's why I know where torches can be found to light the way. Most of them, I put there. I used these passages to leave the Keep undetected when I was Catcher for Tael Riverine. Sometimes secrecy was best."

He shrugged. "Of course, these tunnels are home to things you don't want to take chances with. That is why I said it is dangerous. We don't have to worry, though. I know what they are and how to avoid them. Mostly. Some are very large, some very small. Some have no eyes, they have been down here so long. Some are things no one but me has ever seen."

Her breathing had steadied enough that she could respond. "This whole world is filled with things I have never seen."

"I suppose that's so." He thought a moment, rubbing his fingers across his wrinkled features. "I will not be sad to leave this world," he said suddenly. "I will be happy to leave."

She nodded, saying nothing.

"I was never meant to be here." He shook his head emphatically. "I was born into this world, but it was a mistake. I should have been born into yours. If I had been, I would not have done the things I did. I would not have eaten my young. I would not have been a Catcher for Tael Riverine. I would have done something important."

He smiled, showing off a frightening display of teeth. "I will be much better when I am living in your world, Grianne of the kind and gentle heart. I will serve you. I will be your friend and helper. Whatever you need me to do, I will do it. I am good at many things. I can find anything. That is why I was such a good Catcher. That is why I was able to find you—both times. Nothing escapes me once I set my mind to finding it. It is a gift. I am lucky to have it."

"I have to sleep," she said.

"When I am in your world, I will not do bad things," he continued, apparently not hearing. "I will not eat things I shouldn't or hurt those I care about. I will work hard. I will become your most trusted companion because I know how important that is. I have never had anyone I could trust before. I have not even had a friend. In the world of the Jarka Ruus, friends are hard to find. Mostly, we have alliances with those we protect or who protect us. Everything hunts or is hunted. It is not safe to have friends."

She was stretched on the ground now, barely aware of what he was saying. She felt his hand touch her arm. "But you are my friend, little Straken. We are friends, you and I. We shall always be friends."

A moment later, she was asleep.

She dreamed of dark creatures and long chases, of being hunted relentlessly, of each pursuit ending in a fall that segued into the next. She never knew exactly where she was. She never knew what it was that was after her. She caught shadowy glimpses of her surroundings and of the things that hunted her, but both changed shape and size so often that she could identify neither.

She woke groggy and out of sorts with Weka Dart shaking her. "Wake up, little Straken!" he hissed. "Something's coming!"

She could hear the fear in his voice, and it brought her all the way awake. "What is it?"

"A Graumth! A cave wyrm!" He glanced over his shoulder quickly, then back at her. "There hasn't been one in these tunnels for years. They live deeper underground; you don't see them ever here. But this one scents us. It comes!"

She scrambled to her feet, still unsteady, still aching and worn. She took a moment to gather her thoughts and test her balance. "What should we do?"

His teeth showed in a glistening line. "Run from it! If it catches us, we will be eaten. Have you ever seen a cave wyrm? Very big. Not afraid of anything. I saw one destroy an entire company of Goblins once. There was nothing left but their armor and their weapons when it had finished feasting on them. Come!"

She didn't require any further urging. Weka Dart was already moving away with the torch, and she hurried after him. They cleared the cavern and plunged into a fresh set of tunnels. But they were going back down into the earth again, and she realized that the Ulk Bog had been forced to alter their escape route to avoid the Graumth. She guessed there was nothing she could do about that, but she wasn't sure how she would hold up if the detour proved lengthy. Her headache and sense of disorientation had returned. The food, water, and sleep had helped, but she was not yet herself.

Behind her, something huffed powerfully, like an angry bull or an explosion of steam. Only much, much, louder.

"This thing is big?" she asked, panting.

"Very big."

"Then it can't get down into these smaller tunnels, can it? We should be safe!"

She saw the glint of his eyes in the torchlight as he glanced back at her. "Graumths can squeeze themselves down to a quarter of their size to get through small spaces. We are not safe anywhere, Straken."

They hurried on, not at running speed, but perhaps at half, which was dangerous enough under the circumstances. Even with the torchlight to guide them, the way was treacherous, strewn with knobs and depressions, spits in the rock floor, outcroppings, and occasional drops. Running was dangerous, but easier for the Ulk Bog than for her. She did not possess his agility or his strength. With her balance already uncertain, she soon found herself unable to keep up.

"Weka Dart!" she called to him. "Not so fast."

As if in response, the Graumth's huffing burst out of the darkness behind her in a wave so unexpectedly loud that she almost screamed. It was much nearer, rapidly closing the distance between them.

Weka Dart rushed back to her and seized her arm. "If it catches us, Grianne of the clever tricks, I have no weapons with which to fight it! Can you bring your Straken magic to bear?"

In truth, she didn't know. She hadn't tried to use her magic since the ordeal with the Furies, and she wasn't sure what part of it would respond in her present condition.

"Keep running!" she said, pushing him ahead.

They cleared the narrower tunnel and emerged into a broader one, its ceiling fully twenty feet high. Ahead, the walls opened wider still, the beginnings of another cavern. There was movement behind them now, a kind of sibilant scraping that suggested something heavy and slick. The huffing was all around them, the sound of breathing, heavy and anxious.

They ran on through the broader tunnel to the entrance to the cavern, and then she grabbed Weka Dart's arm and pulled him around.

"We'll make a stand here."

She was played out. She had nothing left. She pushed him behind her, then summoned her Druid magic. It would not come. It resisted her call, locked away deep down inside her where it refused to budge. She had not had that happen since she was little and in training with the Morgawr during the early years of her life as the Ilse Witch.

In the darkness of the tunnels they had just come through, the Graumth was moving rapidly, sensing their presence. For a moment, she panicked.

"Straken!" Weka Dart hissed suddenly, thrusting the torch at her. "Use this! It cannot see in the light! Graumths live in the dark and never see the sun! Perhaps this torch—"

"Keep it!" she snapped at him, furious with the interruption, her concentration completely broken. "Use it yourself if it gets past me!"

She resumed her efforts at summoning the magic, burrowing down inside herself, breaking down barriers one by one. It was her fear of becoming a Fury again that most resisted her efforts. That fear closed about her as she worked to reach her recalcitrant magic. It threatened to make her lose control completely. She understood its power. She would do anything to avoid becoming a Fury again, anything to escape the terrible madness that becoming one of the cat creatures would cause. If she was to do it again, she did not think she could reverse the effects. The madness would claim her, and she would be lost. That fear permeated everything about her need to call up the magic, and she could not seem to separate it out.

"Straken!" cried Weka Dart.

Writhing and twisting, the Graumth burst from the darkness of the smaller tunnel. It was a huge insectlike creature covered with bony plates that gleamed with an oily lubricant. Mandibles clicked at the center of its flat, featureless head, and short, spiky legs ended in huge claws that supported its narrow, reticulated body. It seemed to grow larger right before her eyes, and the forward part of its body lifted right off the cave floor, filling the tunnel with its bulk, undulating as it advanced on them.

As she fought to bring magic to bear, Weka Dart lost control. Whether from fear or impatience or out of desperation too overpowering to resist, he gave way. With a terrifying howl, he burst past her, waving the torch wildly at the Graumth, sparks flying from the flaming brand in long crimson streamers. The Ulk Bog went right at the monster, a bothersome gnat waiting to be crushed. The Graumth made the familiar huffing sound, then jerked back from its tiny attacker, clearly bothered by the presence of the light from the torch.

"No, don't!" Grianne screamed.

Weka Dart was right underneath the monster, rushing it and then backing quickly away, waving the torch as if it had magical powers, howling as if he were the magician who could make them come alive.

In that instant, driven by her fear for the little Ulk Bog and her rage at her own impotence, she broke down the last of her resistance to the summoning of her magic. She smashed through her hesitancy and her reticence, tore down her fears and doubts, wrenched the magic free, and brought it to bear. The wishsong, its blood heritage both a blessing and a curse to generations of her family, but to no one so much so as to herself, surfaced.

Like a tidal wave.

Release me!

Terrified by its unexpected force, by the immensity of it, she fought to contain it. The magic's powerful response was something new, entirely different. It roiled inside her like the winds of a storm, breaking down everything in its path, threatening massive destruction. She clutched at herself with both hands, trying to contain it, to keep it inside until she could control it. For she had no more control over this than she had over her Fury self. She was enveloped. She was consumed.

Release me!

She could not stop it. The magic exploded out of her. Responding instinctively to her needs, it swept through the dark and the damp like a hammer, slamming into the Graumth, striking it with such force that the creature was lifted off its crooked legs and thrown back against the rock of the tunnel walls. The result was instantaneous and devastating. The Graumth didn't merely collapse on impact; it shattered. Armor plates, legs, and body parts flew everywhere until all that remained were bits and pieces that twitched with slow jerking motions in the faint light of Weka Dart's flickering torch.

Then the magic simply faded until no trace of it remained.

Drained of her strength and stunned by her body's response to the magic's implacable surge, Grianne Ohmsford sank to her knees. The wishsong had come out of her with more power than she had ever experienced. It was as if she had been storing it away for weeks on end, had accumulated and hoarded it, waiting for just that moment to set it free. The wishsong had been put to the test countless times over the years, but she had never seen it respond that way.

What had happened to make it do so?

Weka Dart was standing before her, wizened face bright with unrestrained exultation and wild-eyed glee. Holding out the torch in a kind of salute, he bent his head in crude submission.

"Straken Queen," he whispered, the awe in his voice unmistakable. "Yours is the greatest power. Yours is the supreme magic. I bow to you. I salute you. You have no equal."

She closed her eyes against what she was feeling and made no response. She did not pretend to know if the extent of her power was as vast as it appeared. But she knew without question that it was strong enough to have revealed their presence to the Straken Lord, and that he would be there quickly enough to test it for himself.

ELEVEN

When the rune-carved length of the darkwand began to glow, Pen could sense a shift in place and time almost immediately. It was an odd feeling, a suggestion of movement that felt like a small tremor in the earth coupled with a subtle progression of light toward dark. He knew immediately that the magic was in play and the darkwand was responding to his silent plea for help. There was nothing earthshaking about it, nothing overtly dramatic or astounding, just a hint of things being altered.

He had time to glance once at Khyber, who faced the opening where the doors to the Ard Rhys's sleeping chamber had stood before she collapsed them, her body rigid with concentration, her arms lifted and her fingers extended to meet whatever challenge might appear. He regretted abandoning her to so many enemies—hated himself for it, after everything she had done for him—but there was no time or way to act on it. She had accepted the consequences of her fate by agreeing to bring him there, knowing what must happen. What he could do best for her was what he could do best for them both: cross over into the Forbidding, find the Ard Rhys, and bring her back into the Four Lands.

It happened quickly after that. The runes caught fire beneath his fingers and the staff turned bright with their glow. Then the glow

was all around him, enveloping him, shutting him away from his surroundings. The room and Khyber disappeared. He closed his eyes,
hands tightening on the staff, praying that he would be strong
enough to do what was needed.

A giant fist clutched his body, and all the air disappeared from his
lungs. He gasped in response, trying to breathe, fighting to keep
from choking.

Then he was standing in a twilit clearing of wintry grasses and
barren earth surrounded by sparse woods and a deeply clouded
sky. Paranor was gone. The world of the Four Lands was gone.
Nothing he was looking at reminded him of home. Except, perhaps, for the bleaker places he had visited, like the Slags or the
Klu. He stared blankly for a moment, making the comparisons,
measuring the differences in his head, looking slowly about as he
did so.

What struck him first was how dark things were. It didn't
seem to be nightfall, but the sun was nowhere to be seen, the brightness of the overcast sky like a pale reflection off clouded waters.
The trees and grasses were washed of color, their greens muted
and dulled. He peered into the distance. There wasn't much to
see, the woods fading into shifting walls of mist; the sky and
earth coming together miles away in a grayish haze; the mountains stark and barren; the woods skeletal and empty looking.
He could not imagine what lived there. He had the feeling
that whatever did spent most of the time hunkered down and watchful.

He had a feeling that here you were either pursuer or pursued,
hunter or prey.

I hate this world already, he thought.

He was grasping the darkwand so tightly that his hands hurt.
He loosened his grip on the staff and forced himself to take a
few deep breaths to stay calm. He had made the crossing; the
magic of the staff had done its job, bringing him out of the Four
Lands and into the Forbidding. He could scarcely believe it, and in
truth he might not have if everything did not look and feel exactly
right for what the Forbidding should be. Despite the oppressiveness of his surroundings, he felt an odd sense of relief, as if the hardest part of the task given him by the King of the Silver River

were finished. But he knew that wasn't so, that the hardest part lay ahead. He had accomplished much since he had left Patch Run. He had crossed half the Four Lands to find the darkwand and bring it back to Paranor. He had endured hardships and privations of a sort few survived. He had escaped his enemies time and again.

But just staying alive in this dark place would take all the strength he had and then some.

He finished scanning his surroundings, found nothing useful, stood for a moment longer, and then sat down to gather his thoughts. He wondered briefly about his parents. There was no way for them to know what had happened to him unless Khyber managed to reach them. At least they were free of Paranor and the Druids. They would not be tricked again by Shadea a'Ru and her minions. He was still bothered by the fact that the King of the Silver River had failed to warn them, as he had promised he would. Unless they had ignored that warning, of course, and had determined to help him no matter what the risk. His mother would think like that. His mother would brave anything for him.

As would any of his friends and companions on this journey, he thought. As all of them had. He found himself missing them desperately—steady Tagwen, brave Kermadec, resourceful Khyber, and even the truculent Atalan. But most of all he missed Cinnaminson. Just thinking of her made him ache in a way nothing else ever had. He tried to picture her as he remembered her best—free and alive, smiling at him on the decks of the *Skatelow*, reaching out to take his hand. He tried not to think of where she was and what had become of her. But he couldn't quite manage it.

He compressed his lips in a tight line and forced himself to think instead of other things. He was alone for the moment, at least until he found his aunt, and there was nothing he could do to change that. He hoped the others were all right, that they had found ways to escape their predicaments, but wondering if they had was just another dead end in his thinking.

What he must think about was finding his aunt, the Ard Rhys, and bringing her home safe.

He started as sudden heat flooded through his palms. The runes of the darkwand were glowing, turning the staff warm. He got to his feet quickly and looked around, wondering if the staff were warning him of hidden danger. But he sensed nothing. He stared down at the staff once more, but the runes had dimmed and the wood gone cool.

He frowned in confusion. Something had triggered the reaction, but what was it? He looked around. Nothing.

He looked back at the staff. Was it something inside him? Was the staff responding to him? He knew already that they were connected, sufficiently so that he had been able to find it when it was taken away by Traunt Rowan and had known instinctively how to trigger its magic when crossing from his world into this one.

The staff responded to his needs. Was it doing so here? Was it responding to his need to find Grianne Ohmsford?

Experimenting, he turned his thoughts to his aunt, asking himself where she was and how he could find her. At once, the runes turned fiery, pulsating beneath his hands, enveloping the entire staff in a red glow.

He grinned. Now he knew what the staff could do. But he still didn't know how to make practical use of it.

The grayness of the day was fading rapidly toward night, the sky darkening and shadows beginning to drape the world below. Pen glanced around, thinking that he did not want to be caught out in the open once night arrived. He needed to find shelter, but first he needed to determine which way he should go.

To do that, he needed to figure out how to use the darkwand.

He looked at it again, turning his thoughts away from his quest, watching the brightness of the runes fade. Maybe if he asked it to show him where his aunt was, it would do so. If he thought about a direction to take in the same way he thought about looking for her, perhaps the runes would show him something.

He gave it a try. He thought about his aunt, about his need to find her, watched the runes brighten anew, then started thinking about directions he might take, projecting himself going first one way and then another.

Nothing happened. The runes stayed bright, but did not respond in any way to his silent questions.

He shook his head in disgust. So much for that approach. Still, there had to be a way.

He decided to try something else. Keeping his thoughts focused on his aunt, he started walking toward the last of the light, a direction he assumed might be west, but the runes dimmed almost at once. He stopped and turned around to walk the other way, toward the encroaching darkness, which would be east. Again, the runes darkened. At least he was getting a clear response, he thought.

He turned south, toward the mountains that were closest to where he stood. Instantly, the runes turned fiery.

He felt a surge of elation. He would go that way.

He started walking, the staff held before him in both hands like a compass, the runes glowing brightly, providing him with both light and reassurance. All around, the shadows thickened and the world began to change. What had been indistinct before began to lose all shape and form, until most of what he could see was distinguished by little more than changes in color and brightness. He could still make out the peaks ahead of him, but little else. He would have to find shelter soon.

He was further persuaded of that when he noticed movement in the shadows, movement that hadn't been there earlier. He caught only glimpses of it, sudden dartings, like the scurrying of small furry animals except that there were no small furry animals living within the Forbidding—at least, not ones that were likely to be friendly. In any case, he didn't think he wanted to find out. Other than the dark-wand, all he carried for protection was a long knife he had taken from one of the guards. But he didn't think it would prove much of a weapon against the things that lived in the Forbidding—especially after dark.

He trudged on, keeping as much to the open as he could manage, following the dictates of the staff while keeping close watch on his surroundings. Once, something massive flew overhead, a great winged creature that, had it fallen on him, would have crushed him instantly. He froze when he saw it, distant and indistinct, and he did not move again until he was certain it was gone.

He saw other things, too. He saw catlike creatures leaping through the dead-limbed trees and lizard-things that slithered along the earth through the grasses and scrub. He started to hear hissing and snarling, the sounds of hunters at work. Once a shriek momentarily brought his heart to his throat. In the silence that followed, he could hear the rasp of his own frightened breathing.

I am alone here, he kept thinking. *I am alone, and I have no idea what lives here or how to defend myself.*

He swallowed hard. *I wish I weren't so afraid.*

Darkness was almost complete by then, and he had reached the lower slopes of the mountains that blocked the way forward. Clusters of boulders formed huge barriers that rose before him like sentries to challenge his passage. The bare limbs of trees rose against the sky like the finger bones of giants long dead. He saw that a trail led upward through the maze to a pass that in turn opened toward the mountains, to the land beyond. But the way forward was long and arduous. And with the fall of darkness, he would not get far before he couldn't see at all.

So he moved into the center of the tree trunks and boulder piles, found a shelter in the rocks where he was protected on three sides, and settled in. He quit thinking about his aunt, turned his thoughts away from his search, and watched the light of the runes fade. He had nothing to eat or drink, so he tried not to think about how hungry and thirsty he was. Beyond his shelter, the world was ink black, devoid of light from moon or stars, empty of sky. But there were sounds everywhere, sharp and piercing, low and rumbling, sudden and slow to build and die. There were sounds of every sort, but none of them familiar and none pleasant.

Pen wedged himself into one corner of his shelter, clasped his arms about the darkwand, and took out the long knife and placed it against his chest. He sat staring out into the darkness for a long time before he fell asleep.

When he woke, the dragon was staring at him. He didn't realize it was there at first. He woke slowly and lethargically, still half asleep as he opened his eyes to look around. He didn't know where he was. He was stretched out on the hard ground, his bones aching and his muscles sore. The world was dark and hazy; there was no

sunshine, no bright color, and no welcoming warmth or birdsong
to encourage his rising. The new day was cloaked in sullen stillness and a deep gray wash that made him want to go back to
sleep.

He closed his eyes for a moment, then opened them again as his
head cleared and he remembered that he was inside the Forbidding.
He glanced down. The long knife was still in his hand, his fingers
stiff from gripping it. The darkwand was clutched to his chest, its
runes pulsating softly, come alive with the day.

He stared at the staff doubtfully. Why was it glowing? He
couldn't remember thinking about his search for his aunt or anything
that would have made it brighten.

Then his attention was drawn to a huge cluster of mottled boulders settled squarely in front of him. He didn't remember those boulders being there the night before and wasn't sure how he could have
missed seeing them, even in the dark. It was like having a wall materialize out of nowhere, a great massive barrier that somehow didn't
seem to quite belong.

He stared at them in confusion.

A window-size eye blinked, a lazy lowering and lifting of a scaly
lid.

Pen caught his breath and held it. The cluster of rocks began to
assume shape and take on definition. Limbs studded with spikes
crooked awkwardly at the joints to end in claws that were each the
size of his leg. Scales larger than blankets layered a body that would
dwarf a small cottage. Bony ridges ran in parallel lines down a broad
back and long, reticulated tail. A triangular head was tucked between
its forelegs, encrusted snout and brow thick with armor and blunt
horns.

"Shades," he whispered.

He had never seen a dragon, of course. No one in his lifetime had ever seen a dragon. Most types were extinct. Those that
weren't were consigned to the Forbidding, like the one before
him, or so deeply and thoroughly entrenched in mountain caverns
and wilderness forests that no human had ever ventured in far
enough to encounter them. But he knew what dragons were and
what they looked like, and the creature facing him was clearly a
dragon.

It was easily the biggest living creature that Pen had ever seen. It was bigger than he had imagined anything could be. Fascinated in spite of himself, he stared at it. He wondered what it was doing there. He wondered why it hadn't eaten him.

He wondered if it planned to.

He became aware all at once that it was looking at him. It was watching through half-closed lids with a sleepy, almost dreamy gaze. It seemed mesmerized, like a cat stretched out for a nap, lazy and content, drifting in and out of private reveries. Then it occurred to him, almost as an afterthought, that the dragon wasn't looking at him.

It was looking at the darkwand.

Or, more particularly, at the glow of its runes.

At first, he thought he must be mistaken. After all, why would the dragon be interested in the staff and its runes? Was the beast sentient? It certainly didn't look it. But maybe it understood something of magic and of talismans and recognized the darkwand for what it was.

He didn't think that was right, though. The way the dragon was watching the staff suggested that it was all but hypnotized, that its interest was one of almost primordial attraction. Pen glanced down, watching the way the light played across the runes, how it worked itself up and down the staff in ever-changing patterns, how it brightened and dimmed, pulsed and steadied, reinventing itself over and over. The dragon was watching, too, fascinated by the movement of the light as it danced from rune to rune.

Pen tried an experiment. Taking his cloak, he covered the top half of the staff, blocking the light.

Instantly, the great horn-encrusted head lifted, the triangular snout swung about, and its maw split wide in a hiss that sounded like an explosion. Rows of blackened teeth revealed themselves, some still clotted with bits of flesh, some with bones wedged between them. A gaping throat as black as damp ashes pulsed and shimmered, and the stench of carrion on its breath flattened the boy against the rock wall of his all-too-inadequate shelter. Pen gagged and nearly fainted, but he retained sufficient presence of mind to uncloak the darkwand at once. As the runes began anew their intricate play across the polished surface of the wood, the dragon slowly settled back into place, its maw closing, its eyelids drooping, content.

That was a really bad idea, Pen thought, taking great gulps of air to clear his head.

He remained where he was for a moment, sagging against the wall of his shelter, the darkwand held firmly in front of him, his talisman against a monster with breath that would melt iron. He hung his head for a time, thinking he was going to vomit, but when the nausea had passed, he straightened and looked out again at the dragon, trying to think what to do. He still wasn't certain what was happening with the darkwand, which until then he had assumed would respond only to his thoughts of the Ard Rhys. But it had apparently begun to glow even before he was awake and knew what was happening. How could that be?

He returned his attention to the dragon, saw how its eyes were fixed on the glowing runes, listened to how its breathing came slowly and evenly as it crouched there, waiting. Waiting on what? He didn't know. How long did dragons wait on things, anyway? He wondered suddenly if he was trapped. He hadn't thought of it before, but it might well be that just as the dragon wouldn't let him cover up the light, it wouldn't let him take it away, either. That would mean he was stuck in these rocks until the dragon tired of him and moved on.

Which might take a very long time, he realized. Time he didn't have to spare.

He took a moment to consider his options. He didn't have many to consider. He could stay where he was until the dragon grew bored and went away, or he could try leaving and hope the dragon didn't follow—or if it did follow, that it wouldn't follow for long. And that it wouldn't eat him.

He didn't like where his thinking was taking him, so he abandoned it in favor of trying to decide what else he might do to help himself. The long knife he carried was all but useless against something the size of the dragon, so there was no point in relying on that. Of course, any weapon was all but useless against a beast as big as that one. A whole army was probably useless.

He might try using his magic.

It was a reach. He didn't even know if his magic would work

in the Forbidding. But he didn't have anything else he could look to for help, and he had to do more than sit around waiting for the dragon to decide to eat him. His magic had worked with the moor cat they had encountered in the Slags, well enough that it had saved his life. It was conceivable that it might work here, as well.

But how should he try to use it?

He decided to find out first if it irritated the beast, because if it did, that was the end of the matter. He began by reaching out with his five senses, taking in everything he could discover about the creature, from the sound of its breathing to the baleful look in its sleepy eye. He scoured the monster from head to tail and back again, working at finding a connection, at trying to feel something of what the dragon felt. It was hard work, and in the end it yielded almost nothing.

Dragons, apparently, didn't give much away.

There was nothing for it but to try using the magic in the only way that seemed feasible—as a tool of communication. He had no idea how dragons communicated. All he had learned so far was how they breathed and how they reacted when irritated. Perhaps if he started there, a way might reveal itself. What made his efforts so difficult was that the dragon wasn't really interested in him at all; it was only interested in the darkwand. If it were the darkwand that was trying to communicate, he was certain that he would make better progress. But that wasn't possible, of course, so he would have to settle for using his own voice and hope the dragon gave something back.

He began with an imitation of the dragon's breathing, slow and heavy and raw. Enhancing his efforts with his magic, giving them life, it still took him a while to get it right. Eventually, he was sounding exactly like a miniature version of the larger thing. The dragon blinked—once, twice. When he began alternating the breathing with variations on the disgruntled hissing, the dragon lifted its head off its forefeet and looked at him. But it didn't seem inclined to do anything more than stare. Still, Pen kept at it, hoping for something more.

Nothing happened. Eventually, the dragon lost interest, lowered its head to its forefeet and went back to watching the dancing glow of the runes.

Pen sank back, exhausted. He was getting nowhere. Worse, he was growing weak from the effort. He had not eaten or drunk anything since arriving and could not remember when he had done so before that. It had been more than a day. His throat was parched, and he was feeling light-headed. If he didn't get away soon, he was going to pass out from lack of nourishment.

But what in the world was he supposed to do?

He spent several hours trying to figure that out. He used his small magic in every conceivable way to entice the dragon into communicating, but the beast simply ignored him. It lay there across the opening to his shelter, a great scaly lump that refused to move. With one eye fixed steadily on the darkwand and its intriguing runes, it dozed like a monstrous cat in front of a mouse hole, transfixed by the movement of the light. It barely stirred for the whole of the time it kept watch and then only to shift positions.

After a while, Pen dozed off. He wasn't sure how long he slept, as the gray light that marked daytime in the Forbidding was virtually unchanging from dawn to dusk. But when he awoke, he came to a decision. Rather than experiment further with the magic, he would simply try to leave. He had no idea if the dragon would permit it. But anything was better than doing nothing.

Holding the darkwand in front of him so as not to disturb or obscure the play of the light across its runes, he stood and gathered his strength. He was so weak by then that it took him a few minutes to do so. When he felt sufficiently ready, he took a single step out from his shelter.

The dragon blinked slowly.

He took another step. And then another.

The dragon's head came up, the horn-encrusted snout swung toward him, and a sharp hiss escaped through a pair of wide-flaring nostrils.

Pen stopped at once, held his ground, and waited. The dragon continued to watch him, head lifted, yellow eyes fixed. They stared at each other for long moments, each waiting to see what the other would do. Pen listened to the sound of the dragon's breathing and smelled its fetid stench. He forced himself to ignore the urge to gag. Instead, he focused on his determination to keep going.

When he felt he had waited long enough, he took another step.

This time the dragon slowly extended one great spiked foreleg in the manner of a cat toying with a mouse that had become its favorite plaything. It took its time, reaching out slowly and leisurely until the foreleg was stretched directly across the path Pen had intended to take, blocking it.

Pen stared at the dragon in dismay, then slowly backed into the rocks once more.

He spent the rest of the day hoping for a miracle. If only the dragon would grow bored. If only it would grow hungry. If only it would leave for just a few minutes. Didn't it have something else to do or somewhere else to go? Dragons must have lives like other creatures, habits and patterns of behavior that this one would be compelled to act on eventually. If he was just patient, if he could just wait it out, it would have to move on.

Daylight faded and night set in. It began to rain, a soft steady drizzle. Pen stuck his head far enough out of the shelter to catch a few drops in his open mouth, then used his cloak to gather a little more and sucked the water from the cloth. All the while, the dragon lay there, its scaly hide glistening, its eyes lidded, watching the darkwand and its glowing runes.

Eventually, Pen grew sleepy once more. He worried for a short while about what the staff would do when he closed his eyes, then dismissed the matter. Apparently, it would continue to glow, just as it must have done the previous night when the dragon was first attracted, just as it must have done while he was napping earlier. Otherwise, the dragon would have eaten him already. He wondered again how the staff could function independently of his thoughts when it had seemed before that it relied on them. He was missing something, wasn't picking up on what should have been obvious if he wasn't so hungry and exhausted. He wished he could think more clearly, that he could reason better.

He closed his eyes and dreamed about his home and his parents, about how things had been not two months earlier. He had been so anxious for an adventure, so willing for a change in his mundane existence. He had embraced the chance to go in search of the tanequil with Tagwen and the others. He had relished the excitement that would result.

He wished now that none of it had ever happened. He wished that things were back to the way they had been.

He fell asleep, and his wishes drifted away.

T WELVE

Dreams, bits and pieces of incomplete thoughts and unfinished stories, came and went with the swiftness of shadows and light in a cloud-swept forest. They were bright and bold and filled with promise, and Bek Ohmsford rode them like a bird across landscapes that stretched away forever. Sometimes he was in motion for the duration of the dream without ever touching the earth. Sometimes he felt the solid ground just long enough to be reassured that it was still there before winging away again. Nothing of what he saw was familiar to him. People came and went in the course of his travels, but he did not know who they were or why they were there. He had left his waking life behind; he had gone ahead of those he once knew.

It could have been a time of peace and contentment, but the dreams were interspersed with nightmares, and the nightmares were horrifying. Some were memories of things in his past, of creatures and events that he could never forget. Some were dark prophecies of what lay ahead if he could not turn aside in time. All were populated with predators that pursued him relentlessly, hunters of a sort that lacked recognizable purpose or intent. They came at him in waves, and no matter where he fled or tried to hide, they meant to have him.

Dreams and nightmares. There was no recognizable connection between the one and the other, and he transitioned between light and dark visions with distressing unpredictability. He slept, but his sleep was not sound or restful. The strange mix left him plagued with anxiety over which would appear next and how he would deal with it. He sought to combat them by gaining a measure of control, but his efforts fragmented and failed. He sought to wake, swimming upward through the waters of his sleep toward the bright surface of waking, but the distance was too great. Each time he felt himself getting close, the nightmares would come and drag him down again.

He did not know how long the ordeal continued, but it was a considerable time. At times, he came close to crying out his frustration at being unable to break the chains that bound him to a sleep from which there seemed to be no waking. Perhaps he did cry out. He couldn't be sure. But no one came to help. No one reached to take his hand and pull him clear. He struggled on alone, battling to keep the dark from overshadowing the light.

Then something changed. He did not know what it was or how it came to pass, but suddenly the dreams and the nightmares withdrew, fading like wind-blown dust. He was left wrapped in warm silence, in a quietude he had not experienced before. He found solace in his isolation. He was able to breathe normally, to ease down into a comforting sleep that allowed him to rest in the way he needed, deeply and peacefully.

For he had been injured, he knew. He had suffered damage of some sort, though he could not put a name to it. He slept because his body was trying to heal, but the injuries were severe enough that it was not certain yet that he could do so. He knew that without being able to say how. He knew it without being able to remember the specifics of what had happened to him. What he knew was he was fighting to survive and the battle had been going badly.

But the tide had turned and the storm had receded and his damaged body was healing. He dropped deep into a place in which a sense of calm prevailed and no dark things were allowed. He was so grateful for it that he wanted to cry in happiness and relief. The possibility that he had died occurred to him, but he dismissed it. His physical state did not feel like death, unless death was something very different than he had imagined. It felt like living, as if life had found him again.

Time passed, his sleep stretched away like a deep blue ocean, and the world about him began to take shape again. It assumed color and definition in the way a landscape is revealed by the lifting of a fog. As it did so, he found himself in the most beautiful gardens he had ever seen. The gardens were of varying sorts, different shapes and sizes and formations. Some were carefully cultivated beds, each given over to a flower and a theme. Some were hanging, vines and blankets of moss cascading off walls and trellises. Some were hillside and some meadow. There were flowering plants and bushes and grasses. Great ancient trees with broad leafy canopies shaded portions of the gardens while bright sunshine flooded the rest. The colors were vibrant and shimmering like the bands of a rainbow after a storm, blankets of one color and quilts of many. Amid the radiance rose the buzzing of bees as they pollinated flowers and the bright whistle and chirp of birds as they did all the things birds do. Wisps of cloud floated overhead, passing across the sun, casting strange, fleeting shadows on the earth.

It was a vision of paradise. Bek Ohmsford stood in the center of it and marveled. The gardens weren't real; they couldn't be. They were only dreamed. Yet in his sleep, he found them as real as the flesh of his own body.

"Welcome, Bek Ohmsford," a soft voice whispered from behind him.

He turned and found an old man staring at him, an ancient wearing a white robe and carrying a long, bleached wooden staff. White hair tumbled from his head to his shoulders and from chin to chest. His face was deeply lined and careworn in a way that suggested that he had been waging a long, hard fight. But his blue eyes were the eyes of a child, bright and interested and filled with expectation.

"This is my home," the old man said, a smile deepening the wrinkles of his face.

Bek looked around, confused. He was asleep; he was dreaming. But he felt as if he were awake. Was he?

"You have never been here," the old man continued, as if reading his mind. "But we have met before, a long time ago. Do you remember?"

Bek nodded slowly, realization dawning. "You are the King of the Silver River."

The old man nodded. "I am the last of my kind, the last of the Word's children. I am keeper of these gardens, guardian of the Silver River, and watcher over the Races. I am also friend to the Ohmsfords. Do you remember when I helped you?"

Bek did. He had been only a boy, dispatched on a quest he had barely understood to a land no one had ever visited before. He was called Bek Rowe then, and he did not yet know of his Ohmsford heritage. While his companions slept, the King of the Silver River had come to him to give him glimpses of the truth about himself and his sister, who was then the Ilse Witch and not yet Ard Rhys of the Third Druid Order. It was the beginning of a journey of discovery that would change the lives of brother and sister forever.

That had been a long time ago, in a different life.

"I have come to help you again," the old man said. "I do so because I promised your son that I would, although I am late in keeping that promise."

"Pen?" Bek asked in surprise.

"Penderrin, who has gone to find the Ard Rhys and bring her back to us. Penderrin, who is beyond our reach now." The seamed face dipped momentarily into shadow. "Walk with me."

Bek fell into step beside him, thinking again that what was happening wasn't real, that it was only a dream come to him in his sleep, but knowing instinctively that it was important nevertheless. He was being given a vision, a fever dream. In this vision, he might be shown truths that would help him find his son.

"Why is Pen beyond our reach?" he asked, impatient with waiting for the other to speak.

The aged head lifted slightly, one hand gesturing in a quick, dismissive motion. "It only matters that he is. It only matters that he must be. I would have told you sooner. I would have come to you. I promised him I would, weeks ago, when I first appeared to him in the Black Oaks, while he was fleeing from the Druids. He relied on me to tell you, to warn you of the danger. But I could not risk it. Had I told you, you would have gone in search of him. You would have promised me not to, but you would have gone anyway. Had you found him and rescued him, everything that must happen in its own time would have failed to happen at all."

Bek shook his head. "Are you saying you deliberately stopped me from helping Pen by not telling me what was happening to him?"

"I am saying that I stopped you from *thinking* you were helping him when in truth you would have been doing the opposite."

"I don't understand. Why are you telling me this now, since you chose not to before?"

The childlike eyes fixed on him. "Because now your help is needed. But it is needed in an entirely different way from before. And it will not be so easy to give."

They walked on, not speaking. Bek, floating within his vision, dreaming through his sleep, was a disembodied presence with thoughts and emotions, but a lack of substance. It left him feeling oddly removed from what was happening, even while participating. He experienced a need to grasp on to something hard and strong, something real and true. But the words of the King of the Silver River were all he had.

"This is what has happened, Bek Ohmsford," the old man said finally. "Druids within the order have conspired against the Ard Rhys. They found a way to banish her to a place from which she cannot return without help. Your son has gone to find her. He was asked to do so by me because I knew he was the only one who could make the journey and return. He did not think himself equal to the task, but I convinced him otherwise, and now he has convinced himself. He has crossed a barrier that no other may cross to reach the Ard Rhys. When he finds her, he will bring her back through that barrier, and they must both face their destinies."

He paused, looking over at Bek. The look seemed intended both to measure and to reassure. "Your son and your sister are inside the Forbidding."

Bek turned sharply toward the old man, but the heavy staff struck the earth hard enough that he could feel the blow through his feet. "Don't speak. Just listen. Shadea a'Ru and her minions believe they have orchestrated the imprisonment of the Ard Rhys through their own cleverness and skill, but they are mistaken. They have been tricked by one of the demons that dwell within the Forbidding. That demon is a warlock, a sorcerer of great power. Its goal was to exchange the Ard Rhys for another demon, bringing her into the Forbidding in order to free one of its own to come into this world. That exchange has taken place. The demon set free now seeks to destroy the Forbidding so that all those imprisoned since the time of Faerie will be freed. The demon must be stopped or the Four Lands are lost. You must stop it."

Bek shook his head. The charge weighed on him like a set of chains. "How?"

The old man slowed and turned to face him. The childlike eyes were kind and reassuring. "I did not come to you to tell you of your son or warn you of your own danger before this because Penderrin alone was needed to cross into the Forbidding, and you would have stopped him. Penderrin knows that he must find and rescue his aunt. He has the means and the will to accomplish this. I think he will succeed. But he does not know that when the Ard Rhys was sent into the Forbidding, a demon was sent into our world. He only knows that he must use the talisman he has been given to rescue your sister and bring her out again. He believes that is the extent of what is required of him. This was my decision, too. Telling him the rest would have crushed him."

He turned and began walking again, his steps careful and measured. Bek stayed at his side, waiting impatiently to hear more. All around them, breezes rippled the petals of the flowers and gave the impression that they walked upon the surface of a multihued sea.

"The talisman Pen carries is called a darkwand," the old man said. "Penderrin has already used it to cross into the Forbidding. Once he finds the Ard Rhys, he will use it to cross back again." He paused. "But there is one thing more he must do. What has been done must be undone—not in part, but in whole. In order for matters to be put right, everything that the combined magic of the demons and the Druids has brought to pass must be put back. Therefore, not only must the Ard Rhys be returned to this world, but the demon must be put back inside the Forbidding. The darkwand possesses the magic to do this, but only Pen has the power to wield it. He must find the demon and use the darkwand against it."

He looked at Bek. "You are the one who must see that he has the chance to do so."

"What am I supposed to do?"

The old man looked away again. "Two things. First, you must

find a way to protect your son when he crosses back through the Forbidding with the Ard Rhys. They must return to exactly the same place they went in—her sleeping chamber at Paranor."

"Where Shadea and the others will be waiting," Bek finished.

The old man nodded. "Second, you must find the demon. It will not look like a demon. It will look like something else. It is a changeling and takes the shapes of other creatures. This one is particularly dangerous. It absorbs its victims and becomes them. You must find out which disguise it has assumed and unmask it."

Bek looked down at his feet. He couldn't see them. He didn't seem to have feet, even though he could feel himself walking.

"The darkwand will reveal the demon," the old man said. "The talisman will respond to its presence. It will tell you who or what the demon is. If you get close enough."

The scent of tuberoses filled Bek's nostrils, sweet and heady. He shook off the distraction. "The wishsong told me that Pen was at Taupo Rough in the Upper Anar."

"The wishsong did not lie. But now he is inside the Forbidding."

"So I must go back to Paranor to find my son?"

The King of the Silver River turned to face him. "The path that leads to your son does not begin at Paranor. It begins at Taupo Rough, with Penderrin's companions. The Dwarf, the Rock Troll, and the Elven girl will provide you with keys to the doors that you must open to reach him."

He paused. "It is not within the Forbidding that Penderrin faces his greatest danger; it is here. The Druids will know where he has gone and be waiting for him when he returns. If they reach him before you do, they will kill him."

"Nothing will happen to my son while I am alive," Bek said at once.

He felt a subtle shift in his surroundings as he made that vow, a shimmering in the air, a ripple in the blankets and clusters of flowers, a whispering of breezes, and he knew he had committed himself in a way that could not be undone.

The old man nodded. "Do you feel the weight of your words, Bek Ohmsford? They have sealed your fate."

He stepped aside, an effortless movement that belonged to a much younger man. His ancient face lifted and changed. He was something else now, an old man no longer, another creature entirely, not human, not of this world. Bek backed away involuntarily, hands coming up to ward off the thing that stood before him.

The King of the Silver River had become a monster.

"See the future, human!" the monster rasped, teeth showing, eyes bright with hate. "Look upon it! When the Forbidding falls, your world becomes mine!"

Then the gardens withered before Bek's eyes, the flowers dying, their colors fading and their stalks wilting. The great shade trees lost their leaves, and their branches took on the look of bones blackened by fire. The grasses dried and cracked, and all sights and sounds of life disappeared. Overhead, the sky lost its brightness, its depthless blue becoming as gray as ashes, misted and empty.

Bek knew at once he was being given a glimpse of what his world would become if the demon set loose by the unthinking rebel Druids was successful in bringing down the Forbidding and setting free its denizens. When that happened, his world would become the world of the Forbidding. It would be the end of everything that mattered.

Do not fail.

The words echoed softly in the rapidly diminishing sweep of daylight, and Bek turned swiftly to seek the King of the Silver River, to protest that he would not, to give fresh voice to his promise to do as he had been asked, but found he was alone.

He woke with a gasp, jerked from his sleep by a sense of impending horror, his body racked by pain and fever and his mind roiling with wild, uncontrollable emotions that careened through him like tiny razors, jagged edges cutting. He tried to speak and could not. He tried to see, to discover where he was, but his surroundings were blurred and indistinct. He felt a slight rolling motion beneath him and heard the creak and groan of wood and metal fastenings, of lashings and the wind's steady rush. He was aboard a ship, but he couldn't understand how he had gotten there.

Penderrin is inside the Forbidding!

It was his first thought, and the realization all but stopped his heart. Pen, in that monstrous prison, where so much of what was evil in the world had been banished. That the King of the Silver River would send his son to such a place was impossible for him to understand. How could a mere boy have any chance at all of surviving?

How could he hope to find his aunt and bring her back again when everything he encountered would be looking to kill him?

But it is not inside the Forbidding that Penderrin faces his greatest danger.

"Bek, can you hear me?"

He took a deep, steadying breath and blinked against the haze that clouded his vision. A face swam into view, young and with skin ghostly pale, framed with a helmet of close-cropped black hair. A slender hand reached out to touch his cheek. "Can you hear me?"

He nodded, his mouth too dry to allow him to speak. Seeing his difficulty, she raised his head from the bedding on which he lay, brought a cup of water to his lips, and allowed him to sip.

Intense dark eyes peered into his. "Do you remember me?" she asked. "I'm Bellizen. I'm Trefen Morys's friend."

He nodded weakly, remembering nothing. "Where am I?"

"Aboard *Swift Sure*. You have been very sick, Bek. You were badly hurt. A knife wound deep in your side and an arrow through your shoulder. You have been delirious for two days, fighting off a fever. I think it has broken finally."

It all came back to him in a rush. His escape from Paranor with Rue, helped by the young Druid Trefen Morys, the battle to reach *Swift Sure* with the Gnome Hunters attacking from every quarter in an effort to stop them, his collapse moments after finally managing to reach the rope ladder, and then—nothing. This girl had been aboard the airship waiting for them. He remembered looking up into her face as they placed him on the deck and she bent to tend his wounds.

"You helped me," he said.

"Healing is my Druid skill," she replied, giving him a quick, reassuring smile. "Rue sails the airship, Trefen lends her a hand where it is needed, and I care for you. We each have our task. Mine seemed the harder for a time; I was afraid I was going to lose you."

He thought back to the dreams and nightmares of his sleep, already growing distant and vague in his memory. He thought back to the fever dream, to his vision of the King of the Silver River. He had turned the corner into recovery then, he believed. He had been near death, but the dream had brought him back to life. He shivered at the memory of what the dream had shown him, the images of a desiccated, demon-invaded world still fresh in his mind.

Bellizen gave him another few sips of water from the cup and then laid him back down again. "You still need to rest."

She started to rise, but he reached out for her arm. "Is everyone else all right?"

She turned back. "Rue was hurt, too, though not as badly as you. Several arrow wounds, but they were quick to begin healing once I cleaned them and applied the necessary salves. She moves slowly still, but she is able to sail the airship. Yours was the wound we were most worried about. I did not think we could save you unless we went to Storlock for help from the Healers, but Rue said that was the first place the Druids would look for you. I have some skill with infection and fevers. I worked the front on the Prekkendorran for a year in my early training. We decided not to chance going to Storlock."

She stopped, her face turning somber. "I am talking too much. You need to rest. I will tell Rue you are awake."

"Wait," he said again. He swallowed against the tightness in his throat, against the urgency he was feeling at needing to act on his dream. "How long have I been like this?"

"A little more than three days."

Three days. A lifetime. "Where are we?"

"Above the Streleheim, flying north along the western exposure of the Anar Mountains." She hesitated. "We stopped last night so that I could collect plants to treat your wound. And to allow you a chance to sleep on solid ground for one night. But Rue said we had to go on this morning, that we could not afford to delay longer. The Druids would be after us, and we needed to find your son before they did. That's where we are flying."

"To Taupo Rough?"

"To Taupo Rough. You told us just before you lost consciousness that this was where the scrye waters showed him to be."

But where he no longer was, Bek thought. Still, it was where they must begin their search for his companions, whose help the King of the Silver River had said they would need. Keys that would open doors to reach him—what did that mean?

"Rest now," Bellizen said, touching his arm as she rose.

He exhaled slowly and lay back, and she was gone before he could say anything more. He lay in the ensuing silence and stared up at the beams of his cabin, at the underside of the decking, at the windows through which the heavy streamers of daylight shone. It was all so familiar. But he had the feeling that the familiar was rapidly vanishing, and that what lay ahead would be as strange and new as the idea of Penderrin and Grianne inside the Forbidding.

He closed his eyes for a moment, to rest them, and immediately fell asleep.

THIRTEEN

When Bek Ohmsford woke, he was alone. He lay in his bed staring up at the same patch of the decking's underside that he had been looking at when he fell asleep—crossbeams, rough planking, wooden dowels, and iron nails all fitted into place. He felt the sway of the airship and knew she was still flying. Outside, the light was pale and washed of color. It was twilight, he guessed. Or the gray of a new dawn. He wondered how much time had passed. He wondered how far they had come.

For a while he lay without moving, allowing himself to come fully awake, taking time to test the limits of his strength. He found bound about his waist the compress that protected the knife wound, as well as the bandage to his shoulder. Both wounds ached, but no more than he might have expected them to. He moved his arms and legs without difficulty and even managed to lift himself up on one elbow, although the effort caused a sharp twinge in his injured side.

He lay back, feeling appreciably better than he had when he had first regained consciousness. Still, he accepted that he was not yet at full strength. He reached for the cup of water that Bellizen had left at his bedside and drank deeply. The water was sweet and cool, and it helped clear his head of sleep. He thought he might be able to get out of bed and up on deck if he took his time. But he would have to try standing and he would have to dress. It would not be easy.

He was working his way into a sitting position when the door to his cabin opened and Rue appeared.

"What do you think you're doing?" she snapped, rushing over and pushing him down again. Her face reflected a mix of concern and irritation, but it softened almost at once as she leaned down and kissed him. "Wait a bit. You're not ready yet."

"I feel better," he said.

"Apparently. But how you think you feel doesn't necessarily reflect how you really are." She sat down beside him. "Didn't Bellizen tell you how worried we were? You lied to me about that knife wound. It was much worse than you said."

"I just wanted to get out of there. I wasn't thinking about the wound."

"We almost lost you, Bek."

He smiled. "You can't lose me as easy as that."

"I hope not." She ran the tip of one finger across his cheek. "Losing you would be too much for me."

She kissed him again, and he kissed her back, holding her close, even though it hurt both his side and shoulder to do so. When she pulled away, she brushed back her short-cropped hair and shook her head in despair. "You risk too much, Bek Ohmsford. You take too many chances."

"I must have learned that from you," he answered, laughing. "Let's be honest for a moment. Who in the world ever took more chances than you?"

She nodded, conceding the point. "But you feel better, do you?" She held her hand against his forehead for a moment. "Your fever has broken; you're much cooler. Earlier, you were burning up. And delirious. Thrashing and talking about things none of us could understand. You were dreaming. Or having nightmares. Do you remember any of it?"

"I remember what matters," he said quietly.

Then he told her of his vision and of the words of the King of the Silver River. He was surprised to see her cry when she learned that Pen was inside the Forbidding. But immediately afterward she was angry and quick to blame Grianne. "If not for her, none of this would be happening." Their lives were caught up in hers, snared in her Druid machinations and political maneuverings, held prisoner by her web of intrigues and subterfuges. She might not be the Ilse Witch any longer, but as Ard Rhys she inspired the same hostility and enmity. Anyone connected with her, whether by blood or by alliance, suffered as a result. None of them would ever be free of her entanglements.

Bek tried to reason with her, but there was no doing so while her son was in such terrible danger and her anger so great because of it, so he quickly gave it up, instead turning the discussion a different way.

"You did the right thing by keeping us flying toward Taupo Rough. If the King of the Silver River is to be believed, our chance for helping Pen lies in first finding his companions."

She frowned at him. "*Are* we to believe him, Bek? Are we to believe any of those who harbor secrets? We know better than to trust the Druids. Should we trust a creature like the King of the Silver River any farther?"

Bek shrugged. "I think we have to. Pen trusted him."

"Which put our son inside the Forbidding. You make my point."

"But maybe we have to extend our trust a little farther in order to get him out again. After all, what other choice do we have? We haven't another way of reaching Pen."

"I hate this!" she snapped. "I hate that everything we do is dictated by these secret keepers, Faerie and Druid alike. Everything that has happened is their doing. We are just their pawns!"

He nodded. "I know what we are. But we are thinking pawns, and in the end we will make our own decisions. For now, we have to follow the path we have been put upon and hope that it leads us to where we want to go. That path takes us first to Taupo Rough."

She took a deep breath and exhaled slowly. "All right. Taupo Rough." She looked out the window at the graying light. "Dusk comes. You've been asleep for more than a day, but we traveled on while you slept. We should reach the village before dawn. You should go back to sleep while you can. Or would you like something to eat first?"

He chose to eat, and she sat with him while he did. He was heartened to find that her anger gradually lessened and her mood lightened, and he did not argue with her when she told him to go back to sleep afterward. She kissed him and told him she loved him, and he told her that he loved her, too. It was as much as they needed to say. It was enough to leave things at that.

He slept then, surprised to discover that sleep came again so quickly and easily. He was still sleeping when Rue reappeared to tell him that they were almost at their destination. She helped him sit up and then stand, and when he found he was strong enough to do more, she helped him dress and walked him up on deck. It was night still, but the first tinges of dawn were visible east along the crest of the mountains. The land they sailed through was stark and barren, a vast sweeping plain to the west that climbed into foothills east, which in turn rose to the jagged majesty of the Charnals. Small clumps of trees, tiny silver-web streams, and small lakes that reflected the moonlight brightened an otherwise rocky terrain. Bek knew that country. He had explored it with Rue once upon a time. But few expeditions went that way, and he had not been there in years.

Trefen Morys was at the helm and nodded to him as he climbed into the pilot box. "Good to see you looking well again," he said.

Bellizen came over from the port railing and joined them, her pale oval face shining with moonlight. "Are we close, Rue?"

Rue Meridian nodded, then said to Bek, "Tell them everything you told me. They need to hear it from you."

Bek did so, his words floating away from him as he spoke them in the soft rush of the wind, the night air swift and cool, the world vast and dark about their little circle. He covered everything, making certain to include the words of the King of the Silver River that suggested the Ard Rhys was alive and that Pen could reach her.

When he was finished, Bellizen spoke first. "It sounds so impossible. A boy is the only one who can bring the Ard Rhys back? A boy with no magic, no special skills?" She looked quickly at Rue. "I do not doubt his determination, but I do question the reason for the choosing of him."

"No more than I," Rue said. "But Bek keeps nothing from us; the secrets for which we seek answers belong to the King of the Silver River. If we wish to discover those answers, we will have to discover them another way. Pen might know some of them. The Ard Rhys might know the rest."

"We will seek those answers with you," Trefen Morys assured her quickly. "We will do whatever is necessary to find my mistress. If your son can lead us to her, then we will find him and help him as best we can. But first, it appears, we need to find his companions. Three were named. The Dwarf would be Tagwen. The Rock Troll would be Kermadec. Once, he was Captain of her Guard, and he remains her close friend. Taupo Rough is his home." He paused. "But who is the Elven girl?"

Bek shook his head. "I wish I knew."

He wished he knew as well why the King of the Silver River had made no mention of Ahren Elessedil. The Druids had said Tagwen had gone to him for help first before going to Penderrin. Shouldn't there also have been some reference to him?

But he said nothing of his worry to the others.

He stood at the railing and watched the ground sweep away as *Swift Sure* sped onward along the line of the mountains. Rue took several compass readings and directed Trefen Morys, whom she had allowed to keep the helm. She must have been working with him, Bek thought. The young Druid had no flying skills, no experience with weapons, and he had learned both in a very short time under less-than-ideal circumstances. But he was doing better than many would have.

The sky continued to brighten slowly, the darkness giving way to a silvery wash that gradually turned golden. Ahead, the buildings of a fortified settlement came into view, a village built back against a cliff wall. But there were no fires in the village and no signs of movement. Dark smears dotted the plains fronting the village walls, and the village itself had a ragged, neglected look. As they drew nearer, he saw that sections of the walls had been breached and the greater number of buildings were collapsed and blackened by fire.

"Are we in the right place?" he asked Rue.

She nodded, her face dark with concern. "This is Taupo Rough. Not what we expected, is it? Someone has been here before us."

Bek did not care to speculate on who that someone might have been. It was possible that the Druids had gotten to the village ahead of them, but the destruction did not look recent. There were no fires burning, no lingering curtains of smoke, no battle smells, nothing to suggest that anything had happened here for days.

They landed the airship at the edge of the walls, and while he stayed at the helm, the other three went down the rope ladder to have a look around. He hated being left behind, but as Rue sensibly

pointed out, he was too weak to be making long treks. So he con-
tented himself with watching their progress and trying to fit together
in his own mind the story of what had happened here.

By the time the sun was fully up, white-hot in a cloudless sky,
they were back, grim-faced and empty-handed.

"A battle was fought here perhaps two weeks ago," Rue reported.
"At least one Druid warship was brought down in the fighting and
burned. The remains lie out on the flats. So the battle was probably
between the Rock Trolls of the village and the Druids. There are
Gnome weapons and pieces of armor, so Gnomes probably fought in
the service of the Druids. Hard to tell for certain what happened, but
in the end the Trolls fled into the cliffs. There are caves in those
cliffs, and I would imagine tunnels that connect to the far side of the
mountains."

"This must have all happened because of Pen," Bek said. "This is
Kermadec's home. Pen and the others would have come to him for
help. The Druids tracked them here while we were imprisoned at
Paranor and tried to take Pen prisoner. Kermadec refused to give him
up. So the village was sacked."

Rue nodded, brushing back loose strands of her auburn hair. "But
where did Pen and his protectors go from here? What route did they
take?"

"They went in search of the darkwand," Bellizen answered her.

"Somewhere in these mountains," Trefen Morys added.

"Or somewhere beyond." Bellizen looked at Bek. "Can you track
your son's passage from here as you did at Paranor?"

Bek shook his head doubtfully. The battle had happened days
ago, and Pen had been gone from there a long time. He wasn't in the
mountains anymore; he wasn't even on the same world. In any case,
Bek's connection was with his son, not with those who had accompanied him. His magic might not allow him to track them as he
had Pen.

But he knew he had to try.

"There's nothing here for us," he said. "Not unless we try tracking
them through the tunnels. Why don't we fly to the other side of the
cliffs and see if we can pick up a trail?"

They did so, Rue taking the helm, not trusting anyone else to
navigate in a place where the winds could prove unpredictable and a
moment's inattention could send an airship into the rocks. Keeping

Bek beside her in the pilot box, she sent the young Druids to the starboard and port forward draws to work the lines by hand in case of heavy turbulence. But they were lucky that day. The winds were mild and the way into the mountains clear. *Swift Sure* sailed through gaps in the jagged peaks unhindered and unchallenged, and by midday they had reached a valley that lay between the peaks of the Klu.

While the airship hovered midway across the valley, Bek used the wishsong to seek out some sign of Pen or his companions. He had learned the trick from his sister years earlier. As the Ilse Witch, she had used the wishsong to track him. Later, on the long voyage home, she had showed him how. He would see if it could be made to work the same way for him.

It was something of a gamble to do so. Any use of his magic would alert Shadea and her Druids to their presence and remove any doubt about where they were. On the other hand, she would know already where they were going and what they were trying to do, so he really wasn't giving all that much away. And if she had discovered that Pen was inside the Forbidding, she might have lost all interest in pursuing them anyway. Whatever the case, without the use of the wishsong they had no way of knowing where to go.

Eyes closed for better concentration, he sang the magic, slow and smooth, like a carpet being spread across the valley floor, searching for traces of passage. He found several, all of them more than a week old and none distinct enough to identify. Frustrated, he spread his net a little wider, reaching deeper into the peaks ahead, into the mountains of the Klu that fronted the huge forests of the Inkrim.

There, far beyond anywhere he could see, he found traces of his son, tiny beacons in the ether. But the traces were unlike anything he had ever come across before, and for a moment he didn't trust what the wishsong was telling him. Still, his certainty that it was Penderrin and not someone else was so strong that he could not ignore it.

He broke off his efforts, the wishsong dying into silence. His breathing quieted and his eyes opened once more.

"I found him," he said. "Traces of him, anyway. Deeper into the mountains ahead, east." He paused, looking now at Rue. "But something's wrong. What I found wasn't familiar to me; it wasn't what I know of Pen. What I found of his passing was tinged with magic."

She stared at him. "Magic? Whose magic?"

"His own."

She shook her head. "That isn't possible. He doesn't have any magic. He's never had any magic. We both know that."

He held her gaze. "Nevertheless."

"You must be mistaken. You have to be."

He could tell from the way she said it that she needed him to be wrong, that she was frightened at the prospect that the Ohmsford heritage might have been passed on to her son after all. He could discern her thinking. She had believed Pen safely removed from the wishsong's influence, the bloodline dying out with Bek. What if she had been mistaken? What if the magic had simply lain dormant? It had done so with Bek. Was it so strange that it should do so with his son, as well?

"I don't think we can decide about this until we talk to Pen," he said carefully. "What matters is that I feel certain I've found his route of passage. We can track him now."

"What if what you've found is his passage coming out, rather than going in?" Trefen Morys asked suddenly.

It was an uncomfortable thought. There was no way to determine the answer from where they stood. There might not be a way to determine the answer once they reached the source. It might be a long, dangerous journey to their destination, and the journey might well yield nothing.

But it was all they had to work with. It was the only lead they had been given.

"I think we have to try following it for a time, at least," Bek offered, looking to Rue for support.

His wife studied him, her fine, clear features masking what she was feeling, keeping hidden the wash of doubts and fears he knew she must be experiencing. She stayed silent for a long time, considering. Then she nodded. "Bek is right. We have to try."

They turned *Swift Sure's* bow toward the Klu and flew east for the remainder of the day into peaks wrapped in storm clouds and layers of mist, buffeted by heavy winds. *Swift Sure* was battered and tossed and her occupants thrown from side to side. Bek was sent below to help protect his wounds, and the other three strapped on safety harnesses while on deck. By the end of the day, all three were drenched and freezing, their bodies aching and their minds numb from the effort of holding course and staying aloft. Snow was flying all about them in thick gusts, threatening whiteouts at every turn, cloaking cliff walls and passages alike so that the way forward remained an ever-changing mystery.

As darkness approached, Rue Meridian began to despair. If they did not get clear of the mountains quickly, she would have to set down, and there was nowhere for her to do that. Flying blind at night could have only one result. She called Bek back up on deck and had him use the wishsong again, searching for a way to go. But the magic failed Bek this time, refusing to give up anything at all that would help, leaving them adrift and at risk.

Finally, when it seemed that no help was to be had from any quarter and the outcome of their efforts unavoidable, the storms subsided and the peaks ahead opened into the Valley of the Inkrim. Rue took *Swift Sure* through as the last of the day's light gave way to a scattering of stars and no visible moon, just a faint brightening that allowed her enough illumination to set down at the edge of the trees at the rim of the valley.

They slept then, exhausted from their efforts. All but Bek. Awake and awash in fresh doubts, he sat alone in the pilot box, wrapped in a blanket, thinking about what they were doing. He understood the need for it; he understood as well the reasons. What bothered him was the number of uncertainties. Trefen Morys had been right about tracking Pen's passage. It was probably impossible to determine which way the boy was going, absent some physical evidence. He told himself that if they could locate just one of his companions, they would have a way of finding his son.

But he was bothered most by something he had kept from Rue. The traces of Pen he had found had been infused with wishsong magic. Not just any magic, but wishsong magic. He hadn't thought Rue needed to know that just yet. She was distressed enough about the presence of any magic where their son was concerned and would have been beside herself to learn that the magic had its origins in the Ohmsford bloodline. But there was no mistaking its nature. He should have felt a measure of relief; if Pen had the use of the wishsong, he was in a better position to protect himself. But in fact Bek was as upset about the prospect as his wife. He didn't want Pen to have the burden of the wishsong any more than she did. Too many generations of Ohmsfords had struggled with it. Too many had seen their lives altered irrevocably as a result—and not always for the better. It had been so with him. He had hoped that his son might have an easier road.

He thought about it for a long time. He tried to picture Pen within the Forbidding and failed. How could anyone imagine what that must be like? He knew what sort of creatures the Forbidding contained, but no one knew what it would feel like to be a human trapped there. That Penderrin should have been sent to find and retrieve Grianne was still something he could not fathom. The King of the Silver River had given him no reason for the choice of his son as rescuer. There would be a reason, he knew. And the reason might have something to do with Pen's use of the wishsong. Yet if that was so, why hadn't the Faerie creature come to Bek, who had more experience and better command of the magic? Why had Pen been chosen?

It had to be something else—something about Pen that wasn't true of Bek.

He fell asleep at some point and woke to the sound of the others coming up on deck. He was stiff from sleeping upright, but overall he felt better than he had the day before. He felt stronger, more ready. He was mending; he was coming back to himself.

The day was clear and bright ahead of them, the storms of the Klu left behind. After they had eaten from their steadily dwindling stores, Bek used the wishsong to seek anew the traces of Pen he had found the other day. He found them with little trouble. They were stronger, and he was better able to read them. The magic that had infused them a day earlier was more diverse than he had believed, a mix of couplings that involved his son and someone or something else. The source of the traces lay ahead, deep within the Inkrim.

After checking the radian draws and light sheaths for breaks and tears and finding everything intact, Rue took *Swift Sure* off the ground, pointed her east across the sweep of the forested valley, and sailed in search of Bek's findings.

It was nearing midday when Trefen Morys, who had been keeping watch at the bow for the better part of an hour, called back, "There are ruins down there!"

Rue dropped *Swift Sure* into a slow descent toward the canopy of the trees, following the young Druid's shouted directions. Within minutes, the ruins were visible to them all. Remnants of buildings sprawled for miles, a jumble of broken walls, columns, and battlements. What little remained had been overgrown by trees and scrub, enveloped by the foliage of the jungle. In places, wildflowers formed bright patches amid the blanketing shadows.

"There are people down there!" Trefen Morys shouted suddenly.

Bek went forward at once, picking his way gingerly across the decking to where the Druid stood. They were only a hundred feet above the canopy by then and able to see the whole of the valley clearly. As Bek came up beside him, Trefen Morys pointed. Gnarled, string-thin forms darted about the rubble at the edges of the ruins, creatures similar to Gnomes but clearly something else.

"Urdas," Bek said aloud.

He recognized them from earlier expeditions he had made into the Charnals. He saw them look up as *Swift Sure* hove into view, repositioning themselves to meet the newly perceived threat, brandishing slings and bows and arrows.

"Keep us flying, Rue!" he shouted over his shoulder.

"What are they doing?" Trefen Morys asked him.

He shook his head. "I don't know. Keep your eyes open."

He went back to the pilot box and climbed up beside Rue and Bellizen, telling them what he had seen. "They've ringed the ruins. I think they're looking for something. Maybe the same thing we're looking for."

He decided to use the wishsong again, to seek anew the traces of Pen's passing he had sensed that morning. He found them immediately, strong and clear and just ahead in the ruins. The magic was diffuse and fading, days old and no longer clearly defined. But its use had been powerful and reflected both determination and clear intent. Pen had experienced an epiphany or confrontation of major proportions. If he had survived that, Bek thought, then there was some reason to believe he could survive the Forbidding.

"Ahead, five degrees east southeast," he told Rue, pointing for emphasis.

Swift Sure altered course slightly and flew on, Rue holding the airship's speed down so that they could scan the ruins below for other signs of life. They were flying along the southern perimeter, and there were Urdas scattered all along it. They seemed reluctant to go farther in. Bek remembered that the Urdas were superstitious about places they considered sacred; the ruins might well be one such place. But the Urdas were clearly there for a reason. If they could not enter, then they were waiting for something that had.

"Smoke," Rue said suddenly, pointing off to the right.

From just beyond the main body of the ruins, separated by a series of deep, wooded, rifts, a column of black smoke rose from a crumbling blockhouse and tower. The Urdas were all about it, three and four deep within the cover of trees and rocks, showering the fortifications with darts and arrows and spears.

"I'd say we've found something," Rue offered, giving Bek a quick glance.

But it was not something that tracked to the traces of Pen's passing that Bek had detected. It was something entirely apart. He hesitated, wondering how advisable it was to become distracted by something that might have nothing at all to do with what they were looking for.

"All right," he said finally, "let's have a look."

FOURTEEN

It was like flying into a hornet's nest.

Swift Sure descended in a long, slow spiral, drawing the attention of the band of Urdas below. Bek had hoped that their appearance alone would prove startling enough to these superstitious people to make them withdraw. But instead of bolting back into the trees and seeking cover, the Urdas immediately turned their weapons on the airship. Trefen Morys barely had time to shout a warning from the bow when a hail of spears and darts struck the underside of the vessel and a wash of arrows arced over the railing in a deadly sweep.

Everyone ducked behind the protective railings as Bek took *Swift Sure* back up again, out of reach of the attack. As he did so, Trefen Morys came running back.

"There are Rock Trolls down there in that tower!" he shouted up to Pen. "They were waving to us for help!"

Bek turned to Rue. "Load both the port and starboard rail slings. Maybe we can drive the Urdas far enough back into the trees to gain space to get a ladder down."

The starboard rail sling was still in place from their flight out of Paranor, and with help from Trefen Morys it took Rue only minutes to set up the port weapon and arm them both. Placing the young Druid on the former and herself on the latter, she sent Bellizen amidships to stand ready to lower the rope ladder, then signaled for Bek to take *Swift Sure* down again.

It was trickier going in the second time. The Urdas were waiting, neither awed nor frightened of the airship. Even from high up, Bek could tell that they were aggressively hostile. Whatever had incensed them had stirred their anger to such intensity that they were beyond caring what happened to them so long as they stopped any rescue attempt. They were clustered at every quarter of the tower walls, and as soon as *Swift Sure* came within range, they attacked. Bek kept his hold on the airship steady to give Rue and Trefen Morys a chance to chase them off, but even after both rail slings were emptied twice into the attackers, they held their ground, refusing to fall back. Gnarled, hairy forms swarmed through the wooded ravines, keeping the tower and its occupants besieged.

Bek took the airship out of range once more, trying to think what else they might try.

Rue returned from the railing and climbed into the pilot box. "Our weapons aren't going to work, Bek. If we want to get those Rock Trolls out of that tower, we have to take a different approach."

She leaned close so that only he could hear. "Could you use the wishsong to help?"

He stared at her in surprise. She hated his magic, hated the legacy that went with it—so much so that he had barely used it since coming back from Parkasia. The search for their son had marked his first serious attempt in several years. In truth, he wasn't even sure he knew after so long how to employ it in the way that would be necessary.

"I understand," she said, reading the look on his face. "But we don't have any choice."

She was saying that if they wanted to help Pen, this was what it was going to take. The wind shifted and blew across his face, unexpectedly chill and biting as it came down off the mountains. He held her gaze a moment longer, then nodded. "Take the helm."

He went down on deck to where the young Druids stood waiting and motioned them over to the rope ladder so that both could help with the rescue effort. Then he moved forward to the bow and looked down.

Urdas swarmed through the trees below, too many to count. Rue

was right. Even a dozen rail slings wouldn't be enough to chase them
off. A more effective weapon was needed, and there was nothing
more effective than the wishsong when it was used in the right way.
Grianne had taught him so years ago when she had tried to kill
him. He thought it ironic that he would use that lesson now to try to
save her.

"Take us back down!" he shouted to Rue, a sudden gust of wind
nearly obscuring his words. It was heavy enough that it shook the
airship from bow to stern. "Slowly!"

He glanced north to where huge storm clouds were beginning to
build on the horizon, sifting down through the peaks toward the
Inkrim. A change in the weather was coming, and it did not favor
their efforts. If they failed to get a ladder down soon, given the nature of storms in that region, it might not be possible to try again for
days.

He looked down again at the Urdas, trying to think how to force
them to move back from the walls of the tower. He could do some
things safely with the wishsong, but he did not want to risk trying
too much after so many years of no practice. The magic was powerful and at times unpredictable. Using it the wrong way could prove
disastrous. If it failed to respond as intended, it might send them all
crashing down with the airship.

The wind gusted across his face again, and suddenly he remembered that the Druids favored using the elements as allies in their
wielding of magic. Perhaps he could do the same here.

He brought up the wishsong in a soft hum, calling it to life, feeling it come awake and then flood through him with a slow, rising
heat. He kept his gaze fixed on the scene below as he began to give
the magic a shape and a form, a sense and a purpose. He found the
wind currents that preceded the coming storm and stirred in the
magic. The currents gained force and consistency, and as they gusted
about him they began to take on a new intensity. What had begun as
a series of uneven bursts now became a steady blow. Changes of
pitch evened and slowly built into a howl that suggested the cresting
of a tidal wave.

The Urdas began looking around in confusion and then in fear.
A storm of that kind wasn't something they understood. They were
unfamiliar with winds of such magnitude. They crouched lower, and

then began to back away from the tower toward the deep woods, their superstitious nature warning them that the elements were spirit-driven.

Bek built on the power of his magic, adding fresh layers, giving the wind an extraordinary sound and feel, a roar that began to shake trees and earth alike. He did not look back at Rue, trusting her to continue *Swift Sure's* descent, to understand what he was doing and not be frightened by it. He didn't know what the Druids were thinking, but he couldn't spare time to worry about them. He had the wind tearing across the landscape by then, scattering the Urdas in all directions, their determination to stand fast shattered.

Then the treetops were right below them, and the outer walls of the tower became visible through the gaps. He risked a quick glance back at Trefen Morys and Bellizen and saw them dropping the rope ladder over the side of the railing, down to the besieged Trolls. Almost immediately bulky forms began to emerge, scrambling from their concealment, some helping others, all of them moving swiftly for the ladder. But then they ducked back again, unable to advance. Bek felt his strength beginning to fail, and forced himself to push harder to keep the wind in place. The Trolls had still not begun to climb the ladder, and the Urdas were beginning to reemerge from the trees. Rue was yelling something at him, but he couldn't hear what. He intensified the magic once more, feeling his hold on it slipping away.

Then Bellizen was beside him, frantic. "Your magic is too strong, Bek! The force of the wind is keeping the Trolls from climbing the ladder!"

He realized it was true, that his efforts at keeping the Urdas at bay were keeping the Trolls pinned down, as well. Rue must have been trying to tell him as much. He slowed his efforts, letting the wind diminish. Within the ruins of the tower, the Trolls recognized their opportunity and scrambled for the ladder. The Urdas, in response, rushed to stop them.

There was nothing more Bek could do to help. Any further use of the magic to intensify the wind would do as much damage as good. The Trolls would have to make it on their own. He kept the wind in place a few moments longer, tuning its sound to an earsplitting shriek in an effort to frighten the Urdas. But the Inkrim natives were no longer intimidated, having seen what was happening and become newly enraged at the thought of losing the intruders to an airship rescue. They came at the Trolls in waves, weapons loosing, the air filling with missiles. Two of the Trolls were struck, and one fell to his death. The others pressed on, climbing steadily through the hail of fire, helping each other as they did so. One of them, he saw, carried a smaller figure tucked under one arm, a squat blocky form that could only be a Dwarf.

Then the Trolls were over the side of the railing and on board the ship, and Rue was lifting away, taking them quickly out of range of their attackers. Bek broke off his efforts with the wishsong, now thoroughly spent, and hurried over to the newcomers. Seven Trolls and a Dwarf, he saw. The Dwarf wrestled free of the Troll who was carrying him and stood clinging to the rail, breathing hard.

"Tagwen?" Bek asked, coming up to him.

Tagwen looked over, his face ashen and his mouth a tight line. There was blood on his neck and right arm from wounds, and his clothing was torn and soiled.

He blinked rapidly at Bek. "I don't ever want to come to this place again!" he snapped. "Not ever!"

Then he fainted.

There was no time for an exchange of information or for anything but making a quick escape from the fast-approaching storm. If it caught up with them over the Inkrim, their efforts to get free of the Urdas might come to nothing. With Bek at the helm, Rue and Trefen Morys worked the draws and light sheaths by hand to gain speed and maneuverability, heading south and west toward the relative safety of the mountain peaks below the clouds and winds building north. *Swift Sure* skated hard across the long stretch of the valley, buffeted and tossed as storm winds gusted ahead of rain and dark skies. Lightning began to flash in the heart of the encroaching dark, and thunder rumbled ominously across the heavens in long, crackling peals.

On the decks below the pilothouse, Bellizen worked on the injured Rock Trolls. Two of them were badly hurt, wounded by Urda weapons. According to Kermadec, who had managed to say a few words to Bek before *Swift Sure* set sail, his little company had tried to slip past the Urdas during the night, convinced that any attempt at fighting to get free was useless. By then, Pen had been gone for almost a day, and they were desperate to find a way to help him. But the Urdas, furious at what they perceived to be a deliberate violation of sacred ground, had been keeping close watch on the intruders and had no intention of letting them escape. They reacted swiftly to the attempt, catching them out in the open and killing two outright. The surviving Trolls and Tagwen had fled into the tower, where they had remained, trapped and under attack.

Rain struck *Swift Sure* a broadside blow that sent her scudding sideways across the roof of the forest. Bek righted her quickly, trying not to think about Pen and what had happened in the ruins days earlier, concentrating instead on getting them across the valley to the relative safety of the mountains. Inside the peaks, they could find protection from the storm and cross into the valleys beyond. But the rain descended in torrents, inundating the decks and those clustered on them, leaving the entire ship sodden and dripping. Visibility was dropping fast, and Bek turned the ship farther south in an effort to run before the storm and remain clear of its impenetrable shroud of rain and mist.

Then lightning struck the mainmast, dancing down its length and along the conductors to the hull, sparking and flashing in the near dark. The Trolls flattened themselves against the deck until Bellizen signaled for help to get the injured below. Staggering across the slick wood with their burdens, the Trolls did as she asked, and soon everyone had disappeared below, leaving Bek, Rue, and Trefen Morys to sail the airship.

They were flying dangerously low, trying to slip the stronger winds at the higher elevations. But radian draws, stays, and sails were all giving way, tearing loose or shredding, slowing eroding *Swift Sure's* maneuverability. Bek held the airship as steady as he could, relying on the power stored in the diapson crystals to keep her flying. When that was gone, they were finished. He could make out gaps in the mountain peaks ahead, dark passages to the valleys beyond, and he pointed toward them as the storm closed about.

The winds howled like a living thing. They slammed into *Swift Sure* with devastating impact, knocking her off course, forcing Bek to wrestle her back into line again. Rain descended in sheets, and visibility dropped to nothing. Even the dark gaps for which they were headed began to fade. The storm was sweeping the whole of the Inkrim now, a great roiling mass of wind, rain, and darkness.

Then abruptly the mountains ahead disappeared and the gaps toward which *Swift Sure* had been heading were gone.

We're not going to make it, Bek thought.

For heart-stopping minutes, they hung suspended in a gray, fathomless void, directionless and lost.

Then the curtain of rain lifted and the rock walls loomed out of the rain-soaked darkness once more, massive slabs of stone lifting thousands of feet into the mists. Bek caught sight of a gap between them and banked *Swift Sure* sharply toward its dark maw.

Seconds later, they were inside a craggy split that was as dark and still and windless as a subterranean passage.

"Savages!"

Atalan spit the word out as if to rid himself of its bitter taste. It was a word he had used three times in the last two sentences by Bek's reckoning. Apparently the bitterness had a tendency to linger.

"Killed four of us for no better reason than to punish us for coming into those ruins! A place of dead things! Nothing there but bones and rubble and monsters like that tree!" His blunt Troll features were unreadable, but his eyes were fierce. "We should come back here with the rest of our people and wipe them out!"

He was incensed, even now, hours later. They were seated at the bow—Atalan, Kermadec, Tagwen, the young Druids, Rue, and Bek. They made an odd-looking group. The Trolls were giants with skins of bark and flat, virtually featureless faces. The Druids were much smaller and impossibly young. The Dwarf was squat and solid, his thick beard like a mask. And Bek and Rue, fatigued and weak from the wounds they had received during their flight out of Paranor, had the look of the walking dead. *Swift Sure* hung anchored above a valley floor somewhere deep within the Klu, west almost to the Charnals. The Inkrim and the storm had been left behind. It was nightfall, and the Trolls who had been wounded were sleeping below. Everyone was exhausted.

Kermadec shifted his large frame and leaned back against the ship's railing. His rough face was impassive, his voice calm. "Let it be,

Atalan." He nodded at Bek and Rue. "So young Penderrin has found a way into the Forbidding, after all. Your son is nothing if not resourceful. He has kept his wits about him."

"He has his wits, but does he have the use of magic, as well?" Rue asked, reminded suddenly of what Bek had revealed of the traces of her son's passage.

Kermadec shrugged. "He has some. He has that ability to read the responses of living things. He can discern their thinking from that. Like the lichen. Like that moor cat." He glanced at Tagwen. "It's a magic I wouldn't mind having, Bristle Beard."

"He said it was a small magic," the Dwarf muttered. He scowled at Kermadec. "Having seen nothing to suggest otherwise, I am inclined to take him at his word. Penderrin is not given to exaggeration."

Tagwen had recovered from his faint, though he was still embarrassed about the collapse. Kermadec had spent a long time reassuring the Dwarf that it had nothing to do with his courage, but was a result of exhaustion and stress. Anyone might have suffered the same indignity, and it would not be mentioned again. Tagwen, however, did not appear convinced.

"There is the magic he generated during his encounter with the tanequil, as well," Trefen Morys pointed out. "To create a talisman of such power, a tremendous amount of magic would have to be released. Even if it didn't come from Pen, traces of it would cling to him. And he carries the darkwand with him. Any reading of magic attached to Pen would be influenced by that."

It was a reasonable explanation, and even Rue seemed to accept it. Only Bek knew that the reasoning was wrong. The readings given him by the wishsong had told him that the traces of his son's passage encompassed only magic that belonged to him. The blood connection between father and son was too strong for him to be mistaken. Pen had uncovered a form of magic that was still a mystery, possibly even to himself.

"I am very sorry to hear that Ahren Elessedil is dead," he said to Tagwen, changing the subject.

The Dwarf looked down at his hands and shook his shaggy head slowly. "He was a brave man, Bek Ohmsford. He gave his life so that the rest of us could go on. We would not have reached Kermadec and Taupo Rough, let alone Stridegate and the tanequil, if not for him."

"And the Elven girl is his niece?"

"Khyber Elessedil. Tough as old leather, that girl, though nearly as young as Penderrin. She has the Elfstones. Took them from the Elessedils and brought them to Ahren so that he would teach her how to use them. Turned out he had no choice. She used them in the Slags to sink the *Galaphile*, then again later to help us on our journey here. She had them with her when she disappeared in Stridegate."

"But you think that she boarded one of the Druid airships that took Pen to Paranor?" Rue asked.

Tagwen looked at Kermadec and came to some unspoken agreement. "Something might have happened to her in the ruins after she left us and went in search of Penderrin, but I don't think so," the Dwarf declared. He looked up. "She was very close to the boy and determined to help him reach the Ard Rhys. I think she found a way, and that's why he was able to get into the Forbidding after the Druids took him prisoner."

"Well, the fact that the King of the Silver River told Bek in his dream that an Elven girl is one of the three who will help us reach Pen suggests you are right. But where is she now?"

"She must be at Paranor," Kermadec answered with another shrug. "Waiting for us."

"Then we must go there to help them," Tagwen declared firmly. "It was the promise I made to young Penderrin before they took him, and I intend to fulfill it."

"As do I," Kermadec agreed.

"How, exactly, are you going to go about doing that?" Bellizen asked suddenly. Starlight reflected in her ink-black eyes. "Do you have a plan?"

Neither of them did, of course. No one did. There was a long silence as they pondered her question. They had been so consumed with reaching Paranor that none of them had given much thought to what they would do once they were there. It wasn't at all clear, they realized as they reflected on the possibilities, what their course of action should be.

"What are we up against at Paranor?" Bek asked finally, looking from Bellizen to Trefen Morys. "How much support does my sister have?"

Trefen Morys shook his head. "Very little, I'm afraid. There are a handful of Druids who openly support her and will stand with her when she returns, but most have been dismissed from the order. Those who remain support Shadea. It isn't that they believe so strongly in her; it's more that they mistrust your sister. She has never been able to shed her image as the Ilse Witch, not entirely."

"Some will stand with her when she returns," Bellizen added. "But only some, and I do not think we can count their numbers with any degree of certainty. Some will stand with her because, like us, they believe in her. Some will stand with her because they have seen how badly Shadea a'Ru has dealt with her power. But most will take no stand at all."

"That works both ways, of course," Kermadec pointed out. "They do not choose to stand with her, but will not stand with Shadea, either. That gives us a chance."

"Why do you support her?" Rue asked Bellizen, glancing at Trefen Morys, as well. "Why have you taken her side?"

Bellizen blushed. "It is not easy to explain. I do so in part because she was kind to me when others were not. She brought me to Paranor at the suggestion of another Druid, from a village in the Runne where my talents were considered abnormal and my safety threatened. I do not know how she found out about me, but she told me that I belonged with her. I believed that. She has never given me cause to think badly of her or to want her gone. I think she is the Ard Rhys we need. I think she understands the purposes of magic better than anyone."

"I came from a village close to Bellizen's," Trefen Morys added. "We did not know each other before Paranor, but have become friends since. I came to Paranor on my own, seeking a chance to study with the Druids. My mistress gave me that chance. She gave me responsibilities and taught me herself on more than one occasion."

"She is a great lady." Bellizen bit her lip, glancing quickly at her companion. "Those who follow her are mostly younger and never knew her as the Ilse Witch. The others, the older ones, cannot seem to forget. They think of her still as a dark creature, capable of reverting without warning. They do not know her as Trefen and I do. They are less forgiving because their lives are too deeply rooted in the past."

"They are not alone," Bek said quietly. "Perhaps that is just the way of things." He surveyed the faces of the others. "Very well. We know what we have to do. We have to find a way into the Keep and the sleeping chamber of the Ard Rhys. That is where Penderrin and Grianne will reappear when they return from the Forbidding."

He almost added, *if they can find a way back,* but he caught himself just in time. Rue didn't need to hear him saying anything about the odds. She understood them well enough.

"It is more complicated than that," Trefen Morys interjected quickly. "We have to find a way to be inside the sleeping chamber at just the right time. We have to devise a way of knowing exactly when Pen and my mistress will reappear. If we don't choose the right moment, Shadea and her allies will find us out."

The little company went silent, dismayed at the prospect of being stopped after they had come so far and endured so much. But the task the young Druid had just described seemed impossible.

Bek turned to Tagwen. "The King of the Silver River said that the keys to helping Pen were in the hands of his companions— Kermadec, Khyber Elessedil, and yourself. Maybe we should start there. Can you think what he might have been talking about? Is there some special kind of help that you can give us?"

Tagwen considered the question. "Well, there is one possibility," he said after a moment. "I know a way into Paranor using tunnels that run beneath the bluff to the furnace room and continue all through the walls of the Keep. The Ard Rhys showed them to me once, a maze of passages. She used magic to block those leading to her rooms, but perhaps your own magic can undo hers."

"So we can reach the sleeping chamber unseen if I can remove my sister's safeguards?" Bek asked.

The Dwarf nodded rather reluctantly. "Perhaps. If Shadea hasn't discovered the tunnels as well and set traps of her own."

"We'll have to risk it," Bek declared at once. "We've risked worse already to get where we are. Kermadec, what of you?"

The Rock Troll knotted his great hands and looked at Atalan. "Brother, I think the Trolls need to show the Four Lands where we stand in this business. Marching against the Urdas is a waste of time and purpose. We need to march on Paranor and the Druids instead. They attacked Taupo Rough and drove our people out. The attack was unprovoked. Dismissing the Troll guard while it was still in service to the Ard Rhys is insult enough, although we could have endured it. But attacking our home is beyond acceptable. Perhaps we should repay their visit with one of our own."

Atalan's response was a slow, wicked grin. "Let's pull down the walls around their ears!"

"Or at least pull the wool over their eyes—a distraction to give you time to get into place." Kermadec glanced at the others. "Several thousand Rock Trolls gathered at the gates will be something that not even the Druids can ignore. If we must, we will come through those gates to your aid, but at the very least we will keep those snakes pinned down within their own fortress for the time it takes for our mistress to deal with them as she chooses."

"And deal with them she will, you may be sure," Tagwen grunted, looking almost happy.

"That leaves Khyber Elessedil," Bellizen said. "What of her?"

"Her purpose seems easier to divine," Bek responded quickly. "She carries the Elfstones given her by Ahren Elessedil. They are seeking-stones, and I think finding the demon that has crossed over from the Forbidding will be our first order of business after my sister returns. The Elfstones will make that task much easier."

He looked from face to face in the darkness. "We have at least the beginnings of a plan. I think that is the best we can hope for."

"What I don't understand," Rue declared suddenly, "is why the King of the Silver River didn't make this business of the keys and the companions clearer to you in your dream, Bek. He could have told you what purpose Kermadec and Tagwen and Khyber Elessedil were to serve. Why didn't he do that?"

"Faerie creatures and shades are secretive and seldom speak the whole truth," Bellizen ventured.

But Bek shook his head. "I think it is something else. I think we were given a starting point, but nothing more. The future remains undecided. Things may change as events unfold, and we must be ready to change with them. If the King of the Silver River had told me in my dream exactly what the keys were, we might have become too reliant on his words. As it is, we remain uncertain that we have it right. He wants that. He wants us to find our own way. He wants us to understand that the way is not yet determined."

There was a long silence as the others contemplated his words. They knew where they must go and what they must do, but they still did not know how they would accomplish it. The future was a mystery. It was the way the world had always worked. It was the way it would work here.

"We must leave at once," Tagwen declared. "We have no idea how much time remains before the Ard Rhys and young Penderrin cross back."

But Bek shook his head. "No, Tagwen, we need to rest first. We'll stay where we are until dawn, sleep while we can, and fly north tomorrow to Kermadec's people. Once the Trolls are safely delivered and can begin their preparations for a march on Paranor, the rest of us will go ahead to search for Khyber Elessedil."

"And to discover when my mistress and your son will reappear within the Keep," Bellizen added quietly.

It was a disturbing reminder of how difficult the days ahead were going to be.

One by one the members of the company rose and went off to sleep. Most had not slept in days and were exhausted. Bek was the exception. Better rested than the others, he went back up into the pilot box to keep watch.

He was surprised when he found that Rue was following him.

"You should go to sleep," he said, turning back to stop her, reaching out to touch her cheek. "You've slept less than anyone."

She nodded. "I'll sleep soon enough. But I have to say something to you first. Whatever else happens, Bek, I intend to make certain that once Penderrin gets free of the Forbidding, he is kept safe. I intend to protect him from Shadea a'Ru and the rest of those monsters. I don't care what it takes. I don't even care what happens to me."

She was almost in tears as she finished. He tried to hold her, but she pushed him away, refusing to be comforted, defiance on her features. "Promise me that you will do the same."

"You know you don't have to ask me this," he said. "You know I feel the same way you do."

Tight-lipped, she nodded. "I do know it. But I also know that your sister is involved, and that her interests may conflict with ours. Her plans for Pen may not be acceptable. So I need to hear you say it, just in case that happens. I need to hear you promise that if a choice is necessary, you will choose our son."

A sadness inside left him hollow and sick at heart. He knew he would never be able to resolve his wife's feelings—her mistrust and her suspicions—for his sister. He understood why, and he did not blame her. Had he been in her shoes, he would have felt the same.

He reached for her hands, and this time she did not back away. "I promise," he said. "Nothing bad will happen to Pen. No chances will be taken with his safety. His needs come before those of Grianne and the Druid order."

She came into his arms then, reaching to hold him close, her cheek placed against his, her mouth so close to his ear that he could hear her breathing.

"I'm sorry I had to ask that," she whispered.

"Don't be. Don't be sorry for anything."

"I wish Big Red were here."

"I wish Quentin were here."

But her brother was somewhere off the coast of the Blue Divide, flying his airship in service to whoever had paid him most recently, and Quentin Leah was dead two years, never fully recovered from the wounds he had received in Parkasia. Bek thought often of them both, and thinking of them made him wish he could turn time back far enough for them all to be together just once more. But life didn't give you second chances at such things. Life just swept you along and never took you back to where you had been.

"It will be all right," he whispered.

He had said that to her once before and had not been certain it was true. This time, for reasons he could not explain, he felt that it might be.

FIFTEEN

When he was finished speaking, Shadea a'Ru studied Pyson Wence as if studying an interesting insect, glanced momentarily at Traunt Rowan, and then turned her back to both of them and looked out the window into the fading afternoon light.

"Tell it to me again," she said softly.

She managed to keep the rage from her voice, but it radiated from her body like heat off sunbaked earth in midsummer. She sensed their trepidation, their uncertainty, but she let them live with it as the silence between them lengthened.

"I really don't see the point in going over it a second time," Pyson Wence replied.

She could picture his exchange of looks with Traunt Rowan, could picture as well the sullen, gimlet-eyed stare, the one that waffled between boredom and disdain, he was giving her back. She could picture the way his sharp Gnome features were tightening, eyes narrowing and mouth twisting into a crooked line. She had seen that look often enough to have it memorized. She knew when to expect it. Even thinking of it enraged her further.

"I just want to be sure I didn't miss anything," she said.

She remained turned away so that they couldn't see her face. The silence returned and lengthened slowly as she waited to see which of them would speak next. Until then, Pyson had done all the talking.

That was unusual, given the fact that it was Traunt Rowan who normally did the talking for them both. He was the one who stayed calm when there was bad news to deliver or an untenable position to defend. He was the steady one. Pyson was the weasel, the sly one, the manipulator, and perhaps they had decided that his skills were what would work best in their current predicament.

If they had possessed an ounce of sense between them, they would have realized that nothing would save them.

Pyson cleared his throat. "There is nothing to be gained from going over it all—"

"Tell it to me again!" she screamed, wheeling now to fix him with her white-hot glare.

Her tall, muscular body was taut and flexed, as if she might attack him. He blanched at her words, at her posture; he wilted under her glare. He turned small and insignificant. But he was quick-witted and adaptable, and he could return to form in a moment's time, so she gave him no hint of compassion, no suggestion that his lifeline would extend beyond the next moment.

"Cat got your tongue, Pyson?" she spit, taking a quick step toward him, causing him to take several back. "Is the task too difficult for you? Is repeating the words you just spoke too onerous, too demanding? I want to hear them again, Pyson. I want to hear you tell it all to me again! Now!"

"Let him be," Traunt Rowan said, speaking for the first time.

She shifted her angry gaze instantly. "Oh, so you would speak in his place, then? Do so, Traunt Rowan. Amuse me."

"No one is amused, Shadea. Your sarcasm is wasted. We are as angry as you are about what has happened. But it isn't anything we could have avoided. We thought the boy safely locked away."

"Yes, I'm sure you did!" she snapped. "Very much the way you thought his parents were safely locked away. But they escaped as well, didn't they? In fact, they escaped first! Odd. You were given some indication that your security was not all that tight, but that doesn't seem to have made any difference because you didn't change anything and so the boy escaped, too!"

Traunt Rowan shook his head. "The parents escaped because two of our number, misguided believers in the right of Grianne Ohmsford to be considered Ard Rhys even past all reasonable hope, helped them escape. Young Druids—Trefen Morys, whom we mistrusted already, and a girl about whom I know almost nothing. If not for them, the boy's parents would still be here, locked away. But we will get them back again."

She laughed at him. "You sent out word that you have their son, thinking that they will march right back to Paranor when they hear the news. You are deluded. They know what will happen if they return. Even to save their son, whom we don't, in fact, have anyway! You underestimated them once and you are doing so again! Besides, it makes no difference now whether we have them or not, does it?"

She stalked across the room to where the door to her sleeping chamber stood closed, flung it open, and knocked the Gnome guard who crouched with his ear to the door all the way across the hall and into the wall beyond, where he lay stunned and bleeding.

"Try to listen in on my conversations again, and I will cut your throat," she hissed, speaking to him in his own tongue, her voice thick and guttural in the Gnome way. "No one is to come near this door again until I open it!"

Without waiting for a response, she slammed the door shut, wheeling back on the other two. "They listen to everything, your trusted followers, Pyson. They listen and report to you, but that's going to stop right now."

Terror flickered in Pyson Wence's yellow eyes. She watched it shift into a hint of desperation and shook her head in disgust. "You are hopeless." She glanced disdainfully at Traunt Rowan. "Both of you."

She stalked across the room to the window and stared out into the coming night. She wished it would close around the Keep and swallow up everyone in it who had failed her. She wished it would swallow those traitors who had helped the Ohmsfords escape. She wished it would swallow up those fools who had taken sides against her in the matter, starting with Sen Dunsidan and Iridia Eleri.

She wheeled back around. "The parents escaped because you weren't smart enough to expect them to try!" she snapped at Traunt Rowan. "The boy escaped because you weren't smart enough to learn from the example of the parents! You took away the staff, you locked him in a cell, and you thought that was the end of it. *Wait for Shadea to return*, you thought. That was all that was necessary."

"I thought it sufficient, yes," Traunt Rowan replied tightly.

She gave him a withering glare. "It never occurred to you, I don't suppose, that you were bringing the boy to the one place he should never have been brought."

He frowned. "What do you mean?"

She stared at him without speaking, the weight of her gaze enough to crush another man. "You don't understand anything, do you? Neither of you understands what's happened."

Pyson Wence exhaled sharply. "We understand, Shadea. They've escaped, all of them. If you want to blame us, then do so. But we will get them back again."

"Will you?" she whispered.

She walked over to her writing desk and sat behind it, thinking that it might be time to put an end to them both. Why wait? With Terek Molt dead and Iridia turned traitor and perhaps something worse, these two were the last of those who had conspired with her to eliminate Grianne Ohmsford. Her grip on the Third Druid Order was strong enough now that she could afford to do away with them.

She considered the idea a moment longer before dismissing it. It was still too soon.

"You took a staff from the boy," she said to Traunt Rowan. "It had rune markings carved up and down its length. The boy tried to hide it from you, but you knew it was a talisman." She paused. "Do you know what it does?"

The tall man shook his head. "No."

"You took it away from him and you put it in this room?"

"I used magic to suspend it in a cradle so that it would wait undisturbed for your return."

"Except that the boy or this Elven girl who helped him escape found a way to undo your magic. So now the staff is gone as well as the boy. "

He stared at her wordlessly.

"Where, Traunt Rowan? Where do you think they went?"

He shook his head. "He was trapped in this room with the girl when we found them. The girl has the use of Druid magic. Rudimentary, but effective. She held us off long enough for him to find another way out. Perhaps out one of the windows or maybe into a secret passageway, like the one you used to get access to Grianne Ohmsford while she slept."

"But you searched?"

"Everywhere."

She rose from the desk and came out to stand in front of him. "Think back. That boy has been on a mission from the beginning. He has been searching for something that will help him find his missing aunt, his beloved aunt. Tagwen went with him, then Ahren Elessedil and Kermadec. They all went with him. That suggests they believed in him. What is it that they thought this boy could do? I'll tell you what. They thought he could find a way to get inside the Forbidding."

"That's ridiculous," Pyson Wence snapped.

"They didn't think so," she snapped back. "Ahren Elessedil gave his life to help that boy. We might assume that he had a good reason for doing so. We might even assume he thought the boy's life more important than his own. Why would he think that? Because the boy was the best hope any of them had of reaching Grianne Ohmsford inside the Forbidding! That being so, the one thing we didn't want to do was to bring him anywhere near the place where she went in! Especially after you caught him trying to hide a talisman of unknown origin and power!" She paused, looking from face to face. "But that was exactly what you did. Now both are gone, the boy and his staff, vanished into thin air in this very room."

She took a deep breath. "Take a moment and think it through carefully. Where do you think they are?"

Traunt Rowan's face had gone white. "That isn't possible," he whispered. "No one can get into the Forbidding."

She gave him a tight smile. "We did."

He stared at her, unable to put words to what he was thinking.

"There is one way to find out if I am right," she said softly. "You do still have the Elven girl locked away, don't you? She hasn't escaped with the others, has she?"

Traunt Rowan flushed. "We have her."

"Bring her to me."

He left at once, taking Pyson Wence with him. Eyes straight ahead as they stalked through the doorway, neither of them glanced at her on their way out.

Good, she thought. *Let them think about what they have done. Let them dwell on it a little and consider what might be in store for them if I am right.*

She stood alone in her chambers and despaired over how convoluted things had become. Their plan had been a simple one in the beginning—confine Grianne Ohmsford to the Forbidding and take control of the Druid order. Sen Dunsidan had given them the liquid night, and she had found a way to use it. The plan had worked exactly as it was supposed to work, but since then the situation had spiraled steadily out of control. It had begun with that boy, Penderrin Ohmsford. Why it had begun with him rather than with his more experienced and more deeply talented father, she still didn't know. Nor did she know even now exactly what it was that he had set out to do, even though she was pretty sure that he had found a way to do it. If this Elven girl confirmed her suspicions about where he was, she would have to take new measures to protect herself. She had come too far and suffered too much to think of giving up what she had gained. The rest of them could do as they wished, if she let them live long enough, but she had set her mind on her own course of action and did not intend to deviate from it.

Grianne Ohmsford was powerful, but she was also mortal. By now, she could be dead. By now, she *should* be.

But a nagging certainty whispered that she wasn't.

Better I die than that I concede anything to her. Or to that boy.

She imagined momentarily what she would do to Penderrin Ohmsford if she somehow managed to get her hands on him. The image that came to mind made her shiver.

When Traunt Rowan and Pyson Wence reappeared with the Elven girl, Shadea was surprised to see how small and vulnerable looking she was; she had imagined the girl larger and more imposing. The Gnome Hunter clothing she wore, obviously stolen to provide her with a disguise, was ill fitting, loose, and made her look smaller still. But when she saw Shadea, she displayed a look of such obvious defiance that it instantly infuriated the sorceress.

Little fool!

She walked up to the girl without a word, snatched her by her clothing so that she was off balance, and struck her hard across the face. The blow was delivered open-handed, so as not to break anything, but the sound of it caused Traunt Rowan to flinch. The force of the slap sent the girl sprawling. Without waiting for her to recover, Shadea stalked over to where she lay, grabbed another handful of clothing, and hauled her back to her feet.

Then she placed her face inches from the girl's. "That was to give you some small idea of how I feel about what you have done. It should also indicate what sort of trouble you are in."

The defiance was gone from the girl's face, replaced by a sullen acceptance of her fate. Shadea gave her a moment to recover, to let the words sink in, then struck her again, knocking her to the floor once more.

This time when she stood the girl up again, there were tears in her eyes. "It hurt more this time, didn't it?" Shadea asked softly. "But I haven't begun to hurt you yet. What is your name?"

When the girl didn't answer fast enough, Shadea struck her again, twice, the open-handed blows delivered first to one side of her face and then to the other. The girl's head snapped back and forth with the blows, and she gasped audibly with each one. Shadea gripped her clothing with her free hand so that she couldn't fall, kept her standing upright, sagging slightly from the attack.

"Your name, girl," she repeated. "You are an Elessedil or you are a thief because only one or the other would possess the Elfstones. Which is it?"

"Khyber Elessedil," the girl whispered. Her face was already beginning to redden and swell.

Shadea glanced at her companions, both of whom shook their heads. Neither recognized anything beyond the *Elessedil* part of the name.

"What are you to Kellen Elessedil?" Shadea snapped.

"He is my brother."

"Was," Shadea corrected. "He's dead. Killed on the Prekkendorran almost a week ago."

She watched the girl's gaze lift to meet hers and saw more tears fill her eyes. Good. She was already beginning to come apart. This wouldn't be so hard.

"You are all alone, Khyber Elessedil," she whispered, her voice flat and emotionless. "No one even knows you are here, save those you left stranded in the ruins of Stridegate and the boy you helped escape. I wouldn't expect any help from them, if I were you. Nor from any other source. You no longer possess the Elfstones; I have them safely tucked away. You have no real Druid magic to help you escape; you are a neophyte. Your fate is sealed. If you want to live, you will tell me exactly what I want to know. Are you listening to me?"

The girl nodded, but there was a hint of defiance still in her dark eyes. Shadea smiled. Foolish bravado.

She reached inside the girl's clothing, found a place where the flesh was soft and vulnerable, fastened her fingers like a vise, and twisted. The girl screamed with pain, her body jerking in an effort to get free. Shadea held her fast and twisted harder.

"Are you listening carefully?" she hissed.

The girl nodded, her eyes shut against the pain. "Then be quick to answer when I ask you a question." She withdrew her hand. "I can cause you a great deal more pain than a few slaps across the face and a little twisting of your tender parts. I can hurt you in places you haven't even begun to think about. I can make you beg for me to kill you. I learned how while I served with the Federation army on the Prekkendorran. I learned that and a good deal more that you don't want to know anything about!"

She paused. "Let's try it again. I ask a question, you give me an answer. Where did Penderrin Ohmsford go?"

The girl exhaled sharply, her head sagging. "Into the Forbidding. After the Ard Rhys."

Shadea glanced disdainfully at Traunt Rowan and Pyson Wence. *Hear that?* Her eyes challenged them to say otherwise. "How did he get into the Forbidding? No one can go there without magic. Was it the staff he carried out of Stridegate that let him do so?"

The girl nodded again and swallowed thickly.

"How did he find this staff?" She was furious at the idea of it, enraged that such a talisman even existed. "How did he know what it would do?" She reached down and yanked the girl's chin off her chest, pinching her jaws. "Speak to me, you little fool!"

The dark eyes opened, filled with hate. "The King of the Silver River told him."

Shadea stared at her wordlessly, then let her head drop down again. A Faerie creature was aiding the boy. No wonder he had found a way. She refused to look at her Druid allies, afraid of what she would see in their eyes after hearing that.

She snatched a handful of the girl's close-cropped hair and pulled her head back up again. "Why this boy?" she demanded. "Why him? Why not his father? His father is Bek Ohmsford, brother to Grianne. He is the one with real magic. What does this boy have that brought the King of the Silver River to him?"

The girl shook her head slowly. "I don't know. Something different. Something . . ."

"If he succeeds, if he finds Grianne Ohmsford, what happens then? How does he get back?"

"The staff."

"The staff? The staff what? What does it do?" She shook the girl until she could hear her bones crack. "What does the staff do, little Elven girl? How does it work?"

The girl shuddered. "Brings . . . them back . . . together. To the place . . . they went in."

She sagged heavily, and Shadea realized she had fainted. Too much pain, apparently. She wasn't as strong as she had tried to make herself appear. She looked frail, and she was. A poor ally to the boy. But then they were all poor allies, those who had sought to help him, the living and the dead. He had wasted himself relying on them. Whatever chance he had, it did not lie with the likes of this girl and Tagwen and Kermadec and his Rock Trolls.

She flung the girl to the floor and let her lie. Her mind raced. It didn't matter if the boy had crossed over into the Forbidding. It didn't matter if he had found a temporary ally in a spirit creature. What mattered was that his chances of surviving inside the Forbidding were much less than those of Grianne Ohmsford, and hers were poor. What mattered was that if he somehow got *out* of the Forbidding, she must reduce those chances to zero.

She exhaled sharply, her focus on what was needed sharp and clear. She understood the situation perfectly. If Grianne Ohmsford and the boy must return the same way they went in, then they must come back through the very chamber in which she now stood. That gave her a distinct advantage, and she intended to make use of it.

She turned toward her allies. If either had been startled by what they had heard, they had managed to recover their composure.

Pyson Wence wore his sly, cautious look. Traunt Rowan was steady-eyed and stone-faced against whatever she had to offer.

She surprised them. "What's done is done," she said quietly. "It was as much my fault as it was yours. I am the one who leads; I am the one who must bear responsibility for any failure. I should have taken better precautions before going south to Arishaig. I regret that, but there is nothing to be gained by dwelling on it. Let us consider instead what we must do to compensate."

She moved over to the window and beckoned for them to join her. They did so with a certain degree of hesitation. Neither was convinced that she had undergone a real change of heart.

"The boy is inside the Forbidding searching for his aunt. He might find her, if both can manage to stay alive long enough. He might even manage to bring her back again, through the wall of the Forbidding, using whatever magic it is that this staff gives him. I don't think it is likely or even possible, but I don't want to chance being wrong."

She spoke in a whisper, so that they were forced to bend close. She spoke as if she were in fear of being overheard. In truth, she simply wanted them to think she was taking them into her confidence. Which, in a way, she was. She just wasn't doing so for the reasons they thought.

"We know that the staff's magic will bring them to these chambers. We must be waiting for them if that happens. More to the point, we must find a way to make certain that they will be rendered helpless. Even if we are not here, personally, to intercept them, we must make certain that it doesn't matter, that they are caged and stripped of their power and made prisoners. They must be given no chance to use their magic—especially Grianne Ohmsford. They must be disarmed."

"You make this sound so easy, Shadea," Pyson Wence sneered. "As if disarming a Druid of Grianne Ohmsford's power were easily within our means. But it isn't, is it? Catching her off guard and vulnerable was our best chance. She won't be caught napping a second time. She will come back through that doorway like a whirlwind and we will all be swept away!"

Shadea gave him a pitying smile. "Such dramatics, Pyson. You would think she frightened you. Are you frightened of her?"

"We both have a healthy respect for what she will likely do to us if she gets the chance," Traunt Rowan answered for him. "As should you."

She gave him a quick shake of her head. "I don't respect anyone who misuses power as she has. I don't respect anyone with her history. She is an animal, and I will see her caged or put down."

"Brave words, Shadea." He looked less than convinced. "How do you intend to give them weight?"

She shrugged. "We'll create a triagenel," she said.

For the first time that afternoon, she saw agreement reflected in their eyes.

"First," she declared, when they had finished discussing how the triagenel would be achieved, "we have to dispose of the girl. She's told us what we want to know about the boy. She has no further use. Sooner or later, someone will come looking for her, and I don't want them to find her here."

Pyson Wence shrugged. "What do you want done with her?"

"Have your Gnome Hunters take her down to the furnaces and throw her in." She glanced at the girl, who still lay unconscious on the floor. "She won't be much trouble, but bind her anyway. Here, take these and throw them in, as well."

She handed the pouch with the Elfstones to Traunt Rowan. He stared at them in disbelief. "But, Shadea—"

"They're useless to us," she interrupted quickly. "Only Elves can make use of their magic. We're not Elves. If we can't make use of them, let's see to it that no one else can, either. Besides, they are markers. If anyone finds them on us or at Paranor, they will have found a link to the girl. We don't want that. No, throw them into the furnace and be done with it. Come back here when it is finished, and we will begin building the triagenel."

When they were gone, taking the girl and the Elfstones with them, she slipped from the room and went down through the corridors and stairwells of the Keep to a small guardroom that sat near the back of the north wall. *A triagenel is strong enough to hold even Grianne Ohmsford,* she was thinking as she moved along the passageways. Traunt Rowan and Pyson Wence recognized this and so were willing to offer their talents to form it. Three magics from three separate sources, combined in the right way, created a net that would contain and neutralize even the most powerful magic wielder. It took time and effort to build a triagenel, but she had never heard of anyone who was able to overcome one once caught in it. Stringing it about the perimeters of the room would assure them of snaring anyone who entered. There was no escaping a triagenel, once caught in it. Only its creators could undo it. Grianne Ohmsford and the boy would be snared like rabbits—or more like wolves—but snared nevertheless. By the time the triagenel was released, their lives would be over.

She considered the possibility that the triagenel would disintegrate before they were ready to attempt their return. It enjoyed only a limited lifetime, only a finite period of existence because the magic was so powerful that eventually it became unstable and collapsed. But another could be built. And another after that, should the need arise. At some point, it would be clear that her victims weren't coming back after all, and the effort to create further triagenels could be abandoned.

She was satisfied that her plan would work. She was confident that she could undo the damage that her inept allies had created.

She reached a heavy wooden door at the end of a darkened passageway set in the recesses of the northeast tower. She rapped sharply on it and heard a murmur of voices and a furtive scuffling from the room beyond. Then the lock released and a bearded face thrust into view. Eyes that were mean and piggish fixed on her, then looked quickly away. The man's head disappeared back inside the chamber.

"Gresheren!" he hissed.

She waited until a second man appeared, this one big and hulking, but with a sharper, more cunning look to him. He bowed to her immediately and stepped outside the room and into the hallway, closing the door behind him.

"Mistress," he greeted. "You have need of me?"

She took him away from the door and into the shadows. "I have a job for you. I want you to select four of your best men to dispose of someone. They will have the advantage of numbers and surprise, but that is likely all. They must strike quickly and surely. There will be no second chance. If they succeed and return alive, I will give them a year's pay for their efforts."

"Fair enough, Mistress," he rumbled. "More than fair. Who is it that you want killed?"

"A traitor, Gresheren," she told him. "A Druid traitor."

SIXTEEN

When Traunt Rowan threw her over his shoulder and carried her from the room, Khyber Elessedil was not unconscious. She was pretending to be, as she had pretended to be for most of the time after Shadea had thrown her down. But she was awake.

It was a trick of elemental magic she had learned from Ahren. If she was suffering too much pain, whatever the reason, she could distance herself from her anguish. She could quite literally go outside her body; she could disconnect her emotional self from her physical self. She couldn't do it for long, only a couple of minutes at a time. When the ruse worked, it gave her the appearance of being unconscious or asleep. In the past, the attempt was sometimes unsuccessful because her concentration failed. She had good reason not to let it fail here—the pain Shadea was inflicting on her was excruciating.

Once she appeared unconscious and Shadea lost interest in her, she slipped back inside her pain-racked body, hoping the Druids were preoccupied enough that they would let her be. She listened to what they had to say, though. She listened carefully. Some of it was inaudible to her, the words whispered too softly and from too far away to be heard clearly. But she heard enough to get the gist of what they were deciding, especially when it came to the part about disposing of her.

All she could think about after that was, *They're going to kill me.*

She had to do something to save herself—anything—but she had no idea what that might be. She was without weapons, including the Elfstones, and weak with pain and fear. The ordeal at Shadea's hands, while not breaking her, had left parts of her physically and emotionally drained. She had thought herself tougher than she was; Shadea had been right about that. It was a sobering experience to discover how badly mistaken she had been.

She lay limp over Traunt Rowan's shoulder, her eyes closed, but her mind racing. She heard the tall Druid's breathing as he carried her. She heard the sound of Pyson Wence walking next to them, his gait just different enough from his companion's to be distinctive. There were only the two of them; it was probably the best numerical odds she would get. But she knew that favorable odds alone weren't going to be enough to save her.

At that point, she didn't know what was going to be enough, and she was trying hard not to panic.

She had been confined to a cell in the depths of the Keep since they had broken into the chambers of the Ard Rhys two days earlier and overpowered her. Penderrin was gone into the Forbidding by then, swept away by the magic of the darkwand, and when they discovered she was alone, they tried to make her tell them where he was. She had feigned ignorance, as if his disappearance were as confusing to her as it was to them. She had suggested every false possibility she could think of, and they had seemed all too willing to accept that somewhere in the web of her deceptive explanations they would find the truth.

They had not tortured her or mistreated her in any way to discover if she lied, which had surprised her. She had come to understand why; they had saved her for Shadea a'Ru. They had saved her for someone who understood how to employ torture in the most effective way. Still racked with pain, still humiliated by her collapse, she knew that she would have told the sorceress anything.

In fact, she had told her more than enough. Shadea was now aware that Pen was inside the Forbidding, searching for the Ard Rhys. She knew that if the boy found his aunt, they would return with the aid of the darkwand to the chambers of the Ard Rhys. Shadea would be waiting for them. The damage to the chamber entry in the battle of two days earlier had been repaired. It would be an easy matter to seal off the room. Once that was done, Shadea could implement a triagenel.

Even an apprentice Druid like Khyber understood what a triagenel was. Every practitioner of magic in the Four Lands aspired to a level of excellence that would allow his or her participation in the creation of such a wonder. Triagenels were the most difficult form of magic to employ because they required the talents of not one, but three practitioners of equally advanced abilities. Druids were the only ones she had ever heard of who even thought about trying to create triagenels. Even then, under current Druid law, it could not be done without the authorization and supervision of the Ard Rhys. Few attempts at a triagenel had been made in her lifetime, and she did not know the details of any of them. Most such attempts were little more than forms of practice to give credence to the belief that a Druid had advanced far enough in his or her studies to combine talents with others with similar aspirations. A successful attempt was proof of mastery of a certain level of magic.

There was little doubt in Khyber's mind that Shadea and the other two were sufficiently talented to create a triagenel that could imprison, if not completely incapacitate, even as gifted a magic wielder as Grianne Ohmsford. A combination of three strong magics was just too much for one, even if the one was immensely powerful. If Grianne and Pen returned through the Forbidding after the triagenel had been set in place, they would be caught in a deadly trap.

And she was the only one who could prevent it. Aside from the three who would create the triagenel, she was the only one who knew about it. If she died in the furnace, as they intended, the chances of the Ard Rhys and Pen making a successful return were narrowed to almost nothing.

She had been carried down several levels by them, the Druids taking the back stairs to avoid being seen, keeping to the little-used parts of the Keep. She hung limply over Traunt Rowan's broad shoulder, still pretending at unconsciousness, trying to devise a plan. The idea of challenging two powerful Druids at the same time was not a consideration. She had to wait until they had delivered her to the Gnome Hunters before she could act.

She did not have to wait long. They quickly reached the ground level of the Keep and took her into a room filled with racks of weapons and armor. She risked a quick look around and caught glimpses of heavy wooden benches scarred by blades and fire, boxes of cutting tools, and grinding machines clamped in place. Bits and pieces of metal lay scattered across the worn surfaces of the benches and stone floor, and the air smelled of oil and was thick with dust.

Traunt Rowan slid her off his shoulder and onto the floor and left her in a heap. She lay without moving, eyes closed.

"Wait here," Pyson Wence said to him and went out again.

Khyber waited until she heard the door close, then waited some more in the ensuing silence. She felt Traunt Rowan's eyes on her, as if he was waiting for her to move, to reveal her subterfuge to him. She forced herself to remain exactly as he had left her, limp and unmoving, eyes closed. She let her breathing slow, and she listened for his movements.

When, moments later, she heard him turn away from her, she risked a quick look. He was perusing the room, studying the racks of weapons and armor. She shifted her gaze just enough that she could glimpse the floor about her. She searched for a weapon she could use to protect herself. But there were no weapons to be found, nothing but scraps of metal, leavings from the workbenches. Traunt Rowan moved away a few steps, his hand reaching out to feel the flat of a broadsword. Her eyes skipped across the littered surface of the floor, scanning desperately through the debris. There were blades everywhere, all of them out of reach.

Then she caught sight of something that might prove useful. She eased an outflung arm carefully toward a rough piece of metal, its edge razor-sharp. She pulled the scrap into the palm of her hand and closed her fingers around it carefully.

It was not much of a weapon, but it would have to do.

Traunt Rowan glanced back at her suddenly, but she had her eyes closed again and her body limp. He studied her nevertheless, as if noticing that her position had changed. She held her breath, waiting.

Then the door opened, and Pyson Wence reappeared. Four Gnome Hunters followed him in, then moved over to where she lay, rolled her over, and secured her wrists and ankles with heavy cord. Lying limp and unmoving, she let them do as they wished without signaling that she knew what was happening. Their strong, wiry hands roamed across her body, turning her this way and that, causing a wave of revulsion to run through her. Her instincts screamed at her to fight back, to break free while she still had the chance, before she was trussed so tightly she could not. But she knew that would be a mistake. She clutched the jagged piece of metal in her hand, her only real chance of surviving this, and forced herself to stay quiet.

When they were done binding her, they tied a rag about her mouth, covering it so completely that she was forced to begin breathing through her nose.

The Gnomes stood up, looking back at Pyson Wence. The Druid spoke to them softly, then handed one the pouch that contained the Elfstones. "I don't like giving these up," he said to Traunt Rowan. "It seems such a waste."

"Getting caught with them would be a death sentence," the other replied. "Shadea is right. Better to be rid of them." He paused. "Can we trust these four to do what is needed and keep silent afterward?"

"They understand their orders."

"Then let's be done with it."

Pyson Wence said something further, and one of the four picked Khyber up off the floor, tossed her over his shoulder as if she were no more than a sack of grain, and followed the other three out the door and into the torchlit hallway beyond.

She knew where they were taking her. She knew what they intended to do with her once they got there.

It was all she could do to keep from screaming.

They went deep into the bowels of the Keep, along twisting passageways that grew increasingly narrow and steadily darker, down stairways thick with gloom and heavy with damp. Eventually there were no wall-mounted torches to brighten the way, and the Gnomes were forced to light and carry their own. Khyber heard the drip of water and could smell the minerals the water contained. The gloom was impenetrable after more than a few feet, even with the torchlight to chase it back. In the silence, the only sounds were the labored breathing of the Gnomes and the measured beat of their footfalls.

If she had been afraid before, she was terrified now.

But she fought down her terror because she knew that if she panicked she was finished. She could open her eyes without fear of being discovered and did so. It was too dark for her captors to see her eyes, and she was hanging head-down anyway, her face obscured by the cloak of the guard who bore her. She had gained a fresh measure of anonymity. She was little more than a dark lump. She wondered if the men knew who she was; she wondered if they cared. She tried to imagine what it must have taken to imbue them with such blind obedience. Soldiers did what they were told and did not ask questions, she supposed. It was something she understood but would never accept.

She maneuvered the scrap of metal between her fingers until she had a good grip on it and began to saw at her bonds. She did so slowly and carefully, trying her best to disguise her movements by keeping them small and the rest of her body still. It was harder than she had expected because a certain amount of force was required to make any progress with the cutting. She did not know how long she had to free herself. She felt as if she had no time at all. She wanted to hurry her efforts, to work harder, to throw caution to the winds, to just be free. But Ahren had taught her that haste was your worst enemy when you were threatened, that mistakes were too easily made and chances lost. Patience was what would save you. Every fiber in her body shrieked at her to hurry, to cut faster, but she held herself in check.

Be patient.

Trussed and helpless, on her way to her own death, she wanted to be anything but.

Time slipped away, precious and fluid. She could not hold it back. She worked the metal diligently, even though by then her own fingers were cut and bleeding from the effort and the metal shard dangerously slippery. She almost dropped it several times, and she was forced more than once to cease her efforts long enough to wipe clean the shard and her fingers. She smelled her blood, coppery and rank. She could smell her own fear, the sweat of her body. She found that she was crying and hadn't even been aware of it.

She sawed harder, working diligently against the stubborn bonds as her captors trudged on, dark and silent wraiths in the gloom. Burning pitch hissed and spit at the ends of the brands they carried, the flames glinting in the dark like eyes, throwing shadows everywhere. She would be seen, she kept thinking, if she kept this up much longer. She would be caught out.

The air was growing warmer.

Her eyes snapped up as if to discover the reason, even though she already knew it. They were getting close to the furnace and the fire pits that fed it.

The bonds that secured her wrists snapped, nearly falling away before she caught them in her fingers and held them in place. She was free. She flexed her hands, first one, then the other, careful of her movements. Her ankles were still bound, but there was no help for it. She couldn't wait any longer. She had to act now.

But what was she going to do?

Her eyes skittered everywhere, then stopped. The butt of her captor's long knife protruded from its sheath less than a foot away from where her head hung down.

Momentary panic set in. She had never killed anyone. She had never had to fight for her life, never been threatened with serious harm until these past few weeks. Ahren had taught her how to defend herself, but she had never tested her skills in a situation even remotely like this one. She was just a girl, really. She was barely grown.

But they were going to kill her.

She swallowed hard, the panic deepening, threatening to immobilize her. She shouldn't be here. This shouldn't be happening. If she hadn't been so stubborn about going with Ahren and Pen, if she hadn't insisted on the quest being made in the first place, if she hadn't taken the Elfstones from where they were kept hidden away . . .

Her concentration faltered, and the metal shard slipped from her fingers and fell to the passageway floor with an audible *ping*.

She reacted without thinking, snatching the long knife from its sheath and burying it deep in the back of the Gnome Hunter carrying her. She heard his gasp of dismay and felt his body lurch and then collapse beneath her. She went down with him, rolled clear, and came to rest against one wall, the knife still in her hands, yanked free of the dead man's body. She caught a glimpse of the other three Gnomes as they wheeled back to see what was happening, momentarily confused but already reaching for their weapons. Her legs were still bound, and she could not flee them. She was trapped.

She dropped the knife instantly and began weaving her hands to summon a protective magic.

Please!

The magic responded, and the torches flared and went out, leaving the passageway shrouded in darkness.

Instantly, she was moving, dragging herself along the wall and away from her captors, the long knife clutched in one hand. The Gnome Hunters cursed as they stumbled about in the dark, running up against each other and tripping over their dead companion. She rolled all the way across the passage, trying to get as far away from them as she could manage. She had only moments before they found her, whatever she did, and she had to free her legs before that happened.

Backed against the far wall, she reached down and began cutting frantically at the bonds that wrapped her ankles. The blade of the knife was sharper and more efficient than the metal shard and severed the ropes in seconds.

She was struggling to her feet when the first of them, close enough by that time to hear her movements, thrust his short sword blindly into the rock wall only inches from her head. She reacted instantly, driving her own blade deep into his chest. He roared in pain and fear and staggered away from her, the blade still buried in his body. Weaponless, she backed her way along the wall, hearing the stricken man's grunts and moans mix with the guttural whispers of the two who remained. They would fan out along both walls and come toward her until they found her. But they would be more cautious. She would not get a chance to catch them unawares again.

She kept moving away, trying to think what to do. She could flee, if she chose, but her instincts told her that, unarmed and unfamiliar with the corridors, it would be impossible to get far in the blackness. The Gnomes, more at home in the dark, would hunt her down.

She heard them moving toward her already, their boots and clothing soft rustles and scuffs in the silence.

She needed another magic, she thought. But she did not know killing magic, so whatever she tried, it would only buy her a little more time. Perhaps it would gain her another weapon, but could she use it after what had happened? The memory of her blade sinking into the Gnomes she had killed was fresh and sharp and made her shudder. She wasn't sure she could do that again. She wasn't sure she should even try.

But she must try something.

Tell me what I should do, Ahren!

He couldn't, of course—not even in her memories of all he had taught her—because nowhere in his instruction had he addressed such a situation. He had been teaching her basic elemental magic right up to the moment they had set out for the Lazareen. True, anticipating the dangers they would face, he had given her harder lessons on the way, but none of them seemed useful against furious Gnome Hunters stalking her in pitch-black caverns.

They were closing on her, the sounds of their approach more distinct. She had no time left.

Her back against the passageway wall, she turned toward them, lifted her hands, whispered into the darkness and used her fingers to guide the magic accordingly, then clapped her hands to her head. Instantly, the passageway was filled with blinding light, its brilliance equal to the intensity of the sun at midday. With her hands, Khyber shielded her eyes against the sudden glare, but the Gnomes were caught unprepared and left momentarily blinded. She charged right at them, dodged their groping hands and slashing blades and broke into the clear to race down the corridor in the direction of the furnace, the explosion of light behind her revealing the way.

The Gnomes were after her at once, heavy footfalls echoing thunderously, shouts and curses rising up. She ran faster. She had no plan but to get away from them, to reach the confluence of passageways at the furnace and disappear into them. Let them hunt for her then, if they wished. She would be much harder to find once they could no longer see her.

A wave of heat suddenly washed over her, surging out of the gloom ahead. Pale light flickered from far down at the end of the narrowing passageway, the glow of the pit fires rising into the furnace room. Her goal was in sight.

Then something slammed into her, low on her right side, spinning her around and filling her with a wash of pain and shock. A dagger jutted from the fleshy part of her side. It felt as if a red-hot poker had been jammed into her, but she couldn't afford to take time to stop and pull the dagger free. She ran on instead, fighting down her sudden sense of weakness, hardening her resolve to reach the furnace room. Behind her, the Gnome Hunters were running to catch up, grunting from the effort, their breathing quick and heavy.

She reached the furnace just ahead of them, breaking free of the darkness in a rush that carried her right up against the metal railing of the catwalk that encircled the pit. She caught herself just in time, so close to the fires that she felt her hair singe and her lungs burn. She pushed away hurriedly and began to stagger along the catwalk. The fire pit yawned to one side, a deep, glowing chasm within which the earth's exposed magma burned fiercely, the source of the Keep's underground heat. Even with the fires dampened and the vents to the chamber open wide, the heat was all but unbearable.

She searched frantically for a way out. Several doors were set in the chamber walls, and across the way a spiral staircase wound upward to another. All were closed. She hurried to the nearest and tried to open it. It refused to budge.

Behind her, the Gnome Hunters stumbled into the chamber and caught sight of her. They hesitated for a moment, then split apart, one circling one way about the catwalk, one circling the other, trapping her between them. She moved quickly to the second door and pulled on the handle. It was locked, as well. The heat from the furnace fires and the loss of blood from her wound were making her dizzy. She felt the sticky dampness of blood all down her back. Her strength was fading.

She was in danger of passing out.

Bracing herself against the chamber wall, she reached back and pulled the dagger free. The pain was excruciating, but she managed to keep from collapsing. She had to get out of there, had to get through one of these doors. Even as she thought of doing so, however, she saw that it was too late. They would see where she had gone and come after her. They would have no choice; they could not afford to let her get away. Telling their Druid masters that they had let her escape would cost them their lives. They had to know that. They would keep coming until either she was dead or they were.

She felt a moment of despair. There was no way out. She was no match for the Gnomes. She was barely able to move; her growing weakness was coupled now with light-headedness and a sense of dislocation.

But she was the only one who knew of the triagenel. She was the only one who could warn Pen and Grianne Ohmsford of the danger.

With an effort, she straightened. She had her magic. She had the dagger.

Don't let me fail.

She moved ahead as quickly as she could to the stairway that led up to the single closed door at its head, words and gestures forming tendrils of magic like invisible threads. As she reached the stairs, she pretended to stagger—a pretense that was only partially faked—stumbling and reaching out to catch herself. When she righted herself and moved on again, she left the dagger on the sixth step, at head height, point outward, tucked back against the riser where it wouldn't be seen right away by the Gnome approaching from behind, the one now closest to her. A dozen paces farther on, she turned to face him, her back to the wall, waiting as he crept toward her, his blades glinting wickedly in the glow of the fire pit.

Closer.

When he was even with the step on which the dagger rested, she snapped her hands sideways in a sharp motion that jerked taut the tendrils of magic she had surreptitiously woven and attached and sent the dagger flying off the step and into the Gnome's throat. The blow wasn't enough to kill him, but the shock of it caused him to stagger into the railing, dropping both weapons to clutch at the wound. She was on top of him instantly, snatching up his dagger and jamming it into his unprotected chest, then slamming her elbow against his face with such force that he toppled backwards over the railing and was gone.

She hung on the metal stanchion and stared down into the pit, gasping for breath. One left.

When she straightened, the final Gnome was crouched a dozen yards away, watching her. They stared at each other across the fire pit, measuring their chances. Having witnessed the fate of his companions, he was clearly in no hurry to rush things. He might try to wait her out, she thought. Blood loss and exhaustion would claim her eventually. All he had to do was be patient.

To force him to expose himself, she started toward the chamber doors again, looking as if she intended to make her escape. The Gnome hesitated, then reached for the quiver of javelins strapped to his back, intending to kill her without getting close enough to be killed in turn. She paused at the first of the doors she came to, watching as he freed the first of his darts and hefted it into throwing position. She moved to the railing and crouched down again, making herself as small a target as possible.

It will take magic to save me. Earth magic, elemental magic. A little more of what Ahren worked so hard to teach me.

She gritted her teeth against a fresh wave of pain and began working her hands in subtle motions, drawing on fire to save her. It was there in the pit, all she could ask for, enough to accomplish anything, enough to put an end to this.

If I can remember how to summon it.

Her concentration faltered momentarily as she allowed herself to be distracted by the Gnome's stealthy approach, but she refocused instantly. *Steady your efforts.* Her head swam. She could hear Ahren speaking to her, gently encouraging, guiding her movements and her thoughts, walking her through the exercise. It was only an exercise, after all. It was only a little test to see what she had learned.

Close enough to act, the Gnome came out of his crouch, javelin raised to throw, and she snapped her hands upward in response, a lifting motion that suggested the splashing of water from a basin. But it was fire she was summoning, and it exploded from the furnace in a sudden wave to engulf the Gnome. Her attacker screamed in terror as his clothing caught fire, then his skin, then everything around him. He beat at the flames frantically, dropping his weapons, staggering away from the railing, falling onto the catwalk and rolling over and over. But the magic-summoned fire would not go out, his body the fuel it had been seeking.

In seconds, he stopped moving completely, a blackened husk. The flames died out, and the fire disappeared.

Khyber Elessedil hung on the catwalk railing and closed her eyes.

S E V E N T E E N

Rain, a blessing and a curse, fell in windblown sheets that draped the whole of the wetlands through which the Elves trudged. On the one hand, it kept the Federation airships grounded, lessening considerably the chances that their enemy would discover their intentions. No vessel could fly safely in such weather, not even the little three-man skiffs that both sides preferred for scouting missions and which normally were so reliable. On the other hand, it made foot passage through the northwest bottom country all but impossible. Their enemies might not be able to see them, but they, in turn, could barely see the noses in front of their faces.

Pied Sanderling, at the point of the scouting patrol he led, heard something move just ahead and signaled silently for a halt. The three men spread out behind him froze, weapons ready. Somewhere behind them, lost in the mist and rain, the rest of his makeshift army followed, strung out through the wetlands like a long snake, relying on him to act as its eyes. They had been on the march for the better part of three days with no sleep in the last two. The weather had turned foul the first day and hadn't improved since. It hadn't mattered as much in the beginning, when they were still in the hill country north, the ground rolling but solid beneath their feet. Then the rain provided concealment from those who hunted them. But the wetlands were a treacherous bog that swallowed men whole and through which passage was difficult under the best of circumstances. The decision to go that way had been based on Pied's certainty that the Federation's perception of them as little more than harmless remnants of a defeated Elven army had changed with their destruction of the enemy force sent to track them down and finish them off. The hunt for them now would be intensive. Moreover, it would come from the broader, less congested country west, which persuaded him to choose the more difficult eastern route for his own command.

He just hoped that the veteran scout Whyl, on whom he had relied in making that decision, knew what he was talking about when he had assured Pied that there was passage through. It was his country, and he knew it as well as anyone in the Elven command. But in such miserable weather, it was difficult to find your way out of your own backyard. If Whyl was even a little mistaken or had in any way misjudged . . .

He broke off thinking about it. Doubts would not help them. Whyl was with the patrol and had not seemed confused even in the face of the disorienting weather. Pied had to trust him. He had no one else.

"Captain," the veteran whispered, standing at his elbow and pointing ahead into the rain.

At first, the whole of the landscape was gray and rain-washed, earth and sky looking very much the same. Pied didn't see anything. But then a figure appeared, crouched and hesitant.

Troon.

She gave a quick wave of recognition and hurried up to greet them. She was small and compact with unusual gray eyes and impish features. Her clothing was sodden and muddied, and her short-cropped dark hair had flattened against her head like a helmet. She was the best of his Home Guard Trackers, his first choice even before Acrolace had gone down.

"We are almost through," she whispered as they clustered around her, breaking into a smile in response to theirs.

"You're sure?" Pied pressed. "No mistaking a skirmish line for the real thing?"

"No mistake. The Federation lines are less than half a mile away. They have surrounded the east plateau on three sides, laying siege to Droshen's Free-born, but as yet they haven't broken through. I couldn't tell about the condition of the airship fleet; I couldn't get close enough to make certain. But the Free-born still hold the high ground."

"Then they haven't gotten the *Dechtera* aloft again so they can use that weapon." Pied reached out and gripped her shoulder. "Good work. And you also, Whyl," he added, turning to the veteran scout. "We're where we want to be, thanks to you."

"What happens now?" Troon asked. Rain dripped off her face in steady rivulets.

Pied shook his head. He wasn't sure of that himself. "First, we bring up the army."

He sent one of the members of his patrol back with the news, then hunkered down to wait. He sat apart from the others, giving himself time and space to think things through. At such times he wished he had Drumundoon with him to act as a sounding board. But his aide was still gone, hopefully in Arborlon, breaking the news of the disaster on the Prekkendorran to Arling and seeking the reinforcements Pied had requested. He wondered how successful Drum had been. Under Kellen Elessedil, such a request would have been granted with barely a second thought. But the King was dead, and Arling was Queen. Arling might not be so eager to commit further Elven forces to a cause she had never believed in, particularly when the request was coming from him.

How things changed.

Once, he could have asked her for anything. He had been close to her in ways that he had never been close to anyone else. He had thought they would be together forever. But Arling had grander plans. When she married Kellen, he had been devastated but had understood her reasons. Marrying the King of the Elves offered a chance for advancement that only a fool would refuse, and Arling was no one's fool. She had loved Pied, but not well enough to pass up an opportunity of that sort. She was always ambitious that way; she was always smart about her choices. He thought that her marriage to Kellen had lacked the passion of her relationship with him, but he realized that his perception might be mostly the result of wishful thinking. She had left him to marry his cousin, the King, and that made any sort of reasonable perspective difficult.

But she did not abandon him entirely. She had remained his friend, arranging for him to be named Captain of the Home Guard, advancing his career immeasurably. It was a gesture he did not mistake for anything but what it was, but which he appreciated nevertheless. Over the years, she had come to rely on his advice in difficult situations, seeking it surreptitiously, making it clear that Kellen must never know. By doing so, she revealed the lack of confidence she had in her husband's judgment. It was an attitude Pied shared, though both were loyal to and served him as King. Arling never attempted subterfuge or manipulation of the sort that might threaten the throne, but she was not above blunting Kellen's more impulsive behavior or reshaping his more ill-conceived plans when it was clear he was courting disaster of one sort or another. In most of those efforts, Pied was her willing ally.

It was a strange relationship the three shared, the product of lives that were so closely intertwined that it was impossible to separate out the different threads. Each understood the personal role that had been allotted to them; each accepted the roles of the others. But the emotional entanglements made it difficult for Pied, if not for Arling or the King. He would have preferred a different ending to the story than the one that had been thrust upon him, but that had never seemed possible.

Until now. Now, he wondered if the ending might be changed. Would Arling see him in a different light now that Kellen was dead? Could she feel about him again as she once had? He could barely make himself think about that without cringing. It felt like a betrayal. Arling might see it that way, as well.

Who was responsible for the safety of the King if not the Captain of the Home Guard?

Ti Auberen appeared out of the haze and crouched down next to him, his tall frame bending close as he brushed the rain from his eyes. "Captain, the army is closing ranks behind us. Another half hour and the rear guard will have caught up and we will be ready to move. What are your orders?"

He glanced up at the big man, his thoughts of Arling scattered into the mist. "Ask Troon to come over."

The Elven Tracker came at once in response to his summons and dropped down beside him. They had known each other for most of their lives, friends before they were Elven Hunters, before he was her commander.

She gave him another of those quick, engaging smiles, and he smiled back. It was their way of acknowledging the depth of the relationship. "We're going to have to break through the Federation lines to reach the Free-born on the heights," he said. "Is there a place we might do that?"

She considered. "Breaking through isn't the problem; it's gaining the heights. There is a gate in the Free-born fortifications that wards a drift down off the heights west. That gate offers us our best chance. But Federation soldiers surround it to prevent a breakout."

"They think Vaden Wick might run?"

"I don't know. Maybe they think he might attack."

Pied grinned. "It would be like him. Can you get past the Federation lines and inside the fortifications?"

She shrugged. "Can I try it at night?"

He nodded. He could tell from the glint in her eyes that she relished the challenge. "I want you to tell Vaden Wick we will make our breakthrough tomorrow at sunrise. It would help our effort if he was to create a diversion that would draw attention elsewhere and stand ready to throw open the gates when we reach them."

"Sunrise, tomorrow," she repeated.

"Don't take any unnecessary risks. If you can't get through, come back. We'll find another way."

She reached out impulsively and patted his cheek. "Worry for someone who needs it, Captain. I will get through."

She arched an admonishing eyebrow at him, grinned at his obvious discomfort, then rose and hurried away.

By nightfall, she was gone. She left without saying anything further to anyone, slipping from the Elven camp as if her departure were of no consequence. She was like that, a steady presence who never made much of the dangerous work she did. Pied sometimes wondered why she continued to risk herself after so many years, but he could never bring himself to ask her. He felt the reasons were hers, and she was entitled to keep them private. It was enough that she was there for the Home Guard every time he called on her.

Unable to settle in, he slept poorly that night. With Drum gone, he lacked reassurance that things were in any sort of order and kept wondering what he had overlooked. He awoke well before sunrise, stiff and unrested, still dressed in the clothes he had worn for the past three days, rose from his blankets into the chilly morning air, buckled on his weapons, and walked down through the camp to find a cup of hot ale. It had quit raining, though the air was thick with the smell of damp and mist hung in gauzy blankets across the whole of the wilderness. They would march forward the last half mile when the false dawn began to brighten the eastern sky and would be at the backs of the Federation soldiers by true dawn. It would require that they travel in silence, and he had given the order the previous night that everything was to be lashed down or muffled. Whyl and two other scouts would go on ahead to prevent unexpected encounters. If things worked as he hoped, he would catch the Federation just rising and be on them before they knew what was happening.

He found his Elven Hunters mostly awake or coming awake, as anxious as he was to get on with the effort of breaching the Federation lines and rejoining the Free-born army. Activity marked the whole of the camp, and everywhere he walked he was greeted with whispers and nods. He returned the greetings, aware of what they meant. The men and women had come to believe in themselves again, and he must see that they did not lose that newly rediscovered self-confidence through any failure of his.

At the first indication of a graying in the east, the Elven command set out. They were formed up in units of fifty, with a commander of senior rank assigned to each. Erris Crewer had his archers deployed to either side of the regular units, both Elven Hunter and Home Guard, a screen against whatever they might encounter. They moved forward quickly, trusting to the scouts, who had gone on ahead, making their way through the deep gloom like wraiths.

Elves knew how to stay hidden when it was needed; it was one of the first things they were taught while growing up, a part of their heritage from the Old World. That day, in their approach to the Federation, it served them well. Before the sun crested the horizon, they had reached the rear of the Federation siege lines and were able to see how the enemy was deployed and to analyze what they would have to do to get past. It was a daunting task. The Federation forces easily outnumbered them three to one, even there, at that position, and without regard for reinforcements that might be dispatched from other parts of the siege line once the Elves' presence was discovered. The Federation soldiers were settled in behind fortifications that had been erected over the previous week, when the Elves were driven off the western heights and the rest of the Free-born allies were trapped east. An extended line of pack animals and horses was picketed farther back, blocking the Elven way forward and offering still another obstacle that they must get past.

Pied took a long moment to consider how to proceed, weighing the choice of a breakthrough at a single point in the Federation line versus a breakthrough at several. The former kept things more tightly controlled, and he opted for it. They would all get through together or they would not get through at all.

He put the most dependable and seasoned of his Elven Hunters in the vanguard with Ti Auberen in command, wedged Erris Crewer and his archers in behind them with swordsmen and spear bearers on the flanks, passed the signal back to be ready to make a run for it when the front ranks broke from cover, and settled back to wait for the dawn.

We'll need help to do this, he was thinking as he watched the gray horizon slowly brighten.

Then a Federation picket that they had thought safely turned away wandered back through the lines and stumbled on them. He was dead almost immediately, killed by one of the archers, but not before he had gotten off a warning shout that caused heads to turn.

Pied never hesitated. "Elessedil!" he shouted, and the Elves took up the cry.

They broke from the cover of the gloom and the mist and charged through the Federation camp. Pied had been right in his assessment of the situation: The Federation soldiers were just beginning to stir from their sleep, and the Elves were in their midst before most even knew what was happening. The night watch fought back bravely but was swiftly overrun, and the Elves went through the camp virtually unopposed.

The Federation soldiers who manned the fortifications were better prepared, however, and the battle to get past them was bitter and hot. Trapped against their own walls, they fought like demons, slowing the Elven rush sufficiently that for a moment it nearly stalled. Pied pushed his way to the forefront of the fighting, shouting at Ti Auberen to keep moving, to break through the lines. Home Guard warded him every step of the way, fighting to keep the enemy from getting close. From the center of the rush, Elven archers sent flurries of arrows down the siege lines, forcing the soldiers who manned them to duck for cover. In a concerted rush, the Elves slammed into the fortifications. Sandbags, earthworks, and wooden slats gave way under the crush, and the Elves were through and streaming across the flats separating the siege lines from the heights.

Ahead, the Free-born gates were barely visible, a massive barrier formed of iron-reinforced timbers set into walls that stood twenty feet high. There was activity on those walls; Pied could see the movement from the soldiers manning them as he raced across the grasslands.

But the gates were not opening to them.

For just a moment, Pied considered the possibility that Troon had not reached Vaden Wick. It had never occurred to him that she could fail.

At their backs, Federation soldiers were rallying, archers and javelin throwers trying to bring down the Elves from behind. Some among the pursued fell victim to the missiles, stricken and helpless and lost in the rush. Those in the Elven rear guard stopped to help where they could, but the press forward was intense and there was no time for hesitation. A knot of Federation soldiers swarmed onto the plains in a foolish chase that was brought up short when Erris Crewer wheeled his archers back long enough for them to use their longbows in a sustained volley that dropped the pursuers in their tracks.

Farther down the line, Federation horsemen were riding out to intercept the Elves, charging hard and closing the distance between them with alarming quickness. Pied saw that the horsemen would reach the Elves before the Elves reached the protection of the Free-born, even should the Free-born be aware of what was happening.

Why didn't they open the gates?

They were still a hundred yards from the walls when Pied shouted for Ti Auberen to form up ranks. The Elves wheeled into tri-angle formations and turned to face the approaching riders. Erris Crewer brought the archers into position at the rear, their ranks three deep, and the Elves prepared to stand and fight. Pied felt his heart sink. They could hold for a time, but in the end they would be overrun, caught out in the open with no place to hide and no one to stand with them.

He moved to the front triangle to stand with Auberen. Neither spoke. There was nothing to say.

Then, with the Federation riders almost on top of them and the

Elven archers already letting go with their first volleys, the gates of the Free-born defenses finally swung open and out rode the Red Cloaks, the horse unit of the Bordermen of Callahorn, successors to the fabled Border Legion. They burst through the opening in a wave of crimson and a cacophony of wild cries, charging hard for the Federation cavalry. Clad in heavy armor and wielding lances, they tore through the Federation riders as if they were so many straw men, breaking apart their ranks and shattering the attack. In only minutes, the entire Federation force was in flight, and the Red Cloaks owned the grasslands.

The Elves, meanwhile, were running for the gates once more, the cheers of the defenders urging them on. Pied ran with them, a surge of relief flooding through him. As he passed through the gates and behind the safety of the Free-born defenses, a hand reached out and grabbed his arm. Troon stood at his elbow, grinning broadly.

"You didn't think I got through, did you?" she shouted at him above the din of men and horses. "Admit it, you saw the gates were closed and you thought I'd failed." Her gray eyes danced with glee. "Didn't I tell you not to worry?"

Pied responded by giving her a hug and was surprised when she hugged him back, even more surprised to discover how good it felt.

He moved on, searching for Ti Auberen and Erris Crewer. They had to make arrangements for what would happen next. But his Lieutenants were nowhere to be found in the surge of ebullient soldiers coming in from the grasslands. He found himself carried along by the tide, swept uphill to the heights where the main body of the Free-born was settled. There was a general milling about as the newly arrived were sorted out—the healthy directed to campsites and the wounded taken away for treatment. Pied wandered through the crowd, wondering what had possessed him to hug Troon, something commanding officers did not do to soldiers, no matter the nature of the relationship. It wasn't really the propriety of the action that bothered him; it was the emotions it had stirred. He had known Troon since they were children, but he had never been attracted to her. She was a Tracker in his Home Guard command, the one on whom he could always rely. She was his childhood friend, someone he liked to be around and who made him smile.

But for a minute back there, he had felt like she might be something more.

He forced his thoughts to other things and walked on.

Not an hour later, as he was buckling on his weapons, he heard
his name called. He'd had just enough time to find his command
post, connect with Ti Auberen and Erris Crewer, wash himself from
a basin of warm water, and change into fresh clothes. He looked up
to see a powerfully built Dwarf with long black hair and a beard
braided at the chin and just below both ears approach. Several others of similar size but less flamboyant looks flanked him, hard-eyed
men wearing multiple blades and bearing scars on their hands and
faces. There was not a smile to be found on any of them save for the
leader, but he was smiling broadly enough for them all.

"Captain Sanderling!" he boomed, his voice deep and resonant,
the sound of it strangely compelling, like that of a practiced orator.
"I'm Vaden Wick, Captain. Glad you made it through. We have been
anticipating your arrival ever since your Tracker informed us of your
coming. Heard about your success against the Federation three days
back. That was impressive. Others would simply have kept running."

"I thought about it," Pied said. He reached out to shake the
other's hand.

"I doubt that. You haven't the look." Vaden Wick tugged on the
braid below his right ear, casting quick glances about the Elven
camp, his sharp eyes taking in everything. "We have a lot to talk
about. Can we do it now?"

He walked Pied down to the Free-born fortifications at the
southern edge of the east plateau, exchanging greetings with his soldiers on the way, seemingly relaxed and unconcerned about anything. He had that quality of being able to disconnect from the
burden of leadership when out among those he commanded, lending
a sense of confidence to everyone he passed.

But when they stopped at a watchtower that was hastily vacated
for their use, he abruptly changed. "Captain, we have a problem, and
I need your help in solving it." He looked out across the Prekkendorran to where the Federation lines were dark creases against the
horizon to the south, wrapping east and west about the Free-born

encampment like a snake. "We're trapped here, hemmed in on every side but the one where we don't wish to go. We can't allow that to last much longer. That big airship with the weapon that burned Kellen Elessedil and his fleet out of the skies was airborne yesterday, a practice run that took her just outside the rear lines but was clearly meant as a test of her fitness. Another day, maybe two, and they will come after us. When they do, we're finished."

He looked over at Pied. "We have to find a way to stop that airship. You fought against her and you know her better than any of us. You damaged her or she would have done a good deal more than destroy the Elven fleet. I need to know if there is some way we can disable her when she comes after us again."

Pied shook his head. "I was lucky, that last time. We were in a skiff, too small even to be a threat, but we got behind her and under her and used rail slings to damage the steering. My guess is they won't let that happen again. The next time she comes after us, she'll have armor up all over."

Vaden Wick nodded. "I would guess so, too. So we need something else. Another way to damage her. A way to stop her before she even gets to us."

Pied looked at him, realizing suddenly what he was saying. "You plan on going after her, don't you?"

"If I get the chance. But I have to know how to knock her down before we engage her again. We have our airships ready to go, once we find what her weakness is. You've fought her and lived to tell about it. I thought you might have some insight."

Pied looked off into the distance. If he had any insight, it was eluding him. He wanted to help, but the depth of his knowledge about the *Dechtera* and her weapon was tiny. Mostly, he knew what would happen once the big Federation ship was aloft. Was there a weakness that the Free-born could exploit when that happened? He tried to think of one and failed.

"You think we have today and maybe tomorrow," he repeated.

"At most."

Pied thought about it some more. "They seem to have only one of these weapons," he said. "One ship, one weapon."

"So far."

"A prototype."

Vaden Wick looked at him, waiting.

"Can they even build another?"

The Dwarf shrugged. "Seems that if they could, they would have by now."

Pied took a deep breath, an idea forming. "I think we need to get to her while she is still on the ground," he said. "We need to get to her and destroy her completely. Maybe they really can't build another."

"We've thought of that. But she sits right in the center of the Federation camp, ringed by all sorts of protective barriers and hundreds of Federation soldiers. Neither a ground attack nor an air strike would even get close."

Pied nodded. "Not if they see it coming," he said. "But maybe we can arrange it so they don't."

Pied had been sleeping for several hours when he felt the hand gently shake him. He could tell from the light seeping through the tent flap that the sun had moved west, though it wasn't yet dusk.

He opened one eye and saw Drumundoon bending over him. At first, he thought he was dreaming. "Drum?"

His aide knelt, and Pied could see clearly his young face with its high forehead and deeply slanted eyes. "It's me, Captain," Drum assured him.

He experienced a sudden sinking feeling. "You didn't get through to Arborlon?"

"Oh, yes, Captain, I got through all right." Drum rubbed his fringe of black beard. "I got there much quicker than I expected. I see you got through, as well. Everyone is talking about it. You've accomplished the impossible, if I may say so."

Pied blinked, trying to clear the sleep from his mind. "You may not." He pushed himself up on one elbow. "Have you brought help?"

Drumundoon nodded. "Three warships, several sloops, and two companies of Elven Hunters. They landed a little over an hour ago on the Free-born airfield. More will follow. The Elven High Council was quick to act once they understood the gravity of the situation. Arling was less impressed, but she accepted that their consensus constituted an edict she could not afford to ignore."

Drum hesitated. "Now she wants to talk to you."

Pied pushed himself into a sitting position. "I would expect she does. But she will have to wait. I can't go back there until this is finished."

Drum pursed his lips. "You don't understand, Captain. She's here."

"Here?" Now Pied was fully awake. "She came back with you?"

"She wouldn't have it any other way. The Council tried to dissuade her. Bad enough that we've lost a King. Losing a Queen as well would be too much. I even suggested she would do better to wait. But you know Arling. Once she has her mind set on something, that's pretty much the end of the discussion. She said she was coming or the ships and men were staying."

Pied nodded. That was Arling. Stubborn, though in an entirely different way from Kellen. She thought matters through first before setting her mind. She considered all sides. The war on the Prekkendorran was not an undertaking she would ever willingly support. No matter what the attitude of the High Council, she would look for a way to extricate the Elves. To do that, she would want to get a first-hand look at how things stood. She was Queen now, and she knew how to rule like one.

Of course, she had come to see how things stood with him, too. He could already picture her reaction.

"Where is she?" he asked.

"Right outside the tent," his aide said. He paused while Pied absorbed that information, looking decidedly uncomfortable with having been the one to deliver it. "She is waiting for you to invite her inside. I told her I ought to wake you first."

She would have woken me differently, had she been given the chance, Pied thought. He could already see her angry face, hear her accusatory voice. He knew what was coming with the certainty that he knew his own name.

"Let's not keep her waiting," he said.

He stood up, straightened his clothes, and nodded. Drum gave him a sympathetic look and ducked back outside. Alone, Pied stood staring at the tent flap, trying to compose himself, to think through what he knew he had to say.

Then the flap stirred and parted, and she stepped through, golden light trailing off her gilt-edged dress, her pale amber skin, and her long blond hair. She was so beautiful that it took his breath away, just as it always did, leaving him wishing for things that he suddenly knew he would never have. The revelation left him shocked. Arling was a Queen; she was always meant to be a Queen. To think that he had ever thought there could be anything permanent between them was a fantasy he had indulged with not the slightest consideration for reality.

"Hello, Pied," she greeted, coming up and offering her hand.

He bent to kiss it, bowing deeply out of protocol and deference. "My lady."

She stared at him for a moment, saying nothing. Then she clasped her hands in front of her and lifted her chin slightly, a curiously commanding gesture. "What do you have to say for yourself, Pied?"

He shook his head. "Nothing."

"Nothing? I was hoping you could do better than that. I don't know why, though. Nothing?" She gave him a glacial stare. "When I heard what had happened to Kiris and Wencling, I would have killed you if you had been within striking distance. I would have done so without a second thought. My sons, Pied. You were given responsibility for them."

"I know," he said. "I failed you."

"You failed me. You failed them. You failed your King. And you failed yourself." She paused. "I am angry with you still. Furious. But not for the same reasons as before. Do you know why?"

He shook his head, feeling foolish and slow-witted.

"Because Drumundoon told me what you have apparently failed to tell anyone else. Not that he wanted to, but I see more things than I am given credit for. When he told me my sons and husband were dead and the Elven fleet was destroyed, I asked what had happened to you. He told me you were alive. He told me you had rallied the survivors and achieved a decisive victory against the Federation force sent to crush what remained of our scattered units. He was quite proud of you. He was quick to tell me that without your presence, the Federation might well have succeeded in destroying the entire army."

She paused, studying his face. "I asked him how it was that you were in command of the Elven army. If my husband and sons were dead, why you were still alive? I asked why, as Captain of the Home

Guard and protector of the King and his family, you hadn't died with them. How could that possibly be?"

He nodded. "So he told you Kellen dismissed me from his service just before he set out."

"For insisting that he was making a mistake in attacking the Federation, in misreading the signs of what was clearly a trap, but particularly for insisting that my sons should go with him. For recognizing that Kiris and Wencling were pawns in his stupid, stupid game, pieces to be moved about on a board by a father who was mostly concerned that they grow to be the same sort of man he was, even when it was clear to everyone else that this was a bad idea, that they would never be even remotely like he was."

She lifted a finger and pointed it at him. "But none of that changes the fact that my sons are dead because of you. You failed them because you failed to out-think Kellen, something that should never have happened. You knew his propensity for rash behavior, for ill-considered action. You knew what he was like. Yet you reacted to the moment without thinking it through. You spoke your mind when you should have known better, and you got yourself dismissed from his service. No, don't say anything! Nothing you say will help now. You were given responsibility for my sons! You let them die, Pied! You put them in a position from which they could not extricate themselves and then you put *yourself* in a position where you couldn't help them. It would have been better for you if you had died with them. At least then I might be able to forgive you. That can never happen now. I can never forgive you for this. Never!"

He stood flushed and humiliated before her, the weight of the responsibility she was attributing to him immense and crushing and somehow inescapable. He knew he had done the best he could, but she made him feel as if that was not enough.

"So now you are the hero of the Elven army and my sons are dead," she continued softly. "You have pretended to be Captain of the Home Guard when in truth you were relieved of your command days ago. Shame on you."

He took a deep breath. "I did what I thought I needed to do to save the army. I didn't choose to pretend at what I was; it was thrust upon me by circumstance and need. I don't ask you to forgive me, only to try to understand." He paused. "I will resign my position at once and let another take my place."

"Oh, I think not!" she snapped at him. "Resign so that you can have the entire Elven army begging for your return? Resign, so that you can escape yet another obligation and another duty?"

He stared at her in shock. "It was not my intention—"

"Be quiet!" she snapped. He flinched at the force of her words. She froze him with her glare, with the bitterness reflected in her eyes. "Don't say another word unless I ask for it. Not one word."

His center went so cold that it might have been midwinter on the Prekkendorran instead of summer. He held her gaze and waited.

"You have won the hearts of my Elven Hunters," she said in a voice that was barely above a whisper. "You have won them and now you shall see to it that you do not break them as you have broken mine. Vaden Wick tells me that a counterattack is planned for tonight. What is your part in it?"

"I will go into the Federation camp after darkness with a handful of my Home Guard and destroy the airship and its weapon."

Now it was her turn to stare. "Do you really think you can do this?"

He shook his head wearily. "I will do it or die trying."

"Fair enough," she said. "I will take that as a promise and hold you to it. But hear me. If you survive this, if you manage somehow to come back alive, if you are successful in your efforts to put an end to the threat of this weapon that killed my sons, I will put this entire business behind me. Neither of us will speak of it again. But your service to the throne is finished. You will resign your position as Captain of the Home Guard immediately. You may give any reason you wish so long as my name is not mentioned. You will pack your belongings and leave Arborlon. You may go anywhere within the Westland so long as I never have to see you again. Is that clear?"

He thought of their past, a wisp of a memory turned to frost in the coldness of her voice. "It is."

She held herself very still. "It could have been different for us, Pied. If you had saved my sons as you had sworn you would do, it could have been different."

He said nothing in response. There was nothing to say. She might even believe that what she said was true. But he didn't.

She studied his face a moment longer, then held out her hand for him to kiss, turned, and went back through the tent flap. He stared after her, trying to decide how much of what had just happened was deserved. In the end, he guessed, it didn't really matter.

Two hours later, he stood at the edge of the Free-born airfield looking out over the broad sweep of the Prekkendorran to where the fires of the Federation army were being lit against the growing darkness. Dusk had settled in, deep and gloomy on a night that promised clouds and mist. It was the weather Pied had hoped for, an unexpected gift. He was dressed in black, and Drumundoon was standing in front of him applying lampblack to his face.

"She has no right to blame you," his young aide repeated yet again, scowling.

Pied held himself still as Drum's fingers worked across his face. "She has every right."

"She should be grateful you lived. If you hadn't, she might have lost the whole of her army."

"She isn't looking at it that way."

"Well, she should. She needs to distance herself from her emotions. She needs to exercise better judgment."

"A mother can't always do that."

"A Queen can. And should."

There was no satisfying him on the subject. He refused to consider any alternative but the one that favored Pied. Drum was nothing if not loyal. He had known of the entire conversation and confronted Pied with the whole of it minutes after Arling's departure. He didn't seem bothered in the least by the fact that if he had been caught eavesdropping, he would very likely have been shipped home in shackles. What mattered to him was that the Queen had done Pied an injustice that should be set right, and Pied did not seem inclined to do anything about it.

There were reasons for that, though Pied didn't want to talk about them. He was sick at heart at what had happened to Kellen and his sons and dismayed by Arling's response, even though he understood it and did not fault her for it. Mostly, he was weary. When the mission was finished, he did not want to continue as commander of the Elven army. Nor did he want to go back to being Captain of the Home Guard. Even if Arling had asked him to do so, a response

he did not foresee, he would have refused. His sense of account-
ability for what had happened to Kellen and the boys weighed on
him as if a tree had fallen on his shoulders. Nothing would ever be
the same in his relationship with the Elessedils. He no longer belonged in the position of Captain of the Home Guard. He did not
even think he belonged in Arborlon.

Drum would never understand that. So there was no point in discussing it with him. It was better if Pied simply presented it as settled
and let time do the rest.

Drum stepped back, eyeing him critically. "You're done. As good
as I can make it."

"That will have to be good enough," Pied replied.

They stared at each other for a moment, and then Drumundoon
stuck out his hand. "Good luck to you, Captain. I'll be here when you
return."

Pied took his hand and clasped it tightly. "I count on that, Drum.
I really do."

He turned away and moved to where the *Wayford* was anchored,
signaling to the other dark-clad figures scattered about that they
were leaving. The Free-born ship was rigged for sailing and ready to
fly, her captain already in the pilot box, her crew of six at the lines
and anchor ropes. It was dark enough that they could lift off without
drawing attention. If they flew east, into the darkness, they wouldn't
be seen when they turned south. After that, it would be up to fate
and luck.

Pied climbed the rope ladder with the other twelve members of
his tiny force, taking quick note of the flits that were stacked on both
sides of the mainmast before turning to take a head count. As he did
so, he caught sight of Troon, black-faced and black-clad like the others, levering one leg over the ship's railing and pulling herself aboard.
Breaking off his count, he went over to her at once, took her firmly
by the arm, and drew her aside.

"What are you doing here?" he demanded, trying to keep his
anger in check.

She arched one eyebrow. "I think you can figure that out for
yourself, Captain. I decided I didn't want to be left behind."

"You've just finished one mission. You're not ready for another."

"I'm ready enough. I had time to sleep last night once I was inside the Free-born lines. I told you it wasn't that hard. I slept today, as well."

He shook his head. "I don't want you doing this."

"You left it up to the Home Guard to choose a dozen of us. I volunteered, and I was chosen. A Tracker might prove useful."

"Well, I'm overruling the vote. You're off."

She stood her ground. "Because you are afraid I might not be up to doing what's needed? Or because of something else?" She gave him a moment, then shrugged. "Anyhow, we're already under way."

Pied glanced around hurriedly. She was right. The *Wayford* was lifting off, anchor lines released, her sails catching the evening breezes, the ground falling away below. He watched in frustration as the Free-born camp disappeared into the gloom and the ship swung about to fly east, and then he looked back at her, scowling. "I don't like it that you're here. It's asking too much."

"Of you or of me?" She glanced into the rigging as if the answer lay there. "For my part, I gather I am asking less of you than some. I am only asking to come along and help in whatever way I can. I might not be getting many more chances to do that." She looked back at him. "We've been friends a long time, Pied. Friends are supposed to stand by each other in difficult times. It seems to me, given how things have turned out for you, that standing by you just now is mandatory."

He shook his head in exasperation. "Drum just can't keep quiet about things, can he?"

"It's the army. You know how it works. Word gets around. There aren't any secrets." She glanced down at her weapons belt, and then hitched up her pack on her shoulders. "I don't like flying. I need to sit down. I'll be ready when you are."

He let her go; it was pointless to carry the discussion further because there was no reason to chastise her. She was there because she wanted to be. She was risking her life for him and for her comrades. It was hard to find fault with that.

They flew east until they had reached the far end of the Prekkendorran, then turned south and flew across the flats to the low mountains that buttressed the east end of the Federation lines. Slipping down the far side of those mountains, they got several miles behind the Southlanders, then turned west. In another hour, maybe less, they would reach their destination. It would not yet be mid-night.

He glanced over at the flits. They were little gnats compared to the big ships of the line. But gnats were pesky and difficult to swat. Big ships would have trouble getting close to the *Dechtera*. Flits might have a chance.

A small chance, he thought.

He moved over to the railing and settled down to wait.

It was nearing midnight when the *Wayford*, skimming the tops of trees and hills south of the Federation lines, landed beyond a screen of woods that offered some small concealment from discovery. North, the horizon was lit by the glow of the Federation campfires, a dull yellowish coloring of the night sky. Pied disembarked with his company and began unloading the flits, weapons, and spare crystals for the return trip. A single crystal powered each flit, and the crystal had enough stored power for about two hours of use. After that, the flier was on borrowed time. Two hours would be enough to get them there, even given the necessity of evasive maneuvers. The spare crystal would get them back again.

If there was any getting back to be done.

When the group was assembled and the gear was checked and strapped in place, Pied told them what they were going to do and how they were going to do it. Once aloft, they would not be able to speak to one another; they would have to react on instinct. Knowing what they had to do and how they were supposed to do it was the framework that would hold them together. Acting as a team was what would keep them alive.

No one had to be told what the odds were of them succeeding. No one needed to speak of it and no one did.

"Remember that no matter what happens to us, that ship and her weapon have to be destroyed," Pied finished. "If we fail, thousands of Free-born will die. Don't let that happen."

They strapped themselves into the flits, taking time with the fas-tenings and the lines, bunched together in the center of a clearing that gave them sufficient room to lift off. Then, one by one, led by Pied and Sersen, a Southlander who had volunteered because he knew the country, each flier opened the single parse tube containing the diapson crystal that powered the flits, and soared off into the night.

Shadows against a night sky both clouded and misty, they flew low to the ground in near blackness, the only light coming from ahead of them, where the Federation fires burned through the gloom. Barely able to keep one another in sight, they flew in as tight a formation as possible, following the lead of Sersen, who chose their path and kept them on track for their destination. Pied, locked away in a kaleidoscopic rush of wind and sweeping landscape, found he was surprisingly calm. He was going to his death, in all likelihood, and yet he was at peace. He wished he could hold on to the moment, could stay in it forever.

The fringes of the Federation camp came into view, and Sersen took them right, keeping them within the concealment of the dark, just out of view of the sentries stationed along the backside of the enemy army. The airfield lay farther down the line, cradled by a series of low hills occupied by hundreds of Federation soldiers. They would have to fly right down into the center of that cradle, and when they did so they would come under attack from every side.

Pied took a deep breath and watched the Federation fleet begin to take shape in the harsh glow of the fires that warded the airfield. He found the *Dechtera* at once; her huge bulk was unmistakable. The weapon was mounted on her foredeck, covered over with sailcloth. Dozens of Federation soldiers stood on her decks and on the ground surrounding her hull. Pied's stomach lurched as he made a quick count and realized that they would be outnumbered at least thirty to one. Even without the rail slings on the surrounding hills and the soldiers manning them, even without the Federation camp being so close that it would take only minutes for an organized response to any attack, the odds his little force faced were insurmountable.

We're not coming back from this, he thought suddenly. *Not a one of us.*

Then it was too late to think about anything. Sersen had started his dive toward the airfield, flattening himself to the framework of his flit, trying to make himself as small a target as possible. Pied did the same, dipping his wings so that his flit nosed downward, gathering speed. Out of the corner of his eye, he saw the others follow, one by one, a sweep of flits winging out of the darkness and into the light.

It took the Federation soldiers a moment to react, perhaps because they could not believe the audacity of what they were seeing. It was a moment too long. Before they could bring their weapons to bear, including the rail slings mounted on the decks of the airships and the grounds surrounding, Pied and his Elves were crashing into them like waves off the ocean against rocks. The Elves didn't bother with controlled landings; they simply used whatever buffers were at hand—soldiers, weapons, supplies, and ships alike—to slow them down. Pied had just enough time to see Sersen sweep through the center of the airfield and another flit slam right atop the *Dechtera's* main decking and the sentries who weren't fast enough to get off her in time, and then he was down as well.

He skipped across the airfield in a series of bone-jarring bounces toward the nearest railgun, sending men leaping from his path, including the two who were assigned to man the gun. He had his straps off before the flit had finished its skid, leapt to his feet, and raced for the weapon. He got to it before the Federation soldiers could recover, swung it around on them, the crank already drawn back, and released the sling. Metal fragments sliced through the night with a hissing sound that ended in the death cries of the men in their path. Pied cranked back the handle once more, dropped in another load, swung the weapon toward a different group, and fired again.

Atop the *Dechtera*, two of the Home Guard fought hand-to-hand against a dozen soldiers surrounding the shrouded weapon. They held their own for several minutes before disappearing under the weight of their attackers. At the periphery of his vision, Pied saw a Federation-manned rail sling blow apart a flit that was trying to land, flinging its rider against the side of an airship, broken and lifeless.

Too many of them, too few of us.

Pied reloaded the rail sling and swung it toward the *Dechtera*. Fixing on the remnants of the Federation defenders still aboard, he released the sling and cut them apart. He was bringing the railgun back around when the first dart caught him in the shoulder, knocking him back. A second buried itself in his thigh a moment later. He was too exposed, standing out in the open. Worse, he was too far from the target.

Ignoring the pain of his wounds, he bolted for the *Dechtera*, leaping onto her rope ladder and hauling himself aboard so quickly that he bumped into the last of the defenders, a man who was crouched behind the railing, trying to hide. Pied killed him with one swipe of his long knife and broke for the weapon forward. Arrows and darts whistled past his ears, invisible killers. Elves had commandeered two of the railguns on the next ship over and were firing at clumps of Federation soldiers trying to reach the *Dechtera* and Pied. Another of the Home Guard, small and quick enough that it might be Troon, raced toward the airship with burning brands that streamed sparks and fire like comet tails and flung them onto the big ship's decking where they burned, wild and fierce.

Pied reached the mysterious weapon and yanked off the sailcloth. A ten-foot-long barrel connected to a broad rectangular box sat atop a swivel. Cranks jutted from the swivel, clearly meant for maneuvering the weapon into firing position. Strange rods bored holes into the sides and back of the box. Pied snatched up an iron bar from off the deck and began smashing the hinges of the box, the *ping* of arrows and darts ringing in his ears as they bounced all around him. Sersen appeared beside him, blood streaming from a head wound, picked up a second iron bar, and began hammering at the casing from the other side. Behind them, the Elves from the next ship over abandoned their positions and scrambled aboard the *Dechtera*, fighting their way through smoke and flames to the aft port and starboard rail slings, swinging the deadly weapons around to face the Federation soldiers rushing to stop them.

Pied glanced at the airfield. If there were other Elves still standing, he couldn't see them.

Then the hinges on the casing gave way, snapping apart. Pied flung the casing aside, stared momentarily at the array of diapson crystals settled in their shielded slots, and began smashing them.

"Shades!" he gasped as another arrow caught him high on his wounded shoulder.

Sersen lurched backwards, a javelin protruding from his chest. The Southlander tried to catch himself, was hit again, and went down in a heap, sprawled across the ruined weapon. Pied dropped to one knee, seeking cover, and was surprised when the movement caused him intense pain in his side. He glanced down and saw another arrow protruding. When had that happened? Fire and smoke were all around him now, and he started to crawl across the decking, searching for a way out of the inferno, then stopped.

A trio of tattered and bloody Federation soldiers emerged from

the haze right in front of him, blades unsheathed. As they caught
sight of him, they slowed, weapons lifting. Pied drew his own sword,
bracing for their rush. He didn't have the strength to stop them; he
was weak from loss of blood, and pain was slowing his movements.
He tried to think of how he could disable all three, but his mind was
sluggish and unresponsive.

He tightened his grip on his sword.

Then a compact, black-clad form leapt from the roiling smoke
behind the advancing soldiers, short sword cutting down first one,
then another, quick blows that took both out of the fight before they
even knew what had happened. The third turned, and the attacker
went straight at him, as well, feinting and dodging, forcing him to
swing wildly and thereby lower his guard.

In seconds, all three lay dead.

Troon moved quickly to Pied and slung his arm over her shoulder. "Time to be going, Captain."

She hauled him across the deck of the burning ship to the starboard side, practically dragging him. The flit that had crashed earlier
lay jammed against the railing, its frame twisted and bent. "That
won't hold us both," he said. "Leave me."

She ignored him, pulling the flit around so that it faced the port
side of the airship, then jerking open the diapson crystal housing and
yanking out the depleted crystal. Reaching into her pack, she retrieved her spare and fitted it in place. How she still managed to have
that pack after what she had been through was incomprehensible to
Pied. "What of the others?"

She laid him across the frame, strapping him securely into place.
"As far as I know, all gone."

Thick smoke and flames surrounded them, forming a wall that
closed them away from everything that lay beyond, hiding them
from view. Federation soldiers were shouting wildly from somewhere
close, and they heard the sound of boots thudding across the ship's
decking by the ruined weapon. Troon ignored them, concentrating
on the task at hand, her hands steady and sure. When she was satisfied that he was held fast, she lay down on top of him, wrapping her
arms around his chest and her legs around the back part of the frame.

"Ready, Captain?" she whispered.

"Ready."

"This won't be pleasant. Hold tight."

She opened the parse tube, pulled back on the rudders, and threw the throttle all the way forward. The flit shot ahead as if catapulted from a sling, burrowing a tunnel through the smoke and flames, and lifting off the deck to clear the jagged stanchions of the broken railing with just enough room to spare.

An instant later, they were soaring across the Federation airfield, shouts rising from the throats of those below, missiles whipping past them in swarms. Pied heard Troon grunt, and her grip on him tightened. He felt a stinging in his leg, then another on his neck. He closed his eyes, waiting to die. The flit jerked and twisted as it flew, a victim of its damaged frame, unable to fully right itself. But Troon held the controls steady and kept them flying, moving out of the light to gain the darkness beyond.

They flew on for what seemed like an impossibly long time, wrapped together on the flit, sweeping through the night on an erratic path, the flit repeatedly jerking as if stricken, its frame shuddering. Pied wanted to look back to see if there was any pursuit, but he lacked both strength and maneuverability. He settled instead for staying quiet and balanced, trying to help them stay aloft.

"Are they back there?" he asked finally, the wind whipping the words from his mouth as he spoke them.

She pressed close. "Somewhere, but they haven't found us yet."

He fought to stay awake, but that was growing increasingly difficult. His strength was failing, and he thought that if she hadn't lashed him to the frame, he would not have been able to hang on. He felt the dampness of his own blood all down his body, and the arrows and darts buried in his flesh burned and throbbed.

After he hadn't heard or felt anything from Troon for a long time, he said to her, "Are you all right?"

There was no response. She lay heavily atop him, unmoving.

"Troon?"

"Still here."

"You're hurt?"

"A little. Like you. But we'll get through."

"I think I'm hurt pretty bad."

"Don't say that."

"You should have left me."

"Couldn't do that, Captain."

"You should have saved yourself."

She didn't say anything for a long time, then she put her lips close to his ear and said, "Saving you is the same as saving myself." And then he thought he heard her say, so softly he couldn't be sure, "I love you, Pied."

There was light ahead of them now, a fuzzy ball against the black, dim but growing brighter, and he found himself staring at it, watching it grow. He was a deadweight atop the flit, and Troon was a deadweight atop him. The flit was no longer flying straight, but beginning to slide downward, to dip and sway like a leaf tumbling from a tree.

"Troon?"

No answer. Pied stared at the light ahead. It didn't seem to have a source, didn't seem to be coming from anywhere. It occurred to him that there wasn't any light at all, that the light was inside his head. It occurred to him that he was watching the approach of his own death.

Fascinated, he kept his gaze fixed as it became a huge glowing ball and then swallowed him.

NINETEEN

en Dunsidan was awake long before his guards came to rouse him, dressed and waiting by the time they did. A light sleeper in the best of circumstances, he heard the sounds of the battle being fought on the airfield from inside his tented compound at the center rear of the Federation encampment almost a mile away. At first, he thought the entire camp was under attack, and his sole thought was to reach his private airship and flee. But as he dressed, frightened and angry and confused, standing in the dark to keep from becoming a ready target, he realized that the tumult was much farther away than the site of his compound and that any danger to him was still remote.

Nevertheless, he was edgy and impatient by the time his aide called to him from outside the tent flap. "My lord?"

"What is it?" he snapped, unable to keep his voice from betraying him. "What's happening?"

"The airfield is under attack!"

He knew the truth at once then. He didn't even have to leave his tent. The Free-born had watched him test-fly the *Dechtera* the day before, had taken note of how she performed, and had decided to act on the results. Having already witnessed the devastation wrought to the Elven airfleet, they would not have held anything back in their efforts to destroy her this time. He cursed himself for a fool, waiting one day too long, confident that he had them hemmed in and helpless, waiting for the end. He should have paid better attention to what had happened to the command he had sent to finish off those Elves. He had thought them helpless, too.

Still, why was it that his army, the biggest and most powerful army in the Four Lands, couldn't manage to keep the Free-born from breaking through the siege lines and reaching the airfield, which was miles away? Why was it that his soldiers couldn't manage to protect a single airship?

He pushed through the tent flap into the night and saw the huge blaze east, the flames rising up against the darkened horizon, an inferno. He felt a sinking feeling in his stomach, the last of his hopes fading, his worst fears confirmed. The *Dechtera* was destroyed. His weapon was gone. His plans for a strike against the Free-born on the morrow were ruined. He knew it as surely as he knew his own name. He stood looking at the flickering glow of the fire in stunned silence, his aide hanging back, his guards keeping well away from him until they knew what his reaction was going to be.

He turned to his aide. "Find Etan Orek. Bring him to the airfield."

His aide hurried away, and he signaled to his guards to bring up the carriage. Someone was going to pay for this.

It took them only minutes to reach the airfield, which was filled with soldiers running in every direction, some of them carting off the bodies of the dead and wounded, some of them trying to put out the flames of the fires that burned all across the field. The biggest of the fires was fed by what remained of the charred hulk of the *Dechtera*, a smoking, blackened ruin, as he had known she would be. Several other airships were burning, as well, but it didn't appear that they would be a total loss. Weapons lay scattered everywhere, and he could just barely identify twisted pieces of flits.

Composing himself, putting in place his politician's look, the one that masked his true feelings and left his features devoid of expression, he climbed from the carriage.

One of his field commanders came over, saluted, and started to give his report, but Sen Dunsidan cut him short.

"How many of them were there?"

His commander blinked. "We think about a dozen."

"A dozen." He was filled with sudden rage. A mere dozen had done this. "They used flits?"

His commander nodded. "They flew in from the backside of the camp. A suicide mission. We got all of them but two, and we'll have those two, as well, before dawn. Elves, from what we can tell."

"Elves?" Another remnant of those he had presumed helpless and in flight. He shook his head. "Any movement on the Free-born lines?"

The other man shook his head. "Not as yet."

"There will be. Strengthen the siege lines and be ready for an attack. Without the *Dechtera* to keep them at bay, the Free-born will try to break out. I don't want that to happen. Do you understand me, Commander?"

"Yes, Prime Minister."

"In case you don't, pay close attention to this. I want the watch Captain who was on duty tonight relieved of his command. I want him sent to the very front of our lines. When the Free-born attack, I want to be certain that he is the first soldier they see." He paused, his hard gaze fixed on the other. "Make sure everyone knows the reason."

His commander swallowed hard. "Yes, Prime Minister."

"Get out of my sight."

When he was alone, save for his guards, he walked down through the airfield to examine the damage firsthand. White-haired, magisterial, a commanding presence, he drew attention from all quarters. He let himself be seen, because it was necessary for the army to know he had matters under control. But he did not attempt to interact with the soldiers; he could never be reached by such as them. His guards formed a protective phalanx about him, keeping everyone at bay, and those who looked at him did not try to do more.

He stopped to study the wreck of the *Dechtera*, catching sight of what remained of his precious weapon, a twisted hunk of blackened metal. It was all he could do to keep from screaming his rage aloud, but he was practiced at dispassion.

He was contemplating what he would do to those responsible for what had happened here tonight when Etan Orek appeared at his elbow. "My lord?" he ventured.

Sen Dunsidan glanced at him. "You see for yourself what has happened, Engineer Orek. You see how determined our enemies are." He shook his head. "Their job is made easier by the fact that I am surrounded by incompetents. You and I, we must carry so much of the load ourselves."

The little man nodded eagerly, happy to be included as one of the chosen. "My lord, you can always depend on me."

Sen Dunsidan glanced at the *Dechtera*. "There is no salvaging the weapon now. We must start again. How long will it take?"

Etan Orek grinned conspiratorially. "You told me to build other weapons, my lord. I have been doing so. Another is almost complete." He leaned close. "I have actually tested it. The crystals align as they should to generate the fire rope. It needs only to have the casing made."

Sen Dunsidan felt a flush of satisfaction. He put a hand on the other's shoulder. "You have done well, Engineer Orek. Once again, you have not disappointed me. If I had a dozen of you, this war would be over in a week."

The little man flushed with pride. "Thank you, my lord."

"How many days, then?"

"Oh, end of the week, my lord. The weapon awaits my attention in Arishaig. It needs only a few final touches and a new airship to bear it aloft."

"Then we must spirit you back to Arishaig without further delay. I will have you returned at once. Pack up your things and make ready. I will follow in a day or two with the airship that will bear the weapon." He gave the other a smile. "There will be a reward in this for you, Engineer. Your service to the Federation will not be forgotten."

Flanked by two of Sen Dunsidan's personal guards who were charged with keeping close watch over the little man until he was safely away, Etan Orek scurried off. Nothing must happen to him. Not now, not when he was so close to finishing a second weapon. Wouldn't that be a nice surprise for the Free-born, once it was finished? They believed the danger over and done with, having destroyed the *Dechtera*. They believed him to be in possession of only a single weapon, since only the one had been used against them. They would find out soon enough how badly mistaken they were.

He took a final look around, decided there was nothing more he could do that night, and went back to his carriage. He might even be able to sleep again, he thought. At least until morning, when the Free-born attack came. He was still certain it would. Vaden Wick would take advantage of the opportunity. He would rally his forces in an attempt to break through the siege lines, to reclaim the heights lost by the Elves, and to return the Prekkendorran to a no-man's-land.

He might even succeed. But it wouldn't matter. Not anymore. Not once Sen Dunsidan brought up the new weapon and burned them all to cinders.

He reached the carriage and climbed inside. He was comfortably settled in place before he noticed the shadowy figure seated across from him.

"Prime Minister," Iridia Eleri greeted in her soft, insidious voice.

He started violently, but managed to keep the gasp that rose in his throat from escaping. She was cloaked in black and so deep in the shadows of the carriage interior that she was all but invisible.

"I've been waiting for you."

Shades, he thought. He exhaled sharply. "Come to gloat?"

She lifted her head slightly. "I am your personal Druid adviser, Sen Dunsidan. It is not my place to gloat. It is my place to advise. I have come to do so tonight. My sense of things suggests that you need me to do so."

The coach lurched forward, the team of horses turning it back toward the main compound and his tent. He rubbed at his tired eyes, wishing she would simply disappear. "What sort of advice would you offer, Iridia?"

"You have lost your airship and your weapon because you wasted time on a target of no consequence," she said quietly. "Now you will replace them with a new weapon and a new ship. Perhaps you should take this opportunity to reconsider your strategy for winning the war on the Prekkendorran."

He studied her without speaking for a moment. Odd, how used to her strangeness he had gotten, to the peculiar way she made him feel. It bothered him still that he couldn't define what it was about her that was so troubling, but he had gotten past his queasiness and now found her simply irksome. "My strategy?"

"It is still your intention to attack the Free-born forces on the Prekkendorran, to decimate them and thereby gain your victory," she said softly. "You would waste your time on an effort that will prove meaningless. I have told you this before and you have ignored me. I am telling you again, except that this time I must warn you that you ignore me at your peril. You won't get many more chances at winning this war. If you persist in trying to win it here, on this battlefield, or on any battlefield where soldiers and weapons alone are all that are at stake, the odds will catch up to you."

He folded his arms across his chest defensively. "You want me to attack Arborlon? Is that it?"

"It is what will end the war, Prime Minister. Attack the home city of the Elves, cause damage to their homes and their institutions, take the lives of their young and old, of their sick and crippled, and you take away their heart. They will cede you your victory. They will cede you anything to get you off their doorstep. Battles fought and won far from home make no lasting impression. Lives lost mean nothing when those lives are taken in a distant place. But kill a few thousand Elves in front of the rest of the population, and it will impact them forever."

He sighed. "We have had this discussion. I told you I would do as you advised. But I will do so when I am ready, Iridia."

"Time slips away, Prime Minister." Her words were a snake's hiss in the darkness.

"Does it? Perhaps time works differently for you than for me." He leaned forward. "I don't know why you are so adamant about attacking Arborlon. Why not attack Tyrsis or Culhaven? Why not go after the Bordermen or the Dwarves? We've already smashed the Elves on the battlefield. They are no longer the strongest of the Free-born allies."

"It is the Elves who serve as inspiration for the others. It is the Elves who promise hope in the worst of situations. In spite of the death of Kellen Elessedil, they came back to defeat you in the hills north. They broke the back of your pursuit force. Why do you think it was the Elves who attacked here tonight? Because they will give their lives willingly when they must. The other Races take note. They look to the Elves to see how they, too, must be."

"Well, they can look to their ashes when I am through with them.

They can sift through those and see how much courage they can find to continue the fight!"

The coach rolled to a stop within the Prime Minister's encampment. As Sen Dunsidan reached for the latch on the door, Iridia reached out and grasped his wrist, her hand as cold as ice. "Arborlon is the key to everything—"

"Enough!" he shouted at her, snatching back his wrist, repulsed by the feel of her hand on his skin. He rubbed at his wrist furiously. "You forget your place, Iridia! You are my adviser, but that is all you are! Do not presume to try to think for me! Confine your comments to suggestions and let me make the decisions!"

He threw open the door to the carriage and stalked off into the night.

The Moric waited until he was out of sight then climbed from the coach, as well. It stood looking off in the direction the Prime Minister had taken, thinking that Sen Dunsidan was proving to be more obstinate than anticipated. At first it had seemed a simple thing to twist his thinking in the way that was necessary. Persuade him of the need to attack the Elves on their own ground, to fly to their home city and let them discover firsthand the consequences of a war against the Federation, and the rest would be simple.

But Sen Dunsidan was a politician, first and foremost, and he constantly shifted his position to take advantage of the most favorable winds. He had rethought the matter, it seemed, and found that the attack was perhaps not to his advantage after all. He hadn't said so, but the Moric could tell that his hesitation to act quickly and decisively was governed by his sense that in doing as his adviser had recommended he might be making a mistake. Perhaps it was the visit from Shadea a'Ru that had caused him to back away from his earlier position. Perhaps it was something else. It didn't matter to the Moric. What mattered was that his mind had to be changed back.

The Moric breathed in the human stench, the smell of the Federation camp and its occupants, and was revolted. It was eager to have the matter over and done with. It was anxious to break down the wall of the Forbidding so that its brethren could join it and the killing could begin. It never doubted that this would happen. Superior to humans in every way, it knew it would not fail in its efforts. It would find a way to trick Sen Dunsidan into doing its bidding, fly the fire weapon to Arborlon, turn it on the Ellcrys, and destroy the Forbidding. The Moric would do that because there was no one to stop it. No one even knew it was there, save Tael Riverine, who had sent it. By the time the truth was out, there would be no way back.

Unless the Moric made a serious mistake, which it was thinking it might have done. Perhaps its decision to depend on its ability to influence Sen Dunsidan was such a mistake.

It started walking toward the rear of the Prime Minister's camp, back toward the wetland bog it had discovered on the first night of its arrival from Arishaig. Sen Dunsidan thought it settled somewhere within the larger Federation camp, but the Moric wanted nothing to do with humankind and its mode of dwelling. It thought fondly of its home in the swamps of Brockenthrog Weir in the world of the Jarka Ruus, steamy and fetid and rich with the smell of carrion. This world was too sterile, too clean. That would change when the demonkind reclaimed it.

It was deep in thought, paying little attention to anything around it, when the dart buried itself in its neck.

The Moric slowed, feeling the sting of the poison as it seeped into its flesh. Was the poison meant to kill it or merely to put it to sleep? Already its attackers were separating themselves from the surrounding shadows, coming toward it with knives drawn, crouched and ready. Apparently, they were determined to make certain of its demise. Or more to the point, to make certain of Iridia Eleri's demise. She was the one they had come to kill.

The Moric swung slowly about, counting heads. Four in all, stocky and garbed in black cloaks. Dwarves, perhaps. Assassins, whatever their species. But they had misjudged their quarry. They had come to kill a human. What they had found, unfortunately for them, was a demon.

The Moric waited for them to get closer, revealing nothing of its resistance to the poison, of its ability to shrug it off as nothing more than an irritation. When the closest of them, knife extended, rushed in from behind to finish it, the Moric whipped around swiftly, took hold of the attacker's arm, and yanked it from its socket. The attacker screamed and fell writhing on the earth. The Moric left this one where it lay and moved on to the next, catching it as it hesitated just a moment too long. Fingers twisting tightly into the folds of its cloak, the Moric yanked it off its feet and snapped its neck with a crack that sounded like the breaking of a piece of deadwood. The other two showed courage—or perhaps only foolishness—in choosing not to flee, but to attack as a unit, coming at the Moric from two sides. A foolish, pathetic effort. The demon tore the face off the first and crushed the skull of the second, all so swiftly that the struggle was over almost before it had begun.

A quick glance around assured it that no more attackers lurked in the shadows, that four had been deemed sufficient for the job. It pulled the attacker with the ruined face to its feet. It was still alive, though barely, and the Moric licked the blood from what remained of its face. Sweet. It took a second lick, then snapped the man's neck and threw the carcass down. One by one, it went to each of them and finished the job.

Then it took a moment to identify their species. It was surprised to discover that they were Gnomes.

Gnomes. Who would send Gnomes to kill Iridia Eleri? The answer, of course, was obvious. Finding Iridia's presence at Arishaig and her service to Sen Dunsidan intolerable, Shadea a'Ru had decided to take a hand in matters. The men must have been good at what they did or the Ard Rhys wouldn't have sent them. Too bad for her she didn't realize that Iridia was long since dead and that what they were dealing with was something else entirely.

But Shadea was no fool. She would discover that her assassins had failed, and she would take a closer look at what was really going on. She was already suspicious of Iridia's relationship with the Prime Minister. She would figure out soon enough that something about it was not right. Then she would try again, perhaps coming to do the job herself. The Moric was not afraid of her, but it did not want to become involved in a Druid feud that had nothing to do with its purpose in being in this wretched world in the first place.

What it must do, it decided as it walked away from the dead men, was to put an end to this nonsense. Its disguise had served its purpose, but it was becoming a liability. Its efforts at reaching the Ellcrys and tearing down the Forbidding were running up against obstacles it could not afford to spend time overcoming. Sen Dunsidan was recalcitrant. Shadea a'Ru was vengeful. Everything that lived and breathed in the Four Lands was a potential danger to it. Time, especially, was its enemy.

Its mind made up, the Moric licked a dollop of blood from its fingers as it continued on to its place of sleep. It would have to do something to change things. It would have to do so soon.

TWENTY

When she regained consciousness, Khyber Elessedil was sprawled on the catwalk, her body aching and her clothing soaked with her own blood. She pulled herself into a sitting position, glancing quickly about to be certain that the Gnome Hunter was still dead, lying where she had left him. The furnace room was unbearably hot, the tips of the flames from the pit dancing at the edges of her vision, as if trying to climb out. She felt suddenly dizzy, weakened from loss of blood and fatigue, and took a moment to gather her strength. Then she tore the sleeve of her tunic away, folded it into a compress, slipped it under her clothing, and pressed it against the dagger wound. When she had it in place, she pulled her belt free and used it to bind the compress tightly in place.

The effort took everything she had. She sat staring at the dead man, thinking that she had to move, that staying put was dangerous. Sooner or later, someone would come looking. She did not want to be there when they did.

But where was it that she wanted to be?

It was a question she could not answer easily. She had two choices. She could find her way clear of the Keep and seek help on the outside or she could stay where she was and try to find her way to the chambers of the Ard Rhys. Whichever she did, she had to do something to help Pen and Grianne Ohmsford avoid the triagenel. If she failed, they would be snared and made prisoners and the whole effort to rescue the Ard Rhys would have been for nothing.

She tried to think it through. Getting out of the Keep seemed the safer choice. Put some distance between herself and the rebel Druids and their Gnome Hunter protectors. But what would she do then? What sort of help could she expect to find outside Paranor? There were no communities for miles, no settlements, nothing but the heavy woods that surrounded the Keep. She could not count on Kermadec and his Trolls or Tagwen to find her. She could not even count on them to get free of Stridegate. She had no idea what had become of the Ohmsfords senior; they could be anywhere. And they did not know she was at Paranor in any case.

She knew she could not depend on help from the outside. Staying where she was made better sense, given that she had to come back in any case. But staying inside was also extremely dangerous. Enemies surrounded her. She did not know her way around. Everything about the Keep was a potential trap. No matter how careful she was, sooner or later she would make a mistake.

Either way, she might be done in by her wound, which burned like fire. If she didn't bleed to death, she ran a good risk of infection. Her compress was already soaked through, sticking to her clothing and flesh both.

She closed her eyes against her dilemma, trying to think it through. She would stay, she decided finally. Getting safely out of the Keep risked as much as trying to remain hidden inside. There was no guarantee of any help no matter which way she went. She might as well stay where she could do some good.

How much time did she have? How long before Pen and the Ard Rhys would come back into Paranor? It couldn't happen too quickly; he would have to find her first, and they would have to make their way back to the point of entry. But did time pass in the world of the Forbidding at the same speed it did in the Four Lands? What if the Ard Rhys was still at the place where she had entered, and Pen found her right away? It was possible they might come back much more quickly than she imagined.

She exhaled sharply. Too many questions, and there were no answers to any of them. She would have to do the best she could and hope that was enough.

With both hands grasping the catwalk guardrail, she pulled herself to her feet. She tottered for a moment, leaned against the railing for support, and waited for her head to clear. She was still hanging there when she remembered the Elfstones. In the heat of the struggle, she had forgotten them. Her throat tightened. Traunt Rowan had given them to one of the Gnome Hunters, but which one? What if it was the one she had pushed into the furnace pit? Fighting back against the burn of her fear, she pushed away from the railing and staggered back around the catwalk toward the tunnel through which she had entered. She passed the blackened husk of the third Gnome, turning her face away, trying not to look at him. She could not bring herself to begin her search there.

Instead, she retraced her steps and went back into the darkened passageway until she found the first of the remaining two. In the near darkness, she searched him thoroughly, but she did not find the Stones. Her heart sank. Taking his long knife from his belt so that she would have a weapon, she groped her way over to the second man. *Please*, she prayed, her fingers rummaging frantically through his clothing. This time she found what she was looking for. A surge of relief washed through her as she shoved the pouch into her tunic. Whatever else happened, she could not afford to lose the talismans.

Retrieving one of the torches she had extinguished earlier, she used her magic to relight it, and then started back up the passageway toward the Keep. If she encountered anyone at this point, she knew she was in trouble. There was no place for her to hide and she was too weak to fight. She moved ahead at a steady but painfully slow pace, concentrating on putting one foot in front of the other, conscious that her strength was slowing ebbing away. She knew she would have to treat her injury soon if she was to keep going, but she could not afford to stop and do so until she was someplace safe.

At some point, she lost her way, but she pushed on anyway. Eventually, she reached a confluence of tunnels, brightly lit with the smokeless torches the Druids favored in the Keep proper, and she cast her own aside. A stairway led upward, and she hesitated. She wasn't ready to go back into Paranor's upper regions just yet. Instead, she took one of the passageways leading off the hub. After passing several doors that were locked, she found one that wasn't and slipped inside.

A pair of smokeless torches cast a dim glow over a vaulted ceiling and stone-block walls. She was in a storage room jammed high with casks of ale and wine, the oaken barrels ironbound and tipped on their sides in huge cradles. A carpet of dust lay over everything; the air was thick with it. The room had clearly not been entered in a long time. She found that she could not lock the door from the inside, but she did not think she had the strength to look for another. If no one had been here recently, her odds were pretty good that no one would come soon. She worked her way to the back of the room, into the deep shadows where she could not be seen by anyone entering, and collapsed on a wooden pallet used for storing barrel staves.

She closed her eyes, wanting badly to sleep. But she knew if she did, she might not wake up again. She needed to stop the bleeding. Her healing skills were rudimentary, but Ahren had given her a few basic lessons. She knew she had to cauterize the wound. It would have been better if she were outside the Keep where she could gather some healing herbs and leaves, but there was no help for it. She would have to make do with magic and luck alone. She knew it was going to be painful. She was not brave, and she did not want to do this. But she had no choice if she wanted to go on.

She stripped off her tunic and pulled away the compress, then drew a little of the wine from one of the barrels and used it to wash the wound. The wine burned, and she clenched her teeth. It was a start, but it wasn't enough. For the healing process to begin, she had to close the wound all the way. She sat back down on the pallet and summoned a small magic that would help to numb the area around the wound, applying the dancing bits of colored light with her fingertips in gentle strokes. When the pain began to lessen, she brought out the long knife she had taken from the Gnome Hunter and used her magic-conjured fire to heat the tip of the blade until it glowed.

Then she bit down on a small piece of wood she found in a pile of scraps, summoned an image of Ahren and Emberen and better times to distract her, and laid the flat of the knife against the wound.

The pain was enormous. Trying not to and failing, she screamed into the wood, into the silence, smelling her flesh as it burned and seared. She did not lose consciousness, although she thought it might have been better if she had. When she could stand it no longer, she took the knife away, tears streaming down her cheeks, fire coursing through her body. She summoned more of the numbing magic and applied it with small strokes to the cauterized area. It took her a long time to make a difference, but finally the pain decreased.

She looked down at her side and then quickly away again. At least the wound was closed and the bleeding stopped. She had done what she could.

She pulled her tunic back on, wrapped herself in her cloak, and lay down to sleep, the knife gripped tightly in one hand.

Bek stood at the controls of *Swift Sure,* easing the airship down the line of the Charnals toward the Dragons Teeth and Paranor. The sky was hazy and gray, the midday sun blocked by storm clouds that were building into thunderheads. He watched the approaching weather mostly out of habit; his thoughts were elsewhere. On the deck below the pilot box, Trefen Morys and Bellizen sat together, heads bent close as they conversed. Kermadec, his brother Atalan, and a handful of other Rock Trolls were scattered about the aft decking, wrapped in blankets and asleep. Tagwen was belowdecks, fighting airsickness yet again, apparently unable to come to terms with flight motion even with help from Rue, who had given him herbs and a drink to calm his stomach. Some people were like that; no matter how hard they tried or how hard others tried for them, they simply couldn't make the adjustment.

He glanced over his shoulder. Somewhere behind them, perhaps half a day out, the balance of Taupo Rough's Rock Trolls followed aboard the huge flat transports that Trolls favored for conveying their armies to a place of battle. Slow and cumbersome, they rarely got more than a few hundred feet off the ground. But Kermadec had insisted they would reach Paranor in time to be of help. His job, and the job of the small company he had brought with him, was to get inside the Keep and secure at least one of the gates. Bek wasn't sure that eight or nine Trolls could manage that against a fortress of Druids and Gnome Hunters, but he kept his thoughts to himself. He wasn't sure, after all, that he could do what he intended, either.

He was flying the ship alone at that point, something he enjoyed and was comfortable with. He liked the feeling of satisfaction it gave him to be able to control her all by himself. He liked the way she rose and fell beneath his feet in response to the air currents. He knew *Swift Sure* better than any ship he had ever flown, and he had been flying for more than twenty years, ever since his journey to Parkasia aboard the *Jerle Shannara*, where Redden Alt Mer had taught him his flight skills and Rue Meridian had caused him to fall in love.

If Tagwen was to be believed, "falling in love" appeared to have happened all over again with his son and the blind Rover girl, Cinnaminson. An improbable happening under any circumstance, it seemed particularly strange here. Pen, following in the steps of his father, had fallen in love on a dangerous expedition, at a place and a time when falling in love was not convenient. Of course, that was the way love worked. You couldn't control the where or the when.

So many similarities in their lives. Pen, too, was a flier, although he had learned to fly much earlier and was already as comfortable aboard an airship as his father. It was strange to think of Pen traveling down such a familiar road, but the comparisons were inescapable.

But the strong possibility that, like himself, Pen possessed a secret magic gave Bek pause. He had been wrestling with the idea since the moment he had realized in his efforts to track his son that he was able to do so only because Pen had the use of a magic that neither he nor Rue had known anything about. Still, he could not ignore what reason and common sense told him about his connection to his son and, consequently, what it suggested about the possibility of another similarity in their lives. Bek, too, had possessed magic when he had gone with the Druid Walker to Parkasia, and he hadn't known of it. It was only after they were well out over the Blue Divide and confronted with the barriers of Ice Henge and the Squirm that Walker had revealed the truth about who he really was and how the magic had been passed down to him.

He wondered when Pen had made his discovery. Had he known about it earlier and kept it secret from his parents? There was reason to think he might have done so, given his mother's antipathy toward magic and Bek's own reluctance to make use of it. It might also be that while Pen had known of it, he had not until recently fully explored its uses. It might be that he was still on a journey of discovery.

Of one thing Bek was quite certain. The King of the Silver River had chosen his son to make the journey into the Forbidding for a very specific reason, and it almost certainly had something to do with his heritage of the wishsong magic. The Faerie creature could have come to Bek to do what was needed, but he had gone to Pen instead. That meant that something about Pen made him the more appropriate candidate for going into the Forbidding and rescuing Grianne. A boy, barely grown. It was almost impossible to understand. But the King of the Silver River had come to Ohmsfords since the time of Shea and Flick in the days of Allanon, and had always done so with unerring instincts for what each of them was capable of achieving.

Now it was up to Bek and Rue to find a way to help their son fulfill the charge that had been given to him. History was repeating itself, another instance of a similarity in the lives of the Ohmsfords, and more particularly in the lives of a father and son.

Bek paused in his thinking. Would history repeat itself? Would it repeat in every particular? He had come back alive from the expedition he had embarked upon. Would Pen have the same good fortune?

He hated thinking about such a question, but he could not help himself. In part, it was a reflection of his own sense of responsibility for his son. He had been given the task of seeing that Pen got safely back through the Forbidding. If he failed to do that, he would have failed his son. It was a possibility he refused to consider.

"What are you thinking about?" Rue asked him.

She stepped up into the pilot box and stood beside him, her green eyes inquisitive. When she saw the look that came over his face, she leaned over and kissed him. "What's wrong? Can't you tell me?"

He nodded. "I was thinking about how much Pen depends on us, even though he doesn't know it."

"He is supposed to depend on us. He is our son."

"I don't want to fail him."

"You won't. Neither of us will."

They were silent a moment, watching the land slide away beneath the airship's hull, the heavy weather west continuing to advance. Waterbirds from out of the Malg Swamp screamed eerie cries as they sailed across the skies. Far below, a cluster of Forest Trolls emerged from the trees and stalked in a line across the hills leading up to the mountains east.

"Is Tagwen any better?" he asked.

She shook her head. "He just isn't meant for this."

"I guess not." He paused. "I'm worried about how much he really knows about getting into Paranor without being seen."

"You ought to be," she said. He gave her a sharp look. "I asked him about it, and he admitted that he hadn't been inside those secret tunnels in several years and that his memory of them was sketchy at best."

"So we can't rely on him."

She shook her head again.

"How about Trefen Morys and Bellizen? Do they know anything that might help?"

"I don't think so. They've only been a part of the order for a little over two years. They haven't had time to do much more than complete the lessons assigned them as novice Druids. They are loyal to your sister, but they haven't had the closeness with her that Tagwen has. They didn't even know there were secret tunnels."

He looked off into the distance. "So we have to depend on ourselves in this business."

She nodded. "Pretty much like always."

He didn't say anything to that.

When she awoke, Khyber Elessedil ached from head to foot, as if the cauterization had been applied across her entire body. She was not feverish, but she was disoriented and weak. She sat up, wishing she had something to eat or drink, and then remembered she was surrounded by wine and ale casks. She moved over to the closest barrel, opened the spigot, and took a long, satisfying drink of cool wine. She would have preferred water, but the wine would suffice.

She could do nothing about her hunger, though. She considered the possibility that there might be foodstuffs stored somewhere down in these cellar passageways, but she had no idea where they might be and no time to spend looking for them. She would have to get by on whatever she might scavenge along the way. What mattered just then was reaching the sleeping chamber of the Ard Rhys as quickly as possible.

Something, she realized, she did not know how to do.

It was bad enough that she did not have a clear idea of where she was so that she might have some sense of which direction to go. It was much worse that she had no idea how to reach her destination without being seen. She could find a way to disguise herself, she supposed, just as she had done when she had freed Pen. But that was risky and, besides, even if she got that far the sleeping chamber would be heavily guarded.

Trying to decide where to begin, she considered her alternatives for a moment, but the task was hopeless. Everything she thought about trying was too dangerous. Once they found the dead Gnome Hunters, they would be looking for her anyway. Perhaps they already were. She needed to disappear, to become invisible.

She pondered the idea. There were secret passageways in the walls of Paranor. Ahren had told her so once. The Keep was honeycombed with them. The Druids had used them to reach one another when they wished their conferences kept secret. The Ard Rhys had used them from time to time, as well, to slip from her chamber without being seen when need or discretion warranted it.

If she could find a way into those . . .

She would be lost all over again, she finished dismally.

Unless . . .

Her mind raced. Unless she had a way to keep from getting lost.

Her hand strayed to the pocket in her tunic where the Elfstones were tucked away. The Elfstones could keep her from getting lost. They could show her a way into the sleeping chamber, just as they had shown Ahren the way to Stridegate and the tanequil.

She was suddenly excited, the aches and pains and hunger forgotten. But then she remembered that use of magic as powerful as the Elfstones was likely to be detected by the very people she was trying to avoid. It was the reason she had tried so hard not to use the Stones on the journey into the Charnals. Using them in the Druid's Keep, right beneath their noses, would be madness. Besides, they thought the Elfstones destroyed, thrown into the furnace along with her body. Any release of the magic risked revealing that she was still alive.

Or did it?

If the Elfstones had been thrown into the furnace, would the intense heat and pressure destroy them? Would it serve to release the magic in doing so? No one knew, she suspected. There were no other Elfstones save the ones she carried, and little was known about their properties. It might well be that their destruction would unlock their magic in the same way as a user's summoning.

Anyway, what other choice did she have?

She wondered suddenly how long she had been asleep. Did they know yet that she had escaped? Or did they think her dead and the Elfstones dead with her?

She rose and left the storage room, slipping cautiously through the door, and went back down the passageways of the Keep toward the furnace chamber. She picked up a torch on the way to provide her with the light she needed. She was hurrying by then, anxious to discover if her idea had a chance of working. It all depended on how much time had passed and what had happened in the interim. She moved quietly, listening for voices, for sounds that would indicate the bodies of the dead men had been discovered, that her deception was unworkable. But the passageways were silent and empty, and when she reached the place where the first two Gnomes had died, she found their bodies untouched. Farther down, within the furnace room itself, she found the third, as well. No one had missed them yet. No one had come looking.

She still had a chance.

One by one, she dragged the dead men to the edge of the fire pit and shoved them in. It would not conceal the struggle or the shedding of blood, but it would make it harder for those who eventually came looking to determine exactly what had happened. It might give her a measure of time and distance from discovery. She had to hope so because it was all she had to work with.

Exhausted from her efforts, she sat down with her back against the railing and took out the Elfstones. She had to try to use them, even if the release of the magic alerted Shadea and the other rebel Druids. She had to hope that they would register the source of the magic as the furnace room and attribute its presence to the destruction of the Stones in the fire.

She shook her head. She wished she had a better way. But she was stuck with things as they were, and there was no point wishing for something she couldn't have.

She poured the Elfstones out of their pouch and into the palm of her hand, studying them a moment. Then she closed her fingers tightly about them, held up her hand, and summoned the magic.

It was easier this time than it had been before, perhaps because she was used to the process and more receptive to it. The familiar

warmth spread from her hand through her arm and into her body before looping back again. When she was infused with the magic of the
Stones, her thoughts centered on what she needed, seeking a way
into the secret passages of the Keep, a blue glow formed within her
fist and began to seep through the cracks of her fingers. Then,
abruptly, it shot from her hand in a thin, long streamer, penetrating
the fiery atmosphere of the furnace room, burrowing through stone
and darkness, illuminating the way forward.

She watched as her route revealed itself, a twisting of passages
and stairways, cutting through the walls of the Keep, winding
steadily upward until they ended at a wall that gave secret entry into
the sleeping chambers of the Ard Rhys. A strange glow leaked
through the seams of the hidden door, a suggestion of magic contained within the room.

Then the vision flared and was gone, the blue glow of the Elfstone magic disappeared, and the warmth within her faded away.
She sat again on the catwalk with her back to the railing, her memory of what she had been shown sharp and clear.

High in the north tower, several floors below the sleeping room
draped with the lethal netting of the triagenel, the Druid on watch in
the cold chamber for disturbances triggered by unauthorized uses of
magic noticed a spike on the otherwise smooth surface of the scrye
waters. He leaned forward as the ripples spread outward, wanting to
be certain of what he was seeing.

The source of the spike was the Druid's Keep.

He took a long moment to consider what that meant. Magic was
in frequent use at Paranor, so disturbances of that sort were not unusual. Still, the spike suggested a usage more powerful than the conjuring normally done. He should report it, he knew. But he also knew
that if he chose to do so, he must go before Shadea a'Ru, something
no one wanted to do these days.

He tried to think the matter through. It was possible that the
usage was one the Ard Rhys knew about. It was even possible that
the usage was hers. The Druid on watch did not want to intrude
where he was not welcome. Discretion was well advised where matters involving Paranor and the order were concerned—especially by

those who only served. Drawing attention to oneself was not wise. Others had disappeared from the Keep for much less.

Besides, what sort of magic could be called up within these walls that someone in authority did not know about?

He debated the matter only a moment more, then went back to his seat and resumed his watch.

TWENTY-ONE

D awn was a faint glimmer in the east when Penderrin Ohmsford stirred from his sleep and peered from his shelter into the gray, hazy gloom of a new day. Mist clung to the land in deep pockets. Clouds obscured the sky, thick and dull blankets that formed a canopy from horizon to horizon and refused to reveal the sun. The air was windless and raw with unpleasant smells and the landscape wintry and bleak in the pale first light. The night's rain had ended, leaving dark stains on the bare earth and rocks.

The dragon was right where it had been the night before, stretched in front of his shelter like a wall.

Only now, it was sleeping.

Pen stared at it for a moment, not quite believing. Yes, the dragon was asleep, its eyelids closed, its huge, horn-encrusted snout resting comfortably on its wagon-wheel feet, a steady snoring issuing from its maw, and its nostrils flaring at regular intervals as it inhaled and exhaled.

He waited long moments to be certain, then carefully climbed to his feet, his cloak wrapped close and the darkwand gripped firmly in one hand. A corridor opened to his left, leading just past the dragon's outstretched head, passing wickedly close to those teeth and claws but offering a narrow avenue of escape. He just needed to be very quiet. And lucky.

He took a deep breath and stepped from his shelter into the thin dawn light.

Instantly, one scaly lid slipped open and the dragon's yellow eye stared at him.

He froze, his blood gone cold, waiting to see if maybe, just possibly, the eye might not register his presence and simply close again. But it fixed firmly on him and did not move. He watched it for long moments, debating if he should try to go farther, then backed slowly into his shelter and sat down again.

So much for that.

He sat looking out at the dragon for a long time. He was so hungry he could hear his stomach growl. His nerves were ragged, and his hopes for reaching his aunt fading fast. Somehow, he had to get past the monster. To spend another day trapped in those rocks was unacceptable.

He closed his eyes in despair. Didn't the dragon ever get hungry? Why didn't it leave and go off to find something to eat?

Of course, dragons might not have to eat all that often, he reasoned. Maybe they only ate once a week, like the moor cats in the Four Lands. Maybe it had just eaten before it found him. Maybe it would never want to eat anything again as long as it had him to entertain it.

"Get out of here!" he screamed in a rush of frustration.

The dragon didn't move. It didn't even blink.

But the runes on the darkwand began to dance wildly.

He stared at them in confusion and surprise. The dancing continued for a few seconds more, and then slowed. He furrowed his brow. His voice had disturbed them. They had become more active because he had shouted at the dragon.

He found himself thinking again about how the runes continued to glow even while he was asleep and paying no attention to the staff at all. He had thought at first that the runes only brightened when they were responding to his thoughts. But that didn't seem to be the case. Hadn't been the case ever. From the moment he had encountered the dragon, the runes had acted independently of anything he had done, keeping the monster transfixed and at bay.

Even while he was sleeping.

Why would they do that?

They would do it, he thought suddenly, because the darkwand

was sentient. The tanequil had given him a living piece of itself. That was what had enabled him to carve the runes without seeing what he was doing. That was what had transported him from the Four Lands into the Forbidding. It knew to use the runes to charm the dragon, to mesmerize it so that it would not attack Pen. Just as it knew to guide him to the Ard Rhys, it knew to protect him.

But why had the runes responded to his voice?

Shades!

Because it was a thing of magic and it would always respond to other magic. His magic. Not his little magic, his ability to read the actions and behavior of other creatures in an effort to communicate with them. Not the magic he had grown up with and kept secret even from his parents because he never thought it mattered. No, not that magic.

Another magic. The wishsong magic.

Like father, like son.

He could scarcely believe it. He had always understood there was a possibility of his inheriting such magic. But he had thought that possibility long past, faded with the passing of the years. He was too old. If it was going to happen, it would have happened earlier.

Yet it hadn't happened to his father, either, until he was a few years older than Pen was now. So it was possible that history was repeating itself. The blood heritage was a part of his past. But perhaps it was also a part of his future, its seeds locked deep inside him. He knew that his small communicative magic was born of it, even if it wasn't as powerful.

And now, for reasons he didn't understand, the wishsong had surfaced in him as it had surfaced twenty years earlier in his father. It had awakened in his voice and given him a way to connect to the magic of the darkwand.

Except, he thought excitedly, he *did* understand the reasons for its emergence. The darkwand had awakened the wishsong. His joining to the staff in the carving of its intricate web of runes had brought the magic to life.

He looked into the distance, thinking that he was being foolish, that he had no reason to believe any of his conclusions. He glanced down at the staff, at the softly glowing runes, their patterns changing endlessly, dancing hypnotically across the darkened, burnished wood. He had no proof that the wishsong's magic was what had stirred those runes or, even if it had, that he could implement it in any useful way.

But where was the harm in trying to find out?

He began to hum, soft and steady, shifting tones and pitches, trying anything and everything. He kept at it, not knowing exactly what he was doing, just testing to see if anything he tried would make a difference. The response from the runes was immediate. They throbbed and pulsed, the glow shifting from rune to rune and from row to row, skipping here and there as if a thing alive. Patterns formed and were replaced almost quicker than the eye could follow, a kaleidoscope of brilliant images.

The dragon lifted its head, fascinated.

Pen changed from humming to stringing together words, not singing any specific song, just phrases that seemed to go together, seeking ways to make the runes do other things. But the runes just kept shifting about as they chose with little regard to anything he did. They seemed to respond only to sound and not to specific words or meanings. Frustrated, unable to see how this was helping anything, he tightened his resolve, burrowed down inside himself, and gave a harder push to what he was doing.

Get away from me, he sang in a dozen different ways. *Go far, far away from me.*

Suddenly, there was a different response from the staff. Imprints of the runes literally jumped off the wood and into the air, glowing images that hung like fireflies against the sullen morning light. Still throbbing and pulsing, still shifting about in intricate patterns that kept the dragon mesmerized, the rune images danced about and then flew off into the morning mist. Line after line of glowing symbols broke free of the darkwand and winged away like birds taking flight.

The dragon sniffed at them as they passed, and then licked out at them with its long, mottled tongue, but it could not capture them. Frustrated, it heaved its bulk off the ground and rose on its hind legs, maw splitting wide, scaly lips drawing back to reveal blackened teeth. Hissing and spitting, it snapped wildly at the images as they flitted past. Pen shrank back against the rock of his shelter in terror, but managed to keep singing. The dragon ripped at the images with its forelegs, and then finally, screaming with frustration as they continued to elude it, it spread great leathery wings and took flight, chasing after them.

It happened so fast that Pen barely had time to register his sudden change of fortune before the dragon was gone, a dark speck in the distance, pursuing the still-glowing images. Seconds later, it disappeared completely.

Pen kept singing anyway, sending more flights of glowing runes in the same direction, worried that the dragon would decide to come back. When he finally thought it safe, he went silent. The images faded and the runes on the staff ceased their excited dance and resumed a soft, gentle pulsing against the dark surface of the wood. All about, silence hung deep and pervasive on the hazy morning air.

Pen exhaled sharply. What in the world had happened?

The truth was, he didn't know. Obviously he had tapped into the magic of the wishsong, successfully summoning it from where it lay dormant within him. Probably his link with the darkwand enabled him to do so, to bring the magic to life and to make use of it to save himself. But he had no idea what sort of magic he had conjured. He didn't know how to control it; he didn't really even understand how to use it. All he had managed to do was to make the darkwand's runes respond to him in a way that had lured the dragon away and given him a chance to be free. Beyond that, he hadn't learned a thing.

But that was good enough.

Wrapping his cloak close about him once more and gripping the darkwand firmly in one hand, he stepped out of his shelter and looked about. There was no sign of the dragon or anything else. The day was sullen and dark, and the air smelled of damp and rot. He needed to get out of that place; he needed to find Grianne Ohmsford and go home again.

Turning his thoughts to his aunt and mindful of how he had begun his search two days before, he held up the staff, pointed it south again, and watched the runes brighten.

Then, with a last cautious look skyward, he set out.

He walked all the rest of that day through country so bleak and so heavy with the promise of evil that he found himself constantly looking over his shoulder for what he imagined might be following. He took the trail leading up into the mountains, the passage he had chosen before the dragon trapped him, climbing steadily into the rocks through the morning, and then descending on the other side in

the afternoon. The day stayed dreary, the mountain air of no better quality than what he had found below. The haziness of the landscape was deep and pervasive. Not much grew anywhere he passed
through. Mostly, the terrain was marked by different striations of
earth and rock, a blending of washed-out grays and blacks and
browns.

It rained a little at midday. He cupped his hands to catch the precious liquid and licked the dampness from his palms. Other than
that, he found only stagnant ponds and sediment-fouled trickles
coming out of the rocks. Higher up, he encountered trees that bore
a vivid crimson fruit, but he knew that bright colors in living things
frequently indicated danger, and he passed the fruit by. He found a
flock of crowlike birds eating berries from a bush, and though the
berries looked unpleasant, he tried one anyway and found it edible.
With an eye toward the crow-birds, which were squawking at him
angrily, he ate the rest.

Weary from his ordeal of the past few days, drained of energy in
a way he had not expected, he rested at the crest of the pass for a
time before starting down. Some of that had to do with the stress and
fear that his encounter with the dragon had created, but some had to
do with his not eating or sleeping well. The land had a draining effect on him, its blasted, empty terrain unbearably depressing. How
anything could live in that world escaped him. He guessed that what
lived there was a match for the land. Certainly the dragon was. He
found himself hoping that the dragon was the most dangerous creature he would come across, but what were the chances of that?

After his rest, he descended the far side of the mountains, following the long, winding thread of the pass toward a vast misted plain
that stretched away as far as the eye could see. The plain looked devoid of life, but he knew better than to expect that it was. Mist clung
to its surface, twisting and writhing through deep ravines and skirting broad plateaus that lifted out of the flats like beasts rising from
sleep. Skeletal trees jutted from the plains like bones, and here and
there black pools of water shimmered slickly.

He looked out across the plains in despair. Crossing those flats
was not something he wanted to do.

But what choice did he have?

He had no idea how far he would have to travel to reach his aunt or what he would find when he did. She had been there a long time by then; anything could have happened to her. He took it on faith that she was still alive. He did not think the runes would direct him to her lifeless body. But she could be hurt or damaged mentally or emotionally. She could have been made a captive or forced to endure any number of other unpleasant things. If she required physical assistance to get back to the doorway of the Forbidding, how was he going to manage that? If she required medical help, what could he do to heal her? The more he thought about it, the more daunting the prospects seemed. Too much time had passed for everything to be unchanged in her life. Something would be wrong with her; something would have happened.

He was not looking forward to finding out what that was.

He trudged on, reached the bottom of the pass, and struck out across the plains toward the heavily misted horizon. The darkwand was taking him south and east, turning him slightly from his previous path. The way forward was swathed in encroaching darkness that lifted out of the east like a shroud ready to be laid over a corpse. The land felt and looked like that corpse, and Pen supposed that it would be appropriate to lay a shroud over it. He did not care to be out and about when that happened, however, and he began to look for somewhere to spend the night. The clumps of rocks he had relied upon for protection and shelter the past few nights were missing here. All that was available were promontories, deep ravines, and stands of stunted trees. He chose the latter, thinking that if he could find a suitable clump in which to nest, he could conceal himself from whatever might come hunting by night.

For what must have been the hundredth time, he wished he knew more about the land and its inhabitants, knowledge that might help keep him safe. But there was nothing he could do about his ignorance; he was there, and the only person likely to give him any sort of useful information was the person he was searching for.

The light darkened from misty gray to deep twilight. A fog settled in, a thickening of the mist that slowly shortened visibility to a dozen yards. Pen had been making his way toward a particularly thick stand of broad-limbed trees with branches so thoroughly intertwined it was difficult to tell where one tree stopped and another began. The canopy of limbs provided a shelter that might hide him while he sought to gain a little sleep. He questioned whether he could sleep at all given his uneasiness after the dragon experience, but he knew he had to try.

He entered the woods just as darkness was closing down, found a stand of wintry, gray-barked hardwoods that were virtually bereft of leaves, and settled down in a patch of heavy, coarse grass nestled between a pair of ancient trunks. Wrapped in his cloak, he put his back against one of the trunks and watched the onset of night steal away the last of the light.

When everything turned black, he listened to the ensuing hush. When the hush gave way to night sounds, he sat listening to those. When the sounds grew closer, a mix of clicks and huffs and low growls, he pressed harder against the tree trunk and brought the darkwand around in front of him for whatever protection it might offer.

And then the sounds evened out and smoothed over, surrounding him but not coming so close that he felt the need to move, and his eyes began to grow heavy, his breathing to deepen and slow, and finally, he slept.

When he awoke, dawn had broken in a wash of familiar hazy gray light, and the surface of the surrounding land was covered in layers of vapor that ebbed and flowed across the contours of the terrain like an ocean's waves across a rocky shore. He stared out into the all-but-invisible distance, to horizons that ended much nearer than they had the day before and revealed nothing of what they concealed, and he was immediately depressed.

He was hungry, as well, but there was nothing to eat or drink, or at least nothing on which he wished to take a chance. So he turned his efforts to stretching cramped limbs and aching muscles, to finding fresh ways to make the blood flow sufficiently that he could get to his feet and go on. He could barely tolerate the thought of it, his search beginning to take on the feel of an endless odyssey, one that might not have an attainable destination, but would simply lead him on until he was lost beyond recovery in a trackless wilderness.

He thought he might try to use his magic, to employ it to make contact with some of the vegetation or smaller creatures and see what he could learn. It was all well and good to give himself over to the directional dictates of the darkwand, but it would be better if he could feel that he had some small control over his own destiny. Just being able to know a little something more of the world through which he passed might help. He didn't yet have much confidence in his ability to get out of tight spots, and knowing that his magic could do more than make the darkwand's runes dance about would go a long ways toward changing that.

He rose finally and looked about, peering through the gloom, trying not to breathe in the fetid smells of the deadwood and dank earth. The sky was lower today, more heavily clouded, as if rain threatened, and the mix of clouds and mist gave the sense of a sky and earth become joined. The way forward seemed immeasurable, a thick wall of gray that lacked any sense of up or down or sideways. He peered into it with trepidation and repulsion, then reluctantly set out.

He walked for a time, but could not seem to get clear of the woods. He was certain they did not stretch far and that he had set out in the right direction. But trees continued to materialize through the wall of the mist, their tangled limbs linked weblike overhead.

Finally he stopped, directed his thoughts toward his aunt, and held out the staff.

Nothing.

At first, he couldn't believe it. Then he panicked. Had the magic of the darkwand ceased to respond to him? He shook his head. No, that couldn't be. He turned to his left and tried again. Still nothing. He wheeled back in the direction from which he had come and tried a third time. This time, the runes flashed brightly in response.

He had gotten turned completely around.

Still a little afraid and not wishing to chance getting lost again, he kept the staff raised and his thoughts fixed and began to retrace his steps. He moved ahead carefully, watching where he placed his feet, taking note of the location of the trees, trying to form some sense of direction, even as he relied on the darkwand's magic to keep him from wandering astray.

When he stepped from the woods finally, clear at last, he found himself in a stretch of heavy grasses and rotting logs interspersed with stagnant, scum-laced ponds. The smell was terrible. He wrinkled his nose and glanced about apprehensively, took a quick reading from the staff, and moved ahead.

He had gone only a short distance when he saw the bones. Gray and bare and broken, they lay scattered on a patch of bare earth. He stopped at once and stared at them. He did not know what kind of bones they were, but there were enough of them that he could tell that they came from more than one creature. From the number and their condition, he guessed they had been there for a long time.

He was in the middle of a feeding ground.

He looked about once more, suddenly aware of how quiet it was. *A good idea to move away from this place,* he thought.

Sliding left through the grasses, away from the bones, he walked as silently as he could toward another sparse copse of dead trees, try-ing to breathe evenly, to keep his head clear and his thoughts col-lected. *Don't panic,* he told himself. *Whatever feeds here isn't necessarily about.*

A high-pitched shriek stopped him in his tracks. A second re-sponded to the first, and a third. They came from all sides, piercing and raw. A huge shape descended from the gloom, wings out-stretched as it settled onto the log not twenty feet ahead of him. It was a vulturelike bird, its body as big as his own, its wingspan at least a dozen feet. He watched it land, wings folding against its back, its narrow head lowering.

When the head lifted a moment later, he saw that the bird had the face of a woman. But not any kind of woman he had ever seen. This woman had sharp, bony features, its mouth jutting and pinched in the manner of a beak and its eyes hard and birdlike. Its body and wings were covered with dark feathers, and its feet ended in huge, hooked talons that seemed too big for the rest of it.

Hunched so far over that it looked deformed, it sat on the log and watched him intently but made no move toward him. He held his ground a moment, then started to back away. But another shriek rose, and a second bird-woman swooped down right behind him, blocking his way. Then two more appeared, and two more after that, materializing out of the haze, wings flapping as they landed all about him, some on the ground, some on the limbs of trees. A dozen, at least, he saw, all watching him, gazes hard and fixed.

Harpies.

He swallowed hard. He knew what Harpies were; he had read stories of them in his father's histories of the Four Lands. Vicious and unpredictable creatures, Harpies had been exiled to the Forbidding along with the other dark things in the time of Faerie. If memory served him correctly, Harpies were flesh eaters that were said to have preyed on men and animals alike.

He glanced again at the talons of the one perched on the log in front of him and felt a fresh surge of panic. He needed to be somewhere else right away, but he didn't know how he could manage that, encircled as he was. Some of them had started to edge closer, making small cooing sounds. They seemed pleased. They sounded eager.

"Get away!" he shouted at them, waving his arms threateningly.

Instantly, the runes on the darkwand flared, brightening like bits of fire, dancing up and down the wood. The Harpies shrieked and flapped their leathery wings, and those advancing paused. Pen shouted at them some more and tried to move through them, but they quickly adjusted to keep him in place. He swung the staff at them. The runes danced even more wildly. The Harpies flinched but held their ground.

Pen felt an overwhelming sense of desperation. He had to find something more effective. He remembered the dragon then and how his use of the wishsong had sent the runes flying off into the distance, luring it away. Perhaps that would work with the Harpies, as well. He didn't have much control over how the magic worked, but it was all he could think of.

He began to sing boldly, as if he might force his way through his attackers by the sheer force of his voice. He sang snatches of phrases and bits and pieces of things that just came to him, hoping that something would work. It did. Rune images spun off the staff in a glowing swirl and soared skyward, forming bright, complex patterns against the dark ceiling of the clouds.

The Harpies watched as the images lifted into the sky but they did not follow.

Pen's desperation increased. He didn't know what more he could do. He kept singing, punctuating his increasingly frantic efforts with shouts and cries, looking for something that would drive the Harpies back. But, having seen that his magic was confined to pretty glowing images that danced and flew and did nothing more, the bird-women were advancing again. Their sharp eyes glittered in the dim light and their strange mouths worked slowly up and down, opening and closing hungrily.

Pen gripped the darkwand tightly in both hands and prepared to use it as a club. It was all he had left.

But just when it seemed that he was all out of chances, a dark shape appeared on the horizon, winging toward him, quickly growing larger and taking form. The dragon! It was tracking the rune images once more, following them to their source. How it had seen them from so far away, Pen couldn't know. But it was flying right for where the greatest number circled and danced against the clouds overhead.

Their bright, hard eyes fixed on Pen, the Harpies didn't see the dragon at first. Then the dragon screamed—there was no other word for it—and they swung about swiftly, necks craned, a fresh urgency in their posture. A few took flight immediately, but the rest hesitated, unwilling to abandon their prey.

Plummeting out of the sky with such swiftness that Pen, who had thought he might try to make a run for it, had no chance to do anything but stand and watch, the dragon dropped on them like a stone. It snatched up the Harpies the way a big cat might small birds, tearing them apart and casting them aside as fast as it could reach them. A few flew at the dragon with their wicked talons outstretched, but the beast simply crushed them in its huge jaws and flung them to the ground. The Harpies screamed and hissed and flapped their wings frantically, unable to escape.

One by one, the dragon killed them until only two were left, crawling about the blood-soaked earth and whimpering in despair. The dragon played with them, nudging them this way and that. Pen watched for as long as it took him to realize that he might be next, then slowly backed away. Rune images still danced and soared overhead, and fresh images leapt from the darkwand to whirl about the dragon like fireflies. If the dragon saw them, it gave no indication. For the moment, its attention was fixed on its new toys.

Pen reached the edge of the woods without the dragon taking notice and slipped into the trees. After he was well into them, he put the darkwand beneath his cloak, closed down his thoughts of his aunt, and waited for the runes to go dark.

Soaked in his own sweat, he pushed on, barely able to make himself move. He had thought the dragon safely gone. But it couldn't have been far away if it had seen the rune images. That should have made him happy, since it had saved his life, but it only made him further aware of how vulnerable he was. He might be saved for the moment, but he would remain in peril until he was out of the Forbidding and back in the Four Lands. Until then, his life span probably didn't measure the length of his arm. He had to find his aunt, and he had to find her quickly or his luck would be used up.

He kept walking, refusing to look back, heading in the general direction he knew he had to go. He kept the darkwand lowered and inactive, afraid to do anything that would bring the runes to life.

He was half a mile away before he could no longer hear the crunching of bones.

TWENTY-TWO

No matter how often she scowled at him, he just wouldn't stop talking about it.

"Such power, Straken Queen! Such incredible power! No one can match you—no one who is or ever was! I sensed you were special, I did, Grianne of the trees! When I first saw you from my hiding place and knew you for who you were, I knew, too, *what* you were! It was in your eyes and the way you carried yourself. It was in your voice when you first spoke to me. You awoke in a prison, sent by your enemies to be destroyed, and still you showed no fear! *That* is evidence of real power!"

She let him go on mostly because she didn't know how to shut him up. Weka Dart was a bundle of pent-up energy, bouncing off the cavern walls and skittering across the uneven floor, darting this way and that, rushing ahead and then wheeling back, a wild thing in search of an outlet. She didn't think he could help himself; that was just the way he was, a creature of ungovernable whims and uncontrollable urges. He had been like that on the journey to the Forbidding's version of the Hadeshorn, so his hyperactivity was not a surprise.

In any case, she was too tired to do much more than put one foot in front of the other and press on.

"How much farther?" she asked at one point.

"Not far, not far," he said, dashing back to take her hand, which she yanked away irritably. "The tunnels open onto the Pashanon just ahead, and then we will be back outside in the fresh air and light!"

It was all relative, she supposed, picturing the world that waited with its greasy air and its dingy skies. She would not know true fresh air and light again ever if she did not get back into her own world. She found herself thinking again of the boy who was coming to find her, the salvation she had been promised by the Warlock Lord. He seemed such an impossibility that she could not make herself accept that he was real. But if he wasn't, she was trapped there forever. So she kept alive a faint hope that somehow he would appear, whether that appearance was reflected accurately in the words of the promise or in some less easily discernible way. She just knew it had better happen soon because she was beginning to fail.

She took a moment to measure the truth of that statement and found it accurate. It was happening in subtle ways—ways she did not think she could reverse while trapped within the Forbidding. Her physical strength was eroded, the result of poor food and drink, a lack of sleep, and the debilitating struggles she had waged with Tael Riverine. But her emotional and psychological strengths had been drained, as well, and those in a more direct and damaging way. She had been forced to use the magic several times, and each time she had felt something change inside her. It was bad enough that she was forced to use it at all—worse still that she was forced to use it in such horrifying ways. Assimilating with the Furies had torn apart her psyche. Resisting the power of the conjure collar had all but broken her spirit.

But her confrontation with the Graumth had reduced her to a new level of despair, one so fraught with bad feelings that she was literally afraid of calling up the magic again. It was the way the wishsong had responded. She should have been thankful she still had command of it after all she had been through. She should have welcomed its appearance. But the strength of its response had terrified her. It had been not only greater than she had expected, but also virtually uncontrollable. It hadn't just surfaced on being summoned, ready to do her bidding. It had exploded out of her, so wild and destructive that she couldn't hold it back. She had lived with the wishsong for more than thirty years, and she had known before coming into the Forbidding what to expect from it. But that was changed. The magic had taken on a new feel, becoming something she didn't recognize. It was a strange creature living inside her, threatening her in ways that made her afraid for the first time in years.

What she feared most was that it had evolved because of where she was and that the unforeseen evolution was changing her into something that belonged more to the Forbidding than to her world.

Yet what could she do to stop it?

Weka Dart had probably done as much for her as he could. Debilitated or not, she was the one with the magic. If they were backed into a corner, she was the one who could keep them alive. She would have to put aside her concerns about using the magic. The hunt for them would continue, and it would not end until she was free of the Forbidding or she was dead.

They continued working cautiously through the tunnels below Kraal Reach, and it wasn't long until there was a brightening of the darkness ahead of them. Within minutes, they had reached a fissure in the mountain rock, one that opened into the clouded mistiness of the Pashanon.

They stood in silence for a moment, staring out onto a broad wetlands pocked by dozens of stagnant pools and vast stands of heavy grasses and thick scrub. The waters of the ponds nearest were covered in greenish slime and smelled of decay. Insects buzzed and chirped from every quarter, swarms of gnats and flies hovered above the surface of the ponds, and snakes slid soundlessly through the shadows.

The wetlands spread away for miles in all directions.

Grianne shook her head in dismay. "How do we get through this?"

Weka Dart looked over at her, eyes bright and teeth showing. "Follow me, Grianne of the wondrous magic, and I will show you."

Without pausing, he started out through the swamp. She followed with no small amount of misgiving, not certain she should trust his judgment, yet unwilling to be left behind. But the Ulk Bog seemed to know what he was doing. Even though the hazy light was pale and deceptive, he chose their path without hesitating. Now and then he would change course in midstride, turning another way. More than once he reversed himself entirely, muttering about obstacles that hadn't been there before, that didn't belong, that had appeared merely to vex him. When a snake crossed his path he simply reached down, snatched it up, and tossed it aside. He didn't seem afraid of them. He didn't seem to mind the clouds of insects either. He lapped at them with his tongue, hissed at them to clear his nostrils.

Disgusted by her surroundings, Grianne settled for putting her arm and the sleeve of her tunic across her mouth and nose and lowering her head as far as she could without losing sight of the Ulk Bog. The odor of death permeated the air; she could feel the decay worming its way into her breathing passages. She used a little of the wishsong's magic to keep it all at bay—not enough to give them away to anyone following, but enough to give her a measure of distance from the foulness. She cast quick glances all about as they went, searching for movement that might signal a pursuit. But nothing of that sort showed itself, and she began to wonder if perhaps chase had not yet been given. It seemed unlikely that the dead Goblins hadn't been discovered in a changing of the guard, but it was possible. It was possible, as well, that even if they had been discovered, the search for her was still being conducted inside the walls of Kraal Reach and hadn't yet extended to the Pashanon.

Of course, when it did, she would be tracked down pretty fast if she was still out in the open.

"Is there somewhere we can go to hide?" she asked Weka Dart at one point, hurrying to catch up with him as he slipped eel-like through the swamp.

He gave her an irritated glance, feral features screwed up with concentration, breathing quick and heavy. "A place to hide? Why would we hide, Straken Queen? If we are going to your world, we should go there at once."

She took a quick breath. She had forgotten that she had not told him of the boy, of the need for the boy to find her before she could go anywhere. "We might not be able to do that," she said.

He wheeled on her, his face contorted with fury. "What do you mean, *We might not be able to do that?* What are you saying, Grianne of the broken promises?"

She would not tolerate his insolence or his rebelliousness, not then and not with what was at stake. She snatched his tunic front and yanked him close.

"Don't question me, little Ulk Bog!" she hissed. "I didn't make you a promise about how this would happen. Or even that it would happen. I told you there was a chance I couldn't do anything to help either of us!"

He hissed back at her, then dropped his head and sulked. "I didn't mean anything by it. You just upset me. You frightened me. I thought you had a plan."

She released him. "I do, but it relies on help from my own world. Someone is coming to find me, someone who can get through the Forbidding without help from Tael Riverine. We have to wait until he appears. I don't know when that will be. But if it doesn't happen before we reach the Dragon Line, then we might have to hide for a while. Do you understand?"

He nodded sullenly. "I understand."

"Then think about where we might go to do that and stop being so suspicious!"

She kicked at him, and he started off again, skittering away through the grasses. There was no point in telling him everything. Certainly not that she was waiting for a mysterious boy, for something of which she could barely conceive, for a miracle. She hated having told him she would try to get him out of the Forbidding. She would not have done so if there had been any other way of securing his help. She had no idea if there was a way to free him. Or even if such freedom was a good idea. In fact, it probably wasn't. But she would have said or done anything to escape Tael Riverine and thwart his plan to make her the bearer of his spawn. She shuddered at the thought of that, determined that she would die before she would let herself be taken by him again.

They slogged on through the fading daylight, nightfall tracking them west until, sweeping slowly across the flats, it began to overtake them. They crossed out of the swamp and found dry ground beyond, a wintry plain in which the grasses were as dry as old bones, crackling beneath their feet as they stepped through them. Ahead the land stretched away, bleak and empty, crisscrossed by deep ravines and dotted by hummocks.

After a time, Weka Dart dropped back to walk beside her.

"I didn't mean what I said before." He looked at her with his sharp, restless eyes, and then glanced away quickly. "I know you keep your promises. I know you haven't lied to me. If anyone has lied . . ." He shook his head. "I can't help myself, you know. I have lied about everything all my life because that is how Ulk Bogs are. That is how we live. That is how we stay alive. We lie to keep others from gaining an advantage over us."

"I don't think lying does as much for you as you think," she replied. "Do you know what they say about lies? They say that lies have a way of coming back to haunt you."

He shrugged. "I just want you to know that I will change when you take me to your country. I won't lie anymore. Or, at least, I will try hard not to lie. I will be a good companion for you, Grianne of the kind eyes. I will help you do your work, whatever your work is. You will see that I am always there to do your bidding. Here, I would do the bidding of a Straken to stay alive. I would do it because I would have no choice. But it will not be like that with you. I will do your bidding because I want to. Because I respect you."

She sighed wearily. "You don't know me well enough to promise that, Weka Dart. I am not what you think. I have dark secrets in my life. I have a history that is every bit as bad as that of Tael Riverine. I might not be like the demon now, but I was once, not so long ago." She paused. "I might still be like him in some ways."

But the Ulk Bog shook his head stubbornly. "No, you are not like him. You could never be like him."

But I was like him, she thought, the weight of the admission infusing her with a sadness she could barely stand. *I could be like him again.*

Ahead, the flats turned rocky and were eroded by gullies and pocked by wormholes, the grasses and scrub disappearing entirely, the whole of the landscape changing abruptly to something Grianne hadn't seen before. Weka Dart, who was walking next to her but paying little attention to the land into which they were walking, suddenly caught sight of where they were going and drew up short, putting out his arm urgently.

"Wait, stay where you are!" he snapped.

He scanned the rocky flats, searching for something, then hissed sharply. "This wasn't here before!" he exclaimed. "This is new! They've migrated from somewhere else and set up their colony here! How long, I wonder? Very recent. Very."

She looked down at him. "What are you talking about?"

He gave her one of his frightening grins, the ones that showed all his needle-sharp teeth. "Asphinx! This flat is riddled with them."

"The snakes?"

His head cocked. "Do you know about them?"

She did. Asphinx had been exiled to the Forbidding with the other dark things of Faerie. Except for one that had been sealed in a crevice by the Stone King, Uhl Belk, in the caverns of the Hall of Kings to guard the Black Elfstone. Walker Boh, before he became a Druid, had been bitten while searching for the talisman, and his arm had turned to stone. The story was a part of Bek's histories of the Shannara kin, a story she remembered as crucial to what happened to Walker later in his transformation into Allanon's heir.

She glanced back at the flats. "How many are out there?"

He shrugged. "Thousands. Want to have a look?"

"No, I don't want to have a look. Can we get around them?"

He gestured left. "This way. Stay off the rocks and you won't have to deal with them. But watch your step anyway. If one bites you, you will make a nice statue for the birds to perch on."

They walked carefully around the colony, staying on the grassy fringe and keeping well back from where the rocks began. It took them a long time to get all the way to the other side, and by then darkness had settled in so thoroughly that it was difficult to see more than a dozen feet.

Weka Dart took a quick visual survey of their surroundings and nodded. "We'll camp over there, in that stand of wincies." He gestured toward a small grove of needled trees that looked like diseased pines. "Wincies give us some protection. Snakes don't like their scent, and flying things can't get through the screen of their branches without first landing, which they won't do at night. A good place for us to get some rest."

Grianne glanced back the way they had come, toward Kraal Reach. "Do you think they have begun to track us yet?"

"Oh, yes." Weka Dart sounded indifferent. "The Straken Lord will have found his guards and your discarded collar. He will have determined which way you have gone. He will have sent Hobstull and his minions to bring you back." His dark eyes glittered in the fading light. "His magic is very powerful, Grianne Ohmsford. Very powerful. But not so powerful as yours."

She knelt in front of the Ulk Bog. "Listen to me. I know you want me to take you out of the Forbidding, and I have promised I will try. But if Hobstull and whatever dark things he commands catch up to us, I want you to leave me to deal with them. I want you to find someplace to hide—and don't let them see you. Don't give yourself away." She paused. "They don't know about you yet, do they?"

He snorted. "Of course they know about me. Tael Riverine will have determined my presence as easily as he will have recognized your absence. Running and hiding will do me no good. I settled my fate by coming to you in the dungeons of Kraal Reach, Straken Queen. That is why it is so important that you take me with you. If I remain in the world of the Jarka Ruus, I am dead. Now, come."

She ignored the sinking feeling in her stomach and followed him to the trees he called wincies. They were tall, spidery hardwoods with long, thin, whiplike branches that interlaced and, at some points, knotted together. With Weka Dart leading, they slipped into their midst, ducking more than once to get through, wending their way into the center of the grove. The Ulk Bog made a quick check of their surroundings and determined them safe.

"Now you should sleep while I keep watch," he told her. "We must set out early, and you will need your strength. Go ahead. Sleep."

Too tired to argue, she lay down obediently. She closed her eyes, thinking to do little more than nap. Her mind was awash in doubts and fears, in worries of what they would have to do to stay alive another day. Images of her imprisonment and of the creatures that had threatened her paraded like specters. She felt the magic of the conjure collar even as she slept, ripping her apart, draining her strength, and filling her with pain.

She would never sleep again, she thought, and was asleep in seconds.

Her waking thoughts followed her into her sleep and became her dreams, dark and menacing. The Straken Lord tracked her down shadowy corridors, close behind but just out of sight. He carried in one hand the conjure collar with which he would bind her to him, its fastenings glittering like teeth. Other creatures from the Forbidding appeared in front of her, creatures of all sizes and shapes, their features not entirely distinct, but their intentions clear. Winged monsters clung to the ceiling overhead, with claws that gripped like iron, threatening to drop on top of her if she dared to slow. She ran from all of them, blindly and helplessly, with no destination in mind and no end in sight.

She came awake to the sound of howling wolves, and a terrified gasp escaped her lips.

"Hssstt!" Weka Dart whispered in her ear. He was crouched next to her in the darkness, a vague shape barely distinguishable from the night. "Demonwolves! They've found us!"

She tried to scramble to her feet, but he forced her down again, hissing, "No, no, don't move! Stay still! They don't know exactly where we are and we don't want to tell them. Let them come to us!"

She panicked. "But they'll—"

"They'll go the way I want them to go, Straken Queen. They'll go the way of dead things!"

She forced herself to remain calm while trying to sort through what he was talking about. He didn't seem panicked. He didn't even seem particularly worried. He stared past her east, toward Kraal Reach and the sound of the howling as it drew steadily louder, drawing nearer.

She realized suddenly that she was cold. She glanced down and saw that she was missing her cloak.

Weka Dart glanced over quickly. "They have your scent well and good. But they won't have you, Grianne of the wincie woods!"

The howls were very close, coming fast, and there were other sounds as well, shouts and cries of other creatures as they urged the demonwolves on. The pursuit was heated, a sense of expectancy reverberating in the wildness of its sounds.

Then suddenly, with a swiftness that turned her stomach to ice, everything changed. The howls turned to screams and growls filled with rage. The shouts and cries turned to shrieks filled with terror. The pitch rose and the rawness sharpened, and the night was alive with a cacophony that transcended anything Grianne Ohmsford had ever heard. Her pursuers were under attack themselves and fighting for their lives.

At her side, Weka Dart laughed aloud. "They've found what they were searching for, but not what they expected, Straken Queen! Listen to them! Too bad they weren't paying better attention to what they were doing! I think maybe they've encountered something with teeth sharper than their own!"

She stared at him, and then she remembered. *The Asphinx!*

Her pursuers had stumbled right into the center of the colony, and the snakes were striking at them. She listened anew to the sounds of the struggle, and the sounds told her everything. "You put my cloak out there in the middle of the snakes!" she exclaimed. "You knew!"

His grin was frightening. "I suspected. They came more quickly than I had thought they would. Your cloak was a lure to draw them away from us. The night is dark and visibility poor. Too bad for them."

The sounds were dying out, the growls and screams and shrieks turned to whimpers and moans, to gasps that carried even to where she crouched in the trees next to the Ulk Bog. She tried not to listen, but could not help herself. It was destruction of a sort with which she was familiar and from which she could not turn away.

Then everything went still, save for a single lengthy, ragged sob. And then even that was gone.

Weka Dart bent close. "Isn't the silence beautiful?" he whispered.

When it was light enough to do so, the dawn a faint tinge of pale gray brightness set low against the horizon to the east, they walked back to where the Asphinx colony waited. What Grianne Ohmsford saw left her stunned. Statues filled the flats, sculpted creatures posed in desperate positions of battle and flight. There were demonwolves and Goblins, dozens of each, their bodies and necks twisted, their limbs lifted and crooked, and their mouths open in soundless cries.

In their midst stood Hobstull, his lean body rigid, his narrow face taut, hands closed into fists in recognition of what was happening to him.

All had been turned to stone. Not a one had escaped.

"It happens so quickly when you are bitten repeatedly," Weka Dart ventured. "No waiting around for the inevitable. No false hope that you might somehow find a cure. You haven't got more than a minute before it's over. Better that way."

He walked to the edge of the field, picked up one end of a thin line, and reeled in Grianne's cloak, which had been tossed into the center of the killing field. Shaking it out carefully to make certain no snakes had hidden in its folds, he detached the line and handed the cloak back to her. "There, good as ever."

She took the cloak and stared at him, seeing him in an entirely new light, one that gave her pause.

"I prefer Hobstull as a statue," he declared, his smile wicked and challenging. "Don't you?" He dusted off his hands and looked east. "Time to be on our way. The light is good enough for travel. If others are coming, we don't want to be here to greet them."

He walked away, and Grianne followed. As she did so, she glanced back a final time, reminded suddenly of her past. The Ilse Witch had used snakes to dispose of her enemies. That had been a long time ago, and she was no longer that person. Or didn't want to be. But she had felt herself reverting in her battles with the Straken Lord and the Furies. She had felt the magic turning her dark and hard again. It wasn't so difficult to imagine that, whether she wished it or not, she might be changing into something she had thought safely left behind.

She mulled the possibility as they walked, wondering what she could do to prevent it. It was like trying to hold water in your fingers; you could capture the wetness, but the water itself slipped away. She was that water, and she was running swiftly through the cracks in her determination.

They walked several miles, far enough that she could no longer see the statues and the flats, far enough that she had begun to turn her thoughts again to their destination. She could already see the dark rise of the Dragon Line ahead of them.

Then Weka Dart slowed. "Someone is coming," he said.

She peered into the distance. At first, she didn't see anything. The haze and the gloom obscured everything, blending the features of the landscape together. But finally she saw movement. A solitary figure was coming toward them, cloaked and spectral against the still-dark horizon. She tried to make out its features and failed. She could tell only one thing about it.

It was carrying a staff that glowed like fire.

TWENTY-THREE

Surrounded by the dark, menacing forms of his black-clad guards, Sen Dunsidan stalked onto the airfield and crossed to where the *Zolomach* was anchored at the center of the cordoned-off flats south. Chains ringed the big airship, and dozens of Federation soldiers stood at watch. He had no reason to believe that the Free-born would even know of her yet, let alone think to mount an attack, but since the loss of the *Dechtera* and other recent events he wasn't taking any chances.

He stopped when still some distance off to admire the warship. The *Zolomach* was sleek and smooth, strong enough to withstand an attack by multiple enemy craft if she chose to fight and fast enough to outrun them if she chose not to. She was an improvement over the *Dechtera*, not so cumbersome and unresponsive, better suited to making the maneuvers necessary to bring her weapons into line, more able to adjust to the unexpected. She had not yet been put into service on the Prekkendorran though she had been tested and was ready to fly north.

Which she would do, he promised himself, as soon as Etan Orek confirmed that the casing for the fire launcher was complete and the weapon ready to be installed on the *Zolomach*'s foredeck. All that would happen by "sunrise tomorrow," the little engineer had promised him, and Sen Dunsidan intended to take him at his word.

He moved ahead again, reaching the airship and climbing

aboard to view the swivel base on which the fire launcher would be mounted. It was a simple metal platform that rotated on a bed of gears and bearings activated by a pair of release levers, the whole of the assembly able to swivel forty-five degrees to either side from dead forward. Its mobility was an improvement over the mechanism employed on the *Dechtera*, as well. There would be no mishaps when he sent her out. The *Zolomach* would finish the job the *Dechtera* had started.

"Prime Minister."

He turned to find the Captain of the airship saluting him, eager to make his report. "Captain. Is she ready?"

"Yes, my lord. She awaits only the emplacement of the weapon, and she is on her way."

"You've shielded the rudders and underside controls so that we won't have a repeat of the *Dechtera*'s collapse?"

The Captain nodded. "It will take a good deal more than a rail sling to damage her steering this time."

Sen Dunsidan didn't miss a beat. "What would it take, exactly?"

The Captain hesitated. "Another airship would have to ram her from below. That would be very difficult."

The Prime Minister looked away a moment, considering. There was no preventing every possibility, of course. Still, the Captain's words made him uneasy. "Stores and weapons are all accounted for?"

"Loaded and tied down. We are ready, Prime Minister."

Sen Dunsidan looked back at him. "I want you to post men at the rails during battle to watch for the possibility of an underside attack on the steering. I want you to devise a method of alerting the pilot box of the danger of such an attack so that evasive action can be taken in time to prevent any damage. Use the remainder of the day to train a team of men to do that. Take the *Zolomach* aloft and practice." He paused. "There are to be no mistakes, Captain. Is that understood?"

A shade paler than before, seeing in Sen Dunsidan's eyes his fate should he fail to comply, the other man nodded wordlessly.

"Good. I will get back to you with departure orders this evening." He waved the other off. "Get on with it."

His guard following close on his heels, he climbed back down the ladder, walked to the *Zolomach*'s stern to check the shielding, found it satisfactory, and strolled back out onto the airfield. Turning, he watched the airship's Captain summon his crew to quarters, his Lieutenants shouting out instructions, his men rushing to man their positions for lifting off. Within moments, the anchor ropes were released and the big warship was sailing off into the afternoon sky.

This time, he thought as he watched her fly into the depthless blue void, *I'll use the fire launcher on the Free-born until I can't see anything moving.*

His determination to crush the Free-born was fueled by an unpleasant turn of events. First, those ragtag Elves had crushed his pursuit force in the hills north of the Prekkendorran. Then there had been the midnight raid that resulted in the destruction of the *Dechtera* and her weapon. Less than two days ago, a counterstrike by Freeborn forces under the command of Vaden Wick had smashed his siege lines and driven his Federation soldiers all the way back to their original defenses, putting them right where they had been weeks earlier before the successes against Kellen Elessedil and the Elves. Except that now, after collapsing the right flank of the Federation army during the counterattack, Wick had gained a foothold in the hills east, threatening an assault that would roll up the entire Federation line and drive the army back into the middle Southland.

That last reversal had determined for him his present course of action. Whatever else happened, he did not intend to suffer a defeat of the sort that would result if his defensive line collapsed and was overrun. The members of the Coalition Council were afraid of him, but only so long as he did not show himself to be vulnerable. If he demonstrated any noticeable weakness, they would move quickly to eliminate him. A defeat on the Prekkendorran would give them all the encouragement they needed. No one would support him if the army was thrown back, not after all his promises of imminent victory.

So, in spite of Iridia Eleri's insistence on attacking the Elves and Arborlon, he had decided to use the fire launcher on the Free-born lines first, breaking down their defenses and driving them off the Prekkendorran for good. There would be plenty of time after that to test Iridia's theories about the erosion of Elven morale.

Suddenly uneasy, he glanced around. Even the thought of Iridia's name made him nervous. In spite of the presence of his guards, he found himself looking over his shoulder constantly. He had never been comfortable with her, but after their confrontation three nights earlier, he was much less so. It was something about her eyes or her voice, something in the way she held herself whenever she saw him. Whatever it was, it left him wondering how wise it was to continue to keep her around. He might be better off to get rid of her and go back to the way things were before. He didn't trust Shadea, but at least with her, what you saw was what you got. With Iridia, he wasn't sure.

He started back across the airfield toward his carriage. Iridia had traveled back with him to Arishaig, but he had not seen much of her since. He should have been grateful. Instead he found himself wondering where she was.

Perhaps he should find out.

He reached his carriage and climbed inside, half expecting to find her waiting. But the carriage was empty. He sat motionless, thinking about what he should do next. He was impatient for the departure north, back to the Prekkendorran. He was anxious to watch the destruction of the Free-born, to know that his weapon would put an end to them once and for all. He would not feel comfortable until then, no matter how hard he tried to reassure himself that matters were progressing as well as could be expected.

He glanced out the carriage window. He was aware of the driver sitting atop his seat, waiting for instructions. Let him wait. He began thinking about Iridia again. If his instincts were telling him the truth—and they usually were—he should get rid of her as soon as he could find a way to do so without placing himself in danger.

But what would be the best way?

Then, all at once, he knew. He would give her back to Shadea. He would drug her, bind her, and transport her back to Paranor. Shadea would know what to do with her and would welcome the opportunity. There was no longer any question of allowing Iridia back into the Druid order. There was no chance that Shadea would attempt to repair their shattered friendship. Shadea would eliminate Iridia in the blink of an eye, and that would be that.

Satisfied with his plan, he signaled for the driver to take him over to the engineering buildings and Etan Orek.

He rode slouched down in his seat, pondering his plan. He would have to be very careful how he carried it out. Iridia was no fool. She could smell a trap in the way most Druids could; her magic gave her a sixth sense about treachery. She already knew he didn't trust her; he would have to find a way to seduce her into thinking that he did. Perhaps if he agreed to her plan to fly the *Zolomach* to Arborlon, she would let down her guard. It couldn't hurt to try, to tell her he had decided to do as she advised. He could even pretend he was taking her there; propose a toast after they were on board the airship and let the drug do the rest. She wouldn't know what was happening until it was too late. Then he could fly her to Paranor and leave her in the hands of the Druids, and he would never have to worry about her again.

Calmed, reassured that his plan would work, he relaxed for the rest of the ride and looked out at the buildings of the city, their walls golden with the deepening of the approaching sunset.

When the carriage reached the engineering compound, he climbed down, his guards clustered about him, and waited for Etan Orek to respond to his summons. He did not have to wait long. The little engineer appeared within moments and hurried forward to meet his benefactor, eyes bright with excitement, hands clasped, head lowering deferentially as he scurried up.

"My lord," he said as he bowed so low that Sen Dunsidan thought he might topple over.

"Good day to you, Engineer Orek," he replied. He held himself straight, using his size and the strength of his voice to dominate the other. "How do matters progress with the weapon?"

The deferential gaze lifted marginally. "It is finished, Prime Minister! The casing was completed last night, and this morning I installed the weapon's components. Everything is in order. I tested it and it worked perfectly."

Sen Dunsidan felt a surge of satisfaction. Things were coming together nicely. "The range and power of this weapon are similar to those of the other?"

"Oh, much better! The faceting and alignment of the crystals have enhanced the gathering and expulsion of the fire. Where the first weapon would have burned a hole through metal or wood or set sails afire, the second actually incinerates them. It will bring down an airship or explode a defensive wall with virtually no effort at all."

Sen Dunsidan was nodding with approval. "Once again, Engineer, well done. Have we others in the making?"

The little man beamed. "We do. Two more, in fact. I need time to finish them, but they will be ready within a few weeks. Is that soon enough?"

Nothing sooner than tomorrow was soon enough, but Sen Dunsidan knew better than to press the matter. Completion of one weapon was all he needed, and he had that.

"Yes, two weeks is fine," he replied.

"My lord," Etan Orek said softly, moving a step closer. "Before you leave for the airfield, I have something new to show you."

"Something new?"

"I have made a fresh discovery." The bright eyes darted restlessly, looking right and left. "I think you need to see it."

Sen Dunsidan was excited all over again. A new discovery? What could it be? He remembered when Etan Orek had come to him in his bedchamber with news of the discovery of the fire launcher. He remembered his pleasure at finding out what the launcher did. And now there was something else?

"What have you found?" he demanded. He inclined his leonine head slightly, keeping the conversation just between them. "Tell me."

But Etan Orek shook his head. "No, Prime Minister, I need to show you." He glanced around some more. "Alone. Like before. You don't want anyone else to see this right away. For now, this information should belong only to you."

Sen Dunsidan thought about that a moment. He had gone down that road before with the little engineer. During his first visit, Orek had insisted he come into the workroom alone to view the fire launcher, leaving his guards outside. He had proved he was no threat. Nothing had changed where that was concerned. It wouldn't hurt to indulge him. He glanced at the burly, black-clad soldiers surrounding him. He would station them right outside the door, just as he had done before, safely within call.

"Very well," he agreed. "Show me."

With Orek leading the way, they moved over to the building in which the little engineer had been confined for the past few weeks. Sen Dunsidan was impatient to discover what it was the other had stumbled across. Perhaps this time he had found a way to increase airship thrust through enhanced effectiveness in the placement of the diapson crystals. It was while working on employing combinations of crystals that he had made his discovery of the fire launcher. Perhaps something similar had happened here.

He brushed back his mane of white hair and walked a little faster.

Inside the building, they filed down a broad central corridor to the workroom assigned to Orek, the engineer leading, Sen Dunsidan just behind, and his bodyguards following in a knot. At the door to the room, Etan Orek turned to him expectantly.

Sen Dunsidan glanced back at his Captain of the Guard. "Wait here for me, just outside the door. Come if I call."

He felt foolish asking even that. The odds of the little engineer turning treacherous were almost nonexistent. After all, Etan Orek's elevation in the ranks of Sen Dunsidan's subordinates depended entirely on him.

He went through the door, which the little man closed carefully behind them, and stood looking at the workbenches and clutter. Everything was just as he remembered it. His gaze drifted across the scattering of projects and scraps to the back table and the long metal box that held the newest discovery. Without waiting for the other man, he walked quickly to where the sleek casing was stretched across a pair of workbenches. He ran his hands lovingly over the smooth metal, and then lifted the top to peek inside at the array of crystals and shields. So perfect! He smiled broadly, already imagining the destruction he would be witness to in the days ahead.

He turned back to his engineer. "What is it that you wanted to show me?"

Etan Orek smiled and pointed off to his right to another workbench. "There, Prime Minister."

Sen Dunsidan turned and looked. He didn't see what the other was pointing at. He walked forward a few steps and stopped, still not seeing.

"What is it I am supposed to be looking at?" he asked.

Then everything went dark.

When he regained consciousness, he was stripped naked and tied down so securely to one of the workbenches that he couldn't move at all. Pain washed through his limbs and body, and his throat burned as if it were on fire.

He tried to speak and found he couldn't.

Etan Orek appeared next to him and bent close. "Don't bother trying to say anything, Sen Dunsidan. I removed your vocal cords while you were unconscious."

Sen Dunsidan stared. Etan Orek was speaking, but it wasn't the engineer's voice he was hearing. It was a voice he had never heard before, a raw and whispery croak that seemed dredged up from the rough depths of a rock quarry. The eyes weren't right, either. They were Iridia's eyes. Or were they? They reminded him of eyes he had seen somewhere else, somewhere he had all but forgotten. Eyes that belonged to the Ilse Witch. Or to the Morgawr.

Suddenly, he was more afraid than he had ever been in his life. He was terrified. It wasn't Etan Orek he was looking at. It was someone or something else entirely. In spite of what he had been told, he tried to scream. He opened his mouth wide and screamed with everything he could muster. But no sound came forth—only a tiny bubbling and a spray of his own blood.

"You waste your energy," his captor whispered. "Better save what is left. You will need it." He smiled. "You have no idea what has happened to you, do you? No idea at all. Listen to me, then, for the time you have left. I am not Etan Orek, and I was not Iridia Eleri, either. I killed them both and took their skins to hide what I really am. I am something from another place, Prime Minister. I am what you and your foolish Druids released from the Forbidding when you sent your Ard Rhys there to be imprisoned. It was not your fault that you did so; how could you know what you were doing when we were so careful not to let you discover the truth?"

He glanced over his shoulder at the door, and then bent close again. "Your fate is your own doing, Prime Minister. You could have avoided this if you hadn't been so insistent on attacking the Prekkendorran. Had you done as I suggested and gone to Arborlon, you would have preserved your life for at least a little while longer."

Sen Dunsidan stared at the other in horror, the full impact of those words settling in. Desperate to free himself, he surged upward violently against his bonds, but he might as well have been wrestling against iron chains.

"It is time for you to die, Sen Dunsidan. I doubt that many will miss you. I have watched how you are received, and there is no love for you. There is only hatred and fear and a sense it would be better for everyone if you simply disappeared."

His captor moved to the head of the workbench, standing where Sen Dunsidan could not see what he was doing. His mind fought to accept what was happening, to make sense of his situation, but all he could think about was getting free. He jerked his head back and forth violently, hammering it up and down against the table, trying to draw the attention of his guards who waited for his call from just outside the doorway of the workroom. Why had he left them out there? Why had he been so confident that he was safe?

Fool!

Hands grasped his head and held it firmly in place. The hands were scaly and clawed, and he shuddered at their touch. A face bent close, a face like none he had ever seen.

"Hold still," the creature whispered. "Breathe deeply, and it will all go much easier for you."

It leaned forward slowly, still holding Sen Dunsidan's head firmly in place. The clawed fingers reached into the corners of his mouth and pried it open. Sen Dunsidan tried again to scream and again failed. The creature's face was dissolving as it lowered toward his own, and he felt something bitter and sharp fill his mouth and worm its way down his throat. It was like inhaling a steaming mist thick with the taste of iron and sulfur. He gagged, but the mist continued down his throat and into his body, working its way all through him.

When the pain started, he began to shriek soundlessly, over and over again. His body heaved and bucked and twisted in a futile effort to gain relief. Nothing helped. The invasion continued until the pain became unbearable.

He never knew if his heart or his sanity gave out first, but either way, it was the end of him.

It was well after sunset, the sky beginning to fill with stars, a quarter moon rising in the east and the lights of the city of Arishaig glittering in the distance, when the Prime Minister reached the air-field. Accompanied by his personal guard and a wagon with its bed covered in a canvas, he arrived in his carriage. The Captain of the *Zolomach* was waiting for him, his airship ready and his crew trained as ordered to prevent against attacks on the vessel's steering. All that was needed was the order to depart.

The Prime Minister strode over wordlessly, wrapped and hooded in a heavy travel cloak, his face concealed in shadow.

The Captain came to attention and saluted. "My lord."

"Ready, Captain?"

"Yes, my lord."

"The weapon is in the wagon. Carry it aboard and set it in place. Make sure it is properly tightened down and the swivel mechanism working as it should. Take as much time as you need. Our departure is at dawn. Any questions?"

His guards were already unloading the weapon from the wagon bed and setting it carefully on the ground. "No questions, my lord," the Captain replied. "We will be ready at dawn." He paused. "You will be sailing with us?"

"I will."

"Engineer Orek?"

"Engineer Orek will not be coming back with us. He met with an accident. A fire. His workroom and all of his projects and plans were destroyed. A terrible loss. He was careless, and it cost him dearly. A good lesson for us all. Let's remember it when we set sail tomorrow. We can't afford any mistakes on the Prekkendorran."

"No, Prime Minister, of course." The Captain didn't like the way the other's eyes glinted from within the hood. "There will be no mistakes."

"I will hold you to your word," the Moric advised from within the skin of Sen Dunsidan, and turned away.

TWENTY-FOUR

She had intended to close her eyes for only a few moments, but Khyber Elessedil knew she must have fallen asleep for much longer. When she woke her thinking was fuzzy and lethargic and her mouth dry. She was slumped down against the railing where she had taken the reading with the Elfstones some time earlier, and the Stones were still clutched in her hand. She looked around, trying to get her bearings, trying to clear her head, and slowly her memory returned.

The Ard Rhys. Penderrin.

She reached down and touched her wounded side gingerly. The bleeding had stopped, but the entire area burned and throbbed. She tried not to think about what that meant, and instead shoved the Elfstones back in her pocket. Then, using the railing for support, she hauled herself to her feet. She had no idea how much time had passed; inside the furnace room of the Druid's Keep, there was no change of daylight for night from which to tell. At least no one had discovered her. Perhaps, if she was lucky, no one even knew she had escaped.

But time was slipping away.

She closed her eyes and in her mind retraced the hidden passageway that led to the sleeping chambers of the Ard Rhys. She had to get there quickly if she was to find a way to help Pen and Grianne Ohmsford before they attempted their return from the Forbidding.

Whether by warning them or by damaging the triagenel, she must give them a chance to escape the Druids waiting for them.

She looked down at herself and saw rags and dirt and blood. She saw that her hands were shaking. It had taken almost all her energy to get so far. She didn't have much strength left, and there was still a long way to go. She wanted to go back to sleep, but she knew that if she did, she might not wake up.

She had to get out of there. She had to keep moving.

She looked around the room. Her journey began at the door at the top of the stone stairway behind her. She took a deep breath, tottered from the pit railing to the steps, and began to climb, leaning against the wall on her left as she did so. Climbing made her feel even dizzier, and she was constantly in danger of losing her balance. She stopped at one point and shut her eyes, trying to muster her strength. But closing her eyes just made her feel worse, so she opened them quickly and forced herself to continue on.

At the door, she pulled downward on the handle, but it wouldn't move. The door was locked.

She paused a moment, then summoned a small bit of her magic to force the lock. A little pressure, carefully applied, would release it from the catch. She heard it open with a sharp *snick*, pulled down on the handle again to be sure, and was through.

The passageway beyond was dark and musty and narrow. She had to go back out to retrieve a pair of torches from the hallway leading into the furnace room, one to light the way, one to serve as a backup. It took an enormous effort just to do that, and she began to wonder how in the world she was going to muster enough strength to make the climb into the Keep. She wished she had some food and water, but there would be nothing to eat or drink inside these walls.

She lit the first of the torches with her magic and started ahead.

The passageway wound through a series of short, disjoined segments that ended at a stairway. The stairway took her upward in a series of switchbacks for several hundred steps to a door. The door opened, and a second passageway continued from there. At first, there were no choices to be made about which way to go; there were only forward and back. But when she had successfully navigated the second passageway and climbed another set of stairs to a third passageway, things changed. That passageway and those that followed branched out repeatedly, and the stairways she passed led both upward and downward. She still knew where she was meant to go, but she had to stop and think about it more than once.

When finally she reached a branch in the maze of corridors about which she was uncertain, the temptation to use the Elfstones was almost overpowering. She was afraid that if she didn't and made the wrong choice, she would become hopelessly lost. Her feverish mind made her frightened of doing so, eroding what little confidence remained to her, and for a moment she was sure that she was about to make a mistake. But she forced herself to stay calm, gave herself a moment to think, and resisted the impulse to act in haste. When she started walking again, she felt that she was going the right way.

Soon enough, the first of her two torches sputtered out. If the second one gave out as well, she would be left in blackness. By then, she was deep inside the upper reaches of Paranor, passing doors in the walls whose seams were outlined by light from the other side. She had no idea what rooms these secret doors opened into and did not care to find out. The passageways branched off in dozens of directions at each level she passed through. It was a disquieting discovery. Paranor's walls, like her occupants, were rife with secrets.

She stopped several times to rest, to give her head a few moments to clear and her fever and pain time to diminish. Her body ached, and she was so tired that she half believed she might simply collapse at some point.

She wished she knew more about healing magic. She had used what little she did know to cleanse her body of infection and to restore some of her rapidly diminishing strength. But it was hard going. Her injuries were eroding both her strength and her concentration. Determination and adrenaline would get her only so far. If she didn't reach her destination soon, she would not reach it at all.

Time dragged on, and she continued through the darkness, the smoky light of the torch illuminating her way. She felt as if she were entombed, buried in the earth beneath tons of rock. The blackness of the passageways and stairwells never changed. Her torch was all she had for light. In her head, she was seeing movement and hearing noises everywhere.

I can do this, she kept telling herself.

She encountered the first strands of Druid magic not long after the passageway narrowed so far that there was only room for a single person to pass through. She detected them at once, the skills that Ahren Elessedil had imparted warning her they were in place. But in fact the strands were just that: bits and pieces of webbing that had been severed and were hanging loose and forgotten, remnants of some more elaborate magic from an earlier time. She was careful to study them only with her senses; touching them might still serve to alert the one who had placed them. She could not yet tell who that was.

She discovered soon enough that more than one set of magic users had left imprints in those wormholes. One had visited more recently than the other and had severed the other's earlier efforts all along the route she was following. That suggested that the second user was Shadea or one of her minions, while the earlier was Grianne Ohmsford. If magic had been used to transport the Ard Rhys into the Forbidding from her sleeping chamber, that was the way it would have happened. To reach her victim undetected, Shadea would have broken down the protective barriers Grianne had installed.

Khyber moved ahead cautiously, keeping close watch for traps, but it appeared that Shadea's efforts to reach the Ard Rhys had been her sole concern. None of the earlier snares and warning webs had been reset.

Khyber slowed further as she realized she was getting close to her goal. The last part of the Elfstones' vision was playing itself out in her mind, and she knew that the corridor she was following would twist and turn through the Keep's walls a bit more before ending just ahead at the secret door leading into the sleeping chamber. She breathed a long sigh of relief, grateful to have reached her destination, even if she wasn't sure yet what she was going to do about it.

Then she sensed the clipps.

She stopped at once, holding herself perfectly still as she sought out their hiding places. Clipps were little bits of reactive magic that magic users embedded in walls and floors and, sometimes, even in ceilings to give warning of intruders. They were not as powerful or as difficult to bypass as strands of webbing, but they were effective enough. She could tell they had been placed quite recently, a new form of magic layered over the old. Apparently Shadea had decided to protect this approach to the sleeping chamber as well.

She would have to remove or disable the clipps, and that would take time she didn't have. But there was no help for it.

On hands and knees she edged forward and, one by one, began searching them out.

Bek Ohmsford crouched at the edge of the forest abutting the rocky promontory on which Paranor rested, studying its steep walls through the screen of trees and scrub. The walls were cleft in a dozen visible places and many dozens more beyond his plane of view. Any of them could be the secret entrance they were looking for, but they all looked pretty much the same.

He glanced over at Tagwen, who knelt next to him, his bearded face screwed up in a knot of indecision. "Any idea which one it is?" he asked softly.

The Dwarf sighed. "It was only once she took me there, and it was several years ago. I wasn't really paying much attention to the location." He shook his head. "But there was something about it . . ."

He trailed off, lips compressing into a tight line. "I know it was right around here."

Bek wasn't sure Tagwen knew anything at all, that he hadn't forgotten everything. But he didn't have much else to work with. Rue, the young Druids, and the Rock Trolls were all crouched farther back in the trees, hiding until they were summoned to go in. They had arrived at dawn, and after anchoring *Swift Sure* in a place of deep concealment they had made their way in through the shadowed forest to Paranor. The day was gray and hazy, and mist snaked through the trees in long trailers, giving the woods an otherworldly feel that threatened to make them lose their way. But it was Pen who was in the other world and in need of finding.

"I don't think this is exactly right," Tagwen said after a moment's further thought. "Let's try left a bit."

They moved silently through the trees, Bek determined to give the Dwarf whatever leeway he needed to find the entrance. As a last resort, he might try his own magic, although that was a stretch at best. His magic couldn't locate hidden entrances. It might track traces of magic, but there was little chance that such could be found down there. Worse, if the Keep was protected by Druid magic, his own use might give them away. It was an untenable situation at best, and unless they found the entry quickly, it was only going to get worse.

"This looks familiar," Tagwen was saying, muttering to himself as he worked his way through the heavy undergrowth.

It looks familiar because it is familiar, Bek was thinking. They had been that way less than half an hour ago. He exhaled softly. How much longer could he afford to let Tagwen wander about?

"Wait!" The Dwarf grabbed his arm tightly. "This is it! This is the way in!"

He pointed at a rift in the cliff wall that was barely visible through a heavy screen of undergrowth, just a slantwise break in the rocks. "Through that opening?" Bek asked.

"No, through the wall next to it!" Tagwen grinned. "That was why I couldn't find it! I kept thinking it had to be a split in the rocks, but the entrance is through a section of the rock that swings open when you do something to it!"

Bek stared. "Do something to it?"

"Yes, you have to touch it in a certain way. That was exactly what the Ard Rhys did when she opened it!"

He looked so pleased that Bek could not bring himself to point out that without knowing where and how Grianne touched the rock, they were no better off than they had been. Thinking about what to do to find where it was, he glanced at the section of rock where the entrance was concealed.

Then he had a sudden flash of inspiration and got to his feet hurriedly. "Wait here," he said.

He crept forward, keeping to the shadows and the concealment of the tree branches until he was at the cliff wall. Looking back at the Dwarf, he pointed to the section of the wall he thought the other had indicated, and received a firm nod. Turning back again, he worked his way forward through the undergrowth to where the wall blocked his way.

Carefully, he ran his hands over the rock, using just a shading of the wishsong's magic to test for Grianne's presence. His connection to her was so strong that any usage in the immediate past would reveal where she had touched the stone. Because she came and went secretly from the Keep all the time, he thought it reasonable to expect that she had come and gone that way at least once.

He was right. He found her invisible fingerprints on the stone right away. Placing his own fingers over the four places where he sensed Grianne, he tried different combinations of touching, one right after the other, little presses against the rock.

On his ninth try, the concealed door swung open and the entrance was revealed.

He looked back at Tagwen, who was already moving from his hiding place to fetch the others. Bek stayed where he was in the opening, waiting impatiently. No one else had seen him find the entrance, of that he was fairly sure. The cliff wall hid him from the Keep above and from any within it. Nor did there seem to be any protective measures in place below the Keep. He had detected no foreign magic at the entrance, just the lingering presence of the magic used by his sister. He suspected that while the walls of Paranor were carefully warded, the rock on which it rested was not. It was likely that no one other than Grianne and Tagwen even knew about this entrance.

Tagwen was back quickly with Rue, the young Druids, and the Rock Trolls. All of them bristled with weapons and protective leathers, and the Trolls wore chain mail. No one thought they would escape what lay ahead without a fight. Bek herded them through the opening quickly, found torches stacked against one wall, waited long enough for Kermadec to light several using flint and tinder, then touched the rock facing of the secret door a second time in the same combination as before and ducked inside as it swung silently shut.

They moved into the tunnels quickly, Tagwen in the lead with one of the torches, Atalan bringing up the rear with the other. Bek stayed close to Tagwen, worried that he might lose his way if he was left to his own devices. But the passageway burrowed straight ahead until it reached a stairway leading up. They climbed the stairs cautiously, and even the footsteps of the ponderous Rock Trolls were barely audible in the silence.

But as they ascended, the silence was slowly replaced by a deep thrumming sound, and the air grew steadily warmer. Bek unsheathed his long knife and held it ready.

At the head of the stairs, they came up against a huge, ironbound wooden door that looked to have been in place for centuries. When Tagwen pulled down on the handle, though, the door swung open easily.

They stood inside Paranor's furnace room, a cavernous chamber

with a pit at its center that opened down into the earth's core. Firelight flickered within the pit walls, thrown from the burning magma
deep within. The slow ooze and bubbling of the magma accounted
for the thrumming sound. A walkway ringed by an iron railing encircled the pit. Conduits for the heat given off by the fire looked like
black wormholes in the stone ceiling.

Bek looked around quickly. The chamber was empty. They had
to act quickly.

He turned to the others. "This is what I think we should do. Rue
and I will go with Tagwen to find the sleeping chamber of the Ard
Rhys and set up watch for her return. Kermadec, you and your men
will go with Trefen Morys and Bellizen and wait for the rest of your
army to arrive." He paused. "I don't know what to tell you to do after
that, whether you should lie in wait or come right through the gates.
We won't have any way to communicate with each other. You won't
know how things are going with us."

Kermadec nodded, his impassive face crimson in the light from
the pit. "It doesn't matter, Bek Ohmsford. Our course is decided. The
Trolls owe something to Shadea and her Druids for what they did to
us at Taupo Rough. I don't think we will bother waiting on anything.
I think we will do what Atalan has already suggested—pull the walls
down about their ears. We will force the gates and take the Keep.
Then we will come in search of you."

"That won't be easy," Bek pointed out. "The Druids will fight
back."

Kermadec laughed softly. "Some of them will fight, but most of
them will do what they have wanted to do all along—let Shadea and
her bunch of vipers suffer the fate they deserve."

He came forward and put his hand on Bek's shoulder. "Yours is
the task that matters most. If we can reach you in time to be of help,
that will make any sacrifice worthwhile." He squeezed gently. "We've
come a long way to reach this point, Bek Ohmsford. Your son will
have come even farther, once he returns. And the Ard Rhys farther
still. Let's make certain that our efforts are not wasted. Let's put
things back where they belong."

"Let's do that!" Bek said. He put his own hand over the Troll's.
"Good luck to you, Kermadec."

The Maturen stepped back. "And to you."

In a knot of huge bodies, the Rock Trolls trundled away along the catwalk, following the smaller forms of Trefen Morys and Bellizen. When they had disappeared into the dark mouth of the passageway, Bek turned to Tagwen once more.

"I guess we're ready," he said. "Where are the secret passageways that lead to my sister's sleeping chamber?"

Tagwen stared at him with a stricken look. "I have no idea. She never showed me." He glanced helplessly at Rue and back again to Bek. "Can't you find them with your magic?"

Rue Meridian rolled her eyes.

Shadea a'Ru sat at a desk in her new quarters, which were not far down the hallway from the sleeping chamber she had abandoned when she and Traunt Rowan and Pyson Wence had set the triagenel in place. At the sound of the knock on her door, she looked up guardedly.

Who is it? she started to ask, and then simply said, "Come."

The door opened and Traunt Rowan stepped through. "We may have a new problem, Shadea."

She stared at him in a way that suggested she did not want to hear about it. He met her gaze squarely. He had always been better able to do so than the others. "What sort of problem?" she said.

He stood deferentially to one side, knowing his place. "The Gnome Hunters we sent to dispose of the Elessedil girl have disappeared. All of them. Without a trace."

She turned in her chair to face him. "And the girl?"

"Disappeared, as well. The Elfstones, too. We wouldn't have found out at all except that Pyson went back to check with the man he had chosen to lead the squad. He couldn't be found. Further inquiries revealed that the entire squad was gone. It's impossible at this point to say what's happened. Pyson is conducting a search of the Keep, combing all of its passageways and courtyards, every inch. He enlisted more than a hundred of his Gnome Hunters to help."

She thought it through. "But there is no sign of the girl?" She paused. "Has there been any unexplained usage of magic within these walls?"

"Nothing that's been reported."

"Go up to the cold room and see if there has been any disturbance of the scrye waters. Anything at all. Especially here at Paranor.
Anything. Make sure you speak with everyone who has kept watch
for the last twenty-four hours." Her finger came up, pointing at him.
"Don't let them lie to you."

She got to her feet. "If that girl escaped, she might try to go back
to the sleeping chamber."

But Traunt Rowan was already shaking his head. "No, I've been
there already. I stood outside the door and checked to see if the triagenel was still in place. It was. It has not been disturbed in any way.
If she's alive, I don't think that is where she is."

"Perhaps she's gone to Arborlon for help. But how did she escape
a squad of Gnome Hunters when she was bound and gagged? She
doesn't have the magic for that! She's just a girl!"

"Well, maybe she didn't escape. Maybe there's another explanation."

She looked at him as if he were an idiot. "If the Gnomes are missing, she's escaped. But we can deal with that." She gestured toward
the door. "Go. See what the watch in the cold room has to say. Then
come tell me."

He went out the door without a word. She stood looking after
him a moment, considering what she should do. She would check
the triagenel herself, of course. She would not rely on him. Her own
magic was the more powerful and the more capable; it would give
a more sensitive reading. In any case, she no longer cared to rely
on anyone else in matters of importance—even her confederates.
Maybe especially her confederates. They hadn't shown her anything
yet that suggested she should rely on them.

Nor had anyone else, she reminded herself, thinking suddenly of
Iridia.

She paused a moment to ponder the disappearance of the assassins she had dispatched to Arishaig to dispose of the sorceress.
Those Gnomes had vanished as well, which would suggest that they
had failed. Iridia was dangerous, the most capable of those who had
conspired with her to lock Grianne Ohmsford within the Forbidding, but the men sent to kill her should have been equal to the task.

She shook her head. Sooner or later, she would have to deal with
Iridia herself. Perhaps Sen Dunsidan, too. It might be better if she rid

herself of both of them. Let the Federation choose a new Prime Minister. She would take her chances. Sen Dunsidan was becoming more trouble than he was worth.

For the moment, however, she needed to find out if the Elessedil girl was still inside Paranor's walls.

Pulling her dark robes close about her, she went out the door and down the hall toward the Ard Rhys's sleeping chambers.

It took Khyber a while to figure out how to disable the clipps, but in the end she managed. She did so by masking them with her own magic, a small covering that closed down their ability to read the presence of intruders in the passageway and left them useless. The magic she used was small, but sufficiently strong to last for several days. That should be long enough, she decided. It would have to be.

She fell asleep again after that, not meaning to, unable to help herself; she was so exhausted that just resting her eyes for a moment was sufficient to send her off. She awoke feeling a little better, although her wound still throbbed and her face felt hot and tight. She couldn't risk using any further magic to heal herself, couldn't risk anything that might give her away unless it had to do with helping Pen and Grianne, and so she did her best to turn her thoughts away from the pain and to the task at hand.

She slipped the rest of the way down the passage, checking carefully as she went for traps, and reached the doorway at the end. She saw the faint glow of the triagenel's magic as it seeped through the cracks in the doorway from the chamber beyond, a wicked green light that cut through the darkness like a razor's edge. She crouched down in the gloom and studied the doorway for a moment, then inched forward until she was close enough to touch the light seeping through. She kept herself from doing so; some magic could convey disturbances even from something as minuscule as the brush of fingertips. Sitting to one side of the doorway, she tried to plan her next actions.

Warning Pen and the Ard Rhys after they had reentered Paranor would do no good. The trap would be sprung by then, and they would be prisoners. She could try to help them, but she knew she lacked the kind of magic that could break them free. Whatever she was going to do, she had to do it before they attempted their return.

Which meant that she couldn't afford to wait since she didn't know how long she had. Which meant that she had to do something soon.

But what?

The only real magic she possessed was the Elfstones. But if she used them, she would give herself away in a heartbeat. She would be captured anew, and Shadea a'Ru and her allies would simply rebuild the triagenel. Besides, the Elfstones could only serve two purposes— to discover what was hidden and to defend against enemy magic. Neither usage seemed right for what was needed.

She leaned back against the passage wall, thinking. She was still thinking when she heard a noise in the darkness behind her. The hair at the back of her neck prickled and her throat tightened in fear.

Someone was coming.

TWENTY-FIVE

Willing herself to disappear, Khyber pressed back against the rough wall of the darkened passage. She had nowhere to run or to hide, nowhere at all to go. She was trapped, and unless whoever or whatever approached changed direction quickly, she would be caught out. She tried to remember how far back down the passage diverged, but she couldn't. The sounds continued to advance toward her. There was no mistaking the inevitable.

She reached into her tunic and brought out the Elfstones. If Shadea or one of the other Druids had found her, she would have to fight. If magic was used, the Elfstones would give her some protection.

Then a shadowy form appeared from out of the gloom, squat and heavy, too small to be anything other than a Gnome or a Dwarf. One of the Hunters she had feared would come searching, she thought in despair. The Elfstones would do her no good against him. She would have to rely on the long knife she had used to cauterize her wound. She tucked the Stones away swiftly and brought it out.

Not a dozen feet away, the approaching figure paused. Two more figures, cloaked and hooded and much larger than the first, appeared as well. Dizziness washed through her, triggered by the sudden surge of adrenaline that the new threat brought. She could not fight all three. She did not think she could fight one. She was weak and feverish and holding herself together through sheer determination.

Could she use magic to mask her presence? It was a possibility, and she grasped at it as she would a lifeline. Using magic was dangerous, but she was all out of choices.

She brought up her hands in front of her and was beginning to conjure a masking spell when a familiar voice said, "Khyber Elessedil, is that you?"

She was so astonished that she stopped what she was doing and stared at the speaker, realizing as she did so that the light from the triagenel magic was giving him a clear view of her silhouette. "Tagwen?" she whispered in disbelief.

He hurried forward, knelt in front of her, and took her hands in his own. "Shades, Elven girl! We didn't know what had become of you! I must say, I thought the worst more than once. But here you are." He reached out impulsively and hugged her. "Look, I've brought help!" He gestured to the two figures that had joined him. "These are Pen's parents, Bek and Rue."

The older couple knelt as well, and whispered greetings were quickly exchanged in the greenish cast of the magic's light. "How did you find me?" Khyber asked.

"By accident," Bek said, keeping his voice low. "We came looking for my sister's sleeping chamber so that we would be here when she and Pen came through the Forbidding."

Quickly, he explained how Rue and he had escaped the Druids and the Keep more than a week earlier, then flown north aboard *Swift Sure* in search of Pen and his companions, not realizing that Pen was already a prisoner. After finding Tagwen and the others at Stridegate and learning what had become of their son, they had flown back again, determined to rescue him.

"Is Kermadec with you?" she asked excitedly.

"Somewhere in the Keep with Atalan and a few others," Tagwen answered. "The rest of the Trolls of Taupo Rough are following us. They might not be more than a day out. Then we'll see how Shadea and those other weasels handle things."

"We'll need their help," Khyber said. She explained what had befallen after her successful attempt at freeing Pen and helping him to enter the Forbidding. "But Shadea and her allies have constructed a triagenel in the sleeping chamber. If we can't disable it in some way, it will trap Pen and the Ard Rhys the moment they come back through the Forbidding. I've been trying to think of something to do, but I haven't had much luck."

Rue Meridian, who had been listening silently in the background, moved forward and put her hand on Khyber's forehead. "You're burning up, Khyber. We have to do something about that or we're going to lose you." She glanced at the seams of greenish light leaking from the secret door and said, "Let's move you back down the passageway a little."

Khyber was too weak to put up much of a protest. She allowed herself to be stretched out on the passage floor while Rue opened her soiled tunic and began working on the wound. From a sealed pouch, she produced a salve. She spread it on the wound, then rebound the wound with fresh cloth from her own pack. Rue's fingers were cool and soft, and Khyber closed her eyes in momentary relief. The pain began to lessen and the ache subsided.

"Drink this," Rue ordered.

She gave Khyber a bitter-tasting liquid and some water to wash it down. Khyber drank it all, after telling her, "I haven't had anything to eat or drink in a long time."

"You need better care than we can give you here," Rue replied, holding Khyber's face in her hands and looking into her eyes. "You have some infection in you; that wound needs to be reopened and cleaned out. But that will have to wait."

She looked at Bek. "That's the best I can do for her right now."

Her husband nodded. "Tell me about the triagenel, Khyber."

She did so, sitting up again and explaining how it worked. "I still have the Elfstones, but I don't know how I can use them to help."

Bek thought a moment. "Is the strength of the triagenel uniform? Is it the same everywhere or does it vary from strand to strand?"

"There will be some variation in the strands. The building of each by the three magic users necessarily involves some ebb and flow." She hesitated. "At least, that was what Uncle Ahren told me. The more skilled the users, the more uniform the magic. But even with the most accomplished users, there would be weaknesses."

"Ahren would have known." Bek looked toward the concealed

door and the thin shafts of green light leaking through the cracks. "How is the triagenel attached? Your description makes it seem like a net. Does it hang from the ceiling?"

Khyber nodded. "It does. It is gathered at the corners of the room so that when the magic is triggered, it collapses about its victims and seals them away. It happens very fast, too fast for anyone to avoid, even if they are warned immediately."

"What triggers the magic?"

"What do you mean?"

"What does it take to cause the triagenel to collapse?"

"A human presence in the room. Any human presence."

"But not the presence of another magic?"

She hesitated. "What are you thinking?"

Bek leaned forward slightly, brow furrowed. "What if you and I were to weaken a few of the strands that make up the triagenel? Would that give a magic user as powerful as my sister a way of breaking through the net once it collapsed on her?"

Khyber hesitated, thinking. "I don't think the triagenel can heal itself, so yes, I suppose if enough strands were weakened, a captive could break free. But how in the world are you going to do that, Bek? If you go into that room, the magic will be triggered and the triagenel will collapse on you."

"I'm not talking about going into the room. What I want to try requires using two different forms of magic, one yours, one mine. That's why I asked if the presence of another magic would trigger its release. Will it?"

She considered the question, and then shook her head. "I don't think so. I think only the presence of a flesh-and-blood body will do that."

"Then this might work. We don't need much of our own magic to get the job done, and if we're lucky, we won't be detected. The magic of the triagenel is pretty strong, you said?" She nodded. "Then perhaps it will help mask our own."

"What are you thinking about doing?" Rue said as Tagwen pressed close.

Bek sat back on his heels. "What if Khyber were to use the Elfstones to search out weaknesses in the triagenel? The Elfstones are seeking-stones; they should be able to do that. If she can pinpoint, oh, maybe a dozen, I think I can use the wishsong to weaken them further—enough so that any sort of force applied to them after the net collapses will break them apart."

Rue shook her head doubtfully. "That's very delicate work, isn't it? If you weaken even one of those strands too much, it will break through before you want it to. If that happens, won't Shadea detect it? In fact, won't she detect any kind of interference with the triagenel?"

Seeing the possibilities, Khyber leaned forward. "Maybe not. Yes, if Bek breaks one of the strands, that creates a flaw in the netting and anyone looking for it will know right away. But a weakening might not be detected so easily; over time the net erodes anyway. The magic slowly fails and the triagenel has to be rebuilt. So an erosion of the sort Bek is suggesting probably wouldn't draw attention."

The four looked at each other. "Is there another way?" Tagwen asked bluntly.

No one said anything. They all knew the answer.

The Dwarf grunted. "You better get started."

Much farther down and deeper into the bowels of the Keep, Kermadec and his Trolls crept through the passageways of the lower levels, following the cautious lead of Trefen Morys and Bellizen. Seeking to reach Paranor's north walls, they had worked their way steadily upward from the furnace chamber. Kermadec's plan was to get close enough to the outermost of those walls that he could take control of one of the smaller gates, one that would not be heavily manned.

Kermadec knew something that neither Shadea nor her Gnome Hunters knew. There were too many gates for all of them to be guarded all the time, and many of the smaller gates had been permanently sealed over the years to prevent a surprise breach. But the Maturen had unsealed one of them long ago to give the Ard Rhys a means of leaving the castle secretly without having to go all the way down to the furnace chamber and the tunnels below. When he visited, she slipped from the Keep through that gate, to the meeting places outside Paranor's walls they had prearranged over the years.

That unsealed lesser gate was their best chance of breaching Paranor's defenses. It was small, nothing more than a single door. It would not permit a massive rush, but if enough Trolls sneaked through before they were discovered, they could mass within the walls and take one of the main gates. In Kermadec's view, that was how Paranor would fall.

But reaching the north wall undetected, not to mention the gate in question, would have been difficult for any one person, let alone ten. It had become clear early on that some sort of search was under way within the Keep. Twice they had narrowly avoided being discovered, the first time because they had heard the search party approaching and doubled back to another corridor and the second because they were warier after the first.

So they were proceeding much more cautiously, keeping to seldom-used passageways and back stairs, tactics that were slowing them down considerably. It had taken them several hours to get that far, what with hiding and doubling back, and it was beginning to look as if even getting to where they wanted to go was in doubt.

But Trefen Morys seemed to know his way about Paranor even better than Kermadec, and under his guidance they worked their way forward, slowly getting closer.

Then, just when it seemed they would make it safely through the search parties, they slipped from a side corridor into a main passageway and ran right into one. A group of five Gnome Hunters rounded a corner right in front of them and came to an uncertain stop. Trefen Morys tried to bluff their way past, hailing the Gnomes, pretending that everything was as it should be. But the Gnomes were on guard, and they knew that Trolls were forbidden entry into the Keep. Before Kermadec or the other Trolls could stop them, the Gnomes had given the alarm.

Atalan was on top of them quickly, and three were dead before they could defend themselves. The remaining two fled, and Kermadec called his brother back so that they could do the same.

"Where can we go?" he shouted at Trefen Morys as they ran down the corridor toward a stairway leading up.

They rounded the corner of the stairway and were immediately in a second fight, this one with a much larger party. The Gnomes drove the Trolls and the young Druids backwards into the corridor, calling for reinforcements as they did so. Bigger and stronger, and with a great deal more to lose, the Trolls fought back and, after a concerted rush, broke through the Gnome crush and charged up the stairway to the next floor.

"Keep going!" Trefen Morys shouted, pointing to the next set of stairs. "Two more floors!"

They did as he directed, rushing ahead heedlessly, trusting that he knew what he was doing. At the top of the third set of stairs, he reached out and grabbed Kermadec's arm, pointing to a wide set of double doors.

"In there!"

The entire party rushed into a cavernous meeting room filled with chairs and tables stacked all about, the ceiling high and dark with shadows, the room brightened only by a pair of narrow windows on their left.

The young Druid went straight to the windows and released the catch on the nearest. "Go outside," he told them as they rushed up to him. His breath came in short gasps, and there was blood on one arm. "Follow the ledge to the third set of windows. Inside the room beyond, you will find a door that opens onto a narrow stairway. It leads directly down two flights to the base of the north wall. You will know where your gate is once you get there."

"You're not coming with us?" Kermadec asked, realizing what the young Druid had decided.

Trefen Morys shook his head. "We're of no further use to you, Bellizen and I. We're not fighters; we'll just hold you back. Maybe we can do something from up here. Another distraction, perhaps." He stretched out his hand. "Don't fail us, Kermadec. Don't fail our mistress. She isn't the monster they try to make her seem. She has done much good with the order. We need her back."

The Maturen gripped his hand tightly. "Get out of this room, Trefen. If they find you somewhere else, they might think you are just another pair of Druids."

"They're coming," Bellizen hissed from where she kept watch at the door.

"Keep safe," Trefen Morys said. He released the big Troll's hand and hurried over to stand next to her.

Kermadec climbed through the window without another word, the other Trolls following, and disappeared onto the ledge.

With Rue Meridian and Tagwen keeping watch from just down the darkened passageway, Bek Ohmsford and Khyber Elessedil placed themselves, one on each side of the hidden door, keeping clear of the greenish glow that seeped from the sleeping chamber, staying back from the opening itself. They were going to have to use their magic in entirely new ways. Bek, in particular, was going to test himself as he never had. The wishsong was a powerful magic, and he had never spent much time trying to master it. Now he was going to attempt something that even a practiced user would have thought twice about.

But he had no choice if he wanted to save his sister and his son.

"Are you ready?" he asked the Elven girl.

She nodded, and he released the catch that held the door in place. The door swung slowly toward her.

Beyond, the sleeping chamber was bathed in a deep greenish glow. A complex webbing was strung all across the ceiling, thousands of strands of magic carefully joined together, the whole of it secured at the corners and center.

Placing herself to one side, staying carefully out of the magic's steady glow as it flooded the passageway, Khyber brought out the Elfstones. Cradling them in the palm of her hand, she stared at the triagenel, concentrating on what she wanted revealed. She had never seen a triagenel; she had only heard about them. So it was difficult for her to know exactly what to look for. She relied on the Elfstones to respond to her need, and they did. Within seconds, they flared to life, their blue glow spreading all through the chamber, bathing the triagenel in a new brightness. At perhaps twenty-five or thirty places, the webbing burned faintly crimson, mostly where the strands connected to one another.

"Those red spots are the weaknesses," Khyber whispered.

Bek took a long moment to study them, and then whispered back, "Good work, Khyber. Now hold the Elfstone magic steady."

He called up the wishsong in a soft, barely audible hum. Building it slowly, he honed it to a cutting edge, a trick he had learned twenty years earlier from Grianne. When he had the edge sharp enough, he eased it up to the ceiling to where the brightest of the crimson spots could be found and began to cut. He was slow and careful, weakening each strand just a little at a time. Relying on his magic to give him a sense of its strength, he would cut the strand as deeply as he felt he could, and then move on to the next. The process took him a little longer each time, his concentration faltering; his strength was still not back after the injuries suffered in the escape from Paranor two weeks earlier.

"Hurry," Khyber whispered, the word evidence that her own efforts were beginning to fail.

He continued until he had cut into ten strands. It was tedious, demanding work. His eyes watered and his body cramped, but it was his mind that screamed for release. Still, he was afraid to stop, afraid that starting up again would be too dangerous, that it risked discovery through the sheer repetitiveness of the magical activity. Too much of anything would be noticed in a place like Paranor, especially with the scrye waters able to detect any usage of magic at all.

Bek cut two more strands, making his tally an even dozen. When he had finished with the twelfth, he was too tired to go on. He withdrew the cutting edge of his magic and let the wishsong go still. He closed his eyes wearily and leaned back against the passageway wall. "That's all I can do," he whispered to Khyber.

She exhaled sharply, and when he opened his eyes again, the Elfstones had gone dark. She was slumped down across from him, her fingers closed tightly about the talismans. "Do you think it was enough? Will it break apart for your sister and Pen? I couldn't tell. I couldn't feel the weakening at all. All I could do was make out the places where it might give way."

He shook his head. "I don't know."

He reached over from behind the open door and pushed against it. The door closed softly, and the latch caught. They were left in darkness again save for where greenish light leaked through the cracks, blade-thin and knife-sharp. In the ensuing silence, they stared at each other wordlessly, wondering if they had done enough.

Shadea a'Ru had finished rechecking the strength and positioning of the triagenel and was on her way back down the hall when Traunt Rowan reappeared from the cold chamber. She noticed for the first time how much he had aged over the past few weeks. His strong face was lined and gray, the way he held himself was less confident and erect. He had been the most dependable of her allies, the strongest-minded if not the strongest wielder of magic, and she was dismayed that he had not held up better. It pointed up again a truth she regretted.

In the end, she was the only one she could depend on. In the end, she was in the battle alone.

"You were right to have me check the scrye waters," he announced perfunctorily. "The Druid on watch said there was a noticeable disturbance perhaps eight or ten hours ago, one that clearly indicated the presence of a powerful magic. He said he failed to report it because he thought it was Druid magic. The truth is he was afraid he would stumble into something he shouldn't know about and pay the price for doing so."

"What does that mean?"

His laugh was bitter. "It means our decision to keep everyone guessing about who is expendable is having unavoidable consequences. We have created a climate of fear, Shadea, in which no one wants to risk drawing attention. Better to keep silent than to make a mistake and become another unfortunate example."

She glared at him, then looked away. He was right, of course. What was the purpose in getting mad at him for pointing out something she already knew? She had the Druids well in line and working to complete their tasks, but they were frightened and uncertain. Her early, unexplained dismissals had made them that way. Now she was in danger of losing them all.

She was no better than Grianne Ohmsford.

But that would change, she promised herself. She would make it change.

She looked back at him. "What was the source of the disturbance?"

"The furnace chamber, where we sent the Elven girl to be killed. I think we must assume she is still alive. Pyson sent an armed unit to search that whole area. They found evidence of blood, but nothing else."

Shadea shook her head. "What is she up to? What does she think she can accomplish?" Her hard gaze fixed on him. "I want her found, Traunt. I want her found and killed. I don't care how it's done or who knows. We have to put an end to this business."

He nodded wordlessly. There was nothing for him to say.

They walked back down the hall toward her chamber. "I received word from our spies in Arishaig," he said quietly. "Iridia has disappeared."

She looked over in surprise. "How long ago?"

"Several days, at least. She simply vanished. Sen Dunsidan doesn't seem bothered, though. That leads me to believe he may have had something to do with it."

She nodded, thinking that Sen Dunsidan couldn't have gotten rid of Iridia on the best day of his life. It was far more likely that her Gnome assassins had been more successful than she had believed, even if they hadn't gotten word back to her yet.

They reached her door. "Find that girl," she repeated, turning to face him. "And anyone else she might have brought with her into Paranor. Tell Pyson to have his Gnome Hunters sweep the Keep again—every passageway, every room."

She paused. "And double the guard on the sleeping chamber. I have a feeling that Grianne Ohmsford is about to reappear. I want to be sure we are ready for her when she does."

She saw the stricken look on his face and smiled. "What's the trouble? Don't you think we are a match for her? We dispatched her once; we can do so again. Only this time, I intend to make sure she won't ever come back."

She turned away. "I need to rest. Wake me when something happens." She glanced back at him. "And make sure that something happens soon."

He was still standing there in the hallway when she closed the door.

Bek was sitting next to Khyber in the darkened passageway off the sleeping chamber of the Ard Rhys. They had slept for several hours, and now Tagwen and Rue were sleeping. Bek wasn't sure how much time had passed. Not that it mattered; there was nothing they could do but wait. He found himself wondering how long that might be. They couldn't wait indefinitely. Sooner or later, someone would find them. They would need food and drink, as well, although they had brought a little of each with them into the Keep. He guessed that the waiting would end either when Grianne and Pen reappeared out of the Forbidding or Paranor fell to Kermadec and his Trolls.

He wondered about the chances of the latter. The Trolls were formidable, but no one had taken Paranor since it had been betrayed to the Warlock Lord in the time of Jerle Shannara. The Druids were a powerful order, even if dissatisfied with their leadership and their present situation. Their command of magic gave them an edge that no one else possessed. Bek hoped that Kermadec was right when he said that most of them would not support Shadea a'Ru, but he had a feeling that if faced with an assault on Paranor, they might.

But he couldn't do anything about that. He could only do something about the things he had control over.

He leaned close to Khyber. "There is something I have to tell you," he whispered. "About Pen and the staff."

She glanced up. "The darkwand?"

He nodded. "The King of the Silver River came to me in a fever dream while I was flying north in search of Pen. In that dream, he told me that demons from the Forbidding had manipulated Shadea and her Druid allies. Their purpose in helping Shadea had nothing to do with getting their hands on Grianne; their purpose was to release a demon into our world. That demon's mission is to destroy the Ellcrys and tear down the Forbidding."

He felt her fingers dig into his arm. "Let me finish. Pen can stop this from happening. He can send the demon back through the Forbidding. The purpose of the darkwand is not only to bring Grianne out, but also to send the demon back. But Pen has to find it first. It is a changeling, and it will be in disguise."

"What if it reaches Arborlon before Pen gets back?" She looked at him as if she wasn't sure she wanted to hear the answer.

He shook his head. "The Elves guard the Ellcrys day and night. Arborlon has defenses to keep anything from getting close. We have to hope that's enough. There's only so much we can do."

He put his hand over hers. "Now, listen to me. I don't know what will happen once Grianne and Pen reappear in the Four Lands. We are all at risk. But whatever happens, you and Pen have only one concern. You have to find that demon. Escape back through the secret passageway and get outside Paranor's walls. Then go after it. Take *Swift Sure*. Use the Elfstones to track it down and then send it back into the Forbidding."

He paused. "Pen doesn't know about any of this. You might have to be the one to tell him, if Rue and I can't. If so, make sure he understands what he is supposed to do. He can't worry about us or about what happens here. You know the way out; you have to make certain he uses it."

She stared at him doubtfully. "He won't want to leave you. I don't know if he will listen to me."

Bek took her hands and held them. "He will listen to reason. You will find the words."

He wished he had something more to offer. But what he had just given her was the best he had.

TWENTY-SIX

On the wide night-shadowed plains of the Pashanon, Grianne Ohmsford stared in shock as the approaching figure came into the light and its features were revealed.

It was a boy.

At first, she thought she must be mistaken, even though she had been told the boy would come for her, even though she had been looking for him all this time. It was the unexpectedness of his appearance that gave her pause, the way he simply materialized out of the receding night, the ease with which he had found her in the middle of nowhere. But it was more than that. She had just left a killing field, a slaughterhouse of the Forbidding's creatures turned to stone. She thought the figure must be something come out of that madness. She thought she was seeing a ghost.

"Shades," she whispered, and stopped walking altogether.

At her side, Weka Dart growled. "What is it, Straken? Who is this creature?"

The boy approached as if there were no hurry, as if he had all the time in the world. He looked haggard and beaten down. He looked to her, she thought suddenly, as she must look to him. His clothing was ragged and his face dirty and careworn. He walked in a way that suggested his journey had been long and hard, and indeed, if he had come from her world, from the world of the Four Lands, it must have been. Though he was clearly young, everything about him was dark and weathered.

Except for the odd staff he carried, which was made of a wood that was polished and smooth and glowed red with bits of fire.

He walked right up to her and stopped. "Hello, Aunt Grianne."

It was Penderrin. Of all the boys she might have imagined, he was the last. She couldn't say why, but he was. Maybe it was because he was Bek's son, and it would never have occurred to her that Pen would come for her rather than Bek. Maybe it was just her certainty that if a boy was indeed coming, he would be extraordinary, and Pen was not. He was just an average boy. He lacked his father's magic; he lacked his mother's experience. She had met him only a couple of times, and while he was goodhearted and interested in her, he had never seemed special.

Yet there he was, come to her from a place no one else could have come, there when no one else was.

"Penderrin," she whispered.

She stepped forward, placed her hands on his shoulders, and looked into his eyes to make sure. Then she hugged him to her, holding on to him with a mix of disbelief and gratitude. He was the one; just the fact of his being there was confirmation of what the shade of the Warlock Lord had foretold. She felt his arms come around her as well, and he hugged her back. In that instant, they were bonded in a way that could only have happened under the circumstances of that improbable meeting. Whatever befell her, she would never feel the same way about him again.

She released him and stepped back. "How did you find me? How did you get here?"

He smiled faintly. "It might take a while to explain that." He held up the glowing staff. "This is what brought me and what will take us both back, once we return to the place I came in at. The runes carved in its surface glow brighter when it gets nearer to you. I just followed their lead."

She shook her head in disbelief. "I had no idea it could be you. I was told that a boy would come for me, but I never thought it would be Bek's son." She gave him another hug. There were tears in her eyes, and she wiped them away quickly. "I am so grateful to you."

Weka Dart was standing off to one side, a mix of emotions mirrored in his feral features, suspicion fighting with curiosity and hope. She glanced at him, and then turned Pen about to face him. "This is Weka Dart, Pen. He is an Ulk Bog, a creature of the Forbidding. He calls this the world of the Jarka Ruus—the banished ones. What you should know is that he is my friend. He, alone, of all the creatures I have encountered, has tried to help me. Without him, I would be . . ."

She trailed off. "I don't know where I would be," she finished quietly.

Weka Dart beamed. "I am honored to have served the Straken Queen," he announced, and bowed deeply. He looked up again quickly. "If you are her savior, then perhaps you will be mine, as well. I wish to continue to protect Grianne of the kind heart and powerful magic. I have pledged myself to do so for as long as she needs me. Can you help me? Are you a Straken, too?"

"No," Grianne said quickly. "Pen is family. He is not a Straken, Weka Dart. He comes only to take me home again."

"And take me, too?" the Ulk Bog pressed.

"What do you mean?" Pen asked, and then looked at Grianne. "What is he talking about?"

"Leave it alone for now. I have to know more about what you are doing here. I don't understand why you've come instead of your father. Is he all right? He hasn't been harmed, has he?"

She listened then as he told her everything that had happened since Tagwen had appeared in Patch Run to seek his father's help. He told her of the little company that had come together in Emberen to start the quest for the tanequil. She learned of the death of Ahren Elessedil and of the dark creatures that had been enlisted by Shadea to hunt Pen down. He told her of the fate of the *Skatelow* and the Rovers who crewed her and of star-crossed Cinnaminson's transformation into one of the aeriads. He told her of brave Kermadec and his Rock Trolls. He told her of the tanequil, of its dual nature and of the shaping of the darkwand. By listening, she came to understand how desperate the struggle had been to reach her and how much had been sacrificed so that Pen could find a way to bring her back into the Four Lands.

"I would have thought my father a better choice for this, too," he finished. "But the King of the Silver River said that I was the one who was needed. I guess it was because my magic allowed me to communicate with the tanequil. Perhaps my father's couldn't do that. I don't know. I only know that I had to come looking for you, that it was important that I try, even if I really didn't think I could succeed."

Grianne smiled in spite of herself. "Perhaps the King of the Silver River saw something in you that you didn't see in yourself, Penderrin Ohmsford, because here you are, whether you believed it could happen or not."

He smiled back. "I'm glad I found you, Aunt Grianne."

Weka Dart was dancing around again, looking agitated, his craggy features twisting and knotting. "We should leave this place," he whined anxiously. He glanced back in the direction of the Asphinx colony and the stone statues. "It is dangerous to remain here."

Grianne nodded. "He is right, Pen. We can continue talking while we travel. We must go as quickly as possible to the doorway out of the Forbidding. Time slips away."

They began retracing Pen's steps, walking west toward the receding darkness, the dim gray brightening of the dawn at their backs. The vast sweep of the Pashanon stretched away before them, its stunted, broken landscape empty of movement. Far distant still to the north, the Dragon Line lifted in stark relief against the horizon. The sky remained clouded and the air hazy as the daylight brightened only marginally the world of the Jarka Ruus.

"I am very sorry to hear about Ahren Elessedil," she said to Pen after a time. "He was the best of my Druids, the one I could always depend upon. It proved to be so here, at the end, too. But I will miss him."

In truth, she felt as if her heart would break. Only losing Bek could hurt worse. Ahren had been with her since the formation of the Third Druid Order, the linchpin she had relied upon time and time again. He had committed to her during their return to the Four Lands from Parkasia, and she had come to respect him deeply. She looked off into the distance, took a deep breath, and exhaled wearily.

"I am sorry about your father and mother, too," she continued, glancing over at him. "It isn't fair that they should have been brought into this. It isn't fair that any of you should have—Tagwen, Kermadec, the Rover girl, any who tried to help. I won't forget. I will try to make things right again, as much as I can."

"It was their choice," Pen said. "Just as it was mine. We all wanted to help."

She shook her head dismissively. "Shadea," she said softly. "I should have done what Kermadec told me to do a long time ago; I should have rid myself of her. I should have rid myself of them all. Pyson Wence, Terek Molt, Iridia. Even Traunt Rowan. I am the most disappointed in him. I never thought he would turn against me, no matter how bad things got. I let my judgment be clouded. A bad thing for an Ard Rhys to do."

She was silent for a moment. "How many of my Druids stand with Shadea and those others, Pen?" she asked. "Do you know?"

He shook his head. "Some, I guess. She is Ard Rhys now. The Druids all answer to her. But I don't know how loyal they are." He paused. "When I was a prisoner, she was away in Arishaig. She has an alliance with the Prime Minister."

"Sen Dunsidan," she whispered. "Another viper. I would expect him to be involved somehow. Shadea would not act without some sort of outside support, and Sen Dunsidan has always hated me."

With reason, she thought. As the Ilse Witch, she had made his life nightmarish. But he had allied himself with the Morgawr and tried to have her killed. So she had reason to hate him, too. Yet she had forgiven him his maliciousness and thought he had done the same. Clearly, she had shown poor judgment there, as well.

"Are there any I can count upon within the order to support me?"

Pen shook his head. "I don't know of any. No one came to help me but Khyber."

She dropped the matter, and they walked in silence for a time. It was wrong of her to ask such things of Pen. He had no way of knowing the answers. Since her disappearance, his time had been spent in flight. The machinations of those at Paranor and elsewhere would not have been his concern; his concern would have been in trying to stay alive. Her answers to questions of that kind would have to wait until she was back in the Four Lands. Then it would be up to her to find them quickly.

Weka Dart was back to skittering about, crisscrossing the land ahead, dashing first this way and then that, chattering to himself, anxious to get where they were going. But she had a feeling about that. Something Pen had said when the Ulk Bog had mentioned him as being savior not only to her but also to him nagged at her.

"Weka Dart!" she called.

He came racing over, eyes bright with excitement. "I am here, Straken Queen."

"No sign of further pursuit?" she asked. "No sign of Tael Riverine or his creatures?"

The Ulk Bog grinned wickedly. "He won't have learned of Hobstull's new employment as a resting post for birds quite yet," he said. "It will take time for word to reach him. Too much time for him to do anything about it. We will be well away and out of his reach by then."

"Run on ahead a distance and see if the land is clear that way. I want to turn north soon toward the mountains."

He glanced in that direction. "Nothing lies there. What is the point of wasting my time . . . ?"

"Don't argue, little man!" she snapped. "Remember your promise to serve and protect."

He was gone without another word, a dark spot rapidly disappearing into the haze. She felt bad about snapping at him, but he responded better when she did, and she needed to talk with Pen alone.

"A word, Pen," she said to him when Weka Dart was safely away. "I made a promise to the Ulk Bog in return for his help in getting free of the Straken Lord's prisons. I'll explain about that later. My promise was that I would do what I could to get him out of the Forbidding and into the Four Lands. He wants to come with us."

Pen gave her an anxious look. "I thought that was what he meant. But I don't think we can do it. The darkwand will take only you and me out of the Forbidding. It will not allow anyone else to go with us. The King of the Silver River told me so."

She had suspected as much. Creatures consigned to the Forbidding by Faerie magic could not be set free without a disruption of the wall that separated the two worlds. The darkwand was not created for that purpose. It was created for putting things back the way they were meant to be.

"I'll have to tell him," she said quietly, already wondering how she was going to do that. "I can't let him think he still has a chance of getting out when I know he doesn't."

They walked on, the boy keeping pace with her, his head lowered, his staff serving as a walking stick, its runes glowing softly in the dusky light.

Her thoughts stayed with Weka Dart. He was so convinced that she could do anything, that her Straken powers were omnipotent. He had already made up his mind that she would be able to break him free of the Forbidding and bring him back into the Four Lands. She had warned him not to expect too much, but after the encounter with the Graumth, he had ceased believing there was anything to worry about.

Now she was going to have to disappoint him in the way she had disappointed so many others—by not being able to do enough, by being less able than he needed her to be. She felt shackled by her inability, by her weakness, by her humanity. It was almost better not to have any power than to have a lot. Having a lot always created expectations, and somewhere along the way those expectations would not be met because that was the way the world worked.

"Do you remember when you asked me once if I had any of my father's magic?" Pen asked her suddenly.

She glanced over at him, happy for the distraction. "I remember."

"I told you I hadn't. But that wasn't entirely true. I hadn't any of the wishsong's magic. But I had another kind. It was such a small magic that I didn't think it worth mentioning. It allowed me to sense what animals and plants and birds were thinking or why they were acting as they were. I didn't think it was worth anything. I never even told my parents about it. Especially my mother, who is afraid of the Ohmsford magic."

Grianne nodded. "I know. She is right to be afraid."

He sighed. "Well, now I think maybe my magic does come from the wishsong. It changed when I took the limb from the tanequil and shaped it into the darkwand. It changed when I began to bond with the darkwand so that it responded to me. I found I could make it do things by humming and singing, in the way of the wishsong."

"It came late to your father, too," she said. "He was older than you before he discovered he had use of it. Walker let him see by giving him the Sword of Shannara and telling him he would have to use it. That bonding triggered a surfacing. Just as with you."

"I sense it changing still. I think I am just beginning to understand what's there."

"There is a history of that in our family. It happened with Jair Ohmsford. Do you know the story? His sister had full use of the wishsong, the first of the Ohmsfords to have it. Jair, the brother, had a magic that gave the appearance of being wishsong magic, but was only illusion. Except that some years after their quest to destroy the Ildatch, he discovered that it had evolved and he had the same use of it as she had, even though it had started out as something else."

She gave him a questioning look. "What's bothering you?"

He ran his fingers through his shock of reddish hair, tangling it further. "I just thought that since it is my connection with the darkwand that allows us to cross through the Forbidding, maybe there is still a chance for Weka Dart to come with us. If my magic is still changing, if I don't know what it will do yet, it might turn out that it can help."

He looked over at her. "So maybe you should wait to tell him. Until we're sure, I mean."

She stared at him for a moment, surprised. "I don't know if that's such a good idea, Pen," she said finally.

He looked off in the direction the Ulk Bog had gone. "I just don't think anyone should have to stay here if they don't want to. I know he is a descendant of one of those consigned to the Forbidding. But that was a long time ago. Things can change. He doesn't seem so bad to me."

She smiled to herself. She liked the way he wanted to help Weka Dart, even without knowing anything about him. It spoke volumes about the kind of boy he was, and it made her feel still closer to him. She was glad he was like that. She hoped she would get a chance later to tell her brother so.

"He isn't so bad," she said finally.

She tried to tell herself that was so, that being imprisoned in the demon world did not necessarily indicate that the Ulk Bog was beyond redemption. No one was beyond redemption, after all. Wasn't she proof of that?

Then a scream, a mix of shriek and roar, blew past them like a windstorm, and Pen's dragon dropped out of the sky and settled to the ground directly in front of them.

High in the towers of Paranor, Trefen Morys turned another corner on another passageway, Bellizen at his heels, and looked for a way out. They had been running ever since they had helped Kermadec escape through the windows of the meeting chamber. Surrounded by Gnome Hunters, they had been lucky to get away themselves. They'd been able to climb up through the heating vents and crawl down the shaft to another room before the Gnomes could discover what they had done.

But the hunt had gone on, and their time and space were running out. The Gnomes knew they were trapped on the upper levels of the Keep, and had blocked all the passageways down. All that was left to the young Druids were the towers above, and even those were being closed off, one by one.

"In here!" he hissed at Bellizen, pulling her through an open door into a storage room filled with Druid cloaks and soft slippers.

The sounds of pursuit already drawing near, he shut the door quietly behind them. He slid the locking bolt into place and looked around wearily. It was just another in an endless series of rooms into which they had fled and tried to hide. This one had a connecting door that led to a second room, and after determining there was no other way out of the one they were in, he took Bellizen with him into the second and locked its door, as well.

The room was tiny, a chamber he had never seen before. It had no other door than the one they had come through. A single narrow window was set in the far wall. When he crossed to open it, he found himself peering out at the north wall and the woods beyond. They were five stories up, and the wall dropped straight down.

He looked at Bellizen, who stood waiting for his assessment. "They might not think to look here."

But they already had. He could hear them at the door of the first chamber, trying to break through. Eventually, they would. Then they would break through the second door.

He scanned the room from wall to wall, from floor to ceiling, and then looked out through the window again to see if he had missed anything. But there was no help to be found anywhere.

They were trapped.

Bellizen read it in his eyes and nodded. He walked back to her. "I won't let them take me," he said. "I know what will happen if they do."

She nodded, her pale, round face calm, her gaze clear and steady. "I won't let them take me, either."

"But they will take us," he said. "There's too many of them. We'll be overwhelmed."

She gave him a small smile. "Not if we don't wait around for that to happen."

She reached for his hands and led him over to the window. She looked out into the afternoon, and then stepped up onto the windowsill. "Come up with me, Trefen."

He did so, deliberately keeping his eyes on her face, refusing to look down. He stood with her in the opening, holding her hands, feeling the cool wind blow over him in a soothing wash.

In the room beyond, the door began to splinter and break.

"It's only a short jump," she said. "It won't take long."

"I wish we could be here when our mistress returns," he said. "I would like her to know how much she means to us."

"Someone will tell her," she replied. She glanced back at the door to their room. "Are you ready?"

"I think so," he said.

He took a deep breath. They waited quietly, listening to the sounds without, to the breaking down of the door in the far chamber and then to the thudding of booted feet as the Gnomes rushed to the door that led into their room.

"It helps that you are with me," he said softly.

Bellizen gave him a small smile.

Then a horn sounded, its wail deep and ominous, reverberating off the walls and through the rooms of the Keep. Shouts rose from below, and abruptly Paranor came alive in a new and terrible way.

Outside their door, the Gnomes turned and ran, abandoning their efforts. Trefen Morys and Bellizen stared at each other in disbelief, and then they looked out the window where the sounds of activity were loudest.

Thousands of Rock Trolls were striding out of the trees, armored giants forming up battle lines at the gates to the fortress of the Druids.

TWENTY-SEVEN

Grianne Ohmsford took a quick step back as the dragon set-tled into place on the flats, its wings folding against its huge, scaly body. Steam rose off its back in clouds, and she could feel the heat of it from fifty feet away. The dragon flexed and undulated from head to tail, the spikes that ridged its back shivering like great stalks of grass blown in a wind. It coughed once and then exhaled a huge gout of fire and smoke.

An eerie silence settled over the landscape, and it felt to her in that instant as if everything living had disappeared from the earth save the dragon, the boy, and herself.

Then the head swung toward her and the maw parted to reveal rows of blackened teeth. The stench of its breath sent her backwards another few steps. Its yellow eyes narrowed and fixed on her.

Except they weren't fixed on her, she realized suddenly. They were fixed on Pen, who was standing next to her.

"It's the darkwand," he said quietly. "It's fascinated by the glowing runes."

He was right. The dragon had settled down into a comfortable crouch and was staring intently at the staff. The runes carved into its surface were pulsating with hypnotic consistency in the gray misti-ness of the afternoon.

"It's been following me ever since I arrived," Pen said.

She blinked at him. "You've encountered it before?"

"Twice." He looked chagrined. "The first time was after I had walked into the passes leading down from the heights where I came into the Forbidding. I fell asleep, and it was there when I awoke, staring at me. Or at the staff. I couldn't get rid of it at first, but finally I did. I thought I was done with it, but yesterday it reappeared here on the flats while I was trying to reach you. It came to my rescue, actually."

"Your rescue?" She couldn't hide her disbelief.

"I was trying to find somewhere to spend the night and I wandered into a nest of Harpies. They wouldn't let me out again. They were going to eat me. But the dragon reappeared and ate them, instead."

He saw the look on her face and shook his head. "It doesn't have any interest in me. It doesn't care about me one way or the other. It's the runes." He glanced over at the dragon, which was watching them contentedly. "Something about watching the glow of the runes makes it happy. Or fascinates it. I don't know, Aunt Grianne. I just know that I can't get rid of it."

"Well, you managed to do so twice now," she pointed out.

"It was the wishsong magic," he said. "It surfaced after my bonding with the darkwand, but it was the dragon's appearance that gave me a reason to test it. I didn't know if the magic would work, but I was desperate. So I tried it out. I used it to send images of the runes off into the distance, like a lure. The dragon went after them, and I escaped."

He paused for a moment, frowning. "The second time it was too busy eating the Harpies to pay much attention to me. I just slipped away. But I guess it came looking for me."

"I guess it did." She looked at the monster, at its huge bulk and great, hooked claws and muscular body. She stared into its yellowed eyes and found them glazed and unfocused. A dragon mesmerized by bits of light—she would never have believed it. "Can you get rid of it now?"

"I don't know. I can try."

He began to hum softly, connecting with the wishsong, and as he did so the runes of the darkwand danced in response, growing brighter and more active as the music increased. Soon their glow was racing across the length of the staff in ever-changing and increasingly complex patterns. She glanced at the dragon. It was staring at the staff, satisfaction and delight mirrored in its lidded eyes. It was sitting up straight, head bent forward, as still as if it had been carved from stone.

Then the runes began to cast their images into the air, a kaleidoscope of fire bits whirling this way and that. The images spun and wove together, leaving tiny trails of light in the wake of their passing. The dragon's jaws widened, and its breath came in grunts and snorts. Claws dug into the earth, and its tail coiled and uncoiled rhythmically. The images danced toward it, closing on it like tiny fireflies, then leapt away into the sky, speeding off into the horizon, a long line of them, beckoning with their comet light.

But the dragon didn't move. It sat watching them intently for a moment, then turned back to Pen and the staff once more.

Pen kept at it a few moments longer then gave up. "It's not working," he said, breaking off with a tired gasp. "I don't understand. Before, it would have flown after the images. Now it's only watching them."

Grianne studied the dragon a moment. "It's learned that flying after the images doesn't do it any good. The images don't last. It's figured out that the source is the staff and that staying close to the staff is the best way to keep the images coming." She shook her head. "It's a brute, but it isn't stupid."

They stared at the dragon in silence. The dragon stared back. In Pen's hand, the darkwand continued to glow and its runes to dance and pulse.

"What are we going to do?" Pen asked finally.

Grianne didn't know. She could use the wishsong's magic, but she was afraid of the reaction she would trigger. If she didn't kill the dragon, it would be on them in a heartbeat. Even if she did kill it, using so much magic would draw the Straken Lord to them like a beacon of firelight in darkest night. Either result would be horrendous.

She was beginning to think she wasn't going to be given a choice in the matter when a strange, barking cough sounded from somewhere in the distance, off toward the Dragon Line. It was rough and made her think of scraping metal and of old saws cutting green wood. She flinched in spite of herself.

But the dragon sat up immediately, head swinging away from the darkwand and its glowing runes, eyes peering out toward the sound.

Several minutes passed, and no one moved. Then the sound came again, farther away this time and more to the east. The dragon's head swung toward it, lifting alertly. It huffed, and steam poured out of its nostrils. When the sound came a third time, the dragon roared with such ferocity that Grianne and Pen dropped to their knees in shock.

Seconds later, the monster was airborne, winging away in the direction of the sound, flying off without a backwards glance.

"What happened?" Pen breathed in confusion.

Grianne shook her head. "I don't know, but let's not stand around talking about it." She glanced over. "Can you do something to quiet those runes? Can you stop them from glowing? If it comes back, I don't want the staff to help it find us."

"I'll try," he said. He slipped off his cloak and wrapped it carefully about the darkwand so that the glow of the runes was hidden. "There," he said, satisfied.

They began walking again, heading toward the mountains, changing direction just enough that they were moving more north than west. More than once, Grianne peered off into the distance in the direction the dragon had taken, but there was no sign of it. No more than a mile ahead were hills that would offer them better cover. If they hurried, they would reach the hills before the dragon decided to come looking for them.

She wondered how far it was to where they could try to get back through the Forbidding. She glanced skyward. Night was approaching.

"Pen, why do the runes continue to glow even when you're not using the wishsong?"

He shrugged. "They just do. They were glowing that first morning when I woke and the dragon was sitting there. They respond to me in a way that doesn't involve me telling them what to do. I'm not even sure how much control I have over them. Not much, I think."

Odd, she thought. The magic of the wishsong did not have a history of independent response. It came only when summoned and did only what it was asked to do. Its behavior here must have something to do with Pen's bonding with the darkwand, with the melding of two magics. In some way, the wishsong had developed the ability to activate itself, to respond to the boy's needs even when the boy wasn't aware of exactly what they were.

Her magic, she thought, though far more powerful than his, had never been able to do that.

They had walked until they were almost into the hills when Weka Dart reappeared, arms flailing excitedly as he sprang out from behind a stand of heavy brush.

"Did you see? Did you see?" He jumped up and down and cackled as if gone mad. "It was completely fooled! I told you I would protect you, Straken Queen! I could see what would happen if I did not act, and so I used my brain and tricked it!"

She realized he was talking about the dragon. "What did you do, Weka Dart? What was that sound?"

He shrieked with laughter. "A mating call! What better way to get its attention than to give it something more important to think about than the two of you!"

"You know how to give a dragon mating call?"

"I was Catcher for Tael Riverine a long time! I learned how to give many kinds of calls! I would have been a poor Catcher otherwise, and I was the best that ever was! Did you like it? You had no idea what it was, did you? Did it make you wonder if maybe something was dying? That's how dragons sound when they're in love!"

He danced about wildly, and then started away. "Hurry, come, come! We have to reach the Dragon Line by nightfall! We need to keep moving!" He wheeled back a moment. "It was good that I was close by and watching out for you, wasn't it? I saved you both!"

Then he was off again, racing into the distance, a small, crook-limbed blur against the haze.

Grianne stared after him and thought in despair, *There must be a way.*

When the battle horns sounded, Kermadec was crouched in the shadow of a half-wall atop the gatehouse where Atalan and the other Rock Trolls were hiding. He hesitated only long enough to make certain he was not mistaken about what was happening, then leapt from his place of concealment to the floor below and raced for the gatehouse door.

After leaving Trefen Morys and Bellizen, the Trolls had made it down from the parapets and found their way to the base of the north wall and the gate that Grianne had always kept open for meetings.

But the gate was closed and sealed, and Kermadec could tell at a glance that it would take too much effort and make entirely too much noise to force it. Someone had taken a good deal of time and trouble to make certain that it would not be used again. More than likely it had been discovered by Shadea and her allies after they had dispatched the Ard Rhys into the Forbidding and assumed control of the Keep. Shadea would have been quick to recognize its significance.

So for the better part of two hours, the Trolls had hidden in the gatehouse next to it, a less-than-satisfactory location given what they were now faced with doing, but one that was unlikely to be visited anytime soon. But, with the gate of choice stoutly sealed, Kermadec and his Trolls would have to breach another gate. Since the next closest gate was some distance from where they hid, there was every possibility that they would be spotted long before they reached it.

There was nothing they could do about that. The only way the Trolls were going to take Paranor was by breaching the Druid defenses from the inside. That meant seizing and holding a gate long enough for the Trolls outside the walls to get inside.

Kermadec burst through the gatehouse door. All around him, the fortress of the Druids was erupting in a frenzy of wild shouts and charging men.

"They've arrived," he informed the other Trolls, putting his back to the door and facing them across the tiny, shadow-streaked room.

Atalan's face was a mask of excitement. "Now we'll see how strong these walls really are!" he hissed. "Let's go!"

"Not yet." His brother blocked his way. "Give it a moment more. Let them get to the walls and settle in place. Let them all be looking at what threatens from without so they won't be looking at us. Then we'll take them."

Atalan came right up against him. "Why wait, brother? Confusion serves us better than it serves them. Delay is for cowards and weaklings. We should take them now!"

Kermadec held his ground, his gaze steady. "You are too impatient, Atalan. You rush to do everything too quickly."

Atalan spit. "If I am too impatient, you are too cautious. You delay everything too long. Move more quickly, and we might have better success. Are we here to help the Ard Rhys or not?"

"Don't push too hard on me," Kermadec said softly. "And do not question my commitment to the Ard Rhys. It is not your place to do so."

"Shhh," Barek hissed at them. He was standing at the shuttered window, keeping watch as dozens of Gnome Hunters charged past on their way to the parapets. "You'll be heard if you keep this up!"

The brothers faced each other a moment longer, then Atalan turned away with a shrug. "You are Maturen, Kermadec. You are leader. The responsibility for what happens here is yours. Who am I to question you?"

He slouched back to the far wall and slumped down, staring at nothing. Seething with anger and embarrassment, Kermadec turned back to the door and ignored him.

It was dark by the time Grianne and Pen began the climb into the Dragon Line. Shadows thrown by the skeletal trees and distant peaks draped the land. West, the light was fading from gray to black, and the twilight hush that marked the transition from day to night was retiring the creatures of one and bringing out the creatures of the other. Sounds faded as if swallowed beneath the surface of an endless sea, and the world became a place for the quick and the dead.

Grianne's eyes roamed the landscape on a ceaseless scour, alert for things that might be hunting them. The boy walked quietly beside her. They had not seen Weka Dart since he had departed, but she felt certain he was close, watching their progress, ready to save them once more should the need arise. Or save himself, perhaps. She knew enough of the Ulk Bog to appreciate that whatever his good intentions, he would always look after himself first.

Still, it seemed petty of her to think of him that way after he had lured off the dragon. She wished she could form a better opinion of the Ulk Bog, but she was too familiar with how he managed to get through life to do so.

It seemed only moments later that Weka Dart appeared out of the black, materializing so suddenly that she almost struck out at him.

"Straken!" he hissed at her in a clear tone of reprimand. "You cannot continue in the dark! Too many things hunt at night, and even I cannot see them all! We must stop and wait for morning!"

She was anxious to reach their destination and get out of the Forbidding for good. But the urgency in his voice gave her pause. "Is it really so dangerous? We are almost there."

"You are not as close as you think. This is a different pass than the one you took down. Best not to repeat your steps when Tael Riverine is looking for you. No, Grianne of the powerful magic, you must stop now. You and the boy. Rest here. Wait for dawn."

So they did, taking shelter in a cluster of boulders that gave them protection on three sides and provided an overhang as well. They would take turns keeping watch, they agreed. When first light appeared, they would set out again. The remainder of the journey would take only a couple of hours.

Then, Grianne told herself once again, she would be free.

"Weka Dart," she said after they had settled into the rocks. She could barely see him in the hazy darkness, a dim shadow hunched down to one side. Only his eyes gleamed, watchful and steady. "I have something to tell you."

She heard Pen exhale in anticipation of what was coming. She ran her fingers through her hair, pushing it back from her face, wondering how to put what she must say into words, and then deciding she should just say it.

"Penderrin tells me that the darkwand will not take you out of the Forbidding. It will only take him and me. No one else."

Weka Dart snorted. "He is mistaken. Or if not mistaken, he underestimates the power of your magic. You can find a way to take me even if the staff does not wish it."

She sighed. "I don't think so. This is old magic, older than I am, and more powerful. The wall of the Forbidding cannot be broken by ordinary means. That is why it was so difficult for Tael Riverine to get his demon into the Four Lands. He had to work a switch to make that happen. You told me so yourself."

"Perhaps you can switch the Moric back again in exchange for me," he said brightly.

His enthusiasm was frustrating. "No, I can't. I don't know how. I don't even know how this staff works. It responds to Pen, not to me. What matters is that the Faerie creature who told Pen about the staff was very explicit—it cannot bring anyone out of the Forbidding but us."

Weka Dart was on his feet in an instant, arms pinwheeling. "But you promised! You said you would take me with you if I got you out of Tael Riverine's prisons! You said you would! Did you lie? Is it true that all Strakens lie? Even you?"

She held up her hands. "I told you that I would do what I could to help you but that I didn't even know if I could help myself! That was what I said. It was the truth, not a lie. If Pen hadn't come with the staff, I couldn't escape the Forbidding, either. I would be trapped here, as well."

"Now you won't be, will you?" he shrieked.

"No."

"But I will! I will!"

"Not if we can—"

"You lied, you lied, you lied!"

Spitting at Penderrin, as if the situation were his fault, the Ulk Bog rushed out of the shelter, screaming invectives at both of them, and then disappeared into the night. But he was back again within minutes, trudging out of the inky black and flinging himself down where he had been sitting before. For a long time, he didn't say anything. Grianne waited.

"Who will protect you from dragons, Grianne of the broken promises?" he whispered finally.

He said it with such sadness that it made her throat tighten in response. "There are no dragons in my world," she answered.

"No dragons?" His head lifted from the cradle of his arms. "Well, who will protect you from the Furies, then? Or the giants, and ogres and Graumths? Who will warn you of their coming? Who will keep you from stumbling into their lairs?"

"There are no Furies, ogres, giants, or Graumths. All of those are here. They were all sent here in the time of Faerie, when the Forbidding was created." She paused. "My world is nothing like yours, little Ulk Bog. It is a very different kind of place."

"Are there Ulk Bogs like me?"

"No. There are no Faerie kind at all, save Elves."

"I hate Elves," he muttered. "Elves enslaved the Jarka Ruus."

"Weka Dart," she said quietly. "We will try to take you with us, just as I promised. I will keep my word. I just want you to know that I may not be able to break you free. I may not have the power to do that."

He was silent a long time. "No Ulk Bogs?"

"No."

He squirmed around in the dark, shifting positions, trying first one, then another, so restless that she thought there was something wrong with him. "Are you all right?"

"I might not come with you after all," he said suddenly. "I might stay here. Your world sounds boring. It sounds as if there is nothing to do. I might be better off staying right where I am."

She stared at him. "I thought you said you couldn't do that. I thought you said Tael Riverine would kill you if you stayed."

"He might take me back, now that Hobstull is dead." Weka Dart's voice was small and contemplative. "He will need a new Catcher."

"No!" she said at once. "The Straken Lord will have you killed, Weka Dart! He will find out what you have done and that will be the end of you!"

"He might not. He might think me too valuable now."

She wanted to shake him so hard his teeth rattled. "If this is a threat meant to get back at me for telling you the truth, for telling you what I thought you had a right to know, then it is a poor one! Don't be such a fool! You cannot talk about going back to Tael River-ine! Going back is suicide!"

"Or maybe I will go west, where I said I wanted to go when we met." He shrugged. "Maybe I will go to Huka Flats and find a place where I will be accepted."

She didn't know what to say. She wanted him to quit talking the way he was. She wanted to tell him that they would find a way to get him out of the Forbidding. She wanted him to wait until they knew for sure what was going to happen when they used the darkwand. But Weka Dart was already sifting his expectations in his mind, re-thinking his life and his plans for the future, accepting better than she, perhaps, the realities.

"Don't decide anything tonight," she said to him. "Wait until we have a chance to test the staff. Will you do that?"

He was silent for a long time. "I will sleep on it, Straken Queen. I will give it the thought it deserves."

"I wouldn't ask for more than that," she said.

"I would be a good Catcher for you. Is there was anything to catch over there? Or to protect you from? There must be some-thing."

"There are enemies," she assured him. "There are always enemies."

She watched him lie down and curl into a ball. "I will keep you
safe from your enemies," he said softly. "I will protect you."

"I know."

She sat staring out into the night, her thoughts dark and threatening, pushing back her weariness. She should be able to do more
for him than what she believed she could. She should be able to help
him. But she didn't know where to start. She didn't know how to do
what was needed. She felt weak and impotent.

"I will be there for you," he whispered.

Then he said nothing more.

She awoke with the dawn, the silvery tinge of its breaking a
faint blush on the eastern horizon. The sky was overcast and the
clouds thick and roiling across the Pashanon. A storm was building
to the southwest, and there was a screen of rain where it swept eastward out of Huka Flats.

She looked around. Pen was sound asleep at her side, the darkwand cradled in his arms. Weka Dart was nowhere to be found. She
took a moment to scan the countryside, but didn't see him. Apparently, he had left early to scout the pass.

She roused Pen, and after eating the remainder of the roots Weka
Dart had provided for their evening meal, they set off. She felt an urgency about doing so, a need to reach their destination quickly. She
was aware of how fragile she was. Still unhealed from her experiences at the hands of Tael Riverine, her strength came mostly from
the knowledge that she was close to being free of him for good. If
she could escape the Forbidding, as well, she might recover herself.
If she could put enough distance between herself and what had been
done to her, she might be able to shore up her uncertain psyche. The
memories would never leave her but, perhaps, she could take the
edge off them. She was holding herself together mostly through
cobbled-together bits and pieces of determination, stubbornness,
and pride. She was still Ard Rhys, but to become anything like whole
again, she must regain her hold on the position as well as the title.

She looked around with haunted eyes. The oppressiveness of the
world of the Jarka Ruus closed about her. Another day in the Forbid-

ding, and she could not say for certain that she would not give way to the madness that had threatened to claim her ever since her arrival. Time was growing increasingly short for her. She could listen to the sound of its passing in the beating of her heart.

They climbed steadily into the pass, frequently looking back over their shoulders to the plains, which were disappearing in the sweep of the storm. But there appeared to be no pursuit and no indication of anything dangerous coming their way.

And there was still no sign of Weka Dart.

It was nearing midday when they gained the forested heights of the Dragon Line and began to head west, toward the place where they had entered the Forbidding. The day had gone very dark as the storm clouds continued to roll eastward. The wind had picked up, and the first sprinkles of rain blew into their faces. Not wanting to be caught in the storm, they pressed on. Grianne chose their path; her sense of where she was stronger now. The boy walked silently beside her, the staff covered and out of sight.

In the distance, thunder rumbled in long, rolling peals and lightning flashed on the plains.

Then, quite unexpectedly, they emerged from the trees into a clearing, and Grianne recognized it as the place they had been searching for. She took Pen's arm and nodded to him without speaking. The boy grinned, a disarming response that made her smile, as well. It was almost over.

She looked around for Weka Dart, but still he wasn't there.

Pen saw the look on her face. "Where is he, Aunt Grianne? I thought he would be waiting for us."

She took a long moment to study the trees, to peer through the gloom not only of the day but also of her own realization of what had happened.

"He isn't coming," she said.

The boy stared at her. "Why wouldn't he come? Doesn't he want to get out of here?"

She shook her head. "I don't know. I'm not sure he knows. I think he's afraid. Of failing to get out, if the darkwand won't take him. Of getting out and finding it isn't what he expects. Maybe something else altogether."

Penderrin looked away. "I wouldn't stay here if I were him. I would take the chance that there might be something better."

She took a deep breath. She could use her magic to try to find the Ulk Bog. He might be close still, waiting to see if they would look for him. He might be testing her. But she knew in her heart that he wasn't, that he was far away, that he had put her behind him. She would be someone he had known and helped, someone he could brag about. But she would be only a memory.

Would he try to go back to Tael Riverine and become his Catcher once more? Would he take the chance that the Straken Lord either did not know of his participation in her escape or would forgive him for it? With the Ulk Bog, it was impossible to tell.

Weka Dart.

She spoke his name in her mind, conjuring up images of him that she thought she would carry with her to the grave.

"We have to go," she told Pen abruptly. "We can't wait on him. Use the staff."

The boy brought out the darkwand and set it butt-downward against the earth, his hands wrapped around its carved surface. The runes were glowing softly, pulsing bright red in the darkness of the midday storm.

"Place your hands with mine," he said.

She started to do so, and then stopped. "Pen, listen to me. They will be waiting for us when we come through—Shadea a'Ru and those who have allied themselves with her. They will have figured out where you went and be prepared for the possibility that you might get back again and bring me with you. They will know where to look for us. They will attack the moment they see us. They will try to put an end to both of us. So I want you to be ready. I want you to get behind me and stay there until you have a chance to get clear. Any chance. As soon as you see one, you are to take it. Don't wait for me. Don't even think about me. Just run and keep running. Do you understand?"

He nodded, but looked uncertain.

She put her hands on his shoulders. "You showed great courage in coming here to save me. I don't know anyone else who could have done what you did, except perhaps your father. I owe it to him to do for you what you have done for me. I want you safe and sound when this business is finished, Penderrin. Tell me you will do as I have asked."

He nodded again, more firmly this time. "I will, Aunt Grianne."

She took her hands from his shoulders. "Are you ready?"

He took a deep breath. "I am."

"Then let's go home."

She wrapped her hands on the staff and held tight.

TWENTY-EIGHT

The transition happened quickly. The runes began to glow more intensely, gaining strength from her touch. Grianne blinked against the sudden brightness, and then felt a kind of shifting in the space she occupied. The grayness of the Forbidding grew slowly darker, as if the storm had caught up to them and they were about to be engulfed. All that took place in seconds, barely giving her time enough to register what was transpiring. She glanced over at Pen, who held on to the darkwand from the other side, his eyes closed.

But she did not close hers. She wanted to see what was going to happen to her.

Even so, she did not. The runes suddenly burst into fiery brightness, and it appeared as if the staff itself was aflame. It was all she could do to keep holding on to it, to persuade herself that the fire was an illusion. The glow grew steadily, cocooning her away, shutting off her surroundings, from the world of the Jarka Ruus, from everything but the staff and herself and Pen.

Then everything was gone, and she was fighting for air as a massive fist closed about her body, crushing her, squeezing the air from her lungs with relentless pressure. She fought back against it, struggling to breathe, to stay alive. *Something has gone wrong,* she thought in desperation. *Something isn't right.*

Then the light dimmed, the runes darkened, and she was standing once more in the familiar surroundings of her sleeping chamber, returned safe and whole to Paranor. She still had a death grip on the staff, but the runes had gone dark.

She exhaled sharply in relief.

In the next instant, the triagenel collapsed about her.

She knew what it was immediately. She had caught a glimpse of the magic's glow in the few seconds it took for her passage out of the Forbidding to become complete, but had failed to recognize its significance until it was too late. The glow disappeared as the triagenel dropped into place, becoming an invisible presence that hemmed her in on all sides, an unbreakable cage.

"Don't move, Penderrin," she said to him.

He stood across from her, still smiling happily at having escaped the Forbidding. The smile faded slowly, and he looked around in surprise.

"We're caught in a triagenel," she informed him. A quick sweep of her hand illuminated the strands of their prison. "I told you they would be waiting. But I didn't foresee this."

"What is it?"

"A very powerful form of magic. It takes three magic users to create it, a combination of their skills to bring it to life."

But the glow was not uniform, she saw. In some places it was very nearly dark. In a properly constructed triagenel, the magic should be equally distributed. "There's something wrong here," she murmured. "See?"

She pointed at a couple of the weaker spots, at the obvious darknesses, and as she did so the door to the concealed passageway on the far side of the chamber swung inward and her brother's face appeared in the opening. "Grianne?"

"Bek!" she exclaimed in shock. "How in the world . . . ?"

"Listen to me," he interrupted, cutting her short. "I've used the wishsong to weaken several of the triagenel's strands. I think you can break free, if you try."

"Close the door!" she said.

He did so, and she pushed Pen down on the floor and stood over him. "Cover your head. Don't look up until I tell you."

She would not have much time. Shadea and the others would be coming. Perhaps they were already just outside. She would have to hurry. She was afraid of the wishsong after what had happened inside the Forbidding, but she had no other choice. She was going to have to use it anyway when she faced Shadea.

So she summoned the magic boldly, and when it surfaced she formed it into razor-sharp edges that would cut and sever and then sent them screaming into the weakened places in the net. The wishsong spun and ripped through the netting, overcoming momentary resistance from the enabling magic and slicing through strands until the cage sagged like soft rope. She kept at it, working at first one place and then another, and when she had the entire structure sufficiently weakened, she attacked it with such force that the triagenel disintegrated, and she blew out the entire north wall of the sleeping chamber. Stone blocks and debris exploded outward, and a huge cloud of dust mushroomed through the room.

Grianne covered her face, waited for the dust to settle, and then pulled Pen back to his feet. "Bek!" she shouted.

Her brother burst into the room with Rue Meridian, Tagwen, and an Elven girl she took to be Khyber Elessedil right behind. There was a quick exchange of grateful hugs between Pen and his parents and Khyber. Only Bek hugged her. Grianne saw dismay and shock reflected in their faces when they looked at her. She could even see pity.

"I'm all right," she said to them.

Her brother shook his head. "You are not all right. Shadea a'Ru and all those others who betrayed you will pay for this. We will hunt them down. We will find out everything. But we have something else we have to talk about now, something that won't wait. A demon was set free when you were taken. It's still here, and it's trying to break down the Forbidding."

"I know of this," she said.

"I thought as much. What you don't know is that the only way to stop it is for Pen to find it and use the darkwand to return it, just as he used the staff to return you."

"Penderrin has to do this?" she asked in surprise.

"The King of the Silver River said he must. Only the darkwand can complete the transfer from one world to the other, and only Pen can command the magic. I have to take him with us to find the demon."

In the hallway outside the sleeping chamber door, there was new activity, the sound of running and of shouts.

"They're coming," she said to the others. She brought up her hands, summoned her magic once more, and sealed the door from the inside. "That will hold them for a few minutes, no more." She turned back to Bek. "Take the others and go. You found your way here through the secret passageways—can you find your way back again?"

He nodded. "Between us, Tagwen and I can manage."

"I'm not coming," the Dwarf declared almost belligerently. "I belong here with the Ard Rhys."

Grianne moved over to him quickly and knelt. "Yes, you do. But you must leave anyway. All of you must. There's nothing you can do for me by staying. I have to face Shadea and the others alone. I am the one who can deal with them best. Only Bek might be able to help, but his place is with Pen, finding that demon and dispatching it. Listen to me." She gripped the Dwarf's shoulders tightly. "I've seen the inside of the Forbidding, Tagwen. It is a horror beyond anything you can imagine. If the creatures that live there were to be set free in this world, it would be the end of us all. You have to stop that from happening. Whatever becomes of me, you have to stop that."

She held his gaze. Finally, he gave her a small nod, his bearded face twisted into an unhappy knot. "I will do this because you ask it," he said quietly. "But not willingly."

She turned at once to Pen. "This won't be easy. You won't know what you have to do until you find the demon. Perhaps you will have to find a way to get it to touch the staff. Perhaps it will take more. I wish I could tell you something helpful, but you know as much as I do about how it works. Trust your instincts, Pen. They won't betray you."

The boy nodded. "I don't want to leave you, either."

She smiled. "I'll see you again. Just go. Do what you must. Do what is needed." She looked around. "All of you. Go, now."

They did so, one by one, disappearing through the door into the secret passageway, glancing back at her as they did, a mix of reluctance and dismay mirrored on their faces. Bek was the last to depart.

"Don't let anything happen to you," he said. "It's taken too much

out of us getting you back to bear the thought of losing you again."
He paused. "I love you, Grianne."

Then he pulled the door shut behind him and was gone, his
words still echoing in her mind.

I love you, too, she thought.

She turned back to the sleeping chamber and looked at the
sealed door. She had come a long way to face what awaited her on
the other side. She had fought hard for a chance to put things right.
But all of a sudden, she was unsure if she could do so.

How odd, she thought.

On the floor in front of her, the last strands of the ruined triagenel were slowly dissolving as their magic leached away. She stared
for a moment, then caught sight of herself in the mirror and saw
what Bek and the others had seen: a ghost, a tattered imitation of
herself.

She walked to the closet on the other side of the room, opened
it, and took out one of the robes hanging there, clean and sleekly
black. She draped it around her shoulders and fastened it in place
with the clasp she had fashioned in the shape of the Eilt Druin, the
Druid chain of office, the symbol of their order.

Her enemies would see her this last time, she told herself, as she
meant for them to see her. As leader. As Ard Rhys.

She fingered the clasp, tracing the raised image of a hand holding forth a burning torch. The meaning of the Elfish words came
back to her. THROUGH KNOWLEDGE, POWER.

Perhaps. This day, she would see.

Then she crossed the room and swept the air in front of the
chamber door with one hand to remove the magic that sealed it.
Tightening her resolve, she flung open the door.

Shadea a'Ru stood on the battlements of Paranor's north wall
with Traunt Rowan and looked down at the army of Rock Trolls
amassed before the gates. On hearing of this new threat, she had
come at once, determined that she would deal with it herself, that
she would not leave it up to her less-than-reliable allies. But having seen for herself how many Trolls were gathered—in excess of a
thousand—she was unsure of what to do.

"Have they made any sort of demand?" she asked Traunt Rowan.

He shook his head. "Not a word out of any of them. They simply walked out of the trees and formed up in ranks and haven't moved or said anything since."

"This must have something to do with Kermadec," she said quietly. "Those Trolls bear the banner of Taupo Rough. They wouldn't be here if it wasn't for him. Are you sure you left him safely behind at Stridegate? After all, that girl managed to find a way onto one of the ships."

"He was on the ground with the others when we lifted off. He was trapped by thousands of Urdas. Even if he got past them, he would have had to walk out. It would have taken days." Traunt Rowan shook his head, and then gestured toward the Troll army. "Maybe they've come looking for him. Maybe they think he's here."

She considered the possibility. "Maybe."

But that suggestion didn't feel right. A few might come, but not an entire army. It was something else, something much more dangerous. She glanced at the lower walls, where the Gnome Hunters were hiding behind the battlements. They could hold against an attack if the Trolls did not get past the walls. But there were too few of them to withstand an assault if the attackers broke through.

She had already ordered that the gates be reinforced. There was nothing more she could think of to do at that point. She would let the Trolls stand out there all day if that was what they wanted to do. If they were still standing there the next day, she might consider using her magic to disperse them. But that would require an enormous drain on her reserves, a last resort when all else failed. She would need a good reason to commit herself to such an action.

She was considering the possibility of sending word to the Eastland Gnomes that they needed reinforcements when Pyson Wence came flying down the stairs from the north tower, his black robes billowing wildly, his sharp features stricken.

"The triagenel has collapsed!" he shouted to them.

She's back, Shadea thought instantly.

"You're sure about this?" she snapped, exchanging a quick glance with Traunt Rowan.

Pyson Wence sneered, trying to hide the fear in his eyes. "Do you think me a fool? The magic's gone dark. What else could it mean?"

She ignored the taunt, brushing past him as she moved quickly toward the tower stairs, her strong features hard and set. "Let's finish this," she said softly.

They went up the stairs in a rush. Already, Shadea felt the magic building inside her in anticipation of the battle ahead. She smiled fiercely. This time there would be no mistakes.

They had gained the head of the stairs and were turning down the hallway leading to the sleeping chamber when its north wall blew apart.

Deep in the hidden passageways in the walls of the Keep, the Ohmsfords, Khyber Elessedil, and a grumbling Tagwen descended toward the furnace room. In a somber mood, the group moved ahead in silence.

"I don't like it that we left her back there alone," the Dwarf repeated over and over again.

"You know we couldn't stay, Tagwen," Rue Meridian said finally. "You know she wouldn't let us."

"There are too many of them for her to have a chance."

Rue shook her head. "I wouldn't wager against her, whatever the odds."

Tagwen went silent for a time as the little band continued through the darkness using a small light provided by Khyber's elemental magic as a beacon. They could not tell what was happening behind them. The stone-block walls were thick and massive and muffled all sounds from the other side. The chambers of the Druid's Keep were tombs, and they kept their secrets well.

"We could still go back," Tagwen muttered under his breath. "It isn't too late."

Bek wheeled back on him furiously. "Stop it, Tagwen! None of the rest of us likes this any better than you do! How do you think I feel about leaving her? She's my sister! But if the Forbidding comes down, it really won't make any difference what happens to Grianne, will it?"

"Bek," Rue admonished softly.

Tagwen went crimson with shame at the rebuke, his lips compressing into a tight line. He tried to say something in response, but failed. Trembling, he pushed past Bek and went on alone.

It was Pen who went after him, hurrying to catch up as he wandered blindly ahead into the darkness. "Wait, Tagwen!"

When he was even with the Dwarf, Pen slowed and walked at his side. They were descending a stairway that was broad enough for two to pass together, so the boy was able to stay on his shoulder.

"He didn't mean it, Tagwen. He just thinks like you do; he's afraid he will lose her."

Tagwen didn't say anything.

"We all want to go back and help her," Pen continued. "We are all afraid for her. I saw what sort of place the Forbidding is. I saw what she had to survive for all those weeks. She has been though a lot more than you think. I don't even know it all; she wouldn't talk about it with me. But I sensed it, anyway."

"All the more reason we should be back there helping her," Tagwen said furiously. "She's not strong enough to face Shadea and those others. She'll try to stand up to them, to reclaim the order, but she might not have the strength to do it."

Pen nodded. "I know. But if we're not there, Tagwen, she doesn't have to worry about us getting hurt. She only has to worry about herself. I think that's all she can manage just now. She sent us away to find the demon, but she sent us away to keep us safe, too."

He paused. "And if something bad does happen to her, we won't be there to see it happen. I think she wants that, too."

The Dwarf looked over at him, but made no response.

Kermadec had been waiting for the right moment, and when he heard the explosion from high in the north tower, he knew it had arrived. He took his little band of Rock Trolls from the gatehouse in which they had been hiding and moved toward the main gates securing the north wall. They advanced at a trot, bunched close together for protection, prepared to fight their way through any resistance. But they were lucky. The Gnome Hunters guarding the Keep were all on the walls or at the gates themselves, and the corridors between were empty.

The Trolls got to within fifty feet of the north gates before the Gnome Hunters standing guard at the huge crossbar securing the gates caught sight of them and shouted a warning to those on the walls. Kermadec responded by ordering his Trolls to charge. They rushed the Gnomes at the gates and fought their way through them. A hail of arrows and darts rained down from the walls, but once the Trolls were past the defenders and up against the gates, the men on the walls couldn't see them anymore.

"Atalan!" Kermadec shouted to his brother. "Take the others! Watch our backs!"

With Barek to aid him, he turned to the crossbar. It was too heavy for even a dozen men to lift and had to be rolled in and out of a series of iron clasps by a pulley system. With attackers coming at Atalan and the remaining Trolls from every direction, Kermadec and Barek heaved against the levers that engaged the pulleys and began to slide the crossbar free.

Shouts turned to screams of rage and fear as the Gnomes realized what was happening, and they flung themselves on the Trolls heedlessly. Atalan's small line held for a moment, and then broke apart under the rush. Dozens of Gnome Hunters converged on Kermadec and Barek. The latter fought to protect his Maturen, but was overwhelmed. Kermadec threw aside the Gnomes who reached him, still leaning into the pulley levers. The crossbar grated slowly out of its metal fastenings, the pulley wheels squealing from the strain.

"Atalan!" Kermadec shouted again as his attackers tore him away from the levers.

His brother reached him instantly, hammering aside the Gnomes who sought to bar his way, roaring the Taupo Rough battle cry, which was instantly taken up by the Trolls without. The gates sagged inward as Kermadec's soldiers outside pressed up against them. The crossbar was drawn halfway out by then, a single fastening securing it on its farthest end. Gnome Hunters clinging to him, Atalan threw himself against the levers and the crossbar slid all the way free.

An instant later, the gates heaved open behind the crush of armored giants pressing inward, and the Trolls of Taupo Rough poured through. The remaining defenders held their ground for a moment longer, then broke and ran, looking for somewhere farther inside the Keep to regroup.

Kermadec waited just long enough to be certain that entry into Paranor was secure, then broke free of the others and began to climb the stairs to the north tower.

Although his brother didn't see him, Atalan was right behind.

TWENTY-NINE

When Shadea a'Ru reached the sleeping chamber door and pushed her way through the knot of Gnome Hunters that surrounded it, the first thing she recognized was that the door was magic-sealed.

"She's free!" she hissed at Traunt Rowan and Pyson Wence as they came up next to her.

"Free? Of the triagenel?" The Gnome looked stricken. "That's impossible! No one can break out of a triagenel!"

Traunt Rowan smiled faintly, almost as if he had expected as much. "Perhaps we failed to build it properly."

Shadea didn't know and didn't care. What mattered was that their worst enemy was no longer a captive in any sense. She would have to be dealt with in a more direct and immediate manner or they were all finished.

She motioned for the Gnome Hunters to move behind her, thinking to put some space between all of them and the closed door. "To my left," she told Pyson, pulling Traunt Rowan to her right. "When she comes through that door, burn her. Don't hesitate. Don't think about it. Just do it. We'll catch her from three sides. Even Grianne Ohmsford isn't impervious to Druid magic!"

They backed away, Shadea all the way across the hall to the far wall, where she pressed her back up against the stone and summoned her magic to her fingertips. She glanced left and right to the other two, standing perhaps twenty feet away on either side in the middle of the hallway. The Gnome Hunters were crouched behind them, swords drawn, arrows noched into bows.

Thirty, perhaps forty strong, they waited.

Then the door flew open, banging hard against the wall, and a specter emerged, a black and impenetrable wraith backlit by light that poured through a ragged hole in the sleeping chamber wall. Its robes billowed out from its slender form, and light from the flameless hallway lamps reflected off the shiny surface of a clasp fashioned in the shape of the Eilt Druin, a hand holding forth a burning torch.

For a second, in spite of their combined resolve, no one among those who obeyed Shadea a'Ru moved. The sight of the ghostly form froze even the sorceress herself.

But then Shadea broke free of her momentary shock and sent Druid Fire streaking into the black-cloaked form, burning it to ash. Fire from the other two Druids followed on the heels of her own, disintegrating even the ash. Shouts of encouragement rose from the Gnome Hunters, who leapt up and down in response to the destruction.

Then silence settled over the hallway, and everyone went still again. Shadea moved out to the center of the corridor, peering cautiously through the haze.

"I am not where you thought me to be," Grianne Ohmsford said from somewhere off to the right.

All three rebel Druids froze where they were, staring at nothing but wall and smoke and ash as they tried to find her.

"You are not my equal, Shadea," Grianne continued quietly. "You never were. You never will be. You are banished from the order and from these walls. All of you are. If you leave now, I will let you live. I have seen enough of killing and vengeance and do not wish to see more. You deserve much worse than banishment, but if you go now, that will be the end of it. You have my word."

A dozen responses went through Shadea a'Ru's mind, all of them pointless. "I don't think banishment will suit me," she said finally. "And it remains to be seen if I am your equal or not. Show yourself, and let's find out."

But Grianne Ohmsford stayed invisible, speaking out of shadows and smoke. "Do you have any idea of what you have done? Do you have any idea at all? You sought to confine me to the Forbidding. To do so, you enlisted the aid of demons. One demon, in particular. You never stopped to consider why that demon would want to help you. You never thought that it might be using you as you were using it. What you did, Shadea—what all of you did—was to release a demon into this world by imprisoning me in the Forbidding. That demon remains free. It has a purpose in coming here. It seeks to destroy the wall of the Forbidding and set free all the demons it contains."

What nonsense, Shadea thought at once. "Where is your proof of that, Grianne?" she snapped angrily. "Do you think us fools to believe such lies?"

"I think you fools not to. You have set free a changeling, Shadea. You have set free a creature that can disguise itself as anything or anyone. It will have already assumed the identity of another and begun seeking ways to destroy the Ellcrys. If we don't stop it, it will succeed."

"We? You would enlist us? Even as we are banished?" Shadea straightened to her full height. "Come out of hiding and persuade us better, Grianne."

But even as she spoke, she was thinking of Iridia. Iridia, who had not seemed herself in that last encounter and who had gone to Sen Dunsidan to be his adviser when Shadea would have bet anything against that happening. Iridia, who had subsequently disappeared completely.

Could it be?

In an impulsive response to a possibility she could not bring herself to face, and disregarding her own safety, Shadea sent a scattering of illumination specks all across the facing of the wall fronting the bedchamber, trying to uncover Grianne's hiding place. The glittering specks coated everything, leaving a clear outline of what lay concealed within the shadows and smoke.

Grianne Ohmsford was nowhere to be found.

"Show yourself, you coward!" Shadea screamed in fury.

"Turn around."

Shadea stiffened, and then did so. Grianne Ohmsford stood a few yards away against the wall behind Shadea and to the right. She mirrored the wraith that had appeared in the doorway, cloaked and hooded in black, the Eilt Druin clasp at her throat. Her face and hands were pale and ravaged. She looked beaten and tired; she did not look up to a confrontation. Shadea took her measure and recognized the truth. The demon business and the offer of banishment were all a bluff.

"You don't look well, Grianne," she said. "You look as if a strong breeze might topple you. I don't imagine it was very pleasant inside the Forbidding, was it?"

Her enemy said nothing, but those strange blue eyes never left her own. They were watching her, waiting to see which way she would go. Whatever else Grianne was, she wasn't a fool.

"I think you have come to Paranor for the last time," Shadea continued softly. "I think you have just wasted your one chance at escaping with your life."

"Don't mistake what you see," the other whispered. "Take my offer. Go now. Banishment is not the worst of what can happen to you."

"I'll burn your eyes out first," Shadea responded.

"Shadea, wait!" Traunt Rowan stepped forward, hands stretched out in a gesture of supplication. "Enough of this. It's over. We've lost. Don't you see?"

"Be silent!" she hissed.

"To what end? The time for silence is past. Look at what's before us. Anyone who can survive the Forbidding and come back alive to the Four Lands and then break free of a triagenel is no one I care to challenge. If she can do all she has done to get back here and confront us like this, she has magic and luck beyond anything we possess."

He looked at Grianne. "I told you once that you should resign for the good of the order. I have not changed my mind about that. I still think you should. I still think you are too divisive to ever bring the order together in the way that will serve the greater good. I took sides against you because of it. Maybe I was wrong to do so, but I was not wrong about you."

He shook his head. "You must make your own decision. I have made mine. I accept this offer. I accept banishment. I've had enough."

He gave Shadea a hard, searching look, and she returned it with enough venom to poison a city. But he would not look away, and he did not blink. "Do the right thing, Shadea. Give it up."

He turned away from her and stalked down the hall, brushing aside a cluster of Gnomes that barred his way.

Shadea stared after him in disbelief, and then screamed in rage. "Traitor!"

She sent an explosion of Druid Fire into his back, white-hot and corrosive. The force of the blow lifted him off his feet and flung him against the far wall, where he slid to the floor, a lifeless, burning wreck.

In the next instant, Pyson Wence attacked Grianne Ohmsford.

Kermadec had climbed almost two flights into the Keep before he realized Atalan was following him. He wheeled back instantly. "What are you doing?" he shouted at his brother in dismay. "Go back and wait with the others!"

Atalan kept coming and shoved past him as if he weren't there. "Go back yourself, brother."

Kermadec reached for him angrily and then stopped himself. Getting into a fight with his brother would serve no useful purpose. If Atalan wanted to come, it was because he wanted to help. What was the point in being angry with that?

The point, he knew, was that he was afraid for Atalan. But he also knew that their relationship was well beyond a time and place where he could do anything about that.

He forced his concerns aside, caught up with Atalan, and without looking at him said, "We'll go back together when this business is finished and done with."

They passed knots of Druids who stood looking at them in surprise, books and scrolls cradled in their hands, dark robes gathered close. A few recognized him and nodded. They didn't seem to know what was happening. One or two moved quickly away when they realized he had been in a fight, and he shouted after them to go to the Assembly and stay there. He assumed that most of them would; he was still convinced that they would not fight for Shadea if they were not threatened themselves.

The hallways came and went as the two Rock Trolls raced ahead. Only once did they encounter anything resembling resistance, and that was an unexpected run-in with a knot of Gnome Hunters who fled the moment they saw what they were up against. Kermadec had not been inside the Keep in years, but he remembered it well from his time as Captain of the Druid Guard, and he found his way without difficulty. Almost all of the Gnomes were on the walls, fighting to hold against the onslaught of Rock Trolls pouring through the north gates.

As they neared the upper reaches of the north tower, Kermadec grew increasingly uneasy. He did not like the Keep's empty feeling. He did not like the unusual quiet. His battle instincts were finely tuned from years of fighting, and he knew better than to ignore them. There was an edge to his anticipation this time that was unusual. He had the strange sensation of wanting to hurry and at the same time needing to slow down. Perhaps it was the nature of the mission or what was at stake. Perhaps it was the place and time. He could not explain it. But he did not slow. His concerns must be for his mistress. She had come back to them, he believed. She had escaped the Forbidding. The explosion in the north tower told him Penderrin had succeeded. She was there, and he knew in his heart that she needed him.

As he neared the upper hallway and the sleeping chamber of the Ard Rhys, the sounds of a desperate struggle convinced him that he was right.

Grianne Ohmsford was caught off guard by Pyson Wense's attack. She had assumed that any attack would begin with Shadea, to whom the others clearly looked. On coming out of the sleeping chamber and using the false image to distract the Druids, she had placed herself in a position where she could best defend herself against the sorceress. She had not forgotten about Pyson or Traunt Rowan, but she had focused her attention principally on Shadea.

But Shadea's unexpected attack on Traunt Rowan had surprised her, and for just a moment she had taken her attention away from the Gnome. Perhaps he had been watching for that. His attack came just as she realized the danger, but she was too slow to deflect it entirely. The Druid Fire slammed into her, nearly shattering her defenses. It scorched her hair and the skin of her face, and if not for the protective magic already in place, including that woven through her Druid robes, she would have been incinerated.

Even so, the force of the attack knocked her off her feet and sent her sprawling down the hall, tangled in her black robes. Furious at herself for her inattention and desperate to regain control of the sit-

uation, she sprang up again, but a second explosion immediately
knocked her down once more. Pyson was moving toward her by
then, leveling a steady barrage of incendiary magic, trying to keep
her down long enough to finish her. She rolled and twisted, using the
wall to lever herself back to her knees, and launched her own Druid
Fire in response. But her efforts were weak and unsustained, and the
Gnome kept advancing.

Then Shadea wheeled back, and Grianne was forced to turn her
attention to the new threat, lashing out at the sorceress before she
had a chance to join the attack. Shadea screamed in fury as the magic
of the wishsong knocked her backwards. But Shadea was physically
much stronger than Grianne and was quick to regain her balance.
Within seconds, Grianne was under attack from two sides.

Just as it seemed that she had exposed herself too quickly and
would pay the price for her impatience, Kermadec came charging
down the hallway with a second Troll right behind, slamming into a
cluster of Gnome Hunters that tried to slow him, scattering the
gnarled figures as if they were made of paper. Roaring with a fero-
ciousness that froze the blood, the big Troll went right at Shadea.

But Shadea a'Ru had fought on the Prekkendorran and was no
stranger to hand-to-hand combat. Moreover, she was very nearly as
strong as the Troll. She met his rush with a howl as ferocious as his
own, slipped his grasp, and let his momentum carry him into the
wall. Then she wheeled back on him, able to bring her magic to bear
now, and sent the Druid Fire burning into him.

Just as she did so, the second Troll came at her, as well. "Kermadec!" he roared in what seemed more a battle cry than a warning.

Down went Shadea a'Ru and the second Troll in a tangled,
thrashing knot, rolling over and over on the stone floor. Kermadec
was struggling to rise, but Pyson Wence joined the attack and searing Druid Fire slammed Kermadec back against the wall, knocking
the breath out of him and leaving his thick hide steaming from the
heat. The Gnome struck at him again and again, shouting for his
Hunters to move in and finish him.

But Pyson made the same mistake now with Grianne that she had
made earlier with him. He forgot about her. She surged to her feet in
a white-hot fury, summoned the power of the wishsong, and struck
out at him with every ounce of strength she could manage. Sensing
his danger, the Gnome turned from Kermadec toward her just in

time to receive the full brunt of the attack. She had a glimpse of his terrified face as he fought to protect himself. For just a second, his defenses held. Then they fell apart, and Pyson Wence simply exploded.

So damaged by the Gnome Druid's attack that flames were licking at the burned places on his body, Kermadec was trying to get up again. "Atalan!" he called desperately.

Shadea a'Ru broke free of Kermadec's brother, wheeled away, and went into a crouch. When she came out of it, she was holding a long knife at waist level. Atalan came at her fearlessly, his massive arms reaching out to crush her, but she sidestepped him easily in a practiced, fluid movement and drove the knife hilt-deep into his chest. Atalan sagged from the blow and dropped to his knees, gasping.

Shadea kicked his body aside and turned back to Grianne. Hands lifting, she attacked anew, sending a hail of Druid Fire into her enemy. Grianne was able to fight off the attack, but only barely. The force of it knocked her backwards once more, and she struggled to keep her feet as she sought to defend herself, trying in vain to mount a counterattack.

She felt her defenses crumbling. She felt the heat of the Druid Fire beginning to break through.

Suddenly, out of the corner of her eye, she saw Kermadec, his great body bloodied and steaming, lurch to his feet. One hand grasped a spear he had taken from one of his Gnome attackers. Bracing himself against the wall, he gripped the spear in one huge fist, set himself, and heaved it at Shadea.

Too late the sorceress realized the danger. She wheeled to protect herself, but the spear caught her in the chest and drove her back against the wall, the force of the throw pinning her fast. Her body jerked and her head snapped back. Her eyes went wide with shock and disbelief. She screamed and flailed, trying to break free. She sprayed Druid Fire everywhere. But the blow was fatal, and a moment later she collapsed and did not move again.

The remaining Gnome Hunters were already in flight, disappearing down the hallway as fast as they could manage. Grianne stood alone among the wounded and the dead. She lowered her hands, dispersed the magic she had summoned to defend herself, and stared at Shadea a'Ru. The sorceress was staring back at her, eyes blank and unseeing, face twisted in a death mask. Grianne looked away, sickened, then walked quickly over to Kermadec. The big Rock Troll slid down the wall into a sitting position, his chin sunk on his chest. Blood and burned patches were everywhere on his massive body.

She knelt before him and gently raised his head. "Kermadec?" she whispered. "Can you hear me?"

His eyes opened and fixed on her. "Mistress," he replied, his voice thin and reedy. "I told you they were vipers."

She bent forward and kissed his face, and then cradled him against her and whispered, "You great bear."

THIRTY

Pen Ohmsford, his parents, Khyber Elessedil, and Tagwen descended through the corridors of Paranor to the furnace room, then back down along the hidden passageway that led to the outside world. They encountered no one on their way. The silence of the Druid's Keep was deep and pervasive and gave the false impression that it was deserted save for them.

But once they were outside, they heard the sounds of the battle being fought at the north wall, and although they hadn't seen the Trolls arrive, they could pretty well guess at what was happening.

"That will give Shadea something else to think about!" Tagwen grunted, a smile on his bearded face. "Kermadec won't rest until he has the Ard Rhys safely out of there!"

That knowledge seemed to give him some sense of peace, and he quit muttering about how he should be back in the north tower trying to help her. Pen was grateful for that because, given that he was the only one sympathetic enough to permit it, most of the muttering was being done in his ear. While he appreciated Tagwen's concern for his mistress, he was struggling with his own problems.

Pen was beginning to contemplate in some detail the task that lay ahead of him. He had thought he would be safely out of danger once he returned to Paranor with his aunt, so the news that he must go off and find a changeling demon and confront it with the darkwand had come as an unpleasant surprise. Once again, he was being asked to do something without being told exactly how he was supposed to do it. Only this time, he was being asked to confront a very dangerous creature. It was one thing to go into the Forbidding and bring back the Ard Rhys, who was ready and willing to come. It was another to force a demon to go back into a place it did not wish to go.

At least he had his parents to help him. And Khyber, as well. They were much more self-possessed and experienced than he was. His father and Khyber had the use of magic, as well. That should give them an edge once they found the demon. Still, it was his responsibility to use the darkwand to return the demon to the Forbidding, and no amount of reassurance could disguise the fact that he didn't know how to do that.

As they moved away from the base of the cliffs on which Paranor rested, slipping quickly and quietly into the forest toward *Swift Sure*, Pen found himself wondering what demons were like. He hadn't really seen any in the Forbidding, unless you counted Weka Dart, and he didn't. The Ulk Bog didn't seem like a demon to him; he envisioned demons as being something much more fearsome and threatening.

In any case, he didn't know what he was going to do once he met a real one, but he thought it might be a good idea to figure out something before the moment arrived.

They passed through the trees to the clearing where *Swift Sure* was tethered, climbed up the rope ladder, and set about releasing the anchor ropes. His parents did most of the work, his mother taking the helm and his father working the lines. In minutes they were airborne, lifting away from the woods, rising swiftly into the air. He stood with Tagwen and Khyber at the railing and looked down on Paranor. The north wall of the Druid's Keep was under attack by huge numbers of Rock Trolls, their size and build unmistakable from any height. The Trolls were spread out all along the wall, but the greatest number were bunched together at the gates, and from the surge pushing inward it seemed clear that the gates had been taken.

Then *Swift Sure* was moving away too rapidly for them to follow the action below any further, and Bek was calling out to Khyber as he moved toward the ship's bow. The trio moved away from the railing in response and joined the elder Ohmsford in front of the fore-mast.

"Will you use the Elfstones now?" he asked Khyber.

"What am I looking for?" She already had the Stones out and was holding them in the palm of her hand. "I don't know what a demon looks like. I don't know what sort of creature I ought to tell the Stones to find."

Perplexed by the problem, they stared at each other in silence for a moment. None of them, after all, had ever seen a demon or had any clear idea of what one looked like. If they didn't know what they were looking for, how were they supposed to find it?

Then Pen said, "Try holding on to the staff, Khyber. It helped me find Grianne in the Forbidding. If its purpose now is to find the demon, it might help you here."

He handed her the darkwand, which she took from him and held out in front of her in one hand while gripping the Elfstones in the other, summoning their magic. The moments crept by. Nothing happened.

"It isn't working," she said, a hint of panic in her dark eyes.

Pen took the staff back from her. "I guess it only responds to me. Let me try. If it showed me how to find Grianne, it should show me how to find the demon, as well."

He gripped the darkwand and turned his thoughts to the demon and the Forbidding. Instantly, the runes began to brighten all up and down the length of the staff, their glow soft at first and then building in intensity. When they began to dance off the staff like fireflies, Pen said quickly, "Now, Khyber! Put your hand over mine and use the Elf-stones!"

She did so, gripping the staff with her left hand and lifting her right fist to call forth the magic. The response was immediate. The Elfstones brightened like blue fire, their light flooding from between her fingers in brilliant shards and exploding away toward the south-west. The light showed miles and miles of plains and hills, green ex-panses of grasslands and farms, then tightened to a point where a single airship sailed steadily west across the landscape. The craft was huge, a great warship, its decks thick with the black-and-silver uni-forms of the Federation but stripped of any visible weapons. The vi-sion tightened and settled on one man, an imposing patriarch with flowing white hair and a strong, imperious face, who stood in the pilot box as if to oversee its workings, his arms folded across his chest as he stared off into the distance where the thick forests of the Westland spread away from the broad, gleaming surface of a sunlit lake.

Seconds later, the image flared once and went dark, and the magic faded.

"Sen Dunsidan," Tagwen declared, loathing in his voice. Then he realized the implications of what that meant. "Shades!" he breathed, his face going pale.

"You're sure about this?" Bek asked, putting a hand on the Dwarf's broad shoulder.

Tagwen nodded firmly. "There's no mistaking him. He's come to Paranor enough times that I should know. Prime Minister of the Federation, but a snake of the first order. I would have been willing to bet everything I own that he was Shadea's ally in sending the Ard Rhys into the Forbidding. He's always hated her, ever since she manipulated him as the Ilse Witch. She made it up to him, but he never forgave her. He isn't the type to forgive anyone."

"But now he's the demon?" Rue interrupted. "What's going on?"

Bek shook his head. "The demon crossed over when Grianne was sent into the Forbidding. It must have taken another form right away. It probably switched identities more than once. Now it pretends to be Sen Dunsidan. A good choice; it gives the demon tremendous power."

"It's going into the Westland," Khyber said. "That lake was the Myrian and those forests the Tirfing. It must think it's found a way to destroy the Ellcrys."

Bek nodded. "Flying west below Callahorn, away from the Prekkendorran and the normal routes of travel. It's trying to sneak in from below. It knows it will be seen eventually, but perhaps not right away. It must have a plan for what it will do when the Elves intercept it. Negotiation first, perhaps, then force if all else fails. That warship looks formidable, even if it doesn't seem to be carrying any weapons. There must be something aboard that will allow the demon to destroy the Ellcrys."

"The Elves will never let it get close enough to threaten the tree," Khyber insisted.

"Not if they know it is a demon. But as Sen Dunsidan, it will get closer than it would otherwise. At any rate, we have to stop it. If we fly all night, we should intercept it by dawn."

"I might remind you," said Rue Meridian, who had come up quietly behind them while they were discussing what to do, "that we don't have any weapons on this ship except for a pair of rail slings. How are we supposed to intercept anything?"

Pen's father didn't seem to have an answer to that, saying that he would think about it.

Bek went back with Rue into the pilot box, leaving Pen with Khyber and Tagwen. Unable to get past his susceptibility to airsickness even on the calmest of days, the Dwarf was already starting to look a little green, and after grunting something about taking a nap he disappeared below. Pen talked with Khyber for a time, catching up on what had happened to her after he had gone into the Forbidding and telling her in turn what he had seen there. When they were finished with that, neither one wanted to talk about much of anything. They were exhausted from their struggles and in need of nourishment and rest. Khyber left to find something for them to eat, and Pen moved over to the bow and settled in.

Looking out over the countryside, he thought anew about what he was going to do when they found that warship and its demon commander. He was aware of how uncertain things were becoming once again, and the particulars of his own role in what lay ahead were the most nebulous of all. He had survived the Forbidding and a good deal more, but that didn't make him feel any better about his chances. He wished he had some idea of how the darkwand would work on the demon, but there was no one to tell him and no way for him to find out until the moment he was using it. He wasn't very reassured.

He found himself thinking about his aunt. Events at Paranor were in all likelihood already over. She had either regained control of the Druid order or she was dead. He didn't want to think like that, but he knew it was true. Thinking of what they had left her to face made him sick at heart. She seemed so frail and so vulnerable that he couldn't conceive of her surviving a battle with the rebel Druids. He told himself that she had survived in the Forbidding, so she might find a way to survive at Paranor. It would have been better, though, if they could have stayed to help. It would have been better if she weren't so alone.

Khyber returned with food and drink, and after Pen had consumed both, he went below and slept. His sleep was deep and untroubled until sometime around midnight, when he dreamed of a dark presence enfolding him so tightly that he couldn't breathe, and he woke sweating with fear.

After that, he didn't sleep at all.

It was two hours past dawn when the Moric saw the other airship approaching. By then, the *Zolomach* had turned north along the silver ribbon of the Mermidon and was approaching the Valley of Rhenn on a day that was bright and clear and warm. The Moric didn't care what kind of day it was; it only cared that it was to be the last day it would have to spend in an unpleasant world. It hated the brightness and the smells. It hated the humans it was forced to live among. It was worse aboard this airship, where it was in proximity to them all the time and could not escape to its sewer refuge. Worse still, it had assumed the identity of a human who was never left alone for more than a few moments, even when sleeping.

It couldn't change the conditions of this world quickly enough.

But time was running out on the Moric. In spite of its success in avoiding detection by Elven airships, the atmosphere aboard this vessel was poisonous. Two days earlier, the Free-born army had overrun the Federation defensive lines on the Prekkendorran and sent that once seemingly invincible force fleeing back into the deep Southland in a reprise of what the Federation had done to the Elves some days earlier. Matters had turned about completely, and there was no changing them back. All attempts at rallying the remnants of the battered Southland army had failed, and the war, after decades of indecision, had turned decisively in favor of the allied Free-born. The Coalition Council was furious with Sen Dunsidan and had summoned him to appear before it, but the Moric was no fool. It knew, as Sen Dunsidan would have known, what that summoning meant.

So it simply ignored the Council, boarded the *Zolomach*, and set sail for Arborlon. Its own plans were settled and in no way affected by anything that had happened on the Prekkendorran. Those aboard ship knew of their army's defeat, but had been assured that what they were doing would carry the war to the Elves and turn things around. They accepted that because they were soldiers and because they had no choice. No one wanted to question Sen Dunsidan, even when he was in disfavor with the Coalition Council. Sen Dunsidan had come back before; there was no reason to think he would not come back again.

They had been forced to travel cautiously, choosing a route that would keep them from being spotted by Free-born airships and would get them close enough to Arborlon and the Ellcrys that the Moric could implement its plan to get closer still. In a way, the defeat of the Federation army on the Prekkendorran had made its task easier. When finally intercepted by the Elves, the demon would say, in its guise as Sen Dunsidan, that it had come to discuss a plan for peace, to accede to conditions that would assure that the war would not resume. It would ask permission to fly to Arborlon to speak to the Elven High Council. It would give assurances that no treachery was intended and offer hostages as a show of good faith. It would demand that they let it remain aboard the *Zolomach* because, in the face of so many of the enemy, no right-thinking commander would leave the only protection available. The Elves would accept his condition. The Federation ship would display no weapons and pose no visible threat. They would feel confident that they could deal with anything the Prime Minister might attempt.

If persuasion failed to win them over, then the demon would use the fire launcher, which was concealed inside what appeared to be a storage cabin on the foredeck. In the event of an attack, the front section of the cabin could be dropped away and the weapon armed and fired in seconds. The Elven airships would be burned out of the sky before they knew what was happening, and the *Zolomach* would continue on its way. Once within range of the Ellcrys, a single direct hit was all it would take. It would be over before the Elves had a chance to do anything to stop it. In spite of having the fire launcher, the *Zolomach* would be destroyed and its crew killed in reprisal, but the demon would escape because it would shed Sen Dunsidan's skin and take a new form. In the chaos, it would slip over the side of the ship. Once it was on the ground, they would never find it.

But now an unfamiliar airship was approaching, and they were still too far away from Arborlon for it to be an Elven vessel. It was flying alone, as well, which suggested it had another purpose. The demon watched it grow larger, closing steadily, in no apparent hurry and with no indication that it meant any harm.

"Captain?" the demon said to the tall man on his right. "What ship is this?"

The *Zolomach's* Captain, who had been studying the vessel through his spyglass, shook his head. "No ship I know. Not a ship of the line. Not a warship." He looked again. "Wait. Her insignia is of a burning torch on a field of black." He trailed off. "She's a Druid ship."

The Moric stiffened. Shadea a'Ru? Come looking for him out here? The idea seemed preposterous. "Who's aboard her? Tell me what you see."

The Captain put the spyglass up again and studied the ship. "Two Druids standing at the bow. A pilot. Someone else. A boy, it looks like."

"Let me see."

The demon took the spyglass from the Captain and scanned the decks of the approaching airship. It was just as the Captain had said—four figures were visible on deck and no one else. No railguns were mounted, and no other weapons were to be seen. The demon lowered the spyglass and made a quick scan of the decks of the *Zolomach*, reassured by the presence of Federation soldiers at every turn. There was no reason to be worried.

Still, it was uneasy. What was a Druid airship doing way out there by itself? It was not there by chance. The encounter was not a coincidence.

"They're signaling to us," the Captain advised.

The demon glanced over at him in confusion. "Signaling?"

The Captain pointed to the line of pennants being raised along the other ship's foremast. "They wish to come aboard and speak with you. See the pennant with the silver and black on it? That's your pennant, Prime Minister. They must know you are aboard."

The demon's first impulse was to turn on the approaching airship and attack it at once. But the demon was trapped inside Sen Dunsidan's skin, and an unprovoked aggression against an ally would not be well received by the officers and men who crewed the ship. Worse, it might result in a battle they could not win. Although the Druid airship was not armed, the Druids themselves were formidable. If they were to damage the *Zolomach* and force another delay, it might prove fatal to the demon's plans to reach the Ellcrys.

White-hot fury fed the Moric's sense of frustration, but it kept calm outwardly. It would have to deal with the situation in a diplomatic way. "Move alongside them and ask what they wish to speak to us about," he ordered.

The Captain raised his own line of pennants, then maneuvered the *Zolomach* until she was close by her counterpart. The Druids stood at the railing, black-cloaked and hooded. The Moric glanced at the name carved into the ship's bow. *SWIFT SURE.*

"Sen Dunsidan!" shouted one of the Druids, the taller of the two, a woman by the sound of her voice. She kept her hood raised. "Shadea a'Ru sends greetings."

The Moric felt a twinge of panic. If Shadea had sent this ship and these Druids, then nothing good could come of it. After all, the Ard Rhys had already tried to kill it once. There was nothing to say that she was not about to try to do so again.

But then the demon remembered that it was no longer in the guise of Iridia Eleri, and it was the sorceress whom Shadea had sent assassins to kill. Sen Dunsidan was Shadea's ally. So far as the demon knew, nothing had happened to change that.

It calmed itself. "What does Shadea wish of me?" it shouted back in Sen Dunsidan's deep, resonant voice. "How can I be of service to the Ard Rhys?"

"She wishes to be of service to you," the speaker replied. "She wishes to present you with a gift that will be of use in negotiating with the Elves. She knows of the disaster on the Prekkendorran and wishes to mitigate the consequences. May I come over and present it?"

The Moric had no use for such a gift, but it understood that it could not afford to cast aside the offer out of hand. To do so would look suspicious. Worse, it would suggest that its motives in coming to the Westland were not peaceful. Shadea had allied herself and the Druids with Sen Dunsidan and the Federation. It made sense that she would want to aid the Prime Minister in his efforts at resolving the Federation dispute with the Free-born. She was as much at risk in this business as he was. The Moric wondered fleetingly how she had found out about where Sen Dunsidan was going and why, but it assumed she had spies at Arishaig who told her everything.

The Moric steeled itself. It would have to suppress its impulses and act as Sen Dunsidan would. This would only take a few minutes, and then it could be on its way. Better to placate the Druids than to irritate them.

"Let them board, Captain," it said to the *Zolomach's* commander. "But watch them closely in the event this is something other than what it seems."

The Captain nodded wordlessly, and the Moric climbed down from the pilot box and walked over to the railing to await its visitors.

It won't work, Pen kept thinking. *It will never work.*

But it did. He could scarcely believe it when the *Zolomach's* Captain ran up the line of signal pennants that invited the Druids aboard. He had been convinced that permission would be refused and they would be turned away without a second thought. But his father, who had conceived of the plan during the night and worked the details through carefully with his mother, had assured them all that the demon would relent. In its guise as Sen Dunsidan, it would be forced to do what Sen Dunsidan would do. It might want to turn them away, but it would realize that to do so would create suspicion and risk disruption of its efforts to reach the Ellcrys. Its overriding goal was to reach Arborlon as quickly as possible, Bek reminded them. It would do whatever was necessary to make that happen.

Under his father's steady hand, *Swift Sure* eased closer to the *Zolomach,* and lines were thrown from the latter to the former and secured by Pen to the anchor stanchions so that the two vessels were joined. Pen glanced up and down at the soldiers lining the other ship's railings and tried to reassure himself that they didn't matter, that the plan would work out as his father intended. His mother and Khyber, cloaked in the Druid robes his mother had stolen from Paranor and stowed aboard some weeks earlier, stood together at the bow, waiting patiently. They kept their hoods up and their features concealed. Sen Dunsidan didn't know any of them by sight save Tagwen, who was hiding belowdecks, but it didn't hurt to be cautious.

As he finished tying off the lines, Pen went over in his mind one last time the details of what was about to happen. If they were mistaken in any way about how the darkwand would react or if his aunt had guessed wrong about what he needed to do or, worst of all, if the King of the Silver River had deceived his father in his fever dream, then none of them were likely to return from the *Zolomach* alive. But it was mostly up to him to make the plan succeed, and it was his own judgment that was likely to determine how things turned out.

His mother and Khyber were moving along the railing toward the ramp that had been lowered from the *Zolomach* to allow them to board. Unbidden, he fell into step behind them, carrying the dark-wand in his right hand, the almost black, rune-carved surface gleaming in the sunlight. He sensed Sen Dunsidan's gaze—his demon's gaze—drawn to it. Cold and dead as deep winter, those blue eyes flared with sudden interest, and Pen felt a chill run up and down his spine.

Fighting down his repulsion and fear, he took a deep, steadying breath and stepped up onto the ramp behind his mother and Khyber as they walked slowly across to the other vessel. His father stood silently in the pilot box, showing no particular interest in the proceedings, a mercenary paid to do his job. But he would have already summoned the magic of the wishsong and be holding it at his fingertips. He would be watching carefully for any sign of treachery.

Pen paused to glance down. Below, the countryside spread away in a broad tapestry of mixed greens and mottled browns. They were several hundred feet in the air, suspended above the world with no place to run. Trapped, if things went wrong. But things would not go wrong, he told himself. He tightened his resolve and moved quickly off the ramp and onto the *Zolomach's* decks.

Federation soldiers and crew surrounded him, crowding in until there was nowhere left to stand. Seeing what was happening, Khyber lowered her hood to reveal her Elven features, glanced disdainfully at the men, made a quick warding motion with one hand, and watched in satisfaction as they fell backwards like stalks of grass in a heavy wind. Only the demon was left untouched. It smiled Sen Dunsidan's smile, gave Khyber a small nod of approval, and came forward until it was only steps away.

The smile froze. "We have not yet met."

Khyber bowed. "I am a servant to my mistress, Shadea a'Ru, the true Ard Rhys. My name is of no consequence. Shadea sends greetings and asks that you accept her gift of this staff. She would have come herself, but her presence at Paranor is required while matters remain so unsettled within the order. She sends my sister and myself in her place to offer reassurances of her commitment to the Federation. The staff is a demonstration of her support for your alliance."

She gestured dramatically past Rue, who was still cloaked and hooded, to where Pen waited with the darkwand. As prearranged, Pen lifted the staff and held it out so that it could be clearly seen.

"The staff," Khyber said to the demon, whose eyes were riveted on it, "has a special use."

She nodded to Pen, who turned his thoughts to the Forbidding and the creatures that lived within it. At once, his connection with the staff took hold and the runes blazed to life, a crimson glow that was blinding even in the bright morning sunshine. He saw that glow mirrored in the demon's gaze, hot and intense.

Khyber stepped close to the demon so that only it could hear. "The staff gives the holder the ability to command the attention of all who come into its presence. You can see that this is so. It also gives the holder small insights into the thinking of those with whom he negotiates, a window on their attitudes and concerns. It can be useful in knowing how best to persuade."

By now, images of the runes were dancing off the staff in wild patterns that flitted in the air all about Pen. The Federation soldiers and crew muttered excitedly. The demon blinked and its eyes took on a new look, one both hungry and anticipatory. It wanted the staff; it needed to possess it.

"Will you accept my mistress's gift?" Khyber pressed gently.

Sen Dunsidan's anxious features tightened, and the demon's eyes glittered. "I would be honored to accept it."

Khyber looked once more at Pen, who came forward obediently, eyes lowered as much out of fear for what was about to happen as for the demon itself. When he got to within three feet, he stretched out his arm and canted the glowing staff toward the demon. The demon reached for it, and then, for just a second, hesitated. Pen felt his heart stop.

Then Sen Dunsidan's face broke into a broad smile and his fingers closed about the staff.

From the moment it saw the staff, the demon knew it had to possess it. It was not a rational craving. It was a compulsion that defied explanation and transcended reason. It was so overpowering that the demon barely heard what the Druid was saying as she explained the staff's uses. And when the boy held the staff forth and the runes carved into its burnished surface flared with hypnotic brilliance, the demon was lost. The staff must be claimed. The demon was its rightful owner and must possess it. Nothing else mattered. Not the destruction of the Ellcrys. Not its plans to bring down the Forbidding. Nothing.

Even so, it hesitated for just a second when the staff was extended, a glimmer of suspicion aroused by recognition of the intensity of its inexplicable attraction.

But it took the staff anyway, and the moment it did so it realized it had made a mistake. The runes blazed like tiny flames as the demon's hand closed about the carved wood, and another kind of fire exploded through the demon in response. It was a fire of possession, of transference and of magic, a fire meant to cleanse and to purify. The demon felt it instantly, and tried to pull away. But its fingers would not release. They had taken on a separate existence, and no matter how hard it tried to loosen its grip, it could not.

It screamed then, a sound that rent the air and caused even the most hardened of the Federation soldiers to shrink away. It threw back its head and shrieked its defiance and fury. Some among the crew, the Captain included, came racing to its aid. The demon lashed out in response, its claws splitting the concealing skin of the human fingers, slashing and tearing at them until they fell bleeding on the deck of the airship.

The boy still gripped the other end of the darkwand, eyes wide and staring. He knew something of what was happening, the demon saw. Enraged, it snatched at him, trying to draw him close. But the boy ducked away, and one of the Druid women shouted at him to let go of the staff. They understood what was happening, as well, the demon realized. It stumbled toward them, its limbs leaden and unresponsive, filled with the fire of the magic, throbbing with the molten heat of its workings. The boy backed away, stubbornly keeping hold of the staff, and finally the taller of the women flung herself atop him, dragged him to the deck, pried loose his fingers from the staff, and pulled him clear.

Instantly, the light of the staff bloomed until the demon was enveloped by its glow. It fought furiously to free itself, slamming the staff against the deck, twisting and flailing futilely. The skin of the human Dunsidan split wide and the clothes of the human Dunsidan ripped and tore. Both fell away, leaving it fully revealed. Gasps and sharp hisses issued from the mouths of all who saw what it was, and there was a rush of booted feet on the wooden decks as men fled in all directions. The demon would have given chase, if it could have. It would have ripped their throats out. It would have drunk their blood. But it was consumed by its struggle with the staff and could do nothing but thrash and scream its hatred of them.

Then the light closed about it completely, and the world it had sought to subvert, together with the inhabitants it had come to despise, disappeared. The demon felt a crushing pressure on its chest and fought to breathe. It felt a shifting in time and place and realized in horror what was happening. It was going back into the Forbidding, back into the prison from which it had escaped. It was being returned to the world of the Jarka Ruus, a victim of the staff's magic, and there was nothing it could do to prevent it from happening.

It fought anyway, shrieking and spitting and thrashing, an insane thing, right up until the moment it blacked out.

A board the *Zolomach*, Federation soldiers and crew alike stared in shocked silence at the space Sen Dunsidan—or whatever had played at being Sen Dunsidan—had occupied only seconds before. Nothing remained but blood and shredded clothing and pieces of skin. None of them knew what had happened, and most didn't care to find out. All they wanted to know was whether there was any risk that the thing that had been the Prime Minister of the Federation was coming back.

Khyber swept the air in front of her with a sparkle of elemental magic to gain their attention, black Druid robes billowing out. "Back away!" she shouted at them, moving forward threateningly, occupying the space directly in front of what remained of Sen Dunsidan. She glanced down at those remains, and then up at dozens of frozen stares. "You didn't want him for a leader anyway, did you?"

Rue Meridian was hugging Pen, her face fierce. "What were you thinking, Penderrin?" she whispered. "It would have taken you with it if I hadn't broken your grip on the staff!"

Pen was white-faced, both from the pressure of his mother's grip and the realization of how narrow his escape had been. He took a deep breath. "I wasn't sure what would happen if I let go."

She hugged him tighter still. "Well, whatever the reason, you hung on too long to suit me. You scared me to death!"

"I wonder if it worked," he said softly.

"You wonder if what worked?"

"Something I tried, right there at the end. The staff and I were joined. We were communicating. I was telling it things. I was trying to make it understand me." He drew back and looked at her. "That was what I was doing, when I was hanging on, before you made me let go."

"Trying to tell the darkwand something?"

He smiled and nodded. "But I don't know if it understood."

It took a while for the Moric to regain consciousness after its struggle to resist being sent back into the Forbidding. As a result, it did not see the bright images projected into the air by the runes of the darkwand as it pulsated with light on the barren ground next to it. It did not see those images rise skyward to form intricate patterns that danced across the sullen clouds. By the time the demon stirred, the images had faded and the fire had gone out of the runes.

The Moric sat up slowly, knowing at once from the taste of the air and the smell of the earth that it was back inside its prison. It stared down at the staff, the once-gleaming surface become dusty and scarred. The runes had gone dark and the magic had disappeared. It was just a length of wood, a useless thing.

When it became aware of the shadow looming over it and looked up to find the dragon, the demon had to stifle a gasp. A huge, scaly, armored monster, it was easily the biggest the demon had ever seen. Freezing in place, the demon tried to figure out what to do, casting about in vain for a way to escape. The dragon was studying it intently, its lidded yellow eyes gleaming with a strange fascination.

And then it saw that the dragon wasn't looking at it, but at the staff that lay at its feet. The demon snatched up the staff and held it out to the beast, offering it eagerly. But the dragon didn't move. It was waiting for something. The demon laid the staff close by one of its huge, clawed feet and started to move away. But the dragon hissed at it in warning, freezing it in place.

The Moric turned back slowly, not knowing what to do, unable to determine what it was the dragon wanted.

The dragon, in no hurry, waited for the demon to figure it out.

THIRTY-ONE

The day was drenched in sunlight, and from high in the air where she rode aboard the Druid airship *Bremen*, Grianne Ohmsford could see the countryside for fifty miles in all directions. Huge, cottony clouds floated against the western horizon far out on the flats of the Streleheim, distant and remote, a soft promise of good weather. The airship sailed north on the first day of its expedition, and the woman who had once been Ard Rhys of the Third Druid Order was at peace.

She had known for a long time what she would do, she supposed. She had known from before she had come back through the Forbidding what must happen. The order would never heal while she was Ard Rhys, no matter how much she wanted to make it well, no matter how hard she tried to mend its wounds. The past is always with us, and more so with her than with most. She had accepted that she would never be free of that past.

She could chart the important phases of her life: as a child of six hiding in the cellar of her home with her baby brother while her parents were slaughtered in the rooms above; as a young girl subverted by the Morgawr into believing that the Druid Walker Boh had been responsible; as the Ilse Witch working to destroy Walker until a chance meeting with the brother she had thought dead revealed the truth; and as Ard Rhys of the Third Druid Order struggling to find a way to gain acceptance as a force for good within the Four Lands.

She could see the path her life had taken and comprehend the reasons for all that she had done. But she could never explain it satisfactorily to anyone else. She could try, but most would dismiss her words as clever attempts at self-justification or worse.

She understood the truth of things. Some would always see her as the Ilse Witch, and would worry that beneath the surface of the image she projected, a monster lurked. That would never change; the roots of mistrust had grown too deep. Traunt Rowan had been right about that. Had he been more patient and less foolish, he would have lived to see her admit it.

She glanced back at the pilot box, where one of Kermadec's Rock Trolls stood at the helm. Kermadec himself was seated on a box below the side wall, deep in conversation with Penderrin. She wondered what they were talking about. Even in the short time since the big Troll's recovery from the battle in the north tower, the two had grown close. After returning the Moric to the Forbidding, the boy had come back to Paranor with his parents and had remained to help her restore some semblance of order to the Druid's Keep. His parents had stayed, too, for a little while. But they had grown uncomfortable, as they always did with Paranor, and—seeing that she had matters well enough in hand, and missing their home and their old life—they had decided to go home to Patch Run.

But Pen had stayed on, his friendships with Kermadec, Tagwen, and Khyber Elessedil influencing his decision at least in part. All were aware of the transition Grianne was working; all were anxious to help her see it through. Pen could do no less, he told his parents. Bek understood; Rue accepted. They made him promise he would not stay past the end of the month. They wished Grianne and the others well, said good-bye, and flew *Swift Sure* home. Grianne never told them all of what she intended, although she would have liked to tell Bek. But it was best if she didn't, she told herself. It would be easier on them if they didn't know.

She had dissolved the order and dismissed those still in her service. As Ard Rhys, she had the power to do this, and there was no one who would question her now. She gave Paranor into the keeping of Khyber, Bellizen, and Trefen Morys. When the time was right and when they had found a way to do so, they would re-form the order. A handful of others who had remained loyal were invited to stay, as well. But she charged the three she trusted most with spearheading the task of carrying on, the ones she believed would work the hardest. All three had asked her to reconsider. All had pleaded inexperience and limited skills. They were not equal to the task. Others could do better.

But there were no others she could rely on, and there were covenants to monitor, a part of the agreement that she had forged with the Federation and the Free-born. Her young successors would struggle at first, but they would learn from their mistakes and they would grow from their experiences. They would survive, protected as they were by Paranor and their magic, by the mystique of the Druids, and by their own perseverance and determination. She had thought this through carefully after talking with each. It was the right choice.

In the end, persuaded that she would not accept their refusals, they had acquiesced. They would select those men and women who would make up the next generation of Druids at Paranor. Perhaps, in time, the governments and peoples of the Four Lands would come to accept them as a good and necessary force for the furtherance of peace and cooperation among the Races. Certainly, they would have a better chance of achieving that goal than Grianne did.

Just then the Elves and the Federation were in the difficult process of putting themselves back together. Arling Elessedil would serve as Queen regent until her eldest daughter grew to adulthood and assumed the throne. There was a rumor she would remarry and seek to put a son on the throne instead, that she would never permit her daughters to follow in the footsteps of their father and grandfather. She was a strong-willed, at times intractable woman, and she did not look back fondly on her marriage to Kellen Elessedil. With the war on the Prekkendorran ended, she was seeking ways to assure that madness of the sort he had displayed as King would never happen again. She would never achieve that goal, of course. Perhaps she knew that. But it did not stop her from trying.

Battered and disheartened by their defeat on the Prekkendorran, the Federation had withdrawn its armies, ceding to Callahorn and its people the lands to which it had laid claim during the war. After more than thirty years, the Southlanders had lost their taste for fighting a war that had netted them nothing. Sen Dunsidan was dead, and a new Prime Minister ruled the Coalition Council—a man who did not favor expansion as a goal and war as a means to an end. His people appeared to agree. There were those on both sides who believed that the war should be fought to the bitter end, those who would never accept any resolution short of victory on the battlefield, but they represented a small minority. A peace accord was swiftly brokered.

The threat presented by the deadly fire launcher was blunted, at least for the time being. As a condition to the peace she had brokered between the Federation and the Free-born, Grianne had won a single concession: There would be no further use of diapson crystals in the making of weapons. Diapson crystals would be used to power airships, and that would be all. The last fire launcher had been destroyed. The man who had invented it had disappeared and was believed dead, and his plans for building other weapons had been lost in a fire along with his models and designs. She had made certain of those things. She had assured herself that the matter was settled.

Her price for winning the agreement and assistance of all parties in enforcing covenants regarding the future use of diapson crystals was her promise to relinquish her place as head of the Druid order. Those who sought that did not know she had already made the decision to step down. It did not hurt to let them believe they had been responsible for persuading her. They were as frightened of her as they were of any weapon, and the bargain was easily struck.

She could not know if the bargain would be kept, but for the moment, at least, there was a fresh outlook in the governing bodies of the Races and a chance that common sense might prevail. Her successors would do their best to see that it did. Tagwen would serve as their adviser. Kermadec, who had re-formed the Druid Guard from among his own people, would see that they were protected. It was as much as anyone could hope for. It was the best she could do.

"Aunt Grianne?"

Penderrin stood at her elbow. She gave him a quick smile, her reflections and musings scattering like dust motes. "It's a beautiful day, Pen. Perhaps that is a good omen."

He smiled back guardedly. "Do you really think you can do something to help?" he asked. "Do you think there is a chance you can get her back?"

"I think maybe there is. Don't you?"

He bit his lip. "I think that if anyone can do it, you can."

"That is high praise, coming from a boy who found his way into the Forbidding and back again." She paused. "Perhaps when we get there, you will discover that you don't really need me after all, that you can do this by yourself."

She saw the unsettled look that crossed his face. "No," he said. "I've seen what's down there, how she's bound by the tree roots with the others. I don't think I would be strong enough to free her on my own."

They were flying to Stridegate and the island of the tanequil, where they would attempt to reclaim Cinnaminson. She thought that perhaps she had made the decision to do so even before coming out of the Forbidding, that she knew even then that she owed the boy that much. She understood from what he had told her how much the girl meant to him and how hard it had been to give up trying to free her and come looking for Grianne instead. That sort of sacrifice deserved more than a simple thank-you. She had waited until things were settled with the order and the treaties between the Federation and Free-born signed before acting. She had waited until his parents had returned home. It wasn't that she didn't think they would support their son's efforts to free Cinnaminson; indeed, they would want to help. But making the attempt was something she had decided she must do with Pen alone, for reasons she had kept to herself. Only Kermadec and his Trolls were invited to come along.

She put a hand on Pen's shoulder. "You are a lot stronger than you think," she said. "I want you to remember that. Don't make the mistake of underestimating what you can do."

He shrugged. "I'm not very strong, really." He hesitated. "I think that you are wonderful for doing this. I won't ever forget, even if we don't get her back."

She almost hugged him, but couldn't bring herself to do so. She had been distanced from others for too long, and although she might feel affection toward them, she was not comfortable with demonstrating it. She still saw herself as an outcast, as someone who didn't really belong anywhere and would never be close to anyone. Worse, she saw herself as dangerous, more so since the events that had taken place inside the Forbidding. The workings of the wishsong's magic when she had transformed herself into a Fury and when she had destroyed the Graumth had left her shaken. For the first time since she was a child, she was uncertain of the magic. Something about it was changed—perhaps still changing—and she was not sure how well she could control it.

She looked off into the horizon. "Strength comes to us through belief and determination, Pen. The trick is in recognizing how to use it."

"You've done that better than I have," he said quietly.

She glanced over at him and smiled.

How I wish that were true.

The grave diggers arrived around midday on their way south, and the old man invited them to eat with him. He set out ale and cheese and bread and sat with the three men around an old wooden table that occupied one corner of the porch and looked out over the fields of wheat he farmed as his family had farmed them for five generations.

"How is it up there?" he asked, after food and drink were consumed and the men were smoking.

The stocky one shook his head. "Bad. A lot of bodies. We did the best we could, along with the others. But they'll be finding the bones of those we missed for years."

"At least it's over," the old man said.

The tall one shook his head in reproof. "Should have been over years ago. Didn't accomplish anything, did it? Years and years gone and nothing's changed. Except a lot of good men are dead."

"And women," the stocky one added.

The tall one grunted. "Treaty with the Free-born gives us just exactly what we had before the war started. The only good thing that's come of all this is we have a new Prime Minister. Maybe he won't be as stupid as Sen Dunsidan was."

He looked at the old man. "Did you hear what happened with that one?"

The old man shook his head.

"I heard it from one of the soldiers on the *Zolomach*. He was there and saw it all. They were flying Dunsidan to Arborlon, maybe to make peace, maybe not. There's some debate. They had that weapon aboard, the one that shot down the Elven King and his whole fleet. Anyway, some Druids intercepted the ship. One of them had a staff with markings that glowed like fire. Soldier who told me this said Sen Dunsidan couldn't take his eyes off it. The Druids offered it to him, but when he took it, he changed into some sort of monster. Split right out of his skin, like a snake, then disappeared. No one's seen him since."

"Druid magic at work there," the stocky one declared softly. "More of it later, too, if you ask me. The *Zolomach* sailed back to Arishaig, was there maybe a day, caught fire, and burned to her keel. Everything destroyed. Took that weapon with her."

"A fire took the place where they built that weapon and the plans for it, too," the tall one said. "Nothing left but ash and smoke. You're right about those Druids. They were involved in it. Happened right after the witch reappeared. They thought she was gone, but she won't ever be gone, that one. Not her. What is it they called her before she was Ard Rhys? Ilse Witch. She comes back and all this happens? Not by chance, I don't think."

"Doesn't matter what you or I think," the third man said. "What matters is that the war is over, and we can get on with living our lives. There's been enough madness. I lost a brother and two cousins out there on the Prekkendorran. Everyone lost someone. For what? Tell me that. For what?"

"For Sen Dunsidan and his kind," the stocky man declared. "For the politicians and their stupid schemes." He took a long pull on his ale. "This is good," he said to the old man, smiling. "Good enough to help me forget the smell of all those dead men. Can I trouble you for another glass?"

When they were gone, the old man went back into the house, pulled aside the rug to the storm cellar, and let the two Elves out. They'd been in hiding down there for several weeks, too damaged at first to do much more than sleep and eat, and then too weak to travel. He'd nursed them as best he could, using the remedies and skills he had acquired from his mother when she was still alive and working the fields with him. The man was the worse of the two, shot through with arrows and cut with blades in a dozen places. But the woman wasn't much better. He'd helped them because they were hurt and that was the kind of man he was. The war on the Prekkendorran was not his war and not his concern. No Federation war ever had been.

"They're gone," he said as the two climbed back into the light.

Pied Sanderling glanced around, and then reached back for

Troon's hand. The day was clouded, but warm and calm, and it felt good to come back into the light. The old man brought them up whenever it was safe to do so, but that hadn't been often until now. They all knew before the treaty what would happen if they were caught out.

"Did you hear what they said?" the old man asked them.

Pied nodded. He was thinking of those who had gone with him into the Federation camp. He was thinking that their efforts had been worth something after all. The tide of war might have turned on the destruction of the *Dechtera* and her deadly weapon. Twenty-four hours later, Vaden Wick had broken the siege, counterattacked, and driven the Federation off the heights. In the end, the Free-born had prevailed.

Now, it seemed, any danger of fresh weapons of the sort the *Dechtera* had carried was ended, as well. If the Druids had intervened, the chances were good that whatever remained of those weapons had been hunted down and destroyed.

"Sit, and I'll bring you a glass of ale," the old man offered.

He had saved their lives. He had cared for and protected them while they recovered. He had asked nothing about them, nothing from them. He had been kind to them in a place and time when some would have wished them dead and worked to make the wish a reality. They were Elves and enemy soldiers. The old man didn't seem to care.

They took chairs at the table while the old man brought the glasses and set them down. When he left to feed the animals in the barn, Pied looked at Troon. "I guess it's finally over."

She nodded. They were mirror images of each other, their faces cut and bruised, their limbs bandaged, and their bodies so sore that every movement hurt. But they were alive, which was more than they could say about any of the others who had gone with them that night. They would have been dead, too, if not for the old man. He had been burning off a field he had partially cleared, the fire still bright even after darkness fell, and they had homed in on that beacon. The old man had seen the flit come down, found them in the wreckage, and taken them in. He had thrown what remained of the flit into the fire, and then lied to the Federation soldiers who came looking the next morning. Neither of them knew why. Maybe he was just like that. Maybe, like the grave diggers, he'd had enough of war.

"We can go home now," he said to her.

She gave him a bitter smile. "To Arborlon? Where Arling is Queen?"

She was reminding him that he was forbidden to return to Arborlon, that Arling had dismissed him from her service.

They stared at each other wordlessly.

"Let's not go home," she said finally. She held his gaze. "Let's go somewhere else. They think we are dead. Let's leave it that way. Have you anyone waiting for you?"

He thought about Drum for a moment and shook his head. "No."

"Nor I." She took a quick breath and exhaled sharply. "Let's start over. Let's make a new home."

He studied her face, appreciating the straightforward, uncomplicated way it revealed her. With Troon, there was never any question about what she was feeling. Certainly, there wasn't any question there. She was in love with him. She had told him that night on the flit. She had told him any number of times since. The revelation had surprised him, but pleased him, too. Eventually, while they recovered from their wounds, he realized he was in love with her, too.

She reached out for his hands and took them in her own. "I want to spend the rest of my life with you. But I don't want to do it in a place that reminds me of the past. I want to do it where we can start over again and leave behind what we've known. Do you love me enough to do that?"

He smiled. "You know I do."

They smiled at each other across the table, sharing feelings that shouldn't be put into words because words would only get in the way.

They set the *Bremen* down in the gardens that fronted the bridge to the island of the tanequil, anchoring her well back, but safely within walking distance. Stridegate's ruins were empty and still on an afternoon filled with sunshine and blue sky. They had flown into the Inkrim that morning, sailing out of night's departing darkness into dawn's bright promise, the boy and she standing together at the bow and looking down at the world. They had not spoken a word, lost in their separate thoughts. She thought she could probably guess at his but that he could not possibly know hers.

The Urdas were not in evidence on that visit, but Kermadec and his Trolls kept careful watch for them, even after they were anchored and on the ground. Urdas would not enter the ruins, it was said. They would not come into any place they considered sacred. Kermadec was taking no chances, and sent scouts in all directions with instructions to make sure.

Grianne turned to him. "Keep watch for us, Old Bear," she said with a smile. "This won't take long."

He shook his great, impassive face in disagreement. "I wish you would let this wait for a while longer, Mistress. You have been through too much already. If there is a confrontation down there—"

"There will be no confrontation," she said quickly, putting a reassuring hand on his armored wrist. She glanced over to where Penderrin stood at the bridgehead, looking over at the island. "This isn't to be an encounter of that sort."

She took her hand away. "You were the best of them all," she told him. "No one was more faithful or gave more to me when it was needed. I will never forget that."

He looked away. "You should go now, so that you can be back before dark." There was resignation in his eyes. He knew. "Go, Mistress."

She nodded and turned away, walking over to join the boy. He glanced at her as she came up beside him, but said nothing. "Are you ready?" she asked.

He shook his head. "I don't know. What if the tanequil won't let us cross?"

"Why don't we see?"

She walked out onto the bridge, the boy following, and called up the magic of the wishsong, humming softly to let it build, working on the message she wanted it to convey. She stopped perhaps a quarter of the way across until she had it just right, then released the magic into the afternoon silence and let it drift downward into the ravine. She gave it the whole of what she thought was needed, taking her time, content to be patient if patience was what was required.

It was not. A response came almost immediately, a shifting of heavy roots within the earth, a rustle of leaves and grasses, a whisper of wind. Voices, soft and lilting, that only she could hear. She understood what it meant.

"Come, Pen," she said.

They crossed untroubled to the other side of the bridge and walked to the trail that had led the boy into the ravine weeks earlier in his search for Cinnaminson. The island forest was deep and still, the air cooler, the light diffuse, and the earth dappled with layered shadows. She watched Pen cast about, eyes shifting left and right, searching. He was looking for the aeriads, but she already knew they would not come. Nothing would come to them now. Everything was waiting.

They found the trailhead and stopped. The path wound downward in a steep descent that gradually faded into a mix of mist and shadows. It was so dark within the ravine that they could not see the bottom. It was the sort of place she had entered many times. It was a mirror of her heart.

She turned to him. "You are to wait here for me, Pen. I will do this best if I am alone. I know what is needed. I will bring Cinnaminson back to you."

He studied her face carefully, unable to keep the hope from his eyes. "I know you will try, Aunt Grianne."

She reached out impulsively and hugged the boy. It was something she had seldom done, and it felt awkward, but the boy was quick to hug her back, and that made her feel better about it.

"Be careful," he whispered.

She broke away, moving slowly down the trail toward the shadows.

"Thank you," he called after her. "For doing this."

She gave him a small wave in response, but did not look back.

The afternoon eased toward evening, and the light shifted and began to fade. Pen stood until he grew tired, then sat with his back against an ancient trunk, staring down into the ravine, keeping watch. He listened for sounds he did not care to think of too carefully, but no sounds came. Silence cloaked the ravine and the forest and, for all he knew, the entire world. He watched patterns of light and shadows form and re-form, slow-moving kaleidoscopic images against the earth. He smelled the scents released into air by the for-

est and the things that lived there. He rubbed the blunted tips of his
damaged fingers and remembered how they had gotten that way. He
remembered what it had felt like to become joined to the tanequil
through the carving of the runes. He remembered night in the island
forest and his terrifying encounter with Aphasia Wye.

Mostly, he remembered Cinnaminson. He could picture her face
and the way she smiled. He could remember the way she moved. He
could hear her voice. She was there, alive and well within his mind,
and it made him want to cry for his loss.

But he smiled instead. He knew she was coming back to him. He
believed in his aunt Grianne. He had faith in her magic and her
skills, in her promise that she would find a way. He loved Cinnaminson, although he had never loved a girl before and had no frame of
reference from which to draw a comparison. But love seemed to him
to be a state of mind peculiar to each, and there was no set standard
by which you could measure its strength. He knew what he felt for
Cinnaminson, and if the difference between what he felt when he
had her with him and when he did not was an accurate measure, then
he could not imagine how love could be any stronger.

Time slipped away, and at last, when no one had appeared and
darkness had begun to close about, he found himself wondering
what he would do if his aunt failed and Cinnaminson didn't come
back to him.

He dozed then, made sleepy-eyed by the warmth and brightness
of the late afternoon sun slanting down through breaks in the
branches of the trees. He did not fall deeply asleep, but hovered at
the edge of wakefulness, arms about his drawn-up knees, head sunk
on his chest.

Eyes closed, he drifted.

Then something stirred him awake—a whisper of sound, a hint
of movement, a sense of presence—and he looked up to find Cinnaminson standing before him. She was more ghost than flesh and
blood, pale and thin and disheveled in her tattered clothes. He got
to his feet slowly and stood looking at her, afraid that he was mistaken, that he might be hallucinating.

"It's me, Pen," she said, tears welling in her eyes.

He didn't rush to her, didn't grasp her and hold her close, although he wanted to do that, to make certain of her. Instead, he
walked up to her as if time didn't matter. He took her hands and held

them, studying her face, the spray of freckles and the milky eyes. The musty smell of earth and damp emanated from her body, and tendrils of root ends still clung to her arms.

He reached out and touched her face.

"I'm all right," she said. She touched his face. "I missed you. Even when I was one of them and thought I couldn't possibly be happier, I remembered you and missed you. I don't think that ever would have stopped."

She put her arms around him and held on to him as if she was afraid she would be taken away again, and he could feel her crying against his shoulder. He started to speak, then gave it up and just hugged her, closing his eyes and losing himself in the warmth of her body.

"Who was it who came down for me?" she asked him finally, her voice muffled. She lifted her head from his shoulder put her mouth close to his ear. "I don't understand it," she whispered. "Why did she do it? Why did she trade herself for me?"

Pen thought his heart would stop.

In the air above them, the aeriads hummed and sang and danced on the breeze, invisible and soundless. Heedless of time's passage, they played in the soft glow of the sunset's red and gold and the evening's deep indigo. They were spirits unfettered by the restrictions of the human body and the limitations of the human existence. They were sisters and friends, and the whole of the world was their playground.

One strayed momentarily, the newest of them, looking down on the young couple that stood at the edge of the ravine and spoke in soft, comforting tones, their heads bent close. The girl was telling the boy about her, and the boy was trying to understand. She knew it would be hard, that he might never come to terms with what she had done for the girl. But she had done it for herself, too—to give herself a new life, to set herself on a different path, to be reborn. She had known what she would do almost from the time the boy had spoken of the girl's transformation and of her joy at what she had experienced. She had wanted that for herself. That the boy and the girl would make a better life together than apart was incentive to take the chance. Offer herself for the girl, a woman not so young, but deeply talented and magically enhanced, a creature Mother Tanequil could not help but covet.

The trade was simple; the change of places was done in a heartbeat and a small balance to things was set in place.

Come, sister, the others called to her.

She lingered a moment longer, thinking of what she had given up and finding she had no regrets. There was nothing of her old life that was so precious to her, nothing so compelling as even the first few moments of this new one. Too many years of struggle and travail, of heartbreaking loss and backbreaking responsibility, of failure, ruin, and death had marked the path of her life. She would never escape from it in human form. She knew that; she accepted it. But as a creature of the air she had left it all behind, a part of another life.

She watched the boy and the girl turn away and start back through the woods toward the stone bridge. Maybe they would find in their lives something of what she had failed to find in hers. She had already found something precious in her new form, something she had not known since she was six years old and living still in the house of her parents with her baby brother.

She had found freedom.

ABOUT THE AUTHOR

TERRY BROOKS is the *New York Times* bestselling author of more than thirty books, including the Legends of Shannara novels *Bearers of the Black Staff* and *The Measure of the Magic;* the Genesis of Shannara novels *Armageddon's Children, The Elves of Cintra,* and *The Gypsy Morph; The Sword of Shannara;* the Voyage of the Jerle Shannara trilogy: *Ilse Witch, Antrax,* and *Morgawr;* the High Druid of Shannara trilogy: *Jarka Ruus, Tanequil,* and *Straken;* the nonfiction book *Sometimes the Magic Works: Lessons from a Writing Life;* and the novel based upon the screenplay and story by George Lucas, *Star Wars*®: Episode I *The Phantom Menace*™. His novels *Running with the Demon* and *A Knight of the Word* were selected by the *Rocky Mountain News* as two of the best science fiction/fantasy novels of the twentieth century. The author was a practicing attorney for many years but now writes full-time. He lives with his wife, Judine, in the Pacific Northwest.

ABOUT THE TYPE

This book was set in Weiss, a typeface designed by a German artist, Emil Rudolf Weiss (1875–1942). The designs of the roman and italic were completed in 1928 and 1931 respectively. The Weiss types are rich, well-balanced, and even in color, and they reflect the subtle skill of a fine calligrapher.